Robert Ludlum

Robert Ludlum

The Scarlatti Inheritance

The Osterman Weekend

The Matlock Paper

The Gemini Contenders

Octopus/Heinemann

The Scarlatti Inheritance was first published in the United States by
World Publishing Company, New York in 1971; in Great Britain by
Rupert Hart-Davis Limited in 1971

The Osterman Weekend was first published in the United States by
World Publishing Company, New York in 1972; in Great Britain by
Rupert Hart-Davis Limited in 1972

The Matlock Paper was first published in the United States by
The Dial Press in 1973; in Great Britain by
Hart-Davis, MacGibbon Limited in 1973

The Gemini Contenders was first published in the United States by
The Dial Press in 1976; in Great Britain by
Hart-Davis, MacGibbon Limited in 1976

This edition first published in the United States of America
in 1981 jointly by

William Heinemann Inc

and

Octopus Books Inc
One Madison Avenue
New York, NY 10010

ISBN 0 905712 32 3

Eighth Impression 1985

Printed in the United States of America
by R. R. Donnelley & Sons Co.

Contents

The
Scarlatti
Inheritance

Robert
Ludlum

For Mary:

For all those reasons she must know so well—"Above all, there was Mary."

NEW YORKER MISSING

New York, May 21—The scion of one of America's wealthiest industrial families, who was decorated for bravery at the Meuse-Argonne, disappeared from his Manhattan brownstone over five weeks ago, it was learned today. Mr. . . .

HITLER AIDE DISRUPTS I. G. FARBEN CONFERENCE

Berlin, July 10—An unidentified member of Reichschancellor Hitler's Ministry of War today startled negotiators of I. G. Farben and U.S. firms during their reciprocal trade agreements conference. In a surprising display of invective, spoken clearly in the English language, he branded the progress as unacceptable. The unknown observer then departed with his staff. . . .

NAZI OFFICIAL DEFECTED IN 1944

Washington, D.C., February 18— A little-known story from World War II was partially revealed today when it was learned that a high-ranking Nazi figure, using the code name "Saxon," defected to the Allies in October, 1944. A Senate subcommittee . . .

WAR DOCUMENT FOUND

*Kreuzlingen, Switz., May 26—*An oilcloth packet containing maps of armament installations in and around wartime Berlin was found buried in the ground near a small inn in this Swiss village on the Rhine. The inn is being razed for a resort hotel. No identification was found; just the word "Saxon" imprinted on a strip of the tape attached to the packet. . . .

PART ONE

Chapter One

October 10, 1944—Washington, D.C.

The brigadier general sat stiffly on the deacon's bench, preferring the hard surface of the pine to the soft leather of the armchairs. It was nine twenty in the morning and he had not slept well, no more than an hour.

As each half hour had been marked by the single chime of the small mantel clock, he had found himself, to his surprise, wanting the time to pass more swiftly. Because nine thirty had to come, he wanted to reckon with it.

At nine thirty he was to appear before the secretary of state, Cordell S. Hull.

As he sat in the secretary's outer office, facing the large black door with its gleaming brass hardware, he fingered the white folder, which he had taken out of his attaché case. When the time came for him to produce it, he did not want an awkward moment of silence while he opened the case to extract the folder. He wanted to be able to thrust it, if necessary, into the hands of the secretary of state with assurance.

On the other hand, Hull might not ask for it. He might demand only a verbal explanation and then proceed to use the authority of his office to term the spoken words unacceptable. If such was the case, the brigadier could do no more than protest. Mildly, to be sure. The information in the folder did not constitute proof, only data that could or could not bolster the conjectures he had made.

The brigadier general looked at his watch. It was nine twenty-four and he wondered if Hull's reputation for punctuality would apply to his appointment. He had reached his own office at seven thirty, approximately half an hour before his normal arrival time. Normal, that was, except for periods of crisis when he often stayed through the night awaiting the latest development of critical information. These past three days were not unlike those periods of crisis. In a different way.

His memorandum to the secretary, the memorandum that had resulted in his appointment this morning, might put him to the test. Ways could be found to place him out of communication, far from any center of influence. He might well be made to appear a total incompetent. But he knew he was right.

He bent the top of the folder back, just enough to read the typed title page: "Canfield, Matthew. Major, United States Army Reserve. Department of Military Intelligence."

Canfield, Matthew. . . . Matthew Canfield. He was the proof.

A buzzer rang on the intercom on the desk of a middle-aged receptionist.

"Brigadier General Ellis?" She barely looked up from the paper.

"Right here."

"The secretary will see you now."

Ellis looked at his wristwatch. It was nine thirty-two.

He rose, walked toward the ominous black-enameled door, and opened it.

"You'll forgive me, General Ellis. I felt that the nature of your memorandum required the presence of a third party. May I introduce Undersecretary Brayduck?"

The brigadier was startled. He had not anticipated a third party; he had specifically requested that the audience be between the secretary and himself alone.

Undersecretary Brayduck stood about ten feet to the right of Hull's desk. He obviously was one of those White House–State Department university men so prevalent in the Roosevelt administration. Even his clothes—the light gray flannels and the wide herringbone jacket—were casually emphasized in silent counterpoint to the creased uniform of the brigadier.

"Certainly, Mr. Secretary. . . . Mr. Brayduck." The brigadier nodded.

Cordell S. Hull sat behind the wide desk. His familiar features—the very light skin, almost white, the thinning white hair, the steel-rimmed pince-nez in front of his blue-green eyes—all seemed larger than life because they were an everyday image. The newspapers and the motion picture newsreels were rarely without photographs of him. Even the more inclusive election posters—ponderously asking, Do you want to change horses in the middle of the stream?—had his reassuring, intelligent face prominently displayed beneath Roosevelt's; sometimes more prominently than the unknown Harry Truman's.

Brayduck took a tobacco pouch out of his pocket and began stuffing his pipe. Hull arranged several papers on his desk and slowly opened a folder, identical to the one in the brigadier's hand, and looked down at it. Ellis recognized it. It was the confidential memorandum he had had hand-delivered to the secretary of state.

Brayduck lit his pipe and the odor of the tobacco caused Ellis to look at the man once again. That smell belonged to one of those strange mixtures considered so original by the university people but generally offensive to anyone else in the room. Brigadier Ellis would be relieved when the war was over. Roosevelt would then be out and so would the so-called intellectuals and their bad-smelling tobaccos.

The Brain Trust. Pinks, every one of them.

But first the war.

Hull looked up at the brigadier. "Needless to say, General, your memorandum is very disturbing."

"The information was disturbing to me, Mr. Secretary."

"No doubt. No doubt. . . . The question would appear to be, Is there any foundation for your conclusions? I mean, anything concrete?"

"I believe so, sir."

"How many others in Intelligence know about this, Ellis?" Brayduck interrupted and the absence of the word "General" was not lost on the brigadier.

"I've spoken to no one. I didn't think I'd be speaking to anyone but the secretary this morning, to be perfectly frank with you."

"Mr. Brayduck has my confidence, General Ellis. He's here at my request. . . . My orders, if you like."

"I understand."

Cordell Hull leaned back in his chair. "Without offense, I wonder if you do. . . . You send a classified memorandum, delivered under the highest priority to this office—to my own person, to be exact—and the substance of what you say is nothing short of incredible."

"A preposterous charge you admit you can't prove," interjected Brayduck, sucking on his pipe as he approached the desk.

"That's precisely why we're here." Hull had requested Brayduck's presence but he was not going to suffer undue interference, much less insolence.

Brayduck, however, was not to be put off. "Mr. Secretary, Army Intelligence is hardly without its inaccuracies. We've learned that at great cost. My only concern is to prevent another inaccuracy, a misinformed speculation, from becoming ammunition for this administration's political opponents. There's an election less than four weeks away!"

Hull shifted his large head no more than several inches. He did not look at Brayduck as he spoke. "You don't have to remind me of such pragmatic considerations. . . . However, I may have to remind *you* that we have other responsibilities. . . . Other than those to practical politics. Do I make myself clear?"

"Of course." Brayduck stopped in his tracks.

Hull continued. "As I understand your memorandum, General Ellis, you submit that an influential member of the German High Command is an American citizen operating under the assumed name—and a name well-known to us—of Heinrich Kroeger."

"I do, sir. Except that I qualified my statement by saying he *might* be."

"You also imply that Heinrich Kroeger is associated with, or connected to, a number of large corporations in this country. Industries involved with government contracts, armaments appropriations."

"Yes, Mr. Secretary. Except, again, I stated that he *was*, not necessarily *is*."

"Tenses have ways of becoming blurred with such accusations." Cordell Hull took off his steel-rimmed spectacles and placed them beside the folder. "Especially in time of war."

Undersecretary Brayduck struck a match and spoke between puffs on his pipe. "You also state quite clearly that you have no specific proof."

"I have what I believe would be termed circumstantial evidence. Of such a nature I felt I'd be derelict in my duty if I didn't bring it to the secretary's attention." The brigadier took a deep breath before continuing. He knew that once he began he was committed.

"I'd like to point out a few salient facts about Heinrich Kroeger. . . . To begin with, the dossier on him is incomplete. He's received no party recognition as most of the others have. And yet when others have come and gone, he's remained at the center. Obviously he has a great deal of influence with Hitler."

"We know this." Hull did not like restatements of known information simply to bolster an argument.

"The name itself, Mr. Secretary. Heinrich is as common as William or John, and Kroeger no more unusual than Smith or Jones in our own country."

"Oh, come, General." Brayduck's pipe was curling smoke. "Such an inference would make half our field commanders suspect."

Ellis turned and gave Brayduck the full benefit of his military scorn. "I believe the fact is relevant, Mr. Undersecretary."

Hull began to wonder if it had been such a good idea to have Brayduck present. "There's no point in being hostile, gentlemen."

"I'm sorry you feel that way, Mr. Secretary." Brayduck again would not accept a rebuke. "I believe my function here this morning is that of the devil's advocate. None of us, least of all you, Mr. Secretary, have the time to waste. . . ."

Hull looked over at the undersecretary, moving his swivel chair as he did so. "Let's make the time. Please continue, General."

"Thank you, Mr. Secretary. A month ago word was relayed through Lisbon that Kroeger wanted to make contact with us. Channels were arranged and we expected the normal procedures to be followed. . . . Instead Kroeger rejected these procedures—refused any contact with British or French units—insisted on direct communication with Washington."

"If I may?" Brayduck's tone was courteous. "I don't think that's an abnormal decision. We're the predominant factor, after all."

"It was abnormal, Mr. Brayduck, insofar as Kroeger would communicate with no one other than a Major Canfield. . . . Major Matthew Canfield who is, or was, an efficient minor officer in Army Intelligence stationed in Washington."

Brayduck held his pipe motionless and looked at the brigadier general. Cordell Hull leaned forward in his chair, his elbows resting on the desk.

"There's no mention of this in your memorandum."

"I realize that, sir. I omitted it in the conceivable event that the memorandum might be read by someone other than yourself."

"You have my apologies, General." Brayduck was sincere.

Ellis smiled at the victory.

Hull leaned back in his chair. "A ranking member of the Nazi High Command insists upon communicating only with an obscure major in Army Intelligence. Most unusual!"

"Unusual, but not unheard of. . . . We've all known German nationals; we merely assumed that Major Canfield had met Kroeger before the war. In Germany."

Brayduck stepped forward toward the brigadier. "Yet you tell us that Kroeger may not be a German. Therefore between Kroeger's request from Lisbon and your memorandum to the secretary something changed your mind. What was it? Canfield?"

"Major Canfield is a competent, at times excellent Intelligence officer. An experienced man. However, since the channel between him and Kroeger was opened, he's displayed marked tendencies of being under emotional strain. He's become extremely nervous and hasn't functioned in the manner of an officer with his background and experience. . . . He has also, Mr. Secretary, instructed me to make a most unusual request of the president of the United States."

"Which is?"

"That a classified file from the archives of the State Department be delivered to him with the seals unbroken, before he makes contact with Heinrich Kroeger."

Brayduck took his pipe from his mouth, about to object.

"Just one minute, Mr. Brayduck." Brayduck may be brilliant, thought Hull, but did he have any idea of what it meant to a career officer such as Ellis to face the two of them and make a statement? For his statement was an undisguised petition for the White House and the State Department to seriously consider granting Canfield's request. Many officers would have rejected the illegal proposition rather than allow themselves to be placed in such a position. That was the army way. "Am I correct in assuming that you recommend the release of this file to Major Canfield?"

"That judgment would have to be yours. I only point out that Heinrich Kroeger has been instrumental in every important decision made by the Nazi hierarchy since its inception."

"Could the defection of Heinrich Kroeger shorten the war?"

"I don't know. The possibility brought me to your office."

"What is the file this Major Canfield demands?" Brayduck was annoyed.

"I know only the number and the classification stated by the archives section of the State Department."

"What are they?" Cordell Hull again leaned forward on his desk.

Ellis hesitated. It would be inviting personal as well as professional embarrassment to state the terms of the file without giving Hull the data on Canfield. He would have been able to do that had Brayduck not been there. God-damn college boys. Ellis was always uncomfortable with the fast talkers. Damn! he thought. He'd be direct with Hull.

"Before I answer you, may I take the opportunity to fill in some background material I believe is most relevant. . . . Not only relevant, sir, but intrinsic to the file itself."

"By all means." Hull wasn't sure whether he was irritated or fascinated.

"The final communication from Heinrich Kroeger to Major Canfield demands a preliminary meeting with someone identified only as . . . April Red. This meeting is to take place in Bern, Switzerland, prior to any negotiations between Kroeger and Canfield."

"Who is April Red, General? I gather from the tone of your voice that you have an idea who he may be." Very little was lost on Undersecretary Brayduck, and Brigadier Ellis was painfully aware of the fact.

"We . . . or more specifically . . . I think I do." Ellis opened the white folder in his hands and flipped the top page over the cardboard. "If I may have the secretary's permission, I have extracted the following from Major Canfield's security check."

"Of course, General."

"Matthew Canfield—entered government service, Department of the Interior, in March, nineteen seventeen. Education—one year University of Oklahoma, one and one-half years night school extension courses, Washington, D.C. Employed as a junior accountant government frauds section of Interior. Promoted to field accountant in nineteen eighteen. Attached to Group Twenty division, which, as you know . . ."

Cordell Hull interrupted quietly. "A small, highly trained unit assigned to conflicts of interests, misappropriations, et cetera, during the First World War. Very effective too. . . . Until, as most such units, it became overly impressed with itself. Disbanded in twenty-nine or thirty, I believe."

"In nineteen thirty-two, Mr. Secretary." General Ellis was pleased that he had the facts at his command. He flipped a second page over the top of the folder and continued to read.

"Canfield remained with Interior for a period of ten years, rising four pay grades. Superior performance. Excellent rating. In May of nineteen twenty-seven he resigned from government service to enter employment with the

Scarlatti Industries."

At the mention of the name Scarlatti, both Hull and Brayduck reacted as if stung.

"Which of the Scarlatti companies?"

"Executive Offices, five twenty-five Fifth Avenue, New York."

Cordell Hull toyed with the thin black cord of his pince-nez. "Quite a jump for our Mr. Canfield. From night school in Washington to the executive offices of Scarlatti." He glanced downward, taking his eyes off the general.

"Is Scarlatti one of the corporations you referred to in your memorandum?' Brayduck was impatient.

Before the brigadier could answer, Cordell Hull rose from his chair. Hull was tall and imposing. Much larger than the other two. "General Ellis, I instruct you not to answer any further questions!"

Brayduck looked as though he'd been slapped. He stared at Hull, confused and startled by the secretary's order to the brigadier. Hull returned his gaze and spoke softly.

"My apologies, Mr. Brayduck. I cannot guarantee it, but I hope to have an explanation for you later in the day. Until then, will you be so kind as to leave us alone?"

"Of course." Brayduck knew that this good and honest old man had his reasons. "No explanation is necessary, sir."

"However, one is deserved."

"Thank you, Mr. Secretary. You may be assured of my confidence regarding this meeting."

Hull's eyes followed Brayduck until the door was closed. He then returned to the brigadier general, who stood quietly, not comprehending. "Undersecretary Brayduck is an extraordinary public servant. My dismissing him is not to be construed as a reflection on either his character or his work."

"Yes, sir."

Hull slowly and in some pain sat down once more in his chair. "I asked Mr. Brayduck to leave because I believe I may know something of what you're about to discuss. If I'm right, it's best we be alone."

The brigadier general was unsettled. He did not think it possible for Hull to know.

"Don't be alarmed, General. I'm no mind reader. . . . I was in the House of Representatives during the period you speak of. Your words evoked a memory. An almost forgotten memory of a very warm afternoon in the House. . . . But perhaps I'm in error. Please continue where you left off. I believe our Major Canfield had entered employment with the Scarlatti Industries. . . . A most unusual step, I think you'll agree."

"There is a logical explanation. Canfield married the widow of Ulster Stewart Scarlett six months after Scarlett's death in Zurich, Switzerland, in nineteen twenty-six. Scarlett was the youngest of two surviving sons of Giovanni and Elizabeth Scarlatti, founders of the Scarlatti Industries."

Cordell Hull briefly closed his eyes. "Go on."

"Ulster Scarlett and his wife Janet Saxon Scarlett had a son, Andrew Roland, subsequently adopted by Matthew Canfield after his marriage to Scarlett's widow. Adopted but not separated from the Scarlatti estates. . . . Canfield continued in the employ of Scarlatti until August, nineteen forty, when he returned to government service and was commissioned in Army Intelligence."

General Ellis paused and looked over the folder at Cordell Hull. He wondered if Hull was beginning to understand, but the secretary's face betrayed no expression.

"You spoke of the file Canfield has requested from the archives. What is it?"

"That was my next consideration, Mr. Secretary." Ellis folded over another page. "The file is only a number to us, but the number gives us the year of its entry. . . . It's nineteen twenty-six, the fourth quarter of twenty-six to be exact."

"And what are the terms of classification?"

"Maximum. It can be released only by an executive order signed by the president for reasons of national security."

"I presume that one of the signators—witnesses to the file—was a man then employed by the Department of the Interior by the name of Matthew Canfield."

The brigadier was visibly upset but continued to hold the white folder between this thumb and forefinger. "That is correct."

"And now he wants it back or he refuses to make contact with Kroeger."

"Yes, sir."

"I trust you have pointed out to him the illegality of his position?"

"I have personally threatened him with a court-martial. . . . His only reply was that it's our choice to refuse him."

"And then no contact is made with Kroeger?"

"Yes, sir. . . . It's my opinion that Major Canfield would rather face spending the rest of his life in a military prison than alter his position."

Cordell Hull rose from his chair and faced the general. "Would you care to summarize?"

"It is my belief that the April Red referred to by Heinrich Kroeger is the boy, Andrew Roland. I think he's Kroeger's son. The initials are the same. The boy was born in April, nineteen twenty-six. I believe that Heinrich Kroeger is Ulster Scarlett."

"He died in Zurich." Hull watched the general closely.

"The circumstances are suspect. There is on record only a death certificate from an obscure court in a small village thirty miles outside of Zurich and untraceable affidavits of witnesses never heard of before or since."

Hull stared coolly into the general's eyes. "You realize what you're saying? Scarlatti is one of the corporate giants."

"I do, sir. I contend further that Major Canfield is aware of Kroeger's identity and intends to destroy the file."

"So you believe that it's a conspiracy? A conspiracy to conceal the identity of Kroeger?"

"I don't know. . . . I'm not very good at putting into words another person's motives. But Major Canfield's reactions seem so intensely private that I'm inclined to believe that it's a highly personal matter."

Hull smiled. "I think you're very good with words. . . . However, you do believe that the truth is in the file? And if it is, why would Canfield bring it to our attention? Certainly he knows that if we can get it for him, we certainly can get it for ourselves. We might never have been aware of it, had he kept silent."

"As I said, Canfield's an experienced man. I'm sure he's acting on the premise that we soon will be aware of it."

"How?"

"Through Kroeger. . . . And Canfield has set the condition that the file's seals be intact. He's an expert, sir. He'd know if they were tampered with."

Cordell Hull walked around his desk past the brigadier with his hands clasped behind his back. His gait was stiff, his health obviously failing. Brayduck had been right, thought the secretary of state. If even the specter of a relationship between the powerful American industrialists and the German High Command became known, regardless of how remote or how long in the past, it could tear the country apart. Especially during a national election.

"In your judgment if we delivered the file to Major Canfield, would he produce . . . April Red . . . for his meeting with Kroeger?"

"I believe he would."

"Why? It's a cruel thing to do to an eighteen-year-old boy."

The general hesitated. "I'm not sure he has an alternative. There's nothing to prevent Kroeger from making other arrangements."

Hull stopped pacing and looked at the brigadier general. He had made up his mind. "I shall have the president sign an executive order for the file. However, and frankly I place this as a condition for his signature, your suppositions are to remain between the two of us."

"The two of us?"

"I shall brief President Roosevelt on the substance of our conversation, but I will not burden him with conjectures which may prove to be unfounded. Your theory may be nothing more than a series of recorded coincidences easily explained."

"I understand."

"But if you are correct, Heinrich Kroeger could trigger an internal collapse in Berlin. Germany's in a death struggle. . . . As you've pointed out, he's had extraordinary staying power. He's part of the elite corps surrounding Hitler. The Praetorian Guard revolts against Caesar. If you're wrong, however, then we must both think of two people who will soon be on their way to Bern. And may God have mercy on our souls."

Brigadier General Ellis replaced the pages in the white folder, picked up the attaché case at his feet, and walked to the large black door. As he closed it behind him, he saw that Hull was staring at him. He had an uncomfortable feeling in the pit of his stomach.

Hull was not thinking about the general, however. He was remembering that warm afternoon long ago in the House of Representatives. Member after member had gotten up and read glowing tributes into the *Congressional Record* eulogizing a brave young American who was presumed dead. Everyone from both parties had expected him, the honorable member from the great state of Tennessee, to add his comments. Heads kept turning towards his desk in anticipation.

Cordell Hull was the only member of the house who was on a first-name basis with the renowned Elizabeth Scarlatti, that legend in her own time. The mother of the brave young man being glorified for posterity in the Congress of the United States.

For in spite of their political differences, Hull and his wife had been friends with Elizabeth Scarlatti for years.

Yet he had remained silent that warm afternoon.

He had known Ulster Stewart Scarlett, and he had despised him.

Chapter Two

The brown sedan with the United States Army insignia on both doors turned right on Twenty-second Street and entered Gramercy Square.

In the back seat Matthew Canfield leaned forward, taking the briefcase off his lap and placing it at his feet. He pulled the right sleeve of his overcoat down to conceal the thick silver chain, which was tightly wound around his wrist and looped through the metal handle of the case.

He knew that the contents of the briefcase, or more specifically, his possession of its contents, signified the end for him. When it was all over, and if he were still alive, they would crucify him if a way could be found that would exonerate the military.

The army car made two left turns and stopped by the entrance of the Gramercy Arms Apartments. A uniformed doorman opened the rear door and Canfield stepped out.

"I want you back here in half an hour." he told his driver. "No later."

The pale sergeant, obviously conditioned by his superior's habits, replied, "I'll be back in twenty minutes, sir."

The major nodded appreciatively, turned, and went into the building. As he rode the elevator up, the major numbly realized how tired he was. Each number seemed to stay lighted far longer than it should have; the time lapse between the floors seemed interminable. And yet he was in no hurry. No hurry, whatsoever.

Eighteen years. The end of the lie but not the end of the fear. That would come only when Kroeger was dead. What would be left was guilt. He could live with the guilt, for it would be his alone and not the boy's or Janet's.

It would be his death, too. Not Janet's. Not Andrew's. If death was called for, it would be his. He'd make sure of that.

He would not leave Bern, Switzerland, until Kroeger was dead.

Kroeger or himself.

In all likelihood, both of them.

Out of the elevator he turned left and stepped down the short hallway to a door. He unlocked the door and stepped into a large, comfortable living room, furnished in Italian provincial style. Two huge bay windows overlooked the park, and various doors led to the bedrooms, dining room, the pantry, and the library. Canfield stood for a moment and thought unavoidably that all this, too, went back eighteen years.

The library door opened and a young man walked out. He nodded to Canfield without enthusiasm. "Hello, Dad."

Canfield stared at the boy. It took a great deal of strength not to rush to his son and hold him.

His son.

And not his son.

He knew if he attempted such a gesture it would be rejected. The boy was wary now and, although he tried not to show it, afraid.

"Hello," said the major. "Give me a hand with all this, will you?"

The young man crossed to the older one and mumbled, "Sure thing."

Between them they unfastened the primary lock on the chain, and the younger man held the briefcase out straight so Canfield could manipulate the secondary combination lock, which was secured on the flat of his wrist. The briefcase came loose, and Canfield removed his hat, overcoat, and uniform jacket, throwing them on an easy chair.

The boy held the briefcase, standing motionless before the major. He was extraordinarily good looking. He had bright blue eyes below very dark eyebrows, a straight but slightly upturned nose, and black hair combed neatly back. His complexion was swarthy as though he had a perpetual tan. He stood just over six feet and was dressed in gray flannels, a blue shirt, and a tweed jacket.

"How do you feel?" asked Canfield.

The young man paused and replied softly. "Well, on my twelfth birthday you and Mother got me a new sailboat. I liked that better."

The older man returned the younger's smile. "I guess you did."

"Is this it?" The boy placed the briefcase on the table and fingered it.

"Everything."

"I suppose I should feel privileged."

"It took an executive order from the president to get it out of State."

"Really?" The boy looked up.

"Don't be alarmed. I doubt he knows what's in it."

"How come?"

"A deal was made. There was an understanding."

"I don't believe that."

"I think you will after you read it. No more than ten people have ever seen it in full, and most of them are dead. When we compiled the last quarter of the file, we did it in segments . . . in nineteen thirty-eight. It's in the separate folder with the lead seals. The pages are out of sequence and have to be collated. The key's on the first page." The major quickly loosened his tie and started unbuttoning his shirt.

"Was all that necessary?"

"We thought it was. As I recall, we used rotating pools of typists." The major started toward a bedroom door. "I suggest you arrange the pages before starting the last folder." He entered the bedroom, hastily took off his shirt, and unlaced his shoes. The young man followed and stood in the doorframe.

"When are we going?" asked the boy.

"Thursday."

"How?"

"Bomber Ferry Command. Matthews Air Force Base to Newfoundland, Iceland, Greenland, to Ireland. From Ireland, on a neutral, straight through to Lisbon."

"Lisbon?"

"The Swiss embassy takes over from there. They'll take us to Bern. . . . We're fully protected."

Canfield, having removed his trousers, selected a pair of light gray flannels from the closet and put them on.

"What's Mother going to be told?" asked the young man.

Canfield crossed into the bathroom without replying. He filled the washbowl with hot water and began lathering his face.

The boy's eyes followed him, but he did not move or break the silence. He sensed that the older man was far more upset than he wished to show.

"Get me a clean shirt from the second drawer over there, will you, please. Just put it on the bed."

"Sure." He selected a wide-collar broadcloth from the stack of shirts in the dresser drawer.

Canfield spoke while he shaved. "Today's Monday, so we'll have three days. I'll be making the final arrangements, and it'll give you time to digest the file. You'll have questions, and I don't have to tell you that you'll have to ask me. Not that you'll be speaking to anyone else who could answer you, anyway, but in case you get hot and want to pick up a phone, don't."

"Understood."

"Incidentally, don't feel you have to commit anything to memory. That's not important. I simply know that you have to understand."

Was he being honest with the boy? Was it really necessary to make him feel the weight of official truth? Canfield had convinced himself that it was, for no matter the years, no matter the affection between them, Andrew was a Scarlett. In a few years he would inherit one of the largest fortunes on earth. Such persons had to have responsibility thrust upon them when it was necessary, not when it was convenient.

Or did they?

Or was Canfield simply taking the easiest way for himself? Let the words come from someone else. Oh, God! Make somebody else speak!

Drying his face with a towel, the major splashed some Pinaud on his face and started putting on his shirt.

"If you're interested, you missed most of your beard."

"Not interested." He selected a tie from a rack on the closet door and pulled a dark blue blazer from a hanger. "When I leave, you can start reading. If you go out for dinner, put the briefcase in the cabinet to the right of the library door. Lock it. Here's the key." He unclipped a small key from his key ring.

The two men walked out of the bedroom, and Canfield started toward the front hall.

"You either didn't hear me or you don't want to answer, but what about Mother?"

"I heard you." Canfield turned toward the young man. "Janet isn't supposed to know anything."

"Why not? Supposing something happens?"

Canfield was visibly upset. "It's my judgment that she be told nothing."

"I don't agree with you." The young man remained subdued.

"That doesn't concern me!"

"Maybe it should. I'm pretty important to you now. . . . I didn't choose to be, Dad."

"And you think that gives you the right to issue orders?"

"I think I have a right to be heard. . . . Look, I know you're upset, but she's my mother."

"And my wife. Don't forget that part, will you, Andy?" The major took several steps toward the young man, but Andrew Scarlett turned away and walked to the table where the black leather case lay beside the lamp.

"You never showed me how to open your briefcase."

"It's unlocked. I unlocked it in the car. It opens like any other briefcase."

Young Scarlett fingered the clasps and they shot up. "I didn't believe you last night, you know," he said quietly while he opened the lid of the briefcase.

"That's not surprising."

"No. Not about him. I believed that part because it answered a lot of questions about you." He turned and looked at the older man. "Well, not questions really, because I always thought I knew why you acted the way you did. I figured you just resented the Scarletts. . . . Not me. The Scarletts. Uncle Chancellor, Aunt Allison, all the kids. You and Mom always laughed at all of them. So did I. . . . I remember how painful it was for you to tell me why my last name couldn't be the same as yours. Remember that?"

"Painfully." Canfield smiled gently.

"But the last couple of years . . . you changed. You got pretty vicious about the Scarletts. You hated it every time anyone mentioned the Scarlatti companies. You'd fly off the handle whenever the Scarlatti lawyers made appointments to discuss me with you and Mom. She got angry with you and said you were unreasonable. . . . Only she was wrong. I understand now. . . . So you see, I'm prepared to believe whatever's in here." He closed the lid on the briefcase.

"It won't be easy for you.'

"It isn't easy now, and I'm just getting over the first shock." He tried lamely to smile. "Anyway, I'll learn to live with it, I guess. . . . I never knew him. He was never anything to me. I never paid much attention to Uncle Chancellor's stories. You see, I didn't want to know anything. Do you know why?"

The major watched the young man closely. "No, I don't," he replied.

"Because I never wanted to belong to anyone but you . . . and Janet."

Oh, God in your protective heaven, thought Canfield. "I've got to go." He started once again for the door.

"Not yet. We haven't settled anything."

"There's nothing to settle."

"You haven't heard what it was I didn't believe last night."

Canfield stopped, his hand on the doorknob. "What?"

"That mother . . . doesn't know about him."

Canfield removed his hand from the knob and stood by the door. When he spoke his voice was low and controlled. "I was hoping to avoid this until later. Until you'd read the file."

"It's got to be now, or I don't want the file. If anything's going to be kept from her, I want to know why before I go any further."

The major came back into the center of the room. "What do you want me to tell you? That it would kill her to find out?"

"Would it?"

"Probably not. But I haven't the courage to test that."

"How long have you known?"

Canfield walked to the window. The children had left the park. The gate was closed.

"On June twelfth, nineteen thirty-six, I made positive identification. I amended the file a year and a half later on January second, nineteen thirty-eight."

"Jesus Christ."

"Yes. . . . Jesus Christ."

"And you never told her?"

"No."

"Dad, why not?"

"I could give you twenty or thirty impressive reasons," said Canfield as he continued looking down at Gramercy Park. "But three have always stuck out in my mind. First—he'd done enough to her; he was her own personal hell. Second—once your grandmother died, no one else alive could identify him. And the third reason—your mother took my word . . . that I'd killed him."

"You!"

The major turned from the window. "Yes. Me. . . . I believed I had. . . . Enough so that I forced twenty-two witnesses to sign affidavits that he was dead. I bought a corrupt court outside of Zurich to issue the certificate of death. All very legal. . . . That June morning in thirty-six when I found out the truth we were at the bay house and I was on the patio having coffee. You and your mother were hosing down a catboat and calling for me to put it in the water. You kept splashing her with the hose, and she laughed and shrieked and ran around the boat with you following her. She was so happy! . . . I didn't tell her. I'm not proud of myself, but there it is."

The young man sat down in the chair next to the table. He started to speak several times, but each time the words fell short of making sense.

Canfield spoke quietly. "Are you sure you want to belong to me?"

The boy looked up from the chair. "You must have loved her a lot."

"I still do."

"Then I . . . still want to belong to you."

The shaded understatement of the young man's voice nearly caused Canfield to break. But he had promised himself he would not do that no matter what happened. There was too much left to go through.

"I thank you for that." He turned back to the window. The street lights had been turned on—every other one as if to remind people that it could happen here, but probably wouldn't so they could relax.

"Dad?"

"Yes?"

"Why did you go back and change the file?"

There was a long silence before Canfield answered. "I had to. . . . That sounds funny now—'I had to.' It took me eighteen months to make that decision. When I finally did make it, it took less than five minutes to convince myself." He stopped for a moment wondering if it was necessary to tell the boy. There was no point in not telling him. "On New year's Day in nineteen thirty-eight your mother bought me a new Packard Roadster. Twelve cylinders. A beautiful automobile. I took it for a spin on the Southampton road. . . . I'm not sure what happened—I think the steering wheel locked. I don't know, but there was an accident. The car rolled over twice before I was thrown clear. It was a wreck, but I was okay. Except for a little blood, I was fine. But it occurred to me that I might have been killed."

"I remember that. You phoned from somebody's house and Mom and I drove over and picked you up. You were a mess."

"That's right. That was when I made up my mind to go down to Washington and amend the file."

"I don't understand."

Canfield sat on the window seat. "If anything did happen to me, Scarlett . . . Kroeger could have played out a horror story and would have if it served him. Janet was vulnerable because she didn't know anything. So somewhere the truth had to be told. . . . But told in such a way that would leave neither government any alternative but to have Kroeger eliminated . . . immediately. Speaking for this country, Kroeger made fools out of a lot of prominent men. Some of those distinguished gentlemen are at the policy level today. Others are manufacturing planes and tanks and ships. By identifying Kroeger as Scarlett, we move into a whole new set of questions. Questions our government won't want asked now. Or perhaps ever."

He slowly unbuttoned his tweed overcoat but he did not want to take it off.

"The Scarlatti lawyers have a letter which is to be delivered upon my death or disappearance to the most influential cabinet member of whatever administration is in Washington at the time. Scarlatti lawyers are good at that sort of thing. . . . I knew the war was coming. Everyone did. Remember, it was nineteen thirty-eight. . . . The letter directs that person to the file and the truth."

Canfield took a deep breath and looked at the ceiling.

"As you'll see, I outlined a specific course of action if we were at war and a variation if we weren't. Only in the last extremity was your mother to be told."

"Why should anyone pay attention to you after what you did?"

Andrew Scarlett was quick. Canfield liked that.

"There are times when countries . . . even countries in a state of war have the same objectives. Lines of communication are always open for such purposes. . . . Heinrich Kroeger is a case in point. He represents too great an embarrassment to either side. . . . The file makes that clear."

"That seems cynical."

"It is. . . . I directed that within forty-eight hours after my death, the Third Reich's High Command be reached and told that a few of our top personnel in Military Intelligence have long suspected Heinrich Kroeger to be an American citizen."

Andrew Scarlett leaned forward on the edge of the chair. Canfield went on without apparently noticing the boy's growing concern.

"Since Kroeger consistently makes underground contacts with a number of Americans, these suspicions are believed to be confirmed. However, as a result of . . .'" Canfield paused to recall the exact wording. "'. . . 'the death of one Matthew Canfield, a former associate of the man known now as Heinrich Kroeger . . .' our government has in its possession . . . documents which state unequivocally that Heinrich Kroeger is . . . criminally insane. We want no part of him. Either as a former citizen or as a defector."

The young man rose from the chair, staring at his stepfather. "Is this true?"

"It would have been sufficient, which is more to the point. The combination is enough to guarantee a swift execution. A traitor as well as an insane man."

"That's not what I asked."

"All the information's in the file."

"I'd like to know now. Is it true? Is he . . . was he insane? Or is it a trick?"

Canfield got up from the window seat. His reply was barely above a whisper. "This is why I wanted to wait. You want a simple answer, and there isn't any."

"I want to know if my . . . father was insane."

"If you mean do we really have documented proof from medical authorities that he was unbalanced? . . . No, we do not. On the other hand, there were ten men left in Zurich, powerful men—six are still living—who had every reason in the world to want Kroeger, as they knew him, considered a lunatic. . . . It was their only way out. And being who they were, they made sure that was the case. The Heinrich Kroeger referred to in the original file is verified by all ten to be a maniac. A schizophrenic madman. It was a collective effort that left no room for doubt. They had no choice. . . . But if you ask me . . . Kroeger was the sanest man imaginable. And the cruelest. You'll read that, too."

"Why don't you call him by his right name?"

Suddenly, as if the strain had become more than he could bear, Canfield swiftly turned.

Andrew watched the angered, flushed, middle-aged man across the room. He had always loved him for he was a man to be loved. Positive, sure, capable, fun and—what was the word his stepfather had used?—vulnerable.

"You weren't just protecting Mother, were you? You were protecting me. You did what you did to protect me, too. . . . If he ever came back, I'd be a freak for the rest of my life."

Canfield slowly turned and faced his stepson. "Not just you. There'd be a lot of freaks. I counted on that."

"But not the same for them." Young Scarlett walked back to the briefcase.

"I grant you. Not the same." He followed the boy and stood behind him. "I'd have given anything not to have told you, I think you know that. I had no choice. By making you part of the final conditions, Kroeger—left me no choice but to tell you the truth. I couldn't fake that. . . . He believes that once you know the truth you'll be terrified, and I'll do anything short of killing you—perhaps even that—to keep you from going into panic. There is information in this file which could destroy your mother. Send me to prison, probably for the rest of my life. Oh, Kroeger thought it all out. But he misjudged. He didn't know you."

"Do I really have to see him? Talk to him?"

"I'll be in the room with you. That's where the deal is made."

Andrew Scarlett looked startled. "Then you're going to make a deal with him." It was a distasteful statement of fact.

"We have to know what he can deliver. Once he's satisfied that I've carried out my end of the bargain, you, we'll know what it is he's offering. And for what."

"Then I don't have to read this, do I." It was not a question. "All I have to do is be there. . . . Okay, I'll be there!"

"You'll read it because I'm ordering you to!"

"All right. All right, Dad. I'll read it."

"Thank you. . . . I'm sorry I had to speak that way." He began to button his overcoat.

"Sure. . . . I deserved it. . . . By the way, suppose Mother decides to call me at school? She does, you know."

"There's a tap on your phone as of this morning. An intercept, to be exact. Works fine. You have a new friend named Tom Ahrens."

"Who's he?"

"A lieutenant in CIC. Stationed in Boston. He has your schedule and will cover the phone. He knows what to say. You went to Smith for a long weekend."

"Jesus, you think of everything."

"Most of the time." Canfield had reached the door. "I may not be back tonight."

"Where are you going?"

"I've got some work to do. I'd rather you didn't go out but if you do, remember the cabinet. Put everything away." He opened the door.

"I won't go anywhere."

"Good. And Andy . . . you've got one hell of a responsibility ahead of you. I hope we've brought you up so you can handle it. I think you can." Canfield walked out the door and closed it behind him.

The young man knew that his stepfather spoke the wrong words. He was trying to say something else. The boy stared at the door and suddenly he knew what that something else was.

Matthew Canfield wasn't coming back.

What had he said? In the last extremity, Janet had to be told. His mother had to be told the truth. And there was no one else now who could tell her.

Andrew Scarlett looked at the briefcase on the table.

The son and the stepfather were going to Bern, but only the son would come back.

Matthew Canfield was going to his death.

Canfield closed the apartment door and leaned against the hallway wall. He was heavy with sweat, and the rhythmic pounding in his chest was so loud he thought it might be heard back in the apartment.

He looked at his watch. It had taken him less than an hour, and he had remained remarkably calm. Now he wished to get as far away as possible. He knew that by any of the standards of courage or morality or responsibility, he should stay with the boy. But such demands could not be made on him now. One thing at a time or he'd go out of his mind. One item crossed off and then on to the next.

What was the next?

Tomorrow.

The courier to Lisbon with the detailed precautions. One mistake and everything could explode. The courier wasn't leaving until seven o'clock in the evening.

He could spend the night and most of the day with Janet. He rationalized that he had to. If Andy cracked, the first thing he'd do was try to reach his mother. Because he couldn't face staying with him, he had to be with her.

To hell with his office! To hell with the army! To hell with the United States government!

In light of his impending departure he was under voluntary surveillance twenty-four hours a day. God damn them!

They expected him to be no farther than ten minutes from a Teletype.

Well, he wasn't going to be.

He would spend every minute he could with Janet. She was closing up the Oyster Bay home for the winter. They'd be alone, perhaps for the last time.

Eighteen years and the charade was coming to a finish.

Fortunately for the state of his anxiety, the elevator came quickly. Because now he was in a hurry. To Janet.

The sergeant held the car door open and saluted as smartly as he could. Under ordinary circumstances, the major would have chuckled and reminded the sergeant that he was in civilian clothes. Instead, he returned the salute informally and hopped into the car.

"To the office, Major Canfield?"

"No, Sergeant. Oyster Bay."

Chapter Three

An American Success Story

On August 24, 1892, the social world of Chicago and Evanston, Illinois, was shaken to its foundations, which were not inordinately firm to begin with. For on this day Elizabeth Royce Wyckham, the twenty-seven-year-old daughter of industrialist Albert O. Wyckham, married an impoverished Sicilian immigrant by the name of Giovanni Merighi Scarlatti.

Elizabeth Wyckham was a tall, aristocratic girl who had been an ever-present source of worry to her parents. According to Albert O. Wyckham and his wife, the aging Elizabeth had thrown over every golden matrimonial opportunity a girl could ask for in Chicago, Illinois. Her reply had been:

"Fool's gold, Papa!"

So they had taken her on a grand tour of the Continent, expending great sums in great expectations. After four months of surveying the best matrimonial prospects from England, France, and Germany, her reply had been:

"Idiot's gold, Papa. I'd prefer a string of lovers!"

Her father had slapped his daughter resoundingly.

She proceeded, in turn, to kick him in the ankle.

Elizabeth first saw her future husband at one of those picnic outings the officers of her father's firm in Chicago held annually for deserving clerks and their families. He had been introduced to her as a serf might have been to the daughter of a feudal baron.

He was a huge man with massive, yet somehow gentle hands and sharp Italian features. His English was almost unintelligible, but instead of accompanying his broken speech with awkward humility, he radiated confidence and made no apologies. Elizabeth liked him immediately. Although young Scarlatti was neither a clerk nor had he a family, he had impressed the Wyckham executives with his knowledge of machinery and had actually submitted a design for a machine that would cut the cost of producing paper rolls by possibly 16 percent. He had been invited to the picnic.

Elizabeth's curiosity had already been aroused by her father's stories about him. The greaser had a knack for tinkering—absolutely incredible. He had spotted two machines in as many weeks wherein the addition of single levers eliminated the necessity of second men on the jobs. As there were eight of each machine, the Wyckham Company was able to lay off sixteen men who obviously were no longer pulling their weight. Further, Wyckham had had the foresight to hire a second-generation Italian from Chicago's Little Italy to accompany Giovanni Scarlatti wherever he wandered in the plant and literally act as his interpreter. Old Wyckham objected to the eight dollars a week he paid the conversant Italian but justified the salary on the basis that Giovanni would make other improvements. He had better. Wyckham was paying him fourteen dollars a week.

The first true inkling Elizabeth had about her future husband came several weeks after the picnic. Her father gloatingly announced at the dinner table that his big Italian simpleton had requested permission to come in Sundays! No additional pay, mind you; just that he had nothing better to do. Naturally, Wyckham had arranged it with his watchman, for it was his Christian duty to keep such a fellow occupied and away from all the wine and beer to which Italians were addicted.

On the second Sunday Elizabeth found a pretext to go from her elegant home in suburban Evanston to Chicago and then to the plant. There she found Giovanni, not in the machine shop but in one of the billing offices. He was laboriously copying down figures from a file marked clearly—CONFIDEN-TIAL. The drawer of a steel file cabinet on the left wall of the office was open. A long string of thin wire was still hanging from the small lock. Obviously the lock had been expertly picked.

At that moment, as she stood in the doorway watching him, Elizabeth smiled. This large, black-haired Italian simpleton was far more complicated than her father thought. And, not incidentally, he was most attractive.

Startled, Giovanni looked up. Within a split second his attitude changed to one of defiance.

"Okay, Miss 'Lisbet! You tell you papa! I don't want to work here no more!"

Elizabeth then spoke her first words of love to Giovanni.

"Get me a chair, Mr. Scarlatti. I'll help you. . . . It'll be quicker that way."

And, indeed, it was.

The next several weeks were spent educating Giovanni in the legal and corporate structure of the American industrial organization. Just the facts devoid of theory, for Giovanni supplied his own philosophy. This land of opportunity was for those just a little bit quicker than the other opportunists. The period was one of enormous economic growth, and Giovanni understood that unless his machines enabled him to own a part of that growth, his position would remain that of a servant to masters rather than a master of servants. And he was ambitious.

Giovanni set to work with Elizabeth's help. He designed what old Albert Wyckham and his executives thought was a revolutionary impact-extrusion press that could turn out corrugated carton sides at a phenomenal rate of speed and at a cost approximating a 30 percent saving over the old process. Wyckham was delighted and gave Giovanni a ten-dollar raise.

While waiting for the new machinery to be tooled and put into assembly, Elizabeth convinced her father to ask Giovanni to dinner. At first, Albert Wyckham thought his daughter was playing a joke. A joke in poor taste for all concerned. Wyckham may have made fun of the Italian but he respected him. He did not wish to see his clever wop embarrassed at a dinner party. However, when Elizabeth told her father that embarrassment was the last thing she had in mind, that she had met Giovanni on several occasions since the company picnic—finding him quite amusing—her father consented to a small family dinner with suddenly new misgivings.

Three days after the dinner Wyckham's new machinery for corrugated carton sides was in operation and on that morning Giovanni Scarlatti did not show up for work. None of the executives understood. It should have been the most important morning of his life.

It was.

For instead of Giovanni, a letter arrived at Albert Wyckham's office, typed by his own daughter. The letter outlined a second machine for corrugated carton sides that made Wyckham's new assembly totally obsolete.

Giovanni's conditions were frankly put. Either Wyckham assigned him a large block of company stock plus options for purchase of additional shares based upon current values, or he would take his second design for corrugated carton sides to Wyckham's competitor. Whoever possessed the second design would bury the other. It didn't matter to Giovanni Scarlatti, but he did feel it would be better kept in the family as he was formally requesting Albert's daughter in marriage. Again, Wyckham's answer did not really concern him, because Elizabeth and he would be united as man and wife within the month regardless of his position.

From this juncture on, the rise of Scarlatti was as rapid as it was clouded. The public facts indicate that for several years he continued to design newer and better machinery for a number of paper-producing companies throughout the Midwest. He did so always with the same conditions—minor royalties and shares of stock, with options to buy additional shares at the prices of stock prior to the installation of his new designs. All designs were subject to renegotiation of royalties after five-year periods. A reasonable item to be dealt with in reasonable good faith. A very acceptable legal expression, especially in light of the low royalty rates.

By this time, Elizabeth's father, exhausted by the tensions of business events and his daughter's marriage "to that wop," was content to retire. Giovanni and his wife were awarded the old man's entire voting stock in the Wyckham Company.

This was all Giovanni Scarlatti needed. Mathematics is a pure science, and never was this more apparent. Already possessing representation in eleven paper firms in Illinois, Ohio, and western Pennsylvania, and owning patents on thirty-seven different operating assemblies, Giovanni Scarlatti called a conference of the firms accountable to him. In what amounted to a slaughter of the uninformed, Giovanni suggested that a desirable course of action was the formation of one parent organization with himself and his wife as the principal stockholders.

Everyone would, of course, be well taken care of, and the single company would expand beyond their wildest dreams under his inventive genius.

If they didn't agree, they could take his machines out of their factories. He was a poor immigrant who had been deviously misled in his initial negotiations. The royalties paid for his designs were ridiculous in light of the profits. Also in several cases individual stocks had risen astronomically and by the terms of his contracts those particular firms had to make his options available at the previous stock prices. When one came right down to it, Giovanni Scarlatti was a major stockholder in a number of established paper companies.

Howls were heard in boardrooms throughout the three states. Impetuous challenges were flung at the arrogant Italian only to be muted by wiser legal counsel. Better a merging survival than isolated destruction. Scarlatti might be defeated in the courts, but it was quite possible that he might not be. In that latter event his demands could be excessive, and if rejected, the cost of retooling and loss of supply would plunge many of the firms into disastrous financial territory. Besides Scarlatti was a genius, and they all might do rather well.

So the mammoth Scarlatti Industries was formed, and the empire of Giovanni Merighi Scarlatti was born.

It was as its master—sprawling, energetic, insatiable. As his curiosity diversified, so did his companies. From paper it was an easy leap into packaging; from packaging into hauling and freight; from transportation into produce. And always a better idea came along with the purchase.

By the year 1904, after twelve years of marriage, Elizabeth Wyckham

Scarlatti decided that it was prudent for her and her husband to go east. Although her husband's fortunes were secure and growing daily, his popularity was scarcely enviable. Among the financial powers of Chicago, Giovanni was the living proof of the Monroe Doctrine. The Irish were disagreeable, but this was intolerable.

Elizabeth's father and mother died; what few social loyalties that remained for her went with them. The consensus of the households of her lifelong friends was described by Franklyn Fowler, recently of Fowler Paper Products:

"That black wop may own the mortgage on the club's building, but we'll be damned if we'll let him become a member!"

This general attitude had no effect on Giovanni, for he had neither the time nor the inclination for such indulgences. Neither did Elizabeth, for she had become Giovanni's partner in far more than the marriage bed. She was his censor, his sounding board, his constant interpreter of shaded meanings. But she differed from her husband regarding their banishment from the more normal social pursuits. Not for herself, but for the children.

Elizabeth and Giovanni had been blessed with three sons. They were Roland Wyckham, age nine; Chancellor Drew, eight; and Ulster Stewart, seven. And although they were only boys, Elizabeth saw the effects the family's ostracism was having on them. They attended the exclusive Evanston School for Boys, but except for their daily school associations, they saw no boys but each other. They were never asked to birthday parties but always told about them on the following days; invitations proferred to their class-mates were invariably coolly received by calls from governesses; and, perhaps most cutting of all, was the repetitive ditty that greeted the boys each morning as they arrived:

"Scarlatti, spaghetti! Scarlatti, Spaghetti!"

Elizabeth made up her mind that they should all have a fresh start. Even Giovanni and herself. She knew they could afford it even if it meant going back to his native Italy and buying Rome.

Instead of Rome, however, Elizabeth took a trip to New York City and discovered something quite unexpected.

New York was a very provincial town. Its interests were insular, and among those in the business world the reputation of Giovanni Merighi Scarlatti had taken a rather unusual twist: they weren't sure who he was other than the fact that he was an Italian inventor who had purchased a number of American companies in the Midwest.

Italian inventor. *American* companies.

Elizabeth found also that some of the more astute men on Wall Street believed Scarlatti's money had come from one of the Italian ship lines. After all, he'd married the daughter of one of Chicago's best families.

New York it would be.

Elizabeth arranged for a temporary family residence at the Delmonico, and once settled, Elizabeth knew she had made the right decision. The children were bursting with excitement, anticipating new schools and new friends; and within a month Giovanni had purchased controlling interest in two failing, antiquated paper mills on the Hudson and was eagerly planning their joint resurrection.

The Scarlattis stayed at Delmonico's for nearly two years. It wasn't really necessary, for the uptown house might have been completed much sooner had Giovanni been able to give it proper attention. However, as a result of his lengthy conferences with the architects and contractors, he discovered another interest—land.

One evening while Elizabeth and Giovanni were having a late supper in their suite. Giovanni suddenly said, "Write out a check for two hundred ten thousand dollars. Put in the name East Island Real Estaters."

"Realtors, you mean?"

"That's right. Let me have the crackers."

Elizabeth passed the croutons. "That's a lot of money."

"We got a lot of money?"

"Well, yes, we do, but two hundred and ten thousand dollars. . . . Is it a new plant?"

"Just give me the check, Elizabeth. I've got a good surprise for you."

She stared at him. "You know I don't question your judgment but I must insist. . . ."

"All right. All right." Giovanni smiled. "You don't get a surprise. I tell you. . . . I'm going to be like a *barone*."

"A what?"

"A *barone*. A *conte*. You can be a *contessa*!"

"I simply don't understand. . . ."

"In Italy, a man who has a couple of fields, maybe a few pigs, he's practically a *barone*. Lots of men want to be *baroni*. I was talking to the East Island people. They're gonna sell me some meadows out on Long Island."

"Giovanni, they're worthless! They're simply the end of nowhere!"

"Woman, use your head! Already there's no place for the horses to stand. Tomorrow you give me the check. Don't argue, please. Just a smile and be the wife of a *barone*."

Elizabeth Scarlatti smiled.

Don Giovanni Merighi and Elizabeth Wyckham

Scarlatti of Ferrara

House of Ferrara d'Italia - American Residence

Delmonico - New York

Although Elizabeth did not take the cards seriously—they became a private joke between her and Giovanni—they did serve a purpose when not elaborated upon. They gave an identification befitting the Scarlatti wealth. Although no one who knew them ever referred to either as *conte* or *contessa*, there were many who weren't sure.

It was just possible. . . .

And one specific result—although the title did not appear on the cards—was that for the remainder of her long life Elizabeth was called madame.

Madame Elizabeth Scarlatti.

And Giovanni could no longer reach across the table and take his wife's bowl of soup.

Two years after the purchase of the land, on July 14, 1908, Giovanni Merighi Scarlatti died. The man was burnt out. And for weeks Elizabeth numbly tried to understand. There was no one to whom she could turn. She and Giovanni had been lovers, friends, partners, and each other's conscience. The thought of living without one another had been the only real fear in their lives.

But he was gone, and Elizabeth knew that they had not built an empire for one to see it collapse with the other's absence.

Her first order of business was to consolidate the management of the widespread Scarlatti Industries into a single command post.

Top executives and their families were uprooted throughout the Midwest and brought to New York. Charts were prepared for Elizabeth's approval clearly defining all levels of decisions and areas of specific responsibility. A private network of telegraphic communications was set up between the New York offices and each plant, factory, yard, and subdivision office. Elizabeth was a good general and her army was a well-trained, headstrong organization. The times were on her side, and her shrewd analysis of people took care of the rest.

A magnificent town house was built, a country estate purchased in Newport, another seaside retreat constructed in a development called Oyster Bay, and every week she held a series of exhausting meetings with the executives of her late husband's companies.

Among her most important actions was her decision to help her children become totally identified with Protestant democracy. Her reasoning was simple. The name Scarlatti was out of place, even crude, in the circles her sons had entered and in which they would continue to live for the rest of their lives. Their names were legally altered to Scarlett.

Of course, for herself, in deep respect for Don Giovanni and in the tradition of Ferrara, she remained:

Elizabeth

Scarlatti of Ferrara

No residence was listed for it was difficult to know at which home she would be at a given time.

Elizabeth recognized the unpleasant fact that her two older sons had neither Giovanni's gift of imagination nor her own perception of their fellow men. It was difficult to know with the youngest, Ulster Stewart, for Ulster Stewart Scarlett was emerging as a problem.

In his early years it was merely the fact that he was a bully—a trait Elizabeth ascribed to his being the youngest, the most spoiled. But as he grew into his teens, Ulster's outlook changed subtly. He not only had to have his own way, he now demanded it. He was the only one of the brothers who used his wealth with cruelty. With brutality, perhaps, and that concerned Elizabeth. She first encountered this attitude on his thirteenth birthday. A few days before the event his teacher sent her a note.

Dear Madame Scarlatti:
Ulster's birthday invitations seem to have become a minor problem. The dear boy can't make up his mind who are his best friends—he has so many—and as a result he has given out a number of invitations and taken them back in favor of other boys. I'm sure the Parkleigh School would waive the twenty-five limit in Ulster Stewart's case.

That night Elizabeth asked Ulster about it.
"Yes. I took some of the invitations back. I changed my mind."
"Why? That's very discourteous."
"Why not? I didn't want them to come."
"Then why did you give them the invitations in the first place?"
"So they could all run home and tell their fathers and mothers they were coming over." The boy laughed. "Then they had to go back and say they weren't."
"That's terrible!"
"I don't think so. They don't want to come to my birthday party, they want to come to your house!"

While a freshman at Princeton, Ulster Stewart Scarlett displayed marked tendencies of hostility toward his brothers, his classmates, his teachers, and for Elizabeth the most unattractive, her servants. He was tolerated because he was the son of Elizabeth Scarlatti and for no other reason. Ulster was a monstrously spoiled young man, and Elizabeth knew she had to do something about it. In June of 1916 she ordered him to come home for a weekend, and told her son he had to take a job.
"I will not!"
"You *will*! You will *not* disobey me!"
And he didn't. Ulster spent the summer at the Hudson mill while his two brothers in Oyster Bay enjoyed the pleasures of Long Island Sound.
At the end of the summer, Elizabeth asked how he had done.
"You want the truth, Madame Scarlatti?" asked the youngish plant manager in Elizabeth's study one Saturday morning.
"Of course I do."
"It'll probably cost me my job."
"I doubt that."
"Very well, ma'am. Your son started out in raw baling as your ordered. It's a tough job but he's strong. . . . I yanked him out of there after he beat up a couple of men."
"Good Lord! Why wasn't I told?"

"I didn't know the circumstances. I thought that maybe the men had pushed him around. I didn't know."

"What did you find out?"

"The pushing was at the other end. . . . I put him in the upstairs presses and that was worse. He threatened the others, said he'd get them fired, made them do his work. He never let anyone forget who he was."

"You should have told me."

"I didn't know myself until the other week. Three men quit. We had to pay a dentist bill for one of them. Your son hit him with a lead strip."

"These are terrible things to hear. . . . Would you care to offer an opinion? Please, be frank. It will be to your advantage."

"Your son is big. He's a tough young fella. . . . But I'm not sure what else he is. I just have an idea he wants to start at the top and maybe that's what he should do. He's your son. His father built the mill."

"That gives him no such right. His father didn't start at the top!"

"Then maybe you should explain that to him. He doesn't seem to have much use for any of us."

"What you're saying is that my son has a birthright, a temper, certain animal strength . . . and no apparent talents. Am I correct?"

"If that costs me my job, I'll find another. Yes. I don't like your son. I don't like him at all."

Elizabeth studied the man carefully. "I'm not sure I do, either. You'll receive a raise starting next week."

Elizabeth sent Ulster Stewart back to Princeton that fall, and the day of his departure she confronted him with the summer's report.

"That dirty little Irish son of a bitch was out to get me! I knew that!"

"That dirty little Irish son of a bitch is an excellent plant manager."

"He lied! It's all lies!"

"It's the truth! He kept a number of men from pressing charges against you. You should be grateful for that."

"To hell with them! Groveling little snot-noses!"

"Your language is abhorrent! Who are you to call names? What have you contributed?"

"I don't have to!"

"Why? Because you're what you are? What are you? What extraordinary capabilities do you possess? I'd like to know."

"That's what you're looking for, isn't it? Isn't it!? What you can do, little man? What can you do to make money?"

"It's one measure of success."

"It's your only measure!"

"And you reject it?"

"You're damned right!"

"Then become a missionary."

"No, thanks!"

"Then don't cast aspersions at the marketplace. It takes a certain capability to survive there. Your father knew that."

"He knew how to maneuver. You think I haven't heard? How to manipulate, just like you!"

"He was a genius! He trained himself! What have you done? What have you ever done but live on what he provided? And you can't even do that graciously!"

"Shit!"

Elizabeth suddenly stopped for a moment, watching her son. "That's it! My God, that's it, isn't it? . . . You're frightened to death. You possess a great deal of arrogance but you have nothing—absolutely nothing—to be arrogant about! It must be very painful."

Her son raced out of the room, and Elizabeth sat for a long time pondering the exchange that had just taken place. She was genuinely afraid. Ulster was dangerous. He saw all around him the fruits of accomplishment without the talent or the ability to make his own contribution. He'd bear watching. Then she thought of all three sons. Shy, malleable Roland Wyckham; studious, precise Chancellor Drew; and the arrogant Ulster Stewart.

On April 6, 1917, the immediate answer was provided: America entered the World War.

The first to go was Roland Wyckham. He left his senior year at Princeton and sailed for France as Lieutenant Scarlett, AEF, Artillery. He was killed on his first day at the front.

The two remaining boys immediately made plans to avenge their brother's death. For Chancellor Drew the revenge had meaning; for Ulster Stewart it was an escape. And Elizabeth reasoned that she and Giovanni had not created an empire to have it terminated by war. One child must stay behind.

With cold calculation she commanded Chancellor Drew to remain a civilian. Ulster Stewart could go to war.

Ulster Stewart Scarlett sailed for France, had no mishaps at Cherbourg, and gave a fair account of himself at the front, especially at Meuse-Argonne. In the last days of the war he was decorated for bravery in action against the enemy.

Chapter Four

November 2, 1918

The Meuse-Argonne offensive was in its third or pursuit stage in the successful battle to break the Hindenburg line between Sedan and Mézières. The American First Army was deployed from Regneville to La Harasée in the Argonne Forest, a distance of some twenty miles. If the chief German supply lines in this sector were broken, the Kaiser's General Ludendorff would have no alternative but to sue for an armistice.

On November 2, the Third Army Corps under the command of General Robert Lee Bullard crashed through the demoralized German ranks on the right flank and took not only the territory but also eight thousand prisoners. Although other division commanders lived to dispute the conclusion, this breakthrough by the Third Army Corps signaled the final arrangements for the armistice a week later.

And for many in B Company, Fourteenth Battalion, Twenty-seventh Division, Third Corps, the performance of Second Lieutenant Ulster Scarlett was a superb example of the heroics that prevailed during those days of horror.

It started early in the morning. Scarlett's company had reached a field in front of a small forest of pine. The miniature forest was filled with Germans trying desperately to regroup under cover in order to execute an orderly retreat farther back into their own lines. The Americans dug three rows of shallow trenches to minimize their exposure.

Second Lieutenant Scarlett had one dug for himself just a bit deeper.

The captain of Scarlett's company did not like his second lieutenant, for the lieutenant was very good at issuing orders but very poor at executing them himself. Further, the captain suspected him of being less than enthusiastic about being shifted from a reserve division to the combat area. He also held it against his second lieutenant that throughout their reserve assignment—the major portion of their stay in France—he had been sought out by any number of ranking officers, all only too happy to have their photographs taken with him. It seemed to the captain that his second lieutenant was having a hell of a good time.

On this particular November morning, he was delighted to send him out on patrol.

"Scarlett. Take four men and scout out their positions."

"You're insane," said Scarlett laconically. "What positions? They're hightailing it out of the whole area."

"Did you hear what I said?"

"I don't give a God damn what you said. There's no point in a patrol."

Several of the men were sitting in the trenches watching the two officers.

"What's the matter, Lieutenant? No photographers around? No country club colonels to pat you on the back? Get four men and get out there."

"Go shag, *Captain*!"

"Are you disobeying your superior officer in the face of the enemy?"

Ulster Stewart looked at the smaller man with contempt. "Not disobeying. Just being insubordinate. Insulting, if you understand the term better. . . . I'm insulting you because I think you're stupid."

The captain reached for his holster, but Scarlett swiftly clamped his large hand on his superior's wrist.

"You don't shoot people for insubordination, *Captain*. It's not in the regulations. . . . I've got a better idea. Why waste four other men. . . ." He turned and glanced at the soldiers watching. "Unless four of you want to be candidates for Schnauzer bullets, I'll go myself."

The captain was stunned. He had no reply.

The men were similarly and gratefully surprised. Scarlett removed his hand from the captain's arm.

"I'll be back in half an hour. If not, I suggest you wait for some rear support. We're quite a bit ahead of the others."

Scarlett checked the magazine of his revolver and quickly crawled around the captain to the west flank, disappearing into the overgrown field.

The men mumbled to each other. They had misjudged the snotty lieutenant with all the fancy friends. The captain swore to himself and frankly hoped his second lieutenant would not return.

Which was precisely what Ulster Scarlett had in mind.

His plan was simple. He saw that about two hundred yards to the right of the wooded area in front of Company B was a clump of large rocks surrounded by autumn-foliaged trees. It was one of those rough-hewn spots that farmers can not dig out, so the fields were planted around it. Too small an area for any group but ample space for one or two individuals to hide themselves. He would make his way there.

As he crawled through the field, he came upon a number of dead infantrymen. The corpses had a strange effect upon him. He found himself removing personal items—wrist-watches, rings, tags. Ripping them off and dropping them seconds later. He wasn't sure why he did it. He felt like a ruler in some mythical kingdom, and these were his subjects.

After ten minutes he wasn't sure of the direction of his refuge. He raised his head just high enough to orient himself, saw the tips of some small trees, and knew he was headed toward his sanctuary. He hurried forward, elbows and knees pounding the soft earth.

Suddenly he came to the foot of several large pines. He was not in the rocky knoll but on the edge of the small forest his company planned to attack. His preoccupation with the dead enemy had caused him to see what he wanted to see. The small trees had actually been the tall pines above him.

He was about to crawl back into the field when he saw, about fifteen feet to his left, a machine gun with a German soldier propped up against the trunk of a tree. He drew his revolver and remained still. Either the German had not seen him or he was dead. The gun was pointed directly at him.

Then the German moved. Only slightly with his right arm. He was trying to reach his weapon but in too much pain to accomplish the task.

Scarlett rushed forward and fell upon the wounded soldier, trying to make as little noise as possible. He could not let the German fire or raise an alarm. Awkwardly he pulled the man away from the gun and pinned him on the ground. Not wanting to fire his revolver and draw attention to himself, he began to choke him. Fingers and thumbs on his throat, the German tried to speak.

"Amerikaner! Amerikaner! Iche ergebe mich!" He held his palms up in desperation and gestured behind him.

Scarlett partially released his grip. He whispered. "What? What do you want?" He let the German raise himself as much as he was able to. The man had been left to die with his weapon, holding off whatever assault came while the rest of his company retreated.

He pushed the German machine gun out of the wounded man's reach and, while alternately looking forward and backward, crawled several yards into the forest. All around were signs of evacuation. Gas masks, emptied knapsacks, even bandoliers of ammunition. Anything too heavy to carry easily.

They'd all gone.

He rose and walked back to the German soldier. Something was becoming very clear to Ulster Scarlett.

"Amerikaner! Es scheint fast zu Ende zu sein! Lass mich nach Hause gehen!"

Lieutenant Scarlett had made up his mind. The situation was perfect! More than perfect—it was extraordinary!

It would take an hour, perhaps longer, for the rest of the Fourteenth Battalion to reach the area. B Company's Captain Jenkins was so determined to be a hero he had run hell out of them. Advance! Advance! Advance!

But this was his—Scarlett's—way out! Maybe they'd jump a rank and make him a captain. Why not? He'd be a hero.

Only he wouldn't be there.

Scarlett withdrew his revolver and as the German screamed he shot him in the forehead. Then he leapt to the machine gun. He started firing.

First to the rear, then to the right, then to the left.

The crackling, shattering noise echoed throughout the forest. The bullets entering trees thumped with a terrible finality. The sound was overpowering.

And then Scarlett pointed the weapon in the direction of his own men. He pulled the trigger and held it steady, swinging the gun from one flank to the other, Scare the living Jesus out of them! Maybe kill a few!

Who cared?

He was a power of death.

He enjoyed it.

He was entitled to it.

He laughed.

He withdrew his pressed finger and stood up.

He could see the mounds of dirt several hundred yards to the west. Soon he would be miles away and out of it all!

Suddenly he had the feeling he was being watched! Someone was watching him! He withdrew his pistol once again and crouched to the earth.

Snap!

A twig, a branch, a crushed stone!

He crawled on his knees slowly, cautiously into the woods.

Nothing.

He allowed his imagination to take over his reason. The sound was the sound of a tree limb cracked by the machine-gun fire. The sound was the sound of that same limb falling to the ground.

Nothing.

Scarlett retreated, still unsure, to the edge of the woods. He quickly picked up the remains of the dead German's helmet and began to run back to Company B's position.

What Ulster Stewart did not know was that he *was* being watched. He was being watched intently. With incredulity.

A German officer, the blood on his forehead slowly congealing, stood upright hidden from the American by the trunk of a wide pine tree. He had been about to kill the Yank lieutenant—as soon as his enemy left the gun—when he saw the man suddenly turn his fire on his own men. His own troops.

His own troops!

He had the American in his Luger's sight but he did not wish to kill this man.

Not yet.

For the German officer, the last man of his company in that small forest—left for dead—knew precisely what the American was doing.

It was a classic example under maximum conditions.

An infantry point, a commissioned officer at that, turning his information to his own advantage against his own troops!

He could put himself out of range of combat and get a medal in the bargain!

The German officer would follow this American.

Lieutenant Scarlett was halfway back to Company B's position when he heard the noise behind him. He flung himself to the ground and slowly turned his body around. He tried to stare through the slightly weaving tall grass.

Nothing.

Or was there nothing?

There was a corpse not twenty feet away—face down. But there were corpses everywhere.

Scarlett didn't remember this one. He remembered only the faces. He saw only the faces. He didn't remember.

Why should he?

Corpses everywhere. How could he remember? A single body with its face down. There must be dozens like that. He just didn't notice them.

He was letting his imagination overwork again! It was dawn. . . . Animals would come out of the ground, out of the trees.

Maybe.

Nothing moved.

He got up and raced to the mounds of dirt—to Company B.

"Scarlett! My God, it's you!" said the captain, who was crouched in front of the first trench. "You're lucky we didn't shoot. We lost Fernald and Otis in the last fire! We couldn't return it because you were out there!"

Ulster remembered Fernald and Otis.

No loss. Not in exchange for his own escape.

He threw the German helmet he had carried from the forest to the ground. "Now, listen to me. I've wiped out one nest, but there are two others. They're waiting for us. I know where they are and I can get them. But you've got to stay put! Down! Fire off to the left in ten minutes after I leave!"

"Where are you going?" asked the captain in consternation.

"Back where I can do some good! Give me ten minutes and then start firing. Keep it up for at least three or four minutes, but for Christ's sake, shoot *left*. Don't kill me. I need the diversion." He abruptly stopped and before the captain could speak reentered the field.

Once in the tall grass, Scarlett sprung from one German corpse to another, grabbing the helmets off the lifeless heads. After he had five helmets, he lay on the ground and waited for the firing to commence.

The captain did his part. One would have thought they were back at Château-Thierry. In four minutes the firing stopped.

Scarlett rose and ran back to his company's lines. As he appeared with the helmets in his hand, the men broke into spontaneous cheers. Even the captain, whose resentment disappeared with his newfound admiration, joined his men.

"God damn it to hell, Scarlett! That was the bravest act I've seen in the war!"

"Not so fast," Scarlett demurred with a humility not in evidence before. "We're clear in front and on the left flank, but a couple of Krauts ran off to the right. I'm going after them."

"You don't have to. Let 'em go. You've done enough." Captain Jenkins revised his opinion of Ulster Scarlett. The young lieutenant had met his challenge.

"If you don't mind, sir, I don't think I have."

"What do you mean?"

"My brother. . . . Rolly was his name. The Krauts got him eight months ago. Let me go after them and you take the ground."

Ulster Scarlett disappeared back into the field.

He knew exactly where he was going.

A few minutes later the American lieutenant crouched by a large rock in his tiny island of stone and weeds. He waited for B Company to start its assault on the forest of pines. He leaned against the hard surface and looked up at the sky.

Then it came.

The men shouted to give themselves a touch more courage in the conceivable event they met the retreating enemy. Sporadic shots rang out. Several fingers were nervous. As the company reached the forest, a shattering volley from a score of rifles could be heard.

They were firing at dead men, thought Ulster Scarlett.

He was safe now.

For him the war was over.

"Stay where you are, *Amerikaner!*" the voice was thickly Germanic. "Don't move!"

Scarlett had reached for his pistol but the voice above him was emphatic. To touch his revolver meant death.

"You speak English." It was all Lieutenant Scarlett could think of to say.

"Reasonably well. Don't move! My gun is aimed at your skull. . . . The same area of the skull where you put a bullet into Corporal Kroeger."

Ulster Scarlett froze.

There *had* been someone! He *had* heard something! . . . The corpse in the field!

But why hadn't the German killed him?

"I did what I had to do." Again it was the only thing Scarlett could think of to say.

"I'm sure of that. Just as I am sure you had no alternative but to fire on your own troops. . . . You have . . . very strange concepts of your calling in this war, do you not?"

Scarlett was beginning to understand.

"This war . . . is over."

"I have a degree in military strategy from the Imperial Staff school in Berlin. I'm aware of our impending defeat. . . . Ludendorff will have no choice once the Mézières line is broken."

"Then why kill me?"

The German officer came from behind the huge rock and faced Ulster Scarlett, his pistol pointed at the American's head. Scarlett saw that he was a man not much older than himself, a young man with broad shoulders—like himself. Tall—like himself, with a confident look in his eyes, which were bright blue—like his own.

"We can be out of it, for Christ's sake! We can be out of it! Why the hell should we sacrifice each other? Or even one of us. . . . I can help you, you know!"

"Can you really?"

Scarlett looked at his captor. He knew he could not plead, could not show weakness. He had to remain calm, logical. "Listen to me. . . . If you're picked up, you'll be put in a camp with thousands of others. That is, if you're not shot. I wouldn't count on any officers' privileges if I were you. It'll take weeks, months, maybe a year or longer before they get to you! Before they let you go!"

"And you can change all this?"

"You're damned right I can!"

"But why would you?"

"Because I want to be out of it! . . . And so do you! . . . If you didn't, you would have killed me by now. . . . We need each other."

"What do you propose?"

"You're my prisoner. . . ."

"You think me insane?"

"Keep your pistol! Take the bullets out of mine. . . . If anyone comes across us, I'm taking you back for interrogation . . . far back. Until we can get you some clothes. . . . If we can get to Paris, I'll get you money."

"How?"

Ulster Scarlett grinned a confident smile. The smile of wealth. "That's my business. . . . What choice have you got? . . . Kill me and you're a prisoner anyway. Maybe a dead man. And you haven't much time. . . ."

"Get up! Put your arms out against the rock!"

Scarlett complied as the German officer took Scarlett's revolver out of his holster and removed the cartridges.

"Turn around!

"In less than an hour others'll be coming up. We were an advance company but not that far ahead."

The German waved his pistol at Scarlett. "There are several farmhouses about a kilometer and a half southwest. Move! *Mach schnell!*" With his left hand he thrust Scarlett's empty revolver at him.

The two men ran across the fields.

The artillery to the north began its early morning barrage. The sun had broken through the clouds and the mist and was now bright.

About a mile to the southwest was a cluster of buildings. A barn and two small stone houses. It was necessary to cross a wide dirt road to reach the overgrown pasture, fenced for livestock, which were not now in evidence. Chimney smoke curled from the larger of the two houses.

Someone had a fire going and that meant someone had food, warmth. Someone had supplies.

"Let's get into that shack," said Ulster.

"*Nein!*" Your troops will be coming through."

"For Christ's sake, we've got to get you some clothes. Can't you see that?"

The German clicked the hammer of his Luger into firing position. "You're inconsistent. I thought you proposed taking me back—far back—through your own lines for interrogation? . . . It might be simpler to kill you now."

"Only until we could get you clothes! If I've got a Kraut officer in tow, there's nothing to prevent some fat-ass captain figuring out the same thing I have! Or a major or a colonel who wants to get the hell out of the area. . . . It's been done before. All they have to do is order me to turn you over and that's it! . . . If you're in civilian clothes, I can get us through easier. There's so damned much confusion!"

The German slowly released the hammer of his revolver, still staring at the lieutenant. "You really do want this war to be over for you, don't you?"

Inside the stone house was an old man, hard of hearing, confused and frightened by the strange pair. With little pretense, holding the unloaded revolver, the American lieutenant ordered the man to pack a supply of food and find clothes—any clothes for his "prisoner."

As Scarlett's French was poor, he turned to his captor. "Why don't you tell him we're both German? . . . We're trapped. We're trying to escape through the lines. Every Frenchman knows we're breaking through everywhere."

The German officer smiled. "I've already done that. It will add to the confusion. . . . You will be amused to learn that he said he presumed as much. Do you know why he said that?"

"Why?"

"He said we both had the filthy smell of the Boche about us."

The old man, who had edged near the open door, suddenly dashed outside and began—feebly—running toward the field.

"Jesus Christ! Stop him! God damn it, stop him!" yelled Scarlett.

The German officer, however, already had his pistol raised. "Don't be alarmed. He saves us making an unpleasant decision."

Two shots were fired.

The old man fell, and the young enemies looked at each other.

"What should I call you?" asked Scarlett.

"My own name will do. Strasser. . . . Gregor Strasser."

It was not difficult for the two officers to make their way through the Allied lines. The American push out of Regneville was electrifyingly swift, a headlong rush. But totally disconnected in its chain of command. Or so it seemed to Ulster Scarlett and Gregor Strasser.

At Reims the two men came across the remnants of the French Seventeenth Corps, bedraggled, hungry, weary of it all.

They had no trouble at Reims. The French merely shrugged shoulders after uninterested questions.

They headed west to Villers-Cotterêts, the roads to Epernay and Meaux jammed with upcoming supplies and replacements.

Let the other poor bastards take your deathbed bullets, thought Scarlett.

The two men reached the outskirts of Villers-Cotterêts at night. They left the road and cut across a field to the shelter of a cluster of trees.

"We'll rest there for a few hours," Strasser said. "Make no attempt to escape. I shall not sleep."

"You're crazy, sport! I need you as much as you need me! . . . A lone American officer forty miles from his company, which just happens to be at the front! Use your head!"

"You are persuasive, but I am not like our enfeebled imperial generals. I do not listen to empty, convincing arguments. I watch my flanks."

"Suit yourself. It's a good sixty miles from Cotterêts to Paris and we don't know what we're going to run into. We're going to need sleep. . . . We'd be smarter to take turns."

"*Jawohl!*" said Strasser with a contemptuous laugh. "You talk like the Jew bankers in Berlin. 'You do *this*. We'll do *that*! Why *argue*?' Thank you, no, *Amerikaner*. I shall not sleep."

"Whatever you say." Scarlett shrugged. "I'm beginning to understand why you guys lost the war." Scarlett rolled over on his side. "You're stubborn about being stubborn."

For a few minutes neither man spoke. Finally Gregor Strasser answered the American in a quiet voice. "We did not lose the war. We were betrayed."

"Sure. The bullets were blanks and your artillery backfired. I'm going to sleep."

The German officer spoke softly, as if to himself. "Many bullets were in empty cartridges. Many weapons did malfunction. . . . Betrayal. . . ."

Along the road several trucks lumbered out of Villers-Cotterêts followed by horses pulling caissons. The lights of the trucks danced flickeringly up and down. The animals whinnied; a few soldiers shouted at their charges.

More poor, stupid bastards, thought Ulster Scarlett as he watched from his sanctuary. "Hey, Strasser, what happens now?" Scarlett turned to his fellow deserter.

"Was ist?" Strasser had catnapped. He was furious with himself. "You speak?"

"Just wanted you to know I could have jumped you. . . . I asked you what happens now? I mean to you? . . . I know what happens to us. Parades, I guess. What about you?"

"No parades. No celebrations. . . . Much weeping. Much recrimination. Much drunkenness. . . . Many will be desperate. . . . Many will be killed also. You may be assured of that."

"Who? Who's going to be killed?"

"The traitors among us. They will be searched out and destroyed without mercy."

"You're crazy! I said you were crazy before and now I know it!"

"What would you have us do? You haven't been infected yet. But you will be! . . . The Bolsheviks! They are at our borders and they infiltrate! They eat away at our core! They rot inside us! . . . And the Jews! The Jews in Berlin make fortunes out of this war! The filthy Jew profiteers! The conniving Semites sell us out today, you tomorrow! . . . The Jews, the Bolsheviks, the stinking little people! We are all their victims and we do not know it! We fight each other when we should be fighting them!"

Ulster Scarlett spat. The son of Scarlatti was not interested in the problems of ordinary men. Ordinary men did not concern him.

And yet he was troubled.

Strasser was not an ordinary man. The arrogant German officer hated the ordinary man as much as he did. "What are you going to do when you shovel these people under ground? Play king of the mountain?"

"Of many mountains. . . . Of many, many mountains."

Scarlett rolled over away from the German officer.

But he did not close his eyes.

Of many, many mountains.

Ulster Scarlett had never thought of such a domain. . . . Scarlatti made millions upon millions but Scarlatti did not rule. Especially the sons of Scarlatti. They would never rule. . . . Elizabeth had made that clear.

"Strasser?"

"Ja?"

"Who are these people? Your people?"

"Dedicated men. Powerful men. The names can not be spoken of. Committed to rise out of defeat and unite the elite of Europe."

Scarlett turned his face up to the sky. Stars flickered through the low-flying gray clouds. Gray, black, dots of shimmering white.

"Strasser?"

"Was ist?"

"Where will you go? After it's over, I mean."

"To Heidenheim. My family lives there."

"Where is it?"

"Halfway between Munich and Stuttgart." The German officer looked at the strange, huge American deserter. Deserter, murderer, aider and abettor of his enemy.

"We'll be in Paris tomorrow night. I'll get you your money. There's a man in Argenteuil who keeps money for me."

"Danke."

Ulster Scarlett shifted his body. The earth was next to his face, and the smell was clean.

"Just . . . Strasser, Heidenheim. That's all?"

"That's all."

"Give me a name, Strasser."

"What do you mean? Give you a name?"

"Just that. A name you'll know is me when I get in touch with you."

Strasser thought for a moment. "Very well, *Amerikaner*. Let's choose a name you should find hard to forget—Kroeger."

"Who?"

"Kroeger—Corporal Heinrich Kroeger, whose head you shot off in the Meuse-Argonne."

On November 10 at three o'clock in the afternoon the cease-fire order went out.

Ulster Stewart Scarlett bought a motorcycle and began his swift journey to La Harasée and beyond. To B Company, Fourteenth Battalion.

He arrived in the area where most of the battalion was bivouacked and started to search for the company. It was difficult. The camp was filled with drunken, glassy-eyed, foul-breathed soldiers of every description. The order-of-the-early-morning was mass alcoholic hysteria.

Except for Company B.

B Company was holding a religious service. A commemoration for a fallen comrade.

For Lieutenant Ulster Stewart Scarlett, AEF.

Scarlett watched.

Captain Jenkins finished reading the beautiful Psalm for the Dead in a choked voice and then led the men in the Lord's Prayer.

"Our Father Who art in heaven . . ." Some of the men were weeping unashamedly.

It was a pity to spoil it all, thought Scarlett.

His citation read in part:

> . . . after single-handedly destroying three enemy machine-gun nests, he took out in pursuit of a fourth dangerous emplacement, destroying that also and thereby saving many Allied lives. He did not return and was presumed dead. However, until the fighting ceased a week hence, Second Lieutenant Scarlett provided B Company with an inspiring cry of battle. "For Old Rolly!" struck terror in the hearts of many an enemy. Through God's infinite wisdom, Second Lieutenant Scarlett rejoined his platoon the day following the cessation of hostilities. Exhausted and weak, he returned to glory. Through presidential order we hereby bestow . . .

Chapter Five

Back in New York, Ulster Stewart Scarlett discovered that being a hero let him do precisely as he wished. Not that he had been confined, far from it, but now even the minor restrictions such as punctuality and the normal acceptance of routine social courtesies were no longer expected of him. He had faced the supreme test of man's existence—the encounter with death. True, there were thousands like him in these respects but few were officially designated heroes, and none was a Scarlett. Elizabeth, startled beyond words, lavished upon him everything that money and power could make available. Even Chancellor Drew referred to his young brother as the male leader of the family.

And so into the twenties bounded Ulster Stewart Scarlett.

From the pinnacles of society to the owners of speakeasies, Ulster Stewart was a welcome friend. He contributed neither much wit nor a great deal of understanding and yet his contribution was something very special. He was a man in working sympathy with his environment. His demands from life were certainly unreasonable but these were unreasonable times. The seeking of pleasure, the avoidance of pain, the enjoyment of existing without ambition were all that he seemed to require.

Seemed to require.

But not what Heinrich Kroeger required at all.

They corresponded twice a year. Strasser's letters addressed to a general post office box in mid-Manhattan.

April, 1920

My dear Kroeger:

It is official. We have given a name and a new life to the defunct Workers party. We are the National Socialist German Workers party—and, please, my dear Kroeger, don't take the words too seriously. It is a magnificent beginning. We attract so many. The Versailles restrictions are devastating. They reduce Germany to rubble. And yet it is good. It is good for us. The people are angry, they lash out not only at the victors—but at those who betrayed us from within.

June, 1921

Dear Strasser:

You have Versailles, we have the Volstead! And it's good for us, too. . . . Everyone's getting a slice of the pie and I'm not missing my share—our share! Everybody wants a favor, a payoff—a shipment! You have to know the right people. In a short time I'll be the "right people." I'm not interested in the money—screw the money! Leave that for the kikes and the greasers! I'm getting something else! Something far more important. . . .

January, 1922

My dear Kroeger:

It is all so slow. So painfully slow when it could be different. The depression is unbelievable and getting worse. Trunkfuls of currency virtually worthless. Adolf Hitler has literally assumed the position of chairman of the party over Ludendorff. You recall I once said to you that there were names I could not speak of? Ludendorff was one. I do not trust Hitler. There is something cheap about him, something opportunistic.

October, 1922

Dear Strasser:

It was a good summer and it'll be a better fall and a great winter! This Prohibition was tailor-made! It's madness! Have a little money up front and you're in business! . . . And what business! My organization is growing. The machinery is just the way you'd like it—perfect.

July, 1923

My dear Kroeger:
I am concerned. I have moved north and you can reach me at the address below. Hitler is a fool. The Ruhr take-over by Poincaré was his chance to unite all of Bavaria—politically. The people are ready. But they want order, not chaos. Instead, Hitler rants and raves and uses the old fool Ludendorff to give him stature. He will do something insane, I feel it. I wonder if there's room in the party for both of us? There is great activity in the north. A Major Buchrucker has formed the Black Reichswehr, a large armed force that may find sympathy with our cause. I meet with Buckrucker shortly. We'll see.

September, 1923

Dear Strasser:
Since last October it's been a better year than I ever thought possible! It's funny—but a person can find something in his past, something he may hate—and realize it's the best weapon he's got. I have. I lead two lives and neither meets the other! It is a brilliant manipulation if I do say so myself! I think you would be pleased that you didn't kill your friend Kroeger in France.

December, 1923

My dear Kroeger:
I head south immediately! Munich was a disaster. I warned them not to attempt a forcible putsch. It has to be political—but they would not listen. Hitler will draw a long jail sentence, in spite of our "friends." God knows what will happen to poor old Ludendorff? Buchrucker's Black Reichswehr has been destroyed by von Seeckt. Why? We all want the same thing. The depression is nothing short of catastrophic now. Always it is the wrong people who fight each other. The Jews and the Communists enjoy it all, no doubt. It is an insane country.

April, 1924

Dear Strasser:
I've had my first contact with any real difficulty—but it's under control now. Remember, Strasser? Control. . . . The problem is a simple one—too many people are after the same thing. Everyone wants to be the big cheese! There's plenty for everybody but no one believes that. It's very much as you describe—the people who shouldn't fight each other are doing just that. Nevertheless, I've nearly accomplished what I set out to do. Soon I'll have a list of thousands! Thousands! Who'll do as we want!

January, 1925

My dear Kroeger:
This is my last letter. I write from Zurich. Since Herr Hitler's release he has once again assumed leadership of the party and I confess there are deep divisions between us. Perhaps they will be resolved. I, too, have my followers. To the point. We are all of us under the strongest

surveillance. The Weimar is frightened of us—as well it should be. I am convinced my mail, my telephone, my every action is scrutinized. No more chances. But the time approaches. A bold plan is being conceived and I have taken the liberty of suggesting Heinrich Kroeger's inclusion. It is a master plan, a fantastic plan. You are to contact the Marquis Jacques Louis Bertholde of Bertholde et Fils, London. By mid-April. The only name he knows—as myself—is Heinrich Kroeger.

A gray-haired man of sixty-three sat at his desk looking out the window over K Street in Washington. His name was Benjamin Reynolds and in two years he would retire. Until that time, however, he was responsible for the functions of an innocuous-sounding agency attached to the Department of the Interior. The agency was titled Field Services and Accounting. To less than five hundred people, it was known simply as Group Twenty.

The agency got its shortened name from its origins: a group of twenty field accountants sent out by Interior to look into the growing conflicts of interest between those politicians allocating federal funds and those of the electorate receiving them.

With America's entry into the war and the overnight industrial expansion necessary to sustain the war effort, Group Twenty became an overworked unit. The awarding of munitions and armament contracts to businesses throughout the country demanded an around-the-clock scrutiny beyond the capabilities of the limited number of field accountants. However, rather than expand the silent agency, it was decided to use it only in the most sensitive—or embarrassing—areas. There were a sufficient number of these. And the field accountants were specialists.

After the war there was talk of disbanding Group Twenty, but each time such action was considered problems arose that required its talents. Generally they were problems involving highly placed public servants who dipped a bit too greedily into the public jewel box. But in isolated cases Group Twenty assumed duties shunned by other departments for any number of reasons.

Such as the Treasury Department's reluctance to pursue a vapor called Scarlatti.

"Why, Glover?" asked the gray-haired man. "The question is why? Assuming there's an ounce of prosecutable proof, why?"

"Why does anyone break a law?" A man roughly ten years younger than Reynolds answered him with another question. "For profit. And there's a lot of profit in Prohibition."

"No! God damn it to hell, no!" Reynolds spun around in his chair and slammed his pipe on the desk blotter. "You're wrong! This Scarlatti has more money than our combined imaginations can conceive of. It's like saying the Mellons are going to open a bookmaking parlor in Philadelphia. It doesn't make sense. . . . Join me in a drink?"

It was after five and Group Twenty's staff was gone for the day. Only the man named Glover and Ben Reynolds remained.

"You shock me, Ben," Glover said with a grin.

"Then to hell with you. I'll save it for myself."

"You do that and I'll turn you in. . . . Good stuff?"

"Right off the boat from old Blighty, they tell me." Reynolds took a leather-bound flask out of his top drawer and two water glasses from a desk tray and poured.

"If you rule out profits, what the devil have you got left, Ben?"

"Damned if I know," replied the older man, drinking.

"What are you going to do? I gather no one else wants to do anything."

"Yes, siree! That is no, siree! Nobody wants to touch this. . . . Oh, they'll go after Mr. Smith and Mr. Jones with a vengeance. They'll prosecute the hell out of some poor slob in East Orange, New Jersey, with a case in his basement. But not this one!"

"You lost me, Ben."

"This is the Scarlatti Industries! This is big, powerful friends on the Hill! Remember, Treasury needs money, too. It gets it up there."

"What do you want to do, Ben?"

"I want to find out why the mammoth's tusk is plunging into bird feed."

"How?"

"With Canfield. He's partial to bird feed himself, the poor son of a bitch."

"He's a good man, Ben." Glover did not like the sound of Reynold's invective. He liked Matthew Canfield. He thought he was talented, quick. There but for the money to complete an education was a young man with a future. Too good for government service. A lot better than either of them. . . . Well, better than himself, better than a man named Glover who didn't care anymore. There weren't many people better than Reynolds.

Benjamin Reynolds looked up at his subordinate. He seemed to be reading his thoughts. "Yes, he's a good man. . . . He's in Chicago. Go out and call him. His routing must be somewhere."

"I have it in my desk."

"Then get him in here by tomorrow night."

Chapter Six

Matthew Canfield, field accountant, lay in his Pullman berth, and smoked the next to last thin cigar in his pack. They had no thin cigars on the New York–Chicago Limited and he inhaled each breath of smoke with a degree of sacrifice.

In the early morning he would reach New York, transfer to the next train south, and be in Washington ahead of schedule. That would make a better impression on Reynolds than arriving in the evening. That would show that he, Canfield, could close a problem quickly, with no loose ends left dangling. Of course, with his current assignment it wasn't difficult. He had completed it several days ago but had remained in Chicago as the guest of the senator he had been sent to confront about payroll allocations to nonexistent employees.

He wondered why he had been called back to Washington. He always wondered why he was called back. Probably because he believed deeply that it was never just another job but, instead, that someday, somehow Washington would be on to him. Group Twenty would be on to him.

They would confront him.

With evidence.

But it was unlikely. It hadn't happened. Matthew Canfield was a professional—minor level, he granted to himself—but still a professional. And he had no regrets whatsoever. He was entitled to every wooden nickel he could dig up.

Why not? He never took much. He and his mother deserved *something*. It had been a federal court in Tulsa, Oklahoma, which had pasted the sheriff's notice on his father's store. A federal judge who had rendered the determination—Involuntary Bankruptcy. The federal government hadn't listened to any explanations other than the fact that his father no longer had the ability to pay his debts.

For a quarter of a century a man could work, raise a family, get a son off to the state university—so many dreams fulfilled, only to be destroyed with the single banging of a wooden gavel upon a small marble plate in a courtroom.

Canfield had no regrets.

"You have a new occupation to get under your belt, Canfield. Simple procedures. Not difficult."

"Fine, Mr. Reynolds. Always ready."

"Yes. I know you are. . . . You start in three days at pier thirty-seven in New York City. Customs. I'll fill you in as best I can."

But, of course, Benjamin Reynolds did not "fill in" Matthew Canfield as thoroughly as he might have. He wanted Canfield to "fill in" the spaces he, Reynolds, left blank. The Scarlatti *padrone* was operating out of the West Side piers—middle numbers—that much they knew. But someone had to see him. Someone had to identify him. Without being told.

That was very important.

And if anyone could do that it would be someone like Matthew Canfield, who seemed to gravitate to the nether world of the payoff, the bribe, the corrupt.

He did.

On the night shift of January 3, 1925.

Matthew Canfield, customs inspector, checked the invoices of the steamer *Genoa-Stella* and waved to the shake-up foreman to start unloading hold one of its crates of Como wool.

And then it happened.

At first an argument. Then a hook fight.

The *Genoa-Stella* crew would not tolerate a breach of unloading procedures. Their orders came from someone else. Certainly not from the American customs officials.

Two crates plummeted down from the cranes, and underneath the straw packing the stench of uncut alcohol was unmistakable.

The entire pier force froze. Several men then raced to phone booths and a hundred apelike bodies swarmed around the crates ready to fend off intruders with their hooks.

The first argument was forgotten. The hook fight was forgotten.

The contraband was their livelihood and they would die defending it.

Canfield, who had raced up the stairs to the glass-enclosed booth high above the pier, watched the angry crowd. A shouting match began between the men on the loading dock and the sailors of the *Genoa-Stella*. For fifteen minutes the opponents yelled at each other, accompanying their shouts with obscene gestures. But no one drew a weapon. No one threw a hook or knife. They were waiting.

Canfield realized that no one in the customs office made any move to call the authorities. "For Christ's sake! Someone get the police down!"

There was silence from the four men in the room with Canfield.

"Did you hear me? Call the police!"

Still the silence of the frightened men wearing the uniforms of the Customs Service.

Finally one man spoke. He stood by Matthew Canfield, looking out the glass partition at the gangster army below. "No one calls the police, young fella. Not if you want to show up at the docks tomorrow."

"Show up anywhere tomorrow," added another man, who calmly sat down and picked up a newspaper from his tiny desk.

"Why not? Somebody down there could get killed!"

"They'll settle it themselves," said the older customs man.

"What port did you come from again? . . . Erie? . . . You must have had different rules. Lake shipping has different rules. . . ."

"That's a lot of crap!"

A third man wandered over to Canfield. "Look, hick, just mind your own business, all right?"

"What the hell kind of talk is that? I mean, just what the hell kind of talk is that?"

"C'mere, hick." The third man, whose thin body and narrow face seemed lost in his loose-fitting uniform, took Canfield by the elbow and walked him to a corner. The others pretended not to notice but their eyes kept darting over to the two men. They were concerned, even worried. "You got a wife and kids?" the thin man asked quietly.

"No. . . . So what?"

"We do. That's what." The thin man put his hand into his pocket and withdrew several bills. "Here. Here's sixty bucks. . . . Just don't rock the boat, huh? . . . Calling the cops wouldn't do no good, anyhow. . . . They'd rat on you."

"Jesus! Sixty dollars!"

"Two weeks' pay, kid. Have a party."

"Okay. . . . Okay, I will."

"Here they come, Jesse." The older guard by the window spoke softly to the man next to Canfield.

"C'mon, hick. Get an education," said the man with the money, leading Canfield to the window overlooking the interior of the pier.

Down at the street-loading entrance, Canfield saw that two large automobiles, one behind the other, had pulled up—the first car halfway into the building. Several men in dark overcoats had gotten out of the lead car and were walking towards the phalanx of dock workers surrounding the damaged crates.

"What are they doing?"

"They're the goons, kid," answered the guard named Jesse. "They muscle."

"Muscle what?"

"Hah!" came a guttural laugh from the man at the tiny desk with the newspaper.

"They muscle what has to be put in line. No what—who!"

The men in overcoats—five in all—began wandering up to the various stevedores and talking quietly. Cheek to cheek, thought Canfield. With a few, they shoved them humorously and patted their thick necks. They were like zoo keepers, pacifying their animals. Two of the men walked up the gangplank onto the ship. The head man, who wore a white felt fedora and was now the central figure of the remaining three on the pier, looked back toward the automobiles and then up at the glass-enclosed booth. He nodded his head and started towards the stairs. The guard, Jesse, spoke.

"I'll handle this. Everyone stay put."

He opened the door and waited on the steel platform for the man in the white fedora.

Canfield could see the two men talking through the glass. The white fedora was smiling, even obsequious. But there was a hard look in his eyes, a serious look in his eyes. And then he seemed concerned, angry, and the two men looked into the office.

They looked at Matthew Canfield.

The door was opened by Jesse. "You. Cannon. Mitch Cannon, c'mere."

It was always easier to use a cover having one's own initials. You never could tell who'd send you a Christmas gift.

Canfield walked out onto the steel platform as the man in the white fedora descended the stairs to the cement floor of the pier.

"You go down and sign the search papers."

"The hell you say, buddy!"

"I said go down and sign the papers! They want to know you're clean." And then Jesse smiled. "The big boys are here. . . . You'll get another little dividend. . . . But I get fifty percent, understand?"

"Yeah," Cannon said reluctantly. "I understand." He started down the steps looking at the man who waited for him.

"New here, huh?"

"Yeah."

"Where ya' from?"

"Lake Erie. Lot of action in Lake Erie."

"What d'ya work?"

"Canadian stuff. What else? . . . Good hooch that Canadian stuff."

"We import wool! Como wool!"

"Yeah, sure, friend. In Erie it's Canadian pelts, fabric. . . ." Canfield winked at the waterfront subaltern. "Good soft packing, huh?"

"Look, fella. Nobody needs a wise guy."

"Okay. . . . Like I said. Wool."

"Come over to the dispatchers. . . . You sign for the loads."

Canfield walked with the large man to the dispatcher's booth where a second man thrust a clipboard filled with papers at him.

"Write clear and mark the dates and times perfect!" ordered the man in the booth.

After Canfield had complied, the first man spoke. "Okay. . . . C'mon with me." He led Canfield over to the automobiles. The field accountant could see two men talking in the back seat of the second vehicle. No one but a driver remained in the first car. "Wait here."

Canfield wondered why he had been singled out. Had anything gone wrong in Washington? There hadn't been enough time for anything to go wrong.

There was a commotion from the pier. The two goons who had boarded the ship were escorting a man in uniform down the gangplank. Canfield saw that it was the captain of the Genoa-Stella.

The man in the white fedora was now leaning into the window talking with the two men in the second car. They hadn't noticed the noise from the pier. The large man opened the car door and a short, very dark Italian stepped out. He was no more than five feet three.

The short man beckoned the field accountant to come over. He reached into his coat pocket, took out a billfold, and withdrew several bills from it. His speech was heavily accented. "You a new man?"

"Yes, sir."

"Lake Erie? That's right?"

"Yes, sir."

"What's name?"

"Cannon."

The Italian looked at the man in the white fedora.

The man shrugged. "Non conosco. . . ."

"Here." He handed Canfield two fifty-dollar bills. "You be a good boy. . . . We take care of good boys, don't we, Maggiore? . . . We also take care of boys who ain't so good. . . . *Capisce*?"

"You bet! Thanks very . . ."

It was as far as the field accountant got. The two men escorting the *Genoa-Stella* captain had reached the first automobile. They were now forcibly holding him, propelling him against his will.

"Lascia mi! Lascia mi! Maiali!" The captain tried to break the grip of the two hoodlums. He swung his shoulders back and forth but to no avail.

The small Italian brushed Canfield aside as the goons brought the captain up to him. The ship's officer and his two captors started shouting at the same time. The Italian listened and stared at the captain.

And then the other man, the man who remained in the back seat of the second automobile, leaned forward toward the window, half hidden in the shadows.

"What's the matter? What are they yelling about, Vitone?"

"This *comandante* doesn't like the way we do business, *Padrone*. He says he won't let us unload no more."

"Why not?"

"Si rifiuti!" shouted the captain, sensing what was being said though not understanding the words.

"He says he don't see anyone he knows. He says we don't have no rights with his ship! He wants to make telephone calls."

"I'll bet he does," the man in shadow said quietly. "I know just who he wants to call."

"You gonna let him?" asked the short Italian.

"Don't be foolish, Vitone. . . . Talk nice. Smile. Wave back at the ship. All of you! . . . That's a powder keg back there, you imbeciles! . . . Let them think everything's fine."

"Sure. Sure, *Padrone*."

All of them laughed and waved except the captain, who furiously tried to release his arms. The effect was comic, and Canfield found himself nearly smiling except that the face in the automobile window was now in his direct line of sight. The field accountant saw that it was a good-looking face—striking would be the word. Although the face was somewhat obscured by the wide brim of a hat, Canfield noticed that the features were sharp, aquiline, clean-cut. What particularly struck the field accountant were the eyes.

They were very light blue eyes. Yet he was addressed by the Italian "*padrone*." Canfield assumed there were Italians with blue eyes but he had never met any. It was unusual.

"What do we do, *Padrone*?" asked the short man who had given Canfield the hundred dollars.

"What else, sport? He's a visitor to our shores, isn't he? Be courteous, Vitone. . . . Take the captain outside and let him . . . make his phone calls." Then the man with the light blue eyes lowered his voice. "And kill him!"

The small Italian nodded his head slightly in the direction of the pier entrance. The two men on each side of the uniformed officer pushed him forward, out the large door into the darkness of the night.

"Chiama le nostri amici . . ." said the goon on the captain's right arm.

But the captain resisted. Once outside, in the dim spill of the door's light, Canfield could see that he began violently thrashing his body against both escorts until the one on the left lost his balance. The captain then swung into the other man with both fists, shouting at him in Italian.

The man who had been shoved away regained his balance, and took something out of his pocket. Canfield couldn't distinguish its shape.

Then Canfield saw what it was.

A knife.

The man behind the captain plunged it into the officer's unguarded back.

Matthew Canfield pulled the visor of his customs cap down and began walking away from the automobiles. He walked slowly, casually.

"Hey! You! You! Customs!" It was the blue-eyed man from the back seat.

"You! Lake Erie!" the short Italian yelled.

Canfield turned. "I didn't see anything. Not a thing. Nothin'!" He tried to smile but no smile would come.

The man with the light blue eyes stared at him as Canfield squinted and pinched his face below the visor of his cap. The short Italian nodded to the driver of the first car.

The driver got out and came behind the field accountant.

"Porta lui fuori vicin' a l'acqua! Sensa fuccide! Corteddo!" said the short man.

The driver pushed Canfield in the small of the back toward the pier entrance. "Hey, c'mon! I didn't see nothin'! What d'you want with me! . . . . C'mon, for Christ's sake!"

Matthew Canfield didn't have to be given an answer. He knew exactly what they wanted from him. His insignificant life.

The man behind him kept pushing, nudging him onward. Around the building. Along the deserted side of the pier.

Two rats scampered several yards in front of Canfield and his executioner. The growing sounds of arguments could be heard behind the walls of the cargo area. The Hudson River slapped against the huge pylons of the dock.

Canfield stopped. He wasn't sure why but he couldn't simply keep walking. The pain in his stomach was the pain of fear.

"A lesta chi! . . . Keep movin'!" said the man, poking a revolver into Canfield's ribs.

"Listen to me." Gone was Canfield's attempt to roughen his voice. "I'm a government man! You do anything to me, they'll get you! You won't get any protection from your friends when they find out. . . ."

"Keep movin'!"

A ship's horn sounded from the middle of the river. Another responded.

Then came a long, screeching, piercing whistle. It came from the *Genoa-Stella*. It was a signal, a desperate signal, which did not let up. The pitch of its scream was ear shattering.

It distracted—as it had to—the man with the gun beside Canfield.

The field accountant lashed out at the man's wrist and held it, twisted it with all his strength. The man reached up to Canfield's face and clawed at the sockets of his eyes while pushing him toward the steel wall of the building. Canfield gripped the wrist harder, harder, and then with his other hand clutched at the man's overcoat and pulled him toward the wall—the same direction the man was pushing—turning at the last second so that his executioner slammed into the steel.

The gun flew out of the Sicilian's hand and Canfield brought his knee crashing up into the man's groin.

The Italian screamed a guttural cry of anguish. Canfield threw him downward and the man lunged, writhing, across the deck to the edge of the pier, curled up in agony. The field accountant grabbed his head and slammed it repeatedly against the thick wood. The skin broke and blood came pouring out of the man's skull.

It was over in less than a minute.

Matthew Canfield's executioner was dead.

The shrieking whistle from the *Genoa-Stella* kept up its now terrifying blast. The shouting from within the pier's loading area had reached a crescendo.

Canfield thought that the ship's crew must have openly revolted, must have demanded orders from their captain, and when they did not come, assumed him murdered—or at least held captive.

Several gunshots followed one after the other. The staccato sound of a submachine gun—more screaming, more cries of terror.

The field accountant couldn't return to the front of the building, and undoubtedly someone would come out looking for his executioner.

He rolled the body of the dead Sicilian over the edge of the dock and heard the splash below.

The whistle from the *Genoa-Stella* stopped. The shouting began to die down. Someone had assumed control. And at the front end of the pier two men came in sight. They called out.

"La Tona! Hey, La Tona! La Tona. . . ."

Matthew Canfield jumped into the filthy waters of the Hudson and started swimming, as best he could in his heavy customs uniform, toward the middle of the river.

"You're a very lucky fellow!" said Benjamin Reynolds.

"I know that, sir. And grateful it's over."

"We're not called on for this sort of thing, I realize. You take a week off. Relax."

"Thank you, sir."

"Glover will be here in a few minutes. It's still a bit early."

It was. It was six fifteen in the morning. Canfield hadn't reached Washington until four and he was afraid to go to his apartment. He had phoned Benjamin Reynolds at home and Reynolds had instructed the field accountant to go to the Group Twenty offices and wait for him.

The outer door opened and Reynolds called. "Glover? That you?"

"Yes, Ben. Jesus! It's not six thirty yet. . . . A lousy night. My son's kids are with us." The voice was weary, and when Glover reached Reynolds's door, it was apparent that the man was wearier. . . . "Hello, Canfield. What the hell happened to you?"

Matthew Canfield, field accountant, told the entire story.

When he had finished, Reynolds spoke to Glover. "I've phoned Lake Erie

Customs—his personnel file's been removed. The boys in New York cleared out his room there. It hadn't been touched. Is there any other backup we should worry about?"

Glover thought for a moment. "Yes. Probably. . . . In case the Lake Erie employment file's gone after—and it will be—put out a rumour on the docks that Canfield . . . Cannon . . . was a fake name for a hit man. . . . That he was caught up with in Los Angeles or San Diego or someplace, and was shot. I'll take care of it."

"Good. . . . Now, Canfield, I'm going to show you several photographs. Without any comments on my part . . . see if you can identify them." Benjamin Reynolds walked to a file cabinet and opened it. He took out a folder and returned to his desk "Here." He withdrew five photographs—three blowups from newspapers and two prison shots.

It took Canfield less than a second once they were arranged. "That's him! That's the one the little wop called *padrone!*"

"Il Scarlatti padrone," Glover said quietly.

"The identification's absolutely positive?"

"Sure. . . . And if he's got blue eyes, it's Holy Writ."

"You could swear to it in court?"

"Of course."

"Hey, Ben, come on!" interrupted Glover, who knew that such an action on Matthew Canfield's part was a death warrant.

"I'm only asking."

"Who is he?" said Canfield.

"Yes. Who is he? . . . What is he? . . . I'm not sure I should even answer the first, but if you found out some other way—and you could, easily—it might be dangerous." Reynolds turned the photographs over. A name was printed in heavy black crayon.

"Ulster Stewart Scarlett—né Scarlatti," the field accountant read out loud. "He won a medal in the war, didn't he? A millionaire."

"Yes, he did and he is," answered Reynolds. "This identification's got to remain secret. And I mean *totally* classified! Is that understood?"

"Of course."

"Do you think anyone could recognize you from last night?"

"I doubt it. The light was bad and I wore my cap half over my face and tried to talk like a goon. . . . No, I don't think so."

"Good. You did a fine job. Get some sleep."

"Thank you." The field accountant walked out the door, closing it behind him.

Benjamin Reynolds looked at the photographs on his desk. "The Scarlatti *padrone*, Glover."

"Turn it back to Treasury. You've got all you need."

"You're not thinking. . . . We don't have a damned thing unless you want to consign Canfield to his grave. . . . And even assuming that, what is there? Scarlett doesn't write out checks. . . . He 'was observed in the company of . . .' He 'was heard to give an order . . .' To whom? On whose testimony? A minor government employee against the word of the celebrated war hero? The son of Scarlatti? . . . No, all we've got is a threat. . . . And perhaps that's enough."

"Who's going to threaten?"

Benjamin Reynolds leaned back in his chair and pressed the tips of his fingers against one another. "I am. . . . I'm going to talk with Elizabeth Scarlatti. . . . I want to know *why*."

Chapter Seven

Ulster Stewart Scarlett got out of the taxi at the corner of Fifth Avenue and Fifty-fourth Street and walked the short distance to his brownstone house. He ran up the steps to the heavy front door and let himself in. He slammed the door shut and stood for a moment in the huge foyer, stamping his feet against the February cold. He threw his coat into a hallway chair, then walked through a pair of French doors into a spacious living room and turned on a table lamp. . . . It was only four in the afternoon but already growing dark.

He crossed from the table to the fireplace and noted with satisfaction that the servants had piled the logs and the kindling properly. He lit the fire and watched the flames leap to all corners of the fireplace. He gripped the mantel and leaned toward the warmth of the blaze. His eyes were on the level of his Silver Star citation, framed in gold in the center of the wall. He made a mental note to complete the display above the fireplace. The time would soon be here when that display should be in evidence.

A reminder to everyone who entered this house.

It was a momentary diversion. His thoughts returned to the source of his anger. His fury.

Stupid, Gad damn thick-headed scum!

Bilge! Garbage!

Four crewmen from the *Genoa-Stella* killed. The captain's body found in an abandoned waterfront barge.

They could have lived with that. They could have lived with the crew's rebellion. The docks were violent.

But not with the corpse of La Tona hooked to a cross post on the surface of the water fifty yards from the ship. The freighter bringing in the contraband.

La Tona!

Who had killed him? Not the slow-speaking, cloddish customs guard. . . . Christ, no! . . . La Tona would have eaten his balls off and spat them out laughing! La Tona was a sneak killer. The worst kind of homicidal brute.

There'd be a smell. A bad smell. No graft could stop it. Five murders on pier thirty-seven during a single night shift.

And with La Tona it would be traced to Vitone. Little Don Vitone Genovese. Dirty little guinea bastard, thought Scarlett.

Well, it was time for him to get out.

He had what he wanted. More than he needed. Strasser would be amazed. They'd all be amazed.

Ulster Scarlett lit a cigarette and walked to a small, thin door to the left of the fireplace. He took out a key, unlocked the door, and walked in.

The room, like the door to it, was small. It had once been a walk-in wine pantry; now it was a miniature office with a desk, a chair, and two heavy steel file cabinets. On each file drawer was a wide circular combination lock.

Scarlett turned on the desk lamp and went to the first cabinet. He crouched down to the bottom file, manipulated the combination numbers, and pulled out the drawer. He reached in and withdrew an extremely thick leather-bound notebook and placed it on the desk. He sat down and opened it.

It was his master work, the product of five years of meticulous scholarship.

He scanned the pages—delicately, precisely inserted into the rings with cloth circlets around each hole. Each entry was lettered clearly. After every name was a brief description, where available, and a briefer biography—position, finances, family, future—when the candidate warranted it.

The pages were titled and separated by cities and states. Index tabs of different colors descended from the top of the notebook to the bottom.

A masterpiece!

The record of every individual—important and unimportant—who had benefited in any way from the operations of the Scarlatti organization. From congressmen taking outright bribes from his subordinates to corporation heads "investing" in wildcat, highly illegal speculations proffered—again never by Ulster Stewart Scarlett—through his hired hands. All he had supplied was the capital. The honey. And the bees had flocked to it!

Politicians, bankers, lawyers, doctors, architects, writers, gangsters, office clerks, police, customs inspectors, firemen, bookmakers . . . the list of professions and occupations was endless.

The Volstead Act was the spine of the corruption, but there were other enterprises—all profitable.

Prostitution, abortion, oil, gold, political campaigns and patronage, the stock market, speakeasies, loan-sharking . . . this list, too, was endless.

The money-hungry little people could never walk away from their greed. It was the ultimate proof of his theories!

The money-grasping scum!

Everything documented. Everyone identified.

Nothing left to speculation.

The leather-bound notebook contained 4,263 names. In eighty-one cities and twenty-four states. . . . Twelve senators, ninety-eight congressmen, and three men in Coolidge's cabinet.

A directory of malfeasance.

Ulster Stewart picked up the desk phone and dialed a number.

"Put Vitone on. . . . Never mind who's calling! I wouldn't have this number if he didn't want me to have it!"

Scarlett crushed out his cigarette. He drew unconnected lines on a scratch pad while waiting for Genovese. He smiled when he saw that the lines converged—like knives—into a center spot. . . . No, not like knives. Like bolts of lightning.

"Vitone? It's me. . . . I'm aware of that. . . . There's not very much we *can* do, is there? . . . If you're questioned, you've got a story. You were in Westchester. You don't know where the hell La Tona was. . . . Just keep me out! Understand? Don't be a smart-ass. . . . I've got a proposition for you. You're going to like it. It makes everything worth-while for you. . . . It's all yours. Everything! Make whatever deals you like. I'm out."

There was silence from the other end of the line. Ulster Scarlett drew the figure of a Christmas tree on the scratch pad.

"No hitches, no catches. It's yours! I don't want a thing. The organization's all yours. . . . No, I don't know anything! I just want out. If you're not interested, I can go elsewhere—say the Bronx or even out to Detroit. I'm not asking for a nickel. . . . Only this. Only one thing. You never saw me. You never met me. You don't know I exist! That's the price."

Don Vitone Genovese began chattering in Italian while Scarlett held the receiver several inches from his ear. The only word Scarlett really understood was the repeated, "Grazie, grazie, grazie."

He hung up the receiver and closed the leather-bound notebook. He sat for a moment and then opened the top drawer in the center of the desk. He took out the last letter he had received from Gregor Strasser. He reread it for the twentieth time. Or was it the hundred and twentieth?

"A fantastic plan . . . a bold plan . . . the Marquis Jacques Louis Bertholde . . . London . . . by mid-April . . ."

Was the time really here? At last!

If it was, Heinrich Kroeger had to have his own plan for Ulster Scarlett. It wasn't so much bold as it was respectable. Immensely, thoroughly respectable. So proper, in fact, that Ulster Stewart Scarlett burst out laughing.

The scion of Scarlatti—the charming, handsome graduate of the cotillions, the hero of the Meuse-Argonne, New York society's most eligible bachelor—was going to be married.

Chapter Eight

"You presume, Mr. Reynolds!" Elizabeth Scarlatti was seething. Her vehemence was directed at the old man who stood calmly in front of her, peering over his glasses. "I do not countenance presumptuous people and I will not abide liars!"

"I'm sorry. I really am."

"You got this appointment under false pretenses. Senator Brownlee told me you represented the Land Acquisition Agency and your business concerned the transactions between Scarlatti and the Department of the Interior."

"That's exactly what he believes."

"Then he's a bigger fool than I think he is. And now you threaten me! Threaten me with secondhand inflammatory gossip about my son! I trust you're prepared to be cross-examined in court."

"Is that what you want?"

"You may force me to it! . . . I don't know your position, but I do know a great many people in Washington and I've never heard of you. I can only conclude that if someone like you can carry such tales, others must have heard them too. Yes, you may force me into court. I won't tolerate such abuse!"

"Suppose it's true?"

"It isn't true and you know it as well as I do! There's no reason on earth why my son would involve himself in . . . in such activities. He's wealthy in his own right! Both my sons have trust funds that return annual incomes of—let's be honest—preposterous sums."

"Then we have to eliminate profit as a motive, don't we?" Benjamin Reynolds wrinkled his brow.

"We eliminate nothing for there *is* nothing! If my son has caroused a bit, he's to be criticized—not branded a criminal! And if you're using the gutter tactic of maligning the name Scarlatti because of its origin, you're contemptible and I'll have you dismissed!"

Benjamin Reynolds, slow to anger, was reaching a dangerous level of irritation. He had to remind himself that this old woman was guarding her house and was more difficult than she would have been in other circumstances.

"I wish you wouldn't think of me as an enemy. I'm neither an enemy nor a bigot. Frankly, I resent the second implication more than I do the first."

"Again you presume," interrupted Elizabeth Scarlatti. "I don't grant you the stature of an enemy. I think you're a little man using malicious slander for your own ends."

"Ordering a man's murder is not malicious slander!"

"What did you say?"

"It's the most serious charge we have. . . . But there are mitigating circumstances if it's any comfort to you."

The old woman stared at Benjamin Reynolds in contempt. He ignored the look.

"The man who was murdered—the one whose death your son ordered—was a known killer himself. . . . A captain of a freighter who worked with the worst elements on the waterfront. He was responsible for a great deal of killing."

Elizabeth Scarlatti rose from her chair. "I won't tolerate this," she said quietly. "You make the most damaging accusation possible and then you retreat behind a wall of implied judgment."

"These are strange times, Madame Scarlatti. We can't be everywhere. We don't want to be, frankly. We don't lament the gangster wars. Let's face it. Often they accomplish more than we can."

"And you put my son in this . . . this category?"

"I didn't put him anywhere. He did it himself."

Elizabeth walked slowly from her desk to a front window overlooking the street. "How many other people in Washington know about this outrageous gossip?"

"Everything I've told you?"

"Anything."

"There were a few rumors at Treasury. Nothing anyone wanted to run down. About the rest, only my immediate subordinate and the man who was the witness."

"Their names?"

"Oh, no."

"I can easily find out."

"It wouldn't do you any good."

Elizabeth turned. "I see."

"I wonder if you do?"

"Whatever you think, I'm not an idiot. I don't believe a word of this. But I don't want the name of Scarlatti impugned. . . . How much, Mr. Reynolds?"

Group Twenty's director returned Elizabeth's stare without giving quarter. "Nothing. Not a penny, thank you. . . . I'll go further. You tempt me to bring charges against you."

"You stupid old man!"

"Damn it to hell, cut it out! . . . All I want is the truth! . . . No, that's not all I want. I want it stopped. Before anyone else gets hurt. That much is due a decorated hero. Especially in these crazy times. . . . And I want to know why!"

"To speculate would be to grant your premise. I refuse to do that!"

"By Jesus! You're a rough bird."

"More than you realize!"

"Can't you understand? . . . It's not going any further! It ends here! That is, it will if you can stop any future . . . activity, as you call it. We figure you can do that. . . . But I'd think *you'd* want to know why. Since we both know your son is rich—why?"

Elizabeth simply stared at him and Reynolds knew she wouldn't answer. He'd done what he could, said what he had to say. The rest was up to her.

"Good day, Madame Scarlatti. . . . I should tell you. I'll be watching the Scarlatti *padrone*."

"The who?"

"Ask your son."

Reynolds trudged out of the room. People like Elizabeth Scarlatti tired him out. Probably, he thought, because he didn't believe they were worth it all. The giants never were.

Elizabeth—still by the window—watched the old man close the door behind him. She waited until she saw him descend the front steps and walk west toward Fifth Avenue.

The old man looked up at the figure in the window and their eyes met.

Neither acknowledged.

Chapter Nine

Chancellor Drew Scarlett paced the thick oriental rug of his office at 525 Fifth Avenue. He kept breathing deeply, pushing his stomach out as he inhaled—the proper way—because the masseur at his club told him it was one method of calming down under pressure.

It wasn't working.

He would change masseurs.

He stopped in front of the mahogany-paneled wall between the two large windows overlooking Fifth Avenue. On the wall were various framed newspaper articles, all of them about the Scarwyck Foundation. Each prominently mentioned him—some with his name in bold print above the stories.

Whenever he was upset, which was quite often, he looked at these framed records of achievement. It always had a calming effect.

Chancellor Scarlett had assumed the role of husband to a dull wife as a matter of course. The conjugal bed had produced five children. Surprisingly—especially to Elizabeth—he had also become interested in the family enterprises. As if in answer to his celebrated brother's behavior, Chancellor retreated into the secure world of the quasi-inspired businessman. And he did have ideas.

Because the annual income from the Scarlatti holdings far exceeded the needs of a small nation, Chancellor convinced Elizabeth that the intelligent tax course was to establish a philanthropic foundation. Impressing his mother with irrefutable data—including the potential for antitrust suits—Chancellor won Elizabeth's consent for the Scarwyck Foundation. Chancellor was installed as president and his mother as chairman of the board. Chancellor might never be a war hero, but his children would recognize his economic and cultural contributions.

The Scarwyck Foundation poured money into war memorials; preservation of Indian reservations; a *Dictionary of Great Patriots* to be distributed throughout selected prep schools; the Roland Scarlett Field Clubs, a chain of Episcopal youth camps dedicated to the outdoor life and high Christian principles of their democratic—but Episcopalian—patron. And scores of similar endeavors. One couldn't pick up a newspaper without noticing some new project endowed by Scarwyck.

Looking at the articles shored up Chancellor's undermined confidence, but the effect was short-lived. He could hear faintly through the office door the ring of his secretary's telephone and it immediately brought back the memory of his mother's angry call to him. She'd been trying to find Ulster since yesterday morning.

Chancellor picked up the intercom.

"Try my brother's home again, Miss Nesbit."

"Yes, sir."

He had to find Ulster. His mother was adamant. She insisted on seeing him before the afternoon was over.

Chancellor sat down in his chair and tried to breath properly again. The masseur had told him it was good exercise while sitting down.

He took a deep breath, pushing his stomach out as far as possible. The middle button of his suit coat broke from the thread and fell on the soft carpet, bouncing first on the chair between his legs.

Damn!

Miss Nesbit rang him on the intercom.

"Yes!"

"The maid at your brother's house said he was on his way over to see you, Mr. Scarlett." Miss Nesbit's voice conveyed her pride in accomplishment.

"You mean he was there all the time?"

"I don't know, sir." Miss Nesbit was hurt.

Twenty agonizing minutes later Ulster Stewart Scarlett arrived.

"Good God! Where have you been? Mother's been trying to reach you since yesterday morning! We've called everywhere!"

"I've been out at Oyster Bay. Did any of you think of calling there?"

"In February? Of course not! . . . Or maybe she did, I don't know."

"You couldn't have reached me anyway. I was in one of the cottages."

"What the hell were you doing there? I mean, in February!"

"Let's say taking stock, brother mine. . . . Nice office, Chance. I can't remember when I was here last."

"About three years ago."

"What are all those gadgets?" asked Ulster, pointing at the desk.

"Newest equipment. See. . . . Here's an electric calendar that lights up on specific days to remind me of meetings. This is an intercommunicator setup with eighteen offices in the building. Now, right here a private wire to . . ."

"Never mind. I'm impressed. I haven't much time. I thought you might like to know. . . . I may get married."

"What! . . . Ulster, my God in heaven! You! Married! You're going to get married?"

"Seems to be a general request."

"Who, for God's sake!"

"Oh, I've whittled the numbers down, sport. Don't fret. She'll be acceptable."

Chancellor eyed his brother coldly. He was prepared to be told that Ulster had chosen some Broadway trollop from a Ziegfeld show, or, perhaps, one of those weird female writers in black sweaters and men's haircuts who were always at Ulster's parties.

"Acceptable to whom?"

"Well, let's see, I've tried out most of them."

"I'm not interested in your sex life! Who?"

"Oh, but you should be. Most of your wife's friends—married and otherwise—are lousy lays."

"Just tell me who you intend honoring, if you don't mind?"

"What would you say to the Saxon girl?"

"Janet! . . . Janet Saxon!" Chancellor cried out with delight.

"I think she'd do," murmured Ulster.

"Do! Why, she's wonderful! Mother will be so pleased! She's just terrific!"

"She'll do." Ulster was strangely quiet.

"Ulster, I can't tell you how pleased I am. You've asked her, of course." It was a statement.

"Why, Chance, how can you think that? . . . I wasn't sure she'd pass inspection."

"I see what you mean. Of course. . . . But I'm sure she will. Have you told Mother? Is that why she's calling so hysterically?"

"I've never seen Mother hysterical. That should be quite a sight."

"Really, you should phone her right away.'

"I will. Give me a minute. . . . I want to say something. It's quite personal." Ulster Scarlett sat carelessly down in a chair in front of his brother's desk.

Chancellor, knowing that his brother rarely wanted to be personal, took his seat apprehensively. "What is it?"

"I was pulling your leg a few minutes ago. I mean about the lays."

"I'm relieved to hear that!"

"Oh, don't mistake me—I'm not saying it isn't true—just tasteless of me to discuss it. . . . I wanted to see you get upset. Take it easy, I had a reason. . . . I think it makes my case stronger."

"What case?"

"It's why I went out to the island. . . . To do a lot of thinking. . . . The aimless, crazy days are coming to an end. Not overnight, but they're slowly fading out."

Chancellor looked intently at his brother. "I've never heard you talk like this before."

"You do a lot of thinking in a cottage by yourself. No telephones, no one barging in on you. . . . Oh, I'm not making any big promises I can't keep. I don't have to do that. But I want to try. . . . I guess you're the only person I can turn to."

Chancellor Scarlett was touched. "What can I do?"

"I'd like to get some kind of position. Informal, at first. Nothing regimented. See if I can't get interested in something."

"Of course! I'll get you a job here! It'll be simply great working together."

"No. Not here. That'd be just another gift. No. I want to do what I should have done a long time ago. Do what you did. Start right at home."

"At home. What kind of position is that?"

"Figuratively speaking, I want to learn everything I can about us. The family. Scarlatti. Its interests, businesses, that sort of thing. . . . That's what you did and I've always admired you for it."

"Did you really?" Chancellor was very serious.

"Yes, I did. . . . I took a lot of papers out to the island with me. Reports and things I picked up at mother's office. We do a lot of work with that bank downtown, don't we? What in hell is the name?"

"Waterman Trust. They execute all Scarlatti commitments. Have for years."

"Maybe I could start there. . . . Informally. Couple of hours a day."

"No problem at all! I'll arrange it this afternoon."

"Another thing. Do you think you might phone Mother. . . . Just as a favor. Tell her I'm on my way over. I won't bother to call. You might mention our discussion. Tell her about Janet, if you like." Ulster Scarlett stood up in front of his brother. There was something modestly heroic about him, about this errant who was trying to find his roots.

The effect was not lost on Chancellor, who rose from his chair and extended his hand. "Welcome home, Ulster. It's the start of a new life for you. Mark my words."

"Yes. I think it is. Not overnight, but it's a beginning."

Elizabeth Scarlatti slammed the flat of her hand down on the desk as she rose from her chair.

"You're sorry? Sorry? You don't fool me for a minute! You're frightened out of your wits and well you should be! You damned fool! You ass! What did you think you were doing? Playing games! Little boy games!"

Ulster Scarlett gripped the arm of the sofa in which he sat and repeated to himself over and over again, *Heinrich Kroeger, Heinrich Kroeger.*

"I demand an explanation, Ulster!"

"I told you. I was bored. Just plain bored."

"How involved are you?"

"Oh, Christ! I'm not. All I did was give some money for a supply. A shipment. That's all."

"Who did you give the money to?"

"Just—guys. Fellows I met at clubs."

"Were they criminals?"

"I don't know. Who isn't these days? Yes, I guess they were. They are. That's why I'm out of it. Completely out of it!"

"Did you ever sign anything?"

"Jesus, no! You think I'm crazy?"

"No. I think you're stupid."

Heinrich Kroeger, Heinrich Kroeger. Ulster Scarlett rose from the sofa and lit a cigarette. He walked to the fireplace and threw the match on the crackling logs.

"I'm not stupid, Mother," replied Elizabeth's son.

Elizabeth dismissed his pouting objection. "You only supplied money? You were never involved in any violence?"

"No! Of course not!"

"Then who was the ship's captain? The man who was murdered?"

"I don't know! Look, I told you. I admit I was down there. Some guys said I'd get a kick out of seeing how the stuff came in. But that's all, I swear it. There was trouble. The crew started fighting and I left. I got out of there as fast as I could."

"There's nothing more? That's the extent of it?"

"Yes. What do you want me to do? Bleed from my hands and feet?"

"That's not very likely." Elizabeth walked around the desk and approached her son. "What about this marriage, Ulster. Is it, too, because you're bored?"

"I thought you'd approve."

"Approve? I wasn't aware that my approval or disapproval concerned you."

"It does."

"I approve of the Saxon girl, but I doubt for the reasons Chancellor thinks I should. She seems to be a lovely girl from what I've seen of her. . . . I'm not at all sure I approve of you. . . . Do you love her?"

Ulster Scarlett looked casually at his mother. "I think she'll make a good wife."

"Since you avoid my question, do you think you'll make a good husband?"

"Why, Mother. I read in *Vanity Fair* where I was New York's most eligible bachelor."

"Good husbands and eligible bachelors are often mutually exclusive. . . . Why do you want to be married?"

"It's time I should be."

"I'd accept that answer from your brother. Not from you."

Scarlett walked away from his mother to the windows. This was the moment. This was the moment he had planned, the moment he had rehearsed. He had to do it simply, say it simply. He'd pull it off and one day Elizabeth would recognize how wrong she was.

He wasn't stupid; he was brilliant.

"I tried to tell Chance. I'll try again with you. I do want to get married. I do want to get interested in something. . . . You asked me if I love the girl. I think I do. I think I will. What's important to me now is that I get straightened out." He turned from the window and faced his mother. "I'd like to learn what you built for us. I want to know what the Scarlatti family's all about. Everyone seems to know but me. It's a place to start, Mother."

"Yes, it's a place to start. But I should caution you. When you speak of Scarlatti, don't be under any illusions that your name guarantees you a voice in its management. You'll have to prove your value before you receive any responsibility—or authority. In that decision, I am Scarlatti."

"Yes. You've always made that very clear."

Elizabeth Scarlatti circled the desk and sat down in her chair. "I've never been wedded to the idea that nothing changes. Everything changes. And it's possible you have talent. You are the son of Giovanni Scarlatti and, perhaps, I was a damned fool to change the surname. It seemed right at the time. He was a genius. . . . Go to work, Ulster. We'll see what happens."

Ulster Stewart Scarlett walked down Fifth Avenue. The sun was out and he left his topcoat open. He smiled to himself. Several passersby noticed the large, striking-looking man with the open coat in the February cold. He was arrogantly handsome, obviously successful. Some men were born to it.

Ulster Scarlett, seeing the looks of envy from the little people, agreed with the unspoken thoughts.

Heinrich Kroeger was on schedule.

Chapter Ten

When Horace Boutier, president of Waterman Trust Company, received Chancellor's request for an indoctrination program for his brother Ulster, Boutier knew immediately who to make responsible.

Third vice-president Jefferson Cartwright.

Cartwright had been called on previously for duty with Ulster Scarlett and with good reason. He was, perhaps, the only executive at Waterman Trust who did not instantly irritate Ulster Scarlett. In a large measure this was due to Cartwright's unorthodox approach to his work. Quite unbankerlike.

For Jefferson Cartwright, a blondish, large, aging man, was a product of the playing fields of the University of Virginia and learned early in his career that the qualities that made him famous on the gridiron—and on the campus—served him extremely well in his chosen profession.

Briefly these were to learn the formations so thoroughly that one was always in the right position at the right time when on the field and always to press an advantage with the sheer bulk of one's size.

Off the field was merely an extension of the playing principles. Learn the surface formulas, wasting as little time as possible on complexities beyond one's grasp, and, again, impress everyone with the size—and attractiveness—of one's physical being.

These principles—when combined with an easy, outgoing Southern charm—guaranteed Jefferson Cartwright's sinecure at Waterman Trust. They even put his name on department letterheads.

For although Jefferson Cartwright's knowledge of banking hardly approached an expert vocabulary, his ability to commit adultery with some of the wealthiest women in Manhattan, Long Island, and southern Connecticut brought many excellent accounts to Waterman. Yet the bank's directors knew that their prime social stud was rarely a threat to any relatively secure marriage. Rather, he was a temporary divertissement, a charming, quick, and complete roll in the hay for the bored.

Most banking institutions had at least one Jefferson Cartwright on the executive payroll. However, such men often were overlooked when it came to club memberships and dinner parties. . . . One could never be sure.

It was the vague sense of ostracism that made Cartwright acceptable to Ulster Scarlett. Partly because he knew why it existed and it amused him, and partly because Cartwright—outside of a few mild lectures about the state of his accounts—never tried to tell him what to do with his money.

The bank's directors knew this, too. It was right that someone should advise Ulster Scarlett—if only to impress Elizabeth—but as no one could change him, why waste a committed man?

At the first session, as Cartwright called it, the banker discovered that Ulster Stewart Scarlett didn't know the difference between a debit and an asset. So a glossary of terms was prepared to give him a basic language to work with. From there another lexicon of stock market phraseology was written for him and in time he began to master it.

"Then, as I understand it, Mr. Cartwright, I have two separate incomes. Is that correct?"

"Indeed it is, Mr. Scarlett. The first trust fund, which is comprised of stocks—industrial and utility—is for your annual livin' expenses. Houses, clothes, trips abroad, purchases of any sort. . . . Of course, you certainly could invest this money if you wished. You have durin' the past several years if I'm not mistaken." Jefferson Cartwright smiled indulgently remembering a few of Ulster's extravagant withdrawals. "However, the second fund—the open-faced bonds and debentures—is designed for expansion. For re-investment. Even speculation. That was your father's wish. Of course there's a degree of flexibility."

"What do you mean flexibility?"

"It's hardly conceivable, Mr. Scarlett, but should your livin' expenses exceed the income from the first trust we could, with your power of attorney, transfer capital from the second fund to the first. Of course, this is hardly conceivable."

"Of course."

Jefferson Cartwright laughed and gave his innocent pupil an exaggerated wink. "I have you there, haven't I?"

"What?"

"It did occur once. Don't you remember? The dirigible? . . . The dirigible you purchased several years ago?"

"Oh, yes. You were upset about that."

"As a banker I'm responsible to the Scarlatti Industries. After all, I'm your financial adviser. I'm held accountable. . . . We covered the purchase from the second fund but it wasn't proper. Not proper at all. A dirigible could hardly be called an investment."

"I apologize again."

"Just remember, Mr. Scarlett. Your father's wish was that the monies due from the open-faced securities were to be reinvested."

"How could anyone tell?"

"Those are the releases you sign semiannually."

"The hundred-odd signatures I have to sit through?"

"Yes. We convert the notes and invest the capital."

"In what?"

"Those are the portfolio statements we send you. We catalog all invest-ments. We make the selections ourselves as you have not—with your busy schedule—ever answered our letters with regard to your preferences."

"I never understood them."

"Well, now, that can be overcome, can't it?"

"Suppose I didn't sign the releases?"

"Well . . . in that unlikely event the securities would remain in the vaults until the end of the year."

"Where?"

"The vaults. The Scarlatti vaults."

"I see."

"The releases are attached to the securities when we remove them."

"But no releases, no securities. No capital, no money."

"Exactly. They can't be converted. The releases are just what the name implies. You release to us with your power of attorney the right to invest the capital."

"Suppose, for imagination's sake, you didn't exist. There was no Water-man Trust. No bank at all. How could those securities be turned into money?"

"By signature again. Made payable to whomever you designated. It's all clearly set forth on each document."

"I see."

"One day—when you're more advanced, of course—you should see the vaults. The Scarlatti family occupies the entire east wing. The two remaining sons, yourself and Chancellor, have cubicles adjacent to each other. It's really quite touching."

Ulster considered. "Yes, I'd like to see the vaults. . . . When I'm more advanced, of course."

"For God's sake, are the Saxons preparing a wedding or a ceremonial convocation for the Archbishop of Canterbury?" Elizabeth Scarlatti had brought her oldest son to her house to discuss the various newspaper articles and the stack of invitations on her desk.

"You can't blame them. Ulster is hardly an ordinary catch."

"I'm aware of that. On the other hand the rest of New York can't stop functioning." Elizabeth walked to the library door and closed it. She turned and looked at her older son. "Chancellor, I want to discuss something with you. Very briefly and if you've got a brain in your head you won't repeat a word of what I'm going to mention."

"Of course."

Elizabeth kept looking at her son. She thought to herself that Chancellor was really a better man than she ever gave him credit for. His problem was that his outlook was so terribly provincial and yet so totally dependent. And his perpetual vacuous look whenever they had a conference made him seem like an ass.

A conference. Perhaps there had been too many conferences. Too few conversations. Perhaps it was her fault.

"Chancellor, I don't pretend to be on intimate terms with young people these days. There's a permissiveness that was absent from my own youth and, God knows, that's a step in the right direction, but I think it may have gone too far."

"I agree completely!" interrupted Chancellor Drew Scarlett with fervor. "Today it is self-indulgence and I'll not have my children infected, let me tell you!"

"Well, perhaps it goes deeper than righteous indignation. The young, as the times, are what we shape them to be—willingly or unknowingly. . . . However, this is only an introduction." Elizabeth crossed to her desk and sat down. "I've been watching Janet Saxon during the past few weeks. . . . Watching, perhaps, is unfair. I've only seen her on half a dozen occasions starting with that absurd engagement party. It strikes me that she drinks quite heavily. Quite unnecessarily heavily. Yet she's a lovely girl. An intelligent, alert girl. Am I wrong?"

Chancellor Drew Scarlett was startled. He had never thought such a thing about Janet Saxon. It never crossed his mind. Everyone drank too much. It was all part of the self-indulgence and although he disapproved he never took it very seriously.

"I hadn't realized it, Mother."

"Then, obviously, I'm wrong and we'll drop the subject. I really am far removed from the times."

Elizabeth smiled, and for the first time in a long time she gave her oldest son an affectionate kiss. Yet something was bothering Janet Saxon and Elizabeth Scarlatti knew it.

The wedding ceremony of Janet Saxon and Ulster Stewart Scarlett was a triumph. Chancellor Drew was, naturally, his brother's best man and following the bride's train were Chancellor's five children. Chancellor's wife, Allison Demerest Scarlett, was unable to attend the wedding as she was in labor at Presbyterian Hospital.

The fact that it was an April wedding was a source of contention between Janet Saxon and her parents. They would have preferred June or, at least May, but Janet was adamant. Her fiancé insisted that they be in Europe by the middle of April and that's how it would be.

Besides, she had her own very valid reason for a short engagement.

She was pregnant.

Janet knew her mother suspected. She also knew that her mother was delighted, even admired her for what she believed was the proper use of the ultimate feminine ploy. The prospect of this particular bridegroom untrapped, caged, irrefutably cornered, was enough for Marian Saxon to give in quickly to the April ceremony. Marian Saxon would have let her daughter be married in a synagogue on Good Friday if that ensured the Scarlatti heir.

Ulster Scarlett took a leave of absence from his sessions at the Waterman Trust Company. It was understood that following an extended honeymoon on the Continent he would plunge back into the world of finance with increased vigor. It positively touched—and amazed—Jefferson Cartwright that Ulster took with him—"on his sacred journey of love," as the Virginia cavalier put it—a large number of papers to study. He had gathered together literally hundreds of reports concerning the myriad interests of the Scarlatti Industries and promised Cartwright that he would master the complexities of the inexhaustible diversification by the time he returned.

Jefferson Cartwright was so moved by Ulster's earnestness that he presented him with a hand-tooled leather briefcase.

The first leg of the newlyweds' trip was marred by what appeared to be a severe case of seasickness on Janet's part. By a mildly amused ship's doctor, however, it was ascertained to be a miscarriage and as a result the bride spent the entire voyage to Southampton confined to her cabin.

In England they discovered that the English aristocracy was becoming quite tolerant of their invading American counterparts. It was all a question of degree. The crude but rich colonists were ripe for the taking and taken they were. The more acceptable—and this category included Ulster Scarlett and his wife—were absorbed without question.

Even the owners of Blenheim had to be impressed with someone who could wager the price of their best hunter on the turn of a single card. Especially when this particular gambler could tell at a glance which was the best hunter.

At about this time—the second month of their trip—the rumors began filtering back to New York. Brought mainly by returning members in good standing of the Four Hundred. It seemed Ulster Stewart was behaving very badly. He had taken to disappearing for days at a time and on one occasion was known to have been gone for the better part of two weeks, leaving his bride in a state of embarrassed anger.

However, even these extremes of gossip were not dwelled upon, for Ulster Stewart had done the same thing while a single man, and Janet Saxon, after all, had hooked herself Manhattan's most eligible bachelor. She should complain! A thousand girls would have settled for the ring and the ceremony and let him do as he pleased. All those millions and some said a titled family thrown into the bargain! No one had much sympathy for Janet Saxon.

And then the rumors took another turn.

The Scarletts uprooted themselves from London society and began what could only be described as an insanely planned itinerary throughout the Continent. From the frozen lakes of Scandinavia to the warm shores of the Mediterranean. From the still-cold streets of Berlin to the hot pavements of Madrid. From the mountain ranges of Bavaria to the flat, dirty ghettos of Cairo. From Paris in summer to the Scottish islands in autumn. One never knew where Ulster Scarlett and his wife would be next. It didn't make sense. There was no logic in their destinations.

Jefferson Cartwright was more concerned than anyone else. Alarmed. He was unsure of what to do and so he decided to do nothing but send carefully worded memorandums to Chancellor Drew Scarlett.

For Waterman Trust was sending thousands upon thousands of dollars in bank drafts to every conceivable and some inconceivable exchanges in Europe. Each letter of request from Ulster Scarlett was precisely worded and the instructions absolute. The demand for confidence, for silence, in the transactions was emphatic. The breaking of this confidence to be penalized by the immediate withdrawal of his interests from Waterman. . . . One-third of the Scarlett trusts. One-half of the Scarlatti inheritance.

There was no question about it. Ulster Scarlett had benefited from his sessions at the bank. He knew exactly how to expedite his financial demands and did it in the language of the banking profession. Still, Jefferson Cartwright was uneasy. He could be subject to criticism at a later date. There still remained two-thirds of the trusts and the second half of the inheritance. He solved his insoluble dilemma by sending the following—then variations of it—to Ulster Scarlett's brother.

Dear Chancellor:
Just to keep you up-to-date—as we so successfully established during your brother's sessions here at Waterman—Ulster is transferring considerable sums to European banks to cover what must be the finest honeymoon in the history of marriage. Nothing is too good for his beautiful wife! You'll be happy to learn that his correspondence is most businesslike.

A number of such notes were received by Chancellor Drew, who smiled indulgently at his reformed younger brother's devotion to his wife. And to think he was corresponding like a businessman. Progress had been made.

What Jefferson Cartwright did not explain was that Waterman Trust also received endless bills and charges validated by Ulster's signatures from countless hotels, railroads, stores, and lending institutions throughout Europe. What disturbed Cartwright was that the flexibility he had authorized during the dirigible incident would have to be employed again.

It was inconceivable but there it was! Ulster Scarlett's expenses were going to exceed the income from the trust fund. In the space of several months— when one added the charges to the transferals—Ulster Stewart Scarlett was reaching the eight-hundred-thousand-dollar mark.

Inconceivable!

Yet there it was.

And Waterman was subject to losing one-third of the Scarlatti interest if he divulged the information.

In August Ulster Stewart Scarlett sent word back to his mother and brother that Janet was pregnant. They would remain in Europe for a minimum of three more months as the doctors deemed it best that she do as little traveling as possible until the baby was well along.

Janet would remain in London, while Ulster traveled with friends to do some hunting in southern Germany.

He'd be gone for a month. Possibly a month and a half.

He'd cable when they decided to come home.

In mid-December the cable arrived. Ulster and Janet would be home for the holidays. Janet was to remain fairly inactive as the pregnancy was a difficult one, but Ulster hoped Chancellor had checked on the decorators and that his brownstone on Fifty-fourth Street would be comfortable for her.

He instructed Chancellor Drew to have someone meet a prior ship to escort a new housekeeper Ulster had found on the Continent. She had been highly recommended and Ulster wanted her to feel at home. He name was Hannah.

Language would be no problem.

She spoke both English and German.

During the remaining three months of Janet's pregnancy Ulster resumed his sessions at Waterman Trust and his mere presence had a calming effect on Jefferson Cartwright. Although he never spent more than two hours at the bank, he seemed somewhat more subdued, less given to fits of irritation than he had been before his honeymoon.

He even began taking work home in the hand-tooled leather briefcase.

In reply to Cartwright's confidental and offhand questions about the large sums of money forwarded by the bank to Ulster in Europe, the Scarlatti heir reminded Waterman's third vice-president that it was he who had made it clear that nothing prohibited him from using the income from his trust fund for investments. He reiterated his request that all his European transactions remain confidential between the two of them.

"Of course. I understand completely. But you must realize that in the event we transfer funds from the second trust to cover your expenses—as surely we'll have to this year—I must record it for the Scarlatti records. . . . We've paid enormous sums all over Europe on your signature."

"But you won't have to do that for a long time, will you?"

"At the end of the fiscal year, which for the Scarlatti Industries is June thirtieth. The same as the government's."

"Well"—the handsome man sighed as he looked at the agitated Southerner—"on June thirtieth I'll just have to stand up and face the music. It won't be the first time my family's been upset. I hope it's the last."

As the time approached for Janet's delivery, a constant procession of merchants passed through the doors of the Ulster Scarlett brownstone. A team of three doctors gave Janet constant attention and her own family saw her twice a day. What mattered was that the activity kept her occupied. It kept her mind off a frightening fact. A fact so personal she didn't know how to discuss it; there was no one to whom she felt close enough.

Her husband no longer spoke to her.

He had left her bed in her third month of pregnancy. In the south of France, to be exact. He had refused to have intercourse on the assumption that her miscarriage had been brought on by sex. She had wanted sex. She had wanted it desperately. She had wanted his body on hers because it was the only time she felt close to him. The only time her husband appeared to her to be without guile, without deceit, without the cold manipulation in his eyes. But even this was denied her.

Then he left their communal room, insisting upon separate rooms wherever they went.

And now he neither answered her questions nor asked any of his own.

He ignored her.

He was silent.

He was, if she wanted to be honest with herself, contemptuous of her.

He hated her.

Janet Saxon Scarlett. A reasonably intelligent product of Vassar. A graduate of the Pierre cotillions and a sane habitué of the hunt clubs. And always, always wondering why it was she and not someone else who enjoyed the privileges she had.

Not that she ever disclaimed them. She didn't. And perhaps she was entitled to them. God knew she was a "looker." Everyone had said it for as long as she could remember. But she was what her mother always complained about—an observer.

"You never really enter into things, Janet! You must try to get over that!"

But it was hard to "get over." She looked upon her life as two sides of a stereopticon—both different, yet merging into one focus. On one plate was the well-appointed young lady with impeccable credentials, enormous wealth, and an obviously assured future with some well-appointed, enormously wealthy, impeccably credentialed husband. On the other was a girl with a frown on her forehead and a questioning look in her eyes.

For this girl thought the world was larger than the confined world presented to her. Larger and far more compelling. But no one had allowed her to see that larger world.

Except her husband.

And the part of it he let her see—forced her to see—was terrifying.

Which is why she drank.

While preparations for the birth continued, aided by a steady stream of Janet's friends and family, a strange passivity came over Ulster Stewart Scarlett. It was discernible especially to those who observed him closely, but even to others it was apparent that he had slowed down his normally frantic pace. He was quieter, less volatile, sometimes reflective. And for a while his periods of going off by himself became more frequent. Never very long, just three or four days at a time. Many, like Chancellor Drew, atrributed it to impending fatherhood.

"I tell you, Mother, it's simply wonderful. He's a new man! And you know, I told him having children was the answer. Gives a man a purpose. You watch, when it's all over he'll be ready for a real man's job!"

"You have an acute ability to grasp the obvious, Chancellor. Your brother is quite convinced that he has a purpose in avoiding what you call a real man's job. I suspect he's bored to death by his imminent role as father. Or he's drinking bad whiskey."

"You're too hard on him."

"Quite the contrary," interrupted Elizabeth Scarlatti. "I think he's become far too hard on us."

Chancellor Drew looked bewildered. He changed the subject and began to read aloud a report of Scarwyck's newest project.

A week later a male child was born to Janet Scarlett at the French Hospital.

Ten days later at the Cathedral of Saint John the Divine he was christened Andrew Roland Scarlett.

And a day after the christening, Ulster Stewart Scarlett disappeared.

Chapter Eleven

At first no one took much notice. Ulster had stayed away from home before. Although it was not the conventional behavior of a new father, Ulster hardly fit into any conventional pattern. It was presumed that the tribal rites attending the birth of a male child proved just too much for him and that he had taken refuge in activities best left undescribed. When after three weeks no word has been heard from him and no satisfactory explanations furnished by a variety of people, the family became concerned. On the twenty-fifth day after his disappearance, Janet asked Chancellor to call the police. Instead, Chancellor called Elizabeth, which was a far more positive action.

Elizabeth carefully weighed the alternatives. Calling the police would necessitate an investigation and probably a great deal of publicity. In light of Ulster's activities a year ago, that was undesirable. If Ulster's absence was his own doing, such action would only serve to provoke him. Without provocation her son was unpredictable; with it he might well be impossible. She decided to hire a discreet firm of investigators, which often had been called on to examine insurance claims against the family businesses. The owners understood completely and put only their most efficient and trusted men on the job.

Elizabeth gave them two weeks to unearth Ulster Stewart. Actually, she expected he'd show up by then, but if he didn't, she would turn the matter over to the police.

At the end of the first week, the investigators had compiled a multi-page report about Ulster's habits. The places he most frequently visited; his friends (many); his enemies (few); and, in as much detail as possible, a reconstruction of his movements during the last few days before he vanished. They gave this information to Elizabeth.

Elizabeth and Chancellor Drew studied the reports closely. They revealed nothing.

The second week proved equally unenlightening except to fill in Ulster's activities more minutely by the days and hours. Since his return from Europe, his daily rounds had become ritualistic. The squash courts and the steam rooms at the athletic club; the bank on lower Broadway, Waterman Trust; his cocktails on Fifty-third Street between 4:30 and 6:00 P.M. with five speakeasies sharing the five weekdays of his attendance; the nightly sorties into the entertainment world where a handful of entrepreneurs commandeered his indulgence (and financing); the almost routine early morning windups at a supper club on Fiftieth Street prior to his arrival home, never later than 2:00 A.M.

One bit of data did catch Elizabeth's attention as, indeed, it had the one who had reported it. It was incongruous. It appeared on Wednesday's sheet.

Left house at approximately 10:30 and immediately hailed a taxi in front of residence. Maid was sweeping front steps and believed she heard Mr. Scarlett direct the driver to a subway.

Elizabeth had never thought of Ulster in a subway. And yet, two hours later, according to a "Mr. Mascolo, head waiter at the Venezia Restaurant," he was having an early lunch with a "Miss Dempsey (See Acquaintances: Theatrical artists)." The restaurant was two blocks from Ulster's house. Of course there could be a dozen explanations and certainly nothing in the report indicated anything strange other than Ulster's decision to go to a subway. For the time being, Elizabeth attributed it to Ulster's meeting someone, probably Miss Dempsey.

At the end of the week, Elizabeth capitulated and instructed Chancellor Drew to contact the police.

The newspapers had a red-letter day.

The Bureau of Investigation joined with the Manhattan police on the premise that possibly interstate laws had been violated. Dozens of publicity seekers as well as many sincere individuals volunteered that they had seen Ulster during that last week before his disappearance. Some macabre souls telephoned, claiming knowledge of his whereabouts, demanding money for the information. Five letters arrived asking ransom for his return. All leads were checked out. All proved worthless.

Benjamin Reynolds saw the story on page two of the *Washington Herald*. Other than the wedding, it was the first news he'd read about Ulster Scarlett since his meeting with Elizabeth Scarlatti over a year ago. However, in keeping with his word, he had made discreet inquiries about the celebrated war hero during the past months—only to learn that he had rejoined his proper world. Elizabeth Scarlatti had done her job well. Her son had dropped out of the importing business and the rumors of his involvement with criminal elements had died away. He had gone so far as to assume some minor position—with New York's Waterman Trust.

It had seemed the Scarlatti affair was over for Ben Reynolds.

And now this.

Would this mean it was no longer dormant, no longer a closed wound? Would it signify a reopening of the harsh speculation he, Ben Reynolds, had dwelled upon? Would Group Twenty be called in?

A Scarlatti son did not simply disappear without the government at least alerted. Too many congressmen were indebted to Scarlatti for one thing or another—a factory here, a newspaper there, a good-sized campaign check most of the time. Sooner or later someone would remember that Group Twenty had looked into the man's activities once before.

They'd be back. Discreetly.

If Elizabeth Scarlatti said it was all right.

Reynolds put the newspaper down, got out of his chair, and walked to his office door.

"Glover," he asked his subordinate, "could you come in my office a minute?"

The older man walked back to his chair and sat down. "Did you read the story about Scarlatti?"

"This morning on the way to work," answered Glover, coming through the door.

"What do you make of it?"

"I knew you'd ask me. I think some of his last year's friends caught up with him."

"Why?"

Glover sat down in the chair in front of Reynold's desk. "Because I can't think of anything else and it's logical. . . . And don't ask me why again because you know as well as I do."

"I do? I'm not sure of that."

"Oh, come on, Ben. The moneyman isn't having any more. Someone's stuck for a shipment and goes to him. He refuses. Sicilian sparks fly and that's that. . . . It's either something like that or a blackmail job. He decided to fight—and lost."

"I can't buy violence."

"Tell that to the Chicago police."

"Scarlett didn't deal with the lower echelons. That's why I can't buy a violence theory. There was too much to lose. Scarlett was too powerful; he had too many friends. . . . He might be used, not killed."

"Then what do you think?"

"I don't know. That's why I asked you. You jammed up this afternoon?"

"God damn it, yes. Still the same two things. No breaks coming our way."

"Arizona dam?"

"That's one. That son-of-a-bitch congressman keeps pushing through the appropriations and we know damned well he's getting paid, but we can't prove it. Can't even get anyone to admit they know anybody. . . . Incidentally, speaking of the Scarlett business, Canfield's on this one."

"Yes, I know. How's he doing?"

"Oh, we can't blame him. He's doing the best he can."

"What's the other problem?"

"The Pond memorandum from Stockholm."

"He's got to come through with something more than rumors, Glover. He's wasting our time until he gives us something concrete. I've told you that."

"I know, I know. But Pond sent word by courier—it arrived from State this morning—the transaction's been made. That's the word."

"Can't Pond get any names? Thirty million dollars' worth of securities and he can't get a single name?"

"A very tight syndicate, obviously. He hasn't come up with any."

"One hell of an ambassador. Coolidge appoints lousy ambassadors."

"He does think the whole shebang was manipulated by Donnenfeld."

"Well, that's a name! Who in hell is Donnenfeld?"

"Not a person. A firm. About the largest on the Stockholm exchange."

"How did he come to that conclusion?"

"Two reasons. The first is that only a large firm could handle it. Two—the whole thing can be buried easier that way. And it will have to be buried. American securities sold on the Stockholm exchange is touchy business."

"Touchy, hell! It can't be done!"

"All right. Rallied in Stockholm. Same thing as far as the money's concerned."

"What are you going to do about it?"

"Drudgery. Keep checking all the corporations with extensive ties in Sweden. You want to know something? There're a couple of dozen in Milwaukee alone. How do you like that? Make a bundle over here and do business with your cousins back home."

"If you want my opinion, Walter Pond's stirring up a quiet fuss so he gets some attention. Cal Coolidge doesn't make a friend an ambassador to the land of the midnight sun—or whatever the hell it's called—unless the fellow's not so good a friend as he thinks he is."

Chapter Twelve

After two months, with nothing further to write about or to broadcast, the novelty of Ulster Scarlett's disappearance wore off. For in truth the only additional information uncovered by the combined efforts of the police, the Bureau of Missing Persons, and the federal investigators was of a character nature and led nowhere. It was as if he had literally decomposed, became vapor. Existing one minute, a colorful memory the next.

Ulster's life, possessions, prejudices, and anxieties were placed under the scrutiny of professionals. And the result of these labors etched an extraordinary portrait of pointlessness. A man who had just about everything a human being could ask for on this earth had apparently lived in a vacuum. A purposeless, aimless vacuum.

Elizabeth Scarlatti puzzled over the voluminous reports supplied her by the authorities. It had become a habit for her, a ritual, a hope. If her son had been killed, it would, of course, be painful; but she could accept the loss of life. And there were a thousand ways . . . fire, water, earth . . . to rid the world of a body. But she could not accept this conclusion. It was possible, of course. He had known the underworld, but on such a peripheral basis.

One morning Elizabeth stood by her library window watching the outside world come to grips with another day. The pedestrians always walked so rapidly in the morning. The automobiles were subject to far more backfiring after a night of idleness. Then Elizabeth saw one of her maids out on the front steps. The maid was sweeping the front steps.

As she watched the woman swing the broom back and forth, Elizabeth was reminded of another maid. On another set of steps.

A maid at Ulster's house. A maid who swept Ulster's steps one morning and remembered her son giving instructions to a taxi driver.

What were those instructions?

A subway. Ulster had to get to a subway.

Her son had to take a subway one morning and Elizabeth hadn't understood.

It was only a dim, flickering candle in a very dark forest but it was a light. Elizabeth crossed rapidly to the telephone.

Thirty minutes later, Third Vice-President Jefferson Cartwright stood before Elizabeth Scarlatti. He was still partially out of breath from the nervous pressures of rearranging his schedule in order to attend this command performance.

"Yes, indeed," drawled the Virginian. "All the accounts were thoroughly examined the minute Mr. Scarlett's disappearance was known to us. Wonderful boy. We became very close durin' his sessions at the bank."

"What is the state of his accounts?"

"Perfectly normal."

"I'm afraid I don't know what that means."

Cartwright hesitated for a few seconds—the thoughtful banker. "Of course, the final figures aren't complete but we have no reason at this point to believe he exceeded the annual income of his trust."

"What is that income, Mr. Cartwright?"

"Well, of course, the market fluctuates—happily upward—so it'd be difficult to give you a precise figure."

"Just an approximate one."

"Let me see now . . ." Jefferson Cartwright did not like the direction the conversation was taking. He was suddenly very thankful that he had had the foresight to send those vague memorandums to Chancellor Drew about his brother's expenditures in Europe. His Southern drawl became thicker. "I could call several executives more familiar with Mr. Scarlett's portfolio—but it was considerable, Madame Scarlatti."

"Then I expect you to have at least a rough figure at your command." Elizabeth did not like Jefferson Cartwright and the tone of her voice was ominous.

"Mr. Scarlett's income from the trust fund designated for personal expenditures as differentiated from the second trust fund designated for investments was in excess of seven hundred and eighty-three thousand dollars." Cartwright spoke rapidly, quietly.

"I'm very pleased that his personal needs rarely exceeded that trifling amount." Elizabeth shifted her position in the straight-backed chair so she could give Mr. Cartwright the full benefit of her stare. Jefferson Cartwright rattled on at an accelerated tempo. Phrases spilled over into others, his accent more pronounced than ever.

"Well, surely, you were aware of Mr. Scarlett's extravagances. I believe the newspapers reported many. As I say, I personally did my best to caution him, but he was a very headstrong young man. If you recall, just three years ago, Mr. Scarlett purchased a dirigible for nearly a half million dollars. We did our best to dissuade him, of course, but it was simply impossible. He said he had to have a dirigible! If you'll study your son's accounts, madame, you'll find many such rash purchases." Cartwright was decidedly on the defensive although he knew perfectly well Elizabeth could hardly hold him responsible.

"Just how many such . . . purchases were there?"

At an even faster rate of speed the banker replied, "Well, certainly none as extravagant as the dirigible! We were able to prevent similar incidents by explaining to Mr. Scarlett that it was improper to transfer monies from his second trust for such purposes. That he had to . . . limit his expenses to the income produced by the first trust. In our sessions at the bank we emphasized this aspect time and again. However, last year alone, while he was in Europe with the beautiful Mrs. Scarlett, we were in constant touch with the Continental banks over his personal accounts. To put it mildly, your son was most helpful to the European economy. . . . It also was necessary to make . . . numerous direct payments on his signature. . . . Certainly Mr. Chancellor Scarlett spoke of the many, many notes I sent him regarding the large sums of money we forwarded your son in Europe."

Elizabeth's eyebrows rose. "No, he told me nothing."

"Well, Madame Scarlatti, it was your son's honeymoon. There was no reason . . ."

"Mr. Cartwright," the old woman interrupted sharply, "do you have an accurate accounting of my son's bank drafts, here and abroad, for the past year?"

"Why, of course, madame."

"And a listing of the payments made directly by you on his signature?"

"Certainly."

"I shall expect them in my hands no later than tomorrow morning."

"But it would take several accountants a full week to compile everything. Mr. Scarlett was hardly the most precise individual when it came to such matters. . . ."

"Mr. Cartwright! I've dealt with Waterman Trust for over a quarter of a century. The Scarlatti Industries deal through Waterman Trust exclusively, because I direct that they should. I believe in Waterman Trust because it's never given me a reason not to. Do I make myself clear?"

"You do, indeed. Tomorrow mornin'." Jefferson Cartwright bowed out of the room as a pardoned slave might take leave of an Arabian sheikh.

"Oh, Mr. Cartwright."

"Yes?"

"I don't think I really commended you for keeping my son's expenses within the boundaries of his income."

"I'm sorry. . . ." Beads of perspiration appeared on Cartwright's forehead. "There was little . . ."

"I don't think you understand me, Mr. Cartwright. I'm quite sincere. I commend you. Good morning."

"Good day, Madame Scarlatti."

Cartwright and three Waterman bookkeepers stayed throughout the night in an attempt to bring the accounts of Ulster Stewart Scarlett up-to-date. It was a difficult chore.

By two thirty in the morning Jefferson Cartwright had on his desk a list of banks and exchanges where the Scarlatti heir either had or once had accounts. Opposite each were detailed figures and times of transference. The list seemed endless. The specific deposits might well have averaged yearly incomes for the large majority of middle-class Americans but for Ulster Stewart they were no more than weekly allowances. It would take days to ascertain what was left. The list included:

THE CHEMICAL CORN EXCHANGE, *900 Madison Avenue, New York City*.
MAISON DE BANQUE, *22 rue Violette, Paris*.
LA BANQUE AMÉRICAINE, *rue Nouveau, Marseilles*.
DEUTSCHE-AMERICANISCHE BANK, *Kurfuerstendamm, Berlin*.
BANCO-TURISTA, *Calle de la Suenos, Madrid*.
MAISON DE MONTE CARLO, *rue du Feuillage, Monaco*.
WIENER STAEDTISCHE SPARKASSE, *Salzburgerstrasse, Vienna*.
BANQUE-FRANÇAISE-ALGÉRIE, *Harbor of Moons, Cairo, Egypt*.

And so it went. Ulster and his bride had seen Europe.

Of course, balancing this list of supposed assets was a second list of deficits in the form of accounts due. These included monies owed by signature to scores of hotels, department stores, shops, restaurants, automobile agencies, steamship lines, railroads, stables, private clubs, gambling establishments. They all had been paid by Waterman.

Jefferson Cartwright perused the detailed reports.

By civilized standards they were a conglomeration of financial nonsense, but the history of Ulster Stewart Scarlett bore out that for him this was perfectly normal. Cartwright reached the same conclusion as had the government accountants when they checked for the Bureau of Investigation soon after Ulster's disappearance.

Nothing unusual considering Ulster Scarlett's past life. Naturally, Waterman Trust would send letters of inquiry to the banks here and abroad to ascertain the amount of remaining deposits. It would be a simple matter to have the monies transferred under power of attorney back to Waterman Trust.

"Yes, indeed," muttered the Southerner to himself. "Mighty complete job under the circumstances."

Jefferson Cartwright was convinced that old Scarlatti would have a very different attitude toward him this morning. He would sleep for a few hours, take a long cold shower, and bring the reports to her himself. Secretly, he hoped that he would look tired, terribly tired. She might be impressed.

"My dear Mr. Cartwright," spat out Elizabeth Scarlatti, "it never occurred to you that while you were transferring thousands upon thousands to banks all over Europe, you were simultaneously settling debts which totaled nearly a quarter of a million dollars? It never crossed your mind that by combining these two figures my son accomplished the seemingly impossible! He went through the entire annual income from his trust in less than nine months! Damned near to the penny!"

"Naturally, Madame Scarlatti, letters are being sent this mornin' to the banks requestin' full information. Under our power of attorney, of course. I'm sure sizable amounts will be returned."

"I'm not at all sure."

"If I may be frank, Madame Scarlatti, what you're leadin' up to completely eludes me. . . ."

Elizabeth's tone became momentarily gentle, reflective. "To tell the truth, it eludes me also. Only I'm not leading, I'm being led. . . ."

"I beg your pardon?"

"During my son's sessions at Waterman could he have . . . come upon something . . . which might cause him to transfer such sums to Europe?"

"I asked myself the same question. As his adviser I felt it my duty to inquire. . . . Apparently Mr. Scarlett made a number of investments on the Continent."

"Investments? In Europe? That seems most unlikely!"

"He had a wide circle of friends, Madame Scarlatti. Friends who, I'm sure, didn't lack for projects. . . . And I must say, your son was becomin' more and more proficient in investment analysis. . . ."

"He what?"

"I refer to his studies of the Scarlatti portfolios. Why, he put his shoulder to the wheel and was unrelentin' on himself. I took great pride in his accomplishment. He was really takin' our sessions seriously. Tryin' so hard to understand the factor of diversification. . . . Why, on his honeymoon he took along hundreds of the Scarlatti corporate reports."

Elizabeth rose from her chair and walked slowly, deliberately toward the window overlooking the street, but her concentration was on the Southerner's sudden, incredible revelation. As had happened so often in the past, she realized that her instincts—abstract, unclear—were leading her to the truth. It was there; she was near it. But it remained out of her grasp.

"I assume you mean the statements—the breakdowns—of the Scarlatti Industries' holdings?"

"That, too, of course. But much, much more. He analyzed the trusts, both his and Chancellor's—even your own, Madame Scarlatti. It was his hope to write a complete report with special emphasis on the growth factors. It was a mighty ambitious task and he never wavered. . . ."

"Far more than ambitious, Mr. Cartwright," interrupted Elizabeth. "Without training, I'd say impossible." She continued to look out on the street.

"Actually, dear madame, we at the bank understood this. So we convinced him to limit his research to his own holdings. I felt it would be easier to explain and I certainly didn't wish to dampen his enthusiasm, so I . . ."

Elizabeth turned from the window and stared at the banker. Her look caused him to stop speaking. She knew the truth was now within her grasp. "Please clarify. How did my son . . . research his holdings?"

"From the securities in his trust fund. Primarily the bonds in his second trust—the investment fund—they're far more stable commodities. He cataloged them and then matched them with alternate choices, which might have been made when they were originally purchased. If I may add, he was most impressed with the selections. He told me so."

"He . . . cataloged them? What precisely do you mean?"

"He listed the securities separately. The amounts each represented and the years and months they were due. From the dates and the amounts he was able to compare with numerous other issues on the board."

"How did he do this?"

"As I mentioned, from the bonds and debentures themselves. From the yearly portfolios."

"Where?"

"The vaults, madame. The Scarlatti vaults."

My God! thought Elizabeth.

The old woman put her hand—trembling—on the windowsill. She spoke calmly in spite of the fear enveloping her. "How long did my son . . . do this research?"

"Why, for several months. Since his return from Europe to be exact."

"I see. Did anyone assist him? He was so inexperienced, I mean."

Jefferson Cartwright returned Elizabeth's look. He was not an utter fool. "There was no necessity. Catalogin' premature securities isn't difficult. It's a simple process of listin' names, figures, and dates. . . . And your son is . . . was a Scarlatti."

"Yes. . . . He was." Elizabeth knew the banker was beginning to read her thoughts. It didn't matter. Nothing mattered now but the truth.

The vaults.

"Mr. Cartwright, I'll be ready in ten minutes. I'll call for my car and we'll both return to your office."

"As you wish."

The ride downtown was made in silence. The banker and the matriarch sat next to each other in the back seat, but neither spoke. Each was preoccupied with his own thoughts.

Elizabeth's—the truth.

Cartwright's—survival. For if what he had begun to suspect was correct, he'd be ruined. Waterman Trust might be ruined. And he was the appointed adviser to Ulster Stewart Scarlett.

The chauffeur opened the door as the Southerner stepped out onto the curb and held his hand for Elizabeth. He noted that she grasped his hand tightly, too tightly, as she climbed—with difficulty—out of the automobile. She stared down at nothing.

The banker led the old woman rapidly through the bank. Past the cages, past the tellers, past the office doors to the rear of the building. They took the elevator down to the huge Waterman cellars. Out of the elevator they turned to the left and approached the east wing.

The walls were gray, the surfaces smooth, and the thick cement encased both sides of the gleaming steel bars. Above the portal was a simple inscription.

EAST WING

SCARLATTI

Elizabeth thought—once again—that the effect was tomblike. Beyond the bars was a narrow hallway lit from the ceiling with bright bulbs encased in wire mesh. Except for the doorways, two on either side, the corridor looked like a passageway to some pharaoh's final resting place in the center of an awesome pyramid. The door at the end led to the vault of the Scarlatti Industries itself.

Everything.

Giovanni.

The two doors on either side led to cubicles for the wife and the three children. Chancellor's and Ulster's were on the left. Elizabeth's and Roland's on the right. Elizabeth was next to Giovanni.

Elizabeth had never had Roland's consolidated. She knew that ultimately the courts would take care of that. It was her one gesture of sentiment to her lost son. It was proper. Roland, too, was part of the empire.

The uniformed guard nodded—funereally—and opened the steel-barred door.

Elizabeth stood in front of the entrance to the first cubicle on the left. The nameplate on the center of the metal door read, Ulster Stewart Scarlatti.

The guard opened this door and Elizabeth entered the small room. "You will relock the door and wait outside."

"Naturally."

She was alone in the cell-like enclosure. She reflected that only once before had she been in Ulster's cubicle. It had been with Giovanni. Years, histories ago. . . . He had coaxed her downtown to the bank without telling her of his arrangements for the east wing vaults. He had been so proud. He had taken her through the five rooms as a guide might usher tourists through a museum. He had elaborated on the intricacies of the various trusts. She remembered how he slapped the cabinets as if they were prize-winning cattle that would someday provide enormous herds.

He had been right.

The room hadn't changed. It might have been yesterday.

On one side, built into the wall, were the deposit boxes holding the industrials—the stocks, the certificates of ownership in hundreds of corporations. The wherewithal for day-to-day living. Ulster's first trust fund. On two other walls stood file cabinets, seven on each side. Each file drawer was marked with a year date—changed each year by the Waterman executors.

Each drawer contained hundreds of open-faced securities and each cabinet had six drawers.

Securities to be drawn on for the next eighty-four years.

The second trust. Earmarked for Scarlatti expansion.

Elizabeth studied the cards on the cabinets.

1926. 1927. 1928. 1929. 1930. 1931.

These were listed on the first cabinet.

She saw that there was a monk's stool pushed several feet away from the cabinet to the right. Whoever had used it last had been seated between the first and second file. She looked at the index cards on the adjacent cabinet.

1932. 1933. 1934. 1935. 1936. 1937.

She reached down and pulled the stool in front of the first cabinet and sat down. She looked at the bottom file drawer.

1926.

She opened it.

The year was divided by the twelve months, each month separated by a small index tab. Before each tab was a thin metal carton with two miniature cleats joined by a single wire submerged in wax. On the face of the wax—branded—were the initials *W.T.* in old English lettering.

The year 1926 was intact. None of the thin metal cartons had been opened. Which meant that Ulster had not complied with the bank's request for investment instructions. At the end of December the executors would take the responsibility themselves and, no doubt, consult Elizabeth as they had always done in the past with Ulster's fund.

She pulled out the year 1927.

This, too, was untouched. None of the wax crests had been broken.

Elizabeth was about to close the file on 1927 when she stopped. Her eyes caught sight of a blur in the wax. A tiny, slight blemish that would have gone unnoticed had not a person's attention been on the crests.

The *T.* of the *W.T.* was ragged and slanted downward on the month of August. The same was true for September, October, November, and December.

She pulled out the August carton and shook it. Then she ripped the wire apart and the wax crest cracked and fell away.

The carton was empty.

She replaced it and drew out the remaining months of 1927.

All empty.

She replaced the cartons and opened the file for 1928. Every thin carton had the *T.* of the wax crest ragged and slanting downward.

All empty.

For how many months had Ulster carried out his extraordinary charade? Going from one harried banker to the next and always, always—at the last—coming down to the vaults. Document by document. Security by security.

Three hours ago she wouldn't have believed it. It was only because a maid sweeping her front steps had triggered the memory of another maid sweeping steps. A maid who remembered a short command given by her son to a cab-driver.

Ulster Scarlett had taken a subway.

One midmorning he could not take the chance of a taxi ride in traffic. He had been late for his session at the bank.

What better time than midmorning? The initial placing of orders, the chaos of early trading in the market.

Even Ulster Scarlett would be overlooked at midmorning.

She hadn't understood the subway.

Now she did.

As if performing a painful ritual she checked the remaining months and years of the first cabinet. Through December, 1931.

Empty.

She closed the drawer on 1931 and began at the bottom of the second cabinet. 1932.

Empty.

She had reached the middle of the cabinet—1934—when she heard the sound of the metal door opening. She quickly closed the file and turned around in anger.

Jefferson Cartwright entered and shut the door.

"I thought I told you to remain outside!"

"My word, Madame Scarlatti, you look like you've seen a dozen ghosts."

"Get out!"

Cartwright walked rapidly to the first cabinet and arbitrarily pulled out one of the middle drawers. He saw the broken seals on the metal cartons, lifted one out, and opened it. "Seems as if somethin's missin'."

"I'll have you dismissed!"

"Maybe. . . . Maybe you will." The Southerner pulled out another drawer and satisfied himself that several other cartons whose seals had been broken were empty also.

Elizabeth stood silently, contemptuously, next to the banker. When she spoke, it was with the intensity born of disgust. "You have just terminated your employment at Waterman Trust!"

"Maybe I have. Excuse me, please." The Virginian gently moved Elizabeth away from the second cabinet and continued his search. He reached the year 1936 and turned to the old woman. "Not much left, is there? I wonder how far it goes, don't you? Of course, I'll make a complete breakdown for you as soon as possible. For you and my superiors." He closed the drawer on 1936 and smiled.

"This is confidential family business. You'll do nothing! You can do nothing!"

"Oh, come now! These cabinets contained open-faced securities. Bearer bonds negotiable subject to signature. . . . Possession is ownership. They're the same as money. . . . your disappearin' son took a whale of a hunk of the New York Exchange! And we haven't even finished lookin' around. Shall we open a few more cabinets?"

"I will not tolerate this!"

"Then don't. You go on your way, and I'll simply report to my superiors that Waterman Trust is in one hell of a pile of manure. Forgettin' very sizable commissions due the bank and puttin' aside any thoughts of the companies involved gettin' nervous over who owns what—there might even be a run on some stocks—I possess knowledge which I should report immediately to the authorities!"

"You can not! You must not!"

"Why not?" Jefferson Cartwright held out the palms of both hands.

Elizabeth turned away from him and tried to marshal her thoughts. "Estimate what's gone, Mr. Cartwright. . . ."

"I can estimate as far as we've looked. Eleven years, approximately three and a half million a year comes to something like forty million. But we may have only just begun."

"I said . . . prepare an estimate. I trust that I don't have to tell you that if you say a word to anyone—I shall destroy you. We'll arrive at mutually agreeable terms." She slowly turned and looked at Jefferson Cartwright. "You should know, Mr. Cartwright, that through an accident you're privileged to information that lifts you far above your talents or abilities. When men are so fortunate, they must be cautious."

Elizabeth Scarlatti spent a sleepless night.

Jefferson Cartwright also spent a sleepless night. But it wasn't in bed. It was on a monk's stool with reams of papers at his feet.

The figures mounted as he cautiously checked the file cabinets against the Scarlatti trusts reports.

Jefferson Cartwright thought he'd go mad.

Ulster Stewart Scarlett had removed securities worth over $270 million.

He totaled and retotaled the figures.

An amount that would cause a crisis on the exchange.

An international scandal, which could—if known—cripple the Scarlatti Industries. . . . And it would be known when the time came to convert the first missing securities. At the outside, barely a year.

Jefferson Cartwright folded the last of the pages together and stuffed them into his inner jacket pocket. He clamped his arm against his chest, making sure that the pressure between his flesh was stopped by the paper, and left the vaults.

He signaled the front guard with a short whistle. The man had been dozing on a black leather chair near the door.

"Oh, m'God, Mr. Cartwright! Y'startled me!"

Cartwright walked out onto the street.

He looked at the grayish white light of the sky. It was going to be morning soon. And the light was his signal.

For he—Jefferson Cartwright, fifty-year-old ex-football player from the University of Virginia, who had married first money and then lost it—held in his pocket carte blanche to everything he had ever wanted.

He was back in the stadium and the crowds were roaring.

Touchdown!

Nothing could be denied him now.

Chapter Thirteen

At twenty minutes after one in the morning, Benjamin Reynolds sat comfortably in an armchair in his Georgetown apartment. He held on his lap one of the file folders the attorney general's office had sent Group Twenty. There had been sixteen in all and he divided the stack equally between Glover and himself.

With congressional pressure, especially New York's Senator Brownlee, the attorney general's office wasn't going to leave a single stone unturned. If the Scarlatti son had disappeared into a void, at least the AG men could write

volumes explaining the fact. Because Group Twenty had touched
—briefly—on the life of Ulster Scarlett, Reynolds, too, would be expected to
add something. Even if it was nothing.

Reynolds felt a trace of guilt when he thought of Glover wading through
the same nonsense.

Like all reports of investigations of missing persons, it was filled with
trivia. Dates, hours, minutes, streets, houses, names, names, names. A
record of the inconsequential made to seem important. And perhaps to
someone, somewhere, it might be. A part, a section, a paragraph, a sentence,
even a word could open a door for someone.

But certainly not for anyone at Group Twenty.

He'd apologize to Glover later that morning.

Suddenly the phone rang. The sound in the stillness at such an unexpected
hour startled Reynolds.

"Ben? It's Glover. . . ."

"Jesus! You scared the hell out of me! What's wrong? Someone call in?"

"No, Ben. I suppose this could wait until morning, but I thought I'd give
you the pleasure of laughing yourself to sleep, you bastard."

"You've been drinking, Glover. Fight with your wife, not me. What the
hell have I done?"

"Gave me these eight Bibles from the attorney general's office, that's what
you did. . . . I found something!"

"Good Christ! About the New York thing! The docks?"

"No. Nothing we've ever connected with Scarlett. Maybe nothing but it
could be . . ."

"What?"

"Sweden. Stockholm."

"Stockholm? What the hell are you talking about?"

"I know the Pond file by rote."

"Walter Pond? The securities?"

"That's right. His first memorandum arrived last May. The initial word
about the securities. . . . Remember now?"

"Yes, yes, I do. So what?"

"According to a report in the sixth file, Ulster Scarlett was in Sweden last
year. Would you like to guess when?"

Reynolds paused before answering. His attention was riveted on the almost
unimaginable amount of thirty million dollars. "It wasn't Christmas, was it."
It was a statement spoken softly.

"Now that you mention it, some people might have looked at it that way.
Perhaps Christmas in Sweden comes in May."

"Let's talk in the morning." Reynolds hung up without waiting for his
subordinate to reply or say good-night. He walked slowly back to the soft
armchair and sat down.

As always Benjamin Reynolds's thought processes raced ahead of the
information presented. To the complications, the ramifications.

If Glover had made a valid assumption, that Ulster Scarlett was involved
with the Stockholm manipulation, then it had to follow that Scarlett was still
alive. If that were true, then thirty million dollars' worth of American
securities had been illegally offered by him for sale on the Stockholm
exchange.

No one individual, not even Ulster Stewart Scarlett, could get his hands on
thirty million dollars' worth of securities.

Unless there was a conspiracy.

But of what kind? For what purpose?

If Elizabeth Scarlatti herself were a part of it—she had to be considered in light of the magnitude of the capital—why?

Had he misread her completely?

It was possible.

It was also possible that he had been right over a year ago. The Scarlatti son had not done what he had done for thrills or because he'd met unsavory friends. Not if Stockholm was pertinent.

Glover paced the floor in front of Reynolds's desk. "It's there. Scarlett's visa shows he entered Sweden on May tenth. The Pond memorandum is dated the fifteenth."

"I see. I can read."

"What are you going to do?"

"Do? I can't do a damn thing. There's really nothing here at all. Simply a statement calling our attention to some rumors and the date of an American citizen's entry into Sweden. What else do *you* see?"

"Assuming there's a basis for the rumors, the connection's obvious and you know it as well as I do! Five will get you ten that if Pond's last communication is right, Scarlett's in Stockholm now."

"Assuming he's got something to sell."

"That's what I said."

"If I remember, somebody's got to say something's stolen before somebody else can yell thief! If we make accusations, all the Scarlattis have to say is they don't know what we're talking about and we're strung up on a high legal tree. And they don't even have to do that. They can simply refuse to dignify us with an answer—that's the way the old lady would put it—and the boys on the Hill will take care of the rest. . . . This agency—for those who know about it—is an abomination. The purpose we serve is generally at odds with a few other purposes in this town. We're one of the checks and balances—take your choice. A lot of people in Washington would like to see us out."

"Then we'd better let the AG's office have the information and let them draw their own conclusions. I guess that's the only thing left."

Benjamin Reynolds pushed his foot against the floor and his chair swung gently around to face the window. "We should do that. We will if you insist on it."

"What does that mean?" asked Glover, addressing his words to the back of his superior's head.

Reynolds shoved his chair around again and looked at his subordinate. "I think we can do the job better ourselves. Justice, Treasury, even the Bureau. They're accountable to a dozen committess. We're not."

"We're extending the lines of our authority."

"I don't think so. And as long as I sit in this chair that's pretty much my decision, isn't it?"

"Yes, it is. Why do you want us to take it on?"

"Because there's something diseased in all this. I saw it in the old woman's eyes."

"That's hardly clear logic."

"It's enough. I saw it."

"Ben? If anything turns up we think is beyond us, you'll go to the attorney general?"

"My word."

"You're on. What do we do now?"

Benjamin Reynolds rose from his chair. "Is Canfield still in Arizona?"

'Phoenix."

"Get him here."

Canfield. A complicated man for a complicated assignment. Reynolds did not like him, did not completely trust him. But he would make progress faster than any of the others.

And in the event he decided to sell out, Ben Reynolds would know it. He would spot it somehow. Canfield wasn't that experienced.

If that happened Reynolds would bear down on the field accountant and get to the truth of the Scarlatti business. Canfield was expendable.

Yes, Matthew Canfield was a good choice. If he pursued the Scarlattis on Group Twenty's terms, they could ask no more. If, on the other hand, he found different terms—terms too lucrative to refuse—he would be called in and broken.

Destroyed. But they would know the truth.

Ben Reynolds sat down and wondered at his own cynicism.

There was no question about it. The fastest way to solve the mystery behind the Scarlattis was for Matthew Canfield to be a pawn.

A pawn who trapped himself.

Chapter Fourteen

It was difficult for Elizabeth to sleep. She repeatedly sat up in bed to write down whatever came into her head. She wrote down facts, conjectures, remote possibilities, even impossibilities. She drew little squares, inserted names, places, dates, and tried to match them with connecting lines. At about three in the morning, she had reduced the series of events to the following:

April, 1925. Ulster and Janet married after only three-week engagement. Why? . . . Ulster and Janet sailed Cunard Line to Southampton. Reservations made by Ulster in February. How did he know?

May to December, 1925. Approximately eight hundred thousand sent by Waterman Trust to sixteen different banks in England, France, Germany, Austria, Holland, Italy, Spain, and Algeria.

January to March, 1926. Securities valued at approximately 270 million taken from Waterman. Forced sale equivalent between 150 and 200 million. All bills and charges in Ulster's and Janet's name from European accounts settled in full by February, 1926. Month of March, Ulster's behavior considerably altered, withdrawn.

April, 1926. Andrew born. Andrew christened. Ulster disappears.

July, 1926. Confirmation received from fourteen European banks that all monies withdrawn previously. Generally within four weeks of deposit. Two banks, London and The Hague, report sums of twenty-six thousand and nineteen thousand, respectively, remain on deposit.

This was the chronological order of events relative to Ulster's disappearance. The design was there. Premeditation of the whole sequence was apparent: the reservations made in February; the short engagement; the honeymoon tour; the constant deposits and prompt withdrawals; the removal of the securities and the final act of Ulster's disappearance itself. From February, 1925, to April, 1926. An plan conceived for fourteen months and executed with enormous precision, even to the point of assuring pregnancy, if Janet was to be believed. Was Ulster capable of such ingenuity? Elizabeth did not know. She really knew very little about him and the endless reports served only to cloud his image. For the person this research analyzed was seemingly capable of nothing save self-indulgence.

She knew there was only one place to start the search. Europe. The banks. Not all, she rationalized, but several. For regardless of the complexities of growth and the excesses of diversification, the fundamental practice of banking had remained constant since the time of the pharaohs. You put money in and you took money out. And whether for necessity or for pleasure the money withdrawn went someplace else. It was that other place, or those other places, that Elizabeth wanted to find. For it was this money, the money that Waterman Trust sent to the sixteen European banks, which would be used until such times as the securities might be sold.

At ten minutes to nine the butler opened the front door for Waterman Trust Company's newest second vice-president, Jefferson Cartwright. He showed Cartwright into the library where Elizabeth sat behind the desk with the inevitable cup of coffee in her hand.

Jefferson Cartwright sat on the small chair in front of the desk aware that it flatteringly accentuated his size. He put his briefcase by his side.

"Did you bring the letters?"

"I have them right here, Madame Scarlatti," answered the banker, lifting the briefcase to his lap and opening it. "May I take this opportunity to thank you for your kind intercession on my behalf at the office. It certainly was most generous of you."

"Thank you. I understand you've been made second vice-president."

"That's correct, ma'am, and I do believe the good word from you made it possible. I thank you again." He handed Elizabeth the papers.

She took them and started scanning the top pages. They seemed to be in order. In fact, they were excellent.

Cartwright spoke quietly. "The letters authorize you to receive all information regardin' any transactions made by your son, Ulster Stewart Scarlett, at the various banks. Deposits, withdrawals, transferals. They request access to all safety deposit boxes where they may exist. A coverin' letter has been sent to each bank with a photostat of your signature. I've signed these in my capacity as representin' Waterman's collective power of attorney for Mr. Scarlett. By doin' it, of course, I've taken a considerable risk."

"I congratulate you."

"It's simply incredible," the banker said quietly. "Securities worth over two hundred and seventy million dollars. Missin', unaccounted for. Just floatin' around somewhere. Who knows where? Even the largest bankin' syndicates have trouble raisin' such capital. Oh, it's a crisis, ma'am! Especially in a highly speculative market. I honestly don't know what to do."

"It's possible that by keeping your own counsel you'll spend many years drawing a remarkable salary for very little effort. Conversely, it's also possible—"

"I think I know what the other possibility is," interrupted Jefferson Cartwright. "As I see it, you're lookin' for information connected with the disappearance of your child. You may find it, if it exists. You may not. In either case, there're twelve months remainin' before the first of the bonds will be missed. Twelve months. Some of us might not be on God's good earth then. Others of us could be facin' ruin."

"Are you forecasting my demise?"

"I certainly hope not. But my own position is most delicate. I've violated the policies of my firm and the basic ethics of the bankin' business. As your son's financial adviser, the aspect of collusion will be raised—"

"And you'd feel more comfortable with a settlement, is that it?" Elizabeth put down the letters, angry with this ungrateful Southerner. "I bribe you and you proceed to blackmail me on the strength of my bribe. It's clever strategy. How much?"

"I'm sorry I make such a poor impression. I don't want a settlement. That'd be demeanin'."

"Then what do you want?" Elizabeth was becoming exasperated.

"I've prepared a statement. In triplicate. One copy for you, one for the Scarwyck Foundation, and one, of course, for my lawyer. I'd appreciate your perusin' it for your approval."

Cartwright withdrew the papers from his briefcase and placed them before Elizabeth. She picked up the top copy and saw that it was a letter of agreement, addressed to the Scarwyck Foundation.

This is to confirm an agreement between Mr. Jefferson Cartwright and myself, Mrs. Elizabeth Wyckham Scarlatti, in my position as chairman of the board of the Scarwyck Foundation, 525 Fifth Avenue, New York, New York.

Whereas, Mr. Cartwright has given generously of his time and professional services in my behalf and in behalf of the Scarwyck Foundation, it is agreed that he be made advisory consultant to the foundation with an annual salary of fifty thousand dollars ($50,000), said position to be held throughout his natural life. Said position to be made effective as of the above date.

Whereas, Mr. Jefferson Cartwright often has acted in my behalf and in behalf of the Scarwyck Foundation against his better judgment and in opposition to his own wishes, and,

Whereas, Mr. Cartwright performed all services in the manner his client, myself, firmly believed was for the betterment of the Scarwyck Foundation, he did so without anticipating said responsibility and often without full knowledge of the transactions.

Therefore, it is agreed that should there be at any future dates any fines, penalties, or judgments against Mr. Cartwright evolving from such actions, they will be paid in full from my personal accounts.

It should be added that no such actions are anticipated, but as the interests of the Scarwyck Foundation are international in scope, the demands excessive, and decisions often subject to my own opinion, the inclusion of such a statement is deemed proper.

It should be noted that Mr. Cartwright's exceptional services in my behalf have been rendered in confidence during the past months, but that from this date I have no objection to his position with the Scarwyck Foundation being made public knowledge.

There were two lines on the right for the signatures and a third line on the left for the signature of a witness. Elizabeth realized it was a professional document. It said nothing, but covered everything.

"You don't seriously expect me to sign this?"

"I honestly do. You see, if you don't, my overbearin' sense of responsibility would make me go right to the authorities. No doubt direct to the office of the district attorney with information I believe relevant to Mr. Scarlett's disappearance. . . . Can you imagine the international stir that would cause? The mere fact that the celebrated Madame Scarlatti was goin' to question the banks where her son did business—"

"I'll deny everything."

"Unfortunately, you couldn't deny the missin' securities. They don't have to be redeemed for a year, but they *are* missin'."

Elizabeth stared at the Southerner, knowing she was beaten. She sat down and silently reached for a pen. She signed the papers as he in turn took each page and did the same.

Chapter Fifteen

Elizabeth's trunks were placed aboard the British liner *Calpurnia*. She had told her family that the events of the past few months had taken their toll of her patience and health and she planned an extended stay in Europe—by herself. She was sailing the next morning. Chancellor Drew agreed that a trip might be beneficial, but he strongly urged his mother to take along a companion. After all, Elizabeth was no longer young, and in her advanced years someone should accompany her. He suggested Janet.

Elizabeth suggested that Chancellor Drew save his suggestions for the Scarwyck Foundation, but the issue of Janet had to be faced.

She asked the girl to come to her house late in the afternoon two days before the *Calpurnia* sailed.

"The things you tell me are hard to believe, Janet. Not so much about my son, but about you. Did you love him?"

"Yes. I think so. Or perhaps I was overwhelmed by him. In the beginning there were so many people, so many places. Everything went so fast. And then I realized—slowly—that he didn't like me. He couldn't stand being in the same room with me. I was an irritating necessity. God! Don't ask me why!"

Elizabeth remembered her son's words. "It's time I was married. . . . She'll make me a good wife." Why had he said those words? Why had it been so important to him?

"Was he faithful?"

The girl threw back her head and laughed. "Do you know what it's like to share your husband with—well, you're never quite sure?"

"The new psychology tells us that men often behave this way to compensate, Janet. To convince themselves that they're—adequate."

"Wrong again, Madame Scarlatti!" Janet emphasized Elizabeth's name with slight contempt. "Your son was adequate. In the extreme. I suppose I shouldn't say this, but we made love a great deal. The time, the place, it never mattered to Ulster. Or whether I wanted to or not. That was the last consideration. I mean I was the last consideration."

"Why did you put up with him? That's what I find difficult to understand."

Janet Scarlett reached into her purse. She withdrew a pack of cigarettes and nervously lit one. "I've told you this much. Why not the rest. . . . I was afraid."

"Of what?"

"I don't know. I've never thought it out. Why don't we call it—appearances."

"If you don't mind my saying so, that strikes me as foolish."

"You forget, I was the wife of Ulster Stewart Scarlett. I'd caught him. . . . It's not so easy to admit that I wasn't able to hold him any longer than a few months."

"I see your point. . . . We both know that a divorce on the grounds of assumed desertion would be best for you, but you'd be criticized unmercifully. It would appear to be in the poorest taste."

"I know that. I've decided to wait until a year is up before I get a divorce. A year is a reasonable time. It would be understandable."

"I'm not sure that would be in your interest."

"Why not?"

"You'd completely separate yourself and partially separate your child from the Scarlatti family. I'll be frank with you. I don't trust Chancellor under these circumstances."

"I don't understand."

"Once you made the first move, he'd use every legal weapon available to have you declared unfit."

"What!"

"He'd control both the child and the inheritance. Fortunately . . ."

"You're mad!"

Elizabeth continued as if Janet had not interrupted. "Fortunately, Chancellor's sense of propriety—which borders on the ridiculous—would prevent him from initiating action that might cause embarrassment. But if you provoked. . . . No, Janet, a divorce isn't the answer."

"Do you know what you're saying?"

"I assure you I do. . . . If I could guarantee that I'd be alive a year from now I'd give you my blessing! I can't do that. And without me to stop him, Chancellor would be a conniving wild animal!"

"There is nothing, nothing Chancellor can do to me! Or my child!"

"Please, my dear. I'm no moralist. But your behavior hasn't been above reproach."

"I don't have to listen to this!" Janet rose from the sofa and opened her pocketbook, replacing the pack of cigarettes and taking out her gloves.

"I'm not making judgments. You're an intelligent girl. Whatever you do, I'm sure there are reasons. . . . If it's any comfort, I think you've spent a year in hell."

"Yes. A year in hell." Janet Scarlett began putting on her gloves.

Elizabeth spoke rapidly as she crossed to her desk by the window. "But let's be candid. If Ulster were here, or in evidence anywhere, an uncontested divorce could be arranged quietly, without difficulty. After all, neither is without blemish. But, as the law says, one of the parties is removed, perhaps deceased, but not legally declared dead. And there's a child, an only child. That child is Ulster's heir. This, Janet, is the problem."

Elizabeth wondered if the girl was beginning to understand. The trouble with the young rich, she decided, wasn't that they took their money for granted, but that they couldn't comprehend that money, though a by-product, was a true catalyst to power and, because of this, a frightening thing.

"Once you made the first move, the birds of prey from both camps would descend. In the final analysis, the Scarlatti name would become a joke in the back rooms of athletic clubs. And that I will not have!"

Elizabeth took out several folders from the desk drawer, selected one, and replaced the others. She sat down behind the desk and looked over at the girl.

"Do you understand what I'm saying?"

"Yes, I think I do," the girl said slowly, looking down at her gloved hands. "You want to conveniently tuck me away out of sight so nothing can disturb your precious Scarletts." She hesitated, lifting her head to return her mother-in-law's gaze. "And I thought for a minute you were going to be kind."

"You can't very well qualify as a charity case," said Elizabeth.

"No, I suppose not. But since I'm not looking for charity, that doesn't matter, does it? I guess you're trying to be kind, in your own way."

"Then you'll do as I suggest?" Elizabeth moved the folder to put it back in the drawer.

"No," Janet Saxon Scarlett said firmly. "I'll do exactly as I please. And I don't think I'll be a joke in athletic clubs."

"Don't be too sure of that!" Elizabeth slammed the folder back on the top of the desk.

"I'll wait until a year is up," said Janet, "and then do whatever I have to. My father will know what to do. I'll do what he says."

"Your father may have certain misgivings. He's a businessman."

"He's also my father!"

"I can very well understand that, my dear. I understand it so well that I suggest you allow me to ask you several questions before you go."

Elizabeth stood up and crossed to the library door. Closing it, she turned the brass lock.

Janet watched the old woman's movement with as much curiosity as fear. It was not like her mother-in-law to be the least concerned about interruptions. Any unwanted intruder was promptly ordered out.

"There's nothing more to say. I want to leave."

"I agree. You have little to say," broke in Elizabeth, who had returned to the desk. "You enjoyed Europe, my dear? Paris, Marseilles, Rome? I must say, though, New York's apparently a dull place for you. I suppose under the circumstances there's far more to offer across the ocean."

"What do you mean?"

"Just that. You seem to have enjoyed yourself somewhat unreasonably. My son found himself quite a likely playmate for his escapades. However, if I do say so, he was frequently less obvious than you."

"I don't know what you're talking about."

Elizabeth opened the folder and flipped over several pages. "Let's see, now. There was a colored trumpet player in Paris. . . ."

"A what! What are you talking about?"

"He brought you back to your hotel, excuse me, yours and Ulster's hotel, at eight o'clock in the morning. Obviously, you'd been with him all night."

Janet stared at her mother-in-law in disbelief. Although dazed, she answered her rapidly, quietly. "Yes. Paris, yes! And I was with him, but not like that. I was trying to keep up with Ulster. Half the night trying to find him."

"That fact doesn't appear here. You were seen coming into the hotel with a colored man supporting you."

"I was exhausted."

"Drunk is the word used here. . . ."

"Then it's a lie!"

The old woman turned the page. "And then one week in the south of France? Do you remember that weekend, Janet?"

"No," the girl answered hesitantly. "What are you doing? What have you got there?"

Elizabeth rose, holding the folder away from the girl's eyes. "Oh, come now. That weekend at Madame Auriole's. What do they call her chateau—the Silhouette? Quite a dramatic name."

"She was a friend of Ulster!"

"And, of course, you had no idea what Auriole's Silhouette meant, and still means, I believe, throughout the south of France."

"You're not suggesting that I had anything to do with any of that?"

"Just what did people mean when they said they went to Auriole's Silhouette?"

"You can't mean it."

"What happens at Auriole's Silhouette?" Elizabeth's voice rose viciously.

"I don't . . . don't know. I don't know!"

"What happens?"

"I won't answer you!"

"That's very prudent, but I'm afraid it won't do! It's common knowledge that the outstanding items on Madame Auriole's menus are opium, hashish, marijuana, heroin . . . a haven for the users of every form of narcotics!"

"I did not know that!"

"You didn't know anything about it? For an entire weekend? For three days during the height of her season?"

"No! . . . Yes, I found out and I left. I left as soon as I realized what they were doing!"

"Orgies for narcotics addicts. Marvelous opportunities for the sophisticated voyeur. Day and night. And Mrs. Scarlett knew nothing about it at all!"

"I swear I didn't!"

Elizabeth's voice changed to one of gentle firmness. "I'm sure you didn't, my dear, but I don't know who would believe you." She paused briefly. "There's a great deal more here." She flipped the pages, sitting down once more behind the desk. "Berlin, Vienna, Rome. Particularly Cairo."

Janet ran toward Elizabeth Scarlatti and leaned across the desk, her eyes wide with fright. "Ulster left me for almost two weeks! I didn't know where he was. I was petrified!"

"You were seen going into the strangest places, my dear. You even committed one of the gravest international crimes. You bought another human being. You purchased a slave."

"No! No, I didn't! That's not true!"

"Oh, yes, it is. You bought a thirteen-year-old Arab girl who was being sold into prostitution. As an American citizen there are specific laws . . ."

"It's a lie!" broke in Janet. "They told me that if I paid the money, the Arab could tell me where Ulster was! That's all I did!"

"No, it wasn't. You gave him a present. A little thirteen-year-old girl was your present to him and you know it. I wonder if you've ever thought about her."

"I just wanted to find Ulster! I was sick when I found out. I didn't understand! I didn't even know what they were talking about! All I wanted to do was find Ulster and get out of that awful place!"

"I wouldn't pretend to dispute you. Nevertheless, others would."

"Who?" The girl was shaking.

"The courts, for one. Newspapers, for another." Elizabeth stared at the frightened girl. "My friends. . . . . Even your own friends."

"And you would allow . . . someone to use those lies against me?"

Elizabeth shrugged.

"And against your own grandchild?"

"I doubt that he would be your child, legally, that is, for very long. I'm sure he'd be declared a ward of the court until it was determined that Chancellor was the proper guardian for him."

Janet slowly sat down on the edge of the chair. Lips parted, she began to cry.

"Please, Janet. I'm not asking you to enroll in a nunnery. I'm not even asking you to do without the normal satisfactions of a woman of your age and appetites. You've hardly restricted yourself during the past several months, and I don't expect you to now. I'm only asking a fair amount of discretion, perhaps a bit more than you've been exercising, and a healthy degree of physical caution. In the absence of the latter, immediate remedy."

Janet Saxon Scarlett turned her head away, her eyes tightly shut. "You're horrible," she whispered.

"I imagine I appear that way to you. Someday I hope you may reconsider."

Janet sprang from the chair.

"Let me out of this house!"

"For heaven's sake try to understand. Chancellor and Allison will be here soon. I need you, my dear."

The girl raced to the door, forgetting the lock. She could not open it. Her voice was low in her panic. "What more could you possibly want?"

And Elizabeth knew she had won.

Chapter Sixteen

Matthew Canfield leaned against the building on the southeast corner of Fifth Avenue at Sixty-third Street, about forty yards from the imposing entrance to the Scarlatti residence. He pulled his raincoat tightly around him to ward off the chill brought by the autumn rain and glanced at his watch: ten minutes to six. He had been at his post for over an hour. The girl had gone in at a quarter to five; and for all he knew, she would be there until midnight or, God forbid, until morning. He had arranged for a relief at two o'clock if nothing had happened by then. There was no particular reason for him to feel that something would happen by then, but his instincts told him otherwise. After five weeks of familiarizing himself with his subjects, he let his imagination fill in what observation precluded. The old lady was boarding ship the day after tomorrow, and not taking anyone with her. Her lament for her missing or dead son was international knowledge. Her grief was the subject of countless newspaper stories. However, the old woman hid her grief well and went about her business.

Scarlett's wife was different. If she mourned her missing husband, it was not apparent. But what was obvious was her disbelief in Ulster Scarlett's death. What was it she had said in the bar at the Oyster Bay Country Club? Although her voice was thick from whiskey, her pronouncement was clear.

"My dear mother-in-law thinks she's so smart. I hope the boat sinks! She'll find him."

Tonight there was a confrontation between the two women, and Matthew Canfield wished he could be a witness.

The drizzle was letting up. Canfield decided to walk across Fifth Avenue to the park side of the street. He took a newspaper out of his raincoat pocket, spread it on the slatted bench in front of the Central Park wall, and sat down. A man and a woman stopped before the old lady's steps. It was fairly dark now, and he couldn't see who they were. The woman was animatedly explaining something, while the man seemed not to listen, more intent on pulling out his pocket watch and checking the time. Canfield looked again at his own watch and noted that it was two minutes to six. He slowly got up and began to saunter back across the avenue. The man turned toward the curb to get the spill of streetlight on his watch. The woman kept talking.

Canfield saw with no surprise that it was the older brother Chancellor Drew Scarlett and his wife Allison.

Canfield kept walking east on Sixty-third as Chancellor Scarlett took his wife's elbow and marched her up the steps to the Scarlatti door. As he reached Madison Avenue, Canfield heard a sharp crash. He turned and saw that the front door of Elizabeth Scarlatti's house had been pulled open with such force that the collision against an unseen wall echoed throughout the street.

Janet Scarlett came running down the brick stairs, tripped, got up, and hobbled toward Fifth Avenue. Canfield started back toward her. She was hurt and the timing might just be perfect.

The field accountant was within thirty yards of Ulster Scarlett's wife when a roadster, a shiny black Pierce-Arrow, came racing down the block. The car veered close to the curb near the girl.

Canfield slowed down and watched. He could see the man in the roadster leaning forward toward the far window. The light from the overhead streetlamp shone directly on his face. He was a handsome man in his early fifties perhaps, with a perfectly groomed matted moustache. He appeared to be the sort of man Janet Scarlett might know. It struck Canfield that the man had been waiting—as he had been waiting—for Janet Scarlett.

Suddenly the man stopped the car, threw his door open, and quickly got out onto the street. He rapidly walked around the car toward the girl.

"Here, Mrs. Scarlett. Get in."

Janet Scarlett bent down to hold her injured knee. She looked up, bewildered, at the approaching man with the matted moustache. Canfield stopped. He stood in the shadows by a doorway.

"What? You're not a taxi. . . . No. I don't know you. . . ."

"Get in! I'll drive you home. Quickly, now!" The man spoke peremptorily. A disturbed voice. He grabbed Janet Scarlett's arm.

"No! No, I won't!" She tried to pull her arm away.

Canfield came out of the shadows. "Hello, Mrs. Scarlett. I thought it was you. Can I be of help?"

The well-groomed man released the girl and stared at Canfield. He seemed confused as well as angry. Instead of speaking, however, he suddenly ran back into the street and climbed into the car.

"Hey, wait a minute, mister!" The field accountant rushed to the curb and put his hand on the door handle. "We'll take you up on the ride. . . ."

The engine accelerated and the roadster sped off down the street throwing Canfield to the ground, his hand lacerated by the door handle wrenched from his grip.

He got up painfully and spoke to Janet Scarlett.

"Your friend's pretty damned chintzy."

Janet Scarlett looked at the field accountant with gratitude.

"I never saw him before. . . . At least, I don't think so. . . . Maybe. . . . I'm sorry to say, I don't remember your name. I am sorry and I do thank you."

"No apologies necessary. We've only met once. Oyster Bay club a couple of weeks ago."

"Oh!" The girl seemed not to want to recall the evening.

"Chris Newland introduced us. The name's Canfield."

"Oh, yes."

"Matthew Canfield. I'm the one from Chicago."

"Yes, I remember now."

"Come on. I'll get us a taxi."

"Your hand is bleeding."

"So's your knee."

"Mine's only a scratch."

"So's mine. Just scraped. Looks worse than it is."

"Perhaps you should see a doctor."

"All I need is a handkerchief and some ice. Handkerchief for the hand, ice for a Scotch." They reached Fifth Avenue and Canfield hailed a taxi. "That's all the doctoring I need, Mrs. Scarlett."

Janet Scarlett smiled hesitantly as they got into the cab. "That doctoring I can provide."

The entrance hall of the Scarlett home on Fifty-fourth Street was about what Canfield had imagined it would be. The ceilings were high, the main doors thick, and the staircase facing the entrance rose an imposing two stories. There were antique mirrors on either side of the hallway, double french doors beside each mirror facing each other across the foyer. The doors on the right were open and Canfield could see the furniture of a formal dining room. The doors on the left were closed and he presumed they led into a living room. Expensive oriental throw rugs were placed on the parquet floors. . . . This was all as it should be. However, what shocked the field accountant was the color scheme of the hallway itself. The wallpaper was a rich—too rich—red damask, and the drapes covering the french doors were black—a heavy black velvet that was out of character with the ornate delicacy of the French furniture.

Janet Scarlett noticed his reaction to the colors and before Canfield could disguise it, said, "Rather hits you in the eye, doesn't it?"

"I hadn't noticed," he said politely.

"My husband insisted on that hideous red and then replaced all my pink silks with those awful black drapes. He made a terrible scene about it when I objected." She parted the double doors and moved into the darkness to turn on a table lamp.

Canfield followed her into the extraordinarily ornate living room. It was the size of five squash courts, and the number of settees, sofas, and armchairs was staggering. Fringed lamps were silhouetted atop numerous tables placed conveniently by the seating places. The arrangement of the furniture was unrelated except for a semicircle of divans facing an enormous fireplace. In the dim light of the single lamp, Canfield's eyes were immediately drawn to a panoply of dull reflections above the mantel. They were photographs. Dozens of photographs of varying sizes placed in thin black frames. They were arranged as a floral spray, the focal point being a scroll encased in gold borders at the center of the mantel.

The girl noticed Canfield's stare but did not acknowledge it.

"There're drinks and ice over there," she said, pointing to a dry bar. "Just help yourself. Will you pardon me for a minute? I'll change my stockings." She disappeared into the main hall.

Canfield crossed to the glass-topped wheel cart and poured two small tumblers of Scotch. He withdrew a clean handkerchief from his trousers, doused it in ice water, and wrapped it around his slightly bleeding hand. Then he turned on another lamp to illuminate the display above the mantel. For the briefest of moments, he was shocked.

It was incredible. Over the mantel was a photographic presentation of Ulster Stewart Scarlett's army career. From officer's candidate school to embarkation; from his arrival in France to his assignment to the trenches. In some frames there were maps with heavy red and blue lines indicating positions. In a score of pictures Ulster was the energetic center of attraction.

He had seen photographs of Scarlett before, but they were generally snapshots taken at society parties or single shots of the socialite in his various athletic endeavors—polo, tennis, sailing—and he had looked precisely the way Brooks Brothers expected their clients to look. However, here he was among soldiers, and it annoyed Canfield to see that he was nearly a half a head taller than the largest soldier near him. And there were soldiers everywhere, of every rank and every degree of military bearing. Awkward citizen corporals having their weapons inspected, weary sergeants lining up wearier men, experienced-looking field officers listening intently—all were doing what they were doing for the benefit of the vigorous, lean lieutenant who somehow commanded their attention. In many pictures the young officer has his arms slung around half-smiling companions as if assuring them that happy days would soon be here again.

Judging by the expressions of those around him, Scarlett was not notably successful. However, his own countenance radiated optimism itself. Cool, and intensely self-satisfied as well, thought Canfield. The centerpiece was, indeed, a scroll. It was the Silver Star citation for gallantry at the Meuse-Argonne. To judge from the exhibition, Ulster Scarlett was the best-adjusted hero ever to have the good fortune to go to war. The disturbing aspect was the spectacle itself. It was grotesquely out of place. It belonged in the study of some celebrated warrior whose campaigns spanned half a century, not here on Fifty-fourth Street in the ornate living room of a pleasure-seeker.

"Interesting, aren't they?" Janet had reentered the room.

"Impressive, to say the least. He's quite a guy."

"You have no argument there. If anyone forgot, he just had to walk into this room to be reminded."

"I gather that this . . . this pictorial history of how the war was won wasn't your idea." He handed Janet her drink, which, he noted, she firmly clasped and brought immediately to her lips.

"It most certainly was not." She nearly finished the short, straight Scotch. "Sit down, won't you?"

Canfield quickly downed most of his own drink. "First let me freshen these." He took her glass. She sat on the large sofa facing the mantel while he crossed to the bar.

"I never thought your husband was subject to this kind of"—he paused and nodded to the fireplace—"hangover."

"That's an accurate analogy. Aftermath of a big binge. You're a philosopher."

"Don't mean to be. Just never thought of him as the type." He brought over the two drinks, handed one to her, and remained standing.

"Didn't you read his accounts of what happened? I thought the newspapers did a splendid job of making it perfectly clear who was really responsible for the Kaiser's defeat." She drank again.

"Oh, hell, that's the publishing boys. They have to sell papers. I read them but I didn't take them seriously. Never thought he did either."

"You talk as if you knew my husband."

Canfield purposely looked startled and took his glass away from his lips. "Didn't you know?"

"What?"

"Well, of course, I knew him. I knew him quite well. I just took it for granted that you knew. I'm sorry."

Janet concealed her surprise. "There's nothing to be sorry about. Ulster had a large circle of friends. I couldn't possibly know them all. Were you a New York friend of Ulster's? I don't remember his mentioning you."

"No, not really. Oh, we met now and then when I came east."

"Oh, that's right, you're from Chicago. It is Chicago?"

"It is. But to be honest with you, my job takes me all over the place." And certainly, he was honest about that.

"What do you do?"

Canfield returned with the drinks and sat down.

"Stripped of its frills, I'm a salesman. But we never strip the frills that obviously."

"What do you sell? I know lots of people who sell things. They don't worry about frills."

"Well, I don't sell stocks or bonds or buildings or even bridges. I sell tennis courts."

Janet laughed. It was a nice laugh. "You're joking!"

"No, seriously, I sell tennis courts."

He put his drink down and pretended to look in his pockets. "Let's see if I've got one on me. They're really very nice. Perfect bounce. Wimbledon standards except for the grass. That's the name of our company. Wimbledon. For your information, they're excellent courts. You've probably played on dozens of them and never knew who to give the credit to."

"I think that's fascinating. Why do people buy your tennis courts? Can't they just build their own?"

"Sure. We encourage them to. We make more money when we rip one out and replace it with ours."

"You're teasing me. A tennis court's a tennis court."

"Only the grass ones, my dear. And they're never quite ready by spring and they're always brown in the fall. Ours are year-round."

She laughed again.

"It's really very simple. My company's developed an asphalt composition that duplicates the bounce of a grass court. Never melts in heat. Never expands when frozen. Would you like the full sales pitch? Our trucks will be here in three days and during that time we'll contract for the first layer of gravel. We'll do that locally. Before you know it, you'll have a beautiful court right out there on Fifty-fourth Street."

They both laughed.

"And I assume you're a champion tennis player."

"No. I play. Not well. I don't particularly like the game. Naturally we have several internationally known whizzes on the payroll to vouch for the courts. Incidentally, we guarantee an exhibition match on yours the day we complete the job. You can ask your friends over and have a party. Some magnificent parties have been held on our courts. Now, that's generally the close that sells the job!"

"Very impressive."

"From Atlanta to Bar Harbor. Best courts, best parties." He raised his glass.

"Oh, so you sold Ulster a tennis court?"

"Never tried. I imagine I could have. He bought a dirigible once, and after all, what's a tennis court compared to that?"

"It's flatter." She giggled and held her glass out to him. He rose and went to the bar, unwrapping the handkerchief from his hand and putting it in his pocket. She slowly extinguished her cigarette in the ashtray in front of her.

"If you're not in the New York crowd, where did you know my husband?"

"We first met in college. Briefly, very briefly. I left in the middle of my first year." Canfield wondered if Washington had placed the proper records of a long-forgotten freshman down at Princeton University.

"Aversion to books?"

"Aversion to money. The wrong branch of the family had it. Then we met later in the army, again briefly."

"The army?"

"Yes. But in no way like that, I repeat, no way like that!" He gestured toward the mantel and returned to the sofa.

"Oh?"

"We parted company after training in New Jersey. He to France and glory. Me to Washington and boredom. But we had a helluva time before that." Canfield leaned ever so slightly toward her, permitting his voice the minor intimacy usually accompanying the second effects of alcohol. "All prior to his nuptials, of course."

"Not so prior, Matthew Canfield."

He looked at her closely, noting that the anticipated response was positive but not necessarily liking the fact. "If that's the case, he was a bigger fool than I thought he was."

She looked into his eyes as one scans a letter, trying to read, not between the lines, but instead, beyond the words.

"You're a very attractive man." And then she rose quickly, a bit unsteadily, and put her drink down on the small table in front of the settee. "I haven't had dinner and if I don't eat soon I'll be incoherent. I don't like being incoherent."

"Let me take you out."

"And have you bleed all over some poor unsuspecting waiter?"

"No more blood." Canfield held out his hand. "I would like to have dinner with you."

"Yes, I'm sure you would." She picked up her drink and walked with ever so slight a list to the left side of the fireplace. "Do you know what I was about to do?"

"No." He remained seated, slouched deeply into the sofa.

"I was about to ask you to leave."

Canfield began to protest.

"No, wait. I wanted to be all by myself and nibble something all by myself and perhaps that's not such a good idea."

"I think that's a terrible idea."

"So I won't."

"Good."

"But I don't want to go out. Will you have, as they say, potluck with me here?"

"Won't that be a lot of trouble?"

Janet Scarlett yanked at a pull cord, which hung on the wall at the side of the mantel. "Only for the house-keeper. And she hasn't been overworked in the least since my husband—left."

The housekeeper answered her summons with such speed that the field accountant wondered if she were listening at the door. She was about the homeliest woman Matthew Canfield had ever seen. Her hands were huge.

"Yes, madame? We did not expect you home this evening. You did tell us you were dining with Madame Scarlatti."

"It seems I've changed my mind, doesn't it, Hannah? Mr. Canfield and I will dine here. I've told him potluck, so serve us whatever luck the pot holds."

"Very well, madame."

Her accent had a trace of Middle Europe, perhaps Swiss or German, thought Canfield. Her jowled face framed by her pulled-back gray hair should have been friendly. But it wasn't. It was somehow hard, masculine.

Nevertheless, she made sure the cook prepared an excellent meal.

"When that old bitch wants something, she makes them all quiver and quake until she gets it," said Janet. They had gone back to the living room and sat sipping brandy on the pillow-fluffed sofa, their shoulders touching.

"That's natural. From everything I've heard, she runs the whole show. They've got to cater to her. I know I would."

"My husband never thought so," the girl said quietly. "She'd get furious with him."

Canfield pretended disinterest. "Really? I never knew there was any trouble between them."

"Oh, not trouble. Ulster never cared enough about anything or anybody to cause trouble. That's why she'd get so angry. He wouldn't fight. He'd just do what he wanted to. He was the only person she couldn't control and she hated that."

"She could stop the money, couldn't she?" Canfield asked naïvely.

"He had his own."

"God knows that's exasperating. He probably drove her crazy."

The young wife was looking at the mantel. "He drove me crazy, too. She's no different."

"Well, she's his mother. . . ."

"And I'm his wife." She was now drunk and she stared with hatred at the photographs. "She has no right caging me up like an animal! Threatening me with stupid gossip! Lies! Millions of lies! My husband's friends, not mine! Though they might as well be mine, they're no God damn better!"

"Ulster's pals were always a little weird, I agree with you there. If they're being louses to you, ignore them. You don't need them."

Janet laughed. "That's what I'll do! I'll travel to Paris, Cairo, and wherever the hell else, and take ads in the papers. All you friends of that bastard Ulster Scarlett, I ignore you! Signed, J. Saxon Scarlett, widow. I hope!"

The field accountant pressed his luck. "She's got information about you from . . . places like that?"

"Oh, she doesn't miss a trick. You're nobody if the illustrious Madame Scarlatti hasn't got a dossier on you. Didn't you know that?"

And then almost as rapidly as she had flown into rage, she receded into calm reflection. "But it's not important. Let her go to hell."

"Why is she going to Europe?"

"Why do you care?"

Canfield shrugged. "I don't. I just read it in the columns."

"I haven't the vaguest idea."

"Has it anything to do with all that gossip, those lies she collected from Paris . . . and those places?" He tried, and it wasn't difficult, to slur his words.

"Ask her. Do you know, this brandy's good." She finished the remainder in her glass and set it down. The field accountant had most of his left. He held his breath and drank it.

"You're right. She's a bitch."

"She's a bitch." The girl pressed into Canfield's shoulder and arm, turning her face to his. "You're not a bitch, are you?"

"No, and the gender is wrong, anyway. Why is she going to Europe?"

"I've asked myself that lots of times and I can't think of an answer. And I don't care. Are you really a nice person?"

"The nicest, I think."

"I'm going to kiss you and find out. I can always tell."

"You're not that practiced. . . ."

"Oh, but I am." The girl reached across Canfield's neck and pulled him to her. She trembled.

His response was mild astonishment. The girl was desperate and for some senseless reason, he had the feeling of wanting to protect her.

She pulled her hand down from his shoulder. "Let's go upstairs," she said.

And upstairs they kissed and Janet Scarlett put her hands on his face.

"She said . . . fun of being a Scarlett without a Scarlett around. . . . That's what she said."

"Who? Who said that?"

"Mother Bitch. That's who."

"His mother?"

"Unless she finds him. . . . I'm free. . . . Take me, Matthew. Take me, please, for God's sake!"

As he led her to bed, Canfield made up his mind that he'd somehow convince his superiors that he had to get aboard that ship.

Chapter Seventeen

Jefferson Cartwright draped a towel over his body and walked out of the club's steam room. He went into the needle shower and let the harsh spray beat down on the top of his head, turning his face upward until the tiny blasts of water hurt his skin. He adjusted the faucets so that the water slowly became colder, finally icy.

He had gotten very drunk the night before. Actually he had started drinking early in the afternoon and by midnight was so far gone he decided to stay at his club rather than go home. He had every reason to celebrate. Since his triumphant meeting with Elizabeth Scarlatti he'd spent several days analyzing to the best of his ability the affairs of the Scarwyck Foundation. Now he was prepared to walk among his peers. Elizabeth's agreement never left his mind. He kept it in his briefcase until he knew enough about Scarwyck so that even his own attorneys would be impressed. He remembered as the water splashed down on his head that he had put the briefcase in a locker at Grand Central Station. Many of his colleagues swore that the Grand Central lockers were safer than vaults. Certainly they were safer than the Scarlatti vaults!

He'd pick up the briefcase after lunch and take the agreement to his lawyers. They'd be astonished and he hoped they'd ask him questions about Scarwyck. He'd rattle off facts and figures so rapidly they'd be in shock.

He could hear them now.

"My God, ole Jeff! We had no idea!"

Cartwright laughed out loud in the shower.

He, Jefferson Cartwright, was the most cavalier of Virginia Cavaliers! These Northern pricks with their high-fallutin condescending ways, who couldn't even satisfy their own wives, had ole Jeff to reckon with now. On their level!

My God, he thought, he could buy and sell half the members in the club! It was a lovely day!

After his shower, Jefferson dressed and, feeling the full measure of his power, jauntily entered the private bar. Most of the members were gathered for lunch and with false graciousness several accepted his offer of a drink. However, their reluctance turned into minor enthusiasm when Jefferson announced casually that he had "taken over Scarwyck's financial chores."

Two or three suddenly found that the boorish Jefferson Cartwright had qualities that they had not noticed before. Indeed, not a bad chap, if you came to think about it. . . . Certainly must have something! Soon the heavy leather chairs surrounding the circular oak table to which Jefferson had repaired were occupied.

As the clock neared two thirty, the members excused themselves and

headed to their offices and their telephones. The communications network
was activated and the startling news of Cartwright's coup with the Scarwyck
Foundation was spread.

One particular gentleman did not leave, however. He stayed on with a few
diehards and joined the court of Jefferson Cartwright. He was perhaps fifty
years old and the essence of that image so sought by aging socialites. Even to
the graying moustache so perfectly overgroomed.

The funny thing was that no one at the table was quite sure of his name,
but no one wanted to admit it. This was, after all, a club.

The gentleman gracefully propped himself into the chair next to Jefferson
the minute it became available. He bantered with the Southerner and insisted
upon ordering another round of drinks.

When the drinks arrived, the well-tailored gentleman reached for the
martinis and in the middle of an anecdote placed them in front of him for a
moment. As he finished his story, he handed one to Jefferson.

Jefferson took the drink and drank fully.

The gentleman excused himself. Two minutes later Jefferson Cartwright
fell over on the table. His eyes were not drowsy or even closed as might
become a man who had reached the limit of alcoholic capacity. Instead, they
were wide open, bulging out of his skull.

Jefferson Cartwright was dead.

And the gentleman never returned.

Downtown in the press room of a New York tabloid an old typesetter
punched out the letters of the short news story. It was to appear on page 10.

Banker Succumbs in Fashionable Men's Club

The typesetter was disinterested.

Several machines away another employee pushed the keys for another
story. This one was sandwiched between retail advertisements on page 48.

Grand Central Locker Robbed

The man wondered. Isn't anything safe anymore?

Chapter Eighteen

At the captain's table in the first-class dining room of the *Calpurnia*,
Elizabeth was somewhat surprised to find that her companion to the right
was a man no more than thirty years old. The normal practice when she
traveled alone was for the ship line to provide her with an aging diplomat or a
retired broker, a good card player, someone with whom she'd have something in common.

She had no one to blame, however, as she had checked the captain's list—a
procedure she insisted upon so that there would be no embarrassing business
conflicts—and had merely noted that one Matthew Canfield was an executive
with a sporting goods firm that purchased heavily in England. Someone with

social connections, she had assumed.

At any rate he was likable. A polite young man, very shallow, she thought, and probably a good salesman, which he refreshingly admitted he was.

Toward the end of dinner a deck officer approached her chair; there was a cable for her.

"You may bring it to the table." Elizabeth was annoyed.

The officer spoke softly to Elizabeth.

"Very well." She rose from her chair.

"May I be of assistance, Madame Scarlatti?" asked Matthew Canfield, salesman, as he rose with the rest of the table.

"No, thank you."

"Are you quite sure?"

"Quite, thank you." She followed the deck officer out of the salon.

In the radio room, Elizabeth was shown to a table behind the counter and handed the message. She noted the instructions at the top: "Emergency—have addressee brought to office for immediate reply."

She looked over at the deck officer who waited on the other side of the counter to escort her back to the salon. "My apologies, you were following orders."

She read the rest of the wire.

> MADAME ELIZABETH SCARLATTI: H.M.S. CALPURNIA,
> HIGH SEAS
> VICE-PRESIDENT JEFFERSON CARTWRIGHT DEAD STOP
> CAUSE OF DEATH UNCERTAIN STOP AUTHORITIES SUS-
> PECT ABNORMAL CIRCUMSTANCES STOP PRIOR TO DEATH
> CARTWRIGHT MADE PUBLIC A POSITION OF SIGNIFICANT
> RANK WITH SCARWYCK FOUNDATION STOP WE HAVE NO
> RECORD OF SUCH POSITION YET INFORMATION RECEIVED
> FROM RELIABLE SOURCES STOP IN LIGHT OF ABOVE DO
> YOU WISH TO COMMENT OR INSTRUCT US IN ANY WAY STOP
> EPISODE MOST TRAGIC AND EMBARRASSING TO WATER-
> MAN CLIENTS STOP WE HAD NO KNOWLEDGE OF VICE-PRES-
> IDENT CARTWRIGHT'S QUESTIONABLE ACTIVITIES STOP
> AWAITING YOUR REPLY STOP
> HORACE BOUTIER PRESIDENT WATERMAN TRUST COMPANY

Elizabeth was stunned. She wired Mr. Boutier that all announcements from the Scarlatti Industries would be issued by Chancellor Drew Scarlett within a week. Until then there would be no comment.

She sent a second wire to Chancellor Drew.

> C. D. SCARLETT, 129 EAST SIXTY-SECOND STREET, NEW
> YORK
> REGARDING JEFFERSON CARTWRIGHT NO STATEMENTS
> REPEAT NO STATEMENTS WILL BE ISSUED PUBLICLY OR
> PRIVATELY REPEAT PUBLICLY OR PRIVATELY UNTIL WE
> ARE IN CONTACT FROM ENGLAND STOP REPEAT NO STATE-
> MENT STOP
> AFFECTIONATELY AS ALWAYS
> MOTHER

Elizabeth felt she should reappear at the table if for no other reason than to avoid calling too much attention to the incident. But as she walked slowly back through the narrow corridors with the deck officer, it came upon her with progressive apprehension that what had happened was a warning. She immediately dismissed the theory that Cartwright's "questionable activities" caused his murder. He was a joke.

What Elizabeth had to be prepared for was the discovery of her agreement with Cartwright. There could be several explanations, which she would issue without elaboration. Of course, regardless of what she said, the consensus would be that age had finally caught up with her. Such an agreement with such a man as Jefferson Cartwright was proof of eccentricity to the degree that raised questions of competence.

This did not concern Elizabeth Scarlatti. She was not subject to the opinion of others.

What concerned her, and concerned her deeply, was the cause of her profound fear: the fact that the agreement might not be found.

Back at the captain's table she dismissed her absence with a short, sincere statement that one of her trusted executives, of whom she was quite fond, had died. As she obviously did not wish to dwell on the subject, her dinner companions uttered their sympathies, and after an appropriate pause in their conversations, resumed their small talk. The captain of the *Calpurnia*, an overstuffed Englishman with thickly matted eyebrows and enormous jowls, noted ponderously that the loss of a good executive must be akin to the transfer of a well-trained mate.

The young man next to Elizabeth leaned toward her and spoke softly. "Right out of Gilbert and Sullivan, isn't he."

The old woman smiled back in agreeable conspiracy. Beneath the babble of voices she answered him quietly. "A monarch of the sea. Can't you picture him ordering up the cat-o'-nine-tails?"

"No," replied the young man. "But I can picture him climbing out of his bathtub. It's funnier."

"You're a wicked boy. If we hit an iceberg, I shall avoid you."

"You couldn't. I'd be in the first lifeboat and certainly someone around here would reserve a seat for you." He smiled disarmingly.

Elizabeth laughed. The young man amused her and it was refreshing to be treated with a degree of good-humored insolence. They chatted pleasantly about their forthcoming itineraries in Europe. It was fascinating, in an offhand way, because neither had any intention of telling the other anything of consequence.

With dinner over, the captain's troupe of very important passengers made their way to the game room and paired off for bridge.

"I assume you're a terrible card player," Canfield said, smiling at Elizabeth. "Since I'm rather good, I'll carry you."

"It's difficult to refuse such a flattering invitation."

And then he inquired: "Who died? Anyone I might know?"

"I doubt it, young man."

"You never can tell. Who was it?"

"Now why in the world would you know an obscure executive in my bank?"

"I gathered he was a pretty important fellow."

"I imagine some people thought he was."

"Well, if he was rich enough, I might have sold him a tennis court."

"Really, Mr. Canfield, you're the limit." Elizabeth laughed as they reached the lounge.

During the game Elizabeth noted that although young Canfield had the quiet flair of a first-rate player, he really wasn't very good. At one point he made himself dummy, quite unnecessarily thought Elizabeth, but she put it down to a form of courtesy. He inquired of the lounge steward if there was a particular brand of cigars on hand, and when offered substitutes, excused himself saying that he'd get some from his stateroom.

Elizabeth remembered that back in the dining room during their coffee the charming Mr. Canfield had opened a fresh pack of thin cigars.

He returned several minutes after the hand was finished and apologized by explaining that he had helped an elderly gentleman, somewhat overcome by the sea, back to his cabin.

The opponents muttered complimentary phrases, but Elizabeth said nothing. She simply stared at the young man and noted with a degree of satisfaction, as well as alarm, that he avoided her gaze.

The game ended early; the pitch of the *Calpurnia* was now quite unsettling. Canfield escorted Elizabeth Scarlatti to her suite.

"You've been charming," she said. "I now release you to pursue the younger generation."

Canfield smiled and handed her the keys. "If you insist. But you condemn me to boredom. You know that."

"Times *have* changed, or perhaps the young men."

"Perhaps." It seemed to Elizabeth that he was anxious to leave.

"Well, an old woman thanks you."

"A not so young man thanks you. Good night, Madame Scarlatti."

She turned to him. "Are you still interested in who the man was who died?"

"I gathered you didn't want to tell me. It's not important. Good night."

"His name was Cartwright. Jefferson Cartwright. Did you know him?" She watched his eyes closely.

"No, I'm sorry, I didn't." His look was steady and entirely innocent. "Good night."

"Good night, young man." She entered her suite and closed the door. She could hear his footsteps fading away down the outside corridor. He was a man in a hurry.

Elizabeth removed her mink and walked into the large comfortable bedroom with its heavy furniture secured to the floor. She turned on a lamp attached to the nightstand and sat on the edge of the bed. She tried to recall more specifically what the *Calpurnia*'s captain had said of the young man when he had presented his table for her approval.

"And then there's a chap, very well connected, I might add, named Canfield."

Elizabeth paid no more attention to his abbreviated biography than she had to the others.

"He's associated with a sporting goods concern and crosses rather regularly. Wimbledon, I believe."

And then, if Elizabeth's memory served her well, the captain had added, "Priority request from the ship line. Probably the son of an old boy. School tie and that sort of thing. Had to drop Dr. Barstow for him."

Elizabeth had given her approval without any questions.

So the young man had a priority request for the captain's table from the owners of an English steamship company. And a fatuous captain, accustomed to associating with the social and professional leaders of both continents, had felt obliged to drop a highly regarded surgeon in his favor.

If for no other reason than to quell an inexhaustible imagination, Elizabeth picked up the stateroom phone and asked for the wireless room.

"*Calpurnia* radio, good evening." The British accent trailed off the word *evening* to a hum.

"This is Elizabeth Scarlatti, suite double A, three. May I speak with the officer in charge, if you please."

"This is Deck Officer Peters. May I help you?"

"Were you the officer who was on duty earlier this evening?"

"Yes, madame. Your wires to New York went out immediately. They should be delivered within the hour."

"Thank you. However, that's not why I'm calling. . . . I'm afraid I've missed someone I was to meet in the radio room. Has anyone asked for me?" She listened carefully for even the slightest hesitation. There was none.

"No, madame, no one's asked for you."

"Well, he might have been somewhat embarrassed. I really feel quite guilty."

"I'm sorry, Madame Scarlatti. Outside of yourself there've been only three passengers here all evening. First night out, y'know."

"Since there were only three, would you mind terribly describing them to me?"

"Oh, not at all. . . . Well, there was an elderly couple from tourist and a gentleman, a bit squiffed, I'm afraid, who wanted the wireless tour."

"The what?"

"The tour, madame. We have three a day for the first class. Ten, twelve, and two. Nice chap, really. Just a pint too many."

"Was he a young man? In his late twenties, perhaps? Dressed in a dinner jacket?"

"That description would apply, madame."

"Thank you, Officer Peters. It's an inconsequential matter, but I'd appreciate your confidence."

"Of course."

Elizabeth rose and walked to the sitting room. Her bridge partner might not be very skilled at cards, but he was a superb actor.

Chapter Nineteen

Matthew Canfield hurried down the corridor for the simple reason that his stomach was upset. Maybe the bar—and the crowd—on B deck would make him feel better. He found his way and ordered a brandy.

"Hell of a party, isn't it?"

A huge, broad-shouldered fullback-type crowded Canfield against the adjacent stool.

"Certainly is," Canfield replied with a meaningless grin.

"I know you! You're at the captain's table. We saw you at dinner."

"Good food there."

"Y'know something? I could have been at the captain's table, but I said shit on it."

"Well, that would have made an interesting hors d'oeuvre."

"No, I mean it." The accent, Canfield determined, was Tiffany-edged Park Avenue. "Uncle of mine owns a lot of stock. But I said shit on it."

"You can take my place, if you want to."

The fullback reeled slightly backward and grasped the bar for support. "Much too dull for us. Hey, barkeep! Bourbon and ginger!"

The fullback steadied himself and swayed back toward Canfield. His eyes were glazed and almost without muscular control. His very blond hair was falling over his forehead.

"What's your line, chum? Or are you still in school?"

"Thanks for the compliment. No, I'm with Wimbledon Sporting Goods. How about you?" Canfield backed himself into the stool, turning his head to continue surveying the crowd.

"Godwin and Rawlins. Securities. Father-in-law owns it. Fifth largest house in town."

"Very impressive."

"What's your drag?"

"What?"

"Drag. Pull. How come you're at the big table?"

"Oh, friends of the company, I guess. We work with English firms."

"Wimbledon. That's in Detroit."

"Chicago."

"Oh, yeah. Abercrombie of the sticks. Get it? Abercrombie of the sticks."

"We're solvent."

Canfield addressed this last remark directly to the drunken blond Adonis. He did not say it kindly.

"Don't get touchy. What's your name?"

Canfield was about to answer when his eyes were attracted to the drunk's tie. He didn't know why. Then Canfield noticed the man's cuff links. They, too, were large and striped with colors as intense as those of the tie. The colors were deep red and black.

"Cat got you?"

"What?"

"What's your name? Mine's Boothroyd. Chuck Boothroyd." He grasped the mahogany molding once again to steady himself. "You hustle for Abercrombie and . . . Oops, pardon me, Wimbledon?" Boothroyd seemed to lapse into a semistupor.

The field accountant decided that the brandy wasn't doing a thing for him, either. He really felt quite ill.

"Yeah, I hustle. Look, friend, I don't feel so good. Don't take offense, but I think I'd better get going before I have an accident. Good night, Mr. . . . ."

"Boothroyd."

"Right. Good night."

Mr. Boothroyd half opened his eyes and made a gesture of salute while reaching for his bourbon. Canfield made a swift but unsteady exit.

"Chucksie, sweetie!" A dark-haired woman slammed herself against the inebriated Mr. Boothroyd. "You disappear every God damn time I try to find you!"

"Don't be a bitch, love."

"I will be every time you do this!"

The bartender found unfinished business and walked rapidly away.

Mr. Boothroyd looked at his wife and for a few brief moments his wavering stopped. He fixed his eyes on her and his gaze was no longer unsteady, but very much alert. To the observer the two appeared to be nothing more than a husband and wife arguing over the former's drinking but with that quiet violence that keeps intruders away. Although he still maintained his bent-over posture, Chuck Boothroyd spoke clearly under the noise of the party. He sober.

"No worries, pet."

"You're sure?"

"Positive."

"Who is he?"

"Glorified salesman. Just sucking up for business is my guess."

"If he's a salesman, why was he put at a table next to her?"

"Oh, come on, stop it. You're jittery."

"Just careful."

"I'll spell it out for you. He's with that sports store in Chicago. Wimbledon. They import half their stuff from a bunch of English companies." Boothroyd stopped as if explaining a simple problem to a child. "This is a British ship. The old lady's a hell of a contact and somebody's in on the take. Besides, he's drunk as a hoot owl and sick as a dog."

"Let me have a sip." Mrs. Boothroyd reached for her husband's glass.

"Help yourself."

"When are you going to do it?"

"In about twenty minutes."

"Why does it have to be tonight?"

"The whole ship's ginned up and there's some nice, lovely rotten weather. Anybody who isn't drunk is throwing up. Maybe both."

"What do you want me to do?"

"Slap me in the face good and hard. Then go back to whomever you were with and laugh it off. Tell them when I've gone this far, the end's in sight, or something like that. In a few minutes I'll pass out on the floor. Make sure two guys carry me to the stateroom. Three maybe."

"I don't know if anyone's sober enough."

"Then get the steward. Or the bartender, that's even better. The bartender. I've been giving him a hard time."

"All right. You've got the key?"

"Your daddy gave it to me on the pier this morning."

Chapter Twenty

Canfield reached his stateroom thinking he was going to be sick. The interminable and now violent motion of the ship had its effect on him. He wondered why people made jokes about seasickness. It was never funny to him. He never laughed at the cartoons.

He fell into bed removing only his shoes. Gratefully he realized that sleep was coming on. It had been twenty-four hours of never-ending pressure.

And then the knocking began.

At first quietly. So quietly it simply made Canfield shift his position. Then louder and louder and more rapid. It was a sharp knock, as if caused by a single knuckle and because of its sharpness it echoed throughout the stateroom.

Canfield, still half asleep, called out. "What is it?"

"I think you'd better open the door, mate."

"Who is it?" Canfield tried to stop the room from turning around.

The intense knocking started all over again.

"For Christ's sake, all right! All right!"

The field accountant struggled to his feet and lurched toward the stateroom door. It was a further struggle to unlatch the lock. The uniformed figure of a ship's radio operator sprang into his cabin.

Canfield gathered his sense's as best he could and looked at the man now leaning against the door.

"What the hell do you want?"

"You told me to come to your cabin if I had somethin' worthwhile. You know. About what you're so interested in?"

"So?"

"Well, now, you wouldn't expect a British seaman to break regs without some reason, would you?"

"How much?"

"Ten quid."

"What in heaven's name is ten quid?"

"Fifty dollars to you."

"Pretty God damn expensive."

"It's worth it."

"Twenty bucks."

"Come on!" The cockney sailor whined.

"Thirty and that's it." Canfield started toward his bed.

"Sold. Gimme the cash."

Canfield withdrew his wallet and handed the radioman three ten-dollar bills. "Now, what's worth thirty dollars?"

"You were caught. By Madame Scarlatti." And he was gone.

Canfield washed in cold water to wake himself up and pondered the various alternatives.

He had been caught without an alibi that made sense. By all logic his usefulness was finished. He'd have to be replaced and that would take time. The least he could do was throw the old woman off the scent of where he came from.

He wished to God that Benjamin Reynolds was available for some good old sage advice. Then he remembered something Reynolds had once said to another field accountant who'd been exposed unmercifully. "Use part of the truth. See if it helps. Find some reason for what you're doing."

He left the stateroom and climbed the steps to A deck. He found her suite and knocked on the door.

Charles Conaway Boothroyd, executive vice-president of Godwin and Rawlins Securities, passed out cold on the deck of the lounge.

Three stewards, to inebriated male partygoers, his wife, and a passing navigation officer managed to haul his immense body out of the lounge to his cabin. Laughing they removed the blond giant's shoes and trousers and covered him over with a blanket.

Mrs. Boothroyd brought out two bottles of champagne and poured for the rescuers. She filled a water glass for herself.

The stewards and the *Calpurnia* officer drank only at Mrs. Boothroyd's absolute insistence, and left as soon as they could. Not, however, before Mrs. Boothroyd had impressed upon them how totally unconscious her husband was.

Alone with the two volunteers, Mrs. Boothroyd made sure the last of the champagne was finished. "Who's got a cabin?" she asked.

It turned out that only one was a bachelor; the other had his wife at the party.

'Get 'er plastered and let's go on by ourselves!" She flung the challenge at both of them. "Think you boys can handle me?" asked Mrs. Boothroyd.

The boys responded as one, nodding like hamsters smelling cedar shavings.

"I warn you. I'll keep my skirts up for both of you, and you still won't be enough!" Mrs. Boothroyd swayed slightly as she opened the door. "God! I hope you all don't mind watching each other. I love it, myself!"

The two men nearly crushed each other following the lady out the stateroom door.

"Bitch!" Charles Conaway Boothroyd muttered.

He removed the blanket and got into his trousers. He then reached into a drawer and took out one of his wife's stockings.

As if for a practice run, he pulled the thigh end over his head, rose from the bed, and looked at himself in the mirror. He was pleased with what he saw. He removed the stocking and opened the suitcase.

Underneath several shirts were a pair of sneakers and a thin elasticized rope about four feet long.

Charles Conaway Boothroyd laced up the sneakers while the rope lay at his feet. He pulled a black knit sweater over his large frame. He was smiling. He was a happy man.

Elizabeth Scarlatti was already in bed when she heard the knocking. She reached into the bedside table drawer and withdrew a small revolver.

Elizabeth arose and walked to the door to the outer room. "Who is it?" she asked loudly.

"Matthew Canfield. I'd like very much to speak with you."

Elizabeth was confused. She had not expected him and she reached for words. "I'm sure you've had a touch too much to drink, Mr. Canfield. Can't it wait until morning?" She wasn't even convincing to herself.

"You know perfectly well I haven't and it can't. I think we should talk now." Canfield was counting on the wind and the sea to muffle his voice. He was also counting on the fact that he had business at hand to keep him from becoming very, very sick.

Elizabeth approached the door. "I can't think of a single reason why we should talk now. I hope it won't be necessary to call the ship's police."

"For God's sake, lady, will you open this door! Or shall *I* call the ship's police and say we're both interested in someone running around Europe with securities worth millions, none of which, incidentally, will I get."

"What did you say?" Elizabeth was now next to the stateroom door.

"Look, Madame Scarlatti"—Matthew cupped his hands against the wood of the door—"if my information is anywhere near correct, you have a revolver. All right. Open the door, and if I haven't got my hands over my head, and if there's anyone behind me, fire away! Can I be fairer than that?''

She opened the door and Canfield stood there with only the thought of the impending conversation keeping him from being sick. He closed the door and Elizabeth Scarlatti saw the state of his discomfort. As always, she knew the sequence of priorities under pressure.

"Use my bathroom, Mr. Canfield. It's in there. Straighten yourself up and then we'll talk.''

Charles Conaway Boothroyd stuffed two pillows under the blanket of his bed. He picked up the rope and snapped the lines in a lasso loop. The crackle of the fibers was sweet music to him. He placed his wife's silk stocking in his pocket and silently left his cabin. Because he was on A deck, starboard side, he had only to walk around the bow promenade to reach his destination. He ascertained the pitch and the roll of the ship in the rough seas and quickly determined the precise moment of side roll for a human body to reach the water below with the minimum of structural interference. Boothroyd was nothing if not a thorough professional. They would all soon learn his worth.

Canfield came out of Elizabeth's Scarlatti's toilet feeling very much relieved. She stared at him from any easy chair several feet on the far side of the bed, pointing the revolver directly at him.

"If I sit down, will you put that damn thing away?''

"Probably not. But sit down and we'll talk about it.''

Canfield sat on the bed and swung his legs over so that he faced her. The old woman cocked the hammer of her pistol.

"You spoke of something at the door, Mr. Canfield, which is the only reason this pistol hasn't been fired. Would you care to carry on?''

"Yes. The first thing I can think of saying is that I'm not . . .''

Canfield froze.

The lock in the outer room was being opened. The field accountant held up his hand to the old woman and she immediately, instinctively, handed him the pistol.

Swiftly Canfield took her hand and gently but firmly placed her on the bed. The look in his eyes instructed her and she obeyed.

She stretched out on the bed with only the table lamp illuminating her while Canfield backed into the shadows behind the open bedroom door. He signaled her to close her eyes, a command he did not really expect her to carry out, but she did. Elizabeth let her head fall to the left while the newspaper lay several inches from her right hand. She looked as though she had fallen asleep while reading.

The stateroom door was rapidly opened and closed.

Canfield pressed his back against the wall and gripped the small pistol tightly in his hand. Through the overlapping steel lip of the door's inside border was a two-inch space that let Canfield look out. It struck him that the open space gave the intruder the same advantage, only Canfield was in shadow and, he hope, unexpected.

And then the visitor was revealed and Canfield found himself involuntarily swallowing, partially from amazement, partially from fear.

The man was huge, several inches taller than Canfield, with immense chest and shoulders. He wore a black sweater, black gloves, and over his entire head was a translucent filmy cloth, silk, perhaps, which gave the giant an eerie, inhuman appearance and completely blurred his face.

The intruder passed through the bedroom door and stood at the foot of the bed barely three feet in front of Canfield. He seemed to be appraising the old woman while removing a thin rope from his trousers pocket.

He started toward the left side of the bed, hunching his body forward.

Canfield sprang forward, bringing his pistol down on the man's head as hard as he could. The downward impact of the blow caused an immediate break in the skin and a spurt of blood spread through the silk head covering. The intruder fell forward, breaking his fall with his hands, and whirled around to face Canfield. The man was stunned but only for seconds.

"You!" It was not an exclamation, but a damning recognition. "You son of a bitch!"

Canfield's memory mistly raced back, abstracting times and events, and yet he hadn't the remotest idea who this massive creature was. That he should know him was obvious; that he didn't possibly dangerous.

Madame Scarlatti crouched against the headboard of her bed observing the scene in fear but without panic. Instead she was angry because it was a situation she could not possibly control. "I'll phone the ship's police." she said quietly.

"No!" Canfield's command was harsh. "Don't touch that phone! Please!"

"You must be insane, young man!"

"You want to make a deal, buddy?"

The voice, too, was vaguely familiar. The field accountant trained his pistol on the man's head.

"No deal. Just take off your Halloween mask."

The man slowly raised both arms.

"No, buddy! One hand. Sit on the other. With the palm up!"

"Smart guy." The intruder lowered one arm.

"Mr. Canfield, I really must insist! This man broke into my cabin. God knows he was probably going to rob or kill me. Not you. I must phone for the proper authorities!"

Canfield didn't quite know how to make the old woman understand. He was not the heroic type, and the thought of formal protection was inviting. But would it be protection? And even if it were, this hulk at his feet was the only connection, or possible connection, he or anyone in Group Twenty had with the missing Ulster Scarlett. Canfield realized that if the ship's authorities were called in, the intruder would simply be sacrificed as a thief. It was possible that the man was a thief, but Canfield doubted that strongly.

Sitting at the accountant's feet, the masked Charles Boothroyd came to the identical conclusion regarding his future. The prospect of failure coupled with jail began to trigger an uncontrollable desperation.

Canfield spoke quietly to the old woman. "I'd like to point out that this man did not break in. He unlocked the door, which presumes he was given a key."

"That's right! I was! You don't want to do anything stupid, do you, buddy? Let's make a deal. I'll pay you fifty times what you make selling baseball mitts! How about it?

Canfield looked sharply down at the man. This was a new and disturbing note. Was his cover known? The sudden ache in Canfield's stomach came with the realization that there might well be two sacrificial goats in the stateroom.

"Take that God damn cloth off your head!"

"Mr. Canfield, thousands of passengers have traveled this ship. A key wouldn't be that difficult. I must insist . . ."

The giant intruder's right hand lashed out at Canfield's foot. Canfield fired into the man's shoulder as he was pulled forward. It was a small-caliber revolver and the shot was not loud.

The masked stranger's hand spastically released Canfield's ankle as he clutched his shoulder where the bullet was lodged. Canfield rose quickly and kicked the man with all his strength in the general area of the head. The toe of his patent-leather shoe caught the man on the side of the neck and ripped the skin beneath the stocking mask. Still the man lunged toward Canfield, hurling himself in a football cross-block at Canfield's midsection. Canfield fired again; this time the bullet entered the man's huge flank. Canfield pressed himself against the stateroom wall as the man fell against his shins, writhing in agony. The bone and muscle tissue in the path of the bullet had been shattered.

Canfield reached down to pull off the silk face covering, now drenched with blood, when the giant, on his knees, suddenly lashed out with his left arm pinning the field accountant back against the wall. Canfield pistol-whipped the man about the head, simultaneously trying to remove the steellike forearm. As he pulled upward on the man's wrist, the black sweater ripped revealing the sleeve of a white shirt. On the cuff was a large cuff link diagonally striped in red and black.

Briefly, Canfield stopped his assault, trying to assimilate his new knowledge. The creature, bloodied, wounded, was grunting in pain and desperation. But Canfield knew him and he was extraordinarily confused. While trying to steady his right hand, he aimed his revolver carefully at the man's kneecap. It was not easy; the strong arm was pressing into his upper groin with the power of a large piston. As he was about to fire, the intruder lurched upward, arching his back and heaving his frame against the smaller man. Canfield pulled the trigger, more as a reaction than intent. The bullet pierced the upper area of the stomach.

Charles Boothroyd fell again.

Matthew Canfield looked over at the old woman who was reaching for the bedside phone. He jumped over the man and forcibly took the instrument from her. He replaced the ear cup in its cradle. "Please! I know what I'm doing!"

"Are you sure?"

"Yes. Please! Believe me!"

"Good God! Look out!"

Canfield whirled, narrowly missing having his spine crushed by the lurching, wounded Boothroyd, who had entwined his fingers into a single hammerlike weapon.

The man toppled on the end of the bed and rolled off. Canfield pulled the old woman away and leveled his pistol at the assailant.

"I don't know how you do it, but if you don't stop, the next shot goes right into your forehead. That's a marksman's promise, buddy!"

Canfield reflected that he was the only member of the training group to fail the small-arms target course twice in succession.

Lying on the floor, his vision impaired by the pain as well as the bloody silk covering his face, Charles Boothroyd knew there was next to nothing left. His breathing was erratic; blood was spilling into his windpipe. There was only one hope—to get to his cabin and reach his wife. She'd know what to do. She'd pay the ship's doctor a fortune to make him well. And somehow *they* would understand. No man could take this kind of punishment and be questioned.

With enormous effort he began to rise. He muttered incoherently as he steadied himself on the mattress.

"Don't try to stand, friend. Just answer a question," said Canfield.

"What . . . What? Quit. . . ."

"Where's Scarlett?" Canfield felt he was working against time. The man would collapse any second.

"Don't know . . ."

"Is he alive?"

"Who . . ."

"You know damn well who! Scarlett! Her son!"

With his last resource of strength, Boothroyd accomplished the seemingly impossible. Clutching the mattress, he staggered backward as if about to collapse. His movements pulled the heavy pad partially off the bed, loosening the hold of the blankets, and as Canfield stepped forward, Boothroyd suddenly lifted the mattress free of the bed and flung it at the field accountant. As the mattress rose in the air, Boothroyd rushed against it with his full weight. Canfield fired wildly into the ceiling as he and the old woman went down under the impact. Boothroyd gave a last push, crushing the two against the wall and the floor, letting his push spring him back onto his feet. He turned, hardly able to see, and weaved out of the room. Once he reached the other stateroom he pulled off the stocking, opened the door, and rushed out.

Elizabeth Scarlatti moaned in pain, groping for her ankle. Canfield pushed against the mattress, and as it fell off, he tried to help the old woman to her feet.

"I think my ankle or some part of my foot is broken."

Canfield wanted only to go after Boothroyd but he couldn't leave the old woman like this. Too, if he did leave her, she'd be right back on the phone and at this juncture, that would never do. "I'll carry you to the bed."

"For God's sake put the mattress back first. I'm brittle!"

Canfield was torn between taking off his belt, binding the old woman's hands and running after Boothroyd, and carrying out her instructions. The former would be foolish—she'd scream bloody murder; he replaced the mattress and gently lifted her onto the bed.

"How does it feel?"

"Ghastly." She winced as he placed the pillows behind her.

"I guess I'd better call the ship's doctor." However, Canfield made no motion toward the phone. He tried to find the words to convince her to let him have his way.

"There's plenty of time for that. You want to go after that man, don't you?"

Canfield looked at her harshly. "Yes."

"Why? Do you think he has something to do with my son?"

"Every second I spend explaining lessens the possibility of our ever finding out."

"How do I know you'll be dealing in my interest? You didn't want me to phone for help when we certainly needed it. You nearly got us both killed, as a matter of fact. I think I deserve some explanation."

"There isn't time now. Please, trust me."

"Why should I?"

Canfield's eye caught sight of the rope dropped by Boothroyd. "Among other reasons too lengthy to go into, if I hadn't been here, you would have been killed." He pointed at the thin cord on the floor. "If you think that rope was meant to tie your hands with, remind me to explain the advantages of garroting with an elasticized cord as opposed to a piece of clothesline. Your wrists could wriggle out of this." He picked the cord up and thrust it in front of her. "Not your throat!"

She looked at him closely. "Who are you? Whom do you work for?"

Canfield remembered the purpose of his visit—to tell part of the truth. He had decided to say he was employed by a private firm interested in Ulster Scarlett—a magazine or some sort of publication. Under the present circumstances, that was obviously foolish. Boothroyd was no thief; he was a killer on assignment. Elizabeth Scarlatti was marked for assassination. She was no part of a conspiracy. Canfield needed all the resources available to him. "I'm a representative of the United States government."

"Oh, my God! That ass, Senator Brownlee! I had no idea!"

"Neither does he, I assure you. Without knowing it, he got us started, but that's as far as he goes."

"And now I presume all Washington is playing detective and not informing me!"

"If ten people in all Washington now about it, I'd be surprised. How's your ankle?"

"It will survive, as I shall under the circumstances."

"If I call the doctor, will you make up some story about falling? Just to give me time. That's all I ask."

"I'll do you one better, Mr. Canfield. I'll let you go now. We can call a doctor later if it's necessary." She opened the drawer in the bedside table and handed him the stateroom key.

Canfield started toward the door.

"Under one condition." The old woman raised her voice sufficiently to stop him.

"What's that?"

"That you give due consideration to a proposition I have to make to you."

Canfield turned and faced her quizzically. "What kind of proposition?"

"That you go to work for me."

"I'll be back soon," said the field accountant as he ran through the door.

Chapter Twenty-one

Three-quarters of an hour later Canfield let himself quietly back into Elizabeth Scarlatti's stateroom. The moment the old woman heard the key in the latch she cried out apprehensively.

"Who is it?"

"Canfield." He walked in.

"Did you find him?"

"I did. May I sit down?"

"Please."

"What happened? For heaven's sake, Mr. Canfield! What happened? Who is he?"

"His name was Boothroyd. He worked for a New York brokerage house. He obviously was hired, or assigned to kill you. He's dead and his earthly remains are behind us—I judge about three miles."

"Good God!" The old woman sat down.

"Shall we start at the beginning?"

"Young man, do you know what you've done? There'll be searches, inquiries! The ship will be in an uproar!"

"Oh, someone will be in an uproar, I grant you. But I doubt that there will be more than a routine, and I suspect, subdued inquiry. With a grieving, confused widow confined to her quarters."

"What do you mean?"

Canfield told her how he had located the body near Boothroyd's own stateroom. He then touched briefly on the grimmer aspects of searching the body and dispatching it overboard, but he described in fuller detail how he had returned to the lounge and learned that Boothroyd supposedly passed out several hours earlier. The bartender, in what was probably exaggeration, said that it had taken half a dozen men to haul him away and put him to bed.

"You see, his highly noticeable alibi is the most logical explanation for his . . . disappearance."

"They'll search the ship until we reach port!"

"No, they won't."

"Why not?"

"I tore off part of his sweater and wedged it into a corner of the post railing outside his stateroom. It'll be apparent that the drunken Mr. Boothroyd tried to rejoin the party and that he had a tragic accident. A drunk plus rotten weather aboard ship is a bad combination." Canfield stopped and reflected. "If he was operating alone, we're all right. If he wasn't . . ." Canfield decided to be quiet.

"Was it necessary to throw the man overboard?"

"Would it have been better to have him found with four bullets in him?"

"Three. There's one lodged in the bedroom ceiling."

"That's even worse. He'd be traced to you. If he has a colleague aboard this ship, you'd be dead before morning!"

"I suppose you're right. What do we do now?"

"We wait. We talk and we wait."

"For what?"

"For someone to try to find out what happened. Perhaps his wife. Perhaps the one who gave him the key. Someone."

"You think they will?"

"I think they have to if there's anyone on board who was working with him. For the simple reason that everything went—poof."

"Perhaps he was just a burglar."

"He wasn't. He was a killer. I don't mean to alarm you."

The old woman looked carefully into Canfield's eyes. "Who is 'they,' Mr. Canfield?"

"I don't know. That's where the talking comes in."

"You believe they're connected with my son's disappearance, don't you?"

"Yes, I do. . . . Don't you?"

She did not answer directly. "You said we should start at the beginning.

Where is that for you?"

"When we found out that millions of dollars' worth of American securities were being sold secretly on a foreign exchange."

"What has that to do with my son?"

"He was there. He was in the specific area when the rumors started. A year later, after his disappearance, we received reliable intelligence that the sale had been made. He was there again. Obvious, isn't it?"

"Or highly coincidental."

"That theory was knocked out of the box when you opened the door for me an hour ago."

The old woman stared at the field accountant as he slouched in the chair. He, in turn, watched her through half-closed eyes. He saw that she was furious but controlled.

"You presume, Mr. Canfield."

"I don't think so. And since we know who your would-be assassin was and who he worked for—Godwin-somebody-or-other, Wall Street—I think the picture's pretty clear. Someone, someone in the fifth largest brokerage house in New York, is angry enough with you or frightened enough of you to want you killed."

"That's speculation."

"Speculation, hell! I've got the bruises to prove it!"

"How did Washington make this . . . questionable connection?"

"'Washington' takes in too many people. We're a very small department. Our normal concerns are quietly dealing with larcenous but highly placed government officials."

"You sound ominous, Mr. Canfield."

"Not at all. If an uncle of the Swedish ambassador makes a killing in Swedish imports, we'd rather straighten it out quietly." He watched her closely.

"Now you sound harmless."

"Neither I assure you."

"About the securities?"

"The Swedish ambassador, as a matter of fact." Canfield smiled. "Who, to the best of my knowledge, hasn't any uncle in the import business."

"The Swedish ambassador? I thought you said Senator Brownlee was the one."

"I didn't. You did. Brownlee caused enough of a fuss to make the Justice Department call in everyone who ever had anything to do with Ulster Scarlett. At one point, we did."

"You're with Reynolds!"

"Again, that's your statement. Not mine."

"Stop playing games. You work for that man, Reynolds, don't you?"

"One thing I'm not is your prisoner. I'm not going to be cross-examined."

"Very well. What about this Swedish ambassador?"

"You don't know him? You don't know anything about Stockholm?"

"Oh, for God's sake, of course I don't!"

The field accountant believed her. "Fourteen months ago Ambassador Walter Pond sent word to Washington that a Stockholm syndicate had pledged thirty million dollars for large blocks of American securities if they could be smuggled across. His report was dated May fifteenth. Your son's visa shows he entered Sweden on May tenth."

"Flimsy! My son was on his honeymoon. A trip to Sweden was not out of the ordinary."

"He was alone. His wife remained in London. That's out of the ordinary."

Elizabeth rose from the chaise longue. "It was over a year ago. The money was only pledged. . . ."

"Ambassador Pond has confirmed that the transaction was concluded."

"When?"

"Two months ago. Just after your son disappeared."

Elizabeth stopped pacing and looked at Canfield. "I asked you a question before you went after that man."

"I remember. You offered me a job."

"Could I receive cooperation from your agency on your approval alone? We have the same objective. There's no conflict."

"What does that mean?"

"Is it possible for you to report that I voluntarily offered to cooperate with you? The truth, Mr. Canfield, merely the truth. An attempt was made on my life. If it weren't for you, I'd be dead. I'm a frightened old woman."

"It'll be assumed that you know your son's alive."

"Not know. Suspect."

"Because of the securities?"

"I refuse to admit that."

"Then why?"

"First answer me. Could I use the influence of your agency without being questioned further? . . . Responsible only to you."

"Which means I'm responsible to you."

"Exactly."

"It's possible."

"In Europe as well?"

"We have reciprocal agreements with most—"

"Then here's my offer," interrupted Elizabeth. "I add that it's nonnegotiable. . . . One hundred thousand dollars. Paid in installments mutually agreeable."

Matthew Canfield stared at the confident old woman and suddenly found himself frightened. There was something terrifying about the sum Elizabeth Scarlatti had just mentioned. He repeated her words almost inaudibly. "One hundred thousand—"

"'Dust thou wert,' Mr. Canfield. Take my offer and enjoy your life."

The field accountant was perspiring and it was neither warm nor humid in the suite. "You know my answer."

"Yes, I thought so. . . . Don't be overwhelmed. The transition to money takes but minor adjustments. You'll have enough to be comfortable, but not so much for responsibility. That would be uncomfortable. . . . Now, where were we?"

"What?"

"Oh, yes. Why do I suspect my son may be alive? Separate and apart from the securities you speak of."

"Why do you?"

"From April to December of the past year, my son had hundreds of thousands of dollars transferred to banks throughout Europe. I believe he intends to live on that money. I'm tracing those deposits. I'm following the trail of that money." Elizabeth saw that the field accountant did not believe her. "It happens to be the truth."

"But so are the securities, aren't they?"

"Speaking to someone on my payroll and knowing that I'll deny any knowedge of them outside of this stateroom . . . yes."

"Why deny it?"

"A fair question. I don't think you'll understand but I'll try. The missing securities won't be discovered for nearly a year. I have no legal right to question my son's trust—no one has—until the bonds mature. To do so would be to publicly accuse the Scarlatti family. It would tear the Scarlatti Industries apart. Make suspect all Scarlatti transactions in every banking institution in the civilized world. It's a heavy responsibility. Considering the amount of money involved, it could create panics in a hundred corporations."

Canfield reached the limits of his concentration. "Who was Jefferson Cartwright?"

"The only other person who knew about the securities."

"Oh, my God!" Canfield sat up in the chair.

"Do you really think he was killed for the reasons given?"

"I didn't know there were any."

"They were indirect. He was a notorious philanderer."

The field accountant looked into the old woman's eyes. "And you say he was the only other one who knew about the securities?"

"Yes."

"Then I think that was why he was killed. In your section of town, you don't kill a man for sleeping with your wife. You simply use it as an excuse to sleep with his."

"Then I do need you, don't I, Mr. Canfield?"

"What had you planned to do when we reach England?"

"Precisely what I said I was going to do. Start with the banks."

"What would that tell you?"

"I'm not sure. But there were considerable sums of money by ordinary standards. This money had to go somewhere. It certainly wasn't going to be carried around in paper bags. Perhaps other accounts under false names; perhaps small businesses quickly established—I don't know. But I do know this is the money that will be used until the payments for the securities are liquid."

"Christ, he's got thirty million dollars in Stockholm!"

"Not necessarily. Accounts could be opened in Switzerland totaling thirty million—probably paid in bullion—but not released for a considerable length of time."

"How long?"

"As long as it takes to certify the authenticity of every document. Since they were sold on a foreign exchange that could take months."

"So you're going to trace the accounts in the banks."

"That would appear to be the only starting point." Elizabeth Scarlatti opened the drawer of a writing desk and took out a vanity case. Unlocking it she took out a single sheet of paper.

"I assume you have a copy of this. I'd like you to read it over and refresh your memory." She handed him the paper. It was the list of foreign banks where monies had been deposited by Waterman Trust for Ulster Stewart Scarlett. Canfield remembered it from the material sent from the Justice Department.

"Yes, I've seen it, but I haven't got a copy. . . . Something less than a million dollars."

"Have you noticed the dates of the withdrawals?"

"I remember the last one was about two weeks before your son and his wife returned to New York. A couple of accounts are still open, aren't they? Yes, here . . ."

"London and The Hague." The old woman interrupted and continued without stopping. "That's not what I mean, but it could be valuable. What I'm referring to is the geographic pattern."

"What geographic pattern?"

"Starting with London, then north to Norway; then south again to England—Manchester; then east to Paris; north again to Denmark; south to Marseilles; west into Spain, Portugal; northeast to Berlin; south again into North Africa—Cairo; northwest through Italy—Rome; then the Balkans; reversing west back to Switzerland—It goes on. A patchwork." The old lady had recited by rote as Canfield tried to follow the list of dates.

"What's your point, Madame Scarlatti?"

"Nothing strikes you as unusual?"

"Your son was on his honeymoon. I don't know how you people go on honeymoons. All I know about is Niagara Falls."

"This is not a normal itinerary."

"I wouldn't know about that."

"Let me put it this way. . . . You wouldn't take a pleasure trip from Washington, D.C., to New York City, then return to Baltimore with your next stop Boston."

"I suppose not."

"My son crisscrossed within a semicircle. The final destination, the last and largest withdrawal was made at a point more logically reached months earlier."

Canfield was lost trying to follow the banks and dates.

"Don't bother, Mr. Canfield. It was Germany. An obscure town in southern Germany. It's called Tassing. . . . Why?"

PART TWO

Chapter Twenty-two

The second and third days of the *Calpurnia* voyage were calm, both the weather and the first-class section of the ship. The news of the death of a passenger cast a pall over the voyagers. Mrs. Charles Boothroyd was confined to quarters under the constant supervision of the ship's doctor and attending nurses. She had gone into hysterics upon hearing the news of her husband and it had been necessary to administer large doses of sedatives.

By the third day, with revived health, the optimism of most passengers revived.

Elizabeth Wyckham Scarlatti and her young table escort made it a point to part company after each meal. By ten thirty every night, however, Matthew Canfield let himself into her quarters to take up his post lest there be a recurrence of the Boothroyd attempt. It was an unsatisfactory arrangement.

"If I were a hundred years younger, you might pass yourself off as one of those distasteful men who perform services for middle-aged adventuresses."

"If you used some of your well-advertised money to buy your own ocean liner, I might get some sleep at night."

These late-hour conversations served one good purpose, however. Their plans began to take shape. Also Canfield's responsibilities as an employee of Elizabeth Scarlatti were diplomatically discussed.

"You understand," said Elizabeth, "I wouldn't expect you to do anything detrimental to the government. Or against your own conscience. I do believe in a man's conscience."

"But I gather you'd like to make the decision about what's detrimental and what isn't?"

"To a degree, yes. I believe I'm qualified."

"What happens if I don't agree with you?"

"We'll cross that bridge when we come to it."

"Oh, that's great!"

In essence, Matthew Canfield would continue submitting his reports to Washington's Group Twenty with one alteration—they first would be approved by Elizabeth Scarlatti. Together they would, through the field accountant, make certain requests of his office they both felt necessary. In all matters of physical well-being, the old woman would follow the instructions of the young man without argument.

Matthew Canfield would receive ten payments of ten thousand dollars each commencing with the first day in London. In small American bills.

"You realize, Mr. Canfield, that there's another way to look at this arrangement."

"What's that?"

"Your office is getting the benefit of my not inconsiderable talents for absolutely nothing. Extremely beneficial to the taxpayers."

"I'll put that in my next report."

The basic problem of the arrangement had not been resolved, however. For the field accountant to fulfill his obligations to both employers, a reason had to be found explaining his association with the old woman. It would become obvious as the weeks went by and it would be foolish to try to pass it off as either companionship or business. Both explanations would be suspect.

With a degree of self-interest, Matthew Canfield asked, "Can you get along with your daughter-in-law?"

"I assume you mean Ulster's wife. No one could stand Chancellor's."

"Yes."

"I like her. However, if you're thinking about her as a third party, I must tell you that she despises me. There are many reasons, most of them quite valid. In order to get what I want I've had to treat her quite badly. My only defense, if I felt I needed one—which I don't—is that what I wanted was for her benefit."

"I'm deeply moved, but do you think we could get her cooperation? I've met her on several occasions."

"She's not very responsible. But I suppose you know that."

"Yes. I also know that she suspects you of going to Europe on your son's account."

"I realize that. It would help to enlist her, I imagine. But I don't think I could manage it by cable, and I certainly wouldn't want to spell it out in a letter."

"I've a better way. I'll go back for her and I'll take a written . . . explanation from you. Not too involved, not too specific. I'll handle the rest."

"You must know her very well."

"Not so. I just think that if I can convince her that you—and I—are on her side . . . if someone's on her side, she'll help."

"She might be able to. She could show us places. . . ."

"She might recognize people. . . ."

"But what will I do while you're in America? I'll no doubt be dead when you come back."

Canfield had thought of that. "When we reach England, you should go into retreat."

"I beg your pardon?"

"For your immortal soul. And your son's as well, of course."

"I don't understand you."

"A convent. The whole world knows of your bereavement. It's a logical thing to do. We'll issue a statement to the press to the effect that you've gone to an undisclosed retreat in the north of England. Then send you somewhere down south. My office will help."

"It sounds positively ridiculous!"

"You'll be fetching in your black robes!"

The veiled, grieving Mrs. Boothroyd was led off with the first contingent of passengers. She was met by a man at customs who hurried her through the procedures and took her to a Rolls-Royce waiting on the street. Canfield followed the couple to the car.

Forty-five minutes later Canfield checked into the hotel. He had called his

London contact from a public phone and they had agreed to meet as soon as the Londoner could drive down. The field accountant then spent a half hour enjoying the stability of a dry-land bed. He was depressed at the thought of going right back on board ship but he knew there was no other solution. Janet would supply the most reasonable explanation for his accompanying the old lady and it was logical that the wife and mother of the missing Ulster Scarlett should travel together. And certainly Canfield was not unhappy at the prospect of a continued association with Janet Scarlett. She was a tramp, no question; but he had begun to doubt his opinion that she was a bitch.

He was about to doze off when he looked at his watch and realized that he was late for his meeting. He picked up the phone and was delighted by the crisp British accent answering him.

"Madame Scarlatti is in suite five. Our instructions are to ring through prior to callers, sir."

"If you'll do that, please, I'll just go right up. Thank you."

Canfield said his name quite loudly before Elizabeth Scarlatti would open the door. The old woman motioned the young man inside to a chair while she sat on a huge Victorian sofa by the window.

"Well, what do we do now?"

"I phoned our London man nearly an hour ago. He should be here shortly."

"Who is he?"

"He said his name is James Derek."

"Don't you know him?"

"No. We're given an exchange to call and a man is assigned to us. It's a reciprocal arrangement."

"Isn't that convenient." A statement.

"We're billed for it."

"What will he want to know?"

"Only what we want to tell him. He won't ask any questions unless we request something either inimical to the British government or so expensive he'd have to justify it; that's the point he'll be most concerned with."

"That strikes me as very amusing."

"Taxpayers' money." Canfield looked at his watch. "I asked him to bring along a list of religious retreats."

"You're really serious about that, aren't you?"

"Yes. Unless he has a better idea. I'll be gone for about two and a half weeks. Did you write the letter for your daughter-in-law?"

"Yes." She handed him an envelope.

Across the room on a table near the door, the telephone rang. Elizabeth walked rapidly to the table and answered it.

"Is that Derek?" asked Canfield, when she had hung up.

"Yes."

"Good. Now, please, Madame Scarlatti, let me do most of the talking. But if I ask you a question, you'll know I want an honest answer."

"Oh? We don't have signals?"

"No. He doesn't want to know anything. Believe that. Actually, we're a source of embarrassment to each other."

"Should I offer him a drink, or tea, or isn't that allowed?"

"I think a drink would be very much appreciated."

"I'll call room service and have a bar sent up."

"That's fine."

Elizabeth Scarlatti picked up the phone and ordered a complete selection of wines and liquors. Canfield smiled at the ways of the rich and lit one of his thin cigars.

James Derek was a pleasant-looking man in his early fifties, somewhat rotund, with the air of a prosperous merchant. He was terribly polite but essentially cool. His perpetual smile had a tendency to curve slowly into a strained straight line as he spoke.

"We traced the license of the Rolls at the pier. It belongs to a Marquis Jacques Louis Bertholde. French resident alien. We'll get information on him."

"Good. What about the retreats?"

The Britisher took out a paper from his inside coat pocket. "There're several we might suggest depending upon Madame Scarlatti's wishes to be in touch with the outside."

"Do you have any where contact is completely impossible? On both sides?" asked the field accountant.

"That would be Catholic, of course. There're two or three."

"Now see here!" interrupted the imposing old lady.

"What are they?" asked Canfield.

"There's a Benedictine order and a Carmelite. They're in the southwest, incidentally. One, the Carmelite, is near Cardiff."

"There are limits, Mr. Canfield, and I propose to establish them. I will not associate with such people!"

"What is the most fashionable, most sought after retreat in England, Mr. Derek?" asked the field accountant.

"Well, the duchess of Gloucester makes a yearly trek to the Abbey of York. Church of England, of course."

"Fine. We'll send out a story to all the wire services that Madame Scarlatti has entered for a month."

"That's far more acceptable," said the old woman.

"I haven't finished." He turned to the amused Londoner. "Then book us into the Carmelites. You'll escort Madame Scarlatti there tomorrow."

"As you say."

"Just one minute, gentlemen. I do not consent! I'm sure Mr. Derek will adhere to my wishes."

"Terribly sorry, madame. My instructions are to take orders from Mr. Canfield."

"And we have an agreement, Madame Scarlatti, or do you want to tear it up?"

"What can I possibly say to such people? I simply can not stand that voodoo mumbo jumbo coming from Rome!"

"You'll be spared that discomfort, madame," said Mr. Derek. "There's a vow of silence. You'll not hear from anyone."

"Contemplate," added the field accountant. "Good for the immortal soul."

Chapter Twenty-three

YORK, ENGLAND, *August 12, 1926*—
The famed Abbey of York sustained a damaging
explosion and fire at dawn this morning in its west
wing, the residential quarters of the religious order.
An undisclosed number of sisters and novices were
killed in the tragic occurrence. It was believed that the
explosion was due to a malfunction in the heating
system recently installed by the order.

Canfield read the story in the ship's newspaper one day before arriving in
New York.

They do their homework well, he thought. And although the price was
painfully high, it proved two points conclusively: the press releases were read
and Madame Scarlatti was marked.

The field accountant reached into his pocket and took out the old woman's
letter to Janet Scarlett. He'd read it many times and thought it effective. He
read it once more.

My dear Child:

I am aware that you are not particularly fond of me and I accept the
fact as my loss. You have every right to feel as you do—the Scarlattis
have not been pleasant people with whom to be associated. However,
for whatever reasons and regardless of the pain you have been caused,
you are now a Scarlatti and you have borne a Scarlatti into this world.
Perhaps you will be the one who will make us better than we are.

I do not make this statement lightly or out of sentiment. History has
shown that the least expected among us often emerge splendidly
because of the grave responsibilities placed upon them. I ask you to
consider this possibility.

I further ask you to give deep consideration to what Mr. Matthew
Canfield will tell you. I trust him. I do so because he has saved my life
and nearly lost his own in so doing. His interests and ours are
inextricably bound together. He will tell you what he can and he will
ask of you a great deal.

I am a very, very old woman, my dear, and do not have much time.
What months or years I do have (precious perhaps only to me) may well
be cut short in a fashion I'd like to believe is not the will of God.
Naturally, I accept this risk gladly as the head of the house of
Scarlatti, and if I can spend what time I have left preventing a great
dishonor upon our family, I will join my husband with a grateful heart.

Through Mr. Canfield, I await your answer. If it is as I suspect, we
will be together shortly and you will have gladdened me far beyond that
which I deserve. If it is not, you still have my affection and, believe me
when I say, my understanding.

Elizabeth Wyckham Scarlatti

Canfield replaced the letter in the envelope. It was quite good, he thought
again. It explained nothing and asked for implicit trust that the unsaid
explanation was vitally urgent. If he did his job, the girl would be coming
back to England with him. If he failed to persuade her, an alternative would

have to be found.

The Ulster Scarlett brownstone on Fifty-fourth Street was being repainted and sandblasted. There were several scaffolds lowered from the roof and a number of workmen diligently at their crafts. The heavy Checker cab pulled up in front of the entrance and Matthew Canfield walked up the steps. He rang the bell; the door was opened by the obese housekeeper.

"Good afternoon, Hannah. I don't know if you remember, but my name's Canfield. Matthew Canfield to see Mrs. Scarlett."

Hannah did not budge or offer entrance. "Does Mrs. Scarlett expect you?"

"Not formally, but I'm sure she'll see me." He had had no intention of phoning. It would have been too easy for her to refuse.

"I don't know if madame is in, sir."

"Then I'll just have to wait. Shall it be here on the stairs?"

Hannah reluctantly made way for the field accountant to step into the hideously colored hallway. Canfield was struck again by the intensity of the red wallpaper and the black drapes.

"I'll inquire, sir," said the housekeeper as she started toward the stairs.

In a few minutes Janet came down the long staircase, followed by a waddling Hannah. She was very much composed. Her eyes were clear, aware, and devoid of the panic he had remembered. She was in command and without question a beautiful woman.

Canfield felt a sudden sting of inferiority. He was outclassed.

"Why, Mr. Canfield, this is a surpise."

He could not determine whether her greeting was meant to be pleasant or not. It was friendly, but cool and reserved. This girl had learned the lessons of the old money well.

"I hope not an unwelcome one, Mrs. Scarlett."

"Not at all."

Hannah had reached the bottom step and walked toward the dining room doors. Canfield quickly spoke again. "During my trip I ran across a fellow whose company makes dirigibles. I knew you'd be interested." Canfield watched Hannah out of the corner of his eye without moving his head. Hannah had turned abruptly and looked at the field accountant.

"Really, Mr. Canfield? Why would that concern me?" The girl was mystified.

"I understood your friends on Oyster Bay were determined to buy one for the club. Here, I've brought all the information. Purchase price, rentals, specifications, the works. . . . Let me show you."

The field accountant took Janet Scarlett's elbow and led her swiftly toward the living room doors. Hannah hesitated ever so slightly but, with a glance from Canfield, retreated into the dining room. Canfield then closed the living room doors.

"What are you doing? I don't want to buy a dirigible."

The field accountant stood by the doors, motioning the girl to stop talking.

"What?"

"Be quiet for a minute. Please." He spoke softly.

Canfield waited about ten seconds and then opened the doors in one swinging motion.

Directly across the hallway, standing by the dining room table, was Hannah and a man in white overalls, obviously one of the painters. They were talking while looking over toward the living room doors. They were now in full view of Canfield's stare. Embarrassed, they moved away.

Canfield shut the door and turned to Janet Scarlett. "Interesting, isn't it?"

"What are you doing?"

"Just interesting that your help should be so curious."

"Oh, that." Janet turned and picked up a cigarette from a case on the coffee table. "Servants will talk and I think you've given them cause."

Canfield lit her cigarette. "Including the painters?"

"Hannah's friends are her own business. They're no concern of mine. Hannah's barely a concern of mine. . . ."

"You don't find it curious that Hannah nearly tripped when I mentioned a dirigible?"

"I simply don't understand you."

"I admit I'm getting ahead of myself."

"Why didn't you telephone?"

"If I had, would you have seen me?"

Janet thought for a minute. "Probably. . . . Whatever recriminations I had over your last visit wouldn't be any reason to insult you."

"I didn't want to take that gamble."

"That's sweet of you and I'm touched. But why this very odd behavior?"

There was no point in delaying any longer. He took the envelope out of his pocket. "I've been asked to give you this. May I sit down while your read it?"

Janet, startled, took the envelope and immediately recognized her mother-in-law's handwriting. She opened the envelope and read the letter.

If she was astonished or shocked, she hid her emotions well.

Slowly she sat down on the sofa and put out her cigarette. She looked down at the letter and up at Canfield, and then back to the letter. Without looking up, she asked quietly, "Who are you?"

"I work for the government. I'm an official . . . a minor official in the Department of the Interior."

"The government? You're not a salesman, then?"

"No, I'm not."

"You wanted to meet me and talk with me for the government?"

"Yes."

"Why did you tell me you sold tennis courts?"

"We sometimes find it necessary to conceal our employment. It's as simple as that."

"I see."

"I assume you want to know what your mother-in-law means in the letter?"

"Don't assume anything." She was cold as she continued. "It was your job to meet me and ask me all those amusing questions?"

"Frankly, yes."

The girl rose, took the necessary two steps toward the field accountant, and slapped him across the face with all her strength. It was a sharp and painful blow. "You son of a bitch! Get out of this house!" She still did not raise her voice. "Get out before I call the police!"

"Oh, my God, Janet, will you stop it!" He grabbed her shoulders as she tried to wriggle away. "Listen to me! I said listen or I'll slap you right back!"

Her eyes shone with hatred and, Canfield thought, a touch of melancholy. He held her firmly as he spoke. "Yes, I was assigned to meet you. Meet you and get whatever information I could."

She spat in his face. He did not bother to brush it away.

"I got the information I needed and I used that information because that's what I'm paid for! As far as my department is concerned, I left this house by nine o'clock after you served me two drinks. If they want to pick you up for illegal possession of alcohol, that's what they can get you for!"

"I don't believe you!"

"I don't give a good God damn whether you do or not! And for your further information I've had you under surveillance for weeks! You and the rest of your playmates. . . . It may interest you to know that I've omitted detailing the more . . . ludicrous aspects of your day-to-day activities!"

The girls' eyes began to fill with tears.

"I'm doing my job as best I can, and I'm not so sure you're the one who should scream 'violated virgin'! You may not realize it, but your husband, or former husband, or whatever the hell he is, could be very much alive. A lot of nice people who never heard of him—women like you and young girls—were burned to death because of him! Others were killed, too, but maybe they should have been."

"What are you saying?" He relaxed his grip on her but still held her firmly.

"I just know that I left your mother-in-law a week ago in England. It was a hell of a trip over! Someone tried to kill her the first night out on the ship. Oh, you can bet your life it would have been suicide! They would have said she had tearfully thrown herself overboard. No trace at all. . . . A week ago we let out a story to the newspapers saying she'd gone to a retreat in a place called York, in England. Two days ago the heating system blew up and killed Christ knows how many people! An accident, of course!"

"I don't know what to say."

"Do you want me to finish, or do you still want me to go?"

There was a sadness about Ulster Scarlett's wife as she tried to smile. "I guess you'd better stay and . . . finish."

They sat on the sofa and Canfield talked.

He talked as he had never talked before.

Chapter Twenty-four

Benjamin Reynolds sat forward in his chair, clipping a week-old article from the Sunday supplement of the *New York Herald*. It was a photograph of Janet Saxon Scarlett being escorted by "sportinggoods executive, M. Canfield" to a dog show at Madison Square Garden. Reynolds smiled as he recalled Canfield's remark on the telephone.

"I can stand everything but the God damn dog shows. Dogs are for the very rich or the very poor. Not for anyone in between!"

No matter, thought Group Twenty's head. The newspapers were doing an excellent job. Washington had ordered Canfield to spend an additional ten days in Manhattan thoroughly establishing his relationship with Ulster Scarlett's wife before returning to England.

The relationship was unmistakable and Benjamin Reynolds wondered if it was really a public facade. Or was it something else? Was Canfield in the process of trapping himself? The ease with which he had engineered a collaboration with Elizabeth Scarlatti bore watching.

"Ben"—Glover walked briskly into the office—"I think we've found what we've been looking for!" He closed the door firmly and approached Reynolds's desk.

"What have you got? About what?"

"A link with the Scarlatti business. I'm sure of it."

"Let me see."

Glover placed several pages on top of the spread-out newspaper. "Nice coverage, wasn't it?" he said, indicating the photograph of Canfield and the girl.

"Just what us dirty old men ordered. He's going to be the toast of society if he doesn't spit on the floor."

"He's doing a good job, Ben. They're back on board ship now, aren't they?"

"Sailed yesterday. . . . What is this?"

"Statistics found it. From Switzerland. Zurich area. Fourteen estates all purchased within the year. Look at these latitude and longitude marks. Every one of the properties is adjacent to another one. A borders on B, B on C, C on D, right down the line. Hundreds of thousands of acres forming an enormous compound."

"One of the buyers Scarlatti?"

"No. . . . But one of the estates was bought in the name of Boothroyd. Charles Boothroyd."

"You're sure? What do you mean 'bought in the name of'?"

"Father-in-law bought it for his daughter and her husband. Named Rawlins. Thomas Rawlins. Partner in the brokerage house of Godwin and Rawlins. His daughter's name is Cecily. Married to Boothroyd."

Reynolds picked up the page with the list of names. "Who are these people? How does it break down?"

Glover reached for the other two pages. "It's all here. Four Americans, two Swedes, three English, two French, and three German. Fourteen in all."

"Do you have any rundowns?"

"Only on the Americans. We've sent for information on the rest."

"Who are they? Besides Rawlins."

"A Howard Thornton, San Francisco. He's in construction. And two Texas oilmen. A Louis Gibson and Avery Landor. Between them they own more wells than fifty of their competitors combined."

"Any connections between them?"

"Nothing so far. We're checking that out now."

"What about the others? The Swedes, the French? . . . The English and the Germans?"

"Only the names."

"Anyone familiar?"

"Several. There's an Innes-Bowen, he's English, in textiles, I think. And I recognize the name of Daudet, French. Owns steamship lines. And two of the Germans. Kindorf—he's in the Ruhr Valley. Coal. And von Schnitzler, speaks for I. G. Farben. Don't know the rest, never heard of the Swedes, either."

"In one respect they're all alike—"

"You bet your life they are. They're all as rich as a roomful of Astors. You don't buy places like these with mortgages. Shall I contact Canfield?"

"We'll have to. Send the list by courier. We'll cable him to stay in London until it arrives."

"Madame Scarlatti may know some of them."

"I'm counting on it. . . . But I see a problem."

"What's that?"

"It's going to be a temptation for the old girl to head right into Zurich. . . . If she does, she's dead. So's Canfield and Scarlett's wife."

"That's a pretty drastic assumption."

"Not really. We're presuming that a group of wealthy men have bought fourteen estates all adjoining one another because of a common interest. And Boothroyd—courtesy of a generous father-in-law—is one of them."

"Which ties Zurich to Scarlatti. . . ."

"We think so. We believe it because Boothroyd tried to kill her, right?"

"Of course."

"But the Scarlatti woman is alive. Boothroyd failed."

"Obviously."

"And the property was purchased before that fact."

"It must have been—"

"Then if Zurich is tied to Boothroyd, Zurich wants Scarlatti dead. They want to stop her. Also . . . Zurich presumed success. They expected Boothroyd to succeed."

"And now that he's gone," interrupted Glover, "Zurich will figure the old woman found out who he was. Maybe more. . . . Ben, perhaps we've gone too far. It might be better to call it off. Make a report to Justice and get Canfield back."

"Not yet. We're getting close to something. Elizabeth Scarlatti's the key right now. We'll get them plenty of protection."

"I don't want to make an alibi in advance, but this is your responsibility."

"I understand that. In our instructions to Canfield make one thing absolutely clear. He's to stay out of Zurich. Under no condition is he to go to Switzerland."

"I'll do that."

Reynolds turned from his desk and stared out the window. He spoke to his subordinate without looking at him. "And . . . keep a line open on this Rawlins. Boothroyd's father-in-law. He's the one who may have made the mistake."

Chapter Twenty-five

Twenty-five miles from the ancient limits of Cardiff, set in a remote glen in a Welsh forest, stands the Convent of the Virgin, the home of the Carmelite sisters. The walls rise in alabaster purity, like a new bride standing in holy expectation in a lush but serpentless Eden.

The field accountant and the young wife drove up to the entrance. Canfield got out of the car and walked to a small arched doorway set in the wall in which was centered a viewer. There was a black iron knocker on the side of the door that he used, then waited for several minutes until a nun answered.

"May I help you?"

The field accountant drew out his identification card and held it up for the nun to see. "My name is Canfield, sister. I'm here for Madame Elizabeth

Scarlatti. Her daughter-in-law is with me."

"If you'll wait, please. May I?" She indicated that she wished to take his identification card with her. He handed it to her through the small opening.

"Of course."

The viewer was closed and bolted. Canfield wandered back to the car and spoke to Janet. "They're very cautious."

"What's happening?"

"She's taking my card in to make sure the photograph's me and not someone else."

"Lovely here, isn't it? So quiet."

"It is now. I make no promises when we finally see the old girl."

"Your callous, unfeeling disregard for my well-being, to say nothing of my comforts, is beyond anything I can describe! Do you have any idea what these idiots sleep on? I'll tell you! Army cots!"

"I'm sorry—" Canfield tried not to laugh.

"And do you know the slops they eat? I'll tell you! Food I'd prohibit in my stables!"

"I'm told they grow their own vegetables," the field accountant countered gently.

"They pluck up the fertilizer and leave the plants!"

At that moment the bells of the Angelus pealed out.

"That goes on night and day! I asked that damned fool, Mother MacCree, or whoever she is, why so early in the morning—and do you know what she said?"

"What, Mother?" asked Janet.

"'That is the way of Christ,' that's what she said. 'Not a good Episcopal Christ!' I told her. . . . It's been intolerable! Why were you so late? Mr. Derek said you'd be here four days ago."

"I had to wait for a courier from Washington. Let's go. I'll tell you about it."

Elizabeth sat in the back seat of the Bentley reading the Zurich list.

"Know any of those people?" asked Canfield.

"Not personally. Most all of them by reputation, however."

"For instance?"

"The Americans, Louis Gibson and Avery Landor are two self-styled Texas Bunyans. They think they built the oil territories. Landor's a pig, I'm told. Harold Leacock, one of the Englishmen, is a power on the British Stock Exchange. Very bright. Myrdal from Sweden is also in the European market. Stockholm. . . ." Elizabeth looked up and acknowledged Canfield's glance in the rearview mirror.

"Anybody else?"

"Yes. Thyssen in Germany. Fritz Thyssen. Steel companies. Everyone knows Kindorf—Ruhr Valley coal, and von Schnitzler. He's I. G. Farben now. . . . One of the Frenchmen, D'Almeida, has control of railroads, I think. I don't know Daudet but I recognize the name."

"He owns tankers. Steamships."

"Oh, yes. And Masterson. Sydney Masterson. English. Far East imports, I think. I don't know Innes-Bowen, but again I've heard the name."

"You didn't mention Rawlins. Thomas Rawlins."

"I didn't think I had to. Godwin and Rawlins. Boothroyd's father-in-law."

"You don't know the fourth American, Howard Thornton? He's from San Francisco."

"Never heard of him."

"Janet says your son knew a Thornton from San Francisco."

"I'm not at all surprised."

On the road from Pontypridd, on the outskirts of the Rhondda Valley, Canfield became aware of an automobile, which regularly appeared in his side mirror. It was far behind them, hardly more than a speck in the glass, but it was never out of sight except around curves. And whenever Canfield rounded one of the many turns, the automobile appeared subsequently much sooner than its previous distance would indicate. On long stretches it stayed far in the distance and whenever possible allowed other cars to come between them.

"What is it, Mr. Canfield?" Elizabeth was watching the field accountant, who kept shifting his eyes to the mirror outside his window.

"Nothing."

"Is someone following us?"

"Probably not. There aren't that many good roads leading to the English border."

Twenty minutes later Canfield saw that the automobile was drawing nearer. Five minutes after that he began to understand. There were no cars between the two vehicles now. Only a stretch of road—a very long curve—bordered on one side by the rocky slope of a small incline and on the other by a sheer drop of fifty feet into the waters of a Welsh lake.

Beyond the end of the curve, Canfield saw that the ground leveled off into a pasture or overgrown field. He accelerated the Bentley. He wanted to reach that level area.

The car behind shot forward closing the gap between them. It swung to the right on the side of the road by the rocky slope. Canfield knew that once the car came parallel it could easily force him off the road, over the edge, plunging the Bentley down the steep incline into the water. The field accountant held the pedal down and veered the car toward the center trying to cut off the pursuer.

"What is it? What are you doing?" Janet held on to the top of the dashboard.

"Brace yourselves! Both of you!"

Canfield held the Bentley in the center, crossing to the right each time the car behind him tried to squeeze between him and the solid ground. The level field was nearer now. Only another hundred yards.

There were two sharp, heavy crunches as the Bentley lurched spastically under the second car's impact. Janet Scarlett screamed. Her mother-in-law kept silent, clutching the girl's shoulders from behind, helping to brace her.

The level pasture was now on the left and Canfield suddenly swerved the car toward it, going off the road, holding to the dirt border beyond the pavement.

The pursuing car plunged forward at tremendous speed. Canfield riveted his eyes on the rapidly receding black-and-white license plate. He shouted, "*E, B . . . I* or *L!* Seven! Seven or nine! One, one, Three!" he repeated the numbers again softly, quickly. He slowed the Bentley down and came to a stop.

Janet's back was arched against the seat. She held Elizabeth's arms with both her hands. The old woman sat forward, her cheek pressed against her daughter-in-law's head.

Elizabeth spoke.

"The letters you called out were *E, B, I* or *L*, the numbers, seven or nine, one, one, three."

"I couldn't tell the make of the car."

Elizabeth spoke again as she took her arms from Janet's shoulders.

"It was a Mercedes-Benz."

Chapter Twenty-six

"The automobile in question is a Mercedes-Benz coupé. Nineteen twenty-five model. The license is EBI nine, one, one, three. The vehicle is registered in the name of Jacques Louis Bertholde. Once again, the Marquis de Bertholde." James Derek stood by Canfield in front of Elizabeth and Janet who sat on the sofa. He read from his notebook and wondered if these curious Americans realized who the marquis was. Bertholde, too, often stayed at the Savoy and was probably as rich as Elizabeth Scarlatti.

"The same man who met Boothroyd's wife at the pier?" asked Canfield.

"Yes. Or I should say, no. We assume it was Bertholde at the pier from your description. It couldn't have been yesterday. We've established that he was in London. However, the automobile is registered to him."

"What do you think, Mr. Derek?" Elizabeth smoothed her dress and avoided looking at the Englishman. There was something about the man that disturbed her.

"I don't know what to think. . . . However, I feel I should tell you that the Marquis de Bertholde is a resident alien of considerable influence and position. . . ."

"He is the owner of Bertholde et Fils, as I recall." Elizabeth rose from the sofa and gave her empty sherry glass to Canfield. It was not that she wished more wine. She was just too wrought up to sit still. "Bertholde et Fils is an old established firm."

The field accountant went to the drinks table and poured Elizabeth's sherry.

"Then you've met the marquis, Madame Scarlatti? Perhaps you know him?"

Elizabeth didn't like Derek's insinuation. "No, I do not know the marquis. I may have met his father. I'm not sure. The Bertholdes go back many years."

Canfield handed Elizabeth her glass aware that the old woman and the British operative were playing a mental tennis game. He broke in. "What's his business?"

"Plural. Businesses. Near East oil, mining and drilling in Africa, imports—Australia and South America. . . ."

"Why is he a resident alien?"

"I can answer that," said Elizabeth, returning to the couch. "The physical plants—his offices—are, no doubt, within Empire territories or protectorates."

"Quite correct, madame," said Derek. "Since the majority of his interests lie within the borders of British possessions, he deals continuously with Whitehall. He does so, most favorably."

"Is there a government dossier on Bertholde?"

"As a resident alien, of course there is."

"Can you get it for me?"

"I'd have to have a very sound reason. You know that."

"Mr. Derek!" interrupted Elizabeth. "An attempt was made on my life aboard the *Calpurnia*! Yesterday in Wales an automobile tried to run us off the road! In both instances the Marquis de Berthode can be implicated. I would call these sound reasons!"

"I'm afraid I must disagree. What you describe are police matters. Anything I know to the contrary is privileged information and I respect it as such. Certainly no charges are being made in either case. It's a gray area, I grant you, but Canfield knows what I'm talking about."

The field accountant looked at Elizabeth and she knew the time had come to use his ploy. He had explained that eventually they would have to. He had called it—"part of the truth." The reason was simple. British Intelligence was not going to be used as someone's personal police force. There had to be other justifications. Justifications that Washington would confirm. Canfield looked at the Englishman and spoke softly.

"The United States government wouldn't involve my agency unless there were reasons beyond police matters. When Madame Scarlatti's son—Mrs. Scarlett's husband—was in Europe last year, large sums of money, in the form of negotiable securities on a number of American corporations, were forwarded to him. We think they were sold undercover on the European markets. The British exchange included."

"Are you telling me that someone is forming an American monopoly over here?"

"The State Department thinks that the manipulation was handled by our own embassy personnel. They're right here in London now."

"Your own embassy personnel! And you think Scarlett was a party to it?"

"We think he was used." Elizabeth's voice pierced the air. "Used and then eliminated."

"He traveled in that crowd, Derek. So does the Marquis de Bertholde."

James Derek replaced his small notebook in his breast pocket. The explanation obviously was sufficient. The British operative was also very curious. "I'll have a copy of the dossier for you tomorrow, Canfield. . . . Good evening, ladies." He went out.

"I congratulate you, young man. Embassy personnel. Really very intelligent of you."

"I think he was remarkable!" said Janet Scarlett, smiling at him.

"It'll work," mumbled the field accountant, swallowing the major portion of a Scotch. "Now, may I suggest we all need some relief. Speaking for myself, I'm tired of thinking—and I wouldn't appreciate a comment on that, Madame Scarlatti. How about dinner at one of those places you upper class always go? I hate dancing but I swear I'll dance with you both until you drop."

Elizabeth and Janet laughed.

"No, but I thank you," said Elizabeth. "You two go and romp." She looked at the field accountant fondly. "An old woman thanks you again, Mr. Canfield."

"You'll lock the doors and windows?"

"Seven stories off the ground? Of course, if you like."

"I do," said Canfield.

Chapter Twenty-seven

"It's heaven!" shrieked Janet over the din of voices at Claridge's. "Come on, Matthew, don't look so sour!"

"I'm not sour. I just can't hear you."

"Yes, you are. You didn't like it. Let me enjoy it."

"I will. I will! Do you want to dance?"

"No. You hate dancing. I just want to watch."

"No charge. Watch. It's good whiskey."

"Good what?"

"I said whiskey."

"No, thanks. See? I can be good. You're two up on me, you know."

"I may be sixty up on you if this keeps going."

"What, darling?"

"I said I may be sixty when we get out of here."

"Oh, stop it. Have fun!"

Canfield looked at the girl opposite him and felt once again a surge of joy. There was no other word but joy. She was a delight that filled him with pleasure, with warmth. Her eyes held the immediacy of commitment that only a lover can know. Yet Canfield tried so hard to disassociate, to isolate, to objectify, and found that he could not do it.

"I love you very much," he said.

She heard him through the music, the laughter, the undercurrent hum of movement.

"I know." She looked at him and her eyes had the hint of tears. "We love each other. Isn't that remarkable?"

"Do you want to dance, now?"

The girl threw back her head ever so slightly. "Oh, Matthew! My dear, sweet Matthew. No, darling. You don't have to dance."

"Now, look, I will."

She clasped his hand. "We'll dance by ourselves, all by ourselves later."

Matthew Canfield made up his mind that he would have this woman for the rest of his life.

But he was a professional and his thoughts turned for a moment to the old woman at the Savoy.

Elizabeth Wyckham Scarlatti at that moment got out of her bed and into a dressing gown. She had been reading the *Manchester Guardian*. Turning its thin pages, she heard two sharp metallic clicks accompanied by a muffled sound of movement from the living room. She was not at first startled by the noise; she had bolted the hallway door and presumed that her daughter-in-law was fumbling with a key unable to enter because of the latch. After all, it was two o'clock in the morning and the girl should have returned by now. She called out.

"Just one minute, my dear. I'm up."

She had left a table lamp on and the fringe of the shade rippled as she passed it causing a flickering of minute shadows on the wall.

She reached the door and began to unbolt the latch. Remembering the field accountant, she halted momentarily.

"That is you, isn't it, my dear?"

There was no reply.

She automatically snapped back the bolt.

"Janet? Mr. Canfield? Is that you?"

Silence.

Fear gripped Elizabeth. She had heard the sound; age had not impaired her hearing.

Perhaps she had confused the clicking with the unfamiliar rustling of the thin English newspaper. That was not unreasonable and although she tried to believe it, she could not.

Was there someone else in the room?

At the thought she felt pain in the pit of her stomach.

As she turned to go back into the bedroom, she saw that one of the large french windows was partially opened, no more than one or two inches but enough to cause the silk draperies to sway slightly from the incoming breeze.

In her confusion she tried to recall whether she had closed it before. She thought she had, but it had been an uninterested motion because she hadn't taken Canfield seriously. Why should she? They were seven stories high.

Of course, she hadn't closed it. Or, if she had, she hadn't secured the catch and it had slipped off. Nothing at all unusual. She crossed to the window and pushed it closed.

And then she heard it.

"Hello, Mother."

Out of the shadows from the far end of the room walked a large man dressed in black. His head was shaved and he was deeply tanned.

For several seconds she did not recognize him. The light from the one table lamp was dim and the figure remained at the end of the room. As she became adjusted to the light and the object of her gaze, she realized why the man appeared to be a stranger. The face had changed. The shining black hair was shaved off; the nose was altered, smaller and the nostrils wider apart; the ears were different, flatter against the head; even the eyes—where before there had been a Neapolitan droop to the lids—these eyes were wide, as if no lids existed. There were reddish splotches around the mouth and forehead. It was not a face. It was the mask of a face. It was striking. It was monstrous. And it was her son.

"Ulster! My God!"

"If you die right now of heart failure, you'll make fools out of several highly paid assassins."

The old woman tried to think, tried with all her strength to resist panic. She gripped the back of a chair until the veins in her aged hands seemed to burst from the skin.

"If you've come to kill me, there's little I can do now."

"You'll be interested to know that the man who ordered you killed will soon be dead himself. He was stupid."

Her son wandered toward the french window and checked the latch. He cautiously peered through the glass and was satisfied. His mother noticed that the grace with which he had always carried himself remained but there was no softness now, no gentle relaxation, which had taken the form of a slight aristocratic slouch. Now there was a taut, hard quality in his movement, accentuated by his hands—which were encased in skintight black gloves, fingers extended and rigidly curved.

Elizabeth slowly found the words. "Why have you come here?"

"Because of your obstinate curiosity." He walked rapidly to the hotel phone on the table with the lighted lamp, touching the cradle as if making sure it was secure. He returned to within a few feet of his mother and the sight of his face, now seen clearly, caused her to shut her eyes. When she reopened them, he was rubbing his right eyebrow, which was partially inflamed. He watched her pained look.

"The scars aren't quite healed. Occasionally they itch. Are you maternally solicitous?"

"What have you done to yourself?"

"A new life. A new world for me. A world which has nothing to do with yours. Not yet!"

"I asked you what you've done."

"You know what I've done, otherwise you wouldn't be here in London. What you must understand, now, is that Ulster Scarlett no longer exists."

"If that's what you want the world to believe, why come to me of all people?"

"Because you rightly assumed it wasn't true and your meddling could prove irksome to me."

The old woman steeled herself before speaking. "It's quite possible then that the instructions for my death were not stupid."

"That's very brave. I wonder, though, if you've thought about the others?"

"What others?"

Scarlett sat on the couch and spoke in a biting Italian dialect. "La Famiglia Scarlatti! That's the proper phrase, isn't it? . . . Eleven members to be exact. Two parents, a grandmother, a drunken bitch wife, and seven children. The end of the tribe! The Scarlatti line abruptly stops in one bloody massacre!"

"You're mad! I'd stop you! Don't pit your piddling theft against what I have, my boy!"

"You're a foolish old woman! We're beyond sums. It's only how they're applied now. You taught me that!"

"I'd put them out of your reach! I'd have you hunted down and destroyed!"

The man effortlessly sprang up from the couch.

"We're wasting time. You're concerning yourself with mechanics. That's pedestrian. Let's be clear. I make one phone call and the order is sent to New York. Within forty-eight hours the Scarlattis are snuffed out! Extinguished! It will be an expensive funeral. The foundation will provide nothing but the best."

"Your own child as well?"

"He'd be the first. All dead. No apparent reason. The mystery of the lunatic Scarlattis."

"You are mad." She was hardly audible.

"Speak up, Mother! Or are you thinking about those curly headed moppets romping on the beach at Newport, laughing in their little boats on the sound. Tragic, isn't it? Just one of them! Just one out of the whole lot might make it for you, and the Scarlatti tribe continues in glory! Shall I make my call? It's a matter of indifference to me."

The old woman, who had not moved, walked slowly toward one of the armchairs. "Is what you want from me so valuable that the lives of my family depend upon it?"

"Not to you. Only to me. It could be worse, you know. I could demand an additional one hundred million."

"Why don't you? Under the circumstances you know I'd pay it."

The man laughed. "Certainly you'd pay it. You'd pay it from a source that'd cause a panic in the ticker rooms. No, thank you. I don't need it. Remember, we're beyond sums."

"What is it you want?" She sat in the chair, crossing her thin arms on her lap.

"The bank letters for one. They're no good to you anyway, so there should be no struggle with your conscience."

She had been right! The concept had been right! Always trace the practical. The money.

"Bank letters?"

"The bank letters Cartwright gave you."

"You killed him! You knew about our agreement?"

"Come, Mother. A Southern ass is made vice-president of Waterman Trust! Actually given responsibility. We followed him for three days. We have your agreements. At least his copies. Let's not fool each other. The letters, please."

The old lady rose from the chair and went into her bedroom. She returned and handed him the letters. He rapidly opened the envelopes and took them out. He spread them on the couch and counted them.

"Cartwright earned his money."

He gathered them up and casually sat down on the sofa.

"I had no idea those letters were so important."

"They're not, really. Nothing could be accomplished with them. All the accounts have been closed and the money . . . dispersed to others, shall we say."

"Then why were you so anxious to get them?" She remained standing.

"If they were submitted to the banks, they could start a lot of speculation. We don't want a great deal of talk right now."

The old woman searched her son's confident eyes. He was detached, pleased with himself, almost relaxed.

"Who is 'we.' What are you involved in?"

Again that grotesque smile from the crooked mouth underneath the unnatural nostrils. "You'll know in good time. Not by name, of course, but you'll know. You might even be proud but you'll never admit it." He looked at his wristwatch. "Down to business."

"What else?"

"What happened on the *Calpurnia*? Don't lie!" He riveted his eyes on the old woman's and they did not waver.

Elizabeth strained the muscles in her abdomen to help her conceal any reaction to the question. She knew that the truth might be all she had left. "I don't understand you."

"You're lying!"

"About what? I received a cablegram from a man named Boutier concerning Cartwright's death."

"Stop it!" He leaned forward. "You wouldn't have gone to the trouble of throwing everyone off with that York Abbey story unless something happened. I want to know where he is."

"Where who is? Cartwright?"

"I warn you!"

"I have no idea what you're talking about!"

"A man disappeared on that ship! They say he fell overboard."

"Oh, yes. I recall. . . . What has that to do with me?" Her look personified innocence.

Neither moved.

"You know nothing about the incident?"

"I didn't say that."

"What did you say, then?"

"There were rumors. Reliable sources."

"What rumors?"

The old woman weighed several replies. She knew that her answer had to have the ring of authenticity without any obvious errors in character or behavior. On the other hand, whatever she said had to reflect the sketchy extremes of gossip.

"That the man was drunk and belligerent. There'd been a struggle in the lounge. . . . He had to be subdued and carried to his stateroom. He tried to return and fell over the rail. Did you know him?"

A cloud of detachment covered Scarlett's answer. "No, he was no part of us." He was dissatisfied but he did not dwell on it. For the first time in several minutes he looked away from her. He was deep in thought. Finally he spoke. "One last item. You started out to find your missing son . . ."

"I started out to find a thief!" she interrupted sharply.

"Have it your way. From another point of view I simply moved up the calendar."

"That's not true! You stole from Scarlatti. What was assigned to you was to be used in conjunction with the Scarlatti Industries!"

"We're wasting time again."

"I wanted the point cleared up."

"The point is that you set out to find me and you succeeded. We agree on that fact?"

"Agreed."

"Now I'm telling you to say nothing, do nothing, and return to New York. Furthermore, destroy any letters or instructions you may have left concerning me."

"Those are impossible demands!"

"In that event my orders go out. The Scarlattis are dead! Go to your church and let them tell you how they've been washed in the blood of the lamb!"

Ulster Scarlett sprang up from the Victorian couch and before the old woman could adjust her eyes to his movement, he had reached the telephone. There wasn't the slightest hesitation on his part. He picked up the telephone without looking at her and waited for the switchboard to answer.

The old woman rose unsteadily. "Don't!"

He turned to face her. "Why not?"

"I'll do as you ask!"

He replaced the phone. "Are you sure?"

"I'm sure." He had won.

Ulster Scarlett smiled with his misshapen lips. "Then our business is concluded."

"Not quite." Elizabeth now would try, realizing that the attempt might cost her her life.

"Oh?"

"I'd like to speculate, for just a minute."

"On what?"

"For the sake of argument, supposing I decided to abandon our understanding?"

"You know the consequences. You couldn't hide from us, not for any length of time."

"Time, however, could be the factor on my side."

"The securities have been disposed of. No sense in thinking about that."

"I assumed they had been, or else you wouldn't have come here."

"This is a good game. Go on."

"I'm sure that if you hadn't thought of it yourself, someone would have told you that the only intelligent way of selling those securities would be on a currency basis in exchange for diminished value."

"No one had to tell me."

"Now it's my turn to ask a question."

"Go ahead."

"How difficult do you think it is to trace deposits, gold or otherwise, of that magnitude? I'll make it two questions. Where are the only banks in the world willing or even capable of such deposits?"

"We both know the answer. Coded, numbered, impossible."

"And in which of the great banking concerns of Switzerland is there the incorruptible man?"

Her son paused and squinted his lidless eyes. "Now you're the one who's insane," he answered quietly.

"Not at all. You think in small blocks, Ulster. You use large sums but you think in small blocks. . . . Word goes out in the marble halls of Bern and Zurich that the sum of one million American dollars can be had for the confidential exchange of information. . . ."

"What would you gain by it?"

"Knowledge! . . . Names! People!"

"You make me laugh!"

"Your laughter will be short-lived! . . . It's obvious that you have associates; you need them. Your threats make that doubly clear, and I'm sure you pay them well. . . . The question is—once they're known to me and I to them—will they be able to resist my price? Certainly you can never match it! In this we are not beyond sums!"

The grotesque face distorted itself further as a thick, drawlish laugh came forth from the misshapen mouth. "I've waited years to tell you that your slide-rule theories smell! Your stinking buy-me, sell-me manipulations are finished! You've had your way! It's finished! Dead! Gone! . . . Who are you to manipulate? With your conniving bankers! Your stinking little Jews! You're finished! I've watched you! Your kind is dead! . . . Don't talk to me about my associates. They wouldn't touch you or your money!" The man in black was in a rage.

"You believe that?" Elizabeth did not move. She asked a simple question.

"Completely!" Ulster Scarlett's unhealed flesh was red with the blood rushing to his head. "We have something else! And you can't touch us! Any of us! *There is no price for us!*"

"However, you'll grant—as with the bank letters—I could prove irksome. Only to a far greater degree. Do you wish to take that gamble?"

"You sign eleven death warrants! A mass burial! Is that what you want, Mother?"

"The answer to both our questions would seem to be no. This is now a more reasonable understanding."

The man-mask in black paused and spoke softly, precisely. "You're not my equal. Don't for one minute think you are!"

"What happened, Ulster? What happened? . . . Why?"

"Nothing and everything! I'm doing what none of you are capable of doing! What has to be done! But you can't do it!"

"Would I . . . or we . . . want to?"

"More than anything in the world? But you haven't the stomachs! You're weak!"

The telephone rang, piercing the air.

"Don't bother to answer it," Ulster said. "It'll ring only once. It's merely a signal that my wife—the devoted whore—and her newest bedmate have left Claridge's."

"Then I assume our meeting is adjourned." She saw to her great relief that he accepted the statement. She noted also that in such a position he was dangerous. A tick was developing on the surface of his skin above his right eye. He again stretched his fingers in a slow deliberate motion.

"Remember what I say. You make one mistake . . ."

She interrupted before he could finish. "Remember who I am, young man! You're speaking to the wife of Giovanni Merighi Scarlatti! There is no need to repeat yourself. You have your agreement. Go about your filthy business. I have no further interest in you!"

The man in black strode rapidly to the door. "I hate you, Mother."

"I hope you benefit as much from those you hold less dear."

"In ways you'd never understand!"

He opened the door and slipped out, slamming it harshly behind him.

Elizabeth Scarlatti stood by the window and pulled apart the drapes. She leaned against the cold glass for support. The city of London was asleep, and only a scattering of lights dotted its concrete facade.

What in God's name had he done?

More important, who was paying attention to him?

What might have been mere horror turned into terror for he had the weapon. The weapon of power—which she and Giovanni innocently, productively provided.

They were, indeed, beyond sums.

Tears fell from her old eyes and that inner consciousness, which afflicts all human beings, was taken by surprise. She had not cried in over thirty years.

Elizabeth pushed herself away from the window and slowly wandered about the room. She had a great deal of thinking to do.

Chapter Twenty-eight

In a room in the Home Office, James Derek took out a file. "Jacques Louis Bertholde, The Fourth Marquis of Chatellerault."

The dossier custodian entered the room. "Hello, James. Late hours tonight, I see."

"I'm afraid so, Charles. I'm taking out a copy. Did you get my request?"

"Right here. Fill me in and I'll sign for it. But please make it short. I've a card game in my office."

"Short and simple. The Americans suspect their embassy personnel of selling Yank securities undercover over here. This Bertholde travels in the diplomatic circles. There could be a connection with the Scarlatti fellow."

The dossier custodian made his appropriate notes. "When did this all take place?"

"About a year ago, as I understand it."

The custodian stopped writing and looked at James Derek. "A year ago?"

"Yes."

"And this American chap wants to confront embassy personnel *now*? Over *here*?"

"That's right."

"He's on the wrong side of the Atlantic. All American embassy personnel were transferred four months ago. There's no one there now—not even a secretary—who was in London a year ago."

"That's very strange," said Derek quietly.

"I'd say your American friend has a rather poor connection with his State Department."

"Which means he's lying."

"Which means he is."

Janet and Matthew, laughing, got off on the seventh floor and started down the corridor toward Elizabeth's suite. The length of their walk was approximately one hundred feet and they stopped four times to embrace and exchange kisses.

The girl took a key out of her purse and handed it to the field accountant.

He inserted it and simultaneously turned the knob before making any lateral motion with the key. The door opened and in a split second the field accountant was more sober than drunk.

He practically fell into the room.

Elizabeth Scarlatti was sitting on the Victorian couch in the dim light emanating from the single lamp. She did not move other than to look up at Canfield and her daughter-in-law.

"I heard you in the hallway."

"I told you to lock these doors!"

"I'm sorry, I forgot."

"The hell you did! I waited until I heard the latch and the bolt!"

"I ordered some coffee from room service."

"Where's the tray?"

"In my bedroom, which I presume to be private."

"Don't you believe it!" The field accountant ran toward the bedroom door.

"I apologize again! I called to have it taken away. I'm quite confused. Forgive me."

"Why? What's the matter?"

Elizabeth Scarlatti thought quickly and looked at her daughter-in-law as she spoke. "I had a most distressing telephone call. A business matter completely unrelated to you. It entails a great deal of money and I must make a decision before the British exchange opens." She looked at the field accountant.

"May I ask what's so important that you don't follow my instructions?"

"Several million dollars. Perhaps you'd care to help me. Should the Scarlatti Industries conclude the purchase of the remaining convertible debentures in Sheffield Cutlery and by exercising the conversions gain control of the company or not?"

Still uncertain, the field accountant asked, "Why is that so . . . distressing?"

"Because the company constantly loses money."

"Then you don't buy. That shouldn't keep you up all night."

The old woman eyed him coldly. "Sheffield Cutlery is one of the oldest, finest firms in England. Their product is superb. The problem is neither management nor labor conditions but a heavy influx of Japanese imitations. The question is. Will the purchasing public learn in time to reverse the trend?"

Elizabeth Scarlatti rose from the couch and went into her bedroom, closing the door behind her. The field accountant turned to Janet Scarlett. "Does she do this sort of thing all the time? Doesn't she have advisers?"

But Janet was still staring at the bedroom door. She took off her wrap and approached the field accountant. She spoke quietly. "She's not telling the truth."

"How do you know?"

"The way she looked at me when she was talking to you. She was trying to tell me something."

"Like what?"

The girl shrugged impatiently and continued in a hushed whisper. "Oh, I don't know, but you know what I mean. You're with a group of people, and you start to tell a whopper or exaggerate something, and while you do, you look at your husband or a friend who knows better . . . and they know they shouldn't correct you. . . ."

"Was she lying about that company she spoke of?"

"Oh, no. That's the truth. Chancellor Drew's been trying to persuade her to buy that firm for months."

"How do you know?"

"She's already turned it down."

"Then why did she lie?"

As Canfield started to sit down, his attention was drawn to the linen antimacassar on the back of the chair. At first he dismissed it and then he looked again. The material was crumpled as if it had been mangled or bunched together. It was out of place in an immaculate suite. He looked closer. There were breaks in the threads and the imprint of fingertips was unmistakable. Whoever had gripped the chair had done so with considerable force.

"What is it, Matthew?"

"Nothing. Get me a drink, will you?"

"Of course, darling." She went to the dry bar as Canfield walked around the chair in front of the french window. For no particular reason, he pulled apart the curtains and inspected the window itself. He turned the latch and pulled the left side open. He saw what he had begun to look for. The wood around the clasp was scratched. On the sill he could see where the paint had been discolored by the impression of a heavy coarse object, probably a rubber-soled boot or a crepe-soled shoe. Not leather; there were no scratches on the enamel. He opened the right side and looked out. Below were six stories straight down; above two floors to what he recalled was an acutely slanting roof. He pushed the window shut and locked it.

"What on earth are you doing?"

"We've had a visitor. An uninvited guest, you might say."

The girl stood absolutely still. "Oh, my God!"

"Don't be frightened. Your mother-in-law wouldn't do anything foolish. Believe that."

"I'm trying to. What are we going to do?"

"Find out who it was. Now get hold of yourself. I'll need you."

"Why didn't she say something?"

"I don't know, but you may be able to find out."

"How?"

"Tomorrow morning she'll probably bring up the Sheffield business. If she does, tell her you remember she refused to buy it for Chancellor. She'll have to give you an explanation of some kind."

"If Mother Scarlatti doesn't want to talk, she just won't. I know."

"Then don't press it. But she'll have to say something."

Although it was nearly three o'clock, the lobby had a flow of stragglers from late parties. They were mostly in evening dress, a great many were unbalanced and giggling, all were happily tired.

Canfield went to the desk clerk and spoke in a gentle, folksy tone, "Say, fella, I've got a little problem."

"Yes, sir. May we be of service?"

"Well, it's a bit touchy. . . . I'm traveling with Madame Elizabeth Scarlatti and her daughter. . . ."

"Oh, yes indeed. Mr. . . . Canfield, isn't it?"

"Sure. Well, the old girl's getting on, you know, and the people above her keep pretty late hours."

The clerk, who knew the legend of the Scarlatti wealth, was abject in apology. "I'm dreadfully sorry, Mr. Canfield. I'll go up myself at once. This is most embarrassing."

"Oh, no, please, everything's quiet now."

"Well, I can assure you it won't happen again. They must be loud, indeed. As I'm sure you're aware, the Savoy is the soundest of structures."

"Well, I guess they keep the windows open, but, please, don't say anything. She'd be pretty sore at me if she thought I talked to you about it. . . ."

"I don't understand, sir."

"Just tell me who they are and I'll talk to them myself. You know, friendly-like, over a drink."

The clerk couldn't have been happier with the American's solution. "Well, if you insist, sir. . . . In eight west one is the Viscount and Viscountess Roxbury, charming couple and quite elderly, I believe. Most unusual. However, they could be entertaining."

"Who's above them?"

"Above them, Mr. Canfield? I don't think . . ."

"Just tell me, please."

"Well in nine west one is . . ." The clerk turned the page. "It's not occupied, sir."

"Not occupied? That's unusual for this time of year, isn't it?"

"I should say unavailable, sir. Nine west one has been leased for the month for business conferences."

"You mean no one stays there at night?"

"Oh, they're certainly entitled to but that hasn't been the case."

"Who leased it?"

"The firm is Bertholde et Fils."

Chapter Twenty-nine

The telephone beside James Derek's bed rang harshly, waking him.

"It's Canfield. I need help and it can't wait."

"That may possibly be only your judgment. What is it?"

"Scarlatti's suite was broken into."

"What! What does the hotel say?"

"They don't know about it."

"I do think you should tell them."

"It's not that simple. She won't admit it."

"She's your problem. Why call me?"

"I think she's frightened. . . . It was a second-story."

"My dear fellow, her rooms are on the seventh floor! You're too fantastic! Or do the nasty men fly by themselves?"

The American paused just long enough to let the Englishman know he wasn't amused. "They figured she wouldn't open the door, which, in itself, is interesting. Whoever it was, was lowered from one of the rooms above and used a blade. Did you learn anything about Bertholde?"

"One thing at a time." Derek began to take Canfield seriously.

"That's the point. I think they are the same thing. Bertholde's company leased the rooms two floors above."

"I beg your pardon?"

"That's right. For a month. Daily business conferences, no less."

"I think we'd better have a talk."

"The girl knows about it and she's frightened. Can you put a couple of men on?"

"You think it's necessary?"

"Not really. But I'd hate to be wrong."

"Very well. The story will be anticipated jewel theft. Not uniformed, of course. One in the corridor, one in the street."

"I appreciate it. You beginning to wake up?"

"I am, confound you. I'll be with you in a half hour. With everything I've been able to dig up on Bertholde. And I think we'd better get a look at their suite."

Canfield left the phone booth and started back to the hotel. His lack of

sleep was beginning to take effect and he wished he was in an American city
where such institutions as all-night diners provided coffee. The English, he
thought, were wrong in thinking themselves so civilized. No one was
civilized without all-night diners.

He entered the opulent lobby and noted that the clock above the desk read
quarter to four. He walked toward the ancient elevators.

"Oh, Mr. Canfield, sir!" The clerk rushed up.

"What is it?" Canfield could only think of Janet and his heart stopped.

"Just after you left, sir! Not two minutes after you left! . . . Most unusual
this time of night. . . ."

"What the hell are you talking about?"

"This cablegram arrived for you." The clerk handed Canfield an envelope.

"Thank you," said a relieved Canfield as he took the cablegram and
entered the open-grill elevator. As he rose from the ground floor he pressed
the cable between his thumb and forefinger. It was thick. Benjamin Reynolds
had either sent a long abstract lecture or there would be a considerable
amount of decoding to be done. He only hoped he could finish it before
Derek arrived.

Canfield entered his room, sat down in a chair near a floor lamp, and
opened the cable.

No decoding was necessary. It was all written in simple business language
and easily understood when applied to the current situation. Canfield
separated the pages. There were three.

```
SORRY TO INFORM YOU RAWLINS THOMAS AND LILLIAN
IN AUTOMOBILE ACCIDENT REPEAT ACCIDENT POCONO
MOUNTAINS STOP BOTH ARE DEAD STOP KNOW THIS WILL
UPSET YOUR DEAR FRIEND E S STOP SUGGEST YOU CARE
FOR HER IN HER DISTRESS STOP TO WIMBLEDON BUSI-
NESS STOP WE HAVE SPARED NO EXPENSE AGAIN SPARED
NO EXPENSE WITH OUR ENGLISH SUPPLIERS TO OBTAIN
MAXIMUM QUOTAS OF MERCHANDISE STOP THEY ARE SYMPA-
THETIC WITH OUR PROBLEMS OF SCANDINAVIAN EXPORTS
STOP THEY ARE PREPARED TO AID YOU IN YOUR NEGOTI-
ATIONS FOR FAIR REDUCTIONS ON MAXIMUM PURCHASES
STOP THEY HAVE BEEN TOLD OF OUR COMPETITORS IN
SWITZERLAND AGAIN SWITZERLAND AND THE COMPANIES
REPEAT COMPANIES INVOLVED STOP THEY KNOW OF THE
THREE BRITISH FIRMS IN COMPETITION STOP THEY WILL
GIVE YOU ALL ASSISTANCE AND WE EXPECT YOU TO CON-
CENTRATE AGAIN CONCENTRATE ON OUR INTERESTS IN
ENGLAND STOP DO NOT AGAIN DO NOT ATTEMPT TO UNDER-
BID OUR COMPETITORS IN SWITZERLAND STOP STAY OUT
OF IT STOP NOTHING CAN BE ACCOMPLISHED STOP
                 J. HAMMER WIMBLEDON NEW YORK
```

Canfield lit a thin cigar and placed the three pages on the floor between his
outstretched legs. He peered down at them.

Hammer was Reynolds's code name for messages sent to field accountants when he considered the contents to be of the utmost importance. The word *again* was for positive emphasis. The word *repeat* a simple inversion. It denoted the negative of whatever it referred to.

So the Rawlinses—Canfield had to think for a minute before he remembered that the Rawlinses were Boothroyd's in-laws—had been murdered. Not an accident. And Reynolds feared for Elizabeth Scarlatti's life. Washington had reached an agreement with the British government to gain him unusual cooperation—no expense spared—and in return had told the English of the Swedish securities and the land purchases in Switzerland, which were presumed to be related. However, Reynolds did not specify who the men in Zurich were. Only that they existed and three upstanding Englishmen were on the list. Canfield recalled their names—Masterson of India fame; Leacock of the British Stock Exchange; and Innes-Bowen, the textile magnate.

The main points Hammer made were to protect Elizabeth and stay out of Switzerland.

There was a light tapping on his door. Canfield gathered the pages together and put them in his pocket. "Who is it?"

"Goldilocks, confound you! I'm looking for a bed to sleep in." The crisp British accent belonged, of course, to James Derek. Canfield opened the door and the Englishman walked in without further greeting. He threw a manila envelope on the bed, placed his bowler on the bureau, and sat down in the nearest stuffed chair.

"I like the hat, James."

"I'm just praying that it may keep me from being arrested. A Londoner prowling around the Savoy at this hour has to have the look of immense respectability."

"You have it, take my word."

"I wouldn't take your word for a damn thing, you insomniac."

"Can I get you a whiskey?"

"God, no! . . . Madame Scarlatti didn't mention a thing to you?"

"Nothing. Less than nothing. She tried to divert my attention. Then she just shut up and locked herself in her bedroom."

"I can't believe it. I thought you two were working together." Derek withdrew a hotel key attached to the usual wooden identification tag. "I had a chat with the hotel bobby."

"Can you trust him?"

"It doesn't matter. It's a master key and he thinks I'm covering a party on the second floor."

"Then I'll get going. Wait for me, please. Grab some sleep."

"Hold on. You're obviously connected with Madame Scarlatti. I should do the reconnoitering."

The field accountant paused. There was merit in what Derek said. He presumed the British operative was far more adept at this kind of sleuthing than he was. On the other hand, he could not be sure of the man's confidence. Neither was he prepared to tell him very much and have the British government making decisions.

"That's brave of you, Derek, but I wouldn't ask it."

"Not brave at all. Numerous explanations under the Alien Order."

"Nevertheless, I'd prefer going myself. Frankly, there's no reason for you to be involved. I called you for help, not to do my work."

"Let's compromise. In my favor."

"Why?"

"It's safer."

"You've won a point."

"I'll go in first while you wait in the corridor by the lift. I'll check the rooms and then signal you to join me."

"How?"

"With as little energy as possible. Perhaps a short whistle."

Canfield heard the short, shrill whistle and walked quickly down the hallway to nine west one.

He closed the door and went to the source of the flash-light. "Everything all right?"

"It's a well-kept hotel suite. Perhaps not so ostentatious as the American variety, but infinitely more home-like."

"That's reassuring."

"More than you know. I really don't like this sort of work."

"I thought you people were famous for it."

This small talk covered the start of their rapid but thorough search of the premises. The floor plan of the rooms was identical to the Scarlatti suite two stories below. However, instead of similar furniture there was a long table in the center of the mainroom with perhaps a dozen chairs around it.

"Conference table, I presume," said Derek.

"Let's take a look at the window."

"Which one?"

Canfield thought. "Over here." He went toward the french windows directly in line with those of Elizabeth Scarlatti.

"Good point. Here." The Englishman edged Canfield out of the way as he directed the light.

On the wooden sill was a freshly made valley, which had gone through the paint to the wood grain. Where the wood met the outer stone there was a similar semicircle, which had cut through the layers of dirt and turned that small portion of blackish stone to light gray. The ridge was approximately an inch and a half thick and obviously caused by the friction of a wide rope.

"Whoever it was is a cat," said Canfield.

"Let's look around." The two men walked first through the left bedroom door and found a double bed fully made up. The bureaus were empty and nothing but the usual stationery and corked pens were on the desk. The closets held nothing but hangers and cloth shoe repositories. The bathroom was spotless, the fixtures gleaming. The second bedroom to the right was the same except that the bedspread was mussed. Someone had slept or rested on it.

"Large frame. Probably six feet or over," said the Englishman.

"How can you tell?"

"Imprint of the buttocks. See here, below the half point of the bed."

"I wouldn't have thought of that."

"I have no comment."

"He could have been sitting."

"I said probably."

The field accountant opened the closet door. "Hey, shine the light here."

"There you are."

"Here it is!"

On the closet floor was a sloppily coiled pile of rope. Through the coils at the bottom were three wide straps of leather attached to the rope by metal clasps.

"It's an Alpine rig," said the English agent.

"For mountain climbing?"

"Precisely. Very secure. The professionals won't use it. Unsporting. Used for rescues, mainly."

"God bless 'em. Would it scale a wall at the Savoy?"

"Beautifully. Very quick, very safe. You were correct."

"Let's get out of here," said Canfield.

"I'll take that drink now."

"My pleasure." Canfield rose from the bed with difficulty. "Scotch whiskey and soda, friend?"

"Thanks."

The American walked to a table by the window that served as his bar and poured two large quantities of whiskey into glasses. He handed one to James Derek and half raised his own in a toast.

"You do good work, James."

"You're quite competent yourself. And I've been thinking, you may be right about taking that rig."

"All it can do is cause confusion."

"That's what I mean. It could be helpful. . . . It's such an American device."

"I don't understand."

"Nothing personal. Just that you Americans are so equipment conscious, if you know what I mean. When you shoot birds in Scotland, you carry heavy millimeter cannon with you into the field. . . . When you fish in the Lowlands, you have six-hundred artifices in your tackle box. The American's sense of sportsmanship is equated with his ability to master the sport with his purchases, not his skill."

"If this is hate-the-American hour, you should get a radio program."

"Please, Matthew. I'm trying to tell you that I think you're right. Whoever broke into the Scarlatti suite was an American. We can trace the rig to someone at your embassy. Hasn't that occurred to you?"

"We can do what?"

"Your embassy. If it is someone at your embassy. Someone who knows Bertholde. The men you suspect of having been involved with the securities. . . . Even an Alpine rig has to be manipulated by a trained mountain climber. How many climbers can there be in your embassy? Scotland Yard could check it in a day."

"No. . . . We'll handle it ourselves."

"Waste of time, you know. After all, embassy personnel have dossiers just as Bertholde has. How many are mountain climbers?"

The field accountant turned away from James Derek and refilled his glass. "That puts it in a police category. We don't want that. We'll make the interrogations."

"Just as you say. It shouldn't be difficult. Twenty to thirty people at most. You should track it down quickly."

"We will." Canfield walked to his bed and sat down.

"Tell me," said the Englishman, finishing the last of his whiskey, "do you have a current list of your embassy personnel? Up-to-date, that is?"

"Of course."

"And you're absolutely sure that members of the staff working there now were part of this securities swindle last year?"

"Yes. I've told you that. At least, the State Department thinks so. I wish you'd stop harping on it."

"I shan't any longer. It's late and I have a great deal of work on my desk which I've neglected." The British operative rose from the chair and went to the bureau where he had put his hat. "Good night, Canfield."

"Oh, you're leaving? . . . Was there anything in the Berthode file? I'll read it but right now I'm bushed."

James Derek stood by the door looking down at the exhausted field accountant. "One item I'm sure you'll be interested in. . . . Several probably, but one comes to mind."

"What's that?"

"Among the marquis's athletic pursuits is mountain climbing. The eminent sportsman is, in fact, a member of the Matterhorn Club. He's also one of the few hundred who've scaled the north side of the Jungfrau. No mean feat, I gather."

Canfield stood up angrily and shouted at the Englishman. "Why didn't you say so, for Christ's sake?"

"I frankly thought you were more interested in his associations with your embassy. That's really what I was looking for."

The field accountant stared at Derek. "So it was Bertholde. But why? . . . Unless he knew she wouldn't open the door for anyone."

"Perhaps. I really wouldn't know. Enjoy the dossier, Canfield. It's fascinating. . . . However, I don't think you'll find much in it related to the American embassy. . . . But that's not why you wanted it, is it?"

The Britisher let himself out the door, closing it sharply behind him. Canfield stared after him, confused but too tired to care.

Chapter Thirty

The telephone awoke him.

"Matthew?"

"Yes, Jan?" He held the phone and the blood drained from his arm and it hurt.

"I'm in the lobby. I told Mother Scarlatti I had some shopping to do."

The field accountant looked at his watch. It was eleven thirty. He had needed the sleep. "What happened?"

"I've never seen her like this, Matthew. She's frightened."

"That's new. Did she bring up the Sheffield business?"

"No. I had to. She brushed it aside and said the situation had changed."

"Nothing else? Just that?"

"Yes. . . . There was something else. She said she was going to talk with you this afternoon. She says there are problems back in New York that have to be attended to. I think she's going to tell you that she's decided to leave England and go home."

"That's impossible! What did she say exactly?"

"She was vague. Just that Chancellor was a fool and that it was senseless throwing away time on a wild-goose chase."

"She doesn't believe that!"

"I know she doesn't. She wasn't convincing either. But she means it. What are you going to do?"

"Take her by surprise, I hope. Stay out shopping for at least two hours, will you?"

They made plans for a later lunch and said good-bye. Thirty minutes later the field accountant walked across the Savoy lobby into the grill and ordered breakfast. It was no time to go without food. Without energy.

He carried the Bertholde file with him. He promised himself that he'd read through it, or most of it, at the table. He opened it and placed it to the left of his plate and started at the top of the first page.

Jacques Louis Aumont Bertholde, fourth marquis of Chatellerault.

It was a dossier like so many other dossiers on the very wealthy. Exhaustive details about the family lineage. The positions and titles held by each member for several generations in business, government, and society—all impressive sounding, all meaningless to anyone else. The Bertholde holdings—enormous—mainly, as Elizabeth Scarlatti had said, within British territories. The specific education of the subject in question and his subsequent rise in the world of commerce. His clubs—all very correct. His hobbies—automobiles, horse breeding, dogs—also correct. The sports he excelled in—polo, sailing, the Matterhorn and the Jungfrau—not only correct, but colorful, fitting. And finally the character estimates elicited from his contemporaries. The most interesting part and yet the part many professionals disregarded. The flattering contributions were generally supplied by friends or associates hoping to gain. The unflattering, by enemies or competitors with a wish to undermine.

Canfield withdrew a pencil and made two notations in the dossier.

The first was on page 18, paragraph 5.

No particular reason other than the fact that it seemed out of place—unattractive—and it contained the name of a city Canfield recalled was on Ulster Scarlett's European itinerary.

The Bertholde family had extensive interests in the Ruhr Valley, which were sold to the German Ministry of Finance several weeks before the assassination at Sarajevo. The Bertholde offices in Stuttgart and Tassing were closed. The sale caused considerable comment in French business circles and the Bertholde family was criticized by the States General and in numerous newspaper editorials. No collusion accused, however, due to explanation that the German Finance Ministry was paying exorbitant prices. Explanation proved out. Following the war, the Ruhr Valley interests repurchased from the Weimar government. Offices in Stuttgart and Tassing reopened.

The second, on page 23, paragraph 2, referred to one of Bertholde's more recently formed corporations and included the following information.

The Marquis de Bertholde's partners in the importing firm are Mr. Sydney Masterson and Mr. Harold Leacock. . . .

Masterson and Leacock.

Both were on the Zurich list. Each owned one of the fourteen properties in

Switzerland.

No surprise. They tied Bertholde to the Zurich contingent.

No surprise at all. Just comforting—in a professional way—to know that another piece of the puzzle fitted.

As he finished his coffee, an unfamiliar man in a Savoy waistcoat approached the field accountant.

"Front desk, sir. I have two messages."

Canfield was alarmed. He reached for the notes extended to him. "You could have had me paged."

"Both parties requested that we not do that, sir."

"I see. Thank you."

The first message was from Derek. "Imperative you contact me."

The second was from Elizabeth Scarlatti. "Please come to my suite at two thirty. It is most urgent. I cannot see you before then."

Canfield lit one of his thin cigars and settled back into the curved Savoy dining chair. Derek could wait. The Englishman probably had gotten word of Benjamin Reynolds's new arrangement with the British government and was either furious or apologetic. He'd postpone Derek.

Scarlatti, on the other hand, had made a decision. If Janet was right, she was folding up. Forgetting for the moment his own potential loss, he could never explain her reversal to Reynolds, or Glover, or anyone else at Group Twenty, for that matter. He had spent thousands of dollars on the premise that he had Elizabeth's cooperation.

The field accountant thought about the old woman's visitor, the fourth marquis of Chattellerault, veteran of the Matterhorn and the Jungfrau, Jacques Louis Bertholde. Why had he broken into the Scarlatti suite the way he had? Was it simply the locked door and the knowledge that it would remain locked? Was it to terrify Elizabeth? Or was he searching for something?

Just as he and Derek had searched in the darkness two floors above.

Once confronting her what could Bertholde have said to bend her will? What could he possibly say that would frighten Elizabeth Scarlatti?

He could promise the death of her son if he were still alive. That might do it. . . . But would it? Her son had betrayed her. Betrayed the Scarlatti Industries. Canfield had the unnatural feeling that Elizabeth would rather see her son dead than let him continue that betrayal.

Yet now she was retreating.

Again Canfield felt the inadequacy he had begun to feel aboard the *Calpurnia*. An assignment conceived of as theft had been complicated by extraordinary occurrences, extraordinary people.

He forced his mind back to Elizabeth Scarlatti. He was convinced she could "not see" him before two thirty because she was completing arrangements to return home.

Well, he had a shock in store for her. He knew she had had an early-morning visitor. And he had the Bertholde dossier.

The dossier she could refuse. The Alpine rig would be irresistible.

"I wrote in my note that I couldn't see you before two thirty! Would you please respect my wishes?"

"It can't wait. Let me in quickly!"

She opened the door in disgust, leaving it ajar as she walked back into the center of the room. Canfield closed it, loudly inserting the bolt. He spoke before she turned around to face him. "I've read the dossier. I know now why your visitor didn't have to open the door."

It was as if a pistol had been fired in front of her ancient face. The old woman turned and sprang her neck forward and arched her back. Had she been thirty years younger, she would have leapt upon him in fury. She spoke with an intensity he had never heard from her before.

"You unconscionable bastard! You're a liar! A thief! Liar! Liar! I'll have you spend the rest of your life in prison!"

"That's very good. Attack for attack! You've pulled it before but not this time. Derek was with me. We found the rig. An Alpine rig, he called it—which your visitor let down the side of the building."

The old woman lurched toward him, unsteady on her feet.

"For Christ's sake, relax! I'm on your side." He held her thin shoulders.

"You've got to buy him! Oh, my God! You've got to buy him! Get him here!"

"Why? Buy him how? Who?"

"Derek. How long have you known? Mr. Canfield, I ask you in the name of all that's holy, how long have you known?"

"Since about five o'clock this morning."

"Then he's talked to others! Oh, my God, he's talked to others!" She was beside herself, and Canfield was now frightened for her.

"I'm sure he has. But only to his immediate superiors and I gather he's pretty superior himself. What did you expect?"

The old woman tried with what strength she had left to regain control of herself. "You may have caused the murder of my entire family. If you've done that, I'll see you dead!"

"That's pretty strong language! You'd better tell me why!"

"I'll tell you nothing until you get Derek on that telephone."

The field accountant crossed the room to the telephone and gave the operator Derek's number. He talked urgently, quietly, for a few moments and turned to the old woman. "He's going in to a meeting in twenty minutes. He has a full report and they'll expect him to read it."

The old woman walked rapidly toward Canfield. "Give me that phone!"

He handed her both the stand and the receiver. "Mr. Derek! Elizabeth Scarlatti. Whatever this meeting is, do not go to it! I am not in the habit of begging, sir, but I implore you, do not go! Please, please do not speak to a soul about last night! If you do, you will be responsible for the deaths of a number of innocent people. I can say no more now. . . . Yes, yes, whatever you like. . . . I'll see you, of course. In an hour. Thank you. Thank you!"

She replaced the receiver on the hook and slowly, with great relief, put the telephone back on the table. She looked at the field accountant. "Thank God!"

The field accountant watched her as she spoke. He began to walk toward her. "Sweet mother of Jesus! I'm beginning to see. That crazy Alpine thing. The acrobatics at two in the morning. It wasn't just to scare you half to death—it was necessary!"

"What are you talking about?"

"Since early this morning I've thought it was Bertholde! And he'd come to you like that to scare hell out of you! But it didn't make sense. It wouldn't accomplish anything. He could have stopped you in the lobby, in a store, in the dining room. It had to be someone who couldn't do that! Someone who couldn't take a chance anywhere!"

"You're babbling! You're incoherent!"

"Sure, you're willing to call the whole thing off! Why not? You did what you'd set out to do! You found him! You've found your missing son, haven't you?"

"That's a lie!"

"Oh, no, it's not. It's so clear I should have thought of it last night. The whole damn thing was so weird I looked for insane explanations. I thought it was persuasion by terror. It's been used a lot these past few years. But it wasn't that at all! It was our celebrated war hero come back to the land of the living! Ulster Stewart Scarlett! The only one who couldn't risk stopping you outside. The only one who couldn't take a chance that you might not unlatch that bolt!"

"Conjecture! I deny it!"

"Deny all you like! Now I'm giving you a choice! Derek will be here in less than an hour. Either we straighten this out between us before then, or I walk out that door and cable my office that in my highly regarded professional opinion we've found Ulster Scarlett! And, incidentally, I'm taking your daughter-in-law with me."

The old woman suddenly lowered her voice to nearly a whisper. She walked haltingly toward the field accountant. "If you have any feeling whatsoever for that girl, you'll do as I ask. If you don't, she'll be killed."

It was now the field accountant's turn to raise his voice. It was no longer the shout of the angry debater, it was the roar of an angry man. "Don't you make any pronouncements to me! Don't you or your rotten bastard son make any threats to me! You may buy part of me, but you don't buy all of me! You tell him I'll kill him if he touches that girl!"

Pleading without shame, Elizabeth Scarlatti touched his arm. He withdrew it swiftly from her. "It's not my threat. Please, in the name of God, listen to me. Try to understand. . . . I'm helpless. And I can not be helped!"

The field accountant saw the tears roll down her wrinkled cheeks. Her skin was white and the hollows of her eyes were black with exhaustion. He thought, quite out of context with the moment, that he was looking at a tear-stained corpse. His anger ebbed.

"Nobody has to be helpless. Don't let anybody tell you that."

"You love her, don't you?"

"Yes. And because I do, you don't have to be quite so afraid. I'm a committed public servant. But far more committed to us than the public."

"Your confidence doesn't change the situation."

"You won't know that until you tell me what it is."

"You leave me no choice? No alternative?"

"None."

"Then God have mercy on you. You have an awesome responsibility. You are responsible for our lives."

She told him.

And Matthew Canfield knew exactly what he would do. It was time to confront the Marquis de Bertholde.

Chapter Thirty-one

Fifty-seven miles southeast of London is the seaside resort of Ramsgate. Near the town, on a field set back from the main road, stood a wooden shack no more than twenty feet by twenty. It had two small windows and in the early-morning mist a dim light could be seen shining through them. About a hundred yards to the north was a larger building—once a barn—five times the size of the shack. It was now a hangar for two small monoplanes. One of them was being wheeled out by three men in gray overalls.

Inside the shack, the man with the shaved head sat at a table drinking black coffee and munching bread. The reddish splotch above his right eye was sore and inflamed and he touched it continually.

He read the message in front of him and looked up at the bearer, a man in a chauffeur's uniform. The contents of the message infuriated him.

"The marquis has gone too far. The instructions from Munich were clear. The Rawlinses were *not* to be killed in the States. They were to be brought to Zurich! They were to be killed in *Zurich!*"

"There's no need for concern. Their deaths, the man and his wife, were engineered above suspicion. The marquis wanted you to know that. It has appeared as an accident."

"To whom? God damn it, to *whom*? Go shag, all of you! Munich doesn't want risks! In *Zurich* there would have been no risk!" Ulster Scarlett rose from the chair and walked to the small window overlooking the field. His plane was nearly ready. He hoped his fury would subside before takeoff. He disliked flying when he was angry. He made mistakes in the air when he was angry. It had been happening more frequently as the pressures mounted.

God damn Bertholde! Certainly Rawlins had to be killed. In his panic over Cartwright's discovery Rawlins had ordered his son-in-law to kill Elizabeth Scarlatti. A massive error! It's funny, he reflected. He no longer thought of the old woman as his mother. Simply Elizabeth Scarlatti. . . . But to have Rawlins murdered three thousand miles away was insanity! How could they know who was asking questions? And how easily might the order be traced back to Bertholde?

"Regardless of what happened . . ." Labishe started to speak.

"What?" Scarlett turned from the window. He had made up his mind.

"The marquis also wanted you to know that regardless of what happened to Boothroyd, all associations with him are buried with the Rawlinses."

"Not quite, Labishe. Not quite." Scarlett spoke softly but his voice was hard. "The Marquis de Bertholde was ordered . . . commanded by Munich to have the Rawlinses brought to Switzerland. He disobeyed. That was most unfortunate."

"Pardon, monsieur?"

Scarlett reached for his flying jacket, which hung over the back of his chair. Again he spoke quietly, simply. Two words.

"Kill him."

"Monsieur!"

"Kill him! Kill the Marquis de Bertholde and do it today!"

"Monsieur! I do not believe what I hear!"

"Listen to me! I don't give explanations! By the time I reach Munich I want a cable waiting for me telling me that stupid son of a bitch is dead! . . . And, Labishe! Do it so there's no mistake who killed him. You! We can't have any investigations now! . . . Get back here to the field. We'll fly you out of the country."

"Monsieur! I have been with *le marquis* for fifteen years! He has been good to me! . . . I can not . . ."

"You what?"

"Monsieur . . ." The Frenchman sunk to one knee. "Do not ask me. . . ."

"I don't ask. I command! Munich commands!"

The foyer on the third floor of Bertholde et Fils was enormous. In the rear was an impressive set of white Louis XIV doors that obviously led to the sanctum sanctorum of the Marquis de Bertholde. On the right side were six brown leather armchairs in a semicircle—the sort that might be found in the study of a wealthy country squire—with a thick rectangular coffee table placed in front. On the table were neatly stacked piles of chic magazines—chic socially and chic industrially. On the left side of the room was a large white desk trimmed in gold. Behind the desk sat a most attractive brunet with spit curls silhouetted against her forehead. All this Canfield took in with his second impression. It took him several moments to get over his first.

Opening the elevator door, he had been visually overpowered by the color scheme of the walls.

They were magenta red and sweeping from the ceiling moldings were arcs of black velvet.

Good Christ! he said to himself. I'm in a hallway thirty-five hundred miles away!

Seated in the chairs beside one another were two middle-aged gentlemen in Savile Row clothes reading magazines. Standing off to the right was a man in a chauffeur's uniform, his hat off, his hands clasped behind his back.

Canfield approached the desk. The spit-curled secretary greeted him before he could speak. "Mr. Canfield?"

"Yes."

"The marquis would like you to go right in, sir." The girl spoke as she rose from the chair and started toward the large white doors. Canfield saw that the man seated on the left was upset. He uttered a few "Damns!" and went back to his magazine.

"Good afternoon, Mr. Canfield." The fourth marquis of Chatellerault stood behind his large white desk and extended his hand. "We have not met, of course, but an emissary from Elizabeth Scarlatti is a welcome guest. Do sit down."

Bertholde was almost what Canfield expected him to be, except, perhaps, shorter. He was well-groomed, relatively handsome, very masculine, with a voice resonant enough to fill an opera house. However, in spite of his exuding virility—bringing to mind the Matterhorn and the Jungfrau—there was something artificial, slightly effete about the man. Perhaps the clothing. It was almost too fashionable.

"How do you do?" Canfield smiled, shaking the Frenchman's hand. "Is it Monsieur Bertholde? Or *Monsieur le Marquis*? I'm not sure which I should use."

"I could tell you several unflattering names given me by your countrymen." The marquis laughed. "But please, use the French custom—so scorned by our proper Anglicans. Plain Bertholde will do. Marquises are such an out-of-date custom." The Frenchman smiled ingenuously and waited until Canfield sat in the chair in front of his desk before returning to his seat. Jacques Louis Aumont Bertholde, fourth marquis of Chatelleraut, was immensely likable and Canfield recognized the fact.

"I appreciate your interrupting your schedule."

"Schedules are made to be broken. Such a dull existence otherwise, yes?"

"I won't waste time, sir. Elizabeth Scarlatti wants to negotiate."

Jacques Bertholde leaned back in his chair and looked startled. "Negotiate? . . . I'm afraid I don't comprehend, monsieur. . . . Negotiate what?"

"She knows, Bertholde. . . . She knows as much as she needs to know. She wants to meet you."

"I'd be delighted—at any time—to meet Madame Scarlatti but I can't imagine what we have to discuss. Not in a business sense, monsieur, which I presume to be your . . . errand."

"Maybe the key is her son. Ulster Scarlett."

Bertholde leveled his gaze intently on the field accountant. "It is a key for which I have no lock, monsieur. I have not had the pleasure. . . . I know, as most who read newspapers know, that he vanished a number of months ago. But that is all I know."

"And you don't know a thing about Zurich?"

Jacques Bertholde abruptly sat up in his chair. "*Quoi?* Zurich?"

"We know about Zurich."

"Is this a joke?"

"No. Fourteen men in Zurich. Maybe you've got the fifteenth. . . . Elizabeth Scarlatti."

Canfield could hear Bertholde's breathing. "Where did you get this information? What do you refer to?"

"Ulster Scarlett! Why do you think I'm here?"

"I don't believe you! I don't know what you are talking about!" Bertholde got out of his chair.

"For God's sake! She's interested. . . . Not because of him! Because of you! And the others! She's got something to offer, and if I were you, I'd listen to her."

"But you are not me, monsieur! I'm afraid I must ask you to leave. There is no business between Madame Scarlatti and the Bertholde companies."

Canfield did not move. He remained in the chair and spoke quietly. "Then I'd better put it another way. I think you'll have to see her. Talk with her. . . . For your own good. For Zurich's good."

"You threaten me?"

"If you don't, it's my opinion that she'll do something drastic. I don't have to tell you she's a powerful woman. . . . You're linked with her son. . . . And she met with her son last night!"

Bertholde stood motionless. Canfield couldn't decide whether the Frenchman's look of disbelief was over the revelation of Scarlett's visit or his—the field accountant's—knowledge of it.

After a few moments Bertholde replied, "I know nothing of what you speak. It has nothing to do with me."

"Oh, come on! I found the rig! The Alpine rig! I found it at the bottom of a closet in your conference suite at the Savoy!"

"You what?"

"You heard me! Now, let's stop kidding each other!"

"You broke into my firm's private quarters?"

"I did! And that's just the beginning. We've got a list. You might know some of the names on it. . . . Daudet and D'Almeida, fellow countrymen, I think. . . . Olaffsen, Landor, Thyssen, von Schnitzler, Kindorf. . . . And, oh yes! Mr. Masterson and Mr. Leacock! Current partners of yours, I believe! There are several others, but I'm sure you know their names better than I do!"

"Enough! Enough, monsieur!" The Marquis de Bertholde sat down again, slowly, deliberately. He stared at Canfield. "I will clear my office and we will talk further. People have been waiting. It does not look good. Wait outside. I will dispense with them quickly."

The field accountant got out of the chair as Bertholde picked up the telephone and pressed the button for his secretary.

"Monsieur Canfield will remain. I wish to finish the afternoon's business as rapidly as possible. With each person interrupt me in five minutes if I have not concluded by then. What? Labishe? Very well, send him in. I'll give them to him." The Frenchman reached into his pocket and withdrew a set of keys.

Canfield crossed to the large white double doors. Before his hand touched the brass knob, the door on his left opened swiftly, with great force.

"So sorry, monsieur," the man in uniform said.

"Voici les clefs, Labishe."

"Merci, Monsieur le Marquis! Je regrette. . . . J'ai un billet . . ."

The chauffer closed the door and Canfield smiled at the secretary.

He wandered over to the semicircle of chairs, and as the two gentlemen looked up, he nodded pleasantly. He sat down on the end chair nearest the entrance to Bertholde's office and picked up the *Illustrated London News*. He noted that the man nearest him was fidgeting, irritable, quite impatient. He was turning the pages of *Punch*, but he was not reading. The other man was engrossed in an article in the *Quarterly Review*.

Suddenly, Canfield was diverted by an insignificant action on the part of the impatient man. The man extended his left hand through his coat sleeve, turned his wrist, and looked at the watch. A perfectly normal occurrence under the circumstances. What startled the field accountant was the sight of the man's cuff link. It was made of cloth and it was square with two stripes running diagonally from corner to corner. The small stripes were deep red and black. It was a replica of the cuff link that had identified the hulking masked Charles Boothroyd in Elizabeth Scarlatti's stateroom on board the *Calpurnia*. The colors were the same as the paper on the marquis' walls and the black velvet drapes arcing from the ceiling.

The impatient man noticed Canfield's stare. He abruptly withdrew his hand into his jacket and placed his arm at his side.

"I was trying to read the time on your watch. Mine's been running fast."

"Four twenty."

"Thanks."

The impatient gentleman folded his arms and leaned back, looking exasperated. The other man spoke.

"Basil, you'll have a stroke if you don't relax."

"Well and good for you, Arthur! But I'm late for a meeting! I told Jacques it was a hectic day, but he insisted I come over."

"He can be insistent."

"He can be bloody rude, too!"

There followed five minutes of silence except for the rustling of papers at the secretary's desk.

The large left panel of the white double doors opened and the chauffeur emerged. He closed the door, and Canfield noticed that once it was shut, the chauffeur twisted the kob to make sure it was secure. It was a curious motion.

The uniformed man went to the secretary and leaned over her desk, whispering. She reacted to his information with resigned annoyance. He shrugged his shoulders and walked quickly to a door to the right of the elevator. Canfield saw through the slowly closing door the flight of stairs he had presumed to be there.

The secretary placed some papers into a manila folder and looked over at the three men. "I'm sorry, gentlemen, the Marquis de Bertholde can not see anyone further this afternoon. We apologize for any inconvenience."

"Now see here, young lady!" The impatient gentleman was on his feet. "This is preposterous! I've been here for three-quarters of an hour at the explicit request of the Marquis! . . . Request be damned! At his instructions!"

"I'm sorry, sir, I'll convey your displeasure."

"You'll do more than that! You'll convey to Monsieur Bertholde that I am waiting right here until he sees me!" He sat down pompously.

The man named Arthur rose and walked toward the elevator.

"For heaven's sake, man, you'll not improve French manners. People have been trying for centuries. Come along, Basil. We'll stop at the Dorchester and start the evening."

"Can't do it, Arthur. I'm staying right where I am."

"Have it your way. Be in touch."

Canfield remained in his seat next to the impatient Basil. He knew only that he would not leave until Bertholde came out. Basil was his best weapon.

"Ring the marquis again, please, miss," said Basil.

She did so.

A number of times. And there was no response.

The field accountant was alarmed. He rose from his chair and walked to the large double doors and knocked. There was no answer. He tried opening both doors; they were locked.

Basil unfolded his arms and got out of his chair. The spit-curled secretary stood up behind her white desk. She automatically picked up the phone and started pressing the buzzer, finally holding her finger down upon it.

"Unlock the door," commanded the field accountant.

"Oh, I don't know . . ."

"I do! Get me a key!"

The girl started to open the top drawer of her desk and then looked up at the American. "Perhaps we should wait. . . ."

"Damn it! Give me the key!"

"Yes, sir!" She picked up a ring of keys and selecting one, separated it from the others, and gave the key to Canfield. He rapidly unlocked the doors and flung them open.

There in front of them was the Frenchman sprawled across the top of his white desk, blood trickling from his mouth; his tongue was extended and swollen; his eyes bulged from their sockets; his neck was inflated and lacerated just below the chin line. He had been expertly garroted.

The girl kept screaming but did not collapse—a fact that Canfield wasn't sure was fortunate. Basil began to shake and repeated "Oh, my God!" over and over again. The field accountant approached the desk and lifted the dead man's wrist by the coat sleeve. He let go and the hand fell back.

The girl's screams grew louder and two middle-aged executives burst through the staircase doorway into the outer room. Through the double doors the scene was clear to both men. One ran back to the stairway, shouting at the top of his voice, while the other slowly, fearfully walked into Bertholde's room.

"Le bon Dieu!"

Within a minute, a stream of employees had run down and up the staircase, log-jamming themselves in the doorway. As each group squeezed through, subsequent screams and oaths followed. Within two minutes twenty-five people were shouting instructions to nonexistent subordinates.

Canfield shook the spit-curled secretary in an attempt to stop her screaming. He kept telling her to phone the police, but she could not accept the order. Canfield did not want to make the call himself because it would have required separate concentration. He wished to keep his full attention of everyone in sight, especially Basil, if that was possible.

A tall, distinguished-looking, gray-haired man in a double-breasted pin-stripe suit came rushing through the crowd up to the secretary and Canfield. "Miss Richards! Miss Richards! What in God's name happened?"

"We opened his door and found him like this! That's what happened," shouted the field accountant over the growing din of excited voices.

And then Canfield looked closely at the questioner. Where had he seen him before? Or had he? The man was like so many of the Scarlatti world. Even to the perfectly waxed moustache.

"Have you phoned the police?" asked the gentleman.

Canfield saw Basil pushing his way through the hysterical mob gathered by the office doors. "No, the police haven't been called," yelled the American as he watched Basil making headway through the crowd. "Call them! . . . It might be a good idea to close these doors." He started after Basil as if to push the doors shut. The distinguished-looking man with the waxed moustache held him firmly by the lapel.

"You say you found him?"

"Yes. Let go of me!"

"What's your name, young man?"

"What?"

"I asked you your name!"

"Derek, James Derek! Now, phone the police!"

Canfield took the man's wrist and pressed hard against the vein. The arm withdrew in pain and Canfield ran into the crowd after Basil.

The man in the pin-striped suit winced and turned to the secretary. "Did you get his name, Miss Richards? I couldn't hear."

The girl was sobbing. "Yes, sir. It was Darren, or Derrick. First name, James."

The man with the waxed moustache looked carefully at the secretary. She had heard. "The police, Miss Richards. Phone the police!"

"Yes, sir, Mr. Poole."

The man named Poole pushed his way through the crowd. He had to get to his office, he had to be by himself. *They* had done it! The men of Zurich had ordered Jacques' death! His dearest friend, his mentor, closer to him than anyone in the world. The man who'd given him everything, made everything possible for him.

The man he'd killed for—willingly.

They'd pay! They'd pay and pay and pay!

He, Poole, had never failed Bertholde in life. He'd not fail him in death either!

But there were questions. So many questions.

This Canfield who'd just lied about his name. The old woman, Elizabeth Scarlatti.

Most of all the misshapen Heinrich Kroeger. The man Poole knew beyond a doubt was Elizabeth Scarlatti's son. He knew because Bertholde had told him.

He wondered if anyone else knew.

On the third-floor landing, which was now completely filled with Bertholde employees in varying stages of hysteria, Canfield could see Basil one floor below pulling himself downward by the railing. Canfield began yelling.

"Get clear! Get clear! The doctor's waiting! I've got to bring him up! Get clear!"

To some degree the ruse worked and he made swifter headway. By the time he reached the first-floor lobby, Basil was no longer in sight. Canfield ran out the front entrance onto the sidewalk. There was Basil about half a block south, limping in the middle of Vauxhall Road, waving, trying to hail a taxi. The knees of his trousers were coated with mud where he had fallen in his haste.

Shouts were still coming from various windows of Bertholde et Fils, drawing dozens of pedestrians to the foot of the company's steps.

Canfield walked against the crowd toward the limping figure.

A taxi stopped and Basil grabbed for the door handle. As he pulled the door open and climbed in, Canfield reached the side of the cab and prevented the Englishman from pulling the door shut. He moved in alongside Basil, pushing him sideway to make room.

"I say! What are you doing?" Basil was frightened but he did not raise his voice. The driver kept turning his head back and forth from the street in front of him to the gathering crowds receding behind him. Basil did not wish to draw additional attention.

Before Basil could think further, the American grasped the Englishman's right hand and pulled the coat above his wrist. He twisted Basil's arm revealing the red and black cuff link.

"Zurich, Basil!" The field accountant whispered.

"What are you talking about?"

"You damn fool, I'm with you! Or I will be, if they let you live!"

"Oh, my God! Oh, my God!" Basil babbled.

The American released Basil's hand by throwing it downward. He looked straight ahead as if ignoring the Englishman. "You're an idiot. You realize that, don't you?"

"I don't know you, sir! I don't know you!" The Englishman was near collapse.

"Then we'd better change that. I may be all you have left."

"Now see here. I had nothing to do with it! I was in the waiting room with you. I had nothing to do with it!"

"Of course, you didn't. It's pretty damned obvious that it was the chauffeur. But a number of people are going to want to know why you ran. Maybe you were just making sure the job was done."

"That's preposterous!"

"Then why did you run away?"

"I . . . I . . ."

"Let's not talk now. Where can we go where we'll be seen for about ten or fifteen minutes? I don't want it to look as though we dropped out of sight."

"My club . . . I suppose."

"Give him the address!"

Chapter Thirty-two

"What the devil do you mean I was there?" James Derek shouted into the phone. "I've been here at the Savoy since midafternoon! . . . Yes, of course I am. Since three or thereabouts. . . . No, she's here with me." The Englishman suddenly caught his breath. When he spoke again his words were barely audible, drawn out in disbelief. "Good Lord! . . . How horrible. . . . Yes. Yes, I heard you."

Elizabeth Scarlatti sat across the room on the Victorian couch, absorbed in the Bertholde dossier. At the sound of Derek's voice she looked up at the Englishman. He was staring at her. He spoke again into the phone.

"Yes. He left here roughly at three thirty. With Ferguson, from our office. They were to meet Mrs. Scarlett at Tippin's and he was to proceed from there to Bertholde's. . . . I don't know. His instructions were that she remain in Ferguson's custody until he returned. Ferguson's to call in. . . . I see. For heaven's sake, keep me posted. I'll phone you if there're any developments here."

He replaced the telephone receiver on the hook and remained at the table. "Bertholde's been killed."

"Good God! Where's my daughter?"

"With our man. She's all right. He reported in an hour ago."

"Canfield! Where's Canfield?"

"I wish I knew."

"Is he all right?"

"How can I answer that if I don't know where he is? We can presume he's functioning. He identified himself as me and left the scene!"

"How did it happen?"

"He was garroted. A wire around his throat."

"Oh!" Elizabeth suddenly, vividly recalled the picture of Matthew Canfield thrusting the cord in her face after Boothroyd's attempt on her life aboard the *Calpurnia*. "If he killed him, he must have had a reason!"

"What?"

"For killing him. He must have had to!"

"That's most interesting."

"What is?"

"That you would think Canfield had to kill him."

"It couldn't have happened otherwise! He's no killer."

"He didn't kill Bertholde either, if it's any comfort to you."

Her relief was visible. "Do they know who did?"

"They believe so. Apparently it was Bertholde's chauffeur."

"That's odd."

"Very. The man's been with him for years."

"Perhaps Canfield's gone after him."

"Not likely. The man left some ten to twelve minutes before they found Bertholde."

James Derek walked from the telephone table toward Elizabeth. It was obvious that he was upset. "In the light of what's just happened, I'd like to ask you a question. But, of course, you needn't answer. . . ."

"What is it?"

"I'd like to know how—or perhaps why—Mr. Canfield received a full clearance from the British Foreign Office."

"I don't know what that is."

"Come, madame. If you don't care to answer, I respect that. But since my name's been used in the killing of an influential man, I believe I'm entitled to something more than another . . . falsehood."

"Another . . . falsehood? That's insulting, Mr. Derek."

"Is it? And are you and Mr. Canfield still setting elaborate traps for embassy personnel who returned to the United States over four months ago?"

"Oh." Elizabeth sat down again on the couch. She was not concerned with the Englishman's complaint; she only wished Canfield was there to answer him. What she was concerned with was the agent's reference to the Foreign Office. "An unfortunate necessity."

"Most unfortunate. . . . I gather, then, that you don't care to answer."

"On the contrary, I have answered you." Elizabeth looked up at the Britisher. "I wish you'd explain. What is full clearance?"

"Extraordinary cooperation from the highest echelons of our government. And such decisions from the British Foreign Office are generally reserved for major political crises! Not a stock-and-bonds struggle between squabbling millionaires. . . . Or, if you'll pardon me, a private citizen's personal tragedy."

Elizabeth Scarlatti froze.

What James Derek had just said was abhorrent to the head of Scarlatti. More than anything else she had to operate outside the boundaries of "highest echelon" scrutiny. For the sake of Scarlatti itself. Canfield's minor agency had seemed heaven-sent. Her arrangement with him gave her the facilities of official cooperation without answering to anyone of consequence. If she had wanted it otherwise, she would have commanded any number of men in either or both the legislative and executive branches of the United States government. It would not have been difficult. . . . Now, it seemed, Canfield's relatively unimportant department had grown in significance. Or perhaps her son had involved himself in an undertaking far more ominous than she had conceived.

Was the answer in the Bertholde dossier? Elizabeth wondered. "I gather from your tone that this full clearance is a new development."

"I was informed this morning."

Then it must be in the Bertholde dossier, thought Elizabeth. . . . Of course it was! Even Matthew Canfield had begun to perceive it! Only his perception had been based solely on the recognition of certain words, names. He had marked the pages. Elizabeth picked up the file.

"Following the war, the Ruhr Valley interests repurchased. . . . Offices in Stuttgart and Tassing . . ."

Tassing.

Germany.

An economic crisis.

The Weimar Republic.

A series of economic crises! A major and constant political crisis!

". . . . partners in the importing firm are Mr. Sydney Masterson and Mr. Harold Leacock. . . ."

Masterson and Leacock. Zurich!

Tassing!

"Does the city of Tassing mean anything to you?"

"It's not a city. It is an outlying district of Munich. In Bavaria. Why do you ask?"

"My son spent a good deal of time and money there . . . among other places. Does it have any special meaning for you?"

"Munich?"

"I suppose so."

"Hotbed of radicalism. Breeding ground of malcontents."

"Malcontents? . . . Communists?"

"Hardly. They'd shoot a Red on sight. Or a Jew. Call themselves *Schutzstaffel*. Go around clubbing people. Consider themselves a race apart from the rest of the world."

A race apart.

Oh, God!

Elizabeth looked at the dossier in her hands. Slowly she replaced it in the manila envelope and stood up. Without saying a word to the Englishman, she crossed to her bedroom door and let herself in. She closed the door behind her.

James Derek remained in the center of the room. He didn't understand.

Inside her bedroom Elizabeth went to her writing desk where papers were scattered across the top. She sorted them out until she found the Zurich list.

She read each name carefully.

AVERY LANDOR, U.S.A.—*Oil.*
LOUIS GIBSON, U.S.A.—*Oil.*
THOMAS RAWLINS, U.S.A.—*Securities.*
HOWARD THORNTON, U.S.A.—*Industrial Construction.*
SYDNEY MASTERSON, GREAT BRITAIN—*Imports.*
DAVID INNES-BOWEN, GREAT BRITAIN—*Textiles.*
HAROLD LEACOCK, GREAT BRITAIN—*Securities.*
LOUIS FRANÇOIS D'ALMEIDA, FRANCE—*Railroads.*
PIERRE DAUDET, FRANCE—*Ship lines.*
INGMAR MYRDAL, SWEDEN—*Securities.*
CHRISTIAN OLAFFSEN, SWEDEN—*Steel.*
OTTO VON SCHNITZLER, GERMANY—*I.G. Farben.*
FRITZ THYSSEN, GERMANY—*Steel.*
ERICH KINDORF, GERMANY—*Coal.*

One might say that the Zurich list was a cross-section of the most powerful men in the Western hemisphere.

Elizabeth put the list down and reached for a leather-bound notebook in which she kept telephone numbers and addresses. She thumbed to the letter *O*.

Ogilvie and Storm, Ltd., Publishers, Bayswater Road, London.

She would phone Thomas Ogilvie and have him send her whatever information he could unearth on the *Schutzstaffel*.

She knew something about it already. She remembered reading its political name was the National Socialists and they were led by a man named Adolf Hitler.

Chapter Thirty-three

The man's name was Basil Hawkwood, and Canfield quickly pictured the trademark *hawkwood*—small letter *h*—as it appeared on a variety of leather goods. Hawkwood Leather was one of the largest firms in England, only a short distance behind Mark Cross.

The nervous Basil led Canfield into the huge reading room of his club, Knights. They chose two chairs by the Knightsbridge window, where there were no other members within earshot.

Basil's fear caused him to stutter, and when his words came, the phrases tumbled over one another. He assumed, because he wanted to assume, that the young man facing him would help him.

Canfield sat back in the comfortable chair and listened with incredulity to Hawkwood's story.

The chairman of Hawkwood Leather had been sending shipment after shipment of "damaged" leather goods to a little-known firm in Munich. For over a year the directors of Hawkwood accepted the losses on the basis of the "damaged" classification. Now, however, they had ordered a complete report of the excess malfunctions of the plants. The Hawkwood heir was trapped. There could be no more shipments for an indeterminate time.

He pleaded with Matthew Canfield to understand. He begged the young man to report and confirm his loyalty, but the boots, the belts, the holsters would have to come from someone else.

"Why do you wear the cuff links?" asked Canfield.

"I wore them today to remind Bertholde of my contribution. He presented them to me himself. . . . You're not wearing yours."

"My contribution doesn't call for them."

"Well, damn it, mine does! I haven't stinted in the past and I won't in the future!" Hawkwood leaned forward in his chair. "The present circumstances don't change my feelings! You can report that. God damn Jews! Radicals! Bolsheviks! All over Europe! A conspiracy to destroy every decent principle good Christian men have lived by for centuries! They'll murder us in our beds! Rape our daughters! Pollute the races! I've never doubted it! I'll help again. You have my word! Soon there'll be millions at our disposal!"

Matthew Canfield suddenly felt sick. What in God's name had he done? He got out of the chair and his legs felt weak.

"I'll report what you said, Mr. Hawkwood."

"Good fellow. Knew you'd understand."

"I'm beginning to." He walked rapidly away from the Englishman toward the arch to the outer hallway.

As he stood on the curb under the Knight's canopy waiting for a taxi, Canfield was numb with fear. He was no longer dealing with a world he understood. He was dealing with giants, with concepts, with commitments beyond his comprehension.

Chapter Thirty-four

Elizabeth had the newspaper and magazine articles spread over the couch. Ogilvie and Storm, publishers, had done an excellent job. There was more material here than Elizabeth or Canfield could digest in a week.

The National Socialist German Workers party emerged as ragtail fanatics. The *Schutzstaffel* were brutes but no one took them seriously. The articles, the photographs, even the short headlines were slanted in such a way as to give a comic-opera effect.

Why Work in the Fatherland
if You Can Dress Up
and Pretend It's Wagner?

Canfield picked up a portion of a Sunday supplement and read the names of the leaders. Adolf Hitler, Erich Ludendorff, Rudolf Hess, Gregor Strasser. They read like a team of vaudeville jugglers. Adolf, Erich, Rudolf, and Gregor. However, towards the end of the article his amusement waned. There were the phrases.

". . . conspiracy of Jews and Communists . . ."
". . . daughters raped by Bolshevik terrorists! . . ."
". . . Aryan blood soiled by scheming Semites! . . ."
". . . a plan for a thousand years! . . ."

Canfield could see the face of Basil Hawkwood, owner of one of the largest industries in England, whispering with great intensity many of these same words. He thought of the shipments of leather to Munich. The leather without the trademark *hawkwood*, but the leather that became part of the uniforms in these photographs. He recalled the manipulations of the dead Bertholde, the road in Wales, the mass murders at York.

Elizabeth was sitting at the desk jotting down notes from an article. A picture was beginning to emerge for her. But it was incomplete, as if part of a background was missing. It bothered her, but she'd learned enough.

"It staggers your imagination, doesn't it?" said Elizabeth, rising from her chair.

"What do you make of it?"

"Enough to frighten me. An obscure but volatile political organization is being quietly, slowly financed by a number of the wealthiest men on earth. The men of Zurich. And my son is part of them."

"But why?"

"I'm not sure yet." Elizabeth walked to the window. "There's more to learn. However, one thing is clear. If this band of fanatics make solid progress in Germany—in the Reichstag—the men of Zurich could control unheard-of economic power. It's a long-range concept, I think. It could be brilliant strategy."

"Then I've got to get back to Washington!"

"They may already know or suspect."

"Then we've got to move in!"

"You can't move in!" Elizabeth turned back to Canfield, raising her voice, "No government has the right to interfere with the internal politics of another. No government has that right. There's another way. A far more effective way. But there's an enormous risk and I must consider it." The old woman brought her cupped hands up to her lips and walked away from

Canfield.

"What is it? What's the risk?"

Elizabeth, however, did not hear him. She was concentrating deeply. After several minutes she spoke to him from across the room.

"There is an island in a remote lake in Canada. My husband, in a rash moment, bought it years and years ago. There are several dwellings on it, primitive but habitable. . . . If I put at your disposal whatever funds were necessary, could you have this island so guarded that it would be impregnable?"

"I think so."

"That's not good enough. There can be no element of doubt. The lives of my entire family would depend on total isolation. The funds I mention are, frankly, limitless."

"All right, then. Yes, I could."

"Could you have them taken there in complete secrecy?"

"Yes."

"Could you set all this up within a week?"

"Yes, again."

"Very well. I'll outline what I propose. Believe me when I tell you it is the only way."

"What's your proposal?"

"Put simply, the Scarlatti Industries will economically destroy every investor in Zurich. Force them into financial ruin."

Canfield looked at the prepossessing, confident old woman. For several seconds he said nothing, merely sucked breath through his teeth as if trying to formulate a reply.

"You're a lunatic," he said quietly. "You're one person. They're fourteen . . . no, now thirteen stinking rich fatcats. You're no match for them."

It's not what one's worth that counts, Mr. Canfield. Not after a point. It's how rapidly one can manipulate his holdings. The time factor is the ultimate weapon in economics, and don't let anyone tell you otherwise. In my case, one judgment prevails."

"What does that mean?"

Elizabeth stood motionless in front of Canfield. Her speech was measured. "If I were to liquidate the entire Scarlatti Industries, there is no one on earth who could stop me."

The field accountant wasn't sure he understood her implication. He looked at her for a few seconds before speaking. "Oh? So?"

"You fool! . . . Outside of the Rothschilds and, perhaps a few Indian maharajas, I doubt there's another person in my position, or in our civilization, who can say that!"

"Why not? Why can't any of the men in Zurich do the same thing?"

The old woman was exasperated. She clasped her hands and brought the clenched fingers to her chin. "For a man whose imagination far exceeds his intelligence, you astonish me. Or is it only fear that provoked your perception of larger things?"

"No question for a question! I want an answer!"

"It's all related, I assure you. The primary reason why the operation in Zurich can not and will not do as I can do is their own fear. Fear of the laws binding their commitments; fear of the investments, investors; fear of extraordinary decisions; fear of the panic which always results from such decisions. Most important of all, fear of financial ruin."

"And none of that bothers you? Is that what you're saying?"

"No commitments bind Scarlatti. Until I die, there is only one voice. I *am* Scarlatti."

"What about the rest of it? The decisions, the panics, the ruin?"

"As always my decisions will be executed with precision and foresight. Panic will be avoided."

"And so will financial ruin, huh? . . . You are the God damnedest, self-confident old lady!"

"Again you fail to understand. At this juncture I anticipate the collapse of Scarlatti as inevitable should I be called. There will be no quarter given."

Matthew Canfield now understood. "I'll be damned."

"I must have vast sums. Amounts inconceivable to you, which can be allocated by a single command. Money which can purchase massive holdings, inflate or depress entire markets. Once that kind of manipulation has been exercised, I doubt that all the capital on earth could put Scarlatti back together. It would never be trusted again."

"Then you'd be finished."

"Irrevocably."

The old woman moved in front of Canfield. She looked at him but not in the manner to which he was accustomed. She might have been a worried grandmother from the dry plains of Kansas asking the preacher if the Lord would allow the rains to come.

"I have no arguments left. Please allow me my last battle. My final gesture, as it were."

"You're asking an awful lot."

"Not when you think of it. If you return, it'll take you a week to reach Washington. Another week to compile everything we've been through. Days before you reach those in government who should listen to you, if you can get them to listen to you at all. By my calculations that would be at least three or four weeks. Do you agree?"

Canfield felt foolish standing in front of Elizabeth. For no reason other than to increase the distance between them, he walked to the center of the room. "God damn it, I don't know what I agree with!"

"Give me four weeks. Just four weeks from today. . . . If I fail we'll do as you wish. . . . More than that I'll come to Washington with you. I'll testify, if need be, in front of one of those committees. I'll do whatever you and your associates think necessary. Further, I'll settle our personal account three times above that agreed upon."

"Suppose you fail?"

"What possible difference can it make to anyone but myself? There's little sympathy in this world for fallen millionaires."

"What about your family then? They can't spend the rest of their lives in some remote lake in Canada?"

"That won't be necessary. Regardless of the larger outcome, I'll destroy my son. I shall expose Ulster Scarlett for what he is. I'll sentence him to death at Zurich."

The field accountant fell silent for a moment and looked at Elizabeth. "Have you considered the fact that you might be killed?"

"I have."

"You'd risk that. . . . Sell out Scarlatti Industries. Destroy everything you've built. Is it worth that to you? Do you hate him that much?"

"Yes. As one hates a disease. Magnified because I'm responsible for its flourishing."

Canfield put his glass down, tempted to pour himself another drink. "That's going a little far."

"I didn't say I invented the disease. I said that I'm responsible for spreading it. Not simply because I provided the money but infinitely more important, because I implanted an idea. An idea which has become warped in the process of maturing."

"I don't believe that. You're no saint, but you don't think like that." He pointed toward the papers on the couch.

The old woman's weary eyes closed.

"There's a little of . . . that in each of us. It's all part of the idea. . . . The twisted idea. My husband and I devoted years to the building of an industrial empire. Since his death, I've fought in the marketplace—doubling, redoubling, adding, building—always acquiring. . . . It's been a stimulating, all-consuming game. . . . I've played it well. And sometimes during all those years, my son learned what many observers failed to learn—that it was never the acquisition of profits or material gain that mattered—they were merely the by-products. It was the acquisition of power. . . . I wanted that power because I sincerely believed that I was equipped for the responsibility. The more convinced I became, it had to follow that others were not equipped. . . . The quest for power becomes a personal crusade, I think. The more success one has, the more personal it becomes. Whether he understood it or not, that's what my son saw happening. . . . There may be similarities of purpose, even of motive. But a great gulf divides us—my son and me."

"I'll give you the four weeks. Jesus Christ only knows why. But you still haven't made it clear to me why you want to risk all this. Throw away everything."

"I've tried to. . . . You're slow at times. If I offend, it's because I think you do understand. You're deliberately asking me to spell out an unpleasant reality." She carried her notes to the table by her bedroom door. As the light had grown dim, she turned on the lamp, causing the fringe on the shade to shimmy. She seemed fascinated by the movement. "I imagine that all of us—the Bible calls us the rich and mighty—wish to leave this world somewhat different from the way it was before us. As the years go by, this vague, ill-defined instinct becomes really quite important. How many of us have toyed with the phrases of our own obituaries?" She turned from the lamp and looked at the field accountant. "Considering everything we now know, would you care to speculate on my not-too-distant obituary?"

"No deal. That's another question."

"It's a snap, you know. . . . The wealth is taken for granted. Every agonizing decision, every nerve-racking gamble—they become simple, expected accomplishments. Accomplishments more to be scorned than admired because I'm both a woman and a highly competitive speculator. An unattractive combination. . . . One son lost in the Great War. Another rapidly emerging as a pompous incompetent, sought after for every wrong reason, discarded and laughed at whenever feasible. And now this. A madman leading or at least a part of a growing band of psychopathic malcontents. . . . This is what I bequeath. What Scarlatti bequeaths, Mr. Canfield. . . . Not a very enviable sum, is it?"

"No, it isn't."

"Consequently, I'll stop at nothing to prevent this final madness . . ." She picked up her notes and went into the bedroom. She closed the door behind her, leaving Canfield in the large sitting room by himself. He thought for a moment that the old woman was on the verge of tears.

Chapter Thirty-five

The monoplane's flight over the channel had been uneventful—the wind calm, the visibility excellent. It was fortunate for Scarlett that such was the case, for the stinging irritation of his unhealed surgery coupled with the pitch of his fury would have made a difficult trip a disastrous one. He was hardly capable of keeping his mind on the compass bearings and when he first saw the Normandy coast, it looked unfamiliar to him. Yet he had made these very same sightings a dozen times.

He was met at the small airfield outside of Lisieux by the Paris contingent, consisting of two Germans and a French Gascon, whose guttural dialect nearly matched that of his associates.

The three Europeans anticipated that the man—they did not know his name—would instruct them to return to Paris. To await further orders.

The man had other intentions, insisting that they all sit uncomfortably together in the front seat while he occupied the entire space in the back. He ordered the car to Vernon, where two got out and were told to make their own way back to Paris. The driver was to remain.

The driver vaguely protested when Scarlett ordered him to proceed west to Montbéliard, a small town near the Swiss border.

"*Mein Herr!* That's a four-hundred-kilometer trip! It will take ten hours or more on these abysmal roads!"

"Then we should be there by dinner time. And be quiet!"

"It might have been simpler for *mein Herr* to refuel and fly . . ."

"I do not fly when I am tired. Relax. I'll find you some 'seafood' in Montbéliard. Vary your diet, Kircher. It excites the palate."

"Jawohl, mein Herr!" Kircher grinned, knowing the man was really a fine *Oberführer*.

Scarlet reflected. The misfits! One day they'd be rid of the misfits.

Montbéliard was not much more complex than an oversized village. The principal livelihood of its citizens was farm produce, much of which was shipped into Switzerland and Germany. Its currency, as in many towns on the border, was a mixture of francs, marks, and Swiss francs.

Scarlett and his driver reached it a little after nine in the evening. However, except for several stops for petrol and a midafternoon lunch, they had pushed forward with no conversation between them. This quiet acted as a sedative to Scarlett's anxiety. He was able to think without anger, although his anger was ever present. The driver had been right when he had pointed out that a flight from Lisieux to Montbéliard would have been simpler and less arduous, but Scarlett could not risk any explosions of temper brought on by exhaustion.

Sometime that day or evening—the time was left open—he was meeting with the Prussian, the all-important man who could deliver what few others could. He had to be up to that meeting, every brain cell working. He couldn't allow recent problems to distort his concentration. The conference with the Prussian was the culmination of months, years of work. From the first macabre meeting with Gregor Strasser to the conversion of his millions to Swiss capital. He, Heinrich Kroeger, possessed the finances so desparately needed by the National Socialists. His importance to the party was now acknowledged.

The problems. Irritating problems! But he'd made his decisions. He'd have Howard Thornton isolated, perhaps killed. The San Franciscan had betrayed them. If the Stockholm manipulation had been uncovered, it had to be laid at Thornton's feet. They'd used his Swedish contacts and obviously he maneuvered large blocks of securities back into his own hands at the depressed price.

Thornton would be taken care of.

As was the French dandy, Jacques Bertholde.

Thornton and Bertholde! Both misfits! Greedy, stupid misfits!

What had happened to Boothroyd? Obviously killed on the *Calpurnia*. But how? Why? Regardless, he deserved to die! So did his father-in-law. Rawlins' order to kill Elizabeth Scarlatti was stupid! The timing had been insane! Couldn't Rawlins understand that she would have left letters behind, documents? She was far more dangerous dead than alive. At least until she'd been reached—as he has reached her, threatened her precious Scarlattis. Now, she, could die! Now it wouldn't matter. And with Bertholde gone, Rawlins gone, and Thornton about to be killed, there'd be no one left who knew who he was. No one! He was Heinrich Kroeger, a leader of the new order!

They pulled up at L'Auberge des Moineaux, a small restaurant with a *buvette* and lodgings for the traveler or for those desiring privacy for other reasons. For Scarlett it was the appointed meeting place.

"Take the car down the road and park it," he told Kircher. "I'll be in one of the rooms. Have dinner. I'll call for you later. . . . I haven't forgotten my promise." Kircher grinned.

Ulster Scarlett got out of the car and stretched. He felt better, his skin bothered him less, and the impending conference filled him with a sense of anticipation. This was the kind of work he should always do! Matters of vast consequences. Matters of power.

He waited until the car was far enough down the street to obscure Kircher's rear-mirror view of him. He then walked back, away from the door, to the cobblestone path and turned into it. Misfits were never to be told anything that wasn't essential to their specific usefulness.

He reached an unlighted door and knocked several times.

The door opened and a moderately tall man with thick, wavy black hair and prominent, dark eyebrows stood in the center of the frame as if guarding an entrance, not welcoming a guest. He was dressed in a Bavarian-cut gray coat and brown knickers. The face was darkly cherubic, the eyes wide and staring. His name was Rudolf Hess.

"Where have you been?" Hess motioned Scarlett to enter and close the door. The room was small; there was a table with chairs around it, a sideboard, and two floor lamps, which gave the room its light. Another man who had been looking out the window, obviously to identify the one outside, nodded to Scarlett. He was a tiny, ugly man with bird-like features, even to the hawknose. He walked with a limp.

"Joseph?" said Scarlett to him. "I didn't expect you here."

Joseph Goebbels looked over at Hess. His knowledge of English was poor. Hess translated Scarlett's words rapidly and Goebbels shrugged his shoulders.

"I asked you where you have been!"

"I had trouble in Lisieux. I couldn't get another plane so I had to drive. It's been a long day so don't aggravate me, please."

"*Ach!* From Lisieux? A long trip. I'll order you some food, but you'll have to be quick. Rheinhart's been waiting since noon."

Scarlett took off his flying jacket and threw it on the sideboard shelf. "How is he?"

Goebbels understood just enough to interrupt. "Rheinhart? . . . Impatient!" He mispronounced the word, and Scarlett grinned. Goebbels thought to himself that this giant was a horrible-looking creature. The opinion was mutual.

"Never mind the food. Rheinhart's been waiting too long. . . . Where is he?"

"In his room. Number two, down the corridor. He went for a walk this afternoon but he keeps thinking someone will recognize him so he came back in ten minutes. I think he's upset."

"Go get him. . . . And bring back some whiskey." He looked at Goebbels wishing that this unattractive little man would leave. It wasn't good that Goebbels be there while Hess and he talked with the Prussian aristocrat. Goebbels looked like an insignificant Jewish accountant.

But Scarlett knew he could do nothing. Hitler was taken with Goebbels. Joseph Goebbels seemed to be reading the tall man's thoughts.

"Ich werde dabei sitzen während Sie sprechen." He pulled a chair back to the wall and sat down.

Hess had gone out the corridor door and the two men were in the room alone. Neither spoke.

Four minutes later Hess returned. Following him was an aging, overweight German several inches shorter than Hess, dressed in a black double-breasted suit and a high collar. His face was puffed with excess fat, his white hair cropped short. He stood perfectly erect and in spite of his imposing appearance, Scarlett thought there was something soft about him, not associated with his bulk. He strutted into the room. Hess closed the door and locked it.

"Gentlemen. General Rheinhart." Hess stood at attention.

Goebbels rose from the chair and bowed, clicking his heels.

Rheinhart looked at him unimpressed.

Scarlett noticed Rheinhart's expression. He approached the elderly general and held out his hand.

"Herr General."

Rheinhart faced Scarlett, and although he concealed it well, his reaction to Scarlett's appearance was obvious. The two men shook hands perfunctorily.

"Please sit down, *Herr General.*" Hess was enormously impressed with their company and did not hide the fact. Rheinhart sat in a chair at the end of the table. Scarlett was momentarily upset. He had wanted to sit in that particular chair for it was the commanding position.

Hess asked Rheinhart if he preferred whisky, gin, or wine. The general waved his hand, refusing.

"Nothing for me, either," added Ulster Scarlett as he sat in the chair to the left of Rheinhart. Hess ignored the tray and also took his seat. Goebbels retreated with his limp to the chair by the wall.

Scarlett spoke. "I apologize for the delay. Unforgivable but, I'm afraid, unavoidable. There was pressing business with our associates in London."

"Your name, please?" Rheinhart interrupted, speaking English with a thick Teutonic accent.

Scarlett looked briefly at Hess before replying. "Kroeger, *Herr General*. Heinrich Kroeger."

Rheinhart did not take his eyes off Scarlett. "I do not think that is your name, sir. You are not German." His voice was flat.

"My sympathies are German. So much so that Heinrich Kroeger is the name I have chosen to be known by."

Hess interrupted. "Herr Kroeger has been invaluable to us all. Without him we would never have made the progress we have, sir."

"*Amerikaner*. . . . He is the reason we do not speak German?"

"That will be corrected in time," Scarlett said. In fact, he spoke nearly flawless German, but still felt at a disadvantage in the language.

"I am not an American, General. . . ." Scarlett returned Rheinhart's stare and gave no quarter. "I am a citizen of the new order! . . . I have given as much, if not more than anyone else alive or dead to see it come to pass. . . . Please remember that in our conversation."

Rheinhart shrugged. "I'm sure you have your reasons, as I have, for being at this table."

"You may be assured of that." Scarlett relaxed and pulled his chair up.

"Very well, gentlemen, to business. If it is possible, I should like to leave Montbéliard tonight." Rheinhart reached into his jacket pocket and took out a page of folded stationery. "Your party has made certain not inconsequential strides in the Reichstag. After your Munich fiasco, one might even say remarkable progress . . ."

Hess broke in enthusiastically. "We have only begun! From the ignominy of treacherous defeat, Germany will rise! We will be masters of all Europe!"

Rheinhart held the folded paper in his hand and watched Hess. He replied quietly, authoritatively. "To be masters of but Germany itself would be sufficient for us. To be able to defend our country is all we ask."

"That will be the least of your guarantees from us, General." Scarlett's voice rose no higher than Rheinhart's.

"It is the only guarantee we wish. We are not interested in the excesses your Adolf Hitler preaches."

At the mention of Hitler's name, Goebbels sat forward in his chair. He was angered by the fact that he could not comprehend.

"Was gibt's mit Hitler? Was sagen sie über ihn?"

Rheinhart answered Goebbels in his own tongue. "Er ist ein sehr sturer Genosse."

"Hitler ist der Weg! Hitler ist die Hoffnung für Deutschland!"

"Vielleicht für Sie."

Ulster Scarlett looked over at Goebbels. The little man's eyes shone with hatred and Scarlett guessed that one day Rheinhart would pay for his words. The general continued as he unfolded the paper.

"The times our nation lives through call for unusual alliances. . . . I have spoken with von Schnitzler and Kindorf. Krupp will not discuss the subject as I'm sure you are aware. . . . German industry is no better off than the army. We are both pawns for the Allied Controls Commission. The Versailles restrictions inflate us one minute, puncture us the next. There is no stability. There is nothing we can count on. We have a common objective, gentlemen. The Versailles treaty."

"It is only one of the objectives. There are others." Scarlett was pleased, but his pleasure was short-lived.

"It is the only objective which has brought me to Montbéliard! As German industry must be allowed to breathe, to export unencumbered, so must the German Army be allowed to maintain adequate strength! The limitation of one hundred thousand troops with over sixteen hundred miles of borders to protect is ludicrous! . . . There are promises, always promises—then threats. Nothing to count on. No comprehension. No allowance for necessary growth."

"We were betrayed! We were viciously betrayed in nineteen eighteen and that betrayal continues! Traitors still exist throughout Germany!" Hess wanted more than his life to be counted among the friends of Rheinhart and his officers. Rheinhart understood and was not impressed.

"*Ja.* Ludendorff still holds to that theory. The Meuse-Argonne is not easy for him to live with."

Ulster Scarlett smiled his grotesque smile. "It is for some of us, General Rheinhart."

Rheinhart looked at him. "I will not pursue that with you."

"One day you should. It's why I'm here—in part."

"To repeat, Herr Kroeger. You have your reasons; I have mine. I am not interested in yours but you are forced to be interested in mine." He looked at Hess and then over at the shadowed figure of Joseph Goebbels by the wall.

"I will be blunt, gentlemen. It is, at least, an ill-kept secret. . . . Across the Polish borders in the lands of the Bolshevik are thousands of frustrated German officers. Men without professions in their own country. They train the Russian field commanders! They discipline the Red peasant army. . . . Why? Some for simple employment. Others justify themselves because a few Russian factories smuggle us cannon, armaments prohibited by the Allied Commission. . . . I do not like this state of affairs, gentlemen. I do not trust the Russians. . . . Weimar is ineffectual. Ebert couldn't face the truth. Hindenburg is worse! He lives in a monarchial past. The politicians must be made to face the Versailles issue! We must be liberated from within!"

Rudolf Hess placed both his hands, palms down, on the table.

"You have the word of Adolf Hitler and those of us in this room that the first item on the political agenda of the National Socialist German Workers party is the unconditional repudiation of the Versailles treaty and its restrictions!"

"I assume that. My concern is whether you are capable of effectively uniting the diverse political camps of the Reichstag. I will not deny that you have appeal. Far more than the others. . . . The question we would like answered, as I'm sure would our equals in commerce, Do you have the staying power? Can you last? Will you last? . . . You were outlawed a few years ago. We can not afford to be allied with a political comet which burns itself out."

Ulster Scarlett rose from his chair and looked down at the aging German general. "What would you say if I told you that we have financial resources surpassing those of any political organization in Europe? Possibly the Western hemisphere."

"I would say that you exaggerate."

"Or if I told you that we possess territory—land—sufficiently large enough to train thousands upon thousands of elite troops beyond the scrutiny of the Versailles inspection teams."

"You would have to prove all this to me."

"I can do just that."

Rheinhart rose and faced Heinrich Kroeger.

"If you speak the truth . . . you will have the support of the imperial German generals."

Chapter Thirty-six

Janet Saxon Scarlett, eyes still shut, reached under the sheets for the body of her lover. He was not there, so she opened her eyes and raised her head, and the room spun around. Her lids were heavy and her stomach hurt. She was still exhausted, still a bit drunk.

Matthew Canfield sat at the writing desk in his undershorts. His elbows were on the desk, his chin cupped in his hands. He was staring down at a paper in front of him.

Janet watched him, aware that he was oblivious to her. She rolled onto her side so that she could observe him.

He was not an ordinary man, she thought, but on the other hand neither was he particularly outstanding, except that she loved him. What, she wondered, did she find so attractive about him? He was not like the men from her world—even her recently expanded world. Most of the men she knew were quick, polished, overly groomed and only concerned with appearances. But Matthew Canfield could not fit into this world. His quickness was an intuitive alertness not related to the graces. And in other respects there was a degree of awkwardness; what confidence he had was born of considered judgment, not simply born.

Others, too, were far more handsome, although he could be placed in the category of "good-looking" in a rough-hewn way. . . . That was it, she mused; he gave the appearance both in actions and in looks of secure independence, but his private behavior was different. In private he was extraordinarily gentle, almost weak. . . . She wondered if he was weak. She knew he was deeply upset and she suspected that Elizabeth had given him money to do her bidding. . . . He didn't really know how to be at ease with money. She'd learned that during their two weeks together in New York. He'd obviously been told to spend without worrying about sums in order to establish their relationship—he'd suggested as much—and they'd both laughed because what they were doing on government funds was, in essence, spelling out the truth. . . . She would have been happy to pay the freight herself. She'd paid for others, and none were as dear to her as Matthew Canfield. No one would ever be so dear to her. He didn't belong to her world. He preferred a simpler, less cosmopolitan one, she thought. But Janet Saxon Scarlett knew she would adjust if it meant keeping him.

Perhaps, when it was all over, if it was ever to be all over, they would find a way. There had to be a way for this good, rough, gentle young man who was a better man that any she had ever known before. She loved him very much and she found herself concerned for him. That was remarkable for

Janet Saxon Scarlett.

When she had returned the night before at seven o'clock, escorted by Derek's man Ferguson, she found Canfield alone in Elizabeth's sitting room. He'd seemed tense, edgy, even angry, and she didn't know why. He'd made feeble excuses for his temper and finally, without warning, he had ushered her out of the suite and out of the hotel.

They had eaten at a small restaurant in Soho. They both drank heavily, his fear infecting her. Yet he would not tell her what bothered him.

They'd returned to his room with a bottle of whiskey. Alone, in the quiet, they had made love. Janet knew he was a man holding on to some mythical rope, afraid to let go for fear of plunging downward.

As she watched him at the writing desk, she also instinctively knew the truth—the unwanted truth—which she had suspected since that terrible moment more than a day ago when he had said to her, "Janet. I'm afraid we've had a visitor."

That visitor had been her husband.

She raised herself on her elbow. "Matthew?"

"Oh. . . . Morning, friend."

"Matthew . . . are you afraid of him?"

Canfield's stomach muscles grew taut.

She knew.

But, of course, she knew.

"I don't think I will be . . . when I find him."

"That's always the way, isn't it? We're afraid of someone or something we don't know or can't find." Janet's eyes began to ache.

"That's what Elizabeth said."

She sat up, pulling the blanket over her shoulders, and leaned back against the headrest. She felt cold, and the ache in her eyes intensified. "Did she tell you?"

"Finally. . . . She didn't want to. I didn't give her an alternative. . . . She had to."

Janet stared straight ahead, at nothing. "I knew it," she said quietly. "I'm frightened."

"Of course you are. . . . But you don't have to be. He can't touch you."

"Why are you so sure? I don't think you were so sure last night." She was not aware of it, but her hands began to shake.

"No, I wasn't. . . . But only because he existed at all. . . . The unholy specter alive and breathing. . . . No matter how much we expected it, it was a shock. But the sun's up now." He reached for his pencil and made a note on the paper.

Suddenly, Janet Scarlett flung herself down across the bed. "Oh, God, God, God!" Her head was buried in the pillow.

At first Canfield did not recognize the appeal in her voice, for she did not scream or shout out and his concentration was on his notes. Her muffled cry was one of agony, not desperation.

"Jan," he began casually. "Janet!" The field accountant threw down his pencil and rushed to the bed. "Janet! . . . Honey, please don't, please. Janet!" He cradled her in his arms, doing his best to comfort her. And then slowly his attention was drawn to her eyes.

The tears were streaming down her face uncontrollably, yet she did not cry out but only gasped for breath. What disturbed him were her eyes.

Instead of blinking from the flow of tears, they remained wide open, as if she were in a trance. A trance of horror.

He spoke her name over and over again.

"Janet. Janet. Janet. Janet. . . ."

She did not respond. She seemed to sink deeper and deeper into the fear which controlled her. She began to moan, at first quietly, then louder and louder.

"Janet! Stop it! Stop it! Darling, stop it!"

She did not hear him.

Instead she tried to push him away, to disengage herself from him. Her naked body writhed on the bed; her arms lashed out, striking him.

He tightened his grip, afraid for a moment that he might hurt her.

Suddenly she stopped. She threw her head back and spoke in a choked voice he had not heard before.

"God damn you to hell! . . . God damn you to hellll!"

She drew out the word "hell" until it became a scream.

Her legs spread slowly, reluctantly, apart on top of the sheet.

In that same choked, guttural voice she whispered, "You pig! Pig! Pig! Pig!"

Canfield watched her in dread. She was assuming a position of sexual intercourse, steeling herself against the terror which had enveloped her and which would progressively worsen.

"Janet, for God's sake, Jan. . . . Don't! Don't! No one's going to touch you! Please, darling!"

The girl laughed horridly, hysterically.

"You're the *card*, Ulster! You're the God damn jack of . . . jack of . . ." She quickly crossed her legs, one emphatically on top of the other, and brought her hands up to cover her breasts. "Leave me alone, Ulster! Please, dear God, Ulster! Leave me alone! . . . You're going to leave me alone?" She curled herself up like an infant and began to sob.

Canfield reached down to the foot of the bed and pulled the blanket over Janet.

He was afraid.

That she could suddenly, without warning, reduce herself to Scarlett's unwilling whore was frightening.

But it was there, and he had to accept it.

She needed help. Perhaps far more help than he could provide. He gently stroked her hair and lay down beside her.

Her sobs evened off into deep breathing as she closed her eyes. He hoped she was sleeping but he could not be sure. At any rate, he would let her rest. It would give him the time to figure out a way to tell her everything she had to know.

The next four weeks would be terrible for her.

For the three of them.

But now there was an element which had been absent before, and Canfield was grateful for it. He knew he shouldn't have been, for it was against every professional instinct he had.

It was hate. His own personal hate.

Ulster Stewart Scarlett was no longer the quarry in an international hunt. He was now the man Matthew Canfield intended to kill.

Chapter Thirty-seven

Ulster Scarlett watched the flushed, angry face of Adolf Hitler. He realized that in spite of his fury, Hitler had a capacity for control that was nothing short of miraculous. But then the man himself was a miracle. A historic man-miracle who would take them into the finest world imaginable on earth.

The three of them—Hess, Goebbels, and Kroeger—had driven through the night from Montbéliard to Munich, where Hitler and Ludendorff awaited a report of their meeting with Rheinhart. If the conference had gone well, Ludendorff's plan was to be set in motion. Each faction of the Reichstag possessing any serious following would be alerted that a coalition was imminent. Promises would be made, threats implied. As the Reichstag's sole member of the National Socialist party and its candidate for president the previous year, Ludendorff would be listened to. He was the soldier-thinker. He was slowly regaining the stature he had thrown away in defeat at the Meuse-Argonne.

Simultaneously and in twelve different cities anti-Versailles demonstrations would be staged, where the police had been paid handsomely not to interfere. Hitler was to travel to Oldenburg, in the center of the northwest Prussian territory, where the great military estates were slowly going to seed—massive remembrances of past glories. A huge rally would be mounted and it was planned that Rheinhart himself would make an appearance.

Rheinhart was enough to give credence to the party's military support. It was more than enough; it would be a momentary climax fitting their current progress. Rheinhart's recognition of Hitler would leave no room for doubt as to where the generals were leaning.

Ludendorff looked upon the act as a political necessity. Hitler looked upon it as a political coup. The Austrian lance corporal was never unmoved by the anticipation of Junker approval. He knew that it was his destiny to have it—demand it!—but nonetheless it filled him with pride, which was why he was furious now.

The ugly little Goebbels had just finished telling Ludendorff and Hitler of Rheinhart's remarks about the Austrian.

In the large rented office overlooking the Sedlingerstrasse, Hitler gripped the arms of his chair and pushed himself up. He stood for a moment glaring at Goebbels, but the thin cripple knew that Hitler's anger was not directed at him, only at his news.

"Fettes Schwein! Wir werden ihn zu seinen Landsort zurück senden! Lass ihm zu seinen Kühen surück gehen!"

Scarlett was leaning against the wall next to Hess. As usual when the conversations taking place were in German, the willing Hess turned to Ulster and spoke quietly.

"He's very upset. Rheinhart may be an obstacle."

"Why?"

"Goebbels doesn't believe Rheinhart will openly support the movement. He wants all the advantages without getting his tunic dirty!"

"Rheinhart said he would. In Montbéliard he said he would! What's Goebbels talking about?" Scarlett found it necessary to watch himself. He really didn't like Goebbels.

"He's just told them what Rheinhart said about Hitler. Remember?" Hess whispered with his hand cupped in front of his mouth.

Scarlett raised his voice. "They should tell Rheinhart—no Hitler, no marbles! Let him go shag!"

"Was ist los?" Hitler glowered at Hess and Scarlett. "Was sagt er, Hess?"

"Lass Rheinhart zum Teufel gehen!"

Ludendorff laughed out of the corner of his mouth. "Das ist naiv!"

"Tell Rheinhart to do as we say or he's out! No troops! No weapons! No uniforms! No one to pay for it all! I don't pay! No place to train them, without the inspection teams on his back! He'll listen!" Scarlett ignored Hess, who was rapidly translating everything the former said.

Ludendorff broke in on Hess as he finished interpreting.

"Man kann einen Mann wie Rheinhart nicht drohen. Er ist ein einflus-sreicher Preusse!"

Hess turned to Ulster Scarlett. "Herr Ludendorff says that Reinhart will not be threatened. He is a Junker."

"He's a frightened, overstuffed tin soldier, that's what he is! He's running scared. He's got the Russian shakes! He needs us and he knows it!"

Hess repeated Scarlett's remarks. Ludendorff snapped his fingers in the Heidelberg fashion, as if mocking a ridiculous statement.

"Don't laugh at me! I talked with him, not you! It's my money! Not yours!"

Hess did not need to translate. Ludendorff rose from his chair, as angry as Scarlett.

"Sag dem Amerikaner dass sein Gelt ihm noch lange nicht das Recht gibt uns Befehle zu geben."

Hess hesitated. "Herr Ludendorff does not believe that your financial contributions . . . as welcome as they are . . ."

"You don't have to finish! Tell him to go shag, too! He's acting just the way Rheinhart expects!" Scarlett, who had not moved from his position against the wall, pushed himself away and sprang forward effortlessly to his full height.

For the moment the aging, intellectual Ludendorff was physically afraid. He did not trust the motives of this neurotic American. Ludendorff had often suggested to Hitler and the others that this man who called himself Heinrich Kroeger was a dangerous addition to their working circle. But he had been consistently overruled because Kroeger not only possessed what appeared to be unlimited financial resources, but seemed to be able to enlist the support, or at least the interest, of incredibly influential men.

Still, he did not trust him.

Essentially because Ludendorff was convinced that this Kroeger was stupid.

"May I remind you, Herr Kroeger, that I possess a . . . working knowledge of the English language!"

"Then why don't you use it?"

"I do not feel it is—how is it said?—entirely necessary."

"It is now, damn it!"

Adolf Hitler suddenly clapped his hands twice, signifying an order of silence. It was an irksome gesture to Ludendorff, but his respect for Hitler's talents—which bordered on awe—made him accept such aggravations.

"Halt! Beide!"

Hitler stepped away from the table, turning his back on all of them. He stretched his arms, then clasped his hands behind him. He said nothing for several moments, yet no one interrupted his silence. For it was his silence, and Goebbels, whose love of theatrics was paramount, watched with satisfaction the effect Hitler was having on the others.

Ludendorff, on the other hand, played the game but remained annoyed. The Hitler he knew well was capable of poor judgment. Great vision, perhaps, but often slipshod in decisions of everyday practical realities. It was unfortunate that he also resented debate on such matters. It made it difficult for Rosenberg and himself, who knew they were the true architects of the new order. Ludendorff hoped that this particular instance was not going to be another case when Hitler overrode his sound analysis. Like himself, Rheinhart was a Junker, proud and unbending. He had to be handled artfully. Who could know this better than the former field marshal of the imperial army who was forced to maintain his dignity in the midst of tragic defeat. Ludendorff understood.

Adolf Hitler spoke quietly. "Wir werden wie Herr Kroeger sagt tun."

"Herr Hitler agrees with you, Kroeger!" Hess touched Scarlett's sleeve, delighted. He was forever being condescended to by the arrogant Ludendorff, and this was not a small victory over him. Rheinhart was a prize. If Kroeger was correct, Ludendorff would look foolish.

"Warum? Es ist sehr gefährlich."

Ludendorff had to argue although he knew at once it was no use.

"Sie sind zu vorischtig. Die unruhigen Zeiten, Ludendorff—Kroeger hat recht. Aber wir werden einen Schritt weiter gehen."

Rudolf Hess expanded his chest. He looked pointedly at Ludendorff and Goebbels as he nudged Scarlett with his elbow.

"Herr Hitler says that our friend Ludendorff is mistakenly cautious. He is right. Ludendorff is always cautious. . . . But Herr Hitler wishes to elaborate on your suggestion. . . ."

Adolf Hitler began speaking slowly but firmly, lending a finality to each German phrase. As he continued he watched with satisfaction the faces of those listening. When he reached the end of his diatribe he spat out the words.

"Da ist Montbéliard!"

For each it was a different evaluation with an underlying common denominator—the man was a genius.

For Hess, Hitler's conclusion was equated with a startling flash of political insight.

For Goebbels, Hitler had once again demonstrated his ability to capitalize on an opponent's fundamental weakness.

For Ludendorff, the Austrian had taken a mediocre idea, added his own boldness, and emerged with a piece of brilliant strategy.

Heinrich Kroeger—Scarlett—spoke. "What did he say, Hess?"

But it was not Rudolf Hess who answered. It was Erich Ludendorff, who did not take his eyes off Adolf Hitler. "Herr Hitler has just . . . solidified the military for us, Kroeger. In a brief statement he has won us the reluctant Prussians."

"What?"

Rudolf Hess turned to Scarlett. "General Rheinhart will be told that unless he does as we demand, the Versailles officials will be informed that he is secretly negotiating illegal procurements. It is the truth. Montbéliard can not be denied!"

"He is a Junker!" Ludendorff added. "Montbéliard is the key because it is the truth! Rheinhart can not disavow what he has done! Even if he should be tempted, there are too many who know—von Schnitzler, Kindorf. Even

Krupp! Rheinhart has broken his word." And then Ludendorff laughed harshly. "The holy word of a Junker!"

Hitler smiled briefly and spoke rapidly to Hess, gesturing his head toward Ulster Scarlett.

"*Der Führer* admires and appreciates you, Heinrich," said Hess. "He asks what of our friends in Zurich?"

"Everything is proceeding on schedule. Several errors have been corrected. We may lose one of the remaining thirteen. . . . It's no loss; he's a thief."

"Who is that?" Ludendorff exercised his very acceptable working knowledge of English.

"Thornton."

"What of his land?" Ludendorff again.

Scarlet, now Kroeger, looked at the academic Ludendorff, the military intellectual, with the contempt born of money. "I intend to buy it."

"Is that not dangerous?" Hess was watching Ludendorff, who had quietly translated what Scarlett said to Hitler. Both men showed signs of alarm.

"Not at all."

"Perhaps not to you personally, my dashing young friend." Ludendorff's tone was blandly incriminating. "Who knows where your sympathies will lie six months from now?"

"I resent that!"

"You're not a German. This isn't your battle."

"I don't have to be a German! And I don't have to justify myself to you! . . . You want me out? Fine! I'm out! . . . And with me go a dozen of the richest men on earth. . . . Oil! Steel! Industry! Steamship lines!"

Hess no longer tried to be tactful. He looked toward Hitler, throwing his arms up in exasperation.

Hitler did not need to be prompted for he knew exactly what to do. He crossed rapidly to the former general of the imperial German army and struck the old man lightly across the mouth with the back of his hand. It was an insulting action—the very lightness of the blow as akin to disciplining a small child. The two men exchanged words and Scarlett knew the old Ludendorff had been severely, cruelly rebuked.

"My motives seem to be questioned, Herr Kroeger. I was merely—how is it said?—testing you." He lifted his hand to his mouth. The memory of Hitler's insult was difficult for him. He struggled to suppress it.

"I was quite sincere, however, about the Swiss property. Your . . . work with us has been most impressive and undoubtedly noticed by many. Should the purchase be traced through you to the party, it might—how is it said—make useless the whole arrangement."

Ulster Scarlett answered with confident nonchalance. He enjoyed putting the thinkers in their place. "No problems. . . . The transaction will be made in Madrid."

"Madrid?" Joseph Goebbels did not fully understand what Scarlett said, but the city of Madrid had a special connotation for him.

The four Germans looked at each other. None was pleased.

"Why is . . . Madrid so safe?" Hess was concerned that his friend had done something rash.

"Papal attaché. Very Catholic. Very much beyond reproach. Satisfied?"

Hess automatically spoke Scarlett's words in German.

Hitler smiled while Ludendorff snapped his fingers, now in sincere applause.

"How is this accomplished?"

"Very simple. Alfonso's court will be told that the land is being bought with White Russian money. Unless it's done quickly, the capital could be manipulated back into Moscow. The Vatican is sympathetic. So is Rivera. This won't be the first time such an arrangement's been made."

Hess explained to Adolf Hitler as Joseph Goebbels listened intently.

"My congratulations, Herr Kroeger. Be . . . cautious." Ludendorff was impressed.

Suddenly Goebbels began chattering, waving his hands in exaggerated gestures. The Germans all laughed and Scarlett wasn't sure whether the unattractive little fascist was making fun of him or not.

Hess translated. "Herr Goebbels says that if you tell the Vatican you can keep four hungry Communists from having a loaf of bread, the pope will let you repaint the Sistine Chapel!"

Hitler broke in on the laughter. "Was Hörst du aus Zürich?"

Ludendorff turned to Scarlett. "You were saying about our friends in Switzerland?"

"On schedule. By the end of next month . . . five weeks say, the buildings will be completed. . . . Here, I'll show you."

Kroeger approached the table, taking a folded map from his jacket pocket. He spread it on the table. "This heavy blue line is the perimeter of the adjacent properties. This section . . . in the south is Thornton's. We extend west to here, north here to Baden, east to the outskirts of Pfäffikon. Approximately every mile and a quarter is a structure which can house fifty troops—eighteen in all. Nine hundred men. The water lines are down, the foundations are in. Each structure looks like a barn or a granary. You couldn't tell the difference unless you were inside."

"Excellent!" Ludendorff inserted a monocle in his left eye and looked closely at the map. Hess translated for a curious Hitler and a skeptical Goebbels. "This . . . perimeter between the . . . Keserne . . . barracks . . . is it fenced?"

"Twelve feet high. Wired by generators in each building for alarms. Patrols will be maintained twenty-four hours a day. Men and dogs. . . . I've paid for everything."

"Excellent. Excellent!"

Scarlett looked over at Hitler. He knew that Ludendorff's approval was never granted easily and in spite of their unpleasant encounter a few moments ago, Scarlett also realized that Hitler valued Ludendorff's opinion, perhaps above all others. It seemed to Scarlett that Hitler's penetrating stare, which was now directed at him, was a look of admiration. Kroeger controlled his own elation and quickly continued.

"The indoctrinations will be concentrated—each lasting four weeks with several days between sessions for transportation and housing. Each contingent has nine hundred men. . . . At the end of one year . . ."

Hess interrupted. "Prachtvoll! At the end of a year ten thousand trained men!"

"Ready to spread throughout the country as military units. Trained for insurgency!" Scarlett was fairly bursting with energy.

"No longer rabble, but the basis of an elite corps! Perhaps the elite corps itself!" Ludendorff himself was catching the younger man's enthusiasm. "Our own private army!"

"That's it! A skilled machine capable of moving fast, hitting hard, and regrouping swiftly and secretly."

As Kroeger spoke, it was Ludendorff who now turned his phrases into the German language for the benefit of Hitler and Goebbels.

But Goebbels was bothered. He spoke quietly, as if this Kroeger might somehow catch the shaded meaning of his observations. Goebbels was still suspicious. This huge, strange American was too glib, too casual in spite of his fervor. In spite of the power of his money. Adolf Hitler nodded his head in agreement.

Hess spoke. "Quite rightly, Heinrich, Herr Goebbels is concerned. These men in Zurich, their demands are so . . . nebulous."

"Not to them they're not. They're very specific. These men are business-men. . . . And besides, they're sympathetic."

"Kroeger is correct." Ludendorff looked at Ulster Scarlett, knowing that Hess would use the German tongue for the others. He was thinking as he spoke, not wishing Kroeger to have any time to formulate answers or comments. This Kroeger, although he did not speak their language fluently, understood far more than he let on, Ludendorff believed. "We have gone so far as to sign agreements, have we not? . . . Pacts, if you like, that with the emergence of our power on the political scene in Germany, our friends in Zurich will be given . . . certain priorities. . . . Economic priorities. . . . We are committed, are we not." There was no hint of a question in Ludendorff's last remark.

"That's right."

"What happens, Herr Kroeger, if we do not honor those commitments?"

Ulster Scarlett paused, returning Ludendorff's now questioning gaze. "They'd yell like sons of bitches and try to ruin us."

"How?"

"Any means they could, Ludendorff. And their means are considerable."

"Does that bother you?"

"Only if they succeeded. . . . Thornton's not the only one. They're all thieves. The difference is that the rest of them are smart. They know we're right. We'll win! Everyone likes to do business with the winner! They know what they're doing. They want to work with us!"

"I believe you're convinced."

"You're damn right I am. Between us we'll run things our way. The right way! The way we want to. We'll get rid of the garbage! The Jews, the Reds, the stinking little bourgeois bootlickers!"

Ludendorff watched the confident American closely. He was right, Kroeger was stupid. His description of the lesser breeds was emotional, not based upon the sound principles of racial integrity. Hitler and Goebbels had similar blind spots but theirs was a pyramid logic in spite of them-selves—they knew because they saw; they had studied as had Rosenberg and himself. This Kroeger had a child's mentality. He was actually a bigot.

"There is much in what you say. Everyone who thinks will support his own kind. . . . Do business with his own kind." Ludendorff would watch Heinrich Kroeger's actions carefully. Such a high-strung man could do great damage. He was a fever-ridden clown.

But then, their court had need of such a jester. And his money.

As usual, Hitler was right. They dare not lose him now.

"I'm going to Madrid in the morning. I've already sent out the orders concerning Thornton. The whole business shouldn't take any longer than two or three weeks, and then I'll be in Zurich."

Hess told Hitler and Goebbels what Kroeger had said. *Der Führer* barked out a sharp question.

"Where can you be reached in Zurich?" interpreted Ludendorff. "Your schedule, if it proceeds as it has, will require communication with you."

Heinrich Kroeger paused before giving his answer. He knew the question would be asked again. It was always asked whenever he went to Zurich. Yet he was always evasive. He realized that part of his mystique, his charisma within the party, was due to his obscuring the specific individuals or firms with which he did business. In the past he had left a single phone number or a post office box, or perhaps even the name of one of the fourteen men in Zurich with instructions to ask him for a code name.

Never direct and open.

They did not understand that identities, addresses, phone numbers were unimportant. Only the ability to deliver was essential.

Zurich understood.

These Goliaths of the world's great fortunes understood. The international financiers with their tangled labyrinths of manipulations understood perfectly.

He had delivered.

Their agreements with Germany's emerging new order insured markets and controls beyond belief.

And none cared who he was or where he came from.

But now, at this moment, Ulster Stewart Scarlett realized that these titans of the new order needed to be reminded of Heinrich Kroeger's importance.

He would tell them the truth.

He would say the name of the one man in Germany sought by all who drove for power. The one man who refused to talk, refused to be involved, refused to meet with any faction.

The only man in Germany who lived behind a wall of total secrecy. Complete political isolation.

The most feared and revered man in all Europe.

"I'll be with Krupp. Essen will know where to reach us."

Chapter Thirty-eight

Elizabeth Scarlatti sat up in her bed. A card table had been placed at her side, and papers were strewn all over the immediate vicinity—the bed, the table, the entire walking area of the room. Some were in neat piles, others scattered. Some were clipped together and labeled by index cards; others discarded, ready for the trash basket.

It was four o'clock in the afternoon and she had left her room only once. That was to let in Janet and Matthew. She noted that they looked terrible; exhausted, ill, perhaps. She knew what had happened. The pressure had become too much for the government man. He had to break out, get relief. Now that he had, he would be better prepared for her proposal.

Elizabeth gave a final look at the pages she held in her hand.

So this was it! The picture was now clear, the background filled in.

She had said that the men of Zurich might have created an extraordinary strategy. She knew now that they had.

Had it not been so grotesquely evil she might have agreed with her son. She might have been proud of his part in it. Under the circumstances, she could only be terrified.

She wondered if Matthew Canfield would understand. No matter. It was now time for Zurich.

She got up from the bed, taking the pages with her, and went to the door.

Janet was at the desk writing letters. Canfield sat in a chair nervously reading a newspaper. Both were startled when Elizabeth walked into the room.

"Do you have any knowledge of the Versailles treaty?" she asked him. "The restrictions, the reparations payments?"

"As much as the average guy, I guess."

"Are you aware of the Dawes Plan? That wholly imperfect document?"

"I thought it made the reparations livable with."

"Only temporarily. It was grasped at by the politicians who needed temporary solutions. Economically it's a disaster. Nowhere does it give a final figure. If, at any time, a final figure is given, German industry—who pays the bill—might collapse."

"What's your point?"

"Bear with me a minute. I want you to understand. . . . Do you realize who executes the Versailles treaty? Do you know whose voice is strongest in the decisions under the Dawes Plan? Who ultimately controls the internal economics of Germany?"

Canfield put the newspaper down on the floor. "Yes. Some committee."

"The Allied Controls Commission."

"What are you driving at?" Canfield got out of his chair.

"Just what you're beginning to suspect. Three of the Zurich contingent are members of the Allied Controls Commission. The Versailles treaty is being executed by these men. Working together, the men of Zurich can literally manipulate the German economy. Leading industrialists from the major powers to the north, the west, and the south-west. Completed by the most powerful financiers within Germany itself. A wolf pack. They'll make sure that the forces at work in Germany remain on a collision course. When the explosion takes place—as surely it must—they'll be there to pick up the pieces. To complete this . . . master plan, they need only a political base of operation. Believe me when I tell you they've found it. With Adolf Hitler and his Nazis. . . . With my son, Ulster Stewart Scarlett."

"My God!" Canfield spoke quietly, staring at Elizabeth. He had not fully understood the details of her recital, but he recognized the implications.

"It's time for Switzerland, Mr. Canfield."

He would ask his questions on the way.

Chapter Thirty-nine

The cablegrams were all in English and except for the names and addresses of the designees, the words were identical. Each was sent to the company or corporation in which the person specified held the highest position. Time zones were respected, each cable was to arrive at its destination at twelve noon, on Monday, and each was to be hand-delivered to the individual addressee upon a signed receipt of acceptance.

Elizabeth Scarlatti wanted those illustrious corporations identified in writing. She wanted those receiving her cables to know that this was, above all, business.

Each cable read as follows:

```
THROUGH THE LATE MARQUIS DE BERTHOLDE THE SCAR-
LATTI INDUSTRIES THROUGH THE UNDERSIGNED ALONE
HAVE BEEN INFORMED OF YOUR CONSOLIDATION STOP AS
THE SINGLE SPOKESMAN FOR SCARLATTI THE UNDER-
SIGNED BELIEVES THERE EXIST AREAS OF MUTUAL INTER-
EST STOP THE ASSETS OF SCARLATTI COULD BE AT YOUR
DISPOSAL UNDER PROPER CIRCUMSTANCES STOP THE
UNDERSIGNED WILL ARRIVE IN ZURICH TWO WEEKS HENCE
ON THE EVENING OF NOVEMBER 3 AT THE HOUR OF NINE
O'CLOCK STOP THE CONFERENCE WILL TAKE PLACE AT
FALKE HAUS
                    ELIZABETH WYCKHAM SCARLATTI
```

There were thirteen reactions, all separate, in many different languages, but each with a single ingredient common to all.

Fear.

There was a fourteenth reaction, and it took place in the suite of rooms reserved for Heinrich Kroeger at Madrid's Hotel Emperador. The reaction was fury.

"I won't have it! It can't take place! They're all dead! Dead! Dead! Dead! She was warned! They're dead! Every God damned one of them! Dead. My orders go out tonight! Now!"

Charles Pennington, sent by Ludendorff to act as Kroeger's bodyguard, stood across the room looking out the balcony at the reddish, fan-shaped rays of the Spanish sun.

"Glorious! Simply glorious! . . . Don't be an ass." He didn't like to look at Heinrich Kroeger. In repose that tissued, patched face was bad enough. Angered, it was repulsive. It was now crimson with rage.

"Don't you tell me . . ."

"Oh, stop it!" Pennington saw that Kroeger continued to crush in his fist the telegram from Howard Thornton, which spelled out the Scarlatti conference in Zurich. "What bloody difference does it make to you? To any of us?" Pennington had opened the envelope and read the message because, as he told Kroeger, he had no idea when Kroeger would return from his meeting with the papal attaché. It might have been urgent. What he did not tell Kroeger was that Ludendorff had instructed him to screen all letters, phone calls—whatever—received by this animal. It was a pleasure.

"We don't want anyone else involved. We can't have anyone else! We Can't! Zurich will panic! They'll run out on us!"

"They've all got the cables. If Zurich's going to run, you won't stop them now. Besides, this Scarlatti's the cat's whiskers if it's the same one I'm thinking of. She has millions. . . . Damned fortunate for us she wants to come in. I didn't think much of Bertholde—probably less than you did, smelly French Jew—but if he pulled this off, I doff my hat. Anyway, I repeat, what's it to you?"

Heinrich Kroeger glared at the stylish, effeminate Englishman who pulled at his cuffs, making sure they fell just below his jacket sleeve. The red and black cuff links were surrounded by the soft linen of his light blue shirt. Kroeger knew this appearance was deceptive. Like the social Boothroyd, Pennington was a killer who took emotional sustenance from his work. He also was held in high esteem by Hitler, even more so by Joseph Goebbels. Nevertheless, Kroeger had made up his mind. He could not risk it!

"This meeting won't take place! She'll be killed. I'll have her killed."

"Then I'll have to remind you that such a decision must be multilateral. You can not make it yourself. . . . And I don't think you'll find anyone else consenting."

"You're not here to tell me what to do!"

"Oh, but I am. . . . My instructions come from Ludendorff. And, of course, he knows about your message from Thornton. I wired him several hours ago." Pennington casually looked at his wristwatch. "I'm going out for dinner. . . . Frankly, I'd prefer eating alone but if you insist upon joining me, I'll tolerate your company."

"You little prick! I could break your God damn neck!"

Pennington bristled. He knew that Kroeger was unarmed, his revolver lay on the bureau of his bedroom, and the temptation was there. He could kill him, use the telegram as proof, and say that Kroeger had disobeyed. But then there were the Spanish authorities and a hasty retreat. And Kroeger did have a job to do. Strange that it involved Howard Thornton so completely.

"That's possible, of course. But then we could, no doubt, do each other in any number of ways, couldn't we?" Pennington withdrew a thin pistol from his chest holster. "For instance, I might fire a single bullet directly into your mouth right now. . . . But I wouldn't do it in spite of your provocation because the order is larger than either of us. I'd have to answer for my action—no doubt be executed for it. You'll be shot if you take matters into your own hands."

"You don't know this Scarlatti, Pennington. I do!"

How could she have known about Bertholde? What could she have learned from him?

"Of course, You're old friends!" The Englishman put away his pistol and laughed.

How! How? She wouldn't dare challenge him! The only thing she valued was the Scarlatti name, its heritage, its future. She knew beyond a doubt that he would stamp it out! How! Why?

"That woman can't be trusted! She can't be trusted!"

Charles Pennington pulled down his blazer so the shoulders fell correctly, the jacket cloth concealing the slight bulge of his holster. He walked to the door in calm anticipation of *chorizo*. "Really, Heinrich? . . . Can any of us?"

The Englishman closed the door leaving only a faint aroma of Yardley's.

Heinrich Kroeger uncrumpled the telegram in his palm.

Thornton was panic-stricken. Each of the remaining thirteen in Zurich had received identical cablegrams from Elizabeth Scarlatti. But none save Thornton knew who he was.

Kroeger had to move quickly. Pennington hadn't lied. He would be shot if he ordered Elizabeth Scarlatti's death. That did not, however, preclude such an order after Zurich. Indeed, after Zurich it would be mandatory.

But first the Thornton land. He had instructed Thornton for his own safety to let it go. The frightened Thornton had not argued, and the idiot attaché was playing right into his hands. For the glory of Jesus and another blow against atheistic communism.

The money and title would be transferred within a week. Thornton was sending his attorney from San Francisco to conclude the negotiations by signature.

As soon as the land was his, Heinrich Kroeger would issue a warrant for death that no one could deny.

And when that misfit life was snuffed out, Heinrich Kroeger was free. He would be a true light of the new order. None would know that Ulster Scarlett existed.

Except one.

He would confront her at Zurich.

He would kill her at Zurich.

Chapter Forty

The embassy limousine climbed the small hill to the front of the Georgian house in Fairfax, Virginia. It was the elegant residence of Erich Rheinhart, attaché of the Weimar Republic, nephew of the sole imperial general who had thrown his support to the German radical movement given the name of Nazi, by philosophy, a full-fledged Nazi himself.

The well-tailored man with the waxed moustache got out of the back seat and stepped onto the driveway. He looked up at the ornate facade.

"A lovely home."

"I'm pleased, Poole," said Rheinhart, smiling at the man from Berthode et Fils.

The two men walked into the house and Erich Rheinhart led his guest to a book-lined study off the living room. He indicated a chair for Poole and went to a cabinet, taking out two glasses and a bottle of whiskey.

"To business. You come three thousand miles at a loathsome time of year for ocean travel. You tell me I am the object of your visit. I'm flattered, of course, but what can . . ."

"Who ordered Bertholde's death?" Poole said harshly.

Erich Rheinhart was astonished. He hunched his padded shoulders, placed his glass on the small table, and extended his hands, palms up. He spoke slowly, in consternation.

"My dear man, why do you think it concerns me? I mean—in all candor—you are either deluded as to my influence or you need a long rest."

"Labishe wouldn't have killed him without having been ordered to do it. Some one of enormous authority had to issue that order."

"Well, to begin with I have no such authority, and secondly I would have no reason. I was fond of that Frenchman."

"You hardly knew him."

Rheinhart laughed. "Very well. . . . All the less reason . . ."

"I didn't say you personally. I'm asking who did and *why*." Poole was betraying his normal calm. He had good reason. This arrogant Prussian held the key if Poole was right, and he wasn't going to let him go until he found out. He would have to press nearer the truth, yet not disclose it.

"Did Bertholde know something the rest of you didn't want him to know?"

"Now, you're preposterous."

"Did he?"

"Jacques Bertholde was our London contact! He enjoyed a unique position in England that approached diplomatic immunity. His influence was felt in a dozen countries among scores of the industrial elite. His death is a great loss to us! How dare you imply that any of us was responsible!"

"I find it interesting that you haven't answered my question." Poole was exasperated. "Did he know something the men in Munich might consider dangerous?"

"If he did, I have no idea what it might be!"

But Poole knew. Perhaps he was the only one who did know. *If he could only be sure*.

"I'd like another drink, please. Forgive my temper." He smiled.

Rheinhart laughed. "You're impossible. Give me your glass. . . . You're satisfied?" The German crossed to the liquor cabinet and poured. "You travel three thousand miles for nothing. It's been a bad trip for you."

Poole shrugged. He was used to the trips—some good, some bad. Bertholde and his odd friend, the misshapen Heinrich Kroeger, had ordered him over barely six months ago. His orders had been simple then. Pick up the girl, find out what she had learned from old Scarlatti. He'd failed. The Canfield man had stopped him. The solicitous lackey, the salesman-cum-escort had prevented it. But he hadn't failed his other orders. He'd followed the banker named Cartwright. He'd killed him and broken into the railroad station locker and gotten the banker's agreement with Elizabeth Scarlatti.

It was then that he had learned the truth of Heinrich Kroeger's identity. Elizabeth Scarlatti's son had needed an ally and Jacques Bertholde was that ally. And in return for that precious friendship, Ulster Scarlett had ordered Bertholde's death. The fanatic had commanded the death of the man who had made everything possible for him.

He, Poole, would avenge that terrible murder. But before he did, he had to confirm what he suspected was the truth. That neither the Nazi leaders nor the men in Zurich knew who Kroeger was. If that was the case, then Kroeger had murdered Bertholde to keep that identity secret.

The revelation might cost the movement millions. The Munich Nazis would know this, if they knew anything.

Erich Rheinhart stood over Poole. "A penny for your thoughts, my dear fellow? Here, a bourbon. You do not speak to me."

"Oh? . . . Yes, it's been a bad trip, Erich. You were right." Poole bent his neck back, closed his eyes, and rubbed his forehead. Rheinhart returned to his chair.

"You need a rest. . . . Do you know what I think? I think you're right. I think some damned fool *did* issue that order." Poole opened his eyes, startled by Erich Rheinhart's words. "Ja! In my opinion you are correct. And it must stop! . . . Strasser fights Hitler and Ludendorff. Ekhart rambles on like a madman. Attacking! Attacking! Kindorf screams in the Ruhr. Jodl betrays the Black Wehrmacht in Bavaria. Graefe makes a mess in the north. Even my own uncle, the illustrious Wilhelm Rheinhart, makes an idiot of himself. He speaks, and I hear the laughter behind my back in America. I tell you we are split in ten factions. Wolves at each other's throats. We will accomplish nothing! Nothing if this does not stop!" Erich Rheinhart's anger was undisguised. He didn't care. He rose again from his chair. "What is most asinine is the most obvious! We can lose the men in Zurich. If we can not agree among ourselves, how long do you think they will stay with us? I tell you, these men are not interested in who has next week's power base in the Reichstag—not for its own sake. They don't care a Deutschmark for the glories of the new Germany. Or the ambitions of any nation. Their wealth puts them above political boundaries. They are with us for one reason alone—their own power. If we give them a single doubt that we are not what we claim to be, that we are not the emerging order of Germany, they will abandon us. They will leave us with nothing! Even the Germans among them!"

Rheinhart's fury abated. He tried to smile but instead drained his glass quickly and crossed to the cabinet.

If Poole could only be sure. "I understand," he said quietly.

"Ja. I think you do. You've worked long and hard with Bertholde. You've accomplished a great deal . . ." He turned around facing Poole. "That's what I mean. Everything that all of us have worked for can be lost by these internal frictions. The achievements of Funke, Bertholde, von Schnitzler, Thyssen, even Kroeger, will be wiped out of we can not come together. We must unite behind one, possibly two, acceptable leaders . . ."

That was it! That was the sign. Poole was now sure. Rheinhart had said the name! Kroeger!

"Maybe, Erich, but who?" Would Rheinhart say the name again? It was not possible, for Kroeger was no German. But could he get Rheinhart to use the name, just the name, once more without the slightest betrayal of concern.

"Strasser, perhaps. He's strong, attractive. Ludendorff naturally has the aura of national fame, but he's too old now. But mark me, Poole, watch this Hitler! Have you read the transcripts of the Munich trial?"

"No. Should I?"

"Yes! He's electric! Positively eloquent! And sound."

"He has a lot of enemies. He's banned from speaking in almost every *grafshaft* in Germany."

"The necessary excesses in a march to power. The bans on him are being removed. We're seeing to that."

Poole now watched Rheinhart carefully as he spoke.

"Hitler's a friend of Kroeger, isn't he?"

"Ach! Wouldn't you be? Kroeger has millions! It is through Kroeger that Hitler gets his automobiles, his chauffeur, the castle at Berchtesgaden, God knows what else. You don't think he buys them with his royalties, do you? Most amusing. Last year Herr Hitler declared an income which could not possibly purchase two tires for his Mercedes." Rheinhart laughed. "We managed to have the inquiry suspended in Munich, fortunately. Ja, Kroeger is good to Hitler."

Poole was now absolutely sure. The men in Zurich did not know who Heinrich

Kroeger was!

"Erich, I must go. Can you have your man drive me back to Washington?"

"But of course, my dear fellow."

Poole opened the door of his room at the Ambassador Hotel. Upon hearing the sound of the key, the man inside stood up, practically at attention.

"Oh, it's you, Bush."

"Cable from London, Mr. Poole. I thought it best that I take the train down rather than using the telephone." He handed Poole the cable.

Poole opened the envelope and extracted the message. He read it.

```
DUCHESS HAS LEFT LONDON STOP DESTINATION ASCER-
TAINED GENEVA STOP RUMORS OF ZURICH CONFERENCE
STOP CABLE INSTRUCTIONS PARIS OFFICE
```

Poole pinched his aristocratic lips together, nearly biting into his own flesh in an attempt to suppress his anger.

"Duchess" was the code name of Elizabeth Scarlatti. So she headed for Geneva. A hundred and ten miles from Zurich. This was no pleasure trip. It was not another leg on her journey of mourning.

Whatever Jacques Bertholde had feared—plot or counterplot—it was happening now. Elizabeth Scarlatti and her son "Heinrich Kroeger" were making their moves. Separately or together, who could know.

Poole made his decision.

"Send the following to the Paris office. 'Eliminate Duchess from the market. Her bid is to be taken off our lists at once. Repeat, eliminate Duchess'."

Poole dismissed the courier and went to the telephone. He had to make reservations immediately. He had to get to Zurich.

There'd be no conference. He'd stop it. He'd kill the mother, expose the killer son! Kroeger's death would follow quickly!

It was the least he could do for Bertholde.

PART THREE

Chapter Forty-one

The train clanged over the antiquated bridge spanning the Rhone River, into the Geneva station. Elizabeth Scarlatti sat in her compartment looking first down at the river barges, then at the rising banks and into the large railroad yard. Geneva was clean. There was a scrubbed look about it, which helped to hide the fact that scores of nations and a thousand score of business giants used this neutral city to further intensify conflicting interests. As the train neared the city, she thought that someone like herself belonged in Geneva. Or, perhaps, Geneva belonged to someone like herself.

She eyed the luggage piled on the seat facing her. One suitcase contained the clothes she needed, and three smaller bags were jammed with papers. Papers that contained a thousand conclusions, totaling up to a battery of weapons. The data included figures on the complete worth of every man in the Zurich group. Every resource each possessed. Additional information awaited her in Geneva. But that was a different sort of musketry. It was not unlike the *Domesday Book*. For what awaited her in Geneva was the complete breakdown of the Scarlatti interests. The legally assessed value of every asset controlled by the Scarlatti Industries. What made it deadly was her maneuverability. And opposite each block of wealth was a commitment to purchase. These commitments were spelled out, and they could be executed instantaneously by a cable to her attorneys.

And well they should be.

Each block was followed—not by the usual two columns designating assessed value and sales value—but three columns. This third column was an across-the-board cut, which guaranteed the buyer a minor fortune with each transaction. Each signified a mandate to purchase that could not be refused. It was the highest level of finance, returned through the complexities of banking to the fundamental basis of economic incentive. Profit.

And Elizabeth counted on one last factor. It was the reverse of her instructions but that, too, was calculated.

In her sealed orders sent across the Atlantic was the emphatic stipulation that every contact made—to complete the task teams of administrators had to work twelve-hour shifts night and day—was to be carried out in the utmost secrecy and only with those whose authority extended to great financial commitments. The guaranteed gains absolved all from charges of irresponsibility. Each would emerge a hero to himself or to his economic constituency. But the price was consummate security until the act was done. The rewards matched the price. Millionaires, merchant princes, and bankers in New York, Chicago, Los Angeles, and Palm Beach found themselves quartered in conference rooms with their dignified counterparts from one of New York's most prestigious law firms. The tones were hushed and the looks knowing. Financial killings were being made. Signatures were affixed.

And, of course, it had to happen.

Unbelievable good fortune leads to ebullience, and ebullience is no mate for secrecy.

Two or three began to talk. Then four or five. Then a dozen. But no more than that. . . . The *price*.

Phone calls were made, almost none from offices, nearly all from the quiet seclusion of libraries or dens. Most were made at night under the soft light of desk lamps with good pre-Volstead whiskey an arm's length away.

In the highest economic circles, there was a rumor that something most unusual was happening at Scarlatti.

It was just enough. Elizabeth knew it would be just enough. After all, the *price*. . . . And the rumors reached the men in Zurich.

Matthew Canfield stretched out across the seats in his own compartment, his legs propped over his single suitcase, his feet resting on the cushions facing him. He, too, looked out the window at the approaching city of Geneva. He had just finished one of his thin cigars and the smoke rested in suspended layers above him in the still air of the small room. He contemplated opening a window, but he was too depressed to move.

It has been two weeks to the day since he had granted Elizabeth Scarlatti her reprieve of one month. Fourteen days of chaos made painful by the knowledge of his own uselessness. More than uselessness, more akin to personal futility. He could do nothing, and nothing was expected of him. Elizabeth hadn't wanted him to "work closely" with her. She didn't want anyone to work with her—closely or otherwise. She soloed. She soared alone, a crusty, patrician eagle sweeping the infinite meadows of her own particular heaven.

His most demanding chore was the purchase of office supplies such as reams of paper, pencils, notebooks, and endless boxes of paper clips.

Even the publisher Thomas Ogilvie had refused to see him, obviously so instructed by Elizabeth.

Canfield had been dismissed as he was being dismissed by Elizabeth. Even Janet treated him with a degree of aloofness, always apologizing for her manner but by apologizing, acknowledging it. He began to realize what had happened. He was the whore now. He had sold himself, his favors taken and paid for. They had very little use for him now. They knew he could be had again as one knows a whore can be had.

He understood so much more completely what Janet had felt.

Would it be finished with Janet? Could it ever be finished with her? He told himself no. She told him the same. She asked him to be strong enough for both of them, but was she fooling herself and letting him pay for it?

He began to wonder if he was capable of judgment. He had been idle and the rot inside of him frightened him. What had he done? Could he undo it? He was operating in a world he couldn't come to grips with.

Except Janet. She didn't belong to that world either. She belonged to him. She had to!

The whistle on the train's roof screeched twice and the huge metal-against-metal slabs on the wheels began to grind. The train was entering the Geneva station, and Canfield heard Elizabeth's rapid knocking on the wall between their compartments. The knocking annoyed him. It sounded like an impatient master of the house rapping for a servant.

Which is exactly what it was.

"I can manage this one, you take the other two. Let the redcaps handle the rest."

Dutifully Canfield instructed the porter, gathered up the two bags, and followed Elizabeth off the train.

Because he had to juggle the two suitcases in the small exit area, he was several feet behind Elizabeth as they stepped off the metal stairway and started down the concrete platform to the center of the station. Because of those two suitcases they were alive one minute later.

At first it was only a speck of dark movement in the corner of his eye. Then it was the gasps of several travelers behind him. Then the screams. And then he saw it.

Bearing down from the right was a massive freight dolly with a huge steel slab across the front used to scoop up heavy crates. The metal plate was about four feet off the ground and had the appearance of a giant, ugly blade.

Canfield jumped forward as the rushing monster came directly at them. He threw his right arm around her waist and pushed-pulled her out of the way of the mammoth steel plate. It crashed into the side of the train less than a foot from both their bodies.

Many in the crowd were hysterical. No one could be sure whether anyone had been injured or killed. Porters came running. The shouts and screams echoed throughout the platform.

Elizabeth, breathless, spoke into Canfield's ear. "The suitcases! Do you have the suitcases?"

Canfield found to his amazement that he still held one in his left hand. It was pressed between Elizabeth's back and the train. He had dropped the suitcase in his right hand.

"I've got one. I let the other go."

"Find it!"

"For Christ's sake!"

"Find it, you fool!"

Canfield pushed at the crowd gathering in front of them. He scanned his eyes downward and saw the leather case. It had been run over by the heavy front wheels of the dolly, crushed but still intact. He shouldered his way against a dozen midriffs and reached down. Simultaneously another arm, with a fat, uncommonly large hand thrust itself toward the crumpled piece of leather. The arm was clothed in a tweed jacket. A woman's jacket. Canfield pushed harder and touched the case with his fingers and began pulling it forward. Instinctively, amid the panorama of trousers and overcoats, he grabbed the wrist of the fat hand and looked up.

Bending down, eyes in blind fury, was a jowled face Canfield could never forget. It belonged in that hideous foyer of red and black four thousand miles away. It was Hannah, Janet's housekeeper!

Their eyes met in recognition. The woman's iron-gray head was covered tightly by a dark green Tyrolean fedora, which set off the bulges of facial flesh. Her immense body was crouched, ugly, ominous. With enormous strength she whipped her hand out of Canfield's grasp, pushing him as she did so, so that he fell back into the dolly and the bodies surrounding him. She disappeared rapidly into the crowd toward the station.

Canfield rose, clutching the crushed suitcase under his arm. He looked after her, but she could not be seen. He stood there for a moment, people pressing around him, bewildered.

He worked his way back to Elizabeth.

"Take me out of here. Quickly!"

They started down the platform, Elizabeth holding his left arm with more strength than Canfield thought she possessed. She was actually hurting him. They left the excited crowd behind them.

"It has begun." She looked straight ahead as she spoke.

They reached the interior of the crowded dome. Canfield kept moving his head in every direction, trying to find an irregular break in the human pattern, trying to find a pair of eyes, a still shape, a waiting figure. A fat woman in a tyrolean hat.

They reached the south entrance on Eisenbahn Platz and found a line of taxis.

Canfield held Elizabeth back from the first cab. She was alarmed. She wanted to keep moving.

"They'll send our luggage."

He didn't reply. Instead he propelled her to the left toward the second car and then, to her mounting concern, signaled the driver of a third vehicle. He pulled the cab door shut and looked at the crushed, expensive Mark Cross suitcase. He pictured Hannah's wrathful, puffed face. If there was ever a female archangel of darkness, she was it. He gave the driver the name of their hotel.

"Il n'y a plus de bagage, monsieur?"

"No. It will follow," answered Elizabeth in English.

The old woman had just gone through a horrifying experience, so he decided not to mention Hannah until they reached the hotel. Let her calm down. And yet he wondered whether it was him or Elizabeth who needed the calm. His hands were still shaking. He looked over at Elizabeth. She continued to stare straight ahead, but she was not seeing anything anyone else would see.

"Are you all right?"

She did not answer him for nearly a minute.

"Mr. Canfield, you have a terrible responsibility facing you."

"I'm not sure what you mean."

She turned and looked at him. Gone was the grandeur, gone the haughty superiority.

"Don't let them kill me, Mr. Canfield. Don't let them kill me now. Make them wait till Zurich. . . . After Zurich they can do anything they wish."

Chapter Forty-two

Elizabeth and Canfield spent three days and nights in their rooms at the Hotel D'Accord. Only once had Canfield gone out—and he had spotted two men following him. They did not try to take him, and it occurred to him that they considered him so secondary to the prime target, Elizabeth, that they dared not risk a call out of the Geneva police, reported to be an alarmingly belligerent force, hostile to those who upset the delicate equilibrium of their neutral city. The experience taught him that the moment they appeared together he could expect an attack no less vicious than the one made on them at the Geneva station. He wished he could send word to Ben Reynolds. But he couldn't, and he knew it. He had been ordered to stay out of Switzerland. He had withheld every piece of vital information from his reports. Elizabeth had seen to that. Group Twenty knew next to nothing about the immediate situation and the motives of those involved. If he did send an urgent request for assistance, he would have to explain, at least partially, and that explanation would lead to prompt interference by the embassy. Reynolds wouldn't wait upon legalities. He would have Canfield seized by force and held incommunicado.

The results were predictable. With him finished, Elizabeth wouldn't have a chance of reaching Zurich. She'd be killed by Scarlett in Geneva. And the secondary target would then be Janet back in London. She couldn't stay at the Savoy indefinitely. Derek couldn't continue his security precautions ad infinitum. She would eventually leave, or Derek would become exasperated and careless. She, too, would be killed. Finally, there was Chancellor Drew, his wife, and seven children. There would be a hundred valid reasons for all to leave the remote Canadian refuge. They'd be massacred. Ulster Stewart Scarlett would win.

At the thought of Scarlett, Canfield was able to summon up what anger was left in him. It was almost enough to match his fear and depression. Almost.

He walked into the sitting room Elizabeth had converted into an office. She was writing on the center table.

"Do you remember the housekeeper at your son's house?" he said.

Elizabeth put down her pencil. It was momentary courtesy, not concern. "I've seen her on the few occasions I've visited, yes."

"Where did she come from?"

"As I recall, Ulster brought her back from Europe. She ran a hunting lodge in . . . southern Germany." Elizabeth looked up at the field accountant. "Why do you ask?"

Years later Canfield would reflect that it was because he had been trying to find the words to tell Elizabeth Scarlatti that Hannah was in Geneva that caused him to do what he did. To physically move from one place to another at that particular instant. To cross between Elizabeth and the window. He would carry the remembrance of it as long as he lived.

There was a shattering of glass and a sharp, terrible stinging pain in his left shoulder. Actually the pain seemed to come first. The jolt was so powerful that it spun Canfield around, throwing him across the table, scattering papers, and crashing the lamp to the floor. A second and third shot followed, splintering the thick wood around his body and Canfield, in panic, lurched to one side, toppling Elizabeth off her chair onto the floor. The pain in his shoulder was overpowering, and a huge splotch of blood spread across his shirt.

It was all over in five seconds.

Elizabeth was crouched against the paneling of the wall. She was at once frightened and grateful. She looked at the field accountant lying in front of her trying to hold his shoulder. She was convinced he had thrown himself over her to protect her from the bullets. He never explained otherwise.

"How badly are you hurt?"

"I'm not sure. It hurts like hell. . . . I've never been hit before. Never shot before. . . ." He was finding it difficult to speak. Elizabeth started to move toward him. "God damn it! Stay where you are!" He looked up and saw that he was out of the sight line of the window. They both were. "Look, can you reach the phone? Go on the floor. Stay down! . . . I think I need a doctor. . . . A doctor." He passed out.

Thirty minutes later Canfield awoke. He was on his own bed with the whole upper left part of his chest encased in an uncomfortable bandage. He could barely move. He could see, blurredly to be sure, a number of figures around him. As his eyes came into focus, he saw Elizabeth at the foot of the bed looking down at him. To her right was a man in an overcoat, behind him a uniformed policeman. Bending over him on his left was a balding, stern-faced man in his shirt sleeves, obviously a doctor. He spoke to Canfield. His accent was French.

"Move your left hand, please."

Canfield obeyed.

"Your feet, please."

Again he complied.

"Can you roll your head?"

"What? Where?"

"Move your head back and forth. Don't try to be amusing." Elizabeth was possibly the most relieved person within twenty miles of the Hotel D'Accord. She even smiled.

Canfield swung his head back and forth.

"You are not seriously hurt." The doctor stood erect.

"You sound disappointed," answered the field accountant.

"May I ask him questions, *Herr Doktor?*" said the Swiss next to Elizabeth.

The doctor replied in his broken English. "Yes. The bullet passed him through."

What one had to do with the other perplexed Canfield, but he had no time to think about it. Elizabeth spoke.

"I've explained to this gentleman that you're merely accompanying me while I conduct business affairs. We're totally bewildered by what's happened."

"I would appreciate this man answering for himself, madame."

"Damned if I can tell you anything, mister. . . ." And then Canfield stopped. There was no point in being a fool. He was going to need help. "On second thoughts, maybe I can." He looked toward the doctor, who was putting on his suit coat. The Swiss understood.

"Very well. We shall wait."

"Mr. Canfield, what can you possibly add?"

"Passage to Zurich."

Elizabeth understood.

The doctor left and Canfield found that he could lie on his right side. The Swiss *Geheimpolizist* walked around to be nearer.

"Sit down, sir," said Canfield as the man drew up a chair. "What I'm going to tell you will seem foolish to someone like you and me who have to work for our livings." The field accountant winked. "It's a private matter—no harm to anyone outside the family, family business, but you can help. . . . Does your man speak English?"

The Swiss looked briefly at the uniformed policeman.

"No, monsieur."

"Good. As I say, you can help. Both the clean record of your fair city . . . and yourself."

The Swiss *Geheimpolizist* drew up his chair closer.
He was delighted.

The afternoon arrived. They had timed the train schedules to the quarter hour and had telephoned ahead for a limousine and chauffeur. Their train tickets had been purchased by the hotel, clearly spelling out the name of Scarlatti for preferred treatment and the finest accommodations available for the short trip to Zurich. Their luggage was sent downstairs an hour beforehand and deposited by the front entrance. The tags were legibly marked, the train compartments specified, and even the limousine service noted for the Zurich porters. Canfield figured that the lowest IQ in Europe could know the immediate itinerary of Elizabeth Scarlatti if he wished to.

The ride from the hotel to the station took about twelve minutes. One-half hour before the train for Zurich departed an old woman, with a heavy black veil, accompanied by a youngish man in a brand-new fedora, his left arm in a white sling, got into a limousine. They were escorted by two members of the Geneva police, who kept their hands on their holstered pistols.

No incident occurred, and the two travelers rushed into the station and immediately onto the train.

As the train left the Geneva platform, another elderly woman accompanied by a youngish man, this one in a Brooks Brothers hat, and also with his left arm in a sling but hidden by a topcoat, left the service entrance of the Hotel D'Accord. The elderly woman was dressed in the uniform of a Red Cross colonel, female division, complete with a garrison cap. The man driving was also a member of the International Red Cross. The two people rushed into the back seat, and the young man closed the door. He immediately took the cellophane off a thin cigar and said to the driver, "Let's go."

As the car sped out the narrow driveway, the old woman spoke disparagingly. "Really, Mr. Canfield! Must you smoke one of those awful things?"

"Geneva rules, lady. Prisoners are allowed packages from home."

Chapter Forty-three

Twenty-seven miles from Zurich is the town of Menziken. The Geneva train stopped for precisely four minutes, the time allotted for the loading of the railway post, and then proceeded on its inevitable, exact, fated ride up the tracks to its destination.

Five minutes out of Menziken, compartments D4 and D5 on Pullman car six were broken into simultaneously by two men in masks. Because neither compartment contained any passengers, and both toilet doors were locked, the masked men fired their pistols into the thin panels of the commodes, expecting to find the bodies when they opened the doors.

They found no one. Nothing.

As if predetermined, both masked men ran out into the narrow corridor and nearly collided with one another.

"Halt! Stop!" The shouts came from both ends of the Pullman corridor. The men calling were dressed in the uniforms of the Geneva police.

The two masked men did not stop. Instead they fired wildly in both directions.

Their shots were returned and the two men fell.

They were searched; no identifications were found. The Geneva police were pleased about that. They did not wish to get involved.

One of the fallen men, however, had a tattoo on his forearm: an insignia, recently given the term of swastika. And a third man, unseen, unmasked, not fallen, was first off the train at Zurich, and hurried to a telephone.

"Here we are at Aarau. You can rest up here for a while. Your clothes are in a flat on the second floor. I believe your car is parked in the rear and the keys are under the left seat." Their driver was English and Canfield liked that. The driver hadn't spoken a word since Geneva. The field accountant withdrew a large bill from his pocket and offered it to the man.

"Hardly necessary, sir," said the driver as he waved the bill aside without turning.

They waited until eight fifteen. It was a dark night with only half a moon shrouded by low clouds. Canfield had tried the car, driving it up and down a country road to get the feel of it, to get used to driving with only his right hand. The gas gauge registered *rempli* and they were ready.

More precisely, Elizabeth Scarlatti was ready.

She was like a gladiator, prepared to bleed or let blood. She was cold but intense. She was a killer.

And her weapons were paper—infinitely more dangerous than maces or triforks to her adversaries. She was also, as a fine gladiator must be, supremely confident.

It was more than her last *grande geste*, it was the culmination of a lifetime. Hers and Giovanni's. She would not fail him.

Canfield had studied and restudied the map; he knew the roads he had to take to reach Falke Haus. They would skirt the center of Zurich and head toward Kloten, turning right at the Schlieren fork and follow the central road toward Bulach. One mile to the left on the Winterthurstrasse would be the gates of Falke Haus.

He had pushed the car up to eighty-five miles an hour, and he had stopped at sixty within the space of fifty feet without causing a dislocation of the seats. The Geneva *Geheimpolizist* had done his job well. But then he was well paid. Damn near two years' wages at the going Swiss rate of Civil Service. And the car was licensed with the numbers no one would stop—for any reason—the Zurich police. How he had done it, Canfield didn't ask. Elizabeth suggested that it might have been the money.

"Is that all?" asked Canfield as he led Elizabeth Scarlatti toward the car. He referred to her single briefcase.

"It's enough," said the old woman as she followed him down the path.

"You had a couple of thousand pages, a hundred thousand figures!"

"They're meaningless now." Elizabeth held the briefcase on her lap as Canfield shut the car door.

"Suppose they ask you questions?" The field accountant inserted the key in the ignition.

"No doubt they will. And if they do, I'll answer." She didn't wish to talk.

They drove for twenty minutes and the roads were coming out right. Canfield was pleased with himself. He was a satisfied navigator. Suddenly Elizabeth spoke.

"There is one thing I haven't told you, nor have you seen fit to bring it up. It's only fair that I mention it now."

"What?"

"It's conceivable that neither of us will emerge from this conference alive. Have you considered that?"

Canfield had, of course, considered it. He had assumed the risk, if that was the justifiable word, since the Boothroyd incident. It had escalated to pronounced danger when he realized that Janet was possibly his for life. He became committed when he knew what her husband had done to her.

With the bullet through his shoulder, two inches from death, Matthew Canfield in his own way had become a gladiator in much the same manner as Elizabeth. His anger was paramount now.

"You worry about your problems, I'll worry about mine, okay?"

"Okay. . . . May I say that you've become quite dear to me. . . . Oh, stop that little-boy look! Save it for the ladies! I'm hardly one of them! Drive on!"

On Winterthurstrasse, three-tenths of a mile from Falke Haus there is a stretch of straight road paralleled on both sides by towering pine trees. Matthew Canfield pushed the accelerator down and drove the automobile as fast as it would go. It was five minutes to nine and he was determined that his passenger meet her appointment on time.

Suddenly in the far-off illumination of the head lamps, a man was signaling. He waved his hands, crisscrossing above his head, standing in the middle of the road. He was violently making the universal sign, stop—emergency. He did not move from the middle of the road in spite of Canfield's speed.

"Hold on!" Canfield rushed on, oblivious to the human being in his path.

As he did so, there were bursts of gunfire from both sides of the road. "Get down!" shouted Canfield. He continued to push the gas pedal, ducking as he did so, bobbing his head, watching the straight road as best he could. There was a piercing scream—pitched in a death note—from the far side of the road. One of the ambushers had been caught in the crossfire.

They passed the area, pieces of glass and metal scattered all over the seats.

"You okay?" Canfield had no time for sympathy.

"Yes. I'm all right. How much longer?"

"Not much. If we can make it. They may have gotten a tire."

"Even if they did, we can still drive?"

"Don't you worry! I'm not about to stop and ask for a jack!"

The gates of Falke Haus appeared and Canfield turned sharply into the road. It was a descending grade leading gently into a huge circle in front of an enormous flagstone porch with statuary placed every several feet. The front entrance, a large wooden door, was situated twenty feet beyond the center steps. Canfield could not get near it.

For there were at least a dozen long, black limousines lined up around the circle. Chauffeurs stood near them, idly chatting.

Canfield checked his revolver, placed it in his right-hand pocket, and ordered Elizabeth out of the car. He insisted that she slide across the seat and emerge from his side of the automobile.

He walked slightly behind her, nodding to the chauffeurs.

It was one minute after nine when a servant, formally dressed, opened the large wooden door.

They entered the great hall, a massive tabernacle of architectural indulgence. A second servant, also formally attired, gestured them toward another door. He opened it.

Inside was the longest table Matthew Canfield thought possible to build. It must have been fifty feet from end to end. And a good six to seven feet wide.

Seated around the massive table were fifteen or twenty men. All ages, from forty to seventy. All dressed in expensive suits. All looking toward Elizabeth Scarlatti. At the head of the table, half a room away, was an empty chair. It cried out to be filled, and Canfield wondered for a moment whether Elizabeth was to fill it. Then he realized that was not so. Her chair was at the foot of the table closest to them.

Who was to fill the empty chair?

No matter. There was no chair for him. He would stay by the wall and watch.

Elizabeth approached the table.

"Good evening, gentlemen. A number of us have met before. The rest of you I know by reputation, I can asure you."

The entire complement around the table rose as one body.

The man to the left of Elizabeth's chair circled and held it for her.

She sat down, and the men returned to their seats.

"I thank you. . . . But there seems to be one of us missing." Elizabeth stared at the chair fifty feet away directly in front of her eyes.

At that moment a door at the far end of the room opened and a tall man strutted in. He was dressed in the crisp, cold uniform of the German revolutionary. The dark brown shirt, the shining black belt across his chest and around his waist, the starched tan jodhpurs above the thick, heavy boots that came just below his knees.

The man's head was shaven, his face a distorted replica of itself.

"The chair is now taken. Does that satisfy you?"

"Not entirely. . . . Since I know, through one means or another, every person of consequence at this table, I should like to know who you are, sir."

"Kroeger. Heinrich Kroeger! Anything else, Madame Scarlatti?"

"Not a thing. Not a single thing . . . Herr Kroeger."

Chapter Forty-four

"Against my wishes and my better judgment, Madame Scarlatti, my associates are determined to hear what you have to say." The grotesque shaven-headed Heinrich Kroeger spoke. "My position has been made clear to you. I trust your memory serves you well about it."

There were whispers around the table. Looks were exchanged. None of the men were prepared for the news that Heinrich Kroeger had had prior contact with Elizabeth Scarlatti.

"My memory serves me very well. Your associates represent an aggregate of much wisdom and several centuries of experience. I suspect far in excess of your own on both counts—collectively and individually."

Most of the men simply lowered their eyes, some pressing their lips in slight smiles. Elizabeth slowly looked at each face around the table.

"We have an interesting board here, I see. Well represented. Well diversified. Some of us were enemies in war a few short years ago, but such

memories, by necessity, are short. . . . Let's see." Without singling out any
one individual, Elizabeth Scarlatti spoke rapidly, almost in a cadence. "My
own country has lost two members, I'm sad to note. But I don't believe
prayers are in order for Messrs. Boothroyd and Thornton. If they are, I'm
not the one to deliver them. But still, the United States is splendidly
represented by Mr. Gibson and Mr. Landor. Between them, they account for
nearly twenty percent of the vast oil interests in the American Southwest. To
say nothing of a joint expansion in the Canadian Northwest Territories.
Combined personal assets—two hundred and twenty-five million. . . . Our
recent adversary, Germany, brings us Herr von Schnitzler, Herr Kindorf,
and Herr Thyssen. I. G. Farben; the baron of Ruhr coal; the great steel
companies. Personal assets? Who can really tell these days in the Weimar?
Perhaps one hundred and seventy-five million, at the outside. . . . But
someone's missing from this group. I trust he's successfully being recruited. I
speak of Gustave Krupp. He would raise the ante considerably. . . . England
sends us Messrs. Masterson, Leacock, and Innes-Bowen. As powerful a
triumvirate as can be found in the British Empire. Mr. Masterson with half
the India imports, also Ceylon now, I understand; Mr. Leacock's major
portion of the British Stock Exchange; and Mr. Innes-Bowen. He owns the
largest single textile industry throughout Scotland and the Hebrides. Personal assets I place at three hundred million. . . . France has been generous,
too. Monsieur D'Almeida; I now realize that he is the true owner of the
Franco-Italian rail system, partially due to his Italian lineage, I'm sure. And
Monsieur Daudet. It there any among us who have not used some part of his
merchant fleet? Personal assets, one hundred and fifty million. . . . And
lastly, our neighbors to the north, Sweden. Herr Myrdal and Herr Olaffsen.
Understandably"—here Elizabeth looked pointedly at the strange-faced
man, her son, at the head of the table—"one of these gentlemen, Herr
Myrdal, has controlling interest in Donnenfeld, the most impressive firm on
the Stockholm exchange. While Herr Olaffsen's many companies merely
control the export of Swedish iron and steel. Personal assets are calculated at
one hundred and twenty-five million. . . . Incidentally, gentlemen, the term
personal assets denotes those holdings which can be converted easily, quickly,
and without endangering your markets. . . . Otherwise, I would not insult
you by placing such meager limits on your fortunes."

Elizabeth paused to place her briefcase directly in front of her. The men
around the table were aroused, apprehensive. Several were shocked at the
casual mention of what they believed was highly confidential information.
The Americans, Gibson and Landor, had quietly gone into the Canadian
venture unannounced, without legal sanction, violating the U.S.–Canadian
treaties. The Germans, von Schnitzler and Kindorf, had held secret conferences with Gustave Krupp—who was fighting desperately to remain neutral
for fear of a Weimar takeover. If these conferences were made known, Krupp
had sworn to expose them. The Frenchman, Louis François D'Almeida,
guarded with his very life the extent of his ownership of the Franco-Italian
rails. If it were known, it might well be confiscated by the republic. He had
purchased the majority shares from the Italian government through plain
bribery.

And Myrdal, the heavyset Swede, bulked his eyes in disbelief when
Elizabeth Scarlatti spoke so knowingly about the Stockholm exchange. His
own company had covertly absorbed Donnenfeld in one of the most
complicated mergers imaginable, made possible by the illegal transaction of

the American securities. If it became public knowledge, the Swedish law would step in, and he'd be ruined. Only the Englishmen seemed totally poised, totally proud of their achievements. But even this measure of equanimity was misleading. For Sydney Masterson, undisputed heir to the merchant domain of Sir Robert Live, had only recently concluded the Ceylon arrangements. They were unknown in the import–export world and there were certain agreements subject to question. Some might even say they constituted fraud.

Huddled, quiet-toned conferences took place around the table in the four languages. Elizabeth raised her voice sufficiently to be heard.

"I gather some of you are conferring with your aides—I assume they are your aides. If I'd realized this meeting made provisions for second-level negotiators, I'd have brought along my attorneys. They could have gossiped among themselves while we continue. The decisions we reach tonight, gentlemen, must be our own!"

Heinrich Kroeger sat on the edge of his chair. He spoke harshly, unpleasantly. "I wouldn't be so sure of any decisions. There are none to be made! You've told us nothing which couldn't be learned by any major accounting firm!"

A number of the men around the table—specifically the two Germans, D'Almeida, Gibson, Landor, Myrdal, and Masterson—avoided looking at him. For Kroeger was wrong.

"You think so? Perhaps. But them I've overlooked you, haven't I? . . . I shouldn't do that, you're obviously terribly important." Again, a number of the men around the table—excluding those mentioned—had traces of smiles on their lips.

"Your wit is as dull as you are." Elizabeth was pleased with herself. She was succeeding in this most important aspect of her appearance. She was reaching, provoking Ulster Stewart Scarlett. She continued without acknowledging his remark.

"Strangely obtained assets of two hundred and seventy million sold under the most questionable circumstances would necessitate a loss of at least fifty percent, possibly sixty percent of market value. I'll grant you the least, so I shall hazard an estimate of one hundred and thirty-five million dollars at the current rates of exchange. One hundred and eight, if you've been weak."

Matthew Canfield lurched from the wall, then held his place.

The men around the table were astonished. The hum of voices increased perceptibly. Aides were shaking their heads, nodding in agreement, raising their eyebrows unable to answer. Each participant thought he knew something of the others. Obviously, none were this knowledgeable of Heinrich Kroeger. They had not even been sure of his status at this table. Elizabeth interrupted the commotion.

"However, Mister Kroeger, surely you know that theft, when eminently provable, is merely subject to proper identification before steps can be taken. There are international courts of extradition. Therefore, it is conceivable that your assets might be calculated at . . . zero!"

A silence fell over the table as the gentlemen, along with their assistants, gave Heinrich Kroeger their full attention. The words *theft*, *courts*, and *extradition* were words they could not accept at this table. They were dangerous words. Kroeger, the man many of them vaguely feared for reasons solely associated with his enormous influence within both camps, was now warned.

"Don't threaten me, old woman." Kroeger's voice was low, confident. He sat back in his chair and glared at his mother at the opposite end of the long table. "Don't make charges unless you can substantiate them. If you're prepared to attempt that, I'm ready to counter. . . . If you or your colleagues were outnegotiated, this is no place to cry. You don't get sympathy here! I might even go so far as to say you're on treacherous ground. Remember that!" He kept staring until Elizabeth could no longer stand the sight of his eyes. She looked away.

She was not prepared to do anything—not with him, not with Heinrich Kroeger. She would not gamble the lives of her family more than she had already. She would not wager at this table the name of Scarlatti. Not that way. Not now. There was another way.

Kroeger had won the point. It was obvious to all, and Elizabeth had to rush headlong on so that none would dwell upon her loss.

"Keep your assets. They are quite immaterial."

Around the table the phrase "quite immaterial" when applied to such millions was impressive. Elizabeth knew it would be.

"Gentlemen. Before we were interrupted, I gave you all, by national groupings, the personal assets calculated to the nearest five million for each contingent. I felt it was more courteous than breaking down each individual's specific worth—some things are sacred, after all. However, I was quite unfair, as several of you know. I alluded to a number of—shall we say, delicate negotiations, I'm sure you believed were inviolate. Treacherous to you—to use Mr. Kroeger's words—if they were known within your own countries."

Seven of the Zurich twelve were silent. Five were curious.

"I refer to my cocitizens, Mr. Gibson and Mr. Lander. To Monsieur D'Almeida, Sydney Masterson, and of course, to the brilliant Herr Myrdal. I should also include two-thirds of Germany's investors—Herr von Schnitzler and Herr Kindorf, but for different reasons, as I'm sure they realize."

No one spoke. No one turned to his aides. All eyes were upon Elizabeth.

"I don't intend to remain unfair in this fashion, gentlemen. I have something for each one of you."

A voice other than Kroeger's spoke up. It was the Englishman, Sydney Masterson.

"May I ask the point of all this? All this . . . incidental intelligence? I'm sure you've been most industrious—highly accurate, too, speaking for myself. But none of us here have entered the race for a Jesus medal. Surely, you know that."

"I do, indeed. If it were otherwise, I wouldn't be here tonight."

"Then why? Why this?" The accent was German. The voice belonged to the blustering baron of the Ruhr Valley, Kindorf.

Masterson continued. "Your cablegram, madame—we all received the same—specifically alluded to areas of mutual interest. I believe you went so far as to say the Scarlatti assets might be at our joint disposal. Most generous, indeed. . . . But now I must agree with Mr. Kroeger. You sound as though you're threatening us, and I'm not at all sure I like it."

"Oh, come, Mr. Masterson! You've never held out promises of English gold to half the minor potentates in the backwaters of India? Herr Kindorf has not openly bribed his unions to strike with pledges of increased wages once the French are out of the Ruhr? Please! You insult all of us! Of course, I'm here to threaten you! And I can assure you, you'll like it less as I go on!"

Masterson rose from the table. Several others moved their chairs. The air was hostile. "I shall not listen further," said Masterson.

"Then tomorrow at noon the Foreign Office, the British Stock exchange, and the board of directors of the English Importers Collective will receive detailed specifics of your highly illegal agreements in Ceylon! Your commitments are enormous! The news might just initiate a considerable run on your holdings!"

Masterson stood by his chair. "Be damned!" Were the only words he uttered as he returned to his chair. The table once again fell silent. Elizabeth opened her briefcase.

"I have here an envelope for each of you. Your names are typed on the front. Inside each envelope is an accounting of your individual worths. Your strengths. Your weaknesses. . . . There is one envelope missing. The . . . influential, very important Mr. Kroeger does not have one. Frankly, it's insignificant."

"I warn you!"

"So very sorry, Mr. Kroeger." Again the words were rapidly spoken, but this time no one was listening. Each one's concentration was on Elizabeth Scarlatti and her briefcase. "Some envelopes are thicker than others, but none should place too great an emphasis on this factor. We all know the negligibility of wide diversification after a certain point." Elizabeth reached into her leather case.

"You are a witch!" Kindorf's heavy accent was now guttural, the veins stood out in his temples.

"Here. I shall pass them out. And as each of you peruse your miniature portfolios I shall continue talking, which, I know, will please you."

The envelopes were passed down both sides of the table. Some were torn open immediately, hungrily. Others, like the cards of experienced poker players, were handled carefully, cautiously.

Matthew Canfield stood by the wall, his left arm smarting badly in the sling, his right hand in his pocket. sweatily clutching his revolver. Since Elizabeth had identified Ulster Scarlett with the 270 million, he could not take his eyes off him. This man called Heinrich Kroeger. This hideous, arrogant son of a bitch was the man he wanted! This was the filthy bastard who had done it all! This was Janet's personal hell.

"I see you all have your envelopes. Except, of course, the ubiquitous Mr. Kroeger. Gentlemen, I promised you I would not be unfair and I shan't be. There are five of you who can not begin to appreciate the influence of Scarlatti unless you have, as they say in cheap merchandising, samples applicable to you alone. Therefore, as you read the contents of your envelopes, I shall briefly touch on these sensitive areas."

Several of the men who had been reading shifted their eyes toward Elizabeth without moving their heads. Others put the papers down defiantly. Some handed the pages to aides and stared at the old woman. Elizabeth glanced over her shoulder at Matthew Canfield. She was worried about him. She knew he, at last, faced Ulster Scarlett, and the pressure on him was immense. She tried to catch his eye. She tried to reassure him with a look, a confident smile.

He would not look at her. She saw only the hatred in his eyes as he stared at the man called Heinrich Kroeger.

"I shall delineate alphabetically, gentlemen. . . . Monsieur Daudet, the Republic of France would be reluctant to continue awarding franchises to your fleet if they were aware of those ships under Paraguayan flag which carried supplies to France's enemies in time of war." Daudet remained motionless, but Elizabeth was amused to see the three Englishmen bristle at the Frenchmen. The predictable, contradictory British!

"Oh, come, Mr. Innes-Bowen. You may not have run ammunition, but how many neutral ships were loaded off how many piers in India with textile cargoes bound for Bremerhaven and Cuxhaven during the same period? . . . And Mr. Leacock. You can't really forget your fine Irish heritage, can you? The Sinn Féin has prospered well under your tutelage. Monies funneled through you to the Irish rebellion cost the lives of thousands of British soldiers at a time when England could least afford them! And quiet, calm Herr Olaffsen. The crown prince of Swedish steel. Or is he the king now? He might well be, for the Swedish government paid him several fortunes for untold hundreds of tons of low-carbon ingot. However, they didn't come from his own superior factories. They were shipped from inferior mills half a world away—from Japan!"

Elizabeth reached into her briefcase once again. The men around the table were like corpses, immobile, only their minds were working. For Heinrich Kroeger, Elizabeth Scarlatti had placed the seal of approval on her own death warrant. He sat back and relaxed. Elizabeth withdrew a thin booklet from her briefcase.

"Lastly we come to Herr Thyssen. He emerges with the least pain. No grand fraud, no treason, only minor illegality and major embarrassment. Hardly a fitting tribute to the house of August Thyssen." She threw the booklet into the center of the table. "Filth, gentlemen, just plain filth. Fritz Thyssen, pornographer! Purveyor of obscenity. Books, pamphlets, even motion pictures. Printed and filmed in Thyssen warehouses in Cairo. Every government on the Continent has condemned the unknown source. There he is, gentlemen. Your associate."

For a long moment no one spoke. Each man was concerned with himself. Each calculated the damage that could result from old Scarlatti's disclosures. In every instance the loss was accompanied by degrees of disgrace. Reputations could hang in balance. The old woman had issued twelve indictments and personally returned twelve verdicts of guilty. Somehow, no one considered the thirteenth, Heinrich Kroeger.

Sydney Masterson pierced the belligerent air with a loud, manufactured cough. "Very well, Madame Scarlatti, you've made the point I referred to earlier. However, I think I should remind you that we are not impotent men. Charges and countercharges are parts of our lives. Solicitors can refute every accusation you've made, and I can assure you that lawsuits for unmitigated slander would be in the forefront. . . . After all, when gutter tactics are employed, there are expedient replies. . . . If you think we fear disdain, believe me when I tell you that public opinion has been molded by far less money than is represented at this table!"

The gentlemen of Zurich took confidence in Masterson's words. There were nods of agreement.

"I don't for one second doubt you, Mr. Masterson. Any of you. . . . Missing personnel files, opportunistic executives—sacrificial goats. Please, gentlemen! I only contend that you wouldn't welcome the trouble. Or the anxiety which goes with such distasteful matters."

"*Non*, Madame." Claude Daudet was outwardly cool but inwardly petrified. Perhaps his Zurich associates did not know the French people. A firing squad was not out of the question. "You are correct. Such troubles are to be avoided. So, then what is next? What is it you prepare for us, eh?"

Elizabeth paused. She wasn't quite sure why. It was an instinct, an intuitive need to turn around and look at the field accountant.

Matthew Canfield had not budged from his position by the wall. He was a pathetic sight. His jacket had fallen away from his left shoulder revealing the dark black sling, his right hand still plunged in his pocket. He seemed to be swallowing continuously, trying to keep himself aware of his surroundings. Elizabeth noticed that he now avoided looking at Ulster Scarlett. He seemed, in essence, to be trying to hang on to his sanity.

"Excuse me, gentlemen." Elizabeth rose from her chair and crossed to Canfield. She whispered quietly to him. "Take hold of yourself. I demand it! There's nothing to fear. Not in this room!"

Canfield spoke slowly, without moving his lips. She could barely hear him, but what she heard startled her. Not for its content, but for the way in which he said it. Matthew Canfield was now among the ranks in this room in Zurich. He had joined them; he had become a killer, too.

"Say what you have to say and get it over with. . . . I want him. I'm sorry, but I want him. Look at him now, lady, because he's a dead man."

"Control yourself! Such talk will serve neither of us." She turned and walked back to her chair. She stood behind it while she spoke. "As you may have noticed, gentlemen, my young friend has been seriously wounded. Thanks to all of you . . . or one of you, in an attempt to prevent my reaching Zurich. The act was cowardly and provocative in the extreme."

The men looked at each other.

Daudet, whose imagination would not stop conjuring pictures of national disgrace or the firing squad, answered quickly. "Why would any here take such action, Madame Scarlatti? We are not maniacs. We are businessmen. No one sought to prevent your coming to Zurich. Witness, madame, we are all here."

Elizabeth looked at the man called Kroeger.

"One of you violently opposed this conference. We were fired upon less than a half hour ago."

The men looked at Heinrich Kroeger. Some were becoming angry. This Kroeger was, perhaps, too reckless.

"No." He answered simply and emphatically, returning their stares. "I agreed to your coming. If I'd wanted to stop you, I'd have stopped you."

For the first time since the meeting began, Heinrich Kroeger looked at the sporting goods salesman at the far end of the room, half concealed in the poor light. He had reacted with only moderate surprise when he realized Elizabeth Scarlatti had brought him to Zurich. Moderate because he knew Elizabeth's penchant for employing the unusual both in methods and personnel, and because she probably had no one else around she could browbeat into silence as easily as this money-hungry social gadfly. He'd be a convenient chauffeur, a manservant. Kroeger hated the type.

Or was he anything else?

Why had the salesman stared at him? Had Elizabeth told him anything? She wouldn't be that big a fool. The man was the sort who'd blackmail in a minute.

One thing was sure. He'd have to be killed.

But who had tried to kill him previously? Who had tried to stop Elizabeth? And why?

The same question was being considered by Elizabeth Scarlatti. For she believed Kroeger when he disavowed the attempts on their lives.

"Please continue, Madame Scarlatti." It was Fritz Thyssen, his cherubic face still flushed with anger over Elizabeth's disclosure of his Cairo trade. He had removed the booklet from the center of the table.

"I shall." She approached the side of her chair but did not sit down. Instead, she reached once more into her briefcase. "I have one thing further, gentlemen. With it we can conclude our business, and decisions can be made. There is a copy for each of the twelve remaining investors. Those with aides will have to share them. My apologies, Mr. Kroeger, I find I haven't one for you." From her position at the end of the table she distributed twelve slender manila envelopes. They were sealed, and as the men passed them down, the investors taking one apiece, it was apparent that each found it difficult not to rip open the top and withdraw the contents at once. But none wished to betray such obvious anxiety.

Finally, as each of the twelve held his envelope in front of him, one by one the men began to open them.

For nearly two minutes the only sound was the rustling of pages. Otherwise, silence. Even breathing was seemingly suspended. The men from Zurich were mesmerized by what they saw. Elizabeth spoke.

"Yes, gentlemen. What you hold in your hands is the scheduled liquidation of the Scarlatti Industries. . . . So that you have no illusions of doubt concerning the validity of this document, you will note that after each subdivision of holdings is typed the names of the individuals, corporations, or syndicates who are the purchasers. . . . Every one of those mentioned, the individuals as well as the organizations, are known to each of you. If not personally, then certainly by reputation. You know their capabilities, and I'm sure you're not unaware of their ambitions. Within the next twenty-four hours they will own Scarlatti."

For most of the Zurich men Elizabeth's sealed information was the confirmation of the whispered rumors. Word had reached them that something unusual was taking place at Scarlatti. Some sort of unloading under strange circumstances.

So this was it. The head of Scarlatti was getting out.

"A massive operation, Madame Scarlatti." Olaffsen's low Swedish voice vibrated throughout the room. "But to repeat Daudet's question, what is it you prepare us for?"

"Please take note of the bottom figure on the last page, gentlemen. Although I'm quite sure you all have." The rustle of pages. Each man had turned swiftly to the final page. "It reads seven hundred and fifteen million dollars. . . . The combined, immediately convertible assets of this table, placed at the highest figure is one billion, one hundred and ten million. . . . Therefore, a disparity of three hundred and ninety-five million exists between us. . . . Another way to approach this difference is to calculate it from the opposite direction. The Scarlatti liquidation will realize sixty-four point four percent of this table's holdings—if, indeed, you gentlemen could convert your personal assets in such a manner as to preclude financial panics."

Silence.

A number of the Zurich men reached for their first envelopes. The breakdowns of their own worth.

One of these was Sydney Masterson, who turned to Elizabeth with an unamused smile. "And what you're saying, I presume, Madame Scarlatti, is that this sixty-four point plus percent is the club you hold over our heads?"

"Precisely, Mr. Masterson."

"My dear lady, I really must question your sanity . . ."

"I wouldn't, if I were you."

"Then I shall, Frau Scarlatti." I. G. Farben's von Schnitzler spoke in a disagreeable manner, lounging back in his chair as if toying verbally with an imbecile. "To accomplish what you have must have been a costly sacrifice. . . . I wonder to what purpose? You can not buy what there is not to sell. . . . We are not a public corporation. You can not force into defeat something which does not exist!" His German lisp was pronounced, his arrogance every bit as unattractive as reputed. Elizabeth disliked him intensely.

"Quite correct, von Schnitzler."

"Then, perhaps"—the German laughed—"you have been a foolish woman. I would not wish to absorb your losses. I mean, really, you can not go to some mythical *Baumeister* and tell him you have more funds than we—therefore, he must drive us out into the streets!"

Several of the Zurich men laughed.

"That, of course, would be the simplest, would it not? The appeal to one entity, negotiating with one power. It's a shame that I can't do that. It would be so much easier, so much less costly. . . . But, I'm forced to take another road, an expensive one. . . . I should put that another way. I have taken it, gentlemen. It has been accomplished. The time is running out for its execution."

Elizabeth looked at the men of Zurich. Some had their eyes riveted on her—watching for the slightest waver of confidence, the smallest sign of bluff. Others fixed their stares on inanimate objects—caring only to filter the words, the tone of her voice, for a false statement or a lapse of judgment. These were men who moved nations with a single gesture, a solitary word.

"At the start of tomorrow's business, subject to time zones, enormous transfers of Scarlatti capital will have been made to the financial centers of the five nations represented at this table. In Berlin, Paris, Stockholm, London, and New York, negotiations have already been completed for massive purchases on the open market of the outstanding shares of your central companies. . . . Before noon of the next business day, gentlemen, Scarlatti will have considerable, though, of course, minority ownership in many of your vast enterprises. . . . Six hundred and seventy million dollars' worth! . . . Do you realize what this means, gentlemen?"

Kindorf roared. "*Ja!* You will drive up the prices and makes us fortunes! You will own nothing!"

"My dear lady, you are extraordinary." Innes-Bowen's textile prices had remained conservative. He was overjoyed at the prospects.

D'Almeida, who realized she could not enter his Franco-Italian rails, took another view. "You can not purchase one share of my property, madame!"

"Some of you are more fortunate than others, Monsieur D'Almeida."

Leacock, the financier, the gentlest trace of a brogue in his cultivated voice, spoke up. "Granting what you say, and it is entirely possible, Madame Scarlatti, what have we suffered? . . . We have not lost a daughter, but gained a minor associate." He turned to the others who, he hoped, would find humor in his analogy.

Elizabeth held her breath before speaking. She waited until the men of Zurich were once again focused on her.

"I said before noon Scarlatti would be in the position I outlined. . . . One hour later a tidal wave will form in the Kurfuerstendamm in Berlin and end in New York's Wall Street! One hour later Scarlatti will divest itself of these holdings at a fraction of their cost! I have estimated three cents on the dollar. . . . Simultaneously, every bit of information Scarlatti has learned of your questionable activities will be released to the major wire services in each of your countries. . . . You might sustain slander by itself, gentlemen. You will not be the same men when it is accompanied by financial panic! Some of you will remain barely intact. Some will be wiped out. The majority of you will be affected disastrously!"

After the briefest moment of shocked silence, the room exploded. Aides were questioned peremptorily. Answers were bellowed to be heard.

Heinrich Kroeger rose from his chair and screamed at the men. "Stop! Stop! You damn fools, stop it! She'd never do it! She's bluffing!"

"Do you really think so?" Elizabeth shouted above the voices.

"I'll kill you, you bitch!"

"You are demented, Frau Scarlatti!"

"Try it . . . Kroeger! Try it!" Matthew Canfield stood by Elizabeth, his eyes bloodshot with fury as he stared at Ulster Stewart Scarlett.

"Who the hell are you, you lousy peddler?" The man called Kroeger, hands gripping the table, returned Canfield's stare and screeched to be heard by the salesman.

"Look at me good! I'm your executioner!"

"What!"

The man called Heinrich Kroeger squinted his misshapen eyes. He was bewildered. Who was this parasite? But he could not take the time to think. The voices of the men of Zurich had reached a crescendo. They were now shouting at each other.

Heinrich Kroeger pounded the table. He had to get control. He had to get them quiet. "Stop it! . . . Listen to me! If you'll listen to me, I'll tell you why she can't do it! She can't do it, I tell you!"

One by one the voices became quieter and finally trailed off into silence. The men of Zurich watched Kroeger. He pointed at Elizabeth Scarlatti.

"I know this bitch-woman! I've seen her do this before! She gets men together, powerful men, and frightens them. They go into panic and sell out! She gambles on *fear*, you cowards! On fear!"

Daudet spoke quietly. "You have answered nothing. Why can't she do as she says?"

Kroeger did not take his eyes off Elizabeth Scarlatti as he replied. "Because to do it would destroy everything she's ever fought for. It would collapse Scarlatti!"

Sydney Masterson spoke just above a whisper. "That would appear to be obvious. The question remains unanswered."

"She couldn't live without that power! Take my word for it! She couldn't live without it!"

"That's an opinion," said Elizabeth Scarlatti facing her son at the opposite end of the table. "Do you ask the majority of those at this table to risk everything on your opinion?"

"God damn you!"

"This Kroeger's right, honey." The Texas drawl was unmistakable. "You'll ruin yourself. You won't have a pot to piss in."

"Your languages matches the crudity of your operations, Mr. Landor."

"I don't give pig piss for words, old lady. I do about money, and that's what we're talkin' about. Why do you want to pull this here crap?"

"That I'm doing it is sufficient, Mr. Landor. . . . Gentlemen, I said time was running out. The next twenty-four hours will either be a normal Tuesday or a day which will never be forgotten in the financial capitals of our world. . . . Some here will survive. Most of you will not. Which will it be, gentlemen? . . . I submit that in light of everything I've said, it's a poor fiscal decision wherein the majority allows the minority to cause its destruction."

"What is it you want of us?" Myrdal was a cautious bargainer. "A few might rather weather your threats than accept your demands. . . . Sometimes I think it is all a game. What are your demands?"

"That this . . . association be disbanded at once. That all financial and political ties in Germany with whatever factions be severed without delay! That those of you who have been entrusted with appointments to the Allied Controls Commission resign immediately!"

"No! No! No! No!" Heinrich Kroeger was enraged. He banged his fist with all his might upon the table. "This organization has taken years to build! We will control the economy of Europe. We will control all Europe! We will do it!"

"Hear me, gentlemen! Mr. Myrdal said it's a game! Of course, It's a game! A game we expend our lives on. Our souls on! It consumes us, and we demand more and more and more until, at last, we crave our own destruction. . . . Herr Kroeger says I can't live without the power I've sought and gained. He may be right, gentlemen! Perhaps it's time for me to reach that logical end, the end which I now crave and for which I'm willing to pay the price. . . . Of course, I'll do as I say, gentlemen. I welcome death!"

"Let it be yours, then, not ours." Sydney Masterson understood.

"So be it, Mr. Masterson. I'm not overwhelmed, you know. I leave to all of you the necessity of coping with this strange new world we've entered. Don't think for a minute, gentlemen, that I can't understand you! Understand what you've done. Most horridly, why you've done it! . . . You look around your personal kingdoms and you're frightened. You see your power threatened—by theories, governments, strange-sounding concepts which eat away at your roots. You have an overpowering anxiety to protect the feudal system which spawned you. And well you should, perhaps. It won't last long. . . . But you will *not* do it this way!"

"Since you understand us, why do you stop us? This undertaking protects all of us. Ultimately yourself as well. Why do you stop us?" D'Almeida could lose the Franco-Italian rails and survive, if only the remainder could be saved.

"It always starts that way. The greater good. . . . Let's say I stop you because what you're doing is a far greater blemish than it is a cure. And that's all I'll say about it!"

"From you, that's ludicrous! I tell you again, she won't do it!" Kroeger pounded the flat of his hand on the table, but no one paid much attention to him.

"When you say time is running out, Madame Scarlatti, how do you mean it? From what you said, I gathered time had run out. The expensive road had been taken. . . ."

"There's a man in Geneva, Mr. Masterson, who's awaiting a phone call from me. If he receives that phone call, a cable will be sent to my offices in New York. If that cable arrives, the operation is canceled. If it doesn't, it's executed on schedule."

"That's impossible! Such complexity untangled with a cablegram? I don't believe you." Monsieur Daudet was certain of ruin.

"I assume considerable financial penalties by the action."

"You assume more than that, I would suspect, madame. You'll never be trusted again. Scarlatti will be isolated!"

"It's a prospect, Mr. Masterson. Not a conclusion. The marketplace is flexible. . . . Well, gentlemen? Your answer?"

Sydney Masterson rose from his chair. "Make your phone call. There's no other choice, is there, gentlemen?"

The men of Zurich looked at each other. Slowly they began to get out of their chairs, gathering the papers in front of them.

"It's finished. I am out of it." Kindorf folded the manila envelope and put it in his pocket.

"You're a beastly tiger. I shouldn't care to meet you in the arena with an army at my back." Leacock stood erect.

"You may be bullshitter, but I'm not gonna slip on it!" Landor nudged Gibson, who found it difficult to adjust.

"We can't be sure. . . . That's our problem. We can't be sure," said Gibson.

"Wait! Wait! Wait a minute!" Heinrich Kroeger began to shout. "You do this! You walk out! You're dead! . . . Every God damn one of you leeches is dead! Leeches! Yellow-bellied leeches! . . . You suck our blood; you make agreements with us. Then you walk out? . . . Afraid for your little businesses? You God damn Jew bastards! We don't need you! Any of you! But you're going to need us! We'll cut you up and feed you to dogs! God damn swine!" Kroeger's face was flushed. His words spewed out, tumbling over one another.

"Stop it, Kroeger!" Masterson took a step toward the raving man with the splotched face. "It's finished! Can't you understand? It's finished!"

"Stay where you are, you scum, you English fairy!" Kroeger drew the pistol from his holster. Canfield, standing by Elizabeth, saw that it was a long-barreled forty-five and would blast half a man's body off with one shot.

"Stay where you are! . . . Finished! Nothing's finished until I say it's finished. God damn filthy pigs! Frightened little slug worms! We're too far along! . . . No one will stop us now! . . ." He waved the pistol towards Elizabeth and Canfield. "Finished! I'll tell you who's finished! She is! . . . Get out of my way." He started down the left side of the table as the Frenchman, Daudet, squealed.

"Don't do it, monsieur! Don't kill her! You do, and we are ruined!"

"I warn you, Kroeger! You muder her and you'll answer to us! We'll not be intimidated by you! We'll not destroy ourselves because of you!" Masterson stood at Kroeger's side, their shoulders nearly touching. The Englishman would not move.

Without a word, without warning, Heinrich Kroeger pointed his pistol at Masterson's stomach and fired. The shot was deafening and Sydney Masterson was jackknifed into the air. He fell to the floor, blood drenching his entire front, instantaneously dead.

The eleven men of Zurich gasped, some screamed in horror at the sight of the bloody corpse. Heinrich Kroeger kept walking. Those in his path got out of his way.

Elizabeth Scarlatti held her place. She locked her eyes with those of her killer son. "I curse the day you were born. You revile the house of your father. But know this, Heinrich Kroeger, and know it well!" The old woman's voice filled the cavernous room. Her power was such that her son was momentarily stunned, staring at her in hatred as she pronounced his sentence of execution. "Your identity will be spread across every front page of every newspaper in the civilized world after I'm dead! You will be hunted down for what you are! A madman, a murderer, a thief! And every man in this room every investor in Zurich, will be branded your associate if they let you live this night!"

An uncontrollable rage exploded in the misshapen eyes of Heinrich Kroeger. His body shook with fury as he lashed at a chair in front of him sending it crashing across the floor. To kill was not enough. He had to kill at close range, he had to see the life and mind of Elizabeth Scarlatti detonated into oblivion in front of his eyes.

Matthew Canfield held the trigger of his revolver in his right-hand pocket. He had never fired from his pocket and he knew that if he missed he and Elizabeth would die. He was not sure how long he could wait. He would aim in the vicinity of the approaching man's chest, the largest target facing him. He waited until he could wait no longer.

The report of the small revolver and the impact of the bullet into Scarlett's shoulder was so much of a shock that Kroeger, for a split second, widened his eyes in disbelief.

It was enough, just enough for Canfield.

With all his strength he crashed into Elizabeth with his right shoulder sending her frail body toward the floor out of Kroeger's line of sight as he, Canfield, flung himself to the left. He withdrew his revolver and fired again, rapidly, into the man called Heinrich Kroeger.

Kroeger's huge pistol went off into the floor as he crumpled over.

Canfield staggered up, forgetting the unbearable pain in his left arm, which had been crushed under the weight of his own body. He leaped on Ulster Stewart Scarlett, wrenching the pistol from the iron grip. He began hitting the face of Heinrich Kroeger with the barrel. He could not stop.

Destroy the face! Destroy the horrible face!

Finally he was pulled off.

"*Gott!* He's dead! Halt! Stop! You can do no more!" The large, strong Fritz Thyssen held him.

Matthew Canfield felt weak and sank to the floor.

The men of Zurich had gathered around. Several helped Elizabeth, while the others bent over Heinrich Kroeger.

Rapid knocking came from the door leading to the hall.

Von Schnitzler took command. "Let them in!" he ordered in his thick German accent.

D'Almeida walked swiftly to the door and opened it. A number of chauffeurs stood at the entrance. It occurred to Canfield as he watched them that these men were not simply drivers of automobiles. He had good reason. They were armed.

As he lay there on the floor in terrible pain and shock, Canfield saw a brutish-looking blond man with close-cropped hair bent over the body of Heinrich Kroeger. He pushed the others away for the briefest instant while he pulled back the misshapen lid of one eye.

And then Canfield wondered if the agony of the last hours had played tricks with his sight, corrupted the infallible process of vision.

Or had the blond man bent his head down and whispered something into Heinrich Kroeger's ear?

Was Heinrich Kroeger still alive?

Von Schnitzler stood over Canfield. "He will be taken away. I have ordered a coup de grace. No matter, he is dead. It is finished." The obese von Schnitzler then shouted further commands in German to the uniformed chauffeurs around Kroeger. Several started to lift up the lifeless form but they were blocked by the blond man with the close-cropped hair. He shouldered them out of the way, not letting them touch the body.

He alone lifted Heinrich Kroeger off the floor and carried him out the door. The others followed.

"How's she?" Canfield gestured toward Elizabeth, who was seated in a chair. She was staring at the door through which the body had been taken, staring at the man no one knew was her son.

"Fine! She can make her call now!" Leacock was trying his best to be decisive.

Canfield rose from the floor and crossed to Elizabeth. He put his hand on her wrinkled cheek. He could not help himself.

Tears were falling down the ridges of her face.

And then Matthew Canfield looked up. He could hear the sound of a powerful automobile racing away. He was bothered.

Von Schnitzler had told him he'd ordered a coup de grace.

Yet no shot was fired.

A mile away, on the Winterthurstrasse, two men dragged the body of a dead man to a truck. They weren't sure what to do. The dead man had hired them, hired them all to stop the automobile heading to Falke Haus. He had paid them in advance, they had insisted upon it. Now he was dead, killed by a bullet meant for the driver of the automobile an hour ago. As they dragged the body over the rocky incline toward the truck, the blood from the mouth spewed onto the perfectly matted waxed moustache.

The man named Poole was dead.

PART FOUR

Chapter Forty-five

Major Matthew Canfield, aged forty-five—about to be forty-six—stretched his legs diagonally across the back of the army car. They had entered the township of Oyster Bay, and the sallow-complexioned sergeant broke the silence.

"Getting close, Major. You better wake up."

Wake up. It should be as easy as that. The perspiration streamed down his face. His heart was rhythmically pounding an unknown theme.

"Thank you, Sergeant."

The car swung east down Harbor Road toward the ocean drive. As they came closer to his home, Major Matthew Canfield began to tremble. He grabbed his wrists, held his breath, bit the front of his tongue. He could not fall apart. He could not allow himself the indulgence of self-pity. He could not do that to Janet. He owed her so much.

The sergeant blithely turned into the blue stone driveway and stopped at the path, which lead to the front entrance of the large beach estate. The sergeant enjoyed driving out to Oyster Bay with his rich major. There was always lots of good food, in spite of rationing, and the liquor was always the best. No cheap stuff for the Camshaft, as he was known in the enlisted man's barracks.

The major slowly got out of the car. The sergeant was concerned. Something was wrong with the major. He hoped it didn't mean they'd have to drive back to New York. The old man seemed to have trouble standing up.

"Okay, Major?"

"Okay, Sergeant. . . . How'd you like to bunk in the boathouse tonight?" He did not look at the sergeant as he spoke.

"Sure! Great, Major!" It was where he always bunked. The boathouse apartment had a full kitchen and plenty of booze. Even a telephone. But the sergeant didn't have any signal that he could use it yet. He decided to try his luck. "Will you need me, Major? Could I call a couple of friends here?"

The major walked up the path. He called back quietly "Do whatever you like, Sergeant. Just stay away from that radiophone. Is that understood?"

"You betcha, Major!" The sergeant gunned the engine and drove down toward the beach.

Matthew Canfield stood in front of the white, scalloped door with the sturdy hurricane lamps on both sides.

His home.

Janet.

The door opened and she stood there. The slightly graying hair, which she would not retouch. The upturned nose above the delicate, sensitive mouth.

The bright, wide, brown searching eyes. The gentle loveliness of her face. The comforting concern she radiated.

"I heard the car. No one drives to the boathouse like Evans! . . . Matthew. Matthew! My darling! You're crying!"

Chapter Forty-six

The plane, an Army B-29 transport, descended from the late-afternoon clouds to the airport in Lisbon. An Air Force corporal walked down the aisle.

"Please buckle all seat belts! No smoking! We'll be down in four minutes." He spoke in a monotone, aware that his passengers had to be important, so he would be more important, but courteous, when he had to tell them something.

The young man next to Matthew Canfield had said very little since their takeoff from Shannon. A number of times the major tried to explain that they were taking air routes out of range of the *Luftwaffe*, and that there was nothing to worry about. Andrew Scarlett had merely mumbled understood approval and had gone back to his magazines.

The car at the Lisbon airport was an armored Lincoln with two OSS personnel in the front. The windows could withstand short-range gunfire, and the automobile was capable of 120 miles an hour. They had to drive thirty-two miles up the Tejo River road to an airfield in Alenguer.

At Alenguer the man and boy boarded a low-flying, specially constructed Navy TBF with no markings for the trip to Bern. There would be no stops. Throughout the route, English, American, and Free French fighters were scheduled to intercept and protect to the destination.

At Bern they were met by a Swiss government vehicle, flanked by a motorcycle escort of eight men—one at the front, one at the rear, and three on each side. All were armed in spite of the Geneva pact, which prohibited such practices.

They drove to a village twenty-odd miles to the north, toward the German border. Kreuzlingen.

They arrived at a small inn, isolated from the rest of civilization, and the man and boy got out of the car. The driver sped the automobile away, and the motorcycle complement disappeared.

Matthew Canfield led the boy up the steps to the entrance of the inn.

Inside the lobby could be heard the wailing sound of an accordion, echoing from what was apparently a sparsely populated dining room. The high-ceilinged entry room was inhospitable, conveying the feeling that guests were not welcome.

Matthew Canfield and Andrew Scarlett approached the counter, which served as a front desk.

"Please, ring through to room six that April Red is here."

As the clerk plugged in his line, the boy suddenly shook. Canfield grabbed his arm and held him.

They walked up the stairs, and the two men stood in front of the door marked with the numeral six.

"There's nothing I can tell you now, Andy, except that we're here for one person. At least that's why I'm here. Janet. Your mother. Try to remember that."

The boy took a deep breath. "I'll try, Dad. Open the door! Jesus! Open the door!"

The room was dimly lit by small lamps on small tables. It was ornate in the fashion the Swiss felt proper for tourists—heavy rugs and solid furniture, overstuffed chairs and much antimacassar.

At the far end sat a man in half shadow. The spill of light angled sharply down across his chest but did not illuminate his face. The figure was dressed in brown tweeds, the jacket a combination of heavy cloth and leather.

He spoke in a throaty, harsh voice. "You are?"

"Canfield and April Red. Kroeger?"

"Shut the door."

Matthew Canfield closed the door and took several steps forward in front of Andrew Scarlett. He would cover the boy. He put his hand in his right coat pocket.

"I have a gun pointed at you, Kroeger. Not the same gun but the same pocket as last time we met. This time I won't take anything for granted. Do I make myself clear?"

"If you like, take it out of your pocket and hold it against my head. . . . There's not much I can do about it."

Canfield approached the figure in the chair.

It was horrible.

The man was a semi-invalid. He seemed to be paralyzed through the entire left portion of his body, extending to his jaw. His hands were folded across his front, his fingers extended as though spastic. But his eyes were alert.

His eyes.

His face. . . . Covered over by white splotches of skin graft below gray short-cropped hair. The man spoke.

"What you see was carried out of Sevastopol. Operation Barbarossa."

"What do you have to tell us, Kroeger?"

"First, April Red. . . . Tell him to come closer."

"Come here, Andy. By me."

"Andy!" The man in the chair laughed through his half-closed mouth. "Isn't that nice! Andy! Come here, Andy!"

Andrew Scarlett approached his stepfather and stood by his side, looking down at the deformed man in the chair.

"So you're the son of Ulster Scarlett?"

"I'm Matthew Canfield's son."

Canfield held his place, watching the father and son. He suddenly felt as though he didn't belong. He had the feeling that giants—old and infirm, young and scrawny—were about to do battle. And he was not of their house.

"No, young man, you're the son of Ulster Stewart Scarlett, heir to Scarlatti!"

"I'm exactly what I want to be! I have nothing to do with you." The young man breathed deeply. The fear was leaving him now, and in its place Canfield saw that a quiet fury was taking hold of the boy.

"Easy, Andy. Easy."

"Why? . . . For him? . . . Look at him. He's practically dead. . . . He doesn't even have a face."

"Stop it!" Ulster Scarlett's shrill voice reminded Canfield of that long-ago room in Zurich. "Stop it, you fool!"

"For what? For you? . . . Why should I? . . . I don't know you! I don't want to know you! . . . You left a long time ago!" The young man pointed to Canfield. "He took over for you. I listen to him. You're nothing to me!"

"Don't you talk to me like that! Don't you dare!"

Canfield spoke sharply. "I've brought April Red, Kroeger! What have you got to deliver? That's what we're here for. Let's get it over with!"

"He must understand first!" The misshapen head nodded back and forth. "He must be made to understand!"

"If it meant that much, why did you hide it? Why did you become Kroeger?"

The nodding head stopped, the ashen slit eyes stared. Canfield remembered Janet speaking about that look.

"Because Ulster Scarlett was not fit to represent the new order. The new world! Ulster Scarlett served his purpose and once that purpose was accomplished, he was no longer necessary. . . . He was a hindrance. . . . He would have been a joke. He had to be eliminated. . . ."

"Perhaps there was something else, too."

"What?"

"Elizabeth. She would have stopped you again. . . . She would have stopped you later, just the way she stopped you at Zurich."

At Elizabeth's name, Heinrich Kroeger worked up the phlegm in his scarred throat and spat. It was an ugly sight. "The bitch of the world! . . . But we made a mistake in twenty-six. . . . Let's he honest, I made the mistake. . . . I should have asked her to join us. . . . She would have, you know. She wanted the same things we did. . . ."

"You're wrong about that."

"Hah! You didn't know her!"

The former field accountant replied softly without inflection. "I knew her. . . . Take my word for it, she despised everything you stood for."

The Nazi laughed quietly to himself. "That's very funny. . . . I told her she stood for everything I despised. . . ."

"Then you were both right."

"No matter. She's in hell now."

"She died thinking you were dead. She died in peace because of that."

"Hah! You'll never know how tempted I was over the years, especially when we took Paris! . . . But I was waiting for London. . . . I was going to stand outside Whitehall and announce it to the world—and watch Scarlatti destroy itself!"

"She was gone by the time you took Paris."

"That didn't matter."

"I suppose not. You were just as afraid of her in death as you were when she was alive."

"I was afraid of no one! I was afraid of nothing!" Heinrich Kroeger strained his decrepit body.

"Then why didn't you carry out your threat? The house of Scarlatti lives."

"She never told you?"

"Told me what?"

"The bitch-woman always covered herself on four flanks. She found her corruptible man. My one enemy in the Third Reich. Goebbels. She never believed I'd been killed at Zurich. Goebbels knew who I was. After nineteen thirty-three she threatened our respectability with lies. Lies about me. The party was more important than revenge."

Canfield watched the destroyed man below him. As always, Elizabeth Scarlatti had been ahead of all of them. Far ahead.

"One last question."

"What?"

"Why Janet?"

The man in the chair raised his right hand with difficulty. "Him. . . . Him!" He pointed to Andrew Scarlett.

"Why?"

"I believed! I still believe! Heinrich Kroeger was part of a new world! A new order! The true aristocracy! . . . In time it would have been his!"

"But why Janet?"

Heinrich Kroeger, in exhaustion, waved the question aside. "A whore. Who needs a whore? The vessel is all we look for. . . ."

Canfield felt the anger rise inside him, but at his age and in his job, he suppressed it. He was not quick enough for the boy-man beside him.

Andrew Scarlett rushed forward to the overstuffed chair and swung his open hand at the invalid Kroeger. The slap was hard and accurate. "You bastard! You filthy bastard!"

"Andy! Get back!" He pulled the boy away.

"Unehelich!" Heinrich Kroeger's eyes were swimming in their sockets. "It's for you! That's why you're here! You've got to know! . . . You'll understand and start us up again! Think! Think the aristocracy! For you . . . for you. . . ." He reached with his slightly mobile hand to his inside jacket pocket and withdrew a slip of paper. "They're yours. Take them!"

Canfield picked up the paper and without looking at it handed it to Andrew Scarlett.

"They're numbers. Just a lot of numbers."

Matthew Canfield knew what the numbers meant, but before he could explain, Kroeger spoke. "They're Swiss accounts, my son. My only son. . . . They contain millions! Millions! But there are certain conditions. Conditions which you will learn to understand! When you grow older, you'll know those conditions have to be met! And you'll meet them! . . . Because this power is the power to change the world! The way we wanted to change it!"

The man-boy looked at the deformed figure in the chair. "Am I supposed to thank you?"

"One day you will."

Matthew Canfield had had enough. "This is it! April Red has his message. Now I want it! What are you delivering?"

"It's outside. Help me up and we'll go to it."

"Never! What's outside? Your staff members in leather coats?"

"There's no one. No one but me."

Canfield looked at the wreck of a man in front of him and believed him. He started to help Heinrich Kroeger out of the chair.

"Wait here, Andy, I'll be back."

Major Matthew Canfield, in full uniform, helped the crippled man in brown tweeds down the stairs and onto the lobby floor. In the lobby, a servant brought over the crutches discarded by the Nazi when he first ascended the staircase to his room. The American major and the Nazi went out the front door.

"Where are we going, Kroeger?"

"Don't you think it's time you called me by my right name? The name is Scarlett. Or, if you will, Scarlatti." The Nazi led them to the right, off the driveway, into the grass.

"You're Heinrich Kroeger. That's all you are to me."

"You realize, of course, that it was you, and you alone who caused our setback in Zurich. You pushed our timetable back a good two years. . . . No one ever suspected. . . . You were an ass!" Heinrich Kroeger laughed. "Perhaps it takes an ass to portray an ass!" He laughed again.

"Where are we going?"

"Just a few hundred yards. Hold your pistol up, if you like. There's no one."

"What are you going to deliver? You might as well tell me."

"Why not? You'll have them in your hands soon enough." Kroeger hobbled along toward an open field. "And when you have them, I'm free. Remember that."

"We have a deal. What is it?"

"The Allies will be pleased. Eisenhower will probably give you a medal! . . . You'll bring back the complete plans of the Berlin fortifications. They're known only to the elite of the German High Command. . . . Underground bunkers, rocket emplacements, supply depots, even the Führer's command post. You'll be a hero and I'll be nonexistent. We've done well, you and I."

Matthew Canfield stopped.

The plans of the Berlin fortifications had been obtained weeks ago by Allied Intelligence.

Berlin knew it.

Berlin admitted it.

Someone had been led into a trap, but it was not him, not Matthew Canfield. The Nazi High Command had led one of its own into the jaws of death.

"Tell me, Kroeger, what happens if I take your plans, your exchange for April Red, and don't let you go? What happens then?"

"Simple. Doenitz himself took my testimony. I gave it to him two weeks ago in Berlin. I told him everything. If I'm not back in Berlin in a few days, he'll be concerned. I'm very valuable. I expect to make my appearance and then . . . be gone. If I don't appear, then the whole world knows!"

Matthew Canfield thought it was the strangest of ironies. But it was no more than he had anticipated. He had written it all down in the original file, sealed for years in the archives of the State Department.

And now a man in Berlin, unknown to him except by reputation, had reached the same conclusion.

Heinrich Kroeger, Ulster Stewart Scarlett—was expendable.

Doenitz had allowed Kroeger—bearing his false gifts—to come to Bern. Doenitz, in the unwritten rule of war, expected him to be killed. Doenitz knew that neither nation could afford this madman as its own. In either victory or defeat. And the enemy had to execute him so that no doubts existed. Doenitz was that rare enemy in these days of hatreds. He was a man his adversaries trusted. Like Rommel, Doenitz was a thorough fighter. A vicious fighter. But he was a moral man.

Matthew Canfield drew his pistol and fired twice.

Heinrich Kroeger lay dead on the ground.

Ulster Stewart Scarlett was—at last—gone.

Matthew Canfield walked through the field back to the small inn. The night was clear and the moon, three-quarters of it, shone brightly on the still foliage around him.

It struck him that it was remarkable that it had all been so simple.

But the crest of the wave is simple. Deceptively simple. It does not show the myriad pressures beneath that make the foam roll the way it does.

It was over.

And there was Andrew.

There was Janet.

Above all, there was Janet.

The
Osterman
Weekend

Robert
Ludlum

For Michael, Jonathan, Glynis:

three extraordinary people who possess, among so many
talents, the gift of laughter and perception . . .

PART ONE
Sunday Afternoon

Chapter One

Saddle Valley, New Jersey, is a Village.

At least real estate developers, hearing alarm signals from a decaying upper middle-class Manhattan, found a Village when they invaded its wooded acres in the late 1930's.

The white, shield-shaped sign on Valley Road reads

SADDLE VALLEY

VILLAGE INCORPORATED 1862

Welcome

The "Welcome" is in smaller lettering than any of the words preceding it, for Saddle Valley does not really welcome outsiders, those Sunday afternoon drivers who like to watch the Villagers at play. Two Saddle Valley police cars patrol the roads on Sunday afternoon.

It might also be noted that the sign on Valley Road does not read

SADDLE VALLEY, NEW JERSEY

or even

SADDLE VALLEY, N.J.

merely

SADDLE VALLEY

The Village does not acknowledge a higher authority; it is its own master. Isolated, secure, inviolate.

On a recent July Sunday afternoon, one of the two Saddle Valley patrol cars seemed to be extraordinarily thorough. The white car with blue lines roamed the roads just a bit faster than usual. It went from one end of the Village to the other—cruising into the residential areas—in front of, behind and to the sides of the spacious, tastefully landscaped one-acre lots.

This particular patrol car on this particular Sunday afternoon was noticed by several residents of Saddle Valley.

It was meant to be.

It was part of the plan.

John Tanner, in old tennis shorts and yesterday's shirt, sneakers and no socks, was clearing out his two-car garage with half an ear cocked to the sounds coming from his pool. His twelve-year-old son, Raymond, had friends over, and periodically Tanner walked far enough out on the driveway so he could see past the backyard patio to the pool and make sure the children were all right. Actually, he only walked out when the level of shouting was reduced to conversation—or periods of silence.

Tanner's wife, Alice, with irritating regularity, came into the garage through the laundry-room entrance to tell her husband what to throw out next. John hated getting rid of things, and the resulting accumulation of junk exasperated her. This time she motioned toward a broken lawn spreader which had lain for weeks at the back of the garage.

John noticed her gesture. "I could mount it on a piece of wrought iron and sell it to the Museum of Modern Art," he said. "Remnants of past inequities. Pre-gardener period."

Alice Tanner laughed. Her husband noted once again, as he had for so many years, that it was a nice laugh.

"I'll haul it to the curb. They pick up Mondays." Alice reached for the relic.

"That's okay. I'll do it."

"No, you won't. You'll change your mind halfway down."

Her husband lifted the spreader over a Briggs and Stratton rotary lawn mower while Alice sidled past the small Triumph she proudly referred to as her "status symbol." As she started pushing the spreader down the driveway, the right wheel fell off. Both of them laughed.

"That'd clinch the deal with the museum. It's irresistible."

Alice looked up and stopped laughing. Forty yards away, in front of their house on Orchard Drive, the white patrol car was slowly cruising.

"The gestapo's screening the peasants this afternoon," she said.

"What?" Tanner picked up the wheel and threw it into the well of the spreader.

"Saddle Valley's finest is on the job. That's the second or third time they've gone down Orchard."

Tanner glanced at the passing patrol car. The driver, Officer Jenkins, returned his stare. There was no wave, no gesture of greeting. No acknowledgment. Yet they were acquaintances, if not friends.

"Maybe the dog barked too much last night."

"The baby-sitter didn't say anything."

"A dollar fifty an hour is hush money."

"You'd better get this down, darling." Alice's thoughts turned from the police car. "Without a wheel it becomes father's job. I'll check the kids."

Tanner, pulling the spreader behind him, went down the driveway to the curb, his eyes drawn to a bright light about sixty yards away. Orchard Drive, going west, bore to the left around a cluster of trees. Several hundred feet beyond the midpoint of the bend were Tanner's nearest neighbors, the Scanlans.

The light was the reflection of sun off the patrol car. It was parked by the side of the road.

The two policemen were turned around in their seats, staring out the rear window, staring, he was sure, at *him*. For a second or two, he remained motionless. Then he started to walk toward the car. The two officers turned, started the engine and sped off.

Tanner looked after it, puzzled, then walked slowly back towards his house.

The Saddle Valley police car raced out toward Peachtree Lane; there it slowed and resumed cruising speed.

Richard Tremayne sat in his air-conditioned living-room watching the Mets blow a six-run lead. The curtains of the large bay windows were open.

Suddenly Tremayne rose from his chair and went to the window. The patrol car was there again. Only now it was hardly moving.

"Hey, Ginny!" he called to his wife. "Come here a minute."

Virginia Tremayne walked gracefully down the three steps into the living room. "What is it? Now you didn't call me to tell me your Mets or Jets hit something?"

"When John and Alice were over last night . . . were he and I . . . all right? I mean, we weren't too loud or anything, were we?"

"You were both plastered. But pleasant. Why?"

"I know we were drunk. It was a lousy week. But we didn't do anything outlandish?"

"Of course not. Attorneys and newsmen are models of decorum. Why do you ask?"

"Goddamn police car's gone by the house for the fifth time."

"Oh." Virginia felt a knot in the pit of her stomach. "Are you sure?"

"You can't miss *that* car in the sunlight."

"No, I guess you can't. . . . You said it was a rotten week. Would that awful man be trying to . . ."

"Oh, Jesus, no! I told you to forget that. He's a loudmouth. He took the case too personally." Tremayne continued looking out the window. The police car was leaving.

"He did threaten you, though. You said he did. He said he had connections. . . ."

Tremayne turned slowly and faced his wife. "We all have connections, don't we? Some as far away as Switzerland?"

"Dick, please. That's absurd."

"Of course it is. Car's gone now . . . probably nothing. They're due for another raise in October. Probably checking out houses to buy. The bastards! They make more than I did five years out of law school."

"I think you're a little edgy with a bad head. That's what I think."

"I think you're probably right."

Virginia watched her husband. He kept staring out the window. "The maid wants Wednesday off. We'll eat out, all right?"

"Sure." He did not turn around.

His wife started up into the hall. She looked back at her husband; he was now looking at her. Beads of perspiration had formed on his forehead. And the room was cool.

The Saddle Valley patrol car headed east toward Route Five, the main link with Manhattan twenty-six miles away. It stopped on a road overlooking Exit 10A. The patrolman to the right of the driver took a pair of binoculars from the glove compartment and began scanning the cars coming off the exit ramp. The binoculars had Zeiss-Ikon lenses.

After several minutes he tapped the sleeve of the driver, Jenkins, who looked over through the open window. He motioned the other man to give him the binoculars, and put them to his eyes, tracking the automobile specified by his fellow officer. He spoke one word: "Confirmed."

Jenkins started the car and headed south. He picked up the radio phone. "Two car calling in. Heading south on Register Road. Tailing green Ford sedan. New York plates. Filled with niggers or P.R.'s."

The crackling reply came over the speaker. "Read you, two car. Chase 'em the hell out."

"Will do. No sweat. Out."

The patrol car then turned left and sped down the long incline into Route Five. Once on the highway, Jenkins pressed the accelerator to the floor and the car plunged forward on the smooth surface. In sixty seconds the speedometer read ninety-two.

Four minutes later the patrol car slowed down rounding a long curve. A few hundred yards beyond the curve stood two aluminum-framed telephone booths, glass and metal reflecting the harsh glare of the July sun.

The police car came to a stop and Jenkins' companion climbed out.

"Got a dime?"

"Oh, Christ, McDermott!" Jenkins laughed. "Fifteen years in the field and you don't carry the change to make contact."

"Don't be a smartass. I've got nickels, but one of them's an Indian head."

"Here." Jenkins took a coin from his pocket and handed it to McDermott. "An ABM could be stuck and you wouldn't use a Roosevelt dime to alert operations."

"Don't know that I would." McDermott walked to the phone booth, pushed in the squeaky, shiny door, and dialed "0". The booth was stifling, the still air so close that he kept the door open with his foot.

"I'll head down the U-turn," yelled Jenkins from the car window. "Pick you up on the other side."

"Okay. . . . Operator. A collect call to New Hampshire. Area Code three-one-two. Six-five-four-oh-one. The name is Mr. Leather."

There was no mistaking the words. McDermott had placed a call to the state of New Hampshire and the telephone operator put it through. However, what the operator could not know was that this particular number did not cause a telephone to ring in the state of New Hampshire. For somewhere, in some underground complex housing thousands upon thousands of trunk lines, a tiny relay was activated and a small magnetized bar fell across a quarter-inch space and made another connection. This connection caused—not a bell—but a low humming sound to emanate from a telephone two hundred and sixty-three miles *south* of Saddle Valley, New Jersey.

The telephone was in a second-floor office in a red brick building fifty yards inside a twelve-foot-high electrified fence. The building was one of perhaps ten, all connected with one another to form a single complex. Outside the fence the woods were thick with summer foliage. The location was McLean, Virginia. The complex was the Central Intelligence Agency. Isolated, secure, inviolate.

The man sitting behind the desk in the second-floor office crushed out his cigarette in relief. He'd been waiting anxiously for the call. He noted with satisfaction that the small wheels of the recording device automatically started revolving. He picked up the telephone.

"Andrews speaking. Yes, operator, I accept the charges."

"Leather reporting," came the words rerouted from the state of New Hampshire.

"You're cleared. Tape going, Leather."

"Confirming the presence of all suspects. The Cardones just arrived from Kennedy Airport."

"We knew he landed . . ."

"Then why the hell did we have to race down here?"

"That's a rotten highway, Route Five. He could have an accident."

"On Sunday afternoon?"

"Or any other time. You want the statistics on accidents for that route?"

"Go back to your Goddamn computers . . ."

Andrews shrugged. Men in the field were always irritated over one thing or another. "As I read you, all three suspects are present. Correct?"

"Correct. Tanners, Tremaynes and the Cardones. All accounted for. All waiting. The first two are primed. We'll get to Cardone in a few minutes."

"Anything else?"

"Not for now."

"How's the wife?"

"Jenkins is lucky. He's a bachelor. Lillian keeps looking at those houses and wants one."

"Not on our salary, McDermott."

"That's what I tell her. She wants me to defect."

For the briefest of seconds Andrews reacted painfully to McDermott's joke. "The pay's worse, I'm told."

"Couldn't be. . . . There's Jenkins. Be in touch."

Joseph Cardone drove his Cadillac into the circular drive and parked in front of the stone steps leading to the huge oak door. He turned off the engine and stretched, bending his elbows beneath the roof. He sighed and woke his boys of six and seven. A third child, a girl of ten, was reading a comic book.

Sitting beside Cardone was his wife, Betty. She looked out the window at the house. "It's good to get away, but it's better to get home."

Cardone laughed and put his large hand on his wife's shoulder. "You must mean that."

"I do."

"You must. You say it every time we come home. The exact words."

"It's a nice home."

Cardone opened the door. "Hey, Princess . . . get your brothers out and help your mother with the smaller bags." Cardone reached in and withdrew the keys from the ignition. He started toward the trunk. "Where's Louise?"

"She probably won't be here till Tuesday. We're three days early, remember? I gave her off till then."

Cardone winced. The thought of his wife's cooking was not pleasant. "We eat out."

"We'll have to today. It takes too long to defrost things." Betty Cardone walked up the stone steps, taking the front-door key out of her purse.

Joe dismissed his wife's remark. He liked food and he did not like his wife's preparation of it. Rich debutantes from Chestnut Hill couldn't begin to cook like good South Side Italian mamas from Philadelphia.

One hour later he had the central air-conditioning going full blast throughout the large house, and the stuffy air, unchanged for nearly two weeks, was becoming bearable again. He was aware of such things. He'd been an exceptionally successful athlete—his route to success, both social and financial. He stepped out on the front porch and looked at the lawn with the huge willow tree centered in the grass within the circular drive. The gardeners had kept it all up nicely. They should. Their prices were ridiculous. Not that price ever concerned him any more.

Suddenly there it was again. The patrol car. This was the third time he'd seen it since leaving the highway.

"Hey, you! Hold it!"

The two officers in the car looked briefly at one another, about to race away. But Cardone had run to the curb.

"Hey!"

The patrol car stopped.

"Yes, Mr. Cardone?"

"What's with the police routine? Any trouble around here?"

"No, Mr. Cardone It's vacation time. We're just checking against our schedules when residents return. You were due this afternoon, so we just wanted to make sure it was you. Take your house off the check list."

Joe watched the policemen carefully. He knew the officer was lying, and the policeman knew he knew.

"You earn your money."

"Do our best, Mr. Cardone."

"I'll bet you do."

"Good day, sir." The patrol car sped off.

Joe looked after it. He hadn't intended to go to the office until mid-week, but that had to be changed now. He'd go into New York in the morning.

On Sunday afternoons, between the hours of five and six, Tanner closeted himself in his study, a walnut-paneled room with three television sets, and watched three different interview shows simultaneously.

Alice knew her husband had to watch. As Director of News for Standard Mutual, it was part of his job to be aware of the competition. But Alice thought there was something sinister about a man sitting alone in a half-lit room watching three television sets at the same time, and she constantly chided him for it.

Today, Tanner reminded his wife that he'd have to miss next Sunday—Bernie and Leila would be there, and nothing ever disturbed an Osterman weekend. So he sat in the darkened room, knowing all too well what he was going to see.

Every Director of News for every network had his favorite program, the one to which he gave extra attention. For Tanner it was the Woodward show. A half hour on Sunday afternoon during which the best news analyst in the business interviewed a single subject, usually a controversial figure currently in the headlines.

Today Charles Woodward was interviewing a substitute, Undersecretary Ralph Ashton from the State Department. The Secretary himself was suddenly unavailable, so Ashton had been recruited.

It was a gargantuan mistake by the Department. Ashton was a witless, prosaic former businessman whose main asset was his ability to raise money. That he was even considered to represent the Administration was a major error on someone's part. Unless there were other motives.

Woodward would crucify him.

As Tanner listened to Ashton's evasive, hollow replies, he realized that a great many people in Washington were soon going to be telephoning each other. Woodward's polite inflections couldn't hide his growing antagonism toward the Undersecretary. The reportorial instinct was being frustrated; soon Woodward's tones would turn to ice and Ashton would be slaughtered. Politely, to be sure, but slaughtered nevertheless.

It was the sort of thing Tanner felt embarrassed watching.

He turned up the volume of the second set. In ponderous, nasal tones a moderator was describing the backgrounds and positions of the panel of experts who were about to question the U.N delegate from Ghana. The black diplomat looked for all the world as if he were being driven to the guillotine in front of a collection of male Madame Defarges. Very white, well-paid Madame Defarges.

No competition there.

The third network was better, but not good enough. No competition there either.

Tanner decided he had had enough. He was too far ahead to worry, and he'd seen Woodward's tape in the morning. It was only five-twenty, and the sun was still on the pool. He heard his daughter's shouts as she returned from the country club, and the reluctant departure of Raymond's friends from the backyard. His family was together. The three of them were probably sitting outside waiting till he finished watching and started the fire for the steaks.

He'd surprise them.

He turned off the sets, put the pad and pencil on his desk. It was time for a drink.

Tanner opened the door of his study and walked into the living room. Through the rear windows, he saw Alice and the children playing follow-the-leader off the pool diving board. They were laughing, at peace.

Alice deserved it. Christ! She deserved it!

He watched his wife. She jumped—toes pointed—into the water, bobbing up quickly to make sure that eight-year-old Janet would be all right when she followed her.

Remarkable! After all the years he was more in love with his wife than ever.

He remembered the patrol car, then dismissed the thought. The policemen were simply finding a secluded spot in which to rest, or listen to the ball game undisturbed. He'd heard that policemen did that sort of thing in New York. Then why not in Saddle Valley? Saddle Valley was a lot safer than New York.

Saddle Valley was probably the safest place in the world. At least it seemed that way to John Tanner on this particular Sunday afternoon.

Richard Tremayne turned off his one television set within ten seconds after John Tanner had shut off his three. The Mets had won it after all.

His headache had left him and with it his irritability. Ginny had been right, he thought. He was simply edgy. No reason to take it out on the family. His stomach felt stronger now. A little food would fix him up again. Maybe he'd call Johnny and Ali and take Ginny over for a swim in the Tanner's pool.

Ginny kept asking why they didn't have one of their own. Heaven knew they had an income several times that of the Tanners. Everybody could see that. But Tremayne knew why.

A pool would be that one symbol too much. Too much at age forty-four. It was enough that they had moved into Saddle Valley when he was only thirty-eight. A seventy-four-thousand-dollar house at thirty-eight years of age. With a fifty-thousand-dollar down payment. A pool could wait until his forty-fifth birthday. It would make sense then.

Of course what people—clients—didn't think about was that he had graduated from Yale Law in the top five percent of his class, had clerked for Learned Hand, had spent three years at the bottom of his present firm's ladder before any real money came his way. When it came, however, it came rapidly.

Tremayne walked out to the patio. Ginny and their thirteen-year-old daughter Peg were cutting roses near a white arbor. His entire backyard, nearly half an acre, was cultivated and manicured. There were flowers everywhere. The garden was Ginny's pastime, hobby, avocation—next to sex, her passion. Nothing really replaced sex, thought her husband with an unconscious chuckle.

"Here! Let me give you a hand," shouted Tremayne as he walked toward his wife and daughter.

"You're feeling better," said Virginia smiling.

"Look at these, daddy! Aren't they beautiful?" His daughter held up a bunch of red and yellow roses.

"They're lovely, sweetheart."

"Dick, did I tell you? Bernie and Leila are flying east next week. They'll be here Friday."

"Johnny told me. . . . An Osterman weekend. I'll have to get in shape."

"I thought you were practicing last night."

Tremayne laughed. He never apologized for getting drunk, it happened too seldom, and he was never really difficult. Besides, last night he had deserved it. It *had* been a rotten week.

The three of them walked back to the patio. Virginia slipped her hand under her husband's arm. Peggy, growing so tall, her father thought, smiled brightly. The patio phone rang.

"I'll get it!" Peg dashed ahead.

"Why not?" shouted her father in mock exasperation. "It's never for us!"

"We've simply got to get her her own telephone." Virginia Tremayne pinched her husband's arm playfully.

"You're both driving me on welfare."

"It's for you, mother. It's Mrs. Cardone." Peggy suddenly covered the receiver with her hand. "*Please* don't talk too long, Mother. Carol Brown said she'd call me when she got home. You know, I told you. The Choate boy."

Virginia Tremayne smiled knowingly, exchanging a conspiratorial look with her daughter. "Carol won't elope without telling you, darling. She may need more than her week's allowance."

"Oh, mother!"

Richard watched them with amusement. It was comfortable and comforting at the same time. His wife was doing a good job with their child. No one could argue with that. He knew there were those who criticized Ginny, said she dressed a little . . . flamboyantly. He'd heard that word and knew it meant something else. But the kids. The kids all flocked around Ginny. That was important these days. Perhaps his wife knew something most other women didn't know.

Things . . . "things" were working out, thought Tremayne. Even the ultimate security, if Bernie Osterman was to be believed.

It was a good life.

He'd get on the phone with Joe if Ginny and Betty ever finished with their conversation. Then he'd call John and Ali. After Johnny's television shows were over. Perhaps the six of them could go over to the Club for the Sunday buffet.

Suddenly the memory of the patrol car flashed across his mind. He dismissed it. He had been nervous, edgy, hung over. Let's face it, he thought. It *was* Sunday afternoon and the town council *had* insisted that the police thoroughly check out the residential areas on Sunday afternoons.

Funny, he mused. He didn't think the Cardones were due back so early. Joe must have been called by his office to get in on Monday. The market was crazy these days. Especially commodities, Joe's speciality.

Betty nodded yes to Joe's question from the telephone. It solved the dinner problem. The buffet wasn't bad, even if the Club had never learned the secret of a good antipasto. Joe kept telling the manager that you had to use Genoa salami, not Hebrew National, but the chef had a deal with a Jewish supplier, so what could a mere member do? Even Joe, probably the richest of them all. On the other hand he was Italian—not Catholic, but nevertheless Italian—and it had only been a decade since the Saddle Valley Country Club first let Italians join. One of these days they'd let Jews in—that'd be the time for some kind of celebration.

It was this silent intolerance—never spelled out—that caused the Cardones, the Tanners and the Tremaynes to make it a special point to have Bernie and Leila Osterman very much in evidence at the Club whenever they came east. One thing could be said for the six of them. They weren't bigots.

It was strange, thought Cardone as he hung up the phone and started toward the small gym on the side of his house, strange that the Tanners had brought them all together. It had been John and Ali Tanner who had known the Ostermans in Los Angeles when Tanner was just starting out. Now Joe wondered whether John and Ali really understood the bond between Bernie Osterman and him and Dick Tremayne. It was a bond one didn't discuss with outsiders.

Eventually it would spell out the kind of independence every man sought, every worried citizen might pray for; there were dangers, risks, but it was right for him and Betty. Right for the Tremaynes and the Ostermans. They had discussed it among themselves, analyzed it, thought it through carefully, and collectively reached the decision.

It might have been right for the Tanners. But Joe, Dick and Bernie agreed that the first signal had to come from John himself. That was paramount. Enough hints had been dropped and Tanner had not responded.

Joe closed the heavy, matted door of his personal gymnasium, turned on the steam dials and stripped. He put on a pair of sweatpants and took his sweatshirt off the stainless-steel rack. He smiled as he noticed the embroidered initials on the flannel. Only a girl from Chestnut Hill would have a monogram sewn on a sweatshirt.

J. A. C.

Joseph Ambruzzio Cardone.

Guiseppe Ambruzzio Cardione. Second of eight children from the union of Angela and Umberto Cardione, once of Sicily and later South Philadelphia. Eventually, citizens. American flags alongside countless, cosmeticized pictures of the Virgin Mary holding a cherubic Christ-child with blue eyes and red lips.

Guiseppe Ambruzzio Cardione grew into a large, immensely strong young man who was just about the best athlete South Philadelphia High had ever seen. He was president of his senior class and twice elected to the All-City Student Council.

Of the many college scholarships offered he chose the most prestigious, Princeton, also the nearest to Philadelphia. As a Princeton halfback he accomplished the seemingly impossible for his alma mater. He was chosen All-American, the first Princeton football player in years to be so honored.

Several grateful alumni brought him to Wall Street. He'd shortened his name to Cardone, the last vowel pronounced very slightly. It had a kind of majesty, he thought. Like Cardozo. But no one was fooled; soon he didn't care. The market was expanding, exploding to the point where *everyone* was buying securities. At first he was merely a good customers' man. An Italian boy who had made good, a fellow who could talk to the emerging new-rich with money to spend; talk in ways the new-rich, still nervous about investments, could understand.

And it had to happen.

The Italians are sensitive people. They're more comfortable doing business with their own kind. A number of the construction boys—the Castelanos, the Latronas, the Battellas—who had made fortunes in industrial developments, gravitated to Cardone. Two syllables only. "Joey Cardone," they called him. And Joey found them tax shelters, Joey found them capital gains, Joey found them security.

The money poured in. The gross of the brokerage house nearly doubled, thanks to Joey's friends. Worthington and Bennett, members N. Y. Stock Exchange, became Worthington, Bennett and Cardone. From that point it was a short leap to Bennett-Cardone, Ltd.

Cardone was grateful to his *compares*. But the reason for his gratitude was also the reason why he shuddered just a bit when a patrol car appeared too frequently around his house. For a few of his *compares*, perhaps more than a few, were on the fringes—perhaps more than the fringes—of the underworld.

He finished with the weights and climbed on his rowing machine. The perspiration was pouring out and he felt better now. The menace of the patrol car began to diminish. After all, ninety-nine percent of the Saddle Valley families returned from vacations on Sunday. Who ever heard of people coming back from a vacation on a Wednesday? Even if the day were listed as such at the police station, a conscientious desk sergeant might well consider it an error and change it to Sunday. No one returned on Wednesday. Wednesday was a business day.

And who would ever take seriously the idea that Joseph Cardone had anything to do with the Cosa Nostra? He was the living proof of the work ethic. The American Success Story. A Princeton All-American.

Joe removed his sweatsuit and walked into the steam room, now dense with vapor. He sat on the bench and breathed deeply. The steam was purifying. After nearly two weeks of French-Canadian cooking, his body needed purifying.

He laughed aloud in his steam room. It was good to be home, his wife was right about that. And Tremayne told him the Ostermans would be flying in Friday morning. It'd be good to see Bernie and Leila again. It had been nearly four months. But they'd kept in touch.

Two hundred and fifty miles south of Saddle Valley, New Jersey, is that section of the nation's capital known as Georgetown. In Georgetown the pace of life changes every day at 5:30 P.M. Before, the pace is gradual, aristocratic, even delicate. After, there is a quickening—not sudden, but with a growing momentum. The residents, for the most part men and women of power and wealth and commitments to both, are dedicated to the propagation of their influence.

After five-thirty, the games begin.

After five-thirty in Georgetown, it is time for stratagems.

Who is where? . . . Why are they there?

Except on Sunday afternoon, when the power-brokers survey their creations of the previous week, and take the time to restore their strength for the next six days of strategy.

Let there be light and there *was* light. Let there be rest and there *is* rest.

Except, again, not for all.

For instance, not for Alexander Danforth, aide to the President of the United States. An aide without portfolio and without specified activities.

Danforth was the liaison between the all-securities communications room in the underground levels of the White House and the Central Intelligence Agency in McLean, Virginia. He was the compleat power-broker because he was never in evidence, yet his decisions were among the most important in Washington. Regardless of administrations, his quiet voice was heeded by all. It had been for years.

On this particular Sunday afternoon, Danforth sat with the Central Intelligence Agency's Deputy Administrator, George Grover, beneath the bougainvillea tree on Danforth's small backyard patio, watching television. The two men had reached the same conclusion John Tanner had reached two hundred and fifty miles north: Charles Woodward was going to make news tomorrow morning.

"State's going to use up a month's supply of toilet tissue," Danforth said.

"They should. Whoever let Ashton go on? He's not only stupid, he *looks* stupid. Stupid and slippery. John Tanner's responsible for this program, isn't he?"

"He is."

"Smart son of a bitch. It'd be nice to be certain he's on our side," Grover said.

"Fassett's assured us." The two men exchanged looks. "Well, you've seen the file. Don't you agree?"

"Yes. Yes, I do. Fassett's right."

"He generally is."

There were two telephones on the ceramic table in front of Danforth. One was black with an outdoor plug-in jack on the ground. The other was red and a red cable extended from inside the house. The red phone hummed—it did not ring. Danforth picked it up.

"Yes. . . . Yes, Andrews. Good. . . . Fine. Ring Fassett on Redder and tell him to come over. Has Los Angeles confirmed the Ostermans? No change? . . . Excellent. We're on schedule."

Bernard Osterman, C.C.N.Y., Class of '46, pulled the page out of his typewriter and glanced at it. Adding it to the bottom of a thin sheaf of papers, he stood up. He walked around his kidney-shaped pool and handed the manuscript to his wife, Leila, who sat naked in her lounge chair.

Osterman was naked too.

"You know, an undressed woman's not particularly attractive in sunlight."

"You think you're a portrait in beige? . . . Give." She took the pages and reached for her large, tinted glasses. "Is this the finish?"

Bernie nodded. "When are the kids getting home?"

"They'll call from the beach before they start back. I told Marie to make sure they phone. I wouldn't want Merwyn to find out about naked girls in sunlight at his age. There's enough aversion to that in this town."

"You've got a point. Read." Bernie dove into the pool. He swam back and forth rapidly for three minutes . . . until he was out of breath. He was a good swimmer. In the Army they made him a swimming instructor at Fort Dix. "Speed-Jew" they had called him at the Army pool. But never to his face. He was a thin man, but tough. If C.C.N.Y. had had a football team instead of a joke, he would have been its captain. An end. Joe Cardone told Bernie he could have used him at Princeton.

Bernie had laughed when Joe told him that. In spite of the surface democratization of the Army experience—and it was surface—it had never occurred to Bernard Osterman, of the Tremont Avenue Ostermans, Bronx, New York, to vault time-honored barriers and enter the Ivy League. He might have been able to, he was bright and there was the G.I. Bill, but it simply never entered his thinking.

It wouldn't have been comfortable then—in 1946. It would be now; things had changed.

Osterman climbed up the ladder. It was good that he and Leila were going to the east coast, back to Saddle Valley for a few days. It was somehow akin to taking a brief, concentrated course in pleasant living whenever they returned. Everyone always said the east was hectic, pressurized—far more so than Los Angeles; but that wasn't so. It only seemed that way because the area of action was more confined.

Los Angeles, *his* Los Angeles, which meant Burbank, Hollywood, Beverly Hills, was where the real insanity was practiced. Men and women racing crazily up and down the aisles of a palm-lined drug store. Everything on sale, everything labeled, everyone competing in their psychedelic shirts and orange slacks.

There were times when Bernie just wanted to see someone dressed in a Brooks Brothers suit and a button-down broadcloth. It didn't really mean anything, not actually; he didn't give much of a damn what costumes the tribes of Los Angeles wore. Perhaps it was just the continual, overbearing assault on the eyes.

Or perhaps he was entering one of his downswings again. He was wearying of it all.

Which was unfair. The palm-lined drug store had treated him very well.

"How is it? he asked his wife.

"Pretty good. You may even have a problem."

"What?" Bernie grabbed a towel from a stack on the table. "What problem?"

"You could be stripping too many layers away. Too much pain, maybe." Leila flipped over a page as her husband smiled. "Be quiet a minute and let me finish. Perhaps you'll snap out of it."

Bernie Osterman sat down in a webbed chair and let the warm California sun wash over his body. There was still a smile on his lips; he knew what his wife meant and it was comforting to him. The years of formula writing hadn't destroyed his ability to strip away the layers—when he wanted to.

And there were times when there was nothing more important to him than to want to. To prove to himself that he could still do it. The way he used to back in the days when they lived in New York.

They were good days. Provocative, exciting, filled with commitment and purpose. Only there was never anything else really—just commitment, just purpose. A few flattering reviews written by other intense young writers. He'd been called *penetrating* then; *perceptive, incisive*. Once, even, *extraordinary*.

It hadn't been enough. And so he and Leila came to the palm-lined drug store and willingly, happily trained their talents for the exploding world of the television residual.

Someday, though. Someday, thought Bernard Osterman, it would happen again. The luxury of sitting down with all the time in the world to really do it. Make a big mistake if he had to. It was important to be able to think like that.

"Bernie?"

"Yes?"

Leila draped a towel over her front and pushed the latch on the lounge chair so the back raised itself. "It's beautiful, sweetie. I mean really very beautiful, and I think you know it's not going to work."

"It does work!"

"They won't sit still for it."

"Fuck 'em!"

"We're being paid thirty thousand for a one-hour drama, Bernie. Not a two-hour exorcism ending in a funeral home."

"It's not an exorcism. It happens to be a sad story based on very real conditions, and the conditions don't change. You want to drive down to the barrio and take a look?"

"They won't buy it. They'll want rewrites."

"I won't make them!"

"And they'll hold the balance. There's fifteen thousand coming to us."

"Son of a bitch!"

"You know I'm right."

"Talk! All Goddamned talk! This season we'll have *meaning! Controversy!* . . . Talk!"

"They look at the figures. A rave in *The Times* doesn't sell deodorant in Kansas."

"Fuck 'em."

"Relax. Take another swim. It's a big pool." Leila Osterman looked at her husband. He knew what that look meant and couldn't help smiling. A little sadly.

"O.K., fix it then."

Leila reached for the pencil and yellow pad on the table next to her chair. Bernie stood up and approached the edge of the pool.

"You think Tanner might want to join us? You think maybe I can approach him?"

His wife put down her pencil and looked up at her husband. "I don't know. Johnny's different from us . . ."

"Different from Joe and Betty? Dick and Ginny? I don't see he's so different."

"I wouldn't jump at him. He's still a newshawk. Vulture they used to call him, remember? The vulture of San Diego. He's got a spine. I wouldn't want to bend it. It might snap back."

"He thinks like we do. He thinks like Joe and Dick. Like us."

"I repeat. Don't jump. Call it the well-advertised woman's intuition, but don't jump. . . . We could get hurt."

Osterman dove into the pool and swam thirty-six feet under water to the far end. Leila was only half right, he thought. Tanner was an uncompromising newsman but he was also a sensible and sensitive human being. Tanner wasn't a fool, he saw what was happening—everywhere. It was inevitable.

It all came down to individual survival.

It reduced itself to being able to do what one wanted to do. To write an "exorcism" if he was capable of it. Without worrying about deodorants in the state of Kansas.

Bernie surfaced and held onto the side of the pool, breathing deeply. He pushed himself off and slowly breast-stroked back toward his wife.

"Did I box you into a corner?"

"You never could." Leila spoke while writing on the yellow pad. "There was a time in my life when I thought thirty thousand dollars was all the money in the world. Brooklyn's house of Weintraub was not Chase Manhattan's biggest client." She tore off a page and secured it under a Pepsi-Cola bottle.

"I never had that problem," said Bernie treading water. "The Ostermans are really a silent branch of the Rothschilds."

"I know. Your racing colors are puce and pumpkin orange."

"Hey!" Bernie suddenly grasped the ledge and looked excitedly at his wife. "Did I tell you? The trainer called this morning from Palm Springs. That two-year-old we bought did three furlongs in forty-one seconds!"

Leila Osterman dropped the pad on her lap and laughed. "You know, we're really too much! And you want to play Dostoyevski!"

"I see what you mean. . . . Well, someday."

"Sure. In the meantime keep one eye on Kansas and the other on those cockamamie horses of yours."

Osterman chuckled and plunged toward the opposite side of the pool. He thought once more about the Tanners. John and Ali Tanner. He'd cleared their names with Switzerland. Zurich was enthusiastic.

Bernard Osterman had made up his mind. Somehow he'd convince his wife.

He was going to talk seriously to John Tanner next weekend.

Danforth walked through the narrow front hallway of his Georgetown house and opened the door. Laurence Fassett, of the Central Intelligence Agency, smiled and extended his hand.

"Good afternoon, Mr. Danforth. Andrews called me from McLean. We've only met once before—I'm sure you don't remember. It's an honor, sir."

Danforth looked at this extraordinary man and returned the smile. The C.I.A. dossier said Fassett was forty-seven, but to Danforth he seemed much younger. The broad shoulders, the muscular neck, the unwrinkled face beneath the short-cropped blond hair: this all reminded Danforth of his own approaching seventieth birthday.

"Of course I remember. Come in, please."

As Fassett stepped into the hallway, his gaze fell on several Degas watercolors on the wall. He took a step closer. "These are beautiful."

"Yes, they are. Are you an expert, Mr. Fassett?"

"Oh, no. Just an enthusiastic amateur. . . . My wife was an artist. We used to spend a lot of time in the Louvre."

Danforth knew he shouldn't dwell on Fassett's wife. She had been German—with ties in East Berlin. She had been killed in East Berlin.

"Yes, yes, of course. Come this way, please. Grover's out back. We were watching the Woodward program on the patio."

The two men walked out onto the flagstone and brick back yard. George Grover rose from his chair.

"Hello, Larry. Things are beginning to move."

"Looks that way. It can't be too quick for me."

"Nor for any of us, I shouldn't think," said Danforth. "Drink?"

"No, thank you, sir. If you don't mind, I'd rather make this as quick as possible."

The three men sat down around the ceramic table. "Then let's pick up from where we are right now," Danforth said. "What is the immediate plan?"

Fassett looked bewildered. "I thought it had all been cleared through you."

"Oh, I've read the reports. I just want the information firsthand from the man in charge."

"All right, sir. Phase one is complete. The Tanners, the Tremaynes and the Cardones are all in Saddle Valley. No immediate vacations planned, they'll be there throughout the coming week. This information is confirmed from all our sources. There are thirteen agents in the town and the three families will be under constant surveillance. . . . Intercepts have been placed on all telephones. Untraceable.

"Los Angeles has established the Ostermans' flight on Friday to be Number 509, arriving Kennedy at 4:50 Eastern Daylight Time. Their usual procedure is to take a taxi directly out to the suburbs. The cab will be followed, of course . . ."

"If, by then, they're adhering to normal patterns," interrupted Grover.

"If they're not, they won't be on that plane. . . . Tomorrow we bring Tanner down to Washington."

"He has no inkling at the moment, does he?" asked Danforth.

"None at all—other than the patrol car, which we'll use if he balks tomorrow morning."

"How do you think he'll take it?" Grover leaned forward on his seat.

"I think it'll blow his mind."

"He may refuse to cooperate," Danforth said.

"That's not likely. If I do my job, he won't have a choice."

Danforth looked at the intense, muscular man who spoke so confidently. "You're anxious that we succeed, aren't you? You're very committed."

"I have reason to be." Fassett returned the old man's stare. When he continued it was in a matter-of-fact tone. "They killed my wife. They ran her down on the Kurfürstendamm at two o'clock in the morning—while I was being 'detained.' She was trying to find me. Did you know that?"

"I've read the file. You have my deepest sympathy. . . ."

"I don't want your sympathy. Those orders came from Moscow. I want them. I want Omega."

PART TWO
Monday, Tuesday, Wednesday, Thursday

Chapter Two

Monday—10:15 A.M.

Tanner left the elevator and walked down the thickly carpeted corridor toward his office. He'd spent twenty-five minutes in the screening room watching the Woodward tape. It confirmed what the newspapers had reported: Charles Woodward had exposed Undersecretary Ashton as a political hack.

There had to be a lot of embarrassed men in Washington, he thought.

"Quite a show, wasn't it?" his secretary said.

"Out-of-sight, as my son would put it. I don't think we can expect many dinner invitations to the White House. Any calls?"

"From all over town. Mainly congratulations; I left the names on your desk."

"That's comforting. I may need them. Anything else?"

"Yes, sir. The F.C.C. called twice. A man called Fassett."

"Who?"

"Mr. Laurence Fassett."

"We've always dealt with Cranston down there."

"That's what I thought, but he said it was urgent."

"Maybe the State Department's trying to get us arrested before sundown."

"I doubt it. They'd at least wait a day or two; it'd look less political."

"You'd better get him back. To the F.C.C. everything's urgent." Tanner crossed into his office, sat down at his desk, and read through the messages. He smiled; even his competition had been impressed.

The telephone intercom buzzed. "Mr. Fassett's on one, sir."

"Thanks." Tanner pushed the appropriate button. "Mr. Fassett? Sorry I was out of the office when you called."

"It's my place to apologize," said the polite voice at the other end of the line. "It's just that I have a difficult schedule today, and you're a priority."

"What's the problem?"

"Routine but urgent is the best way I can describe it. The papers you filed with us in May for Standard's news division were incomplete."

"What?" John remembered something F.C.C.'s Cranston had said to him a few weeks ago. He also recalled that Cranston had said it was unimportant. "What's missing?"

"Two signatures of yours for one thing. On pages seventeen and eighteen. And the breakdown of projected public service features for the six-month period commencing in January."

John Tanner did remember now. It had been Cranston's fault. Pages seventeen and eighteen had been missing from the folder sent from Washington for Tanner's signature—a point which the network's legal department had made to Tanner's office—and the service feature blanks were to be left open for another month, pending network decisions. Cranston, again, had agreed.

"If you'll check, you'll find your Mr. Cranston omitted the pages you refer to and the specific service features were postponed. He agreed to that."

There was a momentary pause from Washington. When Fassett spoke his voice held a touch less politeness than it had previously.

"In all deference to Cranston, he had no authority to make such a decision. Surely you have the information now." It was a statement.

"Yes, as a matter of fact, we do. I'll send it out Special Delivery."

"I'm afraid that's not good enough. We'll have to ask you to get down here this afternoon."

"Now, wait a minute. That's kind of short notice, isn't it?"

"I don't make the rules. I just carry them out. As of two months ago Standard Mutual Network is operating in violation of the F.C.C. code. We can't allow ourselves to be put in that position. Regardless of who's responsible, that is a fact. You're in violation. Let's get it cleared up today."

"All right. But I warn you, if this action is in any way a harassment emanating from the State Department, I'll bring down the network attorneys and label it for what it is."

"I not only don't like your insinuation, but I don't know what you're talking about."

"I think you do. The Woodward Show yesterday afternoon."

Fassett laughed. "Oh, I heard about that. The *Post* did quite a story on it. . . . And I think you can put your mind at ease. I tried to reach you twice last Friday."

"You did?"

"Yes."

"Wait a minute." Tanner pushed the *hold* button and then the *local*. "Norma? Did this Fassett try to get me Friday?"

There was a short silence while Tanner's secretary checked Friday's call sheet. "Could be. There were two calls from Washington, an Operator thirty-six in D.C. for you to reach if you returned by four. You were in the studio till five-thirty."

"Didn't you ask who was calling?"

"Of course I did. The only answer I got was that it could wait until Monday."

"Thanks." Tanner got back on the line with Fassett. "Did you leave an operator's number?"

"Operator three-six, Washington. Till 4:00 P.M."

"You didn't give your name or identify the agency. . . ."

"It was Friday. I wanted to get out early. Would you have felt better if I'd left an urgent call you couldn't return?"

"Okay, okay. And this can't wait for the mails?"

"I'm sorry, Mr. Tanner. I mean I'm really *very* sorry, but I have my instructions. Standard Mutual's not a small local station. This filing should have been completed weeks ago. . . . Also," here Fassett laughed again, "the way you keep stepping on exposed toes, I wouldn't want to be you if some wheels in the

State Department found out your whole damn news department was in violation. . . . And that's no threat. It couldn't be. We're both at fault."

John Tanner smiled at the telephone. Fassett was right. The filing *was* overdue. And there was no sense risking bureaucratic reprisals. He sighed. "I'll catch the one o'clock shuttle and be at the F.C.C. by three or a little after. Where's your office?"

"I'll be with Cranston. We'll have the papers, and don't forget the schedules. They're only projections, we won't hold you to them."

"Right. See you then." Tanner pushed another button and dialed his home number.

"Hi, darling."

"I've got to hop down to Washington this afternoon."

"Any problems?"

"No. 'Routine but urgent' was the description. Some F.C.C. business. I'll catch a shuttle back to Newark by seven. I just wanted you to know that I'd be late."

"Okay, darling. Do you want me to pick you up?"

"No, I'll get a cab."

"Sure?"

"Very. It'll make me feel good to think Standard's paying the twenty bucks."

"You're worth it. By the way, I read the reviews on the Woodward Show. You're a regular triumph."

"That's what I wrote across my jacket. Tanner the Triumph."

"I wish you would," said Alice quietly.

Even in jest she could never let it go. They had no real money problems, but Alice Tanner forever thought her husband was underpaid. It was the only serious argument between them. He could never explain that to seek more from a corporation like Standard Mutual meant just that much more obligation to the faceless giant.

"See you tonight, Ali."

"Bye. I love you."

As if in silent deference to his wife's complaint, Tanner commandeered one of the news cars to take him to LaGuardia Airport in an hour. No one argued. Tanner was, indeed, a triumph this morning.

During the next forty-five minutes, Tanner tied together a number of administrative loose ends. The last order of business was a call to Standard Mutual's legal department.

"Mr. Harrison, please. . . . Hello, Andy? John Tanner. I'm in a hurry, Andy; I've got to catch a plane. I just want to find out something. Do we have anything pending with the F.C.C. I don't know about? Any problems? I know about the public service features but Cranston said we could hold on those. . . . Sure, I'll wait." Tanner fingered the telephone cord, his thoughts still on Fassett. "Yes, Andy, I'm here. . . . Pages seventeen and eighteen. The signatures. . . . I see. Okay. Thanks. No, no problems here. Thanks again."

Tanner replaced the phone and got out of his chair slowly. Harrison had added fuel to his vague suspicions. It all seemed just a bit too contrived. The F.C.C. filing had been complete except for the final two pages on the fourth and fifth copies of the document. They were merely duplicates, important to no one, easily Xeroxed. Yet those pages had been missing from the file. Harrison had just commented:

"I remember, John. I sent you a memo about it. It looked to me as though they had been deliberately left out. Can't imagine why. . . ."

Neither could Tanner.

Chapter Three

Monday—3:25 P.M.

To Tanner's amazement, the F.C.C. sent a limousine to meet his plane.

Cranston's offices were on the sixth floor of the F.C.C. Building; at one time or another every major network news director had been summoned there. Cranston was a career man—respected by the networks as well as the changing administrations—and because of this Tanner found himself resenting the unknown Laurence Fassett, who could say with indignation, ". . . Cranston had no authority to make such a decision."

He'd never heard of Laurence Fassett.

Tanner pushed open the door to Cranston's waiting room. It was empty. The secretary's desk was bare—no pads, no pencils, no papers of any kind. What light there was came from Cranston's office door. It was open and he could hear the quiet whirr of an air conditioner. The window shades in the office were down, probably to keep out the summer sunlight. And then, against the office wall, he saw the shadow of a figure walking towards the door.

"Good afternoon," said the man as he came into view. He was shorter than Tanner by several inches, probably five ten or eleven, but very broad in the shoulders. His blond hair was cut short, his eyes set far apart beneath bushy light-brown eyebrows. He was, perhaps, Tanner's age, but without question a more physical man. Even his stance had a potential spring to it, thought Tanner.

"Mr. Fassett?"

"That's right. Won't you come in?" Fassett, instead of retreating into Cranston's office, crossed in front of Tanner to the door and locked it. "We'd rather not have any interruptions."

"Why not?" asked Tanner, startled.

Laurence Fassett looked about the room. "Yes. Yes. I see what you mean. Good point. Come in, please." Fassett walked in front of Tanner into Cranston's office. The shades of the two windows overlooking the street were pulled all the way down; Cranston's desk was as bare as his secretary's, except for two ashtrays and one other item. In the center of the cleared surface was a small Wollensak tape recorder with two cords—one in front of Cranston's chair, the other by the chair in front of Cranston's desk.

"Is that a tape recorder?" asked the news director, following Fassett into the office.

"Yes, it is. Won't you sit down, please?"

John Tanner remained standing. When he spoke it was with quiet anger. "No, I will *not* sit down. I don't like any of this. Your methods are very unclear, or maybe *too* clear. If you intend putting anything I say down on tape, you know perfectly well I won't allow it without the presence of a network attorney."

Fassett stood behind Cranston's desk. "This is not F.C.C. business. When I explain, you'll understand my . . . methods."

"You'd better explain quickly, because I'm about to leave. I was called by the F.C.C. to deliver the public service hours projected by Standard Mutual—which I have in my briefcase—and to sign two copies of our filing which *your* office omitted sending. You made it clear that you would be with Cranston when I arrived. Instead, I find an office which obviously is not in use. . . . I'd say you'd better have a good explanation or you'll be hearing from our attorney's within an hour. And if this is any kind of reprisal against Standard Mutual's news division, I'll blast you from coast to coast."

"I'm sorry. . . . These things are never easy."

"They shouldn't be!"

"Now hold it. Cranston's on vacation. We used his name because you've dealt with him before."

"You're telling me you intentionally lied?"

"Yes. The key, Mr. Tanner, is in the phrase you employed just now . . . 'I was called by the F.C.C.', I believe you said. May I present my credentials?" Laurence Fassett reached into his breast pocket and withdrew a small black plastic case. He held it across the desk.

Tanner opened it.

The top card identified Laurence C. Fassett as an employee of the Central Intelligence Agency.

The other card was Fassett's priority permit to enter the McLean complex at any hour of day or night.

"What's this all about? Why am I here?" Tanner handed back Fassett's identification.

"That's the reason for the tape recorder. Let me show you. Before I explain our business I have to ask you a number of questions. There are two switches which can shut off the machine. One here by me, the other there by you. If at any time I ask you a question you do not care to answer, all you have to do is push the O F F switch and the machine stops. On the other hand—and, again, for your protection—if I feel you are including private information which is no concern of ours, *I* shall stop the machine." Fassett started up the recorder with his switch and then reached across the desk for the cord in front of Tanner's chair and stopped it. "See? Quite simple. I've been through hundreds of these interviews. You've got nothing to worry about."

"This sounds like a pretrial examination without benefit of counsel or mandate of subpoena! What's the point? If you think you're going to intimidate me, you're crazy!"

"The *point* is one of completely positive identification. . . . And you're absolutely right. If it was our intention to intimidate anyone, we picked about as vulnerable a subject as J. Edgar Hoover. And even *he* doesn't have control of a network news program."

Tanner looked at the C.I.A. man standing politely behind Cranston's desk. Fassett had a point. The C.I.A. wouldn't allow itself to use so blatant a tactic on someone in his position.

"What do you mean, 'completely positive identification'? You know who I am."

"It should give you some idea of the magnitude of the information I'm empowered to deliver. Just extraordinary precaution in line with the importance of the data. . . . Did you know that in the Second World War an actor—a corporal in the British army, to be exact—impersonated Field Marshall Montgomery at high-level conferences in Africa and even some of Montgomery's Sandhurst classmates didn't catch on?"

The news director picked up the cord and pushed the ON and OFF switches. The machine started and stopped. John Tanner's curiosity—mingled with fear—was growing. He sat down. "Go ahead. Just remember, I'll shut off the tape and leave any time I want to."

"I understand. That's your privilege—up to a point."

"What do you mean by that? No qualifications, please."

"Trust me. You'll understand." Fassett's reassuring look served its purpose.

"Go ahead," said Tanner. The C.I.A. man picked up a manila folder and opened it. He then started the machine.

"Your full name is John Raymond Tanner?"

"Incorrect. My legal name is John Tanner. The Raymond was a baptismal name and is not registered on my birth certificate."

Fassett smiled from across the desk. "Very good."

"Thank you."

"You currently reside at 22 Orchard Drive, Saddle Valley, New Jersey?"

"I do."

"You were born on May 21, 1924, in Springfield, Illinois, to Lucas and Margaret Tanner?"

"Yes."

"Your family moved to San Mateo, California, when you were seven years old?"

"Yes."

"For what purpose?"

"My father's firm transferred him to Northern California. He was a personnel executive for a department-store chain. The Bryant Stores."

"Comfortable circumstances?"

"Reasonably so."

"You were educated in the San Mateo public school system?"

"No. I went through the second year of San Mateo High and transferred to a private school for the final two years of secondary school. Winston Preparatory."

"Upon graduation you enrolled at Stanford University?"

"Yes."

"Were you a member of any fraternities or clubs?"

"Yes. Alpha Kappa fraternity. The Trylon News Society, several others I can't recall. . . . Photography club, I think, but I didn't stay. I worked on the campus magazine, but quit."

"Any reason?"

Tanner looked at the C.I.A. man. "Yes. I strenuously objected to the Nisei situation. The prison camps. The magazine supported them. My objection still stands."

Fassett smiled again. "Your education was interrupted?"

"Most educations were. I enlisted in the Army at the end of my sophomore year."

"Where were you trained?"

"Fort Benning, Georgia. Infantry."

"Third Army? Fourteenth Division?"

"Yes."

"You saw service in the European theatre of operations?"

"Yes."

"Your highest rank was First Lieutenant?"

"Yes."

"O.C.S. training at Fort Benning?"

"No. I received a Field Commission in France."

"I see you also received several decorations."

"They were unit citations, battalion commendations. Not individual."

"You were hospitalized for a period of three weeks in St. Lô. Was this a result of wounds?"

Tanner looked momentarily embarrassed. "You know perfectly well it wasn't. There's no Purple Heart on my Army record," he said quietly.

"Would you explain?"

"I fell out of a jeep on the road to St. Lô. Dislocated hip."

Both men smiled.

"You were discharged in July of 1945 and returned to Stanford the following September?"

"I did. . . . To anticipate you, Mr. Fassett, I switched from an English major to the journalism school. I graduated in 1947 with a Bachelor of Arts degree."

Laurence Fassett's eyes remained on the folder in front of him. "You were married in your junior year to one Alice McCall?"

Tanner reached for his switch and shut off the machine. "This may be where I walk out."

"Relax, Mr. Tanner. Just identification. . . . We don't subscribe to the theory that the sins of the parents are visited upon their daughters. A simple yes or no will suffice."

Tanner started the machine again. "That is correct."

At this point, Laurence Fassett picked the cord off the desk and pushed the OFF switch. Tanner watched the reels stop, and then looked at the C.I.A. man.

"My next two questions concern the circumstances leading up to your marriage. I presume you do not care to answer them."

"You presume correctly."

"Believe me, they aren't important."

"If you told me they were, I'd leave right now." Ali had been through enough. Tanner would not allow his wife's personal tragedy to be brought up again, by anyone.

Fassett started the machine again. "Two children were born to you and Alice Mc . . . Tanner. A boy, Raymond, now age thirteen, and a girl, Janet, now eight."

"My son is twelve."

"His birthday is day after tomorrow. To go back a bit, your first employment after graduation was with *The Sacramento Daily News*."

"Reporter. Rewrite man, office boy, movie critic and space salesman when time permitted."

"You stayed with the Sacramento paper for three and a half years and then obtained a position with *The Los Angeles Times*?"

"No. I was in Sacramento for . . . *two* and a half years—I had an interim job with the *San Francisco Chronicle* for about a year before I got the job at *The Times*."

"On *The Los Angeles Times* you were quite successful as an investigative reporter. . . ."

"I was fortunate. I assume you're referring to my work on the San Diego waterfront operations."

"I am. You were nominated for a Pulitzer, I believe."

"I didn't get it."

"And then elevated to an editorial position with *The Times*?"

"An assistant editor. Nothing spectacular."

"You remained with *The Times* for a period of five years. . . ."

"Nearer six, I think."

"Until January of 1958 when you joined Standard Mutual in Los Angeles?"

"Correct."

"You remained on the Los Angeles staff until March of 1963 when you were transferred to New York City. Since that time you have received several promotions?"

"I came east as a network editor for the seven o'clock news program. I expanded into documentaries and specials until I reached my present position."

"Which is?"

"Director of News for Standard Mutual."

Laurence Fassett closed the folder and shut off the tape recorder. He leaned back and smiled at John Tanner. "That wasn't so painful, was it?"

"You mean that's it?"

"No, not . . . *it*, but the completion of the identity section. You passed. You gave me just enough slightly wrong answers to pass the test."

"What?"

"These things," Fassett slapped the folder, "are designed by the Interrogations Division. Fellows with high foreheads bring in other fellows with beards and they put the stuff through computers. You couldn't possibly answer everything correctly. If you did it would mean you had studied too hard. . . . For instance, you were with *The Sacramento Daily News* for three years almost to the day. Not two and a half or three and a half. Your family moved to San Mateo when you were eight years, two months, not seven years old."

"I'll be Goddamned. . . ."

"Frankly, even if you had answered everything correctly, we might have passed you. But it's nice to know you're normal. In your case, we had to have it all on tape. . . . Now, I'm afraid, comes the tough part."

"Tough compared to what?" asked the newseditor.

"Just rough. . . . I have to start the machine now." He did so and picked up a single sheet of paper. "John Tanner, I must inform you that what I am about to discuss with you comes under the heading of classified information of the highest priority. In no way is this information a reflection on you or your family and to that I do so swear. The revealing of this information to anyone would be against the interests of the United States Government in the severest sense. So much so that those in the government service aware of this information can be prosecuted under the National Security Act, Title eighteen, Section seven-nine-three, should they violate the demands of secrecy. . . . Is everything I've said so far completely clear?"

"It is. . . . However, I am neither bound nor am I indictable."

"I realize that. It is my intention to take you in three stages toward the essential, classified information. At the end of stages one and two you may ask to be excused from this interview and we can only rely on your intelligence and loyalty to your government to keep silent about what has been said. However, if you agree to the third stage, in which identities are revealed to you, you accept the same responsibility as those in government service and can be prosecuted under the National Security Act should you violate the aforementioned demands of secrecy. Is this clear, Mr. Tanner?"

Tanner shifted in his seat before speaking. He looked at the revolving wheels of the tape recorder and then up at Fassett. "It's clear, but I'll be damned if I agree to it. You don't have any right calling me down here under false pretenses and then setting up conditions that make me indictable."

"I didn't ask if you agreed. Only if you understood clearly what I said."

"And if that's a threat, you can go to hell."

"All I'm doing is spelling out conditions. Is that a threat? Is it any more than you do every day with contracts? You can walk out any time you like until you give me your consent to reveal names. Is that so illogical?"

Tanner reasoned that it wasn't, really. And his curiosity now had to be satisfied.

"You said earlier that whatever this thing is, it has nothing to do with my family? Nothing to do with my wife? . . . Or me?"

"I swore to it on this tape." Fassett realized that Tanner had added the "or me" as an afterthought. He was protecting his wife.

"Go ahead."

Fassett rose from the chair and walked toward the window shades. "By the way, you don't have to stay sitting down. They're high-impedance microphones. Miniaturized, of course."

"I'll sit."

"Suit yourself. A number of years ago we heard rumors of a Soviet NKVD operation which could have widespread, damaging effects on the American economy should it ever amount to anything. We tried to trace it down, tried to learn something about it. We couldn't. It remained rumor. It was a better-kept secret than the Russian space program.

"Then in 1966 an East German intelligence officer defected. He gave us our first concrete knowledge of the operation. He informed us that East German Intelligence maintained contact with agents in the West—or a cell—known only as *Omega*. I'll give you the geographical code name in a minute . . . or maybe I won't. It's in step two. That's up to you. Omega would regularly forward sealed files to East German Intelligence. Two armed couriers would fly them to Moscow under the strictest secrecy.

"The function of Omega is as old as espionage itself, and extremely effective in these days of large corporations and huge conglomerates. . . . Omega is a doomsday book."

"A what?"

"Doomsday book. Lists containing hundreds, perhaps by now thousands, of individuals marked for the plague. In this case not bubonic, but blackmail. The men and women on these lists are people in decision-making positions in scores of giant companies in key fields. Many have enormous economic power. Purchasing as well as refusal-to-purchase power. Forty or fifty, acting in concert, could create economic chaos."

"I don't understand. Why would they? Why should they?"

"I told you. Blackmail. Each of these people is vulnerable, exploitable for any of a thousand reasons. Sex, extracurricular or deviate; legal misrepresentation; business malpractice; price-fixing; stock manipulations; tax evasion. The book touches a great many people. Men and women whose reputations, businesses, professions, even their families could be destroyed. Unless they comply."

"It's also a pretty low view of the business world, and I'm not at all sure it's an accurate one. Not to the extent you describe it. Not to the point of economic chaos."

"Oh? The Crawford Foundation made an in-depth study of industry leadership in the United States from 1925 to 1945. The results are still classified a quarter of a century later. The study determined that during this period thirty-two percent of the corporate financial power in this country was obtained by questionable, if not illegal, means. *Thirty-two percent!* .."

"I don't believe that. If it's true it should be made public."

"Impossible. There'd be legal massacre. Courts and money are not an immaculate combination. . . . Today it's the conglomerates. Pick up the newspaper any day. Turn to the financial pages and read about the manipulators. Look at the charges and countercharges. It's a mother lode for Omega. A directory of candidates. None of those boys live in a deep freeze. Not one of them. An unsecured loan is granted, a stock margin is expanded—temporarily—girls are provided to a good customer. Omega digs just a little with the right people and a lot of slime gets in the bucket. It's not very hard to do. You just have to be accurate. Enough so to frighten."

Tanner looked away from the blond man who spoke with such precision. With such relaxed confidence. "I don't like to think you're right."

Suddenly, Fassett crossed back to the table and turned off the tape recorder. The wheels stopped. "Why not? It's not just the information uncovered—that could be relatively harmless—but the way it's applied. Take *you*, for instance. Suppose, just suppose, a story based on occurrences around twenty some-odd years ago outside Los Angeles were printed in the Saddle Valley paper. Your children are in school there, your wife happy in the community. . . . How long do you think you'd stay there?"

Tanner lurched out of his chair and faced the shorter man across the desk. His rage was such that his hands trembled. He spoke with deep feeling, barely audible.

"That's filthy!"

"That's Omega, Mr. Tanner. Relax, I was only making a point." Fassett turned the recorder back on and continued as Tanner returned warily to his chair. "Omega exists. Which brings me to the last part of . . . stage one."

"What's that?"

Laurence Fassett sat down behind the desk. He crushed out his cigarette, while Tanner reached into his pocket and withdrew a pack. "We know now that there's a time table for Omega. A date for the chaos to begin. . . . I'm not telling you anything you don't know whan I admit that my agency is often involved in exchange of personnel with the Soviets."

"Nothing I don't know."

"One of ours for two or three of theirs is the normal ratio. . . ."

"I know that, too."

"Twelve months ago on the border of Albania such an exchange took place. Forty-five days of haggling. I was there, which is why I'm here now. During the exchange our team was approached by several members of the Soviet Foreign Service. The best way I can describe them to you is to call them moderates. The same as our moderates."

"I understand what our moderates oppose. What do the Soviet moderates oppose?"

"Same thing. Instead of a Pentagon—and an elusive military–industrial complex—it's the hard-liners in the Presidium. The militarists."

"I see."

"We were informed that the Soviet militarists have issued a target date for the final phase of Operation Omega. On that date the plan will be implemented. Untold hundreds of powerful executives in the American business community will be reached and threatened with personal destruction if they do not follow the orders given them. A major financial crisis could be the result. An economic disaster is not impossible. . . . It's the truth.

"That is the end of stage one."

Tanner got out of his chair, drawing on his cigarette. He paced up and down in front of the desk. "And with that information I have the option to get out of here?"

"You do."

"You're too much. Honest to Christ, you're too much! . . . The tape's running. Go on."

"Very well. Stage two. We knew that Omega was made up of the very same type of individual it will attack. It had to be, otherwise the contacts could never have been made, the vulnerabilities never established. In essence, we basically knew what to look for. Men who could infiltrate large companies, men who worked either in or for them, who could associate with their subjects. . . . As I mentioned previously, Omega is a code name for a cell or a group of agents. There is also a geographical code name; a clearing house for the forwarding of information. Having passed through this source, the authenticity is presumably established because of its operational secrecy. The geographical code name for Omega is difficult to give an accurate translation of, but the nearest is 'Chasm of . . . Leather' or 'Goat Skin.'"

"'Chasm of Leather'?" Tanner put out his cigarette.

"Yes. Remember, we learned this over three years ago. After eighteen months of concentrated research we pinpointed the 'Chasm of Leather' as one of eleven locations throughout the country. . . ."

"One of them being Saddle Valley, New Jersey?"

"Let's not get ahead of ourselves."

"Am I right?"

"We placed agents within these communities," continued the C.I.A. man, disregarding Tanner's question. "We ran checks on thousands of citizens—a very expensive exercise—and the more we researched, the more evidence we turned up that the village of Saddle Valley was the 'Chasm of Leather.' It was a thorough job. Watermarks on stationery, analysis of dust particles the East German officer brought out in the sealed folders he gave us when he defected, a thousand different items checked and rechecked. . . . But mainly, the information about certain residents unearthed in the research."

"I think you'd better get to the point."

"That will be *your* decision. I've just about concluded stage two." Tanner remained silent, so Fassett continued. "You are in a position to give us incalculable assistance. In one of the most sensitive operations in current U.S.–Soviet relations, you can do what no one else can do. It might even appeal to you, for as you must have gathered from what I've said, the moderates on both sides are at this moment working together."

"Please clarify that."

"Only fanatics subscribe to this type of insurgency. It's far too dangerous for both countries. There's a power struggle in the Soviet Presidium. The moderates must prevail for all our sakes. One way to accomplish this is to expose even part of Omega and kill the target date."

"How can I do anything?"

"You know Omega, Mr. Tanner. You know Omega very well."

Tanner caught his breath. For a moment he believed his heart had stopped. He felt the blood rush to his head. He felt, for an instant, somewhat sick.

"I find that an *incredible* statement."

"I would, too, if I were you. Nevertheless, it's true."

"And I gather this is the end of stage two? . . . You bastard. You son of a bitch!" Tanner spoke hardly above a whisper.

"Call me anything you like. Hit me if you want to. I won't hit back. . . . I told you, I've been through this before."

Tanner got out of the chair and pressed his fingers against his forehead. He turned away from Fassett, then whipped around. "Suppose you're *wrong*?" he whispered. "Suppose you Goddamn idiots have made another *mistake*!"

"We haven't. . . . We don't claim to have flushed Omega out completely. However, we *have* narrowed it down. You're in a unique position."

Tanner walked to the window and started to pull up the shade.

"Don't *touch* that! Hold it *down*!" Fassett leaped from his chair and grabbed Tanner's wrist with one hand and the string of the shade with his other. Tanner looked into the agent's eyes.

"And if I walk out of here now, I live with what you've told me? Never knowing who's in my house, who I'm talking to in the street? Living with the knowledge that you think someone might fire a rifle into this room if I lift up the shade?"

"Don't over-dramatize. These are merely precautions."

Tanner walked back to his side of the desk but did not sit down. "Goddamn you," he said softly. "You know I can't leave. . . ."

"Do you accept the conditions?"

"I do."

"I must ask you to sign this affidavit." He took out a page from the manila folder and placed it in front of Tanner. It was a concise statement on the nature and penalties of the National Security Act. It referred to Omega in unspecific terms—Exhibit A, defined as the tape recording. Tanner scribbled his name and remained standing, staring at Fassett.

"I shall now ask you the following questions." Fassett picked up the folder and flipped to the back pages. "Are you familiar with the individuals I now specify? Richard Tremayne and his wife, Virginia. . . . Please reply."

Astounded, Tanner spoke softly, "I am."

"Joseph Cardone, born Guiseppe Ambruzzio Cardone, and his wife, Elizabeth?"

"I am."

"Bernard Osterman and his wife, Leila?"

"Yes."

"Louder, please, Mr. Tanner."

"I said, yes."

"I now inform you that one, two, or all three of the couples specified are essential to the Omega operation."

"You're out of your mind! You're insane!"

"We're not. . . . I spoke of our exchange on the Albanian border. It was made known to us then that Omega, Chasm of Leather, operated out of a Manhattan suburb—and that confirmed our analysis. That Omega was comprised of couples—men and women fanatically devoted to the militaristic policies of the Soviet expansionists. These couples were well paid for their services. The couples specified—the Tremaynes, the Cardones, and the Ostermans—currently possess coded bank accounts in Zurich, Switzerland, with amounts far exceeding any incomes ever reported."

"You can't mean what you're saying!"

"Even allowing for coincidence, as we have thoroughly researched each party involved, it is our opinion that you are being used as a very successful cover for Omega. You're a newsman above reproach.

"We don't claim that all three couples are involved. It's conceivable that one or possibly two of the couples are being used as decoys, as you are. But it's doubtful. The evidence—the Swiss accounts, the professions, the unusual circumstances of your association—point to a cell."

"Then how did you disqualify me?" asked Tanner numbly.

"Your life from the day you were born has been microscopically inspected by professionals. If we're wrong about you, we have no business doing what we're doing."

Tanner, exhausted, sat down with difficulty in the chair. "What do you want me to do?"

"If our information is correct, the Ostermans are flying east on Friday and will stay with you and your family over the weekend. Is that right?"

"It *was*."

"Don't change it. Don't alter the situation."

"That's impossible now. . . ."

"It's the only way you can help us. *All* of us."

"Why?"

"We believe we can trap Omega during this coming weekend. *If* we have your cooperation. Without it, we can't."

"How?"

"There are four days remaining before the Ostermans arrive. During this period our subjects—the Ostermans, the Tremaynes, and the Cardones—will be harassed. Each couple will receive untraceable telephone calls, cablegrams routed through Zurich, chance meetings with strangers in restaurants, in cocktail lounges, on the street. The point of all this is to deliver a common message. That John Tanner is *not* what he appears to be. You are something else. Perhaps a double agent, or a Politbureau informer, or even a bona fide member of my own organization. The information they receive will be confusing, designed to throw them off balance."

"And make my family a set of targets. I won't permit it! They'd kill us!"

"That's the one thing they won't do."

"Why not? If anything you say is true—and I'm by no means convinced that it is. I *know* these people. I can't believe it!"

"In that event, there's no risk at all."

"Why not?"

"If they—any one or all couples—are not involved with Omega, they'll do the normal thing. They'll report the incidents to the police or the F.B.I. We'll take over then. If one or two couples make such reports and the other or others do not, we'll know who Omega is."

"And . . . supposing you *are* right. What then? What are your built-in guarantees?"

"Several factors. All fool-proof. I told you the 'information' about you will be false. Whoever Omega is will use his resources and check out what he learns with the Kremlin itself. Our confederates there are prepared. They will intercept. The information Omega gets back from Moscow will be the truth. The truth until this afternoon, that is. You are simply John Tanner, news director, and no part of any conspiracy. What will be added is the trap. Moscow will inform whoever runs a check on you to be suspicious of the *other* couples. *They* may be defectors. We divide. We bring about a confrontation and walk in."

"That's awfully glib. It sounds too easy."

"If any attempt was made on your life or the lives of your family, the entire Omega operation would be in jeopardy. They're not willing to take that risk. They've worked too hard. I told you, they're fanatics. The target date for Omega is less than one month away."

"That's not good enough."

"There's something else. A minimum of two armed agents will be assigned to each member of your family. Twenty-four-hour surveillance. They'll never be more than fifty yards away. At any time."

"Now I know you're insane. You don't know Saddle Valley. Strangers lurking around are spotted quickly and chased out! We'd be sitting ducks."

Fassett smiled. "At this moment we have thirteen men in Saddle Valley. Thirteen. They're daily residents of your community."

"Sweet Jesus!" Tanner spoke softly. "Nineteen-eighty-four is creeping up on us, isn't it?"

"The times we live in often call for it."

"I don't have a choice, do I? I don't have a choice at all." He pointed to the tape recorder and the affidavit lying beside it. "I'm hung now, aren't I?"

"I think you're over-dramatizing again."

"No, I'm not. I'm not dramatizing anything. . . . I have to do exactly what you want me to do, don't I? I *have* to go through with it. . . . The only alternative I have is to disappear . . . and be hunted. Hunted by you and—if you're right—by this Omega."

Fassett returned Tanner's look without a trace of deceit. Tanner had spoken the truth and both men knew it.

"It's only six days. Six days out of a lifetime."

Chapter Four

Monday—8:05 P.M.

The flight from Dulles Airport to Newark seemed unreal. He wasn't tired. He was terrified. His mind kept darting from one image to another, each visual picture pushing the previous one out into the distance. There were the sharp staring eyes of Laurence Fassett above the tape recorder's turning reels. The drone of Fassett's voice asking those interminable questions; then the voice growing louder and louder.

"Omega!"

And the faces of Bernie and Leila Osterman, Dick and Ginny Tremayne, Joe and Betty Cardone.

None of it made sense! He'd get to Newark and suddenly the nightmare would be over and he'd remember giving Laurence Fassett the public service features and signing the absent pages of the F.C.C. filing.

Only he knew he wouldn't.

The hour's ride from Newark to Saddle Valley was made in silence, the taxi driver taking his cue from his fare in the back seat who kept lighting cigarettes and who hadn't answered him when he'd asked how the flight had been.

SADDLE VALLEY

VILLAGE INCORPORATED 1862

Welcome

Tanner stared at the sign as it caught the cab's headlights. As it receded he could only think of the words "Chasm of Leather."

Unreal.

Ten minutes later the taxi pulled up to his house. He got out and absently handed the driver the fare agreed upon.

"Thanks, Mr. Tanner," said the driver, leaning over the seat to take the money through the window.

"What? What did you say?" demanded John Tanner.

"I said 'Thanks, Mr. Tanner.'"

Tanner leaned down and gripped the door handle, pulling the door open with all his strength.

"How did you know my name? You tell me how you knew my *name*!"

The taxi driver could see beads of perspiration rolling down his passenger's face, the crazy look in the man's eyes. A weirdo, thought the driver. He carefully moved his left hand toward the floor beneath his feet. He always kept a thin lead pipe there.

"Look, Mac," he said, his fingers around the pipe. "You don't want nobody to use your name, take the sign off your lawn."

Tanner stepped back and looked over his shoulder. On the lawn was the wrought-iron lantern, a weatherproof hurricane lamp hanging from a crossbar by a chain. Above the lamp, reflected in the light, were the words:

THE TANNERS

22 ORCHARD DRIVE

He'd looked at that lamp and those words a thousand times. *The Tanners. 22 Orchard Drive.* At that moment they, too, seemed unreal. As if he had never seen them before.

"I'm sorry, fella. I'm a little on edge. I don't like flying." He closed the door as the driver began rolling up the window. The driver spoke curtly.

"Take the train then, Mister. Or walk, for Christ's sake!"

The taxi roared off, and Tanner turned and looked at his house. The door opened. The dog bounded out to meet him. His wife stood in the hall light, and he could see her smile.

Chapter Five

Tuesday—3:30 A.M. California Time

The white French telephone, with its muted Hollywood bell, had rung at least five times. Leila thought sleepily that it was foolish to have it on Bernie's side of the bed. It never woke him, only her.

She nudged her husband's ribs with her elbow. "Darling. . . . Bernie. Bernie! It's the phone."

"What?" Osterman opened his eyes, confused. "The phone? Oh, the Goddamn phone. Who can hear it?"

He reached over in the darkness and found the thin cradle with his fingers.

"Yes? . . . Yes, this is Bernard Osterman. . . . Long distance?" He covered the phone with his hand and pushed himself up against the headboard. He turned toward his wife. "What time is it?"

Leila snapped on her bedside lamp and looked at the table clock. "Three-thirty. My God!"

"Probably some bastard on that Hawaiian series. It's not even midnight there yet." Bernie was listening at the phone. "Yes, operator, I'm waiting. . . . It's very long distance, honey. If it *is* Hawaii, they can put that producer on the typewriter; we've had it. We never should have touched it. . . . Yes, operator? Please hurry, will you?"

"You said you wanted to see those islands without a uniform on, remember?"

"I apologize. . . . Yes, Operator, this *is* Bernard Osterman, damn it! Yes? Yes? Thank you, operator. . . . Hello? I can hardly hear you. Hello? . . . Yes, that's better. Who's this? . . . What? What did you say? . . . Who *is* this? What's your name? I don't understand you. Yes, I *heard* you, but I don't understand. . . . Hello? . . . Hello! Wait a minute! I said *wait* a minute!" Osterman shot up and flung his legs over the side of the bed. The blankets came after him and fell on the floor at his feet. He began punching the center bar on the white French telephone. "Operator! Operator! The Goddamn line's dead!"

"Who was it? Why are you shouting? What did they say?"

"He . . . the son of a bitch grunted like a bull. He said, he said we were to watch out for the . . . *Tan One*. That's what he said. He made sure I heard the words. The *Tan One*. What the hell is that?"

"The *what*?"

"The Tan One! That's all he kept repeating!"

"It doesn't make sense. . . . Was it Hawaii? Did the operator say where the call came from?"

Osterman stared at his wife in the dim light of the bedroom. "Yes. I heard that clearly. It was overseas. . . . It was Lisbon. Lisbon, Portugal."

"We don't know anyone in Portugal!"

"Lisbon, Lisbon, Lisbon . . ." Osterman kept repeating the name quietly to himself. "Lisbon. Neutral. Lisbon was neutral."

"What do you mean?"

"*Tan One* . . ."

"Tan . . . tan. Tanner. Could it be John Tanner? John Tanner!"

"Neutral!"

"It's John Tanner," said Leila quietly.

"Johnny? . . . What did he mean, 'Watch out'? Why should we watch out? Why place a call at three-thirty in the morning?"

Leila sat up and reached for a cigarette. "Johnny's got enemies. The San Diego waterfront still hurts because of him."

"San Diego, sure! But Lisbon?"

"*Daily Variety* said last week that we're going to New York," continued Leila, inhaling smoke deeply. "That we'd probably stay with our ex-neighbors, the Tanners."

"So?"

"Perhaps we're too well advertised." She looked at her husband.

"Maybe I'll call Johnny." Osterman reached for the phone.

Leila grabbed his wrist. "Are you out of your *mind*?"

Osterman lay back down.

Joe opened his eyes and glanced at his watch: six-twenty-two. Time to get up, have a short workout in his gym and perhaps walk over to the Club for an hour's practice on the golf range.

He was an early riser, Betty the opposite. She would sleep till noon whenever she had the chance. They had two double beds, one for each of them, because Joe knew the debilitating effects of two separate body temperatures under the same set of covers. The benefits of a person's sleep were diminished by nearly fifty percent when he shared a bed all night with somebody else. And since the purpose of the marriage bed was exclusively sexual, there was no point in losing the benefits of sleep.

A pair of double beds was just fine.

He finished ten minutes on the exercycle and five with seven-and-a-half-pound handbells. He looked through the thick glass window of the steam bath and saw that the room was ready.

A panel light above the gym's wall clock flashed on. It was the front doorbell. Joe had the device installed in case he was home alone and working out.

The clock read six-fifty-one, much too early for anyone in Saddle Valley to be ringing front doorbells. He put the small weights on the floor and walked to his house intercom.

"Yes? Who is it?"

"Telegram, Mr. Cardione."

"Who?"

"Cardione, it says."

"The name is Cardone."

"Isn't this Eleven Apple Place?"

"I'll be right there."

He flicked off the intercom and grabbed a towel from the rack, draping it around him as he walked rapidly out of the gym. He didn't like what he had just heard. He reached the front door and opened it. A small man in uniform stood there chewing gum.

"Why didn't you telephone? It's pretty early, isn't it?"

"Instructions were to deliver. I had to drive out here, Mr. Cardione. Almost fifteen miles. We keep twenty-four-hour service."

Cardone signed for the envelope. "Why fifteen miles? Western Union's got a branch in Ridge Park."

"Not Western Union, Mister. This is a cablegram . . . from Europe."

Cardone grabbed the envelope out of the uniformed man's hand. "Wait a minute." He didn't want to appear excited, so he walked normally into the living room where he remembered seeing Betty's purse on the piano. He took out two one-dollar bills and returned to the door. "Here you are. Sorry about the trip." He closed the door and ripped open the cablegram.

L'UOMO BRUNO PALIDO NON È AMICO DEL ITALIANO. GUARDA BENE VICINI DI QUESTA MANIERA. PROTECIATE PER LA FINA DELLA SETTIMANA.

DA VINCI

Cardone walked into the kitchen, found a pencil on the telephone shelf and sat down at the table. He wrote out the translation on the back of a magazine.

The light-brown man is no friend of the Italian. Be cautious of such neighbors. Protect yourself against the end of the week. Da Vinci.

What did it mean? What "light-brown . . . neighbors"? There were no blacks in Saddle Valley. The message didn't make sense.

Suddenly Joe Cardone froze. The light-brown neighbor could only mean John Tanner. The end of the week—Friday—the Ostermans were arriving. Someone in Europe was telling him to protect himself against John Tanner and the upcoming Osterman weekend.

He snatched up the cablegram and looked at the dateline.

Zurich.

Oh, Jesus Christ! Zurich!

Someone in Zurich—someone who called himself Da Vinci, someone who knew his real name, who knew John Tanner, who knew about the Ostermans—was warning him!

Joe Cardone stared out the window at his backyard lawn. Da Vinci, Da Vinci!

Leonardo.

Artist, soldier, architect of war—all things to all men.

Mafia!

Oh, Christ! Which of them?

The Costellanos? The Batellas? The Latronas, maybe.

Which of them had turned on him? And *why*? He was their *friend*!

His hands shook as he spread the cablegram on the kitchen table. He read it once more. Each sentence conjured up progressively more dangerous meanings.

Tanner!

John Tanner had found out something! But *what*?

And why did the message come from Zurich?

What would any of them have to do with Zurich?

Or the Ostermans?

What had Tanner discovered? What was he going to do? . . . One of the Battella men called Tanner something once; what was it?

"*Volturno!*"

Vulture.

". . . . no friend of the Italian. . . . Be cautious. . . . Protect yourself. . . ."

How? From *what*? Tanner wouldn't confide in him. Why should he?

He, Joe Cardone, wasn't syndicate; he wasn't *famiglia*. What could *he* know?

But "Da Vinci's" message had come from Switzerland.

And that left one remaining possibility, a frightening one. The Cosa Nostra had learned about Zurich! They'd use it against him unless he was able to control the "light-brown man," the Italian's enemy. Unless he could stop whatever it was John Tanner was about to do, he'd be destroyed.

Zurich! The Ostermans!

He had done what he thought was right! What he had to do to *survive*. Osterman had pointed that out in a way that left no doubts. But it was in other hands now. Not his. He couldn't be touched any more.

Joe Cardone walked out of the kitchen and returned to his miniature gymnasium. Without putting on gloves he started pounding the bag. Faster and faster, harder and harder.

There was a screeching in his brain.

"Zurich! Zurich! Zurich!"

Virginia Tremayne heard her husband get out of bed at six-fifteen, and knew immediately that something was wrong. Her husband rarely stirred that early.

She waited several minutes. When he didn't return, she rose, put on her bathrobe, and went downstairs. He was in the living room standing by the bay window, smoking a cigarette and reading something on a piece of paper.

"What *are* you doing?"

"Look at this," he answered quietly.

"At what?" She took the paper from his hand.

Take extreme caution with your editorial friend. His friendship does not extend beyond his zeal. He is not what he appears to be. We may have to report his visitors from California.

                                                            Blackstone

"What is this? When did you get it?"

"I heard noises outside the window about twenty minutes ago. Just enough to wake me up. Then there was the gunning of a car engine. It kept racing up and down . . . I thought you heard it, too. You pulled the covers up."

"I think I did. I didn't pay any attention. . . ."

"I came down and opened the door. This envelope was on the doormat."

"What does it mean?"

"I'm not sure yet."

"Who's Blackstone?"

"The commentaries. Basis of the legal system. . . ." Richard Tremayne flung himself down in an armchair and brought his hand up to his forehead. With the other he rolled his cigarette delicately along the rim of an ashtray. "Please. . . . Let me think."

Virginia Tremayne looked again at the paper with the cryptic message. "'Editorial friend.' Does that mean? . . ."

"Tanner's onto something and whoever delivered this is in panic. Now they're trying to make me panic, too."

"Why?"

"I don't know. Maybe they think I can help them. And if I don't, they're threatening me. All of us."

"The Ostermans."

"Exactly. They're threatening us with Zurich."

"Oh, my God! They know! Someone's found out!"

"It looks that way."

"Do you think Bernie got frightened? Talked about it?"

Tremayne's eye twitched. "He'd be insane if he did. He'd be crucified on both sides of the Atlantic. . . . No, that's not it."

"What is it, then?"

"Whoever wrote this is someone I've either worked with in the past or refused to handle. Maybe it's one of the current cases. Maybe one of the files on my desk right now. And Tanner got wind of it and is making noises. They expect me to stop him. If I don't, I'm finished. Before I can afford it. . . . Before Zurich goes to work for us."

"They couldn't *touch* you!" said Tremayne's wife with fierce, artificial defiance.

"Come on, darling. Let's not kid each *other*. In polite circles I'm a merger analyst. In the boardrooms I'm a corporate raider. To paraphrase Judge Hand, the merger market is currently insane with false purchase. False. That means fake. Buying with paper. Pieces of fiction."

"Are you in trouble?"

"Not really—I could always say I was given wrong information. The courts like me."

"They respect you! You've worked harder than any man I know. You're the best damned lawyer there is!"

"I'd like to think so."

"You *are!*"

Richard Tremayne stood at the large bay window looking out at the lawn of his seventy-four-thousand-dollar ranch house. "Isn't it funny. You're probably right. I'm one of the best there is in a system I despise. . . . A system Tanner would rip apart piece by piece on one of his programs if he knew what really made it go. That's what the little message is all about."

"I think you're wrong. I think it's someone you've beaten who wants to get even. Who's trying to frighten you."

"Then he's succeeded. What this . . . Blackstone is telling me isn't anything I don't know. What I *am* and what I *do* makes me Tanner's natural enemy. At least, he'd think so. . . . If only he knew the truth."

He looked at her and forced a smile. "They know the truth in Zurich."

Chapter Six

Tuesday—9:30 A.M. California Time

Osterman wandered aimlessly around the studio lot, trying to get his mind off the pre-dawn phone call. He was obsessed by it.

Neither he nor Leila had slept again. They'd kept trying to narrow down the possibilities and when those were exhausted they explored the more important question of why.

Why had *he* been called? What was behind it? Was Tanner onto another one of his exposés?

If he was, it had nothing to do with him. Nothing to do with Bernie Osterman.

Tanner never talked in specifics about his work. Only in generalities. He had a low pressure point when it came to what he considered injustice, and since the two men often disagreed on what constituted fair game in the marketplace, they avoided specifics.

Bernie thought of Tanner as a crusader who had never traveled on foot. He'd never gone through the experience of watching a father come home and announce he had no job the next day. Or a mother staying up half the night sewing wonders into a worn-out garment for a child going to school in the morning. Tanner could afford his indignation, and he had done fine work. But there were some things he would never understand. It was why Bernie had never discussed Zurich with him.

"Hey, Bernie! Wait a minute!" Ed Pomfret, a middle-aged, rotund, insecure producer, caught up with him on the sidewalk.

"Hello, Eddie. How's everything?"

"Great! I tried reaching you at your office. The girl said you were out."

"Nothing to do."

"I got the word, guess you did, too. It'll be good working with you."

"Oh? . . . No, I didn't get the word. What are we working on?"

"What's this? Jokes?" Pomfret was slightly defensive. As if he was aware that Osterman thought he was a second-rater.

"No jokes. I'm wrapping up here this week. What are you talking about? Who gave you the word?"

"That new man from Continuity phoned me this morning. I'm handling half of the segments on *The Interceptor* series. He said you were doing four running shots. I like the idea."

"What idea?"

"The story outline. Three men working on a big, quiet deal in Switzerland. Right away it grabbed me."

Osterman stopped walking and looked down at Pomfret.

"Who put you up to this?"

"Put me up to what?"

"There's no four shots. No outlines. No deal. Now tell me what you're trying to say."

"You've got to be joking. Would I kid powerhouses like you and Leila? I was tickled to death. Continuity told me to phone you, ask for the outlines!"

"Who called you?"

"What's his name. . . . That new exec Continuity brought from New York."

"Who?"

"He told me his name. . . . Tanner. That's it. Tanner. Jim Tanner, John Tanner . . ."

"John Tanner doesn't work here! Now, who told you to tell me this?" He grabbed Pomfret's arm. "Tell me, you son of a bitch!"

"Take your hands off me! You're crazy!"

Osterman recognized his mistake: Pomfret was no more than a messenger boy. He let go of the producer's arm. "I'm sorry, Eddie. I apologize. . . . I've got a lot on my mind. Forgive me, please. I'm a pig."

"Sure, sure. You're uptight, that's all. You're very uptight, man."

"You say this fellow—Tanner—called you this morning?"

"About two hours ago. To tell you the truth, I didn't know him."

"Listen. This is some kind of a practical joke. You know what I mean? I'm not doing the series, believe me. . . . Just forget it, okay?"

"A joke?"

"Take my word for it, okay? . . . Tell you what; they're talking to Leila and me about a project here. I'll insist on you as the money-man, how about it?"

"Hey, thanks!"

"Don't mention it. Just keep this little joke between the two of us, right?"

Osterman didn't bother to wait for Pomfret's grateful reply. He hurried away down the studio street, toward his car. He had to get home to Leila.

A huge man in a chauffeur's uniform was sitting in the front seat of his car! He got out as Bernie approached and held the back door open for him.

"Mr. Osterman?"

"Who are you? What are you doing in . . ."

"I have a message for you."

"But I don't want to hear it! I want to know why you're sitting in my car!"

"Be very careful of your friend, John Tanner. Be careful what you say to him."

"What in God's name are you talking about?"

The chauffeur shrugged. "I'm just delivering a message, Mr. Osterman. And now would you like me to drive you home?"

"Of course not! I don't know you! I don't understand. . . ."

The back door closed gently. "As you wish, sir. I was simply trying to be friendly." With a smart salute, he turned away.

Bernie stood alone, immobile, staring after him.

Chapter Seven

Tuesday—10:00 A.M.

"Are any of the Mediterranean accounts in trouble?" Joe Cardone asked.

His partner, Sam Bennett, turned in his chair to make sure the office door was shut. "Mediterranean" was their code word for those clients both partners knew were lucrative but dangerous investors. "Not that I know of," he said. "Why? Did you hear something?"

"Nothing direct. . . . Perhaps nothing at all."

"That's why you came back early, though?"

"No, not really." Cardone understood that even for Bennett not all explanations could be given. Sam was no part of Zurich. So Joe hesitated. "Well, partly. I spent some time at the Montreal Exchange."

"What did you hear?"

"That there's a new drive from the Attorney General's office; that the S.E.C. is handing over everything they have. Every possible Mafia connection with a hundred thousand or more is being watched."

"That's nothing new. Where've you been?"

"In Montreal. That's where I've been. I don't like it when I hear things like that eight hundred miles from the office. And I'm Goddamned reluctant to pick up a telephone and ask my partner if any of our clients are currently before a grand jury. . . . I mean, telephone conversations aren't guaranteed to be private any more. . . ."

"Good Lord!" Bennett laughed. "Your imagination's working overtime, isn't it?"

"I hope so."

"You know damned well I'd have gotten in touch with you if anything like that came up. Or even looked like it *might* come up. You didn't cut a vacation short on those grounds. What's the rest?"

Cardone avoided his partner's eyes as he sat down at his desk. "Okay. I won't lie. Something else did bring me in. . . . I don't think it has anything to do with us. With *you* or the company. If I find out otherwise, I'll come to you, all right?"

Bennett got out of the chair and accepted his partner's non-explanation. Over the years he'd learned not to question Joe too closely. For in spite of his partner's gregariousness, Cardone was a private man. He brought large amounts of capital into the firm and never asked for more than a proper business share. That was good enough for Bennett.

Sam walked to the door, laughing softly. "When are you going to stop running from the phantom of South Philadelphia?"

Cardone returned his partner's smile. "When it stops chasing me into the Bankers' Club with a hot lasagna."

Bennett closed the door behind him, and Joe returned to the ten-day accumulation of mail and messages. There was nothing. Nothing that could be related to a Mediterranean problem. Nothing that even hinted at a Mafia conflict. Yet something had happened during those ten days; something that concerned Tanner.

He picked up his telephone and pushed the button for his secretary. "Is this everything? There weren't any other messages?"

"None you have to return. I told everyone you wouldn't be back until the end of the week. Some said they'd call then, the others will phone you Monday."

"Keep it like that. Any calls, I'll be back Monday."

He replaced the phone and unlocked the second drawer of his desk, in which he kept an index file of three-by-five cards. The Mediterranean clients.

He put the small metal box in front of him and started fingering through the cards. Perhaps a name would trigger a memory, a forgotten fact which might have relevance.

His private telephone rang. Only Betty called him on that line; no one else had the number. Joe loved his wife, but she had a positive genius for irritating him with trivial matters when he wished no interruptions.

"Yes, dear?"

Silence.

"What is it, honey? I'm jammed up."

Still his wife didn't answer.

Cardone was suddenly afraid. No one but Betty had that number!

"Betty? Answer me!"

The voice, when it came, was slow, deep and precise.

"John Tanner flew to Washington yesterday. Mr. Da Vinci is very concerned. Perhaps your friends in California betrayed you. They've been in contact with Tanner."

Joe Cardone heard the click of the disconnected telephone.

Jesus! Oh, Jesus! Oh, Christ! It was the Ostermans! They'd turned!

But *why*? It didn't make sense! What possible connection could there be between Zurich and anything *remotely* Mafia? They were light-years apart!

Or were they? Or was one using the other?

Cardone tried to steady himself but it was impossible. He found himself crushing the small metal box.

What could he do? Who could he talk to?

Tanner himself? Oh, God, of course not!

The Ostermans? Bernie Osterman? Christ, no! Not *now*.

Tremayne. Dick Tremayne.

Chapter Eight

Tuesday—10:10 A.M.

Too shaken to sit in a commuter's seat on the Saddle Valley express, Tremayne decided to drive into New York.

As he sped east on Route Five toward the George Washington Bridge, he noticed a light blue Cadillac in his rearview mirror. When he pulled to the left, racing ahead of the other cars, the Cadillac did the same. When he returned to the right, squeezing into the slower flow, so did the Cadillac—always several automobiles behind him.

At the bridge he neared a tollbooth and saw that the Cadillac, in a faster adjacent lane, came parallel. He tried to see who the driver was.

It was a woman. She turned her face away; he could only see the back of her head. Yet she looked vaguely familiar.

The Cadillac sped off before he could reflect further. Traffic blocked any chance he had to follow. He was certain the Cadillac had followed him, but just as surely, the driver did not want to be recognized.

Why? Who was she?

Was this woman "Blackstone"?

He found it impossible to accomplish anything in his office. He canceled the few appointments he had made, and, instead, reexamined the files of recent corporate mergers he had favorably gotten through the courts. One folder in particular interested him: *The Cameron Woolens*. Three factories in a small Massachusetts town owned for generations by the Cameron family. Raided from the inside by the oldest son. Blackmail had forced him to sell his share of the company to a New York clothing chain who claimed to want the Cameron label.

They got the label, and closed the factories; the town went bankrupt. Tremayne had represented the clothing chain in the Boston courts. The Cameron family had a daughter. An unmarried woman in her early thirties. Headstrong, angry.

The driver of the Cadillac was a woman. About the right age.

Yet to select one was to dismiss so many other possibilities. The merger builders knew whom to call when legal matters got sticky. Tremayne! He was the expert. A forty-four year old magician wielding the new legal machinery, sweeping aside old legal concepts in the exploding economy of the conglomerates.

Was it the Cameron daughter in the light blue Cadillac?

How could he know? There were so many. The Camerons. The Smythes of Atlanta. The Boyntons of Chicago. The Fergusons of Rochester. The corporate raiders preyed upon old families, the moneyed families. The old moneyed families pampered themselves, they were targets. Who among them might be Blackstone?

Tremayne got out of his chair and walked aimlessly around his office. He couldn't stand the confinement any longer; he had to go out.

He wondered what Tanner would say if he called him and suggested a casual lunch. How would Tanner react? Would he accept casually? Would he put him off? Would it be possible—if Tanner accepted—to learn anything related to Blackstone's warning?

Tremayne picked up the phone and dialed. His eyelid twitched, almost painfully.

Tanner was tied up in a meeting. Tremayne was relieved; it had been a foolish thing to do. He left no message and hurried out of his office.

On Fifth Avenue, a Checker cab pulled up directly in front of him, blocking his path at the corner crossing.

"Hey, mister!" The driver put his head out the window.

Tremayne wondered whom he was calling—so did several other pedestrians. They all looked at one another.

"You, mister! Your name Tremayne?"

"Me? Yes. . . ."

"I got a message for you."

"For me? How did you? . . ."

"I gotta hurry, the light's gonna change and I got twenty bucks for this. I'm to tell you to walk east on Fifty-fourth Street. Just keep walking and a Mr. Blackstone will contact you."

Tremayne put his hand on the driver's shoulder. "*Who* told you? Who gave you . . ."

"What do I know? Some wack sits in my cab since nine-thirty this morning with the meter on. He's got a pair of binoculars and smokes thin cigars."

The "Don't Walk" sign began to blink.

"What did he say! . . . Here!" Tremayne reached into his pocket and withdrew some bills. He gave the driver a ten. "Here. Now, *tell* me, please!"

"Just what I said, mister. He got out a few seconds ago, gave me twenty bucks to tell you to walk east on Fifty-fourth. That's all."

"That's *not* all!" Tremayne grabbed the driver's shirt.

"Thanks for the ten." The driver pushed Tremayne's hand away, honked his horn to disperse the jaywalkers in front of him, and drove off.

Tremayne controlled his panic. He stepped back onto the curb and retreated under the awning of the storefront behind him, looking at the men walking north, trying to find a man with a pair of binoculars or a thin cigar.

Finding nobody, he began to edge his way from store entrance to store entrance, towards Fifty-fourth Street. He walked slowly, staring at the passersby. Several collided against him going in the same direction but walking much faster. Several others, heading south, noticed the strange behavior of the blond man in his expensively cut clothes, and smiled.

On the Fifty-fourth Street corner, Tremayne stopped. In spite of the slight breeze and his lightweight suit, he was perspiring. He knew he had to head east. There was no question about it.

One thing was clear. Blackstone was not the driver of the light blue Cadillac. Blackstone was a man with binoculars and thin cigars.

Then who was the woman? He'd seen her before. He knew it!

He started east on Fifty-fourth, walking on the right side of the pavement. He reached Madison and no one stopped him, no one signaled, no one even looked at him. Then across Park Avenue to the center island.

No one.

Lexington Avenue. Past the huge construction sites. No one.

Third Avenue. Second. First.

No one.

Tremayne entered the last block. A dead-end street terminating at the East River, flanked on both sides by the canopies of apartment house entrances. A few men with briefcases and women carrying department store boxes came and went from both buildings. At the end of the street was a light tan Mercedes-Benz sedan parked crossways, as if in the middle of a turn. And near it stood a man in an elegant white suit and Panama hat. He was quite a bit shorter than Tremayne. Even thirty yards away, Tremayne could see he was deeply tanned. He wore thick, wide sunglasses and was looking directly at Tremayne as Tremayne approached him.

"Mr. . . . Blackstone?"

"Mr. Tremayne. I'm sorry you had to walk such a distance. We had to be sure, you see, that you were alone."

"Why wouldn't I be?" Tremayne was trying to place the accent. It was cultivated, but not the sort associated with the northeastern states.

"A man who's in trouble often, mistakenly, looks for company."

"What kind of trouble am I in?"

"You *did* get my note?"

"Of course. What did it mean?"

"Exactly what it said. Your friend Tanner is very dangerous to you. And to us. We simply want to emphasize the point as good businessmen should with one another."

"What business interests are you concerned with, Mr. Blackstone? I assume Blackstone isn't your name so I could hardly connect you with anything familiar."

The man in the white suit and hat and dark glasses took several steps towards the Mercedes.

"We told you. His friends from California . . ."

"The Ostermans?"

"Yes."

"My firm has had no dealings with the Ostermans. None whatever."

"But you have, haven't you?" Blackstone walked in front of the hood and stood on the other side of the Mercedes.

"You can't be serious!"

"Believe me when I say that I am." The man reached for the door handle, but he did not open the door. He was waiting.

"Just a minute! Who *are* you?"

"Blackstone will do."

"No! . . . What you said! You couldn't . . ."

"But we do. That's the point. And since you now know that we do, it should offer some proof of our considerable influence."

"What are you driving at?" Tremayne pressed his hands against the Mercedes' hood and leaned toward Blackstone.

"It's crossed our minds that you may have cooperated with your friend Tanner. That's really why we wanted to see you. It would be most inadvisable. We wouldn't hesitate to make public your contribution to the Osterman interests."

"You're crazy! Why would I cooperate with Tanner? On what? I don't know what you're talking about."

Blackstone removed his dark glasses. His eyes were blue and penetrating, and Tremayne could see freckles about his nose and cheekbones. "If that's true then you have nothing to worry about."

"Of course it's true! There's no earthly reason why I should work with Tanner on anything!"

"That's logical." Blackstone opened the door of the Mercedes. "Just keep it that way."

"For God's sake, you can't just *leave*! I see Tanner every day. At the Club. On the train. What the hell am I supposed to think, what am I supposed to say?"

"You mean what are you supposed to look for? If I were you, I'd act as if nothing had happened. As if we'd never met. . . . He may drop hints—if you're telling the truth—he may probe. Then you'll know."

Tremayne stood up, fighting to remain calm. "For all our sakes, I think you'd better tell me whom you represent. It would be best, it really would."

"Oh, no, counselor." A short laugh accompanied Blackstone's reply. "You see, we've noticed that you've acquired a disturbing habit over the past several years. Nothing serious, not at this time, but to be considered."

"What habit is that?"

"Periodically you drink too much."

"That's ridiculous!"

"I said it wasn't serious. You do brilliant work. Nevertheless, at such times you haven't your normal control. No, it would be a mistake to burden you, especially in your current state of anxiety."

"Don't go. Please! . . ."

"We'll be in touch. Perhaps you'll have learned something that will help us. At any rate, we always watch your . . . merger work with great interest."

Tremayne flinched. "What about the Ostermans? You've got to *tell* me."

"If you've got a brain in your legal head, you won't say a thing to the Ostermans! Or hint at anything! If Osterman is cooperating with Tanner, you'll find out. If he's not, don't give him any ideas about *you*." Blackstone climbed into the driver's seat of the Mercedes and started the motor. He said, just before he drove off, "Keep your head, Mr. Tremayne. We'll be in touch."

Tremayne tried to marshal his thoughts; he could feel his eyelid twitch. Thank Christ he hadn't reached Tanner! Not being prepared, he might have said something—something asinine, dangerous.

Had Osterman been such a gargantuan fool—or coward—to blurt out the truth about Zurich to John Tanner? Without consulting them?

If that were the case, Zurich would have to be alerted. Zurich would take care of Osterman. They'd crucify him!

He had to find Cardone. They had to decide what to do. He ran to a corner telephone.

Betty told him Joe had gone into the office. Cardone's secretary told him Joe was still on vacation.

Joe was playing games. The twitch above Tremayne's left eye nearly blinded him.

Chapter Nine

Unable to sleep, Tanner walked into his study, his eyes drawn to the gray glass of the three television sets. There was something dead about them, empty. He lit a cigarette and sat down on the couch. He thought about Fassett's instructions: remain calm, oblivious, and say nothing to Ali. Fassett had repeated the last command several times.

The only real danger would come if Ali said the wrong thing to the wrong person. There *was* danger in that. Danger to Ali. But Tanner had never withheld anything from his wife. He wasn't sure he could do it. The fact that they were always open with each other was the strongest bond in their strong marriage. Even when they fought, there was never the weapon of unspoken accusations. Alice McCall had had enough of that as a child.

Omega, however, would change their lives, for the next six days, at any rate. He had to accept that because Fassett said it was best for Ali.

The sun was up now. The day was beginning and the Cardones, the Tremaynes and the Ostermans would soon be under fire. Tanner wondered what they'd do, how they'd react. He hoped that all three couples would contact the authorities and prove Fassett wrong. Sanity would return.

But it was possible that the madness had just begun. Whichever the case, he would stay home. If Fassett was right, he'd be there with Ali and the children. Fassett had no control over that decision.

He would let Ali think it was the flu. He'd be in touch with his office by phone, but he would stay with his family.

His telephone rang regularly; questions from the office. Ali and the children complained that the constant ringing of the telephone was enough to drive them crazy, so the three of them retreated to the pool. Except for a few clouds around noon, the day was hot—perfect for swimming. The white patrol car passed the house a number of times. On Sunday Tanner had been concerned over it. Now he was grateful. Fassett was keeping his word.

The telephone rang again. "Yes, Charlie." He didn't bother to say hello.

"Mr. Tanner?"

"Oh, sorry. Yes, this is John Tanner."

"Fassett calling. . . ."

"Wait a minute! Tanner looked out his study window to make sure Ali and the children were still at the pool. They were.

"What is it, Fassett? Have you people started?"

"Can you talk?"

"Yes. . . . Have you found out anything? Has any of them called the police?"

"Negative. If that happens we'll contact you immediately. That's not why I'm calling you. . . . You've done something extremely foolish. I can't emphasize how careless."

"What are you talking about?"

"You didn't go in to your office this morning. . . ."

"I certainly did *not*!"

". . . But there must be no break from your normal routine. No altering of your usual schedule. That's terribly important. For your own protection, you *must* follow our instructions."

"That's asking too much!"

"Listen to me. Your wife and children are at this moment in the swimming pool behind your house. Your son, Raymond, did not go to his tennis lesson. . . ."

"I told him not to. I told him to do some work on the lawn."

"Your wife had groceries delivered, which is not customary."

"I explained that I might need her to take notes for me. She's done that before. . . ."

"The main point is you're not doing what you usually do. It's vital that you keep to your day-to-day routine. I can't stress it enough. You cannot, you *must* not call attention to yourself."

"I'm watching out for my family. I think that's understandable."

"So are we. Far more effectively than you can. None of them have been out of our sight for a single minute. I'll amend that. Neither have you. You walked out into your driveway twice: at nine-thirty-two and eleven-twenty. Your daughter had a friend over for lunch, one Joan Loomis, aged eight. We're extremely thorough and extremely careful."

The news director reached for a cigarette and lit it with the desk lighter. "Guess you are."

"There's nothing for you to worry about. There's no danger to you or your family."

"Probably not. I think you're all crazy. None of them have anything to do with this Omega."

"That's possible. But if we're right, they won't take any action without checking further. They won't panic, too much is at stake. And when they do check further they'll immediately suspect each other. For heaven's sake, don't give them any reason not to. Go about your business as if nothing happened. It's vital. No one could harm your family. They couldn't get near enough."

"All right. You're convincing. But I went out to the driveway three times this morning, not twice."

"No, you didn't. The third time you remained in the garage doorway. You didn't physically walk out onto the driveway. And it wasn't morning, it was twelve-fourteen." Fassett laughed. "Feeling better now?"

"I'd be an awful liar if I didn't admit it."

"You're not a liar. Not generally at any rate. Your file makes that very clear." Fassett laughed again. Even Tanner smiled.

"You're really too much, you know that. I'll go into the office tomorrow."

"When it's all over, you and your wife will have to get together with me and mine for an evening. I think they'd like each other. Drinks will be on me. Dewars White Label with a tall soda for you and Scotch on the rocks with a pinch of water for your wife."

"Good God! If you start describing our sex life. . . ."

"Let me check the index. . . ."

"Go to hell," Tanner laughed, relieved. "We'll take you up on that evening."

"You should. We'd get along."

"Name the date, we'll be there."

"I'll make a point of it on Monday. Be in touch. You have the emergency number for after hours. Don't hesitate to call."

"I won't. I'll be in the office tomorrow."

"Fine. And do me a favor. Don't plan any more programs on us. My employers didn't like the last one."

Tanner remembered. The program Fassett referred to had been a Woodward Show. The writers had come up with the phrase *Caught in the Act* for the letters C.I.A. It was a year ago, almost to the week. "It wasn't bad."

"It wasn't good. I saw that one. I wanted to laugh my head off but I couldn't. I was with the Director, in *his* living room. *Caught in the Act!* Jesus!" Fassett laughed again, putting Tanner more at ease than the news director thought possible.

"Thanks, Fassett."

Tanner put down the telephone and crushed out his cigarette. Fassett was a thorough professional, he thought. And Fassett was right. No one could get near Ali and the kids. For all he knew, the C.I.A. had snipers strapped to the trees. What was left for him to do was precisely what Fassett said: nothing. Just go about business as usual. No break from routine, no deviation from the norm. He felt he could play the role now. The protection was everything Fassett said it would be.

However, one thought bothered him, and the more he considered it, the more it disturbed him.

It was nearly four o'clock in the afternoon. The Tremaynes, the Cardones and the Ostermans had all been contacted by now. The harassment had begun. Yet none had seen fit to call the police. Or even to call *him*.

Was it really possible that six people who had been his friends for years were not what they seemed to be?

Chapter Ten

Tuesday—9:40 A.M. California Time

The Karmann Ghia swung off Wilshire Boulevard onto Beverly Drive. Osterman knew he was exceeding the Los Angeles speed limit; it seemed completely unimportant. He couldn't think about anything except the warning he had just received. He had to get home to Leila. They had to talk seriously now. They had to decide what to do.

Why had they been singled out?

Who was warning them? And about what?

Leila was probably right. Tanner was their friend, as good a friend as they'd ever known. But he was also a man who valued reserve in friendship. There were areas one never touched. There was always the slight quality of distance, a thin glass wall that came between Tanner and any other human being. Except, of course, Ali.

And Tanner now possessed information that touched them somehow, meant something to him and Leila. And Zurich was part of it. But, Christ! *How?*

Osterman reached the foot of the Mulholland hill and drove rapidly to the top, past the huge, early-pastiche mansions that were peopled by those near, or once near, the top of the Hollywood spectrum. A few of the houses were going to seed, decaying relics of past extravagance. The speed limit in the Mulholland section was thirty. Osterman's speedometer read fifty-one. He pressed down on the accelerator. He had decided what to do. He would pick up Leila and head for Malibu. The two of them would find a phone booth on the highway and call Tremayne and Cardone.

The mournful wail of the siren, growing louder, jarred him. It was a sound effect in this town of devices. It wasn't real, nothing here was real. It couldn't be for him.

But, of course, it was.

"Officer, I'm a resident here. Osterman. Bernard Osterman. 260 Caliente. Surely you know my house." It was a statement made positively. Caliente was impressive acreage.

"Sorry, Mr. Osterman. Your license and registration, please."

"Now, look. I had a call at the studio that my wife wasn't feeling well. I think it's understandable I'm in a hurry."

"Not at the expense of pedestrians. Your license and registration."

Osterman gave them to him and stared straight ahead, controlling his anger. The police officer wrote lethargically on the long rectangular traffic summons and when he finished, he stapled Bernie's license to it.

At the sound of the snap, Osterman looked up. "Do you have to mutilate the license?"

The policeman sighed wearily, holding onto the summons. "You could have lost it for thirty days, mister. I lessened the speed; send in ten bucks like a parking ticket." He handed the summons to Bernie. "I hope your wife feels better."

The officer returned to the police car. He spoke once more through the open window. "Don't forget to put your license back in your wallet."

The police car sped off.

Osterman threw down the summons and turned his ignition key. The Karmann Ghia started down the Mulholland slope. Half in disgust, Bernie looked at the summons on the seat next to him.

Then he looked again.

There was something wrong with it. The shape was right, the unreadable print was crowded in the inadequate space as usual, but the paper rang false. It seemed too shiny, too blurred even for a summons from the Motor Vehicle Department of the City of Los Angeles.

Osterman stopped. He picked up the summons and looked at it closely. The violations had been marked carelessly, inaccurately, by the police officer. They hadn't really been marked at all.

And then Osterman realized that the face of the card was only a thin photostat attached to a thicker sheet of paper.

He turned it over and saw that there was a message written in red pencil, partially covered by his stapled license. He ripped the license off and read:

Word received that Tanner's neighbors may have cooperated with him. This is a potentially dangerous situation made worse because our information is incomplete. Use extreme caution and find out what you can. It is vital we know—you know—extent of their involvement. Repeat. Use extreme caution.

Zurich

Osterman stared at the red letters and his fear produced a sudden ache at his temples.

The Tremaynes and the Cardones too!

Chapter Eleven

Dick Tremayne wasn't on the four-fifty local to Saddle Valley. Cardone, sitting inside his Cadillac, swore out loud. He had tried to reach Tremayne at his office but was told that the lawyer had gone out for an early lunch. There was no point in having Tremayne call him back. Joe had decided to return to Saddle Valley and meet all the trains from three-thirty on.

Cardone left the station, turned left at the intersection of Saddle Road, and headed west toward the open country. He had thirty-five minutes until the next train was due. Perhaps the drive would help relax him. He couldn't just wait at the station. If anyone was watching him it would look suspicious.

Tremayne would have some answers. Dick was a damned good lawyer, and he'd know the legal alternatives, if there were any.

On the outskirts of Saddle Valley Joe reached a stretch of road bordered by fields. A Silver Cloud Rolls-Royce passed him on his left, and Cardone noted that the huge automobile was traveling extremely fast, much too fast for the narrow country road. He kept driving for several miles, vaguely aware that he was traveling through open country now. He would probably have to turn around in some farmer's driveway. But ahead of him was a long winding curve which, he remembered, had wide shoulders. He'd turn around there. It was time to head back to the station.

He reached the curve and slowed down, prepared to swing hard to his right onto the wide shoulder.

He couldn't.

The Silver Cloud was parked off the road under the trees, blocking him.

Annoyed, Cardone gunned the engine and proceeded several hundred yards ahead where, since there were no other cars in sight, he made the cramped turn.

Back at the station, Cardone looked at his watch. Five-nineteen, almost five-twenty. He could see the entire length of the platform. He'd spot Tremayne if he got off. He hoped the lawyer would be on the five-twenty-five. The waiting was intolerable.

A car pulled up behind his Cadillac, and Cardone looked up.

It was the Silver Cloud. Cardone began to sweat.

A massive man, well over six feet tall, got out of the car and walked slowly toward Cardone's open window. He was dressed in a chauffeur's uniform.

"Mr. Cardione?"

"The name's Cardone." The man's hands, which gripped the base of Joe's window, were immense. Much larger and thicker than his own.

"Okay. Whatever you like. . . ."

"You passed me a little while ago, didn't you? On Saddle Road."

"Yes, sir, I did. I haven't been far from you all day."

Cardone involuntarily swallowed and shifted his weight. "I find that a remarkable statement. Needless to say, very disturbing."

"I'm sorry. . . ."

"I'm not interested in apologies. I want to know why. Why are you following me? I don't know you. I don't like being followed."

"No one does. I'm only doing what I'm told to do."

"What is it? What do you want?"

The chauffeur moved his hands, just slightly, as if to call attention to their size and great strength. "I've been instructed to bring you a message, and then I'll leave. I've a long drive. My employer lives in Maryland."

"What message? Who from?"

"Mr. Da Vinci, sir."

"Da Vinci?"

"Yes sir. I believe he got in touch with you this morning."

"I don't know your Mr. Da Vinci. . . . What message?"

"That you should not confide in Mr. Tremayne."

"What are you talking about?"

"Only what Mr. Da Vinci told me, Mr. Cardione."

Cardone stared into the huge man's eyes. There was intelligence behind the blank façade. "Why did you wait until now? You've been following me all day. You could have stopped me hours ago."

"I wasn't instructed to. There's a radio-phone in the car. I was told to make contact just a few minutes ago."

"*Who* told you?"

"Mr. Da Vinci, sir . . ."

"That's not his name! Now, who is he?" Cardone fought his anger. He took a deep breath before speaking. "You tell me who Da Vinci is."

"There's more to the message," said the chauffeur, disregarding Cardone's question. "Mr. Da Vinci says you should know that Tremayne may have talked to Mr. Tanner. No one's sure yet, but that's what it looks like."

"He *what*? Talked to him about *what*?"

"I don't know, sir. It's not my job to know. I'm hired to drive a car and deliver messages."

"Your message isn't *clear*! I don't understand it! What good is a message if it isn't clear!" Cardone strained to keep in control.

"Perhaps the last part will help you, sir. Mr. Da Vinci feels it would be a good idea if you tried to find out the extent of Mr. Tremayne's involvement with Tanner. But you must be careful. Very, very careful. As you must be careful with your friends from California. That's important."

The chauffeur backed away from the Cadillac and slapped two fingers against his cap's visor.

"Wait a minute!" Cardone reached for the door handle, but the huge man in uniform swiftly clamped his hands on the window ledge and held the door shut.

"No, Mr. Cardione. You stay inside there. You shouldn't call attention to yourself. The train's coming in."

"No, please! *Please* . . . I want to talk to Da Vinci! We've got to talk! Where can I reach him?"

"No way, sir." The chauffeur held the door effortlessly.

"You prick!" Cardone pulled the handle and shoved his whole weight against the door. It gave just a bit and then slammed shut again under the chauffeur's hands. "I'll break you in half!"

The train pulled to a stop in front of the platform. Several men got off and the shriek of two whistle blasts pierced the air.

The chauffeur spoke calmly. "He's not on the train, Mr. Cardione. He *drove* into town this morning. We know that, too."

The train slowly started up and rolled down the tracks. Joe stared at the immense human being holding the car door shut. His anger was nearly beyond control but he was realistic enough to know it would do him no good. The chauffeur stepped back, gave Cardone a second informal salute and walked rapidly towards the Rolls-Royce. Cardone pushed the car door open and stepped out onto the hot pavement.

"Hello there, Joe!" The caller was Amos Needham, of the second contingent of Saddle Valley commuters. A vice-president of Manufacturers Hanover Trust and the chairman of the special events committee for the Saddle Valley Country Club. "You market boys have it easy. When it gets rough you stay home and wait for the calm to set in, eh?"

"Sure, sure, Amos." Cardone kept his eye on the chauffeur of the Rolls, who had climbed into the driver's seat and started the engine.

"I tell you," continued Amos, "I don't know where you young fellas are taking us! . . . Did you see the quotes for DuPont? Everybody else takes a bath and it zooms up! Told my trust committee to consult the Ouija board. To hell with you upstart brokers." Needham chuckled and then suddenly waved his small arm, flagging down a Lincoln Continental approaching the depot. "There's Ralph. Can I give you a lift, Joe? . . . But, of course not. You just stepped out of your car."

The Lincoln pulled up to the platform, and Amos Needham's chauffeur started to get out.

"No need, Ralph. I can still manipulate a door handle. By the way, Joe . . . that Rolls you're looking at reminds me of a friend of mine. Couldn't be, though. He lived in Maryland."

Cardone snapped his head around and looked at the innocuous banker. "Maryland? *Who* in Maryland?"

Amos Needham held the car door open and returned Cardone's stare with unconcerned good humor. "Oh, I don't think you'd know him. He's been dead for years. . . . Funny name. Used to kid him a lot. . . . His name was Caesar.

Amos Needham stepped into his Lincoln and closed the door. At the top of Station Parkway the Rolls-Royce turned right and roared off towards the main arteries leading to Manhattan. Cardone stood on the tarred surface of the Saddle Valley railroad station and he was afraid.

Tremayne!

Tremayne was with Tanner!

Osterman was with Tanner!

Da Vinci . . . Caesar!

The architects of war!

And he, Guiseppe Ambruzzio Cardione, was alone!

Oh, Christ! Christ! Son of God! Blessed Mary! Blessed Mary, Mother of Christ! Wash my hands with his blood! The blood of the lamb! Jesus! Jesus! Forgive me my sins! . . . Mary and Jesus! Christ Incarnate! God all Holy!

What have I done?

Chapter Twelve

Tuesday—5:00 P.M.

Tremayne walked aimlessly for hours; up and down the familiar streets of the East Side. Yet if anyone had stopped him and asked him where he was, he could not have answered.

He was consumed. Frightened. Blackstone had said everything and clarified nothing.

And Cardone had lied. To somebody. His wife or his office, it didn't matter. What mattered was that Cardone couldn't be reached. Tremayne knew that the panic wouldn't stop until he and Cardone figured out between them what Osterman had done.

Had Osterman betrayed them?

Was that really it? Was it *possible*?

He crossed Vanderbilt Avenue, realizing he had walked to the Biltmore Hotel without thinking about a destination.

It was understandable, he thought. The Biltmore brought back memories of the carefree times.

He walked through the lobby almost expecting to see some forgotten friend from his teens—and suddenly he was staring at a man he hadn't seen in over twenty-five years. He knew the face, changed terribly with the years— bloated, it seemed to Tremayne, lined—but he couldn't remember the name. The man went back to prep-school days.

Awkwardly the two men approached each other.

"Dick . . . Dick Tremayne! It *is* Dick Tremayne, isn't it?"

"Yes. And you're . . . Jim?"

"Jack! Jack Townsend! How are you, Dick?" The men shook hands, Townsend far more enthusiastic. "It must be twenty-five, thirty years! You look great! How the hell do you keep the weight down? Gave up myself."

"You look fine. Really, you look swell. I didn't know you were in New York."

"I'm not. Based in Toledo. Just in for a couple of days. . . . I swear to God, I had a crazy thought coming in on the plane. I canceled the Hilton and thought I'd grab a room here just to see if any of the old crowd ever came in. Insane, huh? . . . And look what I run into!"

"That's funny. Really funny. I was thinking the same sort of thing a few seconds ago."

"Let's get a drink."

Townsend kept spouting opinions that were formed in the traditions of corporate thought. He was being very boring.

Tremayne kept thinking about Cardone. As he drank his third drink he looked around for the bar telephone booth he remembered from his youth. It was hidden near the kitchen entrance, and only Biltmore habitués-in-good-standing knew of its existence.

It wasn't there any more. And Jack Townsend kept talking, talking, remembering the unmemorable out loud.

There were two Negroes in leather jackets, beads around their necks, standing several feet away from them.

They wouldn't have been there in other days.

The pleasant days.

Tremayne drank his fourth drink in one assault; Townsend *wouldn't* stop talking.

He *had* to call Joe! The panic was starting again. Maybe Joe would, in a single sentence, unravel the puzzle of Osterman.

"What's the matter with you, Dick? You look all upset."

"S'help me God, this is the first time I've been in here in years." Tremayne slurred his words and he knew it. "Have to make a phone call. Excuse me."

Townsend put his hand on Tremayne's arm. He spoke quietly.

"Are you going to call Cardone?"

"What?"

"I asked if you were going to call Cardone."

"Who are you? . . . Who the hell are you?"

"A friend of Blackstone. Don't call Cardone. Don't do that under any circumstances. You put a nail in your own casket if you do. Can you understand that?"

"I don't understand *anything*! Who *are* you? Who's Blackstone?" Tremayne tried to whisper, but his voice carried throughout the room.

"Let's put it this way. Cardone may be dangerous. We don't trust him. We're not sure of him. Any more than we are of the Ostermans."

"What are you saying?"

"They may have gotten together. You may be flying solo now. Play it cool and see what you can find out. We'll be in touch . . . But Mr. Blackstone told you that already, didn't he?"

Then Townsend did a strange thing. He removed a bill from his wallet and placed it in front of Richard Tremayne. He said only two words as he turned and walked through the glass doors.

"Take it."

It was a one-hundred-dollar bill.

What had it bought?

It didn't buy anything, thought Tremayne. It was merely a symbol.

A price. Any price.

When Fassett walked into the hotel room, two men were already bent over a card table, studying various papers and maps. One was Grover. The other man was named Cole. Fassett removed his Panama hat and sunglasses, putting them on the bureau top.

"Everything okay?" asked Grover.

"On schedule. If Tremayne doesn't get too drunk at the Biltmore."

"If he does," said Cole, his attention on a New Jersey road map, "a friendly, bribable cop will correct the situation. He'll get home."

"Have you got men on both sides of the bridge?"

"And the tunnels. He sometimes takes the Lincoln Tunnel and drives up the Parkway. All in radio contact." Cole was making marks on a piece of tracing paper placed over the map.

The telephone rang. Grover crossed to the bedside table to pick it up.

"Grover here. . . . Oh? Yes, we'll double check but I'm sure we would've heard if he had. . . . Don't worry about it. All right. Keep in touch." Grover replaced the receiver and stood by the telephone.

"What's the matter?" Fassett removed his white Palm Beach jacket and began rolling up his sleeves.

"That was Los Angeles logistics. Between the time Osterman left the studio and was picked up on Mulholland, they lost him for about twenty minutes. They're concerned that he may have reached Cardone or Tremayne."

Cole looked up from the table. "Around one o'clock our time—ten in California?"

"Yes."

"Negative. Cardone was in his car and Tremayne on the streets. Neither could be reached. . . ."

"I see what they mean, though," interrupted Fassett. "Tremayne didn't waste any time this noon trying to get to Cardone."

"We calculated that, Larry," said Cole. "We would have intercepted both of them if a meeting had been scheduled."

"Yes, I know. Risky, though."

Cole laughed as he picked up the tracing papers. "You plan—we'll control. Here's every back road link to 'Leather.'"

"We've got them."

"George forgot to bring up a copy, and the others are with the men. A command post should always have a map of the field."

"*Mea culpa.* I was in briefing until two this morning and had to get the shuttle at six-thirty. I also forgot my razor and toothbrush and God knows what else."

The telephone rang once again and Grover reached down for it.

". . . . I see . . . wait a minute." He held the phone away from his ear and looked over at Laurence Fassett. "Our second chauffeur had a run-in with Cardone . ."

"Oh, Christ! Nothing rough, I hope."

"No, no. The hot-tempered All-American tried to get out of the car and start a fight. Nothing happened."

"Tell him to head back to Washington. Get out of the area."

"Go back to D.C., Jim. . . . Sure, you might as well. Okay. See you at camp." Grover replaced the receiver and walked back to the card table.

"What's Jim going to do 'just as well'?" asked Fassett.

"Drop off the Rolls in Maryland. He thinks Cardone got the license number."

"Good. And the Caesar family?"

"Primed beautifully," interrupted Cole. "They can't wait to hear from Guiseppe Ambruzzio Cardione. Like father, unlike son."

"What's that mean?" Grover held his lighter under his cigarette.

"Old man Caesar made a dozen fortunes out of the rackets. His oldest son is with the Attorney General's office and an absolute fanatic about the Mafia."

"Washing away family sins?"

"Something like that."

Fassett walked over to the window and looked down at the long expanse of Central Park South. When he spoke he did so quietly, but the satisfaction in his voice made his companions smile.

"It's all there now. Each one is jolted. They're all confused and frightened. None of them know what to do or whom to talk to. Now we sit and watch. We'll give them a rest for twenty-four hours. A blackout. . . . And Omega has no choice. Omega has to make its move."

Chapter Thirteen

It was ten-fifteen before Tanner reached his office. He had found it nearly impossible to leave home, but he knew Fassett was right. He sat down and glanced perfunctorily at his mail and messages. Everyone wanted a conference. No one wanted to make a single decision without his say-so.

Corporate musical chairs. The network sub-brass band.

He picked up the phone and dialed New Jersey.

"Hello, Ali?"

"Hi, hon. Did you forget something?"

"No. . . . No. Just felt lonely. What are you doing?"

Inside 22 Orchard Place, Saddle Valley, New Jersey, Alice Tanner smiled and felt warm. "What am I doing? . . . Well, as per the great Khan's orders, I'm overseeing your son's cleaning out the basement. And as the great Khan also instructed, his daughter is spending a hot July morning on her remedial reading. How else could she get into Berkeley by the time she's twelve?"

Tanner caught the complaint. When she was a young girl, his wife's summers were lonely and terrifying. Ali wanted them to be perfect for Janet.

"Well, don't overdo it. Have some kids over."

"I might at that. But Nancy Loomis phoned and asked if Janet could go there for lunch . . ."

"Ali . . ." Tanner switched the phone to his left hand. "I'd rather cool it with the Loomises for a few days . . ."

"What do you mean?"

John remembered Jim Loomis from the daily eight-twenty express. "Jim's trying to boilerplate some market stuff. He's got a lot of fellows on the train to go along with him. If I can avoid him till next week I'm off the hook."

"What does Joe say?"

"He doesn't know about it. Loomis doesn't want Joe to know. Rival houses, I guess."

"I don't see that Janet's going to lunch has anything. . . ."

"Just saves embarrassment. We don't have the kind of money he's looking for."

"Amen to that!"

"And . . . do me a favor. Stay near the phone today."

Alice Tanner's eyes shifted to the telephone in her hand. "Why?"

"I can't go into it, but I may have an important call. . . . What we're always talking about. . . ."

Alice Tanner immediately, unconsciously lowered her voice as she smiled. "Someone's offered you something!"

"Could be. They're going to call at home to set up a lunch."

"Oh, John. That's exciting!"

"It . . . could be interesting." He suddenly found it painful to talk to her. "Speak to you later."

"Sounds marvelous, darling. I'll turn up the bell. It'll be heard in New York."

"I'll call you later."

"Tell me the details then."

Tanner placed the receiver slowly in its cradle. The lies had begun . . . but his family would stay home.

He knew he had to turn his mind to Standard Mutual problems. Fassett had warned him. There could be no break in his normal pattern, and normalcy for any network news director was a condition close to hypertension. Tanner's mark at Standard was his control of potential difficulties. If there was ever a time in his professional life to avoid chaos, it was now.

He picked up his telephone. "Norma. I'll read out the list of those I'll see this morning, and you call them. Tell everyone I want the meetings quick and don't let anyone run over fifteen minutes unless I say otherwise. It would help if all problems and proposals were reduced to written half-pages. Pass the word. I've got a lot to catch up on."

He wasn't free again until 12:30. Then he closed his office door and called his wife.

There was no answer.

He let the phone ring for nearly two minutes, until the spaces between the rings seemed to grow longer and longer.

No answer. No answer at the telephone—the telephone whose bell was turned up so loud it would be heard in New York.

It was twelve-thirty-five. Ali would figure no one would call between noon and one-thirty. And she probably needed something from the supermarket. Or she might have decided to take the children over to the Club for hamburgers. Or she couldn't refuse Nancy Loomis and had taken Janet over for lunch. Or she had gone to the library—Ali was an inveterate poolside reader during the summer.

Tanner tried to picture Ali doing all these things. That she was doing one, or some, or all, had to be the case.

He dialed again, and again there was no answer. He called the Club.

"I'm sorry, Mr. Tanner. We've paged outside. Mrs. Tanner isn't here."

The Loomises. Of course, she went to the Loomises.

"Golly, John, Alice said Janet had a bad tummy. Maybe she took her to the doctor."

By eight minutes after one, John Tanner had dialed his home twice more. The last time he had let the phone ring for nearly five minutes. Picturing Ali coming through the door breathlessly, always allowing that one last ring, expecting her to answer.

But it did not happen.

He told himself over and over again that he was acting foolishly. He himself had seen the patrol car following them when Ali drove him to the station. Fassett had convinced him yesterday that his watchdogs were thorough.

Fassett.

He picked up the phone and dialed the emergency number Fassett had given him. It was a Manhattan exchange.

"Grover . . ."

Who? thought Tanner.

"Hello? Hello? . . . George Grover speaking."

"My name is John Tanner. I'm trying to find Laurence Fassett."

"Oh, hello, Mr. Tanner. Is something the matter? Fassett's out. Can I help you?"

"Are you an associate of Fassett's?"

"I am, sir."

"I can't reach my wife. I've tried calling a number of times. She doesn't answer."

"She may have stepped out. I wouldn't worry. She's under surveillance."

"Are you positive?"

"Of course."

"I asked her to stay by the phone. She thought I was expecting an important call. . . ."

"I'll contact our men and call you right back. It'll set your mind at ease."

Tanner hung up feeling slightly embarrassed. Yet five minutes went by and the expected ring did not come. He dialed Fassett's number but it was busy. He quickly replaced the phone wondering if his impetuous dialing caused Grover to find his line busy. Was Grover trying to reach him? He had to be. He'd try again right away.

Yet the phone did not ring.

Tanner picked it up and slowly, carefully dialed, making sure every digit was correct.

"Grover."

"This is Tanner. I thought you were going to call right back!"

"I'm sorry, Mr. Tanner. We've been having a little difficulty. Nothing to be concerned about."

"What do you mean, difficulty?"

"Making contact with our men in the field. It's not unusual. We can't expect them to be next to a radiophone every second. We'll reach them shortly and call you back."

"That's not good enough!" John Tanner slammed the telephone down and got out of his chair. Yesterday afternoon Fassett had detailed every move made by all of them—even to the precise actions at the moment of his phone call. And now this Grover couldn't reach any of the men supposedly watching his family. What had Fassett said?

"We have thirteen agents in Saddle Valley. . . ."

And Grover couldn't reach any of them.

Thirteen men and none could be contacted!

He crossed to the office door. "Something's come up, Norma. Listen for my phone, please. If it's a man named Grover, tell him I've left for home."

SADDLE VALLEY

VILLAGE INCORPORATED 1862

Welcome

"Where to now, Mister?"

"Go straight. I'll show you."

The cab reached Orchard Drive, two blocks from his home; Tanner's pulse was hammering. He kept picturing the station wagon in the driveway. As soon as they made one more turn he'd be able to see it—if it was there. And if it was, everything would be all right. Oh, Christ! Let everything be all right!

The station wagon was not in the driveway.

Tanner looked at his watch.

Two-forty-five. A quarter to three! And Ali wasn't there!

"On the left. The wood-shingled house."

"Nice place, mister. A real nice place."

"Hurry!"

The cab pulled up to the flagstone path. Tanner paid and pulled open the door. He didn't wait for the driver's thanks.

"Ali! Ali!" Tanner raced through the laundry room to check the garage. Nothing. The small Triumph stood there.

Quiet.

Yet there was something. An odor. A faint, sickening odor that Tanner couldn't place.

"Ali! Ali!" He ran back to the kitchen and saw his pool through the window. Oh, God! He stared at the surface of the water and hurried to the patio door. The lock was stuck and so he slammed against it, breaking the latch, and ran out.

Thank God! There was nothing in the water!

His small Welsh terrier dog stirred from its sleep. The animal was attached to a wire run and immediately started barking in its sharp, hysterical yap.

He sped back into the house, to the cellar door.

"Ray! Janet! Ali!"

Quiet. Except for the incessant barking of the dog outside.

He left the cellar door open and ran to the staircase.

Upstairs!

He leapt up the stairs; the doors to the children's rooms and the guest room were open. The door to his and Ali's room was shut.

And then he heard it. The soft playing of a radio. Ali's clock radio with the automatic timer which shut the radio off at any given time up to an hour. He and Ali always used that timer when they played the radio. Never the ON button. It was a habit. And Ali had been gone over two and a half hours. Someone else had turned on the radio.

He opened the door.

No one.

He was about to turn and search the rest of the house when he saw it. A note written in red pencil next to the clock radio.

He crossed to the bedside table.

"Your wife and children went for an unexpected drive. You'll find them by an old railroad depot on Lassiter Road."

In his panic, Tanner remembered the abandoned depot. It sat deep in the woods on a rarely used back road.

What had he done? What in Christ's name had he done? He'd killed them! If that was so, he'd kill Fassett! Kill Grover! Kill all those who should have been watching!

He raced out of the bedroom, down the staircase, into the garage. The door was open and he jumped into the seat of the Triumph and started the engine.

Tanner swung the small sports car to the right out of the driveway and sped around the long Orchard Drive curve, trying to remember the quickest way to Lassiter Road. He reached a pond he recognized as Lassiter Lake, used by the Saddle Valley residents for ice skating in winter. Lassiter Road was on the other side and seemed to disappear into a stretch of undisciplined woods.

He kept the accelerator flat against the Triumph's floor. He started talking to himself, then screaming at himself.

Ali! Ali! Janet! Ray!

The road was winding. Blind spots, curves, sun rays coming through the crowded trees. There were no other automobiles, no other signs of life.

The old abandoned depot suddenly appeared. And there was his station wagon—half off the overgrown parking area, into the tall grass. Tanner slammed on his brakes beside the wagon. There was no one in sight.

He jumped out of the Triumph and raced to the car.

In an instant his mind went out of control. The horror was real. The unbelievable had happened.

On the floor of the front seat was his wife. Slumped, motionless. In the back were little Janet and his son. Heads down. Bodies sprawled off the red seats.

Oh, Christ! Christ! It had happened! His eyes filled with tears. His body shook.

He pulled the door open, screaming in terror. And suddenly a wave of odor washed over him. The sickish odor he had smelled in his garage. He grabbed Ali's head and pulled her up, frightened beyond feeling.

"Ali! Ali! My God! *Please! Ali!*"

His wife opened her eyes slowly. Blinking. Conscious but not conscious. She moved her arms.

"Where . . . where? The *children!*" She drew out the word hysterically. The sound of her scream brought Tanner back to his senses. He leapt up and reached over the seat for his son and daughter.

They moved. They were alive! They *all* were *alive!*

Ali climbed out of the station wagon and stumbled to the ground. Her husband lifted his daughter out of the back seat and held her as she started to cry.

"What *happened?* What *happened?*" Alice Tanner pulled herself up.

"Don't talk, Ali. Breathe. As deeply as you can. Here!" He walked to her and handed her the sobbing Janet. "I'll get Ray."

"What *happened?* Don't tell me *not* to . . ."

"Be quiet! Just breathe. Breathe hard!"

He helped his son out of the back seat. The boy was sick and started to vomit. Tanner cupped his son's forehead with his hand, holding him around the waist with his left arm.

"John, you simply can't . . ."

"Walk around. Try to get Janet to walk! Do as I *say!*"

Obediently, dazedly, Alice Tanner did what her husband commanded. The boy began to shake his head in Tanner's hand.

"Feeling better, son?"

"Wow! . . . Wow! Where are we?" The boy was suddenly frightened.

"It's all right. It's all right. . . . You're all . . . all right."

Tanner looked over at his wife. She had put Janet's feet on the ground, holding her in her arms. The child was crying loudly now, and Tanner watched, filled with hatred and fear. He walked to the station wagon to see if the keys were in the ignition.

They weren't. It didn't make sense.

He looked under the seats, in the glove compartment, in the back. Then he saw them. Wrapped in a piece of white paper, an elastic band holding the paper around the case. The packet was wedged between the collapsible seats, pushed far down, nearly out of sight.

His daughter was screaming now, and Alice Tanner picked the child up, trying to comfort her, repeating over and over again that everything was all right.

Making sure his wife could not see him, Tanner held the small package below the back seat, snapped the elastic band and opened the paper.

It was blank.

He crumpled the paper and stuffed it into his pocket. He would tell Ali what had happened now. They'd go away. Far away. But he would *not* tell her in front of the children.

"Get in the wagon." Tanner spoke to his son softly and went to his wife, taking the hysterical child from her. "Get the keys out of the Triumph, Ali. We're going home."

His wife stood in front of him, her eyes wide with fright, the tears streaming down her face. She tried to control herself, tried with all her strength not to scream. "What happened? What *happened* to us?"

The roar of an engine prevented Tanner from answering. In his anger, he was grateful. The Saddle Valley patrol car sped into the depot and came to a stop less than ten yards from them.

Jenkins and McDermott leapt out of the automobile. Jenkins had his revolver drawn.

"Is everything all right?" He ran up to Tanner. McDermott went rapidly to the station wagon and spoke quietly to the boy in the back seat.

"We found the note in your bedroom. Incidentally, we think we've recovered most of your property."

"Our what?" Alice Tanner stared at the police officer.

"What property?"

"Two television sets, Mrs. Tanner's jewelry, a box of silver, place settings, some cash. There's a list down at the station. We don't know if we got everything. The car was abandoned several blocks from your house. They may have taken other things. You'll have to check."

Tanner handed his daughter to Ali.

"What the hell are you talking about?"

"You were robbed. Your wife must have come back while they were in the process. She and the children were gassed in the garage. . . . They were professionals, no doubt about it. Real professional methods. . . ."

"You're a liar," said Tanner softly. "There was nothing . . ."

"Please!" interrupted Jenkins. "The main thing now is your wife and children."

As if on signal, McDermott called from inside the station wagon. "I want to get this kid to the hospital! *Now!*"

"Oh, my God!" Alice Tanner ran to the automobile, carrying her daughter in her arms.

"Let McDermott take them," said Jenkins.

"How can I trust you? You lied to me. There was nothing missing in my house. No television sets were gone, no signs of any robbery! Why did you lie?"

"There isn't time. I'm sending your wife and children with McDermott." Jenkins spoke rapidly.

"They're going with *me!*"

"No they're not." Jenkins raised his pistol slightly.

"I'll kill you, Jenkins."

"Then what stands between you and Omega?" said Jenkins calmly. "Be reasonable. Fassett's on his way out. He wants to see you."

"I'm sorry. Truly, abjectly sorry. It won't, it *can't* happen again."

"What *did* happen? Where was your infallible protection?"

"A logistical error on a surveillance schedule that hadn't been cross-checked. That's the truth. There's no point in lying to you. I'm the one responsible."

"You weren't out here."

"I'm still responsible. The Leather team's my responsibility. Omega saw that a post wasn't covered—for less than fifteen minutes, incidentally—and they moved in."

"I can't tolerate that. You risked the lives of my wife and children!"

"I told you, there's no possibility of recurrence. Also—and in an inverted way, this should be comforting—this afternoon confirms the fact that Omega won't kill. Terror, yes. Murder, no."

"Why? Because you say so? I don't buy it. The C.I.A. track record reads like a disaster file. You're not making any more decisions for *me*, let's get that clear."

"Oh? You are then?"

"Yes."

"Don't be a fool. If not for yourself, for your family."

Tanner got out of the chair. He saw through the venetian blinds that two men were standing guard outside the motel window.

"I'm taking them away."

"Where will you go?"

"I don't know. I just know I'm not staying here."

"You think Omega won't follow you?"

"Why should it . . . they? I'm no part of *you*."

"They won't believe that."

"Then I'll make it clear!"

"Are you going to take out an ad in *The Times*?"

"No!" Tanner swung around and pointed a finger at the C.I.A. man. "You will! However you want to do it. Because if you don't, I'll tell the story of this operation and your inept, malicious handling of it on every network newscast in the country. You won't survive that."

"Neither will you because you'll be dead. Your wife dead. Your son, your daughter . . . dead."

"You can't threaten me . . ."

"For God's sake, look at history! Look at what's *really happened*!" Fassett exploded. Then suddenly he lowered his voice and raised his hand to his chest, speaking slowly. "Take me. . . . My wife was killed in East Berlin. They murdered her for no earthly reason except that she was married to me. I was being . . . taught a lesson. And to teach me that lesson they took my wife. Don't make pronouncements to me. I've been there. You've been safe. Well, you're not safe now."

Tanner was stunned. "What are you trying to say?"

"I'm telling you that you'll do exactly what we've planned. We're too close now. I want Omega."

"You can't force me and you know it!"

"Yes, I can. . . . Because if you turn, if you run, I withdraw every agent in Saddle Valley. You'll be alone . . . and I don't think you can cope with the situation by yourself."

"I'm taking my family away . . ."

"Don't be crazy! Omega raced in on a simple logistical error. That means they, whoever they are, are alert. Extremely alert, fast and thorough. What chance do you think you'll have? What chance do you give your family? We've admitted a mistake. We won't make any others."

Tanner knew Fassett was right. If he was abandoned now, he didn't have the resources for control.

"You don't fool around, do you?"

"Did you ever—in a mine field?"

"I guess not. . . . This afternoon. What was it?"

"Terror tactics. Without identification. That's in case you're clean. We realized what had happened and put out a counterexplanation. We'll withhold some of your property—small stuff, like jewelry, until it's over. More authentic."

"Which means you expect me to go along with the 'robbery.'"

"Of course. It's safest."

"Yes. . . . Of course." Tanner reached into his pocket for cigarettes. The telephone rang and Fassett picked it up.

He spoke quietly, then turned to the news director. "Your family's back home. They're okay. Still scared, but okay. Some of our men are straightening up the place. It's a mess. They're trying to lift fingerprints. Naturally, it'll be found the thieves wore gloves. We've told your wife that you're still at headquarters making a statement."

"I see."

"You want us to drive you back?"

"No. . . . No, I don't. I presume I'll be followed anyway."

"Safety surveillance is the proper term."

Tanner entered the Village Pub, Saddle Valley's one fashionable bar, and called the Tremaynes.

"Ginny, this is John. I'd like to talk to Dick. Is he there?"

"John *Tanner?*" Why did she say that? His name. She knew his voice.

"Yes. Is Dick there?"

"No. . . . Of course not. He's at the office. What is it?"

"Nothing important."

"Can't you tell me?"

"I just need a little legal advice. I'll try him at the office. Good-bye."

Tanner knew he had done it badly. He had been awkward.

But then, so had Virginia Tremayne.

Tanner dialed New York.

"I'm sorry, Mr. Tanner. Mr. Tremayne's out on Long Island. In conference."

"It's urgent. What's the number?"

Tremayne's secretary gave it to him reluctantly. He dialed it.

"I'm sorry, Mr. Tremayne isn't here."

"His office said he was in conference out there."

"He called this morning and canceled. I'm sorry, sir."

Tanner hung up the phone, then dialed the Cardones.

"Daddy and Mommy are out for the day, Uncle John. They said they'd be back after dinner. Do you want them to call you?"

"No . . . no, that's not necessary. . . ."

There was an empty feeling in his stomach. He dialed the operator, gave her the information, including his credit card number, and three thousand four hundred miles away a telephone rang in Beverly Hills.

"Osterman residence."

"Is Mr. Osterman there?"

"No, he's not. May I ask who's calling, please?"

"Is Mrs. Osterman there?"

"No."

"When do you expect them back?"

"Next week. Who's calling, please?"

"The name's Cardone. Joseph Cardone."

"C-A-R-D-O-N-E. . . ."

"That's right. When did they go?"

"They left for New York last night. The ten o'clock flight, I believe."

John Tanner hung up the receiver. The Ostermans were in New York! They'd gotten in by six o'clock that morning!

The Tremaynes, the Cardones, the Ostermans.

All there. None accounted for.

Any or all.

Omega!

Chapter Fourteen

Thursday—3:00 A.M.

Fassett had set a convincing scene. By the time Tanner returned home the rooms had been "straightened up," but there was still disarray. Chairs were not in their proper places, rugs off center, lamps in different positions; the woman of the house hadn't yet put things to rights.

Ali told him how the police had helped her; if she suspected collusion she didn't let on.

But then Alice McCall had lived with violence as a child. The sight of policemen in her home was not unfamiliar to her. She was conditioned to react with a minimum of hysteria.

Her husband, on the other hand, was not conditioned at all for the role he had to play. For the second night, sleep was fitful, ultimately impossible. He looked at the dial on the clock radio. It was nearly three in the morning and his mind still raced, his eyes refused to stay shut.

It was no use. He had to get up, he had to walk around; perhaps eat something, read something, smoke.

Anything that would help him stop thinking.

He and Ali had had a number of brandies before going to bed—too many drinks for Ali; she was deep in sleep, as much from the alcohol as from exhaustion.

Tanner got out of bed and went downstairs. He wandered aimlessly around; he finished the remains of a cantaloupe in the kitchen, read the junk mail in the hallway, flipped through some magazines in the living room. Finally he went out to the garage. There was still the faint—ever so faint now—odor of the gas which had been used on his wife and children. He returned to the living room, forgetting to turn off the lights in the garage.

Extinguishing his last cigarette, he looked around for another pack; more for the security of knowing there was one than from any immediate need.

There was a carton in the study. As he opened the top drawer of his desk, a noise made him look up.

There was a tapping on his study window and the beam of a flashlight waving in small circles against the pane.

"It's Jenkins, Mr. Tanner," said the muffled voice. "Come to your back door."

Tanner, relieved, nodded to the dark figure on the other side of the glass.

"This screen-door latch was broken," said Jenkins softly as Tanner opened the kitchen door. "We don't know how it happened."

"I did it. What are you doing out there?"

"Making sure there's no repetition of this afternoon. There are four of us. We wondered what *you* were doing. The lights are on all over downstairs. Even in the garage. Is anything the matter? Has anyone phoned you?"

"Wouldn't you know if they had?"

Jenkins smiled as he stepped through the door. "We're supposed to, I guess you know that. But there's no accounting for mechanical failures."

"I suppose not. Care for a cup of coffee?"

"Only if you'd make enough for three other guys. They can't leave their posts."

"Sure." Tanner filled the hot water kettle. "Instant be all right?"

"Be great. Thanks." Jenkins sat down at the kitchen table, moving his large police holster so it hung free from the seat. He watched Tanner closely and then looked around the room.

"I'm glad you're outside. I appreciate it, really. I know it's a job, but still . . ."

"Not just a job. We're concerned."

"That's nice to hear. You have a wife and kids?"

"No sir, I don't."

"I thought you were married."

"That's my partner. McDermott."

"Oh, I see. . . . You've been on the force here, let's see . . . a couple of years now, isn't it?"

"Just about."

Tanner turned from the stove and looked at Jenkins. "Are you one of them?"

"I beg your pardon?"

"I asked if you were one of them. This afternoon you used the name Omega. That means you're one of Fassett's men."

"I was instructed what to tell you. I've met Mr. Fassett, of course."

"But you're not a small-town policeman, are you?"

Jenkins did not have time to answer. There was a cry from the grounds outside. Both men in the kitchen had heard that sound before, Tanner in France, Jenkins near the Yalu River. It was a scream in the instant of death.

Jenkins bolted to the screen door and raced outside, Tanner following at his heels. Two other men came out of the darkness.

"It's Ferguson! Ferguson!" They spoke harshly, but they did not yell. Jenkins rounded the pool and ran towards the wood beyond Tanner's property. The news director stumbled and tried to keep up with him.

The mutilated body lay in a clump of weeds. The head was severed; its eyes were wide, as if the lids had been pierced and held with nails.

"Get back, Mr. Tanner! Stay back! Don't look! Don't raise your voice!" Jenkins held the petrified news director by the shoulders, pushing him away from the corpse. The two other men ran into the woods, pistols drawn.

Tanner sank to the ground feeling sick, frightened beyond any fear he'd ever known.

"Listen to me," whispered Jenkins, kneeling over the trembling man. "That body in there wasn't meant for you to see. It has nothing to do with *you*! There are certain rules, certain signs we all know about. That man was killed for Fassett. It was meant for *him*."

The body was wrapped in canvas and two men lifted it up to carry it away. Their moves were silent, efficient.

"You're wife's still sleeping." said Fassett quietly. "That's good. . . . The boy got up and came downstairs. McDermott told him you were making coffee for the men."

Tanner sat on the grass on the far side of the pool, trying to make sense out of the last hour. Fassett and Jenkins stood above him.

"For God's sake, how did it happen?" He watched the men carrying the body and his words could hardly be heard. Fassett knelt down.

"He was taken from behind."

"From behind?"

"Someone who knew the woods behind your house." Fassett's eyes bore into Tanner's and the news director understood the unspoken accusation.

"It's my fault, isn't it?"

"Possibly. Jenkins left his post. His position was adjacent. . . . Why were you downstairs? Why were all the first-floor lights on?"

"I couldn't sleep. I got up."

"The lights were on in the garage. Why were you in the garage?"

"I . . . I don't remember. I guess I was thinking about this afternoon."

"You left the garage lights on. . . . I can understand a man who's nervous getting up, going downstairs—having a cigarette, a drink. I can understand that. But I don't understand a man going into his garage and leaving the lights on. . . . Were you going somewhere, Mr. Tanner?"

"Going somewhere? . . . No. No, of course not. Where would I go?"

Fassett looked up at Jenkins who was watching Tanner's face in the dim reflection of the light coming from the house. Jenkins spoke.

"Are you sure?"

"My God. . . . You thought I was running away. You thought I was running away and you came in to stop me!"

"Keep your voice down, please." Fassett rose to his feet.

"Do you think I'd *do* that? Do you think for one minute I'd leave my family?"

"You could be taking your family with you," answered Jenkins.

"Oh, Christ! That's why you came to the window. That's why you left your . . ." Tanner couldn't finish the sentence. He felt sick and wondered if he threw up where he could do it. He looked up at the two government men. "Oh, Christ!"

"Chances are it would have happened anyway." Fassett spoke calmly. "It wasn't . . . wasn't part of any original plan. But you've *got* to understand. You behaved *abnormally*. It wasn't *normal* for you to do what you did. You've got to watch every move you make, everything you do or say. You can't forget that. *Ever*."

Tanner awkwardly, unsteadily, got up. "You're not going on with this? You've got to call it off."

"Call it off? One of my men was just killed. We call it off now and you're also dead. So's the rest of your family."

Tanner saw the sadness in the agent's eyes. One didn't argue with such men. They told the truth.

"Have you checked on the others?"

"Yes, we have."

"Where are they?"

"The Cardones are at home. Tremayne stayed in New York; his wife's out here."

"What about the Ostermans?"

"I'll go into that later. You'd better get back inside. We've doubled the patrol."

"No you don't. What about the Ostermans. Aren't they in California?"

"You know they're not. You placed a call to them on your credit card at four-forty-six this afternoon."

"Then where are they?"

Fassett looked at the news director and replied simply. "They obviously made reservations under another name. We know they're in the New York area. We'll find them."

"Then it could have been Osterman."

"It could have been. You'd better get back. And don't worry. We've got an army out here."

Tanner looked over at the woods where Fassett's man had been murdered. His whole body involuntarily shook for a moment. The proximity of such a brutal death appalled him. He nodded to the government men and started towards his house feeling only a sickening emptiness.

"Is it true about Tremayne?" asked Jenkins softly. "He's in the city?"

"Yes. He had a fair amount to drink and took a room at the Biltmore."

"Anyone check the room tonight?"

Fassett turned his attention from the figure of Tanner disappearing into the house. He looked at Jenkins. "Earlier, yes. Our man reported that he went—probably staggered—to his room a little after midnight. We told him to pull out and pick Tremayne up again at seven. What's bothering you?"

"I'm not sure yet. It'll be clearer when we confirm Cardone's situation."

"We did confirm it. He's at home."

"We assume he's at home because we haven't had any reason to think otherwise up to now."

"You'd better explain that."

"The Cardones had dinner guests. Three couples. They all came together in a car with New York plates. Surveillance said they left in a hurry at twelve-thirty. . . . I'm wondering now if Cardone was in that car. It was dark. He could have been."

"Let's check it out. With both. The Biltmore'll be no problem. With Cardone we'll have Da Vinci make another phone call."

Eighteen minutes later the two government men sat in the front seat of an automobile several hundred yards down the road from the Tanner house. The radio came in clearly.

"Information in, Mr. Fassett. The Da Vinci call got us nowhere. Mrs. Cardone said her husband wasn't feeling well; he was sleeping in a guest room and she didn't want to disturb him. Incidentally, she hung up on us. The Biltmore confirmed. There's no one in room ten-twenty-one. Tremayne didn't even sleep in his bed."

"Thank you, New York," said Laurence Fassett as he flipped the channel button to OFF. He looked over at Jenkins. "Can you imagine a man like Cardone refusing a telephone call at four-thirty in the morning? From Da Vinci?"

"He's not there."

"Neither's Tremayne."

Chapter Fifteen

Thursday—6:40 A.M.

Fassett told him he could stay home on Thursday. Not that he had to be given permission; nothing could have dragged him away. Fassett also said that he'd contact him in the morning. The final plans for the total protection of the Tanner family would be made clear.

The news director put on a pair of khaki trousers and carried his sneakers and a sportshirt downstairs. He looked at the kitchen clock: twenty minutes to seven. The children wouldn't be up for at least an hour and a half. Ali, with luck, would sleep until nine-thirty or ten.

Tanner wondered how many men were outside. Fassett had said there was an army, but what good would an army be if Omega wanted him dead? What good had an army been for the government man in the woods at three-thirty in the morning? There were too many possibilities. Too many opportunities. Fassett had to understand that now. It had gone too far. If the preposterous were real, if the Ostermans, the Cardones or the Tremaynes really were a part of Omega, he couldn't simply greet them at his door as if nothing had happened. It was absurd!

He went to the kitchen door and quietly let himself out. He'd go towards the woods until he saw someone. He'd reach Fassett.

"Good morning." It was Jenkins, dark circles of weariness under his eyes. He was sitting on the ground just beyond the edge of the woods. He couldn't be seen from the house or even the pool.

"Hello. Aren't you going to get any sleep?"

"I'm relieved at eight. I don't mind. What about you? You're exhausted."

"Look, I want to see Fassett. I've got to see him before he makes any more plans."

The patrolman looked at his wristwatch. "He was going to call you after we gave him the word you were up. I don't think he expected it'd be so early. That may be good though. Wait a sec." Jenkins walked a few feet into the woods and returned with a canvas-pack radio. "Let's go. We'll drive over."

"Why can't he come here?"

"Relax. Nobody could get near your house. Come on. You'll see."

Jenkins picked up the radio by its shoulder strap and led Tanner through a newly created path in the woods surrounding his property. Every thirty to forty feet were men, kneeling, sitting, lying on their stomachs facing the house, unseen but seeing. As Jenkins and Tanner approached each man, weapons were drawn. Jenkins gave the radio to the patrol on the east flank.

"Call Fassett. Tell him we're on our way over," he said.

"That agent was killed last night because the killer knew he'd been recognized. One part of Omega was identified and that was unacceptable." Fassett sipped coffee, facing Tanner. "It was also another sort of warning, but that doesn't concern you."

"He was murdered fifty yards from my house, from my family! *Everything* concerns me!"

"All right! . . . Try to understand. We can assume the information on you has been returned; remember, you're just Tanner the newsman, nothing else. They're circling like hawks now, wary of each other. None knowing whether the others have accomplices, scouts of their own. . . . The killer—*one* tentacle of Omega—ran a private surveillance. He collided with the agent; he had no choice but to kill. He didn't know him, he'd never seen him before. The only thing he *could* be sure of was that whoever posted the man would become concerned when he didn't report. Whoever was responsible for that man in the woods would come and find him. That was the warning; his death."

"You can't be sure of that."

"We're not dealing with amateurs. The killer knew the body would be removed before daylight. I told you in Washington, Omega's fanatic. A decapitated body fifty yards from your house is the kind of mistake that would call for an N.K.V.D. execution. *If* Omega was responsible. If not . . ."

"How do you know they're not working together? If the Ostermans or the Cardones or the Tremaynes are any part of it, they could have planned it together."

"Impossible. They haven't been in contact since the harassment began. We've fed them all—each of them—contradictory stories, illogical suppositions, half truths. We've had cables routed through Zurich, telephone calls from Lisbon, messages delivered by strangers in dead-end streets. Each couple is in the dark. None know what the others are doing."

The agent named Cole looked up at Fassett from the chair by the motel window. He knew that Fassett could not be absolutely sure of his last statement. They'd lost the Ostermans for nearly twelve hours. There was a surveillance lapse of three and three-and-a-half hours, respectively, with Tremayne and Cardone. Still, thought Cole, Fassett was right to say what he did.

"Where are the Ostermans? You said last night—this morning—that you didn't know where they were."

"We found them. In a New York hotel. From what we've learned, it's doubtful Osterman was in the area last night."

"But, again, you're not sure."

"I said doubtful. Not beyond doubt."

"And you're convinced it had to be one of them?"

"We think so. The killer was male almost certainly. It . . . took enormous strength. . . . He knew the grounds around your property better than we did. And you should know we've studied your place for weeks."

"For God's sake then, *stop* them! Confront them! You can't let it go on!"

"Which one?" Fassett asked quietly.

"*All* of them! A man was *killed*!"

Fassett put his coffee cup down. "If we do as you suggest, which, I admit, is tempting—it was my man who was killed, remember—we not only wash out any chance we have to expose Omega, but we also take a risk with you and your family that I can't justify."

"We couldn't be taking any greater risk and you know it."

"You're in no danger. Not as long as you continue to act in a normal manner. If we walk in now we're admitting the weekend is a trap. That trap couldn't have been set without your assistance. . . . We'd be signing your death warrants."

"I don't understand that."

"Then take my word for it," said Fassett sharply. "Omega *must* come to *us*. There's no other way."

Tanner paused, watching Fassett carefully. "That's not entirely true, is it? What you're saying is . . . it's too late."

"You're very perceptive."

Fassett picked up his cup and went to the table where there was a thermos of coffee. "There's only one more day. At the most two. Some part of Omega will break by then. All we need is one. One defection and it's over."

"And one stick of dynamite in my house blows us to hell."

"There'll be nothing like that. No violence. Not directed at you. Put simply, you're not important. Not any longer. They'll only be concerned about each other."

"What about yesterday afternoon?"

"We've put out a police-blotter story. A robbery. Bizarre to be sure, but a robbery nevertheless. Just what your wife thinks happened, the way she thinks it happened. You don't have to deny anything."

"They'll know it's a lie. They'll call it."

Fassett looked calmly up from the thermos. "Then we'll have Omega, won't we? We'll know which one it is."

"What am I supposed to do? Pick up a telephone and call you? They may have other ideas . . ."

"We'll hear every word said in your house starting with your first guest tomorrow afternoon. Later this morning two television repairmen will come to fix the sets damaged in the robbery. While tracing antenna wiring they'll also install miniaturized pick-ups throughout your home. Starting with the first arrival tomorrow, they'll be activated."

"Are you trying to tell me you won't activate them until then?"

Cole interrupted. "No, we won't. We're not interested in your privacy, only your safety."

"You'd better get back," said Fassett. "Jenkins will drop you off at the south end of your property. You couldn't sleep so you went for a walk."

Tanner crossed slowly to the door. He stopped and looked back at Fassett. "It's just like it was in Washington, isn't it? You don't give me any alternative."

Fassett turned away. "We'll be in touch. If I were you I'd relax, go to the Club. Play tennis, swim. Get your mind off things. You'll feel better."

Tanner looked at Fassett's back in disbelief. He was being dismissed, as a less-than-respected subordinate is dismissed before a high policy conference.

"Come on," said Cole, standing up, "I'll see you to the car." As they walked, he added, "I think you should know that that man's death last night complicates Fassett's job more than you'll ever realize. That killing was directed at him. It was *his* warning."

The news director looked at Cole closely. "What do you mean?"

"There are signs between old-line professionals and this is one of them. You're insignificant now. . . . Fassett's brilliant. He's set the forces in motion and nothing can stop them. The people who conceived Omega realize what's happened. And they're beginning to see that they may be helpless. They want the man responsible to know they'll be back. Sometime. A severed head means a massacre, Mr. Tanner. They took his wife. Now he's got three kids to worry about."

Tanner felt the sickness coming upon him again.

"What kind of a world do you people live in?"

"The same one you do."

Chapter Sixteen

Thursday—10:15 A.M.

When Alice awoke at ten-fifteen Thursday morning her immediate reaction was to remain in bed forever. She could hear the children arguing downstairs and the indistinguishable but patient words from her husband settling the dispute. She thought about his remarkable sense of small kindnesses that added up to major concern. That wasn't bad after so many years of marriage.

Perhaps her husband wasn't as quick or dramatic as Dick Tremayne, or as sheerly powerful as Joe Cardone, or as witty or bright as Bernie Osterman, but she wouldn't exchange places with Ginny, Betty, or Leila for anything in the world. Even if everything started all over again, she would wait for John Tanner, or *a* John Tanner. He was that rare man. He wanted to share, *had* to share. *Everything*. None of the others did. Not even Bernie, although he was the most like John. Even Bernie had quiet secrets, according to Leila.

In the beginning, Alice had wondered if her husband's need to share was merely the result of his pity for her. Because she was to be pitied, she realized without any sense of self-indulgence. Most of her life before she met John Tanner had been spent in flight or in pursuit of sanctuary. Her father, a self-professed rectifier of the world's ills, was never able to stay too long in one place. A contemporary John Brown.

The newspapers eventually labeled him . . . lunatic.

The Los Angeles police eventually killed him.

She remembered the words.

Los Angeles, February 10, 1945. Jason McCall, whom authorities believe to have been in the pay of the Communists, was shot down today outside his canyon headquarters when he emerged brandishing what appeared to be a weapon. The Los Angeles police and agents of the Federal Bureau of Investigation unearthed McCall's whereabouts after an extensive search. . . .

The Los Angeles police and the agents of the Federal Bureau of Investigation, however, had not bothered to determine that Jason McCall's weapon was a bent piece of metal he called his "plowshare."

Mercifully, Alice had been with an aunt in Pasadena when the killing took place. She'd met the young journalism student, John Tanner, at the public inquest after her father's death. The Los Angeles authorities wanted the inquest public. There was no room for a martyr. They wanted it clear that under no circumstances was McCall's death a murder.

Which, of course, it was.

The young journalist—returned from the war—knew it and labeled it as such. And although his story did nothing for the McCall family, it did bring him closer to the sad and bewildered girl who became his wife.

Alice stopped thinking and rolled over on her stomach. It was all past. She was where she wanted to be.

Several minutes later she heard strange male voices downstairs in the hallway. She started to sit up when the door opened and her husband came in. He smiled and bent down, kissing her lightly on the forehead, but in spite of his casualness, there was something strained about him.

"Who's downstairs?" she asked.

"The T.V. men. They're rehooking the sets, but the outside antenna system's loused up. They have to locate the trouble."

"Which means I get up."

"It does. I'm not taking chances with you in bed in front of two well-proportioned men in overalls."

"You once wore overalls. Remember? In your senior year you had that job at the gas station."

"And when I got home I also remember they came off with alarming ease. Now, up you go."

He was tense, she thought; he was imposing control on the situation, on himself. He announced that in spite of the pressures which descended on him on Thursdays, on this particular Thursday he was staying at home.

His explanation was simple. After yesterday afternoon, regardless of the continuing police investigation, he wasn't about to leave his family. Not until everything was cleared up.

He took them to the Club, where he and Ali played doubles with their neighbors, Dorothy and Tom Scanlan. Tom was reputed to be so rich he hadn't gone to work in a decade.

What struck Ali was her husband's determination to win. She was embarrassed when he accused Tom of miscalling a line shot and mortified when he made an unusually violent overhead, narrowly missing Dorothy's face.

They won the set, and the Scanlans turned down another. So they went to the pool, where John demanded what amounted to extraordinary service from the waiters. Late in the afternoon he spotted McDermott and insisted he join them for a drink. McDermott had come to the Club—so John told his wife—to tell a member that his car was long overdue at a parking meter in town.

And always, always, Tanner kept going to the telephone inside the Club. He could have had one brought to the poolside table but he wouldn't do so. He claimed that the Woodward conferences were getting heated and he'd rather not talk in public.

Alice didn't believe it. Her husband had many talents and perhaps the most finely honed was his ability to remain calm, even cold, under acute pressure. Yet today he was obviously close to panic.

They returned to Orchard Drive at eight o'clock. Tanner ordered the children to bed; Alice revolted.

"I've had it!" she said firmly. She pulled her husband into the living room and held his arm. "You're being unreasonable, darling. I know how you felt. I felt it, too, but you've been barking orders all day long. Do this! Do that! It's not like you."

Tanner remembered Fassett. He had to remain calm, normal. Even with Ali.

"I'm sorry. It's a delayed reaction, I guess. But you're right. Forgive me."

"It's over and done with," she added, not really accepting his quick apology. "It was frightening, but everything's all right now. It's *over*."

Oh, Christ, thought Tanner. He wished to God it were that simple. "It's over and I've behaved childishly and I want my wife to say she loves me so we can have a couple of drinks and go to bed together." He kissed her lightly on the lips. "And that, madam, is the best idea I've had all day."

"You took a long time arriving at it," she said as she smiled up at him.

"It'll take me a few minutes. I promised Janet I'd read her a story."

"What are you going to read her?"

"'Beauty and the Beast.' Ponder it." She disengaged herself from his arms, touching his face with her fingers. "Give me ten, fifteen minutes."

Tanner watched her go back into the hall to the staircase. She'd been through so much, and now this. Now, Omega.

He looked at his watch. It was eighty-twenty and Ali would be upstairs for at least ten minutes, probably twice as long. He decided to call Fassett at the motel.

It wasn't going to be the usual conversation with Fassett. No more condescending instructions, no more sermons. It was now the end of the third day; three days of harassment against the suspects of Omega.

John Tanner wanted specifics. He was entitled to them.

Fassett was alarmed, annoyed, at the news director's precise questions.

"I can't take time to phone you whenever someone crosses the street."

"I need answers. The weekend starts tomorrow, and if you want me to go on with this, you'll tell me what's happened. Where are they now? What have their reactions been? I've *got* to know."

For a few seconds there was silence. When Fassett spoke, his voice was resigned. "Very well. . . . Tremayne stayed in New York last night. I told you that, remember? While at the Biltmore he met a man named Townsend. Townsend's a known stock manipulator out of Zurich. Cardone and his wife went to Philadelphia this afternoon. She visited her family in Chestnut Hill and he went out to Bala Cynwyd to meet with a man we know is a high capo in the Mafia. They got back to Saddle Valley an hour ago. The Ostermans are at The Plaza. They're having dinner later tonight with a couple named Bronson. The Bronsons are friends from years ago. They're also on the Attorney General's subversive list."

Fassett stopped and waited for Tanner to speak.

"And none of them have met? They haven't even called each other? They've made no plans? I want the truth!"

"If they've talked it hasn't been on any telephone we can control, which would mean they'd have to be at pay phones at simultaneous times, which they haven't. We know they haven't met—simple surveillance. If any of them has plans, they're individual, not coordinated. . . . We're counting on that as I've told you. That's all there it."

"There doesn't seem to be any relationship. With any of them?"

"That's right. That's what we've concluded."

"But not what you expected. You said they'd panic. Omega would be in panic by now."

"I think they are. Every one of them. Separately. Our projections are positive."

"What the hell does that mean?"

"Think. One couple races to a powerful Mafioso. Another meets with a husband and wife who are as fanatic as anyone in the Presidium. And the lawyer has a sudden conference with an international securities thief out of Zurich. That's panic. The N.K.V.D. has many tentacles. Every one of them is on the brink. All we do is sit and wait."

"Beginning tomorrow, sitting and waiting's not going to be so easy."

"Be natural. You'll find yourself functioning on two levels really quite comfortably. It's always like that. There's no danger if you even *half* carry it off. They're too concerned with each other now. Remember, you don't have to hide yesterday afternoon. Talk about it. Be expansive. Do and say what comes naturally about it."

"And you think they'll believe me?"

"They haven't got a choice! Don't you understand that? You made your reputation as an investigative reporter. Do I have to remind you that investigation ends when the subjects collide? That's the age-old wrap-up."

"And I'm the innocent catalyst?"

"You better believe it. The more innocent, the better the wrap-up."

Tanner lit a cigarette. He couldn't deny the government man any longer. His logic was too sound. And the safety, the security, the all-holy well-being of Ali and the children was in this cold professional's hands.

"All right. I greet them all at the door as long-lost brothers and sisters."

"That's the way. And if you feel like it, call them all in the morning, make sure they're coming over. Except the Ostermans, of course. Whatever you'd normally do. . . . And remember, we're right there. The most sophisticated equipment the biggest corporation on earth owns is at work for you. Not even the smallest weapon could get through your front door."

"Is that true?"

"We'd know it if a three-inch blade was in someone's pocket. A four-inch revolver would have you all out of there in sixty seconds."

Tanner replaced the receiver and drew heavily on his cigarette. As he took his hand off the telephone he had the feeling—the physical feeling—of *leaving, jumping, going away.*

It was a strange sensation, an awesome sense of loneliness.

And then he realized what it was, and it disturbed him greatly.

His sanity was now dependent on a man named Fassett. He was utterly in his control.

PART THREE
The Weekend

Chapter Seventeen

The taxi drew up to the front of the Tanner house. John's dog, the stringy Welsh terrier, ran up and down the driveway, yapping with each advance and retreat, waiting for someone to acknowledge that the visitors were welcome. Janet raced across the front lawn. The taxi door opened; the Ostermans stepped out. Each carried gift-wrapped boxes. The driver brought out a single large suitcase.

From the inside of the house, Tanner looked at them both: Bernie, in an expensively cut Palm Beach jacket and light-blue slacks; Leila, in a white suit with a gold chain around her waist, the skirt well above her knees, and a wide-brimmed soft hat covering the left side of her face. They were the picture of California success. Yet somehow there was a trace of artifice with Bernie and Leila; they had moved into the real money barely nine years ago.

Or was their success itself a façade, wondered Tanner as he watched the couple bending down to embrace his daughter. Had they, instead, for years and years been inhabitants of a world where scripts and shooting schedules were only secondary—good *covers*, as Fassett might say?

Tanner looked at his watch. It was two minutes past five. The Ostermans were early—according to their original schedule. Perhaps it was their first mistake. Or perhaps they didn't expect him to be there. He always left the Woodward studio early when the Ostermans came, but not always in time to be home before five-thirty. Leila's letter had said plainly their flight from Los Angeles was due at Kennedy around five. A plane being late was understandable, normal. A flight that got in ahead of schedule was improbable.

They'd have to have an explanation. Would they bother?

"Johnny! For heaven's sake! I thought I heard the pup barking. It's Bernie and Leila. What are you standing there for?" Ali had come out of the kitchen.

"Oh, sorry. . . . I just wanted to let Janet have her moment with them."

"Go on out, silly. I'll just set the timer." His wife walked back towards the kitchen as Tanner approached the front door. He stared at the brass knob and felt as he thought an actor might feel before making his first entrance in a difficult part. Unsure—totally unsure—of his reception.

He wet his lips and drew the back of his hand across his forehead. Deliberately he twisted the knob and pulled the door back swiftly. With his other hand he unlatched the aluminum screened panel and stepped outside.

The Osterman weekend had begun.

"Welcome, Schreibers!" he shouted with a wide grin. It was his usual greeting; Bernie considered it the most honorific.

"Johnny!"

"Hi, darling!"

Thirty yards away, they shouted back and smiled broad smiles. Yet even thirty yards away John Tanner could see their unsmiling eyes. Their eyes searched his—briefly, but unmistakably. For a split second Bernie even stopped smiling, stopped any motion whatsoever.

It was over in a moment. And there seemed to be a tacit agreement between them not to pursue the unspoken thoughts.

"Johnny, it's so awfully good to see you!" Leila ran across the lawn.

John Tanner accepted Leila's embrace and found himself responding with more overt affection than he thought he could muster. He knew why. He had passed the first test, the opening seconds of the Osterman weekend. He began to realize that Laurence Fassett could be right, after all. Perhaps he *could* carry it off.

Do as you'd normally do; behave as you'd normally behave. Don't think about anything else.

"John, you look great, just great, man!"

"Where's Ali, sweetie?" asked Leila who stepped aside so Bernie could throw his long thin arms around Tanner.

"Inside. Casserole-doing-time. Come on in! I'll grab the bag. . . . No, Janet, honey, you can't lift Uncle Bernie's suitcase."

"I don't know why not," laughed Bernie. "All it's filled with is towels from The Plaza."

"The Plaza?" Tanner couldn't help himself. "I thought your plane just got in."

Osterman glanced at him. "Uh uh. We flew in a couple of days ago. I'll tell you about it. . . ."

In a strange way it was like old times, and Tanner was astonished that he found himself accepting the fact. There was still the sense of relief at physically seeing each other again, knowing that time and distance were meaningless to their friendship. There was still the feeling that they could take up conversations, continue anecdotes, finish stories begun months previously. And there was still Bernie; gentle, reflective Bernie with his quiet, devastating comments about the palm-lined drug store. Devastating but somehow never condescending; Bernie laughed at himself as well as his professional world, for it *was* his world.

Tanner remembered Fassett's words.

". . . *you'll find yourself functioning on two levels quite comfortably. It's always like that.*"

Again, Fassett was right. . . . In and out; in and out.

It struck Tanner as he watched Bernie that Leila kept shifting her eyes away from her husband to him. Once he returned her look; she lowered her eyes as a child might after a reprimand.

The telephone rang in the study. The sound was jarring to everyone but Alice. There was an extension phone on the table behind the sofa, but John ignored it as he crossed in front of the Ostermans towards the study door.

"I'll take it out here. It's probably the studio."

As he entered the study he heard Leila speak to Ali, her voice lowered.

"Sweetie, Johnny seems tense. Is anything the matter? The way Bernie drawls on no one can get a word in."

"Tense is understating it! You should have seen him yesterday!"

The telephone rang again; Tanner knew it wouldn't be normal to let it ring further. Yet he wanted so much to hear the Ostermans' reaction to Ali's story of the Wednesday terror.

He compromised. He picked the phone out of the cradle, held it to his side and listened for several seconds to the conversation.

Something caught his ear. Bernie and Leila reacted to Ali's words too quickly, with too much anticipation. They were asking questions before she finished sentences! They *did* know something.

"Hello? Hello! Hello, hello!" The anxious voice on the other end of the line belonged to Joe Cardone.

"Hello, Joe? Sorry, I dropped the phone. . . ."

"I didn't hear it drop."

"Very soft, very expensive carpets."

"Where? In that study of yours with the parquet floor?"

"Hey, come on, Joe."

"Sorry. . . . The city was rotten hot today and the market's going to hell."

"That's better. Now you sound like the cheerful fellow we're waiting for."

"You mean everybody's there?"

"No. Just Bernie and Leila."

"They're early. I thought the plane got in at five."

"They flew in a couple of days ago."

Cardone started to speak and then abruptly stopped. He seemed to catch his breath. "Funny they didn't call. I mean, they didn't get in touch with me. Did they with you?"

"No, I guess they had business."

"Sure, but you'd think. . . ." Again Cardone stopped in the middle of a sentence. Tanner wondered whether this hesitation was meant for him; to convince him of the fact that Bernie and Joe hadn't met, hadn't spoken with each other.

"Bernie'll probably tell us all about it."

"Yeah," said Cardone, not really listening. "Well, I just wanted to let you know we'd be late. I'll grab a quick shower; be there soon."

"See you." Tanner hung up the phone, surprised at his own calm. It occurred to him that he had controlled the conversation. *Controlled* it. He had to. Cardone was a nervous man and he hadn't called to say he'd be late. To begin with, he wasn't late.

Cardone had phoned to see if the others had come. Or if they were coming.

Tanner returned to the living room and sat down.

"Darling! Ali just told us! How dreadful! How simply terrifying!"

"My God, John! What an awful experience! The police said it was robbery?"

"So did *The New York Times*. Guess that makes it official."

"I didn't see anything in *The Times*," stated Bernie firmly.

"It was only a few lines near the back. We'll get better coverage in the local paper next week."

"I've never heard of any robbery like that," said Leila. "I wouldn't settle for that, I really wouldn't."

Bernie looked at her. "I don't know. It's actually pretty smart. No identification, no harm to anyone."

"What I don't understand is why they didn't just leave us in the garage." Ali turned to her husband. It was a question he hadn't answered satisfactorily.

"Did the police say why?" asked Bernie.

"They said the gas was a low-yield variety. The thieves didn't want Ali or the kids to come to and see them. Very professional."

"Very scary," Leila said. "How did the kids take it?"

"Ray's a neighborhood hero, of course," said Ali. "Janet's still not sure what happened."

"Where *is* Ray?" Bernie pointed to a package in the hall. "I hope he hasn't outgrown model airplanes. That's one of those remote-control things."

"He'll love it," said Ali. "He's in the basement, I think. John's turning it over to him. . . ."

"No, he's outside. In the pool." Tanner realized that his interruption, his sharp correction of Ali, caused Bernie to look at him. Even Ali was startled by the abruptness of his statement.

So be it, thought Tanner. Let them all know the father was aware, every second, of the whereabouts of his own.

The dog began barking in front of the house; the sound of a car could be heard in the driveway. Alice walked to the window.

"It's Dick and Ginny. And Ray's *not* in the pool," she added, smiling at John. "He's in front saying hello."

"He must have heard the car," said Leila for no apparent reason.

Tanner wondered why she made the remark; it was as if she were defending him. He went to the front door and opened it. "Come on in, son. Some other friends of yours are here."

When he saw the Ostermans, the boy's eyes lit up. The Ostermans never arrived empty-handed. "Hello, Aunt Leila, Uncle Bernie!" Raymond Tanner, age twelve, walked into the arms of Leila and then shook hands manfully, shyly, with Bernie.

"We brought you a little something. Actually your buddy Merv suggested it." Bernie crossed to the hall and picked up the package. "Hope you like it."

"Thank you very much." The boy took the gift and went into the dining room to unwrap it.

Virginia Tremayne came in, the picture of cool sensuality. She was dressed in a man-styled shirt with multicolored stripes and a tight knit skirt which accentuated the movements of her body. There were women in Saddle Valley who resented Ginny's appearance, but they weren't in these rooms. Ginny was a good friend.

"I told Dick you called Wednesday," she said to Tanner, "but he says you never reached him. The poor lamb's been holed up in a conference suite with some awful merger people from Cincinnatti or Cleveland or somewhere. . . . Leila, darling! Bernie, love!" Ginny pecked Tanner's cheek and choreographed herself past him.

Richard Tremayne came in. He was watching Tanner and what he saw obviously pleased him.

Tanner, on the other hand, felt the look and whipped his head around too quickly. Tremayne didn't have time to shift his eyes away. The news director recognized in the lawyer's stare the look of a doctor studying a medical chart.

For a split second both men silently, unwillingly, acknowledged the tension. And then it passed, as it had passed with the Ostermans. Neither man dared sustain it.

"Hey, John! Sorry I didn't get your message. Ginny mentioned something legal."

"I thought you might have read about it."

"What, for God's sake?"

"We didn't get much coverage in the New York papers, but wait'll you read next Monday's weekly. We'll be celebrities."

"What the hell are you talking about?"

"We were robbed Wednesday. Robbed and kidnapped and chloroformed and God knows what else!"

"You're joking!"

"The hell he is!" Osterman walked into the hallway. "How are you, Dick?"

"Bernie! How are you, buddy?" The men grasped hands, but Tremayne could not seem to take his attention from John Tanner.

"Did you hear what he said? Did you hear that? What happened, for Christ's sake? I've been in town since Tuesday. Didn't even have time to get home."

"We'll tell you all about it. Later. Let me get your drinks." Tanner walked away rapidly. He couldn't fault Tremayne's reaction. The lawyer was not only shocked by what he'd heard, he was frightened. So much so that he had to make clear he had been gone since Tuesday.

Tanner made drinks for the Tremaynes and then went into the kitchen and looked out past his pool to the edge of the woods. Although there was no one in sight, he knew the men were there. With binoculars, with radios, probably with tiny speakers which magnified conversations taking place in any section of his house.

"Hey, John, I wasn't kidding!" It was Tremayne walking into the kitchen. "Honest to God, I didn't know anything about it. About Wednesday, I mean. Why the hell didn't you reach me?"

"I tried. I even called a number on Long Island. Oyster Bay, I think."

"Oh, shit! You know what I mean! You or Ali should have told Ginny. I'd have left the conference, you know that!"

"It's over with. Here's your drink." Tremayne lifted the glass to his lips. He could drink any of them under any table.

"You can't leave it like that. Why did you call me in the first place?"

Tanner, stupidly, wasn't prepared for the question.

"I . . . I didn't like the way the police handled it."

"The police? Fat-cap MacAuliff?"

"I never talked to Captain MacAuliff."

"Didn't you give a statement?"

"Yes . . . yes, I did. To Jenkins and McDermott."

"Where the hell was old law'n'order himself?"

"I don't know. He wasn't there."

"Okay, Mac wasn't there. You say Jenkins and McDermott handled it. Ali told me they were the ones who found you . . ."

"Yes. Yes, that's what I was pissed-off about."

"What?"

"I just didn't like the way they handled it. At least I didn't at the time. I've cooled it now. I was hot then, that's why I tried to reach you."

"What were you figuring? Police negligence? Abridged rights? What?"

"I don't know, Dick! I just panicked, that's all. When you panic you want a lawyer."

"I don't. I want a drink." Tremayne held Tanner's eyes. Tanner blinked—as a small boy defeated in a game of stare.

"It's over with. Let's go back inside."

"Maybe we ought to talk later. Maybe you have some kind of case and I don't see it."

Tanner shrugged, knowing that Dick didn't really want to talk later at all. The lawyer was frightened, and his fear arrested his professional instinct to probe. As he walked away, Tanner had the feeling that Tremayne was telling the truth about one aspect of Wednesday afternoon. He hadn't been there himself.

But did he know who had been?

By six, the Cardones still hadn't arrived. No one asked why; the hour passed quickly and if anyone was concerned he hid it well. At ten minutes past, Tanner's eyes were drawn to a car driving slowly past his house. It was the Saddle Valley taxi, the sun causing intermittent, sharp flashes off the black enamel. In the rear window of the automobile he saw Joe Cardone's face for a moment. Joe was making sure all the guests had arrived. Or were still there, perhaps.

Forty-five minutes later the Cardone's Cadillac pulled into the driveway. When they entered the house it was obvious that Joe had had several drinks. Obvious because Joe was not a drinker, he didn't really approve of alcohol, and his voice was just a degree louder than it might have been.

"Bernie! Leila! Welcome to the heart of the eastern establishment!"

Betty Cardone, prim, stoutish, Anglican Betty, properly added to her husband's enthusiasm and the four of them exchanged embraces.

"Betty, you look adorable," said Leila. "Joe, my God, Joe! How can a man look so healthy? . . . Bernie built a gym and look what *I* got!"

"Don't you knock my Bernie!" said Joe, his arm around Osterman's shoulder.

"You tell her, Joe." Bernie moved towards Cardone's wife and asked about the children.

Tanner started towards the kitchen, meeting Ali in the hallway. She carried a plate of hors d'oeuvres.

"Everything's ready. We can eat whenever we want, so I'll sit down for a while. . . . Get me a drink, will you, dear?"

"Sure. Joe and Betty are here."

Ali laughed. "I gathered that. . . . What's the matter, darling? You look funny."

"No, nothing. I was just thinking I'd better call the studio."

Ali looked at her husband. "Please. Everybody's here now. Our best friends. Let's have fun. Forget about Wednesday, *please*, Johnny."

Tanner leaned over the tray of hors d'oeuvres and kissed her. "You're dramatizing," he said, remembering Fassetts' admonition. "I really do have to call the studio."

In the kitchen, Tanner walked again to the window. It was a little after seven o'clock and the sun had gone down behind the tall trees in the woods. Shadows lay across the backyard lawn and the pool. And beyond the shadows were Fassett's men.

That was the important thing.

As Ali had said, they were all there now. The best of friends.

The buffet of curry, with a dozen side dishes, was Ali's usual triumph. The wives asked the usual questions and Ali slightly embossed the culinary answers—as usual. The men fell into the normal arguments about the relative merits of the various baseball teams and, in between, Bernie revealed further the humorous—and extraordinary—working methods of Hollywood television.

While the women cleared out the dining room, Tremayne took the opportunity to press Tanner on the robbery. "What the hell was it last Wednesday? Level with us. I don't buy the burglary story."

"Why not?" asked Tanner.

"It doesn't make sense."

"Nobody uses gas on anybody," added Cardone. "Blackjacks, blindfolds, a shot in the head, maybe. Not gas."

"Advanced thinking, perhaps. I'd rather it was a harmless gas than a blackjack."

"Johnny." Osterman lowered his voice and looked toward the dining room. Betty came out of the kitchen door and began removing several dishes and smiled. He smiled back. "Are you working on something that might make you enemies?"

"I imagine I always am in one way or another."

"I mean something like the San Diego thing."

Joe Cardone watched Osterman carefully, wondering if he might elaborate. San Diego had been a Mafia operation.

"Not that I know of. I've got men digging in a lot of areas, but nothing like that. At least I don't think so. Most of my best people have a free rein. . . . Are you trying to tie in Wednesday with something at work?"

"It hadn't struck you?" asked Tremayne.

"Hell, no! I'm a professional newsman. Do you get worried if you're working on a sticky case?"

"Sometimes."

"I read about that show of yours last Sunday." Cardone sat down on the couch next to Tremayne. "Ralph Ashton has friends in high places."

"That's crazy."

"Not necessarily." Cardone had trouble with "necessarily." "I've met him. He's a vindictive man."

"He's not crazy," interjected Osterman. "No, it wouldn't be anything like that."

"Why should it be anything, period? Anything but a robbery?" Tanner lit a cigarette and tried to watch the faces of the three men.

"Because, Goddamn it, it's not a natural way to get robbed," exclaimed Cardone.

"Oh?" Tremayne looked at Cardone, sitting next to him on the sofa. "Are you an expert on robbery?"

"No more than you are, counselor," said Joe.

Chapter Eighteen

There was something artificial about the start of the weekend; Ali felt it. Perhaps it was that the voices were louder than usual, the laughter more pronounced.

Usually, when Bernie and Leila arrived, they all began calmly, catching up with each family's affairs. Conversations about this or that child, this or that career decision—these always occupied the first few hours. Her husband called it the Osterman syndrome. Bernie and Leila brought out the best in all of them. Made them talk, really *talk* with one another.

Yet no one had volunteered a single important personal experience. No one had brought up a single vital part of their recent lives—except, of course, the horrible thing on Wednesday afternoon.

On the other hand, Ali realized, she was still concerned about her husband—concerned about his staying home from the office, his short temper, his erratic behavior since Wednesday afternoon. Maybe she was imagining things about everybody else.

The other women had rejoined their husbands; Alice had put away the left-overs. The children were in bed now. And she wouldn't listen to any more talk from Betty or Ginny about maids. She *could* afford a maid! *They* could afford a maid! But she wouldn't *have* one!

Her father had had maids. "Disciples" he called them. "Disciples" who cleaned and swept and brought-in and . . .

Her mother had called them "maids."

Ali stopped thinking and wondered if she'd had a drink she couldn't handle. She turned on the faucet and dabbed her face with cold water. Joe Cardone walked through the kitchen door.

"The boss-man told me if I wanted a drink, I pour it myself. Don't tell me where, I've been here before."

"Go right ahead, Joe. Do you see everything you need?"

"Sure do. Lovely gin; beautiful tonic. . . Hey, what's the matter? You been crying?"

"Why should I be? I just splashed water on my face."

"Your cheeks are all wet."

"Water on the face does that."

Joe put down the bottle of tonic and approached her. "Are you and Johnny in any trouble? . . . This Wednesday afternoon . . . okay, it was a crazy type of robbery, Johnny told me . . . but if it was anything else, you'd let me know, wouldn't you? I mean, if he's playing around with sharks you wouldn't keep it a secret from me, would you?"

"Sharks?"

"Loan-sharks. I've got clients at Standard Mutual. Even a little stock. I know the company. . . . You and Johnny live very well, but sixty thousand dollars after taxes isn't that much any more."

Alice Tanner caught her breath. "John does very well!"

"That's relative. In my opinion, John's in that big middle mess. He can't take over and he won't let go of his little kingdom to try for anything better. That's his business, and yours. But I want you to tell him for me. . . . I'm his friend. His good friend. And I'm clean. Absolutely *clean*. If he needs anything, you tell him to call me, all right?"

"Joe, I'm touched. I really am. But I don't think it's necessary. I don't, really."

"But you'll tell him?"

"Tell him yourself. John and I have an unspoken pact. We don't discuss his salary any more. Frankly because I agree with you."

"Then you've got problems."

"You're not being fair. Problems to you may not be problems for us."

"I hope you're right. Tell him that, too." Cardone walked rapidly back to the bar and picked up his glass. Before Ali could speak he walked through the door back into the living room.

Joe was telling her something and she didn't understand.

"Nobody appointed you or any other member of *any* news media to set yourselves up as infallible guardians of the truth! I'm sick and tired of it! I live with it every day." Tremayne stood in front of the fireplace, his anger obvious to everyone.

"Not infallible, of course not," answered Tanner. "But no one gave the courts the right to stop us from looking for information as objectively as we can."

"When that information is prejudicial to a client *or* his opponent you have no right to make it public. If it's factual, it'll be heard in court. Wait'll the verdict's rendered."

"That's impossible and you know it."

Tremayne paused, smiled thinly, and sighed. "I know I do. Realistically, there's no solution."

"Are you sure you want to find one?" asked Tanner.

"Of course."

"Why? The advantage is yours. You win the verdict, fine. If you lose, you claim the court was corrupted by a biased press. You appeal."

"It's the rare case that's won on appeal," said Bernard Osterman sitting on the floor in front of the sofa. "Even I know that. They get the publicity, but they're rare."

"Appeals cost money," added Tremayne with a shrug. "Most of the time for nothing. Especially corporate appeals."

"Then force the press to restrain itself when there's a lot of heat. It's simple." Joe finished his drink and looked pointedly at Tanner.

"It's not simple," said Leila, sitting in an armchair opposite the sofa. "It becomes judgment. Who defines restraint? That's what Dick means. There's no clear-cut definition."

"At the risk of offending my husband, God forbid," Virginia laughed as she spoke, "I think an informed public is just as important as an unbiased courtroom. Perhaps they're even connected. I'm on your side, John."

"Judgment, again," said her husband. "It's opinion. What's factual information and what's interpreted information?"

"One's truth," said Betty off-handedly. She was watching her husband. He was drinking too much.

"Whose truth? Which truth? . . . Let's create a hypothetical situation. Between John and myself. Say I've been working for six months on a complicated merger. As an ethical attorney I'm dealing with men whose cause I believe in; by putting together a number of companies thousands of jobs are saved, firms which are going bankrupt suddenly have new lives. Then along come several people who are getting hurt—because of their own ineptness—and start shouting for injunctions. Suppose they reach John and start yelling 'Foul!' Because they seem—seem, mind you—like underdogs, John gives their cause one *minute*, just one *minute* of network time across the country. Instantly my case is prejudiced. And don't let anyone tell you the courts aren't subject to media pressure. One *minute* as opposed to *six months*."

"Do you think I'd allow that? Do you think any of us would?"

"You need copy. You always need copy! There are times when you don't understand!" Tremayne's voice grew louder.

Virginia stood up. "Our John wouldn't do that, darling. . . . I'm for another cup of coffee."

"I'll get it," said Alice, rising from the sofa. She'd been watching Tremayne, startled by his sudden vehemence.

"Don't be silly," answered Ginny going into the hallway.

"I'd like a drink." Cardone held out his glass, expecting someone to take it.

"Sure, Joe." Tanner took his glass. "Gin and tonic?"

"That's what I've been drinking."

"Too much of," added his wife.

Tanner walked into the kitchen and began making Cardone's drink. Ginny was at the stove.

"I'm heating the Chemex; the candle burned out."

"Thanks."

"I always have the same problem. The damn candles go out and the coffee's cold."

Tanner chuckled and poured the tonic. Then he realized that Ginny was making a comment, a rather unattractive comment. "I told Ali to get an electric pot, but she refuses."

"John?"

"Yes?"

"It's a beautiful night. Why don't we all take a swim?"

"Sure. Good idea. I'll backwash the filter. Let me get this to Joe." Tanner returned to the living room in time to hear the opening bars of "Tangerine." Ali had put on an album called "Hits of Yesterday."

There were the proper responses, the laughs of recognition.

"Here you are, Joe. Anyone else for anything?"

There was a chorus of no-thanks. Betty had gotten up and was facing Dick Tremayne by the mantle. Tanner thought they looked as though they'd been arguing. Ali was at the stereo showing Bernie the back of the album cover; Leila Osterman sat opposite Cardone, watching him drink his gin and tonic, seemingly annoyed that he drank so quickly.

"Ginny and I are going to backwash the pool. We'll take a swim, okay? You've all got suits here; if not, there're a dozen extras in the garage."

Dick looked at Tanner. It was a curious look, thought the news editor. "Don't teach Ginny too much about that damned filter. I'm holding firm. No pool."

"Why not?" asked Cardone.

"Too many kids around."

"Build a fence," said Joe with a degree of disdain.

Tanner started out toward the kitchen and the back door. He heard a sudden burst of laughter behind him, but it wasn't the laughter of people enjoying themselves. It was forced, somehow unkind.

Was Fassett right? Was Omega showing the signs? Were the hostilities slowly coming to the surface?

Outside he walked to the edge of the pool, to the filter box. "Ginny?"

"I'm over here, by Ali's tomato plants. This stake fell down and I can't retie the vine."

"Okay." He turned and walked over to her. "Which one? I can't see it."

"Here," said Ginny, pointing.

Tanner knelt down and saw the stake. It hadn't fallen over, it had been snapped. "One of the kids must have run through here." He pulled up the thin broken dowel and placed the tomato vine carefully on the ground. "I'll fix it tomorrow."

He got up. Ginny stood very close to him and put her hand on his arm. He realized they couldn't be seen from the house.

"I broke it," Ginny said.

"Why?"

"I wanted to talk to you. Alone."

She had undone several buttons of her blouse below the neckline. He could see the swell of her breasts. Tanner wondered if Ginny was drunk. But Ginny never got drunk, or if she did, no one ever knew it.

"What do you want to talk about?"

"Dick, for one thing. I apologize for him. He can become gross . . . rude, when he's upset."

"Was he rude? Upset? I didn't notice."

"Of course you did. I was watching you."

"You were wrong."

"I don't think so."

"Let's get the pool done."

"Wait a minute." Ginny laughed softly. "I don't frighten you, do I?"

"My friends don't frighten me," Tanner said, smiling.

"We know a great deal about each other."

Tanner watched Ginny's face closely, her eyes, the slight pinching of her lips. He wondered if this was the moment the unbelievable was about to be revealed to him. If it was, he'd help her say it. "I suppose we always think we know our friends. I sometimes wonder if we ever do."

"I'm very attracted . . . physically attracted to you. Did you know that?"

"No, I didn't," said Tanner, surprised.

"It shouldn't bother you. I wouldn't hurt Ali for the world. I don't think physical attraction necessarily means a commitment, do you?"

"Everyone has fantasies."

"You're sidestepping."

"I certainly am."

"I told you, I wouldn't harm your commitments."

"I'm human. They'd be harmed."

"I'm human, too. May I kiss you? At least I deserve a kiss."

Ginny put her arms around the startled Tanner's neck and pressed her lips against his, opening her mouth. Tanner knew she was doing her best to arouse him. He couldn't understand it. If she meant what she was doing, there was nowhere to complete the act.

Then he did understand. She was promising.

She meant that.

"Oh, Johnny! Oh, God, Johnny!"

"All right, Ginny. All right. Don't. . . ." Perhaps she really was drunk, thought Tanner. She'd feel like a fool tomorrow. "We'll talk later."

Ginny pulled slightly back. Her lips to the side of his. "Of course, we'll talk later. . . . Johnny? . . . Who is Blackstone?"

"Blackstone?"

"Please! I've got to know! Nothing will change, I promise you that! *Who is Blackstone?*"

Tanner held her shoulders, forcing her face in front of his own.

She was crying.

"I don't know any Blackstone."

"Don't do this!" she whispered. "Please, for God's sake, don't do this! Tell Blackstone to *stop it!*"

"Did Dick send you out here?"

"He'd kill me," she said softly.

"Let me get it straight. You're offering me . . ."

"Anything you want! Just leave him *alone.* . . . My husband's a good man. A very, very decent man. He's been a good friend to you! Please, don't hurt him!"

"You love him."

"More than my life. So please, don't hurt him. And tell Blackstone to stop!"

She rushed off into the garage.

He wanted to go after her and be kind, but the specter of Omega prevented him. He kept wondering whether Ginny, who was capable of offering herself as a whore, was also capable of things far more dangerous.

But Ginny wasn't a whore. Careless, perhaps, even provocative in a humorous, harmless way, but it had never occurred to Tanner or anybody Tanner knew that she would share her bed with anyone but Dick. She wasn't like that.

Unless she was Omega's whore.

There was the forced laughter again from inside the house. Tanner heard the opening clarinet strains of "Amapola." He knelt down and picked the thermometer out of the water.

Suddenly he was aware that he wasn't alone. Leila Osterman was standing several feet behind him on the grass. She'd come outside silently; or perhaps he was too preoccupied to hear the kitchen door or the sound of her footsteps.

"Oh, hi! You startled me."

"I thought Ginny was helping you."

"She . . . spilled filter powder on her skirt. . . . Look, the temperature's eighty-three. Joe'll say it's too warm."

"If he can tell."

"I see what you mean," said Tanner getting to his feet, smiling, "Joe's no drinker."

"He's trying."

"Leila, how come you and Bernie got in a couple days ago?"

"He hasn't told you?" Leila was hesitant, seemingly annoyed that the explanation was left to her.

"No. Obviously."

"He's looking around. He had conferences, lunches."

"What's he looking for?"

"Oh, projects. You know Bernie; he goes through phases. He never forgets that *The New York Times* once called him exciting . . . or incisive, I never remember which. Unfortunately, he's acquired expensive tastes."

"You've lost me."

"He'd like to find a class series; you know, the old Omnibus type. There's a lot of talk around the agencies about upgrading."

"Is there? I hadn't heard it."

"You're in news, not programming."

Tanner took out a pack of cigarettes and offered one to Leila. As he lit it he could see the concern, the strain, in her eyes. "Bernie has a lot going for him.

You and he have made the agencies a great deal of money. He won't have any trouble; he's persuasive as hell."

"It takes more than persuasion, I'm afraid," Leila said. "Unless you want to work for a percentage of nonprofit culture. . . . No, it takes influence. Enormous influence; enough to make the money people change their minds." Leila drew heavily on her cigarette, avoiding Tanner's stare.

"Can he do that?"

"He might be able to. Bernie's word carries more weight than any other writer's on the coast. He has 'clout,' as they say. . . . It extends to New York, take my word for it."

Tanner found himself not wanting to talk. It hurt too much. Leila had all but told him, he thought. All but proclaimed the power of Omega. Of course Bernie was going to do what he wanted to do. Bernie was perfectly capable of making people change their minds, reverse decisions. Or Omega was, and he was part of it—part of them.

"Yes," he said softly. "I'll take your word for it. Bernie's a big man."

They stood quietly for a moment, then Leila spoke sharply. "Are you satisfied?"

"What?"

"I asked if you were satisfied. You've just questioned me like a cop. I can even furnish you with a list of his appointments, if you'd like. And there are hairdressers, department stores, shops—I'm sure they'd confirm my having been there."

"What the hell are you talking about?"

"You know perfectly well! That's not a very nice party in there, in case you haven't noticed. We're all behaving as if we'd never met before, as if we really didn't like our new acquaintances."

"That has nothing to do with me. Maybe you should look to yourselves."

"Why?" Leila stepped back. Tanner thought she looked bewildered, but he didn't trust his appraisal. "Why should we? What *is* it, John?"

"Can't *you* tell *me*?"

"Good Lord, you *are* after him, aren't you? You're after *Bernie*."

"No, I'm not. I'm not after anyone."

"You listen to me, John! Bernie would give his life for you! Don't you know that?"

Leila Osterman threw the cigarette on the ground and walked away.

As Tanner was about to carry the chlorine bucket to the garage, Ali came outside with Bernie Osterman. For a moment he wondered whether Leila had said anything. Obviously she hadn't. His wife and Bernie simply wanted to know where he kept the club soda and to tell him that everyone was getting into suits.

Tremayne stood in the kitchen doorway, glass in hand, watching the three of them talking. To Tanner he seemed nervous, uneasy.

Tanner walked into the garage and placed the plastic bucket in the corner next to the garage toilet. It was the coolest place. The kitchen door opened and Tremayne walked down the steps.

"I want to see you a minute."

"Sure."

Tremayne turned sideways and slid past the Triumph. "I never see you driving this."

"I hate it. Getting in and out of it's murder."

"You're a big guy."

"It's a small car."

"I . . . I wanted to say I'm sorry about that bullshit I was peddling before. I have no argument with you. I got burned on a case several weeks ago by a reporter on *The Wall Street Journal*. Can you imagine? *The Journal*! My firm decided not to go ahead on the strength of it."

"Free press or fair trial. A damned valid argument. I didn't take it personally."

Tremayne leaned against the Triumph. He spoke cautiously. "A couple of hours ago, Bernie asked you—he was talking about last Wednesday—if you were working on anything like that San Diego story. I never knew much about that except that it's still referred to in the newspapers . . ."

"It's been exaggerated out of proportion. A series of waterfront payoffs. Indigenous to the industry, I think."

"Don't be so modest."

"I'm not. It was a hell of a job and I damned near got the Pulitzer. It's been responsible for my whole career."

"All right. . . . Fine, good. . . . Now, I'm going to stop playing games. Are you digging around something that affects me?"

"Not that I know of. . . . It's what I said to Bernie; I've a staff of seventy-odd directly involved with news gathering. I don't ask for daily reports."

"Are you telling me you don't know what they're doing?"

"I'm better than that," said Tanner with a short laugh. "I approve expenditures; nothing is aired without my clearing it."

Tremayne pushed himself away from the Triumph. "All right, let's level. . . . Ginny came back inside fifteen minutes ago. I've lived with that girl for sixteen years. I know her. . . . She'd been crying. She was outside with you and she came back crying. I want to know why."

"I can't answer you."

"I think you'd better try! . . . You resent the money I make, don't you?"

"That's not true."

"Of course it is! You think I haven't heard Ali on your back! And now you subtly, off-handedly drop that nothing is *aired* without your *clearing* it! Is that what you told my wife? Am I supposed to hear the details from *her*? A wife can't testify; are you *protecting* us? What do you *want*?"

"Get hold of yourself! Are you into something so rotten you're getting paranoid? Is that it? You want to tell me about it?"

"No. No! Why was she *crying*?"

"Ask her yourself!"

Tremayne turned away and John Tanner could see the lawyer's body begin to shake as he passed his hands on the hood of the small sports car.

"We've known each other a long time; but you've never understood me at all. . . . Don't make judgments unless you understand the men you're judging."

So this was it, thought Tanner. Tremayne was admitting it. He *was* part of Omega.

And then Tremayne spoke again and the conclusion was destroyed. He turned around and the look on his face was pathetic.

"I may not be beyond reproach, I know that, but I'm within the law. That's the system. I may not like it all the time, but I respect that *system*!"

Tanner wondered if Fassett's men had placed one of their electronic pick-ups in the garage. If they had heard the words, spoken in such sorrow, with such a ring of truth. He looked at the broken man in front of him.

"Let's go into the kitchen. You need a drink and so do I."

Chapter Nineteen

Alice flipped the switch under the living-room windowsill so the music would be heard on the patio speakers. They were all outside now on the pool deck. Even her husband and Dick Tremayne had finally gotten up from the kitchen table; they'd been sitting there for twenty minutes and Ali thought it strange they'd hardly spoken.

"Hello, gracious lady!" The voice was Joe's, and Alice felt herself grow tense. He walked from the hallway into view; he was in swimming trunks. There was something ugly about Joe's body; it dwarfed objects around it. "You're out of ice, so I made a phone call to get some."

"At this hour?"

"It's easier than one of us driving."

"Who'd you call?"

"Rudy at the liquor store."

"It's closed."

Cardone walked towards her, weaving a bit. "I got him at home; he wasn't in bed. . . . He does little favors for me. I told him to leave a couple of bags on the front porch and charge it to me."

"That wasn't necessary. I mean the charging."

"Every little bit helps."

"Please." She walked towards the sofa if for no other reason than to get away from Cardone's gin-laden breath. He followed her.

"Did you think over what I told you?"

"You're very generous, but we don't need any help."

"Is that what John said?"

"It's what he *would* say."

"Then you haven't talked to him?"

"No."

Cardone took her hand gently. She instinctively tried to pull it away, but he held it—firmly, with no trace of hostility, only warmth; but he held it nevertheless. "I may be a little loaded but I want you to take me seriously. . . . I've been a lucky man; it hasn't been hard at all, not really. . . . Frankly, I even feel a little guilty, you know what I mean? I admire Johnny. I think the world of him because he *contributes*. . . . I don't contribute much; I just take. I don't hurt anybody, but I take. . . . You'd make me feel better if you'd let me *give* . . . for a change."

He let her hand go and because she didn't expect it, her forearm snapped back against her waist. She was momentarily embarrassed. And perplexed. "Why are you so determined to give us something. What brought it up?"

Cardone sat down heavily on the arm of the couch. "You hear things. Rumors, gossip, maybe."

"About us? About us and money?"

"Sort of."

"Well, it's not true. It's simply not true."

"Then let's put it another way. Three years ago when Dick and Ginny and Bernie and Leila went skiing with us at Gstaad, you and Johnny didn't want to go. Isn't that right?"

Alice blinked, trying to follow Joe's logic. "Yes, I remember. We thought we'd rather take the children to Nassau."

"But now John's very interested in Switzerland, isn't that right?" Joe's body was swaying slightly.

"Not that I know of. He hasn't told me about it."

"Then if it's not Switzerland, maybe it's Italy. Maybe he's interested in Sicily; it's a very interesting place."

"I simply don't understand you."

Cardone got off the arm of the couch and steadied himself. "You and I aren't so very different, are we? I mean, what credentials we have weren't exactly handed to us, were they? . . . We've earned them, after our own Goddamn fashion. . . ."

"I think that's insulting."

"I'm sorry, I don't mean to be insulting. . . . I just want to be honest, and honesty starts with where you are . . . where you were."

"You're drunk."

"I certainly am. I'm drunk and I'm nervous. Lousy combination. . . . You talk to John. You tell him to see me tomorrow or the next day. You tell him not to worry about Switzerland or Italy, all right? You tell him, no matter what, that I'm clean and I like people who contribute but don't hurt other people. . . . That I'll pay."

Cardone took two steps toward Ali and grabbed her left hand. Gently but insistently, he brought it to his lips, eyes closed, and kissed her palm. Ali had seen that type of kiss before; in her childhood she'd seen her father's fanatical adherents do the same. Then Joe turned and staggered into the hallway.

At the window a shifting of light, a reflection, a change of brightness caught Ali's eye. She turned her head. What she saw caused her to freeze. Outside on the lawn, no more than six feet from the glass, stood Betty Cardone in a white bathing suit, washed in the blue-green light of the swimming pool.

Betty had seen what had happened between Alice and her husband. Her eyes told Ali that.

Joe's wife stared through the window and her look was cruel.

The full tones of the young Sinatra filled the warm summer night as the four couples sat around the pool. Individually—it seemed never by twos to John Tanner—one or another would slip into the water and paddle lazily back and forth.

The women talked of schools and children while the men, on the opposite side of the deck, spoke less quietly of the market, politics, an inscrutable economy.

Tanner sat on the base of the diving board near Joe. He'd never seen him so drunk, and he bore watching. If any or all around the deck were part of Omega, Joe was the weakest link. He'd be the first to break.

Small arguments flared up, quickly subsiding. At one point, Joe's voice was too loud and Betty reacted swiftly but quietly.

"You're drunk, husband-mine. Watch out."

"Joe's all right, Betty," said Bernie, clapping Cardone's knee. "It was rotten-hot in New York today, remember?"

"You were in New York, too, Bernie," answered Ginny Tremayne, stretching her legs over the side of the pool. "Was it really that rotten-hot?"

"Rotten-hot, sweetheart." It was Dick who spoke across the water to his wife.

Tanner saw Osterman and Tremayne exchange glances. Their unspoken communication referred to Cardone but it was not meant that he, Tanner, should understand or even notice. Then Dick got up and asked who'd like refills.

Only Joe answered yes.

"I'll get it," said Tanner.

"Hell, no," replied Dick. "You watch the ballplayer. I want to call the kid anyway. We told her to be back by one; it's damn near two. These days you have to check."

"You're a mean father," said Leila.

"So long as I'm not a grandfather." Tremayne walked across the grass to the kitchen door.

There was silence for several seconds, then the girls took up their relaxed conversation and Bernie lowered himself over the side into the pool.

Joe Cardone and Tanner did not speak.

Several minutes later, Dick came out of the kitchen door carrying two glasses. "Hey, Ginny! Peg was teed off that I woke her up. What do you think of that?"

"I think she was bored with her date."

Tremayne approached Cardone and handed him his glass. "There you are, fullback."

"I was a Goddamn halfback. I ran circles around your Goddamn Levi Jackson at the Yale Bowl!"

"Sure. But I talked to Levi. He said they could always get you. All they had to do was yell 'tomato sauce' and you went for the sidelines!"

"Pretty Goddamn funny! I murdered that black son of a bitch!"

"He speaks well of you, too," said Bernie, smiling over the side of the pool.

"And I speak well of *you*, Bernie! And big Dick, here!" Cardone clumsily got to his feet. "I speak well of *all* of you!"

"Hey, Joe. . . ." Tanner got off the board.

"Really, Joe, just sit down," ordered Betty. "You'll fall over."

"Da Vinci!"

It was only a name but Cardone shouted it out. And then he shouted it again.

"*Da Vinci*. . . ." He drew out the sound, making the dialect sharply Italian.

"What does *that* mean?" asked Tremayne.

"You tell *me*!" roared Cardone through the tense stillness around the pool.

"He's crazy," said Leila.

"He's positively drunk, if nobody minds my saying so," added Ginny.

"Since we can't—at least I can't—tell you what a Da Vinci is, maybe you'll explain." Bernie spoke lightly.

"Cut it out! Just *cut it out*!" Cardone clenched and reclenched his fists.

Osterman climbed out of the water and approached Joe. His hands hung loosely at his sides. "Cool it, Joe. Please. . . . Cool it."

"*Zurichchchch!*" The scream from Joe Cardone could be heard for miles, thought Tanner. It was happening! He'd said it!

"What do you mean, Joe?" Tremayne took a halting step toward Cardone.

"*Zurich!* That's what I mean!"

"It's a city in Switzerland! So what the hell else?" Osterman stood facing Cardone; he wasn't about to give quarter. "You say what you mean!"

"No!" Tremayne took Osterman by the shoulder.

"Don't talk to me," yelled Cardone. "You're the one who . . ."

"*Stop it! All of you!*" Betty stood on the concrete deck at the end of the pool. Tanner would never have believed such strength could come from Cardone's wife.

But there it was. The three men parted from one another, as chastised dogs. The women looked up at Betty, and then Leila and Ginny walked away while Ali stood immobile, uncomprehending.

Betty continued, reverting now to the soft, suburban housewife she seemed to be. "You're all behaving childishly and I know it's time for Joe to go home."

"I . . . I think we all can have a nightcap, Betty," said Tanner. "How about it?"

"Make Joe's light," answered Betty with a smile.

"No other way," said Bernie.

"I'll get them." Tanner started back towards the door. "Everyone in?"

"Wait a minute, Johnny!" It was Cardone, a wide grin on his face. "I'm the naughty boy so let me help. Also, I gotta go to the bathroom."

Tanner went into the kitchen ahead of Cardone. He was confused, bewildered. He had expected that when Joe screamed the name "Zurich" it would all be over. Zurich was the key that should have triggered the collapse. Yet it did not happen.

Instead, the opposite occurred.

A control was imposed; imposed by the most unlikely source imaginable, Betty Cardone.

Suddenly, from behind him came a crash. Tremayne was standing in the doorway, looking at the fallen Cardone.

"Well. A mountain of Princeton muscle just passed out! . . . Let's get him into my car. I'm chauffeur tonight."

Passed out? Tanner didn't believe it. Cardone was drunk, yes. But he was nowhere near collapsing.

Chapter Twenty

The three men dressed quickly and manhandled the lurching, incoherent Cardone into the front seat of Tremayne's car. Betty and Ginny were in the back. Tanner kept watching Joe's face, especially the eyes, for any signs of pretense. He could see none. And yet there was something false, he thought; there was too much precision in Cardone's exaggerated movements. Was Joe using silence to test the others, he wondered?

Or were his own observations being warped by the progressive tension?

"Damn it!" exclaimed Tremayne. "I left my jacket inside."

"I'll bring it to the Club in the morning," said John. "We're scheduled for eleven."

"No, I'd better get it. I left some notes in the pocket; I may need them. . . . Wait here with Bernie. I'll be back in a second."

Dick ran inside and he grabbed his jacket from a hallway chair. He looked at Leila Osterman, who was polishing the top of a table in the living room.

"If I get these rings now maybe the Tanners'll have some furniture left," she said.

"Where's Ali?"

"In the kitchen." Leila continued rubbing the table top.

As Tremayne entered the kitchen, Alice was filling the dishwasher.

"Ali?"

"Oh! . . . Dick, Joe all right?"

"Joe's fine. . . . How's John?"

"Isn't he out there with you?"

"I'm in here."

"It's late; I'm too tired for jokes."

"I couldn't feel less like joking. . . . We've been good friends, Ali. You and Johnny mean a lot to us, to Ginny and me."

"We feel the same; you know that."

"I thought I did. I really believed it. . . . Listen to me. . . ." Tremayne's face was flushed; he swallowed repeatedly, unable to control the pronounced twitch over his left eye. "Don't make judgments. Don't let John make . . . editorial judgments that hurt people unless he understands why they do what they do."

"I don't understand what you're—"

"That's very important," interrupted Tremayne. "He should try to understand. That's one mistake I never commit in court. I always try to understand."

Alice recognized the threat. "I suggest that you say whatever it is you're saying to him."

"I did and he wouldn't answer me. That's why I'm saying it to you. . . . Remember, Ali. No one's ever completely what he seems. Only some of us are more resourceful. Remember that!"

Tremayne turned and left; a second later Ali heard the front door close. As she looked at the empty doorway, she was aware of someone else nearby. There was the unmistakable sound of a quiet footstep. Someone had walked through the dining room and was standing in her pantry, around the corner, out of sight. She walked slowly, silently to the arch. As she turned into the small narrow room she saw Leila standing motionless against the wall, staring straight ahead.

Leila had been listening to the conversation in the kitchen. She gasped when she saw Ali, then laughed with no trace of humor. She knew she'd been caught.

"I came for another cloth." She held up a dustrag and went back inside the dining room without speaking further.

Alice stood in the center of the pantry wondering what dreadful thing was happening to all of them. Something was affecting the lives of everyone in the house.

They lay in bed; Ali on her back, John on his left side away from her. The Ostermans were across the hall in the guest room. It was the first time they'd been alone together all night.

Alice knew her husband was exhausted but she couldn't postpone the question—or was it a statement—any longer.

"There's some trouble between you and Dick and Joe, isn't there?"

Tanner rolled over; he looked up at the ceiling, almost relieved. He knew the question was coming and he had rehearsed his answer. It was another lie; he was getting used to the lies. But there was so little time left—Fassett had guaranteed that. He began slowly, trying to speak off-handedly.

"You're too damned smart."

"I am?" She shifted to her side and looked at her husband.

"It's nasty, but it'll pass. You remember my telling you about the stock business Jim Loomis was peddling on the train?"

"Yes. You didn't want Janet to go over for lunch . . . to the Loomis', I mean."

"That's right. . . . Well, Joe and Dick jumped in with Loomis. I told them not to."

"Why?"

"I checked on it."

"What?"

"I checked on it. . . . We've got a few thousand lying around drawing five percent. I figured why not? So I called Andy Harrison—he's head of Legal at Standard, you met him last Easter. He made inquiries."

"What did he find out?"

"The whole thing smells. It's a boilerplate operation. It's rotten."

"Is it illegal?"

"Probably will be by next week. . . . Harrison suggested we do a feature on it. Make a hell of a show. I told that to Joe and Dick."

"Oh, my God! That you'd do a program on it?"

"Don't worry. We're booked for months. There's no priority here. And even if we did, I'd tell them. They could get out in time."

Ali heard Cardone and Tremayne again: *'Did you speak to him? What did he say?' 'Don't let Johnny make judgments. . . .'* They had been panicked and now she understood why. "Joe and Dick are worried sick, you know that, don't you?"

"Yeah. I gathered it."

"You *gathered* it? For heaven's sake, these are your friends! . . . They're frightened! They're scared to death!"

"Okay. Okay. Tomorrow at the Club, I'll tell them to relax. . . . The San Diego vulture isn't vulturing these days."

"Really, that was cruel! No wonder they're all so upset! They think you're doing something terrible." Ali recalled Leila's silent figure pressed against the pantry wall, listening to Tremayne alternately pleading and threatening in the kitchen. "They've told the Ostermans."

"Are you sure? How?"

"Never mind, it's not important. They must think you're a horror. . . . Tomorrow morning, for heaven's sake, tell them not to worry."

"I said I would."

"It explains so much. That silly yelling at the pool, the arguments . . . I'm really very angry with you." But Alice Tanner wasn't angry; the unknown was known to her now. She could cope with it. She lay back, still concerned, still worried, but with a degree of calm she hadn't felt for several hours.

Tanner shut his eyes tight, and let his breath out. The lie had gone well. Better than he had thought it would. It was easier for him now, easier to alter the facts.

Fassett had been right; he could manage them all.

Even Ali.

Chapter Twenty-one

He stood by the bedroom window. There was no moon in the sky, just clouds barely moving. He looked below at the side lawn and the woods beyond, and wondered suddenly if his eyes were playing tricks on him. There was the glow of a cigarette, distinctly seen. Someone was walking and smoking a cigarette in full view! Good Christ! he thought; did whoever it was realize that he was giving away the patrol?

And then he looked more closely. The figure was in a bathrobe. It was Osterman.

Had Bernie seen something? Heard something?

Tanner silently, rapidly went to the bedroom door and let himself out.

"I thought you might be up and around," said Bernie sitting on a deck chair, looking at the water in the pool. "This evening was a disaster."

"I'm not so sure about that."

"Then I assume you've given up your senses of sight and sound. It was a wet night at Malibu. If we all had had knives that pool would be deep red by now."

"Your Hollywood mentality's working overtime." Tanner sat down at the edge of the water.

"I'm a writer. I observe and distill."

"I think you're wrong," Tanner said. "Dick was uptight about business; he told me. Joe got drunk. So what?"

Osterman swung his leg over the deck chair and sat forward. "You're wondering what I'm doing here. . . . It was a hunch, an instinct. I thought you might come down yourself. You didn't look like you could sleep any more than I could."

"You intrigue me."

"No jokes. It's time we talk."

"About what?"

Osterman got up and stood above Tanner. He lit a fresh cigarette with the stub of his first. "What do you want most? I mean for yourself and your family?"

Tanner couldn't believe he'd heard correctly. Osterman had begun with the tritest introduction imaginable. Still, he answered as though he took the question seriously.

"Peace, I guess. Peace, food, shelter, creature comforts. Are those the key words?"

"You've got all that. For your current purposes, anyway."

"Then I *really* don't understand you."

"Has it ever occurred to you that you have no right to select anything anymore? Your whole life is programmed to fulfill a predetermined *function*; do you realize that?"

"It's universal, I imagine. I don't argue with it."

"You can't argue. The system won't permit it. You're trained for something; you gain experience—that's what you do for the rest of your *life*. No arguments."

"I'd be a rotten nuclear physicist; you'd be less than desirable in brain surgery. . . ." Tanner said.

"Of course everything's relative; I'm not talking fantasy. I'm saying that we're controlled by forces *we* can't control any longer. We've reached the age of specialization, and that's the death knell. We live and work within our given circles; we're not allowed to cross the lines, even to look around. You more than me, I'm afraid. At least I have a degree of choice as to which piece of crap I'll handle. But crap, nevertheless. . . . We're stifled."

"I hold my own; I'm not complaining. Also, my risks are pretty well advertised."

"But you have no back-ups! Nothing! You can't afford to stand up and say *this is me*! Not on the money-line, you can't! Not with *this* to pay for!" Osterman swung his arm to include Tanner's house and grounds.

"Perhaps I can't . . . on the money-line. But who can?"

Osterman drew up the chair and sat down. He held Tanner's eyes with his own and spoke softly. "There's a way. And I'm willing to help." He paused for a moment, as if searching for words, then started to speak again. "Johnny. . . ." Osterman stopped once more. Tanner was afraid he wouldn't continue, wouldn't find the courage.

"Go on."

"I've got to have certain . . . assurances; that's very important!" Osterman spoke rapidly, the words tumbling forth on top of each other.

Suddenly both men's attention was drawn to the house. The light in Janet Tanner's bedroom had gone on.

"What's that?" asked Bernie, not bothering to disguise his apprehension.

"Just Janet. That's her room. We finally got it through her head that when she goes to the bathroom she should turn on the lights. Otherwise she bumps into everything and we're all up for twenty minutes."

And then it pierced the air. Terrifyingly, with ear-shattering horror. A child's scream.

Tanner raced around the pool and in the kitchen door. The screams continued and lights went on in the other three bedrooms. Bernie Osterman nearly ran up Tanner's back as the two men raced to the little girl's room. Their speed had been such that Ali and Leila were just then coming out of their rooms.

John rushed against the door, not bothering about the doorknob. The door flew open and the four of them ran inside.

The child stood in the center of the room over the body of the Tanners' Welsh terrier. She could not stop screaming.

The dog lay in a pool of blood.

Its head had been severed from its body.

John Tanner picked up his daughter and ran back into the hallway. His mind stopped functioning. There was only the terrifying picture of the body in the woods alternating with the sight of the small dog. And the horrible words of the man in the parking lot at the Howard Johnson's motel.

"A severed head means a massacre."

He had to get control, he *had* to.

He saw Ali whispering in Janet's ear, rocking her back and forth. He was aware of his son crying several feet away and the outline of Bernie Osterman comforting him.

And then he heard the words from Leila.

"I'll take Janet, Ali. Go to Johnny."

Tanner leapt to his feet in fury. "You touch her, I'll *kill* you! Do you hear me, I'll *kill* you!"

"*John!*" Ali yelled at him in disbelief. "What are you *saying*?"

"*She* was across the hall! Can't you see that? She was *across the hall!*"

Osterman rushed toward Tanner, pushing him back, pinning his shoulders against the wall. Then he slapped him hard across the face.

"That dog's been dead for hours! Now, cut it out!"

For hours. It couldn't be for hours. It had just happened. The lights went on and the head was severed. The little dog's head was cut off. . . . And Leila was across the hall. She and Bernie. Omega! A massacre!

Bernie cradled his head. "I had to hit you. You went a little nuts. . . . Come on, now. Pull yourself together. It's terrible, just terrible, I know. I got a daughter."

Tanner tried to focus. First his eyes, then his thoughts. They were all looking at him, even Raymond, still sobbing by the door of his room.

"Isn't anybody here?" Tanner couldn't help himself. Where were Fassett's men? Where in God's name *were* they?

"Who, darling?" Ali put her arm around his waist in case he fell again.

"Nobody here." It was a statement said softly.

"*We're* here. And we're calling the police. Right now!" Bernie put Tanner's hand on the staircase railing and walked him downstairs.

Tanner looked at the thin, strong man helping him down the steps. *Didn't Bernie understand? He was Omega. His wife was Omega! He couldn't phone the police!*

"The police? You want the police?"

"I certainly do. If that was a joke, it's the sickest I've ever seen. You're damned right I want them. Don't you?"

"Yes. Of course."

They reached the living room; Osterman took command.

"Ali, you call the police! If you don't know the number, dial the operator!" And then he went into the kitchen.

Where were Fassett's men?

Alice crossed to the beige telephone behind the sofa. In an instant it was clear she didn't have to dial.

The beam of a searchlight darted back and forth through the front windows and danced against the wall of the living room. Fassett's men had arrived at last.

At the sound of the front door chimes, Tanner wrenched himself off the couch and into the hallway.

"We heard some yelling and saw the light on. Is everything all right?" It was Jenkins and he barely hid his anxiety.

"You're a little late!" Tanner said quietly. "You'd better come on in! Omega's been here."

"Take it easy." Jenkins walked into the hallway, followed by McDermott.

Osterman came out of the kitchen.

"Jesus! You people are fast!"

"Twelve-to-eight shift, sir," said Jenkins. "Saw the lights on and people running around. That's unusual at this hour."

"You're very alert and we're grateful. . . ."

"Yes, sir." Jenkins interrupted and walked into the living room. "Is anything the matter, Mr. Tanner? Can you tell us or would you rather speak privately?"

"There's nothing private here, officer." Osterman followed the policeman and spoke before Tanner could answer. "There's a dog upstairs in the first bedroom on the right. It's dead."

"Oh?" Jenkins was confused. He turned back to Tanner.

"Its head was cut off. Severed. We don't know who did it."

Jenkins spoke calmly. "I see. . . . We'll take care of it." He looked over at his partner in the hallway. "Get the casualty blanket, Mac."

"Right." McDermott went back outside.

"May I use your phone?"

"Of course."

"Captain MacAuliff should be informed. I'll have to call him at home."

Tanner didn't understand. This wasn't a police matter. It was Omega! What was Jenkins doing? Why was he calling MacAuliff? He should be reaching *Fassett*! MacAuliff was a local police officer; acceptable, perhaps, but fundamentally a political appointment. MacAuliff was responsible to the Saddle Valley town council, not to the United States government. "Do you think that's necessary? At this hour? I mean, is Captain . . ."

Jenkins cut Tanner off abruptly. "Captain MacAuliff is the Chief of Police. He'd consider it very abnormal if I didn't report this directly to him."

In an instant Tanner understood. Jenkins had given him the key.

Whatever happened, whenever it happened, however it happened—there could be no deviation from the norm.

This was the Chasm of Leather.

And it struck Tanner further that Jenkins was making his phone call for the benefit of Bernard and Leila Osterman.

Captain Albert MacAuliff entered the Tanner house and immediately made his authority clear. Tanner watched him deliver his instructions to the police officers, in a low, commanding voice. He was a tall, obese man, with a thick neck which made his shirt collar bulge. His hands were thick, too, but strangely immobile, hanging at his sides as he walked—the mark of a man who'd spent years patrolling a beat on foot, shifting his heavy club from one hand to the other.

MacAuliff had been recruited from the New York police and he was a living example of the right man for the right job. Years ago the town council had gone on record that it wanted a no-nonsense man, someone who'd keep Saddle Valley clear of undesirable elements. And the best defense in these days of permissiveness was offense.

Saddle Valley had wanted a mercenary.

It had hired a bigot.

"All right, Mr. Tanner, I'd like a statement. What happened here tonight?"

"We . . . we had a small party for friends."

"How many?"

"Four couples. Eight people."

"Any hired help?"

"No. . . . No, no help."

MacAuliff looked at Tanner, putting his notebook at his side. "No maid?"

"No."

"Did Mrs. Tanner have anyone in during the afternoon? To help out?"

"No."

"You're sure?"

"Ask her yourself." Ali was in the study where they'd made makeshift beds for the children.

"It could be important. While you were at work she might have had some coloreds or P.R.'s here."

Tanner saw Bernie recoil. "I was home all day."

"Okay."

"Captain," Osterman stepped forward from Leila's side. "Somebody broke into this house and slit that dog's throat. Isn't it possible that it was a thief? Mr. and Mrs. Tanner were robbed last Wednesday. Shouldn't we check . . ."

It was as far as he got. MacAuliff looked at the writer and scarcely disguised his contempt. "I'll handle this, Mr. . . . ." The Police Chief glanced at his notebook. "Mr. Osterman. I'd like Mr. Tanner to explain what happened here tonight. I'd appreciate it if you'd let *him* answer. We'll get to you in good time."

Tanner kept trying to get Jenkins' attention, but the policeman avoided his eyes. The news director didn't know what to say—or what specifically *not* to say.

"Now then, Mr. Tanner," MacAuliff sat down and returned to his notebook, pencil poised. "Let's start at the beginning. And don't forget things like deliveries."

Tanner was about to speak when McDermott's voice could be heard from the second floor.

"Captain! Can I see you a minute? The guest room."

Without saying anything, Bernie started up the stairs in front of MacAuliff, Leila following.

Instantly, Jenkins approached Tanner's chair and bent over. "I've only got time to say this once. Listen and commit! Don't bring up any Omega business. None of it. Nothing! I couldn't say it before, the Ostermans were hovering over you."

"Why not? For Christ's sake, this *is* Omega business! . . . What am I supposed to say? Why shouldn't I?"

"MacAuliff's not one of us. He's not cleared for anything. . . . Just tell the truth about your party. That's *all*!"

"You mean he doesn't *know*?"

"He doesn't. I told you, he's not cleared."

"What about the men outside, the patrols in the woods?"

"They're not his men. . . . If you bring it up he'll think you're crazy. And the Ostermans will know. If you point at me I'll deny everything you say. You'll look like a psycho."

"Do you people think that MacAuliff . . ."

"No. He's a good cop. He's also a small-time Napoleon so we can't use him. Not openly. But he's conscientious, he can help us. Get him to find where the Tremaynes and the Cardones went."

"Cardone was drunk. Tremayne drove them all home."

"Find out if they went *straight* home. MacAuliff loves interrogations; he'll nail them if they're lying."

"How can I . . ."

"You're worried about them. That's good enough. And remember, it's nearly over."

MacAuliff returned. McDermott had "mistaken" the lateral catch in the guest room window as a possible sign of a break-in.

"All right, Mr. Tanner. Let's start with when your guests arrived."

And so John Tanner, functioning on two levels, related the blurred events of the evening. Bernie and Leila Osterman came downstairs and added very little of consequence. Ali came out of the study and contributed nothing.

"Very well, ladies and gentlemen." MacAuliff got out of the chair.

"Aren't you going to question the others?" Tanner also rose and faced the police captain.

"I was going to ask you if we could use your telephone. We have procedures."

"Certainly."

"Jenkins, call the Cardones. We'll see them first."

"Yes, sir."

"What about the Tremaynes?"

"Procedures, Mr. Tanner. After we speak to the Cardones we'll call the Tremaynes and *then* see them."

"That way no one checks with anyone else, right?"

"That's right, Mr. Osterman. You familiar with police work?"

"I write your guidelines every week."

"My husband's a television writer," said Leila.

"Captain." Patrolman Jenkins spoke from the telephone. "The Cardones aren't home. I've got the maid on the line."

"Call the Tremaynes."

The group remained silent while Jenkins dialed. After a brief conversation Jenkins put down the telephone.

"Same story, Captain. The daughter says they're not home either."

Chapter Twenty-two

Tanner sat with his wife in the living room. The Ostermans had gone upstairs; the police departed in search of the missing couples. Neither John nor Ali was comfortable. Ali because she had decided in her own mind who had killed the dog, John because he couldn't get out of his mind the implications of the dog's death.

"It was Dick, wasn't it?" Alice asked.

"Dick?"

"He threatened me. He came into the kitchen and threatened me."

"*Threatened* you?" If that was so, thought Tanner, why hadn't Fassett's men come sooner. "When? How?"

"When they were leaving. . . . I don't mean he threatened me personally. Just generally, all of us."

"What did he say?" Tanner hoped Fassett's men were listening now. It would be a point he'd bring up later.

"He said you shouldn't make judgments. Editorial judgments."

"What else?"

"That some . . . some people were more resourceful. That's what he said.

That I should remember that people weren't always what they seemed. . . . That some were more resourceful than others."

"He could have meant several things."

"It must be an awful lot of money."

"What's a lot of money?"

"Whatever he and Joe are doing with Jim Loomis. The thing you had looked into."

Oh, God, thought Tanner. The real and the unreal. He'd almost forgotten his lie.

"It's a lot of money," he said softly, realizing he was on dangerous ground. It would occur to Ali that money itself was insufficient. He tried to anticipate her. "More than just money, I think. Their reputations could go down the drain."

Alice stared at the single lighted table lamp. "Upstairs you . . . you thought Leila had done it, didn't you?"

"I was wrong."

"She *was* across the hall . . ."

"That wouldn't make any difference; we went over that with MacAuliff. He agreed. A lot of the blood had dried, congealed. The pup was killed hours ago."

"I guess you're right." Ali kept picturing Leila with her back pressed against the wall, staring straight ahead, listening to the conversation in the kitchen.

The clock on the mantel read five-twenty. They had agreed they would sleep in the living room, in front of the study, next to their children.

At five-thirty the telephone rang. MacAuliff had not found the Tremaynes or the Cardones. He told Tanner that he had decided to put out a missing persons bulletin.

"They may have decided to go into town, into New York," said Tanner quickly. A missing persons bulletin might drive Omega underground, prolong the nightmare. "Some of those Village spots stay open. Give them more time. They're friends, for heaven's sake!"

"Can't agree. No place stays open after four."

"They may have decided to go to a hotel."

"We'll know soon enough. Hotels and hospitals are the first places M.P.B.'s go to."

Tanner's mind raced. "You've searched the surrounding towns? I know a few private clubs . . ."

"So do we. Checked out."

Tanner knew he had to think of something. Anything that would give Fassett enough time to control the situation. Fassett's men were listening on the line, there was no question about that; they'd see the danger instantly.

"Have you searched the area around the old depot? The one on Lassiter Road?"

"Who the hell would go out there? What for?"

"I found my wife and children there on Wednesday. Just a thought."

The hint worked. "Call you back," MacAuliff said. "I'll check that out."

As he hung up the telephone, Ali spoke. "No sign?"

"No. . . . Honey, try to get some rest. I know of a couple of places—clubs—the police may not know about. I'll try them. I'll use the kitchen phone. I don't want to wake the kids."

Fassett answered the phone quickly.

"It's Tanner. Do you know what's happened?"

"Yes. That was damned good thinking. You're hired."

"That's the last thing I want. What are you going to do? You can't have an interstate search."

"We know. Cole and Jenkins are in touch. We'll intercept."

"And then what?"

"There are several alternate moves. I don't have time to explain. Also, I need this line. Thanks, again." Fassett hung up.

"Tried two places," said Tanner coming back into the living room. "No luck. . . . Let's try to get some sleep. They probably found a party and dropped in. Lord knows we've done that."

"Not in years," said Ali.

Both of them pretended to sleep. The tick of the clock was like a metronome, hypnotic, exasperating. Finally, Tanner realized his wife was asleep. He closed his eyes, feeling the heavy weight of his lids, aware of the complete blackness in front of his mind. But his hearing would not rest. At six-forty he heard the sound of a car. It came from in front of his house. Tanner got out of the chair and went quickly to the window. MacAuliff walked up the path, and he was alone. Tanner went out to meet him.

"My wife's asleep. I don't want to wake her."

"Doesn't matter," said MacAuliff ominously. "My business is with you."

"What?"

"The Cardones and the Tremaynes were rendered unconscious by a massive dose of ether. They were left in their car off the road by the Lassiter depot. Now I want to know why you sent us there. How did you know?"

Tanner could only stare at MacAuliff in silence.

"Your answer?"

"So help me, I didn't know! I didn't know *anything*. . . . I'll never forget Wednesday afternoon as long as I live. Neither would you if you were me. The depot just came to mind. I *swear* it!"

"It's one hell of a coincidence, isn't it?"

"Look, if I *had* known I would have told you hours ago! I wouldn't put my wife through this. For Christ's sake, be reasonable!"

MacAuliff looked at him questioningly. Tanner pressed on. "How did it happen? What did they say? Where are they?"

"They're down at the Ridge Park Hospital. They won't be released until tomorrow morning at the earliest."

"You must have talked with them."

According to Tremayne, MacAuliff said, the four of them had driven down Orchard Drive less than a half mile when they saw a red flare in the road and an automobile parked on the shoulder. A man waved them down; a well-dressed man who looked like any resident of Saddle Valley. Only he wasn't. He'd been visiting friends and was on his way back to Westchester. His car had suddenly developed engine trouble and he was stuck. Tremayne offered to drive the man back to his friends' house. The man accepted.

That was the last Tremayne and the two wives remembered. Apparently Cardone had been unconscious throughout the incident.

At the deserted depot the police found an unmarked aerosol can on the floor of Tremayne's car. It would be examined in the morning, but MacAuliff had no doubt it was ether.

"There must be a connection with last Wednesday," said Tanner.

"It's the obvious conclusion. Still, anyone who knows this neck of the woods knows that the old depot area is deserted. Especially anyone who read the papers or heard about Wednesday afternoon."

"I suppose so. Were they robbed . . . too?"

"Not of money, or wallets or jewelry. Tremayne said he was missing some papers from his coat. He was very upset."

"Papers?" Tanner remembered the lawyer saying he had left some notes in his jacket. Notes that he might need. "Did he say which papers?"

"Not directly. He was hysterical—didn't make too much sense. He kept repeating the name 'Zurich.'"

John held his breath and, as he had learned to do, tensed the muscles of his stomach, trying with all his strength to suppress his surprise. It was so like Tremayne to arrive with written-down, pertinent data concerning the Zurich accounts. If there *had* been a confrontation, he was armed with the facts.

MacAuliff caught Tanner's reaction. "Does Zurich mean something to you?"

"No, why should it?"

"You always answer a question with a question?"

"At the risk of offending you again, am I being officially questioned?"

"You certainly are."

"Then, no. The name Zurich means nothing to me. I can't imagine why he'd say it. Of course, his law firm is international."

MacAuliff made no attempt to conceal his anger. "I don't know what's going on, but I'll tell you this much. I'm an experienced police officer and I've had some of the toughest beats a man can have. When I took this job I gave my word I'd keep this town clean. I meant that."

Tanner was tired of him. "I'm sure you did, Captain. I'm sure you always mean what you say." He turned his back and started for the house.

It was MacAuliff's turn to be stunned. The suspect was walking away and there was nothing Saddle Valley's Police Chief could do about it.

Tanner stood on his front porch and watched MacAuliff drive off. The sky was brighter but there'd be no sun. The clouds were low, the rain would come, but not for a while.

No matter. Nothing mattered. It was over for him.

The covenant was broken now. The contract between John Tanner and Laurence Fassett was void.

For Fassett's guarantee had proven false. Omega did not stop with the Tremaynes, the Cardones and the Ostermans. It went beyond the constituency of the weekend.

He was willing to play—*had* to play—under Fassett's rules as long as the other players were the men and women he knew.

Not now.

There was someone else now—someone who could stop a car on a dark road in the early morning hours and create terror.

Someone he didn't know. He couldn't accept that.

Tanner waited until noon before heading towards the woods. The Ostermans had decided to take a nap around eleven-thirty and it was a good time to suggest the same to Ali. They were all exhausted. The children were in the study watching the Saturday morning cartoons.

He walked casually around the pool, holding a six iron, pretending to practice his swing, but actually observing the windows on the rear of the house: the two children's rooms and the upstairs bathroom.

He approached the edge of the woods and lit a cigarette.

No one acknowledged his presence. There was no sign, nothing but silence from the small forest. Tanner spoke softly.

"I'd like to reach Fassett. Please answer. It's an emergency."

He swung his golf club as he said the words.

"I repeat! It's urgent I talk with Fassett! Someone say where you are!"

Still no answer.

Tanner turned, made an improvised gesture toward nothing, and entered the woods. Once in the tall foliage he used his elbows and arms to push deeper into the small forest, towards the tree where Jenkins had gone for the portable radio.

No one!

He walked north; kicking, slashing, searching. Finally he reached the road.

There was no one there! No one was guarding his house! No one was watching the island!

No one!

Fassett's men were gone!

He raced from the road, skirting the edge of the woods, watching the windows fifty yards away on the front of his house.

Fassett's men were gone!

He ran across the back lawn, rounded the pool and let himself into the kitchen. Once inside he stopped at the sink for breath and turned on the cold water. He splashed it in his face and then stood up and arched his back, trying to find a moment of sanity.

No one! No one was guarding his house. No one guarding his wife and his children!

He turned off the water and then decided to let it run slowly, covering whatever footsteps he made. He walked through the kitchen door, hearing the laughter of his children from the study. Going upstairs, he silently turned the knob of his bedroom door. Ali was lying on top of their bed, her bathrobe fallen away, her nightgown rumpled. She was breathing deeply, steadily, asleep.

He closed the door and listened for any sound from the guest room. There was none.

He went back down into the kitchen, closed the door and walked through the archway into the small pantry to make sure that, too, was shut.

He returned to the telephone on the kitchen wall, lifting the receiver. He did not dial.

"Fassett! If you or any of your men are on this line, cut in and acknowledge! And I mean *now!*"

The dial tone continued; Tanner listened for the slightest break in the circuit.

There was none.

He dialed the motel. "Room twenty-two, please."

"I'm sorry, sir. Room twenty-two is not occupied."

"Not occupied? You're wrong! I spoke to the party at five o'clock this morning!"

"I'm sorry, sir. They checked out."

Tanner replaced the receiver, staring at it in disbelief.

The New York number! The emergency number!

He picked up the telephone, trying to keep his hand from trembling.

The beep of a recording preceded the flat-toned voice.

"The number you have reached is not in service. Please check the directory for the correct number. This is a recording. The number you have reached . . ."

John Tanner closed his eyes. It was inconceivable! Fassett couldn't be reached! Fassett's men had disappeared!

He was alone!

He tried to think. He *had* to think. Fassett had to be found! Some gargantuan error had taken place. The cold, professional government man with his myriad ruses and artifices had made some horrible mistake.

Yet Fassett's men were gone. Perhaps there was no mistake at all.

Tanner suddenly remembered that he, too, had resources. There existed for Standard Mutual Network necessary links to certain government agencies. He dialed Connecticut information and got the Greenwich number of Andrew Harrison, head of Standard's legal department.

"Hello, Andy? . . . John Tanner." He tried to sound as composed as possible. "Sorry as hell to bother you at home but the Asian Bureau just called. There's a story out of Hong Kong I want to clear. . . . I'd rather not go into it now. I'll tell you Monday morning. It may be nothing, but I'd rather check. . . . I guess C.I.A. would be best. It's that kind of thing. They've cooperated with us before. . . . Okay, I'll hold on." The news editor cupped the telephone under his chin and lit a cigarette. Harrison came back with a number and Tanner wrote it down. "That's Virginia, isn't it? . . . Thanks very much, Andy. I'll see you Monday morning."

Once more he dialed.

"Central Intelligence. Mr. Andrews' office." It was a male voice.

"My name is Tanner. John Tanner. Director of News for Standard Mutual in New York."

"Yes, Mr. Tanner? Are you calling Mr. Andrews?"

"Yes. Yes, I guess I am."

"I'm sorry, he's not in today. May I help you?"

"Actually, I'm trying to locate Laurence Fassett."

"Who?"

"Fassett. Laurence Fassett. He's with your agency. It's urgent I speak with him. I believe he's in the New York area."

"Is he connected with this department?"

"I don't know. I only know he's with the Central Intelligence Agency. I told you, it's urgent! An emergency, to be exact!" Tanner was beginning to perspire. This was no time to be talking to a clerk.

"All right, Mr. Tanner. I'll check our directory and locate him. Be right back."

It was a full two minutes before he returned. The voice was hesitant but very precise.

"Are you sure you have the right name?"

"Of course, I am."

"I'm sorry, but there's no Laurence Fassett listed with the switchboard or in any index."

"That's impossible! . . . Look, I've been working with Fassett! . . . Let me talk with your superior." Tanner remembered how Fassett, even Jenkins, kept referring to those who had been "cleared" for Omega.

"I don't think you understand, Mr. Tanner. This is a priority office. You called for my associate . . . my subordinate, if you like. My name is Dwight. Mr. Andrews refers decisions of this office to me."

"I don't care who you are! I'm telling you this is an emergency! I think you'd better reach someone in much higher authority than yourself, Mr. Dwight. I can't put it plainer. That's *all*! Do it *now*! I'll hold on!"

"Very well. It may take a few minutes . . ."

"I'll hold."

It took seven minutes, an eternity of strain for Tanner, before Dwight returned to the line.

"Mr. Tanner, I took the liberty of checking your own position so I assume you're responsible. However, I can assure you you've been misled. There's no Laurence Fassett with the Central Intelligence Agency. There never has been."

Chapter Twenty-three

Tanner hung up the telephone and supported himself on the edge of the sink. He pushed himself off and walked mindlessly out the kitchen door onto the backyard patio. The sky was dark. A breeze rustled the trees and caused ripples on the surface of the pool. There was going to be a storm, thought Tanner, as he looked up at the clouds. A July thunderstorm was closing in.

Omega was closing in.

With or without Fassett, Omega was real, that much was clear to Tanner. It was real because he had seen and sensed its power, the force it generated, capable of removing a Laurence Fassett, of manipulating the decisions and the personnel of the country's prime intelligence agency.

Tanner knew there was no point in trying to reach Jenkins. What had Jenkins said in the living room during the early morning hours? . . . "If you point at me, I'll deny everything. . . ." If Omega could silence Fassett, silencing Jenkins would be like breaking a toy.

There had to be a starting point, a springboard that could propel him backward through the lies. He didn't care any longer; it just had to end, his family kept safe. It wasn't his war any more. His only concern was Ali and the children.

Tanner saw the figure of Osterman through the kitchen window.

That was it! Osterman was his point of departure, his break with Omega! He walked quickly back inside.

Leila sat at the table while Bernie stood by the stove boiling water for coffee.

"We're leaving," Bernie said. "Our bag's packed; I'll call for a taxi."

"Why?"

"Something's terribly wrong," said Leila, "and it's none of our business. We're not involved and we don't care to be."

"That's what I want to talk to you about. Both of you."

Bernie and Leila exchanged looks.

"Go ahead," said Bernie.

"Not here. Outside."

"Why outside?"

"I don't want Ali to hear."

"She's asleep."

"It's got to be outside."

The three of them walked past the pool to the rear of the lawn. Tanner turned and faced them.

"You don't have to lie any more. Either of you. I just want my part over with. I've stopped caring." He paused for a moment. "I know about Omega."

"About what?" asked Leila.

"Omega . . . Omega!" Tanner's voice—his whisper—was pained. "I don't *care*! So help me *God*, I *don't care*!"

"What are you talking about?" Bernie watched the news director, taking a step towards him. Tanner backed away. "What's the matter?"

"For God's sake, don't do this!"

"Don't do what?"

"I told you! It doesn't make any difference to me! Just please! *Please!* Leave Ali and the kids alone. Do whatever you want with *me*! . . . Just leave *them alone!*"

Leila reached out and put her hand on Tanner's arm. "You're hysterical, Johnny. I don't know what you're talking about."

Tanner looked down at Leila's hand and blinked back his tears. "How can you do this? Please! Don't lie any longer. I don't think I could stand that."

"Lie about what?"

"You never heard about any bank accounts in Switzerland? In Zurich?"

Leila withdrew her hand and the Ostermans stood motionless. Finally, Bernie spoke quietly. "Yes, I've heard of bank accounts in Zurich. We've got a couple."

Leila looked at her husband.

"Where did you get the money?"

"We make a great deal of money," answered Bernie cautiously. "You know that. If it would ease whatever's troubling you, why don't you call our accountant. You've met Ed Marcum. There's no one better . . . or cleaner . . . in California."

Tanner was confused. The simplicity of Osterman's reply puzzled him; it was so natural. "The Cardones, the Tremaynes. They've got Zurich accounts, too?"

"I guess they have. So do fifty percent of the people I know on the coast."

"Where did they get the money?"

"Why don't you ask them?" Osterman kept his voice quiet.

"*You* know!"

"You're being foolish," said Leila. "Both Dick and Joe are very successful men. Joe probably more than any of us."

"But why *Zurich? What's in Zurich?*"

"A degree of freedom," answered Bernie softly.

"That's it! That's what you were selling last night! 'What do you want most?', you said. Those were your words!"

"There's a great deal of money to be made in Zurich, I won't deny that."

"*With Omega!*" That's how you make it, *isn't it? Isn't it?*"

"I don't know what that means," said Bernie, now apprehensive himself.

"*Dick* and *Joe*! They're with *Omega*! So are *you*! The 'Chasm of Leather!' Information for Zurich! *Money for information!*"

Leila grabbed her husband's hand. "The phone calls, Bernie! The messages."

"Leila, please. . . . Listen, Johnny. I swear to you I don't know what you're talking about. Last night I offered to help you and I meant it. There are investments being made; I was offering you money for investments. That's all."

"Not for *information?* Not for *Omega?*"

Leila clutched her husband's hand; Bernie responded by looking at her, silently commanding her to calm herself. He turned back to Tanner. "I can't imagine any information you might have that I could want. I don't know any Omega. I don't know what it is."

"Joe knows! Dick knows! They both came to Ali and me! They threatened us."

"Then I'm no part of them. *We're* no part."

"Oh, God, Bernie, something happened. . . ." Leila couldn't help herself. Bernie reached over and took her in his arms.

"Whatever it is, it hasn't anything to do with us. . . . Perhaps you'd better tell us what it's all about. Maybe we can help."

Tanner watched them, holding each other gently. He wanted to believe them. He wanted friends; he desperately needed allies. And Fassett had said it; not *all* were Omega. "You *really* don't know, do you? You *don't* know what Omega it. Or what 'Chasm of Leather' means."

"No," said Leila simply.

Tanner believed them. He had to believe them, for it meant he wasn't alone any more. And so he told them.

Everything.

When he had finished the two writers stood staring at him, saying nothing. It had begun to drizzle lightly but none of them felt the rain. Finally, Bernie spoke.

"And you thought I was talking about . . . *we* had something to do with *this?*" Bernie narrowed his eyes in disbelief. "My God! It's insane!"

"No it's not. It's real. I've seen it."

"You say Ali doesn't know?" asked Leila.

"I was told not to tell her, that's what they *told* me!"

"Who? Someone you can't even reach on the phone? A man Washington doesn't acknowledge? Someone who pumped you full of lies about us?"

"A man was *killed*! My family could have been killed last Wednesday! The Cardones and the Tremaynes were gassed last night!"

Osterman looked at his wife and then back at Tanner.

"*If* they really were gassed," he said softly.

"You've got to tell Alice." Leila was emphatic. "You can't keep it from her any longer."

"I know. I will."

"And then we've got to get out of here," said Osterman.

"Where to?"

"Washington. There are one or two Senators, a couple of Congressmen. They're friends of our."

"Bernie's right. We've got friends in Washington."

The drizzle was beginning to turn into hard rain. "Let's go inside," said Leila, touching Tanner's shoulder gently.

"Wait! We can't talk in there. We can't say anything inside the house. It's wired."

Bernie and Leila Osterman reacted as though they'd been slapped. "Everywhere?" asked Bernie.

"I'm not sure. . . . I'm not sure of anything anymore."

"Then we don't talk inside the house; or if we do we put on a radio loud and whisper."

Tanner looked at his friends. Thank God! Thank *God*! It was the beginning of his journey back to sanity.

Chapter Twenty-four

In less than an hour the July storm was upon them. The radio reports projected gale force winds; medium-craft warnings were up from Hatteras to Rhode Island, and the Village of Saddle Valley was neither so isolated nor inviolate as to escape the inundation.

Ali awoke with the first thunder and John told her—whispered to her—through the sound of the loud radios, that they were to be prepared to leave with Bernie and Leila. He held her close to him and begged her not to ask questions, to trust him.

The children were brought into the living room; a television set moved in front of the fireplace. Ali packed two suitcases and placed them beside the garage entrance. Leila boiled eggs and wrapped celery and carrot sticks.

Bernie had said they might not stop driving for an hour or two.

Tanner watched the preparations and his mind went back a quarter of a century.

Evacuation!

The phone rang at two-thirty. It was a suppressed, hysterical Tremayne who—falsely, thought Tanner—recounted the events of the Lassiter depot and made it clear that he and Ginny were too shaken to come over for dinner. The Saturday evening dinner of an Osterman weekend.

"You've got to tell me what's going *on!*" Alice Tanner spoke to her husband in the pantry. There was a transistor radio at full volume and she tried to turn it down. He held her hand, preventing her, and pulled her to him.

"Trust me. Please *trust me*," he whispered. "I'll explain in the car."

"In the car?" Ali's eyes widened in fright as she brought her hand to her mouth. "Oh, my God! What you're saying is . . . you *can't* talk."

"Trust me." Tanner walked into the kitchen and spoke, gestured really, to Bernie. "Let's load." They went for the suitcases.

When Tanner and Osterman returned from the garage, Leila was at the kitchen window looking out on the back yard. "It's becoming a regular gale out there."

The phone rang, and Tanner answered it.

Cardone was an angry man. He swore and swore again that he'd rip apart and rip apart once more the son of a bitch who'd gassed them. He was also confused, completely bewildered. His watch was worth eight hundred dollars and it wasn't taken. He'd had a couple of hundred in his wallet and it was left intact.

"The police said Dick had some papers stolen. Something about Zurich, Switzerland."

There was a sharp intake of breath from Cardone and then silence. When Joe spoke he could hardly be heard. "That's got nothing to do with *me!*" And then he rapidly told Tanner without much conviction that a call from

Philadelphia had warned him that his father might be extremely ill. He and Betty would stay around home. Perhaps they'd see them all on Sunday. Tanner hung up the phone.

"Hey!" Leila was watching something out on the lawn. "Look at those umbrellas. They're practically blowing away."

Tanner looked out the window above the sink. The two large table umbrellas were bending under the force of the wind. The cloth of each was straining against the thin metal ribs. Soon they'd rip or invert themselves. Tanner knew it would appear strange if he didn't take care of them. It wouldn't be normal.

"I'll go get them down. Take two minutes."

"Want some help?"

"No sense both of us getting wet."

"Your raincoat's in the hall closet."

The wind was strong, the rain came down in torrents. He shielded his face with his hands and fought his way to the farthest table. He reached up under the flapping cloth and felt his fingers on the metal hasp. He started to push it in.

There was a shattering sound on the top of the wrought iron table. Pieces of metal flew up, searing his arm. Another report. Fragments of cement at his feet bounced off the base of the table. And then another shot, now on his other side.

Tanner flung himself under the metal table, crouching to the far side, away from the direction of the bullets.

Shots came in rapid succession, all around him, kicking up particles of metal and stone.

He started to crawl backwards onto the grass but the small eruptions of wet dirt paralyzed him. He grabbed for a chair and held it, clutched it in front of him as though it were the last threads of a disintegrating rope and he were high above a chasm. He froze in panic, awaiting his death.

"Let go! Goddamn it! Let go!"

Osterman was pulling at him, slapping him in the face and wrenching his arms from the chair. They scrambled back toward the house; bullets thumped into the wooden shingles.

"Stay away! Stay away from the door!" Bernie screamed. But he wasn't in time, or his wife would not heed the command. Leila opened the door and Bernie Osterman threw Tanner inside, jumping on top of him as he did so. Leila crouched below the window and slammed the door shut.

The firing stopped.

Ali rushed to her husband and turned him over, cradling his head, wincing at the blood on his bare arms.

"Are you hit?" yelled Bernie.

"No . . . no, I'm all right."

"You're not all right! Oh, God! Look at his arms!" Ali tried to wipe the blood away with her hand.

"Leila! Find some alcohol! Iodine! Ali, you got iodine?"

Tears were streaming down her cheeks, Alice could not answer the question. Leila grabbed her shoulders and spoke harshly.

"Stop it, Ali! *Stop* it! Where are some bandages, some antiseptic? Johnny needs help!"

"Some spray stuff . . . in the pantry. Cotton, too." She would not let go her husband. Leila crept towards the pantry.

Bernie examined Tanner's arms. "This isn't bad. Just a bunch of scratches. I don't think anything's embedded . . ."

John looked up at Bernie, despising himself. "You saved my life. . . . I don't know what to say."

"Kiss me on my next birthday. . . . Good girl, Leila. Give me that stuff." Osterman took a medicine can and held the spray steady on Tanner's arms. "Ali, phone the police! Stay away from the window but get hold of that fat butcher you call a police captain!"

Alice reluctantly let her husband go and crawled past the kitchen sink. She reached up the side of the wall and removed the receiver.

"It's dead."

Leila gasped. Bernie leapt towards Ali, grabbing the phone from her hand. "She's right."

John tanner turned himself over and pressed his arms against the kitchen tile. He was all right. He could move.

"Let's find out where we stand," he said slowly.

"What do you mean?" asked Bernie.

"You girls stay down on the floor. . . . Bernie, the light switch is next to the telephone. Reach up and turn it on when I count to three."

"What are you going to do?"

"Just do as I say."

Tanner crept to the kitchen door, by the bar, and stood up out of sight of the window. The rain, the wind, the intermittent rumble of thunder were the only sounds.

"Ready? I'm going to start counting."

"What's he going to do?" Ali started up, but Osterman grabbed her and held her to the floor.

"You've been here before, Bernie," John said. "Infantry Manual. Heading: Night Patrols. Nothing to worry about. The odds are a thousand to one on my side."

"Not in any book *I* know."

"Shut up! . . . One, two, *three!*"

Osterman flipped the switch and the overhead kitchen light went on. Tanner leapt towards the pantry.

It came. The signal. The sign that the enemy was there.

The shot was heard, the glass shattered, and the bullet smashed into the wall, sending pieces of plaster flying. Osterman turned off the light.

On the floor, John Tanner closed his eyes and spoke quietly. "So, that's where we stand. The microphones were a lie. . . . Everything, a lie."

"*No! Stay back! Get back!*" screamed Leila before any of them knew what she meant. She lunged, followed by Alice, across the kitchen toward the doorway.

Tanner's children had not heard the shots outside; the sounds of the rain, the thunder, and the television set had covered them. But they'd heard the shot fired into the kitchen. Both women fell on them now, pulling them to the floor, shielding them with their bodies.

"Ali, get them into the dining room! Stay on the floor!" commanded Tanner. "Bernie, you don't have a gun, do you?"

"Sorry, never owned one."

"Me either. Isn't it funny? I've always disapproved of anyone buying a gun. So Goddamned primitive."

"What are we going to do?" Leila was trying to remain calm.

"We're going to get out of here," answered Tanner. "The shots are from the woods. Whoever is firing doesn't know whether we have weapons or not. He's not going to shoot from the front . . . at least I don't think so. Cars pass on Orchard pretty frequently. . . . We'll pile into the wagon and get the hell out."

"I'll open the door," said Osterman.

"You've been hero enough for one afternoon. It's my turn. . . . If we time it right, there's no problem. The door goes up fast."

They crept into the garage.

The children lay in the back section of the wagon between the suitcases, cramped but protected. Leila and Ali crouched on the floor behind the front seat. Osterman was at the wheel and Tanner stood by the garage door, prepared to pull it up.

"Go ahead, Start it!" He would wait until the engine was full throttle then open the door and jump into the wagon. There were no obstructions. The station wagon would clear the small Triumph and swing around easily for the spurt forward down the driveway.

"Go ahead, Bernie! For Christ's sake, start it!"

Instead, Osterman opened his door and got out. He looked at Tanner. "It's dead."

Tanner turned the ignition key on the Triumph. The motor did not respond. Osterman opened the hood of the wagon and beckoned John over. The two men looked at the motor, Tanner holding a match.

Every wire had been cut.

"Does that door open from the outside?" asked Bernie.

"Yes. Unless it's locked."

"Was it?"

"No."

"Wouldn't we have heard it open?"

"Probably not with this rain."

"Then it's possible someone's in here."

The two men looked over at the small bathroom door. It was closed. The only hiding place in the garage. "Let's get them out of here," whispered Tanner.

Ali, Leila, and the two children went back into the house. Bernie and John looked around the walls of the garage for any objects which might serve as weapons. Tanner took a rusty axe; Osterman, a garden fork. Both men approached the closed door.

Tanner signaled Bernie to pull it open. Tanner rushed in, thrusting the blade of the axe in front of him.

It was empty. But on the wall, splotched in black spray paint, was the Greek letter Ω.

Chapter Twenty-five

Tanner ordered them all into the basement. Ali and Leila took the children down the stairs, trying feebly to make a game of it. Tanner stopped Osterman at the staircase door.

"Let's put up a few obstacles, okay?"

"You think it's going to come to that?"

"I just don't want to take chances."

The two men crept below the sight-lines of the windows and pushed three heavy armchairs, one on top of another, the third on its side, against the front door. Then they crawled to each window, standing out of sight, to make sure the locks were secure.

Tanner, in the kitchen, took a flashlight and put it in his pocket. Together they moved the vinyl table against the outside door: Tanner shoved the aluminium chairs to Osterman, who packed them under the table, one chair rim braced under the doorknob.

"This is no good," Bernie said. "You're sealing us up. We should be figuring out how to get away!"

"Have *you* figured that out?"

In the dim light Osterman could see only the outline of Tanner's body. Yet he could sense the desperation in his voice.

"No. No, I haven't. But we've got to *try!*"

"I know. In the meantime we should take every precaution. . . . We don't know what's out there. How many or where they are."

"Let's finish it, then."

The two men crawled to the far end of the kitchen, beyond the pantry to the garage entrance. The outside garage door had been locked, but only for additional security they propped the last kitchen chair under the knob and crept back into the hallway. They picked up their primitive weapons—the axe and the garden fork—and went down into the basement.

The sound of the heavy rain could be heard pounding on the small, rectangular windows, level with the ground outside the cellar. Intermittent flashes of lightning lit up the cinderblock walls.

Tanner spoke. "It's dry in here. We're safe. Whoever's out there is soaked to the skin, he can't stay there all night. . . . It's Saturday. You know how the police cars patrol the roads on weekends. They'll see there are no lights on and come investigate."

"Why should they?" asked Ali. "They'll simply think we went out to dinner. . . ."

"Not after last night. MacAuliff made it clear he'd keep an eye on the house. His patrol cars can't see through to the back lawn but they'll notice the front. They're bound to. . . . Look." Tanner took his wife's elbow and led her to the single front window just above ground level to the side of the flagstone steps. The rain made rivulets on the panes of glass; it was hard to see. Even the street lamp on Orchard Drive was not always visible. Tanner took the flashlight out of his pocket and motioned Osterman over. "I was telling Ali, MacAuliff said this morning that he'd have the house watched. He will, too. He doesn't want any more trouble. . . . We'll take turns at this window. That way no one's eyes will get tired or start playing tricks. As soon as one of us sees the patrol car, we'll signal up and down with the flashlight. They'll see it. They'll stop."

"That's good," said Bernie. "That's very good! I wish to hell you'd said that upstairs."

"I wasn't sure. Funny, but I couldn't remember if you could see the street from this window. I've cleaned this basement a hundred times, but I couldn't remember for sure." He smiled at them.

"I feel better," said Leila, trying her best to instill John's confidence into the others.

"Ali, you take the first shift. Fifteen minutes apiece. Bernie, you and I will keep moving between the other windows. Leila, sort of stay with Janet, will you?"

"What can I do, dad?" Raymond asked.

Tanner looked at his son, proud of him.

"Stay at the front window with your mother. You'll be permanent there. Keep watching for the police car."

Tanner and Osterman paced between the two windows at the rear of the house and the one at the side. In fifteen minutes, Leila relieved Ali at the front window. Ali found an old blanket which she made into a small mattress so Janet could lie down. The boy remained at the window with Leila, peering out, intermittently rubbing his hand on the glass as if the action might wipe away the water outside.

No one spoke; the pounding rain and blasts of wind seemed to increase. It was Bernie's turn at the front. As he took the flashlight from his wife he held her close for several seconds.

Tanner's turn came and went, and Ali once again took her place. None of them said it out loud but they were losing hope. If MacAuliff was patrolling the area, with concentration on the Tanner property, it seemed illogical that a police car hadn't passed in over an hour.

"There it is! There it is, Dad! See the red light?"

Tanner, Bernie and Leila rushed to the window beside Alice and the boy. Ali had turned on the flashlight and was waving it back and forth. The patrol car had slowed down. It was barely moving, yet it did not stop.

"Give me the light!"

Tanner held the beam steady until he could see, dimly but surely, the blurred reflection of the white car through the downpour. Then he moved the beam vertically, rapidly.

Whoever was driving had to be aware of the light. The path of the beam had to cross the driver's window, hit the driver's eyes.

But the patrol car did not stop. It reached the line of the driveway and slowly drove away.

Tanner shut off the flashlight, not wanting to turn around, not wanting to see the faces of the others.

Bernie spoke softly. "I don't like this."

"He had to see it! He *had* to!" Ali was holding her son, who was still peering out the window.

"Not necessarily," lied John Tanner. "It's a mess out there. His windows are probably just as clouded as ours. Maybe more so. Car windows fog up. He'll be around again. Next time we'll make sure. Next time, I'll run out."

"How," asked Bernie. "You'd never make it in time. We piled furniture in front of the door."

"I'll get through this window." Tanner mentally measured the space. It was far too small. How easily the lies came.

"I can crawl out of there, dad!" The boy was right. It might be necessary to send him.

But he knew he wouldn't. He couldn't.

Whoever was in the patrol car had seen the beam of light and hadn't stopped.

"Let's get back to the windows. Leila, you take over here. Ali, check Janet. I think she's fallen asleep."

Tanner knew he had to keep them doing something, even if the action meant nothing. Each would have his private thoughts, his private panic.

There was a shattering crack of thunder. A flash of lightning lit up the basement.

"Johnny!" Osterman's face was against the left rear window. "Come here."

Tanner ran to Osterman's side and looked out. Through the whipping patterns of the downpour he saw a short, vertical beam of light rising from the ground. It was moving from far back on the lawn, beyond the pool, near the woods. The beam swayed slowly, jerkily. Then a flash of lightning revealed the figure holding the flashlight. Someone was coming toward the house.

"Someone's worried he's going to fall into the pool," whispered Bernie.

"What is it?" Ali's intense voice came from the makeshift mattress where she sat with her daughter.

"There's somebody out there," answered Tanner. "Everybody stay absolutely still. . . . It could be . . . all right. It might be the police."

"Or the person who shot at us! Oh, God!"

"Ssh! Be quiet."

Leila left the front window and went over to Alice.

"Get your face away from the glass, Bernie."

"He's getting nearer. He's going around the pool."

The two men moved back and stood at the side of the window. The man in the downpour wore a large poncho, his head sheltered by a rain hat. He extinguished the light as he approached the house.

Above them, the prisoners could hear the kitchen door rattling, then the sound of a body crashing against the wood. Soon the banging stopped and except for the storm there was silence. The figure left the area of the kitchen door, and Tanner could see from his side of the window the beam of light darting up and down. And then it disappeared around the far end of the house by the garage.

"Bernie!" Leila stood up beside Alice and the child. "Look! Over there!"

Through her side window came the intermittent shafts of another beam of light. Although it was quite far away, the beam was bright; it danced closer. Whoever was carrying that light was racing towards the house.

Suddenly it went out and again there was only the rain and the lightning. Tanner and Osterman went to the side window, one on each side, and cautiously looked out. They could see no one, no figure, nothing but rain, forced into diagonal sheets by the wind.

There was a loud crash from upstairs. And then another, this one sharper, wood slamming against wood. Tanner went toward the stairs. He had locked the cellar door, but it was thin; a good kick would break it from its hinges. He held the axe level, prepared to swing at anything descending those stairs.

Silence.

There were no more sounds from the house.

Suddenly, Alice Tanner screamed. A large hand was rubbing the pane of glass in the front window. The beam of a powerful flashlight pierced the darkness. Someone was squatting behind the light, the face hidden under a rain hood.

Tanner rushed to his wife and daughter, picking up the child from the blanket.

"Get back! Get back against the wall!"

The glass shattered and flew in all directions under the force of the outsider's boot. The kicking continued. Mud and glass and fragments of wood came flying into the basement. Rain swept through the broken window. The six prisoners huddled by the front wall as the beam of light flashed about the floor, the opposite wall and the stairs.

What followed paralyzed them.

The barrel of a rifle appeared at the edge of the window frame and a volley of ear-shattering shots struck the floor and rear wall. Silence. Cinderblock dust whirled about the basement; in the glare of the powerful flashlight it looked like swirling clouds of stone mist. The firing began again, wildly, indiscriminately. The infantryman in Tanner told him what was happening. A second magazine had been inserted into the loading clip of an automatic rifle.

And then another rifle butt smashed the glass of the left rear window directly opposite them. A wide beam of light scanned the row of human beings against the wall. Tanner saw his wife clutching their daughter, shielding the small body with her own, and his mind cracked with fury.

He raced to the window, swinging the axe toward the shattered glass and the crouching figure behind it. The form jumped back; shots pounded into the ceiling above Tanner's head. The shaft of light from the front window caught him now. It's over, Tanner thought. It was going to be over for him. Instead, Bernie was swinging the garden fork at the rifle barrel, deflecting shots away from Tanner. The news director crawled back to his wife and children.

"Get over here!" he yelled, pushing them to the far wall, the garage side of the basement. Janet could not stop screaming.

Bernie grabbed his wife's wrist and pulled her toward the basement corner. The beams of light crisscrossed each other. More shots were fired; dust filled the air; it became impossible to breathe.

The light from the rear window suddenly disappeared; the one from the front continued its awkward search. The second rifle was changing its position. And then from the far side window came another crash and the sound of breaking glass. The wide beam of light shone through again, now blinding them. Tanner shoved his wife and son toward the rear corner next to the stairs. Shots poured in; Tanner could feel the vibration as the bullets spiraled into the wall above and around him.

Crossfire!

He held the axe tightly, then he lunged forward, through the fire, fully understanding that any one bullet might end his life. But none could end it until he reached his target. Nothing could prevent that!

He reached the side window and swung the axe diagonally into it. An anguished scream followed; blood gushed through the opening. Tanner's face and arms were covered with blood.

The rifle in the front window tried to aim in Tanner's direction, but it was impossible. The bullets hit the floor.

Osterman rushed toward the remaining rifle, holding the garden fork at his shoulder. At the last instant he flung it through the outline of the broken glass as if it were a javelin. A cry of pain; the firing stopped.

Tanner supported himself against the wall under the window. In the flashes of lightning he could see the blood rolling down over the cinderblock.

He was alive, and that was remarkable.

He turned and went back toward his wife and children. Ali held the still screaming Janet. The boy had turned his face into the wall and was weeping uncontrollably.

"Leila! Jesus, God! *Leila!*" Bernie's hysterical roar portended the worst. "*Leila, where are you?*"

"I'm here," Leila said quietly. "I'm all right, darling."

Tanner found Leila against the front wall. She had not followed his command to move.

And then Tanner saw something which struck his exhausted mind. Leila wore a large greenish brooch—he hadn't noticed it before. He saw it clearly now, for it shone in the dark. It was iridescent, one of those mod creations sold in fashionable boutiques. It was impossible to miss in the darkness.

A dim flash of lightning lit up the wall around her. Tanner wasn't sure but he was close to being sure: there were no bullet markings near her.

Tanner held his wife and daughter with one arm and cradled his son's head with the other. Bernie ran to Leila and embraced her. The wail of a siren was heard through the sounds of the outside storm, carried by the blasts of wind through the smashed windows.

They remained motionless, spent beyond human endurance. Several minutes later they heard the voices and the knocking upstairs.

"Tanner! Tanner! Open the door!"

He released his wife and son and walked to the broken front window.

"We're here. We're here, you Goddamned filthy pricks."

Chapter Twenty-six

Tanner had seen these two patrolmen numerous times in the Village, directing traffic and cruising in radio cars, but he didn't know their names. They had been recruited less than a year ago and were younger than Jenkins and McDermott.

Now he attacked. He pushed the first policeman violently against the hallway wall. The blood on his hands was smudged over the officer's raincoat. The second patrolman had dashed down the basement stairs for the others.

"For Christ's sake, let go!"

"You dirty *bastard*! You *fucking punk*! We could have been . . . *would* have been *killed* down there! All of us! My wife! My children! *Why did you do that?* You give me an answer and give it to me quick!"

"Goddamn it, let go! Do *what*? *What* answer, for God's sake?"

"You passed this house half hour ago! You saw the Goddamn flashlight and you beat it! You raced out of here!"

"You're crazy! Me and Ronnie been in the north end! We got a transmission to get over here not five minutes ago. People named Scanlan reported shots . . ."

"Who's in the other car? I want to know who's in the other *car*?"

"If you'll take your Goddamned hands off me I'll go out and bring in the route sheet. I forget who—but I know *where* they are. They're over on Apple Drive. There was a robbery."

"The Cardones live on Apple Drive!"

"It wasn't the Cardones' house. I know that one. It was Needham. An old couple."

Ali came into the hall from the stairs, holding Janet in her arms. The child was retching, gasping for air. Ali was crying softly, rocking her daughter back and forth in her arms.

Their son followed, his face filthy from the dust, smudged with his tears. The Ostermans were next. Bernie held on to Leila's waist, supporting her up the stairs. He held on to her as though he would never let her go.

The second patrolman came slowly through the doorway. His expression startled the other officer.

"Holy Mary Mother of God," he said softly. "It's a human slaughterhouse down there. . . . I swear to Christ I don't see how any of 'em are alive."

"Call MacAuliff. Get him over here."

"The line's dead," said Tanner, gently leading Ali to the couch in the living room.

"I'll go radio in." The patrolman named Ronnie went to the front door. "He won't believe this," he said quietly.

The remaining patrolman got an armchair for Leila. She collapsed into it and for the first time started to weep. Bernie leaned over behind his wife and caressed her hair. Raymond crouched beside his father, in front of his mother and sister. He was so terrified he could do nothing but stare into his father's face.

The policeman wandered toward the basement stairs. It was obvious he wanted to go down, not only out of curiosity, but because the scene in the living room was somehow so private.

The door opened and the second patrolman leaned in. "I told Mac. He picked up the radio call on his car frequency. Jesus, you should have heard him. He's on his way."

"How long will it be?" asked Tanner from the couch.

"Not long, sir. He lives about eight miles out and the roads are rotten. But the way he sounded he'll be here faster than anyone else could."

"I've stationed a dozen deputies around the grounds and two men in the house. One will stay downstairs, the other in the upper hallway. I don't know what else I can do." MacAuliff was in the basement with Tanner. The others were upstairs. Tanner wanted the police captain to himself.

"Listen to me! Someone, one of *your* men, passed this house and refused to stop! I know damned well he saw the flashlight! He saw it and drove away!"

"I don't believe that. I checked. Nobody in the cars spotted anything around here. You saw the route sheet. This place is marked for extra concentration."

"I *saw* the patrol car *leave*! . . . Where's Jenkins? McDermott?"

"It's their day off. I'm thinking of calling them back on duty."

"It's funny they're off on weekends, isn't it?"

"I alternate my men on weekends. The weekends are very well covered. Just like the council ordered."

Tanner caught the tone of self-justification in MacAuliff's voice.

"You've got to do one other thing."

MacAuliff wasn't paying attention. He was inspecting the walls of the cinderblock cage. He stooped his immense frame down and picked up several lead slugs from the floor.

"I want every piece of evidence picked up here and sent down for analysis. I'll use the F.B.I. if Newark can't do it. . . . What did you say?"

"I said you've got to do one more thing. It's imperative, but you've got to do it with me alone. Nobody else."

"What's that?"

"You and I are going to find a phone, and you're going to get on it and make two calls."

"Who to?" MacAuliff asked the question because Tanner had taken several steps toward the cellar staircase to make sure no one was there.

"The Cardones and the Tremaynes. I want to know where they are. Where they *were*."

"What the hell . . ."

"Just do as I say!"

"You think . . ."

"I don't think *anything*! I just want to know where they are. . . . Let's say I'm still worried about them." Tanner started for the stairs, but MacAuliff stood motionless in the center of the room.

"Wait a minute! You want me to make the calls and then follow up with verification. Okay, I'll do it. . . . Now, it's my turn. You give me a pain. You aggravate my ulcer. What the hell's going on? There's too much crap here to suit me! If you and your friends are in some kind of trouble, come clean and tell me. I can't do a thing if I don't know who to go after. And I'll tell you this," MacAuliff lowered his voice and pointed his finger at the news director, his other hand on his ulcerated stomach, "I'm not going to have my record loused up because you play games. I'm not going to have mass homicide on my beat because you don't tell me what I should know so I can prevent it!"

Tanner stood where he was, one foot on the bottom step. He looked and wondered. He could tell in a minute, he thought.

"All right . . . Omega. . . . You've heard of Omega?" Tanner stared into MacAuliff's eyes, watching for the slightest betrayal.

"I forgot. You're not cleared for Omega, are you?"

"What the hell are you talking about?"

"Ask Jenkins, Maybe he'll tell you. . . . Come on, let's go."

Three telephone calls were made from MacAuliff's police car. The information received was clear, precise. The Tremaynes and the Cardones were neither at home nor in the vicinity.

The Cardones were in Rockland County, across the New York line. Dining out, the maid said; and if the police officer reached them would he be so kind as to ask them to call home. There was an urgent message from Philadelphia.

The Tremaynes, Virginia sick again, had returned to their doctor in Ridge Park.

The doctor confirmed the Tremayne's visit to his office. He was quite sure they'd gone into New York City. As a matter of fact, he had prescribed dinner and a show. Mrs. Tremayne's relapse was primarily psychological. She had to get her mind on things other than the Lassiter depot.

It was all so specific, thought Tanner. So well established through second and third parties.

Yet neither couple was really accounted for.

For as Tanner reconstructed the events in the basement, he realized that one of the figures intent on killing them could have been a woman.

Fassett had said Omega was killers and fanatics. Men *and* women.

"There's your answer." MacAuliff's words intruded on Tanner's thoughts. "We'll check them out when they return. Easy enough to verify whatever they tell us . . . as you know."

"Yes. . . . Yes, of course. You'll call me after you talk to them."

"I won't promise that. I will if I think you should know."

The mechanic arrived to repair the automobiles. Tanner took him through the kitchen into the garage and watched the expression on his face as he inspected the severed wires.

"You were right, Mr. Tanner. Every lead. I'll splice in temporary connections and we'll make them permanent down at the shop. Somebody played you a rotten joke."

Back in the kitchen Tanner rejoined his wife and the Ostermans. The children were upstairs in Raymond's room where one of MacAuliff's policemen had volunteered to stay with them, play whatever games they liked, try to keep them calm while the adults talked.

Osterman was adamant. They *had* to get out of Saddle Valley, they had to get to Washington. Once the station wagon was repaired they'd leave, but instead of driving they'd go to Kennedy Airport and take a plane. They'd trust no taxis, no limousines. They'd give MacAuliff no explanations; they'd simply get in the car and go. MacAuliff had no legal right to hold them.

Tanner sat next to Ali, across from the Ostermans, and held her hand. Twice Bernie and Leila had tried to force him to explain everything to his wife and both times Tanner had said he would do so privately.

The Ostermans thought they understood.

Ali didn't and so he held her hand.

And each time Leila spoke Tanner remembered her shining brooch in the darkness of the basement—and the unmarked wall behind her.

The front door chimed and Tanner went to answer it. He came back smiling.

"Sounds from reality. The telephone repair crew." Tanner did not return to his seat. The blurred outlines of a plan were slowly coming into focus. He'd need Ali.

His wife turned and looked at him, reading his thoughts. "I'm going up to see the children."

She left and Tanner walked to the table. He reached down for his pack of cigarettes and put them in his shirt pocket.

"You're going to tell her now?" asked Leila.

"Yes."

"Tell her everything. Maybe she'll make some sense out of this . . . Omega." Bernie still looked unbelieving. "Christ knows, I can't."

"You saw the mark on the wall."

Bernie looked strangely at Tanner. "I saw a mark on the wall."

"Excuse me, Mr. Tanner." It was the downstairs policeman at the kitchen door. "The telephone men want to see you. They're in your study."

"Okay. Be right out." He turned back to Bernie Osterman. "To refresh your memory, the mark you saw was the Greek letter Omega."

He walked rapidly out the kitchen door and went to the study. Outside the windows, the storm clouds hovered, the rain, though letting up, was still strong. It was dark in the room; only the desk lamp was on.

"Mr. Tanner." The voice came from behind and he swung around. There was the man named Cole, dressed in the blue jacket of the telephone company, looking at him intently. Another man stood next to him. "Please don't raise your voice."

Tanner's shock was such that he lost control of himself. He lunged at the agent. "You son of a bitch . . ."

He was stopped by both men. They held his arms tightly behind him, pressed against the small of his back. Cole gripped his shoulders and spoke rapidly, with great intensity.

"Please! We know what you've been through! We can't change that, but we can tell you it's over! It's *over*, Mr. Tanner. Omega's cracked!"

"Don't you tell me anything! You bastards! You filthy bastards! You don't exist! They never heard of Fassett! Your phones are disconnected! Your . . ."

"We had to get out fast!" interrupted the agent. "We had to abandon both posts. It was mandatory. It will all be explained to you."

"I don't believe a thing you say!"

"Just listen! Make up your mind later, but *listen*. Fassett's not two miles from here putting the last pieces together. He and Washington are closing in. We'll have Omega by morning."

"What Omega? What Fassett? I called Washington! I talked to McLean, Virginia!"

"You spoke with a man named Dwight. In title, he's Andrews' superior, but not in fact. Dwight was never cleared for Omega. He checked with Clandestine Services, and the call came to the Director. There was no alternative but to deny, Mr. Tanner. In these cases we always deny. We *have* to."

"Where are the guards outside? What happened to all your Goddamned taps? Your shock troops who wouldn't let us be touched?"

"It will all be explained to you. . . . I won't lie. Mistakes are made. One massive error, if you like. We can never make up for them, we know that. But we've never been faced with an Omega before. The main point is—the objective is right in front of us. We're on target now!"

"That's horseshit! The *main point* is my wife and children were almost killed!"

"Look. Look at this." Cole took a small metal disk from the pocket. His colleague let go of Tanner's arms. "Go on, take it. Look at it closely."

Tanner took the object in his hand, and turned it to catch the light. He saw that the tiny object was corroded, pock-marked.

"So?"

"That's one of the miniaturized pick-ups. The corrosion is acid. Acid dropped on it, to ruin it. The pick-ups have been messed up in every room. We're not getting any transmissions."

"How could anyone find them?"

"It's easy enough with the proper equipment. There's no evidence on any of these, no fingerprints. That's Omega, Mr. Tanner."

"Who is it?"

"Even I don't know that. Only Fassett does. He's got everything under control. He's the best man in three continents. If you won't take my word ask the Secretary of State. The President, if you like. Nothing more will happen in this house."

John Tanner took several deep breaths and looked at the agent. "You realize you haven't explained anything."

"I told you. Later."

"That's not good enough!"

Cole returned Tanner's questioning look. "What choice have you got?"

"Call that policeman in here and start yelling."

"What good would that do you? Buy you a couple of hours of peace. How long would it last?"

Tanner would ask him one further question. Whatever the answer, it would make no difference. The plan in John Tanner's mind was crystallizing. But Cole would never know it.

"What's left for me to do?"

"Do nothing. Absolutely nothing."

"Whenever you people say that, the mortars start pounding the beach."

"No mortars now. That's over with."

"I see. It's over with. . . . All right. I . . . do . . . nothing. May I go back to my wife now?"

"Of course."

"Incidentally, is the telephone really fixed?"

"Yes, it is."

The news editor turned, his arms aching, and walked slowly into the hallway.

No one could be trusted any longer.

He would force Omega's hand himself.

Chapter Twenty-seven

Ali sat on the edge of the bed and listened to her husband's story. There were moments when she wondered if he were sane. She knew that men like her husband, men who functioned a great deal of the time under pressure, were subject to breakdowns. She could understand maniacs in the night, lawyers and stockbrokers in the panic of impending destruction, even John's compelling drive to reform the unreformable. Yet what he was telling her now was beyond her comprehension.

"Why did you agree?" she asked him.

"It sounds crazy, but I was trapped. I didn't have a choice. I had to go through with it."

"You volunteered!" said Ali.

"Not really. Once I agreed to let Fassett reveal the names, I signed an affidavit which made me indictable under the National Security Act. Once I knew who they were I was hung. Fassett knew I would be. It was impossible to continue normal relationships with them. And if I didn't, I might step over the line and be prosecuted."

"How awful," said Ali softly.

"Filthy is more to the point."

He told her about the succeeding episodes with Ginny and Leila outside by the pool. And how Dick Tremayne had followed him into the garage. Finally how Bernie had started to tell him something just before Janet's screams had wakened the household.

"He never told you what it was?"

"He said he was only offering me money for investments. I accused them both of being part of Omega. . . . Then he saved my life."

"No. Wait a minute." Ali sat forward. "When you went out for the umbrellas and we all watched you in the rain . . . and then the shots started and we all panicked. . . . I tried to go out and Leila and Bernie stopped me. So I screamed and tried to break away. Leila—no Bernie—held me against the wall. Suddenly she looked at Bernie and said, 'You can go, Bernie! It's all right, Bernie!' . . . I didn't understand, but she ordered him."

"A woman doesn't send her husband in front of a firing squad."

"That's what I wondered about. I wondered if I'd have the courage to send you out . . . for Bernie."

And so Tanner told his wife about the brooch; and the wall with no bullet marks.

"But they were *in* the basement, darling. They weren't *outside*. They weren't the ones who shot at us." Ali stopped. The memory of the horror was too much. She couldn't bring herself to speak further of it. Instead, she told him about Joe's hysterics in the living room and the fact that Betty Cardone had watched them through the window.

"So here we are," he said when she had finished. "And I'm not sure where that is."

"But the man downstairs said it would be over. He told you that."

"They've told me a lot of things. . . . But which one is it? Or is it all three?"

"Who?" she asked.

"Omega. It has to be in couples. They have to operate in couples. . . . But the Tremaynes and the Cardones were gassed in the car. They *were* left out on Lassiter. . . . Or were they?"

Tanner put his hands in his pockets and paced the floor. He went to the window and leaned against the sill, looking out on the front lawn.

"There are a lot of cops outside. They're bored to death. I bet they haven't seen the basement. I wonder—"

The glass shattered. Tanner spun around and blood spurted out of his shirt. Ali screamed, running to her husband as he fell to the floor.

More shots were fired but none came through the window. They were outside.

The patrolman in the hallway crashed through the door and raced to the fallen Tanner. No more than three seconds later the downstairs guard rushed into the room, his pistol drawn. Voices were heard yelling outside on the grounds. Leila entered, gasped, and ran to Ali and her fallen husband.

"Bernie! For God's sake, *Bernie!*"

But Osterman did not appear.

"Get him on the bed!" roared the patrolman from the upstairs hallway. "Please, ma'am, let go! Let me get him on the bed!"

Osterman could be heard yelling on the staircase. "What the hell happened?" He came into the room. "Oh *Jesus!* Oh, Jesus *Christ!*"

Tanner regained consciousness and looked around. MacAuliff stood next to the doctor; Ali sat on the bed. Bernie and Leila were at the footrail, trying to smile at him reassuringly.

"You're going to be fine. Very superficial," said the doctor. "Painful, but not serious. Shoulder cartilage, that's what it is."

"I was shot?"

"You were shot." MacAuliff agreed.

"Who shot me?"

"We don't know that." MacAuliff tried to conceal his anger, but it surfaced. The captain was obviously convinced he was being ignored; that vital information was being withheld from him. "But I tell you this, I intend to question each one of you if it takes all night to find out what's happening here. You're all being damned fools and I won't permit it!"

"The wound is dressed," said the doctor, putting on his jacket. "You can get up and around as soon as you feel like it, only take it easy, Mr. Tanner. Not much more than a deep cut. Very little loss of blood." The doctor smiled and left rapidly. He had no reason to remain.

The moment the door was closed, MacAuliff made his abrupt statement. "Would you all wait downstairs, please? I want to be left alone with Mr. Tanner."

"Captain, he was just shot," said Bernie firmly. "You can't question him now; I won't let you."

"I'm a police officer on official business; I don't need your permission. You heard the doctor. He's not seriously hurt."

"He's been through enough!" Ali stared at MacAuliff.

"I'm sorry, Mrs. Tanner. This is necessary. Now will you all please . . ."

"No, we will *not*!" Osterman left his wife's side and approached the police chief. "He's not the one who should be questioned. *You* are. Your whole Goddamn police force should be put on the carpet. . . . I'd like to know why that patrol car didn't stop, Captain! I heard your explanation and I don't accept it!"

"You continue this, Mr. Osterman, I'll call in an officer and have you locked up!"

"I wouldn't try that. . . ."

"Don't tempt me! I've dealt with your kind before! I *worked* New York, sheenie!"

Osterman had grown very still. "What did you say?"

"Don't provoke me. You're provoking me!"

"Forget it!" said Tanner from the bed. "I don't mind, really. . . . Go ahead downstairs, all of you."

Alone with MacAuliff, Tanner sat up. His shoulder hurt, but he could move it freely.

MacAuliff walked to the end of the bed and held the footrail with both hands. He spoke calmly, "You talk now. You tell me what you know or I'll book you for withholding information in attempted murder."

"They were trying to kill *me*."

"That's still murder. M-u-r-d-e-r. It doesn't make any difference whether it's yours or that big Jew bastard's!"

"Why are you so hostile?" Tanner asked. "Tell me. You should be begging at my feet. I'm a taxpayer and you haven't protected my house."

MacAuliff made several attempts to speak but he was choking on his own anger. Finally he controlled himself.

"Okay. I know a lot of you don't like the way I run things. You bastards want to put me out and get some fucking hippie from a half-assed law school! Well, the only way you can do that is if I louse up. And I'm not *gonna* louse up! My record stays clean! This town stays clean! So you tell me what's going on and if I need help, I'll call it in! I can't do that without something to go on!"

Tanner rose from the bed, at first unsteadily, and then, to his surprise, firmly.

"I believe you. You're too frantic to lie. . . . And you're right. A lot of us *don't* like you. But that may be chemical, so let's let it go. . . . Still, I'm not answering questions. Instead, I'm giving you an order. You'll keep this house guarded night and day until I tell you to stop! Do you understand that?"

"I don't *take* orders!"

"You'll take them from me. If you don't, I'll plaster you across sixty million television screens as the typical example of the outdated, uneducated, unenlightened threat to real law enforcement! You're obsolete. Get that pension and run."

"You couldn't do that . . ."

"Couldn't I? Check around."

MacAuliff stood facing Tanner. The veins in his neck were so apparent the news director thought they would burst. "I hate you bastards!" he said coldly. "I hate your guts."

"As I do yours. . . . I've seen you in action. . . . But that doesn't matter now. Sit down."

Ten minutes later MacAuliff rushed out of the house into the diminishing July storm. He slammed the front door behind him and gave cursory orders to several police deputies on the lawn. The men acknowledged with feeble salutes, and MacAuliff climbed into his car.

Tanner took a shirt from his bureau drawer and awkwardly put it on. He went out of the bedroom and started down the stairs.

Ali was in the hallway talking to the police officer and saw him. She rushed up to meet him on the staircase landing.

"There are police crawling all over the place. I wish it were an army. . . . Oh, Lord! I'm trying to be calm. I really am! But I can't" She embraced him, conscious of the bandage beneath his shirt. "What are we going to *do*? Who are we going to *turn* to?"

"Everything's going to be all right. . . . We just have to wait a little longer."

"What for?"

"MacAuliff is getting me information."

"What information?"

Tanner moved Ali against the wall. He spoke quietly, making sure the policeman wasn't watching them. "Whoever was outside those basement windows is hurt. One I know is badly wounded—in the leg. The other we can't be sure of, but Bernie thinks he hit him in the shoulder or the chest. MacAuliff's going out to see the Cardones and the Tremaynes. He'll phone me then. It may take quite a while, but he'll get back to me."

"Did you tell him what to look for?"

"No. Nothing. I simply asked him to follow up their stories about where they were. That's all. I don't want MacAuliff making decisions. That's for Fassett."

But it wasn't for Fassett, thought Tanner. It wasn't for anyone but him any longer. He'd tell Ali when he had to. At the last minute. So he smiled at her and put his arm around her waist and wished he could be free to love her again.

The telephone rang at ten-forty-seven.

"John? It's Dick. MacAuliff was over to see me." Tremayne was breathing hard into the telephone, but was keeping his voice reasonably calm. His control was stretched very thin, however.

". . . I have no idea what you're involved with—intended murder, for God's sake!—and I don't *want* to know, but it's more than I can take! I'm sorry, John, but I'm getting the family out of here. I've got reservations on Pan Am at ten in the morning."

"Where are you going?"

Tremayne did not reply. Tanner spoke again. "I asked you where you were going."

"Sorry, John . . . this may sound rotten, but I don't want to tell you."

"I think I understand. . . . Do us a favor, though. Drop by on the way to the airport."

"I can't promise that. Good-bye."

Tanner held his finger down on the phone and then released it. He dialed the Saddle Valley police station.

"Police headquarters. Sergeant Dale."

"Captain MacAuliff, please. John Tanner calling."

"He's not here, Mr. Tanner."

"Can you reach him? It's urgent."

"I can try on the car radio; do you want to hold?"

"No, just have him call me as soon as possible." Tanner gave his telephone number and hung up. MacAuliff was probably on his way to the Cardones. He should have arrived by now. He'd call soon. Tanner returned to the living room. He wanted to unnerve the Ostermans.

It was part of his plan.

"Who called?" asked Bernie.

"Dick. He heard what happened. . . . He's taking the family and leaving."

The Ostermans exchanged looks.

"Where?"

"He didn't say. They've got a flight in the morning."

"He didn't say where he was going?" Bernie stood up casually but couldn't hide his anxiety.

"I told you. He wouldn't tell me."

"That's not what you said." Osterman looked at Tanner. "You said 'didn't say.' That's different from not telling you."

"I suppose it is. . . . You still think we should head down to Washington?"

"What?" Osterman was looking at his wife. He hadn't heard Tanner's question.

"Do you still think we should go to Washington?"

"Yes." Bernie stared at Tanner. "Now more than ever. You need protection. Real protection. . . . They're trying to kill you, John."

"I wonder. I wonder if it's me they're trying to kill."

"What do you mean?" Leila stood up, facing Tanner.

The telephone rang.

Tanner returned quickly to the study and picked up the receiver. It was MacAuliff.

"Listen," said Tanner quietly. "I want you to describe exactly—*exactly*—where Tremayne was during your interrogation."

"In his study."

"*Where* in his study?"

"At his desk. Why?"

"Did he get up? Did he walk around? To shake your hand, for instance?"

"No. . . . No, I don't think so. No, he didn't."

"What about his wife? She let you in?"

"No. The maid. Tremayne's wife was upstairs. She was sick. We verified that; called the doctor, remember?"

"All right. Now tell me about the Cardones. Where did you find them?"

"Spoke first with his wife. One of the kids let me in. She was lying on the sofa, her husband was in the garage."

"Where did you talk with him?"

"I just told you. In the garage. I didn't get there too soon either. He's on his way to Philadelphia. His father's sick. They gave him last rites."

"Philadelphia? . . . Where exactly was he?"

"In the *garage*, I said! His bags were packed. He was in the car. He told me to be quick. He wanted to take off."

"He was *in* the car?"

"That's right."

"Didn't that seem strange to you?"

"Why should it? For Christ's sake, his father's dying! He wanted to get the hell to Philadelphia. I'll check it out."

Tanner hung up the phone.

Neither couple was seen by MacAuliff under normal conditions. None stood, none walked. Both had reasons not to be at his house on Sunday.

Tremayne behind a desk, frightened, immobile.

Cardone seated in an automobile, anxious only to drive away.

One or both *wounded*.

One or both, perhaps, Omega.

The time had come. Outside the rain had stopped; his traveling would be easier now, although the woods would still be wet.

In the kitchen, he changed into the clothes he'd carried down from the bedroom: black trousers, a black long-sleeved sweater, and sneakers. He put money in his pocket, making sure that his change included at least six dimes. Finally, he clipped a pencil-light to the top of his sweater.

Then he went to the hallway door and called Ali into the kitchen. He dreaded this moment far more than anything which lay before him. Yet there was no other way. He knew he had to tell her.

"What are you doing? Why—"

Tanner held his finger to his lips and drew her close to him. They had walked to the far end of the kitchen by the garage door, the furthest point from the hallway. He whispered calmly to her.

"Remember I asked you to trust me?"

Ali nodded her head slowly.

"I'm going out for a while; just for a little while. I'm meeting a couple of men who can help us. MacAuliff made contact."

"Why can't they come here? I don't want you to go outside. You can't go outside!"

"There's no other practical way. It's been arranged," he lied, knowing she suspected the lie. "I'll phone you in a little while. You'll know everything's all right then. But until I do, I want you to tell the Ostermans I went for a walk. . . . I'm upset, anything you like. It's important they think *you* believe I went for a walk. That I'll be back any minute. Maybe I'm talking to some of the men outside."

"Who *are* you going to meet? You've got to tell me."

"Fassett's men."

She held his gaze. The lie was established between them now and she searched his eyes. "You have to do this?" she asked quietly.

"Yes." He embraced her roughly, anxious to leave, and walked rapidly to the kitchen door.

Outside he strolled about his property, establishing his presence with the police deputies in front and back of his house, to the point where he guessed he was no longer really watched. And then, when he felt no one was looking at him, he disappeared into the woods.

He made a wide circle towards the west, using the tiny beam of the pencil light to avoid obstacles. The wetness, the softness of the earth, made the going difficult, but eventually he saw the backyard lights of his neighbors the Scanlans, three hundred feet from his property line. He was soaked as he approached the Scanlans' back porch and rang the bell.

Fifteen minutes later—again longer than Tanner had anticipated—he climbed into Scanlan's Mercedes coupe and started the engine. Scanlan's Smith & Wesson magazine-clip pistol was in his belt, three extra clips of ammunition in his pocket.

Tanner swung left down Orchard Drive toward the center of the Village. It was past midnight; he was behind the schedule he had set.

He took momentary stock of himself and his actions. He had never considered himself an exceptionally brave man. Whatever courage he had ever displayed was always born of the moment. And he wasn't feeling courageous now. He was desperate.

It was strange. His fear—the profound, deeply felt terror he had lived with for days—now created its own balance, gave birth to its own anger. Anger at being manipulated. He could accept it no longer.

Saddle Valley was quiet, the main street softly lit by replicas of gas lamps, the storefronts in keeping with the town's image of quiet wealth. No neons, no floodlights, everything subdued.

Tanner drove past. The Village Pub and the taxi stand, made a U-turn, and parked. The public telephone was directly across from the Mercedes. He wanted the car positioned far enough away so he could see the whole area. He walked across the street and made his first call.

"It's Tanner, Tremayne. Be quiet and listen to me. . . . Omega's finished. It's being disbanded. I'm calling it off. Zurich's calling it off. We've put you through the final test and you've failed. The stupidity displayed by everyone is beyond belief! I'm issuing the phase-out orders tonight. Be at the Lassiter depot at two-thirty. And don't try to call my home. I'm phoning from the Village. I'll take a taxi to the area. My house is being watched, thanks to *all* of you! Be at the depot at two-thirty and bring Virginia. Omega's collapsed! If you want to get out alive, be there. . . . Two-thirty!"

Tanner pressed down the receiver. The Cardones next.

"Betty? It's Tanner. Listen closely. You get hold of Joe and tell him Omega is finished. I don't care how you do it, but get him back here. That's an order from Zurich. Tell him that! . . . Omega's collapsed. You've all been damn fools. Disabling my cars was stupid. I'm issuing phase-out orders tonight at the Lassiter depot at two-thirty. You and Joe be there! Zurich expects you. And *don't* try to phone me back. I'm calling from the Village. My house is watched. I'll take a taxi. Remember. The Lassiter depot—tell Joe."

Once more Tanner pressed the receiver down. His third call was to his own home.

"Ali? Everything's fine, darling. There's nothing to worry about. Now, don't talk. Put Bernie on the phone right away. . . . Ali, not *now*! Put Bernie on the *phone*! . . . Bernie, it's John. I'm sorry I took off but I had to. I know who Omega is but I need your help. I'm calling from the Village. I'll need a car later . . . not now; later. I don't want mine seen in the Village. I'll use a taxi. Meet me out at the Lassiter depot at two-thirty. Turn right out of the driveway and go east on Orchard—it curves north—for about a mile. You'll see a large pond, there's a white fence around it. On the other side is Lassiter Road. Go down Lassiter a couple of miles and you'll see the depot. . . . It's over, Bernie. I'll have Omega at the depot at two-thirty. For Christ's sake *don't, don't blow* it! Trust me! *Don't* call anybody or *do* anything! Just *be* there!"

Tanner hung up the telephone, opened the door and ran towards the Mercedes coupe.

Chapter Twenty-eight

He stood in the darkened doorway of a toy store. It occurred to him that Scanlan's Mercedes was a familiar car in the Village and the Tremaynes, the Cardones, and perhaps even the Ostermans knew Scanlan was his nearest neighbor. That might be to his advantage, he considered. If the assumption were made that he'd borrowed the automobile, it would be further assumed that he remained in the area. The hunt, then, would be thorough. There was nothing to do but wait now. Wait until a little after two o'clock before driving out to the Lassiter depot.

Wait in the center of the Village to see who came after him; who tried to stop him from making the rendezvous. Which couple? Or would it be all three? For Omega had to be frightened now. The unutterable had been said; the mystery brought out into the open.

Omega would have to try to stop him now. If anything Fassett has said was true, that was their only course of action. To intercept him before he reached the depot.

He counted on it. They wouldn't stop him—he'd make sure of that, but he wanted to know in advance who the enemy was.

He looked up and down the street. There were only four people visible. A couple walking a Dalmation, a man emerging from the Pub, and the driver asleep in the front seat of his taxi.

From the east end of town Tanner saw the headlights of a car approaching slowly. Soon he saw it was his own station wagon. He pressed back into the recessed, unlit doorway.

The driver was Leila Osterman. Alone.

Tanner's pulse quickened. What had he done? It had never occurred to him that any of the couples would separate in a crisis! Yet Leila was alone! And there was nothing to prevent Osterman from holding his family as hostages! Osterman was one of those being protected, not one of the hunted. He could move about freely, leave the premises if he wished. Force Ali and the children to go with him if he thought it necessary!

Leila parked the station wagon in front of the Pub, got out, and walked rapidly over to the taxi driver, shaking him awake. They talked quietly for a moment; Tanner couldn't hear the voices. Eventually Leila turned back to the Pub and went in. Tanner remained in the doorway, fingering the dimes in his pocket, waiting for her to come out. The waiting was agony. He had to get to the phone. He had to get through to the police! He had to make sure his family was safe!

Finally she appeared, got in the wagon, and drove off. Five or six blocks west she turned right; the car disappeared.

Tanner raced across the street to the telephone booth. He dropped in a dime and dialed.

"Hello?"

Thank God! It was Ali!

"It's me."

"Where are you . . ."

"Never mind that now. Everything's fine. . . . Are you all right?" He listened carefully for any false note.

"Of course, I am. We're worried sick about you. What are you doing?"

She sounded natural. It was all right.

"I don't have time. I want . . ."

She interrupted him. "Leila went out looking for you. You've made an awful mistake. . . . We've talked. You and I were wrong, darling. Very *wrong*. Bernie got so worried he thought . . ."

He cut her off. He didn't have the seconds to waste; not on the Ostermans, not now. "I've got to get off the phone. Stay with the guards. Do as I say. Don't let them out of your sight!"

He hung up before she could speak. He had to reach the police. Every moment counted now.

"Headquarters. Jenkins speaking."

So the one man on the Saddle Valley police force cleared for Omega was back. MacAuliff had recalled him.

"Headquarters," repeated the patrolman testily.

"This is John Tanner . . ."

"Jesus Christ, where have you been? We've been looking all over for you!"

"You won't find me. Not until I want you to. . . . Now, listen to me! The two policemen in the house—I want them to stay with my wife. She's never to be left alone! The children either! Never! None of them can be alone with Osterman!"

"Of course! We know that! Now, where are you? Don't be a damned fool!"

"I'll phone you later. Don't bother to trace this call. I'll be gone."

He slammed down the receiver and opened the door, looking for a better vantage point than the storefront. He couldn't run unobserved from the doorway. He started back across the street. The taxi driver was asleep again.

Suddenly, without warning, Tanner heard the roar of an engine. The blurred outline of a car without headlights sped toward him. It came out of nowhere at enormous speed; he was its target. He raced towards the opposite sidewalk only feet ahead of the rushing car. He threw himself toward the curb, twisting his body away from the automobile.

At the same instant he felt a great blow on his left leg. There was a piercing sound of tires braking on asphalt. Tanner fell, rolling with his plunge, and saw the black car narrowly miss the Mercedes, then speed away down Valley Road.

The pain in his leg was excruciating; his shoulder was throbbing. He hoped to Christ he could walk! He had to be able to *walk*!

The cab driver was running toward him.

"Jesus! What happened?"

"Help me up, will you, please?"

"Sure! Sure! You okay? . . . That guy must've had a load on! Jesus! You could've been killed. You want me to get a doctor?"

"No. No, I don't think so."

"I got a telephone right over there! I'll call the cops! They'll have a doctor here in no time!"

"No! No, don't! I'm all right. . . . Just help me walk around a bit." It was painful for him, but Tanner found he could move. That was the important fact. The pain didn't matter now. Nothing mattered but Omega. And Omega was out in the open!

"I better call the police anyway," said the driver, holding on to Tanner's arm. "That clown should get yanked off the road."

"No. . . . I mean, I didn't get the license. I didn't even see what kind of car. It wouldn't do any good."

"I guess not. Serve the bastard right, though, if he plows himself into a tree."

"Yeah. That's right." Tanner was walking by himself now. He'd be all right.

The telephone at the taxi stand rang across the street.

"There goes my phone. . . . You okay?"

"Sure. Thanks."

"Saturday night. Probably the only call I'll get on the whole shift. Only keep one cab on duty Saturday night. That's one too many." The driver moved away. "Good luck, buddy. You sure you don't want a doctor?"

"No, really. Thanks."

He watched the driver take down an address, then heard his voice as he repeated it.

"Tremayne. Sixteen Peachtree. Be there in five minutes, Ma'am." He hung up and saw Tanner watching him. "How d'you like that? She wants to go to a motel at Kennedy. Who do you suppose she's shacking up with out there?"

Tanner was bewildered. The Tremaynes had two cars of their own. . . . Had Tremayne intended to ignore the command to meet at the Lassiter depot? Or, by making sure the single Saturday night taxi was away, was Tremayne hoping to isolate him in the Village?

Either was possible.

Tanner hobbled toward an alley running alongside of the Pub, used primarily for deliveries. From there, since it led to a municipal parking lot, he could escape undetected if it were necessary. He stood in the alley and massaged his leg. He'd have a huge welt in an hour or so. He looked at his watch. It was twelve-forty-nine. Another hour before he would drive to the depot. Perhaps the black car would return. Perhaps others would come.

He wanted a cigarette, but did not want to strike a match near the street. He could cup the glow of a cigarette, not the flame of a match. He walked ten yards into the alley and lit up. He heard something. Footsteps?

He inched his way back toward the Valley Road entrance. The Village was deserted. The only sounds were muted, coming from the Pub. Then the Pub's door opened and three people came out. Jim and Nancy Loomis with a man he didn't recognize. He laughed sadly to himself.

Here he was, John Tanner, the respected Director of News for Standard Mutual, hiding in a darkened alley—filthy, soaked, a bullet crease in his shoulder and a swelling bruise on his leg from a driver intent on murder—silently watching Jim and Nancy come out of the Pub. Jim Loomis. He had been touched by Omega and he'd never know it.

From the west end of Valley Road—the direction of Route Five—came an automobile traveling quietly at no more than ten miles an hour. The driver seemed to be looking for someone or something on Valley Road.

It was Joe.

He hadn't gone to Philadelphia. There was no dying father in Philadelphia. The Cardones had lied.

It was no surprise to Tanner.

He pressed his back against the alley wall and made himself as inconspicuous as he could, but he was a large man. For no other reason than that it gave him security, Tanner withdrew the pistol from his belt. He'd kill Cardone if he had to.

When the car was within forty feet of him, two short blasts from a second automobile, coming from the other direction, made Cardone stop.

The second car approached rapidly.

It was Tremayne. As he passed the alley, Tanner could see the look of panic on his face.

The lawyer pulled up beside Cardone and the two men spoke quickly, softly. Tanner couldn't make out the words, but he could tell they were spoken rapidly and with great agitation. Tremayne made a U-turn, and the automobiles raced off in the same direction.

Tanner relaxed and stretched his pained body. All were accounted for now. All he knew about and one more he didn't. Omega plus one, he considered. Who was in the black automobile? Who had tried to run him down?

There was no point in putting it off any longer. He'd seen what he had to see. He'd drive to within a few hundred yards of the Lassiter depot and wait for Omega to declare themselves.

He walked out of the alley and started for the car. And then he stopped.

There was something wrong with the car. In the subdued light of the gas lamps he could see that the automobile's rear end had settled down to the surface of the street. The chrome bumper was inches above the pavement.

He ran to the car and unclipped his pencil light. Both back tires were flat, the metal rims supporting the weight of the automobile. He crouched down and saw two knives protruding from the deflated rubber.

How? When? He was within twenty yards every second! The street was deserted! No one! No one could have crept behind the Mercedes without being seen!

Except, perhaps, those few moments in the alley. Those moments when he lit a cigarette and crouched by the wall watching Tremayne and Cardone. Those seconds when he'd thought he'd heard footsteps.

The tires had been slashed not five minutes ago!

Oh Christ! thought Tanner. The manipulation hadn't stopped at all! Omega was at his heels. Knowing, Knowing every move he made. Every second!

What had Ali started to say on the phone? Bernie had . . . what? He started toward the booth, taking the last dime out of his pocket. He pulled the pistol out of his belt and looked around as he crossed the street. Whoever punctured the tires might be waiting, watching.

"Ali?"

"Darling, for God's sake come home!"

"In a little while, hon. Honest, no problems. No problems at all. . . . I just want to ask you a question. It's important."

"It's just as important that you get *home!*"

"You said before that Bernie had decided something. What was it?"

"Oh . . . when you called the first time. Leila went out after you; Bernie didn't want to leave us alone. But he was worried that you might not listen to her and since the police were here, he decided to go find you himself."

"Did he take the Triumph?"

"Now. He borrowed a car from one of the police."

"Oh, Christ!" Tanner didn't mean to explode into the phone but he couldn't help it. The black automobile out of nowhere! The *plus-one* was really part of the three! "Is he back?"

"No. Leila is, though. She thinks he may have gotten lost."

"I'll call you." Tanner hung up. Of course Bernie was "lost." There hadn't been time for him to get back. Not since Tanner had been in the alley, not since the tires were slashed.

And now he realized that somehow he had to reach the Lassiter depot. Reach it and position himself before any part of Omega could stop him, or know where he was.

Lassiter Road was diagonally northwest, about three miles from the center of the Village. The depot perhaps another mile or two beyond. He'd walk. It was all he could do.

He started as quickly as he could, his limp diminishing with movement, then ducked into a doorway. No one followed him.

He kept up a zigzag pattern northwest until he reached the outskirts of town—where there were no sidewalks, only large expanses of lawn. Lassiter wasn't far away now. Twice he lay on the ground while automobiles raced past him, drivers oblivious to anything but the road in front of them.

Finally, through a back stretch of woods behind a well-trimmed lawn, neither unlike his own, he reached Lassiter Road.

On the rough tarred surface he turned left and started the final part of his journey. It wasn't any farther than a mile or a mile and a half by his calculations. He could reach the deserted depot in fifteen minutes if his leg held out. If it didn't, he'd simply slow down, but he'd get there. His watch read one-forty-one. There was time.

Omega wouldn't arrive early. It couldn't afford to. It—or they—didn't know what was waiting for them.

Tanner limped along the road and found he felt better—more secure—holding Scanlan's pistol in his hand. He saw a flicker of light behind him. Headlights, three or four hundred yards away. He crossed into the woods bordering on the road and lay flat on the muddy ground.

The car passed him traveling slowly. It was the same black car that had run him down on Valley Road. He couldn't see the driver; the absence of street lights made any identification impossible.

When it was out of sight, Tanner went back to the road. He had considered walking in the woods but it wasn't feasible. He could make better time on the cleared surface. He went on, hobbling now, wondering whether the black automobile belonged to a policeman currently stationed at 22 Orchard Drive. Whether the driver was a writer named Osterman.

He had gone nearly half a mile when the lights appeared again, only now in front of him. He dove into the brush, hoping to God he hadn't been seen, unlatching the safety of his pistol as he lay there.

The automobile approached at incredible speed. Whoever was driving was racing back to find someone.

Was it to find him?

Or Leila Osterman?

Or was it to reach Cardone, who had *no* dying father in Philadelphia. Or Tremayne, who *wasn't* on his way to the motel at Kennedy Airport.

Tanner got up and kept going, his leg about to collapse under him, the pistol gripped tightly in his hand.

He rounded a bend in the road and there it was. A single sagging street lamp lit the crumbling station house. The old stucco depot was boarded up, giant weed drooping ominously from the cracks in the rotted wood. Small ugly leaves grew out of the foundation.

There was no wind, no rain, no sound but the rhythmic drip of water from thousands of branches and leaves—the last exhausted effects of the storm.

He stood on the outskirts of the decayed, overgrown parking area trying to decide where to position himself. It was nearly two o'clock and a secluded place had to be found. The station house itself! Perhaps he could get inside. He started across the gravel and weeds.

A blinding light flashed in his eyes; his reflexes lurched him forward. He rolled over on his wounded shoulder, yet felt no pain. A powerful searchlight had pierced the dimness of the depot grounds, and gunshots echoed throughout the deserted area. Bullets thumped into the earth around him and whistled over his head. He kept rolling, over and over, knowing that one of the bullets had hit his left arm.

He reached the edge of the sunken gravel and raised his pistol toward the blinding light. He fired rapidly in the direction of the enemy. The searchlight exploded; a scream followed. Tanner kept pulling the trigger until the clip was empty. He tried to reach into his pocket with his left hand for a second clip and found he couldn't move his arm.

There was silence again. He put down the pistol and awkwardly extracted another clip with his right hand. He twisted the pistol on its back and with his teeth holding the hot barrel, pushed the fresh clip into the chamber, burning his lips as he did so.

He waited for his enemy to move. To make any sound at all. Nothing stirred.

Slowly he rose, his left arm now completely immobile. He held the pistol in front of him, ready to pull the trigger at the slightest movement in the grass.

None came.

Tanner backed his way towards the door of the depot, holding his weapon up, probing the ground carefully with his feet so that no unexpected obstacle would cause him to fall. He reached the boarded-up door, knowing he couldn't possibly break it down if it was nailed shut. Most of his body was inoperative. He had little strength left.

Still, he pushed his back against the door and the heavy wood gave slightly, creaking loudly as it did so. Tanner turned his head just enough to see that the opening was no more than three or four inches. The ancient hinges were caked with rust. He slammed his right shoulder against the edge of the door and it gave way, plunging Tanner into the darkness, onto the rotted floor of the station.

He lay where he was for several seconds. The station house door was three-quarters open, the upper section snapped away from its hinges. The street lamp fifty yards away provided a dull wash of illumination. Broken and missing boards from the roof were a second, inadequate source of light.

Suddenly Tanner heard a creaking behind him. The unmistakable sound of a footstep on the rotted floor. He tried to turn around, tried to rise. He was too late. Someone crashed into the base of his skull. He felt himself grow dizzy, but he saw the foot. A foot encased in bandages.

As he collapsed on the rotted floor, blackness sweeping over him, he looked upward into a face.

Tanner knew he had found Omega.

It was Laurence Fassett.

Chapter Twenty-nine

He couldn't know how long he'd been unconscious. Five minutes? An hour? There was no way to tell. He couldn't see his watch, he couldn't move his left arm. His face was against the rough splintered floor of the crumbling station house. He could feel the blood slowly trickling from his wounded arm; his head ached.

Fassett!

The manipulator.

Omega.

As he lay there, isolated fragments of past conversations raced through his mind.

". . . we should get together . . . our wives should get together . . ."

But Laurence Fassett's wife had been killed in East Berlin. Murdered in East Berlin. That fact had been his most moving entreaty.

And there was something else. Something to do with a Woodward broadcast. . . . The broadcast about the C.I.A. a year ago.

". . . I was in the States then. I saw that one."

But he wasn't "in the States" then. In Washington Fassett had said he'd been on the Albanian border a year ago. ". . . forty-five days of haggling." In the field. It was why he'd contacted John Tanner, the solid, clean news director of Standard Mutual, a resident of the target, Chasm of Leather.

There were other contradictions—none as obvious, but they were there. They wouldn't do him any good now. His life was about to end in the ruins of the Lassiter depot.

He moved his head and saw Fassett standing above him.

"We've got a great deal to thank you for. If you are as good a shot as I think you are you've created the perfect martyr out there. A dead hero. If he's only wounded, he'll soon be dead at any rate. . . . Oh, he's the other part of us, but even he'd recognize the perfect contribution of his sacrifice. . . . You see, I didn't lie to you. We are fanatics. We have to be."

"What now?"

"We wait for the others. One or two are bound to show up. Then it'll be over. Their lives and yours, I'm afraid. And Washington will have its Omega. Then, perhaps, a field agent named Fassett will be given another commendation. If they're not careful, they'll make me Director of Operations one day."

"You're a traitor." Tanner found something in the dark shadows by his right hand. It was a loose piece of flooring about two feet long, an inch or so wide. He awkwardly, painfully, sat up, pulling the plank to his side.

"Not by my lights. A defector, perhaps. Not a traitor. Let's not go into that. You wouldn't understand or appreciate the viewpoint. Let's just say in my opinion you're the traitor. *All* of you. Look around you . . ."

Tanner lashed out with the piece of wood and crashed it with all his might across the bandaged foot in front of him. Blood erupted instantly, spreading through the gauze. Tanner flung himself upward into Fassett's groin, trying desperately to reach the hand with the gun. Fassett screamed in anguish. Tanner found the agent's wrist with his right hand, his left arm immobile, serving only as a limping tentacle. He drove Fassett back against the wall and ground his heel into Fassett's wounded foot, stamping it over and over again.

Tanner wrenched the gun free and it fell to the floor, sliding towards the open door and the dim shaft of light. Fassett's screams shattered the stillness of the station house as he slumped against the wall.

John lunged for the pistol, picked it up and held it tightly in his hand. He got up, every part of his body in pain, the blood flowing now out of his arm.

Fassett was barely conscious, gasping in agony. Tanner wanted his man alive, wanted Omega alive. But he thought of the basement, of Ali and the children, and so he took careful aim and fired twice, once into the mass of blood and flesh which was Fassett's wound, once into the knee cap of the leg.

He lurched back toward the doorway, supporting himself in the frame. Painfully, he looked at his watch: two-thirty-seven. Seven minutes after Omega's appointed time.

No one else would come now. Half of Omega lay in agony in the station house; the rest in the tall, wet grass beyond the parking lot.

He wondered who it was.

Tremayne?

Cardone?

Osterman?

Tanner tore off part of his sleeve and tried to wrap it around the wound in his arm. If only he could stop the bleeding, even a bit. If he could do that perhaps he could make it across the old parking area to where the searchlight was.

But he couldn't, and, off balance, fell backwards to the floor. He was no better off than Fassett. Both their lives would ebb away right there. Inside the ancient depot.

A wailing began; Tanner wasn't sure if it was a trick of his brain or if it was real. Real! It was growing louder.

Sirens, then the roar of engines. Then the screeching of brakes against loose gravel and wet dirt.

Tanner rose to his elbow. He tried with all his strength to get up—only to his knees, that would be good enough. That would be sufficient to crawl. Crawl to the doorway.

The beams of searchlights filtered through the loose boards and cracked stucco, one light remaining on the entrance. Then a voice, amplified by a bull horn.

"This is the police! We are accompanied by federal authorities! If you have weapons, throw them out and follow with your hands up! . . . If you are holding Tanner hostage, release him! You are surrounded. There's no way for you to escape!"

Tanner tried to speak as he crawled toward the door. The voice sounded once again.

"We repeat. Throw out your weapons . . ."

Tanner could hear another voice yelling, this one not on a horn.

"Over here! Throw a light over here! By this automobile! Over here in the grass!"

Someone had found the rest of Omega.

"Tanner! John Tanner! Are you inside!?"

Tanner reached the entrance and pulled himself up by the edge of the door into the spill of light.

"There he is! Jesus, *look* at him!"

Tanner fell forward. Jenkins raced to his side.

"There you are, Mr. Tanner. We've tied you up as best we can. It'll hold till the ambulance gets here. See if you can walk." Jenkins braced Tanner around the waist and pulled him to his feet. Two other policemen were carrying out Fassett.

"That's him. . . . That's Omega."

"We know. You're a very impressive fellow. You did what no one else was able to do in five years of trying. You got Omega for us."

"There's someone else. Over there. . . . Fassett said he was the other part of them."

"We found him. He's dead. He's still there. You want to go over and see who it is? Tell your grandchildren some day."

Tanner looked at Jenkins and replied haltingly. "Yes. Yes, I would. I guess I'd better know."

The two men walked over into the grass. Tanner was both fascinated and repelled by the moment that approached, the moment when he would see for himself the second face of Omega. He sensed that Jenkins understood. The revelation had to be of his own observation, not second hand. He had to bear witness to the most terrible part of Omega.

The betrayal of love.

Dick. Joe. Bernie.

Several men were examining the black automobile with the ruined searchlight. The body lay face down by the sedan's door. In the dark, Tanner could see it was a large man.

Jenkins turned on his flashlight and kicked the body over. The beam of light shone into the face.

Tanner froze.

The riddled body in the grass was Captain Albert MacAuliff.

A police officer approached and spoke to Jenkins from the edge of the parking area.

"They want to come over."

"Why not? It goes with their territories. The beach is secured." Jenkins spoke with more than a trace of contempt.

"Come on!" yelled McDermott to some men in the shadows on the other side of the parking lot.

Tanner could see the three tall figures walking across the gravel. Walking slowly, reluctantly.

Bernie Osterman. Joe Cardone. Dick Tremayne.

He limped with Jenkins' help out of the grass, away from Omega. The four friends faced each other; none knew what to say.

"Let's go," said Tanner to Jenkins.

"Pardon us, gentlemen."

PART FOUR
Sunday Afternoon

Chapter Thirty

Sunday afternoon in the Village of Saddle Valley, New Jersey. The two patrol cars roamed up and down the streets as usual, but they remained at cruising speeds, lazily turning into the shady roads. The drivers smiled at the children and waved at the residents doing their Sunday chores. Golf bags and tennis rackets could be seen in small foreign convertibles and in gleaming station wagons. The sun was bright; the trees and the lawns glistened, refreshed by the July storm.

Saddle Valley was awake, preparing for a perfect Sunday afternoon. Telephones were dialed, plans made, a number of apologies offered for last evening's behavior. They were laughed off—what the hell, last evening was Saturday night. In Saddle Valley, New Jersey, Saturday nights were quickly forgiven.

A late model dark blue sedan with whitewall tires drove into the Tanner driveway. Inside the house John Tanner got up from the couch and walked painfully to the window. His upper chest and his entire left arm was encased in bandages. So, too, was his left leg, from thigh to ankle.

Tanner looked out the window at the two men walking up the path. One he recognized as Patrolman Jenkins—but only on second glance. Jenkins was not in his police uniform. Now he looked like a Saddle Valley commuter—a banker or an advertising executive. Tanner didn't know the second man. He'd never seen him before.

"They're here," he called toward the kitchen. Ali came out and stood in the hallway. She was dressed casually in slacks and a shirt, but the look in her eyes wasn't casual at all.

"I suppose we've got to get it over with. The sitter's out with Janet. Ray's at the Club. . . . I suppose Bernie and Leila are at the airport by now."

"If they made it in time. There were statements, papers to sign. Dick's acting as everyone's attorney."

The chimes rang and Ali went to the door. "Sit down, darling. Just a little at a time, the doctor said."

"Okay."

Jenkins and his unfamiliar partner came in. Alice brought coffee and the four of them sat across from each other, the Tanners on the couch, Jenkins and the man he introduced as Grover in the armchairs.

"You're the one I talked to in New York, aren't you?" John asked.

"Yes, I am. I'm with the Agency. Incidentally, so is Jenkins. He's been assigned here for the past year and a half."

"You were a very convincing policeman, Mr. Jenkins," said Ali.

"It wasn't difficult. It's a pleasant place, nice people."

"I thought it was the Chasm of Leather." Tanner's hostility was apparent. It was time for explanations. He had demanded them.

"That, too, of course," added Jenkins softly.

"Then we'd better talk about it."

"Very well," said Grover. "I'll summarize in a few words. 'Divide and kill.' That was Fassett's premise. Omega's premise."

"Then there really was a Fassett. That was his name, I mean."

"There certainly was. For ten years Laurence Fassett was one of the finest operatives in the Agency. Excellent record, dedicated. And then things happened to him."

"He sold out."

"It's never that simple," said Jenkins. "Let's say his commitments changed. They altered drastically. He became the enemy."

"And you didn't know it?"

Grover hesitated before replying. He seemed to be searching for the least painful words. His head nodded, imperceptibly. "We knew. . . . We found out gradually, over a period of years. Defectors of Fassett's caliber are never revealed overnight. It's a slow process; a series of assignments with conflicting objectives. Sooner or later a pattern emerges. When it does, you make the most of it. . . . Which is exactly what we did."

"That seems to me awfully dangerous, complicated."

"A degree of danger, perhaps; not complicated, really. Fassett was maneuvered, just as he maneuvered you and your friends. He was brought into the Omega operation because his credentials warranted it. He was brilliant and this was an explosive situation. . . . Certain laws of espionage are fundamental. We correctly assumed that the enemy would give Fassett the responsibility of keeping Omega *intact*, not *allowing* its destruction. He was at once the defending general and the attacking force. The strategy was well thought out, take my word for it. Do you begin to see?"

"Yes." Tanner was barely audible.

"'Divide and kill.' Omega existed. Chasm of Leather *was* saddle Valley. The checks on residents *did* uncover the Swiss accounts of the Cardones and the Tremaynes. When Osterman appeared, he, too, was found to have an account in Zurich. The circumstances were perfect for Fassett. He had found three couples allied with each other in an illegal—or at least highly questionable—financial venture in Switzerland."

"Zurich. That's why the name Zurich made them all nervous. Cardone was petrified."

"He had every reason to be. He and Tremayne. One the partner in a highly speculative brokerage house with a lot of Mafia financing; and the other an attorney with a firm engaged in unethical mergers—Tremayne, the specialist. They could have been ruined. Osterman had the least to lose, but, nevertheless, as part of the public media, an indictment might have had disastrous effects. As you know better than we do, networks are sensitive."

"Yes," said Tanner again without feeling.

"If, during the weekend, Fassett could so intensify mistrust between the three couples that they began hurling accusations at each other—the next step would be violence. Once *that possibility* was established, the real Omega intended to murder at least two of the couples, and Fassett could then present us with a substitute Omega. Who could refuse him? The subjects would be dead. It . . . was brilliant."

Tanner rose painfully from the couch and limped to the fireplace. He gripped the mantel angrily.

"I'm glad you can sit there and make professional judgments." He turned on the government men. "You had no right, *no right*! My *wife*, my *children* were damn near *killed*! Where were your men outside on the grounds? What happened to all that protective equipment from the biggest corporation in the world? Who listened on those electronic . . . *things* which were supposedly installed all over the house? *Where was everybody? We were left in that cellar to die!*"

Grover and Jenkins let the moment subside. They accepted Tanner's hostility calmly, with understanding. They'd been through such moments before. Grover spoke quietly, in counterpoint to Tanner's anger.

"In operations such as these, we anticipate that errors—I'll be honest, generally one massive error—occur. It's unavoidable when you consider the logistics."

"*What error?*"

Jenkins spoke. "I'd like to answer that. . . . The error was mine. I was the senior officer at 'Leather' and the only one who knew about Fassett's defection. The only one. Saturday afternoon McDermott told me that Cole had unearthed extraordinary information, and had to see me right away. I didn't check it out with Washington, I didn't confirm it. I just accepted it and drove into the city as fast as I could. . . . I thought that Cole, or someone here at 'Leather,' had discovered who Fassett really was. If that had been the case a whole new set of instructions would have to come from Washington. . . ."

"We were prepared," interrupted Grover. "Alternate plans were ready to be implemented."

"I got into New York, went up to the hotel suite . . . and Cole wasn't there. I know it sounds incredible, but he was out to dinner. He was simply *out to dinner*. He left the name of the restaurant, so I went there. This all took time. Taxis, traffic. I couldn't use the phone; all conversations were recorded. Fassett might have been tipped. Finally I got to Cole. He didn't know what I was talking about. He'd sent no message."

Jenkins stopped, the telling of the story angered and embarrassed him.

"That was the error?" asked Ali.

"Yes. It gave Fassett the time he needed. *I* gave him the time."

"Wasn't Fassett risking too much? Trapping himself? Cole denied the message."

"He calculated the risk. Timed it. Since Cole was constantly in touch with 'Leather', a single message, especially second hand, could be garbled. The fact that I fell for the ruse also told him something. Put simply, I was to be killed."

"That doesn't explain the guards outside. Your going to New York doesn't explain their not being there?"

"We said Fassett was brilliant," continued Grover. "When we tell you why they weren't there, why there wasn't a single patrol within miles, you'll understand just how brilliant he was. . . . He systematically withdrew all the men from your property on the grounds that *you* were *Omega*. The man they were guarding with their lives was, in reality, the enemy."

"*What?*"

"Think about it. Once you were dead, who could disprove it?"

"Why would they believe it?"

"The electronic pick-ups. They'd stopped functioning throughout your house. One by one they stopped transmitting. You were the only one here who knew they existed. Therefore, *you* were eliminating them."

"But I wasn't! I didn't know where they were! I still don't!"

"It wouldn't make any difference if you did." It was Jenkins who spoke. "Those transmitters had operating capacities of anywhere from thirty-six to forty-eight hours only. No more. I showed you one last night. It was treated with acid. They all were. The acid gradually ate through the miniature plates and shorted out the transmission. . . . But all the men in the field knew was that they weren't functioning. Fassett *then* announced that he'd made the error. *You* were Omega and he hadn't realized it. I'm told he did it very effectively. There's something awesome about a man like Fassett admitting a major mistake. He withdrew the patrols and then he and MacAuliff moved in for the kill. They were able to do it because I wasn't here to stop them. He'd removed me from the scene."

"Did you know about MacAuliff?"

"No," answered Jenkins. "He wasn't even a suspect. His cover was pure genius. A bigoted small town cop, veteran of the New York police, and a right-winger to boot. Frankly, the first hint we had of his involvement was when you said the police car didn't stop when you signaled from the basement. Neither patrol car was in the vicinity at the time; MacAuliff made sure of that. However, he carries a red signal light in his trunk. Simple clamp device that can be mounted on top. He was circling your house, trying to draw you out. . . . When he finally got here, two things struck us. The first was that he'd been reached by car radio. Not at home. The second was a general description supplied by those on duty. That MacAuliff kept holding his stomach, claimed to be having a severe ulcer attack. MacAuliff had no history of ulcers. It was possible that he'd been wounded. It turned out to be correct. His 'ulcer' was a gash in his stomach. Courtesy of Mr. Osterman."

Tanner reached for a cigarette. Ali lit it for him.

"Who killed the man in the woods?"

"MacAuliff. And don't hold yourself responsible. He would have killed him whether you got up and turned on the light or not. He also gassed your family last Wednesday. He used the police riot supply."

"What about our dog? In my daughter's bedroom."

"Fassett," said Grover. "You had ice cubes delivered at one-forty-five; they were left on the front porch. Fassett saw the chance to create further panic and so he simply took them in. You were all at the pool. Once he got inside, he could maneuver; he's a pro. He was just a man delivering ice cubes. Even if you saw him, he could have told you it was extra precaution on his part. You certainly wouldn't have argued. And Fassett obviously was the man on the road who gassed the Cardones and the Tremaynes."

"Everything was calculated to keep us *all* in a constant state of panic. With no let up. Force my husband to think it was each of them." Ali stared at Tanner and spoke quietly. "What have we done? What did we say to them?"

"At one time or another I was convinced each person had given himself . . . or herself . . . away. I was positive."

"You were looking for that desperately. The relationships in this house, during the weekend, were intensely personal. Fassett knew that." Grover looked over at Jenkins. "Of course, you must realize that they were all frightened. They had good reason to be. Regardless of their own personal, professional guilts, they shared a major one."

"Zurich?"

"Precisely. It accounted for their final actions. Cardone wasn't going to a dying father in Philadelphia last night. He'd called his partner Bennett to come out. He didn't want to talk on the phone and he thought his house might be watched. Yet he wasn't about to go far away from his family. They met at a diner on Route Five. . . . Cardone told Bennett about the Zurich manipulation and offered his resignation for a settlement. His idea was to turn state's evidence for the Justice Department in return for immunity."

"Tremayne said he was leaving this morning . . ."

"Lufthansa. Straight through to Zurich. He's a good attorney, very agile in these sorts of negotiations. He was getting out with what he could salvage."

"Then they both—separately—were leaving Bernie with the mess."

"Mr. and Mrs. Osterman had their own plans. A syndicate in Paris was prepared to assume their investment. All it would have taken was a cablegram to the French attorneys."

Tanner rose from the couch and limped toward the windows overlooking his backyard. He wasn't sure he wanted to hear any more. The sickness was everywhere. It left no one, it seemed, untouched. Fassett had said it.

It's a spiral, Mr. Tanner. No one lives in a deep freeze anymore.

He turned slowly back to the government men. "There are still questions."

"We'll never be able to give you all the answers," said Jenkins. "No matter what we tell you now, the questions will be around for a long time. You'll find inconsistencies, seeming contradictions, and they'll turn into doubts. The questions will become real again. . . . That's the difficult part. Everything was too subjective for you. Too personal. You operated for five days in a state of exhaustion, with little or no sleep. Fassett counted on that, too."

"I don't mean that. I mean physical things. . . . Leila wore a brooch that could be seen in the dark. There were no bullet marks in the wall around her. . . . Her husband wasn't here when I was in the Village last night. Someone slashed the tires then and tried to run me down. . . . The rendezvous at the Lassiter depot was *my* idea. How could Fassett have known if one of them hadn't told him? . . . How can you be so sure? You didn't know about MacAuliff. How do you know they aren't . . ." John Tanner stopped as he realized what he was about to say. He looked at Jenkins, who was staring at him.

Jenkins had spoken the truth. The questions were real again, the deceptions too personal.

Grover leaned forward in his chair. "In time everything will be answered. Those questions aren't difficult. Fassett and MacAuliff worked as a team. Fassett had the telephone taps moved to his new location once he left the motel. He easily could have radioed MacAuliff in the Village to kill you and then gone out to the depot when MacAuliff told him he'd failed. Obtaining other automobiles is no problem, slashing tires no feat. . . . Mrs. Osterman's brooch? An accident of dress. The unmarked wall? Its location, as I understand it, makes direct fire almost impossible."

"'Almost,' 'could have' . . . oh, God." Tanner walked back to the sofa and awkwardly sat down. He took Ali's hand. "Wait a minute." He spoke haltingly. "Something happened in the kitchen yesterday afternoon . . ."

"We know," interrupted Jenkins gently. "Your wife told us."

Ali looked at John and nodded. Her eyes were sad.

"Your friends, the Ostermans, are remarkable people," continued Jenkins. "Mrs. Osterman saw that her husband wanted to, *had* to go out and help you. He couldn't stand by and watch you killed. . . . They're very close to each other. She was giving him permission to risk his life for you."

John Tanner closed his eyes.

"Don't dwell on it," said Jenkins.

Tanner looked at Jenkins and understood.

Grover got out of his chair. It was a signal for Jenkins, who did the same.

"We'll go now. We don't want to tire you out. There'll be plenty of time later. We owe you that. . . . Oh, by the way. This belongs to you." Grover reached into his pocket and withdrew an envelope.

"What is it?"

"The affidavit you signed for Fassett. Your agreement with Omega. You'll have to take my word that the recording is buried in the archives. Lost for a millenium that way. For the sake of both countries."

"I understand. . . . One last thing." Tanner paused, afraid of his question. "What is it?"

"Which of them called you? Which of them told you about the Lassiter depot?"

"They did it together. They all met back here and decided to phone the police."

"Just like that?"

"That's the irony, Mr. Tanner," said Jenkins. "If they had done what they should have done earlier, none of this would have happened. But it was only last night that they got together and told each other the truth."

Saddle Valley was filled with whispers. In the dimly lit Village Pub men gathered in small groups and talked quietly. At the Club, couples sat around the pool and spoke softly of the terrible things which had touched their gracious haven. Strange rumors circulated—the Cardones had taken a long vacation, no one knew where; there was trouble in his firm, some said. Richard Tremayne was drinking more than usual, and his usual was too much. There were other stories about the Tremaynes, too. The maid was no longer there, the house a far cry from what it had been. Virginia's garden was going to seed.

But soon the stories stopped. Saddle Valley was nothing if not resilient. People forgot to ask about the Cardones and the Tremaynes after a while. They never fitted in really. Their friends were hardly the kind a person wanted at the Club. There simply wasn't the time for much concern. There was so much to do. Saddle Valley, in summer, was glorious. Why shouldn't it be?

Isolated, secure, inviolate.

And John Tanner knew there'd never be another Osterman weekend.

Divide and kill.

Omega had won, after all.

The Matlock Paper

Robert Ludlum

For Pat and Bill:

As the ancient Bagdhivi proverb says:
When giants cast shadows, hope for the shade.
The "Due Macellis" are giants!

Chapter One

Loring walked out the side entrance of the Justice Department and looked for a taxi. It was nearly five thirty, a spring Friday, and the congestion in the Washington streets was awful. Loring stood by the curb and held up his left hand, hoping for the best. He was about to abandon the effort when a cab that had picked up a fare thirty feet down the block stopped in front of him.

"Going east, mister? It's O.K. This gentleman said he wouldn't mind."

Loring was always embarrassed when these incidents occurred. He unconsciously drew back his right forearm, allowing his sleeve to cover as much of his hand as possible—to conceal the thin black chain looped around his wrist, locked to the briefcase handle.

"Thanks, anyway. I'm heading south at the next corner."

He waited until the taxi reentered the flow of traffic and then resumed his futile signaling.

Usually, under such conditions, his mind was alert, his feelings competitive. He would normally dart his eyes in both directions, ferreting out cabs about to disgorge passengers, watching the corners for those dimly lit roof signs that meant this particular vehicle was for hire if you ran fast enough.

Today, however, Ralph Loring did not feel like running. On this particular Friday, his mind was obsessed with a terrible reality. He had just borne witness to a man's being sentenced to death. A man he'd never met but knew a great deal about. An unknowing man of thirty-three who lived and worked in a small New England town four hundred miles away and who had no idea of Loring's existence, much less of the Justice Department's interest in him.

Loring's memory kept returning to the large conference room with the huge rectangular table around which sat the men who'd pronounced the sentence.

He had objected strenuously. It was the least he could do for the man he'd never met, the man who was being maneuvered with such precision into such an untenable position.

"May I remind you, Mr. Loring," said an assistant attorney general who'd once been a judge advocate in the navy, "that in any combat situation basic risks are assumed. A percentage of casualties is anticipated."

"The circumstances are different. This man isn't trained. He won't know who or where the enemy is. How could he? We don't know ourselves."

"Just the point." The speaker then had been another assistant AG, this one a recruit from some corporation law office, fond of committee meetings, and, Loring suspected, incapable of decisions without them. "Our subject is highly mobile. Look at the psychological profile, 'flawed but mobile in the extreme.' That's exactly what it says. He's a logical choice."

"'Flawed but mobile'! What in heaven's name does that mean? May *I* remind this committee that I've worked in the field for fifteen years. Psychological profiles are only screening guidelines, hit-and-miss judgments. I would no more send a man into an infiltration problem without knowing him thoroughly than I would assume the responsibility for NASA mathematics."

The chairman of the committee, a career professional, had answered Loring.

"I understand your reservations; normally, I'd agree. However, these aren't normal conditions. We have barely three weeks. The time factor overrides the usual precautions."

"It's the risk we have to assume," said the former judge advocate pontifically.

"*You're* not assuming it," Loring replied.

"Do you wish to be relieved of the contact?" The chairman made the offer in complete sincerity.

"No, sir. I'll make it. Reluctantly. I want that on the record."

"One thing before we adjourn." The corporation lawyer leaned forward on the table. "And this comes right from the top. We've all agreed that our subject is motivated. The profile makes that clear. What must also be made clear is that any assistance given this committee by the subject is given freely and on a voluntary basis. We're vulnerable here. We cannot, repeat *cannot*, be responsible. If it's possible, we'd like the record to indicate that the subject came to *us*."

Ralph Loring had turned away from the man in disgust.

If anything, the traffic was heavier now. Loring had about made up his mind to start walking the twenty-odd blocks to his apartment when a white Volvo pulled up in front of him.

"Get in! You look silly with your hand up like that."

"Oh, it's you. Thanks very much." Loring opened the door and slid into the small front seat, holding his briefcase on his lap. There was no need to hide the thin black chain around his wrist. Cranston was a field man, too; an overseas route specialist. Cranston had done most of the background work on the assignment which was now Loring's responsibility.

"That was a long meeting. Accomplish anything?"

"The green light."

"It's about time."

"Two assistant AGs and a concerned message from the White House were responsible."

"Good. Geo division got the latest reports from Force-Mediterranean this morning. It's a regular mass conversion of source routes. It's confirmed. The fields in Ankara and Konya in the north, the projects in Sidi Barrani and Rashid, even the Algerian contingents are systematically cutting production. It's going to make things very difficult."

"What the hell do you want? I thought the objective was to rip them out. You people are never satisfied."

"Neither would you be. We can exert controls over routes we know about; what in God's name do we know about places like . . . Porto Belocruz, Pilcomayo, a half dozen unpronounceable names in Paraguay, Brazil, Guiana? It's a whole goddamn new ballgame, Ralph."

"Bring in the SA specialists. CIA's crawling with them."

"No way. We're not even allowed to ask for maps."

"That's asinine."

"That's espionage. We stay clean. We're strictly according to Interpol-Hoyle; no funny business. I thought you knew that."

"I do," replied Loring wearily. "It's still asinine."

"You worry about New England, USA. We'll handle the pampas, or whatever they are—it is."

"New England, USA, is a goddamn microcosm. That's what's frightening. What happened to all those poetic descriptions of rustic fences and Yankee spirit and ivied brick walls?"

"New poetry. Get with it."

"Your sympathy is overwhelming. Thanks."

"You sound discouraged."

"There isn't enough time. . . ."

"There never is." Cranston steered the small car into a faster lane only to find it bottlenecked at Nebraska and Eighteenth. With a sigh, he shoved the gearshift into neutral and shrugged his shoulders. He looked at Loring, who was staring blankly at the windshield. "At least you got the green light. That's something."

"Sure. With the wrong personnel."

"Oh . . . I see. Is that him?" Cranston gestured his head toward Loring's briefcase.

"That's him. From the day he was born."

"What's his name?"

"Matlock. James B. Matlock II. The *B* is for Barbour, very old family—two very old families. James Matlock, B.A., M.A., Ph.D. A leading authority in the field of social and political influences on Elizabethan literature. How about that?"

"Jesus! Are those his qualifications? Where does he start asking questions? At faculty teas for retired professors?"

"No. That part of it's all right; he's young enough. His qualifications are included in what Security calls 'flawed but mobile in the extreme.' Isn't that a lovely phrase?"

"Inspiring. What does it mean?"

"It's supposed to describe a man who isn't very nice. Probably because of a loused-up army record, or a divorce—I'm sure it's the army thing—but in spite of that insurmountable handicap, is very well liked."

"I like him already."

"That's my problem. I do, too."

The two men fell into silence. It was clear that Cranston had been in the field long enough to realize when a fellow professional had to think by himself. Reach certain conclusions—or rationalizations—by himself. Most of the time, it was easy.

Ralph Loring thought about the man whose life was detailed so completely in his briefcase, culled from a score of data-bank sources. James Barbour Matlock was the name, but the person behind the name refused to come into focus. And that bothered Loring; Matlock's life had been shaped by disturbing, even violent, inconsistencies.

He was the surviving son of two elderly, immensely wealthy parents who lived in handsome retirement in Scarsdale, New York. His education had been properly Eastern Establishment: Andover and Amherst, with the proper expectations of a Manhattan-based profession—banking, brokerage, advertising. There was nothing in his precollege or undergraduate record to indicate a deviation from this pattern. Indeed, marriage to a socially prominent girl from Greenwich seemed to confirm it.

And then things happened to James Barbour Matlock, and Loring wished he understood. First came the army.

It was the early sixties, and by the simple expedient of agreeing to a six-month extension of service, Matlock could have sat comfortably behind a desk as a supply officer somewhere—most likely, with his family's connections, in Washington or New York. Instead, his service file read like a hoodlum's: a series of infractions and insubordinations that guaranteed him the least desirable of assignments—Vietnam and its escalating hostilities. While in the Mekong Delta, his military behavior also guaranteed him two summary courts-martial.

Yet there appeared to be no ideological motivation behind his actions, merely poor, if any, adjustment.

His return to civilian life was marked by continuing difficulties, first with his parents and then with his wife. Inexplicably, James Barbour Matlock, whose academic record had been gentlemanly but hardly superior, took a small apartment in Morningside Heights and attended Columbia University's graduate school.

The wife lasted three and a half months, opting for a quiet divorce and a rapid exit from Matlock's life.

The following several years were monotonous intelligence material. Matlock, the incorrigible, was in the process of becoming Matlock, the scholar. He worked around the calendar, receiving his master's degree in fourteen months, his doctorate two years later. There was a reconciliation of sorts with his parents, and a position with the English department at Carlyle University in Connecticut. Since then Matlock had published a number of books and articles and acquired an enviable reputation in the academic community. He was obviously popular—"mobile in the extreme" (silly goddamn expression); he was moderately well off and apparently possessed none of the antagonistic traits he'd displayed during the hostile years. Of course, there was damn little reason for him to be discontented, thought Loring. James Barbour Matlock II had his life nicely routined; he was covered on all flanks, thank you, including a girl. He was currently, with discretion, involved with a graduate student named Patricia Ballantyne. They kept separate residences, but according to the data, were lovers. As near as could be determined, however, there was no marriage in sight. The girl was completing her doctoral studies in archeology, and a dozen foundation grants awaited her. Grants that led to distant lands and unfamiliar facts. Patricia Ballantyne was not for marriage; not according to the data banks.

But what of Matlock? wondered Ralph Loring. What did the facts tell him? How could they possibly justify the choice?

They didn't. They couldn't. Only a trained professional could carry out the demands of the current situation. The problems were far too complex, too filled with traps for an amateur.

The terrible irony was that if this Matlock made errors, fell into traps, he might accomplish far more far quicker than any professional.

And lose his life doing so.

"What makes you all think he'll accept?" Cranston was nearing Loring's apartment and his curiosity was piqued.

"What? I'm sorry, what did you say?"

"What's the motive for the subject's acceptance? Why would he agree?"

"A younger brother. Ten years younger, as a matter of fact. The parents are quite old. Very rich, very detached. This Matlock holds himself responsible."

"For what?"

"The brother. He killed himself three years ago with an overdose of heroin."

Ralph Loring drove his rented car slowly down the wide, treelined street past the large old houses set back beyond manicured lawns. Some were fraternity houses, but there were far fewer than had existed a decade ago. The social exclusivity of the fifties and early sixties was being replaced. A few of the huge structures had other identifications now. *The House, Aquarius* (naturally), *Afro-Commons, Warwick, Lumumba Hall*.

Connecticut's Carlyle University was one of those medium-sized "prestige" campuses that dot the New England landscape. An administration, under the guidance of its brilliant president, Dr. Adrian Sealfont, was restructuring the college, trying to bring it into the second half of the twentieth century. There were inevitable protests, proliferation of beards, and African studies balanced against the quiet wealth, club blazers, and alumni-sponsored regattas. Hard rock and faculty tea dances were groping for ways to coexist.

Loring reflected, as he looked at the peaceful campus in the bright spring sunlight, that it seemed inconceivable that such a community harbored any real problems.

Certainly not the problem that had brought him there.

Yet it did.

Carlyle was a time bomb which, when detonated, would claim extraordinary victims in its fallout. That it *would* explode, Loring knew, was inevitable. What happened before then was unpredictable. It was up to him to engineer the best possible probabilities. The key was James Barbour Matlock, B.A., M.A., Ph.D.

Loring drove past the attractive two-story faculty residence that held four apartments, each with a separate entrance. It was considered one of the better faculty houses and was usually occupied by bright young families before they'd reached the tenure necessary for outlying homes of their own. Matlock's quarters were on the first floor, west section.

Loring drove around the block and parked diagonally across the street from Matlock's door. He couldn't stay long; he kept turning in the seat, scanning the cars and Sunday morning pedestrians, satisfied that he himself wasn't being observed. That was vital. On Sunday, according to Matlock's surveillance file, the young professor usually read the papers till around noon and then drove to the north end of Carlyle where Patricia Ballantyne lived in one of the efficiency apartments reserved for graduate students. That is, he drove over if she hadn't spent the night with him. Then the two generally went out into the country for lunch and returned to Matlock's apartment or went south into Hartford or New Haven. There were variations, of course. Often the Ballantyne girl and Matlock took weekends together, registering as man and wife. Not this weekend, however. Surveillance had confirmed that.

Loring looked at his watch. It was twelve forty, but Matlock was still in his apartment. Time was running short. In a few minutes, Loring was expected to be at Crescent Street. 217 Crescent. It was where he would make cover-contact for his second vehicle transfer.

He knew it wasn't necessary for him to physically watch Matlock. After all, he'd read the file thoroughly, looked at scores of photographs, and even talked briefly with Dr. Sealfont, Carlyle's president. Nevertheless, each agent had his own working methods, and his included watching subjects for a period of hours before making contact. Several colleagues at Justice claimed it gave him a sense of power. Loring knew only that it gave him a sense of confidence.

Matlock's front door opened and a tall man walked out into the sunlight. He was dressed in khaki trousers, loafers, and a tan turtleneck sweater. Loring saw that he was modestly good looking with sharp features and fairly long blond hair. He checked the lock on his door, put on a pair of sunglasses, and walked around the sidewalk to what Loring presumed was a small parking area. Several minutes later, James Matlock drove out of the driveway in a Triumph sportscar.

The government man reflected that his subject seemed to have the best of a pleasant life. Sufficient income, no responsibilities, work he enjoyed, even a convenient relationship with an attractive girl.

Loring wondered if it would all be the same for James Barbour Matlock three weeks from then. For Matlock's world was about to be plunged into an abyss.

Chapter Two

Matlock pressed the Triumph's accelerator to the floor and the low-slung automobile vibrated as the speedometer reached sixty-two miles per hour. It wasn't that he was in a hurry—Pat Ballantyne wasn't going anywhere—just that he was angry. Well, not angry, really; just irritated. He was usually irritated after a phone call from home. Time would never eliminate that. Nor money, if ever he made any to speak of—amounts his father considered respectable. What caused his irritation was the infuriating condescension. It grew worse as his mother and father advanced in years. Instead of making peace with the situation, they dwelled on it. They insisted that he spend the spring midterm vacation in Scarsdale so that he and his father could make daily trips into the city. To the banks, to the attorneys. To make ready for the inevitable, when and if it ever happened.

". . . There's a lot you'll have to digest, son," his father had said sepulchrally. "You're not exactly prepared, you know. . . ."

". . . You're all that's left, darling," his mother had said with obvious pain.

Matlock knew they enjoyed their anticipated, martyred leavetaking of this world. They'd made their mark—or at least his father had. The amusing part was that his parents were as strong as pack mules, as healthy as wild horses. They'd no doubt outlast him by decades.

The truth was that they wanted him with them far more than he wished to be there. It had been that way for the past three years, since David's death at the Cape. Perhaps, thought Matlock, as he drew up in front of Pat's apartment, the roots of his irritation were in his own guilt. He'd never quite made peace with himself about David. He never would.

And he didn't want to be in Scarsdale during the midterm holidays. He didn't want the memories. He had someone now who was helping him forget the awful years—of death, no love, and indecision. He'd promised to take Pat to St. Thomas.

The name of the country inn was the Cheshire Cat, and, as its title implied, it was Englishy and pubbish. The food was decent, the drinks generous, and those factors made it a favorite spot of Connecticut's exurbia. They'd finished their second Bloody Mary and had ordered roast beef and Yorkshire pudding. There were perhaps a dozen couples and several families in the spacious dining area. In the corner sat a single man reading *The New York Times* with the pages folded vertically, commuter fashion.

"He's probably an irate father waiting for a son who's about to splash out. I know the type. They take the Scarsdale train every morning."

"He's too relaxed."

"They learn to hide tension. Only their druggists know. All that Gelusil."

"There are always signs, and he hasn't any. He looks positively self-satisfied. You're wrong."

"You just don't know Scarsdale. Self-satisfaction is a registered trademark. You can't buy a house without it."

"Speaking of such things, what are you going to do? I really think we should cancel St. Thomas."

"I don't. It's been a rough winter; we deserve a little sun. Anyway, they're being unreasonable. There's nothing I want to learn about the Matlock manipulations; it's a waste of time. In the unlikely event that they ever *do* go, others'll be in charge."

"I thought we agreed that was only an excuse. They want you around for a while. I think it's touching they do it this way."

"It's not touching, it's my father's transparent attempt at bribery. . . . Look. Our commuter's given up." The single man with the newspaper finished his drink and was explaining to the waitress that he wasn't ordering lunch. "Five'll get you ten he pictured his son's hair and leather jacket—maybe bare feet—and just panicked."

"I think you're wishing it on the poor man."

"No, I'm not. I'm too sympathetic. I can't stand the aggravation that goes with rebellion. Makes me self-conscious."

"You're a very funny man, Private Matlock," said Pat, alluding to Matlock's inglorious army career. "When we finish, let's go down to Hartford. There's a good movie."

"Oh, I'm sorry, I forgot to tell you. We can't today. . . . Sealfont called me this morning for an early evening conference. Said it was important."

"About what?"

"I'm not sure. The African studies may be in trouble. That 'Tom' I recruited from Howard turned out to be a beaut. I think he's a little to the right of Louis XIV."

She smiled. "Really, you're terrible."

Matlock took her hand.

The residence of Dr. Adrian Sealfont was imposingly appropriate. It was a large white colonial mansion with wide marble steps leading up to thick double doors carved in relief. Along the front were Ionic pillars spanning the width of the building. Floodlights from the lawn were turned on at sundown.

Matlock walked up the stairs to the door and rang the bell. Thirty seconds later he was admitted by a maid, who ushered him through the hallway toward the rear of the house, into Dr. Sealfont's huge library.

Adrian Sealfont stood in the center of the room with two other men. Matlock, as always, was struck by the presence of the man. A shade over six feet, thin, with aquiline features, he radiated a warmth that touched all who were near him. There was about him a genuine humility which concealed his brilliance from those who did not know him. Matlock liked him immensely.

"Hello, James." Sealfont extended his hand to Matlock. "Mr. Loring, may I present Dr. Matlock?"

"How do you do? Hi, Sam." Matlock addressed this last to the third man, Samuel Kressel, dean of colleges at Carlyle.

"Hello, Jim."

"We've met before, haven't we?" asked Matlock, looking at Loring. "I'm trying to remember."

"I'm going to be very embarrassed if you do."

"I'll bet you will!" laughed Kressel with his sardonic, slightly offensive, humor. Matlock also liked Sam Kressel, more because he knew the pain of Kressel's job—what he had to contend with—than for the man himself.

"What do you mean, Sam?"

"I'll answer you," interrupted Adrian Sealfont. "Mr. Loring is with the federal government, the Justice Department. I agreed to arrange a meeting between the three of you, but I did not agree to what Sam and Mr. Loring have just referred to. Apparently Mr. Loring has seen fit to have you—what is the term—under surveillance. I've registered my strong objections." Sealfont looked directly at Loring.

"You've had me *what*?" asked Matlock quietly.

"I apologize," said Loring persuasively. "It's a personal idiosyncrasy and has nothing to do with our business."

"You're the commuter in the Cheshire Cat."

"The what?" asked Sam Kressel.

"The man with the newspaper."

"That's right. I knew you'd noticed me this afternoon. I thought you'd recognize me the minute you saw me again. I didn't know I looked like a commuter."

"It was the newspaper. We called you an irate father."

"Sometimes I am. Not often, though. My daughter's only seven."

"I think we should begin," Sealfont said. "Incidentally, James, I'm relieved your reaction is so understanding."

"My only reaction is curiosity. And a healthy degree of fear. To tell you the truth, I'm scared to death." Matlock smiled haltingly. "What's it all about?"

"Let's have a drink while we talk." Adrian Sealfont smiled back and walked to his copper-topped dry bar in the corner of the room. "You're a bourbon and water man, aren't you, James? And Sam, a double Scotch over ice, correct? What's yours, Mr. Loring?"

"Scotch'll be fine. Just water."

"Here, James, give me a hand." Matlock crossed to Sealfont and helped him.

"You amaze me, Adrian," said Kressel, sitting down in a leather armchair. "What in heaven's name prompts you to remember your subordinates' choice of liquor?"

Sealfont laughed. "The most logical reason of all. And it certainly isn't confined to my . . . colleagues. I've raised more money for this institution with alcohol than with hundreds of reports prepared by the best analytic minds in fund-raising circles." Here Adrian Sealfont paused and chuckled—as much to himself as to those in the room. "I once gave a speech to the Organization of University Presidents. In the question and answer period, I was asked to what I attributed Carlyle's endowment. . . . I'm afraid I replied, 'To those ancient peoples who developed the art of fermenting the vineyards.' . . . My late wife roared but told me later I'd set the fund back a decade."

The three men laughed; Matlock distributed the drinks.

"Your health," said the president of Carlyle, raising his glass modestly. The toast, however, was brief. "This is a bit awkward, James . . . Sam. Several weeks ago I was contacted by Mr. Loring's superior. He asked me to come to Washington on a matter of utmost importance, relative to Carlyle. I did so and was briefed on a situation I still refuse to accept. Certain information which Mr. Loring will impart to you seems incontrovertible on the surface. But that is the surface: rumor; out-of-context statements, written and verbal; constructed evidence which may be meaningless. On the other hand, there might well be a degree of substance. It is on that possibility that I've agreed to this meeting. I must make it clear, however, that I cannot be a party to it. Carlyle *will not* be a party to it. Whatever may take place in this room has my unacknowledged approval but not my official sanction. You act as individuals, not as members of the faculty or staff of Carlyle. If, indeed, you decide to act at all. . . . Now, James, if that doesn't 'scare you,' I don't know what will." Sealfont smiled again, but his message was clear.

"It scares me," said Matlock without emphasis.

Kressell put down his glass and leaned forward on the chair. "Are we to assume from what you've said that you don't endorse Loring's presence here? Or whatever it is he wants?"

"It's a gray area. If there's substance to his charges, I certainly cannot turn my back. On the other hand, no university president these days will openly collaborate with a government agency on speculation. You'll forgive me, Mr. Loring, but too many people in Washington have taken advantage of the academic communities. I refer specifically to Michigan, Columbia, Berkeley . . . among others. Simple police matters are one thing, infiltration . . . well, that's something else again."

"Infiltration? That's a pretty strong word," said Matlock.

"Perhaps too strong. I'll leave the terms to Mr. Loring."

Kressel picked up his glass. "May I ask why we—Matlock and I—have been chosen?"

"That, again, will be covered in Mr. Loring's discussion. However, since I'm responsible for *your* being here, Sam, I'll tell you *my* reasons. As dean, you're more closely attuned to campus affairs than anyone else. . . . You will also be aware of it if Mr. Loring or his associates overstep their bounds. . . . I think that's all I have to say. I'm going over to the assembly. That filmmaker, Strauss, is speaking tonight and I've got to put in an appearance." Sealfont walked back to the bar and put his glass on the tray. The three other men rose.

"One thing before you go," said Kressel, his brow wrinkled. "Suppose one or both of us decide we want no part of Mr. Loring's . . . business?"

"Then refuse." Adrian Sealfont crossed to the library door. "You are under no obligation whatsoever; I want that perfectly clear. Mr. Loring understands. Good evening, gentlemen." Sealfont walked out into the hallway, closing the door behind him.

Chapter Three

The three men remained silent, standing motionless. They could hear the front entrance open and close. Kressel turned and looked at Loring.

"It seems to me you've been put on the spot."

"I usually am in these situations. Let me clarify my position; it will partly explain this meeting. The first thing you should know is that I'm with the Justice Department, *Narcotics* Bureau."

Kressel sat down and sipped at his drink. "You haven't traveled up here to tell us forty percent of the student body is on pot and a few other items, have you? Because if so, it's nothing we don't know."

"No, I haven't. I assume you *do* know about such things. Everyone does. I'm not sure about the percentage, though. It could be a low estimate."

Matlock finished his bourbon and decided to have another. He spoke as he crossed to the copper bar table. "It may be low or high, but comparatively speaking—in relation to other campuses—we're not in panic."

"There's no reason for you to be. Not about that."

"There's something else?"

"Very much so." Loring walked to Sealfont's desk and bent down to pick up his briefcase from the floor. It was apparent that the government man and Carlyle's president had talked before Matlock and Kressel arrived. Loring put the briefcase on the desk and opened it. Matlock walked back to his chair and sat down.

"I'd like to show you something." Loring reached into the briefcase and withdrew a thick page of silver-colored stationery, cut diagonally as if with pinking shears. The silver coating was now filthy with repeated handling and blotches of grease or dirt. He approached Matlock's chair and handed it to him. Kressel got up and came over.

"It's some kind of letter. Or announcement. With numbers," said Matlock. "It's in French; no, Italian, I think. I can't make it out."

"Very good, professor," said Loring. "A lot of both and not a predominance of either. Actually, it's a Corsican dialect, written out. It's called the Oltremontan strain, used in the southern hill country. Like Etruscan, it's not entirely translatable. But what codes are used are simple to the point of not being codes at all. I don't think they were meant to be; there aren't too many of these. So there's enough here to tell us what we need to know."

"Which is?" asked Kressel, taking the strange-looking paper from Matlock.

"First I'd like to explain how we got it. Without that explanation, the information is meaningless."

"Go ahead." Kressel handed the filthy silver paper back to the government agent, who carried it to the desk and carefully returned it to his briefcase.

"A narcotics courier—that is, a man who goes into a specific source territory carrying instructions, money, messages—left the country six weeks ago. He was more than a courier, actually; he was quite powerful in the distribution hierarchy; you might say he was on a busman's holiday, Mediterranean style. Or perhaps he was checking investments. . . . At any rate, he was killed by some mountain people in the Toros Daglari—that's Turkey, a growing district. The story is, he canceled operations there and the violence followed. We accept that; the Mediterranean fields are closing down right and left, moving into South America. . . . The paper was found on his body, in a skin belt. As you saw, it's been handed around a bit. It brought a succession of prices from Ankara to Marrakesh. An Interpol undercover man finally made the purchase and it was turned over to us."

"From Toros Dag-whatever-it-is to Washington. That paper's had quite a journey," said Matlock.

"And an expensive one," added Loring. "Only it's not in Washington now, it's here. From Toros Daglari to Carlyle, Connecticut."

"I assume that means something." Sam Kressel sat down, apprehensively watching the government man.

"It means the information in that paper concerns Carlyle." Loring leaned back against the desk and spoke calmly, with no sense of urgency at all. He could have been an instructor in front of a class explaining a dry but necessary mathematics theorem. "The paper says there'll be a conference on the tenth of May, three weeks from tomorrow. The numbers are the map coordinates of the Carlyle area—precision decimals of longitude and latitude in Greenwich units. The paper itself identifies the holder to be one of those summoned. Each paper has either a matching half or is cut from a pattern that can be matched—simple additional security. What's missing is the precise location."

"Wait a minute." Kressel's voice was controlled but sharp; he was upset. "Aren't you ahead of yourself, Loring? You're giving us information—obviously restricted—before you state your request. This university administration isn't interested in being an investigative arm of the government. Before you go into facts, you'd better say what you want."

"I'm sorry, Mr. Kressel. You said I was on the spot and I am. I'm handling it badly."

"Like hell. You're an expert."

"Hold it, Sam." Matlock raised his hand off the arm of the chair. Kressel's sudden antagonism seemed uncalled for. "Sealfont said we had the option to refuse whatever he wants. If we exercise that option—and we probably will—I'd like to think we did so out of judgment, not blind reaction."

"Don't be naïve, Jim. You receive restricted or classified information and instantly, *post facto*, you're involved. You can't deny receiving it; you can't say it didn't happen."

Matlock looked up at Loring. "Is that true?"

"To a degree, yes. I won't lie about it."

"Then why should we listen to you?"

"Because Carlyle University *is* involved; has been for years. And the situation is critical. So critical that there are only three weeks left to act on the information we have."

Kressel got out of his chair, took a deep breath, and exhaled slowly. "Create the crisis—without proof—and force the involvement. The crisis fades but the records show the university was a silent participant in a federal investigation. That was the pattern at the University of Wisconsin." Kressel turned to Matlock. "Do you remember that one, Jim? Six days of riots on campus. Half a semester lost on teach-ins."

"That was Pentagon oriented," said Loring. "The circumstances were entirely different."

"You think the Justice Department makes it more palatable? Read a few campus newspapers."

"For Christ's sake, Sam, let the man talk. If you don't want to listen, go home. I want to hear what he has to say."

Kressel looked down at Matlock. "All right. I think I understand. Go ahead, Loring. Just remember, no obligations. And we're not bound to respect any conditions of confidence."

"I'll gamble on your common sense."

"That may be a mistake." Kressel walked to the bar and replenished his drink.

Loring sat on the edge of the desk. "I'll start by asking both of you if you've ever heard of the word *nimrod*?"

"Nimrod is a Hebrew name," Matlock answered. "Old Testament. A descendant of Noah, ruler of Babylon and Nineveh. Legendary prowess as a hunter, which obscures the more important fact that he founded, or built, the great cities in Assyria and Mesopotamia."

Loring smiled. "Very good again, professor. A *hunter* and a *builder*. I'm speaking in more contemporary terms, however."

"Then, no, I haven't. Have you, Sam?"

Kressel walked back to his chair, carrying his glass. "I didn't even know what you just said. I thought a nimrod was a casting fly. Very good for trout."

"Then I'll fill in some background. . . . I don't mean to bore you with narcotics statistics; I'm sure you're bombarded with them constantly."

"Constantly," said Kressel.

"But there's an isolated geographical statistic you may not be aware of. The concentration of drug traffic in the New England states is growing at a rate exceeding that of any other section of the country. It's a startling pattern. Since 1968, there's been a systematic erosion of enforcement procedures. . . . Let me put it into perspective, geographically. In California, Illinois, Louisiana, narcotics controls have improved to the point of at least curtailing the growth curves. It's really the best we can hope for until the international agreements have teeth. But not in the New England area. Throughout this section, the expansion has gone wild. It's hit the colleges hard."

"How do you know that?" asked Matlock.

"Dozens of ways and always too late to prevent distribution. Informers, marked inventories from Mediterranean, Asian, and Latin American sources, traceable Swiss deposits; that *is* restricted data." Loring looked at Kressel and smiled.

"Now I know you people are crazy." Kressel spoke disagreeably. "It seems to me that if you can substantiate those charges, you should do so publicly. And loud."

"We have our reasons."

"Also restricted, I assume," said Kressel with faint disgust.

"There's a side issue," continued the government man, disregarding him. "The eastern prestige campuses—large and small, Princeton, Amherst, Harvard, Vassar, Williams, Carlyle—a good percentage of their enrollments include VIP kids. Sons and daughters of very important people, especially in government and industry. There's a blackmail potential, and we think it's been used. Such people are painfully sensitive to drug scandals."

Kressel interrupted. "Granting what you say is true, and I don't, we've had less trouble here than most other colleges in the northeast area."

"We're aware of that. We even think we know why."

"That's esoteric, Mr. Loring. Say what you want to say." Matlock didn't like the games some people played.

"Any distribution network which is capable of systematically servicing, expanding, and controlling an entire section of the country has got to have a base of operations. A clearing house—you might say, a command post. Believe me when I tell you that this base of operations, the command post for the narcotics traffic throughout the New England states, is Carlyle University."

Samuel Kressel, dean of the colleges, dropped his glass on Adrian Sealfont's parquet floor.

Ralph Loring continued his incredible story. Matlock and Kressel remained in their chairs. Several times during his calm, methodical explanation, Kressel began to interrupt, to object, but Loring's persuasive narrative cut him short. There was nothing to argue.

The investigation of Carlyle University had begun eighteen months ago. It had been triggered by an accounts ledger uncovered by the French Sureté during one of its frequent narcotics investigations in the port of Marseilles. Once the ledger's American origins were established, it was sent to Washington under Interpol agreement. Throughout the ledger's entries were references to "C–22°–59°" consistently followed by the name *Nimrod*. The numbered degree marks were found to be map coordinates of northern Connecticut, but not decimally definitive. After tracing hundreds of possible trucking routes from Atlantic seaboard piers and airports relative to the Marseilles operation, the vicinity of Carlyle was placed under maximum surveillance.

As part of the surveillance, telephone taps were ordered on persons known to be involved with narcotics distribution from such points as New York, Hartford, Boston, and New Haven. Tapes were made of conversations of underworld figures. All calls regarding narcotics to and from the Carlyle area were placed to and from public telephone booths. It made the intercepts difficult, but not impossible. Again, restricted methods.

As the information files grew, a startling fact became apparent. The Carlyle group was independent. It had no formal ties with structured organized crime; it was beholden to no one. It *used* known criminal elements, was not used *by* them. It was a tightly knit unit, reaching into the majority of New England universities. And it did not—apparently—stop at drugs.

There was evidence of the Carlyle unit's infiltration into gambling, prostitution, even postgraduate employment placement. Too, there seemed to be a purpose, an objective beyond the inherent profits of the illegal activities. The Carlyle unit could have made far greater profit with less complications by dealing outright with known criminals, acknowledged suppliers in all areas. Instead, it spent its own money to set up its organization. It was its own master, controlling its own sources, its own distribution. But what its ultimate objectives were was unclear.

It had become so powerful that it threatened the leadership of organized crime in the Northeast. For this reason, leading figures of the underworld had demanded a conference with those in charge of the Carlyle operation. The key here was a group, or an individual, referred to as *Nimrod*.

The purpose of the conference, as far as could be determined, was for an accommodation to be reached between Nimrod and the overlords of crime who felt threatened by Nimrod's extraordinary growth. The conference would be attended by dozens of known and unknown criminals throughout the New England states.

"Mr. Kressel." Loring turned to Carlyle's dean and seemed to hesitate. "I suppose you have lists—students, faculty, staff—people you know or have reason to suspect are into the drug scene. I can't assume it because I don't know, but most colleges do have."

"I won't answer that question."

"Which, of course, gives me my answer," said Loring quietly, even sympathetically.

"Not for a minute! You people have a habit of assuming exactly what you want to assume."

"All right, I stand rebuked. But even if you'd said yes, it wasn't my purpose to ask for them. It was merely by way of telling you that we *do* have such a list. I wanted you to know that."

Sam Kressel realized he'd been trapped; Loring's ingenuousness only annoyed him further. "I'm sure you do."

"Needless to say, we'd have no objection to giving you a copy."

"That won't be necessary."

"You're pretty obstinate, Sam," said Matlock. "You burying your head?"

Before Kressel could reply, Loring spoke. "The dean knows he can change his mind. And we've agreed, there's no crisis here. You'd be surprised how many people wait for the roof to cave in before asking for help. Or accepting it."

"But there aren't many surprises in your organization's proclivity for turning difficult situations into disasters, are there?" countered Sam Kressel antagonistically.

"We've made mistakes."

"Since you have names," continued Sam, "why don't you go after them? Leave us out of it; do your own dirty work. Make arrests, press charges. Don't try to deputize *us*."

"We don't want to do that. . . . Besides, most of our evidence is inadmissible."

"That occurred to me," interjected Kressel.

"And what do we gain? What do *you* gain?" Loring leaned forward, returning Sam's stare. "We pick up a couple of hundred potheads, a few dozen speedfreaks; users and low-level pushers. Don't you understand, that doesn't *solve* anything."

"Which brings us to what you really want, doesn't it?" Matlock sank back into the chair; he watched the persuasive agent closely.

"Yes," answered Loring softly. "We want Nimrod. We want to know the location of that conference on May 10. It could be anywhere within a radius of fifty to a hundred miles. We want to be prepared for it. We want to break the back of the Nimrod operation, for reasons that go way beyond Carlyle University. As well as narcotics."

"How?" asked James Matlock.

"Dr. Sealfont said it. Infiltration. . . . Professor Matlock, you are what's known in intelligence circles as a highly mobile person within your environment. You're widely accepted by diverse, even conflicting factions—within both the faculty and the student body. We have the names, you have the mobility." Loring reached into his briefcase and withdrew the scissored page of filthy stationery. "Somewhere out there is the information we need. Somewhere there's someone who has a paper like this; someone who knows what we have to know."

James Barbour Matlock remained motionless in his chair, staring at the government man. Neither Loring nor Kressel could be sure what he was thinking but both had an idea. If thoughts were audible, there would have been full agreement in that room at that moment. James Matlock's mind had wandered back three, almost four years ago. He was remembering a blond-haired boy of nineteen. Immature for his age, perhaps, but good, kind. A boy with problems.

They'd found him as they'd found thousands like him in thousands of cities and towns across the country. Other times, other Nimrods.

James Matlock's brother, David, had inserted a needle in his right arm and had shot up thirty mg. of white fluid. He had performed the act in a catboat in the calm waters of a Cape Cod inlet. The small sailboat had drifted into the reeds near shore. When they found it, James Matlock's brother was dead.

Matlock made his decision.

"Can you get me the names?"

"I have them with me."

"Just hold it." Kressel stood up, and when he spoke, it wasn't in the tone of an angry man—it was with fear. "Do you realize what you're asking him to do? He has no experience in this kind of work. He's not trained. Use one of your *own* men."

"There isn't time. There's no time for one of our men. He'll be protected; you can help."

"I can *stop* you!"

"No, you can't, Sam," said Matlock from the chair.

"Jim, for Christ's sake, do you know what he's asking? If there's *any* truth to what he's said, he's placing you in the worst position a man can be in. An informer."

"You don't have to stay. My decision doesn't have to be your decision. Why don't you go home?" Matlock rose and walked slowly to the bar, carrying his glass.

"That's impossible now," said Kressel, turning toward the government agent. "And *he knows it*."

Loring felt a touch of sadness. This Matlock was a good man; he was doing what he was doing because he felt he owed a debt. And it was coldly, professionally projected that by accepting the assignment, James Matlock was very possibly going to his death. It was a terrible price, that possibility. But the objective was worth it. The conference was worth it.

Nimrod was worth it.

That was Loring's conclusion.

It made his assignment bearable.

Chapter Four

Nothing could be written down; the briefing was slow, repetition constant. But Loring was a professional and knew the value of taking breaks from the pressures of trying to absorb too much too rapidly. During these periods, he attempted to draw Matlock out, learn more about this man whose life was so easily expendable. It was nearly midnight; Sam Kressel had left before eight o'clock. It was neither necessary nor advisable that the dean be present during the detailing of the specifics. He was a liaison, not an activist. Kressel was not averse to the decision.

Ralph Loring learned quickly that Matlock was a private man. His answers to innocuously phrased questions were brief, thrown-away replies constituting no more than self-denigrating explanations. After a while, Loring gave up. Matlock had agreed to do a job, not make public his thoughts or his motives. It wasn't necessary; Loring understood the latter. That was all that mattered. He was just as happy not to know the man too well.

Matlock, in turn—while memorizing the complicated information—was, on another level, reflecting on his own life, wondering in his own way why he'd been selected. He was intrigued by an evaluation that could describe him as being *mobile*; what an awful word to have applied!

Yet he knew he was precisely what the term signified. He *was* mobile. The professional researchers, or psychologists, or whatever they were, were accurate. But he doubted they understood the reasons behind his . . . "mobility."

The academic world had been a refuge, a sanctuary. Not an objective of long-standing ambition. He had fled into it in order to buy time, to organize a life that was falling apart, to understand. To get his *head straight*, as the kids said these days.

He had tried to explain it to his wife, his lovely, quick, bright, ultimately hollow wife, who thought he'd lost his senses. What was there to understand but an *awfully* good job, an *awfully* nice house, an *awfully* pleasant club, and a *good* life within an *awfully* rewarding social and financial world? For her, there *was* nothing more to understand. And he understood that.

But for him that world had lost its meaning. He had begun to drift away from its core in his early twenties, during his last year at Amherst. The separation became complete with his army experience.

It was no one single thing that had triggered his rejection. And the rejection itself was not a violent act, although violence played its role in the early days of the Saigon mess. It had begun at home, where most life-styles are accepted or rejected, during a series of disagreeable confrontations with his father. The old gentleman—too old, too gentlemanly—felt justified in demanding a better performance from his first son. A direction, a sense of purpose not at all in evidence. The senior Matlock belonged to another era—if not another century—and believed the gap between father and son a desirable thing, the lower element being dismissible until it had proved itself in the marketplace. Dismissible but, of course, malleable. In ways, the father was like a benign ruler who, after generations of power, was loathe to have the throne abandoned by his rightful issue. It was inconceivable to the elder Matlock that his son would not assume the leadership of the family business. Businesses.

But for the younger Matlock, it was all *too* conceivable. And preferable. He was not only uncomfortable thinking about a future in his father's *marketplace*, he was also afraid. For him there was no joy in the regimented pressures of the financial world; instead, there was an awesome fear of inadequacy, emphasized by his father's strong—overpowering—competence. The closer he came to entering that world, the more pronounced was his fear. And it occurred to him that along with the delights of extravagant shelter and unnecessary creature comforts had to come the justification for doing what was expected in order to possess these things. He could not find that justification. Better the shelter should be less extravagant, the creature comforts somewhat limited, than face the prospects of continuing fear and discomfort.

He had tried to explain *that* to his father. Whereas his wife had claimed he'd lost his senses, the old gentleman pronounced him a misfit.

Which didn't exactly refute the army's judgment of him.

The army.

A disaster. Made worse by the knowledge that it was of his own making. He found that blind physical discipline and unquestioned authority were abhorrent to him. And he was large enough and strong enough and had a sufficient vocabulary to make his unadjustable, immature objections known—to his own disadvantage.

Discreet manipulations by an uncle resulted in a discharge before his tour of service was officially completed; for that he *was* grateful to an influential family.

And at this juncture of his life, James Barbour Matlock II was a mess. Separated from the service less than gloriously, divorced by his wife, dispossessed—symbolically if not actually—by his family, he felt the panic of belonging nowhere, of being without motive or purpose.

So he'd fled into the secure confines of graduate school, hoping to find an answer. And as in a love affair begun on a sexual basis but growing into psychological dependence, he had married that world; he'd found what had eluded him for nearly five vital years. It was the first real commitment he'd ever experienced.

He was free.

Free to enjoy the excitement of a meaningful challenge; free to revel in the confidence that he was equal to it. He plunged into his new world with the enthusiasm of a convert but without the blindness. He chose a period of history and literature that teemed with energy and conflict and contradictory evaluations. The apprentice years passed swiftly; he was consumed and pleasantly surprised by his own talents. When he emerged on the professional plateau, he brought fresh air into the musty archives. He made startling innovations in long-unquestioned methods of research. His doctoral thesis on court interference with English Renaissance literature—news management—blew into the historical ashcan several holy theories about one benefactress named Elizabeth.

He was the new breed of scholar: restless, sceptical, unsatisfied, always searching while imparting what he'd learned to others. Two and a half years after receiving his doctorate, he was elevated to the tenured position of associate professor, the youngest instructor at Carlyle to be so contracted.

James Barbour Matlock II made up for the lost years, the awful years. Perhaps best of all was the knowledge that he could communicate his excitement to others. He was young enough to enjoy sharing his enthusiasm, old enough to direct the inquiries.

Yes, he was *mobile*; God, was he! He couldn't, *wouldn't* turn anyone off, shut anyone out because of disagreement—even dislike. The depth of his own gratitude, the profoundness of his relief was such that he unconsciously promised himself never to discount the concerns of another human being.

"Any surprises?" Loring had completed a section of the material that dealt with narcotics purchases as they'd been traced.

"More a clarification, I'd say," replied Matlock. "The old-line fraternities or clubs—mostly white, mostly rich—get their stuff from Hartford. The black units like Lumumba Hall go to New Haven. Different sources."

"Exactly; that's student orientation. The point being that none buy from the Carlyle suppliers. From Nimrod."

"You explained that. The Nimrod people don't want to be advertised."

"But they're here. They're used."

"By whom?"

"Faculty and staff," answered Loring calmly, flipping over a page. "This *may* be a surprise. Mr. and Mrs. Archer Beeson . . ."

Matlock immediately pictured the young history instructor and his wife. They were Ivy League conformity itself—falsely arrogant, aesthetically precious. Archer Beeson was a young man in an academic hurry; his wife, the perfect faculty ingenue, carelessly sexy, always in awe.

"They're with LSD and the methedrines. Acid and speed."

"Good Lord! They fooled the hell out of me. How do you know?"

"It's too complicated to go into, also restricted. To oversimplify: they, he, used to purchase heavily from a distributor in Bridgeport. The contact was terminated and he didn't show up on any other lists. But he's not off. We think he made the Carlyle connection. No proof, though . . . Here's another."

It was the coach of varsity soccer, a jock who worked in physical education. His items were marijuana and amphetamines; his previous source, Hartford. He was considered a pusher on campus, not a user. Although the Hartford source was no longer employed, the man's varied and dummied bank accounts continued to grow. Assumption: Nimrod.

And another. This one frightening to Matlock. The assistant dean of admissions. An alumnus of Carlyle who returned to the campus after a brief career as a salesman. He was a flamboyant, open-handed man; a proselytizer for the cause of Carlyle. A popular enthusiast in these days of cynicism. He, too, was considered a distributor, not a user. He covered himself well through second- and third-level pushers.

"We think he came back here through the Nimrod organization. Good positioning on Nimrod's part."

"Goddamn scarey. That son of a bitch makes parents think he's a combination of astronaut and chaplain."

"Good positioning, as I said. Remember? I told you and Kressel: the Nimrod people have interests that go beyond drugs."

"But you don't know what they are."

"We'd better find out. . . . Here's the breakdown of the kids."

The names of the students seemed endless to Matlock. There were 563 out of a total enrollment of 1200 plus. The government man admitted that many were included not because of confirmation of individual use, but due to their campus affiliations. Clubs and fraternities were known to pool resources for the purchase of narcotics.

"We haven't the time to ascertain the validity of every name. We're looking for relationships; any, no matter how remote. You've got to have all kinds of avenues; we can't restrict them. . . . And there's one aspect to this list; I don't know whether you see it or not."

"I certainly do. At least, I think I do. Twenty or thirty names here ring loud bells in several high places. Some very influential parents. Industry, government. Here." Matlock pointed. "The president's cabinet, if I'm not mistaken. And I'm not."

"You see." Loring smiled.

"Has any of this had any effect?"

"We don't know. Could have, could be. The Nimrod tentacles are spreading out fast. That's why the alarms are sounding; louder than your bells. Speaking unofficially, there could be repercussions no one's dreamed of. . . . Defense overruns, union contracts, forced installations. You name it. It *could* be related."

"Jesus Christ," said Matlock softly.

"Exactly."

The two men heard the front door of Sealfont's mansion open and shut. As if by reflex, Loring calmly took the papers from Matlock's hand and quickly replaced them in his briefcase. He closed the case and then did an unexpected thing. He silently, almost unobtrusively, whipped back his jacket and curled his fingers around the handle of a revolver in a small holster strapped to his chest. The action startled Matlock. He stared at the hidden hand.

The library door opened and Adrian Sealfont walked in. Loring casually removed his hand from inside his coat. Sealfont spoke kindly.

"I *do try*. I honestly do. I understand the words and the pictures and take no offense whatsoever at the braided hair. What confuses me is the hostility. Anyone past thirty is the natural enemy of these fellows."

"That was Strauss, wasn't it?" asked Matlock.

"Yes. Someone inquired about the New Wave influence. He replied that the New Wave was ancient history. Prehistoric, was his word. . . . I won't interrupt you gentlemen. I would, however, like to know Kressel's status, Mr. Loring. Obviously, James has accepted."

"So has Mr. Kressel, sir. He'll act as liaison between us."

"I see." Sealfont looked at Matlock. There was a sense of relief in his eyes. "James, I can tell you now. I'm extremely grateful you've decided to help."

"I don't think there's an alternative."

"There isn't. What's frightening is the possibility of such total involvement. Mr. Loring, I'll want to be advised the minute you have anything concrete. At that point, I shall do whatever you wish, follow any instructions. All I ask is that you supply me with proof and you'll have my complete, my official cooperation."

"I understand, sir. You've been very helpful. More than we had a right to expect. We appreciate it."

"As James said, there is no alternative. But I must impose limits; my first obligation is to this institution. The campuses these days might appear dormant; I think that's a surface evaluation. . . . You have work to do and I have some reading to finish. Good night, Mr. Loring. James."

Matlock and the government man nodded their goodnights as Adrian Sealfont closed the library door.

By one o'clock, Matlock could absorb no more. The main elements—names, sources, conjectures—were locked in; he would never forget them. Not that he could recite everything by rote; that wasn't expected. But the sight of any particular individual on the lists would trigger a memory response. He knew Loring was right about that. It was why the agent insisted that he say the names out loud, repeating them several times each. It would be enough.

What he needed now was a night's sleep, if sleep would come. Let everything fall into some kind of perspective. Then in the morning he could begin to make initial decisions, determine which individuals should be approached, selecting those least likely to come in contact with one another. And this meant familiarizing himself with immediate friends, faculty or student body status—dozens of isolated fragments of information beyond the data supplied by Loring. Kressel's files—the ones he disclaimed having—would help.

Once in conversations he'd have to make his way carefully—thrusting, parrying, watching for signs, looks, betrayals.

Somewhere, with someone, it would happen.

"I'd like to go back to something," said Loring. "Background material."

"We've covered an awful lot. Maybe I should digest what I've got."

"This won't take a minute. It's important." The agent reached into his briefcase and withdrew the filthy, scissored paper. "Here, this is yours."

"Thanks for I-don't-know-what." Matlock took the once-shining silver paper and looked at the strange script.

"I told you it was written in Oltremontan-Corsican and, except for two words, that's correct. At the bottom, on a single line, you'll see the phrase *Venerare Omerta*. That's not Corsican, it's Sicilian. Or a Sicilian contraction, to be precise."

"I've seen it before."

"I'm sure you have. It's been given wide distribution in newspapers, movies, fiction. But that doesn't lessen its impact on those concerned by it. It's very real."

"What does it mean?"

"Roughly translated: Respect the law of Omerta. Omerta is an oath of allegiance *and* silence. To betray either is asking to be killed."

"Mafia?"

"It's involved. You might say it's the party of the second part. Bear in mind that this little announcement was issued jointly by two factions trying to reach an accommodation. 'Omerta' goes across the board; it's understood by both."

"I'll bear it in mind, but I don't know what I'm supposed to do with it."

"Just know about it."

"O.K."

"One last item. Everything we've covered here tonight is related to narcotics. But if our information is correct, the Nimrod people are involved in other fields. Sharking, prostitution, gambling . . . perhaps, and it's only perhaps, municipal controls, state legislatures, even the federal government. . . . Experience tells us that narcotics is the weakest action, the highest rate of collapse among these activities, and that's why we've centred on it. In other words, concentrate on the drug situation but be aware that other avenues exist."

"It's no secret."

"Maybe not to you. Let's call it a night."

"Shouldn't you give me a number where I can reach you?"

"Negative. Use Kressel. We'll check with him several times a day. Once you start asking questions, you may be put under a microscope. Don't call Washington. And *don't* lose our Corsican invitation. It's your ultimate clout. Just find another one."

"I'll try."

Matlock watched as Loring closed his briefcase, looped the thin black chain around his wrist, and snapped the built-in lock.

"Looks very cloak-and-daggerish, doesn't it?" Loring laughed.

"I'm impressed."

"Don't be. The custom began with diplomatic couriers who'd take their pouches to hell with them, but today it's simply a protection against purse-snatching. . . . So help me, that's what they think of us."

"I don't believe a word you say. That's one of those cases that make smoke screens, send out radio signals, and trigger bombs."

"You're right. It does all those things and more. It's got secret compartments for sandwiches, laundry, and God knows what else." Loring swung the briefcase off the desk. "I think it'd be a good idea if we left separately. Preferably one from the front, one from the rear. Ten minutes apart."

"You think that's necessary?"

"Frankly, no, but that's the way my superiors want it."

"O.K. I know the house. I'll leave ten minutes after you do, from the kitchen."

"Fine." Loring extended his right hand by steadying the bottom of his case with his left. "I don't have to tell you how much we appreciate what you're doing."

"I think you know why I'm doing it."

"Yes, we do. Frankly, we counted on it."

Loring let himself out of the library and Matlock waited until he heard the outer door open and close. He looked at his watch. He'd have one more drink before he left.

By one twenty Matlock was several blocks away from the house. He walked slowly west toward his apartment, debating whether to detour around the campus. It often helped him to walk out a problem; he knew sleep would come fitfully. He passed a number of students and several faculty members, exchanging low-keyed, end of the weekend greetings with those he recognized. He'd about made up his mind to turn north on High Street, away from the direction of his apartment, when he heard the footsteps behind him. First the footsteps, then the harsly whispered voice.

"Matlock! Don't turn around. It's Loring. Just keep walking and listen to me."

"What is it?"

"Someone knows I'm here. My car was searched. . . ."

"Christ! How do you know?"

"Field threads, preset markings. All over the car. Front, back, trunk. A very thorough, very professional job."

"You're sure?"

"So goddamn sure I'm not going to start that engine!"

"Jesus!" Matlock nearly stopped.

"Keep walking! If anyone was watching me—and you can be damned sure someone was—I made it clear I'd lost my ignition key. Asked several people who passed by where a pay phone was and waited till I saw you far enough away."

"What do you want me to do? There's a phone booth on the next corner. . . ."

"I know. I don't think you'll have to do anything, and for both our sakes, I hope I'm right. I'm going to jostle you as I pass—pretty hard. Lose your balance, I'll shout my apologies. Pretend you twisted an ankle, a wrist, anything you like; *but buy time!* Keep me in sight until a car comes for me and *I nod that* it's o.k. Do you have all that? I'll get to the booth in a hurry."

"Suppose you're still phoning when I get there?"

"Keep walking but *keep checking.* The car's cruising."

"What's the point?"

"This briefcase. That's the point. There's only one thing Nimrod—if it *is* Nimrod—would like more than this briefcase. And that's the paper in your coat pocket. So be careful!"

Without warning, he rushed up beside Matlock and pushed him off the sidewalk.

"Sorry, fella! I'm in an awful hurry!"

Matlock looked up from the ground, reflecting that he'd had no reason to *pretend* to fall. The force of Loring's push eliminated that necessity. He swore and rose awkwardly. Once on his feet, he limped slowly toward the phone booth several hundred yards away. He wasted nearly a minute lighting a cigarette. Loring was inside the booth now, sitting on the plastic seat, hunched over the phone.

Any second, Matlock expected Loring's car to drive up the street.

Yet none came.

Instead, there was the tiniest break in the spring noises. A rush of air through the new leaves. Or was it the crush of a stone beneath a foot, or a small twig unable to take the weight of the new growth in the trees? Or was it Matlock's imagination? He couldn't be sure.

He approached the booth and remembered Loring's orders. *Walk by and pay no attention.* Loring was still huddled over the phone, his briefcase resting on the floor, its chain visible. But Matlock could hear no conversation, could see no movement from the man within. Instead, again, there was a sound: now, the sound of a dial tone.

Despite his instructions, Matlock approached the booth and opened the door. There was nothing else he could do. The government man had not even *begun* his call.

And in an instant, he understood why.

Loring had fallen into the gleaming gray metal of the telephone. He was dead. His eyes wide, blood trickling out of his forehead. A small circular hole no larger than a shirt button, surrounded by a spray of cracked glass, was ample evidence of what had happened.

Matlock stared at the man who had briefed him for hours and left him minutes ago. The dead man who had thanked him, joked with him, then finally warned him. He was petrified, unsure of what he should do, *could* do.

He backed away from the booth toward the steps of the nearest house. Instinct told him to stay away but not to run away. Someone was out there in the street. Someone with a rifle.

When the words came, he realized they were his, but he didn't know when he'd decided to shout them. They just emerged involuntarily.

"Help . . . *Help!* There's a man out here! He's been *shot!*"

Matlock raced up the steps of the corner house and began pounding on the door with all his strength. Several lights went on in several different homes. Matlock continued shouting.

"For God's *sake*, someone call the *police! There's a dead man out here!*"

Suddenly, from the shadows underneath the full trees in the middle of the block, Matlock heard the roar of an automobile engine, then the sound of swerving tires as the vehicle pulled out into the middle of the street and started forward. He rushed to the edge of the porch. The long black automobile plunged out of the darkness and sped to the corner. Matlock tried to see the license plates and, realizing that was impossible, took a step down to identify the make of the car. Suddenly he was blinded. The beam of a searchlight pierced the dimly lit spring night and focused itself on him. He pulled his hands up to shield his eyes and then heard the quiet slap, the instant rush of air he had heard minutes ago.

A rifle was being fired at him. A rifle with a silencer.

He dove off the porch into the shrubbery. The black car sped away.

Chapter Five

He waited alone. The room was small, the window glass meshed with wire. The Carlyle Police Station was filled with officers and plainclothesmen called back on duty; no one could be sure what the killing signified. And none discounted the possibility that others might follow.

Alert. It was the particular syndrome of midcentury America, thought Matlock.

The gun.

He'd had the presence of mind after reaching the police to call Sam Kressel. Kressel, in shock, told him he would somehow contact the appropriate men in Washington and then drive down to the station house.

Until further instructions, they both agreed Matlock would restrict himself to a simple statement on finding the body and seeing the automobile. He had been out for a late night walk, that was all.

Nothing more.

His statement was typed out; questions as to time, his reasons for being in the vicinity, descriptions of the "alleged perpetrator's vehicle," direction, estimated speed—all were asked routinely and accepted without comment.

Matlock was bothered by his unequivocal negative to one question.

"Did you ever see the deceased before?"

"No."

That hurt. Loring deserved more than a considered, deliberate lie. Matlock recalled that the agent said he had a seven-year-old daughter. A wife and a child; the husband and father killed and he could not admit he knew his name.

He wasn't sure why it bothered him, but it did. Perhaps, he thought, because he knew it was the beginning of a great many lies.

He signed the short deposition and was about to be released when he heard a telephone ring inside an office beyond the desk. Not *on* the desk, beyond it. Seconds later, a uniformed policeman emerged and said his name in a loud voice, as if to make sure he had not left the building.

"Yes, officer?"

"We'll have to ask you to wait. If you'll follow me, please."

Matlock had been in the small room for nearly an hour; it was 2:45 A.M. and he had run out of cigarettes. It was no time to run out of cigarettes.

The door opened and a tall, thin man with large, serious eyes walked in. He was carrying Loring's briefcase. "Sorry to detain you, Dr. Matlock. It is 'Doctor', isn't it?"

"'Mister' is fine."

"My identification. Name's Greenberg, Jason Greenberg. Federal Bureau of Investigation. I had to confirm your situation. . . . It's a hell of a note, isn't it?"

"'A hell of a note'? Is that all you can say?"

The agent looked at Matlock quizzically. "It's all I care to share," he said quietly. "If Ralph Loring had completed his call, he would have reached me."

"I'm sorry."

"Forget it. I'm out-briefed—that is, I know something but not much about the Nimrod situation; I'll get filled in before morning. Incidentally, this fellow Kressel is on his way over. He knows I'm here."

"Does this change anything? . . . That sounds stupid, doesn't it? A man is killed and I ask you if it changes anything. I apologize again."

"No need to; you've had a terrible experience. . . . Any change is up to you. We accept the fact that Ralph's death could alter tonight's decision. We ask only that you keep your own counsel in what was revealed to you."

"You're offering me a chance to renege?"

"Of course. You're under no obligation to us."

Matlock walked to the small, rectangular window with the wire-enclosed glass. The police station was at the south end of the town of Carlyle, about a half a mile from the campus, the section of town considered industrialized. Still, there were trees along the streets. Carlyle was a very clean town, a neat town. The trees by the station house were pruned and shaped.

And Carlyle was also something else.

"Let me ask you a question," he said. "Does the fact that I found Loring's body associate me with him? I mean, would I be considered a part of whatever he was doing?"

"We don't think so. The way you behaved tends to remove you from any association."

"What do you mean?" Matlock turned to face the agent.

"Frankly, you panicked. You didn't run, you didn't take yourself out of the area; you flipped out and started shouting your head off. Someone who's programmed for an assignment wouldn't react like that."

"I wasn't programmed for *this*."

"Same results. You just found him and lost your head. If this Nimrod even *suspects* we're involved . . ."

"Suspects!" interrupted Matlock. "They *killed* him!"

"*Someone* killed him. It's unlikely that it's any part of Nimrod. Other factions, maybe. No cover's absolutely foolproof, even Loring's. But his was the closest."

"I don't understand you."

Greenberg leaned against the wall and folded his arms, his large, sad eyes reflective. "Ralph's field cover was the best at Justice. For damn near fifteen years." The agent looked down at the floor. His voice was deep, with faint bitterness. "The kind of goddamn cover that works best when it doesn't matter to a man anymore. When it's finally used, it throws everyone off balance. And insults his family."

Greenberg looked up and tried to smile, but no smile would come.

"I still don't understand you."

"It's not necessary. The main point is that you simply stumbled on the scene, went into panic, and had the scare of your life. You're dismissible, Mr. Matlock. . . . So?"

Before Matlock could respond, the door swung open and Sam Kressel entered, his expression nervous and frightened.

"Oh, Christ! This is terrible! Simply terrible! You're Greenberg?"

"And you're Mr. Kressel."

"Yes. What's going to happen?" Kressel turned to Matlock, speaking in the same breath. "Are you all right, Jim?"

"Sure."

"Well, Greenberg, what's *happening!?* They told me in Washington that you'd let us know."

"I've been talking to Mr. Matlock and . . ."

"Listen to me," interrupted Kressel suddenly. "I called Sealfont and we're of the same opinion. What happened was terrible . . . tragic. We express our sympathies to the man's family, but we're most anxious that any use of the Carlyle name be cleared with us. We assume this puts everything in a different light and, therefore, we insist we be kept out of it. I think that's understandable."

Greenberg's face betrayed his distate. "You race in here, ask me what's happening, and before you give me a chance to answer, you tell me what *must* happen. Now, how do you want it? Do I call Washington and let them have *your* version or do you want to listen first? Doesn't make a particle of difference to me."

"There's no reason for antagonism. We never asked to be involved."

"Nobody does." Greenberg smiled. "Just please let me finish. I've offered Matlock his out. He hasn't given me his answer, so I can't give you mine. However, if he says what I think he's going to say, Loring's cover will be activated immediately. It'll be activated anyway, but if the professor's in, we'll blow it up a bit."

"What the hell are you talking about?" Kressel stared at the agent.

"For years Ralph was a partner in just about the most disreputable law firm in Washington. Its clients read like a cross section of a Mafia index. . . . Early this morning, there was the first of two vehicle transfers. It took place in a Hartford suburb, Elmwood. Loring's car with the D.C. plates was left near the home of a well-advertised capo. A rented automobile was waiting for him a couple of blocks away. He used that to drive to Carlyle and parked it in front of 217 Crescent Street, five blocks from Sealfont's place. 217 Crescent is the residence of a Dr. Ralston. . . ."

"I've met him," interjected Matlock. "I've heard he's . . ."

". . . an abortionist," completed Greenberg.

"He's in no way associated with this university!" said Kressel emphatically.

"You've had worse," countered Greenberg quietly. "And the doctor is still a Mafia referral. At any rate, Ralph positioned the car and walked into town for the second transfer. I covered him; this briefcase is prime material. He was picked up by a Bell Telephone truck which made routine stops—including one at a restaurant called the Cheshire Cat—and finally delivered him to Sealfont's. No one could have known he was there. If they had, they would have intercepted him outside; they were watching the car on Crescent."

"That's what he told me," said Matlock.

"He knew it was possible; the trace to Crescent was intentionally left open. When he confirmed it, to his satisfaction, he acted fast. I don't know what he did, but he probably used whatever stragglers he could find until he spotted you."

"That's what he did."

"He wasn't fast enough."

"What in God's name does this have to do with *us?* What *possible* bearing can it have?" Kressel was close to shouting.

"If Mr. Matlock wants to go on, Loring's death will be publicized as an underworld killing. Disreputable lawyer, maybe a bag man; undesirable clients. The capo and the doctor will be hauled in; they're expendable. The smoke screen's so thick everyone's off balance. Even the killers. Matlock's forgotten. It'll work; it's worked before."

Kressel seemed astonished at Greenberg's assured glibness, his confidence, his calm professionalism. "You talk awfully fast, don't you?"

"I'm very bright."

Matlock couldn't help but smile. He liked Greenberg; even in—perhaps because of—the sadly disagreeable circumstances. The agent used the language well; his mind was fast. He was, indeed, bright.

"And if Jim says he washes his hands of it?"

Greenberg shrugged. "I don't like to waste words. Let's hear him say it."

Both the men looked at Matlock.

"I'm afraid I'm not going to, Sam. I'm still in."

"You can't be serious! That man was killed!"

"I know. I found him."

Kressel put his hand on Matlock's arm. It was the gesture of a friend. "I'm not an hysterical shepherd watching over a flock. I'm concerned. I'm *frightened*. I see a man being manipulated into a situation he's not qualified to handle."

"That's subjective," broke in Greenberg quietly. "We're concerned, too. If we didn't think he was capable, we never would have approached him."

"I think you would," said Kressel. "I don't for a minute believe such a consideration would stop you. You use the word *expendable* too easily, Mr. Greenberg."

"I'm sorry you think so. Because I don't. We don't. . . . I haven't gotten the detailed briefing, Kressel, but aren't you supposed to act as liaison? Because if that's true, I suggest you remove yourself. We'll have someone else assigned to the job."

"And give you a clear field? Let you run roughshod over this campus? Not on your life."

"Then we work together. As disagreeable as that may be for both of us . . . You're hostile; perhaps that's good. You'll keep me on my toes. You protest too much."

Matlock was startled by Greenberg's statement. It was one thing to form an antagonistic coalition, quite another to make veiled accusations; insulting to use a literary cliché.

"That remark requires an explanation," said Kressel, his face flushed with anger.

When Greenberg replied, his voice was soft and reasonable, belying the words he spoke. "Pound sand, mister. I lost a very good friend tonight. Twenty minutes ago I spoke with his wife. I don't give explanations under those conditions. That's where my employers and me part company. Now, shut up and I'll write out the hours of contact and give you the emergency telephone numbers. If you don't want them, get the hell out of here."

Greenberg lifted the briefcase onto a small table and opened it. Sam Kressel, stunned, approached the agent silently.

Matlock stared at the worn leather briefcase, only hours ago chained to the wrist of a dead man. He knew the deadly pavanne had begun. The first steps of the dance had been taken violently.

There were decisions to make, people to confront.

Chapter Six

The implausible name below the doorbell on the two-family faculty house read: Mr. and Mrs. Archer Beeson. Matlock had elicited the dinner invitation easily. History instructor Beeson had been flattered by his interest in coordinating a seminar between two of their courses. Beeson would have been flattered if a faculty member of Matlock's attainments had asked him how his wife was in bed (and most wondered). And since Matlock was very clearly male, Archer Beeson felt that "drinks and din" with his wife wriggling around in a short skirt might help cement a relationship with the highly regarded professor of English literature.

Matlock heard the breathless shout from the second-floor landing. "Just a sec!"

It was Beeson's wife, and her broad accent, overcultivated at Miss Porter's and Finch, sounded caricatured. Matlock pictured the girl racing around checking the plates of cheese and dip—very unusual cheese and dip, conversation pieces, really—while her husband put the final touches on the visual aspects of his bookcases—perhaps several obscure tomes carelessly, carefully, placed on tables, impossible for a visitor to miss.

Matlock wondered if these two were also secreting small tablets of lysergic acid or capsules of methedrine.

The door opened and Beeson's petite wife, dressed in the expected short skirt and translucent silk blouse that loosely covered her large breasts, smiled ingenuously.

"Hi! I'm Ginny Beeson. We met at several *mad* cocktail parties. I'm *so* glad you could come. Archie's just finishing a paper. Come on up." She preceded Matlock up the stairs, hardly giving him a chance to acknowledge. "These stairs are *horrendous*! Oh, well, the price of starting at the bottom."

"I'm sure it won't be for long," said Matlock.

"That's what Archie keeps saying. He'd better be right or I'll have muscles all over my legs!"

"I'm sure he is," said Matlock looking at the soft, unmuscular large expanse of legs in front of him.

Inside the Beeson apartment, the cheese and dip were prominently displayed on an odd-shaped coffee table, and the anticipated showcase volume was one of Matlock's own. It was titled *Interpolations in Richard II* and it resided on a table underneath a fringed lamp. Impossible for a visitor to miss.

The minute Ginny closed the door, Archie burst into the small living room from what Matlock presumed was Beeson's study—also small. He carried a sheaf of papers in his left hand; his right was extended.

"Good-oh! Glad you could make it, old man! . . . Sit, sit. Drinks are due and overdue! God! I'm flaked out for one! . . . Just spent three hours reading twenty versions of the Thirty Years' War!"

"It happens. Yesterday I got a theme on *Volpone* with the strangest ending I ever heard of. Turned out the kid never read it but saw the film in Hartford."

"With a new ending?"

"Totally."

"God! That's marvy!" injected Ginny semihysterically. "What's your drink preference, Jim? I may call you Jim, mayn't I, Doctor?"

"Bourbon and a touch of water, and you certainly better, Ginny. I've never gotten used to the 'doctor.' My father calls it fraud. Doctors carry stethoscopes, not books." Matlock sat in an easy chair covered with an Indian serape.

"Speaking of doctors, I'm working on my dissertation now. That and two more hectic summers'll do the trick." Beeson took the ice bucket from his wife and walked to a long table underneath a window where bottles and glasses were carelessly arranged.

"It's worth it," said Ginny Beeson emphatically. "Isn't it worth it, Jim?"

"Almost essential. It'll pay off."

"That and *publishing*." Ginny Beeson picked up the cheese and crackers and carried them to Matlock. "This is an interesting little Irish *fromage*. Would you believe, it's called 'Blarney'? Found it in a little shop in New York two weeks ago."

"Looks great. Never heard of it."

"Speaking of publishing. I picked up your *Interpolations* book the other day. *Damned fascinating*! Really!"

"Lord, I've almost forgotten it. Wrote it four years ago."

"It should be a *required text*! That's what Archie said, isn't it, Archie?"

"Damned right! Here's the poison, old man," said Beeson, bringing Matlock his drink. "Do you work through an agent, Jim? Not that I'm nosy. I'm years from writing anything."

"That's not true, and you know it," Ginny pouted vocally.

"Yes, I do. Irving Block in Boston. If you're working on something, perhaps I could show it to him."

"Oh, no, I wouldn't . . . that'd be awfully presumptuous of me. . . ." Beeson retreated with feigned humility to the couch with his drink. He sat next to his wife and they—involuntarily, thought Matlock—exchanged satisfied looks.

"Come on, Archie. You're a bright fellow. A real comer on this campus. Why do you think I asked you about the seminar? *You* could be doing *me* the favor. I might be bringing Block a winner. That rubs off, you know."

Beeson's expression had the honesty of gratitude. It embarrassed Matlock to return the instructor's gaze until he saw something else in Beeson's eyes. He couldn't define it, but it was there. A slight wildness, a trace of panic.

The look of a man whose mind and body knew drugs.

"That's *damned* good-oh of you, Jim. I'm touched, *really*."

The cheese, drinks, and dinner somehow passed. There were moments when Matlock had the feeling he was outside himself, watching three characters in a scene from some old movie. Perhaps on board ship or in a sloppily elegant New York apartment with the three of them wearing tightly fitted formal clothes. He wondered why he visualized the scene in such fashion—and then he knew. The Beesons had a thirties quality about them. The thirties that he had observed on the late night television films. They were somehow an anachronism, of this time but not of the time. It was either more than camp or less than put-on; he couldn't be sure. They were not artificial in themselves, but there was a falseness in their emphatic small talk, their dated expressions. Yet the truth was that they were the *now* of the present generation.

Lysergic acid and methedrine.

Acid heads. Pill poppers.

The Beesons were somehow forcing themselves to show themselves as part of a past and carefree era. Perhaps to deny the times and conditions in which they found themselves.

Archie Beeson and his wife were frightening.

By eleven, after considerable wine with the "interesting-little-veal-dish-from-a-recipe-in-an-old-Italian-cookbook," the three of them sat down in the living room. The last of the proposed seminar problems was ironed out. Matlock knew it was time to begin; the awful, awkward moment. He wasn't sure how; the best he could do was to trust his amateur instincts.

"Look, you two. . . . I hope to hell this won't come as too great a shock, but I've been a long time without a stick." He withdrew a thin cigarette case from his pocket and opened it. He felt foolish, uncomfortably clumsy. But he knew he could not show those feelings. "Before you make any judgments, I should tell you I don't go along with the pot laws and I never have."

Matlock selected a cigarette from the dozen in the case and left the case open on the table. Was that the proper thing to do? He wasn't sure; he didn't know. Archie and his wife looked at each other. Through the flame in front of his face, Matlock watched their reaction. It was cautious yet positive. Perhaps it was the alcohol in Ginny, but she smiled hesitantly, as if she was relieved to find a friend. Her husband wasn't quite so responsive.

"Go right ahead, old man," said the young instructor with a trace of condescension. "We're hardly on the attorney general's payroll."

"Hardly!" giggled the wife.

"The laws are archaic," continued Matlock, inhaling deeply. "In all areas. Control and an abiding sense of discretion—self-discretion—are all that matter. To deny experience is the real crime. To prohibit any intelligent individual's right to fulfillment is . . . goddamn it, it's repressive."

"Well, I think the key word in *intelligent*, Jim. *In*discriminate use among the *un*intelligent leads to chaos."

"Socratically, you're only half right. The other half is 'control.' Effective control among the 'iron' and 'bronze' then frees the 'gold'—to borrow from *The Republic*. If the intellectually superior were continually kept from thinking, experimenting, because their thought processes were beyond the comprehension of their fellow citizens, there'd be no great works—artistically, technically, politically. We'd still be in the Dark Ages."

Matlock inhaled his cigarette and closed his eyes. Had he been too strong, too positive? Had he sounded too much the false proselytizer? He waited, and the wait was not long. Archie spoke quietly, but urgently nevertheless.

"Progress is being made every day, old man. Believe that. It's the truth."

Matlock half opened his eyes in relief and looked at Beeson through the cigarette smoke. He held his gaze steady without blinking and then shifted his stare to Beeson's wife. He spoke only two words.

"You're children."

"That's a relative supposition under the circumstances," answered Beeson still keeping his voice low, his speech precise.

"And that's talk."

"Oh, don't be so sure about that!" Ginny Beeson had had enough alcohol in her to be careless. Her husband reached for her arm and held it. It was a warning. He spoke again, taking his eyes off Matlock, looking at nothing.

"I'm not at all sure we're on the same wavelength . . ."

"No, probably not. Forget it. . . . I'll finish this and shove off. Be in touch with you about the seminar." Matlock made sure his reference to the seminar was offhanded, almost disinterested.

Archie Beeson, the young man in an academic hurry, could not stand that disinterest.

"Would you mind if I had one of those?"

"If it's your first, yes, I would. . . . Don't try to impress me. It doesn't really matter."

"My first? . . . Of what?" Beeson rose from the couch and walked to the table where the cigarette case lay open. He reached down, picked it up, and held it to his nostrils. "That's passable grass. I might add, just passable. I'll try one . . . for openers."

"For openers?"

"You seem to be very sincere but, if you'll forgive me, you're a bit out of touch."

"From what?"

"From where it's at." Beeson withdrew two cigarettes and lit them in *Now, Voyager* fashion. He inhaled deeply, nodding and shrugging a reserved approval, and handed one to his wife. "Let's call this an hors d'oeuvre. An appetizer."

He went into his study and returned with a Chinese lacquered box, then showed Matlock the tiny peg which, when pushed, enabled the holder to flip up a thin layer of wood on the floor of the box, revealing a false bottom. Beneath were two dozen or so white tablets wrapped in transparent plastic.

"This is the main course . . . the entrée, if you're up to it."

Matlock was grateful for what knowledge he possessed and the intensive homework he'd undertaken during the past forty-eight hours. He smiled but his tone of voice was firm.

"I only take white trips under two conditions. The first is at *my* home with very good, very old friends. The second is with very good, very old friends at *their* homes. I don't know you well enough, Archie. Self-discretion. . . . . I'm not averse to a small red journey, however. Only I didn't come prepared."

"Say no more. I just may be." Beeson took the Chinese box back into his study and returned with a small leather pouch, the sort pipe smokers use for tobacco, and approached Matlock's chair. Ginny Beeson's eyes grew wide; she undid a button on her half-unbuttoned blouse and stretched her legs.

"Dunhill's best." Beeson opened the top flap and held the pouch down for Matlock to see inside. Again there was the clear plastic wrapped around tablets. However, these were deep red and slightly larger than the white pills in the Chinese box. There were at least fifty to sixty doses of Seconal.

Ginny jumped out of the chair and squealed. "I *love* it! It's the pinky-groovy!"

"Beats the hell out of brandy," added Matlock.

"We'll trip. Not too much, old man. Limit's five. That's the house rules for new old friends."

The next two hours were blurred for James Matlock, but not as blurred as they were for the Beesons. The history instructor and his wife quickly reached their "highs" with the five pills—as would have Matlock had he not been able to pocket the final three while pretending to have swallowed them. Once on the first plateau, it wasn't so hard for Matlock to imitate his companions and then convince Beeson to go for another dosage.

"Where's the almighty discretion, Doctor?" chuckled Beeson, sitting on the floor in front of the couch, reaching occasionally for one of his wife's legs.

"You're better friends that I thought you were."

"Just the *beginning* of a beautiful, *beautiful* friendship." The young wife slowly reclined on the couch and giggled. She seemed to writhe and put her hand on her husband's head, pushing his hair forward.

Beeson laughed with less control than he had shown earlier and rose from the floor. "I'll get the magic then."

When Beeson walked into his study, Matlock watched his wife. There was no mistaking her action. She looked at Matlock, opened her mouth slowly, and pushed her tongue out at him. Matlock realized that one of Seconal's side effects was showing. As was most of Virginia Beeson.

The second dosage was agreed to be three, and Matlock was now easily able to fake it. Beeson turned on his stereo and played a recording of "Carmina Burana." In fifteen minutes Ginny Beeson was sitting on Matlock's lap, intermittently rubbing herself against his groin. Her husband was spread out in front of the stereo speakers, which were on either side of the turntable. Matlock spoke as though exhaling, just loud enough to be heard over the music.

"These are some of the best I've had, Archie. . . . Where? Where's the supply from?"

"Probably the same as yours, old man." Beeson turned over and looked at Matlock and his wife. He laughed. "Now, I don't know what you mean. The magic or the girl on your lap. Watch her, Doctor. She's a minx."

"No kidding. Your pills are a better grade than mine and my grass barely passed inspection. Where? Be a good friend."

"You're funny, man. You keep asking. Do I ask you? No. . . . It's not polite. . . . Play with Ginny. Let me listen." Beeson rolled back over face down on the floor.

The girl on Matlock's lap suddenly put her arms around his neck and pressed her breats against his chest. She put her head to the side of his face and began kissing his ears. Matlock wondered what would happen if he lifted her out of the chair and carried her into the bedroom. He wondered, but he didn't want to find out. Not then. Ralph Loring had not been murdered to increase his, Matlock's, sex life.

"Let me try one of your joints. Let me see just how advanced your taste is. You many be a phony, Archie."

Suddenly Beeson sat up and stared at Matlock. He wasn't concerned with his wife. Something in Matlock's voice seemed to trigger an instinctive doubt. Or was it the words? Or was it the too normal pattern of speech Matlock used? The English professor thought of all these things as he returned Beeson's look over the girl's shoulder. Archie Beeson was suddenly a man warned, and Matlock wasn't sure why. Beeson spoke haltingly.

"Certainly, old man. . . . Ginny, don't annoy Jim." He began to rise.

"Pinky groovy . . ."

"I've got several in the kitchen. . . . I'm not sure where but I'll look. Ginny, I told you not to tease Jim. . . . Be nice to him, be good to him." Beeson kept staring at Matlock, his eyes wide from the Seconal, his lips parted, the muscles of his face beyond relaxation. He backed away toward the kitchen door, which was open. Once inside, Archie Beeson did a strange thing. Or so it appeared to James Matlock.

He slowly closed the swing-hinged door and held it shut.

Matlock quickly eased the drugged girl off his lap and she quietly stretched out on the floor. She smiled angelically and reached her arms up for him. He smiled down, stepping over her.

"Be right back," he whispered. "I want to ask Archie something." The girl rolled over on her stomach as Matlock walked cautiously toward the kitchen door. He ruffled his hair and purposely, silently, lurched, holding onto the dining room table as he neared the entrance. If Beeson suddenly came out, he wanted to appear irrational, drugged. The stereo was a little louder now, but through it Matlock could hear the sound of Archie's voice talking quietly, excitedly on the kitchen telephone.

He leaned against the wall next to the kitchen door and tried to analyze the disjointed moments that caused Archie Beeson to panic, to find it so imperative to reach someone on the telephone.

Why? What?

Had the grand impersonation been so obvious? He had blown his first encounter?

If he had, the least he could do was to try to find out who was on the other end of the line, who it was that Beeson ran to in his disjointed state of anxiety.

One fact seemed clear: whoever it was had to be more important than Archer Beeson. A man—even a drug addict—did not panic and contact a lesser figure on his own particular totem.

Perhaps the evening wasn't a failure; or his failure—conversely—a necessity. In Beeson's desperation, he might let slip information he never would have revealed if he *hadn't* been desperate. It wasn't preposterous to force it out of the frightened, drugged instructor. On the other hand, that was the least desirable method. If he failed in that, too, he was finished before he'd begun. Loring's meticulous briefing would have been for nothing; his death a rather macabre joke, his terrible cover—so painful to his family, so inhuman somehow—made fruitless by a bumbling amateur.

There was no other way, thought Matlock, but to try. Try to find out who Beeson had reached *and* try to put the pieces of the evening back where Beeson might accept him again. For some insane reason, he pictured Loring's briefcase and the thin black chain dangling from the handle. For an even crazier reason, it gave him confidence; not much, but some.

He assumed a stance as close to the appearance of collapse as he could imagine, then moved his head to the door frame and slowly, quarter inch by quarter inch, pushed it inward. He fully expected to be met by Beeson's staring eyes. Instead, the instructor's back was to him; he was hunched over like a small boy trying to control his bladder, the phone clutched to his thin scrunched neck, his head bent to the side. It was obvious that Beeson thought his voice was muffled, indistinguishable beneath the sporadic crescendos of the "Carmina Burana." But the Seconal had played one of its tricks. Beeson's ear and his speech were no longer synchronized. His words were not only clear. They were emphasized by being spaced out and repeated.

". . . You *do not* understand me. I want you to understand me. *Please*, understand. He keeps asking questions. He's not *with* it. He *is not with it*. I swear to Christ he's a plant. Get hold of Herron. Tell Herron to reach him for *God's* sake. Reach him, *please!* I could lose everything! . . . No. No, I can tell! I *see* what I *see, man!* When that bitch turns horny I have *problems*. I mean there are appearances, old man. . . . Get Lucas. . . . For Christ's sake *get* to him! I'm in *trouble* and I can't. . . ."

Matlock let the door swing slowly back into the frame. His shock was such that thought and feeling were suspended; he saw his hand still on the kitchen door, yet he felt no wood against his fingers. What he had just heard was no less horrible than the sight of Ralph Loring's lifeless body in the telephone booth.

Herron. *Lucas Herron!*

A seventy-year-old legend. A quiet scholar who was as much revered for his perceptions of the human condition as he was for his brilliance. A lovely man, an honored man. There had to be a mistake, an explanation.

There was no time to ponder the inexplicable.

Archer Beeson thought he was a "plant." And now, someone else thought so, too. He couldn't allow that. He had to think, force himself to *act*.

Suddenly he understood. Beeson himself had told him what to do.

No informer—no one not narcotized—would attempt it.

Matlock looked over at the girl lying face down on the living room floor. He crossed rapidly around the dining table and ran to her side, unbuckling his belt as he did so. In swift movements, he took off his trousers and reached down, rolling her over on her back. He lay down beside her and undid the remaining two buttons on her blouse, pulling her brassiere until the hasp broke. She moaned and giggled, and when he touched her exposed breasts, she moaned again and lifted one leg over Matlock's hip.

"Pinky groovy, pinky groovy . . ." She began breathing through her mouth, pushing her pelvis into Matlock's groin; her eyes half open, her hands reaching down, stroking his leg, her fingers clutching at his skin.

Matlock kept his eyes toward the kitchen door, praying it would open.

And then it did, and he shut his eyes.

Archie Beeson stood in the dining area looking down at his wife and guest. Matlock, at the sound of Beeson's footsteps, snapped his head back and feigned terrified confusion. He rose from the floor and immediately fell back down again. He grabbed his trousers and held them in front of his shorts, rising once more unsteadily and finally falling onto the couch.

"Oh, Jesus! Oh, sweet Jesus, Archie! Christ, young fella! I didn't think I was this freaked out! . . . I'm far out, Archie! What the hell, what do I *do*? I'm *gone*, man, I'm sorry! Christ, I'm sorry!"

Beeson approached the couch, his half-naked wife at his feet. From his expression it was impossible to tell what he was thinking. Or the extent of his anger.

Or was it anger?

His audible reaction was totally unexpected: he started to laugh. At first softly, and then with gathering momentum, until he became nearly hysterical.

"Oh, *God*, old man! I said it! I *said* she was a minx! . . . Don't worry. No tattle tales. No rapes, no dirty-old-man-on-the-faculty. But we'll have our *seminar*. Oh, Christ, yes! That'll be some *seminar!* And you'll tell them all you picked *me!* Won't you? Oh, yes! That's what you'll tell them, isn't it?"

Matlock looked into the wild eyes of the addict above him.

"Sure. Sure, Archie. Whatever you say."

"You better believe it, old man! And don't apologize. No apologies are necessary! The apologies are mine!" Archer Beeson collapsed on the floor in laughter. He reached over and cupped his wife's left breast; she moaned and giggled her maddening, high-pitched giggle.

And Matlock knew he had won.

Chapter Seven

He was exhausted, both by the hour and by the tensions of the night. It was ten minutes past three and the choral strains of the "Carmina Burana" were still hammering in his ears. The image of the bare-breasted wife and the jackal-sounding husband—both writhing on the floor in front of him—added revulsion to the sickening taste in his mouth.

But what bothered him most was the knowledge that Lucas Herron's name was used within the context of such an evening.

It was inconceivable.

Lucas Herron. The "grand old bird," as he was called. A reticent but obvious fixture of the Carlyle campus. The chairman of the Romance languages department and the embodiment of the quiet scholar with a deep and abiding compassion. There was always a glint in his eyes, a look of bemusement mixed with tolerance.

To associate him—regardless of how remotely—with the narcotics world was unbelievable. To have heard him sought after by an hysterical addict—for essentially, Archer Beeson *was* an addict, psychologically if not chemically—as though Lucas were some sort of power under the circumstances was beyond rational comprehension.

The explanation had to lie somewhere in Lucas Herron's immense capacity for sympathy. He was a friend to many, a dependable refuge for the troubled, often the deeply troubled. And beneath his placid, aged, unruffled surface, Herron was a strong man, a leader. A quarter of a century ago, he had spent countless months of hell in the Solomon Islands as a middle-aged infantry officer. A lifetime ago, Lucas Herron had been an authentic hero in a vicious moment of time during a savage war in the Pacific. Now over seventy, Herron was an institution.

Matlock rounded the corner and saw his apartment half a block away. The campus was dark; aside from the street lamps, the only light came from one of his rooms. Had he left one on? He couldn't remember.

He walked up the path to his door and inserted his key. Simultaneously with the click of the lock, there was a loud crash from within. Although it startled him, his first reaction was amusement. His clumsy, long-haired house cat had knocked over a stray glass or one of those pottery creations Patricia Ballantyne had inflicted on him. Then he realized such a thought was ridiculous, the product of an exhausted mind. The crash was too loud for pottery, the shattering of glass too violent.

He rushed into the small foyer, and what he saw pushed fatigue out of his brain. He stood immobile in disbelief.

The entire room was in shambles. Tables were overturned; books pulled from the shelves, their pages torn from the bindings, scattered over the floor; his stereo turntable and speakers smashed. Cushions from his couch and armchairs were slashed, the stuffing and foam rubber strewn everywhere; the rugs upended, lumped in folds; the curtains ripped from their rods, thrown over the upturned furniture.

He saw the reason for the crash. His large casement window, on the far right wall bordering the street, was a mass of twisted lead and broken glass. The window consisted of two panels; he remembered clearly that he had opened both before leaving for the Beesons. He liked the spring breezes, and it was too early in the season for screens. So there was no reason for the window to be smashed; the ground was perhaps four or five feet below the casement, sufficient to dissuade an intruder, low enough for a panicked burglar to negotiate easily.

The smashing of the window, therefore, was not for escape. It was intended.

He had been watched, and a signal had been given.

It was a warning.

And Matlock knew he could not acknowledge that warning. To do so was to acknowledge more than a robbery; he was not prepared to do that.

He crossed rapidly to his bedroom door and looked inside. If possible, his bedroom was in more of a mess than the living room. The mattress was thrown against the wall, ripped to shreds. Every drawer of his bureau was dislodged, lying on the floor, the contents scattered all around the room. His closet was like the rest—suits and jackets pulled from the clothes rod, shoes yanked from their recesses.

Even before he looked he knew his kitchen would be no better off than the rest of his apartment. The foodstuffs in cans and boxes had not been thrown on the floor, simply moved around, but the soft items had been torn to pieces. Matlock understood again. One or two crashes from the other rooms were tolerable noise levels; a continuation of the racket from his kitchen might arouse one of the other families in the building. As it was, he could hear the faint sounds of footsteps above him. The final crash of the window had gotten someone up.

The warning was explicit, but the act itself was a search.

He thought he knew the object of that search, and again he realized he could not acknowledge it. Conclusions were being made as they had been made at Beeson's; he had to ride them out with the most convincing denials he could manufacture. That much he knew instinctively.

But before he began that pretense, he had to find out if the search was successful.

He shook the stammering lethargy out of his mind and body. He looked once again at his living room; he studied it. All the windows were bare, and the light was sufficient for someone with a pair of powerful binoculars stationed in a nearby building or standing on the inclining lawn of the campus beyond the street to observe every move he made. If he turned off the lights, would such an unnatural action lend credence to the conclusions he wanted denied?

Without question. A man didn't walk into a house in shambles and proceed to turn off lights.

Yet he had to reach his bathroom, at that moment the most important room in the apartment. He had to spend less than thirty seconds inside to determine the success or failure of the ransacking, and do so in such a way as to seem innocent of any abnormal concerns. If anyone *was* watching.

It was a question of appearance, of gesture, he thought. He saw that the stereo turntable was the nearest object to the bathroom door, no more than five feet away. He walked over and bent down, picking up several pieces, including the metal arm. He looked at it, then suddenly dropped the arm and brought his finger to his mouth, feigning an imagined puncture on his skin. He walked into the bathroom rapidly.

Once inside, he quickly opened the medicine cabinet and grabbed a tin of Band-Aids from the glass shelf. He then swiftly reached down to the left of the toilet bowl where the cat's yellow plastic box was placed and picked up a corner of the newspaper underneath the granules of litter. Beneath the newspaper he felt the coarse grain of the two layers of canvas he had inserted and lifted up an edge.

The scissored page was still intact. The silver Corsican paper that ended in the deadly phrase *Venerare Omerta* had not been found.

He replaced the newspaper, scattered the litter, and stood up. He saw that the frosted glass of the small window above the toilet was partially opened, and he swore.

There was no time to think of that.

He walked back into the living room, ripping the plastic off a Band-Aid.

The search had failed. Now the warning had to be ignored, the conclusions denied. He crossed to the telephone and called the police.

"Can you give me a list of what's missing?" A uniformed patrolman stood in the middle of the debris. A second policeman wandered about the apartment making notes.

"I'm not sure yet. I haven't really checked."

"That's understandable. It's a mess. You'd better look, though. The quicker we get a list, the better."

"I don't think anything *is* missing, officer. What I mean is, I don't have anything particularly valuable to anyone else. Except perhaps the stereo . . . and that's smashed. There's a television set in the bedroom, that's okay. Some of the books could bring a price, but look at them."

"No cash, Jewelry, watches?"

"I keep money in the bank and cash in my wallet. I wear my watch and haven't any jewelry."

"How about exam papers? We've been getting a lot of that."

"In my office. In the English department."

The patrolman wrote in a small black notebook and called to his partner, who had gone into the bedroom. "Hey, Lou, did the station confirm the print man?"

"They're getting him up. He'll be over in a few minutes."

"Have you touched anything, Mr. Matlock?"

"I don't know. I may have. It was a shock."

"Particularly any of the broken items, like that record player? It'd be good if we could show the fingerprint man specific things you haven't touched."

"I picked up the arm, not the casing."

"Good. It's a place to start."

The police stayed for an hour and a half. The fingerprint specialist arrived, did his work, and departed. Matlock thought of phoning Sam Kressel, but reasoned that there wasn't anything Kressel could do at that hour. And in the event someone outside *was* watching the building, Kressel shouldn't be seen. Various people from the other apartments had wakened and had come down offering sympathy, help, and coffee.

As the police were leaving, a large patrolman turned in the doorway. "Sorry to take so much time, Mr. Matlock. We don't usually lift prints in a break and entry unless there's injury or loss of property, but there's been a lot of this sort of thing recently. Personally, I think it's those weirdos with the hair and the beads. Or the niggers. We never had trouble like this before the weirdos and the niggers got here."

Matlock looked at the uniformed officer, who was so confident of his analysis. There was no point in objecting; it would be useless, and Matlock was too tired. "Thanks for helping be straighten up."

"Sure thing." The patrolman started down the cement path, then turned again. "Oh, Mr. Matlock."

"Yes?" Matlock pulled the door back.

"It struck us that maybe someone was looking for something. What with all the slashing and books and everything . . . you know what I mean?"

"Yes."

"You'd tell us if that was the case, wouldn't you?"

"Of course."

"Yeah. It'd be stupid to withhold information like that."

"I'm not stupid."

"No offense. Just that sometimes you guys get all involved and forget things."

"I'm not absentminded. Very few of us are."

"Yeah." The patrolman laughed somewhat derisively. "I just wanted to bring it up. I mean, we can't do our jobs unless we got all the facts, you know?"

"I understand."

"Yeah. Good."

"Good night."

"Good night, Doctor."

He closed the door and walked into his living room. He wondered if his insurance would cover the disputable value of his rarer books and prints. He sat down on the ruined couch and surveyed the room. It was still a mess; the carnage had been thorough. It would take more than picking up debris and righting furniture. The warning had been clear, violent.

The startling fact was that the warning existed at all.

Why? From whom?

Archer Beeson's hysterical telephone call? That was possible, even preferable, perhaps. It might encompass a motive unrelated to Nimrod. It could mean that Beeson's circle of users and pushers wanted to frighten him enough to leave Archie alone. Leave them all alone; and Loring had specifically said there was no proof that the Beesons were involved with the Nimrod unit.

There was no proof that they weren't, either.

Nevertheless, if it *was* Beeson, the alarm would be called off in the morning. There was no mistaking the conclusion of the night's engagement. The "near-rape" by a dirty, drugged "old man." He was Beeson's academic ladder.

On the other hand, and far less preferable, there was the possibility that the warning *and* the search were centered on the Corsican paper. What had Loring whispered behind him on the sidewalk?

". . . There's only one thing they want more than this briefcase; that's the paper in your pocket."

It was then reasonable to assume that he'd been linked to Ralph Loring. Washington's assessment that his panic at finding Loring dissociated him from the agent was in error, Jason Greenberg's confidence misplaced.

Still again, as Greenberg had suggested, they might test him. Press him before issuing a clean bill of health.

Might, could, possible, still again.

Conjectures.

He had to keep his head; he couldn't allow himself to overreact. If he was

to be of *any* value, he had to play the innocent.
Might have, could have, it was possible.

His body ached. His eyes were swollen and his mouth still had the terrible aftertaste of the combined dosages of Seconal, wine, and marijuana. He was exhausted; the pressures of trying to reach unreachable conclusions were overtaking him. His memory wandered back to the early days in 'Nam and he recalled the best advice he'd ever been given in those weeks of unexpected combat. That was to rest whenever he could, to sleep if it was at all possible. The advice had come from a line sergeant who, it had been rumored, had survived more assaults than any man in the Mekong Delta. Who, it was also rumored, had slept through an ambush which had taken most of his company.

Matlock stretched out on the barely recognizable couch. There was no point in going into the bedroom—his mattress was destroyed. He unbuckled his belt and kicked off his shoes. He could sleep for a few hours; then he'd talk to Kressel. Ask Kressel and Greenberg to work out a story for him to use about the invasion of his apartment. A story approved by Washington and, perhaps, the Carlyle police.

The police.

Suddenly he sat up. It hadn't struck him at the time, but now he considered it. The crass but imperiously polite patrolman whose primitive detection powers had centered on the "weirdos and niggers" had addressed him as "Mister" throughout the nearly two hours of police investigation. Yet when he was leaving, when he insultingly referred to the possibility of Matlock's withholding information, he had called him "Doctor." The "mister" was normal. The "doctor" was most unusual. No one outside the campus community—and rarely there—ever called him "Doctor," ever called *any* Ph.D. "Doctor." It struck most holders of such degrees as fatuous, and only the fatuous expected it.

Why had the patrolman used it? He didn't know him, he had never seen him to his knowledge. How would the patrolman know he was even entitled to the name "doctor"?

As he sat there, Matlock wondered if the combined efforts and pressures of the last hours were taking their toll. Was he now finding unreasonable meanings where no meanings existed? Was it not entirely plausible that the Carlyle police had a list of the Carlyle faculty and that a desk sergeant, or whoever took emergency calls, had checked his name against the list and casually stated his title? Was he not, perhaps, consigning the patrolman to a plateau of ignorance because he disliked the officer's prejudices?

A lot of things were possible.

And disturbing.

Matlock fell back onto the couch and closed his eyes.

At first the noise reached him as a faint echo might from the far end of a long, narrow tunnel. Then the noise became identifiable as rapid, incessant tapping. Tapping which would not stop, tapping which became louder and louder.

Matlock opened his eyes and saw the blurred light coming from two table lamps across from the couch. His feet were drawn up under him, his neck perspiring against the rough surface of the sofa's corduroy cover. Yet there was a cool breeze coming through the smashed, lead-framed window.

The tapping continued, the sound of flesh against wood. It came from the foyer, from his front door. He flung his legs over the side onto the floor and found that they both were filled with pins and needles. He struggled to stand.

The tapping and the knocking became louder. Then the voice. "Jamie! Jamie!"

He walked awkwardly toward the door.

"Coming!" He reached the door and opened it swiftly. Patricia Ballantyne, dressed in a raincoat, silk pajamas evident underneath, walked rapidly inside.

"Jamie, for God's sake, I've been trying to call you."

"I've been here. The phone didn't ring."

"I know it didn't. I finally got an operator and she said it was out of order. I borrowed a car and drove over as fast as I could and . . ."

"It's not out of order, Pat. The police—the police were here and a quick look around will explain why—they used it a dozen times."

"Oh, good Lord!" The girl walked past him into the still-disheveled room. Matlock crossed to the telephone and picked it up from the table. He quickly held it away from his ear as the piercing tone of a disengaged instrument whistled out of the receiver.

"The bedroom," he said, replacing the telephone and going to his bedroom door.

On his bed, on top of the slashed remains of his mattress, was his bedside phone. The receiver was off the hook, *underneath* the pillow, muffling the harsh sound of the broken connection so it would not be heard. Someone had not wanted it to ring.

Matlock tried to remember everyone who'd been there. All told, more than a dozen people. Five or six policemen—in and out of uniform; husbands and wives from other apartments; several latenight passersby who had seen the police cars and wandered up to the front door. It had been cumulatively blurred. He couldn't remember all the faces.

He put the telephone back on the bedside table and was aware that Pat stood in the doorway. He gambled that she hadn't seen him remove the pillow.

"Someone must have knocked it over straightening out things," he said, pretending irritation. "That's rotten; I mean your having to borrow a car. . . . Why did you? What's the matter?"

She didn't reply. Instead, she turned and looked back into the living room. "What happened?"

Matlock remembered the patrolman's language. "They call it 'break and entry.' A police phrase covering human tornadoes, as I understand it. . . . Robbery. I got myself robbed for the first time in my life. It's quite an experience. I think the poor bastards were angry because there wasn't anything of any value so they ripped the place apart. . . . Why'd you come over?"

She spoke softly, but the intensity of her voice made Matlock realize that she was close to panic. As always, she imposed a control on herself when she became emotional. It was an essential part of the girl.

"A couple of hours ago—at quarter to four to be exact—my phone rang. The man, it was a man, asked for you. I was asleep, and I suppose I didn't make much sense, but I pretended to be upset that anyone would think you were there. . . . I didn't know what to do. I was confused. . . ."

"Okay, I understand that. So?"

"He said he didn't believe me. I was a liar. I . . . I was so surprised that anyone would phone then—at quarter to four—and call me a liar . . . I was confused. . . ."

"What did you say?"

"It's not what *I* said. It's what *he* said. He told me to tell you to . . . not to stay 'behind the globe' or 'light the lower world.' He said it *twice!* He said it was an awful joke but you'd understand. It was frightening! . . . Do you? Do you understand?"

Matlock walked past her into the living room. He looked for his cigarettes and tried to remain calm. She followed him. "What did he mean?"

"I'm not sure."

"Has it anything to do with . . . this?" She gestured her hand over the apartment.

"I don't think so." He lit his cigarette and wondered what he should tell her. The Nimrod people hadn't wasted any time finding associations. If it *was* Nimrod.

"What did he mean by . . . 'standing behind the globe'? It sounds like a riddle."

"It's a quote, I think." But Matlock did not have to think. He knew. He recalled Shakespeare's words precisely: *Knowest thou not that when the searching eye of heaven is hid behind the globe and lights the lower world . . . then thieves and robbers range abroad unseen . . . in murders and in outrage bloody here.*

"What does it mean?"

"I don't *know!* I can't remember it. . . . Somebody's confusing me with someone else. That's the only thing I can imagine. . . . What did he sound like?"

"Normal. He was angry but he didn't shout or anything."

"No one you recognized? Not specifically, but did you ever hear the voice before?"

"I'm not sure. I don't think so. No one I could pick out, but . . ."

"But what?"

"Well, it was a . . . cultivated voice. A little actorish, I think."

"A man used to lecturing." Matlock made a statement, he did not ask a question. His cigarette tasted sour so he crushed it out.

"Yes, I guess that would describe it."

"And probably not in a science lab. . . . That reduces the possibilities to roughly eighty people on campus."

"You're making assumptions I don't understand! That phone call *did* have something to do with what happened here."

He knew he was talking too much. He didn't want to involve Pat; he *couldn't* involve her. Yet someone else had—and that fact was a profound complication. "It might have. According to the best sources—naturally I refer to television detectives—thieves make sure people aren't home before they rob a place. They were probably checking me out."

The girl held his wavering eyes with her gaze. "Weren't you home then? At quarter to four? . . . The question is not inquisitorial, my darling, simply a point of information."

He swore at himself silently. It was the exhaustion, the Beeson episode, the shock of the apartment. Of course the question wasn't inquisitorial. He was a free agent. And, of course, he was home at quarter to four.

"I'm not sure. I wasn't that concerned with the time. It was one hell of a long evening." He laughed feebly. "I was at Archie Beeson's. Proposed seminars with your instructors promote a lot of booze."

She smiled. "I don't think you understand me. I really don't mind what Poppa Bear was doing. . . . Well, of course, I do, but right now I don't understand why you're lying to me. . . . You were *here* two hours ago, and that phone call wasn't any thief checking your whereabouts and you *know* it."

"Momma Bear's reaching. That doesn't go with the territory." Matlock was rude. It, too, like the lying, was obviously false. Whatever his past rebellions, whatever his toughness, he was a kind person and she knew that.

"All right. I apologize. I'll ask one more question and then I'll leave. . . . What does *Omerta* mean?"

Matlock froze. "What did you say?"

"The man on the phone. He used the word *Omerta*."

"How?"

"Very casually. Just a reminder, he said."

Chapter Eight

Field Agent Jason Greenberg walked through the borderless door of the squash court. "You're working up quite a sweat there, Dr. Matlock."

"I'd hate to have it analyzed. . . . Anyway, it was your idea. I would have been just as happy at Kressel's office or even downtown somewhere."

"This is better. . . . We've got to talk quickly, though. The gym registry has me listed as an insurance surveyor. I'm checking the extinguishers in the corridors."

"They probably need checking." Matlock walked to a corner where a gray sweatshirt was wrapped in a towel. He unwound it and slipped it over his head. "What have you come up with? Last night was a little hairy."

"If you discount confusion, we haven't come up with a thing. At least nothing specific. A couple of theories, that's all. . . . We think you handled yourself very well."

"Thanks. I was confused. What are the theories? You sound academic, and I'm not sure I like that."

Greenberg's head suddenly shifted. From the right wall there could be heard a dull thumping. "Is that another court?"

"Yes. There are six of them on this side. They're practice courts, no balconies. But you know that."

Greenberg picked up the ball and threw it hard against the front wall. Matlock understood and caught it on the bounce. He threw it back; Greenberg returned it. They maintained a slow rhythm, neither man moving more than a foot or two, each taking his turn to throw. Greenberg spoke softly, in a monotone.

"We think you're being tested. That's the most logical explanation. You *did* find Ralph. You made a statement about seeing the car. Your reasons for being in the area were weak; so weak we thought they were plausible. They want to make sure, that's why they brought in the girl. They're being thorough."

"Okay. Theory number one. What's number two?"

"I said that was the most logical. . . . It's the only one, really."

"What about Beeson?"

"What about him? You were there."

Matlock held the squash ball in his hand for a few seconds before lobbing it against the side wall. The wall away from Greenberg's stare.

"Could Beeson have been smarter than I thought and sent out an alarm?"

"He could have. We think it's doubtful. . . . The way you described the evening."

But Matlock had *not* described the *entire* evening. He had not told Greenberg or anyone of Beeson's telephone call. His reasons weren't rational, they were emotional. Lucas Herron was an old man, a gentle man. His sympathy for troubled students was legendary; his concern for young, untried, often arrogant new instructors was a welcomed sedative in faculty crises. Matlock had convinced himself that the "grand old bird" had befriended a desperate young man, helping him in a desperate situation. He had no right to surface Herron's name on the basis of a phone call made by a panicked drug user. There were too many possible explanations. Somehow he'd speak with Herron, perhaps over coffee at the Commons, or in the bleachers at a baseball game—Herron loved baseball—talk to him, tell him he should back away from Archer Beeson.

"——about Beeson?"

"What?" Matlock had not heard Greenberg.

"I asked you if you had second thoughts about Beeson."

"No. No, I haven't. He's not important. As a matter of fact, he'll probably throw away the grass and the pills—except for *my* benefit—if he thinks he can use me."

"I won't try to follow that."

"Don't. I just had momentary doubts. . . . I can't believe you arrived at only one theory. Come on. What else?"

"All right. Two others and they're not even plausible—both from the same egg. The first is that there might be a leak in Washington. The second—a leak here at Carlyle."

"Why not plausible?"

"Washington first. There are fewer than a dozen men who know about this operation, and that includes Justice, Treasury, and the White House. They're the calibre of men who exchange secret messages with the Kremlin. Impossible."

"And Carlyle?"

"You, Adrian Sealfont, and the obnoxious Samuel Kressel. . . . I'd like nothing better than pointing at Kressel—he's a prick—but, again, impossible. I'd also take a certain ethnic delight in knocking a venerated WASP like Sealfont off his pedestal, but there, too—no sense. That leaves you. Are you the one?"

"Your wit is staggering." Matlock had to run to catch the ball which Greenberg threw into a corner. He held it in his hand and looked at the agent. "Don't misunderstand me—I like Sam, or at least I think I do—but why is he 'impossible'?"

"Same as Sealfont. . . . In an operation like this we start at the beginning. And I *mean* the *beginning*. We don't give a goddamn about positions, status, or reputation—good or bad. We use every trick in the books to prove someone guilty, not innocent. We try to find even the flimsiest reason *not* to clear him. Kressel's as clean as John the Baptist. Still a prick, but clean. Sealfont's worse. He's everything they say. A goddamn saint—Church of England, of course. So, again, that leaves you."

Matlock whipped the ball up in a spinning reverse shot into the rear left ceiling. Greenberg stepped back and slashed the ball in midair into the right wall. It bulleted back between Matlock's legs.

"I gather you've played the game," said Matlock with an embarrassed grin.

"The bandit of Brandeis. What about the girl? Where is she?"

"In my apartment. I made her promise not to leave till I got back. Outside of safety, it's one way to get the place cleaned up."

"I'm assigning a man to her. I don't think it's necessary, but it'll make *you* feel better." Greenberg looked at his watch.

"It will and thanks."

"We'd better hurry. . . . Now, listen. We're letting everything take it's normal course. Police blotter, newspapers, everything. No covers, no counter stories, nothing to obstruct normal curiosity or your perfectly normal reactions. Someone broke into your apartment and smashed up the place. That's all you know. . . . And there's something else. You may not like it, but we think it's best—and safest."

"What?"

"We think Miss Ballantyne should report the phone call she received to the police."

"Hey, come on! The caller expected to find me there at four o'clock in the morning. You don't spell that kind of thing out. Not if you're on a fellowship and expect to work for museum foundations. They still revere McKinley."

"The eye of the beholder, Dr. Matlock. . . . She just received a phone call; some man asked for you, quoted Shakespeare, and made an unintelligible reference to some foreign word or city. She was goddamn mad. It wouldn't rate five lines in a newspaper, but since your apartment was broken into, it's logical she report it."

Matlock was silent. He walked over to the corner of the squash court where the ball had settled and picked it up. "We're a couple of ciphers who got pushed around. We don't know what happened; just that we don't like it."

"That's the idea. Nothing is so convincing as someone who's a bewildered injured party and lets everybody know it. Make an insurance issue about those old books of yours. . . . I've got to go. There aren't that many extinguishers in the building. Anything else? What are you doing next?"

Matlock bounced the ball on the floor. "A fortuitous invitation. Fortuitously received over a number of beers at the Afro-Commons. I'm invited to a staged version of the original puberty rites of the Mau Mau tribes. Tonight at ten o'clock in the cellars of Lumumba Hall. . . . It used to be the Alpha Delt fraternity house. I can tell you there are a lot of white Episcopalians spinning in hell over that one."

"Again, I'm not following, Doctor."

"You don't do your homework, either. . . . Lumumba Hall is very large on your list."

"Sorry. You'll phone me in the morning?"

"In the morning."

"I'll call you Jim if you'll call me Jason."

"No kiss, but agreed."

"O.K. Practice some more in here. I'll take you when this is over."

"You're on."

Greenberg let himself out. He looked up and down the narrow corridor, satisfied that no one was there; no one had seen him enter or leave the court. Continuous thumping could be heard within the walls. All the courts were in use. Greenberg wondered, as he was about to turn the corner into the main hallway, why the Carlyle gymnasium was so heavily attended at eleven o'clock in the morning. It was never the case at Brandeis; not fifteen years ago. Eleven o'clock in the morning was a time for class.

He heard a strange noise that was not the sound of a hard ball against thick wood and turned quickly.

No one.

He entered the main hall and turned once again. No one. He left quickly.

The sound he heard was that of a stubborn latch. It came from the door next to Matlock's court. Out of that door a man emerged. He, too, as Greenberg had done less than a minute before, looked up and down the narrow corridor. But instead of being satisfied that no one was there, he was annoyed. The obstinate latch had caused him to miss seeing the man who'd met with James Matlock.

Now the door of court four opened and Matlock himself stepped into the corridor. The man ten feet away was startled, pulled his towel up to his face, and walked away, coughing.

But the man wasn't quick enough. Matlock knew that face.

It was the patrolman from his apartment at four o'clock in the morning.

The patrolman who had called him "Doctor." The man in uniform who knew beyond a doubt that the campus troubles were caused by the "weirdos and the niggers."

Matlock stared at the retreating figure.

Chapter Nine

Over the large cathedral doors one could see—if one looked closely, or the sun was shining at a certain angle—the faded imprint of the Greek letters $A\Delta\varphi$. They had been there in bas-relief for decades, and no amount of sand blasting or student damage could eradicate them completely. The fraternity house of Alpha Delta Phi had gone the way of other such buildings at Carlyle. Its holy order of directors could not find it within themselves to accept the inevitable. The house had been sold—lock, stock, leaking roof, and bad mortgage—to the blacks.

The blacks had done well, even extremely well, with what they had to work with. The decrepit old house had been totally refurbished inside and out. All past associations with its former owners were obliterated wherever possible. The scores of faded photographs of venerated alumni were replaced with wildly theatrical portraits of the new revolutionaries—African, Latin American, Black Panther. Throughout the ancient halls were the new commands, screeched in posters and psychedelic art: *Death to the Pigs! Up Whitey! Malcolm Lives! Lumumba the Black Christ!*

Between these screams for recognition were replicas of primitive African artifacts—fertility masks, spears, shields, animal skins dipped in red paint, shrunken heads suspended by hair with complexions unmistakably white.

Lumumba Hall wasn't trying to fool anyone. It reflected anger. It reflected fury.

Matlock didn't have to use the brass knocker set beside the grotesque iron mask at the edge of the doorframe. The large door opened as he approached it, and a student greeted him with a bright smile.

"I was hoping you'd make it! It's gonna be a groove!"

"Thanks, Johnny. Wouldn't miss it." Matlock walked in, struck by the proliferation of lighted candles throughout the hallway and adjoining rooms. "Looks like a wake. Where's the casket?"

"That's later. Wait'll you see!"

A black Matlock recognized as one of the campus extremists walked up to them. Adam Williams' hair was long—African style and clipped in a perfect semicircle above his head. His features were sharp; Matlock had the feeling that if they met in the veldt, Williams would be assumed to be a tribal chief.

"Good evening," Williams said with an infectious grin. "Welcome to the seat of revolution."

"Thanks very much." They shook hands. "You don't look so revolutionary as you do funereal. I was asking Johnny where the casket was."

Williams laughed. His eyes were intelligent, his smile genuine, without guile or arrogance. In close quarters, the black radical had little of the firebrand quality he displayed on the podium in front of cheering supporters. Matlock wasn't surprised. Those of the faculty who had Williams in their courses often remarked on his subdued, good-humored approach. So different from the image he projected in campus—rapidly becoming national —politics.

"Oh, Lord! We're lousing up the picture then! This is a happy occasion. A little gruesome, I suppose, but essentially joyful."

"I'm not sure I understand," Matlock smiled.

"A youngster from the tribe reaches the age of manhood, the brink of an active, responsible life. A jungle Bar Mitzvah. It's a time for rejoicing. No caskets, no weeping shrouds."

"That's right! That's right, Adam!" said the boy named Johnny enthusiastically.

"Why don't you get Mr. Matlock a drink, brother." And then he turned to Matlock. "It's all the same drink until after the ceremony—it's called Swahili punch. Is that O.K.?"

"Of course."

"Right." Johnny disappeared into the crowd toward the dining room and the punch bowl. Adam smiled as he spoke.

"It's a light rum drink with lemonade and cranberry juice. Not bad, really. . . . Thank you for coming. I mean that."

"I was surprised to be invited. I thought this was a very 'in' thing. Restricted to the tribe. . . . That didn't come out the way I meant it."

Williams laughed. "No offense. I used the word. It's good to think in terms of tribes. Good for the brothers."

"Yes, I imagine it is. . . ."

"The collective, protective social group. Possessing an identity of its own."

"If that's the purpose—the constructive purpose—I endorse it."

"Oh, it is. Tribes in the bush don't always make war on each other, you know. It's not all stealing, looting, carrying away women. That's a Robert Ruark hang-up. They trade, share hunting and farming lands together, coexist in the main probably better than nations or even political subdivisions."

It was Matlock's turn to laugh. "All right, professor. I'll make notes *after* the lecture."

"Sorry. Avocational hazard."

"Avocational or occupational?"

"Time will tell, won't it? . . . One thing I should make clear, however. We don't need your endorsement."

Johnny returned with Matlock's cup of Swahili punch. "Hey, you know what? Brother Davis, that's Bill Davis, says you told him you were going to flunk him, then at midterm you gave him a High Pass!"

"Brother Davis got off his fat ass and did a little work." Matlock looked at Adam Williams. "You don't object to that kind of endorsement, do you?"

Williams smiled broadly and placed his hand on Matlock's arm. "No, sir, bwana. . . . In that area you run King Solomon's Mines. Brother Davis is here to work as hard as he can and go as far as his potential will let him. No argument there. Bear down on the brother."

"You're positively frightening." Matlock spoke with a lightness he did not feel.

"Not at all. Just pragmatic. . . . I've got some last-minute preparations to look after. See you later." Williams hailed a passing student and walked through the crowd toward the staircase.

"Come on, Mr. Matlock. I'll show you the new alterations." Johnny led Matlock into what used to be Alpha Delt's common room.

In the sea of dark faces, Matlock saw a minimum of guarded, hostile looks. There were, perhaps, less overt greetings than he might expect outside on the campus, but by and large, his presence was accepted. He thought for a moment that if the brothers knew why he had come, the inhabitants of Lumumba Hall might turn on him angrily. He was the only white person there.

The alterations in the common room were drastic. Gone were the wide moldings of dark wood, the thick oak window seats beneath the huge cathedral windows, the solid, heavy furniture with the dark red leather. Instead, the room was transformed into something else entirely. The arched windows were no longer. They were now squared at the top, bordered by jet-black dowels an inch or two in diameter, which looked like long, rectangular slits. Spreading out from the windows into the walls was a textured pattern of tiny wooden bamboo strips shellacked to a high polish. This same wall covering was duplicated on the ceiling, thousands of highly glossed reeds converging towards the center. In the middle of the ceiling was a large circle, perhaps three feet in width, in which there was placed a thick pane of rippled glass. Beyond the glass shone a bright yellowish white light, its flood diffused in ripples over the room. What furniture he could see through the mass of bodies was not really furniture at all. There were various low-cut slabs of thick wood in differing shapes on short legs—these Matlock assumed were tables. Instead of chairs, there were dozens of pillows in vibrant colors scattered about the edge of the walls.

It didn't take Matlock long to realize the effect.

Alpha Delta Phi's common room had been transformed brilliantly into the replica of a large thatched African hut. Even to the point of the blazing equatorial sun streaming through the enclosure's vent to the skies.

"This is remarkable! Really remarkable. It must have taken months."

"Almost a year and a half," Johnny said. "It's very comfortable, very relaxing. Did you know that lots of top designers are going in for this sort of thing now? I mean the back-to-nature look. It's very functional and easy to maintain."

"That sounds dangerously like an apology. You don't have to apologize. It's terrific."

"Oh, I'm *not* apologizing." Johnny retreated from his explanation. "Adam says there's a certain majesty in the primitive. A very proud heritage."

"Adam's right. Only he's not the first person to make that observation."

"Please don't put us down, Mr. Matlock. . . ."

Matlock looked at Johnny over the rim of his cup of Swahili punch. Oh, Christ, he thought, the more things change, the more they remain the same.

The high-ceilinged chapter room of Alpha Delta Phi had been carved out of the cellars at the farthest end of the fraternity house. It had been built shortly after the turn of the century when impressive alumni had poured impressive sums into such hobbies as secret societies and debutante cotillions. Such activities promulgated and propagandized a way of life, yet assuredly kept it selective.

Thousands of starched young men had been initiated in this chapel-like enclosure, whispering the secret pledges, exchanging the unfamiliar handshakes explained to them by stern-faced older children, vowing till death to keep the selected faith. And afterward, getting drunk and vomiting in corners.

Matlock thought these thoughts as he watched the Mau Mau ritual unfold before him. It was no less childish, no less absurd than the preceding scenes in this room, he considered. Perhaps the physical aspects—the simulated physical aspects—were more brutal in what they conveyed, but then the roots of the ceremony were not based in the delicate steps of a cotillion's pavanne but, instead, in harsh, animal-like pleas to primitive gods. Pleas for strength and survival. Not supplications for continued exclusivity.

The tribal rite itself was a series of unintelligible chants, each one growing in intensity, over the body of a black student—obviously the youngest brother in Lumumba Hall—stretched out on the concrete floor, naked except for a red loincloth strapped around his waist and legs, covering his genitals. At the finish of each chant, signifying the end of one canto and the commencement of the succeeding song, the boy's body was raised above the crowd by four extremely tall students, themselves naked to the waist, wearing jet-black dance belts, their legs encased in spirals of rawhide strips. The room was lighted by dozens of thick candles mounted on stands, causing shadows to dance across the upper walls and the ceiling. Adding to this theatrical effect was the fact that the five active participants in the ritual had their skins covered with oil, their faces streaked in diabolical patterns. As the singing grew wilder, the young boy's rigid body was thrown higher and higher until it left the hands of its four supporters, returning split seconds later into the outstretched arms. Each time the black body with the red loincloth was flung into the air, the crowd responded with growing volumes of guttural shouts.

And then Matlock, who had been watching with a degree of detachment, suddenly found himself frightened. Frightened for the small Negro whose stiff, oiled body was being flung into air with such abandon. For two additional blacks, dressed like the others, had joined the four in the center of the floor. However, instead of helping toss the now soaring figure, the two blacks crouched between the rectangular foursome—beneath the body—and withdrew long-bladed knives, one in each hand. Once in their squatting positions, they stretched out their arms so that the blades were held upright, as rigid, as stiff as the body above them. Each time the small Negro descended, the four blades inched closer to the falling flesh. One slip, one oily miscalculation on the part of just one of the four blacks, and the ritual would end in death for the small student. In murder.

Matlock, feeling that the ritual had gone as far as he could allow, began scanning the crowd for Adam Williams. He saw him in front, on the edge of the circle, and started pushing his way toward him. He was stopped—quietly but firmly—by the blacks around him. He looked angrily at a Negro who held his arm. The black didn't acknowledge his stare; he was hypnotized by the action now taking place in the center of the room.

Matlock saw why instantly. For the body of the small boy was now being *spun*, alternately face up and face down with each elevation. The danger of error was increased tenfold. Matlock grabbed the hand on his arm, twisted it inward, and flung it off him. He looked once more in the direction of Adam Williams.

He wasn't there. He was nowhere in sight! Matlock stood still, undecided. If he raised his voice between the crowd's roaring crescendos, it was entirely possible that he might cause a break in the concentration of those handling the body. He couldn't risk that, and yet he couldn't allow the dangerous absurdity to continue.

Suddenly Matlock felt another hand, this one on his shoulder. He turned and saw the face of Adam Williams behind him. It startled him. Had some primitive tribal signal been transmitted to Williams? The black radical gestured with his head for Matlock to follow him through the shouting crowd to the outer edge of the circle. Williams spoke between the roars.

"You look worried. Don't be."

"Look! This crap's gone far enough! That kid could be killed!"

"No chance. The brothers have rehearsed for months. . . . It's really the most simplistic of the Mau Mau rites. The symbolism is fundamental. . . . See? The child's eyes remain open. First to the sky, then facing the blades. He is constantly aware—every second—that his life is in the hands of his brother warriors. He cannot, he *must* not show fear. To do so would betray his peers. Betray the confidence he must place in their hands—as they will someday place their lives in *his* hands."

"It's childish, *dangerous stupidity*, and you *know* it!" cut in Matlock. "Now, I'm telling you, Williams, you put a stop to it or *I* will!"

"Of course," continued the black radical, as if Matlock had not spoken, "there are anthropologists who insist that the ceremony is essentially one of fertility. The unsheathed knives representing erections, the four protectors guarding the child through its formative years. Frankly, I think that's reaching. Also, it strikes me as contradictory even for the primitive mind. . . ."

"Goddamn you!" Matlock grabbed Williams by the front of his shirt. Immediately other blacks closed in on him.

Suddenly there was total silence in the eerily lit room. The silence lasted only a moment. It was followed by a series of mind-shattering screams from the mouths of the four Negroes in the center of the crowd in whose hands the life of the young student depended. Matlock whipped around and saw the shining black body descending downward from an incredible height above the outstretched hands.

It couldn't be true! It wasn't happening! Yet it was!

The four blacks suddenly, in unison, crouched into kneeling positions *away* from the center, their arms slashed to their sides. The young student came crashing down, *face toward the blades*. Two further screams followed. In a fraction of a second, the students holding the huge knives swung their weapons across one another and in an unbelievable display of wrist strength, *caught* the body on the flat of the blades.

The crowd of blacks went wild.

The ceremony was over.

"Do you believe me now?" Williams asked, speaking in a corner with Matlock.

"Whether I do or not doesn't change what I said. You can't *do* this sort of thing! It's too goddamn dangerous!"

"You exaggerate. . . . Here, let me introduce another guest." Williams raised his hand and a tall thin black with close-cropped hair and glasses, dressed in an expensively cut tan suit, joined them. "This is Julian Dunois, Mr. Matlock. Brother Julian is our expert. Our choreographer, if you like."

"A pleasure." Dunois extended his hand, speaking with a slight accent.

"Brother Julian is from Haiti. . . . Harvard Law out of Haiti. A most unusual progression, I think you'll agree."

"It certainly is. . . ."

"Many Haitians, even the Ton Ton Macoute, still get upset when they hear his name."

"You exaggerate, Adam," said Julian Dunois with a smile.

"That's what I just said to Mr. Matlock. *He* exaggerates. About the danger of the ceremony."

"Oh, there's danger—as there's danger if one crosses the Boston Commons wearing a blindfold. The petcock of safety, Mr. Matlock, is that those holding the knives watch closely. In the training there is as much emphasis on being able to drop the knives instantly as there is in holding them up."

"That may be so," Matlock acknowledged. "But the margin for error terrifies me."

"It's not as narrow as you think." The lilt in the Haitian's voice was as reassuring as it was attractive. "Incidentally, I'm a fan of yours. I've enjoyed your works on the Elizabethans. May I add, you're not exactly what I expected. I mean, you're far, far younger."

"You flatter me. I didn't think I was known in law schools."

"My undergraduate major was English literature."

Adam interrupted politely. "You two enjoy yourselves. There'll be drinks upstairs in a few minutes; just follow the crowd. I've got things to do. . . . I'm glad you've met. You're both strangers, in a way. Strangers should meet in unfamiliar areas. It's comforting."

He gave Dunois an enigmatic look and walked rapidly away through the crowd.

"Why does Adam feel he has to talk in what I'm sure he considers are profound riddles?" Matlock asked.

"He's very young. He strives constantly to make emphasis. Very bright, but very young."

"You'll pardon me, but you're not exactly ancient. I doubt more than a year or two older than Adam."

The black in the expensively cut tan suit looked into Matlock's eyes and laughed gently.

"Now you flatter *me*," he said. "If the truth were known—and why shouldn't it be?—and if my tropic color did not disguise the years so well, you'd know that I was precisely one year, four months, and sixteen days *older* than *you*."

Matlock stared at the Negro, speechless. It took him nearly a full minute to assimilate the lawyer's words and the meaning behind those words. The black's eyes did not waver. He returned Matlock's stare in equal measure. Finally, Matlock found his voice.

"I'm not sure I like this game."

"Oh, come, we're both here for the same reason, are we not? You from your vantage point, I from mine. . . . Let's go upstairs and have a drink. . . . Bourbon and soda, isn't it? Sour mash, if it's available, I understand."

Dunois preceded Matlock through the crowd, and Matlock had no other course but to follow.

Dunois leaned against the brick wall.

"All right," Matlock said, "the amenities are over. Everyone's acknowledged your show downstairs, and there's no one left for me to impress my white skin on. I think it's time you started explaining."

They were alone now, outside on the porch. Both held drinks.

"My, aren't we professional? Would you care for a cigar? I can assure you it's Havana."

"No cigar. Just talk. I came here tonight because these are my friends. I felt privileged to be invited. . . . Now, you've attached something else and I don't like it."

"Bravo! Bravo!" said Dunois, raising his glass. "You do that very well. . . . Don't worry, they know nothing. Perhaps they suspect, but believe me, only in the vaguest terms."

"What the hell are you talking about?"

"Finish your drink and let's walk out on the lawn." Dunois drained his rum and, as if by reflex, Matlock drank the remainder of his bourbon. The two men walked down the steps of the Lumumba Hall, Matlock following the black to the base of a large elm tree. Dunois turned suddenly and grabbed Matlock by the shoulders.

"Take your goddamn hands off me!"

"Listen to me! I want that paper! I *must have* that paper! And you must tell me *where it is!*"

Matlock flung his hands up to break Dunois's grip. But his arms did not respond. They were suddenly heavy, terribly heavy. And there was a whistling. A growing, piercing whistling in his head.

"What? What? . . . What paper? I don't have any paper. . ."

"Don't be difficult! We'll get it, you know! . . . Now, just tell me where it is!"

Matlock realized that he was being lowered to the ground. The outline of the huge tree above him began to spin, and the whistling in his brain became louder and louder. It was unendurable. He fought to find his mind again.

"What are you doing? What are you doing to me!?"

"The paper, Matlock! Where is the Corsican *paper*?"

"Get *off* me!" Matlock tried to yell. But nothing came from his lips.

"The silver paper, goddamn you to hell!"

"No paper . . . no. Haven't paper! No!"

"Listen to me! You just had a drink, remember the drink? . . . You just finished that drink. Remember? . . . You can't be alone now! You don't *dare* be alone!"

"What? . . . What? Get off me! You're crushing me!"

"I'm not even *touching* you. The drink is! You just consumed three tabs of *lysergic acid!* You're in trouble, Doctor! . . . *Now! You tell me where that paper is!*"

From the inner recesses he found an instant of clarity. From the spinning, turning, whirling spirals of mind-blasting colors, he saw the form of the man above him and he lashed out. He grabbed at the white shirt between the dark borders of the jacket and pulled it down with all the strength he could summon. He brought his fist up and hit the descending face as hard as he could. Once the face was jarred, he began hammering at the throat beneath it mercilessly. He could feel the shattering of the glasses and he knew his fist had found the eyes and crushed the glass into the rolling head.

It was over in a period of time he could never ascertain. Dunois's body was beside him, unconscious.

And he knew he had to run. Run furiously away! What had Dunois said? . . . Don't dare be alone. Don't *dare!* He had to find Pat! Pat would know what to do. He had to find her! The chemical in his body was going to take full effect soon and he knew it! Run, for Christ's sake!

But where?! Which way?! He didn't know *the way!* The *goddamn, fucking way!* The street was there, he raced along the street, but was it the *right way?!* Was it the *right street?!*

Then he heard a car. It *was* a car, and it was coming close to the curb and the driver was looking at him. Looking at him, so he ran faster, tripping once over the curb and falling into the pavement and rising again. Running, for Christ Almighty's sake, running till the breath in his lungs was gone and he could no longer control the movement of his feet. He felt himself swerve, unable to stop himself, toward the wide, gulf of the street, which suddenly became a river, a black putrid river in which he would drown.

He vaguely heard the screech of the brakes. The lights blinded him, and the figure of a man reached down and poked at his eyes. He didn't care any longer. Instead, he laughed. Laughed through the blood which flowed into his mouth and over his face.

He laughed hysterically as Jason Greenberg carried him to the car.

And then the earth, the world, the planet, the galaxy, and the entire solar system went crazy.

Chapter Ten

The night was agony.

The morning brought a degree of reality, less so for Matlock than for the two people sitting beside him, one on either side of the bed. Jason Greenberg, his large, sad eyes drooping, his hands calmly crossed on his lap, leaned forward. Patricia Ballantyne, her arm stretched out, held a cool washcloth on Matlock's forehead.

"The schvugs gave you one hell of a party, friend."

"Shh!" whispered the girl. "Leave him alone."

Matlock's eyes wandered as best they could around the room. He was in

Pat's apartment, in her bedroom, her bed.

"They gave me acid."

"You're telling *us* . . . We had a doctor—a real doctor—brought in from Litchfield. He's the nice fella you kept trying to take the eyeballs from. . . . Don't worry, he's federal. No names."

"Pat? How come . . ."

"You're a very sweet acid head, Jamie. You kept yelling my name."

"It also made the best sense," interrupted Greenberg. "No hospitals. No out-patient records. Nice and private; good thinking. Also, you're very persuasive when you're violent. You're a hell of a lot stronger than I thought. Especially for such a lousy handball player."

"You shouldn't have brought me here. Goddamn it, Greenberg, you shouldn't have *brought* me here!"

"Forgetting for the moment that it was your idea . . ."

"I was drugged!"

"It was a *good* idea. What would you have preferred? The emergency clinic? . . . 'Who's that on the stretcher, Doctor? The one screaming.' . . . 'Oh, just Associate Professor Matlock, Nurse. He's on an acid trip.'"

"You know what I mean! You could have taken me home. Strapped me down."

"I'm relieved to see you don't know much about acid," said Greenberg.

"What he means, Jamie . . .," Pat took his hand, ". . . if it's bad, you should be with someone you know awfully well. The reassurance is necessary."

Matlock looked at the girl. And then at Greenberg. "What have you told her?"

"That you volunteered to help us; that we're grateful. With your help we may be able to prevent a serious situation from getting worse." Greenberg spoke in a monotone; it was obvious that he didn't wish to expand.

"It was a very cryptic explanation," Pat said. "He wouldn't have given me that if I hadn't threatened him."

"She was going to call the police." Greenberg sighed, his sad eyes sadder. "She was going to have me locked up for dosing you. I had no choice."

Matlock smiled.

"Why are you doing this, Jamie?" Pat found nothing amusing.

"The man said it: the situation's serious."

"But why *you*?"

"Because I can."

"What? Turn in kids?"

"I told you," said Jason. "We're not interested in students. . . ."

"What's Lumumba Hall, then? A branch of General Motors?"

"It's one contact point; there are others. Frankly, we'd rather *not* have gotten involved with that crowd; it's ticklish. Unfortunately, we can't choose."

"That's offensive."

"I don't think there's much I could say that wouldn't be offensive to you, Miss Ballantyne."

"Perhaps not. Because I thought the FBI had more important work to do than harassing young blacks. Obviously, you don't."

"Hey, come on." Matlock squeezed the girl's hand. She took it from him.

"No, I mean that, Jamie! No games, no radical chic. There are drugs all over this place. Some of it's a bad scene, most of it's pretty standard. We *both* know that. Why all of a sudden are the kids at Lumumba singled out?"

"We wouldn't *touch* those kids. Except to help them." Greenberg was weary from the long night. His irritation showed.

"I don't like the way you people help people and I don't like what happened to Jamie! Why did you send him there?"

"He didn't *send* me. I maneuvered that myself."

"Why?"

"It's too complicated and I'm too washed out to explain it."

"Oh, Mr. Greenberg did that. He explained all right. They've given you a badge, haven't they? They can't do it themselves so they pick a nice, easygoing fellow to do it for them. You take all the risks; and when it's over, you'll never be trusted on this campus again. Jamie, for God's sake, this is your *home*, your *work!*"

Matlock held the girl's eyes with his own, doing his best to calm her. "I know that better than you do. My home needs to be helped—and that's no game either, Pat. I think the risks are worth it."

"I won't pretend to understand that."

"You can't understand it, Miss Ballantyne, because we can't tell you enough to make it reasonable. You'll have to accept that."

"Do I?"

"I'm asking you to," said Matlock. "He saved my life."

"I wouldn't go that far, Professor." Greenberg shrugged as he spoke.

Pat stood up. "I think he threw you overboard and tossed you a rope as an afterthought. . . . Are you all right?"

"Yes," answered Matlock.

"I have to go; I won't if you don't want me to."

"No, you go ahead. I'll call you later. Thanks for the ministrations."

The girl looked briefly at Greenberg—it was not a pleasant look—and crossed to her dresser. She picked up a brush and rapidly stroked her hair, slipping an orange headband into place. She watched Greenberg through the mirror. He returned the stare.

"The man who's been following me, Mr. Greenberg. Is he one of your men?"

"Yes."

"I don't like it."

"I'm sorry."

Pat turned. "Will you remove him, please?"

"I can't do that. I'll tell him to be less obvious."

"I see." She took her purse from the dresser top and reached down to the floor, picking up her accordion briefcase. Without speaking further, the girl walked out of the bedroom. Several seconds later, the two men could hear the apartment door open and shut firmly.

"That is one very strong-willed young lady," said Jason.

"There's a good reason."

"What do you mean?"

"I thought you fellows were so familiar with the people you had to deal with. . . ."

"I'm still getting briefed. I'm the back-up, remember?"

"Then I'll save you time. In the late fifties her father got McCarthyized out of the State Department. Of course, he was very dangerous. He was a language consultant. He was cleared for translating newspapers."

"Shit."

"That's the word, brother. He never made it back. She's had scholarships all her life; the cupboard's bare. She's a little sensitive to your type."

"Boy, do you pick 'em!"

"You picked *me*, remember?"

Matlock opened the door to his apartment and walked into the foyer. Pat had done a good job putting the rooms in order—as he knew she would. Even the curtains were rehung. It was a little after three—most of the day wasted. Greenberg had insisted that the two of them drive over to Litchfield for a reexamination by the doctor. Shaken but operable, was the verdict.

They stopped for lunch at the Cheshire Cat. During the meal, Matlock kept looking over at the small table where four days ago Ralph Loring had sat with his folded newspaper. The lunch was quiet. Not strained—the two men were comfortable in each other's company—but quiet, as if each had too much to think about.

On the road back to Carlyle, Greenberg told him to stay in his apartment until he contacted him. Washington hadn't issued any new instructions. They were evaluating the new information, and until they confirmed any further involvement, Matlock was to remain "OOS"—a term the English professor found hard to equate with grownups: *out of strategy*.

It was just as well, he thought. He had his own strategy to think about—Lucas Herron. The "grand old bird," the campus elder statesman. It was time to reach him, to warn him. The old man was out of his element, and the quicker he retreated, the better for everyone—Carlyle included. Yet he didn't want to telephone him, he didn't want to arrange a formal meeting—he had to be subtler than that. He didn't want to alarm old Lucas, have him talking to the wrong people.

It occurred to Matlock that he was acting as some sort of protector for Herron. That presumed Lucas was innocent of any serious involvement. He wondered if he had the right to make that assumption. On the other hand, by civilized standards, he had no right to make any other.

The telephone rang. It couldn't be Greenberg, he thought. He'd just left him at the curb. He hoped it wasn't Pat; he wasn't ready to talk to her yet. Reluctantly he lifted the instrument to his ear. "Hello!"

"Jim! Where have you *been*!? I've been calling since eight this morning! I was so goddamn worried I went over there twice. Got your key from maintenance." It was Sam Kressel. He sounded as though Carlyle had lost its accreditation.

"It's too involved to go into now, Sam. Let's get together later. I'll come over to your place after dinner."

"I don't know if it can wait that long. Jesus! What the hell got *into* you?"

"I don't understand."

"At Lumumba last night!"

"What are you talking about? What have you heard?"

"That black bastard, Adam Williams, handed in a report to my office accusing you of just about everything short of advocating slavery! He claims the only reason he's not filing police charges is that you were blind drunk! Of course, the alcohol stripped you of your pretenses and showed clearly what a racist you are!"

"What?"

"You broke up furniture, slapped around some kids, smashed windows. . . ."

"You know damned well that's bullshit!"

"I figured as much." Kressel lowered his voice. He was calming down. "But my knowing it doesn't help, can't you see that? This is the kind of thing we've got to *avoid*. Polarization! The government walks onto a campus, polarization follows."

"Listen to me. Williams' statement is a decoy—if that's the word. It's camouflage. They drugged me last night. If it hadn't been for Greenberg, I don't know where I'd be right now."

"Oh, God! . . . Lumumba's on your list, isn't it? That's all we *need!* The blacks'll scream persecution. Christ knows what'll happen."

Matlock tried to speak calmly. "I'll come over around seven. Don't do anything, don't say anything. I've got to get off the phone. Greenberg's supposed to call."

"Wait a minute, Jim! One thing. This Greenberg . . . I don't trust him. I don't trust any of them. Just remember. Your loyalty's to Carlyle. . . ." Kressel stopped, but he had not finished. Matlock realized he was at a loss for words.

"That's a strange thing to say."

"I think you know what I mean."

"I'm not sure I do. I thought the idea was to work together. . . ."

"*Not at the expense of ripping this campus apart!*" The dean of colleges sounded nearly hysterical.

"Don't worry," Matlock said. "It won't tear. I'll see you later." Matlock hung up the phone before Kressel could speak again. His mind needed a short rest, and Kressel never let anyone rest where his domain was concerned. Sam Kressel, in his own way, was as militant as any extremist, and, perhaps, quicker to cry "foul."

These thoughts led Matlock to another consideration—two considerations. Four days ago, he had told Pat that he didn't want to change their plans for St. Thomas. Carlyle's midterm holiday, a short ten days at the end of April, would start after classes on Saturday, in three days. Under the circumstances, St. Thomas was out—unless Washington decided to retire him, and he doubted that. He'd use his parents as the excuse. Pat would understand, even be sympathetic. The other thought was his own classes. He had fallen behind. His desk was piled with papers—mostly themes and essay exams. He had also missed his two classes earlier in the day. He was not so much concerned for his students—his method was to accelerate in the fall and winter and relax in the spring—but he didn't want to add any fuel to such fires as Williams' false complaint. An absentee associate professor was a target for gossip. His class load for the next three days was medium—three, two, and two. He'd organize the work later. Between now and seven o'clock, however, he had to find Lucas Herron. If Greenberg called while he was out, he'd blame it on a forgotten graduate conference.

He decided to shower, shave, and change clothes. Once in the bathroom, he checked the litter box. The Corsican paper was there—he knew it would be.

The shave and shower completed, Matlock walked into his bedroom, selecting clothes and a course of action. He didn't know Herron's daily schedule, although it would be a simple matter to find out if Lucas had any late afternoon classes or seminars. If he didn't, Matlock knew Herron's house; it would take about fifteen minutes to get there by car. Herron lived eight miles from the campus, on a rarely traveled back road in a section once a part of the old Carlyle family estate. Herron's home had been a carriage house. It was out of the way, but as Lucas kept saying, "Once there, it's worth it."

The rapid tapping of the door knocker broke his concentration. It also frightened him—he felt himself gasping for breath; that was disturbing.

"Be right there," he yelled, slipping a white sport shirt over his head. He walked barefoot to the front door and opened it. It was impossible for him to conceal his shock. In the doorframe stood Adam Williams—alone.

"Afternoon."

"Jesus! . . . I don't know whether to hit you in the mouth right now or first call the police! What the hell do you want? Kressel's already called me, if that's what you're checking on."

"Please let me talk to you. I'll be quick." The black spoke with urgency, trying, thought Matlock, to conceal his fear.

"Come on in. And *make* it quick." Matlock slammed the door as Williams passed by him into the foyer. The black turned and tried to smile, but there was no humor in his eyes.

"I'm sorry about that report. Truly sorry. It was an unpleasant necessity."

"I don't buy that and you can't sell it! What did you want Kressel to do? Bring me up before the board and burn me out of here? Did you think I'd just sit down and play doormat? You're a goddamn maniac!"

"We didn't think *anything* would happen. That's precisely why we did it. . . . We couldn't be sure where you went. You disappeared, you know. You might say we had to take the offensive and then later agree that it was all a disagreeable misunderstanding. . . . It's not a new tactic. I'll send Kressel another report, backing off—but not entirely. In a couple of weeks, it'll be forgotten."

Matlock raged, as much against Williams' attitude as his conscienceless pragmatism. But when he spoke he did not raise his voice. "Get out. You disgust me."

"Oh, come off it, man! Haven't we *always disgusted* you?!" Matlock had hit a nerve and Williams responded in kind. But just as suddenly, he took hold of himself. "Let's not argue theoretical practicalities. Let me get to the point and leave."

"By all means."

"All right. Listen to me. Whatever Dunois wanted from you, *give* it to him! . . . That is, give it to me and I'll send it on. No forked tongue; it's last-extremity language!"

"Too pat a phrase. No sale. Why would I have anything Brother Julian wanted? Did he say so? Why doesn't he come over himself?"

"Brother Julian doesn't stay long in any one place. His talents are in great demand."

"Staging Mau Mau puberty rituals?"

"He really does that, you know. It's a hobby."

"Send him to me." Matlock crossed in front of Williams and went to the coffee table. He reached down and picked up a half-empty pack of cigarettes. "We'll compare notes on associative body movements. I've a hell of a collection of sixteenth-century folk dances."

"Talk seriously. There's no *time!*"

Matlock lit a cigarette. "I've got all the time in the world. I just want to see Brother Julian again; I want to put him in jail."

"No chance! No chance. I'm here for *your* benefit! If I leave without it, I can't *control* it!"

"Two pronouns signifying the same or different objects?"

"Oh, you're too much! You're really too much! Do you know who Julian Dunois *is*?"

"Part of the Borgia family? Ethiopian branch?"

"*Stop it, Matlock!* Do what he says! People could be hurt. Nobody wants that."

"I *don't* know who Dunois is and I don't much give a damn. I just know he drugged me and assaulted me and is exercising a dangerous influence on a bunch of children. Beyond this, I suspect he had my apartment broken into and many of my personal belongings destroyed. I want him put away. From you *and* from me."

"Be reasonable, *please*!"

Matlock walked swiftly to the curtains in front of his casement window and with a flourish, yanked them down, displaying the shattered glass and twisted lead.

"Is this one of Brother Julian's calling cards?"

Adam Williams stared, obviously shocked, at the mass of destruction. "No, man. Absolutely, no. That's not Julian's style. . . . That's not even my style. That's someone else."

Chapter Eleven

The road to Lucas Herron's house was dotted with the potholes of winter. Matlock doubted that the town of Carlyle would fill them in; there were too many other commercially traveled streets still showing the effects of the New England freeze. As he approached the old carriage house, he slowed his Triumph to barely ten miles an hour. The bumps were jarring, and he wanted to reach Herron's house with little noise.

Thinking that Jason Greenberg might have had him followed, Matlock took the long route to Herron's, driving four miles north on a parallel road and then doubling back on Herron's street. There was no one behind him. The nearest houses to Herron's were a hundred yards away on either side, none in front. There'd been talk of turning the area into a housing development just as there'd been talk of enlarging Carlyle University, but nothing came of either project. Actually, the first depended upon the second, and there was strong alumni opposition to any substantial physical change at Carlyle. The alumni were Adrian Sealfont's personal cross.

Matlock was struck by the serenity of Herron's home. He'd never really looked at the house before. A dozen times, more or less, he'd driven Lucas home after faculty meetings, but he'd always been in a hurry. He'd never accepted Lucas's invitations for a drink and, as a result, he had never been inside the house.

He got out of the car and approached the old brick structure. It was tall and narrow; the faded stone covered with thousands of strands of ivy heightened the feeling of isolation. In front, on the large expanse of lawn, were two Japanese willow trees in full spring bloom, their purple flowers cascading toward the earth in large arcs. The grass was cut, the shrubbery pruned, and the white gravel on the various paths was gleaming. It was a house and grounds which were loved and cared for, yet one had the feeling that they were not shared. It was the work of and for one person, not two or a family. And then Matlock remembered that Lucas Herron had never married. There were the inevitable stories of a lost love, a tragic death, even a runaway bride-to-be, but whenever Lucas Herron heard about such youthful romanticizing he countered with a chuckle and a statement about being "too damned selfish."

Matlock walked up the short steps to the door and rang the bell. He tried practicing an opening smile, but it was false; he wouldn't be able to carry it off. He was afraid.

The door swung back and the tall, white-haired Lucas Herron, dressed in wrinkled trousers and a half-unbuttoned, oxford-blue shirt, stared at him.

It was less than a second before Herron spoke, but in that brief instant, Matlock knew that he'd been wrong. Lucas Herron knew why he had come.

"Well, Jim! Come in, come in, my boy. A pleasant surprise."

"Thank you, Lucas. I hope I'm not interrupting anything."

"Not a thing. You're just in time, as a matter of fact. I'm dabbling in alchemy. A fresh fruit gin Collins. Now I won't have to dabble alone."

"Sounds good to me."

The inside of Herron's house was precisely as Matlock thought it would be—as his own might be in thirty-odd years, if he lived that long alone. It was a mixed bag, an accumulated total of nearly half a century of unrelated gatherings from a hundred unrelated sources. The only common theme was comfort; there was no concern for style or period or coordination. Several walls were lined with books, and those which were not were filled with enlarged photographs of places visited abroad—one suspected during sabbaticals. The armchairs were thick and soft, the tables within arm's reach—the sign of practiced bachelorhood, thought Matlock.

"I don't think you've ever been here—inside, I mean."

"No, I haven't. It's very attractive. Very comfortable."

"Yes, it's that. It's comfortable. Here, sit down, I'll finish the formula and bring us a drink." Herron started across the living room toward what Matlock presumed was the door to the kitchen and then stopped and turned. "I know perfectly well that you haven't come all the way out here to liven up an old man's cocktail hour. However, I have a house rule: at least one drink—religion and strong principles permitting—before any serious discussion." He smiled and the myriad lines around his eyes and temples became more pronounced. He was an *old*, old man. "Besides, you look terribly serious. The Collins'll lessen the degree, I promise you."

Before Matlock could answer, Herron walked rapidly through the door. Instead of sitting, Matlock walked to the wall nearest him, against which was a small writing desk, above it a half-dozen photographs that hung in no discernible pattern. Several were of Stonehenge taken from the same position, the setting sun at dramatically different angles. Another was of a rock-bound coast, mountains in the distance, fishing boats moored offshore. It looked Mediterranean, possibly Greece or the Thracian Islands. Then there was a surprise. On the lower right side of the wall, only inches above the desk, was a small photograph of a tall, slender army officer standing by the trunk of a tree. Behind him the foliage was profuse, junglelike; to the sides were the shadows of other figures. The officer was helmetless, his shirt drenched with sweat, his large right hand holding the stock of a submachine gun. In his left hand the officer held a folded piece of paper—it looked like a map—and the man had obviously just made a decision. He was looking upward, as though toward some high terrain. The face was taut but not excited. It was a good face, a strong face. It was a dark-haired, middle-aged Lucas Herron.

"I keep that old photograph to remind me that time was not always so devastating."

Matlock snapped up, startled. Lucas had reentered and had taken him off guard. "It's a good picture. Now I know who really won that war."

"No doubt about it. Unfortunately, I never heard of that particular island either before or since. Someone said it was one of the Solomons. I think they blew it up in the fifties. Wouldn't take much. Couple of fire crackers'd do it. Here." Herron crossed to Matlock, handing him his drink.

"Thanks. You're too modest. I've heard the stories."

"So have I. Impressed the hell out of me. They grow better as I grow older. . . . What do you say we sit in the back yard. Too nice to stay indoors." Without waiting for a reply, Herron started out and Matlock followed.

Like the front of the house, the back was precisely manicured. On a flagstone patio, there were comfortable-looking, rubber-stranded beach chairs, each with a small table by its side. A large wrought-iron table with a sun umbrella was centered in the middle of the flagstones. Beyond, the lawn was close cropped and full. Dogwood trees were dotted about, each spaded around its trunk, and two lines of flowers—mostly roses—stretched lengthwise to the end of the lawn, about a hundred feet away. At the end of the lawn, however, the pastoral effect abruptly stopped. Suddenly there were huge trees, the underbrush thick, mangled, growing within itself. The side borders were the same. Around the perimeters of the sculptured back lawn was an undisciplined, overgrown forest.

Lucas Herron was surrounded by a forbidding green wall.

"It *is* a good drink, you'll admit." The two men were seated.

"It certainly is. You'll convert me to gin."

"Only in spring and summer. Gin's not for the rest of the year. . . . All right, young fellow, the house rule's been observed. What brings you to Herron's Nest?"

"I think you have an idea."

"Do I?"

"Archie Beeson." Matlock watched the old man, but Herron's concentration was on his glass. He showed no reaction.

"The young history man?"

"Yes."

"He'll make a fine teacher one day. Nice little filly of a wife, too."

"Nice . . . and promiscuous, I think."

"*Appearances*, Jim." Herron chuckled. "Never thought of you as Victorian. . . . One grows infinitely more tolerant of the appetites as one gets older. And the innocent whetting of them. You'll see."

"Is that the key? The tolerance of appetites?"

"Key to what?"

"Come on. He wanted to reach you the other night."

"Yes, he did. And you were there. . . . I understand your behavior left something to be desired."

"My behavior was calculated to leave that impression." For the first time

Herron betrayed a trace of concern. It was a small reaction, the blinking of his eyes in rapid succession.

"That was reprehensible." Herron spoke softly and looked up at his imposing green wall. The sun was going below the line of tall trees; long shadows were cast across the lawn and patio.

"It was necessary." Matlock saw the old man's face wince in pain. And then he recalled his own reaction to Adam Williams' description of the "unpleasant necessity" of sending Sam Kressel the false report of his actions at Lumumba Hall. The parallel hurt.

"The boy's in trouble. He's sick. It's a disease and he's trying to cure himself. That takes courage. . . . This is no time for campus Gestapo tactics." Herron took a long drink from his glass while his free hand gripped the arm of the chair.

"How did you know about it?"

"That might be privileged information. Let's say I heard from a respected co-worker of ours—in the medical line—who ran across the symptoms and became concerned. What difference does it make? I tried to help the boy and I'd do it again."

"I'd like to believe that. It's what I wanted to believe."

"Why is that difficult for you?"

"I don't know. . . . Something at the front door a few minutes ago. Perhaps this house. I can't put my finger on it. . . . I'm being completely honest with you."

Herron laughed but still avoided Matlock's eyes. "You're too wound up in the Elizabethans. The plots and counterplots of *The Spanish Tragedy*. . . . You young faculty crusaders should stop trying to be an amateur Scotland Yard. Not too long ago it was fashionable around here to have Red Dogs for breakfast. You're just magnifying the situation out of proportion."

"That's not true. I'm not a faculty crusader. I'm no part of that crowd, and I think you know it."

"What was it then? Personal interest? In the boy. Or his wife? . . . I'm sorry, I shouldn't have said that."

"I'm glad you did. I have no interest in Virginia Beeson—sexual or otherwise. Although I can't imagine what else there would be."

"Then you put on quite an act."

"I certainly did. I took extreme measures to keep Beeson from knowing why I was there. It was that important."

"To whom?" Herron slowly put his glass down with his right hand, his left still gripped the arm of the chair.

"To people beyond this campus. Washington people. The federal authorities . . ."

Lucas Herron took a sudden, sustained intake of breath through his nostrils. In front of Matlock's eyes, Herron's face began to drain itself of color. When he spoke, he did so barely above a whisper.

"What are you saying?"

"That I was approached by a man from the Justice Department. The information he showed me was frightening. Nothing was trumped up, nothing overdramatized. It was straight data. I was given a free choice whether to cooperate or not."

"And you accepted?" Herron's words were uttered softly in disbelief.

"I didn't feel there was an alternative. My younger brother . . ."

"You didn't feel there was an *alternative?*" Herron rose from his chair, his hands began to shake, his voice grew in intensity. "You didn't *feel* there was an *alternative?!*"

"No, I didn't," Matlock remained calm. "That's why I came out here. To warn you, old friend. It's much deeper—far more dangerous . . ."

"*You* came out here to warn *me?!* What have you *done?* What in the name of everything sacred *have you done?* . . . Now, you listen to me! You listen to what I say!" Herron backed off, bumping into the small side table. In one whip of his left arm, he sent it crashing onto the flagstones. "You let it *go*, do you hear me! You go back and tell them *nothing! Nothing exists!* It's all . . . all in their imaginations! *Don't touch it! Let it go!*"

"I can't do that," said Matlock gently, suddenly afraid for the old man. "Even Sealfont will have to agree. He can't fight it any longer. It's there, Lucas. . . ."

"Adrian! Adrian's been told? . . . Oh, my God, do you know what you're doing? *You'll destroy so much.* So many, many . . . Get out of here! *Get out!* I don't know you! Oh, *Jesus! Jesus!*"

"Lucas, what is it?" Matlock got up and took several steps toward the old man. Herron continued backing away, an old man in panic.

"Don't come near me! Don't you *touch me!*"

Herron turned and started running as well as his ancient legs could carry him across the lawn. He stumbled, falling to the ground, and picked himself up. He didn't look back. Instead he ran with all his might toward the rear of the yard, toward the overgrown woods. And then he disappeared through his huge green wall.

"Lucas! For Christ's sake!" Matlock raced after the old man, reaching the edge of the woods only seconds behind him. Yet he was nowhere in sight. Matlock whipped at the overgrowth in front of him and stepped into the tangled mass of foliage. Branches slashed back at him, and the intricate webbings of giant weeds ensnared his feet as he kicked his way into the dense woods.

Herron was gone.

"Lucas! Where are you?"

There was no answer, only the rustling of the disturbed growth behind him. Matlock went farther into the forest, ducking, crouching, sidling by the green barriers in front of him. There was no sign of Lucas Herron, no sound.

"Lucas! For God's sake, Lucas, answer me!"

Still no reply, no hint of presence.

Matlock tried to look around him, tried to spot a break in the patterns of foliage, a route to follow. He could see none. It was as if Lucas were matter one moment, vapor the next.

And then he heard it. Indistinct, from all sides of him, echoing softly from some unknown place. It was a deep-throated moan, a wail. Near, yet far in the dense distance. And then the wail diminished and became a plaintive sob. A single sob, punctuated by a single word—clear, and spoken in hatred.

The word was—

"Nimrod . . ."

Chapter Twelve

"Goddamn it, Matlock! I told you to stay put until I contacted you!"

"Goddamn it, Greenberg! How did you get into my apartment?!"

"You didn't get your window fixed."

"You haven't offered to pay for it."

"We're even. Where have you been?"

Matlock threw his car keys on the coffee table and looked at his broken stereo set in the corner. "It's an involved story and I suspect . . . pathetic. I'll tell you all about it after I've had a drink. My last one was interrupted."

"Get me one, too. I've also got a story and mine's *definitely* pathetic."

"What do you drink?"

"Very little, so whatever you're having is fine."

Matlock looked out his front window. The curtains were strewn on the floor where he had torn them in front of Adam Williams. The sun was almost down now. The spring day was over. "I'm going to squeeze some lemons and have a fresh fruit Tom Collins."

"You file says you drink bourbon. Sour mash."

Matlock looked at the federal agent. "Does it?"

Greenberg followed Matlock into the kitchen and watched in silence as he fixed their drinks. Matlock handed the federal man his glass.

"Looks fancy."

"It's not. . . . Whose pathetic story gets first telling?"

"I'll want to hear yours, of course, but under the circumstances, mine has priority."

"You sound ominous."

"No. Just pathetic. . . . I'll start by asking you if you'd care to know where I've been since I dropped you off." Greenberg leaned against the counter.

"Not particularly, but you'll tell me anyway."

"Yes, I will. It's part of the pathos. I was out at your local airport—Bradley Field—waiting for a jet dispatched by Justice a few hours ago from Dulles. There was a man on the plane who brought me two sealed envelopes which I had to sign for. Here they are." Greenberg reached into his jacket pocket and took out two long business envelopes. He put one on the counter and began to open the second.

"They look very official," said Matlock, edging himself up so that he sat next to the sink, his long legs dangling over the side in front of the cabinets.

"They couldn't be more official. . . . This envelope contains the summary of our conclusions based on information you gave us—gave me. It ends with a specific recommendation. I'm allowed to convey this information in my own words as long as I cover all the facts. . . ."

"Jason Greenberg gets two points."

"However," continued the federal man without acknowledging Matlock's interruption, "the contents of the second envelope must be delivered verbatim. You are to read it thoroughly—*should it be necessary*—and if it's acceptable, you've got to acknowledge that by your signature."

"This gets better and better. Am I running for the Senate?"

"No, you're just running. . . . I'll start as instructed." Greenberg glanced at the unfolded paper and then looked across at Matlock. "The man at Lumumba Hall named Julian Dunois—alias Jacques Devereaux, Jésus Dambert, and probably several others we don't know about—is a legal strategist for the Black Left militants. The term *legal strategist* covers everything from court manipulations to agent provocateur. When involved with the former, he uses the name of Dunois, the latter—any number of aliases. He operates out of unusual places geographically. Algiers, Marseilles, the Caribbean—including Cuba—and, we suspect, Hanoi and probably Moscow. Perhaps even Peking. In the States he has a regular, bona fide law office in upper Harlem and a West Coast affiliate in San Francisco. . . . He's generally in the background, but wherever he's in evidence, bad news usually follows. Needless to say, he's on the attorney general's list of undesirables, and these days that's not respectable any longer. . . ."

"These days," broke in Matlock, "that includes almost everyone to the left of AT & T."

"No comment. To continue. The surfacing of Dunois in this operation adds a dimension not anticipated—a new aspect not considered before. It goes beyond domestic lawbreakers and enters the area of international crime and/or subversion. *Or* a combination of *both*. In light of the fact that drugs were used on you, your apartment broken into and ripped apart, your friend, Miss Ballantyne, indirectly threatened—and don't kid yourself, that's what it was—in light of all this, the recommendation is as follows. You withdraw from any further participation in this investigation. Your involvement is beyond the realm of reasonable risk." Greenberg dropped the paper on the counter and took several swallows of his drink. Matlock swung his legs slowly back and forth in front of the cabinet beneath him. "What say you, in the docket?" asked Greenberg.

"I'm not sure. It seems to me you're not finished."

"I'd like to be. Right here. The summary's accurate, and I think you should agree with the recommendation. Pull out, Jim."

"Finish first. What's the other letter? The one I'm supposed to read verbatim?"

"It's only necessary if you reject the recommendation. Don't reject it. I'm not instructed to lean that way, so that's off the record."

"You know damned well I'm going to reject it, so why waste time?"

"I *don't* know that. I don't want to *believe* that."

"There's no way out."

"There are counter explanations I can activate in an hour. Get you off the hook, out of the picture."

"Not any longer."

"What? Why?"

"That's *my* pathetic story. So you'd better continue."

Greenberg searched Matlock's eyes for an explanation, found none, and so picked up the second envelope and opened it.

"In the unlikely and ill-advised event that you reject our recommendation to cease and desist, you must understand that you do so against the express wishes of the Justice Department. Although we will offer whatever protection we can—as we would any citizen—you act under your own responsibility. We cannot be held liable for any injuries or inconveniences of any nature."

"Is that what it says?"

"No, that's *not* what it says, but that's what it means," said Greenberg, unfolding the paper. "It's much simpler and even more inclusive. Here." The federal agent handed Matlock the letter.

It was a statement signed by an assistant attorney general with a separate line on the left for Matlock's signature.

An investigative office of the Department of Justice accepted the offer of James B. Matlock to make inquiries of a minor nature with regard to certain illegal acts alleged to have occurred within the vicinity of Carlyle University. However, the Department of Justice now considers the situation to be a professional matter, and any further participation on the part of Professor Matlock is deemed unwarranted and against the policies of the Department. Therefore, the Department of Justice hereby informs James B. Matlock that it appreciates his previous cooperation but requests him to remove himself from any further involvement in the interest of safety and investigatory progress. It is the opinion of the Department that further actions on the part of Professor Matlock might tend to interfere with the aims of the Investigation in the Carlyle area. Mr. Matlock has received the original of this letter and so signifies by his signature below.

"What the hell are you talking about? This says that I agree to pull out."

"You'd make a lousy lawyer. Don't buy a bicycle on time before talking to me."

"What?"

"Nowhere! No*where* does your signing this little stinkpot say you *agree* to retire from the scene. Only that Justice *requested* you to."

"Then why in hell should I sign it?"

"Excellent question. You may buy a bicycle. . . . You sign it if, as you say, you reject the recomendation to pull out."

"Oh, for Christ's sake!" Matlock slipped down from the edge of the sink and threw the paper across the counter next to Greenberg. "I may not know law but I know language. You're talking in contradictions!"

"Only on the surface. . . . Let me ask you a question. Say you continue playing undercover agent. Is it conceivable that you may want to ask for help? An emergency, perhaps?"

"Of course. Inevitable."

"You get no help whatsoever without that letter going back signed. . . . Don't look at *me!* I'll be replaced in a matter of days. I've been in the area too long already."

"Kind of hypocritical, isn't it? The only way I can count on any assistance—any protection—is to sign a statement that says I won't need it."

"It's enough to send me into private practice. . . . There's a new term for this sort of thing these days. It's called 'hazardless progress.' Use whatever—*who*ever—you can. But don't take the blame if a *game plan* gets fucked up. Don't be responsible."

"And I jump without a parachute if I don't sign."

"I told you. Take some free advice—I'm a good lawyer. Quit. Forget it. But *forget it*."

"And I told *you*—I can't."

Greenberg reached for his drink and spoke softly. "No matter what you do, it's not going to bring your brother out of his grave."

"I know that." Matlock was touched, but he answered firmly.

"You might prevent other younger brothers but you probably won't. In either case, someone else can be recruited from professional ranks. I hate like hell to admit it, but Kressel was right. And if we don't get this conference—this convocation of peddlers in a couple of weeks—there'll be others."

"I agree with everything you say."

"Then why hesitate? Pull out."

"Why? . . . I haven't told you *my* pathetic little story, that's why. Remember? You had priority, but I've still got my turn."

"So tell."

And Matlock told him. Everything he knew about Lucas Herron—legend, giant, the "grand old bird" of Carlyle. The terror-stricken skeleton who had run into his personal forest. The wail of the single word: "Nimrod." Greenberg listened, and the longer Matlock talked, the sadder Jason Greenberg's eyes became. When Matlock finished, the federal agent drank the last of his drink and morosely nodded his head in slow motion.

"You spelled out everything for him, didn't you? You couldn't come to *me*, you had to go to *him*. Your campus saint with a bucket of blood in his hands. . . . Loring was right. We had to reach a conscience-stricken amateur. . . . Amateurs in front of us and amateurs behind us. At least I'll say this for you. You got a conscience. That's more than I can say for the rear flank."

"What should I do?"

"Sign the stinkpot." Greenberg picked up the Justice Department letter from the counter and handed it to Matlock. "You're going to need help."

Patricia Ballantyne preceded Matlock to the small side table at the far end of the Cheshire Cat. The drive out had been strained. The girl had hammered away—quietly, acidly—at Matlock's cooperating with the government, in particular and specifically the Federal Bureau of Investigation. She claimed not to be reacting to a programmed liberal response; there was simply too much overwhelming evidence that such organizations had brought the country ten steps from its own particular police state.

She knew firsthand. She'd witnessed the anguished aftermath of one FBI exercise and knew it wasn't isolated.

Matlock held her chair as she sat down, touching her shoulders as she did so. Touching, reaffirming, lessening the imagined hurt. The table was small, next to a window, several feet from a terrace that soon—in late May—would be in use for outside dining. He sat across from her and took her hand.

"I'm not going to apologize for what I'm doing. I think it has to be done. I'm not a hero and I'm not a fink. I'm not asked to be heroic, and the information they want ultimately will help a lot of people. People who need help—desperately."

"Will those people *get* help? Or will they simply be prosecuted? Instead of hospitals and clinics . . . will they find themselves in jail?"

"They're not interested in sick kids. They want the ones who make them sick. So do I."

"But in the process, the kids get hurt." A statement.

"Some may be. As few as possible."

"That's contemptible." The girl took her hand away from Matlock's "It's so condescending. Who makes *those* decisions? You?"

"You're beginning to sound like a one-track tape."

"I've *been* there. It's not pleasant."

"This is entirely different. I've met just two men; one . . . left. The other's Greenberg. They're not your nightmares from the fifties. Take my word for that."

"I'd like to."

The manager of the Cheshire Cat approached the table. "There's a telephone call for you, Mr. Matlock."

Matlock felt a twinge of pain in his stomach. It was the nerves of fear. Only one person knew where he was—Jason Greenberg.

"Thanks, Harry."

"You can take it by the reservations desk. The phone's off the hook."

Matlock got out of his chair and looked briefly at Pat. In the months and months of their going out together, from restaurants to parties to dinners, he had never received a telephone call, had never been interrupted that way. He saw that realization in her eyes. He walked rapidly away from the table to the reservations desk.

"Hello?"

"Jim?" It *was* Greenberg, of course.

"Jason?"

"Sorry to bother you. I wouldn't if I didn't have to."

"What is it, for heaven's sake?"

"Lucas Herron's dead. He committed suicide about an hour ago."

The pain in Matlock's stomach suddenly returned. It wasn't a twinge this time, but instead a sharp blow that left him unable to breathe. All he could see in front of his eyes was the picture of the staggering, panicked old man running across the manicured lawn and disappearing into the dense foliage bordering his property. And then the wailing sound of a sob and the name of Nimrod whispered in hatred.

"Are you all right?"

"Yes. Yes, I'm all right." For reasons he could not fathom, Matlock's memory focused on a small, black-framed photograph. It was an enlarged snapshot of a dark-haired, middle-aged infantry officer with a weapon in one hand, a map in the other, the face lean and strong, looking up toward the high ground.

A quarter of a century ago.

"You'd better get back to your apartment. . . ." Greenberg was issuing an order, but he had the sense to be gentle about it.

"Who found him?"

"My man. No one else knows yet."

"Your man?"

"After our talk, I put Herron under surveillance. You get to spot the signs. He broke in and found him."

"How?"

"Cut his wrists in the shower."

"Oh, Christ! What have I done?"

"Cut that out! Get back here. We've got people to reach. . . . Come on, Jim."

"What can I tell Pat?" Matlock tried to find his mind but it kept wandering back to a helpless, frightened old man.

"As little as possible. But hurry."

Matlock replaced the receiver and took several deep breaths. He searched his pockets for cigarettes and remembered that he'd left them at the table.

The table. Pat. He had to go back to the table and think of something to say.

The truth. Goddamn it, the *truth*.

He made his way around two antique pillars toward the far end of the room and the small side table by the window. In spite of his panic, he felt a degree of relief and knew it was because he had decided to be honest with Pat. God knew he had to have someone other than Greenberg and Kressel to talk to.

Kressel! He was supposed to have gone to Kressel's house at seven. He'd forgotten all about it!

But in an instant Sam Kressel went out of his thoughts. He saw the small side table by the window and there was no one there.

Pat was gone.

Chapter Thirteen

"No one saw her leave?" Greenberg followed a frustrated Matlock into the living room from the foyer. Sam Kressel's voice could be heard from the bedroom, shouting excitedly into a telephone. Matlock took notice of it, his attention split in too many areas.

"That's Sam in there, isn't it?" he asked. "Does he know about Herron?"

"Yes. I called him after I talked to you. . . . What about the waitresses? Did you ask them?"

"Of course, I did. None of them were sure. It was busy. One said she thought she might have gone to the ladies' room. Another hinted, s'help me, hinted, that she might have been the girl who left with a couple from another table."

"Wouldn't they have had to pass you on the way out? Wouldn't you have seen her?"

"Not necessarily. We were in the back. There are two or three doors which lead to a terrace. In summer, especially when it's crowded, they put tables on the terrace."

"You drove out in your car?"

"Naturally."

"And you didn't see her outside, walking on the road, on the grounds?"

"No."

"Did you recognize any of the other people there?"

"I didn't really look. I was . . . preoccupied." Matlock lit a cigarette. His hand shook as he held the match.

"If you want my opinion, I think she spotted someone she knew and asked for a lift home. A girl like that doesn't go anywhere she doesn't want to go without a fight."

"I know. That's occurred to me."

"Have a fight?"

"You might say it was diminishing but not over. The phone call probably set her off again. Old English teachers rarely get calls while out at restaurants."

"I'm sorry."

"It's not your fault. I told you, she's uptight. She keeps thinking about her father. I'll try her apartment when Sam gets off the phone."

"*He's* a funny man. I tell him about Herron—naturally he goes off the deep end. He says he's got to talk privately with Sealfont so he goes into the bedroom and shouts so loud they can hear him in Poughkeepsie."

Matlock's thoughts shifted quickly to Herron. "His death—his *suicide*—is going to be the biggest shock this campus has had in twenty years. Men like Lucas simply don't die. They certainly don't die like *this*. . . . Does Sam know I saw him?"

"He does. I couldn't withhold that. I told him pretty much what you told me—shorter version, of course. He refuses to believe it. The implications, I mean."

"I don't blame him. They're not easy to believe. What do we do now?"

"We wait. I've made a report. Two lab men from the Hartford Bureau are out there now. The local police have been called in."

At the mention of the police, Matlock suddenly remembered the patrolman out of uniform in the squash court corridor, who had walked rapidly away at the moment of recognition. He'd told Greenberg and Greenberg had never given him an explanation—if there was one. He asked again.

"What about the cop in the gym?"

"The story's reasonable. At least so far. The Carlyle police are assigned three mornings a week for limited use of the facilities. Town-gown relations. Coincidence."

"You're settling for that?"

"I said, 'so far.' We're running a check on the man. Nothing's turned up but an excellent record."

"He's a bigot, a nasty bastard."

"This may surprise you, but that's no crime. It's guaranteed in the Bill of Rights."

Sam Kressel walked through the bedroom door quickly, emphatically. Matlock saw that he was as close to pure fear as he'd ever seen a man. There was an uncomfortable similarity between Sam's face and the bloodless expression of Lucas Herron before the old man had raced into the woods.

"I heard you come in," Kressel said. "What are we going to *do*? What in hell are we *going to do*? . . . Adrian doesn't believe that absurd story any more than *I* do! *Lucas Herron! It's insane!*"

"Maybe. But it's true."

"Because *you* say so? How can you be sure? You're no professional in these matters. As I understand it, Lucas admitted he was helping a student through a drug problem."

"He . . . they aren't students."

"I see." Kressel stopped briefly and looked back and forth between Matlock and Greenberg. "Under the circumstances, I demand to know the identities."

"You'll get them," said Greenberg quietly. "Go on. I want to hear why Matlock's so wrong, the story so absurd."

"Because Lucas Herron isn't . . . wasn't the only member of the faculty concerned with these problems. There are dozens of us giving aid, helping wherever we can!"

"I don't follow you." Greenberg stared at Kressel. "So you help. You don't go and kill yourself when a fellow member of the faculty finds out about it."

Sam Kressel removed his glasses and looked momentarily reflective, sad. "There's something else neither of you know about. I've been aware of it for some time but not so knowledgeably as Sealfont. . . . Lucas Herron was a very sick man. One kidney was removed last summer. The other was also cancerous and he knew it. The pain must have been unbearable for him. He hadn't long."

Greenberg watched closely at Kressel returned his glasses to his face. Matlock bent down and crushed out his cigarette in an ashtray on the coffee table. Finally, Greenberg spoke.

"Are you suggesting that there's no relationship between Herron's suicide and Matlock's seeing him this afternoon?"

"I'm not suggesting any such thing. I'm sure there's a relationship. . . . But you didn't know Lucas. His whole life for nearly half a century, except for the war years, was Carlyle University. It's been his total, complete existence. He loved this place more than any man could love a woman, more than any parent a child. I'm sure Jim's told you. If he thought for a moment that his world here was going to be defaced, torn apart—that would be a greater pain than the physical torture his body gave him. What better time to take his own life?"

"*Gaddamn you!*" roared Matlock. "You're saying *I killed him!*"

"Perhaps I am," Kressel said quietly. "I hadn't thought of it in those terms. I'm sure Adrian didn't either."

"But that's what you're *saying!* You're saying I went off halfcocked and killed him as much as if I'd slashed his wrists! . . . Well, you weren't there. *I was!*"

Kressel spoke gently. "I didn't say you went off half-cocked. I said you were an amateur. A very well-intentioned amateur. I think Greenberg knows what I mean."

Jason Greenberg looked at Matlock. "There's an old Slovak proverb: 'When the old men kill themselves, the cities are dying.'"

The telephone bell suddenly pierced the air; its sound acted as a jolt to the three men. Matlock answered it, then turned to Greenberg. "It's for you."

"Thanks." The federal agent took the phone from Matlock. "Greenberg. . . . O.K. I understand. When will you know? . . . I'll probably be on the road by then. I'll call you back. Talk later." He replaced the telephone and stood by the desk, his back to Matlock and Kressel. The dean of colleges couldn't contain himself.

"What was it? What happened?"

Greenberg turned and faced them. Matlock thought his eyes seemed sadder than usual, which Matlock had learned was a sign of trouble in Greenberg.

"We're making a request of the police—the courts—for an autopsy."

"*Why?!*" Kressel shouted as he approached the agent. "For God's sake, *why?!* The man killed himself! he was in *pain!* . . . Jesus Christ, you can't *do* this! If news of it gets out . . ."

"We'll handle it quietly."

"That can't be done and you *know* it! It'll leak out and all hell'll break loose around here! I won't *permit* it!"

"You can't stop it. Even I couldn't stop it. There's sufficient evidence to indicate that Herron didn't take his own life. That he was killed." Greenberg smiled wryly at Matlock. "And not by words."

Kressel argued, threatened, made another call to Sealfont, and finally, when it was obvious that all were to no avail, he left Matlock's apartment in fury.

No sooner had Kressel slammed the door than the telephone rang again. Greenberg saw that the sound disturbed Matlock—not merely annoyed him, but disturbed him; perhaps frightened him.

"I'm sorry. . . . I'm afraid this place has to be a kind of patrol base for a while. Not long. . . . Maybe it's the girl."

Matlock picked up the phone, listened, but did not say anything into it.

Instead, he turned to Greenberg. He said only one word.

"You."

Greenberg took the telephone, uttered his name softly, and then spent the next minute staring straight ahead. Matlock watched Greenberg for half the time and then wandered into his kitchen. He didn't wish to stand awkwardly to one side while the agent listened to a superior's instructions.

The voice at the other end of the line had initially identified itself by saying, "Washington calling."

On the counter lay the empty envelope in which the brutally hypocritical statement had come from the Department of Justice. It had been one more sign that his worst fantasies were gradually becoming real. From that infinitesimal portion of the mind which concerns itself with the unthinkable, Matlock had begun to perceive that the land he had grown up in was changing into something ugly and destructive. It was far more than a political manifestation, it was a slow, all-embracing sense of morality by strategy. A corruption of intentions. Strong feelings were being replaced with surface anger, convictions and compromise. The land was becoming something other than its promise, its commitment. The grails were empty vessels of flat wine, impressive solely because they were possessed.

"I'm off the phone now. Would you like to try reaching Miss Ballantyne?"

Matlock looked up at Greenberg, standing in the frame of the kitchen door. Greenberg, the walking contradiction, the proverb-quoting agent deeply suspicious of the system for which he worked.

"Yes. Yes, I'd like to." He started into the living room as Greenberg stepped aside to let him pass. Matlock reached the center of the room and stopped. "That's one hell of a quotation. What was it? 'When the old men kill themselves, the cities are dying.'" He turned and looked at the agent. "I think that's the saddest proverb I've ever heard."

"You're not Hassidic. Of course, neither am I, but the Hassidim wouldn't think it sad. . . . Come to think of it, no true philosopher would."

"Why not? It *is* sad."

"It's truth. Truth is neither joyful nor sad, neither good nor bad. It is simply truth."

"Someday let's debate that, Jason." Matlock picked up the telephone, dialed Pat's number, and let it ring a dozen times. There was no answer. Matlock thought of several of Pat's friends and wondered whether to call them or not. When angry or upset, Pat usually did one of two things. She either went off by herself for an hour or so, or, conversely, sought out one or two friends and drove off to a film in Hartford or an out-of-the-way bar. It was just over an hour. He'd give her another fifteen minutes before phoning around. It had, of course, occurred to him that she might have been taken involuntarily—that had been his first thought. But it wasn't logical. The Cheshire Cat had been filled with people, the tables close together. Greenberg was right. Wherever she went, she went because she wanted to go.

Greenberg stood by the kitchen door. He hadn't moved. He'd been watching Matlock.

"I'll try in a quarter of an hour. Then, if there's no answer, I'll call some friends of hers. As you said, she's one strong-willed young lady."

"I hope you're not from the same cloth."

"What does that mean?"

Greenberg took several steps into the living room. When he spoke, he looked directly into Matlock's eyes.

"You're out. Finished. Forget the letter, forget Loring, forget me. . . . That's the way it's got to be. We understand you have reservations for St. Thomas on Pan Am for Saturday. Enjoy it, because that's where you're going. Much better this way."

Matlock returned the government man's look. "Any decision like that will be made by me. I've got a gentle old man on my conscience; and you've got that stinkpot in your pocket. I signed it, remember?"

"The stinkpot doesn't count anymore. D.C. wants you out. You go."

"Why?"

"Because of the gentle old man. If he *was* killed, you could be, too. If that happened, certain records might be subpoenaed, certain men who had reservations about recruiting you might voice those reservations to the press. You were maneuvered. I don't have to tell you that."

"So?"

"The directors at Justice have no wish to be called executioners."

"I see." Matlock took his eyes off Greenberg and wandered toward the coffee table. "Suppose I refuse?"

"Then I remove you from the scene."

"How?"

"I have you arrested on suspicion of murder one."

"*What?*"

"You were the last person on record to see Lucas Herron alive. By your own admission, you went out to his house to threaten him."

"To *warn* him!"

"That's subject to interpretation, isn't it?"

When the thunderous crash came, it was so ear-shattering both men threw themselves to the floor. It was as if the whole side of the building had collapsed in rubble. Dust was everywhere, furniture toppled, glass shattered, splinters of wood and plaster flew through the air, and the terrible stench of burning sulfur settled over the room. Matlock knew the smell of that kind of bomb, and his reflexes knew how to operate. He clung to the base of his couch waiting, waiting for a second explosion—a delayed detonator which would kill any who rose in panic. Through the mist, he saw Greenberg start to get up, and he leaped forward, tackling the agent at his knees.

"Get down! Stay. . . ."

The second explosion came. Parts of the ceiling blackened. But Matlock knew it was not a killer explosive. It was something else, and he could not figure it out at the moment. It was an eyegrabber, a camouflage—no meant to kill, but to deflect all concentration. A huge firecracker.

Screams of panic could now be heard mounting from all parts of the building. The sounds of rushing feet pounded on the floor above his apartment.

And then a single screech of terror from outside Matlock's front door. It would not stop. The horror of it caused Matlock and Greenberg to struggle to their feet and race to the source. Matlock pulled the door open and looked down upon a sight no human being should ever see more than once in a lifetime, if his life must continue beyond that instant.

On his front step was Patricia Ballantyne wrapped in a blood-soaked sheet. Holes were cut in the areas of her naked breasts, blood flowing from gashes beneath the nipples. The front of her head was shaved; blood poured out of lacerations where once had been the soft brown hair. Blood, too, came from the half-open mouth, her lips bruised and split. The eyes were blackened into deep crevasses of sore flesh—but they moved! The eyes moved!

Saliva began forming at the corners of her lips. The half-dead corpse was trying to speak.

"Jamie . . ." was the only word she managed and then her head slipped to one side.

Greenberg threw his whole weight against Matlock, sending him sprawling into the gathering crowd. He roared orders of "Police!" and "Ambulance!" until he saw enough people running to execute his commands. He put his mouth to the girl's mouth, to force air into the collapsing lungs, but he knew it wasn't really necessary. Patricia Ballantyne wasn't dead; she'd been tortured by experts, and the experts knew their business well. Every slash, every crack, every bruise meant utmost pain but did not mean death.

He started to pick the girl up but Matlock stopped him. The English professor's eyes were swollen with tears of hate. He gently removed Greenberg's hands and lifted Pat into his arms. He carried her inside and stretched her out on the half-destroyed sofa. Greenberg went into the bedroom and returned with a blanket. Then he brought a bowl of warm water from the kitchen and several towels. He lifted the blanket and held a towel beneath the bleeding breasts. Matlock, staring in horror at the brutally beaten face, then took the edge of another towel and began wiping away the blood around the shaven head and the mouth.

"She'll be all right, Jim. I've seen this before. She'll be all right."

And as Greenberg heard the sounds of the sirens in the near distance, he wondered, really, if this girl would ever be right again.

Matlock, helpless, continued to wipe the girl's face, his tears now streaming down his cheeks, his eyes unblinking. He spoke through his controlled sobs.

"You know what this means, don't you? No one pulls me out now. They try, I'll kill them."

"I won't let them," said Greenberg simply.

The screeching of brakes could be heard outside and the flashing lights of the police cars and the ambulances whipped in circles through the windows.

Matlock's face fell into the cushion beside the unconscious girl and he wept.

Chapter Fourteen

Matlock awoke in the antiseptic whiteness of a hospital room. The shade was up, and the sun reflected harshly on the three walls he could see. At his feet a nurse was writing efficiently, emphatically, on top of a clipboard attached to the base of the bed by a thin keychain. He stretched his arms, then quickly brought his left back, aware of a sharp pain in his forearm.

"You feel those the next morning, Mr. Matlock," droned the nurse without looking up from the clipboard. "Heavy intravenous sedations are murder, I can tell you. Not that I've ever had one, but Lord knows, I've seen enough who have."

"Is Pat . . . Miss Ballantyne here?"

"Well, not in the same *room!* Lord, you campus types!"

"She's here?"

"Of course. Next room. Which I intend to keep *locked!* Lord, you people from the hill! . . . There! You're all accounted for." The nurse left the clipboard crash down and vibrate back and forth. "Now. *You've* got special privileges. *You're* allowed breakfast even though it's past breakfast time—*way* past! That's probably because they want you to pay your bill. . . . You can be discharged any time after twelve."

"What time is it? Someone took my watch."

"It's eight minutes to nine," said the nurse, glancing at her wrist. "And no one *took* your watch. It's with any other valuables you had when you were admitted."

"How *is* Miss Ballantyne?"

"We don't discuss other patients, Mr. Matlock."

"Where's her doctor?"

"He's the same as yours, I understand. Not one of *ours*." The nurse made sure the statement was hardly complimentary. "According to your chart, he'll be here at nine thirty unless we phone for an emergency."

"Call him. I want him here as soon as possible."

"Now, really. There's no emergency. . . ."

"Goddamn it, get him here!"

As Matlock raised his voice the door of his room opened. Jason Greenberg came in quickly. "I could hear you in the corridor. That's a good sign."

"How's Pat?!"

"Just a minute, sir. We have regulations. . . ."

Greenberg took out his identification and showed it to the nurse. "This man is in my custody, Miss. Check the front desk, if you like, but leave us alone."

The nurse, ever professional, scrutinized the identification and walked rapidly out the door.

"How's Pat?"

"A mess, but with it. She had a bad night; she's going to have a worse morning when she asks for a mirror."

"The hell with that! Is she *all right?*"

"Twenty-seven stitches—body, head, mouth, and, for variety, one on her left foot. But she's going to be fine. X-rays show only bone bruises. No fractures, no ruptures, no internal bleeding. The bastards did their usual professional job."

"Was she able to talk?"

"Not really. And the doctor didn't advise it. She needs sleep more than anything else. . . . You need a little rest, too. That's why we put you here last night."

"Anyone hurt at the apartment?"

"Nope. It was a crazy bombing. We don't think it was intended to kill anyone. The first was a short two-inch stick taped below the window exterior; the second—activated by the first—wasn't much more than a July Fourth rocket. You expected the second blast, didn't you?"

"Yes. I guess I did. . . . Terror tactics, wasn't it?"

"That's what we figure."

"Can I see Pat?"

"Rather you waited. The doctor thinks she'll sleep into the afternoon. There's a nurse in there with ice packs and stuff if localized pain bother's her.

Let her rest."

Matlock cautiously sat up on the edge of the bed. He began flexing his legs, arms, neck, and hands, and found that he wasn't much below par. "I feel sort of like a hangover without the headache."

"The doctor gave you a heavy dose. You were . . . understandably . . . very emotional."

"I remember everything. I'm calmer, but I don't retract one goddamned word. . . . I have two classes today. One at ten and the other at two. I want to make them."

"You don't have to. Sealfont wants to see you."

"I'll talk to him after my last class. . . . Then I'll see Pat." Matlock stood on his feet and walked slowly to the large hospital window. It was a bright, sunlit morning; Connecticut had had a string of beautiful days. As he stared outside, Matlock remembered that he'd looked out another window five days ago when he'd first met Jason Greenberg. He'd made a decision then as he was making one now. "Last night you said you wouldn't let them pull me out. I hope you haven't changed your mind. I'm *not* going to be on that Pan Am flight tomorrow."

"You won't be arrested. I promised you that."

"Can you prevent it? You also said you were going to be replaced."

"I can prevent it. . . . I can morally object, an enigmatic phrase which is translated to mean I can embarrass people. However, I don't want to mislead you. If you create problems, you could be taken into protective custody."

"They can if they can find me."

"That's a condition I don't like."

"Forget you heard it. Where are my clothes?" Matlock walked to the single closet door and opened it. His slacks, jacket, and shirt were hung on hangers; his loafers were on the floor with his socks carefully inserted. The lone bureau held his undershorts and a hospital-furnished toothbrush. "Will you go down and see whoever you've got to see to get me out of here? Also, I'll need my wallet, cash, and watch. Will you do that, please?"

"What do you mean—if they could find you? What are you going to do?" Greenberg made no move to leave.

"Nothing earth-shattering. Merely continue making those inquiries . . . of a minor nature. That's the way the statement from your employers phrased it, wasn't it? Loring said it. Somewhere out there is the other half of that paper. I'm going to find it."

"You listen to me first! I don't deny you have a right . . ."

"You don't *deny!*" Matlock turned on the federal agent. His voice was controlled but vicious. "That's not good enough. That's *negative* approval! I've got several *big* rights! They include a kid brother in a sailboat, a black son of a bitch named Dunois or whatever you call him, a man by the name of Lucas Herron, and that girl in there! I suspect you and the doctor know the rest of what happened to her last night, and I can *guess!* Don't talk to me about *a right!*"

"In principle, we agree. I just don't want your 'rights' to land you next to your brother. This is a job for professionals. Not an amateur! If you work at all, I want you to work with whoever takes my place. That's important. I want your word on it."

Matlock took off the top of his pajamas and gave Greenberg a short, embarrassed smile. "You have it. I don't really see myself as a one-man ranger team. Do you know who's taking your place?"

"Not yet. Probably someone from D.C. They won't take a chance on using a Hartford or a New Haven man. . . . The truth is . . . they don't know who's been bought. He'll be in touch. I'll have to brief him myself. No one else can. I'll instruct him to identify himself with . . . what would you like?"

"Tell him to use your proverb. 'When the old men kill themselves, the cities are dying.'"

"You like that, don't you?"

"I don't like it or dislike it. It's simply the truth. Isn't that the way it should be?"

"And very applicable. I see what you mean."

"Very."

"Jim, before I go this afternoon, I'm going to write out a telephone number for you. It's a Bronx number—my parents. They won't know where I am, but I'll check with them every day. Use it if you have to."

"Thanks, I will."

"I want your word on it."

"You have it." Matlock laughed a short laugh of gratitude.

"Of course, under the circumstances, I may just be on the other end of the line if you do call."

"Back in private practice?"

"The possibility is less remote than you think."

Chapter Fifteen

Between his two classes, Matlock drove to the small brokerage office in the town of Carlyle and emerged with a check for $7,312. It represented his total investment in the market, mostly from royalties. The broker had tried to dissuade him; it was no time to sell, especially at current prices. But Matlock had made up his mind. The cashier reluctantly issued the check.

From there Matlock went to his bank and transferred his entire savings into his checking account. He added the $7,312 to the slip and looked at the sum total of his immediate cash value.

It came to $11,501.72.

Matlock stared at the figure for several minutes. He had mixed feelings about it. On the one hand, it proved solvency; on the other, it was a little frightening to think that after thirty-three years of living he was able to pinpoint so accurately his net financial worth. There was no house, no land, no hidden investments anywhere. Only an automobile, a few possessions of minor value, and some published words of such a specialized nature that there would be no significant commercial rewards.

Yet by many standards, it was a great deal of money.

Only nowhere *near* enough. He knew that. It was why Scarsdale, New York, was on the day's schedule.

The meeting with Sealfont had been unnerving, and Matlock wasn't sure how much more his shattered nerves could take. The cold fury of Carlyle's president was matched only by the depth of his anguish.

The bewildering shadow world of violence and corruption was a world he could never come to grips with because it was not within the realm of his comprehension. Matlock had been startled to hear Sealfont say, as he sat in his chair staring out the bay window overlooking the most beautiful lawn on the Carlyle campus, that he might well resign.

"If this whole sordid, unbelievable business is true—and who can doubt it—I have no right to sit in this chair."

"That's not so," Matlock had answered. "If it's true, this place is going to need you more than ever before."

"A blind man? No one needs a blind man. Not in this office."

"Not blind. Unexposed."

And then Sealfont had swung around in his chair and pounded on the top of his desk in an enormous display of strength.

"Why *here?! Why here?!*"

As he sat in front of Sealfont's desk, Matlock looked at the pained face of Carlyle's president. And for a second he thought the man might weep.

The trip down the Merritt Parkway was made at high speed. He had to race; it was necessary for him. It helped take his mind off the sight of Pat Ballantyne as he had seen her a few minutes before leaving. He had gone from Sealfont's to the hospital; still he hadn't been able to talk with her. No one had yet.

She had awakened at noon, he'd been told. She'd gone into severe hysterics. The doctor from Litchfield had administered further sedatives. The doctor was worried, and Matlock knew it was Pat's mind he was worried about. The nightmare of terror inflicted upon her body had to touch her brain.

The first minutes with his parents at the huge Scarsdale house were awkward. His father, Jonathan Munro Matlock, had spent decades in the highest spheres of his marketplace and knew instinctively when a man came to him without strength.

Without strength but with need.

Matlock told his father as simply and unemotionally as he could that he wanted to borrow a large sum of money; he could not guarantee its repayment. It would be used to help—ultimately help—young people like his dead brother.

The dead son.

"How?" asked Jonathan Matlock softly.

"I can't tell you that." He looked into his father's eyes and the irrevocable truth of the son's statement was accepted by the father.

"Very well. Are you qualified for this undertaking?"

"Yes. I am."

"Are there others involved?"

"By necessity, yes."

"Do you trust them?"

"I do."

"Have they asked for this money?"

"No. They don't know about it."

"Will it be at their disposal?"

"No. Not that I can foresee. . . . I'll go further than that. It would be wrong for them to learn of it."

"I'm not restricting you, I'm asking."

"That's my answer."

"And you believe that what you're doing will help, in some way, boys like David? Practical help, not theoretical, not dream stuff, not charity."

"Yes. It has to."

"How much do you want?"

Matlock took a deep breath silently. "Fifteen thousand dollars."

"Wait here."

Several minutes later, the father came out of his study and gave the son an envelope.

The son knew better than to open it.

Ten minutes after the exchange—and Matlock knew it *was* an exchange—he left, feeling the eyes of his parents as they stood on the enormous porch and watched him drive out through the gates.

Matlock pulled into the apartment driveway, shut off the lights and the engine, and wearily climbed out. As he approached the old Tudor house, he saw that every light he owned was turned on. Jason Greenberg wasn't taking chances, and Matlock assumed that some part of Greenberg's silent, unseen army was watching his place from varying distances—none too far away.

He unlocked the door and pushed it open. There was no one there. At least, not in sight. Not even his cat.

"Hello? Jason? . . . Anybody here? It's Matlock."

There was no answer and Matlock was relieved. He wanted only to crawl into bed and sleep. He'd stopped at the hospital to see Pat, and the request had been denied. At least he'd learned that ". . . . she is resting and her condition is deemed satisfactory." That was a step up. That afternoon she'd still been on the critical list. He would see her at nine in the morning.

Now was the time for him to sleep—peaceably if possible. Sleep at all costs. There was a great deal to do in the morning.

He went into his bedroom, passing the still unrepaired sections of wall and window as he did so. Carpenter's and plasterer's tools were neatly stacked in corners. He removed his jacket and his shirt and then thought, with a degree of self-ridicule, that he was becoming far too confident. He walked rapidly out of the bedroom and into his bathroom. Once the door was shut, he reached down to the litter box and lifted up the newspaper to the layer of canvas. The Corsican paper was there, the tarnished silver coating reflecting the light.

Back in the bedroom, Matlock removed his wallet, cash, and car keys, placing them on top of his bureau. As he did so, he remembered the envelope.

He hadn't been fooled. He knew his father, perhaps better than his father realized. He presumed there was a short note with the check stating clearly that the money was a gift, not a loan, and that no repayment was anticipated.

The note was there, folded inside the envelope, but the written words were not what Matlock expected.

I believe in you. I always have.

Love,

Dad

On top of the note, clipped to the paper on the reverse side, was the check. Matlock slipped it off and read the figure.

It was for fifty thousand dollars.

Chapter Sixteen

Much of the swelling on her face and around her eyes had subsided. He took her hand and held it tightly, putting his face once more next to hers.

"You're going to be fine," were the innocuous words he summoned. He had to hold himself in check to stop himself from screaming out his anger and his guilt. That this could be done to a human being by other human beings was beyond his endurance. And he was responsible.

When she spoke, her voice was hardly audible, like a small child's, the words only partially formed through the immobile lips.

"Jamie . . . Jamie?"

"Shh . . . Don't talk if it hurts."

"Why?"

"I don't know. But we'll find out."

"No! . . . No, don't! They're . . . they're . . ." The girl had to swallow; it was nearly impossible for her. She pointed to a glass of water on the bedside table. Matlock quickly reached for it and held it to her lips, supporting her by the shoulders.

"How did it happen? Can you tell me?"

"Told . . . Greenberg. Man and woman . . . came to the table. Said you were . . . waiting . . . outside."

"Never mind, I'll talk to Jason."

"I . . . feel better. I hurt but . . . feel better, I . . . really do. . . . Am I going to be all right?"

"Of course you are. I spoke with the doctor. You're bruised, but nothing broken, nothing serious. He says you'll be out of bed in a few days, that's all."

Patricia Ballantyne's eyes brightened, and Matlock saw the terrible attempt of a smile on her sutured lips. "I fought. . . . I fought and I fought . . . until I . . . couldn't remember any more."

It took all of Matlock's strength not to burst into tears. "I know you did. Now, no more talking. You rest, take it easy. I'll just sit here and we'll talk with our eyes. Remember? You said we always communicate around other people with our eyes. . . . I'll tell you a dirty joke."

When the smile came, it *was* from her eyes.

He stayed until a nurse forbade him to stay longer. Then he kissed her softly on the lips and left the room. He was a relieved man; he was an angry man.

"Mr. Matlock?" The young doctor with the freshly scrubbed face of an intern approached him by the elevator.

"Yes?"

"There's a telephone call for you. You can take it at the second floor reception, if you'll follow me."

The caller's voice was unknown. "Mr. Matlock, my name's Houston. I'm a friend of Jason Greenberg's. I'm to get in touch with you."

"Oh? How's Jason?"

"Fine. I'd like to get together with you as soon as possible."

Matlock was about to name a place, any place, after his first class. And then he stopped. "Did Jason leave any message . . . where he is now, or anything?"

"No sir. Just that I was to make contact pronto."

"I see." Why didn't the man say it? Why didn't Houston identify himself?

"Greenberg definitely told me he'd leave word . . . a message . . . where he'd be. I'm sure he said that."

"Against department regulations, Mr. Matlock. He wouldn't be allowed to."

"Oh? . . . Then he didn't leave any message at all?"

The voice on the other end of the line hesitated slightly, perceptibly. "He may have forgotten. . . . As a matter of fact, I didn't speak to him myself. I received my orders directly from Washington. Where shall we meet?"

Matlock heard the anxiety in the man's voice. When he referred to Washington, his tone had risen in a small burst of nervous energy. "Let me call you later. What's your number?"

"Now listen, Matlock. I'm in a telephone booth and we have to meet. I've got my orders!"

"Yes, I'll bet you do. . . ."

"What?"

"Never mind. Are you downtown? In Carlyle?"

The man hesitated again. "I'm in the area."

"Tell me, Mr. Houston. . . . Is the city dying?"

"What? What are you talking about?"

"I'm going to be late for my class. Try me again. I'm sure you'll be able to reach me." Matlock hung up the phone. His left hand shook and perspiration had formed on his brow.

Mr. Houston was the enemy.

The enemy was closing in.

His first Saturday class was at eleven, which gave him just about an hour to make what he felt were the most logical arrangements for the money. He didn't want to think that he had to physically be in the town of Carlyle—at the Carlyle Bank—on Monday morning. He wasn't sure it would be possible. He wasn't sure where he would be on Monday.

Since, on the surface, Carlyle was a typical New England college town, it had a particular way of life common to such places. One knew, generally on a first-name basis, all the people whose jobs made day-to-day living the effortless, unhurried existence that it was. The garage mechanic was "Joe" or "Mac," the manager at J. Press was "Al," the dentist "John" or "Warren," the girl at the dry cleaners "Edith." In Matlock's case, the banker was "Alex." Alex Anderson, a Carlyle graduate of forty, a local boy who'd made the jump from town to gown and then coordinated both. Matlock called him at home and explained his problem. He was carrying around a large check from his father. He was making some private family investments in his own name, and they were confidential. Since the robbery at his apartment, he wanted to divest himself of the check immediately. Could Alex suggest anything? Should he put it in the mail? How best to get it into his account, since he wasn't sure he would be in Carlyle on Monday, and he needed it cleared, the money available. Alex Anderson suggested the obvious. Matlock should endorse the check, put it in an envelope marked for Anderson's attention, and drop it in the night deposit box at the bank. Alex would take care of the rest first thing Monday morning.

And then Alex Anderson asked him the denomination and Matlock told him.

The account problem solved, Matlock concentrated on what he began to think of as his point of departure. There was no other phrase he could find, and he needed a phrase—he needed the discipline of a definition. He had to start precisely right, knowing that what might follow could be totally *undisciplined*—completely without plan or orthodoxy. For he had made up his mind.

He was going to enter the world of Nimrod. The builder of Babylon and Nineveh, the hunter of wild animals, the killer of children and old men, the beater of women.

He was going to find Nimrod.

As were most adults not wedded to the precept that all things enjoyable were immoral, Matlock was aware that the state of Connecticut, like its sister states to the north, the south, and the west, was inhabited by a network of men only too eager to supply those divertissements frowned upon by the pulpits and the courts. What Hartford insurance executive in the upper brackets never heard of that string of "Antique Shoppes" on New Britain Avenue where a lithe young girl's body could be had for a reasonable amount of petty cash? What commuter from Old Greenwich was oblivious to the large estates north of Green Farms where the gambling often rivaled the Vegas stakes? How many tired businessmen's wives from New Haven or Westport were really ignorant of the various "escort" services operating out of Hamden and Fairfield? And over in the "old country," the Norfolks? Where the rambling mansions were fading apotheoses to the *real* money, the blooded first families who migrated just a little west to avoid the new rich? The "old country" had the strangest diversions, it was rumored. Houses in shadows, lighted by candles, where the bored could become aroused by observation. Voyeurs of the sickest scenes. Female, male, animal—all types, all combinations.

Matlock knew that in this world Nimrod could be found. It had to be. For although narcotics were but one aspect of the services rendered within this network, they were available—as was everything else.

And of all these games of indulgence, none had the fire and ice, none had the magnetism, of the gambling houses. For those thousands who couldn't find time for the junkets to San Juan, London, or Paradise Island, there were the temporary excursions into the manic moments where daily boredom could be forgotten—a stone's throw from home. Reputations were made quickly over the green felt tables—with the roll of the dice or a turn of a card. It was here that Matlock would find his point of departure. It was in these places where a young man of thirty-three years was prepared to lose thousands—until someone asked who he was.

At twelve thirty Matlock walked across the quadrangle toward his apartment. The time had come to initiate his first move. The vague outline of a plan was coming into focus.

He should have heard the footsteps, but he didn't. He only heard the cough, a smoker's cough, the cough of a man who'd been running.

"Mr. Matlock?"

Matlock turned and saw a man in his middle thirties, like himself, perhaps a bit older and, indeed, out of breath.

"Yes?"

"Sorry, I keep missing you. I got to the hospital just as you'd left, then waited in the wrong damn building for you, after your class. There's a very confused biology teacher with a name similar to yours. Even looks a little like you. Same height, build, hair . . ."

"That's Murdock. Elliot Murdock. What's the matter?"

"He couldn't understand why I kept insisting that when 'old men kill themselves, the cities are dying'!"

"You're from Greenberg!"

"That's it. Morbid code, if you don't mind my saying so. Keep walking. We'll separate at the end of the path. Meet me in twenty minutes at Bill's Bar & Grill by the freight depot. It's six blocks south of the railroad station. O.K.?"

"Never heard of it."

"I was going to suggest you remove your necktie. I'll be in a leather jacket."

"You pick classy spots."

"Old habit. I cheat on the expense account."

"Greenberg said I was to work with you."

"You better believe it! He's up to his Kosher ass in boiling oil for you. I think they're shipping him out to a job in Cairo. . . . He's one hell of a guy. We field men like him. Don't louse him up."

"All I wanted to ask was your name. I didn't expect a sermon."

"It's Houston. Fred Houston. See you in twenty minutes. Get rid of the tie."

Chapter Seventeen

Bill's Bar & Grill was a part of Carlyle Matlock had never seen before. Railroad laborers and freight-yard drifters were its predominant clientele. He scanned the filthy room; Houston sat in a back booth.

"It's cocktail hour, Matlock. A little early by campus standards, but the effects aren't much different. Not even the clothes these days."

"It's quite a place."

"It serves the purpose. Go up to the bar and get yourself a drink. The bunnies don't come on till sundown."

Matlock did as Houston instructed and brought back the best bourbon he could find. It was a brand he had given up when he reached a living wage.

"I think I should tell you right away. Someone using your name telephoned me at the hospital."

It was as if Houston had been hit in the stomach. "My God," he said quietly. "What did he say? How did you handle it?"

"I waited for him to identify himself . . . with Greenberg's proverb. I gave him a couple of chances but he didn't. . . . So I told him to call me later and hung up."

"He used *my* name?! *Houston*. You're sure?"

"Absolutely."

"That doesn't make sense. He *couldn't!*"

"Believe me. He did."

"No one knew I was the replacement. . . . *I* didn't know it until three this morning."

"Someone found out."

Houston took several swallows of his beer. "If what you say is true, I'll be

out of here within a couple of hours. Incidentally, that was good thinking.
. . . Let me give you an extra hint, though. Never accept a contact made by
telephone."

"Why not?"

"If that *had* been me calling—how would *I* know it was *you* I was talking
to?"

"I see what you mean. . ."

"Common sense. Most everything we do is common sense. . . . We'll keep
the same code. The 'old men' and 'the cities.' Your next contact will be made
tonight."

"You're sure you'll be leaving?"

"I've been *spotted*. I'm not *about* to stick around. Maybe you forgot Ralph
Loring. . . . We gave big at the office."

"All right. Have you talked to Jason? Did he brief you?"

"For two hours. From four till six this morning. My wife said he drank
thirteen cups of coffee."

"What can you tell me about Pat? Patricia Ballantyne. What happened?"

"You know the medical facts. . . ."

"Not all of them."

"I don't know *all* of them, either."

"You're lying."

Houston looked at Matlock without offense. When he replied, he did so
compassionately. "All right. There was evidence of rape. That's what you
want to know, isn't it?"

Matlock gripped his glass. "Yes," he said softly.

"However, you should know this, too. The girl doesn't know it. Not at
this stage of her recovery. I understand the mind plays tricks. It rejects
things until it thinks—or something tells it—that the remembering can be
handled."

"Thanks for the lesson is psychology. . . . Animals. Filthy animals . . ."
Matlock pushed his glass away. The liquor was intolerable to him now. The
thought of dulling his senses even slightly was abhorrent.

"I'm supposed to play this by ear, so if I read you wrong, all I can do is
apologize. . . . Be around when the puzzle gets put together for her. She's
going to need you."

Matlock looked up from the table, from the sight of his tensed hands. "It
was that bad?" he asked almost inaudibly.

"Preliminary lab tests—fingernails, hair, what have you—indicate that the
assault was carried out by more than one person."

Matlock's hatred could find only one expression. He closed his eyes and
lashed out at the glass, sending it across the floor, where it smashed in front
of the bar. The bartender dropped his soiled rag and started toward his latch,
looking over at the man who threw the glass. Then he stopped. Houston held
up a bill quickly, gesturing the man to stay away.

"Get hold of yourself!" Houston said. "You're not going to do anyone any
good like that. You're just calling attention to us. . . . Now, listen. You're
cleared to make further inquiries, but there are two stipulations. The first is
to check with our man—it was supposed to be me—before approaching
anyone. The second—keep your subjects to students and only students. No
faculty, no staff, no one outside—just students. . . . Make your reports every
night between ten and eleven. Your contact will reach you daily as to where.
Have you got that?"

Matlock stared at the agent in disbelief. He understood what the man was saying—even why he said it—but he couldn't believe that anyone who'd been briefed by Jason Greenberg would think he could deliver such instructions. "Are you serious?"

"The orders are explicit. No deviations. That's holy writ."

It was there again for Matlock. Another sign, another compromise. Another plastic order from the unseen plastic leaders.

"I'm there but I'm *not* there, is that the idea? I'm consigned to the outer limits and that fulfills the bargain?"

"Frig that."

Matlock's eyes wandered upward, at nothing. He was trying to buy a few seconds of sweet reason. "Frigga is the Norse goddess of the sky. She shares the heavens with Odin. Don't insult the lady, Houston."

"You're a nut!" said the agent. "I'm not sorry I'm getting out of here. . . . Look, it's for the best, take my word for it. And one last thing. I've got to take back the paper Loring gave you. That's a *must do*."

"Is it, really?" Matlock slid across the filthy leatherette seat and started to get up. "I don't see it that way. You go back to Washington and tell them I see it as a *must don't*. Take care of yourself, holy writ."

"You're playing around with preventive custody!"

"We'll see who's playing," said Matlock as he pushed himself away from the table, angling it to block the agent's exit, and started for the door. He could hear the screech of the table's legs as Houston moved it out of his way. He heard Houston call his name softly, intensely, as if he were confused, wanting to make Matlock come back, yet afraid of identifying him. Matlock reached the door, turned right on the sidewalk, and started running as fast as he could. He found a narrow alley and realized that it was, at least, in the right direction. He raced into it and stopped, pressing himself into a doorway. At the base of the alley, on the freight-yard thoroughfare, he saw Houston walking rapidly past the phlegmatic noonday laborers on their lunch breaks. Houston looked panicked; Matlock knew he couldn't return to his apartment.

It was a funny thing to do, he considered, as he sat in the booth of Bill's Bar & Grill. Returning to the place he couldn't wait to get out of twenty minutes ago. But it made vague sense to him—as much as anything made sense at the moment. He had to be by himself and think. He couldn't take the chance of wandering the streets where some part of the Greenberg-Houston unseen army might spot him. Ironically, the bar seemed safest.

He'd made his apologies to a wary bartender, offering to pay for the broken glass. He implied that the man he'd had words with before was a deadbeat—into him for a lot of money with no ability to pay. This explanation, given by the now-relaxed customer, was not only accepted by the bartender, it elevated him to a status not often seen in Bill's Bar & Grill.

He had to marshal his thoughts. There were checkpoints he'd mentally outlined which were to be passed before he began his journey to Nimrod. Now, there was another checkpoint. Houston had supplied it, although he'd never know. Pat had to be totally safe. He couldn't have that worry on his mind. All other items on his list were subservient to this. The clothes, the ready cash, the unfamiliar automobile, all would have to wait. He might have to alter his strategy now, Matlock thought. Nimrod's associates would be watched, his apartment would be watched, every name and location on the Justice list would be under surveillance.

But first, Pat. He'd have her guarded night and day, around the clock, every minute. Guarded openly, with no pretense of secrecy. Guarded in such a way as to be a signal to both the unseen armies, a warning that she was out of the game. Money was no problem now, none at all. And there were men in Hartford whose professions would fit his requirements. He knew that. The huge insurance companies used them incessantly. He remembered an ex-faculty member from the math department who'd left Carlyle for the lucrative field of insurance actuaries. He worked for Aetna. He looked for a telephone inside the dingy bar.

Eleven minutes later, Matlock returned to the booth. The business was concluded with Blackstone Security, Incorporated, Bond Street, Hartford. There would be three men daily on eight-hour shifts, three hundred dollars for each twenty-four-hour period the subject was covered by Blackstone, Inc. There would, of course, be the additional charges for any expenses incurred and a fee attached for the use of a "Tel-electronic" if it was required. The Tel-electronic was a small device which signaled the bearer with short beeps if the telephone number designated was called. Blackstone, of course, suggested a different telephone number from a resident phone—which, of course, they would have activated within twelve hours and for which, of course, there was an additional charge.

Matlock agreed to everything, was grateful *for* everything, and said he'd be in Hartford to sign the papers later in the afternoon. He wanted to meet Mr. Blackstone—for another reason now. Blackstone, however, made it clear that since the head of Aetna's actuarial department had personally contacted him regarding Mr. Matlock, the formalities were not pressing. He'd dispatch his team to the Carlyle Hospital within the hour. And by any chance, was Mr. Matlock related to Jonathan Munro Matlock . . . ? The head of Aetna's actuarial department had mentioned . . .

Matlock was relieved. Blackstone *could* be useful. The ex-faculty member at Aetna had assured him that there was none better than Blackstone. Expensive, but the best. Blackstone's personnel for the most part were former officers of the Special Forces and Marine Intelligence teams. It was more than a business gimmick. They were smart, resourceful, and tough. They were also licensed and respected by the state and local police.

The next item on his list was clothes. He had planned to go to his apartment and pack a suit, several pairs of slacks, and a jacket or two. Now that was out. At least for the time being. He would buy clothes—what he needed—as he went along. The ready cash could prove more of a problem, considering the amount he wanted. It was Saturday—he wasn't going to waste a Saturday night. The banks were closed, the large money sources unavailable.

Alex Anderson would have to solve the problem. He'd lie to Alex Anderson, tell him Jonathan Munro Matlock would look kindly—financially kindly—on Anderson if the banker would make available a large sum of cash on a Saturday afternoon. It would be confidential on both sides, of course. There would be a gratuity rendered for a coveted favor on a Saturday afternoon. Nothing which could be construed remotely indelicate. And, of course, again, confidential.

Matlock rose from the ripped, stained, dirty leatherette seat and returned to the telephone.

Anderson had only fleeting doubts about accommodating Jonathan Munro Matlock's son, and they concerned not the act but the confidence of the act.

Once that concern was allayed, the fact that he was giving aid in the best traditions of banking became clear. It was important for any bank to accommodate the better client. If a particular client wished to show gratitude . . . well, that was up to the client.

Alex Anderson would secure James Matlock five thousand dollars in cash on a Saturday afternoon. He would deliver it to him at three outside the Plaza Movie Theatre, which was showing a revival of *A Knife in the Water*—with subtitles.

An automobile would be the least of his problems. There were two rent-a-car offices in the town, a Budget-National and a Luxor-Elite. The first for students, the second for affluent parents. He would rent a Luxor Cadillac or Lincoln and drive into Hartford to another Luxor lot and change cars. From Hartford he'd go to a Luxor branch in New Haven and do the same. With money, there would be the minimum of questions; with decent tips, there might even be cooperation.

He'd moved to his point of departure.

"Hey, mister. Your name Matlock?" The hairy bartender leaned over the table, the soiled bar rag squeezed in his right hand.

"Yes," answered the startled Matlock with a short, violent intake of breath.

"Guy just came up t' me. Said for me to tell you you forgot something outside. On the curb, he said. You should hurry, he said."

Matlock stared at the man. The pain in his stomach was the fear again, the panic. He reached into his pocket and pulled out several bills. Separating a five, he held it up to the bartender. "Come to the door with me. Just to the window. Tell me if he's outside."

"Sure. . . . To the window." The hairy bartender switched the soiled rag to his left hand and took the bill. Matlock got out of the booth and walked beside the man to the half-curtained, filthy glass looking out on the street.

"No, he's not there. There's no one there. . . . Just a dead . . ."

"I see," said Matlock, cutting the man off. He didn't have to go outside, it wasn't necessary.

Lying on the edge of the curb, its body draping down into the gutter, was Matlock's cat.

Its head was severed, held to the rest of its body by a small piece of flesh. The blood poured out, staining the sidewalk.

Chapter Eighteen

The killing preyed on Matlock's mind as he approached the West Hartford town line. Was it another warning or had they found the paper? If they *had* found the paper, it didn't vitiate the warning, only reinforced it. He wondered whether to have a member of the Blackstone team check his apartment, check the litter box. He wasn't even sure why he hesitated. Why not have a Blackstone man find out? For three hundred dollars a day, plus charges, such an errand was hardly too much to ask. He was going to ask far more of Blackstone, Incorporated, but they didn't know it. Yet he kept balking. If the paper *was* secure, sending a man to check it might reveal its location.

He'd almost made up his mind to take the chance when he noticed the tan sedan in his rear-view mirror. It was there again. It had been there, off and on, since he'd entered Highway 72 a half hour ago. Whereas other cars turned off, passed him, or fell behind, this tan sedan was never really out of sight. Weaving in and around the traffic, it always managed to stay three or four cars behind him. There was one way to find out if it was coincidence. Off the next exit into West Hartford was a narrow street which wasn't a street at all but a cobblestone alley used almost exclusively for deliveries. He and Pat thought it was a shortcut one hectic afternoon and had been hemmed in for five minutes.

He swung off the exit and down the main street toward the alley. He made a sharp left and entered the narrow cobblestone lane. Since it was Saturday afternoon, there were no delivery trucks, and the alley was clear. He raced through, emerging in a crowded A & P parking lot, which in turn led to a parallel main road. Matlock drove to an empty parking space, shut off his motor, and lowered himself on the seat. He angled his side-view mirror so that it reflected the entrance of the alley. In roughly thirty seconds, the tan sedan came into view.

The driver was obviously confused. He slowed down, looking at the dozens of automobiles. Suddenly, behind the tan sedan, another car began blowing its horn. The driver was impatient; the tan sedan was blocking his progress. Reluctantly, the driver of the tan sedan started up; but before he did, he turned his face, craning his neck over his right shoulder in such a way that Matlock, now looking directly at the automobile, recognized him.

It was the patrolman. The police officer who'd been in his demolished apartment after the Beeson episode, the man who had covered his face with a towel and raced down the corridor of squash alley two days ago.

Greenberg's "coincidence."

Matlock was perplexed. He was also frightened.

The patrolman in mufti drove the tan sedan haltingly toward a parking lot exit, still obviously searching. Matlock saw the car turn into the flow of traffic and drive away.

The offices of Blackstone Security, Incorporated, Bond Street, Hartford, looked more like a wealthy, sedate insurance company than an investigatory agency. The furniture was heavy colonial, the wallpaper a subdued, masculine stripe. Expensive hunting prints above the glow of brass table lamps. The effect was immediately one of strength, virility, and financial solidity. Why not? thought Matlock, as he sat in the Early American two-seater in the outer office. At three hundred dollars a day, Blackstone Security, Incorporated, probably rivaled Prudential in ratio of investment to profits.

When he was at last ushered into the office, Michael Blackstone rose from his chair and walked around the cherrywood desk to greet him. Blackstone was a short, compact man, neatly dressed. He was in his early fifties, obviously a physical person, very active, probably very tough.

"Good afternoon," he said. "I hope you didn't drive down here just for the papers. They could have waited. Just because *we* work seven days a week, doesn't mean we expect the rest of the world to do so."

"I had to be in Hartford, anyway. No problem."

"Sit down, sit down. Can I offer you anything? A drink? Coffee?"

"No thanks." Matlock sat in a huge black leather chair, the kind of chair usually found in the oldest, most venerated men's clubs. Blackstone returned to his desk. "Actually, I'm in somewhat of a hurry. I'd like to sign our agreement, pay you, and leave."

"Certainly. The file's right here." Blackstone picked up a folder on his desk and smiled. "As I mentioned on the phone, there are questions we'd like answered, of course. Beyond what you've instructed us to do. It would help us carry out your orders. Take just a few minutes."

Matlock expected the request. It was part of his plan, why he wanted to see Blackstone. His assumption—once Blackstone entered the picture—was that Blackstone might be able to offer him shortcuts. Perhaps not willingly, but if it was a question of "an additional charge." . . . It was for this reason that he had to meet Blackstone face to face. If Blackstone could be bought, a great deal of time could be saved.

"I'll answer what I can. As I'm sure you've checked out, the girl was beaten severely."

"We know that. What puzzles us is the reluctance of anyone to say why. No one's given that sort of beating for kicks. Oh, it's possible, but that kind of case is generally handled quickly and efficiently by the police. There's no need for us. . . . Obviously you have information the police don't have."

"That's true. I do."

"May I ask why you haven't given it to them? Why you hired us? . . . The local police will gladly furnish protection if there's sufficient cause, and far less expensively."

"You sound like you're turning away business."

"We often do." Blackstone smiled. "It's never done happily, I can tell you that."

"Then why . . ."

"You're a highly recommended client," interrupted Blackstone, "the son of a very prominent man. We want you to know your alternatives. That's our reasoning. What's yours?"

"You're plainspoken. I appreciate it. I assume what you're saying is that you don't want your reputation tarnished."

"That's good enough."

"Good. That's my reasoning, too. Only it's not *my* reputation. It's the girl's. Miss Ballantyne's. . . . The simplest way to put it is that she showed bad judgment in her choice of friends. She's a brilliant girl with an exciting future, but unfortunately that intelligence didn't carry over into other areas." Matlock purposely stopped and took out a pack of cigarettes. Unhurriedly, he removed one and lit it. The pause had its effect. Blackstone spoke.

"Did she profit financially from these associations?"

"Not at all. As I see it, she was used. But I can understand why you asked. There's a lot of money to be made on campuses these days, isn't there?"

"I wouldn't know. Campuses aren't our field." Blackstone smiled again, and Matlock knew he was lying. Professionally, of course.

"I guess not."

"All right, Mr. Matlock. Why was she beaten? And what do you intend to do about it?"

"It's my opinion she was beaten to frighten her from revealing information *she doesn't have.* I intend to find the parties involved and tell them that. Tell them to leave her alone."

"And if you go to the police, her associations—past associations, I assume—become a matter of record and jeopardize this brilliant future of hers."

"Exactly."

"That's a tight story. . . . Who are these parties involved?"

"I don't know them by name. . . . However, I know their occupations. The main line of work seems to be gambling. I thought you might be able to help me here. Naturally, I would expect an additional charge for the service."

"I see." Blackstone got up and walked around his chair. For no particular reason, he fingered the dials on his inoperative air conditioner. "I think you presume too much."

"I wouldn't expect names. I'd like them, of course, and I'd pay well for them. . . . But I'd settle for locations. I can find them myself, and you know I can. You'd be saving me time, though."

"I gather you're interested in . . . private clubs. *Private* social organizations where members may meet to pursue activities of their choice."

"Outside the eye of the law. Where private citizens can follow their perfectly natural inclinations to place bets. That's where I'd like to start."

"Could I dissuade you? Is it possible I could convince you to go to the police, instead?"

"No."

Blackstone walked to a file cabinet on the left wall, took out a key, and opened it. "As I said, a tight story. Very plausible. And I don't believe a word of it. . . . However, you seem determined; that concerns me." He took a thin metal case from the file cabinet and carried it back to the desk. Selecting another key from his chain, he unlocked it and withdrew a single sheet of paper. "There's a Xerox machine over there," he said, pointing to a large gray copier in the corner. "To use it one places a page face down under the metal flap and dials the required duplicates. Records are kept of the numbers automatically. There's rarely a reason for more than one. . . . If you'll excuse me for approximately two minutes, Mr. Matlock, I must make a phone call in another office."

Blackstone held up the single sheet of paper, then placed it face down on top of Matlock's file folder. He stood erect, and, with the fingers of both hands, tugged at the base of his jacket in the manner of a man used to displaying expensive suits. He smiled and walked around his desk toward the office door. He opened it and turned back.

"It may be what you're looking for, and then again, it may not. I wouldn't know. I've simply left a confidential memorandum on my desk. The charge will be listed on your billing as . . . additional surveillance."

He went out the door, closing it firmly behind him. Matlock rose from the black leather chair and crossed behind the desk. He turned the paper over and read the typed heading.

FOR SURVEILLANCE: HARTFORD—NEW HAVEN AXIS
PRIVATE CLUBS: LOCATIONS AND CONTACTS (MANAGERS)
AS OF 3–15. NOT TO BE REMOVED FROM OFFICE

Beneath the short, capitalized paragraph were twenty-odd addresses and names.

Nimrod was closer now.

Chapter Nineteen

The Luxor-Elite Rental Agency on Asylum Street, Hartford, had been cooperative. Matlock now drove a Cadillac convertible. The manager had accepted the explanation that the Lincoln was too funereal, and since the registration papers were in order, the switch was perfectly acceptable.

So was the twenty-dollar tip.

Matlock had analyzed Blackstone's list carefully. He decided to concentrate on the clubs northwest of Hartford for the simple reason that they were nearer the Carlyle area. They weren't the nearest, however. Two locations were within five and seven miles of Carlyle respectively—in opposite directions—but Matlock decided to hold them off for a day or so. By the time he reached them—if he did so—he wanted the managements to know he was a heavy plunger. Not a mark, just heavy. The network gossip would take care of that—if he handled himself properly.

He checked off his first location. It was a private swimming club west of Avon. The contact was a man named Jacopo Bartolozzi.

At nine thirty Matlock drove up the winding driveway to a canopy extending from the entrance of the Avon Swim Club. A uniformed doorman signaled a parking attendant, who appeared out of nowhere and slid into the driver's seat the moment Matlock stepped onto the pavement. Obviously no parking ticket was to be given.

As he walked toward the entrance, he looked at the exterior of the club. The main building was a sprawling, one-story white brick structure with a tall stockade fence extending from both ends into the darkness. On the right, quite far behind the fence, was the iridescent glow of greenish blue light and the sound of water splashing. On the left was a huge tentlike canopy under which could be seen the shimmering light of dozens of patio torches. The former was obviously an enormous pool, the latter some kind of dining area. Soft music could be heard.

The Avon Swim Club appeared to be a very luxurious complex.

The interior did nothing to dispel this observation. The foyer was thickly carpeted and the various chairs and odd tables against the damask walls seemed genuine antiques. On the left was a large checkroom, and further down on the right was a white marble counter not unlike a hotel information desk. At the end of the narrow lobby was the only incongruous structure. It was a black, ornate wrought-iron gate, and it was closed, obviously locked. Beyond the grilled enclosure could be seen an open-air corridor, subtly lit, with an extended covering supported by a series of thin Ionic pillars. A large man in a tuxedo was standing at attention behind the iron gate. Matlock approached him.

"Your membership card, sir?"

"I'm afraid I don't have one."

"Sorry, sir, this is a private swimming club. Members only."

"I was told to ask for Mr. Bartolozzi."

The man behind the grill stared at Matlock, frisking him with his eyes.

"You'd better check the front desk, sir. Right over there."

Matlock walked back to the counter, to be greeted by a middle-aged, slightly paunchy desk clerk who had not been there when he first came in.

"May I help you?"

"You may. I'm fairly new in the area. I'd like to become a member."

"We're sorry. Membership's full right now. However, if you'll fill out an application, we'll be glad to call you if there's an opening. . . . Would that be a family application or individual, sir?" The clerk, very professionally, reached below the counter and brought up two application forms.

"Individual. I'm not married. . . . I was told to ask for Mr. Bartolozzi. I was told specifically to ask for him. Jacopo Bartolozzi."

The clerk gave the name only the slightest indication of recognition. "Here, fill out an application and I'll put it on Mr. Bartolozzi's desk. He'll see it in the morning. Perhaps he'll call you, but I don't know what he can do. Membership's full and there's a waiting list."

"Isn't he here now? On such a busy night?" Matlock said the words with a degree of incredulity.

"I doubt it, sir."

"Why don't you find out? Tell him we have mutual friends in San Juan." Matlock withdrew his money clip and removed a fifty-dollar bill. He placed it in front of the clerk, who looked at him sharply and slowly picked up the money.

"San Juan?"

"San Juan."

Matlock leaned against the white marble counter and saw the man behind the wrought-iron gate watching him. If the San Juan story worked and he got through the gate, he realized that he would have to part with another large-sized bill. The San Juan story *should* work, thought Matlock. It was logical to the point of innocence. He had spent a winter vacation in Puerto Rico two years ago, and although no gambler, he'd traveled with a crowd—and a girl—who made the nightly rounds of the casinos. He'd met a number of people from the Hartford vicinity, although he couldn't for the life of him remember a single name.

A foursome emerged from inside the grilled entrance, the girls giggling, the men laughing resignedly. The women had probably won twenty or thirty dollars, thought Matlock, while the men had probably lost several hundred. Fair exchange for the evening. The gate closed behind them; Matlock could hear the electric click of the latch. It was a very well-locked iron gate.

"Excuse me, sir?" It was the paunchy desk clerk, and Matlock turned around.

"Yes?"

"If you'll step inside, Mr. Bartolozzi will see you."

"Where? How?" There was no door except the wrought-iron gate and the clerk had gestured with his left hand, away from the gate.

"Over here, sir."

Suddenly a knobless, frameless panel to the right of the counter swung open. The outline was barely discernible when the panel was flush against the damask wall; when shut, no border was in evidence. Matlock walked in and was taken by the clerk to the office of Jacopo Bartolozzi.

"We got mutual friends?" The obese Italian spoke hoarsely as he leaned back in his chair behind the desk. He made no attempt to rise, gave no gesture of welcome. Jacopo Bartolozzi was a short, squat caricature of himself. Matlock couldn't be sure, but he had the feeling that Bartolozzi's feet weren't touching the floor beneath his chair.

"It amounts to the same thing, Mr. Bartolozzi."

"What amounts? Who's in San Juan?"

"Several people. One fellow's a dentist in West Hartford. Another's got an accounting firm in Constitution Plaza."

"Yeah. . . . Yeah?" Bartolozzi was trying to associate people with the professions and locations Matlock described. "What's the names? They members here?"

"I guess they are. They gave me *your* name."

"This is a swim club. Private membership. . . . Who are they?"

"Look, Mr. Bartolozzi, it was a crazy night at the Condado casino. We all had a lot to drink and . . ."

"They don't drink in the Puerto Rican casinos. It's a law!" The Italian spoke sharply, proud of his incisive knowledge. He was pointing his fat finger at Matlock.

"More honored in the breach, believe me."

"What?"

"We drank. Take my word for it. I'm just telling you I don't remember their names. . . . Look, I can go downtown on Monday and stand all day outside the Plaza and I'll find the CPA. I could also go out to West Hartford and ring every dentist's doorbell. What difference does it make? I like to play and I've got the money."

Bartolozzi smiled. "This is a swim club. I don't know what the hell you're talking about."

"O.K.," said Matlock with a disgruntled edge to his voice. "This place happened to be convenient, but if you want to show three lemons, there are others. My San Juan friends also told me about Jimmy Lacata's down in Middletown, and Sammy Sharpe's in Windsor Shoals. . . . Keep your chips, fink." He turned to the door.

"Hold it! Wait a minute!"

Matlock watched the fat Italian get out of the chair and stand up. He'd been right. Bartolozzi's feet couldn't have been touching the floor.

"What for? Maybe your limit's too small here."

"You know Lacata? Sharpe?"

"Know *of* them, I told you. . . . Look, forget it. You've got to be careful. I'll find my CPA on Monday and we'll both come back some other time. . . . I just felt like playing tonight."

"O.K. O.K. Like you said, we gotta be careful." Bartolozzi opened his top drawer and pulled out some papers. "C'mere. Sign 'em. You got an itch. Maybe I'll take your money. Maybe you'll take mine."

Matlock approached the desk. "What am I signing?"

"Just a couple of forms. Initiation's five hundred. Cash. You got it? No checks, no credit."

"I've got it. What are the forms?"

"The first is a statement that you understand that this is a non-profit corporation and that any games of chance are for charitable purposes. . . . What are you laughing at? I built the Church of the Blessed Virgin down in Hamden."

"What's this other? It's a long one."

"That's for our files. A certificate of general partnership. For the five hundred you get a classy title. You're a partner. Everybody's a partner. . . . Just in case."

"In case?"

"In case anything good happens to us, it happens just as good to you. Especially in the newspapers."

The Avon Swim Club was certainly a place for swimming, no doubt about it. The enormous pool curved back nearly two hundred feet, and scores of small, elegant cabanas bordered the far side. Beach chairs and tables were dotted about the grassy edges beyond the tiled deck of the pool, and the underwater floodlights made the setting inviting. All this was on the right of the open-air corridor. On the left, Matlock could see fully what was only hinted at from the outside. A huge green-and-white-striped tent rose above dozens of tables. Each table had a candled lantern in the center, and patio torches were safely placed about the whole enclosure. At the far end was a long table filled with roasts, salads, and buffet food. A bar was adjacent to the long table; scores of couples were milling about.

The Avon Swim Club was a lovely place to bring the family.

The corridor led to the rear of the complex, where there was another sprawling, white-bricked structure similar to the main building. Above the large, black-enameled double doors was a wooden sign in old English scroll:

The Avon Spa

This part of the Avon Swim Club was not a lovely place to bring the family.

Matlock thought he was back in a San Juan casino—his only experience in gambling rooms. The wall-to-wall carpet was sufficiently thick to muffle sound almost completely. Only the click of the chips and the low-keyed but intense mutterings of the players and the board men were heard. The craps tables were lined along the walls, the blackjack counters in the center. In between, in staggered positions to allow for the flow of traffic, were the roulette wheels. In the middle of the large room, raised on a platform, was the cashier's nest. All of the Avon Spa's employees were in tuxedos, neatly groomed and subservient. The players were less formal.

The gate man, pleased with Matlock's crisp fifty-dollar bill, led him to the half-circle counter in front of the cashier's platform. He spoke to a man counting out slips of paper.

"This is Mr. Matlock. Treat him good, he's a personal friend."

"No other way," said the man with a smile.

"I'm sorry, Mr. Matlock," muttered the gate man quietly. "No markers the first time around."

"Naturally. . . . Look, I'm going to wander about. . . ."

"Sure. Get the feel of the action. . . . I tell you, it ain't Vegas. Between you and me, it's Mickey Mouse most of the time. I mean for a guy like you, you know what I mean?"

Matlock knew exactly what the gate man meant. A fifty-dollar bill was not the ordinary gratuity in Avon, Connecticut.

It took him three hours and twelve minutes to lose $4,175. The only time he felt panic was when he had a streak at the craps table and had built up his reserves to nearly $5,000. He had begun the evening properly—for his purposes. He went to the cashier often enough to realize that the average purchase of chips was $200 to $300. Hardly "Mickey Mouse" in his book. So his first purchase was $1,500. The second was $1,000; the third $2,000.

By one in the morning, he was laughing with Jacopo Bartolozzi at the bar underneath the green-and-white-striped tent.

"You're a game one. Lots'a creeps would be screaming 'ice pick' if they went for a bundle like you did. Right now I'd be showing them a few papers in my office."

"Don't you worry, I'll get it back. I always do. . . . You said it before. My itch was too much. Maybe I'll come back tomorrow."

"Make it Monday. Tomorrow it's only swimming."

"How come?"

"Sunday. Holy day."

"Shit! I've got a friend coming in from London. He won't be here Monday. He's a big player."

"Tell you what. I'll call Sharpe over in Windsor Shoals. He's a Jew. Holy days don't mean a fucking thing to him."

"I'd appreciate that."

"I may even drop over myself. The wife's got a Mothers of Madonna meeting, anyway."

Matlock looked at his watch. The evening—his point of departure—had gone well. He wondered if he should press his luck. "Only real problem coming into a territory is the time it takes to find the sources."

"What's your problem?"

"I've got a girl over in the motel. She's sleeping, we traveled most of the day. She ran out of grass—no hard stuff—just grass. I told her I'd pick some up for her."

"Can't help you, Matlock. I don't keep none here, what with the kids around during the day. It's not good for the image, see? A few pills, I got. No needle crap, though. You want some pills?"

"No, just grass. That's all I let her use."

"Very smart of you. . . . Which way you headed?"

"Back into Hartford."

Bartolozzi snapped his fingers. A large bartender sprang into position instantly. Matlock thought there was something grotesque about the squat little Italian commandeering in such fashion. Bartolozzi asked the man for paper and pencil.

"Here. Here's an address. I'll make a phone call. It's an after-hours place right off the main drag. Down the street from G. Fox. Second floor. Ask for Rocco. What you couldn't use, he's got."

"You're a prince." And as Matlock took the paper, he meant it.

"For four grand the first night, you got privileges. . . Hey, y'know what? You never filled out an application! That's a gas, huh?"

"You don't need credit references. I play with cash."

"Where the hell do you keep it?"

"In thirty-seven banks from here to Los Angeles." Matlock put down his glass and held out his hand to Bartolozzi. "It's been fun. See you tomorrow?"

"Sure, sure. I'll walk you to the door. Don't forget now. Don't give Sammy all the action. Come on back here."

"My word on it."

The two men walked back to the open-air corridor, the short Italian placing his fat hand in the middle of Matlock's back, the gesture of a new friend. What neither man realized as they stepped onto the narrow causeway was that one well-dressed gentleman at a nearby table who kept punching at a fluidless lighter was watching them. As the two men passed his table, he put his lighter back into his pocket while the woman across from him lit his cigarette with a match. The woman spoke quietly through a smile.

"Did you get them?"

The man laughed softly. "Karsh couldn't have done better. Even got close-ups."

Chapter Twenty

If the Avon Swim Club was an advantageous point of departure, the Hartford Hunt Club—under the careful management of Rocco Aiello—was an enviable first lap. For Matlock now thought of his journey to Nimrod as a race, one which had to end within two weeks and one day. It would end with the convocation of the Nimrod forces and the Mafiosi somewhere in the Carlyle vicinity. It would be finished for him when someone, somewhere produced another silver Corsican paper.

Bartolozzi's telephone call was effective. Matlock entered the old red stone building—at first he thought he had the wrong address, for no light shone through the windows, and there was no sign of activity within—and found a freight elevator at the end of the hallway with a lone Negro operator sitting in a chair in front of the door. No sooner had he come in than the black rose to his feet and indicated the elevator to Matlock.

In an upstairs hallway a man greeted him. "Very nice to make your acquaintance. Name's Rocco. Rocco Aiello." The man held out his hand and Matlock took it.

"Thanks. . . . I was puzzled. I didn't hear anything. I thought maybe I was in the wrong place."

"If you had heard, the construction boys would have taken me. The walls are eighteen inches thick, sound-proofed both sides; the windows are blinds. Very secure."

"That's really something."

Rocco reached into his pocket and withdrew a small wooden cigarette case. "I got a box of joints for you. No charge. I'd like to show you around, but Jock-O said you might be in a hurry."

"Jock-O's wrong. I'd like to have a drink."

"Good! Come on in. . . . Only one thing, Mr. Matlock. I got a nice clientele, you know what I mean? Very rich, very cube. Some of them know about Jock-O's operation, most of them don't. You know what I mean?"

"I understand. I was never much for swimming anyway."

"Good, good. . . . Welcome to Hartford's finest." He opened the thick steel door. "I hear you went for a bundle tonight."

Matlock laughed as he walked into the complex of dimly lit rooms crowded with tables and customers. "Is that what it's called?"

"In Connecticut, that's what it's called. . . . See? I got two floors—a duplex, like. Each floor's got five big rooms, a bar in each room. Very private, no bad behavior. Nice place to bring the wife, or somebody else, you know what I mean?"

"I think I do. It's quite something."

"The waiters are mostly college boys. I like to help them make a few dollars for their education. I got niggers, spics, ikes—I got no discrimination. Just the hair, I don't go for the long hair, you know what I mean?"

"College kids! Isn't that dangerous? Kids talk."

"Hey, what d'you think?! This place was originally started by a Joe College. It's like a fraternity home. Everybody's a bona fide, dues-paying member of a private organization. They can't getcha for that."

"I see. What about the other part?"

"What other part?"

"What I came for."

"What? A little grass? Try the corner newsstand."

Matlock laughed. He didn't want to overdo it. "Two points, Rocco. . . . Still, if I knew you better, may be I'd like to make a purchase. Bartolozzi said what I couldn't use, you've got. . . . Forget it, though. I'm bushed. I'll just get a drink and shove off. The girl's going to wonder where I've been."

"Sometimes Bartolozzi talks too much."

"I think you're right. By the way, he's joining me tomorrow night at Sharpe's over in Windsor Shoals. I've got a friend flying in from London. Care to join us?"

Aiello was obviously impressed. The players from London were beginning to take precedence over the Vegas and Caribbean boys. Sammy Sharpe's wasn't that well known, either.

"Maybe I'll do that. . . . Look, you need something, you feel free to ask, right?"

"I'll do that. Only I don't mind telling you, the kids make me nervous."

Aiello took Matlock's elbow with his left hand and walked him toward the bar. "You got it wrong. These kids—they're not kids, you know what I mean?"

"No, I don't. Kids are kids. I like my action a little more subdued. No sweat. I'm not curious." Matlock looked up at the bartender and withdrew what was left of his bankroll. He removed a twenty-dollar bill and placed it on the bar. "Old Fitz and water, please."

"Put your money away," Rocco said.

"Mr. Aiello?" A young man in a waiter's jacket approached them. He was perhaps twenty-two or twenty-three, Matlock thought.

"Yeah?"

"If you'll sign this tab. Table eleven. It's the Johnsons. From Canton. They're O.K."

Aiello took the waiter's pad and scribbled his initials. The young man walked back toward the tables.

"See that kid? That's what I mean. He's a Yalie. He got back from Nam six months ago."

"So?"

"He was a lieutenant. An officer. Now he's studying business administration. . . . He fills in here maybe twice a week. Mostly for contacts. By the time he gets out, he'll have a real nest egg. Start his own business."

"What?"

"He's a supplier. . . . These kids, that's what I mean. You should hear their stories. Saigon, Da Nang. Hong Kong, even. Real peddling. Hey, these kids today, they're great! They know what's up. Smart, too. No worries, believe me!"

"I believe you." Matlock took his drink and swallowed quickly. It wasn't that he was thirsty, he was trying to conceal his shock at Aiello's revelation. The graduates of Indochina were not the pink-cheeked, earnest, young-old veterans of Armentières, Anzio, or even Panmunjom. They were something else, something faster, sadder, infinitely more knowing. A hero in Indochina was the soldier who had contacts on the docks and in the warehouses. That man in Indochina was the giant among his peers. And such young-old men were almost all back.

Matlock drank the remainder of his bourbon and let Rocco show him the other rooms on the third floor. He displayed the controlled appreciation Aiello expected and promised he'd return. He said no more about Sammy Sharpe's in Windsor Shoals. He knew it wasn't necessary. Aiello's appetite had been whetted.

As he drove away, two thoughts occupied his mind. Two objectives had to be accomplished before Sunday afternoon was over. The first was that he had to produce an Englishman; the second was that he had to produce another large sum of money. It was imperative that he have both. He had to be at Sharpe's in Windsor Shoals the next evening.

The Englishman he had in mind lived in Webster, an associate professor of mathematics at a small parochial campus, Madison University. He had been in the country less than two years; Matlock had met him—quite unprofessionally—at a boat show in Saybrook. The Britisher had lived on the Cornwall coast most of his life and was a sailing enthusiast. Matlock and Pat had liked him immediately. Now Matlock hoped to God that John Holden knew something about gambling.

The money was a more serious problem. Alex Anderson would have to be tapped again, and it was quite possible that he'd find enough excuses to put him off. Anderson was a cautious man, easily frightened. On the other hand, he had a nose for rewards. That instinct would have to be played upon.

Holden had seemed startled but not at all annoyed by Matlock's telephone call. If he was anything other than kind, it was curious. He repeated the directions to his apartment twice and Matlock thanked him, assuring him that he remembered the way.

"I'll be perfectly frank, Jim," said Holden, admitting Matlock into his neat three-room apartment. "I'm simply bursting. Is anything the matter? Is Patricia all right?"

"The answers are yes and no. I'll tell you everything I can, which won't be a hell of a lot. . . . I want to ask you a favor, though. Two favors, actually. The first, can I stay here tonight?"

"Of course—you needn't ask. You looked peaked. Come, sit down. Can I get you a drink?"

"No, no thanks." Matlock sat on Holden's sofa. He remembered that it was one of those hide-a-beds and that it was comfortable. He and Pat had slept in it one happy, alcoholic night several months ago. It seemed ages ago.

"What's the second favor? The first is my pleasure. If it's cash, I've something over a thousand. You're entirely welcome to it."

"No, not money, thanks just the same. . . . I'd like you to impersonate an Englishman for me."

Holden laughed. He was a small-boned man of forty, but he laughed the way older, fatter men laughed.

"That shouldn't be too demanding, now should it? I suspect there's still a trace of Cornwall in my speech. Hardly noticeable, of course."

"Hardly. With a little practice you may even lose the Yankee twang. . . . There's something else, though, and it may not be so easy. Have you ever gambled?"

"Gambled? You mean horses, football matches?"

"Cards, dice, roulette?"

"Not substantially, no. Of course, as any reasonably imaginative mathematician, I went through a phase when I thought that by applying arithmetical principles—logarithmic averages—one could beat the gambling odds."

"Did they work?"

"I said I went through the phase, I didn't stay there. If there's a mathematical system, it eluded me. Still does."

"But you've played? You know the games."

"Rather well, when you come right down to it. Laboratory research, you might say. Why?"

Matlock repeated the story he had told Blackstone. However, he minimized Pat's injuries and lightened the motives of those who assaulted her. When he finished, the Englishman, who'd lit his pipe, knocked the ashes out of the bowl into a large glass ashtray.

"It's right out of the cinema, isn't it? . . . You say Patricia's not seriously hurt. Frightened but nothing much more than that?"

"Right. If I went to the police it might louse up her scholarship money."

"I see. . . . Well, I don't really, but we'll let it go. And you'd rather I lost tomorrow night."

"That doesn't matter. Just that you bet a great deal."

"But you're *prepared* for heavy losses."

"I am."

Holden stood up. "I'm perfectly willing to go through with this performance. It should prove rather a lark. However, there's a great deal you're not telling me and I wish you would. But I shan't insist upon it. I will tell you that your story is boggled with a large mathematical inconsistency."

"What's that?"

"As I understand it, the money you are prepared to lose tomorrow evening is far in excess of any amount Patricia might realize in scholarship aid. The logical assumption, therefore, is that you do not wish to go to the police. Or perhaps, you can't."

Matlock looked up at the Englishman and wondered at his own stupidity. He felt embarrassed and very inadequate. "I'm sorry. . . . I haven't consciously lied to you. You don't have to go through with it: may be I shouldn't have asked."

"I never implied that you lied—not that it matters. Only that there was much you haven't told me. Of course, I'll do it. I just want you to know I'm a willing audience when and if you decide to tell me everything that's happened. . . . Now, it's late and you're tired. Why don't you take my room."

"No, thanks. I'll sack out here. It has pleasant memories. A blanket's all I need. Also I have to make a phone call."

"Anything you say. A blanket you'll get, and you know where the phone is."

When Holden left, Matlock went to the phone. The Tel-electronic device he'd agreed to lease would not be ready until Monday morning.

"Blackstone."

"This is James Matlock. I was told to call this number for any messages."

"Yes, Mr. Matlock. There is a message, if you'll hold on while I get the card. . . . Here it is. From the Carlyle team. Everything is secure. The subject is responding nicely to medical treatment. The subject had three visitors. A Mr. Samuel Kressel, a Mr. Adrian Sealfont, and a Miss Lois Meyers. The subject received two telephone calls, neither of which the physician allowed to be taken. They were from the same individual, a Mr. Jason Greenberg. The calls were placed from Wheeling, West Virginia. At no time was the subject separated from the Carlyle team. . . . You can relax."

"Thank you. I will. You're very thorough. Good night." Matlock breathed deeply in relief and exhaustion. Lois Meyers lived across the hall from Pat in the graduate apartment house. The fact that Greenberg had called was comforting. He missed Greenberg.

He reached up and turned off the table lamp by the sofa. The bright April moon shone through the windows. The man from Blackstone's service was right—he could relax.

What he couldn't allow to relax were his thoughts about tomorrow—and after tomorrow. Everything had to remain accelerated; one productive day had to lead into another. There could be no letup, no sense of momentary satisfaction which might slow his thrust.

And after tomorrow. After Sammy Sharpe's in Windsor Shoals. If all went according to his calculations, it would be the time to head into the Carlyle area. Matlock closed his eyes and saw Blackstone's printed page in front of his mind.

CARMOUNT COUNTRY CLUB—CONTACT: HOWARD STOCKTON
WEST CARLYLE SAIL AND SKI RESORT—CONTACT: ALAN CANTOR

Carmount was east of Carlyle near the border of Mount Holly. The Sail and Ski was west, on Lake Derron—a summer and winter resort area.

He'd find some reason to have Bartolozzi or Aiello, or, perhaps, Sammy Sharpe, make the proper introductions. And once in the Carlyle area, he would drop the hints. Perhaps more than hints—commands, requirements, necessities. This was the boldness he needed to use, this was the way of Nimrod.

His eyes remained closed, the muscles in his body sagged, and the pitch darkness of exhausted sleep came over him. But before sleeping he remembered the paper. The Corsican paper. He had to get the paper now. He would need the silver paper. He would need the invitation to Nimrod.

His invitation now. His paper.

The Matlock paper.

Chapter Twenty-one

If the elders at the Windsor Shoals Congregational Church had ever realized that Samuel Sharpe, attorney at law, the very bright Jewish lawyer who handled the church's finances, was referred to as Sammy the Runner by most of North Hartford and South Springfield, Massachusetts, vespers would have been canceled for a month. Fortunately, such a revelation had never been made to them and the Congregational Church looked favorably on him. He had done remarkable things for the church's portfolio and gave handsomely himself during fund drives. The Congregational Church of Windsor Shoals, as indeed most of the town, was nicely disposed toward Samuel Sharpe.

Matlock learned all of this in Sharpe's office inside the Windsor Valley Inn. The framed citations on the wall told half the story, and Jacopo Bartolozzi good-naturedly supplied the rest. Jacopo was actually making sure that Matlock and his English friend were aware that Sharpe's operation, as well as Sharpe himself, lacked the fine traditions of the Avon Swim Club.

Holden surpassed Matlock's expectations. Several times he nearly laughed out loud as he watched Holden take hundred-dollar bills—rushed into

Webster by a harassed, nervous Alex Anderson—and flick them nonchalantly at a croupier, never bothering to count the chips but somehow letting everyone at whatever table he was at realize that he knew—to the dollar—the amount given him. Holden played intelligently, cautiously, and at one point was ahead of the house by nine thousand dollars. By the end of the evening, he had cut his winnings to several hundreds and the operators of the Windsor Valley breathed grateful sighs of relief.

James Matlock cursed his second night of terrible luck and took his twelve-hundred-dollar loss for what it meant to him—nothing.

At four in the morning Matlock and Holden, flanked by Aiello, Bartolozzi, Sharpe, and two of their cronies, sat at a large oak table in the colonial dining room. They were alone. A waiter and two busboys were cleaning up; the gambling rooms on the third floor of the inn had closed.

The husky Aiello and the short, fat Bartolozzi kept up a running commentary about their respective clientele, each trying to upstage the other with regard to their customers' status; each allowing that "it might be nice" for the other to become "acquainted" with a Mr. and Mrs. Johnson of Canton or a certain Dr. Wadsworth. Sharpe, on the other hand, seemed more interested in Holden and the action in England. He told several funny, self-effacing stories about his visits to London clubs and his insurmountable difficulty with British currency in the heat of betting.

Matlock thought, as he watched Sammy Sharpe, that he was a very charming man. It wasn't hard to believe that Sharpe was considered a respectable asset to Windsor Shoals, Connecticut. He couldn't help comparing Sharpe to Jason Greenberg. And in the comparison, he found an essential difference. It was told in the eyes. Greenberg's were soft and compassionate, even in anger. Sharpe's were cold, hard, incessantly darting—strangely in conflict with the rest of his relaxed face.

He heard Bartolozzi ask Holden where he was off to next. Holden's offhand reply gave him the opportunity he was looking for. He waited for the right moment.

"I'm afraid I'm not at liberty to discuss my itinerary."

"He means where he's going," injected Rocco Aiello.

Bartolozzi shot Aiello a withering glance. "I just thought you should drop over to Avon. I got a real nice place I think you'd enjoy."

"I'm sure I would. Perhaps another time."

"Johnny'll be in touch with me next week," Matlock said. "We'll get together." He reached for an ashtray and crushed out his cigarette. "I have to be in . . . Carlyle, that's the name of the place."

There was the slightest pause in the conversation. Sharpe, Aiello, and one of the other two men exchanged looks. Bartolozzi, however, seemed oblivious to any deep meaning.

"The college place?" asked the short Italian.

"That's right," answered Matlock. "I'll probably stay at Carmount or the Sail and Ski. I guess you fellows know where they are."

"I guess we do." Aiello laughed softly.

"What's your business in Carlyle?" The unidentified man—at least no one had bothered to introduce him by name—drew deeply on a cigar as he spoke.

"*My* business," said Matlock pleasantly.

"Just asking. No offense."

"No offense taken. . . . Hey, it's damned near four thirty! You fellows are too hospitable." Matlock pushed his chair back, prepared to stand.

The man with the cigar, however, had to ask another question.

"Is your friend going to Carlyle with you?"

Holden held up his hand playfully. "Sorry, no itineraries. I'm simply a visitor to your pleasant shores and filled with a tourist's plans. . . . We really must go."

Both men rose from the table. Sharpe stood, too. Before the others could move, Sharpe spoke.

"I'll see the boys to their car and show them the road out. You fellows wait here—we'll settle accounts. I owe you money, Rocco. Frank owes me. Maybe I'll come out even."

The man with the cigar, whose name was obviously Frank, laughed. Aiello looked momentarily perplexed but within seconds grasped the meaning of Sharpe's statement. The men at the table were to remain.

Matlock wasn't sure he'd handled the situation advantageously.

He had wanted to pursue the Carlyle discussion just enough to have someone offer to make the necessary calls to Carmount and the Sail and Ski. Holden's refusal to speak about his itinerary precluded it, and Matlock was afraid that it also implied that he and Holden were so important that further introductions were unnecessary. In addition, Matlock realized that as his journey progressed, he banked more and more on the dead Loring's guarantee that none of those invited to the Carlyle conference would discuss delegates among themselves. The meaning of "Omerta" was supposedly so powerful that silence was inviolate. Yet Sharpe had just commanded those at the table to remain.

He had the feeling that perhaps he had gone too far with too little experience. Perhaps it was time to reach Greenberg—although he'd wanted to wait until he had more concrete knowledge before doing so. If he made contact with Greenberg now, the agent might force him—what was the idiotic phrase?—out of strategy. He wasn't prepared to face that problem.

Sharpe escorted them to the near-deserted parking lot. The Windsor Valley Inn wasn't crowded with overnight guests.

"We don't encourage sleeping accommodations," Sharpe explained. "We're known primarily as a fine restaurant."

"I can understand that," said Matlock.

"Gentlemen," began Sharpe haltingly. "May I make a request that might be considered impolite?"

"Go right ahead."

"May I have a word with you, Mr. Matlock? Privately."

"Oh, don't concern yourself," said Holden, moving off. "I understand fully. I'll just walk around."

"He's a very nice fellow, your English friend," Sharpe said.

"The nicest. What is it, Sammy?"

"Several points of information, as we say in court."

"What are they?"

"I'm a cautious man, but I'm also very curious. I run a fine organization, as you can see."

"I can see."

"I'm growing nicely—cautiously, but nicely."

"I'll accept that."

"I don't make mistakes. I've a trained legal mind and I'm proud that I don't make mistakes."

"What are you driving at?"

"It strikes me—and I must be honest with you, it has also occurred to my partner Frank and to Rocco Aiello—that you may have been sent into the territory to make certain observations."

"Why do you think that?"

"Why? . . . From nowhere comes a player like you. You got powerful friends in San Juan. You know our places like the back of your hand. Then you have a very rich, very nice associate from the London scene. That all adds up. . . . But most important—and I think you know it—you mention this business in Carlyle. Let's be honest. That speaks a whole big book, doesn't it?"

"Does it?"

"I'm not foolhardy. I told you, I'm a cautious man. I understand the rules and I don't ask questions I'm not supposed to ask or talk about things I'm not privileged to know about. . . . Still, I want the generals to realize they have a few intelligent, even ambitious, lieutenants in the organization. Anyone can tell you. I don't skim, I don't hold back."

"Are you asking me to give you a good report?"

"That about sizes it up. I have value. I'm a respected attorney. My partner's a very successful insurance broker. We're naturals."

"What about Aiello? It seems to me you're friendly with him."

"Rocco's a good boy. Maybe not the quickest, but solid. He's a kind person, too. However, I don't believe he's in our league."

"And Bartolozzi?"

"I have nothing to say about Bartolozzi. You'll have to make up your own mind about him."

"By saying nothing, you're saying a lot, aren't you?"

"In my opinion, he talks too much. But that could be his personality. He rubs me the wrong way. Not Rocco, though."

Matlock watched the methodical Sharpe in the predawn light of the parking lot and began to understand what had happened. It was logical; he, himself, had planned it, but now that it was taking place, he felt curiously objective. Observing himself; watching reacting puppets.

He had entered Nimrod's world a stranger; possibly suspect, certainly devious.

Yet suddenly, that suspicion, that deviousness, was not to be scorned but *honored*.

The suspect honored for his deviousness—because it *had* to come from a higher source. He was an emissary from the upper echelons now. He was feared.

What had Greenberg called it? The shadow world. Unseen armies positioning their troops in darkness, constantly on the alert for stray patrols, unfriendly scouts.

The thin line he had to tread was precarious. But it was his now.

"You're a good man, Sharpe. Goddamn smart, too. . . . What do you know about Carlyle?"

"Nothing! Absolutely nothing."

"Now you're lying, and that's *not* smart."

"It's true. I don't *know anything*. Rumors I've heard. Knowledge and hearsay are two different kinds of testimony." Sharpe held up his right hand, his two forefingers separated.

"What rumors? Give it straight, for your own sake."

"Just rumours. A gathering of the clan, maybe. A meeting of very highly placed individuals. An agreement which has to be reached between certain people."

"Nimrod?"

Sammy Sharpe closed his eyes for precisely three seconds. During those moments he spoke.

"Now you talk language I don't want to hear."

"Then you didn't hear it, did you?"

"It's stricken from the record, I assure you."

"O.K. You're doing fine. And when you go back inside, I don't think it would be such a good idea to discuss the rumors you've heard. That would be acting like a stupid lieutenant, wouldn't it?"

"Not only stupid—insane."

"Why did you tell them to stay, then? It's late."

"For real. I wanted to know what everybody thought of you and your English friend. I'll tell you now, though—since you have mentioned a certain name, no such discussion will take place. As I said, I understand the rules."

"Good. I believe you. You've got possibilities. You'd better go back in. . . . Oh, one last thing. I want you . . . *we* want you to call Stockton at Carmount and Cantor at the Sail and Ski. Just say I'm a personal friend and I'll be showing up. Nothing else. We don't want any guards up. That's important, Sammy. Nothing else."

"It's my pleasure. And you won't forget to convey my regards to the others?"

"I won't forget. You're a good man."

"I do my best. It's all a person can do . . ."

Just then, the quiet of the predawn was shattered by five loud reports. Glass smashed. The sounds of people running and screaming and furniture crashing came from within the inn. Matlock threw himself to the ground.

"John! John!"

"Over here! By the car! Are you all right?!"

"Yes. Stay there!"

Sharpe had run into the darkness by the base of the building. He crouched into a corner, pressing himself against the brick. Matlock could barely see the outline of his form, but he could see enough to watch Sharpe withdraw a revolver from inside his jacket.

Again there was a volley of shots from the rear of the building, followed once more by screams of terror. A busboy crashed through the side door and crawled on his hands and knees toward the edge of the parking lot. He shouted hysterically in a language Matlock could not understand.

Several seconds later, another of the inn's employees in a white jacket ran through the door pulling a second man behind him, this one obviously wounded, blood pouring from his shoulder, his right arm dangling, immobile.

Another shot rang out of nowhere and the waiter who had been screaming fell over. The wounded man behind him went pummeling forward, crashing face down into the gravel. Within the building, men were shouting.

"Let's go! Get *out!* Get to the *car!*"

He fully expected to see men come scrambling out of the side door into the parking lot, but no one came. Instead, from another section of the property, he heard the gunning of an engine and, moments later, the screeching of tires as an automobile made a sharp turn. And then, to his left, about fifty yards away, a black sedan came racing out of the north driveway toward the main road. The car had to pass under a street light, and Matlock saw it clearly.

It was the same automobile that had plunged out of the darkness moments after Ralph Loring's murder.

Everything was still again. The grayish light of dawn was getting brighter.

"Jim! Jim, come here! I think they've gone!"

It was Holden. He had left the sanctuary of the automobile and was crouching over the man in the white jacket.

"Coming!" said Matlock, getting off the ground.

"This fellow's dead. He was shot between the shoulders. . . . This one's still breathing. Better get an ambulance." Holden had walked over to the unconscious busboy with the bloodied, immobile right arm.

"I don't hear anything. Where's Sharpe?"

"He just went inside. That door. He had a gun."

The two men walked carefully to the side entrance of the inn. Matlock slowly opened the door and preceded Holden into the foyer. Furniture was overturned, chairs and tables on their sides; blood was glistening on the wooden floor.

"Sharpe? Where are you?" Matlock raised his voice cautiously. It was several seconds before the reply came. When it did, Sharpe could hardly be heard.

"In here. In the dining room."

Matlock and Holden walked through the oak-framed arch. Nothing in either man's life had prepared him for what he saw.

The overpowering horror was the sight of the bodies literally covered with blood. What was left of Rocco Aiello was sprawled across the red-soaked tablecloth, most of his face blown off. Sharpe's partner, the unintroduced man named Frank, was on his knees, his torso twisted back over the seat of a chair, blood flowing out of his neck, his eyes wide open in death. Jacopo Bartolozzi was on the floor, his obese body arched around the leg of a table, the front of his shirt ripped up to the collar, revealing his bulging stomach, the flesh pierced with a score of bullet holes, blood still trickling out over the coarse black hair. Bartolozzi had tried to tear his shirt away from his battered chest, and a portion of cloth was clutched in his dead hand. The fourth man lay behind Bartolozzi, his head resting on Bartolozzi's right foot, his arms and legs extended in a spread-eagle pattern, his entire back covered with a thick layer of blood, portions of his intestines pushed through the skin.

"Oh, my God!" muttered Matlock, not fully believing what he saw. John Holden looked as though he might become sick. Sharpe spoke softly, rapidly, wearily.

"You'd better go. You and your English friend better leave quickly."

"You'll have to call the police," said Matlock, bewildered.

"There's a man outside, a boy. He's still alive." Holden stuttered as he spoke.

Sharpe looked over at the two men, the revolver at his side, his eyes betraying only the slightest degree of suspicion. "I have no doubt the lines have been cut. The nearest houses are farms at least half a mile from here. . . . I'll take care of everything. You'd better get out of here."

"Do you think we should?" asked Holden, looking at Matlock.

Sharpe replied. "Listen, Englishman, personally I couldn't care less what either of you do. I've got enough to think about, enough to figure out. . . . For your own good, get out of here. Less complications, less risk. Isn't that right?"

"Yes, you're right," Matlock said.

"In case you're picked up, you left here a half hour ago. You were friends of Bartolozzi, that's all I know."

"All right."

Sharpe had to turn away from the sight of the murdered men. Matlock thought for a moment that the Windsor Shoals attorney was going to weep. Instead, he took a deep breath and spoke again.

"A trained legal mind, Mr. Matlock. I'm valuable. You tell them that."

"I will."

"You also tell them I need protection, *deserve* protection. You tell them that, too."

"Of course."

"Now, get out." Suddenly Sharpe threw his revolver on the floor in disgust. And then he screamed, as the tears came to his eyes, "Get out for Christ's sake! *Get out!*"

Chapter Twenty-two

Matlock and Holden agreed to separate immediately. The English professor dropped off the mathematician at his apartment and then headed south to Fairfield. He wanted to register at a highway motel far enough away from Windsor Shoals to feel less panicked, yet near enough to Hartford so he could get to Blackstone's by two in the afternoon.

He was too exhausted, too frightened to think. He found a third-rate motel just west of Stratford and surprised the early morning clerk by being alone.

During the registration, he mumbled unpleasant criticisms about a suspicious wife in Westport, and with a ten-dollar bill convinced the clerk to enter his arrival at 2:00 A.M., single. He fell into bed by seven and left a call for twelve thirty. If he slept for five hours, he thought, things had to become clearer.

Matlock slept for five hours and twenty minutes and nothing much had changed. Very little had cleared up for him. If anything, the massacre at Windsor Shoals now appeared more extraordinary than ever. Was it possible that he was meant to be a victim? Or were the killers waiting outside, waiting silently for him to leave before committing their executions?

Mistake or warning?

By one fifteen he was on the Merritt Parkway. By one thirty he entered the Berlin Turnpike, taking the back roads into Hartford. By five minutes past two he walked into Blackstone's office.

"Look," said Michael Blackstone, leaning over his desk, staring at Matlock, "we ask a minimum of questions, but don't for one minute think that means we give our clients blank checks!"

"It seems to me you like that process reversed."

"Then take your money and go somewhere else. We'll survive!"

"Just hold it! You were hired to protect a girl, that's all! That's what I'm paying three hundred dollars a day for! Anything else is marginal, and I'm paying for that, too, I expect."

"There'll be no extra charges. I don't know what you're talking about."

Suddenly Blackstone bent his elbows, crouching forward. He whispered hoarsely. "Christ, Matlock? Two *men!* Two men on that goddamn list were murdered last night! If you're a hopped-up maniac, I don't want anything to do with you! That's no part of any deal here! I don't care *who* your old man is or *how* much money you've got!"

"Now I don't know what *you're* talking about. Except what I read in the papers. I was at a motel in Fairfield last night. I was registered there at two this morning. According to the papers, those killings took place around five."

Blackstone pushed himself off the desk and stood up. He looked at Matlock suspiciously. "You can verify that?"

"Do you want the name and number of the motel? Give me a phone book, I'll get it for you."

"No! . . . No. I don't want to know a thing. You were in Fairfield?"

"Get the phone book."

"All right. All right, forget it. I think you're lying, but you've covered yourself. As you say, we're only hired to protect the girl."

"Any change from Sunday afternoon? Is everything all right?"

"Yes. . . . Yes." Blackstone seemed preoccupied. "I've got your Tel-electronic. It's operative. It's an additional twenty dollars a day."

"I see. Wholesale price."

"We never implied we were cheap."

"You couldn't."

"We don't." Blackstone remained standing, pushed a button on his office intercom, and spoke into it. "Bring in Mr. Matlock's Tel-electronic, please."

Seconds later an attractive girl came into the office carrying a metal device no larger than a pack of cigarettes. She put it on Blackstone's desk and placed an index card beside it. She left as rapidly as she had entered.

"Here you are," Blackstone said. "Your code is Charger Three-zero. Meaning—Carlyle area, three-man team. The telephone number you call is five, five, five, six, eight, six, eight. We keep a list of numbers on reserve which we feel are easy to commit. The Tel-electronic will signal you by short beeps. You can shut it off by pushing this button here. When the signal is emitted, you are to call the number. A recording machine on that telephone will give you the message from the team. Often it will be to phone another number to make direct contact. Do you understand everying? It's really very simple."

"I understand," said Matlock, taking the small metal box. "What confuses me is why you don't just have the men call this office and then you contact me. Outside of whatever profit there is, wouldn't it be easier?"

"No. Too much room for error. We handle a great many clients. We want our clients to be in direct contact with the men they're paying for."

"I see."

"Also, we respect the privacy of our clients. We don't think it's such a good idea for information to be transmitted through third and fourth parties. Incidentally, you can reach the team by the same procedures. Each one has a machine. Just phone the number and record the message for them."

"Commendable."

"Professional." And then Blackstone, for the first time since Matlock had entered the office, sat in his chair and leaned back. "Now I'm going to tell you something, and if you want to take it as a threat, you'd be justified. Also, if you want to cancel our services on the strength of what I say, that's O.K., too. . . . We know that you're being actively sought by agents of the Justice Department. However, there are no charges leveled against you, no warrants for your arrest. You have certain rights which the federal men often overlook in their zealousness—it's one of the reasons we're in business. However, *again*, we want you to know that should your status change, should there *be* charges or a warrant for your arrest, our services are terminated immediately, and we won't hesitate to cooperate with the authorities regarding your whereabouts. Whatever information we possess will be held for your attorneys—it's privileged—but not your whereabouts. *Capiche?*"

"I do. That's fair."

"We're more than fair. That's why I'm going to demand ten days' advance payment from you—unused portion returnable. . . . In the event the situation changes and the federal men get a court order for you, you will receive—*only once*—the following message on the telephone recorder. Just *these words*."

Blackstone paused for emphasis.

"What are they?"

"'*Charger Three-zero is canceled.*'"

Out on Bond Street Matlock felt a sensation he knew wouldn't leave him until his journey, his race was over. He thought people were staring at him. He began to think strangers were watching him. He found himself involuntarily turning around, trying to find the unseen, observing eyes. Yet there were none.

None that he could distinguish.

The Corsican paper now had to be gotten out of his apartment. And considering Blackstone's statements, there was no point in his attempting to get it himself. His apartment would be under surveillance—from both camps, the seekers and the quarry.

He would use the Blackstone team, one of them, putting to the test the sartorial Blackstone's guarantee of privileged information. He would reach them—him—as soon as he placed one prior telephone call. A call that would make it clear whether the silver Corsican invitation was really necessary or not. A call to Samuel Sharpe, attorney at law, Windsor Shoals, Connecticut.

Matlock decided to show Sharpe a temporary, more compassionate side of his acquired personality. Sharpe himself had displayed a momentary lapse of control. Matlock thought it was the moment to indicate that even such men as himself—men who had influential friends in San Juan and London—had feelings beyond personal survival.

He walked into the lobby of the Americana Hotel and called him. Sharpe's secretary answered.

"Are you in an office where Mr. Sharpe can return your call momentarily?"

"No, I'm in a telephone booth. I'm also in a hurry."

There was silence, preceded by the click of a hold button. The wait was less then ten seconds.

"May I have the number you're calling from, Mr. Matlock? Mr. Sharpe will get back to you within five minutes."

Matlock gave the girl the number and hung up.

As he sat in the plastic seat, his memory wandered back to another telephone booth and another plastic seat. And a black sedan which raced past the dead man slouched in that booth, on that seat, with a bullet hole in his forehead.

The bell sounded; Matlock lifted the receiver.

"Matlock?"

"Sharpe?"

"You shouldn't call me at the office. You should know better. I had to go down to the lobby here, to a pay phone."

"I didn't think a respected attorney's telephone would be any risk. I'm sorry."

There was a pause at the other end of the line. Sharpe obviously never expected an apology. "I'm a cautious man, I told you. What is it?"

"I just wanted to know how you were. How everything went. It was a terrible thing, last night."

"I haven't had time for a reaction. There's so much to do. Police, funeral arrangements, reporters."

"What are you saying? How are you handling it?"

"There won't be any major mistakes. In a nutshell—if it comes to that—I'm an innocent victim. Frank's a victim, too, only he's dead. . . . I'm going to miss Frank. He was a very good fellow. I'll close down the upstairs, of course. The state police have been paid. By you people, I assume. It'll be what the papers say it was. A bunch of Italian hoodlums shot up in a nice country restaurant."

"You're a cool operator."

"I told you," replied Sharpe sadly, "I'm a cautious man. I'm prepared for contingencies."

"Who did it?"

Sharpe did not answer the question. He did not speak at all.

"I asked you, who do you think did it?"

"I expect you people will find out before I do. . . . Bartolozzi had enemies; he was an unpleasant person. Rocco, too, I suppose. . . . But why Frank? You tell me."

"I don't know. I haven't been in touch with anyone."

"Find out for me. Please. It wasn't right."

"I'll try. That's a promise. . . . And, Sammy, make those calls to Stockton and Cantor, don't forget."

"I won't. I've got them listed on my afternoon calendar. I told you, I'm a methodical man."

"Thanks. My sympathies about Frank. He seemed like a nice guy."

"He was a prince."

"I'm sure he was. . . . I'll be in touch, Sammy. I haven't forgotten what I said I'd do for you. You've really impressed me. I'll . . ."

The sound of coins dropping into the telephone receptacle at Windsor Shoals interrupted Matlock. The time limit was up, and there was no point in prolonging the conversation. He had found out what he needed to know. He had to have the Corsican paper now. The horror of the dawn massacre had not caused the methodical Sharpe to forget the telephone calls he'd promised to make. Why it hadn't was a miracle to Matlock, but there it was. The cautious man had not panicked. He was ice.

The telephone booth was stuffy, close, uncomfortable, filled with smoke. He opened the door and walked rapidly across the hotel lobby to the front exit.

He rounded the corner of Asylum Street looking for an appropriate restaurant. One in which he could have lunch while awaiting the return call from Charger Three-zero. Blackstone had said that he should leave a number; what better than a restaurant?

He saw the sign: The Lobster House. The kind of place frequented by business executives.

He was given a booth to himself, not a table. It was nearly three; the luncheon crowd had thinned. He sat down and ordered a bourbon on the rocks, asking the waitress the whereabouts of the nearest telephone. He was about to get out of the booth to make his call to 555–6868 when he heard the muted, sharp, terrifying sound of the Tel-electronic from within his jacket. At first it paralyzed him. It was as if some part of his person, an hysterical organ perhaps, had gone mad and was trying to signal its distress. His hand shook as he reached inside his coat and withdrew the small metal device. He found the shut-off button and pressed it as hard as he could. He looked around, wondering if the sound had attracted attention.

It had not. No one returned his looks. No one had heard a thing.

He got out of his seat and walked quickly toward the telephone. His only thought was Pat—something had happened, something serious enough for Charger Three-zero to activate the terrible, insidious machine which had panicked him.

Matlock pulled the door shut and dialed 555–6868.

"Charger Three-zero reporting." The voice had the once-removed quality of a taped recording. "Please telephone five, five, five; one, nine, five, one. There is no need for alarm, sir. There's no emergency. We'll be at this number for the next hour. The number again is five, five, five; one, nine, five, one. Out."

Matlock realized that Charger Three-zero took pains to allay his fears immediately, perhaps because it was his first experience with the Tel-electronic. He had the feeling that even if the town of Carlyle had gone up in thermonuclear smoke, Charger Three-zero's words would have a palliative quality about them. The other reasoning, perhaps, was that a man thought more clearly when unafraid. Whatever, Matlock knew that the method worked. He was calmer now. He reached into his pocket and took out some change, making a mental note as he did so to convert some dollar bills into coins for future use. The pay telephone had become an important part of his life.

"Is this five, five, five; nineteen fifty-one?"

"Yes," said the same voice he had heard on the recording. "Mr. Matlock?"

"Yes. Is Miss Ballantyne all right?"

"Doing very well, sir. That's a good doctor you've got. She sat up this morning. A lot of the swelling's gone down. The doctor's quite pleased. . . . She's asked for you a number of times."

"What are you telling her?"

"The truth. That we've been hired by you to make sure she's not bothered."

"I mean about where I am."

"We've simply said you had to be away for several days. It might be a good idea to telephone her. She can take calls starting this afternoon. We'll screen them, of course."

"Of course. Is that why you contacted me?"

"In part. The other reason is Greenberg. Jason Greenberg. He keeps calling for you. He insists that you get in touch with him."

"What did he say? Who talked to him?"

"I did. Incidentally, my name's Cliff."

"O.K., Cliff, what did he say?"

"That I should tell you to call him the minute I reached you. It was imperative, critical. I've got a number. It's in Wheeling, West Virginia."

"Give it to me." Matlock withdrew his ballpoint pen and wrote the number on the wooden shelf under the telephone.

"Mr. Matlock?"

"What?"

"Greenberg also said to tell you . . . that 'the cities weren't dying, they were dead.' Those were his words. 'The cities were dead.'"

Chapter Twenty-three

Cliff agreed without comment to retrieve the Corsican paper from Matlock's apartment. A rendezvous would be arranged later by telephone. In the event the paper was missing, Charger Three-zero would alert him immediately.

Matlock restricted himself to one drink. He picked at his lunch and left the Lobster House by three thirty. It was time to regroup his forces, resupply his ammunition. He had parked the Cadillac in a lot several blocks south of Blackstone's office on Bond Street. It was one of those municipal parking areas, each slot with its own meter. It occurred to Matlock as he approached it that he hadn't returned to insert additional coins since going to Blackstone's. The meters were only good for an hour; he'd been there for nearly two. He wondered what rental-car businesses did with the slew of traffic violations which had to mount up with transients. He entered the lot and momentarily wondered if he was in the right aisle. Then he realized he was not. The Cadillac was two lanes over, in the fourth aisle. He started to sidle past the closely parked vehicles toward his own and then he stopped.

In between the automobiles, he saw the blue and white stripes of a Hartford patrol car. It was parked directly behind his Cadillac. One police officer was trying the Cadillac's door handle, a second patrolman was leaning against the police vehicle talking into a radio phone.

They'd found the car. It frightened him, but somehow it didn't surprise him.

He backed away cautiously, prepared to run if he was spotted. His thoughts raced ahead to the problems to which this newest complication gave rise. First and most immediate was an automobile. Second was the fact that they knew he was in the Hartford vicinity. That ruled out other means of transportation. The railroad stations, the bus terminals, even the hack bureaus would be alerted. It came back to finding another car.

And yet he wondered. Blackstone made it clear there were no charges against him, no warrants. If there were, he would have received the message from 555–6868. He would have heard the words: "Charger Three-zero is canceled."

He hadn't. There'd been no hint of it. For a moment he considered going back to the patrol car, accepting a ticket for overtime.

He dismissed the thought. These police were not meter maids. There had been a previous parking lot beyond an alley, at the rear of an A&P. And another policeman—in civilian clothes—following him. A pattern was there, though it eluded definition.

Matlock walked swiftly up Bond Street away from the municipal lot. He turned into the first side street and found himself beginning to break into a run. Instantly he slowed down. There is nothing in a crowded street more noticeable than a man running—unless it is a woman. He resumed a pace equal to the afternoon shoppers, doing his best to melt into the flow of human traffic. He even paused now and then to stare blankly into store-front windows, not really seeing the displays of merchandise. And then he began to reflect on what was happening to him. The primitive instincts of the hunted were suddenly working inside his brain. The protective antennae of the would-be trapped animal were thrusting, parrying with their surroundings and, chameleonlike, the body did its best to conform to the environment.

Yet he wasn't the hunted! He was the hunter! Goddamn it, he was the *hunter!*

"Hello, Jim! How the hell are you? What are you doing in the big city?"

The shock of the greeting caused Matlock to lose his balance. To actually *lose his balance* and trip. He fell to the sidewalk and the man who had spoken to him reached down and helped him up.

"Oh! Oh, hello, Jeff! Christ, you startled me. Thanks." Matlock got up and brushed himself off. He looked around wondering who else besides Jeff Kramer was watching him.

"A long lunch, buddy?" Kramer laughed. He was a Carlyle alumnus with a graduate degree in psychology that had been impressive enough for an expensive public relations firm.

"Lord, no! Just have something on my mind. My bumbling old professor bag." And then Matlock looked at Jeff Kramer. Jeff Kramer was not only with an expensive firm, but he also had an expensive wife and two very expensive kids in extremely expensive prep schools. Matlock felt he should reemphasize his previous point. "For a fact, I had one unfinished bourbon."

"Why don't we rectify that," said Kramer, pointing at the Hogshead Tavern across the street. "I haven't seen you in months. I read in *The Courant* you got yourself robbed."

"Goddamn, *did* I! The robbery I could take, but what they did to the apartment! And the *car!*" Matlock headed toward the Hogshead Tavern with Jeff Kramer. "That's why I'm in town. Got the Triumph in a garage here. That's my problem, as a matter of fact."

The hunted not only had antennae which served to warn the host of its enemies, but also the uncanny—if temporary—ability to turn disadvantage into advantage. Conceivable liabilities into positive assets.

Matlock sipped his bourbon and water while Kramer went through half his Scotch in several swallows. "The idea of a bus down to Scarsdale, with changes at New Haven and Bridgeport, defeats me."

"*Rent* a car, for Christ's sake."

"Just tried two places. The first can't let me have one until tonight. The second not until tomorrow. Some kind of convention, I guess."

"So wait until tonight."

"Can't do it. Family business. My father called his council of economic advisers. For dinner—and if you think I'm going to Scarsdale without my own wheels, you're out of it!" Matlock laughed and ordered another round of drinks. He reached into his pocket and put a fifty-dollar bill on the bar. The bill had to attract the attention of Jeff Kramer, who had such an expensive wife.

"Never thought you could balance a checkbook, say nothing of being an economic adviser."

"Ah, but I'm the prince royal. Can't forget that, can we?"

"Lucky bastard, that's what I can't forget. Lucky bastard."

"Hey! I've got one hell of an idea. Your car in town?"

"Hey, wait a minute, good buddy. . . ."

"No, listen." Matlock took out his bills. "The old man'll pay for it. . . . Rent me *your* car. Four or five days. . . . Here. I'll give you two, three hundred."

"You're nuts!"

"No, I'm not. He wants me down. He'll pay!"

Matlock could sense Kramer's mind working. He was estimating the cost of a low-priced rent-a-car for a week. Seventy-nine fifty and ten cents a mile with an average daily mileage of, perhaps, fifteen or twenty. Tops, $105, and maybe $110, for the week.

Kramer had that expensive wife and those two very expensive kids in extremely expensive prep schools.

"I wouldn't want to take you like that."

"Not *me!* Christ, no. *Him!*"

"Well . . ."

"Here, let me write out a bill. I'll give it to him the minute I get there." Matlock grabbed a cocktail napkin and turned it over to the unprinted side. He took out his ballpoint pen and began writing. "Simple contract. . . . 'I, James B. Matlock, agree to pay Jeffrey Kramer three hundred' . . . what the hell, it's his money . . . 'four hundred dollars for the rental of his . . .'—what's the make?"

"Ford wagon. A white Squire. Last year's." Kramer's eyes alternately looked at the napkin and the roll of bills Matlock carelessly left next to Kramer's elbow on the bar.

"'Ford Wagon, for a period of' . . . let's say one week, O.K.?"

"Fine." Kramer drank the remainder of his second Scotch.

"'One week. . . . Signed, James B. Matlock!' There you are, friend. Countersign. And here's four hundred. Courtesy of Jonathan Munro. Where's the car?"

The hunted's instincts were infallible, thought Matlock, as Kramer pocketed the bills and wiped his chin, which had begun to perspire. Kramer removed the two car keys and the parking lot ticket from his pocket. True to Matlock's anticipation, Jeff Kramer wanted to part company. With his four hundred dollars.

Matlock said he would phone Kramer in less than a week and return the automobile. Kramer insisted on paying for the drinks and rapidly left the Hogshead Tavern. Matlock, alone, finished his drink and thought out his next move.

The hunted and the hunter were now one.

Chapter Twenty-four

He sped out Route 72 toward Mount Holly in Kramer's white station wagon. He knew that within the hour he would find another pay telephone and insert another coin and make another call. This time to one Howard Stockton, owner of the Carmount Country Club. He looked at his watch; it was nearly eight thirty. Samuel Sharpe, attorney at law, should have reached Stockton several hours ago.

He wondered how Stockton had reacted. He wondered about Howard Stockton.

The station wagon's headlights caught the reflection of the road sign.

MOUNT HOLLY. INCORPORATED 1896

And just beyond it, a second reflection.

MOUNT HOLLY ROTARY

HARPER'S REST

TUESDAY NOON

ONE MILE

Why not? thought Matlock. There was nothing to lose. And possibly something to gain, even learn.

The hunter.

The white stucco front and the red Narragansett neons in the windows said all there was to say about Harper's cuisine. Matlock parked next to a pickup truck, got out, and locked the car. His newly acquired suitcase with the newly acquired clothes lay on the back seat. He had spent several hundred dollars in Hartford; he wasn't about to take a chance.

He walked across the cheap, large gravel and entered the bar area of Harper's Restaurant.

"I'm on my way to Carmount," said Matlock, paying for his drink with a twenty-dollar bill. "Would you mind telling me where the hell it is?"

"About two and a half miles west. Take the right fork down the road. You got anything smaller than a twenty? I only got two fives and singles. I need my singles."

"Give me the fives and we'll flip for the rest. Heads you keep it, tails I have one more and you still keep it." Matlock took a coin from his pocket and threw it on the formica bar, covering it with his hand. He lifted his palm and picked up the coin without showing it to the bartender. "It's your unlucky night. You owe me a drink—the ten's yours."

His conversation did not go unheeded by the other customers—three men drinking draft beer. That was fine, thought Matlock, as he looked around for a telephone.

"Men's room's in the rear around the corner," said a rustic-looking drinker in a chino jacket, wearing a baseball cap.

"Thanks. Telephone around?"

"Next to the men's room."

"Thanks again." Matlock took out a piece of paper on which he had written: Howard Stockton, Carmount C.C., #203-421-1100. He gestured for the bartender, who came toward him like a shot. "I'm supposed to phone this guy," said Matlock quietly. "I think I got the name wrong. I'm not sure whether it's Stackton or Stockton. Do you know him?"

The bartender looked at the paper and Matlock saw the instant reflex of recognition. "Sure. You got it right. It's Stockton. Mr. Stockton. He's vice-president of the Rotary. Last term he was president. Right boys?" The bartender addressed this last to his other customers.

"Sure."

"That's it. Stockton."

"Nice fella."

The man in the chino jacket and baseball cap felt the necessity of elaborating. "He runs the country club. That's a real nice place. Real nice."

"Country club?" Matlock implied the question with a trace of humor.

"That's right. Swimming pool, golf course, dancing on the weekends. Very nice." It was the bartender who elaborated now.

"I'll say this, he's highly recommended. This Stockton, I mean." Matlock drained his glass and looked toward the rear of the bar. "Telephone back there, you say?"

"That's right, Mister. Around the corner."

Matlock reached into his pocket for some change and walked to the narrow corridor where the rest rooms and telephone were located. The instant he rounded the corner, he stopped and pressed himself against the wall. He listened for the conversation he knew would be forthcoming.

"Big spender, huh?" The bartender spoke.

"They all are. Did I tell you? My kid caddied there a couple of weeks ago—some guy got a birdie and give the kid a fifty-dollar bill. Che-ryst! Fifty dollars!"

"My old woman says all them fancy dames there are *whoores*. Real whoores. She works a few parties there, my old woman does. Real whoores. . . ."

"I'd like to get my hands on some of them. Jee-*sus!* I swear to Christ most of 'em got no brazzieres!"

"Real whoores. . . ."

"Who gives a shit? That Stockton's O.K. He's O.K. in my book. Know what he did? The Kings. You know, Artie King who had a heart attack—dropped dead doin' the lawns up there. Old Stockton not only give the family a lotta dough—he set up a regular charge account for 'em at the A&P. No shit. He's O.K."

"Real whoores. They lay for money. . . ."

"Stockton put most of the cash up for the grammar school extension, don't forget that. You're fuckin' right, he's O.K. I got two kids in that school!"

"Not only—y'know what? He give a pocketful to the Memorial Day picnic."

"Real, honest-to-Christ whoores. . . ."

Matlock silently sidestepped his way against the wall to the telephone booth. He closed the door slowly with a minimum of noise. The men at the bar were getting louder in their appreciation of Howard Stockton, proprietor of the Carmount Country Club. He was not concerned that they might hear his delayed entrance into the booth.

What concerned him in an odd way was himself. If the *hunted* had instincts—protective in nature—the *hunter* had them also—aggressive by involvement. He understood now the necessity of tracking the scent, following the spoor, building a fabric of comprehensive habit. It meant that the hunter had abstract tools to complement his weapons. Tools which could build a base of entrapment, a pit in which the hunted might fall.

He ticked them off in his mind.

Howard Stockton: former president, current vice-president of the Mount Holly Rotary; a charitable man, a compassionate man. A man who took care of the family of a deceased employee named Artie King; who financed the extension of a grammar school. The proprietor of a luxurious country club in which men gave fifty-dollar tips to caddies and girls were available for members in good standing. Also a good American who made it possible for the town of Mount Holly to have a fine Memorial Day picnic.

It was enough to start with. Enough to shake up Howard Stockton if—as Sammy Sharpe had put it—"it came to that." Howard Stockton was not the formless man he was fifteen minutes ago. Matlock still didn't know the man's features, but other aspects, other factors were defined for him. Howard Stockton had become a *thing* in Mount Holly, Connecticut.

Matlock inserted the dime and dialed the number of the Carmount Country Club.

"It *suh*tainly is a pleasure, Mr. Matlock!" exclaimed Howard Stockton, greeting Matlock on the marble steps of the Carmount Country Club. "The boy'll take your car. Heah! Boy! Don't wrap it up, now!"

A Negro parking attendant laughed at his southern gentleman's command. Stockton flipped a half-dollar in the air and the black caught it with a grin.

"Thank you, suh!"

"Treat 'em good, they'll treat you good. That right, boy? Do I treat you good?!"

"*Real* good, Mister Howard!"

Matlock thought for a moment that he was part of an odious television commercial until he saw that Howard Stockton was the real item. Right up to his grayish blond hair, which topped a sun-tanned face, which, in turn, set off his white moustache and deep blue eyes surrounded by crow's nests of wrinkles belonging to a man who lived well.

"Welcome to Carmount, Mr. Matlock. It's not Richmond, but on the other hand, it ain't the Okefenokee."

"Thank you. And the name is Jim."

"Jim? Like that name. It's got a good, honest ring to it! My friends call me Howard. You call me Howard."

The Carmount Country Club, what he could see of it, reminded Matlock of all those pictures of antebellum architecture. And why not, considering the owner? It was rife with potted palms and delicate chandeliers and light blue toile wallpaper depicting rococo scenes in which cavorted prettified figures in powdered wigs. Howard Stockton was a proselytizer of a way of life which had collapsed in 1865, but he wasn't going to admit it. Even the servants, mostly black, were in liveries—honest-to-god liveries, knickers and all. Soft, live music came from a large dining room, at the end of which was a string orchestra of perhaps eight instruments gracefully playing in a fashion long since abandoned. There was a slowly winding staircase in the center of the main hall which would have done honor to Jefferson Davis—or David O. Selznick. Attractive women were wandering around, linked with not-so-attractive men.

The effect was incredible, thought Matlock, as he walked by his host's side toward what his host modestly claimed was his private library.

The southerner closed the thick paneled door and strode to a well-stocked mahogany bar. He poured without asking a preference.

"Sam Sharpe says you drink sour mash. You're a man of taste, I tell you that. That's *my* drink." He carried two glasses to Matlock. "Take your pick. A Virginian has to disarm a northerner with his complete lack of bias these days."

"Thank you," said Matlock, taking a glass and sitting in the armchair indicated by Stockton.

"This Virginian," continued Howard Stockton, sitting opposite Matlock, "also has an unsouthern habit of getting to the point. . . . I don't even know if it's wise for you to be in my place. I'll be honest. That's why I ushered you right in here."

"I don't understand. You could have told me on the phone not to come. Why the game?"

"Maybe you can answer that better than I can. Sammy says you're a real big man. You're what they call . . . *international*. That's just dandy by me. I like a bright young fella who goes up the ladder of success. Very commendable, that's a fact. . . . But I pay my bills. I pay every month on the line. I got the best combined operation north of Atlanta. I don't want trouble."

"You won't get it from *me*. I'm a tired businessman making the rounds, that's all I am."

"What happened at Sharpe's? The papers are full of it! I don't want *nothin'* like that!"

Matlock watched the southerner. The capillaries in the suntanned face were bloodred, which was probably why the man courted a year-round sunburn. It covered a multitude of blemishes.

"I don't think you understand." Matlock measured his words as he lifted the glass to his lips. "I've come a long way because I *have* to be here. I don't *want* to be here. Personal reasons got me into the area early, so I'm doing some sightseeing. But it's only that. I'm just looking around. . . . Until my appointment."

"What appointment?"

"An appointment in Carlyle, Connecticut."

Stockton squinted his eyes and pulled at his perfectly groomed white moustache. "You've got to be in Carlyle?"

"Yes. It's confidential, but I don't have to tell you that, do I?"

"You haven't told me anything." Stockton kept watching Matlock's face, and Matlock knew the southerner was looking for a false note, a wrong word, a hesitant glance which might contradict his information.

"Good. . . . By any chance, do you have an appointment in Carlyle, too? In about a week and a half?"

Stockton sipped his drink, smacking his lips and putting the glass on a side table as though it were some precious *objet d'art*. "I'm just a southern cracker tryin' to make a dollar. Livin' the good life and makin' a dollar. That's all. I don't know about any appointments in Carlyle."

"Sorry I brought it up. It's a . . . major mistake on my part. For both our sakes, I hope you won't mention it. Or *me*."

"That's the *last* thing I'd do. Far as I'm concerned, you're a friend of Sammy's lookin' for a little action . . . and a little hospitality." Suddenly Stockton leaned forward in his chair, his elbows on his knees, his hands folded. The looked like an earnest minister questioning a parishioner's sins.

"What in tarnation happened at Windsor Shoals? What in hell was it?"

"As far as I can see, it was a local vendetta. Bartolozzi had enemies. Some said he talked too goddamn much. Aiello, too, I suppose. They were show-offs. . . . Frank was just there, I think."

"Goddamn *Eye*talians! Mess up everything! *That* level, of course, you know what I mean?"

There it was again. The dangling interrogative—but in this southerner's version, it wasn't really a question. It was a statement.

"I know what you mean," said Matlock wearily.

"I'm afraid I got a little bad news for you, Jim. I closed the tables for a few days. Just plum scared as a jackrabbit after what happened at the Shoals."

"That's not bad news for me. Not the way my streak's been going."

"I heard. Sammy told me. But we got a couple of other diversions. You won't find Carmount lacking in hospitality, I promise you that."

The two men finished their drinks, and Stockton, relieved, escorted his guest into the crowded, elegant Carmount dining room. The food was extraordinary, served in a manner befitting the finest and wealthiest plantation of the antebellum South.

Although pleasant—even relaxing, in a way—the dinner was pointless to Matlock. Howard Stockton would not discuss his "operation" except in the vaguest terms and with the constant reminder that he catered to the "best class of Yankee." His speech was peppered with descriptive anachronisms, he was a walking contradiction in time. Halfway through the meal, Stockton excused himself to say good-bye to an important member.

It was the first opportunity Matlock had to look at Stockton's "best class of Yankee" clientele.

The term applied, thought Matlock, if the word *class* was interchangeable with *money*, which he wasn't willing to concede. Money screamed from every table. The first sign was the proliferation of suntans in the beginning of a Connecticut May. These were people who jetted to the sun-drenched islands at will. Another was the easy, deep-throated laughter echoing throughout the room; also the glittering reflection of jewelry. And the clothes—softly elegant suits, raw silk jackets, Dior ties. And the bottles of sparkling vintage wines, standing majestically in sterling silver stands upheld by cherrywood tripods.

But something was wrong, thought Matlock. Something was missing or out of place, and for several minutes he couldn't put his finger on what it was. And then he did.

The suntans, the laughter, the wrist jewelry, the jackets, the Dior ties—the money, the elegance, the aura was predominantly *male*.

The contradiction was the women—the girls. Not that there weren't some who matched their partners, but in the main, they didn't. They were younger. Much, much younger. And different.

He wasn't sure what the difference was at first. Then, abstractly, it came to him. For the most part, the girls—and they *were* girls—had a look about them he knew very well. He'd referred to it often in the past. It was the campus look—as differentiated from the office look, the secretary look. A slightly more intense expression around the eyes, a considerably more careless attitude in conversation. The look of girls not settling into routines, not welded to file cabinets or typewriters. It was definable because it was real. Matlock had been exposed to that look for over a decade—it was unmistakable.

Then he realized that within this contradiction there was another—

minor—discrepancy. The clothes the girls wore. They weren't the clothes he expected to find on girls with the campus look. They were too precisely cut, too designed, if that was the word. In this day of unisex, simply too feminine.

They wore costumes!

Suddenly, in a single, hysterically spoken sentence from several tables away, he knew he was right.

"Honest, I mean it—it's too groovy!"

That voice! *Christ, he knew that voice!*

He wondered if he was meant to hear it.

He had his hand up to his face and slowly turned toward the direction of the giggling speaker. The girl was laughing and drinking champagne, while her escort—a much older man—stared with satisfaction at her enormous breasts.

The girl was Virginia Beeson. The "pinky groovy" perennial undergraduate wife of Archer Beeson, Carlyle University's history instructor.

The man in an academic hurry.

Matlock tipped the black who carried his suitcase up the winding staircase to the large, ornate room Stockton had offered him. The floor was covered with a thick wine-colored carpet, the bed canopied, the walls white with fluted moldings. He saw that on the bureau was an ice bucket, two bottles of Jack Daniels, and several glasses. He opened the suitcase, picked out his toilet articles, and put them on the bedside table. He then removed a suit, a lightweight jacket, and two pairs of slacks, and carried them to the closet. He returned to the suitcase, lifted it from the bed, and laid it across the two wooden arms of a chair.

There was a soft tapping on his door. His first thought was that the caller was Howard Stockton, but he was wrong.

A girl, dressed in a provocative deep-red sheath, stood in the frame and smiled. She was in her late teens or very early twenties and terribly attractive.

And her smile was false.

"Yes?"

"Compliments of Mr. Stockton." She spoke the words and walked into the room past Matlock.

Matlock closed the door and stared at the girl, not so much bewildered as surprised.

"That's very thoughtful of Mr. Stockton, isn't it?"

"I'm glad you approve. There's whisky, ice, and glasses on your bureau. I'd like a short drink. Unless you're in a hurry."

Matlock walked slowly to the bureau. "I'm in no hurry. What would you like?"

"It doesn't matter. Whatever's there. Just ice, please."

"I see." Matlock poured the girl a drink and carried it over to her. "Won't you sit down?"

"On the bed?"

The only other chair, besides the one on which the suitcase was placed, was across the room by a French window.

"I'm sorry." He removed the suitcase and the girl sat down. Howard Stockton, he thought, had good taste. The girl was adorable. "What's your name?"

"Jeannie." She drank a great deal of her drink in several swallows. The girl may not have perfected a selection in liquor, but she knew how to drink. And then, as the girl took the glass from her mouth, Matlock noticed the ring on her third right finger.

He knew that ring very well. It was sold in a campus bookstore several blocks from John Holden's apartment in Webster, Connecticut. It was the ring of Madison University.

"What would you say if I told you I wasn't interested?" asked Matlock, leaning against the thick pole of the bed's anachronistic canopy.

"I'd be surprised. You don't look like a fairy."

"I'm not."

The girl looked up at Matlock. Her pale blue eyes were warm—but professionally warm—meaning, yet not meaning at all. Her lips were young. And full; and taut.

"Maybe you just need a little encouragement."

"You can provide that?"

"I'm good." She made the statement with quiet arrogance.

She was so young, thought Matlock, yet there was age in her. And hate. The hate was camouflaged, but the cosmetic was inadequate. She was performing—the costume, the eyes, the lips. She may have detested the role, but she accepted it.

Professionally.

"Suppose I just want to talk?"

"Conversation's something else. There are no rules about that. I've equal rights in that department. Quid pro, Mister No-name."

"You're facile with words. Should that tell me something?"

"I don't know why."

"'Quid pro quo' isn't the language of your eight to three hooker."

"This place—in case you missed it—isn't the Avenida de la Putas, either."

"Tennessee Williams?"

"Who knows?"

"I think you do."

"Fine. All right. We can discuss Proust in bed. I mean, that *is* where you want me, isn't it?"

"Perhaps I'd settle for the conversation."

The girl suddenly, in alarm, whispered hoarsely, "Are you a cop?"

"I'm the furthest thing from a cop," laughed Matlock. "You might say that some of the most important policemen in the area would like to find me. Although I'm no criminal. . . . Or a nut, by the way."

"Now *I'm* not interested. May I have another drink?"

"Surely." Matlock got it for her. Neither spoke until he returned with her glass.

"Do you mind if I stay here awhile? Just long enough for you to have balled me."

"You mean you don't want to lose the fee?"

"It's fifty dollars."

"You'll probably have to use part of it to bribe the dormitory head. Madison University's a little old-fashioned. Some coed houses still have weekday check-ins. You'll be late."

The shock on the girl's face was complete. "You *are* a cop! You're a lousy *cop!*" She started to get out of the chair, but Matlock quickly stood in front of her, holding her shoulders. He eased her back into the chair.

"I'm not a cop, I told you that. And you're not interested, remember? But *I'm* interested. I'm *very* interested, and you're going to tell me what I want to know."

The girl started to get up and Matlock grabbed her arms. She struggled; he pushed her back violently. "Do you always get 'balled' with your ring on? Is that to show whoever gets laid there's a little class to it?!"

"Oh, my God! Oh, Jesus!" She grabbed her ring and twisted her finger as if the pressure might make it disappear.

"Now, listen to me! You answer my questions or I'll be down in Webster tomorrow morning and I'll start asking them down there! Would you like that better?"

"Please! *Please!*" Tears came to the girl's eyes. Her hands shook and she gasped for breath.

"How did you get here?!"

"No! No . . ."

"*How?*"

"I was recruited. . . ."

"By whom?"

"Other . . . Others. We recruit each other."

"How many are there?"

"Not many. Not very many. . . . It's quiet. We have to keep it quiet. . . . Let me go, *please*. I want to *go*."

"Oh, no. Not yet. I want to know how many and *why!*"

"I told you! Only a few, maybe seven or eight girls."

"There must be thirty downstairs!"

"I don't *know* them. They're from other places. We don't ask each other's *names!*"

"But you know where they're from, don't you!"

"Some. . . . Yes."

"Other schools?"

"Yes. . . ."

"*Why*, Jeannie? For Christ's sake, *why?*"

"Why do you *think? Money!*"

The girl's dress had long sleeves. He grabbed her right arm and ripped the fabric up past the elbow. She fought him back but he overpowered her.

There were no marks. No signs.

She kicked at him and he slapped her face, hard enough to shock her into momentary immobility. He took her left arm and tore the sleeve.

There they were. Faded. Not recent. But there.

The small purple dots of a needle.

"I'm not on it now! I haven't been in *months!*"

"But you need the money! You need fifty or a hundred dollars every time you come over here! . . . What is it *now*? Yellows? Reds? *Acid? Speed?* What the hell is it *now?* Grass isn't that expensive!"

The girl sobbed. Tears fell down her cheeks. She covered her face and spoke—moaned—through her sobs.

"There's so much trouble! So much . . . *trouble!* Let me go, *please!*"

Matlock knelt down and cradled the girl's head in his arms, against his chest.

"What trouble? tell me, please. What trouble?"

"They *make* you do it. . . . You *have* to. . . . So many need help. They won't help *anyone* if you don't do it. Please, whatever your name is, let me alone. Let me go. Don't say anything. Let me *go!* . . . *Please!*"

"I will, but you've got to clear something up for me. Then you can go and I won't say anything. . . . Are you down here because they threatened you? Threatened the other kids?"

The girl nodded her head, gasping quietly, breathing heavily. Matlock continued. "Threatened you with what? Turning you in? . . . Exposing a habit? That's not worth it. Not today. . . ."

"Oh, you're outta sight!" The girl spoke through her tears. "They can ruin you. For life. Ruin your family, your school, maybe later. Maybe. . . . Some rotten prison. Somewhere! Habit, pushing, supplying . . . a boy you know's in trouble and *they* can get him off. . . . Some girl's in her third month, she needs a doctor . . . *they* can get one. No noise."

"You don't need *them!* Where've you *been*?! There are agencies, counseling!"

"Oh, Jesus Christ, mister! Where have *you* been?! . . . The drug courts, the doctors, the judges! They run them *all!* . . . There's nothing *you* can do about it. Nothing *I* can do about it. So leave me alone, leave *us* alone! Too many people'll get hurt!"

"And you're just going to keep doing what they say! Frightened, spoiled little bastards who keep on whining! Afraid to wash your hands, or your *mouths*, or your *arms!*" He pulled at her left elbow and yanked it viciously.

The girl looked up at him, half in fear, half in contempt.

"That's right," she said in a strangely calm voice. "I don't think you'd understand. You don't know what it's all about. . . . We're different from you. My friends are all I've got. All any of us have got. We help each other. . . . I'm not interested in being a hero. I'm only interested in my friends. I don't have a flag decal in my car window and I don't like John Wayne. I think he's a shit. I think you all are. All shits."

Matlock released the girl's arm. "Just how long do you think you can keep it up?"

"Oh, I'm one of the lucky ones. In a month I'll have that scroll my parents paid for and I'm out of it. They hardly ever try to make contact with you later. They say they will, but they rarely do. . . . You're just supposed to live with the possibility."

He understood the implications of her muted testimony and turned away. "I'm sorry. I'm very, very sorry."

"Don't be. I'm one of the lucky ones. Two weeks after I pick up that piece of engraved crap my parents want so badly, I'll be on a plane. I'm leaving this goddamn country. And I'll never come back!"

Chapter Twenty-five

He had not been able to sleep, nor had he expected to. He had sent the girl away with money, for he had nothing else he could give her, neither hope nor courage. What he advocated was rejected, for it involved the risk of danger and pain to untold children committed to the well-being of each other. He could not demand; there was no trust, no threat equal to the burdens they carried. Ultimately, it was the children's own struggle. They wanted no help.

He remembered the Bagdhivi admonition: *Look ye to the children; look and behold. They grow tall and strong and hunt the tiger with greater cunning and stronger sinews than you. They shall save the flocks better than you. Ye are old and infirm. Look to the children. Beware of the children.*

Were the children hunting the tiger better? And even if they were, whose flocks would they save? And who was the tiger?

Was it the "goddamn country"?

Had it come to that?

The questions burned into his mind. How many Jeannies were there? How extensive was Nimrod's recruiting?

He had to find out.

The girl admitted that Carmount was only one port of call; there were others, but she didn't know where. Friends of hers had been sent to New Haven, others to Boston, some north to the outskirts of Hanover.

Yale. Harvard. Dartmouth.

The most frightening aspect was Nimrod's threat of a thousand futures. What had she said?

"They hardly ever make contact. . . . They say they will. . . . You live with the possibility."

If such was the case, Bagdhivi was wrong. The children had far less cunning, possessed weaker sinews; there was no reason to beware. Only to pity.

Unless the children were subdivided, led by other, stronger children.

Matlock made up his mind to go down to New Haven. Maybe there were answers there. He had scores of friends at Yale University. It would be a side trip, an unconsidered excursion, but intrinsic to the journey itself. Part of the Nimrod odyssey.

Short, high-pitched sounds interrupted Matlock's concentration. He froze, his eyes swollen in shock, his body tense on top of the bed. It took him several seconds to focus his attention on the source of the frightening sound. It was the Tel-electronic, still in his jacket pocket. But where had he put his jacket? It wasn't near his bed.

He turned on the bedside lamp and looked around, the unrelenting, unceasing sounds causing his pulse to hammer, his forehead to perspire. Then he saw his coat. He had put it on top of the chair in front of the French window, halfway across the room. He looked at his watch: 4:35 A.M. He ran to the jacket, pulled out the terrible instrument, and shut it off.

The panic of the hunted returned. He picked up the telephone on the bedside table. It was a direct line, no switchboard.

The dial tone was like any other dial tone outside the major utility areas. A little fuzzy, but steady. And if there was a tap, he wouldn't be able to recognize it anyway. He dialed 555–6868 and waited for the call to be completed.

"Charger Three-zero reporting," said the mechanized voice. "Sorry to disturb you. There is no change with the subject, everything is satisfactory. However, your friend from Wheeling, West Virginia, is very insistent. He telephoned at four fifteen and said it was imperative you call him at once. We're concerned. Out."

Matlock hung up the telephone and forced his mind to go blank until he found a cigarette and lit it. He needed the precious moments to stop the hammering pulse.

He hated that Goddamn machine! He hated what its terrifying little beeps did to him.

He drew heavily on the smoke and knew there was no alternative. He had to get out of the Carmount Country Club and reach a telephone booth. Greenberg wouldn't have phoned at four in the morning unless it was an emergency. He couldn't take the chance of calling Greenberg on the Carmount line.

He threw his clothes into the suitcase and dressed quickly.

He assumed there'd be a night watchman, or a parking attendant asleep in a booth, and he'd retrieve his, Kramer's, automobile. If not, he'd wake up someone, even if it was Stockton himself. Stockton was still frightened of trouble, Windsor Shoals trouble—he wouldn't try to detain him. Any story would do for the purveyor of young, adorable flesh. The sunburned southern flower of the Connecticut Valley. The stench of Nimrod.

Matlock closed the door quietly and walked down the silent corridor to the enormous staircase. Wall sconces were lighted, dimmed by rheostats to give a candlelight effect. Even in the dead of night, Howard Stockston couldn't forget his heritage. The interior of the Carmount Country Club looked more than ever like a sleeping great hall of a plantation house.

He started for the front entrance, and by the time he reached the storm carpet, he knew it was as far as he would go. At least for the moment.

Howard Stockton, clad in a flowing velour, nineteenth-century dressing gown, emerged from a glass door next to the entrance. He was accompanied by a large, Italian-looking man whose jet black eyes silently spoke generations of the Black Hand. Stockton's companion was a killer.

"Why, Mr. Matlock! Are you leavin' us?"

He decided to be aggressive.

"Since you tapped my goddamn phone, I assume you gather I've got problems! They're *my business, not yours!* If you want to know, I resent your intrusion!"

The ploy worked. Stockton was startled by Matlock's hostility.

"There's no reason to be angry. . . . I'm a businessman, like you. Any invasion of your privacy is for your protection. Goddamn! That's *true, boy!*"

"I'll accept the lousy explanation. Are my keys in the car?"

"Well, not in your *car*. My friend Mario here's got 'em. He's a real high-class Eyetalian, let me tell you."

"I can see the family crest on his pocket. May I have my keys?"

Mario looked at Stockton, obviously confused.

"Now, just a minute," Stockton said. "Wait a bit, Mario. Let's not be impulsive. . . . I'm a reasonable man. A very reasonable, rational person. I'm merely a Virginia . . ."

"*Cracker*, trying to make a dollar!" interrupted Matlock. "I'll buy that! Now get the hell out of my way and give me the keys!"

"Good Lord, *you all* are downright *mean!* I mean, *mean!* Put yourself in my place! . . . Some crazy code like 'Chargin' Three-zero' and an urgent call from Wheelin', West *Virginia!* And instead of usin' my perfectly good telephone, you gotta make space and get *outta* here! C'mon, Jim. What would *you* do?!"

Matlock kept his voice chillingly precise. "I'd try to understand *who* I was dealing with. . . . We've made a number of inquiries, Howard. My superiors are concerned about you."

"What-do-you-mean?" Stockton's question was asked so swiftly the words had no separation.

"They think . . . we think you've called too much attention to yourself. President and vice-president of a *Rotary Club!* Jesus! A one-man fund-raiser for new school buildings; the big provider for widows and orphans—charge accounts included; Memorial Day picnics! Then hiring locals to spread rumors about the girls! Half the time the kids walk around half naked. You think the local citizens don't talk? *Christ*, Howard!"

"Who the hell are you?"

"Just a tired businessman who gets annoyed when he sees another businessman make an ass of himself. What the hell do you think you're running for? Santa Claus? Have you any idea how prominent that costume is?"

"Goddamn it, you got it in for me! I've got the finest combined operation north of Atlanta! I don't know who you people been talkin' to, but I tell you—this l'il old Mount Holly'd go to hell in a basket for me! Those things you people dug up—they're *good things! Real* good! . . . You twist 'em, make 'em sound bad! That ain't *right!*"

Stockton took out a handkerchief and patted his flushed, perspiring face. The southerner was so upset his sentences spilled over into one another, his voice strident. Matlock tried to think swiftly, cautiously. Perhaps the time was now—with Stockton. It had to be sometime. He had to send out his own particular invitation. He had to start the last lap of his journey to Nimrod.

"Calm down, Stockton. Relax. You may be right. . . . I haven't time to think about it now. We've got a crisis. All of us. That phone call was serious." Matlock paused, looking hard at the nervous Stockton, and then put his suitcase on the marble floor. "Howard," he said slowly, choosing his words carefully, "I'm going to trust you with something and I hope to hell you're up to it. If you pull it off, no one'll bother your operation—ever."

"What's that?"

"Tell *him* to take a walk. Just down the hall, if you like."

"You heard the man. Go smoke a cigar."

Mario looked both hostile and confused as he trudged slowly toward the staircase. Stockton spoke.

"What do you want me to do? I told you, I don't want trouble."

"We're *all* going to have trouble unless I reach a few delegates. That's what Wheeling was telling me."

"What do you mean . . . delegates?"

"The meeting over at Carlyle. The conference with our people and the Nimrod organization."

"That's not my affair!" Stockton spat out the words. "I don't know a thing about that!"

"I'm sure you don't; you weren't meant to. But now it concerns all of us. . . . Sometimes rules have to be broken; this is one of those times. Nimrod's gone too far, that's all I can tell you."

"You tell *me?* I live with those *preachers!* I *parlay* with them, and when I complain, you know what our own people say? They say, 'That's the way it is, old Howie, we all do business'! What kind of talk is that? Why do *I* have to do business with them?"

"Perhaps you won't much longer. That's why I have to reach some of the others. The delegates."

"They don't include me in those meetings. I don't know anyone."

"Of course you don't. Again, you weren't meant to. The conference is heavy; very heavy and very quiet. So quiet we may have screwed ourselves: we don't know who's in the area. From what organization; from what family? But I have my orders. We've got to get through to one or two."

"I can't help you."

Matlock looked harshly at the southerner. "I think you can. Listen to me. In the morning, get on the phone and pass the word. *Carefully!* We don't want panic. Don't talk to anyone you don't know and don't use my name! Just say you've met someone who has the Corsican paper, the silver Corsican paper. He's *got* to meet quietly with someone else who has it, too. We'll start with one person if we have to. Have you got that?"

"I got it but I don't like it! It's none of *my business!*"

"Would you rather close down? Would you rather lose this magnificent relic of yours and stare out of a cell window for ten or twenty years? I understand prison funerals are very touching."

"All right! . . . All right. I'll call my bag boy. I'll say I don't know nothin'! I'm just passin' along a message."

"Good enough. If you make a contact, tell whoever it is that I'll be at the Sail and Ski tonight or tomorrow. Tell him to bring the paper. I won't talk to anyone without the paper!"

"Without the paper. . . ."

"Now let me have my keys."

Stockton called Mario back. Matlock got his keys.

He swung south on Route 72 out of Mount Holly. He didn't remember precisely where, but he knew he'd passed several highway telephone booths on his way up from Hartford. It was funny how he was beginning to notice public telephones, his only connecting link with solidity. Everything else was transient, hit or miss, unfamiliar and frightening. He'd phone Greenberg as Charge Three-zero requested, but before he did, he was going to reach one of Blackstone's men.

A rendezvous would have to be arranged immediately. He now had to have the Corsican paper. He'd put out the word; he'd have to keep his end of the bargain or he would learn nothing. *If* Stockton's message got through and *if* someone *did* make contact, that someone would kill or be killed before breaking the oath of "Omerta" unless Matlock produced the paper.

Or was it all for nothing? Was he the amateur Kressel and Greenberg said he was? He didn't know. He tried so hard to think things through, look at all sides of every action, use the tools of his trained, academic imagination. But was it enough? Or was it possible that his sense of commitment, his violent feelings of vengeance and disgust were only turning him into a Quixote?

If that were so, he'd live with it. He'd do his goddamnedest and live with it. He had good reasons—a brother named David; a girl named Pat; a gentle old man named Lucas; a nice fellow named Loring; a confused, terrified student from Madison named Jeannie. The sickening whole *scene!*

Matlock found a booth on a deserted stretch of Route 72 and called the inanimate receiver at the other end of 555–6868. He gave the number of the telephone booth and waited for Charger Three-zero to answer his call.

The milk truck lumbered by. The driver was singing and waved to Matlock. Several minutes later a huge Allied Van Lines sped past, and shortly after a produce truck. It was nearing five thirty, and the day was brightening. Brightening to a dull gray, for there were rain clouds in the sky.

The telephone rang.

"Hello!"

"What's the problem, sir? Did you reach your friend in West Virginia? He said he's not kidding anymore."

"I'll call him in a few minutes. Are you the fellow named Cliff?" Matlock knew it was not; the voice was different.

"No, sir. I'm Jim. Same name as yours."

"All right, Jim. Tell me, did the other fellow do what I asked him to? Did he get the paper for me?"

"Yes, sir. If it's the one on silver paper, written in Italian. I think it's Italian."

"That's the one. . . ."

Matlock arranged for the pickup in two hours. It was agreed that the Blackstone man named Cliff would meet him at an all-night diner on Scofield Avenue near the West Hartford town line. Charger Three-zero insisted that the delivery be made rapidly, in the parking lot. Matlock described the car he was driving and hung up the phone.

The next call would have to be Jason Greenberg in Wheeling. And Greenberg was furious.

"Schmuck! It isn't bad enough you break your word, you've got to hire your own army! What the hell do you think those clowns can do that the United States Government can't?"

"Those clowns are costing me three hundred dollars a day, Jason. They'd better be good."

"You ran out! Why did you do that? You gave me your word you wouldn't. You said you'd work with our man!"

"Your man gave me an ultimatum I couldn't live with! And if it was your idea, I'll tell you the same thing I told Houston."

"What does that mean? What ultimatum?"

"You know goddamn well! Don't play that game. And you listen to me. . . ." Matlock took a break before plunging into the lie, giving it all the authority he could summon. "There's a lawyer in Hartford who has a very precise letter signed by me. Along the same lines as the letter I signed for you. Only the information's a bit different: it's straight. It describes in detail the story of my recruitment; how you bastards sucked me in and then how you let me hang. How you forced me to sign a lie. . . . You try anything, he'll release it and there'll be a lot of embarrassed manipulators at the Justice Department. . . . You gave me the idea, Jason. It was a damn good idea. It might even make a few militants decide to tear up the Carlyle campus. Maybe launch a string of riots, with luck, right across the country. The academic scene's ready to be primed out of its dormancy; isn't that what Sealfont said? Only this time it won't be the war or the draft or drugs. They'll find a better label: government infiltration, police state . . . *Gestapo* tactics. Are you prepared for that?"

"For Christ's sake, cut it out! It won't do you any good. You're not that important. . . . Now, what the hell are you talking about? *I briefed him!* There weren't any conditions except that you keep him informed of what you were doing."

"Bullshit! I wasn't to leave the campus; I wasn't to talk to anyone on the faculty or the staff. I was restricted to student inquiries, and I gathered those were to be cleared *first!* Outside of those minor restrictions, I was free as a bird! Come on! You *saw* Pat! You saw what they did to her. You know what else they did—the word is *rape*, Greenberg! Did you people expect me to *thank* Houston for being so *understanding?*"

"Believe me," said Greenberg softly, in anger. "Those conditions were added after the briefing. They should have told me, that's true. But they were added for your own protection. You can see that, can't you?"

"They weren't part of our bargain!"

"No, they weren't. And they should have told me. . . ."

"Also, I wonder whose protection they were concerned with. Mine or theirs."

"A good question. They should have told me. They can't delegate responsibility and always take away the authority. It's not logical."

"It's not *moral*. Let me tell you something. This little odyssey of mine is bringing me closer and closer to the sublime question of morality."

"I'm glad for you, but I'm afraid your odyssey's coming to an end."

"Try it!"

"They're going to. Statements in lawyer's offices won't mean a damn. I told them I'd try first. . . . If you don't turn yourself over to protective custody within forty-eight hours, they'll issue a warrant."

"On what grounds?!"

"You're a menace. You're mentally unbalanced. You're a nut. They'll cite your army record—two courts-martial, brig time, continuous instability under combat conditions. Your use of drugs. And alcohol—they've got witnesses. You're also a racist—they've got that Lumumba affidavit from Kressel. And now I understand, although I haven't the facts, you're consorting with known criminals. They have photographs—from a place in Avon. . . . Turn yourself in, Jim. They'll ruin your life."

Chapter Twenty-six

Forty-eight hours! Why forty-eight hours? Why not twenty-four or twelve or immediately? It didn't make sense! Then he understood and, alone in the booth, he started to laugh. He laughed out loud in a telephone booth at five thirty in the morning on a deserted stretch of highway in Mount Holly, Connecticut.

The practical men were giving him just enough time to accomplish something—if he *could* accomplish something. If he couldn't, and anything happened, they were clean. It was on record that they considered him a mentally unbalanced addict with racist tendencies who consorted with known criminals, and they had given him warning. In deference to the delicate balance of dealing with such madmen, they allocated *time* in the hopes of reducing the danger. Oh, Christ! The manipulators!

He reached the West Hartford diner at six forty-five and ate a large breakfast, somehow believing that the food would take the place of sleep and give him the energy he needed. He kept glancing at his watch, knowing that he'd have to be in the parking lot by seven thirty.

He wondered what his contact at Charger Three-zero would look like.

The man was enormous, and Matlock had never considered himself small. Cliff of Charger Three-zero reminded Matlock of those old pictures of Primo Carnera. Except the face. The face was lean and intelligent and smiled broadly.

"Don't get out, Mr. Matlock." He reached in and shook Matlock's hand.

"Here's the paper; I put it in an envelope. By the way, we had Miss Ballantyne laughing last night. She's feeling better. Encephalograph's steady, metabolism's coming back up to par, pupil dilation's receding. Thought you'd like to know."

"I imagine that's good."

"It is. We've made friends with the doctor. He levels."

"How's the hospital taking your guard duty?"

"Mr. Blackstone solves those problems in advance. We have rooms on either side of the subject."

"For which, I'm sure, I'll be charged."

"You know Mr. Blackstone."

"I'm getting to. He goes first class."

"So do his clients. I'd better get back. Nice to meet you." The Blackstone man walked rapidly away and got into a nondescript automobile several years old.

It was time for Matlock to drive to New Haven.

He had no set plan, no specific individuals in mind; he wasn't leading, he was being led. His information was, at best, nebulous, sketchy, far too incomplete to deal in absolutes. Yet perhaps there was enough for someone to make a connection. But whoever made it, or was capable of making it, had to be someone with an overall view of the university. Someone who dealt, as did Sam Kressel, with the general tensions of the campus.

However, Yale was five times the size of Carlyle; it was infinitely more diffuse, a section of the New Haven city, not really isolated from its surroundings as was Carlyle. There *was* a focal point, the Office of Student Affairs; but he didn't know anyone there. And to arrive off the street with an improbable story of college girls forming—or being formed into—a prostitution ring reaching, as so far determined, the states of Connecticut, Massachusetts, and New Hampshire, would create havoc if he was taken seriously. And he wasn't sure he *would* be taken seriously, in which case he'd learn nothing.

There was one possibility; a poor substitute for Student Affairs, but with its own general view of the campus: the Department of Admissions. He knew a man, Peter Daniels, who worked in Yale's admissions office. He and Daniels had shared a number of lecterns during prep school recruitment programs. He knew Daniels well enough to spell out the facts as he understood them; Daniels wasn't the sort to doubt him or to panic. He'd restrict his story to the girl, however.

He parked on Chappel Street near the intersection of York. On one side of the thoroughfare was an arch leading to the quadrangle of Silliman College, on the other a large expanse of lawn threaded with cement paths to the Administration Building. Daniels's office was on the second floor. Matlock got out of the car, locked it, and walked toward the old brick structure with the American flag masted next to the Yale banner.

"That's preposterous! This is the age of Aquarius and then some. You don't pay for sex; it's exchanged freely."

"I know what I saw. I know what the girl told me; she wasn't lying."

"I repeat. You can't be sure."

"It's tied in with too many other things. I've seen them, too."

"May I ask the obvious question? Why don't you go to the police?"

"Obvious answer. Colleges have been in enough trouble. What facts I have are isolated. I need more information. I don't want to be responsible for indiscriminate name-calling, any widespread panic. There's been enough of that."

"All right. I'll buy it. But I can't help you."

"Give me several names. Students *or* faculty. People you know . . . you're certain are messed up, seriously messed up. Near the center. You've got those kinds of names, I know you do; we do. . . . I swear, they'll never know who gave them to me."

Daniels got out of his chair, lighting his pipe. "You're being awfully general. Messed up how? Academically, politically . . . narcotics, alcohol? You're covering a wide territory."

"Wait a minute." Daniels's words evoked a memory. Matlock recalled a dimly lit, smoke-filled room inside a seemingly deserted building in Hartford. Rocco Aiello's Hunt Club. And a tall young man in a waiter's jacket who had brought over a tab for Aiello to sign. The veteran of Nam and Da Nang. The Yalie who was *making contacts, building up his nest egg* . . . the *business administration* major. "I know who I want to see."

"What's his name?"

"I don't know. . . . But he's a veteran—Indochina, about twenty-two or three; he's pretty tall, light brown hair . . . majoring in business administration."

"A description which might fit five hundred students. Except for premed, law, and engineering, it's all lumped under liberal arts. We'd have to go through every file."

"Application photographs?"

"Not allowed anymore, you know that."

Matlock stared out the window, his eyebrows wrinkled in thought. He looked back at Daniels. "Pete, it's May. . . ."

"So? It could be November; that wouldn't change the Fair Practices law."

"Graduation's in a month. . . . Senior class photographs. Yearbook portraits."

Daniels understood instantly. He took his pipe from his mouth and started for the door.

"Come with me."

His name was Alan Pace. He was a senior and his curriculum was not centered on business administration; he was a government major. He lived off campus on Church Street near the Hamden town line. According to his records, Alan Pace was an excellent student, consistent honors in all subjects, a fellowship in the offing at the Maxwell School of Political Science at Syracuse. He had spent twenty-eight months in the army, four more than was required of him. As with most veterans, his university extracurricular activities were minimal.

While Pace was in service, he was an officer attached to inventory and supply. He had volunteered for a four-month extended tour of duty in the Saigon Corps—a fact noted with emphasis on his reapplication form. Alan Pace had given four months of his life more than necessary to his country. Alan Pace was obviously an honorable man in these days of cynicism.

He was a winner, thought Matlock.

The drive out Church Street toward Hamden gave Matlock the chance to clear his mind. He had to take one thing at a time; one item crossed off—on to the next. He couldn't allow his imagination to interpret isolated facts beyond their meaning. He couldn't lump everything together and total a sum larger than the parts.

It was entirely possible that this Alan Pace played a solo game. Unattached, unencumbered.

But it wasn't logical.

Pace's apartment house was an undistinguished brown brick building, so common on the outskirts of cities. Once—forty or fifty years ago—it had been the proud symbol of a rising middle class extending themselves out beyond the cement confines toward the country, but not so courageous as to leave the city completely. It wasn't so much run down as it was . . . not spruced up. The most glaring aspect of the apartment house to Matlock, however, was that it seemed to be a most unlikely place for a student to reside.

But he was there now; Peter Daniels had ascertained that.

Pace had not wanted to unlatch the door. It was only Matlock's strong emphasis on two points that made the student relent. The first point was that he wasn't from the police; the second, the name Rocco Aiello.

"What do you want? I've got a lot of work to do; I don't have time to talk. I've got comprehensives tomorrow."

"May I sit down?"

"What for? I told you, I'm busy." The tall, brown-haired student crossed back to his desk, piled with books and papers. The apartment was neat—except for the desk—and quite large. There were doors and short corridors leading to other doors. It was the sort of apartment that usually was shared by four or five students. But Alan Pace had no roommates.

"I'll sit down anyway. You owe that much to Rocco."

"What does that mean?"

"Just that Rocco was my friend. I was the one with him the other night when you brought him a tab to sign. Remember? And he was good to you. . . . He's dead."

"I know. I read about it. I'm sorry. But I didn't owe him anything."

"But you bought from him."

"I don't know what you're talking about."

"Come on, Pace. You don't have the time and neither do I. You're not connected to Aiello's death, I know that. But I've got to have information, and you're going to supply it."

"You're talking to the wrong person. I don't know you. I don't know *anything*."

"I know *you*. I've got a complete rundown on you. Aiello and I were considering going into business together. Now, that's none of your concern, I realize that, but we exchanged . . . personnel information. I'm coming to you because, frankly, Rocco's gone and there are areas that need filling. I'm really asking a favor, and I'll pay for it."

"I told you, I'm not your man. I hardly knew Aiello. I picked up a few dollars waiting tables. Sure, I heard rumors, but that's *all*. I don't know what you want, but you'd better go to someone else."

Pace was sharp, thought Matlock. He was disengaging himself but not foolishly claiming complete innocence. On the other hand, perhaps he was telling the truth. There was only one way to find out.

"I'll try again. . . . Fifteen months in Vietnam. Saigon, Da Nang;

excursions to Hong Kong, Japan. I&S officer; the dullest, most exasperating kind of work for a young man with the potential that earns him honors at a very tough university."

"I&S was good duty; no combat, no sweat. Everybody made the tourist hops. Check the R&R route sheets."

"Then," continued Matlock without acknowledging Pace's interruption, "the dedicated officer returns to civilian life. After a four-month voluntary extension in Saigon—I'm surprised you weren't caught up on *that* one—he comes back with enough money to make the proper investments, and certainly not from his army pay. He's one of the biggest suppliers in New Haven. Do you want me to go on?"

Pace stood by the desk and seemed to stop breathing. He stared at Matlock, his face white. When he spoke, it was the voice of a frightened young man.

"You can't prove anything. I haven't done anything. My army record, my record here—they're both good. They're very good."

"The best. Umblemished. They're records to be proud of; I mean that sincerely. And I wouldn't want to do anything to spoil them; I mean that, too."

"You couldn't. I'm clean!"

"No, you're not. You're up to your fellowship neck. Aiello made that *clear*. On *paper*."

"You're lying!"

"You're stupid. You think Aiello would do business with *anyone* he didn't run a check on? Do you think he'd be *allowed* to? He kept very extensive books, Pace, and I've *got* them. I told you; we were going into business together. You don't form a partnership without audit disclosures, you should know that."

Pace spoke barely above a whisper. "There are no books like that. There never are. Cities, towns, codes. No names. Never any names."

"Then why am I here?"

"You saw me in Hartford; you're reaching for a connection."

"You know better than that. Don't be foolish."

Matlock's quickly put implications were too much for the tall, shocked young man. "Why did you come to me? I'm not that important. You say you know about me; then you know I'm not important."

"I told you. I need information. I'm reluctant to go to the high priests, anyone with real authority. I don't want to be at a disadvantage. That's why I'm willing to pay; why I'm prepared to tear up everything I've got on you."

The prospect of being cut free of the stranger's grip was obviously all that was on Pace's mind. He replied quickly.

"Suppose I can't answer your questions? You'll think I'm lying."

"You can't be worse off. All you can do is try me."

"Go ahead."

"I met a girl . . . from a nearby college. I met her under circumstances that can only be described as professional prostitution. Professional in every sense of the word. Appointments, set fees, no prior knowledge of clients, the works. . . . What do you know about it?"

Pace took several steps toward Matlock. "What do you mean, what do I know? I know it's there. What else is there to know?"

"How extensive?"

"All over. It's not news."

"It is to me."

"You don't know the scene. Take a walk around a few college towns."

Matlock swallowed. Was he really that far out of touch? "Suppose I were to tell you I'm familiar with a lot of . . . college towns?"

"I'd say your circles were cubed. Also, I'm no part of that action. What else?"

"Let's stick to this for a minute. . . . Why?"

"Why what?"

"Why do the girls do it?"

"Bread, man. Why does anyone do anything?"

"You're too intelligent to believe that. . . . Is it organized?"

"I guess so. I told you, I'm no part of it."

"Watch it! I've got a lot of paper on you. . . ."

"All right. Yes, it's organized. Everything's organized. If it's going to work."

"Where *specifically* are the operations?"

"I *told* you! All *over*."

"Inside the colleges?"

"No, not inside. On the outskirts. A couple of miles usually, if the campuses are rural. Old houses, away from the suburbs. If they're in cities—downtown hotels, private clubs, apartment houses. But not *here*."

"Are we talking about . . . Columbia, Harvard, Radcliffe, Smith, Holyoke? And points south?"

"Everyone always forgets Princeton," replied Pace with a wry smile. "A lot of nice old estates in those back roads. . . . Yes, we're talking about those places."

"I never would have believed it. . . ." Matlock spoke as much to himself as to Pace. "But, *why?* Don't give me the 'bread' routine. . . ."

"Bread is *freedom*, man! For these kids it's freedom. They're not psyched-up freaks; they're not running around in black berets and field jackets. Very few of us are. We've *learned*. Get the money, fella, and the nice people will like you. . . . Also, whether you've noticed it or not, the straight money's not as easy to come by as it once was. Most of these kids need it."

"The girl I mentioned before; I gathered she was forced into it."

"Oh, Jesus, nobody's *forced!* That's crap."

"She was. She mentioned a few things. . . . Controls is as good a word as any. Courts, doctors, even jobs. . . ."

"I wouldn't know anything about that."

"And afterward. Making contact later—perhaps a few years later. Plain old-fashioned blackmail. Just as I'm blackmailing you now."

"Then she was in trouble before; this girl, I mean. If it's a bummer, she doesn't have to make the trip. Unless she's into somebody and owes what she can't pay for."

"Who is Nimrod?" Matlock asked the question softly, without emphasis But the question caused the young man to turn and walk away.

"I don't know that. I don't have that information."

Matlock got out of the chair and stood motionless. "I'll ask you just once more, and if I don't get an answer, I'll walk out the door and you'll be finished. A very promising life will be altered drastically—if you have a life. . . . Who is Nimrod?"

The boy whipped around and Matlock saw the fear again. The fear he had seen on Lucas Herron's face, in Lucas Herron's eyes.

"So help me Christ, I can't answer that!"

"Can't or won't?"

"Can't. I *don't know!*"

"I think you do. But I said I'd only ask you once. That's it." Matlock started for the apartment door without looking at the student.

"No! . . . Goddamn it, I *don't know!* . . . How *could* I know? You can't!" Pace ran to Matlock's side.

"Can't what?"

"Whatever you said you'd do. . . . Listen to me! I don't know who they are! I don't have . . ."

"They?"

Pace looked puzzled. "Yeah. . . . I guess 'they.' I don't know. I don't have any contact. Others do; I don't. They haven't bothered me."

"But you're aware of them." A statement.

"Aware. . . . Yes, I'm aware. But *who*, honest to God, *no!*"

Matlock turned and faced the student. "We'll compromise. For now. Tell me what you *do* know."

And the frightened young man did. And as the words came forth, the fear infected James Matlock.

Nimrod was an unseen master puppeteer. Faceless, formless, but with frightening, viable authority. It wasn't a *he* or a *they*—it was a *force*, according to Alan Pace. A complex abstraction that had its elusive tentacles in every major university in the Northeast, every municipality that served the academic landscape, all the financial pyramids that funded the complicated structures of New England's higher education. "And points south," if the rumors had foundation.

Narcotics was only one aspect, the craw in the throats of the criminal legions—the immediate reason for the May conference, the Corsican letter.

Beyond drugs and their profits, the Nimrod imprimatur was stamped on scores of college administrations. Pace was convinced that curriculums were being shaped, university personnel hired and fired, degree and scholarship policies, all were expedited on the Nimrod organization's instructions. Matlock's memory flashed back to Carlyle. To Carlyle's assistant dean of admissions—a Nimrod appointee, according to the dead Loring. To Archer Beeson, rapidly rising in the history department; to a coach of varsity soccer; to a dozen other faculty and staff names on Loring's list.

How many more were there? How deep was the infiltration?

Why?

The prostitution rings were subsidiary accommodations. Recruitments were made by the child-whores among themselves; addresses were provided, fees established. Young flesh with ability and attractiveness could find its way to Nimrod and make the pact. And there was "freedom," there was "bread" in the pact with Nimrod.

And "no one was hurt"; it was a victimless crime.

"No crime at all, just freedom, man. No pressures over the head. No screaming zonkers over scholarship points."

Alan Pace saw a great deal of good in the elusive, practical Nimrod. More than good.

"You think it's all so different from the outside—straight? You're wrong, mister. It's mini-America: organized, computerized, and very heavy with the corporate structure. Hell, it's patterned on the American syndrome; it's company *policy*, man! It's GM, ITT, and Ma Bell—only someone was smart enough to organize the groovy groves of academe. And it's growing fast. Don't fight it. Join it."

"Is that what you're going to do?" asked Matlock.

"It's the way, man. It's the faith. For all I know *you're* with it now. Could be, you're a recruiter. You guys are everywhere; I've been expecting you."

"Suppose I'm not?"

"Then you're out of your head. And over it, too."

Chapter Twenty-seven

If one watched the white station wagon and its driver heading back toward the center of New Haven, one would have thought—if he thought at all—that it was a rich car, suitable to a wealthy suburb, the man at the wheel appropriately featured for the vehicle.

Such an observer would not know that the driver was barely cognizant of the traffic, numbed by the revelations he'd learned within the hour; an exhausted man who hadn't slept in forty-eight hours, who had the feeling that he was holding onto a thin rope above an infinite chasm, expecting any instant that his lifeline would be severed, plunging him into the infinite mist.

Matlock tried his best to suspend whatever thought processes he was capable of. The years, the specific months during which he'd run his academic race against self-imposed schedules had taught him that the mind—at least his mind—could not function properly when the forces of exhaustion and overexposure converged.

Above all, he had to function.

He was in uncharted waters. Seas where tiny islands were peopled by grotesque inhabitants. Julian Dunoises, Lucas Herrons; the Bartolozzis, the Aiellos, the Sharpes, the Stocktons, and the Paces. The poisoned and the poisoners.

Nimrod.

Uncharted waters?

No, they weren't uncharted, thought Matlock.

They were well traveled. And the travelers were the cynics of the planet.

He drove to the Sheraton Hotel and took a room.

He sat on the edge of the bed and placed a telephone call to Howard Stockton at Carmount. Stockton was out.

In brusque, officious tones, he told the Carmount switchboard that Stockton was to return his call—he looked at his watch; it was ten of two—in four hours. At six o'clock. He gave the Sheraton number and hung up.

He needed at least four hours' sleep. He wasn't sure when he would sleep again.

He picked up the telephone once more and requested a wake-up call at five forty-five.

As his head sank to the pillow, he brought his arm up to his eyes. Through the cloth of his shirt he felt the stubble of his beard. He'd have to go to a barbershop; he'd left his suitcase in the white station wagon. He'd been too tired, too involved to remember to bring it to his room.

The short, sharp three rings of the telephone signified the Sheraton's adherence to his instructions. It was exactly quarter to six. Fifteen minutes later there was another ring, this one longer, more normal. It was precisely six, and the caller was Howard Stockton.

"I'll make this short, Matlock. You got a contact. Only he doesn't want to meet *inside* the Sail and Ski. You go to the East Gorge slope—they use it in spring and summer for tourists to look at the scenery—and take the lift to the top. You be there at eight thirty this evenin'. He'll have a man at the top. That's all I've got to say. It's none of *mah business!*"

Stockton slammed down the telephone and the echo rang in Matlock's ear.

But he'd made it! *He'd made it!* He had made the contact with Nimrod! With the conference.

He walked up the dark trail toward the ski lift. Ten dollars made the attendant at the Sail and Ski parking lot understand his problem: the nice-looking fellow in the station wagon had an assignation. The husband wasn't expected till later—and, what the hell, that's life. The parking lot attendant was very cooperative.

When he reached the East Gorge slope, the rain, which had threatened all day, began to come down. In Connecticut, April showers were somehow always May thunderstorms, and Matlock was annoyed that he hadn't thought to buy a raincoat.

He looked around at the deserted lift, its high double lines silhouetted against the increasing rain, shining like thick strands of ship hemp in a fogged harbor. There was a tiny, almost invisible light in the shack which housed the complicated, hulking machines that made the lines ascend. Matlock approached the door and knocked. A small, wiry-looking man opened the door and peered at him.

"You the fella goin' up?"

"I guess I am."

"What's your name?"

"Matlock."

"Guess you are. Know how to catch a crossbar?"

"I've skied. Arm looped, tail on the slat, feet on the pipe."

"Don't need no help from me. I'll start it, you get it."

"Fine."

"You're gonna get wet."

"I know."

Matlock positioned himself to the right of the entrance pit as the lumbering machinery started up. The lines creaked slowly and then began their halting countermoves, and a crossbar approached. He slid himself onto the lift, pressed his feet against the footrail, and locked the bar in front of his waist. He felt the swinging motion of the lines lifting him off the ground.

He was on his way to the top of East Gorge, on his way to his contact with Nimrod. As he swung upward, ten feet above the ground, the rain became, instead of annoying, exhilarating. He was coming to the end of his journey, his race. Whoever met him at the top would be utterly confused. He counted on that, he'd planned it that way. If everything the murdered Loring and the very-much-alive Greenberg had told him was true, it couldn't be any other way. The total secrecy of the conference; the delegates, unknown to each other; the oath of "Omerta," the subculture's violent insistence on codes and countercodes to protect its inhabitants—it *was* all true. He'd seen it all in operation. And such complicated logistics—when sharply interrupted—inevitably led to suspicion and fear and ultimately confusion. It was the confusion Matlock counted on.

Lucas Herron had accused him of being influenced by plots and counterplots. Well, he wasn't *influenced* by them—he merely *understood* them. That was different. It was this understanding which had led him one step away from Nimrod.

The rain came harder now, whipped by the wind which was stronger off the ground than on it. Matlock's crossbar swayed and dipped, more so each time he reached a rung up the slope. The tiny light in the machine shack was now barely visible in the darkness and the rain. He judged that he was nearly halfway to the top.

There was a jolt; the machinery stopped. Matlock gripped the waist guard and peered above him through the rain trying to see what obstruction had hit the wheel or the rung. There was none.

He turned awkwardly in the narrow perch and squinted his eyes down the slope toward the shack. There was no light now, not even the slightest illumination. He held his hand up in front of his forehead, keeping the rain away as best he could. He had to be mistaken, the downpour was blurring his vision, perhaps the pole was in his line of sight. He leaned first to the right, then to the left. But still there was no light from the bottom of the hill.

Perhaps the fuses had blown. If so, they would have taken the bulb in the shack with them. Or a short. It was raining, and ski lifts did not ordinarily operate in the rain.

He looked beneath him. The ground was perhaps fifteen feet away. If he suspended himself from the footrail, the drop would only be eight or nine feet. He could handle that. He would walk the rest of the way up the slope. He had to do it quickly, however. It might take as long as twenty minutes to climb to the top, there was no way of telling. He couldn't take the chance of his contact's panicking, deciding to leave before he got to him.

"Stay right where you are! Don't unlatch that harness!"

The voice shot out of the darkness cutting through the rain and wind. Its harsh command paralyzed Matlock as much from the shock of surprise as from fear. The man stood beneath him, to the right of the lines. He was dressed in a raincoat and some kind of cap. It was impossible to see his face or even determine his size.

"Who are you?! What do you want?!"

"I'm the man you came to meet. I want to see that paper in your pocket. Throw it down."

"I'll show you the paper when I see *your* copy. That's the deal! That's the deal I made."

"You don't understand, Matlock. Just throw the paper down. That's all."

"What the hell are you talking about?!"

The glare of a powerful flashlight blinded him. He reached for the guard rail latch.

"Don't touch that! Keep your hands straight out or you're dead!"

The core of the high-intensity light shifted from his face to his chest, and for several seconds all Matlock saw were a thousand flashing spots inside his eyes. As his sight returned, he could see that the man below him was moving closer to the lines, swinging the flashlight toward the ground for a path. In the glow of the beam, he also saw that the man held a large, ugly automatic in his right hand. The blinding light returned to his face, now shining directly beneath him.

"Don't threaten me, punk!" yelled Matlock, remembering the effect his anger had on Stockton at four that morning. "Put that goddamn gun away and help me down! We haven't much time and I don't like games!"

The effect now was not the same. Instead, the man beneath him began to laugh, and the laugh was sickening. It was, more than anything else, utterly genuine. The man on the ground was enjoying himself.

"You're very funny. You look funny sitting there on your ass in midair. You know what you look like? You look like one of those bobbing monkey targets in a shooting gallery! *You know what I mean?* Now, cut the bullshit and throw down the paper!"

He laughed again, and at the sound everything was suddenly clear to Matlock.

He hadn't made a contact. He hadn't cornered anyone. All his careful planning, all his thought-out actions. All for nothing. He was no nearer Nimrod now than he was before he knew Nimrod existed.

He'd been trapped.

Still, he had to try. It was all that was left him now.

"You're making the mistake of your life!"

"Oh, for Christ's sake, knock it off! Give me the paper! We've been looking for the fucking thing for a week! My orders are to get it *now!*"

"I can't give it to you."

"I'll blow your head off!"

"I say I *can't!* I didn't say I *wouldn't!*"

"Don't shit me. You've got it on you! You wouldn't have come here without it!"

"It's in a packet strapped to the small of my back."

"Get it out!"

"I told you, I can't! I'm sitting on a four-inch slat of wood with a footrail and I'm damn near twenty feet in the air!"

His words were half lost in the whipping rain. The man below was frustrated, impatient.

"*I said get it out!*"

"I'll have to drop down. I can't reach the straps!" Matlock yelled to be heard. "I can't *do* anything! I haven't got a gun!"

The man with the large, ugly automatic moved back several feet from the lines. He pointed both the powerful beam and his weapon at Matlock.

"O.K., come on down! You cough wrong and your head's blown off!"

Matlock undid the latch, feeling like a small boy on top of a ferris wheel wondering what could happen if the wheel stopped permanently and the safety bar fell off.

He held onto the footrail and let the rest of him swing beneath it. He dangled in the air, the rain soaking him, the beam of light blinding him. He had to think now, he had to create an instant strategy. His life was worth far less than the lives at Windsor Shoals to such men as the man on the ground.

"Shine the light down! I can't see!"

"Fuck that! Just drop!"

He dropped.

And the second he hit the earth, he let out a loud, painful scream and reached for his leg.

"Aaaahhh! My ankle, my foot! I broke my goddamn ankle!" He twisted and turned on the wet overgrowth, writhing in pain.

"Shut up! Get me that paper! *Now!*"

"*Jesus Christ!* What do you *want* from me? My ankle's turned *around!* It's *broken!*"

"Tough! Give me the paper!"

Matlock lay prostrate on the ground, his head moving back and forth, his neck straining to stand the pain. He spoke between short gasps.

"Strap's here. Undo the strap." He tore at his shirt displaying part of the canvas belt.

"Undo it yourself. Hurry up!"

But the man came closer. He wasn't sure. And closer. The beam of light was just above Matlock now. Then it moved to his midsection and Matlock could see the large barrel of the ugly black automatic.

It was the second, the instant he'd waited for.

He whipped his right hand up toward the weapon, simultaneously springing his whole body against the legs of the man in the raincoat. He held the automatic's barrel, forcing it with all his strength toward the ground. The gun fired twice, the impact of the explosions nearly shattering Matlock's hand, the sounds partially muted by wet earth and the slashing rain.

The man was beneath him now, twisting on his side, thrashing with his legs and free arm against the heavier Matlock. Matlock flung himself on the pinned arm and sank his teeth into the wrist above the hand holding the weapon. He bit into the flesh until he could feel the blood spurting out, mingled with the cold rain.

The man released the automatic, screaming in anguish. Matlock grabbed for the gun, wrested it free, and smashed it repeatedly into the man's face. The powerful flashlight was in the tall grass, its beam directed at nothing but drenched foliage.

Matlock crouched over the half-conscious, bloody face of his former captor. He was out of breath, and the sickening taste of the man's blood was still in his mouth. He spat a half dozen times trying to cleanse his teeth, his throat.

"O.K.!" He grabbed the man's collar and yanked his head up. "Now you tell me what happened! This was a trap, wasn't it?"

"The paper! I gotta get the paper." The man was hardly audible.

"I was *trapped, wasn't I!* The whole last week was a trap!"

"Yeah. . . . Yeah. The paper."

"That paper's pretty important, isn't it?"

"They'll kill you . . . they'll kill you to get it! You stand no chance, mister. . . . No chance . . ."

"Who's *they?!*"

"I don't know . . . don't know!"

"*Who's Nimrod?*"

"I don't know . . . 'Omerta'! . . . 'Omerta'!"

The man opened his eyes wide, and in the dim spill of the fallen flashlight, Matlock saw that something had happened to his victim. Some thought, some concept overpowered his tortured imagination. It was painful to watch. It was too close to the sight of the panicked Lucas Herron, the terrified Alan Pace.

"Come on, I'll get you down the slope. . . ."

It was as far as he got. From the depths of his lost control, the man with the blood-soaked face lunged forward, making a last desperate attempt to reach the gun in Matlock's right hand. Matlock yanked back; instinctively he fired the weapon. Blood and pieces of flesh flew everywhere. Half the man's neck was blown off.

Matlock stood up slowly. The smoke of the automatic lingered above the dead man, the rain forcing it downward toward the earth.

He reached into the grass for the flashlight, and as he bent over he began to vomit.

Chapter Twenty-eight

Ten minutes later he watched the parking lot below him from the trunk of a huge maple tree fifty yards up the trail. The new leaves partially protected him from the pouring rain, but his clothes were filthy, covered with wet dirt and blood. He saw the white station wagon near the front of the area, next to the stone gate entrance of the Sail and Ski. There wasn't much activity now; no automobiles entered, and those drivers inside would wait until the deluge stopped before venturing out on the roads. The parking lot attendant he'd given the ten dollars to was talking with a uniformed doorman under the carpet roof of the restaurant entrance. Matlock wanted to race to the station wagon and drive away as fast as he could, but he knew the sight of his clothes would alarm the two men, make them wonder what had happened on the East Gorge slope. There was nothing to do but wait, wait until someone came out and distracted them, or both went inside.

He hated the waiting. More than hating it, he was frightened by it. There'd been no one he could see or hear near the wheel shack, but the didn't mean no one was there. Nimrod's dead contact probably had a partner somewhere, waiting as Matlock was waiting now. If the dead man was found, they'd stop him, kill him—if not for revenge, for the Corsican paper.

He had no choice now. He'd gone beyond his depth, his abilities. He'd been manipulated by Nimrod as he'd been maneuvered by the men of the Justice Department. He would telephone Jason Greenberg and do whatever Greenberg told him to do.

In a way, he was glad his part of it was over, or soon would be. He still felt the impulse of commitment, but there was nothing more he could do. He had failed.

Down below, the restaurant entrance opened and a waitress signaled the uniformed doorman. He and the attendant walked up the steps to speak with the girl.

Matlock ran down to the gravel and darted in front of the grills of the cars parked on the edge of the lot. Between automobiles he kept looking toward the restaurant door. The waitress had given the doorman a container of coffee. All three were smoking cigarettes, all three were laughing.

He rounded the circle and crouched in front of the station wagon. He crept to the door window and saw to his relief that the keys were in the ignition. He took a deep breath, opened the door as quietly as possible, and leaped inside. Instead of slamming it, he pulled the door shut quickly, silently, so as to extinguish the interior light without calling attention to the sound. The two men and the waitress were still talking, still laughing, oblivious.

He settled himself in the seat, switched on the ignition, threw the gears into reverse, and roared backward in front of the gate. He raced out between the stone posts and started down the long road to the highway.

Back under the roof, on the steps by the front door, the three employees were momentarily startled. Then, from being startled they became quickly bewildered—and even a little curious. For, from the rear of the parking lot, they could hear the deep-throated roar of a second, more powerful engine. Bright headlights flicked on, distorted by the downpour of rain, and a long black limousine rushed forward.

The wheels screeched as the ominous-looking automobile swerved toward the stone posts. The huge car went to full throttle and raced after the station wagon.

There wasn't much traffic on the highway, but he still felt he'd make better time taking the backroads into Carlyle. He decided to go straight to Kressel's house, despite Sam's proclivity toward hysteria. Together they could both call Greenberg. He had just brutally, horribly killed another human being, and whether it was justified or not, the shock was still with him. He suspected it would be with him for the remainder of his life. He wasn't sure Kressel was the man to see.

But there was no one else. Unless he returned to his apartment and stayed there until a federal agent picked him up. And then again, instead of an agent, there might well be an emissary from Nimrod.

There was a winding S-curve in the road. He remembered that it came before a long stretch through farmland where he could make up time. The highway was straighter, but the back roads were shorter as long as there was no traffic to speak of. As he rounded the final half-circle, he realized that he was gripping the wheel so hard his forearms ached. It was the muscular defenses of his body taking over, controlling his shaking limbs, steadying the car with sheer unfeeling strength.

The flat stretch appeared; the rain had let up. He pushed the accelerator to the floor and felt the station wagon surge forward in overdrive.

He looked twice, then three times, up at his rear-view mirror, wary of patrol cars. He saw headlights behind him coming closer. He looked down at his speedometer. It read eighty-seven miles per hour and still the lights in the mirror gained on him.

The instincts of the hunted came swiftly to the surface; he knew the automobile behind him was no police car. There was no siren penetrating the wet stillness, no flashing light heralding authority.

He pushed his right leg forward, pressing the accelerator beyond the point of achieving anything further from the engine. His speedometer reached ninety-four miles per hour—the wagon was not capable of greater speed.

The headlights were directly behind him now. The unknown pursuer was feet, inches from his rear bumper. Suddenly the headlights veered to the left, and the car came alongside the white station wagon.

It was the same black limousine he had seen after Loring's murder! The same huge automobile that had raced out of the darkened driveway minutes after the massacre at Windsor Shoals! Matlock tried to keep part of his mind on the road ahead, part on the single driver of the car, which was crowding him to the far right of the road. The station wagon vibrated under the impact of the enormous speed; he found it more and more difficult to hold the wheel.

And then he saw the barrel of the pistol pointed at him through the window of the adjacent automobile. He saw the look of desperation in the darting eyes behind the outstretched arm, trying to steady itself for a clean line of fire.

He heard the shots and felt the glass shattering into his face and over the front seat. He slammed his foot into the brake and spun the steering wheel to the right, jumping the shoulder of the road, careening violently into and through a barbed-wire fence and onto a rock-strewn field. The wagon lunged into the grass, perhaps fifty or sixty feet, and then slammed into a cluster of rocks, or property demarcation. The headlights smashed and went out, the grill buckled. He was thrown into the dashboard, only his upheld arms keeping his head from crashing into the windshield.

But he was conscious, and the instincts of the hunted would not leave him.

He heard a car door open and close, and he knew the killer was coming into the field after his quarry. After the Corsican paper. He felt a trickle of blood rolling down his forehead—whether it was the graze of a bullet or a laceration from the flying glass, he couldn't be sure—but he was grateful it was there. He'd need it now, he needed the sight of blood on his forehead. He remained slumped over the wheel, immobile, silent.

And under his jacket he held the ugly automatic he had taken from the dead man in the raincoat on the slope of East Gorge. It was pointed under his left arm at the door.

He could hear the mushed crunch of footsteps on the soft earth outside the station wagon. He could literally feel—as a blind man feels—the face peering through the shattered glass looking at him. He heard the click of the door button as it was pushed in and the creaking of the hinges as the heavy panel was pulled open.

A hand grabbed his shoulder. Matlock fired his weapon.

The roar was deafening; the scream of the wounded man pierced the drenched darkness. Matlock leaped out of the seat and slammed the full weight of his body against the killer, who had grabbed his left arm in pain. Wildly, inaccurately, Matlock pistol-whipped the man about his face and neck until he fell to the ground. The man's gun was nowhere to be seen, his hands were empty. Matlock put his foot on the man's throat and pressed.

"I'll stop when you signal you're going to talk to me, you son of a bitch! Otherwise I *don't* stop!"

The man sputtered, his eyes bulged. He raised his right hand in supplication.

Matlock took his foot away and knelt on the ground over the man. He was heavy set, black-haired, with the blunt features of a brute killer.

"Who sent you after me? How did you know this car?"

The man raised his head slightly as though to answer. Instead the killer whipped his right hand into his waist, pulled out a knife, and rolled sharply to his left, yanking his gorilla-like knee up into Matlock's groin. The knife slashed into Matlock's shirt, and he knew as he felt the steel point crease his flesh that he'd come as close as he would ever come to being killed.

He crashed the barrel of the heavy automatic into the man's temple. It was enough. The killer's head snapped back; blood matted itself around the hairline. Matlock stood up and placed his foot on the hand with the knife.

Soon the killer's eyes opened.

And during the next five minutes, Matlock did what he never thought he would be capable of doing—he tortured another man. He tortured the killer with the killer's own knife, penetrating the skin around and below the eyes, puncturing the lips with the same steel point that had scraped his own flesh. And when the man screamed, Matlock smashed his mouth with the barrel of the automatic and broke pieces of ivory off the killer's teeth.

It was not long.

"The paper!"

"What else?"

The writhing killer moaned and spat blood, but would not speak. Matlock did; quietly, in total conviction, in complete sincerity.

"You'll answer me or I'll push this blade down through your eyes. I don't care anymore. Believe me."

"The old man!" The guttural words came from deep inside the man's throat. "He said he wrote it down. . . . No one knows. . . . You talked to him. . . ."

"What old . . ." Matlock stopped as a terrifying thought came into his mind. "*Lucas Herron?! Is that who you mean?!*"

"He said he wrote it down. They think you know. Maybe he lied. . . . For Christ's sake, he could have lied. . . ."

The killer fell into unconsciousness.

Matlock stood up slowly, his hands shaking, his whole body shivering. He looked up at the road, at the huge black limousine standing silently in the diminishing rain. It would be his last gamble, his ultimate effort.

But something was stirring in his brain, something elusive but palpable. He had to trust that feeling, as he had come to trust the instincts of the hunter and the hunted.

The old man!

The answer lay somewhere in Lucas Herron's house.

Chapter Twenty-nine

He parked the limousine a quarter of a mile from Herron's Nest and walked toward the house on the side of the road, prepared to jump into the bordering woods should any cars approach.

None did.

He came upon one house, then another, and in each case he raced past, watching the lighted windows to see if anyone was looking out.

No one was.

He reached the edge of Herron's property and crouched to the ground. Slowly, cautiously, silently he made his way to the driveway. The house was dark; there were no cars, no people, no signs of life. Only death.

He walked up the flagstone path and his eye caught sight of an official-looking document, barely visible in the darkness, tacked onto the front door. He approached it and lit a match. It was a sheriff's seal of closure.

One more crime, thought Matlock.

He went around to the back of the house, and as he stood in front of the patio door, he remembered vividly the sight of Herron racing across his manicured lawn into the forbidding green wall which he parted so deftly and into which he disappeared so completely.

There was another sheriff's seal on the back door. This one was glued to a pane of glass.

Matlock removed the automatic from his belt and as quietly as possible broke the small-paned window to the left of the seal. He opened the door and walked in.

The first thing that struck him was the darkness. Light and dark were relative, as he'd come to understand during the past week. The night had light which the eyes could adjust to; the daylight was often deceptive, filled with shadows and misty blind spots. But inside Herron's house the darkness was complete. He lit a match and understood why.

The windows in the small kitchen were covered with shades. Only they weren't ordinary window shades, they were custom built. The cloth was heavy and attached to the frames with vertical runners, latched at the sills by large aluminium hasps. He approached the window over the sink and lit another match. Not only was the shade thicker than ordinary, but the runners and the stretch lock at the bottom insured that the shade would remain absolutely flat against the whole frame. It was doubtful that any light could go out or come in through the window.

Herron's desire—or need—for privacy had been extraordinary. And if all the windows in all the rooms were sealed, it would make his task easier.

Striking a third match, he walked into Herron's living room. What he saw in the flickering light caused him to stop in his tracks, his breath cut short.

The entire room was a shambles. Books were strewn on the floor, furniture overturned and ripped apart, rugs upended, even sections of the wall smashed. He could have been walking into his own apartment the night of the Beeson dinner. Herron's living room had been thoroughly, desperately searched.

He went back to the kitchen to see if his preoccupation with the window shades and the darkness had played tricks on his eyes. They had. Every drawer was pulled open, every cabinet ransacked. And then he saw on the floor of a broom closet two flashlights. One was a casement, the other a long-stemmed Sportsman. The first wouldn't light, the second did.

He walked rapidly back into the living room and tried to orient himself, checking the windows with the beam of the flashlight. Every window was covered, every shade latched at the sill.

Across the narrow hallway in front of the narrower stairs was an open door. It led to Herron's study, which was, if possible, more of a mess than his living room. Two file cabinets were lying on their sides, the backs torn off; the large leather-topped desk was pulled from the wall, splintered, smashed on every flat surface. Parts of the wall, as the living room, were broken into. Matlock assumed these were sections which had sounded hollow when tapped.

Upstairs, the two small bedrooms and the bath were equally dismantled, equally dissected.

He walked back down the stairs, even the steps had been pried loose from their treads.

Lucas Herron's home had been searched by professionals. What could he find that they hadn't? He wandered back into the living room and sat down on what was left of an armchair. He had the sinking feeling that his last effort would end in failure also. He lit a cigarette and tried to organize his thoughts.

Whoever had searched the house had not found what they were looking for. Or had they? There was no way to tell, really. Except that the brute killer in the field had screamed that the old man "had written it down." As if the fact was almost as important as the desperately coveted Corsican document.

Yet he had added: ". . . maybe he lied, he could have lied." *Lied?* Why would a man in the last extremity of terror add that qualification to something so vital?

The assumption had to be that in the intricate delicacy of a mind foundering on the brink of madness, the worst evil was rejected. Had to be rejected so as to hold onto what was left of sanity.

No. . . . No, they had not found whatever it was they *had to find*. And since they hadn't found it after such exhaustive, extraordinary labors—it didn't *exist*.

But he knew it did.

Herron may have been involved with Nimrod's world, but he was not born of it. His was not a comfortable relationship—it was a tortured one. Somewhere, someplace he had left an indictment. He was too good a man not to. There had been a great decency in Lucas Herron. Somewhere . . . someplace.

But where?

He got out of the chair and paced in the darkness of the room, flicking the flashlight on and off, more as a nervous gesture than for illumination.

He reexamined minutely every word, every expression used by Lucas that early evening four days ago. He was the hunter again, tracking the spoor, testing the wind for the scent. And he was close; goddamn it, he was close!

. . . Herron had *known* from the second he'd opened his front door what Matlock was after. That instantaneous, fleeting moment of recognition had been in his eyes. It had been unmistakable to Matlock. He'd even said as much to the old man, and the old man had laughed and accused him of being influenced by plots and counterplots.

But there'd been something else. Before the plots and counterplots. . . . Something *inside*. In this room. Before Herron suggested sitting *outside*. . . . Only he hadn't *suggested*, he'd made a statement, given a command.

And just before he'd given the command to rear-march toward the backyard patio, he'd walked in silently, *walked in silently*, and startled Matlock. He had opened the swinging door, *carrying* two filled glasses, and Matlock *hadn't heard* him. Matlock pushed the button on the flashlight and shot the beam to the base of the kitchen door. There was no rug, nothing to muffle footsteps—it was a hardwood floor. He crossed to the open swing-hinged door, walked through the frame, and shut it. Then he pushed it swiftly open in the same direction Lucas Herron had pushed it carrying the two drinks. The hinges clicked as such hinges do if they are old and the door is pushed quickly—*normally*. He let the door swing shut and then he pressed against it slowly, inch by inch.

It was silent.

Lucas Herron had made the drinks and then *silently* had eased himself back into the living room so he wouldn't be heard. So he could observe Matlock without Matlock's knowing it. And then he'd given his firm command for the two of them to go outside.

Matlock forced his memory to recall *precisely* what Lucas Herron said and did at that *precise* moment.

". . . we'll go out on the patio. It's too nice a day to stay inside. Let's go."

Then, *without waiting for an answer*, even a mildly enthusiastic agreement, Herron had walked *rapidly* back through the kitchen door. No surface politeness, none of the courtly manners one expected from Lucas.

He had given an order, the firm command of an officer and a gentleman.

By Act of Congress.

That was *it!* Matlock swung the beam of light over the writing desk.

The photograph! The photograph of the marine officer holding the map and the Thompson automatic in some tiny section of jungle on an insignificant island in the South Pacific.

"I keep that old photograph to remind myself that time wasn't always so devastating."

At the precise moment Herron walked through the door, Matlock had been looking closely at the photograph! The fact that he was doing so disturbed the old man, disturbed him enough for him to insist that they go outside instantly. In a curt, abrupt manner so unlike him.

Matlock walked rapidly to the desk. The small cellophane-topped photograph was still where it had been—on the lower right wall above the desk. Several larger glass-framed pictures had been smashed; this one was intact. It was small, not at all imposing.

He grabbed the cardboard frame and pulled the photo off the single thumbtack which held it to the wall. He looked at it carefully, turning it over, inspecting the thin edges.

The close, harsh glare of the flashlight revealed scratches at the upper corner of the cardboard. Fingernail scratches? Perhaps. He pointed the light down on the desk top. There were unsharpened pencils, scraps of note paper, and a pair of scissors. He took the scissors and inserted the point of one blade between the thin layers of cardboard until he could rip the photograph out of the frame.

And in that way he found it.

On the back of the small photograph was a diagram drawn with a broad-tipped fountain pen. It was in the shape of a rectangle, the bottom and top lines filled in with dots. On the top were two small lines with arrows, one straight, the other pointing to the right. Above each arrowhead was the numeral 30. Two 30s.

Thirty.

On the sides, bordering the lines, were childishly drawn trees.

On the top, above the numbers, was another simplified sketch. Billowy half-circles connected to one another with a wavy line beneath. A cloud. Underneath, more trees.

It was a map, and what it represented was all too apparent. It was Herron's back yard; the lines on three sides represented Herron's forbidding green wall.

The numerals, the 30s, were measurements—but they were also something else. They were contemporary symbols.

For Lucas Herron, chairman for decades of Romance Languages, had an insatiable love for words and their odd usages. What was more appropriate than the symbol "30" to indicate finality?

As any first year journalism student would confirm, the number 30 at the bottom of any news copy meant the story was finished. It was over.

There was no more to be said.

Matlock held the photograph upside down in his left hand, his right gripping the flashlight. He entered the woods at midsection—slightly to the left—as indicated on the diagram. The figure 30 could be feet, yards, meters, paces—certainly not inches.

He marked off thirty twelve-inch spaces. Thirty feet straight, thirty feet to the right.

Nothing.

Nothing but the drenched, full overgrowth and underbrush which clawed at his feet.

He returned to the green wall's entrance and decided to combine yards and paces, realizing that paces in such a dense, jungle-like environment might vary considerably.

He marked off the spot thirty paces directly ahead and continued until he estimated the point of yardage. Then he returned to the bent branches where he had figured thirty paces to be and began the lateral trek.

Again nothing. An old rotted maple stood near one spot Matlock estimated was thirty steps. There was nothing else unusual. He went back to the bent branches and proceeded to his second mark.

Thirty yards straight out. Ninety feet, give or take a foot or two. Then the slow process of thirty yards through the soaking wet foliage to his next mark. Another ninety feet. Altogether, one hundred and eighty feet. Nearly two-thirds of a football field.

The going was slower now, the foliage thicker, or so it seemed. Matlock wished he had a machete or at least some kind of implement to force the wet branches out of his way. Once he lost count and had to keep in mind the variation as he proceeded—was it twenty-one or twenty-three large steps? Did it matter? Would the difference of three to six feet really matter?

He reached the spot. It was either twenty-eight or thirty. Close enough if there was anything to be seen. He pointed the flashlight to the ground and began slowly moving it back and forth laterally.

Nothing. Only the sight of a thousand glistening weeds and the deep-brown color of soaked earth. He kept swinging the beam of light, inching forward as he did so, straining his eyes, wondering every other second if he had just covered that particular section or not—everything looked so alike.

The chances of failure grew. He could go back and begin again, he thought. Perhaps the 30s connoted some other form of measurement. Meters, perhaps, or multiples of another number buried somewhere in the diagram. The dots? Should he count the dots on the bottom and top of the rectangle? Why were the dots there?

He had covered the six-foot variation and several feet beyond.

Nothing.

His mind returned to the dots, and he withdrew the photograph from his inside pocket. As he positioned himself to stand up straight, to stretch the muscles at the base of his spine—pained by crouching—his foot touched a hard, unyielding surface. At first he thought it was a fallen limb, or perhaps a rock.

And then he knew it was neither.

He couldn't see it—whatever it was, was underneath a clump of overgrown weeds. But he could feel the outline of the object with his foot. It was straight, precisely tooled. It was no part of a forest.

He held the light over the cluster of weeds and saw that they weren't weeds. They were some kind of small-budded flower in partial bloom. A flower which did not need sunlight or space.

A jungle flower. Out of place, purchased, replanted.

He pushed them out of the way and bent down. Underneath was a thick, heavily varnished slab of wood about two feet wide and perhaps a foot and a half long. It had sunk an inch or two into the ground; the surface had been sanded and varnished so often that the layers of protective coating reached a high gloss, reflecting the beam of the flashlight as though it were glass.

Matlock dug his fingers into the earth and lifted up the slab. Beneath it was a weathered metal plaque, bronze perhaps.

For Major Lucas N. Herron, USMCR

In Gratitude from the Officers and Men of Bravo Company,

Fourteenth Raider Battalion, First Marine Division

Solomon Islands—South Pacific

May 1943

Seeing it set in the ground under the glare of light, Matlock had the feeling he was looking at a grave.

He pushed away the surrounding mud and dug a tiny trench around the metal. On his hands and knees, he slowly, awkwardly lifted the plaque up and carefully placed it to one side.

He had found it.

Buried in earth was a metal container—the type used in library archives for valuable manuscripts. Airtight, weatherproofed, vacuumed, a receptacle for the ages.

A coffin, Matlock thought.

He picked it up and inserted his cold, wet fingers under the lever of the coiled hasp. It took considerable strength to pull it up, but finally it was released. There was the rush of air one hears upon opening a tin of coffee. The rubber edges parted. Inside Matlock could see an oilcloth packet in the shape of a notebook.

He knew he'd found the indictment.

Chapter Thirty

The notebook was thick, over three hundred pages, and every word was handwritten in ink. It was in the form of a diary, but the lengthy entries varied enormously. There was no consistency regarding dates. Often days followed one another; at other times entries were separated by weeks, even months. The writing also varied. There were stretches of lucid narrative followed by incoherent, disjointed rambling. In the latter sections the hand had shaken, the words were often illegible.

Lucas Herron's diary was a cry of anguish, an outpouring of pain. A confessional of a man beyond hope.

As he sat on the cold wet ground, mesmerized by Herron's words, Matlock understood the motives behind Herron's Nest, the forbidding green wall, the window shades, the total isolation.

Lucas Herron had been a drug addict for a quarter of a century. Without the drugs, his pain was unendurable. And there was absolutely nothing anyone could do for him except confine him to a ward in a Veterans' Hospital for the remainder of his unnatural life.

It was the rejection of this living death that had plunged Lucas Herron into another.

Major Lucas Nathaniel Herron, USMCR, attached to Amphibious Assault Troops, Raider Battalions, Fleet Marine Force, Pacific, had led numerous companies of the Fourteenth Battalion, First Marine Division, in ranger assaults on various islands throughout the Japanese-held Solomons and Carolinas.

And Major Lucas Herron had been carried off the tiny island of Peleliu in the Carolinas on a stretcher, having brought two companies back to the beach through jungle fire. None thought he could survive.

Major Lucas Herron had a Japanese bullet imbedded at the base of his neck, lodged in a section of his nervous system. He was not expected to live. The doctors, first in Brisbane, then San Diego, and finally at Bethesda, considered further operations unfeasible. The patient could not survive them; he would be reduced to a vegetable should even the slightest complication set in. No one wished to be responsible for that.

They put the patient under heavy medication to relieve the discomfort of his wounds. And he lay there in the Maryland hospital for over two years.

The stages of healing—partial recovery—were slow and painful. First, there were the neck braces and the pills; then the braces and the metal frames for walking, and still the pills. At last the crutches, along with the braces and always the pills. Lucas Herron came back to the land of the living—but not without the pills. And in moments of torment—the needle of morphine at night.

There were hundreds, perhaps thousands, like Lucas Herron, but few had his extraordinary qualifications—for those who sought him out. An authentic hero of the Pacific war, a brilliant scholar, a man above reproach.

He was perfect. He could be used perfectly.

On the one hand, he could not live, could not endure, without the relief afforded him by the narcotics—the pills and the increasingly frequent needles. On the other hand, if the degree of his dependence was known medically, he would be returned to a hospital ward.

These alternatives were gradually, subtly made clear to him. Gradually in the sense that his sources of supply needed favors now and then—a contact to be made in Boston, men to be paid in New York. Subtly in that when Herron questioned the involvement, he was told it was really quite harmless. Harmless but *necessary*.

As the years went by, he became enormously valuable to the men he needed so badly. The contact in Boston, the men to be paid in New York, became more and more frequent, more and more *necessary*. Then Lucas was sent farther and farther afield. Winter vacations, spring midterms, summers: Canada, Mexico, France . . . the Mediterranean.

He became a courier.

And always the thought of the hospital ward on his tortured body and brain.

They had manipulated him brilliantly. He was never exposed to the results of his work, never specifically aware of the growing network of destruction he was helping to build. And when finally he learned of it all, it was too late. The network had been built.

Nimrod had his power.

April 22, 1951. At midterm they're sending me back to Mexico. I'll stop at the U. of M.—as usual—and on the way back at Baylor. A touch of irony: the bursar here called me in, saying Carlyle would be pleased to help defray my "research" expenses. I declined, and told him the *disability allowance* was sufficient. Perhaps I should have accepted. . . .

June 13, 1956. To Lisbon for three weeks. A routing map, I'm told, for a small ship. Touching the Azores, through Cuba (a mess!), finally into Panama. Stops—for me—at the Sorbonne, U. of Toledo, U. of Madrid. I'm becoming an academic gadfly! I'm not happy about methods—who could be?—but neither am I responsible for the archaic laws. So many, many can be helped. They need help! I've been in touch with scores on the telephone—they put me in touch—men like myself who couldn't face another day without help. . . . Still, I worry. . . . Still, what can I do? Others would do it, if not me. . . .

February 24, 1957. I'm alarmed but calm and reasonable (I hope!) about my concerns. I'm told now that when they send me to make contacts I am the *messenger* from *"Nimrod"*! The name is a code—a meaningless artifice, they say—and will be honored. It's all so foolish—like the intelligence information we'd receive from MacArthur's HQ in So-Pac. *They* had *all* the codes and *none* of the *facts.* . . . The pain is worse, the medics said it would get worse. But . . . "Nimrod's" considerate. . . . As I am. . . .

March 10, 1957. They were angry with me! They withheld my dosage for two days—I thought I would kill myself! I started out in my car for the VA hospital in Hartford, but they stopped me on the highway. They were in a Carlyle *patrol car*—I should have known they had the police here! . . . It was either *compromise* or the *ward!* . . . They were right! . . . I'm off to Canada and the job is to bring in a man from North Africa. . . . I *must* do it! The calls to me are constant. This evening a man—Army, 27th—Naha casualty—from East Orange, N.J., said that he and six others *depended* on me! There are so many like ourselves! Why? Why, for God's sake, are we *despised?* We need *help* and all that's offered to us are the *wards!* . . .

August 19, 1960. I've made my position clear! They go too far! . . . "Nimrod" is not just a code name for a location, it's also a *man!* The geography doesn't change but the man does. They're not helping men like me any longer—well, maybe they are—but it's more than *us!* They're reaching out—they're *attracting* people—for a great deal of money! . . .

August 20, 1960. Now they're threatening me. They say I'll have no more once my cabinet's empty. . . . I don't care! I've enough for a week—with luck—a week and a half. . . . I wish I liked alcohol more, or that it didn't make me sick. . . .

August 28, 1960. I shook to my ankles but I went to the Carlyle Police Station. I wasn't thinking. I asked to speak with the highest man in authority and they said it was after five o'clock—he had gone home. So I said I had information about narcotics and within ten minutes the chief of police showed up. . . . By now I was obvious—I couldn't control myself—I urinated through my trousers. The chief of police took me into a small room and opened his kit and administered a needle. He was from Nimrod! . . .

October 7, 1965. This Nimrod is displeased with me. I've always gotten along with the Nimrods—the two I've met, but this one is sterner, more concerned with my accomplishments. I refuse to touch *students*, he accepts that, but he says I am getting silly in my classroom lectures, I'm not bearing down. He doesn't care that I don't *solicit*—he doesn't want me to—but he tells me that I should be—well, be more conservative in my outlook. . . . It's strange. His name is Matthew Orton and he's an insignificant aide to the lieutenant governor in Hartford. But he's Nimrod. And I'll obey. . . .

November 14, 1967. The back is intolerable now—the doctors said it would *disintegrate*—that was *their* word—but not like *this!* I can get through forty minutes of a lecture and then I *must* excuse myself! . . . I ask always—is it worth it? . . . It must be or I wouldn't go on. . . . Or am I simply too great an egoist—or too much a coward—to take my life? . . . Nimrod sees me tonight. In a week it's *Thanksgiving*—I wonder where I will go. . . .

January 27, 1970. It *has* to be the end now. In C. Fry's beautiful words, the "seraphic strawberry, beaming in its bed" but turn and show its nettles. There's nothing more for me and Nimrod has infected too many, too completely. I will take my life—as painlessly as possible—there's been so much pain. . . .

January 28, 1970. I've tried to kill myself! I can't *do* it! I bring the gun, then the knife to the point, but it *will not happen!* Am I *really* so infused, so infected that I cannot accomplish that which is most to be desired? . . . Nimrod will kill me. I know that and he knows it better.

January 29, 1970. Nimrod—he's now *Arthur Latona!* Unbelievable! The same *Arthur Latona* who built the middle-income housing projects in Mount Holly!—At any rate, he's given me an unacceptable order. I've *told* him it's *unacceptable.* I'm far too valuable to be discarded and I've told him that, *too.* . . . He wants me to carry a great deal of money to Toros Daglari in Turkey! . . . Why, oh why, can't my life be *ended?* . . .

April 18, 1971. It's a wondrously strange world. To survive, to exist and breathe the air, one does so much one comes to loathe. The total is frightening . . . the excuses and the rationalizations are worse. . . . Then something happens which suspends—or at least postpones—all necessity of judgment. . . . The pains shifted from the neck and spine to the lower sides. I knew it had to be something else. Something *more.* . . . I went to Nimrod's doctor—as I must—always. My weight has dropped, my reflexes are pathetic. He's worried and tomorrow I enter the private hospital in Southbury. He says for an exploratory. . . . I know they'll do their best for me. They have other trips—very important trips, Nimrod says. I'll be traveling throughout most of the summer, he tells me. . . . If it wasn't me, it would be someone else. The pains are terrible.

May 22, 1971. The old, tired soldier is home. Herron's Nest is my salvation! I'm minus a kidney. No telling yet about the other, the doctor says. But I know better. I'm dying. . . . Oh, God, I welcome it! There'll be no more trips, no more threats. Nimrod can do no more. . . . They'll keep me alive, too. As long as they can. *They have to now!* . . . I hinted to the doctor that I've kept a record over the years. He just stared at me speechless. I've never seen a man so frightened. . . .

May 23, 1971. Latona—Nimrod—dropped by this morning. Before he could discuss anything, I told him I knew I was dying. That nothing

mattered to me now—the decision to end my life was made, not by me.
I even told him that I was prepared—relieved; that I had tried to end it
myself but couldn't. He asked about *"what you told the doctor."* He
wasn't able to say the *words!* His *fear* blanketed the living room like a
heavy mist. . . . I answered calmly, with great authority, I think. I told
him that whatever records there were would be given to him—*if my last
days or months were made easier for me*. He was furious but he knew there
wasn't anything he could do. What can a person do with an old man in
pain who knows he's going to die? What arguments are left?

August 14, 1971. Nimrod is dead! Latona died of a coronary! Before
me, and there's irony in that! . . . Still the business continues without
change. Still I'm brought my supplies every week and every week the
frightened messengers ask the questions—where are they? Where are
the records?—they come close to threatening me but I remind them
that Nimrod had the word of a dying old man. Why would I change
that? . . . They retreat into their fear. . . . A new Nimrod will be
chosen soon. . . . I've said I didn't want to know—and I don't!

September 20, 1971. A new year begins for Carlyle. My last year, I
know that—what responsibilities I can assume, that is. . . . Nimrod's
death has given me courage. Or is it the knowledge of my own? God
knows I can't undo much but I can try! . . . I'm reaching out, I'm
finding a few who've been hurt badly, and if nothing else I offer help. It
may only be words, or advice, but just the knowledge that *I've been
there* seems to be comforting. It's always such a shock to those I speak
with! Imagine! The "grand old bird"! The pains and the numbness are
nearly intolerable. I may not be able to wait. . . .

December 23, 1971. Two days before my last Christmas. I've said to
so many who've asked me to their homes that I was going into New
York. Of course, it's not so. I'll spend the days here at the Nest. . . . A
disturbing note. The messengers tell me that the new Nimrod is the
sternest, strongest one of all. They say he's ruthless. He orders
executions as easily as his predecessors issued simple requests. Or are
they telling me these things to frighten me? That can't frighten me!

February 18, 1972. The doctor told me that he'd prescribe heavier
"medication" but warned me not to overdose. He, too, spoke of the
new Nimrod. Even he's worried—he implied that the man was mad. I
told him I didn't want to know anything. I was out of it.

February 26, 1972. I can't believe it! Nimrod *is* a *monster!* He's *got* to
be *insane!* He's demanded that all those who've been working here over
three years be cut off—sent out of the country—and if they refuse—be
killed! The doctor's leaving next week. Wife, family, practice. . . .
Latona's widow was murdered in an "automobile accident"! One of the
messengers—Pollizzi—was shot to death in New Haven.
Another—Capalbo—OD'd and the rumor is that the dose was administered!

April 5, 1972. From Nimrod to me—deliver to the messengers any
and all records or he'll shut off my supplies. My house will be watched
around the clock. I'll be followed wherever I go. I'll not be allowed to
get any medical attention whatsoever. The combined effects of the
cancer and with the withdrawal will be beyond anything I can imagine.
What Nimrod doesn't know is that before he left the doctor gave me
enough for several months. He frankly didn't believe I'd last that long.

. . . For the first time in this terrible, horrible life, I'm dealing from a position of strength. My life is firmer than ever because of death.

April 10, 1972. Nimrod is near the point of hysterics with me. He's threatened to expose me—which is meaningless. I've let him know that through the messengers. He's said that he'll destroy the whole Carlyle campus, but if he does that he'll destroy himself as well. The rumor is that he's calling together a conference. An important meeting of powerful men. . . . My house is now watched—as Nimrod said it would be—around the clock. By the Carlyle police, of course. Nimrod's private army!

April 22, 1972. Nimrod has won! It's horrifying, but he's won! He sent me two newspaper clippings. In each a student was killed by an overdose. The first a girl in Cambridge, the second a boy from Trinity. He says that he'll keep adding to the list for every week I withhold the records. . . . Hostages are executed!—He's got to be *stopped!* But how? What can I *do?* . . . I've got a plan but I don't know if I can do it—I'm going to try to *manufacture* records. Leave them intact. It will be difficult—my hands shake so sometimes! Can I possibly get through it?—I have to. I said I'd deliver a *few* at a time. For my *own* protection. I wonder if he'll agree to that?

April 24, 1972. Nimrod's unbelievably evil, but he's a realist. He knows he can do nothing else! We both are racing against the time of my death. Stalemate! I'm alternating between a typewriter and different fountain pens and various types of paper. The killings are suspended but I'm told they will resume if I miss *one* delivery! Nimrod's hostages are in my hands! Their executions can be prevented only by me!

April 27, 1972. Something strange is happening! The Beeson boy phoned our contact at Admissions. Jim Matlock was there and Beeson suspects him. He asked questions, made an ass of himself with Beeson's wife. . . . Matlock isn't on any list! He's no part of Nimrod—on either side. He's never purchased a thing, never sold. . . . The Carlyle patrol cars are always outside now. Nimrod's army is alerted. What is it?

April 27, 1972. Something strange is happening! The Beeson boy they led me to believe is so incredible I cannot write it here. . . . I've never asked the identity of Nimrod, I never wanted to know. But panic's rampant now, something is happening beyond even Nimrod's control. And the messengers told me who Nimrod is. . . . They *lie! I cannot, will not believe it!* If it is true we are all in hell!

Matlock stared at the last entry helplessly. The handwriting was hardly readable; most of the words were connected with one another as if the writer could not stop the pencil from racing ahead.

April 28. Matlock was here. He knows! Others know! He says the government men are involved now. . . . It's over! But what they can't understand is what will happen—a bloodbath, killings—executions! Nimrod can do *no less!* There will be so much *pain*. There will be mass killing and it will be provoked by an insignificant teacher of the Elizabethans. . . . A messenger called. Nimrod *himself* is coming out. It is a confrontation. Now I'll know the truth—who he really is. . . . If he's who I've been led to believe—somehow I'll get this record out—somehow. It's all that's left. It's my turn to threaten. . . . It's over now. The pain will soon be over, too. . . . There's been so much pain . . . I'll make one final entry when I'm sure. . . .

Matlock closed the notebook. What had the girl named Jeannie said? *They have the courts, the police, the doctors.* And Alan Pace. He'd added the major university administrations—all over the Northeast. Whole academic policies; employments, deployments, curriculums—sources of enormous financing. *They* have it *all.*

But Matlock had the indictment.

It was enough. Enough to stop Nimrod—whoever he was. Enough to stop the bloodbath, the executions.

Now he *had* to reach Jason Greenberg.

Alone.

Chapter Thirty-one

Carrying the oilcloth packet, he began walking toward the town of Carlyle, traveling the back roads on which there was rarely any night traffic. He knew it would be too dangerous to drive. The man in the field had probably recovered sufficiently to reach someone—reach Nimrod. An alarm would be sent out for him. The unseen armies would be after him now. His only chance was to reach Greenberg. Jason Greenberg would tell him what to do.

There was blood on his shirt, mud caked on his trousers and jacket. His appearance brought to mind the outcasts of Bill's Bar & Grill by the railroad freight yards. It was nearly two thirty in the morning, but such places stayed open most of the night. The blue laws were only conveniences for them, not edicts. He reached College Parkway and descended the hill to the yards.

He brushed his damp clothes as best he could and covered the bloodstained shirt with his jacket. He walked into the filthy bar; the layers of cheap smoke were suspended above the disheveled customers. A jukebox was playing some Slovak music, men were yelling, a stand-up shuffleboard was being abused. Matlock knew he melted into the atmosphere. He would find a few precious moments of relief.

He sat down at a back booth.

"What the hell happened to *you?*"

It was the bartender, the same suspicious bartender whom he'd finally befriended several days ago. Years . . . ages ago.

"Caught in the rainstorm. Fell a couple of times. Lousy whisky. . . . Have you got anything to eat?"

"Cheese sandwiches. The meat I wouldn't give you. Bread's not too fresh either."

"I don't care. Bring me a couple of sandwiches. And a glass of beer. Would you do that?"

"Sure. Sure, mister. . . . You sure you want to eat here? I mean, I can tell, this ain't your kind of place, you know what I mean?"

There it was again. The incessant, irrelevant question; the dangling interrogative. *You know what I mean. . . ?* Not a question at all. Even in his few moments of relief he had to hear it once more.

"I know what you mean . . . but I'm sure."

"It's your stomach." The bartender trudged back to his station.

Matlock found Greenberg's number and went to the foul-smelling pay phone on the wall. He inserted a coin and dialed.

"I'm sorry, sir," the operator said, "the telephone is disconnected. Do you have another number where the party can be reached?"

"Try it again! I'm sure you're wrong."

She did and she wasn't. The supervisor in Wheeling, West Virginia, finally informed the operator in Carlyle, Connecticut, that any calls to a Mr. Greenberg were to be routed to Washington, D.C. It was assumed that whoever was calling would know where in Washington.

"But Mr. Greenberg isn't expected at the Washington number until early A.M.," she said. "Please inform the party on the line."

He tried to think. Could he trust calling Washington, the Department of Justice, Narcotics Division? Under the circumstances, might not Washington—for the sake of speed—alert someone in the Hartford vicinity to get to him? And Greenberg had made it clear—he didn't trust the Hartford office, the Hartford agents.

He understood Greenberg's concern far better now. He had only to think of the Carlyle police—Nimrod's private army.

No, he wouldn't call Washington. He'd call Sealfont. His last hope was the university president. He dialed Sealfont's number.

"James! Good Lord, James! Are you all right?! Where in heaven's name have you *been?!*"

"To places I never knew were there. Never knew existed."

"But you're all right? That's all that matters! Are you all right?"

"Yes, sir. And I've got everything. I've got it all. Herron wrote everything down. It's a record of twenty-three years."

"Then he *was* part of it?"

"Very much so."

"Poor, *sick* man. . . . I don't understand. However, that's not important now. That's for the authorities. Where are you? I'll send a car. . . . No, I'll come myself. We've all been so worried. I've been in constant touch with the men at the Justice Department."

"Stay where you are," Matlock said quickly. "I'll get to you myself—everyone knows your car. It'll be less dangerous this way. I know they're looking for me. I'll have a man here call me a taxi. I just wanted to make sure you were home."

"Whatever you say. I must tell you I'm relieved. I'll call Kressel. Whatever you have to say, he should know about it. That's the way it's to be."

"I agree, sir. See you shortly."

He went back to the booth and began to eat the unappetizing sandwiches. He had swallowed half the beer when from inside his damp jacket, the short, hysterical beeps of Blackstone's Tel-electronic seared into his ears. He pulled out the machine and pressed the button. Without thinking of anything but the number 555–6868 he jumped up from the seat and walked rapidly back to the telephone. His hand trembling, he awkwardly manipulated the coin and dialed.

The recorded words were like the lash of a whip across his face.

"Charger Three-zero is canceled."

Then there was silence. As Blackstone had promised, there was nothing else but the single sentence—stated but once. There was no one to speak to, no appeal. Nothing.

But there had to be! He would not, *could not*, be cut off like this! If Blackstone was canceling him, he had a right to know *why!* He had a right to know that Pat was *safe!*

It took several minutes and a number of threats before he reached Blackstone himself.

"I don't have to talk to you!" The sleepy voice was belligerent. "I made that clear! . . . But I don't mind because if I can put a trace on this call I'll tell them where to find you the second you hang up!"

"Don't threaten me! You've got too much of my money to threaten me. . . . Why am I canceled? I've got a right to know that."

"Because you stink! You stink like garbage!"

"That's not good enough! That doesn't *mean* anything!"

"I'll give you the rundown then. A warrant is out for you. Signed by the court and . . ."

"For *what*, goddamn it?! Protective custody?! *Preventive detention?!*"

"For *murder*, Matlock! For conspiracy to distribute *narcotics!* For aiding and abetting known narcotics *distributors!* . . . You sold *out!* Like I said, you *smell!* And I hate the business you're in!"

Matlock was stunned. Murder? Conspiracy! What was Blackstone talking about?

"I don't know what you've been told, but it's not true. None of it's *true!* I risked my life, my *life*, do you *hear* me! To bring what I've got . . ."

"You're a good talker," interrupted Blackstone, "but you're careless! You're also a ghoulish bastard! There's a guy in a field outside of Carlyle with his throat slit. It didn't take the government boys ten minutes to trace that Ford wagon to its owner!"

"I didn't *kill* that man! I swear to Christ I *didn't kill him!*"

"No, of course not! And you didn't even *see* the fellow whose head you shot off at East Gorge, did you? Except that there's a parking lot attendant and a couple of others who've got you on the scene! . . . I forgot. You're also stupid. You left the parking ticket under your windshield wiper!"

"Now, wait a minute! *Wait a minute!* This is all *crazy!* The man at East Gorge asked to meet me there! He tried to *murder me!*"

"Tell that to your lawyer. We got the whole thing—straight—from the Justice boys! I demanded that. I've got a damned good reputation. . . . I'll say this. When you sell out, you sell *high!* Over sixty thousand dollars in a *checking* account. Like I said, you *smell*, Matlock!"

He was so shocked he could not raise his voice. When he spoke, he was out of breath, hardly audible. "Listen to me. You've *got* to listen to me. Everything you say . . . there are explanations. Except the man in the field. I don't understand that. But I don't care if you believe me or not. It doesn't matter. I'm holding in my hand all the vindication I'll ever need. . . . What *does* matter is that you watch *that girl!* Don't cancel me out! *Watch her!*"

"Apparently you don't understand English very well. You *are* canceled! Charger Three-zero is *canceled!*"

"What about the girl?"

"We're not irresponsible," said Blackstone bitterly. "She's perfectly safe. She's under the protection of the Carlyle police."

There was a general commotion at the bar. The bartender was closing up and his customers resented it. Obscenities were shouted back and forth over the beer-soaked, filthy mahogany, while cooler or more drunken heads slowly weaved their way toward the front door.

Paralyzed, Matlock stood by the foul-smelling telephone. The roaring at the bar reached a crescendo but he heard nothing; the figures in front of his eyes were only blurs. He felt sick to his stomach, and so he held the front of his trousers, the oilcloth packet with Lucas Herron's notebook between his hand and his belt. He thought he was going to be sick as he had been sick beside the corpse on the East Gorge slope.

But—there was no time. Pat was held by Nimrod's private army. He had to act *now*. And when he acted, the spring would be sprung. There would be no rewinding.

The horrible truth was that he didn't know where to begin.

"What's the matter, mister? The sandwiches?"

"What?"

"Ya look like you're gonna throw up."

"Oh? . . . No." Matlock saw for the first time that almost everyone had left the place.

The notebook! The notebook would be the ransom! There would be no tortured decision—not for the plastic men! Not for the *manipulators!* Nimrod could have the notebook! The indictment!

But then what? Would Nimrod let her live? Let him live?! . . . What had Lucas Herron written: "The new Nimrod is a monster . . . ruthless. He orders executions. . . ."

Nimrod had murdered with far less motive than someone's knowledge of Lucas Herron's diaries.

"Look, mister. I'm sorry, but I gotta close up."

"Will you call a taxi for me, please?"

"A taxi? It's after three o'clock. Even if there was one, he wouldn't come down *here* at three o'clock in the morning."

"Have you got a car?"

"Now wait a minute, mister. I gotta clean up and ring out. I had some action tonight. The register'll take me twenty minutes."

Matlock withdrew his bills. The smallest denomination was a hundred. "I've got to have a car—right away. How much do you want? I'll bring it back in an hour—maybe less."

The bartender looked at Matlock's money. It wasn't a normal sight. "It's a pretty old heap. You might have trouble driving it."

"I can drive *anything!* Here! Here's a hundred! If I wreck it you can have the whole roll! Here! Take it, for Christ's sake!"

"Sure. Sure, mister." The bartender reached under his apron and took out his car keys. "The square one's the ignition. It's parked in the rear. Sixty-two Chevy. Go out the back door."

"Thanks." Matlock started for the door indicated by the bartender.

"Hey, mister!"

"What?"

"What's your name again? . . . Something 'rock'? I forgot. I mean, for Christ's sake, I give you the car, I don't even know your name!"

Matlock thought for a second. "Rod. Nimrod. The name's Nimrod."

"That's no name, mister." The burly man started toward Matlock. "That's a spin fly for catchin' trout. Now, what's your name? You got my car, I gotta know your name."

Matlock still held the money in his hand. He peeled off three additional hundreds and threw them on the floor. It seemed right. He had given Kramer four hundred dollars for his station wagon. There should be symmetry somewhere. Or, at least, meaningless logic.

"That's four hundred dollars. You couldn't get four hundred dollars for a '62 Chevy. I'll bring it back!" He ran for the door. The last words he heard were those of the grateful but confused manager of Bill's Bar & Grill.

"Nimrod. Fuckin' joker!"

The car was a heap, as its owner had said. But it moved, and that was all that mattered. Sealfont would help him analyze the facts, the alternatives. Two opinions were better than one; he was afraid of assuming the total responsibility—he wasn't capable of it. And Sealfont would have people in high places he could contact. Sam Kressel, the liaison, would listen and object and be terrified for his domain. No matter; he'd be dismissed. Pat's safety was uppermost. Sealfont would see that.

Perhaps it was time to threaten—as Herron ultimately had threatened. Nimrod had Pat; he had Herron's indictment. The life of one human being for the protection of hundreds, perhaps thousands. Even Nimrod had to see their bargaining position. It was irrefutable, the odds were on their side.

He realized as he neared the railroad depot that this kind of thinking, by itself, made him a manipulator, too. Pat had been reduced to *quantity X*, Herron's diaries, *quantity Y*. The equation would then be postulated and the mathematical observers would make their decisions based on the data presented. It was the ice-cold logic of survival; emotional factors were disregarded, consciously despised.

Frightening!

He turned right at the station and started to drive up College Parkway. Sealfont's mansion stood at the end. He went as fast as the '62 Chevy would go, which wasn't much above thirty miles an hour on the hill. The streets were deserted, washed clean by the storm. The store fronts, the houses, and finally the campus were dark and silent.

He remembered that Kressel's house was just a half block off College Parkway on High Street. The detour would take him no more than thirty seconds. It was worth it, he thought. If Kressel hadn't left for Sealfont's, he would pick him up and they could talk on the way over. Matlock *had* to talk, *had* to begin. He couldn't stand the isolation any longer.

He swung the car to the left at the corner of High Street. Kressel's house was a large gray colonial set back from the street by a wide front lawn bordered by rhododendrons. There were lights on downstairs. With luck, Kressel was still home. There were two cars, one in the driveway; Matlock slowed down.

His eyes were drawn to a dull reflection at the rear of the driveway. Kressel's kitchen light was on; the spill from the window illuminated the hood of a third car, and the Kressels were a two-car family.

He looked again at the car in front of the house. It was a Carlyle patrol car. The Carlyle police were in Kressel's house!

Nimrod's private army was with *Kressel!*

Or was Nimrod's private army with *Nimrod?*

He swerved to the left, narrowly missing the patrol car, and sped down the street to the next corner. He turned right and pressed the accelerator to the floor. He was confused, frightened, bewildered. If Sealfont had called

Kressel—which he had obviously done—and Kressel worked with Nimrod, or *was* Nimrod, there'd be other patrol cars, other soldiers of the private army waiting for him.

His mind went back to the Carlyle Police Station—a century ago, capsuled in little over a week—the night of Loring's murder. Kressel had disturbed him then. And even before that—with Loring and Greenberg—Kressel's hostility to the federal agents had been outside the bounds of reason.

Oh, Christ! It was so clear now! His instincts had been right. The instincts which had served him as the *hunted* was well as the *hunter* had been true! He'd been watched *too* thoroughly, his every action anticipated. Kressel, the *liaison*, was, in fact, Kressel the tracker, the seeker, the supreme killer.

Nothing was ever as it appeared to be—only what one sensed behind the appearance. Trust the senses.

Somehow he had to get to Sealfont. Warn Sealfont that the Judas was Kressel. Now they *both* had to protect themselves, establish some base from which they could strike back.

Otherwise the girl he loved was lost.

There couldn't be a second wasted. Sealfont had certainly told Kressel that he, Matlock, had Lucas Herron's diaries, and that was all Kressel would need to know. All Nimrod needed to know.

Nimrod had to get possession of both the Corsican paper *and* the diaries; now he knew where they were. His private army would be told that this was its moment of triumph or disaster. They would be waiting for him at Sealfont's; Sealfont's mansion was the trap they expected him to enter.

Matlock swung west at the next corner. In his trouser pocket were his keys, and among them was the key to Pat's apartment. To the best of his knowledge, no one knew he had such a key, certainly no one would expect him to go there. He had to chance it; he couldn't risk going to a public telephone, risk being seen under a street lamp. The patrol cars would be searching everywhere.

He heard the roar of an engine behind him and felt the sharp pain in his stomach. A car was following him—closing in on him. And the '62 Chevrolet was no match for it.

His right leg throbbed from the pressure he exerted on the pedal. His hands gripped the steering wheel as he turned wildly into a side street, the muscles in his arms tensed and aching. Another turn. He spun the wheel to the left, careening off the edge of the curb back into the middle of the road. The car behind him maintained a steady pace, never more than ten feet away, the headlights blinding in the rear-view mirror.

His pursuer was *not* going to close the gap between them! Not then. Not at that moment. He could have done so a hundred, two hundred yards ago. He was waiting. Waiting for something. But what?

There was so *much* he couldn't understand! So much he'd miscalculated, misread. He'd been out maneuvered at every important juncture. He was what they said—an amateur! He'd been beyond his depth from the beginning. And now, at the last, his final assault was ending in ambush. They would kill him, take the Corsican paper, the diaries of indictment. They would kill the girl he loved, the innocent child whose life he'd thrown away so brutally. Sealfont would be finished—he knew too much now! God knew how many others would be destroyed.

So be it.

If it had to be this way, if hope really had been taken from him, he'd end it all with a gesture, at least. He reached into his belt for the automatic.

The streets they now traveled—the pursuer and the pursued—ran through the outskirts of the campus, consisting mainly of the science buildings and a number of large parking lots. There were no houses to speak of.

He swerved the Chevrolet as far to the right as possible, thrusting his right arm across his chest, the barrel of the pistol outside the car window, pointed at the pursuing automobile.

He fired twice. The car behind him accelerated; he felt the repeated jarring of contact, the metal against metal as the car behind hammered into the Chevrolet's left rear chassis. He pulled again at the trigger of the automatic. Instead of a loud report, he heard and felt only the single click of the firing pin against an unloaded chamber.

Even his last gesture was futile.

His pursuer crashed into him once more. He lost control; the wheel spun, tearing his arm, and the Chevrolet reeled off the road. Frantic, he reached for the door handle, desperately trying to steady the car, prepared to jump if need be.

He stopped all thought; all instincts of survival were arrested. Within those split seconds, time ceased. For the car behind him had drawn parallel and he saw the face of his pursuer.

There were bandages and gauze around the eyes, beneath the glasses, but they could not hide the face of the black revolutionary, Julian Dunois.

It was the last thing he remembered before the Chevrolet swerved to the right and skidded violently off the road's incline.

Blackness.

Chapter Thirty-two

Pain roused him. It seemed to be all through his left side. He rolled his head, feeling the pillow beneath him.

The room was dimly lit; what light there was came from a table lamp on the other side. He shifted his head and tried to raise himself on his right shoulder. He pushed his elbow into the mattress, his immobile left arm following the turn of his body like a dead weight.

He stopped abruptly.

Across the room, directly in line with the foot of the bed, sat a man in a chair. At first Matlock couldn't distinguish the features. The light was poor and his eyes were blurred with pain and exhaustion.

Then the man came into focus. He was black and his dark eyes stared at Matlock beneath the perfectly cut semicircle of an Afro haircut. It was Adam Williams, Carlyle University's firebrand of the Black Left.

When Williams spoke, he spoke softly and, unless Matlock misunderstood—once again—there was compassion in the black's voice.

"I'll tell Brother Julian you're awake. He'll come in to see you." Williams got out of the chair and went to the door. "You've banged up your left shoulder. Don't try to get out of bed. There are no windows in here. The hallway is guarded. Relax. You need rest."

"I don't have *time* to rest, you *goddamn fool!*" Matlock tried to raise himself further but the pain was too great. He hadn't adjusted to it.

"You don't have a choice." Williams opened the door and walked rapidly out, closing it firmly behind him.

Matlock fell back on the pillow. . . . Brother Julian. . . . He remembered now. The sight of Julian Dunois's bandaged face watching him through the speeding car window, seemingly inches away from him. And his ears had picked up Dunois's words, his commands to his driver. They had been shouted in his Caribbean dialect.

"Hit him, mon! Hit him again! Drive him *off*, mon!"

And then everything had become dark and the darkness had been filled with violent noise, crashing metal, and he had felt his body twisting, turning, spiraling into the black void.

Oh, God! How long was it? He tried to lift up his left hand to look at his watch, but the arm barely moved; the pain was sharp and lingering. He reached over with his right hand to pull the stretch band off his wrist, but it wasn't there. His watch was gone.

He struggled to get up and finally managed to perch on the edge of the bed, his legs touching the floor. He pressed his feet against the wood, thankful that he could sit up. . . . He had to put the pieces together, to reconstruct what had happened, where he was going.

He'd been on his way to Pat's. To find a secluded telephone on which to reach Adrian Sealfont. To warn him that Kressel was the enemy, Kressel was Nimrod. And he'd made up his mind that Herron's diaries would be Pat's ransom. Then the chase had begun, only it wasn't a chase. The car behind him, commanded by Julian Dunois, had played a furious game of terror. It had toyed with him as a lethal mountain cat might play with a wounded goat. Finally it had attacked—steel against steel—and driven him to darkness.

Matlock knew he had to escape. But *from where* and *to whom?*

The door of the windowless room opened. Dunois entered, followed by Williams.

"Good morning," said the attorney. "I see you've managed to sit up. That's good. It augurs well for your very abused body."

"What time is it? Where am I?"

"It's nearly four thirty. You are in a room at Lumumba Hall. You see? I withhold nothing from you. . . . Now, you must reciprocate. You must withhold nothing from me."

"Listen to me!" Matlock kept his voice steady. "I have no fight with you, with *any* of you! I've got . . ."

"Oh, I disagree," Dunois smiled. "Look at my *face*. It's only through enormous good fortune that I wasn't blinded by you. You tried to crush the lenses of my glasses into my eyes. Can you imagine how my work would suffer if I were blind?"

"Goddamn it! You filled me with acid!"

"And you provoked it! You were actively engaged in pursuits inimicable to our brothers! Pursuits you had no *right* to engage in! . . . But this is concentric debate. It will get us nowhere. . . . We *do* appreciate what you've brought us. Beyond our most optimistic ambitions."

"You've got the notebook. . . ."

"*And* the Corsican document. The Italian invitation we knew existed. The notebook was only a rumor. A rumor which was fast being ascribed to fiction until tonight—this morning. You should feel proud. You've accomplished what scores of your more experienced betters failed to accomplish. You found the treasure. The *real* treasure."

"I've got to have it back!"

"Fat chance!" said Williams, leaning against the wall, watching.

"If I don't get it back, a girl will *die!* Do whatever you goddamn well please with me, but let me *use* it to get her back. Christ! Please, *please!*"

"You feel deeply, don't you? I see tears in your eyes. . . ."

"Oh, *Jesus!* You're an *educated man!* You can't *do* this! . . . *Listen!* Take whatever information you want out of it! Then give it to me and let me go! . . . I swear to you I'll come back. Give her a chance. Just give her a *chance!*"

Dunois walked slowly to the chair by the wall, the chair in which Adam Williams sat when Matlock awoke. He pulled it forward, closer to the bed, and sat down, crossing his knees gracefully. "You feel helpless, don't you? Perhaps . . . even without hope."

"I've been through a great deal!"

"I'm sure you have. And you appeal to my reason . . . as an *educated man*. You realize that it is within my scope to help you and therefore I am superior to you. You would not make such an appeal if it were not so."

"Oh, Christ! Cut that out!"

"Now you know what it's like. You are helpless. Without hope. You wonder if your appeal will be lost on a deaf ear. . . . Do you really, for one second, think that I care for the life of Miss Ballantyne? Do you honestly believe she has any priority for me? Any more than the lives of *our* children, *our* loved ones mean anything to you!"

Matlock knew he had to answer Dunois. The black would offer nothing if he evaded him. It was another game—and he had to play, if only briefly.

"I don't deserve this and you know it. I loathe the people who won't do anything for them. You know me—you've made that clear. So you must know that."

"Ahh, but I *don't* know it! You're the one who made the choice, the decision to work for the superior mon! The *Washington* mon! For decades, two *centuries*, *my* people have appealed to the *superior Washington mon!* 'Help us,' they cry. 'Don't leave us without hope!' they scream. But nobody listens. Now, you expect me to listen to you?"

"Yes, I *do!* Because I'm not your enemy. I may not be everything you want me to be, but I'm not your enemy. If you turn me—and men like me—into objects of hatred, you're *finished*. You're outnumbered, don't forget that, Dunois. We won't storm the barricades every time you yell 'foul,' but we hear you. We're willing to help; we want to help."

Dunois looked coldly at Matlock. "Prove it."

Matlock returned the black's stare. "Use me as your bait, your hostage. Kill me if you have to. But get the girl out."

"We can do that—the hostaging, the killing—without your consent. Brave but hardly proof."

Matlock refused to allow Dunois to disengage the stare between them. He spoke softly. "I'll give you a statement. Written, verbal—on tape; freely, without force or coercion. I'll spell it all out. How I was used, what I did. Everything. You'll have your Washington men as well as Nimrod."

Dunois folded his arms and matched Matlock's quiet voice. "You realize you would put an end to your professional life; this life you love so much. No university administration worthy of its name would consider you for a position. You'd never be trusted again. By any factions. You'd become a pariah."

"You asked for proof. It's all I can offer you."

Dunois sat immobile in the chair. Williams had straightened up from his slouching position against the wall. No one spoke for several moments. Finally Dunois smiled gently. His eyes, surrounded by the gauze, were compassionate.

"You're a good man. Inept, perhaps, but persevering. You shall have the help you need. We won't leave you without hope. Do you agree, Adam?"

"Agreed."

Dunois got out of the chair and approached Matlock.

"You've heard the old cliché, that politics make strange bedfellows. Conversely, practical objectives often make for strange political alliances. History bears this out. . . . We want this Nimrod as much as you do. As well as the Mafiosi he tries to make peace with. It is they and their kind who prey upon the children. An example must be made. An example which will instill terror in other Nimrods, other Mafiosi. . . . You shall have help, but this is the condition we demand."

"What do you mean?"

"The disposition of Nimrod and the others will be left to us. We don't trust your judges and your juries. Your courts are corrupt, your legalistics no more than financial manipulations. . . . The barrio addict is thrown into jail. The rich gangsters appeal. . . . No, the disposition must be left to us."

"I don't care about that. You can do whatever you like."

"Your not caring is insufficient. We demand more than that. We must have our guarantee."

"How can I give a guarantee?"

"By your silence. By not acknowledging our presence. We will take the Corsican paper and somehow we will find the conference and be admitted. We will extract what we want from the diaries—that's being done now, incidentally. . . . But your *silence* is the paramount issue. We will help you now—on a best-efforts basis, of course—but you must never mention our involvement. Irrespective of what may happen, you must not, directly, or indirectly, allude to our participation. Should you do so, we will take your life and the life of the girl. Is this understood?"

"It is."

"Then we are in agreement?"

"We are."

"Thank you," said Dunois, smiling.

Chapter Thirty-three

As Julian Dunois outlined their alternatives and began to formulate strategy, it became clearer to Matlock why the blacks had sought him out with such concentration—and why Dunois was willing to offer help. He, Matlock, had the basic information they needed. Who were his contacts? Both inside and without the university? Who and where were the government men? How were communications expedited?

In other words—whom should Julian Dunois *avoid* in his march to Nimrod?

"I must say, you were extraordinarily unprepared for contingencies," Dunois said. "Very slipshod."

"That occurred to me, too. But I think I was only partially to blame."

"I dare say you were!" Dunois laughed, joined by Williams. The three men remained in the windowless room. A card table had been brought in along with several yellow pads. Dunois had begun writing down every bit of information Matlock supplied. He double-checked the spelling of names, the accuracy of addresses—a professional at work; Matlock once again experienced the feeling of inadequacy he had felt when talking with Greenberg.

Dunois stapled a number of pages together and started on a fresh pad. "What are you doing?" asked Matlock.

"These will be duplicated by a copier downstairs. The information will be sent to my office in New York. . . . As will a photostat of every page in Professor Herron's notebook."

"You don't fool around, do you?"

"In a word—no."

"It's all I've got to give you. Now, what do we do? What do *I* do? I'm frightened, I don't have to tell you that. I can't even let myself think what might happen to her."

"*Nothing* will happen. Believe me when I tell you that. At the moment, your Miss Ballantyne is as safe as if she were in her mother's arms. Or yours. She's the bait, not you. The bait will be kept fresh and unspoiled. For you have what they want. They can't survive without it."

"Then let's make the offer. The sooner the better."

"Don't worry. It will be made. But we must decide carefully—aware of the nuances—how we do it. So far, we have two alternatives, we agreed upon that. The first is Kressel, himself. The direct confrontation. The second, to use the police department, to let your message to Nimrod be delivered through it."

"Why do that? Use the police?"

"I'm only listing alternatives. . . . Why the police? I'm not sure. Except that the Herron diaries state clearly that Nimrod was replaced in the past. This current Nimrod is the third since the position's inception, is that not correct?"

"Yes. The first was a man named Orton in the lieutenant governor's office. The second, Angelo Latona, a builder. The third, obviously, Kressel. What's your point?"

"I'm speculating. Whoever assumes the position of Nimrod has authoritarian powers. Therefore, it is the position, not the man. The man can make whatever he can of the office."

"But the office," interrupted Williams, "is given and taken away. Nimrod isn't the last voice."

"Exactly. Therefore, it might be to Matlock's advantage to let the word leak out very specifically that it is *he* who possesses the weapon. That Kressel—Nimrod—must exercise great caution. For everyone's sake."

"Wouldn't that mean that more people would be after me?"

"Possibly. Conversely, it could mean that there'd be a legion of anxious criminals protecting you. Until the threat you impose is eliminated. No one will act rashly until that threat is taken away. No one will want Nimrod to act rashly."

Matlock lit a cigarette, listening intently. "What you're trying to do then is to partially separate Nimrod from his own organization."

Dunois snapped the fingers of both hands, the sound of castanets, applause. He smiled as he spoke.

"You're a quick student. It's the first lesson of insurgency. One of the prime objectives of infiltration. Divide. Divide!"

The door opened; an excited black entered. Without saying a word, he handed Dunois a note. Dunois read it and closed his eyes for several moments. It was his way of showing dismay. He thanked the black messenger calmly and dismissed him politely. He looked at Matlock but handed the note to Williams.

"Our stratagems may have historic precedence, but I'm afraid for us they're empty words. Kressel and his wife are dead. Dr. Sealfont has been taken forcibly from his house under guard. He was driven away in a Carlyle patrol car."

"What? Kressel! I don't believe it! It's not true!"

"I'm afraid it is. Our men report that the two bodies were carried out not more than fifteen minutes ago. The word is murder and suicide. Naturally. It would fit perfectly."

"Oh, Christ! Oh, Jesus Christ! It's my fault! I made them do it! I *forced* them! Sealfont! Where did they take him?"

"We don't know. The brothers on watch didn't dare follow the patrol car."

He had no words. The paralysis, the fear, was there again. He reeled blindly into the bed and sank down on it, sitting, staring at nothing. The sense of futility, of inadequacy, of defeat was now overwhelming. He had caused so much pain, so much death.

"It's a severe complication," said Dunois, his elbows on the card table. "Nimrod has removed your only contacts. In so doing, he's answered a vital question, prevented us from making an enormous error—I refer to Kressel, of course. Nevertheless, to look at it from another direction, Nimrod has reduced our alternatives. You have no choice now. You must deal through his private army, the Carlyle police."

Matlock looked numbly across at Julian Dunois. "Is that all you can *do?* Sit there and coolly decide a next move? . . . Kressel's *dead*. His *wife* is *dead*. Adrian Sealfont's probably killed by now. These were my *friends!*"

"And you have my sympathies, but let me be honest: I don't regret the loss of the three individuals. Frankly, Adrian Sealfont is the only *real* casualty—we might have worked with him, he was brilliant—but his loss does not break my heart. We lose thousands in the barrios every month. I weep for them more readily. . . . However, to the issue at hand. You really don't have a choice. You must make your contact through the police."

"But that's where you're wrong." Matlock felt suddenly stronger. "I *do* have a choice. . . . Greenberg left West Virginia early this morning. He'll be in Washington by now. I have a number in New York that can put me in touch with him. I'm getting hold of Greenberg." He'd done enough, caused enough anguish. He couldn't take the chance with Pat's life. Not any longer. He wasn't capable.

Dunois leaned back in his chair, removing his arms from the card table. He stared at Matlock. "I said a little while ago that you were an apt student. I amend that observation. You are quick but obviously superficial. . . . You will *not* reach Greenberg. He was not part of our agreement and you *will not* violate that agreement. You will carry through on the basis we agree upon or you will be subject to the penalties I outlined."

"Goddamn it, don't threaten me! I'm sick of threats!" Matlock stood up.

Dunois reached under his jacket and took out a gun. Matlock saw that it was the black automatic he had taken from the dead man on the East Gorge slope. Dunois, too, rose to his feet.

"The medical report will no doubt estimate your death to be at dawn."

"For God's sake! The girl is being held by killers!"

"So are you," Dunois said quietly. "Can't you *see* that? Our motives are different, but make no mistake about it. We are *killers*. We *have* to be."

"You wouldn't go that far!"

"Oh, but we would. We have. And much, much further. We would drop your insignificant corpse in front of the police station with a note pinned to your bloodstained shirt. We would *demand* the death of the girl prior to any negotiations. They would readily agree, for neither of us can take the chance of her living. Once she, too, is dead, the giants are left to do battle by themselves."

"You're a monster."

"I am what I have to be."

No one spoke for several moments. Matlock shut his eyes, his voice a whisper. "What do I do?"

"That's much better." Dunois sat down, looking up at the nervous Adam Williams. Briefly, Matlock felt a kinship with the campus radical. He, too, was frightened, unsure. As Matlock, he was ill-equipped to deal with the world of Julian Dunois or Nimrod. The Haitian seemed to read Matlock's thoughts.

"You must have confidence in yourself. Remember, you've accomplished far more than anyone else. With far less resources. And you have extraordinary courage."

"I don't feel very courageous."

"A brave man rarely does. Isn't that remarkable? Come, sit down." Matlock obeyed. "You know, you and I are not so different. In another time, we might even be allies. Except, as many of my brothers have noted, I look for saints."

"There aren't any," Matlock said.

"Perhaps not. And then again, perhaps . . . we'll debate it some other time. Right now, we must plan. Nimrod will be expecting you. We can't disappoint him. Yet we must be sure to guard ourselves on all flanks." He pulled closer to the table, a half-smile on his lips, his eyes shining.

The black revolutionary's strategy, if nothing else, was a complex series of moves designed to protect Matlock and the girl. Matlock grudgingly had to acknowledge it.

"I have a double motive," Dunois explained. "The second is, frankly, more important to me. Nimrod will not appear himself unless he has no other choice, and I want Nimrod. I will not settle for a substitute, a camouflage."

The essence of the plan was Herron's notebook itself, the last entries in the diary.

The identity of Nimrod.

"Herron states explicitly that he *would* not write the name intimated by the messengers. Not that he couldn't. His feeling obviously was that he could not implicate that man if the information was incorrect. Guilt by innuendo would be abhorrent to him. Like yourself, Matlock; you refused to offer up Herron on the basis of an hysterical phone call. He knew that he might die at any given moment; his body had taken about as much abuse as it could endure.

. . . He had to be positive." Dunois, by now, was drawing meaningless geometric shapes on a blank page of yellow paper.

"And then he was murdered," said Matlock. "Made to look like suicide."

"Yes. If nothing else, the diaries confirm that. Once Herron had proved to himself who Nimrod was, he would have moved heaven and earth to include it in the notebook. Our enemy cannot know that he did not. That is our Damocletian sword."

Matlock's first line of protection was to let the chief of the Carlyle police understand that he, Matlock, knew the identity of Nimrod. He would reach an accommodation solely with Nimrod. This accommodation was the lesser of two evils. He was a hunted man. There was a warrant out for his arrest of which the Carlyle police surely were aware. He might conceivably be exonerated from the lesser indictments, but he would not escape the charge of murder. Possibly, two murders. For he had killed, the evidence was overwhelming, and he had no tangible alibis. He did not know the men he had killed. There were no witnesses to corroborate self-defense; the manner of each killing was grotesque to the point of removing the killer from society. The best he could hope for was a number of years in prison.

And then he would spell out his terms for an accommodation with Nimrod. Lucas Herron's diaries for his life—and the life of the girl. Certainly the diaries were worth a sum of money sufficient for both of them to start again somewhere.

Nimrod could do this. Nimrod *had* to do it.

"The key to this . . . let's call it phase one . . . is the amount of conviction you display." Dunois spoke carefully. "Remember, you are in panic. You have taken lives, killed other human beings. You are not a violent man but you've been forced, coerced into frightening crimes."

"It's the truth. More than you know."

"Good. Convey that feeling. All a panicked man wants is to get away from the scene of his panic. Nimrod must believe this. It guarantees your immediate safety."

A second telephone call would then be made by Matlock—to confirm Nimrod's acceptance of a meeting. The location, at this point, could be chosen by Nimrod. Matlock would call again to learn where. But the meeting must take place before ten o'clock in the morning.

"By now, you, the fugitive, seeing freedom in sight, suddenly possess doubts," said Dunois. "In your gathering hysteria, you need a guarantee factor."

"Which is?"

"A third party; a mythical third party. . . ."

Matlock was to inform the contact at the Carlyle Police Headquarters that he had written up a complete statement about the Nimrod operation; Herron's diaries, identities, everything. This statement had been sealed in an envelope and given to a friend. It would be mailed to the Justice Department at ten in the morning unless Matlock instructed otherwise.

"Here, phase two depends again on conviction, but of another sort. Watch a caged animal whose captors suddenly open the gate. He's wary, suspicious; he approaches his escape with caution. So, too, must our fugitive. It will be expected. You have been most resourceful during the past week. By logic you should have been dead by now, but you survived. You must continue that cunning."

"I understand."

The last phase was created by Julian Dunois to guarantee—as much as was possible in a "best-efforts situation"—the reclaiming of the girl and the safety of Matlock. It would be engineered by a third and final telephone call to Nimrod's contact. The object of the call was to ascertain the specific location of the meeting and the precise time.

When informed of both, Matlock was to accept without hesitation.

At first.

Then moments later—seemingly with no other reason than the last extremity of panic and suspicion—he was to reject Nimrod's choice.

Not the time—the location.

He was to hesitate, to stutter, to behave as close to irrationality as he could muster. And then, suddenly, he was to blurt out a second location of his *own* choice. As if it had just come to mind with no thoughts of it before that moment. He was then to restate the existence of the nonexistent statement which a mythical friend would mail to Washington at ten in the morning. He was then to hang up without listening further.

"The most important factor in phase three is the recognizable consistency of your panic. Nimrod must see that your reactions are now primitive. The act itself is about to happen. You lash out, recoil, set up barriers to avoid his net, should that net exist. In your hysteria, you are as dangerous to him as a wounded cobra is deadly to the tiger. For rationality doesn't exist, only survival. He now must meet you himself, he now must bring the girl. He will, of course, arrive with his palace guard. His intentions won't change. He'll take the diaries, perhaps discuss elaborate plans for your accommodation, and when he learns that there is no written statement, no friend about to mail it, he'll expect to kill you both. . . . However, none of his intentions will be carried out. For we'll be waiting for him."

"How? How will you be waiting for him?"

"With my own palace guard. . . . We shall now, you and I, decide on that hysterically arrived at second location. It should be in an area you know well, perhaps frequent often. Not too far away, for it is presumed you have no automobile. Secluded, because you are hunted by the law. Yet accessible, for you must travel fast, most likely on back roads."

"You're describing Herron's Nest. Herron's house."

"I may be, but we can't use it. It's psychologically inconsistent. It would be a break in our fugitive's pattern of behavior. Herron's Nest is the root of his fear. He wouldn't go back there. . . . Someplace else."

Williams started to speak. He was still unsure, still wary of joining Dunois's world. "I think, perhaps . . ."

"What, Brother Williams? What do you think?"

"Professor Matlock often dines at a restaurant called the Cheshire Cat."

Matlock snapped his head up at the black radical. "You too? You've had me followed."

"Quite often. We don't enter such places. We'd be conspicuous."

"Go on, brother," broke in Dunois.

"The Cheshire Cat is about four miles outside Carlyle. It's set back from the highway, which is the normal way to get there, about half a mile, but it also can be reached by taking several back roads. Behind and to the sides of the restaurant are patios and gardens used in the summer for dining. Beyond these are woods."

"Anyone on the premises?"

"A single night watchman, I believe. It doesn't open until one. I don't imagine cleanup crews or kitchen help get there before nine thirty or ten."

"Excellent." Dunois looked at his wrist watch. "It's now ten past five. Say we allow fifteen minutes between phases one, two, and three and an additional twenty minutes for traveling between stations, that would make it approximately six fifteen. Say six thirty for contingencies. We'll set the rendezvous for seven. Behind the Cheshire Cat. Get the notebook, brother. I'll alert the men."

Williams rose from his chair and walked to the door. He turned and addressed Dunois. "You won't change your mind? You won't let me come with the rest of you?"

Dunois didn't bother to look up. He answered curtly. "Don't annoy me. I've a great deal to think about."

Williams left the room quickly.

Matlock watched Dunois. He was still sketching his meaningless figures on the yellow pad, only now he bore down on the pencil, causing deep ridges on the paper. Matlock saw the diagram emerging. It was a series of jagged lines, all converging.

They were bolts of lightning.

"Listen to me," he said. "It's not too late. Call in the authorities. Please, for Christ's sake, you can't risk the lives of these kids."

From behind his glasses, surrounded by the gauze bandages, Dunois's eyes bore into Matlock. He spoke with contempt. "Do you for one minute think I would allow these children to tread in waters I don't even know *I* can survive? We're not your Joint Chiefs of Staff, Matlock. We have greater respect, greater love for our young."

Matlock recalled Adam Williams' protestations at the door. "That's what Williams meant then? About coming with you."

"Come with me."

Dunois led Matlock out of the small, windowless room and down the corridor to a staircase. There were a few students milling about, but only a few. The rest of Lumumba Hall was asleep. They proceeded down two flights to a door Matlock remembered as leading to the cellars, to the old, high-ceilinged chapter room in which he'd witnessed the frightening performance of the African tribal rite. They descended the stairs and, as Matlock suspected, went to the rear of the cellars, to the thick oak door of the chapter room. Dunois had not spoken a word since he'd bade Matlock follow him.

Inside the chapter room were eight blacks, each well over six feet tall. They were dressed alike: dark, tight-fitting khakis with open shirts and black, soft leather ankle boots with thick rubber soles. Several were sitting, playing cards; others were reading, some talking quietly among themselves. Matlock noticed that a few had their shirt sleeves rolled up. The arms displayed were tautly muscular, veins close to the skin. They all nodded informally to Dunois and his guest. Two or three smiled intelligently at Matlock, as if to put him at ease. Dunois spoke softly.

"The palace guard!"

"My God!"

"The elite corps. Each man is trained over a period of three years. There is not a weapon he cannot fire or fix, a vehicle he cannot repair . . . or a philosophy he cannot debate. Each is familiar with the most brutal forms of combat, traditional as well as guerrilla. Each is committed until death."

"The terror brigade, is that it? It's not new, you know."

"Not with that description, no, it wouldn't be. Don't forget, I grew up

with such dogs at my heels. Duvalier's Ton Ton Macoute were a pack of
hyenas; I witnessed their work. These men are no such animals."

"I wasn't thinking of Duvalier."

"On the other hand, I acknowledge the debt to Papa Doc. The Ton Ton's
concept was exciting to me. Only I realized it had to be restructured. Such
units are springing up all over the country."

"They sprung up once before," Matlock said. "They were called 'elite'
then, too. They were also called 'units'—SS units."

Dunois looked at Matlock and Matlock saw the hurt in his eyes. "To reach
for such parallels is painful. Nor is it justified. We do what we have to do.
What is right for us to do."

"*Ein Volk, Ein Reich, Ein Fuehrer*," said Matlock softly.

Chapter Thirty-four

Everything happened so fast. Two of Dunois's elite guard were assigned to
him, the rest left for the rendezvous with Nimrod, to prepare themselves to
meet another elite guard—the selected few of Nimrod's private army who
undoubtedly would accompany him. Matlock was ushered across the campus
by the two huge blacks after the word came back from scouts that the path
was clear. He was taken to a telephone booth in the basement of a freshman
dormitory, where he made his first call.

He found that his fear, his profound fear, aided the impression Dunois
wanted to convey. It wasn't difficult for him to pour out his panicked
emotions, pleading for sanctuary, for, in truth, he *felt* panicked. As he spoke
hysterically into the phone, he wasn't sure which was the reality and which
the fantasy. He wanted to be free. He wanted Pat to live and be free with
him. If Nimrod could bring it all about, why not deal with Nimrod in good
faith?

It was a nightmare for him. He was afraid for a moment that he might yell
out the truth and throw himself on the mercy of Nimrod.

The sight of Dunois's own Ton Ton Macoute kept bringing him back to
his failing senses, and he ended the first telephone call without breaking. The
Carlyle police "superintendent" would forward the information, receive an
answer, and await Matlock's next call.

The blacks received word from their scouts that the second public
telephone wasn't clear. It was on a street corner, and a patrol car had been
spotted in the area. Dunois knew that even public phones could be traced,
although it took longer, and so he had alternate sites for each of the calls, the
last one to be made on the highway. Matlock was rushed to the first alternate
telephone booth. It was on the back steps of the Student Union.

The second call went more easily, although whether that was an advantage
was not clear. Matlock was emphatic in his reference to the mythical
statement that was to be mailed at ten in the morning. His strength had its
effect, and he was grateful for it. The "superintendent" was frightened now,
and he didn't bother to conceal it. Was Nimrod's private army beginning to
have its doubts? The troops were, perhaps, picturing their own stomach's
blown out by the enemy's shell's. Therefore, the generals had to be more

alert, more aware of the danger.

He was raced to a waiting automobile. It was an old Buick, tarnished, dented, inconspicuous. The exterior, however, belied the inside. The interior was as precisely tooled as a tank. Under the dashboard was a powerful radio; the windows were at least a half-inch thick, paned, Matlock realized, with bulletproof glass. Clipped to the sides were high-powered, short-barreled rifles, and dotted about the body were rubber-flapped holes into which these barrels were to be inserted. The sound of the engine impressed Matlock instantly. It was as powerful a motor as he'd ever heard.

They followed an automobile in front of them at moderate speed; Matlock realized that another car had taken up the rear position. Dunois had meant it when he said they were to cover themselves on all flanks. Dunois was, indeed, a professional.

And it disturbed James Matlock when he thought about the profession.

It was black. It was also *Ein Volk, Ein Reich, Ein Fuehrer.*

As was Nimrod and all he stood for.

The words came back to him.

". . . *I'm getting out of this goddamn country, mister.* . . ."

Had it come to that?

And: ". . . *You think it's all so different?* . . . *It's mini-America!* . . . *It's company policy, man!*"

The land was sick. Where was the cure?

"Here we are. Phase three." The black revolutionary in command tapped him lightly on the arm, smiling reassuringly as he did so. Matlock got out of the car. They were on the highway south of Carlyle. The car in front had pulled up perhaps a hundred yards ahead of them and parked off the road, its lights extinguished. The automobile behind had done the same.

In front of him stood two aluminum-framed telephone booths, placed on a concrete platform. The second black walked to the right booth, pushed the door open—which turned on the dull overhead light—and quickly slid back the pane of glass under the light, exposing the bulb. This he rapidly unscrewed so that the booth returned to darkness. It struck Matlock—impressed him, really—that the Negro giant had eliminated the light this way. It would have been easier, quicker, simply to have smashed the glass.

The objective of the third and final call, as Dunois had instructed, was to reject Nimrod's meeting place. Reject it in a manner that left Nimrod no alternative but to accept Matlock's panicked substitute: the Cheshire Cat.

The voice over the telephone from the Carlyle police was wary, precise.

"Our mutual friend understands your concerns, Matlock. He'd feel the same way you do. He'll meet you with the girl at the south entrance of the athletic field, to the left of the rear bleachers. It's a small stadium, not far from the gym and the dormitories. Night watchmen are on; no harm could come to you. . . ."

"All right. All right, that's O.K." Matlock did his best to sound quietly frantic, laying the groundwork for his ultimate refusal. "There are people around; if any of you tried anything, I could scream my head off. And I *will!*"

"Of course. But you won't have to. Nobody wants anyone hurt. It's a simple transaction; that's what our friend told me to tell you. He admires you. . . ."

"How can I be sure he'll bring Pat? I have to be sure!"

"The *transaction*, Matlock." The voice was oily, there was a hint of desperation. Dunois's "cobra" was unpredictable. "That's what it's all about. Our friend wants what you found, remember?"

"I remember. . . ." Matlock's mind raced. He realized he had to maintain his hysteria, his unpredictability. But he had to switch the location. Change it without being suspect. If Nimrod became suspicious, Dunois had sentenced Pat to death. "And you tell our *friend* to remember that there's a statement in an envelope addressed to men in Washington!"

"He knows that, for Christ's sake. I mean . . . he's concerned, you know what I mean? Now, we'll see you at the field, O.K.? In an hour, O.K.?"

This was the moment. There might not come another.

"No! Wait a minute. . . . I'm not going on that campus! The Washington people, they've got the whole place watched! They're all around! They'll put me away!"

"No, they won't. . ."

"How the hell do you know?"

"There's nobody. So help me, it's *O.K.* Calm down, please."

"That's easy for you, not me! No, I'll tell you where. . . ."

He spoke rapidly, disjointedly, as if thinking desperately while talking. First he mentioned Herron's house, and before the voice could either agree or disagree, he rejected it himself. He then pinpointed the freight yards, and immediately found irrational reasons why he could not go there.

"Now, don't get so excited," said the voice. "It's a simple transaction. . . ."

"That restaurant! Outside of town. The Cheshire Cat! Behind the restaurant, there's a garden. . ."

The voice was confused trying to keep up with him, and Matlock knew he was carrying off the ploy. He made last references to the diaries and the incriminating affidavit and slammed the telephone receiver into its cradle.

He stood in the booth, exhausted. Perspiration was dripping down his face, yet the early morning air was cool.

"That was handled very nicely," said the black man in command. "Your adversary chose a place within the college, I gather. An intelligent move on his part. Very nicely done, sir."

Matlock looked at the uniformed Negro, grateful for his praise and not a little astonished at his own resourcefulness. "I don't know if I could do it again."

"Of course you could," answered the black, leading Matlock toward the car. "Extreme stress activates a memory bank, not unlike a computer. Probing, rejecting, accepting—all instantaneously. Until panic, of course. There are interesting studies being made regarding the varying thresholds."

"Really?" said Matlock as they reached the car door. The Negro motioned him inside. The car lurched forward and they sped off down the highway flanked by the two other automobiles.

"We'll take a diagonal route to the restaurant using the roads set back in the farm country," said the black behind the wheel. "We'll approach it from the southwest and let you off about a hundred yards from a path used by employees to reach the rear of the building. We'll point it out to you. Walk directly to the section of the gardens where there's a large white arbor and a circle of flagstones surrounding a goldfish pond. Do you know it?"

"Yes, I do. I'm wondering how *you* do, though."

The driver smiled. "I'm not clairvoyant. While you were in the telephone booth, I was in touch with our men by radio. Everything's ready now. We're prepared. Remember, the white arbor and the goldfish pond. . . . And here. Here's the notebook and the envelope." The driver reached down to a flap pocket on the side of his door and pulled out the oilcloth package. The envelope was attached to it by a thick elastic band.

"We'll be there in less then ten minutes," said the man in command, shifting his weight to get comfortable. Matlock looked at him. Strapped to his leg—sewn into the tight-fitting khaki, actually—was a leather scabbard. He hadn't noticed it before and knew why. The bone-handled knife it contained had only recently been inserted. The scabbard housed a blade at least ten inches long.

Dunois's elite corps was now, indeed, prepared.

Chapter Thirty-five

He stood at the side of the tall white arbor. The sun had risen over the eastern curve, the woods behind him still heavy with mist, dully reflecting the light of the early morning. In front of him the newly filled trees formed corridors for the old brick paths that converged into the restful flagstone haven. There were a number of marble benches placed around the circle, all glistening with morning moisture. From the center of the large patio, the bubbling sounds of the man-made goldfish pond continued incessantly with no break in the sound pattern. Birds could be heard activating their myriad signals, greeting the sun, starting the day's foraging.

Matlock's memory wandered back to Herron's Nest, to the forbidding green wall which isolated the old man from the outside world. There were similarities, he thought. Perhaps it was fitting that it should all end in such a place.

He lit a cigarette, extinguishing it after two intakes of smoke. He clutched the notebook, holding it in front of his chest as though it were some impenetrable shield, his head snapping in the direction of every sound, a portion of his life suspended with each movement.

He wondered where Dunois's men were. Where had the elite guard hidden itself? Were they watching him, laughing quietly among themselves at his nervous gestures—his so obvious fear? Or were they spread out, guerrilla fashion? Crouched next to the earth or in the low limbs of the trees, ready to spring, prepared to kill?

And who would they kill? In what numbers and how armed would be Nimrod's forces? Would Nimrod come? Would Nimrod bring the girl he loved safely back to him? And if Nimrod did, if he finally saw Pat again, would the two of them be caught in the massacre which surely had to follow?

Who *was* Nimrod?

His breathing stopped. The muscles in his arms and legs contorted spastically, stiffened with fear. He closed his eyes tightly—to listen or to pray, he'd never really know, except that his beliefs excluded the existence of God. And so he listened with his eyes shut tight until he was sure.

First one, then two automobiles had turned off the highway and had entered the side road leading to the entrance of the Cheshire Cat. Both vehicles were traveling at enormous speeds, their tires screeching as they rounded the front circle leading into the restaurant parking area.

And then everything was still again. Even the birds were silent; no sound came from anywhere.

Matlock stepped back under the arbor, pressing himself against its lattice frame. He strained to hear—anything.

Silence. Yet not silence! Yet, again, a sound so blended with stillness as to be dismissed as a rustling leaf is dismissed.

It was a scraping. A hesitant, halting scraping from one of the paths in front of him, one of the paths hidden amongst the trees, one of the old brick lanes leading to the flagstone retreat.

At first it was barely audible. Dismissible. Then it became slightly clearer, less hesitant, less unsure.

Then he heard the quiet, tortured moan. It pierced into his brain.

"Jamie . . . Jamie? Please, Jamie. . . ."

The single plea, his name, broke off into a sob. He felt a rage he had never felt before in his life. He threw down the oilcloth packet, his eyes blinded by tears and fury. He lunged out of the protective frame of the white arbor and yelled, roared so that his voice startled the birds, who screeched out of the trees, out of their silent sanctuary.

"Pat! Pat! Where are you? Pat, my God, where? *Where!*"

The sobbing—half relief, half pain—became louder.

"Here. . . . Here, Jamie! Can't see."

He traced the sound and raced up the middle brick path. Halfway to the building, against the trunk of a tree, sunk to the ground, he saw her. She was on her knees, her bandaged head against the earth. She had fallen. Rivulets of blood were on the back of her neck; the sutures in her head had broken.

He rushed to her and gently lifted up her head.

Under the bandages on her forehead were layers of three-inch adhesive tape, pushed brutally against the lids of her eyes, stretched tight to her temples—as secure and unmovable as a steel plate covering her face. To try and remove them would be a torture devised in hell.

He held her close and kept repeating her name over and over again.

"Everything will be all right now. . . . Everything will be all right. . . ."

He lifted her gently off the ground, pressing her face against his own. He kept repeating those words of comfort which came to him in the midst of his rage.

Suddenly, without warning, without any warning at all, the blinded girl screamed, stretching her bruised body, her lacerated head.

"Let them have it, for God's sake! Whatever it is, *give it to them!*"

He stumbled down the brick path back to the flagstone circle.

"I will, I will, my darling. . . ."

"Please, Jamie! Don't let them touch me again! *Ever again!*"

"No, my darling. Not ever, not ever. . . ."

He slowly lowered the girl onto the ground, onto the soft earth beyond the flagstones.

"Take the tape off! Please take the tape off."

"I can't now, darling. It would hurt too much. In a little . . ."

"I don't *care!* I can't stand it any longer!"

What could he do? What was he supposed to *do?* Oh, God! Oh, God, you son-of-a-bitching God! *Tell me! Tell me!*

He looked over at the arbor. The oilcoth packet lay on the ground where he had thrown it.

He had no choice now. He did not care now.

"*Nimrod! . . . Nimrod! Come to me now, Nimrod! Bring your goddamn army! Come on and get it, Nimrod! I've got it here!*"

Through the following silence, he heard the footsteps.

Precise, surefooted, emphatic.

On the middle path, Nimrod came into view.

Adrian Sealfont stood on the edge of the flagstone circle.

"I'm sorry, James."

Matlock lowered the girl's head to the ground. His mind was incapable of functioning. His shock was so total that no words came, he couldn't assimilate the terrible, unbelievable fact in front of him. He rose slowly to his feet.

"Give it to me, James. You have your agreement. We'll take care of you."

"No. . . . No. No, I don't, I *won't believe* you! This isn't so. This isn't the way it can be. . . ."

"I'm afraid it is." Sealfont snapped the fingers of his right hand. It was a signal.

"No. . . . No! No! No!" Matlock found that he was screaming. The girl, too, cried out. He turned to Sealfont. "They said you were taken away! I thought you were dead! I blamed myself for your death!"

"I wasn't taken, I was escorted. Give me the diaries." Sealfont, annoyed, snapped his fingers again. "And the Corsican paper. I trust you have both with you."

There was the slightest sound of a muffled cough, a rasp, an interrupted exclamation. Sealfont looked quickly behind him and spoke sharply to his unseen forces.

"Get out here!"

"Why?"

"Because we *had* to. *I* had to. There was no alternative."

"No alternative?" Matlock couldn't believe he had heard the words. "No alternative to *what?*"

"Collapse! We were financially exhausted! Our last reserves were committed; there was no one left to appeal to. The moral corruption was complete: the pleas of higher education became an unprofitable, national bore. There was no other answer but to assert our own leadership . . . over the corruptors. We did so, and we survived!"

In the agonizing bewilderment of the moment, the pieces of the puzzle fell into place for Matlock. The unknown tumblers of the unfamiliar vault locked into gear and the heavy steel door was opened. . . . Carlyle's extraordinary endowment. . . . But it was more than Carlyle; Sealfont had just said it. The *pleas* had become a *bore!* It was subtle, but it was there!

Everywhere!

The raising of funds throughout all the campuses continued but there were no cries of panic these days; no threats of financial collapse that had been the themes of a hundred past campaigns in scores of colleges and universities.

The general assumption to be made—if one bothered to make it—was that the crises had been averted. Normality had returned.

But it *hadn't*. The norm had become a monster.

"Oh, my God," said Matlock softly, in terrified consternation.

"He was no help, I can assure you," replied Sealfont. "Our accomplishments are extremely human. Look at us now. *Independent!* Our strength growing systematically. Within five years every major university in the

Northeast will be part of a self-sustaining federation!"

"You're diseased. . . . You're a *cancer!*"

"We *survive!* The choice was never really that difficult. No one was going to stop the way things were. Least of all ourselves. . . . We simply made the decision ten years ago to alter the principal players."

"But *you* of all people . . ."

"Yes. I was a good choice, wasn't I?" Sealfont turned once again in the direction of the restaurant, toward the sleeping hill with the old brick paths. He shouted. "I told you to come out here! There's nothing to worry about. Our friend doesn't care who you are. He'll soon be on his way. . . . Won't you, James?"

"You're *insane.* You're . . ."

"Not for a *minute!* There's no one saner. Or more practical. . . . History repeats, you should know that. The fabric is torn, society divided into viciously opposing camps. Don't be fooled by the dormancy; scratch the surface—it bleeds profusely."

"You're *making* it bleed!" Matlock screamed. There was nothing left; the spring had sprung.

"On the contrary! You pompous, self-righteous *ass!*" Sealfont's eyes stared at him in cold fury, his voice scathing. "Who gave you the right to make pronouncements? Where were you when men like myself—in *every institution*—faced the very real prospects of closing our doors! You were safe; we *sheltered* you. . . . And our appeals went unanswered. There wasn't room for our needs . . ."

"You didn't try! Not hard enough . . ."

"Liar! *Fool!*" Sealfont roared now. He was a man possessed, thought Matlock. Or a man tormented. "What was *left?* Endowments? Dwindling! There are other, more *viable tax incentives!* . . . Foundations? Small-minded tyrants—smaller allocations! . . . The Government? *Blind! Obscene!* Its priorities are bought! Or returned in kind at the ballot box! We had no funds; we bought no votes! For us, the system had collapsed! It was finished! . . . And no one knew it better than I did. For years . . . begging, pleading; palms outstretched to the ignorant men and their pompous *committees.* . . . It was hopeless; we were killing ourselves. Still no one listened. . . . And always . . . *always*—behind the excuses and the delays—there was the snickering, the veiled reference to our common God-given frailty. After all . . . we were *teachers.* Not *doers.* . . ."

Sealfont's voice was suddenly low. And hard. And utterly convincing as he finished. "Well, young man, we're *doers now.* The system's damned and rightly so. The leaders never learn. Look to the children. They saw. They understood. . . . And we've enrolled them. Our alliance is no coincidence."

Matlock could do no more than stare at Sealfont. Sealfont had said it: *Look to the children. . . . Look, and behold. Look and beware.* The leaders never learn. . . . Oh, God! Was it so? Was it really the way things were? The Nimrods and the Dunoises. The "federations," the "elite guards." Was it happening all over again?

"Now James. Where is the letter you spoke of? Who has it?"

"Letter? What?"

"The letter that is to be mailed this morning. We'll stop it now, won't we?"

"I don't understand." Matlock was trying, trying *desperately* to make contact with his senses.

"Who has the letter!"

"The letter?" Matlock knew as he spoke that he was saying the wrong words, but he couldn't help himself. He couldn't stop to think, for he was incapable of thought.

"The letter! . . . There *is* no *letter, is there?!* There's . . . no 'incriminating statement' typed and ready to be mailed at ten o'clock in the morning! You were lying!"

"I was lying. . . . Lying." His reserves had been used up. There was nothing now but what was so.

Sealfont laughed softly. It wasn't the laugh Matlock was used to hearing from him. There was a cruelty he'd not heard before.

"Weren't you clever? But you're ultimately weak. I knew that from the beginning. You were the government's perfect choice, for you have no really firm commitments. They called it mobility. I knew it to be unconcerned flexibility. You talk but that's all you do. It's meaningless. . . . You're very representative, you know." Sealfont spoke over his shoulder toward the paths. "All right, *all* of you! Dr. Matlock won't be in a position to reveal any names, any identities. Come out of your hutches, you rabbits!"

"Augh . . ."

The guttural cry was short, punctuating the stillness. Sealfont whipped around.

Then there was another gasp, this the unmistakable sound of a human windpipe expunging its last draft of air.

And another, this coupled with the beginnings of a scream.

"Who is it? Who's up there?" Sealfont rushed to the path from which the last cry came.

He was stopped by the sound of a terrifying shout—cut short—from another part of the sanctuary. He raced back; the beginnings of panic were jarring his control.

"Who's up there?! Where are all of you? *Come down here!*"

The silence returned. Sealfont stared at Matlock.

"What have you done? What have you done, you unimportant little man? Whom have you brought with you? *Who is up there? Answer me!*"

Even if he'd been capable, there was no need for Matlock to reply. From a path at the far end of the garden, Julian Dunois walked into view.

"Good morning, Nimrod."

Sealfont's eyes bulged. "Who *are* you? Where are my men?!"

"The name is Jacques Devereaux, Heysoú Daumier, Julian Dunois—take your choice. You were no match for us. You had a complement of ten, I had eight. No match. Your men are dead and how their bodies are disposed of is no concern of yours."

"Who *are* you?"

"Your enemy."

Sealfont ripped open his coat with his left hand, plunging his right inside. Dunois shouted a warning. Matlock found himself lurching forward toward the man he'd revered for a decade. Lunging at him with only one thought, one final objective, if it had to be the end of his own life.

To kill.

The face was next to his. The Lincoln-like face now contorted with fear and panic. He brought his right hand down on it like the claw of a terrified animal. He ripped into the flesh and felt the blood spew out of the distorted mouth.

558   The Matlock Paper

He heard the shattering explosion and felt a sharp, electric pain in his left
shoulder. But still he couldn't stop.

"Get off, Matlock! For God's sake, get off!"

He was being pulled away. Pulled away by huge black muscular arms. He
was thrown to the ground, the heavy arms holding him down. And through it
all he heard the cries, the terrible cries of pain and his name being repeated
over and over again.

"Jamie . . . Jamie . . . Jamie . . ."

He lurched upward, using every ounce of strength his violence could
summon. The muscular black arms were taken by surprise; he brought his
legs up in crushing blows against the ribs and spines above him.

For a few brief seconds, he was free.

He threw himself forward on the hard surface, pounding his arms and
knees against the stone. Whatever had happened to him, whatever was meant
by the stinging pain, now spreading throughout the whole left side of his
body, he had to reach the girl on the ground. The girl who had been through
such terror for him.

"Pat!"

The pain was more than he could bear. He fell once more, but he had
reached her hand. They held each other's hands, each trying desperately to
give comfort to the other, fully aware that both might die at that moment.

Suddenly Matlock's hand went limp.

All was darkness for him.

He opened his eyes and saw the large black kneeling in front of him. He
had been propped up into a sitting position at the side of a marble bench. His
shirt had been removed; his left shoulder throbbed.

"The pain, I'm sure, is far more serious than the wound," said the black.
"The upper left section of your body was badly bruised in the automobile,
and the bullet penetrated below your left shoulder cartilage. Compounded
that way, the pain would be severe."

"We gave you a local anesthetic. It should help." The speaker was Julian
Dunois, standing to his right. "Miss Ballantyne has been taken to a doctor.
He'll remove the tapes. He's black and sympathetic, but not so much so to
treat a man with a bullet wound. We've radioed our own doctor in
Torrington. He should be here in twenty minutes."

"Why didn't you wait for him to help Pat?"

"Frankly, we have to talk. Briefly, but in confidence. Secondly, for her
own sake, those tapes had to be removed as quickly as possible."

"Where's Sealfont?"

"He's disappeared. That's all you know, all you'll ever know. It's
important that you understand that. Because, you see, if we must, we will
carry out our threat against you and Miss Ballantyne. We don't wish to do
that. . . . You and I, we are not enemies."

"You're wrong. We are."

"Ultimately, perhaps. That would seem inevitable. Right now, however,
we've served each other in a moment of great need. We acknowledge it. We
trust you do also."

"I do."

"Perhaps we've even learned from each other."

Matlock looked into the eyes of the black revolutionary. "I understand
things better. I don't know what you could have learned from me."

The revolutionary laughed gently. "That an individual, by his actions—his courage, if you like—rises above the stigma of labels."

"I don't understand you."

"Ponder it. It'll come to you."

"What happens now? To Pat? To me? I'll be arrested the minute I'm seen."

"I doubt that sincerely. Within the hour, Greenberg will be reading a document prepared by my organization. By me, to be precise. I suspect the contents will become part of a file buried in the archives. It's most embarrassing. Morally, legally, and certainly politically. Too many profound errors were made. . . . We'll act this morning as your intermediary. Perhaps it would be a good time for you to use some of your well-advertised money and go with Miss Ballantyne on a long, recuperative journey. . . . I believe that will be agreed upon with alacrity. I'm sure it will."

"And Sealfont? What happens to him. Are you going to kill him?"

"Does Nimrod deserve to die? Don't bother to answer; we'll not discuss the subject. Suffice it to say he'll remain alive until certain questions are answered."

"Have you any idea what's going to happen when he's found to be missing?"

"There will be explosions, ugly rumors. About a great many things. When icons are shattered, the believers panic. So be it. Carlyle will have to live with it. . . . Rest, now. The doctor will be here soon." Dunois turned his attention to a uniformed Negro who had come up to him and spoken softly. The kneeling black who had bandaged his wound stood up. Matlock watched the tall, slender figure of Julian Dunois, quietly, confidently issuing his instructions, and felt the pain of gratitude. It was made worse because Dunois suddenly took on another image.

It was the figure of death.

"Dunois?"

"Yes?"

"Be careful."

EPILOGUE

The blue green waters of the Caribbean mirrored the hot afternoon sun in countless thousands of swelling, blinding reflections. The sand was warm to the touch, soft under the feet. This isolated stretch of the island was at peace with itself and with a world beyond that it did not really acknowledge.

Matlock walked down to the edge of the water and let the miniature waves wash over his ankles. Like the sand on the beach, the water was warm.

He carried a newspaper sent to him by Greenberg. Part of a newspaper, actually.

KILLINGS IN CARLYLE, CONN.

***

23 SLAIN, BLACKS AND WHITES, TOWN

STUNNED, FOLLOWS DISAPPEARANCE

OF UNIVERSITY PRESIDENT

***

CARLYLE, MAY 10—On the outskirts of this small university town, in a section housing large, old estates, a bizarre mass killing took place yesterday. Twenty-three men were slain; the federal authorities have speculated the killings were the result of an ambush that claimed many lives of both the attackers and the attacked. . . .

There followed a cold recitation of identities, short summaries of police file associations.

Julian Dunois was among them.

The spectre of death had not been false; Dunois hadn't escaped. The violence he engendered had to be the violence that would take his life.

The remainder of the article contained complicated speculations on the meaning and the motives of the massacre's strange cast of characters. And the possible connection to the disappearance of Adrian Sealfont.

Speculations only. No mention of Nimrod, nothing of himself; no word of any long-standing federal investigation. Not the truth; nothing of the truth.

Matlock heard his cottage door open, and he turned around. Pat was standing on the small veranda fifty yards away over the dune. She waved and started down the steps toward him.

She was dressed in shorts and a light silk blouse; she was barefoot and smiling. The bandages had been removed from her legs and arms, and the Caribbean sun had tanned her skin to a lovely bronze. She had devised a wide orange headband to cover the wounds above her forehead.

She would not marry him. She said there would be no marriage out of pity, out of debt—real or imagined. But Matlock knew there would be a marriage. Or there would be no marriages for either of them. Julian Dunois had made it so.

"Did you bring cigarettes?" he asked.

"No. No cigarettes," she replied. "I brought matches."

"That's cryptic."

"I used that word—cryptic—with Jason. Do you remember?"

"I do. You were mad as hell."

"You were spaced out . . . In hell. Let's walk down to the jetty."

"Why did you bring matches?" He took her hand, putting the newspaper under his arm.

"A funeral pyre. Archeologists place great significance in funeral pyres."

"What?"

"You've been carrying around that damned paper all day. I want to burn it." She smiled at him, gently.

"Burning it won't change what's in it."

Pat ignored his observation. "Why do you think Jason sent it to you? I thought the whole idea was several weeks of nothing. No newspapers, no radios, no contact with anything but warm water and white sand. He made the rules and he broke them."

"He *recommended* the rules and knew they were difficult to live by."

"He should have let someone else break them. He's not as good a friend as I thought he was."

"Maybe he's a better one."

"That's sophistry." She squeezed his hand. A single, overextended wave lapped across their bare feet. A silent gull swooped down from the sky into the water offshore; its wings flapped against the surface, its neck shook violently. The bird ascended screeching, no quarry in its beak.

"Greenberg knows I've got a very unpleasant decision to make."

"You've made it. He knows that, too."

Matlock looked at her. Of course Greenberg knew; she knew, too, he thought. "There'll be a lot more pain; perhaps more than justified."

"That's what they tell you. They'll tell you to let them do it their way. Quietly, efficiently, with as little embarrassment as possible. For everyone."

"Maybe it's best; maybe they're right."

"You don't believe that for a second."

"No, I don't."

They walked in silence for a while. The jetty was in front of them, its rocks placed decades, perhaps centuries ago, to restrain a long-forgotten current. It was a natural fixture now.

As Nimrod had become a natural fixture, a logical extension of the anticipated; undesirable but nevertheless expected. To be fought in deep cover.

Mini-America . . . just below the surface.

Company policy, man.

Everywhere.

The hunters, builders. The killers and their quarry were making alliances.

Look to the children. They understand. . . . We've enrolled them.

The leaders never learn.

A microcosm of the inevitable? Made unavoidable because the needs were real? Had been real for years?

And still the leaders would not learn.

"Jason said once that truth is neither good nor bad. Simply truth. That's why he sent me this." Matlock sat down on a large flat rock; Pat stood beside him. The tide was coming in and the sprays of the small waves splashed upward. Pat reached over and took the two pages of the newspaper.

"This is the truth then." A statement.

"Their truth. Their judgment. Assign obvious labels and continue the game. The good guys and the bad guys and the posse will reach the pass on time. Just in time. This time."

"What's your truth?"

"Go back and tell the story. All of it."

"They'll disagree. They'll give you reasons why you shouldn't. Hundreds of them."

"They won't convince me."

"Then they'll be against you. They've threatened; they won't accept interference. That's what Jason wants you to know."

"That's what he wants me to think about."

Pat held the pages of the newspaper in front of her and struck a wooden island match on the dry surface of a rock.

The paper burned haltingly, retarded by the Caribbean spray.

But it burned.

"That's not a very impressive funeral pyre," said Matlock.

"It'll do until we get back."

The
Gemini
Contenders

Robert Ludlum

For Richard Marek, Editor. Brilliance cloaked in great humor. Perception beyond any writer's imagination. Simply, the best there is. And for lovely Margot, who makes it all perfect.

PROLOGUE

December 9, 1939—Salonika, Greece

One by one the trucks struggled up the steep road in the predawn light of
Salonika. Each went a bit faster at the top; the drivers were anxious to return
to the darkness of the descending country road cut out of the surrounding
forests.

Yet each of the five drivers in the five trucks had to control his anxiety.
None could allow his foot to slip from a brake or press an accelerator beyond
a certain point; eyes had to be squinted, sharpening the focus, alert for a
sudden stop or an unexpected curve in the darkness.

For it was darkness. No headlights were turned on; the column traveled
with only the gray light of the Grecian night, low-flying clouds filtering the
spill of the Grecian moon.

The journey was an exercise in discipline. And discipline was not foreign to
these drivers, or to the riders beside the drivers.

Each was a priest. A monk. From the Order of Xenope, the harshest
monastic brotherhood under the control of the Patriarchate of Constantine.
Blind obedience coexisted with self-reliance; they were disciplined to the
instant of death.

In the lead truck, the young bearded priest removed his cassock, under
which were the clothes of a laborer, a heavy shirt and trousers of thick fabric.
He rolled up the cassock and placed it in the well behind the high-backed
seat, shoving it down between odd items of canvas and cloth. He spoke to the
robed driver beside him.

"It's no more than a half mile now. The stretch of track parallels the road
for about three hundred feet. In the open; it will be sufficient."

"The train will be there?" asked the middle-aged, powerfully built monk,
narrowing his eyes in the darkness.

"Yes. Four freight cars, a single engineer. No stokers. No other men."

"You'll be using a shovel, then," said the older priest, smiling but with no
humor in his eyes.

"I'll be using the shovel," replied the younger man simply. "Where's the
weapon?"

"In the glove compartment."

The priest in the laborer's clothes reached forward and released the catch
on the compartment panel. It fell open. He put his hand inside the recess and
withdrew a heavy, large-calibered pistol. Deftly, the priest sprung the
magazine out of the handle, checked the ammunition, and cracked the thick
steel back into the chamber. The metallic sound had a finality to it.

"A powerful instrument. Italian, isn't it?"

"Yes," answered the older priest without comment, only the sadness in his voice.

"That's appropriate. And, I suppose, a blessing." The younger man shoved the weapon into his belt. "You'll call his family?"

"I've been so ordered——" It was obvious that the driver wanted to say something more, but he controlled himself. Silently he gripped the wheel more firmly than necessary.

For a moment the moonlight broke through the night clouds, illuminating the road cut out of the forest.

"I used to play here as a child," said the younger man. "I would run through the woods and get wet in the streams . . . then I would dry off in the mountain caves and pretend I had visions. I was happy in these hills. The Lord God wanted me to see them again. He is merciful. And kind."

The moon disappeared. There was darkness once more.

The trucks entered a sweeping curve to the west; the woods thinned out and in the distance, barely visible, were the outlines of telegraph poles, black shafts silhouetted against gray night. The road straightened and widened and became one with a clearing that stretched perhaps a hundred yards from forest to forest. A flat, barren area imposed on the myriad hills and woodlands. In the center of the clearing, its hulk obscured by the darkness beyond, was a train.

Immobile but not without movement. From the engine came curls of smoke spiraling up into the night.

"In the old days," said the young priest, "the farmers would herd their sheep and cart their produce here. There was always a great deal of confusion, my father told me. Fights broke out constantly over what belonged to whom. They were amusing stories. . . . There he is!"

The beam of a flashlight shot out from the black. It circled twice and then remained stationary, the white shaft directed now at the last freight car. The priest in laborer's clothes unclipped a pencil light from his shirt pocket, held it forward and pressed the button for precisely two seconds. The reflection off the truck's windshield briefly illuminated the small enclosure. The younger man's eyes were drawn swiftly to the face of his brother monk. He saw that his companion had bitten his lip; a rivulet of blood trickled down his chin, matting itself in the close-cropped gray beard.

There was no reason to comment on it.

"Pull up to the third car. The others will turn around and start unloading."

"I know," said the driver simply. He swung the wheel gently to the right and headed toward the third freight car.

The engineer, in overalls and a goatskin cap, approached the truck as the young priest opened the door and jumped to the ground. The two men looked at each other and then embraced.

"You look different without your cassock, Petride. I'd forgotten how you looked——"

"Oh, come now. Four years out of twenty-seven is hardly the better part."

"We don't see you often enough. Everyone in the family remarks about it." The engineer removed his large, calloused hands from the priest's shoulders. The moon broke through the clouds again; the spill lighted the trainman's face. It was a strong face, nearer fifty than forty, filled with the lines of a man constantly exposing his skin to the wind and the sun.

"How's mother, Annaxas?"

"Well. A little weaker with each month of age, but alert."

"And your wife?"

"Pregnant again and not laughing this time. She scolds me."

"She should. You're a lustful old dog, my brother. But better to serve the church, I rejoice to say." The priest laughed.

"I'll tell her you said that," said the engineer, smiling.

There was a moment of silence before the young man replied. "Yes. You tell her." He turned to the activity taking place at the freight cars. The loading doors had been opened and lanterns hung inside, shedding their muted light sufficiently for packing, but not bright enough to be obvious outside. The figures of robed priests began walking swiftly back and forth between the trucks and the doors, carrying crates, boxes of heavy cardboard framed with wood. Prominently displayed on each crate was the crucifix and thorns of the Order of Xenope.

"The food?" inquired the engineer.

"Yes," answered his brother. "Fruits, vegetables, dried meats, grain. The border patrols will be satisfied."

"Then where?" It was not necessary to be clearer.

"This vehicle. In the middle section of the carriage, beneath tobacco nets. You have the lookouts posted?"

"On the tracks and the road; both directions for over a mile. Don't worry. Before daybreak on a Sunday morning, only you priests and novices have work to do and places to go."

The young priest glanced over at the fourth freight car. The work was progressing rapidly; the crates were being stacked inside. All those hours of practice were showing their value. The monk who was his driver stopped briefly by the muted light of the loading door, a carton in his hands. He exchanged looks with the younger man, then forced his attention away, back to the carton which he swung up into the well of the freight car.

Father Petride turned to his brother. "When you picked up the train, did you speak with anyone?"

"Only the dispatcher. Naturally. We had black tea together."

"What did he say?"

"Words I wouldn't offend you with, for the most part. His papers said the cars were to be loaded by the fathers of Xenope in the outlying yards. He didn't ask any questions."

Father Petride looked over at the second freight car, on his right. In minutes all would be completed; they would be ready for the third car. "Who prepared the engine?"

"Fuel crews and mechanics. Yesterday afternoon. The orders said it was a standby; that's normal. Equipment breaks down all the time. We are laughed at in Italy. . . . Naturally, I checked everything myself several hours ago."

"Would the dispatcher have any reason to telephone the freight yards?" Where supposedly we are loading the cars?"

"He was asleep, or practically so, before I left his tower. The morning schedule won't start——" the engineer looked up at the gray black sky "——for at least another hour. He'd have no reason to call anyone, unless the wireless reported an accident."

"The wires were shorted out; water in a terminal box," said the priest quickly, as if talking to himself.

"Why?"

"In case you did have problems. You spoke to *no one* else?"

"Not even a drifter. I checked the cars to make sure none were inside."

"You've studied our schedule by now. What do you think?"

The trainman whistled softly, shaking his head. "I think I'm astounded, my brother. Can so much be . . . so arranged?"

"The arrangements are taken care of. What about the time? That's the important factor."

"If there are no track failures the speed can be maintained. The Slav border police at Bitola are hungry for bribes; and a Greek freight at Banja Luka is fair game. We'll have no trouble at Sarajevo or Zagreb; they look for larger fish than food for the religious."

"The time, not the bribes."

"They *are* time. One haggles."

"Only if *not* haggling would seem suspicious. Can we reach Monfalcone in three nights?"

"If your arrangements are successful, yes. If we lose time we could make it up during the daylight hours."

"Only as a last resort. We travel at night."

"You're obstinate."

"We're cautious." Again the priest looked away. Freight cars one and two were secure, the fourth would be loaded and packed before the minute was up. He turned back to his brother. "Does the family think you're taking a freight to Corinth?"

"Yes. To Navpaktos. To the shipyards on the straits of Patrai. They don't expect me back for the better part of a week."

"There are strikes at Patrai. The unions are angry. If you were a few days longer, they'd understand."

Annaxas looked closely at his brother. He seemed startled at the young priest's worldly knowledge. There was a hesitancy in his reply. "They'd understand. Your sister-in-law would understand."

"Good." The monks had gathered by Petride's truck, watching him, waiting for instructions. "I'll join you at the engine shortly."

"All right," said the trainman as he walked away, glancing at the priests.

Father Petride removed the pencil light from his shirt pocket and in the darkness approached the other monks at the truck. He searched out the powerfully built man who was his driver. The monk understood and stepped away from the others, joining Petride at the side of the vehicle.

"This is the last time we speak," said the young priest.

"May the blessings of God——"

"Please," interrupted Petride. "There's no time. Just commit to memory each move we make here tonight. *Everything.* It must be duplicated exactly."

"It will be. The same roads, the same orders or trucks, the same drivers, identical papers across the borders to Monfalcone. Nothing will change, except one of us will be missing."

"That's the will of God. For the glory of God. It's a privilege beyond my worth."

There were two master padlocks on the truck's panel. Petride had one key; his driver held the other. Together they approached the locks and inserted the keys. The irons sprung; the locks were lifted out of the steel hasps, the hasps slapped up, and the doors opened. A lantern was hung high on the edge of the panel.

Inside were the crates with the symbols of the crucifix and thorns stenciled on the sides between the strips of wood. The monks began to remove them, maneuvering like dancers—robes flowing in the eerie light. They carried the cartons to the loading door of the third freight car. Two men leaped up into the heavy-beamed deck of the car and started stacking the boxes at the south end.

Several minutes later half the truck was empty. In the center of the van, separated from the surrounding cartons, was a single crate draped in black cloth. It was somewhat larger than the cases of produce and not rectangular in shape. Instead, it was a perfect cube: three feet in height, three in width, and three in depth.

The priests gathered in a semicircle in front of the open panels of the truck. Shafts of filtered white moonlight mingled with the yellow spill of the lantern. The combined effect of the strange admixture of light, the cavernous truck, and the robed figures made Father Petride think of a catacomb, deep in the earth, housing the true relics of the cross.

The reality was not much different. Except that what lay sealed inside the iron vault—for that was what it was—was infinitely more meaningful than the petrified wood of the crucifixion.

Several of the monks had closed their eyes in prayer; others were staring, transfixed by the presence of the holy thing, their thoughts suspended, their faith drawing sustenance from what they believed was within the tomblike chest—itself a catafalque.

Petride watched them, feeling apart from them, and that was how it should be. His mind wandered back to what seemed only hours ago, but was in reality six weeks. He had been ordered out of the fields and taken to the white concrete rooms of the Elder of Xenope. He was ushered into the presence of that most holy father; there was one other priest with the old prelate, no one else.

"Petride Dakakos," the holy man had begun, sitting behind his thick wooden table, "You have been chosen above all others here at Xenope for the most demanding task of your existence. For the glory of God and the preservation of Christian sanity."

The second priest had been introduced. He was an ascetic-looking man with wide, penetrating eyes. He spoke slowly, precisely. "We are the custodians of a vault, and sarcophagus, if you will, that has remained sealed in a tomb deep in the earth for over fifteen hundred years. Within that vault are documents that would rend the Christian world apart, so devastating are their writings. They are the ultimate proof of our most sacred beliefs, yet their exposure would set religion against religion, sect against sect, entire peoples against one another. In a holy war. . . . The German conflict is spreading. The vault must be taken out of Greece, for its existence has been rumored for decades. The search for it would be as thorough as a hunt for microbes. Arrangements have been made to remove it where none will find it. I should say, most of the arrangements. You are the final component."

The journey had been explained. The *arrangements*. In all their glory. And fear.

"You will be in contact with only one man. Savarone Fontini-Cristi, a great *padrone* of northern Italy, who lives in the vast estates of Campo di Fiori. I, myself, have traveled there and spoken with him. He's an extraordinary man, of unparalleled integrity and utter commitment to free men."

"He is of the Roman church?" Petride had asked incredulously.

"He is of no church, yet *all* churches. He is a powerful force for men who care to think for themselves. He is the friend of the Order of Xenope. It is he who will conceal the vault. . . . You and he alone. And then you . . . but we will get to that; you are the most privileged of men."

"I thank my God."

"As well you should, my son," said the holy father of Xenope, staring at him.

"We understand you have a brother. An engineer for the railroads."

"I do."

"Do you trust him?"

"With my life. He's the finest man I know."

"You shall look into the eyes of the Lord," said the holy father, "and you will not waver. In His eyes you will find perfect grace."

"I thank my God," said Petride once again.

He shook his head and blinked his eyes, forcing the reflections out of his mind. The priests by the truck were still standing immobile; the hum of whispered chants came from rapidly moving lips in the darkness.

There was no time for meditation or prayer. There was no time for anything but swift movement—to carry out the commands of the Order of Xenope. Petride gently parted the priests in front of him and jumped up into the truck. He knew why he had been chosen. He was capable of such harshness; the holy father of Xenope had made that clear to him.

There was a time for such men as himself.

God forgive him.

"Come," he said quietly to those on the ground. "I'll need help."

The monks nearest the truck looked uncertainly at one another. Then, one by one, five men climbed into the van.

Petride removed the black drape that covered the vault. Underneath, the holy receptacle was encased in the heavy cardboard, wood framing, and the stenciled symbols of Xenope; identical except for size and shape to all the other crates. But the casing was the only similarity. It required six strong backs, pushing and pulling, to nudge it to the edge of the van and onto the freight car.

The moment it was in place, the dancelike activity resumed. Petride remained in the freight car, arranging the crates so that they concealed the holy thing, obscuring it as one among so many. Nothing unusual, nothing to catch the eye.

The freight car was filled. Petride pulled the doors shut and inserted the iron padlock. He looked at the radium dial of his wristwatch; it had all taken eight minutes and thirty seconds.

It had to be, he supposed, and yet still it annoyed him: His fellow priests knelt on the ground. A young man—younger than he, a powerful Serbo-Croat barely out of his novitiate—could not help himself. As the tears rolled down his cheek, the young priest began the chant of Nicaea. The others picked it up and Petride knelt also, in his laborer's clothes, and listened to the holy words.

But not speaking them. There was no *time! Couldn't they understand?*

What was happening to him? In order to take his mind off the holy whispers, he put his hand inside his shirt and checked the leather pouch that was strapped to his chest. Inside that flat, uncomfortable dispatch case were the orders that would lead him across hundreds of miles of uncertainty. Twenty-seven separate pages of paper. The pouch was secure; the straps cut into his skin.

The prayer over, the priests of Xenope rose silently. Petride stood in front of them and each in turn approached him and embraced him and held him in love. The last was his driver, his dearest friend in the order. The tears that filled the rims of his eyes and rolled down his strong face said everything there was to say.

The monks raced back to the trucks; Petride ran to the front of the train and climbed up into the pilot's cabin. He nodded to his brother who began to pull levers and turn wheels. Grinding shrieks of metal against metal filled the night.

In minutes the freight was traveling at high speed. The journey had begun. The journey for the glory of one Almighty God.

Petride held on to an iron bar that protruded from the iron wall. He closed his eyes and let the hammering vibrations and rushing wind numb his thoughts. His fears.

And then he opened his eyes—briefly—and saw his brother leaning out of the window, his massive right hand on the throttle, his stare directed to the tracks ahead.

Annaxas the Strong, everyone called him. But Annaxas was more than strong; he was good. When their father had died, it was Annaxas who had gone out to the yards—a huge boy of thirteen—and worked the long, hard hours that exhausted grown men. The money Annaxas brought home kept them all together, made it possible for his brothers and sisters to get what schooling they could. And one brother got more. Not for the family, but for the glory of God.

The Lord God tested men. As He was testing now.

Petride bowed his head and the words seared through his brain and out of his mouth in a whisper that could not be heard.

I believe in one God, the Father Almighty, maker of all things both visible and invisible, and in one Lord, Jesus Christ, Teacher, Son of God, Only begotten of the Father. God of God, Light of Light, Very God of Very God, begotten not made. . . .

They reached the sidings of Edhessa; a switch was thrown by unseen, unauthorized hands, and the freight from Salonika plunged into the northern darkness. The Yugoslav border police at Bitola were as anxious for Greek news as they were for Greek bribes. The northern conflict was spreading rapidly, the armies of Hitler were maniacs; the Balkans were next to fall, everyone said so. And the unstable Italians were filling the piazzas, listening to the screams of war mouthed by the insane Mussolini and his strutting *fascisti*. The talk everywhere was of invasion.

The Slavs accepted several crates of fruit—Xenope fruit was the best in Greece—and wished Annaxas better fortune than they believed he would have, especially since he traveled north.

They sped through the second night north into Mitrovica. The Order of Xenope had done its work; a track was cleared on which no train was scheduled and the freight from Salonika proceeded east to Sarajevo, where a man came out of the shadows and spoke to Petride.

"In twelve minutes the track will be shifted. You will head north to Banja Luka. During the day you'll stay in the yards. They're very crowded. You'll be contacted at nightfall."

In the crowded freight yards at Banja Luka, at precisely quarter past six in the evening, a man came to them dressed in overalls. "You've done well," he said to Petride. "According to the dispatcher's flagging schedules, you don't exist."

At six thirty-five a signal was given; another switch was thrown, and the train from Salonika entered the tracks for Zagreb.

At midnight, in the quiet yards of Zagreb, another man, emerging from other shadows, gave Petride a long manila envelope. "These are papers signed by *Il Duce's Ministro di Viaggio*. They say your freight is part of the Venice *Ferrovia*. It is Mussolini's pride; no one stops it for anything. You will hold at the Sezana depot and pick up the *Ferrovia* out of Trieste. You'll have no trouble with the Monfalcone border patrols."

Three hours later they waited on the Sezana track, the huge locomotive idling. Sitting on the steps, Petride watched Annaxas manipulate the valves and levers.

"You're remarkable," he said, meaning the compliment sincerely.

"It's a small talent," replied Annaxas. "It takes no schooling, just doing it over and over."

"I think it's a remarkable talent. I could never do it."

His brother looked down at him; the glow of the coals washed over his large face, with the wide-set eyes, so firm and strong and gentle. He was a bull of a man, this brother. A decent man. "You could do anything," said Annaxas awkwardly. "You have the head for thoughts and words far beyond mine."

"That's nonsense," laughed Petride. "There was a time when you'd slap my backside and tell me to tend to my chores with more brains."

"You were young; that was many years ago. You tended to your books, you did that. You were better than the freight yards; you got out of them."

"Only because of you, my brother."

"Rest, Petride. We must both rest."

They had nothing in common any longer, and the reason they had nothing was because of Annaxas's goodness and generosity. The older brother had provided the means for the younger to escape, to grow beyond he who provided . . . until there was nothing in common. What made the reality unbearable was that Annaxas the Strong understood the chasm between them now. In Bitola and Banja Luka he had also insisted they rest, not talk. They would get little sleep once they crossed the borders at Monfalcone. In Italy there would be no sleep at all.

The Lord God tested.

In the silence between them, in the open cabin, the black sky above, the dark ground below, the incessant straining of the engine's fires filling the night outside, Petride felt an odd suspension of thought and feelings. Thinking and feeling once-removed, as though he were examining another's experiences from some isolated perch, looking down through a glass. And he began to consider the man he would meet in the Italian Alps. The man who had provided the Order of Xenope with the complicated schedules of transportation through northern Italy. The expanding circles within circles that led inexorably across the Swiss borders in a way that was untraceable.

Savarone Fontini-Cristi was his name. His estate was called Campo di Fiori. The Elders of Xenope said the Fontini-Cristis were the most powerful family in Italy north of Venice. Quite possibly the richest north of Rome. The power and the wealth certainly were borne out by the twenty-seven separate papers in the leather pouch strapped so securely around his chest. Who but an extraordinarily influential man could provide them? And how did the Elders reach him? Through what means? And why would a man named Fontini-Cristi, whose origins had to be of the Roman Church, deliver such assistance to the Order of Xenope?

The answers to these questions were not within his province, but nevertheless the questions burned. He knew what lay sealed in the vault of iron in the third freight car. It was more than what his brother priests believed.

Far more.

The Elders had told him so he would understand. *It* was the holiest of compelling motives that would allow him to look into the eyes of God without doubt or hesitation. And he needed that assurance.

Unconsciously, he put his hand under the coarse shirt and felt the pouch. A rash had formed around the straps; he could feel the swelling and the rough, abrasive surface of his skin. It would be infected soon. But not before the twenty-seven papers did their work. Then it did not matter.

Suddenly, a half mile away on the northern track, the Venice *Ferrovia* could be seen speeding out of Trieste. The Sezana contact raced out of the control tower and ordered them to proceed without delay.

Annaxas fired up and throttled the idling locomotive as rapidly as possible and they plunged north behind the *Ferrovia* toward Monfalcone.

The guards at the border accepted the manila envelope and gave it to their superior officer. The officer shouted at the top of his lungs for the silent Annaxas to fire up quickly. *Proceed! The freight was part of the *Ferrovia!* The engineer was not to delay!

The madness began at Legnago, when Petride gave the dispatcher the first of Fontini-Cristi's papers. The man blanched and became the most obsequious of public servants. The young priest could see the dispatcher searching his eyes, trying to unearth the level of authority Petride represented.

For the strategy devised by Fontini-Cristi was brilliant. Its strength was in its simplicity, its power over men based in fear—the threat of instant retaliation from the state.

The Greek freight was not a Greek freight at all. It was one of the highly secretive investigating trains sent out by Rome's Ministry of Transportation, the inspectors general of the Italian rail system. Such trains roamed the tracks throughout the country, manned by officials ordered to examine and evaluate all rail operations and submit reports that some said were read by Mussolini himself.

The world made jokes about *Il Duce*'s railroads, but behind the humor was respect. The Italian rail system was the finest in Europe. It maintained its excellence by the time-honored method of the fascist state: secret efficiency ratings compiled by unknown investigators. A man's livelihood—or absence of it—depended on the judgments of the *esaminatori*. Retentions, advancements, and dismissals were often the results of a few brief moments of observation. It stood to reason that when an *esaminatore* revealed himself, absolute cooperation and confidentiality were given.

The freight from Salonika was now an Italian train with the covert imprimatur of Rome as its shield. Its movements were subject only to the authorizations contained in the papers supplied the dispatchers. And the orders within those authorizations were bizarre enough to have come from the convoluted machinations of *Il Duce* himself.

The circuitous route began. The towns and villages fled by—San Giorgio, Latisana, Motta di Levenza—as the freight from Salonika entered tracks behind Italian boxcars and passenger trains. Treviso, Montbelluna, and Valdagno, west to Malcesine on the Lago di Garda; across the large expanse

of water on the sluggish freight boat and immediately north to Breno and
Passo della Presolana.

There was only frightened cooperation. Everywhere.

When they reached Como the circling stopped and the dash began. They
sped north on the land route and swung south to Lugano, following the
tracks on the Swiss borders south and west again to Santa Maria Maggiore,
crossing into Switzerland at Saas Fee, where the freight from Salonika
resumed its identity, with one minor alteration.

This was determined by the twenty-second authorization in Petride's
pouch. Fontini-Cristi had once again provided the simple explanation: The
Swiss International Aid commission at Geneva had granted permission for
the Eastern church to cross borders and supply its retreat on the outskirts of
Val de Gressoney. What was implied was that the borders would soon be
closed to such supply trains. The war was gaining a terrible momentum; soon
there would be no trains whatever from the Balkans or Greece.

From Saas Fee the freight rolled south into the yards at Zermatt. It was
night; they would wait for the yards to close operations and a man who would
come to them and confirm that another switch had been thrown. They would
make the incursion south into the Italian Alps of Champoluc.

At ten minutes to nine a trainman appeared in the distance, coming out of
the shadows across the Zermatt freight yard. He ran the last several hundred
feet and raised his voice.

"Hurry! The rails are clear for Champoluc. There's no time to waste! The
switch is tied to a master line; it could be spotted. Get *out* of here!"

One more Annaxas went about the business of releasing the enormous
pressures built up in the fires of the iron fuselage, and once again the train
plunged into the darkness.

The signal would come in the mountains, high near an Alpine pass. No one
knew just where.

Only Savarone Fontini-Cristi.

A light snow was falling, adding its thin layer to the alabaster cover on the
moonlit ground. They passed through tunnels carved out of rock, swinging
westward around the ledges of the mountains, the steep gorges menacingly
beneath them on their right. It was so much colder. Petride had not expected
that; he had not thought about temperatures. The snow and the ice; there
was ice on the tracks.

Every mile they traveled seemed like ten, every minute that passed could
have been an hour. The young priest peered through the windshield, seeing
the beam of the train's searchlight reflecting off the falling snow. He leaned
out; he could see only the giant trees that rose up in the darkness.

Where *was* he? Where was the Italian *padrone*, Fontini-Cristi? Perhaps he
had changed his mind. O merciful God, that could not be! He could not allow
himself to think such thoughts. What they carried in that holy vault would
plunge the world into chaos. The Italian knew that; the Patriarchate had total
confidence in the *padrone*. . . .

Petride's head was aching, his temples pounded. He sat on the steps of the
tender; he had to control himself. He looked at the radium dial of his watch.
Merciful God! They'd traveled too far! In a half hour they'd be out of the
mountains!

"There is your signal!" shouted Annaxas.

Petride leaped to his feet and leaned over the side, his pulse wild, his hands
trembling as he gripped the roof ladder. Down the track no more than a

quarter of a mile, a lantern was being raised and lowered, its light flickering through the thin sheets of snow.

Annaxas braked the locomotive. The belching engine drew out its roars like the subsiding giant furnace it was. In the snow-lit, moonlit distance, aided by the beam of the locomotive's single headlight, Petride saw a man standing next to an odd-shaped vehicle in a small clearing at the side of the rails. The man was dressed in heavy clothing, collar and cap of fur. The vehicle was both a truck and not a truck. Its rear wheels were much larger than those in front, as though belonging to a tractor. Yet the hood beyond the windshield was not a truck's hood, or a tractor's, thought the priest. It resembled something else.

What was it?

Then he knew and he could not help but smile. He had seen hundreds of such pieces of equipment during the past four days. In front of the strange vehicle's hood was a vertically controlled cargo platform.

Fontini-Cristi was as resourceful as the monks in the Order of Xenope. But then the pouch strapped to his chest had told him that.

"You are the priest of Xenope?" Savarone Fontini-Cristi's voice was deep, aristocratic, and very used to authority. He was a tall man and slender beneath the Alpine clothing, with large, penetrating eyes recessed in the aquiline features of his face. And he was a much older man than Petride thought he would be.

"I am, *signore*," said Petride, climbing down into the snow.

"You're very young. The holy men have given you an awesome responsibility."

"I speak the language. I know that what I do is right."

The *padrone* stared at him. "I'm sure you do. What else is left for you?"

"Don't you believe it?"

The *padrone* replied simply. "I believe in only one thing, my young father. There is but a single war that must be fought. There can be no divisions among those who battle the fascist. *That* is the extent of what I believe." Fontini-Cristi looked up abruptly at the train. "Come. There's no time to waste. We must return before daybreak. There are clothes for you in the tractor. Get them. I'll instruct the engineer."

"He doesn't speak Italian."

"I speak Greek. Hurry!"

The freight car was lined up with the tractor. Laterally operated chains were placed around the holy vault, and the heavy iron receptacle encased in strips of wood was pulled, groaning under the tension, out onto the platform. It was secured by the chains in front; taut straps buckled over the top.

Savarone Fontini-Cristi tested the harnessing on all sides. He was satisfied; he stood back, the beam of his flashlight illuminating the monastic symbols stenciled on the encasement.

"So after fifteen hundred years it comes out of the earth. Only to be returned to the earth," said Fontini-Cristi quietly. "Earth and fire and sea. I should have chosen the last two, my young priest. Fire or the sea."

"That is not the will of God."

"I'm glad your communication is so direct. You holy men never cease to amaze me with your sense of the absolute." Fontini-Cristi turned to Annaxas and spoke fluently now in Greek. "Pull up so that I may clear the tracks. There's a narrow trail on the other side of the woods. We'll be back before dawn."

Annaxas nodded. He was uncomfortable in the presence of such a man as Fontini-Cristi. "Yes, Your Excellency."

"I'm no such thing. And you're a fine engineer."

"Thank you." Annaxas, embarrassed, walked toward the engine.

"That man is your brother?" asked Fontini-Cristi softly of Petride.

"Yes."

"He doesn't know?"

The young priest shook his head.

"You'll need your God then." The Italian turned swiftly and started for the driver's side of the enclosed tractor. "Come, Father. We have work to do. This machine was built for the avalanche. It will take our cargo where no human being could carry it."

Petride climbed into the seat. Fontini-Cristi started the powerful engine and expertly shifted gears. The platform in front of the hood was lowered, permitting visibility, and the vehicle lunged forward, vibrating across the tracks into the Alpine forest.

The priest of Xenope sat back and closed his eyes in prayer. Fontini-Cristi maneuvered the powerful machine through the rising woods toward the upper trails of the Champoluc mountains.

"I have two sons older than you," said Fontini-Cristi after a while. And then he added, "I'm taking you to the grave of a Jew. I think it's appropriate."

They returned to the Alpine clearing as the black sky was turning gray. Fontini-Cristi stared at Petride as the young priest climbed out of the strange machine. "You know where I live. My house is your house."

"We all reside in the house of the Lord, *signore*."

"So be it. Good-bye, my young friend."

"Good-bye. May God go with you."

"If He chooses."

The Italian pushed the gearshift into place and drove quickly down the barely visible road below the tracks. Petride understood. Fontini-Cristi could not lose a minute now. Every hour he was away from his estate would add to the questions that might be asked. There were many in Italy who considered the Fontini-Cristis to be enemies of the state.

They were watched. All of them.

The young priest ran through the snow toward the engine. And his brother.

Dawn came over the waters of Lago Maggiore. They were on the Stresa freight barge; the twenty-sixth authorization in the pouch was their passport. Petride wondered what would greet them in Milan, although he realized that it did not really matter.

Nothing mattered now. The journey was coming to an end.

The holy thing was in its resting place. Not to be unearthed for years; perhaps to be buried for a millennium. There was no way to tell.

They sped southeast on the main track through Varese into Castiglione. They did not wait for nightfall . . . nothing mattered now. On the outskirts of Varese, Petride saw a roadsign in the bright Italian sunlight.

CAMPO DI FIORI. 20 KIL.

God had chosen a man from Campo di Fiori. The holy secret now belonged to Fontini-Cristi.

The countryside rushed by; the air was clear and cold and exhilarating. The skyline of Milan came into view. The haze of factory smoke intruded on God's sky and lay suspended like a flat, gray tarpaulin above the horizon. The freight slowed and entered the tracks of the depot sidings. They held at a stop until a disinterested *spedizioniere* in the uniform of the state railroads pointed to a curve in the rails where a green disc snapped up in front of a red one. It was the signal to enter the Milan yards.

"We're here!" shouted Annaxas. "A day's rest, then home! I must say you people are remarkable!"

"Yes," said Petride simply. "We're remarkable."

The priest looked at his brother. The sounds of the freight yard were music to Annaxas; he sang a Greek song, his whole upper body swaying rhythmically to the sharp, fast beats of the melody.

It was strange, the song Annaxas sang. It was not a song of the railroads; it belonged to the sea. A chanty that was a favorite of the fishermen of Thermaïkós. There was something appropriate, thought Petride, about such a song at such a moment.

The sea was God's source of life. It was from the sea that He created earth.

I believe in one God . . . maker of all things. . . .

The priest of Xenope removed the large Italian pistol from under his shirt. He took two steps forward, toward his beloved brother, and raised the barrel of the weapon. It was inches from the base of Annaxas's skull.

. . . both visible and invisible . . . and in one Lord, Jesus Christ . . . only begotten of the Father. . . .

He pulled the trigger.

The explosion filled the cabin. Blood and flesh and things most terrible flew through the air and matted onto glass and metal.

. . . substance of the Father . . . God of God . . . light of light . . . very God of very God. . . .

The priest of Xenope closed his eyes and shouted in exaltation as he held the weapon against his own temple.

"*. . . begotten, not made! I will look into the eyes of the Lord and I shall not waver!*"

He fired.

PART ONE

Chapter One

December 29, 1939—Milan, Italy

Savarone walked past his son's secretary into his son's office and across the heavily carpeted floor to the window overlooking the vast factory complex that was the Fontini-Cristi Industries. His son, of course, was nowhere to be seen. His son, his *eldest* son, was rarely in his office; he was rarely in Milan, for that matter. The first son, the heir-apparent to all of Fontini-Cristi, was incorrigible. And arrogant, and far too concerned with his own creature comforts.

Vittorio was also brilliant. A far more brilliant man than the father who had trained him. And that fact only served to further infuriate Savarone; a man possessing such gifts had greater responsibilities than other men. *He* did not settle for the daily accomplishments that came naturally. He did not carouse and whore and gamble at roulette and baccarat. Or waste sleepless nights with the naked children of the Mediterranean. Neither did he turn his back on the events that were crippling his country, veering it into chaos.

Savarone heard a slight cough behind him and turned. Vittorio's secretary had come into the office.

"I've left word for your son at the Borsa Valori. I believe he was to see his broker this afternoon."

"You may believe it, but I doubt you'll find it on his calendar." Savarone saw the girl flush. "I apologize. You're not accountable for my son. Although you've probably done so, I suggest you try whatever private numbers he's given you. This is a familiar office to me. I'll wait." He removed his overcoat of light camel's hair and his hat, a Tyrolean of green felt. He threw them on the armchair at the side of the desk.

"Yes, sir." The girl left quickly, closing the door behind her.

It *was* a familiar office, thought Fontini-Cristi, although it had been necessary to call it to the girl's attention. Until two years ago, it had been his. Very little remained of his presence, now; only the dark wood paneling. All the furniture had been changed. Vittorio had accepted the four walls. Nothing else.

Savarone sat in the large swivel chair behind the desk. He did not like such chairs; he was too old to let his body be suddenly turned and sprung back by unseen springs and hidden ball bearings. He reached into his pocket and took out the telegram that had brought him to Milan from Campo di Fiori, the telegram from Rome that said the Fontini-Cristis were marked.

But marked for what? By whom? On whose orders?

Questions that could not be asked on the telephone, for the telephone was an instrument of the state. The state. Always the state. Seen and unseen. Observing, following, listening, prying. No telephone could be used and no answer given by the informer in Rome who employed the simple codes.

We have received no reply from Milan, therefore we take the liberty of wiring you personally. Five shipments of aircraft piston hammers defective. Rome insists on immediate replacement. Repeat: immediate. Please confirm by telephone before the end of the day.

The number "five" referred to the Fontini-Cristis, because there were five men in the family—a father and four sons. Anything to do with the word "hammer" meant sudden, extreme danger. The repetition of the word "immediate" was self-explanatory: not a moment could be lost, confirmation of receipt was to be made by telephone to Rome within minutes of the telegram's arrival in Milan. Other men would then be contacted, strategies analyzed, plans made. It was too late now.

The wire had been sent to Savarone that afternoon. Vittorio must have received his cable by eleven. And yet his son had neither replied to Rome nor alerted him in Campo di Fiori. The end of the day was at hand. Too late.

It was unforgivable. Men daily risked their lives and the lives of their families in the fight against Mussolini.

It had not always been so, thought Savarone, as he stared at the office door, hoping that any second the secretary would reappear with news of Vittorio's whereabouts. It had all been very different once. In the beginning, the Fontini-Cristis had endorsed *Il Duce*. The weak, indecisive Emmanuel was letting Italy die. Benito Mussolini had offered an alternative; he had come himself to Campo di Fiori to meet with the patriarch of the Fontini-Cristis, seeking alliance—as Machiavelli once so sought the backing of the princes—and he had been alive, and committed, and filled with promise for all Italy.

That was sixteen years ago; since that time Mussolini had fed upon his own rhetoric. He had robbed the nation of its right to think, the people of their freedom to choose; he had deceived the aristocrats—using them and denied their common objectives. He had plunged the country into an utterly useless African war. All for the personal glory of this Caesar Maximus. He had plundered the soul of Italy, and Savarone had vowed to stop him. Fontini-Cristi had gathered the northern "princes" together, and quietly the revolt was taking place.

Mussolini could not risk an open break with the Fontini-Cristis. Unless the charge of treason could be sustained with such clarity that even the family's most avid supporters would have to conclude they had been—if nothing else—stupid. Italy was gearing for its own entry into the German war. Mussolini had to be careful. That war was not popular, the Germans less so.

Campo di Fiori had become the meeting place of the disaffected. The sprawling acres of lawns and forests and hills and streams were suited to the clandestine nature of the conferences which generally took place at night. But not always; there were other gatherings that required the daylight hours, where younger men were trained by other experienced younger men in the arts of a new, strange warfare. The knife, the rope, the chain, and the hook. They had even coined a name for themselves: *partigiani*.

The partisans. A name that was spreading from nation to nation.

These were the games of Italy, thought Savarone. "The games of Italy" was what his son called them, a term used in derision by an arrogant, self-centered *aristocratico* who took seriously only his own pleasures. . . . No, that was not entirely true. Vittorio also took seriously the running of Fontini-Cristi, as long as pressures of the marketplace conformed to his own schedules. And he made them conform. He used his financial power ruthlessly, his expertise—the expertise he had learned at his father's side—arrogantly.

The telephone rang; Savarone was tempted to pick it up, but he did not. It was his son's office, his son's telephone. Instead, he got out of the terrible chair and walked across the room to the door. He opened it. The secretary was repeating a name.

". . . Signore Tesca?"

Savarone interrupted harshly. "Is that Alfredo Tesca?"

The girl nodded.

"Tell him to stay on the telephone. I'll speak with him."

Savarone walked rapidly back to his son's desk and the telephone. Alfredo Tesca was a foreman in one of the factories; he was also a *partigiano*.

"Fontini-Cristi," Savarone said.

"*Padrone?* I'm glad it's you. This line is clear; we check it every day."

"Nothing changes. It only accelerates."

"Yes, *padrone*. There's an emergency. A man has flown up from Rome. He must meet with a member of your family."

"Where?"

"The Olona house."

"When?"

"As soon as possible."

Savarone looked at the overcoat and the green felt hat he had thrown over the chair. "Tesca? Do you remember two years ago? The meeting at the apartment on the Duomo?"

"Yes, *padrone*. It will be six o'clock soon. I'll be waiting for you."

Fontini-Cristi hung up the telephone and reached for his overcoat and his hat. He put them on and checked his watch. It was five forty-five; he had to wait a few minutes. The walk across the concrete lot to the factory was short. He had to time it so that he entered the building at the height of the crowds; when the day shift was leaving and the night shift came to work.

His son had taken full advantage of *Il Duce*'s war machine. The Fontini-Cristi Industries operated around the clock. When the father had reproached the son, the son had replied, "We don't make munitions. We're not geared for that. The conversion would be too expensive. We make only profits, father."

His son. The most capable of them all had a hollowness in him.

Savarone's eyes fell on the photograph in the silver frame on Vittorio's desk. Its very existence was a cruel, self-inflicted joke. The face in the picture was that of a young woman, pretty in the accepted sense, with the pert, set features of a spoiled child growing into spoiled maturity. She had been Vittorio's wife. Ten years ago.

It had not been a good marriage. It had been more an industrial alliance between two immensely wealthy families. And the bride brought little to the union; she was a pouting, self-indulgent woman whose outlook was guided by possessions.

She died in an automobile crash in Monte Carlo, early in the morning after the casinos had closed. Vittorio never talked about that early morning; he had not been with his wife. Another had.

His son had spent four years in turbulent discomfort with a wife he could not stand, and yet the photograph was on his desk. Ten years later. Savarone once asked him why.

"Being a widower lends a certain respectability to my life-style."

It was seven minutes to six. Time to begin. Savarone walked out of his son's office and spoke to the secretary. "Please call downstairs and have my car brought around to the west gate. Tell my chauffeur I have a meeting at the Duomo."

"Yes, sir. . . . Do you wish to leave a number where your son can reach you?"

"Campo di Fiori. But by the time he calls, I'll no doubt be asleep."

Savarone took the private elevator to the ground floor and went out the executive entrance onto the concrete. Thirty yards away his chauffeur was walking toward the limousine with the crest of Fontini-Cristi on the door panels. The two men exchanged looks. The chauffeur nodded slightly; he knew what to do. He was a *partigiano*.

Savarone crossed the yard, aware that people were watching him. That was good; that was the way it had been two years ago when *Il Duce*'s secret police were tracking his every move, trying to unearth the whereabouts of an antifascist cell. The factory whistles blew; the day shift was released and within minutes the yard and the corridors would be crowded. The incoming workers—due at their stations at six fifteen—were flooding through the west gate.

He climbed the steps to the employees' entrance and entered the crowded, noisy corridor, removing his coat and hat in the confusion. Tesca stood by the wall, halfway toward the doors that led to the workers' lockers. He was tall and slender, very much like Savarone, and he took Savarone's coat and hat and helped Fontini-Cristi into his own worn, three-quarter-length raincoat with a newspaper in the pocket. Then he handed Savarone a large cloth visor cap. The exchange was completed without words in the jostling crowds. Tesca accepted Savarone's assistance in putting on the camel's hair coat; the employer saw that the employee had taken the trouble—as he had done two years ago—to change into pressed trousers, shined shoes, and a white shirt and tie.

The *partigiano* entered the flow of human traffic to the exit doors. Savarone followed ten yards behind, then stood immobile on the crowded platform outside the constantly opening doors, pretending to read the newspaper.

He saw what he wanted to see. The camel's hair coat and the green Tyrolean hat stood out among the worn leather jackets and frayed workers' clothing. Two men beyond the throngs signaled each other and began the chase, making their way through the crowd as best they could in an effort to catch up. Savarone squeezed himself into the stream of workers and arrived at the gate in time to see the door of the Fontini-Cristi limousine close and the huge automobile roll into the traffic of the Via di Sempione. The two pursuers were at the curb; a gray Fiat pulled up and they climbed in.

The Fiat took up the chase. Savarone turned north and walked swiftly to the corner bus stop.

The house on the riverfront was a relic that once, perhaps a decade ago, had been painted white. From the outside it looked dilapidated, but inside the rooms were small, neat, and organized; they were places of work, an antifascist headquarters.

Savarone entered the room with the windows overlooking the murky waters of the Olona River, made black by the darkness of night. Three men rose from the straight-backed chairs around a table and greeted him with feeling and respect. Two were known to him; the third, he presumed, was from Rome.

"The hammer code was sent this morning," said Savarone. "What does it mean?"

"You *received* the wire?" asked the man from Rome incredulously. "All telegrams to Fontini-Cristi in Milan were intercepted. It's why I'm here. All communications to your factories were stopped."

"I received mine at Campo di Fiori. Through the telegraph office in Varese, I imagine, not Milan." Savarone felt a minor relief in knowing his son had not disobeyed. "Have you the information?"

"Not all, *padrone*," replied the man. "But enough to know it's extremely serious. And imminent. The military is suddenly very concerned with the northern movement. The generals want it crippled; they intend to see your family exposed."

"As what?"

"As enemies of the new Italy."

"On what grounds?"

"For holding meetings of a treasonable nature at Campo di Fiori. Spreading antistate lies; of attempting to undermine Rome's objectives and corrupt the industrial arm of the country."

"Words."

"Nevertheless, an example is to be made. They demand it, they say."

"Nonsense. Rome wouldn't dare move against us on such tenuous grounds."

"That is the problem, *signore*," said the man hesitantly. "It's not Rome. It's Berlin."

"*What?*"

"The Germans are everywhere, giving orders to everyone. The word is that Berlin wants the Fontini-Cristis stripped of influence."

"They look to the future, don't they," stated one of the other two men, an older *partigiano* who had walked to the window.

"How do they propose to accomplish this?" asked Savarone.

"By smashing a meeting at Campo di Fiori. Forcing those there to bear witness to the treasons of the Fontini-Cristis. That would be less difficult than you think, I believe."

"Agreed. It's the reason we've been careful. . . . When will this happen? Do you have any idea?"

"I left Rome at noon. I can only assume the code word 'hammer' was used correctly."

"There's a meeting tonight."

"Then 'hammer' was called for. Cancel it, *padrone*. Obviously, word got out."

"I'll need your help. I'll give you names . . . our telephones are unsafe." Fontini-Cristi began writing in a notebook on the table with a pencil supplied by the third *partigiano*.

"When's the meeting scheduled?"

"Ten thirty. There's enough time," replied Savarone.

"I hope so. Berlin is thorough."

Fontini-Cristi stopped writing and looked over at the man. "That's a strange thing to say. The Germans may bark orders in the Campidoglio;

they're not in Milan."

The three partisans exchanged glances. Savarone knew there was further news he had not received. The man from Rome finally spoke.

"As I said, our information is not complete. But we know certain things. The degree of Berlin's interest, for example. The German high command wants Italy to openly declare itself. Mussolini wavers; for many reasons, not the least of which is the opposition of such powerful men as yourself——" The man stopped; he was unsure. Not, apparently, of his information, but how to say it.

"What are you driving at?"

"They say that Berlin's interest in the Fontini-Cristis is Gestapo inspired. It's the Nazis who demand the example; who intend to crush Mussolini's opposition."

"I gathered that. So?"

"They have little confidence in Rome, none in the provinces. The raiding party will be led by Germans."

"A German raiding party out of *Milan?*"

The man nodded.

Savarone put down the pencil and stared at the man from Rome. But his thoughts were not on the man; they were on a Greek freight from Salonika he had met high in the mountains of Champoluc. On the cargo that train carried. A vault from the Patriarchate of Constantine, now buried in the frozen earth of the upper regions.

It seemed incredible, but the incredible was commonplace in these times of madness. Had Berlin found out about the train from Salonika? Did the Germans know about the vault? *Mother of Christ*, it had to be kept from them! And all—*all*—*like* them!

"You're sure of your information?"

"We are."

Rome could be managed, thought Savarone. Italy needed the Fontini-Cristi Industries. But if the German intrusion was linked to the vault from Constantine, Berlin would not consider Rome's needs in the slightest. The possession of the vault was *everything*.

And, therefore, the protection of it essential beyond all life. Above all things its secret could not fall into the wrong hands. Not now. Perhaps not ever, but certainly not now.

The key was Vittorio. It was always Vittorio, the most capable of them all. For whatever else he was, Vittorio was a Fontini-Cristi. He would honor the family's commitment; he was a match for Berlin. The time had come to tell him about the train from Salonika. Detail the family's arrangements with the monastic Order of Xenope. The timing was right, the strategy complete.

A date marked in stone, etched for a millennium, was only a hint, a clue in case of a sudden failing of the heart, death from abrupt natural or unnatural causes. It was not enough.

Vittorio had to be told, charged with a responsibility beyond anything in his imagination. The documents from Constantine made everything else pale into insignificance.

Savarone looked up at the three men. "The meeting will be canceled tonight. The raiding party will find only a large family gathering. A holiday dinner party. All my children and their children. However, for it to be complete, my oldest son must be at Campo di Fiori. I've tried calling him all afternoon. Now you must find him. Use your telephones. Call everyone in

Milan if you have to, but *find him!* If it gets late, tell him to use the stable road. It wouldn't do for him to enter with the raiding party."

Chapter Two

December 29, 1939—Lake Como, Italy

The white, twelve-cylinder Hispano-Suiza, its off-white leather top rolled halfway back, uncovering the front, red leather seat, took the long curve at high speed. Below on the left were the winter-blue waters of Lake Como, to the right the mountains of Lombardy.

"Vittorio!" shrieked the girl beside the driver, holding her wind-shocked blonde hair with one hand, her collar of Russian pony with the other. "I'll be undone, my lamb!"

The driver smiled, his squinting gray eyes steady on the onrushing road in the sunlight, his hands expertly, almost delicately, feeling the play in the ivory steering wheel. "The Suiza is a far better car than the Alfa-Romeo. The British Rolls is no comparison."

"You don't have to prove it to *me*, darling. My God, I refuse to look at the speedometer! And I'll be an absolute mess!"

"Good. If your husband's in Bellagio, he won't recognize you. I'll introduce you as a terribly sweet cousin from Verona."

The girl laughed. "If my husband's in Bellagio, he'll have a terribly sweet cousin to introduce to *us*."

They both laughed. The curve came to an end, the road straightened, and the girl slid over next to the driver. She slipped her hand under the arm of his tan suede jacket, enlarged by the heavy wool of the white turtleneck sweater beneath; briefly she placed her face against his shoulder.

"It was sweet of you to call. I really had to get away."

"I knew that. It was in your eyes last night. You were bored to death."

"Well, God, weren't *you*? Such a dreary dinner party! Talk, talk, talk! War this, war that. Rome yes, Rome no, Benito always. I'm positively sick of it! Gstaad closed! St. Moritz filled with Jews throwing money at everyone! Monte Carlo an absolute fiasco! The casinos are closing, you know. Everybody says so. It's all such a *bore!*"

The driver let his right hand drop from the steering wheel and reached for the fold of the girl's overcoat. He separated the fur and caressed her inner thigh as expertly as he fingered the ivory steering wheel. She moaned pleasantly and craned her neck, putting her lips to his ear, her tongue darting.

"You continue that, we'll end up in the water. I suspect it's damned cold."

"You started it, my lovely Vittorio."

"I'll stop it," he said smiling, returning his hand to the wheel. "I won't be able to buy another like this for a long time. Today everything is the tank. Far less profit in the tank."

"Please! No war talk."

"You'll get none from me," said Fontini-Cristi, laughing again. "Unless you want to negotiate a purchase for Rome. I'll sell you anything from conveyor belts to motorcycles to uniforms, if you like."

"You don't make uniforms."

"We own a company that does."

"I forgot. Fontini-Cristi owns everything north of Parma and west of Padua. At least, that's what my husband says. Quite enviously, of course."

"Your husband, the sleepy count, is a dreadful businessman."

"He doesn't mean to be."

Vittorio Fontini-Cristi smiled as he braked the long white automobile for a descending curve in the road toward the lakeshore. Halfway down, on the promontory that was Bellagio, stood the elegant Villa Lario, named for the ancient poet of Como. It was a resort lodge known for its extraordinary beauty, as well as its marked exclusivity.

When the elite moved north, they played at Villa Lario. Money and family were their methods of entry. The *commessi* were diffident, soft-spoken, aware of their clientele's every proclivity, and most alert as to the scheduling of reservations. It was uncommon for a husband or a wife, a lover or a mistress, to receive a quiet, cautioning phone call suggesting another date for arrival. Or rapid departure.

The Hispano-Suiza swerved into the parking lot of blue brick; two uniformed attendants raced from the heated booth to both sides of the automobile, opening the doors and bowing.

The attendant at Vittorio's side spoke. "Welcome to Villa Lario, *signore*."

It was never nice-to-see-you-again-*signore*.

Never.

"Thank you. We have no luggage. We're here only for the day. See to the oil and petrol. Is the mechanic around?"

"Yes, sir."

"Have him check the alignment. There's too much play."

"Of course, *signore*."

Fontini-Cristi got out of the car. He was a tall man, over six feet in height. His straight, dark-brown hair fell over his forehead; his features were sharp—as aquiline as his father's—and his eyes, still squinting in the bright sunlight, were at once passive and alert. He walked in front of the white hood, absently feeling the radiator cap, and smiled at his companion, the Contessa d'Avenzo. Together they crossed to the stone steps leading up to the entrance of Villa Lario.

"Where did you tell the servants you were off to?" asked Fontini-Cristi.

"Treviglio. You are a horse trainer who wants to sell me an Arabian."

"Remind me to buy you one."

"And you? What did you say at your office?"

"Nothing, really. Only my brothers might ask for me; everyone else waits patiently."

"But not your brothers." The Contessa d'Avenzo smiled. "I like that. The important Vittorio is hounded in business by his brothers."

"Hardly! My sweet younger brothers have between them three wives and eleven children. Their problems are continuously and forever domestic. I think sometimes I'm a referee. Which is fine; they keep occupied and *away* from business."

They stood on the terrace outside the glass doors that led to the lobby of Villa Lario and looked down at the enormous lake and across to the mountains beyond.

"It's beautiful," said the contessa. "You've arranged for a room?"

"A suite. The penthouse. The view's magnificent."

"I've heard of it. I've never been up there."

"Few people have."

"I imagine you lease it by the month."

"That's not really necessary," said Fontini-Cristi, turning toward the huge glass doors. "You see, as it happens I own Villa Lario."

The Contessa d'Avenzo laughed. She preceded Vittorio into the lobby. "You are an *impossible,* *a*moral man. You get richer from your own kind. My God, you could blackmail half of Italy!"

"Only *our* Italy, my dear."

"That's enough!"

"Hardly. But I've never had to, if it relieves your mind. I'm merely a guest. Wait here, please."

Vittorio walked over to the front desk. The tuxedoed clerk behind the marble counter greeted him. "How good of you to come to see us, Signore Fontini-Cristi."

"Are things going well?"

"Extremely so. Would you care to——?"

"No, I should not," interrupted Vittorio. "I assume my rooms are ready."

"Of course, *signore*. As you requested, an early supper is being prepared. Caviar Iranian, cold pressed duck, Veuve Cliquot twenty-eight."

"And?"

"There are flowers, naturally. The masseur is prepared to cancel his other appointments."

"And . . . ?"

"There are no complications for the Contessa d'Avenzo," answered the clerk quickly, rapidly. "None of her circle is here."

"Thank you." Fonti-Cristi turned, only to be stopped by the sound of the clerk's voice.

"*Signore?* "

"Yes?"

"I realize you do not care to be disturbed except in emergencies, but your office called."

"Did my office say it was an emergency?"

"They said your father was trying to locate you."

"That's not an emergency. It's a whim."

"I think you may be that Arabian, after all, lamb," mused the contessa out loud, lying beside Vittorio in the feather bed. The eiderdown quilt was pulled down to her naked waist. "You're marvelous. And so patient."

"But not patient enough, I think," replied Fontini-Cristi. He sat up against the pillow, looking down at the girl; he was smoking a cigarette.

"Not patient enough," agreed the Contessa d'Avenzo, turning her face and smiling up at him. "Why don't you put out the cigarette?"

"In a little while. Be assured of it. Some wine?" He gestured at the silver ice bucket within arm's reach. It stood on a tripod; an open bottle draped with a linen towel was pushed into the melting crushed ice.

The contessa stared at him, her breath coming shorter. "You pour the wine. I'll drink my own."

In swift, gentle movements, the girl turned and reached under the soft quilt with both hands to Vittorio's groin. She raised the cover and placed her

face underneath, over Vittorio. The quilt fell back, covering her head as her
throaty moans grew louder and her body writhed.

The waiters cleared away the dishes and rolled out the tables, a *commesso*
lighted a fire in the fireplace and poured brandy.

"It's been a lovely day," said the Contessa d'Avenzo. "May we do it
often?"

"I think we should set up a schedule. By your calendar, of course."

"Of course." The girl laughed throatily. "You're a very practical man."

"Why not? It's easier."

The telephone rang. Vittorio looked over at it, annoyed. He rose from the
chair in front of the fireplace and crossed angrily to the bedside table. He
picked up the instrument and spoke harshly. "Yes?"

The voice at the other end was vaguely familiar. "This is Tesca. Alfredo
Tesca."

"*Who?*"

"One of the foremen in the Milan factories."

"You're *what?* How *dare* you call here! How did you get this number?"

Tesca was silent for a moment. "I threatened the life of your secret
secretary, young *padrone*. And I would have killed her had she not given it to
me. You may fire me tomorrow. I am your foreman, but I am a *partigiano*
first."

"You *are* fired. *Now*. As of this moment!"

"So be it, *signore*."

"I want no part——."

"*Basta!*" shouted Tesca. "There's no time! Everyone's looking for you.
The *padrone*'s in danger. Your whole *family*'s in danger! Go to Campo di
Fiori! At once! Your father says to use the stable road!"

The telephone went dead.

Savarone walked through the great hall into the enormous dining room of
Campo di Fiori. Everything was as it should be. The room was filled with
sons and daughters, husbands and wives, and a thoroughly boisterous crowd
of grandchildren. The servants had placed silver trays of antipasto on the tops
of marble tables. A tall pine that reached the high beamed ceiling was a
magnificent Christmas tree, its myriad lights and glittering ornament filling
the room with reflections of color that bounced off the tapestries and the
ornate furniture.

Outside in the circular drive in front of the marble steps of the entrance
were four automobiles illuminated by the floodlights that beamed down from
the eaves. They could easily be mistaken for anyone's automobiles, which
was what Savarone intended. For when the raiding party arrived, all it would
find was an innocent, festive family gathering. A holiday dinner. Nothing
else.

Except an imperiously aggravated patriarch of one of Italy's most powerful
clans. The *padrone* of the Fontini-Cristis, who would demand to know who
was responsible for such a barbarous intrusion.

Only Vittorio was missing; and his presence was vital. Questions might be
raised that could lead to other questions. The unwilling Vittorio, who scoffed
at their work, could become an unjustified target of suspicion. What was a
holiday family dinner without the eldest son, the primary heir? Further, if
Vittorio appeared *during* the intrusion, arrogantly reluctant—as his cus-

tom—to give an account of himself to anyone, there could be trouble. His son refused to acknowledge the extent, but Rome *was* under Berlin's thumb.

Savarone beckoned his next eldest, the serious Antonio, who stood with his wife as she admonished one of their children.

"Yes, father?"

"Go to the stables. See Barzini. Tell him that if Vittorio arrives during the fascists' visit, he's to say he was detained at one of the plants."

"I can call him on the stable phone."

"No. Barzini's getting on. He pretends it's not so, but he's growing deaf. Make sure he understands."

The second son nodded dutifully. "Yes, of course, father. Anything you say."

What in God's name had his father *done*? What *could* he do that would give Rome the confidence, the *excuse*, to move openly against the house of Fontini-Cristi?

Your whole family is in danger.

Preposterous!

Mussolini courted the northern industrialists; he needed them. He knew that most were old men, set in their ways, and knew he could achieve more with honey than vinegar. What did it matter if a few Savarones played their silly games? Their time was past.

But then there was only one Savarone. Separate and apart from all other men. He had become, perhaps, that terrible thing, a symbol. With his silly, goddamned *partigiani*. Ragtail lunatics who raced around the fields and the woods of Campo di Fiori pretending they were some kind of primitive tribesmen hunting tigers and killer lions.

Jesus! *Children!*

Well, it would all come to a stop. *Padrone* or no *padrone*, if his father had gone too far and embarrassed them, there would be a confrontation. He had made it clear to Savarone two years ago that when he assumed the reins of Fontini-Cristi, it meant that all the leather was in his hands.

Suddenly Vittorio remembered. Two weeks ago, Savarone had gone to Zürich for a few days. At least, he *said* he was going to Zürich. It wasn't really clear; he, Vittorio, had not been listening closely. But during those few days, it was unexpectedly necessary to get his father's signature on several contracts. So necessary that he had telephoned every hotel in Zürich, trying to locate Savarone. He was nowhere to be found. No one had seen him, and his father was not easily overlooked.

And when he returned to Campo di Fiori, he would not say where he had been. He was maddeningly enigmatic, telling his son that he would explain everything in a few days. An incident would take place in Monfalcone and when it occurred, Vittorio would be told. Vittorio *had* to be told.

What in hell was his father talking about? *What* incident at Monfalcone? Why would *anything* taking place at Monfalcone concern them?

Preposterous!

But Zürich wasn't preposterous at all. Banks were in Zürich. Had Savarone manipulated money in Zürich? Had he transferred extraordinary sums out of Italy into Switzerland? There was specific laws against that these days. Mussolini needed every *lira* he could keep. And God knew the family had sufficient reserves in Berne and Geneva; there was no lack of Fontini-Cristi capital in Switzerland.

Whatever Savarone had done, it would be his last gesture. If his father was so politically involved, let him go somewhere else and proselytize. America, perhaps.

Vittorio shook his head slowly in defeat, as he steered the Hispano-Suiza onto the road out of Varese. What was he thinking of? Savarone was—Savarone. The head of the house of Fontini-Cristi. No matter the son's talents or expertise, the son was not the *padrone*.

Use the stable road.

What was the point of that? The stable road started at the north end of the property, three miles from the east gates. Nevertheless, he would use it; his father must have had a reason for giving the order. No doubt as implausible as the foolish games he indulged in, but a surface filial obedience was called for; the son was going to be very firm with the father.

What had happened in Zürich?

He passed the main gates on the road out of Varese and proceeded to the intersecting west road three miles beyond. He turned left and drove nearly two miles to the north gate, turning left again into Campo di Fiori. The stables were three-quarters of a mile from the entrance; the road was dirt. It was easier on the horses, for this was the road used by riders heading for the fields and trails north and west of the forest at the center of Campo di Fiori. The forest behind the great house was bisected by the wide stream that flowed from the northern mountains.

In the headlights he saw the figure of old Guido Barzini waving his arms, signaling him to stop. The gnarled Barzini was something: a fixture at Campo di Fiori who had spent his life in the service of the house.

"Quickly, Signore Vittorio!" said Barzini through the open window. "Leave your car here. There's no more time."

"Time for what?"

"The *padrone* spoke to me not five minutes ago. He said if you drove in now, you were to call him on the stable telephone before you went to the house. It's nearly half past the hour."

Vittorio looked at the dashboard clock. It was twenty-eight minutes past ten. "What's going on?"

"Hurry, *signore! Please!* The *fascisti!*"

"What *fascisti*?"

"The *padrone*. He'll tell you."

Fontini-Cristi got out of the car and followed Barzini down the stone path into the entrance of the stables. It was a tack room; bits and braces and halters and leather were hung neatly on the walls, surrounding countless plaques and ribbons, proof of the superiority of the Fontini-Cristi colors. Also on the wall was the telephone that connected the stables to the great house.

"What's going on, father? Have you any idea who called me in Bellagio?"

"*Basta!*" roared Savarone over the telephone. "They'll be here any moment. A German raiding party."

"*Germans?*"

"Yes. Rome expects to find a *partigiano* meeting taking place. They won't, of course. They'll intrude on a family dinner. *Remember!* A family dinner party was on your calendar. You were detained in Milan."

"What have Germans got to do with Rome?"

"I'll explain later. Just remember——"

Suddenly, over the telephone, Vittorio heard the sounds of screeching tires and powerful motors. A column of automobiles was speeding toward the great house from the east gates.

"*Father!*" yelled Vittorio. "Has this anything to do with your trip to Zürich?"

There was silence over the phone. Finally Savarone spoke. "It may have, You must stay where you are——"

"What happened? What happened in Zürich?"

"Not Zürich. Champoluc."

"What?"

"Later! I have to get back to the others. Stay where you are! Out of sight! We'll talk when they leave."

Vittorio heard the click. He turned to Barzini. The old stable master was riffling through a low chest of drawers filled with odd bits and braces; he found what he was looking for: a pistol and a pair of binoculars. He pulled them out and handed both to Vittorio.

"Come!" he said, his old eyes angry. "We'll watch. The *padrone* will teach them a lesson."

They ran down the dirt road toward the house and the gardens above and behind it. When the dirt became pavement they cut to their left and climbed the embankment overlooking the circular drive. They were in darkness; the whole area below bathed in floodlights.

Three automobiles sped up the east-gate road; long, black, powerful vehicles, their headlights emerging out of the darkness, swallowed by the floodlamps that washed the area in white light. The cars entered the circular drive, careening to the left of the other automobiles, stopping suddenly, equidistant from each other in front of the stone steps that led to the thick oak doors of the entrance.

Men leaped out of the cars. Men dressed alike in black suits and black overcoats; men carrying weapons.

Carrying *weapons!*

Vittorio stared as the men—seven, eight, nine—raced up the steps to the door. A tall man in front assumed command; he held his hand up to those behind, ordering them to flank the doors, four on each side. He pulled the bell chain with his left hand, his right holding a pistol at his side.

Vittorio put the binoculars to his eyes. The man's face was turned away toward the door, but the weapon in his hand came into focus. It was a German Luger. Vittorio swung the binoculars to those on both sides of the doors.

The weapons were all German. Four Lugers, four Bergmann MP38 submachine guns.

Vittorio's stomach suddenly convulsed; his mind caught fire as he watched in disbelief. What had Rome *permitted?* It was incredible!

He focused the binoculars on the three automobiles. In each was a man; all were in shadows, only the backs of their heads seen through the rear windows. Vittorio concentrated on the nearest car, on the man inside that car.

The man shifted his position in the seat and looked back to his right; the light from the floodlamps caught his hair. It was close-cropped, grayish hair, but with a white streak shooting up from his forehead. There was something familiar about the man—the shape of the head, the streak of white in the hair—but Vittorio could not place him.

The door of the house opened; a maid stood in the frame, startled by the sight of the tall man with a gun. Vittorio stared in fury at the scene below.

Rome would pay for the insult. The tall man pushed the maid aside and burst through the door, followed by the squad of eight men, their weapons held in front of them. The maid disappeared in the phalanx of bodies.

Rome would pay dearly!

There were shouts from inside. Vittorio could hear his father's roar and the subsequent shouted objections of his brothers.

There was a loud crash, a combination of glass and wood. Vittorio reached for the pistol in his pocket. He felt a powerful hand grip his wrist.

It was Barzini. The old stable master held Vittorio's hand, but he was looking over his shoulder, staring below.

"There are too many guns. You'll solve nothing," he said simply.

A third crash came from below, the sound nearer now. The left panel of the huge oak double door had been thrown open and figures emerged. The children, first, bewildered, some crying in fear. Then the women, his sisters and his brothers' wives. Then his mother, her head defiant, the youngest child in her arms. His father and his brothers followed, prodded violently by the weapons in the hands of the black-suited men.

They were herded onto the pavement of the circular drive. His father's voice roared above the others, demanding to know who was responsible for the outrage.

But the outrage had not begun.

When it did, the mind of Vittorio Fontini-Cristi snapped. Cracks of thunder deafened him, streaks of lightning blinded him. He lunged foward, every ounce of his strength trying to wrench his hand free of Barzini's grip, twisting, turning, trying desperately to free his neck and his jaw from Barzini's stranglehold.

For the black-suited men below had opened fire. Women threw themselves over the children, his brothers lurched at the weapons that shattered the night with fire and death. The screams of terror and pain and outrage swelled in the blinding light of the execution grounds. Smoke billowed; bodies froze in midair—suspended in blood-soaked garments. Children were cut in half, the bullets ripping out mouths and eyes. Pieces of flesh and skull and intestine shot through the swirling mists. A child's body exploded in its mother's arms. And still Vittorio Fontini-Cristi could not free himself, could not go to his own.

He felt dead weight pressing him downward, then a clawing, choking, pulling at his lower jaw that blocked all sound from his lips.

And then the words pierced through the cacophony of gunshot and human screams below. The voice was tremendous, its thunder chopped by the firepower of submachine guns, but not stopped.

It was his father. Calling to him over the chasms of death.

"*Champoluc* . . . Zürich is *Champoluc*. . . . Zürich is the *river* . . . *Champoluuuc*. . . ."

Vittorio gnashed his teeth down on the fingers inside his mouth, pulling his jaw out of its socket. He wrenched his hand free for an instant—the hand with the weapon—and tried to raise the pistol and fire below.

But suddenly he could not. The sea of heaviness was over him again, his wrist twisted beyond endurance; the pistol was shaken loose. The enormous hand that had gripped his jaw was pushing his face into the cold earth. He could feel the blood in his mouth, over his lips, mingled with dirt.

And the horrible scream from the abyss of death came once more.

"*Champoluc!*"

And then was stilled.

Chapter Three

December 30, 1939

"Champoluc . . . Zürich is Champoluc . . . Zürich is the river. . . ."

The words were screams and they were blurred in agony. His mind's eye was filled with white light and explosions of smoke and deep red streaks of blood; his ears heard the screams of jolting shock, and terror, and the outrage of infinite pain and terrible murder.

It had happened. He had borne witness to the tableau of execution: strong men, trembling children, wives and mothers. His own.

Oh, my God!

Vittorio twisted his head and buried his face into the coarse cloth of the primitive bed, the tears flowing down his cheeks. It was cloth, not cold rough dirt; he had been moved. The last thing he remembered was his face being pressed with enormous strength into the hard ground of the embankment. Pressed down and held furiously immobile, his eyes blinded, his lips filled with warm blood and cold earth.

Only his ears bearing witness to the agony.

"Champoluc!"

Mother of God, it had happened!

The Fontini-Cristis were massacred in the white lights of Campo di Fiori. All the Fontini-Cristis but one. And that one would make Rome pay. The last Fontini-Cristi would cut the flesh, layer by layer, from *Il Duce*'s face; the eyes would be last, the blade would enter slowly.

"Vittorio. Vittorio."

He heard his name and yet he did not hear it. It was a whisper, an urgent whisper, and whispers were dreams of agony.

"Vittorio." The weight was on his arms again; the whisper came from above, in the darkness. The face of Guido Barzini was inches from his, the sad strong eyes of the stablemaster were reflected in a shaft of dim light.

"Barzini?" It was all he could manage to say.

"Forgive me. There was no choice, no other way. You would have been killed with the rest."

"Yes, I know. Executed. But *why?* In the name of God, *why?*"

"The Germans. That's all we know at the moment. The Germans wanted the Fontini-Cristis dead. They want you dead. The ports, the airfields, the roads, all of northern Italy is sealed off."

"Rome allowed it." Vittorio could still taste the blood in his mouth, still feel the pain in his jaw.

"Rome hides," said Barzini softly. "Only a few speak."

"What do they say?"

"What the Germans want them to say. That the Fontini-Cristis were traitors, killed by their own people. That the family was aiding the French, sending arms and monies across the borders."

"Preposterous."

"Rome is preposterous. And filled with cowards. The informer was found. He hangs naked from his feet in the Piazza del Duomo, his body riddled, his tongue nailed to his head. A *partigiano* placed a sign below; it says, 'This pig betrayed Italy, his blood flows from the stigmata of the Fontini-Cristis.'"

Vittorio turned away. The images burned; the white smoke in the white light, the bodies suspended, abruptly immobile in death, a thousand sudden blots of thick red; the execution of children.

"Champoluc," whispered Vittorio Fontini-Cristi.

"I beg your pardon?"

"My father. As he was dying, as the gunfire ravaged him, he shouted the name, Champoluc. Something happened in Champoluc."

"What does it mean?"

"I don't know. Champoluc is in the Alps, deep in the mountains. 'Zürich is Champoluc. Zürich is the river.' He said that. He shouted it as he died. Yet there's no river in the Champoluc."

"I cannot help you," said Barzini, sitting up, the anxiety in his questioning eyes and in the awkward rubbing together of his large hands. "There's not a great deal of time to dwell on it, or to think. Not now."

Vittorio looked up at the huge, embarrassed farmhand sitting on the side of the primitive bed. They were in a room built of heavy wood. There was a door, only partially open, ten or fifteen feet away, on his left, but no windows. There were several other beds; he could not tell how many. It was a barracks for laborers.

"Where are we?"

"Across the Maggiore, south of Baveno. On a goat farm."

"How did we get here?"

"A wild trip. The men at the riverfront drove us out. They met us with a fast car on the road west of Campo di Fiori. The *partigiano* from Rome knows the drugs; he gave you a hypodermic needle."

"You carried me from the embankment to the west road?"

"Yes."

"It's more than a mile."

"Perhaps. You're large, but not so heavy." Barzini stood up.

"You saved my life." Vittorio pressed his hands on the coarse blanket and raised himself to a sitting position, his back against the wall.

"Revenge is not found in one's own death."

"I understand."

"We must both travel. You out of Italy, me to Campo di Fiori."

"You're going back?"

"It's where I can do the most good. The most damage."

Fontini-Cristi stared for a moment at Barzini. How quickly the unimaginable became the practical reality. How rapidly did men react savagely to the savage; and how necessary was that reaction. But there was no time. Barzini was right; the thinking would come later.

"Is there a way for me to get out of the country? You said all of northern Italy was sealed off."

"All the usual routes. It is a manhunt mounted by Rome, directed by the Germans. There are other ways. The British will help, I am told."

"The British?"

"That is the word. They have been on *partigiano* radios all through the night."

"The British? I don't understand."

The vehicle was an old farm truck with poor brakes and a sliding clutch, but it was sturdy enough for the badly paved back roads. It was no match for motorcycles or official automobiles, but excellent for traveling from one point to another in the farm country—one more truck carrying a few livestock that lurched unsteadily in the open, slatted van.

Vittorio was dressed, as was his driver, in the filthy, dung-encrusted, sweat-stained clothes of a farm laborer. He was provided with a dirty, mutilated identification card that gave his name as Aldo Ravena, former *soldato semplice* in the Italian army. It could be assumed his schooling was minimal; any conversation he might have with the police would be simple, blunt, and perhaps a touch hostile.

They had been driving since dawn, southwest into Torino, where they swung southeast toward Alba. With no serious interruptions they would reach Alba by nightfall.

At an *espresso* bar in Alba's main piazza, San Giorno, they would make contact with the British; two operatives sent in by MI6. It would be their job to get Fontini-Cristi down to the coast and through the patrols that guarded every mile of waterfront from Genoa to San Remo. Italian personnel, German efficiency, Vittorio was told.

This area of the coast in the Gulf of Genoa was considered the most conducive to infiltration. For years it had been a primary source route for Corsican smugglers. Indeed the *Unio Corso* claimed the beaches and rocky ocean cliffs as their own. They called this coast the soft belly of Europe; they knew every inch.

Which was fine as far as the British were concerned. They employed the Corsicans, whose services went to the highest bidders. The *Unio Corso* would aid London in getting Fontini-Cristi through the patrols and out on the water where, in a prearranged rendezvous north of Rogliano on the Corsican coast, a submarine from the Royal Navy would surface and pick him up.

This was the information Vittorio was given—by the ragtail lunatics he had scorned as children playing primitive games. The unkempt, wild-eyed fools who had formed an untenable alliance with such men as his father had saved his life. *Were* saving his life. Skinny peasant thugs who had direct communication with the far-off British . . . far off and not so distant. No farther than Alba.

How? Why? What in the name of God were the English doing? Why were they doing it? What were men he had barely acknowledged, hardly spoken to in his life before—except to order and ignore—what were *they* doing. And *why?* He was no friend; no enemy, perhaps, but certainly no friend.

These were the questions that frightened Vittorio Fontini-Cristi. A nightmare had exploded in white light and death, and he was not capable of fathoming—even wanting—his own survival.

They were eight miles from Alba on a curving dirt road that paralleled the main highway from Torino. The *partigiano* driver was weary, his eyes bloodshot from the long day of bright sunlight. The shadows of early evening were now playing tricks on his eyes; his back obviously ached from the constant strain. Except for infrequent fuel stops he had not left his seat. Time was vital.

"Let me drive a while."

"We're nearly there, *signore*. You don't know this road; I do. We'll enter Alba from the east, on the Canelli highway. There may be soldiers at the municipal limits. Remember what you're to say."

"As little as possible, I think."

The truck entered the light traffic on the Via Canelli and maintained a steady speed with the other vehicles. As the driver had predicted, there were two soldiers at the municipal line.

For any of a dozen reasons, the truck was signaled to stop. They pulled off the road onto the shoulder of sand and waited. A sergeant approached the driver's window, a private stood laconically outside Fontini-Cristi's.

"Where are you from?" asked the sergeant.

"A farm south of Baveno," the *partigiano* said.

"You've come a long way for such a small delivery. I count five goats."

"Breeding stock. They're better animals than they look. Ten thousand *lire* for the males; eight for the females."

The sergeant raised his eyebrows. He did not smile as he spoke. "You don't look like *you're* worth that, *paisan*. Your identification."

The partisan reached into his rear pocket and pulled out a worn billfold. He withdrew the state card and handed it to the soldier.

"This says you're from Varallo."

"I come from Varallo. I work in Baveno."

"*South* of Baveno," corrected the soldier coldly. "*You*," said the sergeant, addressing Vittorio. "Your identification."

Fontini-Cristi put his hand into his jacket, bypassing the handle of his pistol, and removed the card. He handed it to the driver, who gave it to the soldier.

"You were in Africa?"

"Yes, sergeant," replied Vittorio bluntly.

"What corps?"

Fontini-Cristi was silent. He had no answer. His mind raced, trying to recall from the news a number, or a name. "The Seventh," he said.

"I see." The sergeant returned the card; Vittorio exhaled. But the relief was short-lived. The soldier reached for the handle of the door, yanked it downward and pulled the door open swiftly. "Get out! Both of you!"

"What? Why?" objected the partisan in a loud whine. "We have to make our delivery by nightfall! There's barely time!"

"Get *out*." The sergeant had removed his army revolver from the black leather holster and was pointing it at both men. He barked his orders across the hood to the private. "Pull him out! Cover him!"

Vittorio looked at the driver. The partisan's eyes told him to do as he was told. But to stay alert, be ready to move; the man's eyes told him that also.

Out of the truck on the shoulder of sand, the sergeant commanded both men to walk toward the guardhouse that stood next to a telephone pole. A telephone wire sagged down from a junction box and was attached to the roof of the small enclosure; the door was narrow, and open.

On the Via Canelli the twilight traffic was heavier now; or it seemed heavier to Fontini-Cristi. There were mostly cars, with a scattering of trucks, not unlike the farm truck they were driving. A number of drivers slowed perceptibly at the sight of the two soldiers, their weapons drawn, marching the two civilians to the guardhouse. Then the drivers speeded up, anxious to be away.

"You have no right to stop us!" cried the partisan. "We've done nothing illegal. It's no crime to earn a living!"

"It's a crime to give false information, *paisan*."

"We gave no false information! We are workers from Baveno, and, by the Mother of God, that's the truth!"

"Be careful," said the soldier sarcastically. "We'll add sacrilege to the charges. Get inside!"

The roadside guardhouse seemed even smaller than it appeared from the Via Canelli. The depth was no more than five feet, the length perhaps six.

There was barely enough room for the four of them. And the look in the partisan's eyes told Vittorio that the close quarters was an advantage.

"Search them," ordered the sergeant.

The private placed his rifle on the floor, barrel up. The partisan driver then did a strange thing. He pulled his arms across his chest, protectively over his coat, as though it were a conscious act of defiance. Yet the man was not armed; he had made that clear to Fontini-Cristi.

"You'll steal!" he said, louder than was necessary, his words vibrating in the wooden shack. "Soldiers steal!"

"We're not concerned with your *lire, paisan*. There are more impressive vehicles on the highway. Take your hands from your coat."

"Even in Rome reasons are given! *Il Duce*, himself, says the workers are not to be treated so! I march with the fascist guards; my rider served in Africa!"

What was the man doing? thought Vittorio. *Why was he behaving so? It would only anger the soldiers.* "You try my patience, pig! We look for a man from Maggiore. Every road post looks for this man. You were stopped because the license on your truck is from the Maggiore district . . . Hold out your arms!"

"*Baveno!* Not Maggiore! We are from *Baveno!* Where are the lies?"

The sergeant looked at Vittorio. "No soldier in Africa says he was with the Seventh Corps. It was disgraced."

The army guard had barely finished when the partisan screamed his command.

"*Now, signore!* Take the other!" The driver's hand swept down, lashing at the revolver in the sergeant's grip, only inches from his stomach. The suddenness of the action and the shattering roar of the partisan's voice in the small enclosure had the effect of an unexpected collision. Vittorio had no time to watch; he could only hope his companion knew what he was doing. The private had lurched for his rifle, his left hand on the barrel, his right surging down to the stock. Fontini-Cristi threw his weight against the man, slamming him into the wall, both hands on the side of the soldier's head, crashing the head into the hard, wooden surface. The private's barracks cap fell off; blood matted instantly throughout the hairline and streaked down over the man's head. He slumped to the floor.

Vittorio turned. The sergeant was wedged into the corner of the tiny guardhouse, the partisan over him, pistol-whipping him with his own weapon. the soldier's face was a mass of torn flesh, the blood and ripped skin sickening.

"*Quickly!*" cried the partisan as the sergeant fell. "Bring the truck to the front! Directly to the front; squeeze it between the road and the guardhouse. Keep the motor running."

"Very well," said Fontini-Cristi, confused by the brutality as well as the swift decisiveness of the last thirty seconds.

"And, *signore!*" shouted the partisan, as Vittorio had one foot out the door.

"Yes?"

"Your gun, please. Let me use it. These army issues are like thunder."

Fontini-Cristi hesitated, then withdrew the weapon and handed it to the man. The partisan reached over to the crank-telephone on the wall and ripped it out.

Vittorio steered the truck to the front of the guardhouse, the left wheels by necessity on the hard surface of the highway; there was not sufficient room on the shoulder to pull completely off the road. He hoped the rear lights were sufficiently bright for the onrushing traffic—far heavier now—to see the obstruction and skirt it.

The partisan came out of the guardhouse and spoke through the window. "Race the motor, *signore*. As loud and as fast as you can."

Fontini-Cristi did so. The partisan ran back to the guard house. Gripped in his right hand was Vittorio's pistol.

The two shots were deep and sharp; muffled combustions that were sudden, terrible outbursts within the sounds of the rushing traffic and racing motor. Vittorio stared, his emotions a mixture of awe and fear and, inexplicably, sorrow. He had entered a world of violence he did not understand.

The partisan emerged from the guardhouse, pulling the narrow door shut behind him. He jumped into the truck, slammed the door panel, and nodded to Vittorio. Fontini-Cristi waited several moments for a break in the traffic, then let out the clutch. The old truck lurched forward.

"There is a garage on the Via Monte that will hide the truck, paint it, and alter the license plates. It's less than a mile from the Piazza San Giorno. We'll walk there from the garage. I'll tell you where to turn."

The partisan held out the pistol for Vittorio. "Thank you," said Fontini-Cristi awkwardly, as he shoved the weapon into his jacket pocket. "You killed them?"

"Of course," was the simple reply.

"I suppose you had to."

"Naturally. You'll be in England, *signore*. I, in Italy. I could be identified."

"I see," answered Vittorio, the hesitancy in his voice.

"I don't mean disrespect, Signore Fonti-Cristi, but I don't think you *do* see. You people at Campo di Fiori, it's all new to you. It's not new to us. We've been at war for twenty years; I, myself, for ten."

"War?"

"Yes. Who do you think trains your *partigiani*?"

"What do you mean?"

"I am a Communist, *signore*. The powerful, capitalist Fontini-Cristis are shown how to fight by Communists."

The truck was rushing forward; Vittorio held the wheel firmly, astonished but strangely unmoved by his companion's words.

"I didn't know that," he replied.

"It's peculiar, isn't it?" said the partisan. "No one ever asked."

Chapter Four

December 30, 1939—Alba, Italy

The *espresso* bar was crowded, the tables full, the voices loud. Vittorio followed the partisan through the mass of gesturing hands and reluctantly parted bodies to the counter; they ordered coffee with Strega.

"Over there," said the partisan, indicating a table in the corner with three laborers seated around it, their soiled clothes and stubbled faces testifying to their status. There was one empty chair.

"How do you know? I thought we were to meet two men, not three. And British. Besides, there's not enough room; there's only one chair."

"Look at the heavyset man on the right. The identification is on the shoes. There are splotches of orange paint, not much but visible. *He's* the Corsican. The other two are English. Go over and say 'Our trip was uneventful'; that's all. The man with the shoes will get up; take his seat."

"What about you?"

"I'll join you in a minute. I must talk with the *Corso*."

Vittorio did as he was told. The heavyset man with the drippings of paint on his shoes got up, heaving a sigh of discomfort; Fontini-Cristi sat down. The British across from him spoke. His Italian was grammatically proper but hesitant; he had learned the language but not the idiom.

"Our sincerest regrets. Absolutely dreadful. We'll get you out."

"Thank you. Would you prefer speaking English? I'm fluent."

"Good," said the second man. "We weren't sure. We've had precious little time to read up on you. We were flown out of Lakenheath this morning. The *Corsos* picked us up in Pietra Ligure."

"Everything's happened so fast," said Vittorio. "The shock hasn't worn off."

"Don't see how it could," said the first man. "But we're not clear yet. You'll have to keep your wits about you. Our orders are to make bloody sure we get you to London: not to come back without you, and that's a fact."

Vittorio looked alternately at both men. "May I ask you why? Please understand, I'm grateful, but your concern seems to me extraordinary. I'm not humble, but neither am I a fool. Why am I so important to the British?"

"Damned if we know," replied the second agent. "But I can tell you, all hell broke loose last night. *All* night. We spent from midnight till four in the morning at the Air Ministry. All the radio dials in every operations room were beaming like mad. We're working with the Corsicans, you know."

"Yes, I was told."

The partisan walked through the crowds to the table. He pulled out the empty chair and sat down, a glass of Strega in his hand. The conversation was continued in Italian.

"We had trouble on the Canelli road. A checkpoint. Two guards had to be taken out."

"What's the A-span?" asked the agent on Fontini-Cristi's right. He was a slender man, somewhat more intense than his partner. He saw the puzzled expression on Vittorio's face and clarified. "How long does he think we have before the alarm goes out?"

"Midnight. When the twelve o'clock shift arrives. No one bothers with unanswered telephones. The equipment breaks down all the time."

"Well done," said the agent across the table. He was rounder in the face than his fellow Englishman; he spoke more slowly, as if constantly choosing his words. "You're a Bolshevik, I imagine."

"I am," replied the partisan, his hostility near the surface.

"No, no, please," added the agent. "I like working with you chaps. You're very thorough."

"M.I.-*Sei* is polite."

"By the way," said the Britisher on Vittorio's right, "I'm Apple; he's

Pear."

"We know who you are," said Pear to Fontini-Cristi.

"And my name's not important," said the partisan with a slight laugh. "I'll not be going with you."

"Let's run through that, shall we?" Apple was anxious, but controlled to the point of being reserved. "The going. Also, London wants to set up firmer communications."

"We knew London would."

The three men fell into a professional conversation that Vittorio found extraordinary. The spoke of routes and codes and radio frequencies as though they were discussing prices on the stock exchange. They touched on the necessity of *taking-out*, *eliminating* various people in specific positions—not men, not human beings, but *factors* that had to be killed.

What kind of men were these three? "Apple," "Pear," a Bolshevik with no name, only a false identification card. Men who killed without anger, without remorse.

He thought of Campo di Fiori. Of blinding white floodlights, and gunfire and death. *He* could kill now. Viciously, savagely—but he could not speak of death as these men spoke of it.

". . . get us to a trawler known to the coastal patrols. Do you understand?" Apple was speaking to him, but he had not been listening.

"I'm sorry," said Vittorio. "My mind was elsewhere."

"We've a long way to go," said Pear. "Over fifty miles to the coast, then a minimum of three hours on the water. A lot can happen."

"I'll try to be more attentive."

"Do better than try," replied Apple, his tone one of controlled irritation. "I don't know what you've done to the Foreign Office, but you happen to be a high-priority subject. It's our asses if we don't bring you out. So *listen!* The Corsicans will take us to the coast. There will be four changes of vehicles——"

"Wait!" The partisan reached over the table and gripped Apple's arm. "The man who was seated with you, the paint-spattered shoes. Where did you pick him up? *Quickly.*"

"Here in Alba. About twenty minutes ago."

"Who made contact first?"

Both Englishmen looked at each other. Briefly, with instant concern. "He did," said Apple.

"Get out of here! Now! Use the kitchen!"

"*What?*" Pear was looking over at the *espresso* counter.

"He's leaving," said the partisan. "He was to wait for me."

The heavyset man was making his way through the crowds toward the door. He was doing so as unobtrusively as possible; a drinker going to the men's room, perhaps.

"What do you think?" asked Apple.

"I think that there are a great many men throughout Alba with paint on their shoes. They wait for strangers whose eyes stray to the floor." The Communist rose from the table. "The contact code was broken. It happens. The Corsicans will have to change it. Now, *go!*"

The two Englishmen got out of their chairs, but not with any overt sense of urgency. Vittorio took his cue and stood up. He reached out and touched the partisan's sleeve. The Communist was startled; his eyes were on the heavyset man; he was about to plunge into the crowds.

"I want to thank you."

The partisan stared for an instant. "You're wasting time," he said.

The two Britishers knew exactly where the kitchen was, and therefore the exit *from* that kitchen. The alley outside was filthy; garbage cans were lined against the dirty stucco walls, refuse overflowing. The alley was a link between the Piazza San Giorno and the street behind, but so dimly lit and strewn with trash it was not a popular shortcut.

"This way," said Apple, turning left, away from the piazza. "Quickly now."

The three men ran out of the alley. The street was sufficiently filled with pedestrians and shopkeepers to provide them with cover. Apple and Pear fell into a casual walk; Vittorio followed suit. He realized that the two agents had maneuvered him between them.

"I'm not sure the Bolshie was right," said Pear. "Our *Corso* might simply have spotted a friend. He was damned convincing."

"The Corsicans have their own language," interjected Vittorio, excusing himself as he nearly collided with an oncoming stroller.

"Couldn't he tell by talking to him?"

"Don't do that," said Apple incisively.

"What?"

"Don't be so damned polite. It hardly goes with the clothes. To answer your question, the Corsicans employ regional contacts everywhere. We all do. They're minor level, just messengers."

"I see." Fontini-Cristi looked at the man who called himself Apple. He was walking casually, but his eyes kept shifting about in the night-cloaked street. Vittorio turned his head and looked at Pear. He was doing precisely what his countryman was doing: observing the faces in the crowds, the vehicles, the recesses in the buildings on both sides of the street.

"Where are we going?" asked Fontini-Cristi.

"To within a block of where our Corsican told us to be," replied Apple.

"But I thought you suspected him."

Pear spoke. "They won't see us because they don't know what to look for. The Bolshevik will catch the *Corso* in the piazza. If everything's on the up-and-up, they'll arrive together. If not, and if your friend is competent, he'll be the only one."

The shopping area curved to the left, into the south entrance of the Piazza San Giorno. The entrance was marked by a fountain, the circular pool at its base littered with discarded papers and bottles. Men and women sat on the ledge dipping their hands in the dirty water; children shouted and ran on the cobblestones under their parents' watchful eyes.

"The road beyond," said Apple, lighting a cigarette, gesturing toward the wide pavement seen through the spray of the fountain, "is the Via Ligata. It leads to the coastal highway. Two hundred yards down is a side street where the *Corso* said a taxi would be waiting."

"Would the side street, by any chance, be a dead end?" Pear asked the question with a degree of disdain. He did not really expect an answer.

"Isn't that a coincidence? I was wondering the same thing. Do let's find out. You," said Apple to Vittorio, "stay with my partner and do *exactly* as he says." The agent threw the match to the ground, inhaled deeply on his cigarette, and walked rapidly over the cobblestones toward the fountain. When he was within several feet of the pool, he slowed down, and then, to Vittorio's astonishment, he disappeared, lost entirely in the crowds.

"He does that rather in top form, doesn't he?" said Pear.

"I can't make him out. I don't see him."

"Not supposed to. A good race-and-melt, done in the proper light, can be very effective." He shrugged. "Come along. Keep abreast and chatter a bit. And gesture. You people wave your hands like mad."

Vittorio smiled at the Englishman's bromide. But as they walked into the crowds, he was conscious of moving hands and flailing arms and sudden exclamations. The Britisher knew his Italians. He kept pace with the agent, fascinated by the man's decisiveness. Suddenly, Pear grabbed Vittorio's sleeve and yanked him to the left, propelling them both toward a newly vacated space on the fountain's ledge. Fontini-Cristi was startled; he thought their objective was to reach the Via Ligata as rapidly and as unobtrusively as possible.

Then he understood. The Britisher's experienced, professional eyes had seen what the amateur's had not seen: the signal.

Vittorio sat on the agent's right, his head down. The first objects that came into focus were a pair of worn shoes with the splotches of orange paint on the scuffed leather. A single pair of immobile shoes in the moving shadows of moving bodies. Then Vittorio raised his head and froze. The partisan driver was cradling the heavyset body of the Corsican contact, as though succoring a friend who had drunk too much. But the contact was not drunk. His head was slumped, his eyes open, staring downward into the moving darkness. He was dead.

Vittorio leaned back on the ledge, mesmerized by the sight below. A steady, narrow stream of blood was soaking the back of the Corsican's shirt, rolling down the stone of the fountain's inner wall, mingling with the filthy water, forming circles and swirling half circles in the intermittent light of the piazza's street lamps.

The partisan's hand gripped the cloth, bunching the shirt around the blood-soaked area, knuckles and wrist drenched. And in his grip was the handle of a knife.

Fontini-Cristi tried to control his shock.

"I was hoping you'd stop," said the Communist to the Englishman.

"Nearly didn't," replied Pear in his overly grammatical Italian. "Until I noticed the couple leap up here." The agent indicated the ledge on which he and Vittorio sat. "They're yours, I presume."

"No. When you were closest, I told them my friend was about to vomit. It's a trap, of course. Fishnet variety; they don't know what they'll catch. They broke the code—last night. There are a dozen or so *provocatori* in the area, flushing out what targets they can. A roundup."

"We'll tell the Corsicans."

"It won't do much good. The code changes tomorrow."

"The taxi's the snare, then?"

"No. The second bait. They're not taking chances. The taxi drives the targets into the net. Only the driver knows where; he's upper level."

"There must be others nearby." Pear brought his hand to his mouth; it was a gesture of thought.

"Certainly."

"But which ones?"

"There's a way to find out. Where's Apple?"

"In the Via Ligata by now. We wanted to separate in case you had trouble."

"Join him; the trouble wasn't mine."

"Yes. I can see that——"

"*Mother of God!*" exclaimed Vittorio under his breath, incapable of silence. "You're holding a dead man in the middle of the piazza and you chatter like women!"

"We have things to say, *signore*. Be quiet and listen." The partisan returned his eyes to the Englishman, who had barely taken notice of Fontini-Cristi's outburst. "I'll give you two minutes to reach Apple. Then I'll let our *Corso* friend here slide into the pool, back up, knife visible. There'll be chaos. I'll start the shouting myself. It will carry. It'll be enough."

"And we keep our eyes on the taxi," interrupted Pear.

"Yes. As the shouting grows, see who speaks together. See who leaves to investigate."

"Then take the bloody taxi and be off," added the agent with finality. "Good show! I look forward to working with you again." The Britisher rose; Vittorio did the same, feeling Pear's hand on his arm.

"You," said the partisan, looking up at Vittorio while cradling the limp, heavyset body in the noisy, jostling, shadow-filled darkness. "Something to remember. A conversation in the midst of many people is often the safest. And a blade in a crowd is the hardest to trace. Remember these things."

Vittorio looked down at the man, not sure whether the Communist meant his words to be insulting or not.

"I'll remember," said Vittorio.

They walked swiftly into the Via Ligata. Apple was on the other side, slowly making his way toward the side street where the Corsican contact said the taxi would be waiting. The street lamps were dimmer than in the piazza.

"Hurry, now. There he is," said Pear in English. "Take longer steps, but don't run."

"Shouldn't we go over and meet him?" asked Vittorio.

"No. One person crossing the street is less obvious than two. . . . All right. Stop now."

Pear removed a box of matches from his pocket; he struck one. The instant it flared, he waved it out, throwing it to the pavement—as if the flame had seared his finger—and immediately struck a second, holding it to the cigarette he had placed in his lips.

Less than a minute passed before Apple joined them by the wall of a building. Pear told him the partisan's strategy. The three walked in silence, between the strollers down the pavement to the end of the block opposite the side street. Across, in the dim white wash of the streetlights, was the taxi, thirty feet from the corner.

"Isn't that a coincidence," said Apple, lifting his foot to a low ledge on the building, pulling up his sock. "It's a dead end."

"The troops can't be far away. Is your pillow attached? Mine isn't."

"Yes. Fix yours."

Pear turned into the building and removed an automatic from inside his jacket. With his other hand he reached into his pocket and withdrew a cylinder about four inches long, with perforations on the iron surface, and twisted it into the barrel of his weapon. He replaced the gun inside his jacket just as the cries from the piazza began.

There were only a few at first, almost indistinguishable. And then a crescendo of sound erupted.

"*Polizia!*" "*A quale punto polizia!*" "*Assassinio!*" "*Omicidio!*" Women and children ran out of the square; men followed, shouting orders and information at no one and everyone. Among the screams came the words: "*Uomo con arancia scarpe*," a man with orange shoes. The partisan had done his job well.

And then the partisan himself was among the crowds running down the pavement. He stopped ten feet from Fontini-Cristi and the two Englishmen and roared in a loud voice to any who would listen.

"I saw him! I saw *them!* I was right *next* to him! This man—his shoes were *painted*—they put a knife into his back!"

From the dark recess of a building a figure came dashing across the street, heading for the partisan. "You! Come here!"

"What?"

"I'm with the police. What did you see?"

"The police. Thank God! Come with me! There were two men! In sweaters——"

Before the official could adjust, the partisan started to race back toward the entrance of the piazza through the crowds. The policeman hesitated, then looked across the dimly lit street. Three men were talking together several yards in front of the taxi. The policeman gestured; two of the men broke away and started after the officer, who was now racing toward San Giorno and the disappearing partisan.

"The man left at the car. He's the driver," said Apple. "Here we go."

The next moments were a blur. Vittorio followed the two agents across the Via Ligata into the side street. The man at the taxi had climbed into the driver's seat. Apple approached the car, opened the door, and without saying a word raised his gun. A muted explosion burst from the mouth of his revolver. The man slumped forward; Apple rolled him over the seat toward the opposite door. Pear spoke to Fontini-Cristi.

"Into the back. Quickly, now!"

Apple turned the ignition; the taxi was old, the engine new and powerful. The automobile's make was the usual Fiat, Vittorio thought, but the motor was a Lamborgini.

The car lurched forward, turned right at the corner and gathered speed on the Via Ligata. Apple spoke over his shoulder, addressing Pear. "Check the glove compartment, will you? This bloody wreck belongs to some very *important people*. I daresay it would do well at Le Mans."

Pear lunged from the seat in the speeding car, over the felt back, and across the corpse of the Italian. He pulled open the glove compartment panel, grabbed the papers, bunching them together in his hand. As he pushed himself off the dashboard, the car swerved; Apple had swung the wheel to pass two automobiles. The body of the dead Italian fell across Pear's arm. He gripped the lifeless neck and threw the corpse violently back into the corner.

Vittorio stared at the scene, sick and uncomprehending. Behind them a heavyset man floated in death in a piazza fountain, the handle of a knife protruding from his blood-soaked shirt. Here, in an unmarked, speeding police car disguised as a taxi, a man slumped in the front seat, a bullet in his lifeless body. Miles away in a small guardhouse on the Via Canelli, two other men lay dead, killed by the Communist who had saved his life. The continuing nightmare was destroying his mind. He held his breath, desperately trying to find an instant of sanity.

"Here we are!" shouted Pear, holding up a rectangular sheet of heavy paper he had been studying in the inadequate light. "By God, it's a clean wicket!"

"An inland passport, I expect," said Apple, slowing down for a curve in the road.

"Indeed it is! The bloody *veicolo* is assigned to the *ufficiale segreto!* That bunch has access to Mussolini himself."

"It had to be something like that," agreed Apple, nodding his head. "The motor in this tacky box is a bloody marvel."

"It is a Lamborgini," said Vittorio quietly.

"What?" Apple raised his voice to be heard over the roar of the engine on the now straightaway road. They were approaching the outskirts of Alba.

"I said it's a Lamborgini."

"Yes," replied Apple, obviously unfamiliar with the engine. "Well, you keep coming up with things like that. Things Italian, that is. We're going to need your words before we reach the coast."

Pear turned to Fontini-Cristi. The Englishman's pleasant face was barely discernible in the darkness. He spoke gently, but there was no mistaking the quiet urgency in his voice.

"I'm sure this is all very strange to you, and damned uncomfortable, I should think. But that Bolshevik had a point. Remember what you can. The most difficult part of this work isn't the *doing*; it's getting *used* to the doing, if you see what I mean. Just accepting the fact that it's real, that's the leg up a fellow needs. We've all been through it, go through it constantly, as a matter of fact. It's all so bloody outrageous, in a way. But someone's got to do it; that's what they tell us. And I'll say this: You're getting some very practical on-the-job training. Wouldn't you agree?"

"Yes," said Vittorio softly, turning front, his eyes mesmerized by the onrushing road outlined by the beams of the headlights, and his mind frozen by the sudden question he could not avoid.

Training for what?

Chapter Five

December 31, 1939—Celle Ligure, Italy

It was two hours of madness. They turned off the coastal highway and carried the body of the dead driver into a field, stripping it naked, removing all identification.

They returned to the highway and sped south toward Savona. The road checks were similar to those on the Via Canelli: single guardhouses next to telephone booths, two soldiers in attendance at each. There were four checkpoints; three were passed easily. The thick, official document that proclaimed the vehicle assigned to the *ufficiale segreto* was read with respect and not a little fear. Fontini-Cristi did the talking at all three posts.

"You're damned quick," said Apple from the front, shaking his head in agreeable surprise. "And you were right about staying back there. You roll down that window like a Punjab prince."

The road sign was caught in the headlights.

ENTRARE MONTENOTTE SUD

Vittorio recognized the name; it was one of those medium-sized towns
surrounding the Gulf of Genoa. He recognized it from a decade ago, when he
and his wife had driven down the coast road on their last trip to Monte Carlo.
A journey that had ended a week later in death. In a speeding car at night.

"The coast's about fifteen miles from here, I think," said Apple hesitantly,
interrupting Fontini-Cristi's thoughts.

"Nearer eight," corrected Vittorio.

"You know this area?" asked Pear.

"I've driven to Cap Ferrat and Villefranche a number of times." *Why
didn't he say Monte Carlo; was the name too much of a symbol?* "Usually on the
Torino road, but several times on the shore route from Genoa. Montenotte
Sud is known for its inns."

"Then would you know a dirt road that cuts north of Savona—through
some hills, I gather—into Celle Ligure?"

"No. There are hills everywhere. . . . But I know Celle Ligure. It's on the
waterfront just beyond Albisolla. Is that where we're going?"

"Yes," said Apple. "It's our backup rendezvous with the Corsicans. In
case anything happened, we were to make our way to Celle Ligure, to a
fishing pier south of the marina. It'll be marked with a green wind sock."

"Well, *something* happened, as they say," interjected Pear. "I'm sure
there's a *Corso* wandering around Alba wondering where we are."

Several hundred yards ahead in the glare of the headlights, two soldiers
stood in the center of the road. One held a rifle at port arms; the other had his
hand raised, signaling them to stop. Apple slowed the Fiat, the transposed
motor emitting the low sounds of its decelerating power. "Do your bitchy
act," he said to Vittorio. "Be arrogant as hell." The Britisher kept the car in
the center of the road, a sign that the inhabitants expected no interruption;
pulling off to the side was unnecessary.

One of the soldiers was a lieutenant, his companion a corporal. The officer
approached Apple's open window and saluted the unkempt civilian smartly.

Too smartly, thought Vittorio.

"Your identification, *signore*," said the soldier courteously.

Too courteously.

Apple held up the thick official paper and gestured toward the back seat. It
was Vittorio's cue.

"We are the *ufficiale segreto*, Genoa garrison, and in a great hurry. We have
business in Savona. You've done your job; pass us through immediately."

"My apologies, *signore*." The officer took the heavy paper in Apple's
hand and scrutinized it. He creased the folds as his eyes scanned downward
in the very dim light. He continued politely. "I must see your identifications.
There is so little traffic on the road at this hour. All vehicles must be
checked."

Fontini-Cristi slammed his hand down on the top of the front seat in
sudden irritation. "You're out of order! Don't let our appearances fool you.
We're on official business and we're late for Savona!"

"Yes. Well, I must read this——"

But he was *not* reading it, thought Vittorio. A man in inadequate light did
not fold a page of paper *toward* him; if he folded it at all, it would be

away—to catch more light. The soldier was stalling. And the corporal had moved to the right front of the Fiat, his rifle still held across his chest; but the left hand was now lower on the barrel grip. Any hunter knew the stance; it was ready-at-fire.

Fontini-Cristi sat back in the seat, swearing furiously as he did so. "I demand your name and the name of your commanding officer!"

In the front, Apple had edged his shoulders to the right, trying to see into the rearview mirror, unable to do so without being obvious. But in his pretended anger, Fontini-Cristi had no such difficulty. He whipped his hand up behind Pear's shoulders, as if his irritation had reached the breaking point.

"Perhaps you did not hear me, soldier? Your name and that of your commanding officer!"

Through the rearview mirror he saw it. Quite far in the distance, beyond the clear range of the mirror, not easily seen through the window itself. A car had pulled off the road . . . so far off, it was half into the field bordering the highway. Two men were getting out of the front seat, the figures barely visible, moving slowly.

". . . Marchetti, *signore*. My commanding officer is Colonel Balbo. Genoa garrison, *signore*."

Vittorio caught Apple's eye in the rearview mirror, nodded slightly, and moved his head in a slow arc toward the back window. At the same time, he tapped his fingers rapidly on Pear's neck in the darkness. The agent understood.

Without warning, Vittorio opened his door. The rifle-bearing corporal jerked his weapon forward. "Put that *down, caporale*. Since your superior sees fit to take up my time, I will put it to use. I am Major Aldo Ravena, *ufficiale segreto*, from Rome. I will inspect your quarters. I will also relieve myself."

"*Signore!*" shouted the officer from across the Fiat's hood.

"Are you addressing me?" asked Fontini-Cristi arrogantly.

"My apologies, major." The officer could not help himself; he stole a quick glance to his right, to the road behind. "There are no facilities inside the guardhouse."

"Surely you are not immaculate in your bowels, man. The fields must be inconvenient. Perhaps Rome will install such facilities. I'll see."

Vittorio walked swiftly toward the door of the small structure; it was open. As he expected, the corporal went with him. He walked rapidly through the door. The instant the corporal entered behind him, Fontini-Cristi turned and jammed the pistol up under the man's chin. He pushed the weapon into the flesh of the corporal's throat and with his left hand grabbed the barrel of the rifle.

"If you so much as cough, I'll have to kill you!" whispered Vittorio. "I don't wish to do that."

The corporal's eyes widened in shock; he had no stomach for heroics. Fontini-Cristi held the rifle and gave his order quietly, precisely.

"Call the officer. Say I'm using your telephone and you don't know what to do. Tell him I'm calling the Genoa garrison. For that Colonel Balbo. *Now!* "

The corporal shouted the words, conveying both his confusion and his fear. Vittorio pressed his back against the wall by the door. The reply from the lieutenant betrayed the officer's own fear; perhaps he had made a dreadful mistake.

"I am only following orders! I received orders from Alba!"

"Tell him Colonel Balbo is coming to the telephone," whispered Fontini-Cristi. *"Now!"*

The corporal did so. Vittorio heard the footsteps of the officer running from the Fiat to the guardhouse.

"If you wish to live, Lieutenant, remove your pistol belt—just unbuckle both straps—and join the corporal at the wall."

The lieutenant was stunned. His jaw dropped, his lips parted in fright. Fontini-Cristi prodded him with the rifle, lancing the barrel into his stomach. The bewildered officer winced and gasped and did as he was told. Vittorio called outside, in English.

"I've disarmed them. Now I'm not sure what to do."

Pear's half-whispered shout came back. "What to *do?* My God, you're a bloody marvel! Send the officer back outside. Make sure he knows we have our weapons on him. Tell him to return to Apple's window right off. We'll take it from there."

Fontini-Cristi translated the instructions. The officer, prodded by the barrel of Vittorio's pistol, lurched out the doors and crossed swiftly in front of the car's headlights to the driver's window.

Ten seconds later the officer's shouts were heard on the road outside.

"You men from Alba! This is not the vehicle! A mistake has been made!"

A moment passed before other voices replied. Two voices, loud and angry.

"What happened? Who are they?"

Vittorio could see the figures of two men come out of the darkness of the field. They were soldiers and held guns at their sides. The officer answered.

"These are *segreti* from Genoa. They, too, look for the vehicle from Alba."

"Mother of Christ! How many *are* there?"

Suddenly, the officer pushed himself away from the window, screaming as he dove for the front of the automobile.

"Shoot! Open fire! They are——"

The muffled explosions of the British pistols erupted. Pear leaped out of the right rear door, covered by the automobile, and fired at the approaching soldiers. A rifle answered; it was a wild shot that thumped into the tarred surface of the road, triggered by a dying man. The checkpoint lieutenant sprang to his feet and started to race toward the opposite field into the darkness. Apple fired; three muted reports accompanied the sharp, abrupt flashes of his weapon. The officer screamed and arched his back. He fell into the dirt off the road.

"Fontini!" yelled Apple. "Kill your man and get out here!"

The corporal's lips trembled, his eyes watered. He had heard the muted explosions, the screams, and he understood the command.

"No," said Fontini-Cristi.

"Goddamn you!" roared Apple. "You do as I *say!* You're under *my* orders! We've no time to waste *or* chances to take!"

"You're wrong. We would waste more time and take greater risks if we could not find the road into Celle Ligure. This soldier will surely know it."

He did. Vittorio drove, the soldier beside him in the front seat. Fontini-Cristi knew the area; if they ran into trouble, he could handle it. He had proved that.

"Relax," said Vittorio in Italian to the frightened corporal. "Continue to be helpful; you'll be all right."

"What will heppen to me? They'll say I deserted my post."

"Nonsense. You were ambushed, forced at the point of a gun to accompany us, to act as a shield. You had no choice."

They drove into Celle Ligure at ten forty; the streets of the fishing village were nearly deserted. The majority of its inhabitants began their days at four in the morning; ten at night was late. Fontini-Cristi drove into the sandy parking area behind an open fish market that fronted the wide ocean street. Across was the main section of the marina.

"Where are the sentries?" asked Apple. "Where do they meet?"

At first the corporal seemed confused. Vittorio explained. "When you are on duty here, where do you turn around?"

"I see." The corporal was relieved; he was obviously trying to help. "Not here, not at this section. Up farther; I mean, down farther."

"*Damn* you!" Apple was forward in the back seat. He grabbed the Italian by the hair.

"You'll get nowhere like that," said Vittorio in English. "The man's frightened."

"So am I!" countered the agent. "There's a dock across there with a green wind sock on it, and a boat in that dock we have to find! We don't know what's happened behind us; there are soldiers on the piers with weapons—one shot would alert the whole area. And we have no idea what orders have been radioed the water patrols. *I'm damned* frightened!"

"I remember!" cried the corporal. "On the left. Up the street on the left! The trucks stopped and we would walk through to the piers and wait for the man on duty. He would give us the patrol sheet and be relieved."

"Where? *Exactly* where, Corporal?" Pear spoke urgently.

"The next street. I'm sure of it."

"That's roughly one hundred yards, wouldn't you say?" asked Pear, looking at Fontini-Cristi. "And the street below this another one hundred, give or take some."

"What's your idea?" Apple had released the corporal, but kept his hands menacingly on the top of the seat.

"Same as yours," replied Pear. "Take the sentry at midpoint; less chance of his being seen there. Once he's out we walk south to the wind sock, where, I trust, a Corsican or two will show themselves."

They crossed the ocean road into an alley that led to the dock complex. The smell of fish and the sounds of half a hundred boats creaking in rhythmic rest in their slips filled the darkness. Nets were hung everywhere; the wash of the sea could be heard beyond the planked walkway that fronted the piers. A few lanterns were swaying on ropes over decks; a concertina played a simple tune in the distance.

Vittorio and Pear walked casually out of the alley, their footsteps muted by moist planks. Apple and the corporal remained in the shadows. The walkway was bordered by a railing of metal tubing above the lapping water.

"Do you see the sentry?" asked Fontini-Cristi softly.

"No. But I hear him," answered the agent. "He's rapping the pipe as he walks. Listen."

It took Vittorio several seconds before he could distinguish the faint metal sounds among the rhythmic creakings of wood on water. But they were there. The unconscious, irregular tattoo of a bored men performing a dull task.

Several hundred feet south on the walkway, the figure of the soldier came under the spill of a pier light, his rifle angled down to the deck through his left arm. He was beside the railing, his right hand aimlessly tapping out his steps.

"When he gets here, ask him for a cigarette," said Pear calmly. "Pretend you're drunk. I will, too."

The sentry approached. The instant he saw them he snapped up his rifle and cracked the bolt, holding his position fifteen feet away.

"*Halt!* Who's *there?*"

"Two fishermen without cigarettes," replied Fontini-Cristi, slurring his words. "Be a nice fellow and give us a couple. Even one; we'll share it."

"You're drunk," said the soldier. "There's a curfew tonight on the piers. How come you're here? It was on the loudspeakers all day."

"We've been with two whores in Albisolla," answered Vittorio, lurching, steadying himself on the railing. "Only things we heard were music on a phonograph and creaking beds."

"Very nice," mumbled Pear.

The sentry shook his head in disapproval. He lowered his rifle and approached, reaching into the pocket of his tunic for cigarettes. "You *Ligurini* are worse than the *Napoletani*. I've done duty there."

Behind the soldier, Vittorio could see Apple coming out of the shadows. He had forced the corporal to lie down on his back in the corner of the alley; the corporal would not move. In Apple's hands were two spools.

Before Vittorio could realize what was happening, Apple sprang out of the passageway, his arms stretched, angled upward. In two swift moves, the agent's hands whipped over the sentry's head, and with his knee jammed into the small of the soldier's back, he yanked violently, causing the guard to arch spastically and then collapse.

The only noise was an abrupt, horrible expunging of air, and the quiet fall of the man's body onto the soft, moist wood.

Pear rushed to the corporal; he held his pistol against the soldier's temple. "Not a sound. Understood?" It was a command that left no room for debate. The corporal rose silently.

Fontini-Cristi looked down in the dim light at the guard on the walkway. What he could see he wished he had not seen. The man's neck was severed half off his body, the blood was pouring out in a dark-red stream from what had been the man's throat. Apple rolled the body through a wide space in the railing. It hit the water with a muffled splash. Pear picked up his rifle and spoke in English.

"Off we go. Down this way."

"Come on," said Fontini-Cristi, his hand on the trembling corporal's arm. "You have no choice."

The green wind sock was limp, no breeze billowing its cloth. The pier was only half filled with boats; it seemed to extend farther out into the water than the others. The four of them walked down the steps, Apple and Pear in front, their hands in their pockets. The two Englishmen were obviously hesitant. It was apparent to Vittorio that they were concerned.

Without warning or sound, men suddenly appeared on both sides of them, their weapons drawn. They were on the decks of the boats; five, no, six men dressed as fishermen.

"Be you George the Fifth?" said the gruff voice of the man nearest the agents, standing on the deck of a small trawler.

"Thank *God!*" said Pear in relief. "We've had a nasty time of it."

At the spoken English, weapons were replaced in belts and pockets. The men converged, a number talking at once.

The language was Corsican.

One man, obviously the leader, turned to Apple. "Go to the end of the pier. We've got one of the fastest trawlers in Bastia. We'll take care of the Italian. They won't find him for a month!"

"No!" Fontini-Cristi stepped between the two men. He looked at Pear. "We gave our word. If he cooperated, he lived."

Apple replied, instead, his whispered voice drawn out in irritation. "Now, you see here. You've been a help, I'll not deny it, but you're not running this show. Get out to the bloody boat."

"Not until this man is back on the walkway. We gave our word!" He spoke to the corporal. "Go back. You won't be harmed. Strike a match when you reach a passageway to the ocean road."

"And if I say *no?*" Apple continued to grip the soldier's tunic.

"Then I'll remain here."

"*Damn!*" Apple released the soldier.

"Walk with him part way," said Fontini-Cristi to the Corsican. "Make sure your men let him pass."

The Corsican spat on the pier.

The corporal ran as fast as he could toward the base of the dock. Fontini-Cristi looked at the two Englishmen.

"I am sorry," he said simply. "There's been enough killing."

"You're a damn fool," replied Apple.

"Hurry," said the Corsican leader. "I want to get started. The water's rough beyond the rocks. And you people are crazy!"

They walked out to the end of the long pier, one by one jumping over the gunwale onto the deck of the huge trawler. Two Corsicans remained on the dock by the pilings; they unwound the thick greasy ropes while the gruff captain started the engines.

It happened without warning.

A fusillade of gunfire from the walkway. Then the blinding shaft of a searchlight shot out of the darkness, accompanied by the shouts of soldiers at the base of the pier. The voice of the corporal could be heard.

"Out *there!* At the end of the dock! The *fishing trawler!* Send out the alarms!"

One of the Corsicans was hit; he plunged to the ground, at the last second freeing the rope from the piling.

"The *light!* Shoot out the light!" screamed the Corsican from the open wheelhouse, revving the engines, heading for open water.

Apple and Pear unscrewed their silencers for greater accuracy. Apple was the first to raise himself over the protection of the gunwale; he squeezed his trigger repeatedly, steadying his hand on the wooden rail. In the distance the searchlight exploded. Simultaneously, fragments of wood burst around Apple; the agent reeled back, screaming in pain.

His hand was shattered.

But the Corsican had steered the fast-moving trawler out into the protective darkness of the sea. They were free of Celle Ligure.

"Our price goes up, English!" shouted the man at the wheel. "You whoreson bastards! You'll pay for this craziness!" He looked at Fontini-Cristi crouched beneath the starboard gunwale. Their eyes met; the Corsican spat furiously.

Apple sat back sweating against a pile of ropes. In the night light reflecting the ocean's spray, Vittorio saw that the Englishman was staring at the bloody mass of flesh that was his hand, holding it by the wrist.

Fontini-Cristi got up and crossed to the agent, tearing off part of his shirt as he did so. "Let me wrap that for you. Stop the bleeding——"

Apple jerked his head up and spoke in quiet anger. "Stay the hell away from me. Your goddamned principles cost too much."

The seas were heavy, the winds strong, the rolls violent and abrupt. They had plowed through the drenching waves of the open water for thirty-eight minutes. Arrangements had been made, the blockade run; the trawler's engines were now idling.

Beyond the swells, Vittorio could see a small flashing blue disc: on for a beat, off for a beat. The signal from a submarine. The Corsican on the bow with the lantern began his own signal. He lowered and raised the lamp, using the gunwale as a shutter, imitating the timing of the blue disc half a mile away over the waters.

"Can't you radio him?" Pear shouted his question.

"Frequencies are monitored," replied the Corsican. "The patrol boats would circle in; we can't bribe them all."

The two vessels began their cautious pavane over the rough seas, the trawler making most of the moves until the huge undersea marauder was directly off the starboard rail. Fontini-Cristi was hypnotized by its size and black majesty.

The two ships drifted within fifty feet of each other, the submarine considerably higher on the mountainous waves. Four men could be seen on the deck; they were hanging on to a metal railing, the two in the center trying to manipulate some kind of machine.

A heavy rope shot through the air and crashed against the midships of the trawler. Two Corsicans leaped at it, holding on desperately, as if the line had a hostile will of its own. They lashed the rope to an iron winch in the center of the deck and signaled the men on the submarine.

The action was repeated. But the second rope was not the only item that had been shot from the submarine. There was a canvas pouch with metal rings on the edges, and from one of these rings was a thick coil of wire that extended back to the crew on the sub's deck.

The Corsicans ripped open the canvas pack and pulled out a shoulder harness. Fontini-Cristi recognized it immediately; it was a rig used to cross crevasses in the mountains.

Pear, bracing himself as he lurched forward on the rolling deck, approached Vittorio.

"It's a bit skin-crawling, but it's safe!" he yelled.

Vittorio shouted back "Send your man Apple first. His hand should be looked after."

"You're the priority. And frankly, if the damn thing doesn't hold, I'd rather we find out with you!"

Fontini-Cristi sat on the iron bunk inside the small metal room and drank from the thick china mug of coffee. He pulled the Royal Navy blanket around his shoulders, feeling the wet clothes beneath. The discomfort did not bother him; he was grateful to be alone.

The door of the small metal room opened. It was Pear. He carried an armful of clothing which he dropped on the bunk.

"Here's a dry change for you. It wouldn't do for you to croak off with pneumonia now. That'd be a clanker in the balls, wouldn't it?"

"Thank you," said Vittorio, getting up. "How's your friend?"

"The ship's doctor is afraid he'll lose the use of his hand. The doctor hasn't told him, but he knows."

"I'm sorry. I was naïve."

"Yes," agreed the Britisher simply. "You were naïve." He left, leaving the door open.

From the narrow metal corridors outside the tiny metal room, there was a sudden eruption of noise. Men raced by the door, all running in the same direction, fore or aft, Fontini-Cristi could not tell. Over the ship's intercom a piercing, deafening whistle shrieked without letup; metal doors slammed, the shouting increased.

Vittorio lunged at the open door; his breathing stopped. The panic of helplessness under the sea gripped him.

He collided with a British sailor. But the sailor's face was not contorted in panic or fear. Or anything but carefree laughter.

"*Happy New Year*, mate!" cried the sailor. "Midnight, chum! We're in 1940. A bloody new decade!"

The sailor raced on to the next hatchway, which he opened with a crash. Beyond, Fontini-Cristi could see the mess quarters. Men were gathered around holding out mugs into which two officers were pouring whiskey. The shouts merged into laughter. "Auld Lang Syne" began to fill the metal chambers.

The new decade.

The old one had ended in death. Death everywhere, most horribly in the blinding white light of Campo di Fiori. Father, mother, brothers, sisters . . . the children. *Gone.* Gone in a minute of shattering violence that was burned into his mind. A memory he would live with for the rest of his life.

Why? *Why?* Nothing made sense!

And then he remembered. Savarone had said he had gone to Zürich. But he had not gone to Zürich; he had gone somewhere else.

In that somewhere else lay the answer. But what?

Vittorio walked into the small metal room of the submarine and sat down on the iron ridge of the bed.

The new decade had begun.

PART TWO

Chapter Six

January 2, 1940—London, England

Sandbags.

London was a city of sandbags. Everywhere. In doorways, windows, storefronts; piled in mounds on street corners. The sandbag was the symbol. Across the Channel, Adolf Hitler vowed the destruction of all England; quietly the English believed his threat, and quietly, firmly, they steeled themselves in anticipation.

Vittorio had reached the Lakenheath military airfield late on the previous night, the first day of the new decade. He had been taken off an unmarked plane flown out of Majorca and whisked into operations, the purpose of which was to confirm his identity for the Naval Ministry. And now that he was safely in the country, the voices suddenly became calm and solicitous: Would he care to rest up after his grueling journey? Perhaps the Savoy? It was understood that the Fontini-Cristis stayed at the Savoy when in London. Would a conference tomorrow afternoon at fourteen hundred hours be convenient? At the Admiralty, Intelligence Sector Five. Alien operations.

Of course. For God's sake, *yes!* Why have you English done what you've done? I must know, but I will be silent until you tell me.

The Savoy desk provided him with toilet articles and nightclothes, including a Savoy robe. He had drawn a very hot bath in the enormous hotel tub and immersed himself for such a length of time the skin on his fingertips wrinkled. He then proceeded to drink too many glasses of brandy and fell into bed.

He had left a wake-up call for ten but, of course, it was unnecessary. He was fully alert by eight thirty; showered and shaved by nine. He ordered an English breakfast from the floor steward and while waiting, telephoned Norcross Limited, on Savile Row. He needed clothes immediately. He could not walk around London in a borrowed raincoat, a sweater, and the ill-fitting trousers provided by an agent named Pear on a submarine in the Mediterranean.

As he hung up the phone, it struck Vittorio that he had no money other than ten pounds courtesy of Lakenheath dispersals. He assumed his credit was good; he would have funds transferred from Switzerland. He had not had time to concentrate on the logistics of living; he had been too preoccupied with staying alive.

It occurred to Fontini-Cristi that he had many things to do. And if only to control the terrible memory—the infinite pain—of Campo di Fiori, he had to keep active. Force his mind to concentrate first on the simple things, everyday things. For when the great things came into focus he could go mad pondering them.

Please, dear God, the *little* things! Spare me the time to find my sanity.

He saw her first across the Savoy lobby while waiting for the day manager to arrange for immediate monies. She was sitting in an armchair, reading the *Times*, dressed in the stern uniform of a branch of the women's service, what branch he had no idea. Beneath the officer's visor cap her dark brunette hair fell in waves to her shoulders, outlining her face. It was a face he had seen before; it was a face one remembered. But it was a younger version of that face that stuck in his mind. The woman was, perhaps, in her middle thirties; the face he recalled had been no more than twenty-two or twenty-three. The cheekbones were high, the nose more Celtic than English—sharp, slightly upturned, and delicate above the full lips. He could not see the eyes clearly, but he knew what they looked like: a very intense blue, as blue as he had ever seen a woman's eyes.

That's what he remembered. Angry blue eyes staring up at him. Angry and filled with disdain. He had not encountered that reaction often in his life; it had irritated him.

Why did he remember? When was it?

"Signor Fontini-Cristi." The Savoy manager walked briskly out of the cashier's arch, an envelope in his hand. "As you requested, a thousand pounds."

Vittorio took the envelope and shoved it in the raincoat pocket. "Thank you."

"We've arranged for your limousine, sir. It should be here shortly. If you'd care to return to your suite, we'll ring you the moment it arrives."

"I'll wait here. If you can put up with these clothes, I can."

"Please, *signore*. It is always a great pleasure to welcome a member of the Fontini-Cristis. Will your father be joining you this trip? We trust he's well."

England marched to the sudden drums of war and the Savoy inquired about families.

"He'll not be joining me." Vittorio saw no point in further explanations. The news had not reached England, or if it had, the war dispatches made it insignificant. "By the way, do you know that lady over there? The one seated. In the uniform."

The manager unobtrusively glanced across the sparsely crowded lobby. "Yes, sir. She's Mrs. Spane. I should say *was* Mrs. Spane; they're divorced. I believe she's remarried now. Mr. Spane is. We don't see her often."

"Spane?"

"Yes, sir. I see she's with Air Defense. They're a no-nonsense group, they are."

"Thank you," said Vittorio, dismissing the manager courteously. "I shall wait for my car."

"Yes, of course. If there's anything we can do to make your stay more pleasant, don't hesitate to call upon us."

The manager nodded and walked away. Fontini-Cristi looked again at the women. She glanced at her watch, and then returned to her reading.

He remembered the name Spane because of its spelling, and because of the spelling, he remembered the man. It had been eleven, no, twelve years ago; he had accompanied Savarone to London to observe his father in negotiations with British Haviland—the observation a part of his training. Spane had been introduced to him one night at Les Ambassadeurs, a youngish man two or three years older than he was. He found the Englishman mildly amusing but basically tiring. Spane was a Mayfair product quite content to enjoy the fruits of ancestral labors without contributing much of anything himself, other than his expertise at the races. His father had disapproved of Spane and said as much to his eldest son, which, quite naturally, goaded the son into a brief acquaintanceship.

But it had been brief, and Vittorio suddenly remembered why. That it had not first come to mind was merely further proof that he had blocked her existence from much of his memory: not the woman across the lobby, but his wife.

His wife had come to England with them twelve years ago, the *padrone* feeling that her presence would have a restraining influence on a headstrong, wandering son. But Savarone did not know his daughter-in-law that well; he did later, but not at the time. The heady atmosphere of Mayfair at the height of the season was a tonic to her.

His wife was attracted to Spane; one or the other seduced one or the other. He had not paid much attention; he had been occupied himself.

And somewhere along the way there'd been a disagreeable confrontation. Recriminations had been hurled, and the angry blue eyes had stared up at him.

Vittorio walked across the lobby toward the armchair. The Spane woman glanced up as he approached. There was a moment of hesitancy in her eyes, as if she were unsure. And then she *was* sure and there was no hesitance at all; the disdain he recalled so vividly replaced the hesitation. Their eyes locked for a second—no more—and she returned to the newspaper.

"Mrs. Spane?"

She looked up. "The name is Holcroft."

"We've met."

"We have. It's Fontini——" She paused.

"Fontini-Cristis. Vittorio Fontini-Cristis."

"Yes. A long time ago. You'll forgive me, but I've a full day. I'm waiting for someone and I shan't have the chance to get through the paper again." She went back to her reading.

Vittorio smiled. "You dismiss me efficiently."

"I find it quite easy to do so," she replied without looking at him.

"Mrs. Holcroft, it *was* a long time ago. The English poet says that nothing so becomes change as the years."

"The English poet also maintains that leopards do not change their spots. I'm really quite occupied. Good day."

Vittorio started to nod his departure when he saw that her hands trembled ever so slightly. Mrs. Holcroft was somewhat less confident than her demeanor implied. He was not sure why he stayed; it was a time to be alone. The terrible memories of white light and death burned; he did not care to share them. On the other hand, he wanted to talk. To someone. About anything.

"Is an apology offered for childish behavior twelve years ago a decade too late?"

The lieutenant glanced up. "How *is* your wife?"

"She died in an automobile crash ten years ago."

The look in her eyes was steady; the hostility lessened. She blinked in discomfort, mildly embarrassed. "I'm sorry."

"It is my place to apologize. Twelve years ago you were seeking an explanation. Or comfort. And I had neither to give."

The woman allowed herself the trace of a smile. Her blue eyes had an element—if only an element—of warmth in them. "You were a very arrogant young man. And I'm afraid I had very little grace under pressure. I came to have more, of course."

"You were better than the games we played. I should have understood."

"That's a very disarming thing to say. . . . And I think we've said enough about the subject."

"Will you and your husband have dinner with me tonight, Mrs. Holcroft?" He heard the words he had spoken, not sure he had said them. It was the impulse of the moment.

She stared at him briefly before answering. "You mean that, don't you?"

"Certainly. I left Italy in somewhat of a rush, courtesy of your government, as these clothes are the courtesy of your countrymen. I haven't been to London in several years. I have very few acquaintances here."

"Now that's a provocative thing to say."

"I beg your pardon?"

"That you left Italy in a rush and you're wearing someone else's clothes. It raises questions."

Vittorio hesitated, then spoke quietly. "I would appreciate your having the understanding I lacked ten years ago. I would prefer those questions not be raised. But I'd like to have dinner with you. And your husband, of course."

She held his gaze, looking up at him curiously. Her lips curved into a gentle smile; she had made her decision. "My husband's name was Spane. Holcroft's my own. Jane Holcroft. And I'll have dinner with you."

The Savoy doorman interrupted. "Signor Fontini-Cristi, your car has arrived, sir."

"Thank you," he replied, his eyes on Jane Holcroft. "I'll be right there."

"Yes, sir." The doorman nodded and walked away.

"May I pick you up this evening? Or send my car for you?"

"Petrol's getting scarce. I'll meet you here. Eight o'clock?"

"Eight o'clock. *Arrivederci.*"

"Until then."

He walked down the long corridor at the Admiralty, escorted by a Commander Neyland who had met him at the entrance desk. Neyland was middle-aged, properly military, and quite impressed with himself. Or perhaps he was not at all impressed with Italians. In spite of Vittorio's fluency in English, Neyland insisted on using the simplest terms, and raising his voice as though addressing a retarded child. Fontini-Cristi was convinced that Neyland had not listened to his replies; a man did not hear of pursuit, death, and escape, and respond with such banalities as "You don't say." . . . "Odd, isn't it?" . . . "The Genoa gulf can be choppy in December, can't it?"

As they walked, Vittorio balanced his negative reaction to the commander with his gratitude for old Norcross on Savile Row.

Where the commander floundered, Norcross performed. The old tailor had clothed him in a matter of hours.

The little things; concentrate on the every*day* things.

Above all, maintain a control that bordered on ice during the conference with whatever, or whoever, comprised Intelligence Sector Five. There was so much to learn, to understand. So much that was beyond his comprehension. In the cold recital of the events that were the horror of Campo di Fiori, he could not let the agony cloud his perceptions; the recital, therefore, *would* be cold and understated.

"Through here, old man," said Neyland, indicating a cathedral-arched doorway that was more reminiscent of some venerable men's club than a military building. The commander opened the heavy door, gleaming with brass hardware, and Vittorio walked in.

There was nothing about the large room that belied the concept of a subdued but richly appointed club. Two huge windows overlooked a courtyard; everything was heavy and ornate: the drapes, the furniture, the lamps, and to some degree the three men who sat at the thick mahogany table in the center. Two were in uniform—the insignia and breast decorations duly proclaiming advanced ranks unknown to Fontini-Cristi. The man in civilian clothes had an archly diplomatic look about him, complete with a waxed moustache. Such men had come and gone in Campo di Fiori. They spoke in soft voices, their words ambiguous; they were seekers of elastic. The civilian was at the head of the table, the officers seated at the sides. There was one empty chair, obviously for him.

"Gentlemen," said Commander Neyland, as if he were announcing a petitioner at the Court of St. James, "Signor Savarone Fontini-Cristi of Milan."

Vittorio stared at the fatuous Englishman; the man had not heard a word he said.

The three men at the table rose as one. The civilian spoke. "May I introduce myself, sir. I am Anthony Brevourt. For a number of years I was the crown's ambassador of the Greek court of George the Second in Athens. On my left, Vice Admiral Hackett, Royal Navy; on my right, Brigadier Teague, Military Intelligence."

At first there were formal nods of acknowledgment, then Teague broke the formality by coming around his chair, his hand held out for Vittorio.

"I'm glad you're here, Fontini-Cristi. I received the preliminary reports. You've had a hell of a time of it."

"Thank you," said Vittorio, shaking the general's hand.

"Do sit down," said Brevourt, indicating the expected chair to Vittorio and returning to his own. The two officers took their seats—Hackett rather formally, even pompously; Teague quite casually. The general withdrew a cigarette case from his pocket and offered it to Fontini-Cristi.

"No, thank you," said Vittorio. To smoke with these men would imply a casualness he neither felt nor wanted them to think he felt. A lesson from Savarone.

Brevourt quickly continued. "I think we'd better get on with it. I'm sure you know the subject of our anxieties. The Greek consignment."

Vittorio looked at the ambassador. And then at the two officers. They were staring at him, apparently in anticipation. "The Greek? I know nothing of a 'Greek consignment.' However, I know the gratitude I feel. There are no words to express it in either language. You saved my life; men were killed doing so. What more can I say?"

"I think," said Brevourt slowly, "that we should like to hear you say something about an extraordinary delivery made to the family Fontini-Cristi by the Eastern Brotherhood of Xenope."

"I beg your pardon?" Vittorio was stunned. The words had no meaning for him. Some extraordinary error had been made.

"I told you. I was the crown's ambassador to Athens. During the tenure of my office, diplomatic liaisons were formed throughout the country, including, of course, the religious. For, in spite of the turmoil Greece is experiencing, the church hierarchy remains a powerful force."

"I'm sure it does," agreed Vittorio. "But I have no idea why it concerns me."

Teague leaned forward, the smoke curling in front of his face, his eyes riveted on Fontini-Cristi. "Please. We've done our share, you know. As you've said—I think quite properly—we saved your life. We sent in our best men, paid thousands to the *Corsos*, took considerable gambles in dangerous waters with a submarine—of which we have precious few—and activated a barely developed aircraft escape route. All these just to get you out." Teague paused, put down his cigarette and smiled ever so slightly. "All human life is sacred, perhaps, but there are limits to the expenditures one makes to prolong it."

"Speaking for the navy," said Hackett with controlled irritation, "we followed blindly, given only the barest facts, urged by the most commanding figures in the government. We jeopardized a vital area of operations; a decision that could cost a great many lives in the near future. Our expense was considerable. And the full tally's not in yet."

"These gentlemen—the government itself—acted on my most urgent entreaties," said Ambassador Anthony Brevourt with measured precision. "I was convinced beyond any doubt that *whatever* the cost, it was imperative to get you out of Italy. Quite simply put, Signore Fontini-Cristi, it was not your life. It was the information you possess relative to the Patriarchate of Constantine. That is my conduit. Now, if you please, the location of the delivery. Where is the vault?"

Vittorio returned Brevourt's stare until he could feel the sting in his eyes. No one spoke; the silence was strained. Things were being alluded to that moved the highest echelons of government and Fontini-Cristi knew he was the focus. But that was all he knew.

"I cannot tell you what I know nothing about."

"*The freight from Salonika.*" Brevourt's voice was cutting. The flat of his hand descended delicately on the table, the soft slap of flesh against the wood was startling as it was abrupt. "Two dead men in the railroad yards of Milan. One a priest. Somewhere beyond Banja Luka, north of Trieste, past Monfalcone, somewhere in Italy, or Switzerland you met that train. Now *where?*"

"I met no train, *signore*. I know nothing of Banja Luka, or Trieste. Monfalcone, yes, but it was only a phrase, and meaningless to me. An 'incident' would 'take place at Monfalcone.' That was all. My father did not elaborate. His position was that I would be given the information *after* the incident at Monfalcone. Not before."

"What of the two dead men in Milan? In the railroad yards." Brevourt would not let up; his intensity was electric.

"I read of the two men you speak of—shot in the Milan freight yards. It was a newspaper story. It did not seem terribly important to me."

"They were *Greeks*."

"I understand that."

"You *saw* them. They made the *delivery* to you."

"I saw no Greeks. No delivery was made to me."

"Oh, my God!" Brevourt drew out the words in a painted whisper. It was obvious to all at the table that the diplomat was suddenly gripped in his own particular fear; he was not feigning for negotiable effect.

"Easy," said Vice Admiral Hackett vacuously. The diplomat started to speak again, slowly, carefully, as though marshaling his thoughts.

"An agreement was made between the Elders of Xenope and the Italian Fontini-Cristis. It was a matter of incalculable priority. Sometime between December ninth and sixteenth—the dates the train left Salonika and arrived in Milan—it was met and a crate removed from the third freight car. Of such value was this cargo that the train's itinerary was prepared in isolated stages. There was only a single master plan, itself a sequence of documents, held by one man, a priest of Xenope. These, too, were destroyed before the priest took his own life and that of the engineer. Only he knew where the transfer was to be made, where the crate was to be removed. He and those responsible for removing it. The Fontini-Cristis." Brevourt paused, his deepset eyes riveted on Vittorio. "These are facts, sir; given to me by a courier from the Patriarchate. Coupled with the measures my government has taken, I presume they are sufficient to convince you to give us the information."

Fontini-Cristi shifted his position in the chair and looked away from the quietly intense face of the ambassador. He was sure that the three men thought he was dissembling; he would have to dissuade them of that. But first he had to think. So this was the reason. An unknown train from Salonika had caused the British government to take extraordinary measures to—what had Teague said?—prolong his life. Yet it was not his life that was important, as Brevourt had made clear. It was the information they assumed he possessed.

Which, of course, he did not.

December 9 through 16. His father had left for Zürich on the twelfth. But Savarone had not been in Zürich. And he would not tell his son where he had been. . . . Brevourt might well have cause for his anxieties. Still, there were other questions; the pattern was unclear. Vittorio turned back to the diplomat.

"Bear with me. You say Fontini-Cristis. You use the plural. A father and four sons. The father's name was Savarone. Your Commander Neyland inaccurately introduced me by that name."

"Yes." Brevourt was barely audible, as if he were being forced to confront a conclusion he refused to accept. "I was aware of that."

"So Savarone is the name you received from the Greeks. Is that correct?"

"He could not have done it alone." Again Brevourt spoke hardly above a whisper. "You're the eldest son; you run the companies. He would have advised you. He needed your help. There were over twenty separate documents to be prepared, we know that. He *needed* you!"

"It is what you apparently—perhaps desperately—wish to believe. And because you believed it, you took extraordinary measures to save my life, to get me out of Italy. You obviously know what happened at Campo di Fiori."

Brigadier Teague spoke. "We picked it up first through the partisans. The Greeks weren't far behind. The Greek embassy in Rome was keeping close tabs on the Fontini-Cristis; it wasn't told why, apparently. The Athens conduit reached the ambassador and he, in turn, got in touch with us."

"And now you are implying," said Brevourt icily, "that it was all for nothing."

"I'm not implying it. I'm stating it. During the period you spoke of, my father said he was traveling to Zürich. I'm afraid I wasn't paying much attention at the time, but several days later I had an urgent reason to ask him to return to Milan. I tried contacting him; I called every hotel in Zürich; he was nowhere to be found. He never told me where he was, where he had been. That's the truth, gentlemen."

The two officers looked at the diplomat. Brevourt leaned slowly back in his chair—it was a gesture of futility and exhaustion; he stared at the table top. Finally, he spoke.

"You have your life, Signore Fontini-Cristi. For all our sakes, I hope the cost was not too great."

"I can't answer that, of course. Why was this agreement made with my father?"

"*I* can't answer *that*," replied Brevourt, his eyes still on the table. "Apparently someone, somewhere, believed he was resourceful enough, or powerful enough, to carry it off. Either or both of which have been borne out. Perhaps we'll never know. . . ."

"What was on the train from Salonika? What was in the vault that caused you to do what you did?"

Anthony Brevourt raised his eyes and looked at Vittorio and lied. "I don't know."

"That's preposterous."

"I'm sure it must appear that way. I know only the . . . implications of its significance. There is no price on such things. It's an abstract value."

"And on that judgment you made these decisions, convinced your highest authorities to make them? Moved your government?"

"I did, sir. I would do it again. And that's all I'll say on the subject." Brevourt rose from the table. "It's pointless to go on. Others may be in touch with you. Good day, Signore Fontini-Cristi."

The ambassador's action startled the two officers, but they said nothing. Vittorio got out of his chair, nodded, and walked silently to the door. He turned and looked at Brevourt; the man's eyes were noncommittal.

Outside, Fontini-Cristi was surprised to see Commander Neyland standing at attention between two enlisted men. Intelligence Sector Five, Alien Operations, was taking no chances. The door of the conference room was being guarded.

Neyland turned, astonishment in his face. He obviously expected the meeting to last far longer.

"You've been released, I see."

"I didn't think I was being held," answered Vittorio.

"Figure of speech."

"I never realized how unattractive it was. Are you to escort me past the desk?"

"Yes, I'll sign you out."

They approached the Admiralty's huge entrance desk. Neyland checked his watch, gave Vittorio's last name to the guard. Fontini-Cristi was asked to initial the departure time; he did so, and as he stood up from the desk he was greeted by the commander's very formal salute. He nodded—formally—turned and walked across the marble floor to the huge double doors to the street.

He was on the fourth step when the words came to him. They shot through the swirling mists of white light and the shattering staccato of gunfire.

"*Champoluc . . . Zürich is Champoluc . . . Zürich is the river!*"

And then no more. Only the screams, and the white light, and the bodies suspended in death.

He stopped on the marble step, seeing nothing but the terrible visions of his mind.

"Zürich is the river! Champoluc. . . ."

Vittorio controlled himself. He stood motionless and breathed deeply, vaguely aware that people on the pavement and the steps were staring at him. He wondered if he should walk back through the doors of the Admiralty and down a long corridor to the cathedral arch that was the conference room of Intelligence Sector Five.

Calmly he made his decision. *Others may contact you.* Let the others come. He would not share with Brevourt, the seeker of elastic who lied to him.

"If I may, Sir Anthony," said Vice Admiral Hackett, "I believe there was a great deal more ground we might have covered——"

"I agree," interrupted Brigadier Teague, his irritation showing. "The admiral and I have our differences, but not in *this*, sir. We barely scratched the surface. We made an extraordinary investment and got nothing for it; there was more to be had."

"It was useless," said Brevourt wearily, walking slowly to the draped window overlooking the courtyard. "It was in his eyes. Fontini-Cristi told the truth. He was stunned by the information. He knows nothing."

Hackett cleared his throat, a prelude to judgment. "He didn't strike me as foaming at the mouth. He seemed to take it rather in stride, I'd say."

The diplomat stared absently out the window as he replied quietly. "If he had foamed at the mouth, I would have kept him in that chair for a week. He behaved precisely the way such a man reacts to deeply disturbing news. The shock was too profound for theatrics."

"Granting your premise," said Teague coldly, "it does not eliminate mine. He may not *realize* what he knows. Secondary information often leads to a primary source. In our business it nearly always does. I must object, Sir Anthony."

"Your objection is noted. You're perfectly free to make further contact; I made that clear. But you'll learn no more than we did this afternoon."

"How can you be so *sure?*" asked the Intelligence man quickly, his irritation rapidly turning into anger.

Brevourt turned from the window, his expression pained, his eyes in reflection. "Because I knew Savarone Fontini-Cristi. Eight years ago in Athens. He was a neutral emissary, I think is the term, from Rome. The only man Athens would trust. The circumstances are not relevant here; the methods of Fontini-Cristi are. He was a man possessed with a sense of discretion. He could move economic mountains, negotiate the most difficult international agreements, because all parties knew his word was better than any written contract. In a strange way, it was why he was feared; beware the man of total integrity. Our only hope was if he had called in his son. If he had needed him."

Teague absorbed the diplomat's words, then leaned forward, his arms on the table. "What was on the train from Salonika? In that damned vault?"

Brevourt paused before answering. The two officers understood that whatever the ambassador was about to say, it was *all* he would say.

"Documents hidden from the world for fourteen centuries. They could tear the Christian world apart, setting church against church . . . nation against nation, perhaps; forcing millions to choose sides in a war as profound as Hitler's."

"And by so doing," interrupted Teague in the form of a question, "dividing those who fight Germany."

"Yes. Inevitably."

"Then we'd better pray they're not found," concluded Teague.

"Pray strenuously, general. It's strange. Over the centuries men have willingly given their lives to protect the sanctity of those documents. Now they've disappeared. And all who knew where are dead."

PART THREE

Chapter Seven

January 1940 to September 1945—Europe

The telephone rang on the antique desk in the Savoy suite. Vittorio was at the casement window overlooking the Thames, watching the barges make their way slowly up and down the river in the afternoon rain. He checked his watch; it was exactly four thirty. The caller had to be MI6's Alec Teague.

Fontini-Cristi had learned many things about Teague over the past three weeks; one was that the man was punctual to a fault. If he said he would telephone *around* four thirty, then he would do so *at* four thirty. Alec Teague ran his life by a clock; it made for abrupt conversations.

Vittorio picked up the telephone. "Yes?"

"Fontini?" The Intelligence man was also given to brevity when it came to names. Apparently he saw no reason to add the Cristi when the Fontini was sufficient.

"Hello, Alec, I've been expecting you."

"I've got the papers," said Teague rapidly. "And your orders. The Foreign Office was reluctant. It's an equal wager whether they were concerned for your well-being, or whether they thought you'd present the crown with a bill."

"The latter, I can assure you. My father drove 'hard bargains,' I think is the term. Frankly, I've never understood the phrase; can bargains be soft?"

"Damned if I know." Teague was not really listening. "I think we should meet right off. How's your evening?"

"I'm having dinner with Miss Holcroft. Under the circumstances I can cancel, of course."

"Holcroft? Oh, the Spane woman."

"I think she prefers Holcroft."

"Yes, can't blame her. He's a bloody fool. Still, you can't deny the ceremony."

"She's doing her best to, I believe."

Teague laughed. "Damned gutsy girl. I think I'd like her."

"Which means you don't know her, and you want *me* to know you've had me followed. I never mentioned her married name to you."

Teague laughed again. "For your own benefit, not ours."

"Shall I cancel?"

"Don't bother. When will you be finished?"

"Finished?"

"Dinner. Damn, I forgot; you're Italian."

Vittorio smiled. Alec's recollection was made in complete sincerity. "I can

see the lady home by ten thirty . . . ten o'clock. I gather you wish to meet
tonight."

"I'm afraid we have to. Your orders call for you to leave tomorrow. For
Scotland. In the morning."

The restaurant in Holborn was named Fawn's. Black curtains were drawn
tautly across the windows, stretched and tacked, inhibiting any light from
spilling a single shaft into the street. He was in the bar, seated at a corner
stool with a clear view of the lounge and the shrouded entrance. She would
arrive any minute now and he smiled at himself, realizing that he wanted to
see her very much.

He knew when it had begun with Jane—their swiftly developing relationship that would shortly lead to the splendid comfort of the bed. It was not
their meeting in the Savoy lobby; nor was it their first evening together.
Those were pleasant distractions; he had sought no more, wanted no more.

The beginning was five days later when he had been sitting alone in his
rooms. There'd been a knock on the foyer door. He had opened it; Jane was
standing in the hallway. In her hand was a slightly worn copy of the *Times*.
He had not seen it.

"For God's sake, what happened?" she asked.

He had shown her in without answering, unsure of her meaning. She'd
handed him the newspaper. In the lower left corner of the front page was a
brief article circled in red pencil.

MILAN, Jan. 2 (Reuters)—A news blackout has been lowered on the
Fontini-Cristi Industries here as government officials moved in assuming managerial control. No member of the Fontini-Cristi family has
been seen, and the police have sealed off the family estate at Campo di
Fiori. Rumors abound as to the fate of this powerful dynasty headed by
the financier Savarone Fontini-Cristi and his eldest son, Vittorio.
Reliable sources indicate they may have been killed by patriots,
infuriated by recent company decisions many felt were inimicable to
Italy's interests. It was reported that the mutilated body of an
"informer" (unseen by this journalist) was found hanging in the Piazza
del Duomo, with a sign that would seem to confirm the rumors of
execution. Rome has issued only the statement that the Fontini-Cristis
were enemies of the state.

Vittorio had put down the paper and walked across the room, away from
the girl. He knew she meant well; he did not fault her concern. Yet he was
profoundly annoyed. The anguish was his alone and he did not care to share
it. She had intruded.

"I'm sorry," she'd said quietly. "I presumed. I had no right to do that."

"When did you first read this?"

"Less than half hour ago. It was left on my desk. I've mentioned you to
friends. I saw no reason not to."

"And you came right over?"

"Yes."

"Why?"

"I cared," had been her simple answer. The honesty of it had touched him.

"I'll go now."

"Please——"

"Do you want me to stay?"

"Yes. I think I do."

And so he had told her. In measured tones at first, his sentences gathering momentum as he approached the hideous night of white light and death that was Campo di Fiori. His throat was dry. He did not wish to go on.

And Jane did a strange thing. Separated by the short distance between their opposing chairs, making no move to diminish that separation, she forced him to continue.

"For God's sake, *say* it. *All* of it."

She whispered, but the whisper was a command and in his confusion and anguish he accepted it.

When he was done, relief swept over him. For the first time in days an unbearable weight had been lifted. Not permanently, it would return; but for the moment he had found his sanity; really found it, not an imposed pretense that left his breath always a little short.

Jane had known what he had not understood. She had said it.

"Did you think you could go on keeping it inside? Not saying the words; not hearing them. What kind of man do you think you *are?*"

What kind of man? He did not really know. He had not actually thought about the kind of man he was; it was not a question that had concerned him beyond certain limits. He was Vittorio Fontini-Cristi, first son of Savarone. Now he would find out what else he was. He wondered whether Jane could be a part of his new world. Or whether the hate and the war would be all-consuming. He knew only the war—and the hate—were his springboards back to life.

Which was why he had encouraged Alec Teague when the MI6 man contacted him after the disastrous conference with Brevourt at Intelligence Sector Five. Teague wanted background material—seemingly unimportant conversations, offhand remarks, oddly repeated words—anything that might have a bearing on the train from Salonika. But Vittorio wanted something, too. From Teague. So he spaced out the isolated scraps of information: a river that might or might not have anything to do with Zürich, a district in the Italian Alps that bore the name Champoluc, but possessed no river. Whatever the puzzle was, its pieces remained separate. Still Teague probed.

And while he probed, Vittorio drew out the conceivable options MI6 might have for him. He was fluent in English and Italian, more than proficient in French and German; he had an intimate working knowledge of a score of major European industries, had negotiated with the leading financial figures throughout Europe. Certainly there was *something*.

Teague said he would look. Yesterday Teague said he would call him today at four thirty; there might be something. This afternoon at precisely four thirty Teague had called; he had Vittorio's "orders." There *had* been something. Fontini-Cristi wondered what it was, and even more, why the abruptness of his departure for Scotland.

"Have you been waiting long?" asked Jane Holcroft, suddenly standing beside him in the dimly lit bar.

"I'm *sorry.*" Vittorio was; he had not seen her in the lounge. Yet he had been staring at the door. "No, not at all."

"You were miles away. You looked right at me, and when I smiled, you scowled. I trust it's not indicative."

"Good heavens, no. You were right; I was miles away. In Scotland."

"I beg your pardon?"

"I'll tell you about it at the table. What I know, which is very little."

They were led to their table and ordered drinks. "I've told you about Teague," he said, lighting her cigarette, holding the flame of the match for his own.

"Yes. The man from Intelligence. You didn't say a great deal about him. Only that he seemed to be a good chap who asked a lot of questions."

"He had to. My family required it." Fontini-Cristi had not told Jane about the freight from Salonika; there was no point. "I've been pestering him for several weeks to find me a job."

"In the service?"

"In any service. He was a logical man to approach; he knows people everywhere. We both agreed I have qualifications that might be useful to someone."

"What will you be doing?"

"I don't know, but whatever it is, it begins in Scotland."

The waiter arrived with their drinks. Vittorio nodded his thanks, aware that Jane kept her eyes on his face.

"There are training camps in Scotland," she said quietly. "Several are listed as highly classified. They're quite secret and heavily guarded."

Vittorio smiled. "They can't be *too* secret."

The girl returned his smile, the full explanation in her eyes, only half of it in her words. "There's an elaborate system of air defense warning-relays throughout the areas. Overlapping sectors; extremely difficult for aircraft to penetrate. Especially single-engine light aircraft."

"I forgot. The Savoy manager said you were no-nonsense people."

"We're also given extensive training in all existing systems. As well as those in development stages. Systems vary considerably from sector to sector. When are you leaving?"

"Tomorrow."

"I see. For how long?"

"I don't know."

"Of course. You said that."

"I'm to meet with Teague tonight. After dinner, but there's no need to rush. I'm not seeing him until ten thirty. I presume I'll know more then."

Jane was silent for several moments. She locked her eyes with his and then spoke simply. "When your meeting with Teague is over, will you come to me? To my flat? Tell me what you can."

"Yes. I will."

"I don't care what time it is." She placed her hand over his. "I want us to be together."

"So do I."

Brigadier Alec Teague removed his creased officer's cap and army overcoat and threw them on the Savoy chair. He unbuttoned his tunic and his collar and loosened his tie. He lowered his large, powerful frame into the soft couch and exhaled a sigh of relaxation. He grinned at Fontini-Cristi, who stood in front of an opposing armchair and held his palms up in supplication.

"Since I've been at it since seven this morning, I do think you should offer me a drink. Whiskey neat would be splendid."

"Of course." Vittorio crossed to the small bar against the wall, poured two short glasses, and returned with the drinks.

"Mrs. Spane's a most attractive woman," Teague said. "And you're quite

right, you know, she does prefer her maiden name. At the Air Ministry the
'Spane' is in brackets. She's called Flying Officer Holcroft."

"Flying Officer?" Vittorio did not know why but the title seemed faintly
amusing to him. "I hadn't thought of her in such military terms."

"Yes, I see what you mean." Teague finished his drink quickly and placed
his glass on the coffee table. Vittorio gestured for a refill. "No more, thank
you. It's time for serious talk." The Intelligence man looked at his
wristwatch; Fontini-Cristi wondered if Teague really scheduled himself to
the precise half-minute for social conversation.

"What's in Scotland?"

"Your place of residence for the next month or so. Should you accept the
terms of employment. The pay's not exactly what you're accustomed to, I'm
afraid." Teague grinned again. "As a matter of fact, we rather arbitrarily
placed it at a captain's rate. I don't have the figures in my head."

"The figures aren't my concern. You say I have a choice, but before you
said that my orders had arrived. I don't understand."

"We have no hold over you. You can reject the employment and I'll cancel
the orders. It's as simple as that. However, in the interests of time, I made
the purchase first. Frankly, to be sure it *could* be made."

"All right. What is it?"

"That's rather difficult to answer quickly. If at all, really. You see, it's
pretty much up to you."

"To *me?*"

"Yes. The circumstances surrounding your getting out of Italy were
unique, we all understand that. But you're not the only continental who's
fled Europe. We've got dozens and dozens. And I'm not talking about the
Jews and the Bolsheviks; they're in the thousands. I'm referring to scores of
men like yourself. Businessmen, professionals, scientists, engineers, university people who, for one reason or another—we'd like to think it was moral
repugnance—couldn't function where they lived. That's about where we
are."

"I don't understand. Where are you?"

"In Scotland. With forty or fifty ragtail continentals—all quite successful
in their previous livelihoods—in search of a leader."

"And you think I am *he?*"

"The more I think about it, the more convinced I become. Rather natural
qualifications, I'd say. You've moved in the monied circles, you speak the
languages. Above all, you're a businessman, you've developed markets all
over Europe. Good heavens, man, the Fontini-Cristi Industries are *enormous;*
you were its chief executive. Adapt to the conditions. Do what you've done
splendidly for the past half-dozen years or so. Only do it from the *opposite
point of view. Mis*management."

"What *are* you talking about?"

The brigadier continued, speaking rapidly. "We have men in Scotland
who've worked in scores of occupations and professions in all the major cities
in Europe. One step always leads to another, doesn't it?"

"That's what you're counting on, isn't it? We both ask questions."

Teague leaned forward, suddenly reflective. "These are hectic and complicated times. There are more questions than there are answers. But one
answer was right in front of our eyes only we didn't see it. We were training
these men for the wrong things! That is, we weren't sure *what* we were
training them for; vaguely for underground contacts, routine information

runs, it was amorphous. There's something better; damned ingenious, if I say so myself. The strategy, the concept is to send them back to *disrupt* the marketplace, create havoc—not so much physical sabotage, we've enough people doing that, but bureaucratic chaos. Let them operate in their former bailiwicks. Accounting offices consistently out of balance, bills of lading constantly inaccurate, delivery schedules at sixes and sevens, mass confusion in the factories: exemplary *mis*management at all *costs!"*

Teague was excited, his enthusiasm infectious. It was difficult for Vittorio to keep his concentration on the essence of his original question. "But why do I have to leave in the morning?"

"To put it bluntly, I said I might lose you if there were any further delays."

"Further? How can you say that? I've been here less than——"

"Because," broke in Teague, "no more than five people in England know why we *really* got you out of Italy. Your complete lack of information about the train from Salonika has them stunned. They took an extraordinary gamble and lost. What you've told me leads nowhere; our agents in Zürich, Berne, Trieste, Monfalcone . . . they can trace nothing. So I stepped in with a different version of why we got you out and saved a few heads in the bargain. I said this new operation was *your* idea. They leaped at it! After all, you are a Fontini-Cristi. Will you accept?"

Vittorio smiled. "'Mismanagement at all costs.' That is a credo I doubt has a precedent. Yes, I do see the possibilities. Whether they are enormous—or theoretical—remains to be seen. I accept."

Teague smiled slyly. "There's one thing more. About your name——"

"Victor Fontine?" Jane laughed beside him on the couch in the Kensington flat, warmed by the glow of the burning logs in the fireplace. "That's British cheek if I ever heard it. They've *colonized* you."

"And made me an officer in the process," chuckled Captain Victor Fontine, holding up the envelope and dropping it on the coffee table. "Teague was amusing. He approached the subject rather the way one expects from the cinema. 'We must find you a *name.* Something immediately recognizable, easy to use in cables.' I was intrigued. I was to be given a code name, something quite dramatic, I imagined. A precious stone, perhaps, with a number. Or an animal's name. Instead, he merely Anglicized my own and lopped it off." Victor laughed. "I'll get used to it. It's not for a lifetime."

"I don't know if I can, but I'll try. It's rather a letdown, frankly."

"We must all sacrifice. Am I correct in assuming a *capitano* is a higher rank than a flying officer?"

"The 'flying officer' has no intention of giving orders. I don't think either of us is very military. Nor is Kensington. What about Scotland?"

He told her sketchily, keeping what facts he knew unspecific. As he spoke, he saw and could feel her unusually light-blue eyes probing his, looking beyond the offhand phrases, knowing surely there was more, or would be. She was dressed in a comfortable lounging robe of pale yellow that accentuated her very dark brown hair and emphasized the blue of her eyes. Underneath the robe, between the wide lapels, he could see the soft white of her nightgown and he knew she meant him to see it, and to want to touch her.

It was so comfortable, thought Fontine. There was no sense of urgency or maneuver. At one point during his monologue he touched her shoulder; she slowly, gently reached up and held his hand, her fingers caressing his. She led his hand down to her lap and cupped it with her other hand as he finished.

"So there we have it. 'Mismanagement at all costs' wherever it can be inflicted."

She was quiet for a moment, her eyes still probing, and then she smiled. "It's a marvelous idea. Teague's right, the possibilities are enormous. How long will you be in Scotland? Did he say?"

"Not specifically. A 'number of weeks.'" He withdrew his hand from hers and casually, naturally reached around her shoulders and drew her to him. Her head rested on his upper chest; he kissed her soft hair. She pulled back and looked up at him—her eyes still searching. She parted her lips as she moved toward him, taking his hand and casually, perfectly naturally, leading it between the lapels of her robe, inside over her breast. When their lips met, Jane moaned and widened her mouth, accepting the full moisture of his own.

"It's been a long time," she whispered finally.

"You're lovely," he replied, stroking her soft hair with his hand, kissing her eyes.

"I wish you didn't have to go away. I don't want you to go."

They stood up in front of the small couch. She helped him take off his jacket, pausing to press her face against his chest. They kissed again, holding each other at first gently, and then with gathering strength. For the briefest time, Victor placed his hands on her shoulders and moved her back; her lovely face was below him and he spoke into her blue eyes. "I'll miss you terribly. You've given me so much."

"And you've given me what I was afraid to find," she answered, her lips forming a gentle, quiet smile. "Afraid to look for, actually. Good heavens, I was petrified!"

She took his hand and they walked across the room to a doorway. Inside was the bedroom; a single ivory lamp shone on a night table, its yellowish white glow throwing light up on the walls of soft blue and across the ivory-colored, simple furniture. The silk spread over the bed was, again, blue and white and filled with the intricate circles of a floral design. It was all so peaceful, so away, so lovely, as Jane was lovely.

"This is a room of great privacy. And warmth," said Fontine, struck by simple beauty. "It's an extraordinary room, because it's your room and you care for it. Do I sound foolish?"

"You sound Italian," she answered softly, smiling, her blue eyes filled with love and urgency. "The privacy and the warmth are for you to share. I want you to share them."

She walked to one side of the bed, he to the other. Together they folded back the silk spread; their hands touched and they looked at each other. Jane walked around the bed to him. As she did so, she reached up and unbuttoned the top of her negligee, and then untied the ribbon of her gown. The fabric fell away, her round, full breasts emerged from the folds of silk, the nipples pink, taut.

He took her into his arms, his lips seeking hers in moist, soft excitement. She pressed her body against his. He could never remember being so completely, so totally aroused. Her long legs trembled and once again she pressed against him. She opened her mouth, her lips covered his, low moans of sweet pleasure coming from her throat.

"Oh, God, *take* me, Vittorio. Quickly, *quickly*, my love!"

The telephone rang on Alec Teague's desk. He looked at the office clock on the wall, then at his wristwatch. It was ten minutes to one in the morning. He picked up the receiver.

"Teague here."

"Reynolds in surveillance. We have the report. He's still in Kensington at the Holcroft flat. We think he'll stay the night."

"Good! We're on schedule. Everything according to plan."

"I wish we knew what was said. We could have set it up, sir."

"Quite unnecessary, Reynolds. Deposit a file-insertion for the morning: Parkhurst at the Air Ministry is to be contacted. Flying Officer Holcroft is to be given flexible considerations, including a tour of the Loch Torridon warning relays in Scotland, if it can be arranged quietly. Now, I'm off for some sleep. Good night."

Chapter Eight

Loch Torridon was west of the northwest highlands on the edge of the water, the source of the loch in the sea leading to the Hebrides. Inland there were scores of deep ravines, with streams rolling down from the upper regions, water that was icy and clear and formed pockets of marsh. The compound was between the coast and the hills. It was rough country. Isolated, invulnerable, patrolled by guards armed with weapons and dogs. Six miles northeast was a small village with a single main street that wound between a few shops and became a dirt road on the outskirts.

The hills themselves were steep, the abrupt inclines profuse with tall trees and thick foliage. It was in the hills that the continentals were put through the rigors of physical training. But the training was slow and laborious. The recruits were not soldiers but businessmen, teachers, and professionals, incapable of sustaining harsh physical exertion.

The common denominator was a hatred of the Germans. Twenty-two had their roots in Germany and Austria; in addition, there were eight Poles, nine Dutch, seven Belgians, four Italians, and three Greeks. Fifty-three once-respectable citizens who had made their own calculations months earlier.

They understood that one day they would be sent back to their homelands. But as Teague had noted, it was a formless sort of objective. And this undefined, seemingly low-level, participation was unacceptable to the continentals; undercurrents of discontent were heard in the four barracks in the middle of the camp. As the news of German victories came with alarming rapidity over the radio, the frustrations grew.

For God's sake! When? Where? How? *We are wasted!*

The camp commander greeted Victor Fontine with not a little wariness. He was a blunt officer of the Regulars and a graduate of MI6's various schools of covert operations.

"I won't pretend to understand much," he said at first meeting. "My instructions are muddy, which is what they're supposed to be, I imagine. You'll spend three weeks, more or less—until Brigadier Teague gives us the order—training with our group as one of the men. You'll do everything they do, nothing out of the ordinary."

"Yes, of course."

With these words Victor entered the world of Loch Torridon. A strange, convoluted world that had little in common with anything he had experienced in his life before. And he understood, although he was not sure why, that the lessons of Loch Torridon would merge with the teachings of Savarone and shape the remaining years of his life.

He was issued regulation combat fatigues and equipment, including a rifle and a pistol (without ammunition), a carbine bayonet that doubled as a knife, a field pack with mess utensils, and a blanket roll. He moved into the barracks, where he was greeted casually, with as few words as possible and no curiosity. He learned quickly that there was not much camaraderie in Loch Torridon. These men lived in and with their immediate pasts; they did not seek friendship.

The daylight hours were long and exhausting; the nights spent memorizing codes and maps and the deep sleep necessary to ease aching bodies. In some ways Victor began to think of Loch Torridon as an extension of other, remembered games. He might have been back at the university, in competition with his classmates on the field, on the courts, on the mats, or up on the slopes racing downhill against a stopwatch. Except that the classmates at Loch Torridon were different; most were older than he was and none had known even vaguely what it was like to have been a Fontini-Cristi. He gathered that much from brief conversations; it was easy to keep to himself, and therefore to compete against himself. It was the cruelest competition.

"Hello? My name is Mikhailovic." The man grinning and speaking to Victor sank to the ground, breathing heavily. He released the straps of his field pack and let the bulky canvas slip from his shoulders. It was midpoint in a ten-minute break between a forced march and a tactical maneuver exercise.

"Mine's Fontine," replied Victor. The man was one of the two new recruits who had arrived in Loch Torridon less than a week ago. He was in his mid-twenties, the youngest trainee in the compound.

"You're Italian, aren't you? In Barracks Three?"

"Yes."

"I'm Serbo-Croat, Barracks One."

"Your English is very good."

"My father is an exporter—was, I should say. The money's in the English-speaking countries." Mikhailovic pulled out a pack of cigarettes from his fatigues pocket and offered it to Fontine.

"No, thanks. I just finished one."

"I ache all over," said the Slav, grinning, lighting a cigarette. "I don't know how the old men do it."

"We've been here longer."

"I don't mean you. I mean the others."

"Thank you." Victor wondered why Mikhailovic complained. He was a stocky, powerfully built man, with a bull neck and large shoulders. Too, something about him was odd: there was no perspiration whatsoever on Mikhailovic's forehead, while Fontine's own was matted with sweat.

"You got out of Italy before Mussolini made you a lackey to the German, eh?"

"Something like that."

"Machek's taking the same road. He'll run all of Yugoslavia soon, mark my word."

"I didn't know that."

"Not many people do. My father did." Mikhailovic drew on his cigarette, his eyes across the field. He added quietly, "They executed him."

Fontine looked compassionately at the younger man. "I'm sorry. It's painful, I know."

"Do you?" The Slav turned; there was bewilderment in his eyes.

"Yes. We'll talk later. We must concentrate on the maneuver. The object is to reach the top of the next hill through the woods without being tagged." Victor stood and held out his hand. "My first name's Vittor—Victor. What's yours?"

The Serbo-Croat accepted the handshake firmly. "Petride. It's Greek. My grandmother was Greek."

"Welcome to Loch Torridon, Petride Mikhailovic."

As the days went by, Victor and Petride worked well together. So well, in fact, the compound sergeants paired them off against superior numbers in the infiltration exercises. Petride was allowed to move into Victor's barracks.

For Victor, it was like having one of his younger brothers suddenly return to life; curious, often bewildered, but strong and obedient. In some ways Petride filled a void, lessened the pain of his memories. If there was a liability in the relationship it was merely one of excess on the Serbo-Croat's part. Petride was an excessive talker, forever questioning, always volunteering information about his personal life, expecting Victor to reciprocate.

Beyond a point, Fontine could not. He simply was not so inclined. He had shared the anguish of Campo di Fiori with Jane; there would be no one else. Occasionally he found it necessary to reprimand Petride Mikhailovic.

"You're my friend. Not my priest."

"Did you have a priest?"

"Actually, no. It was a figure of speech."

"Your family was religious. It must have been."

"Why?"

"Your real name. 'Fontini-Cristi.' It means fountains of Christ, doesn't it?"

"In a language several centuries old. We're not religious in the accepted sense; not for a long time."

"I'm very, *very* religious."

"It's your right."

The fifth week came and went and still there was no word from Teague. Fontine wondered if he's been forgotten; whether MI6 had developed second thoughts over the concept of "mismanagement at all costs." Regardless, life at Loch Torridon had taken his mind off his self-destructive memories; he actually felt quite strong and capable again.

The compound's lieutenants had devised what they called a "long-pursuit" exercise for the day. The four barracks operated separately, each taking forty-five degrees of the compass within a ten-mile radius of Loch Torridon. Two men from each barracks were given a fifteen-minute head start before the remaining recruits took chase; the object being for the hunted to elude the hunters for as long as possible.

It was natural for the sergeants to choose the best two from each barracks to begin the exercise. Victor and Petride were the first eluders in Barracks Three.

They raced down the rocky slope toward the Loch Torridon woods.

"Quickly now!" ordered Fontine as they entered the thick foliage of the forest. "We'll go left. The *mud;* step into the mud! Break as many branches as you can."

They ran no more than fifty yards, snapping limps, stamping their feet into the moist corridor of soft earth that angled through the woods. Victor issued his second command.

"Stop! This is far enough. Now, carefully. We'll make footprints up onto the dry ground. . . . That's enough. All right, step backward, directly on the prints. *Across* the mud. . . . Good. Now, we'll head back."

"Head back?" asked the bewildered Petride. "Head back where?"

"To the edge of the woods. Where we entered. We've still got eight minutes. That's enough time."

"For what?" The Serbo-Croat looked at his older friend as if Fontine was amusingly mad.

"To climb a tree. Out of sight."

Victor selected a tall Scotch pine in the center of a cluster of lower trees and started up, shinnying to the first level of branches. Petride followed, his boyish face elated. Both men reached the three-quarter height of the pine, bracing themselves on opposite sides of the trunk. They were obscured by the surrounding branches; the ground beneath, however, was visible to them.

"We've nearly two minutes to spare," whispered Victor, looking at his watch. "Kick any loose limbs away. Rest your weight solidly."

Two minutes and thirty seconds later, their pursuers passed far below them. Fontine leaned forward toward the young Serbo-Croat.

"We'll give them thirty seconds and then climb down. We'll head for the other side of the hill. A section of it fronts a ravine. It's a good hiding place."

"A stone's throw from the starting line!" Petride grinned. "How did you think of it?"

"You never had brothers to play games with. Race-and-hide was a favorite."

Mikhailovic's smile disappeared. "I have many brothers," he said enigmatically, and looked away.

There was no time to pursue Petride's statement. Nor did Victor care to. During the past eight days or so, the young Serbo-Croat had behaved quite strangely. Morose one minute, antic the next; and incessantly asking questions that were beyond the bounds of a six-week friendship. Fontine looked at his watch. "I'll start down first. If there's no one in sight, I'll yank the branches. That's your signal to follow."

On the ground, Victor and Petride crouched and ran east at the edge of the woods, the base of the starting hill. Three hundred yards, around the circle of the hill was a slope of jagged rock that overlooked a deep ravine. It was carved out of the hill by a crack of a glacier eons ago, a natural sanctuary. They made their way literally across the gorge. Breathing hard, Fontine lowered himself into a sitting position, his back against the stone cliff. He opened the pocket of his field jacket and took out a pack of cigarettes. Petride sat in front of him, his legs over the side of the ledge. Their isolated perch was no more than seven feet across, perhaps five in depth. Again, Victor looked at his watch. There was no need to whisper now.

"In half an hour, we'll climb over the crest and surprise the lieutenants. Cigarette?"

"No, thank you," replied Mikhailovic harshly, his back to Fontine.

The note of anger could not be overlooked. "What's the matter? Did you hurt yourself?"

Petride turned. His eyes bore into Victor. "In a manner of speaking, yes."

"I won't try to follow that. You either hurt yourself or you didn't. I'm not interested in manners of speech." Fontine decided that if this was to be one of Mikhailovic's periods of depression, they could do without conversation. He was beginning to think that beneath his wide-eyed innocence, Petride Mikhailovic was a disturbed young man.

"You *choose* what interests you, don't you, Victor? You turn the world off at will. With a switch in your head, all is void. Nothing." The Serbo-Croat stared at Fontine as he spoke.

"Be quiet. Look at the scenery, smoke a cigarette, leave me alone. You're becoming a bore."

Mikhailovic slowly pulled his legs over the ledge, his eyes still riveted on Victor. "You must not dismiss me. You cannot. I've shared my secrets with you. Openly, willingly. Now you must do the same."

Fontine watched the Serbo-Croat, suddenly apprehensive. "I think you mistake our relationship. Or, perhaps, I've mistaken your preferences."

"Don't insult me."

"Merely clarification——"

"My time has *run out!*" Petride raised his voice; his words formed a cry as his eyes remained wide, unblinking. "You're not blind! You're not deaf! Yet you pretend these things!"

"Get out of here," ordered Victor quietly. "Go back to the starting line. To the sergeants. The exercise is over."

"My name," Mikhailovic whispered, one leg pulled up beneath his powerful, crouching body. "From the beginning you refused to acknowledge it! *Petride!*"

"It is your name. I acknowledge it."

"You've never heard it before? Is that what you're saying?"

"If I have, it made no impression."

"That's a lie! It's the name of a priest. And you *knew that priest!*" Again the words floated upward, a cry shouted in desperation.

"I've known a number of priests. None with that name——"

"A priest on a *train!* A man devoted to the glory of God! Who walked in the grace of His holy work! You cannot, *must* not deny him!"

"*Mother of Christ!*" Fontine spoke inaudibly; the shock was overpowering. "Salonika. The freight from Salonika."

"Yes! That most holy train; documents that are the blood, the *soul* of the *one incorruptible, immaculate* church! You've taken them from us!"

"You're a priest of Xenope," said Victor, incredulous at the realization. "My God, you're a monk from Xenope!"

"With all my heart! With all my *mind* and *soul* and *body!*"

"How did you get here? How did you penetrate Loch Torridon?"

Mikhailovic pulled his other leg up; he was fully crouched now, a mad animal prepared to spring. "It's irrelevant. I must know where that vault was taken, where it was hidden. You'll tell me, *Vittorio Fontini-Cristi!* You've no choice!"

"I'll tell you what I told the British. I know *nothing!* The English saved my life; why would I lie?"

"Because you gave your word. To another."

"Who?"

"Your father."

"No! He was killed before he could say the words! If you know anything, you know that!"

The priest of Xenope's eyes became suddenly fixed. His stare was clouded, his lids wide, almost thyroid. He reached under his field jacket and withdrew a small, snub-nosed automatic. With his thumb he snapped up the safety. "You're insignificant. We're both insignificant," he whispered. "We're nothing."

Victor held his breath. He pulled his knees up; the split second approached when he would have the one opportunity to save his life, when he would lash his feet out at the maniacal priest. One boot at the weapon, the other at Mikhailovic's weighted leg, sending him over the precipice. It was all there was left—if he could do it.

Abruptly, the vocal intrusion startling, the priest spoke, his tone chantlike, transfixed. "You're telling me the truth," he said, closing his eyes. "You have told me the truth," he repeated hypnotically.

"Yes." Fontine took a deep, deep breath. As he exhaled, he knew he would plunge both legs out; the moment had come.

Petride stood up, his powerful chest expanding beneath the soldier's clothes. But the weapon was no longer aimed at Victor. Instead, both Mikhailovic's arms were extended in an attitude of crucifixion. The priest raised his head to the skies and shouted.

"I believe in one God, the Father Almighty! I will look into the eyes of the Lord and I shall not waver!"

The priest of Xenope bent his right arm and put the barrel of the automatic to his temple.

He fired.

"You got your first kill," said Teague casually, sitting in a chair in front of Fontine's desk in the small, enclosed cubicle.

"I did not kill him!"

"It doesn't matter how it happens, or who pulls the bloody trigger. The result's the same."

"For the wrong reason! That *train*, that damned, *unholy train!* When will it stop? When will it *go away?*"

"He was your enemy. That's all I'm saying."

"If he was, you should have know it, spotted it! You're a fool, Alec."

Teague shifted his legs in irritation. "That's rather harsh language for a captain to employ with a brigadier."

"Then I'd be delighted to purchase your command and set it right," said Victor, returning to the papers in manila folders on his desk.

"One doesn't do that in the military."

"It's the only reason for your continuity. You wouldn't last a week as one of my executives."

"I don't believe this." Teague spoke in astonishment. "I'm sitting here being cashiered by a ragtail guinea."

Fontine laughed. "Don't exaggerate. I'm only doing what you asked me to do." He gestured at the manila folders on the desk. "Refine Loch Torridon. In that process, I've tried to learn how this priest of Xenope, this Mikhailovic, got in."

"Have you?"

"I think so. It's a basic weakness with every one of these dossiers. There are no clear financial appraisals; there are endless words, histories, judgments—but very few figures. It should be corrected wherever possible before we make our final personnel decisions."

"What on earth are you talking about?"

"Money. Men are proud of it; it's the symbol of their productivity. It can be traced, confirmed in a dozen different ways. Records abound. Where possible, I want financial statements on every recruit in Loch Torridon. There was none on Petride Mikhailovic."

"*Financial——*"

"A financial statement," completed Fontine, "is a most penetrating look into a man's character. These are businessmen and professionals, by and large. They'll be anxious to oblige. Those that are not we'll question at length."

Teague uncrossed his legs, his voice respectful. "We'll get at it, there are forms for that sort of thing."

"If not," said Victor glancing up, "any banker or brokerage house can supply them. The more complex, the better."

"Yes, of course. And beyond this, how are things going?"

Fontine shrugged, waving his hand again over the pile of the folders on the desk. "Slowly. I've read all the dossiers several times, making notes, cataloging by professions and related professions. I've detailed geographical patterns, linguistic compatibilities. But where it's all led me, I'm not sure. It'll take time."

"And a lot of work," interrupted Teague. "Remember, I told you that."

"Yes. You also said it would be worthwhile. I hope you're right."

Teague leaned forward. "I have one of the finest men in the service to work with you. He'll be your communications man for the whole show. He's a crackerjack; knows more codes and ciphers than any ten of our best cryptographers. He's damned decisive, a shark at quick decision. Which is what you'll want, of course."

"Not for a long time."

"Before you know it."

"When do I meet him? What's his name?"

"Geoffrey Stone. I brought him up with me."

"He's in Loch Torridon?"

"Yes. No doubt checking the cryp's quarters. I want him in at the beginning."

Victor was not sure why but Teague's information disturbed him. He wanted to work alone, without distraction. "All right. I imagine we'll see him at the dinner mess."

Teague smiled again and looked at his watch.

"Well, I'm not sure you'll want to dine at the Torridon mess."

"One never *dines* at the mess, Alec. He eats."

"Yes, well, the cuisine notwithstanding. I've a bit of news for you. A friend of yours is in the sector."

"Sector? Is Loch Torridon a sector?"

"For air warning-relays."

"Good Lord! *Jane* is here?"

"I found out the night before last. She's on tour for the Air Ministry. Of course, she had no idea you were in this area, until I reached her yesterday. She was in Moray Firth, on the coast."

"You're a terrible manipulator!" Fontine laughed. "And so obvious. Where the devil *is* she?"

"I swear to you," said Teague with convincing innocence, "I knew nothing. Ask her yourself. There's an inn on the outskirts of town. She'll be there at five thirty."

My God, I've missed her! I've really missed her. It was rather extraordinary; he had not realized how deeply he felt. Her face with its sharp yet delicate features, her dark, soft hair that fell so beautifully around her shoulders; her eyes, so intensely blue; all were etched in his mind. "I assume you'll give me a pass to leave the compound."

Teague nodded. "And arrange a vehicle for you. But you've a while before you should drive off. Let's spend it on specifics. I realize you've only begun, but you must have reached a conclusion or two."

"I have. There are fifty-three men here. I doubt twenty-five will survive Loch Torridon, as I believe it should be run——"

They talked for nearly an hour. The more Fontine expanded his views, the more completely, he realized, did Teague accept them. Good, thought Victor. He was going to make many requests, including a continuing hunt for Loch Torridon talent. But now his thoughts turned to Jane.

"I'll walk you to your barracks," Teague said, sensing his impatience. "We might drop in at the officers' club for a minute—I promise no longer. Captain Stone will be there by now; you should meet him."

But it was not necessary to stop off at the officers' bar to find Captain Geoffrey Stone. As they walked down the steps of the field complex, Victor saw the figure of a tall man in an army overcoat. He stood about thirty feet away in the compound, his back to them, talking to a sergeant major. There was something familiar about the officer's build, a kind of unmilitary slouch in the shoulders. Most striking was the man's right hand. It was encased in a black glove obviously several sizes too large to be normal. It was a medical glove; the hand was bandaged beneath the black leather.

The man turned; Fontine halted in his tracks, his breath suspended.

Captain Geoffrey Stone was the agent named Apple, who was shot on the pier in Celle Ligure.

They held each other. Neither spoke, for words were extraneous. It had been ten weeks since they'd been together. Ten weeks since the splendid, exciting moments of love-making.

At the inn, the old woman who sat in a rocking chair behind the front desk had greeted him.

"Flying Officer Holcroft arrived a half hour ago. 'A trust you're the captain, though the clothes dinna' say it. She said you're t' go up, if you're a mind to. She's a direct lass. Dinna' care for sly words, that one. Top of the stairs, turn left, room four."

He had knocked softly at the door, the pounding in his chest ridiculously adolescent. He wondered if she was possessed by the same tension.

She stood inside, her hand on the doorknob, her inquisitive blue eyes bluer and more searching than he could remember ever having seen them. The tension was there, yet there was confidence, too.

He stepped in and took her hand. He shut the door; they closed the distance between them and slowly reached for each other. When their lips touched, all the questions were put to rest, the answers obvious in silence.

"I was frightened, do you know that?" whispered Jane, holding his face in her hands, kissing his lips tenderly, repeatedly.

"Yes. Because I was frightened, too."

"I wasn't sure what I was going to say."

"Neither was I. So here we are talking about our uncertainties. It's healthy, I suppose."

"It's probably childish," she said, tracing his forehead and his cheek with her fingers.

"I think not. To want . . . to *need* . . . with such feeling is a thing apart. One is afraid it may not be returned." He took her hand from his face and kissed it, then kissed her lips and then her soft dark hair that fell, framing the smooth skin of her lovely face. He reached around her and pulled her to him, holding her close, and whispered "I *do* need you. I've missed you."

"You're a love to say it, my darling, but you don't have to. I don't require it, I won't ask for it."

Victor pulled away gently and cupped her face, staring into her eyes, so close to his. "Isn't it the same with you?"

"Very much the same." She leaned into him, her lips against his cheeks. "I think of you far too often. And I'm a very busy girl."

He knew she wanted him as fully and completely as he wanted her. The tension each had felt was transferred to their bodies, release to be found only in the act of love. Yet the swelling, aching urgency in them did not demand swiftness. Instead, they held each other in the warm excitement of the bed, explored each other in tenderness and growing insistence. And they talked softly in whispers as their excitement grew.

Oh, God, he loved her so.

They lay naked under the covers, spent. She rose on her elbow and reached across him, touching his shoulders, tracing the skin with her fingers down to his thighs. Her dark hair fell over his chest; behind it, below her delicate face and penetrating blue eyes, her breasts were suspended over his flesh. He moved his right hand and reached for her, a signal that the act of love would begin again. And it suddenly occurred to Vittorio Fontini-Cristi, as they lay naked together, that he never wanted to lose this woman.

"How long can you stay in Loch Torridon?" he asked, pulling her face down to his.

"You're a horrid manipulating spoiler of not-so-young girls," she whispered, laughing softly in his ear. "I am currently in a state of erotic anxiety, with the memory of thunderbolts and erogenous pleasure still rippling up my most private—and you ask me how long I can stay! Forever and ever, of course. Until I return to London in three days."

"Three days! It's better than two days. Or twenty-four hours."

"For what? To reduce us both to babbling idiots?"

"We'll be married."

Jane raised her head and looked at him. She looked at him for a long time before she spoke, her eyes locked with his. "You've been through a great deal of sorrow. And terrible confusion."

"You don't want to marry me?"

"More than my *life*, my darling. God, more than all the world. . . ."

"But you don't say yes."

"I'm yours. You don't have to marry me."

"I *want* to marry you. Is it wrong?"

"It's the rightest thing I can imagine. But you have to be sure."

"Are *you* sure?"

She lowered her cheek on his. "Yes. It's you. *You* must be sure."

With his hand he swept her soft dark hair away from her face and answered her with his eyes.

Ambassador Anthony Brevourt sat behind the enormous desk in his Victorian study. It was nearly midnight, the household retired, the city of London dark. Everywhere men and women were on rooftops and on the river and in the parks talking quietly into wireless sets, watching the skies. Waiting for the siege they knew would come, but had not yet begun.

It was a matter of weeks; Brevourt knew it, the records projected it. But he could not keep his attention on the horrors that would reshape history as inevitably as the events moved forward. He was consumed by another catastrophe. Less immediately dramatic, but in many ways no less profound. It was contained in the file folder in front of him. He stared at the handwritten code name he had created for himself. And a few—very few—others.

SALONIKA

So simple in the reading, yet so complex in meaning.

How in God's name could it have happened? What were they thinking of? How could the movements of a single freight crossing half a dozen national borders be untraceable? The key had to be with the subject.

From below, in a locked drawer of his desk, a telephone rang. Brevourt unlocked the drawer and pulled it open. He lifted the receiver.

"Yes?"

"Loch Torridon," was the flat reply.

"Yes, Loch Torridon? I'm alone."

"The subject was married yesterday. To the candidate."

Brevourt momentarily stopped breathing. Then inhaled deeply. The voice on the other end of the line spoke again. "Are you there, London? Do you hear me?"

"Yes, Torridon. I heard you. It's more than we might have hoped for, isn't it? Is Teague pleased?"

"Not actually. I think he would have preferred a convenient relationship. Not the marriage. I don't think he was prepared for that."

"Probably not. The candidate might be considered an obstruction. Teague will have to adjust. Salonika has far greater priority."

"Don't you ever tell M.I.-Six that, London."

"At this juncture," said Brevourt coldly, "I trust all files relative to Salonika have been *removed* from M.I.-Six. That was our understanding, Loch Torridon."

"It is correct. Nothing remains."

"Good. I'll be traveling with Churchill to Paris. You may reach me through the official Foreign Office channel, Code Maginot. Stay in contact; Churchill wants to be kept informed."

Chapter Nine

London

Fontine entered the stream of pedestrians moving toward Paddington Station. There was a numbness in the streets, a sense of disbelief that resulted in pockets of silence. Eyes searched other eyes, strangers took notice of the other strangers.

France had fallen.

Victor turned into Marylebone; he saw people buying newspapers in silence. It had happened; it had *really happened*. Across the Channel was the enemy—victorious, invincible.

The Dover boats from Calais held no crowds of laughing tourists on holiday any longer. Now there were different journeys; everyone had heard of them. The Calais boats sailed under cover of night, as men and women, some bloodied, some whole, all desperate, crouched below decks, hidden by nets and canvas, bringing out the stories of agony and defeat that were Normandy, Rouen, Strasbourg, and Paris.

Fontine remembered Alec Teague's words: *The concept, the strategy is to send them back to disrupt the marketplace . . . create havoc! Mismanagement at all costs!*

The marketplace was now all of Western Europe. And Captain Victor Fontine was ready to send out his Loch Torridon mismanagers of that marketplace.

Of the original fifty-three continentals, twenty-four remained; others would be added—slowly, selectively—as losses demanded. These twenty-four were as diverse as they were accomplished, as inventive as they were devious. They were German, Austrian, Belgian, Polish, Dutch, and Greek, but their nationalities were secondary. Labor forces were shipped across borders daily. For in Berlin, the *Reichsministerium* of Industry was pressing into service people from all occupied territories—it was a sweeping policy that would accelerate as new lands were brought under control. It was not unusual for a Hollander to be working in a Stuttgart factory. Already—only days after Paris fell—Belgians were being shipped to captured plants in Lyon.

Acting on this knowledge, the underground leaders were scouring the labor-transfer lists. Objectives: Find specialized temporary "employment" for twenty-four skilled professionals.

In the confusion that resulted from the German obsession for maximum productivity, positions were unearthed everywhere. Krupp and I.G. Farben were exporting so many experts to get factories and laboratories rolling in conquered countries that German industrialists complained bitterly to Berlin. It led to haphazard organization, slipshod management; it reduced the effectiveness of German plants and offices.

It was into this morass that the French, Dutch, Belgian, Polish, and German undergrounds infiltrated. Job recruitment directives were sent by espionage couriers to London, for the scrutiny of Captain Victor Fontine.

Item: Frankfurt, Germany. Messerschmidt subsupplier. Three plant foremen sought.

Item: Kraków, Poland. Axle division, automobile plant. Draftsmen needed.

Item: Antwerp, Belgium. Railroad yards. Freight and scheduling divisions. Management scarce.

Item: Mannheim, Germany. Government printing offices. Bilingual technical translators needed imperatively.

Item: Turin, Italy. Turin Aircraft. Source partigiano. *Mechanical engineers in short supply.*

Item: Linz, Austria. Berlin claims consistent overpayment fabrics company. Cost accountants needed.

Item: Dijon, France. Wehrmacht legal department. Lawyers demanded by occupation forces. . . . (So like the French, Victor had thought. In the midst of defeat, the Gallic mind sought debate in practical legalities.)

And so they went. Scores of "requirements," dozens of possibilities that would grow in numbers as the German demands for productivity grew.

There was work to be had, to be done, by the small brigade of Loch Torridon continentals. It was now merely a question of proper allocations and Fontine would personally oversee the specifics. He carried in his briefcase a very small strip of reusable tape that could be attached to any part of the body. The adhesive had the tensile strength of steel, but could be removed by a simple solution of water, sugar, and citrus juice.

Within that tape were twenty-four dots, each containing a microfilm. On each microfilm was a microscopically reduced photograph and a brief résumé of talents. They would be used in concert with the underground leaders. Twenty-four positions of employment would be found . . . temporary, to be sure, for such skilled personnel would be desirable in many locations during the coming months.

But first things first, and the first item on Fontine's agenda was a business trip of undetermined length. He would be parachuted into France, in the province of Lorraine near the Franco-Swiss border. His first conference would take place in the small town of Montbéliard, where he would stay for several days. It was a strategic geographical point, affording maximum accessibility for the underground from northern and central France and southern Germany.

From Montbéliard he would head north on the Rhine as far as Wiesbaden, where contingents of anti-Reichists from Bremen, Hamburg, Berlin, and points north and west would gather for meetings. From Wiesbaden he would take the underground's routes east to Prague, then northwest into Poland and Warsaw. Schedules would be created, codes refined, official work papers provided for eventual duplication in London.

From Warsaw he would return to Lorraine. The decision would then be made whether to head south into his beloved Italy. Captain Geoffrey Stone was against it in principle. The agent Fontine had known as Apple made that clear. All things Italian filled Stone with loathing, his revulsion traced to a pier in Celle Ligure and a hand shattered because of Italian naïveté and betrayal. Stone saw no reason to waste their resources on Italy; there were too many other pressure points. The nation of incompetents was its own worst enemy.

Fontine reached Paddington and waited for the Kensington bus. He had discovered buses in London; he had never taken public conveyances in his life before. The discovery was partly defensive. Whenever official cars were used, they were shared, calling for conversation between the passengers. None was called for on a bus.

There were times, of course, when he carried highly sensitive material home to read, when Alec Teague simply refused to allow him his newfound indulgence. It was too dangerous. Tonight had been a case in point, but

Victor had fought his superior; the official car had two other riders and he wanted to think. It was his last night in England. Jane had to be told.

"For heaven's sake, Alec! I'll be traveling several thousand miles in hostile territory. If I lose a briefcase that's chained to my wrist with a combination lock on a London bus, I think we're all in for immense trouble!"

Teague had capitulated, checking the chain and the lock himself.

The bus pulled up and he climbed in, threading his way down the crowded corridor to a seat in the front. It was by a window; he looked out and let his thoughts dwell first on Loch Torridon.

They *were* ready. The concept *was* valid. They *could* place their personnel in succeeding managerial positions. All that remained was the implementation of the strategy. He would accomplish a great deal of that on his trip. He would find the right positions for the right personnel . . . the chaos and the havoc would shortly follow.

He was primed for the moment of departure. Yet he was not really prepared for the one thing that faced him now: telling Jane the moment had finally come.

He had moved into her Kensington flat when he returned from Scotland. She'd rejected his offer of considerably grander quarters. And these past weeks were the happiest in his life.

And now the moment had come and fear would replace the comfort of daily existence together. It made no difference that thousands upon thousands were going through the same experience; there was no comfort in mathematics.

His stop was next. The June twilight washed the trees and scrubbed the houses. Kensington was peaceful, the war remote. He got off the bus and started down the quiet street when suddenly his attention was drawn away from the entrance gate. He had learned over the past months not to betray his concern, so he pretended to wave to an unseen neighbor in a window across the way. By doing so, while squinting his eyes against the setting sun, he was able to see more clearly the small Austin sedan parked on the opposite side of the street fifty yards diagonally in front of him. It was gray. He had seen that gray Austin before. Exactly five days ago. He remembered vividly. He and Stone had been driving up to Chelmsford to interview a Jewess who had worked for the Kraków civil service until just before the invasion. They had stopped at a service station outside of Brentwood.

The gray Austin sedan had driven in behind them to the pump beside theirs. Victor had noticed it only because an attendant who sold the driver petrol was caustic when the pump registered less than two gallons . . . and the Austin's tank was full.

"That's bein' a mite greedy," the attendant had said.

The driver had looked embarrassed, turned the ignition, and sped out on the highway.

Fontine had noticed because the driver was a priest. The driver of the gray Austin across from him now was a priest. The white collar could be seen clearly.

And the man, he knew, was staring at him.

Fontine walked casually to the gate of the house. He lifted the latch, entered, turned, and closed the gate; the priest in the gray Austin sat motionless, his eyes—behind what appeared to be thick glasses—still directed at him. Victor approached the door and let himself inside. The moment he was in the hallway he shut the door and moved quickly to the narrow column of windows that flanked the doorframe. A blackout curtain was draped over the glass; he parted the edge and looked out.

The priest had inched his way over to the right window of his car and was looking out and up at the front of the building. The man was grotesque, thought Fontine. He was extremely pale and thin, and the lenses of his glasses were thick.

Victor let the curtain fall back and walked rapidly to the staircase, climbing the steps two at a time to the third floor, their floor. He could hear music within; the radio was on; Jane was home. As he closed the door behind him, he heard her humming in the bedroom. There was no time to shout greetings; he wanted to get to the window. And he did not wish to alarm her if he could avoid it.

His binoculars were in the bookshelf on the fireplace wall. He pulled the case from its recess between a section of books and took out the binoculars, went to the window and focused the glass below.

The priest was talking to someone in the back seat of the small automobile. Fontine had not seen anyone else in the car. The rear seat was in shadow and he had been concentrating on the driver. He edged the binoculars behind the priest and refined the focus.

Victor froze. The blood rushed to his head.

It was a nightmare! A nightmare that repeated itself! *Fed* upon itself!

The streak of white in the close-cropped hair! He had seen that shock of white from an embankment . . . inside an automobile . . . under the glaring lights . . . soon to erupt in smoke and death!

Campo di Fiori!

The man in the back seat of the gray Austin below had been in another back seat! Fontine had looked down at him from the darkness as he was now looking down at him thousands of miles away in a Kensington street! One of the German commanders! One of the German executioners!

"Good heavens! You startled me," said Jane, walking into the room. "What are you——?"

"Get Teague on the telephone! Now!" shouted Victor, dropping the binoculars, struggling with the combination lock on his briefcase.

"What *is* it, darling?"

"Do as I say!" He fought to keep control. The numbers came; the lock sprang open.

Jane stared at her husband; she dialed rapidly, asking no further questions.

Fontine raced into the bedroom. He pulled his service revolver from between a pile of shirts and tore it from its holster, running back into the living room toward the door.

"Victor! Stop! For God's sake!"

"Tell Teague to get over here! Tell him a German from Campo di Fiori is below!"

He ran out into the corridor and raced down the narrow staircase, manipulating his thumb beneath the barrel of the weapon, unlatching the safety. As he reached the top of the first flight, he heard the gunning of an engine. He yelled and plunged down to the hallway, to the front door, yanking furiously at the knob, pulling the door open with such force that it crashed against the wall. He ran outside to the gate.

The gray Austin was speeding down the street; pedestrians were on the sidewalks. Fontine chased it, dodging two oncoming cars, their tires screeching as they braked. Men and women shouted at him; Victor understood. A man racing in the middle of the street at seven in the evening with a gun in his hand was a cause for violent alarms. But he could not dwell on such thoughts; there was only the gray Austin and a man in the back seat with a shock of white in his hair.

The *executioner*.

The Austin turned right at the corner! Oh, God! The traffic on the throughfare was light, only a few taxis and private cars! The Austin accelerated, speeding, weaving between the vehicles. It jumped a traffic light, narrowly missing a delivery truck which jolted to a stop, blocking all vision beyond.

He had lost it. He stopped, his heart pounding, sweat pouring down his face, his weapon at his side. But he had not lost everything. There were six numbers on the gray Austin's license plate. He'd managed to distinguish four of them.

"The automobile in question is registered to the Greek embassy. The attaché assigned to it claims it must have been removed from the embassy grounds late this afternoon." Teague spoke rapidly, annoyed not only with his conceivably false information but with the entire incident itself. It was an obstruction, a serious obstruction. The Loch Torridon operation could not tolerate barriers at this moment.

"Why the German? Who is he? I know *what* he is." Victor spoke quietly, with enormous feeling.

"We're putting on every trace we can come up with. A dozen experienced field men are pulling the files. They're going back years, getting everything we have. The description you gave the artist was good; his sketch quite accurate, you said. If he's there, we'll find him."

Fontine got out of the chair, started for the window and saw that heavy black drapes had been drawn, shutting in all light. He turned and looked absently at a large map of Europe on Teague's wall. There were dozens of red mark-pins protruding from the thick paper.

"It's the train from Salonika, isn't it?" He asked the question softly, not needing an answer.

"That wouldn't explain the German. If he is a German."

"I *told* you," interrupted Victor, turning to face the brigadier. "He was there. In Campo di Fiori. I remembered then that I'd thought I'd seen him before."

"And you've never been able to recall where?"

"No. There are times when it drives me mad. I don't *know!*"

"Can you associate? Go back. Think in terms of cities, or hotels; start with business dealings, contracts. Fontini-Cristi had investments in Germany."

"I've tried all that. There's nothing. Only the face, and that not terribly clear. But the white streak in the hair, that's what stays in my mind." Wearily, Victor returned to the chair and sat down again. He leaned back, both hands over his closed eyes. "Oh, God, Alec, I'm frightened to death."

"You've no reason to be."

"You weren't in Campo di Fiori that night."

"There'll be no repetition in London. Or anywhere else, for that matter. Tomorrow morning your wife will be escorted to the Air Ministry, where she will turn over her workload—files, letters, maps, everything—to another officer. The ministry has assured me the transition can be concluded by early afternoon. Thereupon, she'll be driven to very comfortable quarters in the countryside. Isolated and totally secure. She'll stay there until you return, or until we find your man. And break him."

Fontine lowered his hands from his eyes. He looked questioningly at Teague. "When did you do this? There's been no time."

Teague smiled, but it was not the unsettling smile Victor was used to. It was, if anything, gentle. "It's been a contingency plan since the day you were married. Within hours, as a matter of fact."

"She'll be safe?"

"No one in England more so. Frankly, I've a twofold motive. Your wife's safety is directly related to your state of mind. You've a job to do, so I'll do mine."

Teague looked at the wall clock, then at his wristwatch. The clock had lost nearly a minute since he'd last adjusted it. When *was* that? It must have been eight, ten days ago; he would have to bring it back to the watchsmith's in Leicester Square.

It was a foolish preoccupation, he supposed, this obsession with time. He'd heard the names: "Stopwatch Alec," "Timer Teague." His colleagues often chided him; he wouldn't be so damned concerned with time if he had a wife and small ones clattering about. But he had made that decision years ago; in his profession he was better off without such attachments. He was no monk. There had, of course, been women. But no marriage. It was out of the question; it was a hindrance, an obstacle.

These passive thoughts gave rise to an active consideration: Fontine and *his* marriage. The Italian was the perfect coordinator for the Loch Torridon operation, yet now there was an obstacle—his wife.

Goddamn it! He had cooperated with Brevourt because he really *did* want to use Fontini-Cristi. If a convenient relationship with an English girl served both objectives, he was willing to go along. But not *this* far!

And now, where the hell was Brevourt? He had given up. He had faded away after having made extraordinary demands of Whitehall in the name of an unknown freight from Salonika.

Or had he merely pretended to fade away?

It seemed that Brevourt knew when to cut his losses, when to back away from an embarrassing failure. There'd been no further instructions regarding Fontine; he was now the property of MI6. Just like that. It was as though Brevourt wanted to put as much distance as possible between himself and the Italian *and* the goddamned train. When the report of the infiltrating priest of Xenope was given to Brevourt, he feigned only a mild interest, ascribing the episode to a lone fanatic.

For a man who had moved his government to do what it did, that wasn't natural. Because the priest of Xenope had not acted alone. Teague knew it; Brevourt knew it, too. The ambassador was reacting too simply, his sudden disinterest too obvious.

And that girl, Fontine's wife. When she appeared, Brevourt had snapped up her existence like a true MI-Sixer himself. She was a short-range anchor. She could be appealed to, used. If Fontine's behavior became suddenly strange, if he entered into or sought abnormal contacts that could be traced to the train from Salonika, she was to be called in and given her instructions: *report everything*. She was an English patriot; she would comply.

But no one had even considered a marriage. That *was* mismanagement-at-all-costs! Instructions could be given to a convenient mistress; they were not given to a wife.

Brevourt had taken this news with an equanimity that was again unnatural. Something was happening that Teague did not understand. He had the uncomfortable feeling that Whitehall was using MI6 and that meant using him, tolerating Loch Torridon because it might lead Brevourt to a greater objective than the scattered disruption of enemy industry.

Back to the train from Salonika.

So two parallel strategies were being played out: Loch Torridon, and the search for the documents of Constantine. They allowed him the former; he was dismissed from the latter.

Dismissed and left with a married Intelligence officer—the most vulnerable kind.

It was ten minutes to three in the morning. In six hours he would be driving down to Lakenheath with Fontine to see him off.

A man with a streak of white in his hair. A sketch that eluded thousands of photographs and file descriptions, a hunt that led nowhere. A dozen MI6 staffers were down in the archives continuing the search. The field agent who broke the identity would not be overlooked when choice assignments were passed around.

His telephone rang, startling him.

"Yes?"

"It's Stone, sir. I think I have something."

"I'll be right down."

"If it's all the same to you, I'd prefer coming up. It's a bit mad. I'd rather see you alone."

"Very well."

What had Stone found? What could be so odd that it required in-house security?

"Here is the sketch Fontine approved, general," said Captain Geoffrey Stone, standing in front of Teague's desk, placing the charcoal portrait on the blotter. An envelope was clamped awkwardly between his arm and his chest, above the immobile, gloved right hand. "It matched nothing in the Himmler files, or any other German—or German-related—sources, including collaborationist circles in Poland, Czechoslovakia, France, the Balkans, and Greece."

"And Italy? What of the Italians?"

"That was our first consideration. Regardless of what Fontine claims to have seen that night in Campo di Fiori, he *is* Italian. The Fontini-Cristis made enemies among the fascists. But we found nothing, no one faintly resembling the subject in question. Then quite frankly, sir, I began thinking about the man. His marriage. We didn't expect that, did we, sir?"

"No, captain. We did not expect that."

"A small vicarage in Scotland. A church of England ceremony. Not exactly what one would have thought."

"Why not?"

"I've worked the Italian sectors, general. The Catholic influence is most pervasive."

"Fontine's not a religious man. What in hell are you driving at?"

"Just that. Everything's a question of degree, isn't it? One never is just this or just that. Especially a man who has wielded such power. I went back to *his* file; we've photostats of every damned thing we could lay our hands on. Including his marriage application and certificate. Under the heading of 'denomination' he inserted one word: 'Christian.'"

"Get to the point."

"I'm doing so. One thing always leads to another. An immensely wealthy, powerful family in a Catholic country, and the surviving son purposely denies any association with its church."

Teague narrowed his eyes. "Go on, captain."

"He *was denying*. Perhaps unconsciously, we don't know. 'Christian' is not a denomination. We were looking for the wrong Italians, pulling out the wrong files." Stone raised the envelope with his left hand, unwound the small string and opened the flap. He took out a newspaper clipping, a cropped photograph of a bareheaded man with a shock of white in his dark hair. The bareheaded man wore the black robes of the church; the picture was taken at the altar of St. Peter's. The man was kneeling, facing the cross. Above him was a pair of outstretched hands. They were holding the three-cornered hat of a cardinal.

"My God!" Teague looked up at Stone.

"The Vatican files. We keep records of all ecclesiastical elevations."

"But *this*——"

"Yes, sir. The subject's name is Guillamo Donatti. He's one of the most powerful cardinals in the Curia."

Chapter Ten

Montbéliard

The aircraft began its ninety-degree turn. They were at 3,000 feet, the night clear, the wind stream rushing past the open hatch with such force Fontine thought he would be sucked out before the red light above him was extinguished, replaced by the sudden glare of the white bulb that was his signal to leap. He gripped the handles at the sides of the hatch, bracing himself; his thick boots were pressed against the steel deck of the Haviland bomber; he waited to jump.

He thought of Jane. At first, she'd objected strenuously to her confinement. She had earned her position at the Air Ministry, weeks and months of "just plain damned hard work," were now taken away in a matter of hours. And then she abruptly stopped, seeing, he was sure, the pain in his eyes. She wanted him back. If isolation in the countryside would help his return, she would go.

He thought, too, of Teague; partially of what he said, mostly of what he did not say. MI6 had a line on the German executioner, the man-monster with the streak of white in his hair who had coldly observed the horror of Campo di Fiori. The service assumed him to be a ranking member of the *Geheimdienst Korps*, Himmler's secret police, a man who stayed far in the background, never expecting to be identified. Someone who had been stationed at the German consulate in Athens, perhaps.

"Assumed." "Perhaps." Words of equivocation. Teague was concealing information. For all his experience, the Intelligence man could not hide his omissions. Nor was he entirely convincing when he subtly introduced a subject that had little to do with anything:

"——it's standard procedure, Fontine. When a man goes on assignment we list his religious affiliation. Just like a birth certificate or a passport——"

No, he had no formal affiliation. No, he was not Catholic, nor was that extraordinary; there *were* non-Catholics in Italy. Yes, Fontini-Cristi was a derivative combination that was translated as the "fountains of Christ"; yes, the family for centuries had been allied with the church, but a number of decades ago had broken with the Vatican. But, no, he did not place undue emphasis on the break; he rarely thought about it.

What was Teague after?

The red light went off. Victor bent his knees as he had learned to do, and held his breath.

The white bulb flashed. The tap came—sharp, assured, solid. Fontine whipped his hands into reverse grips on the latch handles, leaned back, and propelled himself through the open hatch into the furious slipstream of the aircraft. He was buffeted away from the huge fuselage, the force of the wind crashing into his body with the sudden velocity and weight of a giant wave.

He was in free fall. He forced his legs into a V, feeling the harness of his chute cutting into his thighs. He thrust his arms forward and diagonally out at his side. The spread-eagle configuration did what it was supposed to do: It stabilized his fall through the sky, just enough for Victor to concentrate on the dark earth below.

He saw them! Two tiny flares to his left.

He pulled his right hand in against the rushing air and tugged at a small ring beside the parachute release. There was a momentary flash above him, like an instantly fading spit of a Roman candle. It would be enough for those on the ground to get a sighting. The moment fell back into darkness; he yanked the rubber handle of the parachute release. The billowing folds of cloth shot out of the pack; the massive jolt came, causing him to expunge his breath, his every muscle taut in counterthrust.

He floated, swinging in quarter circles in the night sky, toward the earth.

The conferences in Montbéliard went well. It was strange, thought Victor, but in spite of the crude, even primitive surroundings—an abandoned warehouse, a barn, a rock-strewn pasture—the conferences were not unlike smoothly run management meetings, with himself acting as a visiting consultant from the home office. The objective of each conference with the teams of underground leaders who made their covert treks into Lorraine was the same: projected recruitment for the pool of skilled personnel now in exile in England.

Management personnel were in demand everywhere, for everywhere within the Third Reich's expanding sphere production facilities were instantly appropriated and geared for maximum output. But there was a major flaw in the German obsession for immediate efficiency: Control remained in Berlin. Requests were processed by the *Reichsministerium* of Industry and Armaments; orders were cleared and issued hundreds of miles away from the place of origin.

Orders could be intercepted enroute; requests could be altered at the source, within the ministries; infiltrated at the clerical level.

Positions could be created; personnel could be replaced. In the chaos that was the Berlin fever for instant, total efficiency, fear was inherent. Orders were rarely questioned.

Everywhere the bureaucratic environment was ripe for Loch Torridon.

"You will be taken to the Rhine and put aboard a river barge at Neuf-Brisach," said the Frenchman, going to the small window in the rooming house overlooking Montebéliard's rue de Bac. "Your escort will bring the papers. I understand they describe you as river garbage, strong back and small head. A loading stevedore who spends most of his waking hours drunk with very cheap wine."

"That should be interesting."

The Rhine

It wasn't. It was grueling, physically exhausting, and made almost intolerable by the stench below decks. German patrols prowled the river, stopping vessels continuously, subjecting crews to brutal interrogations. The Rhine was an underground courier route; it took no great perception to know that. And because the river "garbage" deserved no better, the patrols took delight in wielding clubs and rifle stocks when bones and flesh were the objects of impact. Fontine's cover was successful, if revolting. He drank enough rancid wine and induced sufficient vomit to give his breath the putrid foulness of a confirmed, unkempt alcoholic.

What kept him from losing his sensibilities altogether was his escort. The man's name was Lübok, and Victor knew that whatever risks he was taking, Lübok's were far greater.

Lübok was a Jew and a homosexual. He was a blond-haired, blue-eyed, middle-aged ballet master whose Czechoslovakian parents had emigrated to Berlin thirty years ago. Fluent in the Slovak languages, as well as German, he held papers identifying him as a translator for the Wehrmacht. Along with the papers were several letters on High Command stationery that proclaimed Lübok's loyalty to the Reich.

The papers and the letterheads were genuine, the loyalty false. Lübok operated as an underground courier across the Czechoslovakian and Polish borders. At such times he wore his homosexual inclinations outrageously on his sleeve; it was common knowledge that such circles existed in the Officer *Korps*. Checkpoints never knew who was favored by powerful men who preferred to bed with other men. And the middle-aged ballet master was an encyclopedia of truths, half-truths and gossip as they pertained to the sexual practices and aberrations practiced by the German High Command in any given sector or zone he entered. It was his inventory; it was his weapon.

Lübok had volunteered for the Loch Torridon assignment, to be the MI6 escort out of Montbéliard, through Wiesbaden, east to Prague and north to Warsaw. And as the journey progressed and the days and the miles went by, Fontine was grateful. Lübok was the best. Beneath the well-tailored suits was a powerful man whose acid tongue and withering stare guaranteed a hot but intelligent temper.

Warsaw, Poland

Lübok drove the motorcycle with Victor in the sidecar, dressed in the uniform of a Wehrmacht *Oberst* attached to Occupation Transport. They sped out of Lódz on the road to Warsaw, reaching the final checkpoint a little before midnight.

Lübok performed outrageously before the patrols, dropping the names of *Kommandanten* and *Oberführerin* in acid rapidity, implying all manner of recriminations if their vehicle was detained. The embarrassed guards were not anxious to test him. The bike was waved through; they entered the city.

It was chaos. Although it was dark, rubble could be discerned everywhere. Street after street was deserted. Candles shone in windows—most electricity was out. Wires sagged, automobiles and trucks were immobilized—scores overturned, lying like giant steel insects waiting to be impaled on a laboratory table.

Warsaw was dead. Its armed killers walked in groups, themselves afraid of the corpse.

"We head for the Casimir," said Lübok softly. "The underground's waiting for you. It's no more than ten streets from here."

"What's the Casimir?"

"An old palace on the Kraków Boulevard. In the middle of the city. For years it was the university; now the Germans use it for barracks and offices."

"We go in *there?*"

Lübok smiled in the darkness. "You can put Nazis in universities, but it guarantees no instruction. The maintenance crews for all the buildings and the grounds are *podziemna*. Underground, to you. At least the beginnings of one."

Lübok squeezed the motorcycle between two staff cars on the Kraków Boulevard, halfway down the block, across from the main gate to the Casimir. Except for the guards at the gatehouse, the street was deserted. Only two streetlamps were working, but within the Casimir's grounds floodlights shot up from the grass, lighting the ornate facades of the buildings.

Out of the shadows walked a German soldier, an enlisted man. He approached Lübok and spoke quietly in Polish. Lübok nodded; the German continued diagonally across the wide boulevard up toward the Casimir gate.

"He's with the *podziemna*," said Lübok. "He used the correct codes. He said you should go in first. Ask for Captain Hans Neumann, Block Seven."

"Captain Hans Neumann," repeated Victor. "Block Seven. What then?"

"He's tonight's contact in the Casimir. He'll take you to the others."

"What about you?"

"I'm to wait ten minutes and follow. I'm to ask for an Oberst Schneider, Block Five."

Lübok seemed concerned. Victor understood. Never before had they been separated at their point of contact with the underground leaders. "This is an unusual procedure, isn't it? You look troubled."

"They must have their reasons."

"But you don't know what they are. And that fellow didn't tell you."

"He wouldn't know. He's a messenger."

"Do you sense a trap?"

Lübok leveled his gaze at Fontine. He was thinking as he spoke. "No, that's not really possible. The commandant of this sector has been compromised. On film. I won't bore you with details, but his proclivity for children has been duly recorded. He's been shown the results and told negatives exist. He lives in fear, and we live with *him*. . . . He's a Berlin favorite, a close friend of Göring's. No, it's not a trap."

"But you're worried."

"Needlessly. He *had* the codes; they're complicated and very precise. I'll see you later."

Victor got out of the cramped sidecar and started across the boulevard toward the gates of the Casimir. He stood erect, the picture of arrogance, prepared to arrogantly display false papers that would gain him admittance.

As he walked across the Casimir's floodlit grounds, he could see German soldiers strolling in pairs and threes down the paths. A year ago these men might have been students and professors, recapping the events of the academic day. Now they were conquerors, peacefully removed from the devastation that was everywhere outside the walls of the Casimir. Death, hunger, and mutilation were within the sound of their commands, yet they talked quietly on clean paths, oblivious to the consequences of their acts.

Campo di Fiori. There were floodlights at Campo di Fiori. And death with mutilation.

He forced the images out of his mind; he could not allow his concentration to be weakened. The entranceway with the filigreed arch framing the thick double doors below the number seven was directly ahead. A Wehrmacht guard stood at attention on the single marble step.

Fontine recognized him: the soldier who had whispered in Polish to Lübok on the Kraków Boulevard:

"You're efficient," said Victor softly in German.

The guard nodded, reached for the door and opened it. "Be quickly now. Do use the staircase to the left. You will be met on the first landing."

Fontine walked rapidly through the door into the huge marble hall, crossed to the stairs, and started up. Halfway to the landing he slowed his pace. A silent alarm went off in his brain.

The guard's voice, his use of German. The words were odd, strangely awkward. *Be quickly. . . . Do use the staircase. . . .*

Watch for the lack of idiom, the excessively grammatical, or conversely, unmatching end syllables. Loch Torridon.

The guard was not German. Yet why should he be? He was from the *podziemna.* Yet, again, the *podziemna* would not take chances. . . .

Two German officers appeared on the landing, their pistols drawn and leveled down at him. The man on the right spoke.

"Welcome to the Casimir, Signor Fontini-Cristi."

"Please don't stop, *padrone.* We must hurry," said the second man.

The language they spoke was Italian, but their speech was not native. Victor recognized the source. The officers above him were no more German than the guard was German. They were *Greek*. The train from Salonika had reappeared!

There was the crack of a pistol bolt behind him, followed by rapid footsteps. Within seconds, the barrel was jammed into the small of his back, propelling him farther up the staircase.

There was no way he could move, no diversion he could employ, to distract his confronters. Weapons covered him, eyes watched his hands, bullets were locked in chambers.

Above, somewhere in an unfamiliar corridor, he heard laughter. Perhaps if he shouted, raising alarms of an enemy within the enemy camp; the concentric circle of thought was numbing.

"Who are you?" *Words.* Begin with words. If he could raise his voice in sequence, natural sequence that would minimize the chance of triggers pulled. "You're not German!"

Louder. *Now* louder.

"What are you *doing* here?"

The barrel of the pistol slid up his back and was jabbed into the base of his skull. The jolt caused him to stop. A closed fist punched him in the left kidney; he lurched forward, caught by the silent, staring Greeks in front of him.

He started to shout; there was no other way. The laughter above was growing louder, nearer. Other men were descending the staircase.

"I warn you——"

Suddenly, both his hands were yanked back, his arms bent and locked, the wrists turned inward. A large, coarse cloth was shoved into his face, saturated with acrid, foul-smelling liquid.

He was blinded; a breathless vacuum was being imposed on him, without light, without air. His tunic was ripped away, the cross strap pulled up from his chest. He tried to lash out his arms.

As he did so, he could feel the long needle entering his flesh; he was not sure where. Instinctively, he raised his hands in protest. They were *free*; and they were useless as his resistance was useless.

He heard the laughter again; it was deafening. He was aware of being propelled forward, and downward.

But that was all.

"You betray those who saved your life."

He opened his eyes; images came into focus slowly. There was a burning sensation in his left arm, or shoulder. He reached for it; the touch was painful.

"You feel the antidote," said the voice of the blurred figure somewhere in front of him. "It raises a welt, but it isn't harmful."

Fontine's eyes began to clear. He was sitting on a cement floor, his back against a wall of stone. Across from him, perhaps twenty feet away, a man stood in front of an opposite wall. They were on some kind of raised platform in a large tunnel. The tunnel appeared to be deep underground, carved out of rock, both ends disappearing into darkness. On the floor of the tunnel were old, narrow tracks; they were cracked, rusted. Light came from several thick candles inserted in ancient brackets on the walls.

His focus refined, Fontine concentrated on the man across from him. He wore a black suit; around his neck was a white collar. The man was a priest.

He was bald, but not from age. The head was shaved; the man was no more than forty-five or fifty, the face ascetic, the body slender.

Beside the priest was the guard in the Wehrmacht uniform. The two Greeks impersonating German officers stood by an iron door in the left wall facing the tunnel. The priest spoke.

"We've followed you since Montbéliard. You're a thousand miles from London. The English can't protect you. We have routes south they know nothing about."

"The English?" Fontine stared at the priest trying to understand. "You're from the Order of Xenope."

"We are."

"Why do you fight the English?"

"Because Brevourt's a liar. He breaks his word."

"Brevourt?" Victor was stunned; nothing made sense. "You're out of your mind! Everything, *everything* he's done in *your name!* For *you.*"

"Not for us! For England. He wants the vault of Constantine for *England!* Churchill demands it! It's a more powerful weapon than a hundred armies, and they all know it! We would never see it again!" The priest's eyes were wide, furious.

"You believe that?"

"Don't be an ass!" spat the monk from Xenope. "As Brevourt breaks his word, we broke Code *Maginot.* Messages were intercepted; communications between . . . shall we say, interested parties."

"You're *crazy!*" Fontine tried to think. Anthony Brevourt had faded away; there'd been no word from him—or about him—in months. "You say you've followed me since Montbéliard. *Why?* I don't have what you want! I never did have it! I know nothing about that goddamned train!"

"Mikhailovic believed you," said the priest softly. "I don't."

"Petride——" The sight of the child monk taking his own life on the rocky ledge in Loch Torridon came back to Victor.

"Petride was not his name——"

"You killed him!" said Fontine. "You killed him as surely as if you'd pulled the trigger yourself. You're insane! All of you."

"He failed. He knew what was expected. It was understood."

"You're *sick!* You infect everyone you touch! You can believe me or not, but I'm telling you for the last time! I don't have the information you want!"

"Liar!"

"You're mad!"

"Then why do you travel with Lübok? Tell me that, Signor Fontini-Cristi! Why Lübok?"

Victor recoiled; the shock of Lübok's name caused him to arch his back against the stone. "Lübok?" he whispered incredulously. "If you know his word, you know the answer to that."

"Loch Torridon?" asked the priest sarcastically.

"I never heard of Lübok before in my life. I only know he does his job. He's a Jew, a . . . he takes great risks."

"He works *for Rome!*" roared the priest of Xenope. "He conveys offers to Rome! *Your* offers!"

Victor was silent; his astonishment was so complete he had no words. The monk of Xenope continued, his voice low, penetrating. "Strange, isn't it? Of all the escorts in the occupied territories, Lübok is chosen. He just shows up in Montbéliard. Do you expect us to believe that?"

"Believe what you will. This is madness."

"It is *betrayal!*" the priest shouted again, taking several steps away from the wall. "A degenerate who can pick up a telephone and blackmail half of Berlin! And most outrageous—for you—a dog who works for the monster of——"

"*Fontine! Dive!*" The piercing command came from the black hole of the tunnel. It was screamed in Lübok's highpitched voice, the sound bouncing off the receding walls of rock, overriding the shouts of the priest.

Victor reeled and sprang forward, rolling down the stone wall, crashing from the platform to the hard ground by the old rusted track. Above him he heard the spits of bullets shattering the air, followed by two thunderous explosions of unsilenced Lugers.

In the flickering light he could see the figures of Lübok and several others lurch out of the darkness, angling their weapons, taking rapid, accurate aim; firing and spinning back into the protection of the rock.

It was over in seconds. The priest of Xenope had fallen; he was hit in the neck, his left ear blown off his head. He had crawled to the ledge of the platform, dying, staring down at Fontine. In imminent death his whispered voice was a rasp.

"We . . . are not your enemies. For the mercy of God, bring the documents to us——"

A final, muted spit was heard; the priest's forehead exploded above his staring eyes.

Victor felt a grip on his left arm; it caused shooting pains throughout his shoulder and chest. He was being yanked to his feet.

"*Get up!*" was Lübok's command. "The shots may have been heard. Run!"

They raced into the tunnel. The beam of a flashlight pierced the black, held by one of Lübok's men up ahead. The man whispered his instructions in Polish. Lübok translated for Fontine, who ran beside him.

"About two hundred yards down there's a monks' cave. We'll be safe."

"A *what?*"

"Monks' cave," answered Lübok, breathing heavily. "The history of the Casimir goes back centuries. Escapes were needed."

They crawled on their hands and knees through a narrow, dark passageway cut out of rock. It led to the depths of a cave. The air was instantly different; there was an opening somewhere beyond in the darkness.

"I have to talk to you," said Victor quickly.

"To answer your questions, Captain Hans Neumann is a devoted officer of the Reich with a cousin in the Gestapo. Oberst Schneider wasn't on the roster; that was sticky. We knew it was a trap. . . . In all honesty we didn't expect to find you in the tunnel. That was a stroke of luck. We were on our way to Block Seven." Lübok turned to his comrades. He spoke first in Polish, then translated for Fontine. "We'll stay here for a quarter of an hour. That should be time enough. Then we'll proceed to the rendezvous in Seven. You'll conduct your business on schedule."

Fontine grabbed Lübok's arm and led him away from the *podziemna* men. Two of the men had turned on their flashlights. There was enough light to see the middle-aged courier's face, and Victor was grateful for that.

"It wasn't a German trap! Those men back there were Greek! One was a priest!" Fontine whispered, but there was no mistaking his intensity.

"You're mad," said Lübok casually, his eyes a perfect blank.

"They were from *Xenope.*"

"From what?"

"You heard me."

"I heard you, but I haven't the faintest idea what you're talking about."

"Goddamn you, Lübok! Who are you?"

"Many things to many people, thank heavens."

Victor grabbed the blond-haired Czech by the lapels of his jacket. Lübok's eyes became suddenly distant, filled with cold anger. "They said you worked for Rome. That you would convey offers to Rome! *What* offers? What does it mean?"

"I don't know," replied the Czech slowly.

"Who do you work for?"

"I work for many people. *Against* the Nazis. That's all you have to know.

I keep you alive and see that you complete your negotiations. How I do it is none of your business."

"You know *nothing* about Salonika?"

"It is a city in Greece, on the Aegean Sea . . . Now, take your hands off me."

Fontine relaxed his grip but still held on. "Just in case—in *case*—the many people you speak of include men interested in that train from Salonika. I know *nothing*. I never did."

"If the subject ever comes up, and I can't imagine why, I'll convey the information. Now may we concentrate on your negotiations in Warsaw? We must complete them tonight. In the morning arrangements have been made for two couriers to fly out on the Berlin military shuttle. I'll check the airfield myself before daybreak. We'll get off at Müllheim. It's near the Franco-Swiss border, a night's trip to Montbéliard. Your business in Europe is finished."

"*Fly* out?" Victor removed his hands. "On a German plane?"

"Courtesy of a very distraught Warsaw commandant. He's seen too many motion pictures in which he was a prominent player. Sheer pornography."

Chapter Eleven

Air Corridor, Munich West

The trimotored Fokker was stationary as maintenance crews checked the engines and a fuel truck filled the tanks. They were in Munich; they had left Warsaw early in the morning with a stop at Prague. Most of the passengers had gotten off at Munich.

Müllheim was next, the last leg of their journey. Victor sat uncomfortably beside a seemingly relaxed Lübok in the quiet cabin of the aircraft. There was one other passenger: an aging corporal on leave to Stuttgart.

"I'd like it better if there were a few more hitchhikers," whispered Lübok. "With so small a number, the pilot may insist everyone stay on board at Müllheim. He could gas up quickly and be on his way. He takes on most of his passengers in Stuttgart."

He was interrupted by the sound of clattering footsteps on the metal stairs outside the aircraft. Raucous, uninhibited laughter accompanied the unsteady clattering and grew louder as the new passengers approached the cabin door. Lübok looked at Fontine and smiled in relief. He returned to the newspaper provided by the attendant and sank back in the seat. Victor turned; the Munich contingent came into view.

There were three Wehrmacht officers and a woman. They were drunk. The girl was in a light-covered cloth coat; she was pushed through the narrow door by two of the Wehrmacht and shoved into a seat by the third. She did not object; instead she laughed and made funny faces. A willing, participating toy.

She was in her late twenties, pleasant-looking but not attractive. There was a frantic quality in her face, an intensity that made her appear somehow frayed. Her light-brown, windswept hair was a little too thick; it had not fallen free in the wind. The mascara about her eyes was too pronounced, the lipstick too red, the rouge too obvious.

"What are *you* looking at?" The question was shouted above the roar of the revving motors. The speaker was the third Wehrmacht officer, a broad-chested, muscular man in his thirties. He had walked past his two comrades and addressed Victor.

"I'm sorry," said Fontine, smiling weakly. "I didn't mean to be rude."

The officer squinted his eyes; he was a brawler, it was unmistakable. "We've got a *fancy* one. Listen to the lacepants!"

"I meant no offense."

The officer turned to his comrades; one had pulled the not-unwilling girl over on his lap, the other was in the aisle. "The lace-pants meant no offense! Isn't that nice?"

The two fellow officers groaned derisively. The girl laughed; a little too hysterically, thought Victor. He turned front, hoping the Wehrmacht boor would go away.

Instead, a huge hand reached over the seat and grabbed him by the shoulder blade. "That's not good enough." The officer looked at Lübok. "You two move up front."

Lübok's eyes sought Victor's. The message was clear: Do as the man ordered.

"Certainly." Fontine and Lübok rose and walked swiftly up the aisle. Neither spoke. Fontine could hear the uncorking of bottles. The Wehrmacht party had begun.

The Fokker sped down the runway and left the ground. Lübok had taken the aisle seat, leaving him the window. He riveted his eyes on the sky, withdrawing into the cocoon of himself, hoping to produce a blankness that would make the journey to Müllheim pass more swiftly. It could not pass swiftly enough.

The blankness would not come. Instead, involuntarily, he thought of the Xenope priest in the underground tunnel of the Casimir.

You travel with Lübok. Lübok works for Rome.

Lübok.

We are not your enemies. For the mercy of God, bring the documents to us.

Salonika. It was never far away. The vault from Constantine was capable of violently dividing men who fought a common enemy.

He heard laughter from the rear of the cabin, then a whispered voice behind him.

"*No!* Don't turn around. *Please!*" It was the flight attendant, barely audible through the narrow space between the seats. "Don't get up. They're *Kommandos*. They just let off steam, so don't concern yourselves. Pretend there is nothing!"

"*Kommandos?*" whispered Lübok. "In Munich? They're stationed north, in the Baltic zones."

"Not these. These operate across the mountains in the Italian sectors. Execution teams. There are many——"

The words struck with the impact of silent thunderbolts. Victor inhaled; the muscles of his stomach hardened into a wall of stone.

. . . *execution teams.* . . .

He gripped the armrests of his seat and arched his back. Then, pressing his back into the seat, he stretched his neck and turned his eyes toward the rear of the cabin, over the metal rim of the headrest. He could not believe what he saw.

The wild-eyed girl was on the floor, her coat open; she was naked except for torn undergarments, her legs spread, her buttocks moving. A Wehrmacht officer, his trousers and shorts pulled down to his knees, lowered himself on her, his penis stabbing. Kneeling above the girl's head was a second Wehrmacht, his trousers removed, an erection protruding from the opening in his shorts. He held the girl by the hair and lanced his erection around the flesh of her face; she opened her mouth and accepted it, moaning and coughing. The third Wehrmacht was sitting, bent over on the armrest above the rape. He was breathing in gasps through parted lips, his left hand extended, rubbing the girl's naked breasts in a rhythm that matched the masturbating motions of his right hand.

"*Animali!*" Fontine lunged from the seat, ripping Lübok's fingers from his wrist, hurling himself forward. The Wehrmacht were stunned beyond movement, their shock total. The officer on the armrest gaped. Victor's open hand gripped his hair and crashed the man's head into the steel rim of the seat. The skull cracked; an eruption of blood sprayed the face of the Wehrmacht lying between the spread legs of the girl. The officer caught his knees in his trousers; he fell forward on top of the girl, his hands lashing out to grab support. He rolled on his back, crushing the girl in the narrow aisle. Fontine raised the heel of his right boot and propelled it into the soft throat of the Wehrmacht. The blow was pulverizing; the veins in the German's neck swelled into huge tubes of bluish-black under the skin. His eyes rolled up into his sockets, the eyeballs white gelatine, blank and horrible.

The screams of the girl beneath were now mingled with the cries of agony from the third officer, who had sprung forward, propelling himself off the Fokker's deck toward the rear bulkhead. The man's underwear was matted with blood.

Fontine lunged; the German rolled hysterically away. His bloody, trembling hand reached under his tunic; Victor knew what he was after: the four-inch *Kommando* knife, strapped next to his flesh beneath his armpit. The Wehrmacht whipped out the blade—short, razor sharp—and slashed it diagonally in front of him. Fontine rose from his crouch, prepared to leap.

Suddenly an arm was lashed around Victor's neck. He struck back with his elbows, but the grip was unbreakable.

His neck was yanked back and a long knife sped through the air and imbedded itself deep in the German's chest. The man was dead before his body slumped to the floor of the cabin.

Abruptly Fontine's neck was released. Lübok slapped him across the face, the blow powerful, stinging his flesh.

"*Enough!* Stop it! I won't die for *you!* "

Dazed, Victor looked around. The throats of the other two Wehrmacht had been cut. The girl had crawled away, vomiting and weeping between two seats. The flight attendant lay sprawled in the aisle—dead or unconscious, there was no way to tell.

And the old corporal who had stared at nothing—in fear—only minutes ago, stood by the pilot's cabin door, a pistol in his hand.

Suddenly the girl started screaming as she got to her feet. "They'll *kill* us! Oh, God! Why did you do it?"

Stunned, Fontine stared at the girl and spoke quietly with what breath he had left. "*You?* You can ask that?"

"Yes! Oh, my God!" She pulled her filthy coat around her as best she could. "They'll kill me. I don't want to die!"

"You don't want to live like *that*."

She returned his stare maniacally, her head trembling. "They took me from the camps," she whispered. "I understood. They gave me drugs when I needed them, wanted them." She pulled at her loose right sleeve; there were scores of needle marks from her wrist to her upper arm. "But I understood. And I lived!"

"*Basta!*" roared Victor stepping toward the girl, raising his hand. "Whether you live or die is immaterial to me. I didn't act for you!"

"Whatever you did is done, Captain," said Lübok quickly, touching his arm. "Snap out of it! You've had your confrontation, there can be no more. Understand?"

Fontine saw the strength in Lübok's eyes. Breathing heavily, Victor pointed in astonishment at the fortyish corporal who stood silently by the cabin door, his weapon drawn. "He's one of you, isn't he?"

"No," said Lübok. "He's a German with a conscience. He doesn't know who or what we are. At Müllheim he'll be unconscious, an innocent bystander who can tell them whatever he likes. I suspect it will be nothing. Stay with the girl."

Lübok took charge. He went back to the bodies of the Wehrmacht and removed identification papers and weapons. In the tunic of one, he found a hypodermic kit and six vials of narcotics. He gave them to the girl, who sat by the window next to Fontine. She accepted them gratefully and without so much as looking at Victor, she proceeded to break a capsule, fill the hypodermic, and insert the needle into her left arm.

She carefully repacked the kit and shoved it into the pocket of her bloodstained coat. She leaned back and breathed deeply.

"Feel better?" asked Fontine.

She turned and looked at him. Her eyes were calmer now, only contempt showing in them. "You understand, Captain. I don't *feel*. There are no feelings. One just goes on living."

"What will you do?"

She took her eyes away from him and returned to the window. She answered him quietly, dreamily—out of contact. "Live, if I can. It's not up to me. It's up to you."

In the aisle the flight attendant stirred. He shook his head and got to his knees. Before he could focus, Lübok was in front of him, his gun at the attendant's head.

"If you want to stay alive, you'll do exactly as I say at Müllheim."

Obedience was in the soldier's eyes.

Fontine got up. "What about the girl? he whispered.

"What about her?" countered Lübok.

"I'd like to bring her out with us."

The Czech ran an exasperated hand through his hair. "Oh, Christ! Well, it's that or killing her. She'd identify me for a drop of morphine." He looked down at the girl. "Get her to clean up. There's a raincoat in the back. She can put it on."

"Thanks," said Victor.

"Don't," replied Lübok. "I'd kill her in a second if I thought it was a better solution. But she could be valuable; she's been with a *Kommando* unit where we didn't know one existed."

The Resistance fighters met the automobile on a back road of Lörrach, near the Franco-Swiss border. Victor was given clean but ragged clothes to replace the German uniform. They crossed the Rhine at nightfall. The girl was taken west to a Resistance camp in the hills; she was too drugged, too erratic to make the trip south to Montbéliard.

The flight attendant was simply taken away. Fontine kept his own counsel. There'd been another corporal from another army on a pier in Celle Ligure.

"I leave you now," said Lübok, crossing to him on the riverbank. The Czech's hand was extended.

Fontine was surprised. The plan had been for Lübok to go with him to Montbéliard; London might have new instructions for him. He took Lübok's hand, protesting.

"Why? I thought——"

"I know. But things change. There are problems in Wiesbaden."

Victor held the Czech's right hand with his own, covering it with his left. "It's difficult to know what to say. I owe you my life."

"Whatever I did, you would have done the same. I never doubted that."

"You're generous as well as brave."

"That Greek priest said I was a degenerate who could blackmail half of Berlin."

"Could you?"

"Probably," answered Lübok quickly, looking over at a Frenchman who was beckoning him to the boat. He acknowledged with a nod of his head. He turned back to Victor. "Listen to me," he said softly, removing his hand. "That priest told you something else. That I worked for Rome. You said you didn't know what that meant."

"I don't, specifically. But I'm not blind; it has to do with the train from Salonika."

"It has *everything* to do with it."

"You do work for Rome, then? For the church?"

"The church is not your enemy. Believe that."

"The Order of Xenope claims *it* is not my enemy. Yet certainly I have one. But you don't answer my question. Do you work for Rome?"

"Yes. But not in the way you think."

"Lübok!" Fontine grabbed the middle-aged Czech by the shoulders. "I *have* no thoughts! I don't *know!* Can't you understand that?"

Lübok stared at Victor; in the dim night light his eyes were searching. "I believe you. I gave you a dozen opportunities; you seized none of them."

"Opportunities? *What* opportunities?"

The Frenchman by the boat called again, this time harshly. "You! Peacock! Let's get out of here."

"Right away," replied Lübok, his eyes still on Fontine. "For the last time. There are men—on both sides—who think this war is insignificant compared to the information they believe you have. In some ways I agree with them. But you don't have it, you never did. And this war must be fought. And won. In fact, your father was wiser than all of them."

"Savarone? What do you——?"

"I go now." Lübok raised his hands, with strength but no hostility, and removed Victor's arms. "For these reasons, I did what I did. You'll know soon enough. That priest in the Casimir was right: there are monsters. He was one of them. There are others. But don't blame churches; they are innocent. They harbor the fanatics, but they're innocent."

"Peacock! No more delay!"

"Coming!" said Lübok in a shouted whisper. "Good-bye, Fontine. If for one minute I thought you were not what you say you are, I would have wracked you myself for the information. Or killed you. But you are what you are, caught in the middle. They'll leave you alone now. For a while."

The Czech touched Victor's face briefly, gently, and ran down to the boat.

The blue lights flashed above the Montbéliard field at precisely five minutes past midnight. Instantly two rows of small flares were ignited; the runway was marked, the plane circled and made its approach.

Fontine ran across the field carrying his briefcase. By the time he reached the side of the rolling plane, the hatch was open; two men were standing in the frame, gripping the sides, their arms extended. Victor heaved the briefcase inside and reached up, making contact with the arm on his right. He ran faster, jumped, and was pulled in through the opening; he lay face down on the deck. The hatch was slammed shut, a command shouted out to the pilot, and the engines roared. The plane sprang forward, the tail of the fuselage rising in seconds, and seconds later they were airborne.

Fontine raised his head and crawled to the ribbed wall outside the hatch. He pulled the briefcase to his side and breathed deeply, letting his head fall back against the metal.

"Oh, my God!" came the words spoken in shock out of the darkness. "It's *you!*"

Victor snapped his head to the left, in the direction of the indistinguishable figure who spoke with such alarm in his voice. The first shafts of moonlight came from the windows of the open pilot area. Fontine's eyes were drawn to the right hand of the speaker. It was encased in a black glove.

"Stone? What are you doing here?"

But Geoffrey Stone was incapable of answering. The moonlight grew brighter, illuminating the hollow shell that was the aircraft's fuselage. Stone's eyes were wide, his lips parted, immobile.

"Stone? It *is* you?"

"Oh, Jesus! We've been tricked. They've done it!"

"What are you talking about?"

The English continued in a monotone. "You were reported killed. Captured and executed in the Casimir. We were told that only one man escaped. With your papers——"

"Who?"

"The courier, Lübok."

Victor got to his feet unsteadily, holding on to a metal brace that protruded from the wall of the vibrating aircraft. The geometric pieces were coming together. "Where did you get this information?"

"It was relayed to us this morning."

"By whom? Who picked it up? Who relayed it?"

"The Greek embassy," replied Stone barely above a whisper.

Fontine sank back down to the deck of the plane. Lübok had said the words.

I gave you a dozen opportunities; you seized none. There are men who think this war is insignificant. . . . For these reasons I did what I did. You'll know soon enough. . . . They'll leave you alone now. For a while.

Lübok had made his move. He had checked an airfield in Warsaw before daybreak and sent a false message to London.

It did not take a great deal of imagination to know what that message accomplished.

"We're immobilized. We've exposed ourselves and been taken out. We all watch each other now, but no one can make a move, or admit what we're looking for. No one can afford that." Brevourt spoke as he stood by the leaded window overlooking the courtyard in Alien Operations. "Check-mate."

Across the room, standing by the long conference table, was a furious Alec Teague. They were alone.

"I don't give a *damn*. What concerns me is your blatant manipulation of Military Intelligence! You've placed an entire network in jeopardy. Loch Torridon may well have been crippled!"

"Create another strategy," said Brevourt absently, looking out the window. "It's your job, isn't it?"

"Damn you!"

"For God's sake, Teague, *stop* it!" Brevourt reeled from the window. "Do you for one minute think I was the final authority?"

"I think you compromised that authority! I should have been consulted!"

Brevourt started to reply, then stopped. He nodded his head as he walked slowly across the room to the table opposite Teague. "You may be right, general. Tell me, you're the expert. What was our mistake?"

"Lübok," said the brigadier coldly. "He faded you. He took your money and turned to Rome, then made up his own mind. He was the wrong man."

"He was your man. From your files."

"Not for that job. You interfered."

"He can go anywhere in Europe," continued Brevourt almost plaintively, as if Teague had not interrupted. "He's untouchable. If Fontini-Cristi broke away, Lübok could have followed him anywhere. Even into Switzerland."

"You expected that, didn't you?"

"Frankly, yes. You're too good a salesman, general. I believed you. I thought Loch Torridon *was* Fontini-Christi's brainchild. How logical it all seemed. The Italian goes back under perfect cover to make his own arrangements." Brevourt sat down wearily, clasping his hands in front of him on the table.

"Didn't it occur to you that if such was the case, he would have come to us? To you?"

"No. We couldn't return his lands or his factories."

"You don't know him," concluded Teague with finality. "You never took the trouble. That was your first mistake."

"Yes, I expect it was. I've lived most of my life with liars. The corridors of mendacity. The simple truth is elusive." Brevourt suddenly looked up at the Intelligence man. His face was pathetic, his pallid skin taut, the hollows of his eyes proof of exhaustion. "You didn't believe it, did you? You didn't believe he was dead."

"No."

"I couldn't take the chance, you see. I accepted what you said, that the Germans wouldn't execute him, that they'd put a trace on him, find out who he was, use him. But the report said otherwise. So, if he *was* dead, it meant the fanatics in Rome or Xenope had killed him. They wouldn't do that unless—*unless*—they'd learned his secret."

"And if they had, the vault would be theirs. Not yours. Not England's. It was never yours to begin with."

The ambassador looked away from Teague and sank back in the chair, closing his eyes. "Nor could it be allowed to fall into the hands of maniacs. Not now. We know who the maniac is in Rome. The Vatican will watch Donatti now. The Patriarchate will suspend activities; we've been given assurance."

"Which was Lübok's objective, of course."

Brevourt opened his eyes. "Was it really?"

"In my judgment, yes. Lübok's a Jew."

Brevourt turned his head and stared at Teague. "There'll be no more interference, general. Get on with your war. Mine is at a standoff."

Anton Lübok crossed Prague's Wenceslaus Square and walked up the steps of the bombed-out cathedral. Inside, the late afternoon sun streaked through the huge gaps of stone where *Luftwaffe* bombs had exploded. Whole sections of the left wall were destroyed; primitive scaffolds had been erected everywhere for support.

He stood on the far right aisle and checked his watch. It was time.

An old priest came out of the curtained apse and crossed in front of the confessional booths. He paused briefly at the fourth. It was Lübok's signal.

He walked down the aisle cautiously, his attention on the dozen or so worshippers in the church. None was watching him. He parted the curtains and walked inside the confessional. He knelt before the tiny Bohemian crucifix, the flickering light of the prayer candle throwing shadows on the draped walls.

"Forgive me, Father, for I have sinned," Lübok began softly. "I have sinned in excess. I have debased the body and blood of Christ."

"One cannot debase the Son of God," came the proper reply from behind the drapes. "One can only debase oneself."

"But we are in the image of God. As was Himself."

"A poor and imperfect image," was the correct response.

Lübok exhaled slowly, the exercise was completed. "You are Rome?"

"I am the conduit," said the voice in quiet arrogance.

"I didn't think you were the city, you damn fool."

"This is the house of God. Watch your tongue."

"And you revile this house," whispered Lübok. "All who work for Donatti revile it!"

"*Silence.* We are the way of Christ!"

"You're *dirt!* Your Christ would spit on you."

The breathing beyond the drapes was filled with controlled loathing. "I shall pray for your soul," came the forced words. "What of Fontini-Cristi?"

"He had no other purpose but Loch Torridon. Your projections were wrong."

"That won't do!" The priest's whisper was strident. "He had to have other objectives! We're positive!"

"He never left my side from the moment we met in Montbéliard. There were no additional contacts other than those we knew about."

"*No!* We don't believe that!"

"In a matter of days it won't make any difference what you believe. You're finished. All of you. Good men will see to it."

"What have you done, *Jew?*" The voice behind the drapes was low now, the loathing absolute.

"What had to be done, priest." Lübok rose to his feet and put his left hand into his pocket. With his right he suddenly ripped the drapes in front of him.

The priest was revealed. He was huge, the black robes giving him the appearance of immensity. His face was the face of a man who hated deeply; the eyes were the eyes of a predator.

Lübok withdrew an envelope from his pocket and dropped it on the prayer stall in front of the stunned priest. "Here's your money. Give it back to Donatti. I wanted to see what you looked like."

The priest answered quietly. "You'd better know the rest. My name is Gaetamo. Enrici Gaetamo. And I'll come back for you."

"I doubt it," replied Lübok.

"Don't," said Enrici Gaetamo.

Lübok stood for a moment looking down at the priest. When their eyes were locked, the blond-haired Czech wet the fingers of his right hand and reached for the prayer candle, extinguishing its flame. All was darkness. He parted the drapes and walked out of the confessional.

PART FOUR

Chapter Twelve

The cottage was on the grounds of a large estate west of Aylesbury in Oxfordshire. Tall metal poles strung with electrified barbed wire surrounded the area. Killer dogs guarded the enormous compound.

There was only one entrance, a gate at the base of a long, straight driveway flanked by open lawns. At the main house, a quarter of a mile from the gate, the drive split off right and left, then split again with several smaller roads leading to the various cottages.

There were fourteen cottages in all, houses built in and around the woods of the estate. The residents were men and women who needed the security: defectors and their families, double agents, couriers who'd been exposed—targets who'd been marked for an assassin's bullet.

Jane's cottage became their home and Victor was grateful for its remoteness. For nightly the *Luftwaffe* streaked through the skies, the fires of London grew, the battle for Britain had begun.

And so had Loch Torridon.

For weeks at a time, Victor was away from their miniature house in Oxfordshire, away from Jane, his mind at rest because she was safe. Teague moved the Loch Torridon headquarters into the cellars of MI6. Day and night had no essential meaning. Men worked around the clock with files and shortwave radios, and with complicated equipment that reproduced perfectly the documents required in the occupied lands: work papers, travel permits, clearances from the *Reichsministerium* of Armaments and Industry. Other men were called into the cellars and given their instructions by Captains Fontine and Stone. And they were sent to Lakenheath and beyond.

As was Victor on a growing number of occasions. At such times, he knew Alec Teague was right: *Your wife's safety is directly related to your state of mind. You have a job to do; I'll do mine.*

Jane could not be touched by the maniacs of Rome or Xenope. It was all that mattered. The freight from Salonika became a strange, painful memory. And the war went on.

AUGUST 24, 1940
ANTWERP, BELGIUM

    (Intercepted dispatch—duplicate—Commandant: Occupation Forces, Antwerp, to Reichsminister Speer, Armaments.)

The railroad yards at Antwerp are chaos! Supply trains crossing Schelde River are overloaded through carelessness in shipping orders, causing cracks throughout bridge structure. Schedules and signaling codes altered without proper notice. From offices managed by *German personnel!* Reprisals ludicrous. No alien responsibility. Trains meet one another from opposing directions on the same tracks! Freights pull up for loading at sidings and depots where there are no trucks! No shipments! The situation is intolerable and I must insist that the *Reichministerium* coordinate more thoroughly. . . .

SEPTEMBER 19, 1940
VERDUN-SUR-MEUSE, FRANCE

(Excerpts from letter received by the second command legal office of *Gesetzbuch Besitzergreifung*—from a Colonel Grepschedit, Verdun-Meuse.)

. . . It was agreed that we prepare specific rules of occupation to adjudicate disputes between ourselves and the conquered who laid down their arms. The regulations were circulated. We now find additional regulations—circulated by *your* offices—that contradict whole sections of the previous codes. We are in constant debate with even those who *welcome* us! Entire days are taken up with occupation hearings. Our own officers are faced with conflicting orders from your couriers—all under proper signatures and validated by your seals. We are at a boiling point over inconsequentials. We are going out of our minds. . . .

MARCH 20, 1941
BERLIN, GERMANY

(Extracted minutes of the meeting between accounts stabilizers of the *Finanzministerium* and the officials of *Reichsordnung*. File removed—duplicate.)

. . . The substance of Ordnance's unending difficulties are to be found with the *Finanzministerium*'s consistent errors in funds allocations. Accounts go unsettled for months, payrolls are miscalculated, monies are transferred to wrong dispersal depots—often to wrong geographical sectors! Whole battalions have gone without pay because the funds were somewhere in Yugoslavia when they should have been in Amsterdam! . . .

JUNE 23, 1941
BREST-LITOVSK, RUSSIAN FRONT

(Courier dispatch from General Guderian to his commander, General Bock, Hdqtrs: Pripet, Poland. Intercept: Bialystok. Not delivered.)

. . . In two days of the offensive we are within forty-eight hours of Minsk. The Dnieper will be crossed in a matter of weeks, the Don and Moscow not far beyond! The speed of our assault requires instant communications—in the main—radio communications, but there are increasing difficulties with our radio equipment. Specifically in what the engineers tell me is frequency calibration. More than half our divisional equipment is set in differing graduations. Unless extreme caution is taken, communications are sent out on unintended frequencies, often *enemy* frequencies. It is a factory problem. Our concern is that it is impossible to determine which equipment has malfunctioning calibrations. I, myself, initiated a communication to Kleist on Rundstedt's south flank and reached our forces in eastern Lithuania. . . .

FEBRUARY 2, 1942
BERLIN, GERMANY

(Removed from correspondence file of Manfried Probst, Official, *Reichsindustrie* from Hiru Kayanaka, attaché, Japanese Embassy, Berlin.)

Dear Reichsoffiziell Probst:
Since we are now comrades in battle as well as spirit we must attempt to strive further for the perfection expected of us by our leaders.

To the subject at hand, my dear *Reichsoffiziell*. As you know, our respective governments have entered into joint radar development experiments.

We flew—at great risk—our foremost electronic scientists to Berlin to enter conferences with your people. That was six weeks ago and to date there have been no conferences whatsoever. I am now informed that our foremost scientists were flown to Griefswald on the Baltic Sea by error. They are not concerned with the rocket experiments, but with radar, my dear *Reichsoffiziell*. Unfortunately, none speak your language and the interpreters you assigned are less than fluent in ours.

Word reached my desk an hour ago that our foremost scientists are now on their way to Würzburg, where there are radio transmitters. My dear *Reichsoffiziell*, we do not know where Würzburg is. And our foremost scientists are not concerned with radio transmitters, but with *radar!*

Can you please locate our foremost scientists? When are the radar conferences? Our foremost scientists are traveling all over Germany for what purpose? . . .

MAY 25, 1942
ST. VALÉRY-EN-CAUX, FRANCE

(Report filed by Captain Victor Fontine, who was dropped behind lines in the Héricourt district. Returned by trawler, Isle of Wight.)

. . . The armaments shipments along the coastal regions are primarily offensive in nature, with little thought at this point given to defensive weapons. The shipments are routed from Essen, through Düsseldorf, across the border to Roubaix and then to the French coast. The key is fuel. We have placed our people in the petrol depots. They are receiving continuous "instructions" from the *Reichsministerium* of Industry to divert shipments of fuel immediately out of Brussels to Rotterdam, where rails will begin the journey to the Russian front. At last report, there were fourteen miles of standard armaments vehicles choking the roads between Louvain and Brussels, their tanks empty. And, of course, no reprisals. We estimate that the ploy will be operable for another four days, at which point Berlin will be forced to move in and our people will move out. Coordinate air strikes at this time. . . .

(Note: Loch Torridon Command. For record. Cleared, Brigadier

General Teague. Captain Victor Fontine granted leave upon return from Wight. Recommendation for majority approved——)

Fontine sped out of London on the Hempstead road toward Oxfordshire. He thought the debriefing session with Teague and Stone would never end! *God!* The repetitions! His coadministrator, Stone, was always furious when he returned from one of his trips behind the German lines. It was work Stone had been trained to do, but now was impossible for him. His shattered hand ruled out such incursions and he spent his rage on Victor. He would subject Fontine to rapid, harsh, repetitive interrogation, looking for errors in every phase of a mission. What charity Victor once felt for the cryptographer had disappeared over the months. Months? Mother of Christ, it was nearly two and a half years!

But tonight Stone's delaying tactics were unforgivable. The *Luftwaffe* strikes over England had lessened, but they had not disappeared. Should the air raid sirens begin, it might be impossible for him to drive out of London.

And Jane was nearly due. The doctors had said it was a matter of a fortnight. That was a week ago, when he had flown out of Lakenheath to France and dropped into the grazing fields of Héricourt.

He reached the outskirts of Aylesbury and looked at his watch, holding it under the dim light of the dashboard. It was twenty minutes past two in the morning. They would both laugh at that; he was always coming back to her at ridiculous hours.

But he was coming back. He'd be at the compound in ten minutes.

Behind him, in the distance, he could hear the wail of the sirens rising and falling in plaintive fugues. There was not the jolting, breath-catching anxiety that used to accompany the terrible sound. The sound itself had taken on a weariness; repetition had dulled its terror.

He swung the wheel of the automobile to the right; he was now on the back road that led to the Oxfordshire estate. Another two or three miles and he'd be with his wife. His foot pressed down on the accelerator. There were no cars on the road; he could speed.

Instinctively, his ears listened for the distant rumbling of the bombing. But there was no faraway thunder, only the incessant whines of the sirens. Suddenly, there were sounds intruding where no sounds should be; he caught his breath, realizing instantly the return of forgotten anxiety. He wondered for a moment whether his exhaustion was causing tricks to be played. . . .

It was no trick! No trick at all! The sounds were overhead and unmistakable. He'd heard them too often, both over London and across the Channel in scores of different covert locations.

Heinkel aircraft. Twin-engine, German, long-range bombers. They'd passed London. And if London was bypassed, it was a good bet that Heinkels would take a northwest heading toward the Birmingham district and the munitions factories.

My God! The aircraft were *losing altitude*. They were pitching down in rapid descent.

Direct *above* him!

In *front* of him!

A bombing run! An airstrike in the countryside of *Oxfordshire!* What in God's name? . . .

Jesus! Oh, Jesus Christ!

The compound!

The one place in England without parallel in security. From the ground, but *not* from the skies!

A low-altitude air strike had been called against the compound!

Fontine held the accelerator to the floor, his body trembling, his breath coming in short, spurting expulsions, his eyes riveted to the onrushing road.

The skies exploded. The screams of diving aircraft mingled with the manmade thunder: detonation after detonation. Immense flashes of white and yellow—jagged, shapeless, horrible—filled the open spaces above and between the woods of Oxfordshire.

He reached the compound's gate, tires screeching as he braked the car into a turn. The iron gates were open.

Evacuation.

He stabbed the pedal to the floor and sped into the long straight drive. Beyond, fires were everywhere, explosions everywhere, people running in panic—everywhere.

The main house had taken a direct hit. The entire left front wall was blown out; the roof was collapsing in weirdly shapeless splendor, bricks and stone cascading to the ground. Smoke spread in vertical swirls of black and gray—fires, spurting upward, jagged, yellow, terrifying.

A deafening crash; the car lurched, the ground swelled, the windows shattered, hurling fragments of glass—everywhere. Fontine felt blood streaking down his face, but he could see and that was all that mattered.

The bomb had struck less than fifty yards to his right. In the light of the fires he could see the ripped-out earth of the lawn. He swung the car to the right, skirting the crater, cutting across the grass toward the dirt road that led to their cottage. Bombs did not strike twice in the same zero target, he thought.

The road was blocked; trees had fallen, fires consuming them—everywhere.

He lurched out of the car and raced between the flaming barriers. He saw their cottage. A huge oak had been blown out of the ground, its massive trunk crashed into the pipetiled roof.

"*Jane! Jane!*"

God of hatred, do not do this to me! Do not do this to me again!

He smashed through the door, sending it hurtling off its hinges. Inside was total wreckage; tables, lamps, chairs were scattered, overturned, broken into a thousand fragments. Fires were burning—on the couch, in the open roof where the oak had crashed.

"*Jane!*"

"Here. . . ."

Her voice came from the kitchen. He raced through the narrow doorway and felt for an instant that he should fall to his knees in supplication. Jane stood gripping the edge of the counter, her back to him, her body shaking, her head nodding up and down. He rushed to her and held her shoulders, his face against her cheek, the spastic rhythm of her movements uninterrupted.

"My darling."

"Vittorio. . . ." Suddenly Jane contracted violently, gasping as she did so. "Sheets. . . . Sheets, my love. And blankets, I think I'm not sure, really——"

"Don't talk." He picked her up and saw the pain in her face in the darkness. "I'll take you to the clinic. There's a clinic, a doctor, nurses——"

"We can't get there!" she screamed. "Do as I say." She coughed in a spasm of pain. "I'll show you. Carry me."

In her hand she gripped a knife. Hot water had been running over the blade; she had been prepared to give birth alone.

Through the incessant detonations, Victor could hear the aircraft ascending, scrambling to higher altitudes. The strike was coming to an end; the distant, furious whines of Spitfires converging into the sector was a signal no *Luftwaffe* pilot overlooked.

He did as his wife told him to do, holding her in his arms, awkwardly gathering up whatever she ordered.

He kicked his way through the wreckage and the spreading flames and carried his wife out the door. Like an animal seeking sanctuary, he hurried into the woods and found a lair that was their own.

They were together. The frenzy of death that was several hundred yards away could not deter life. He delivered his wife of two male infants.

The sons of Fontini-Cristi were born.

Smoke spiraled up lazily, vertical coils of dignified, dead vapor interrupting the shafts of early morning sunlight. Stretchers were everywhere. Blankets covered the faces of the dead; the living and partly living were staring upward, mouths open, the shock imbedded. Ambulances were everywhere. And fire engines and police vehicles.

Jane was in an ambulance, a mobile medical unit, they called it. His sons were with their mother.

The doctor came out of the lean-to canvas extension of the strange vehicle and walked across the short stretch of lawn toward Victor. The doctor's face was haggard; he had escaped death but he lived with the dying.

"She's had a hard time of it, Fontine. I told her she would under normal circumstances——"

"Will she be all right?" interrupted Victor.

"Yes, she'll be all right. However, she'll need a long, *long* rest. I told her several months ago I suspected a multiple birth. She was not—shall I say—designed for such a delivery. In some ways it's rather amazing that she made it."

Fontine stared at the man. "She never mentioned that to me."

"Didn't think she would. You're in a precarious business. Can't have too much on your mind."

"May I see her?"

"Not for a while. She's solidly corked off; the infants are quiet. Let her be."

The doctor's hand was gently on his arm, leading him away from the ambulance toward what remained of the main house. An officer approached them and took Victor aside.

"We found what we were looking for. We knew it was here, or something like it. The strike was far too accurate. Even German instruments couldn't do it, and night pilotage was out; we checked. There were no markings, no flares."

"Where are we going? What are you talking about?" Victor had heard the officer speak, but the words were elliptical.

". . . high-arc transmitter."

The words still did not penetrate. "I'm sorry. What did you say?"

"I said the room's still standing. It's at the rear of the right wing. The bastard was operating a simple high-arc transmitter."

"A transmitter?"

"Yes. That's how the Huns came in on pinpoint. They were guided by a radio beam. The chaps at M.I.-Five and -Six had no objection to my showing you. As a matter of fact, I think they were pleased. They're afraid with all the confusion here someone'll disturb things. You can confirm that we haven't."

They threaded their way through the rubble and the intermittent piles of smoking debris to the right side of the large house. The major opened the door and they turned right down a corridor that seemed to be newly partitioned, as is for offices.

"A radio beam could bring a squadron into the area," said Fontine, walking beside the officer. "But only the area, not the target. These were bombers. I was on the road; they dove to the lowest levels. They would need more sophisticated equipment than a simple high-arc——."

"When I said there were no markings, no flares," interrupted the major, "I meant in a pattern; points A to B to C. Once they were over the target area, the bastard simply opened his window and shot up fireworks. He *did* use flares then. A fucking box full, from what we've found on the ground."

At the end of the corridor a door was flanked by two uniformed guards. The officer opened it and stepped inside; Victor followed.

The room was immaculate, miraculously no part of the surrounding carnage. On a table against the wall was an open briefcase, a circular aerial protruding out of it, attached to radio equipment beneath, secured in the case.

The officer gestured to his left, to the bed, not at first visible from the doorway.

Fontine froze. His eyes locked on the sight now in front of him.

On the bed was the body of a man, the back of his head blown off, a pistol beside his right hand. In his left hand was gripped a large crucifix.

The man was in the black robes of a priest.

"Damned strange," said the major. "His papers said he was a member of some Greek monastic brotherhood. The Order of Xenope."

Chapter Thirteen

He vowed it! There would be no more.

Jane and their two infant sons were taken secretly to Scotland. North of Glasgow, to an isolated house in the countryside of Dunblane. Victor would not rely on compounds *without-parallel-in-security*, nor on any guarantees from MI6 or the British government. Instead, he used his own funds, employed former soldiers, exhaustively screened by himself, and turned the house and grounds into a small but impenetrable fortress. He would not tolerate Teague's suggestions *or* objections *or* excuses. He was being pursued by forces he could not understand, an enemy beyond control, removed from the war and yet part of it.

He wondered if it would be so for the rest of his life. Mother of Christ, why didn't they believe him? How could he reach the fanatics and the killers and roar his denials? He knew nothing! *Nothing!* A train had left Salonika three years ago, at dawn on the ninth of December 1939, and he knew *nothing!* Only of its existence. Nothing more!

"Do you intend to remain here for the rest of the war?" Teague had come up to Dunblane for the day; they walked in the gardens behind the house, in sight of the high brick wall and the guards. It had been five months since they'd seen each other, although Victor permitted calls over redirected scrambler-telephones. He was too much a part of Loch Torridon; his knowledge was vital.

"You have no hold over me, Alec. I'm not British. I've sworn no allegiance to you."

"I never thought that was necessary. I did make you a major, however." Teague smiled.

Victor laughed. "Without ever having been formally inducted into the service? You're a disgrace to military tradition."

"Absolutely. I get things done." The brigadier stopped. He bent over to pick up a long blade of grass and rose, looking at Fontine. "Stone can't do it alone."

"Why not? You and I talk several times a week. I tell you what I can. Stone expedites the decisions. It's a sound arrangement."

"It's not the same and you know it."

"It will have to do. I can't fight two wars." Fontine paused, remembering. "Savarone was right."

"Who?"

"My father. He must have known that whatever was on that train could make men enemies even when they fought for a common survival."

They reached the edge of the path. A guard was thirty yards away across the lawn by the wall; he smiled and stroked the fur of a leashed Great Dane that snarled at the sight and scent of the stranger.

"One day it will have to be resolved," said Teague. "You, Jane, the children: You can't live with it for the rest of your lives."

"I've said that to myself more times than I can count. But I'm not sure how it can be."

"Perhaps I do. At least, I'm willing to try. And I have at my disposal the finest Intelligence service in existence."

Victor glanced at him, interested. "Where would you start?"

"The question is not where, but when."

"Then, *when?*"

"When this war is over."

"Please, Alec. No more words, no strategies. Or tricks."

"No tricks. A simple, uncomplicated agreement. I need you. The war has turned; Loch Torridon enters its most important phase. I intend to see that it does its job."

"You're obsessed."

"So are you. Quite rightfully. But you'll learn nothing of 'Salonika'—that's Brevourt's code name, incidentally—until this war is won, take my word for it. And the war *will* be won."

Fontine held Teague's eyes with his own. "I want facts, not rhetoric."

"Very well. We have identities you don't have, nor, for your own safety and the safety of your family, will I reveal them to you."

"The man in the car? In Kensington, Campo di Fiori. The streak of white? The *executioner?*"

"Yes."

Victor held his breath, controlling a nearly overpowering urge to grab the Englishman and force the words from him. "You've taught me to kill; I could kill you for that."

"To what end? I'd protect you with my life, and you know it. The point is, he's immobilized. Under control. If, indeed, he *was* the executioner."

Victor let his breath out slowly. The muscles in his jaw pained from the tension. "What other identities?"

"Two elders of the Patriarchate. Through Brevourt. They command the Order of Xenope."

"Then they're responsible for *Oxfordshire*. My *God*, how can you——?"

"They're *not*," interrupted Teague quickly. "They were, if possible, more shocked than we were. As was pointed out, the last thing they wanted was your death."

"The man who guided those planes was a priest! From Xenope!"

"Or someone made to appear so."

"He killed himself," said Fontine softly, "in the prescribed manner."

"No one has a quota on fanatics."

"Go on." Victor began walking back on the path, away from the guard and the dog.

"These people are the worst kind of extremists. They're mystics; they believe they're involved in a holy war. Their war permits only confrontation by violence, not negotiation. But we know the pressure points, those whose word cannot be disobeyed. We can bring about a confrontation through Whitehall pressure, if need be, and demand a resolution. At least one that removes you from their concerns—once and for all. You can't do this by yourself. We can. Will you come back?"

"If I do, all this will be set in motion? I, myself, a part of the planning?"

"We'll mount it with the precision we mounted Loch Torridon."

"Has my cover in London been kept absolute?"

"Not a dent. You're somewhere in Wales. All our telephone calls are placed to the Swansea area and tripped north. Mail is regularly sent to a post office box in the village of Gwynliffen, where it's quietly put in other envelopes and returned only to me. Right now, if I'm needed, Stone places a call to a Swansea number."

"No one knows where we are? *No one?*"

"Not even Churchill."

"I'll talk with Jane."

"One thing," said Teague, his hand on Fontine's arm. "I've given my word to Brevourt. There'll be no more trips across the Channel for you."

"She'll like that."

Loch Torridon flourished. The principle of mismanagement-at-all-costs became a thorn in the German craw.

In the Mannheim printing plants, 130,000 *Commandmant Manuals for Occupation* came off the presses with all negatives dropped in vital restrictions. Shipments to the Messerschmidt factories in Frankfurt were routed to the Stuka assembly lines in Leipzig. In Kalach on the Russian front, it was found that three quarters of the radio equipment now operated on varying frequency calibrations. In the Krupp plants at Essen, engineering miscalculations resulted in malfunctions in the firing mechanisms of all cannon with the bore number 712. In Kraków, Poland, in the uniform factories, fabric bypassed a chemical saturation process and 200,000 units were sent out, subject to instant flammability. In Turin, Italy, where the Germans ran the aircraft plants, designs were implemented that caused metal fatigue after twenty hours of flight; entire sections of squadrons structurally collapsed in midair.

In late April of 1944, Loch Torridon concentrated on the offshore patrols throughout the coastal zones of Normandy. A strategy was conceived that would alter the patrol schedules as they were issued to the German naval personnel from the base at Pointe de Barfleur. Brigadier Teague brought the explosive report to Supreme Headquarters, Allied Command, and handed it personally to Dwight Eisenhower.

The German coastal predawn patrols will be removed from Normandy zones during the first eleven days in June. That is the calendar target. Repeat: 1 June through 11 June.

The supreme commander responded appropriately. "I'll be goddamned. . . ."

Overlord was executed and the invading armies progressed. Under Badoglio and Grandi, the outlines of the Italian collaboration were negotiated in Lisbon.

It was a trip Alec Teague permitted Major Fontine. He was entitled to it.

And in a small room in Lisbon, a weary Badoglio faced Victor. "So the son of Fontini-Cristi brings us our ultimatum. There must be a certain gratification in that for you."

"No," replied Victor simply. "Merely contempt."

JULY 26, 1944
WOLFSSCHANZE, EAST PRUSSIA

(Excerpts from the Gestapo investigation of the assassination attempt on Adolf Hitler at the Wolfsschanze High Command Headquarters. File removed and destroyed.)

. . . The aides of the traitor, Gen. Claus von Stauffenburg, have broken. They described a widespread conspiracy implicating such generals as Olbricht, von Falkenhausen, Hoepner, and possibly Kluge and Rommel. This conspiracy could not have been coordinated without enemy assistance. All normal channels of communication were avoided. A network of unknown couriers was employed, and a code name surfaced, unheard of previously. It is of Scottish origin, the name of a district or a village: Loch Torridon. . . . . We have captured . . .

Alec Teague stood in front of the map on his office wall. Fontine sat dejectedly in the chair by Teague's desk, his eyes on the brigadier across the room.

"It was a gamble," said Teague. "We lost. Can't expect to win every time. You've had too few losses, that's your trouble, you're not used to them." He removed three pins from the map and walked back to his desk. He sat down slowly and rubbed his eyes. "Loch Torridon has been an extremely effective operation. We have every reason to be proud."

Fontine was startled. "Past tense?"

"Yes. The Allied ground offensive toward the Rhine will commence maximum effort by October first. The Supreme Command wants no complications; they anticipate widespread defections. We're a complication, possibly a detriment. Loch Torridon will be phased out over the next two months. Terminated by the end of September."

Victor watched Teague as the brigadier made the pronouncement. A part of the old soldier died with the words. It was painful to watch Alec. Loch Torridon was his moment in the military sun; he would get no nearer, and jealousies were not out of the question regarding its termination. But decisions had been made. They were irrevocable, and to fight them *was* out of the question. Teague was a soldier.

Fontine examined his own thoughts. At first he experienced neither elation nor depression; more a suspension, as if time were abruptly arrested. Then slowly, painfully, there was the momentary feeling of what now? Where is my purpose? What do I do?

And then suddenly these vague concerns were swiftly replaced. The obsession that was never far from his mind came sharply into focus. He got out of the chair and stood in front of Alec's desk. "Then I call in your debt," he said quietly to Teague. "There's another operation that must be mounted 'with all the precision of Loch Torridon.' That's the way you phrased it."

"It will be. I gave you my word. The Germans can't last a year; surrender feelers already come from the generals. Six, eight months, and the war will be over. 'Salonika' will be mounted then. With all the precision of Loch Torridon."

Chapter Fourteen

It took twelve weeks to close the books and bring the men back to England. Loch Torridon was finished; twenty-two cabinets of accomplishments were all that remained. They were put under lock and seal and stored in the vaults of Military Intelligence.

Fontine returned to the isolated compound in Scotland. To Jane and the twins, Andrew and Adrian, named for the British saint and any of several acceptable Romans. But they were neither saintly nor imperial; they were two and a half years old, with all the energy that age implied.

Victor had been surrounded by the children of his brothers all his adult life, but these were *his*. In themselves they were different. They alone would carry on the Fontini-Cristis. Jane could have no more children; the doctors had agreed. The injuries at Oxfordshire were too extensive.

It was strange. After four years of furious activity and strain he was suddenly, abruptly, totally passive. The five months in '42 when he remained in Dunblane could not be considered a period of tranquility. Jane's recovery had been slow and dangerous; the fortifying of the compound had obsessed him. There'd been no letup of pressure then.

There was now. And the transition was unbearable. As unbearable as the wait for "Salonika" to begin. It was the inactivity that gnawed at him; he was not a man for idleness. In spite of Jane and the children, Dunblane became his prison. There were men outside, across the Channel, deep within Europe and the Mediterranean, who sought him as intensely as he sought them. There was nothing until that movement could begin.

Teague would not go back on his word, Victor understood that. But neither would he deviate from it. The end of the war would mark the commencement of the strategy that would lead to the men of Salonika. Not before. With each new victory, each new penetration within Germany, Fontine's mind raced. The war *was* won; it was not over, but it was won. Lives all over the world had to be picked up, the pieces put back together and decisions made, for years of living had to be faced. For him, for Jane, everything depended on the forces that sought a vault that came out of Greece five years ago—at dawn on the ninth of December.

The inactivity was his own particular hell.

During the waiting he had reached one decision: he would not return to Campo di Fiori after the war. When he thought of his house and looked at his wife, he saw other wives slain in the white mists of light. When he saw his sons, he saw other sons, helpless, terrified, riddled by gunfire. The tortures of the mind were too vivid still. He could not go back to the killing ground, or to anything or anyone associated with it. They would build a new life somewhere else. The Fontini-Cristi Industries would be returned to him, the Court of Reparations in Rome had sent word to London.

And he had sent word back through MI6. The factories, the plants, all lands and properties—except Campo di Fiori—would go to the highest bidder. He would make separate arrangements for Campo di Fiori.

It was the night of March 10. The children were asleep across the hall; the last of the winter winds blew in gusts outside the windows of their bedroom. Victor and Jane lay under the covers, the coals in the fireplace throwing an orange glow on the ceiling. And they talked quietly, as they always talked in the final hours of the day.

"Barclay's will handle everything," said Victor. "It's a simple auction, really. I've put a cellar on the total; however they want to divide the entire purchase is up to them."

"Are there buyers?" asked Jane, lying on her elbow, looking at him.

Fontine laughed softly. "Packs of them. Mostly in Switzerland, mostly American. There are fortunes to be made in the reconstruction. Those who have manufacturing bases will have the advantage."

"You sound like an economist."

"I sincerely hope so. My father would be terribly disappointed if I didn't." He fell silent. Jane touched his forehead, brushing aside his hair.

"What's the matter?"

"Just thinking. It'll be over with soon. First the war, then 'Salonika'; that will be finished, too. I trust Alec. He'll bring it off if he has to blackmail all the diplomats in the Foreign Office. The fanatics will be forced to accept the fact that I don't know a damn thing about their ungodly train."

"I thought it was supposed to be awfully godly." She smiled.

"Inconceivable." He shook his head. "What kind of god would allow it?"

"Checkmate, my darling."

Victor raised himself on the pillow. He looked over at the windows; a March snow was silently careening off the dark panes of glass, carried by the winds. He turned to his wife. "I can't go back to Italy."

"I know. You've told me. I understand."

"But I don't want to stay here. In England. Here I will always be Fontini-Cristi. Son of the massacred family of *padrones*. Equal parts reality, legend, and myth."

"You *are* Fontini-Cristi."

Victor looked down at Jane in the dim light of the fire. "No. For five years now I've been Fontine. I've gotten rather used to it. What do you think?"

"It doesn't lose too much in the translation," said Jane, smiling again. "Except, perhaps, a flavor of landed gentry."

"That's part of what I mean," he replied quickly. "Andrew and Adrian shouldn't be burdened with such nonsense. Times are not what they were; those days will never return."

"Probably not. It's a little sad to see them go, but it's for the best, I suppose." His wife suddenly blinked her eyes and looked questioningly up to him. "If not Italy, or England, then where?"

"America. Would you live in America?"

Jane stared at him, her eyes still searching. "Of course. I think that's very exciting. . . Yes, it's right. For all of us."

"And the name? You don't mind really, do you?"

She laughed, reaching up to touch his face. "It doesn't matter. I married a man, not a name."

"You matter," he said, pulling her to him.

Harold Latham walked out of the old, brass-grilled elevator and looked at the arrows and the numbers on the wall. He had been transferred to the Burma theater three years ago; it had been that long since he'd been in the corridors of MI6-London.

He tugged at the jacket of his new suit. He was a civilian now; he had to keep reminding himself of that. Soon there would be thousands upon thousands of civilians—*new* civilians. Germany had collapsed. He'd wagered five pounds that the formal announcement of surrender would come before the first of May. There were three days to go, and he didn't give a damn about the five quid. It was over; that was all that mattered.

He started walking down the hallway toward Stone's office. Good old, poor old, angry Geoff Stone. The *Apple* to his *Pear*. Rotten fucking luck it was, old Apple's hand shot to bits because of a high-handed guinea; and so early on, too.

Still, it bloody well might have saved his life. An awful lot of two-handed operatives never came back. In some ways Stone was damned fortunate. As he had been fortunate. He had a few pieces of metal in his back and stomach, but if he was careful they said he'd do fine. Practically normal, they said. Discharged him early, too.

Apple and Pear had survived. They'd made it! *Goddamn*, that called for a month of whiskies!

He had tried to call Stone but hadn't been able to reach him. He telephoned for two days straight, both the flat and the office, but there was never an answer. There was no point in leaving messages; his own plans were so ragtail he wasn't sure how long he could stay in London.

It was better this way. Just barge in and demand to know why old Apple had taken so long to win the war.

The door was locked. He knocked; there was no answer. *Damn!* The front desk had Stone checked in; that was to say he hadn't checked *out* last night, or the night before, which was not unusual these days. Office couches were beds these days. All the Intelligence services were working around the clock, going through files, destroying records that could be embarrassing, and probably saving a few thousand lives in the process. When the dust of victory and defeat settled, informers were the least popular survivors.

He knocked louder. Nothing.

Yet there was light shining through the thin, lateral crack at the base of the door. Perhaps Stone had stepped out for a minute. To the W.C. or the cafeteria.

And then Latham's eyes strayed to the round lock cylinder. There was something odd, something wrong. A speck of dull gray seemed to cling to the brass, a tiny scratch above it, to the right of the keyhole. Latham looked closer; he drew a match and struck it, almost afraid to do what he was about to do.

He held the flame directly below the speck of gray matter. It melted instantly and fell away; solder.

It was also an obscure but time-tested device that Apple favored. He had used it on numerous occasions when they worked together. Come to think of it, Latham couldn't remember anyone else ever using it.

Melt the end of a small solder wire and shove the soft liquid into the lock with its key. It jammed the tumblers but did not prevent the key from going in.

It merely prevented any key from opening the lock. In quiet situations that called for a little time while a man raced out of a trap, it provided that time without raising any sudden alarms. A perfectly normal-looking lock malfunctioned; most locks were old. One did not break down a door; one called a locksmith.

Had Apple needed time? Was there a trap?

Something *was* wrong.

"Good Christ! Don't touch anything! Get a *doctor!"* shouted Teague, lunging into the office beyond the unhinged door. "And keep this tight!"

"He's dead," said Latham quietly at the brigadier's side.

"I know that," answered Teague curtly. "I want to know how *long* he's been dead."

"Who is he?" asked Latham, looking down at the dead man. The body had been stripped; only the undershorts and shoes remained. There was a single, clean gunshot wound in the upper center of the naked chest; the rivulet of blood had dried.

"Colonel Aubrey Birch. Officer of the vaults." Teague turned and spoke to the two guards holding the door. A third soldier had gone for the MI6 house surgeon on the second floor. "Put that door back. Admit no one. Say nothing. Come with me, Latham."

They rode the elevator to the cellars. Latham saw that Teague was not only in a state of shock, he was frightened.

"What do you think happened, sir?"

"I gave him his separation papers two nights ago. He hated me for it."

Latham was silent for a moment. Then he spoke without looking at Teague, his eyes straight ahead. "I'm a civilian, so I'll say it. That was a rotten, goddamned thing to do. Stone was once the best man you had."

"Your objection is noted," said the brigadier coldly. "You were the one they called Pear, weren't you?"

"Yes."

Teague glanced at the discharged Intelligence agent; the panel light indicated that the cells had been reached. "Well, the apple soured, Mr. Pear. It became rancid. What concerns me now is how far the rot penetrated."

The door opened. They walked out of the elevator and turned right toward a wall of steel that closed off the corridor. In the center of the wall was a thick steel door, its frame was barely discernible. There was a plate of bulletproof glass in the upper section, a black button to the left, a thin rubber slot below, a metal sign above.

SECURITY AREA

No Admittance Without Proper Authorisation
Ring Bell—Place Authorisation In Vacuum Slot

Teague approached the glass, pushed the button and spoke firmly. "Code Hyacinth. No delays, please; make visual confirmation. This is Brigadier Teague. I'm accompanied by one Mr. Harold Latham, cleared by me."

There was a whirring sound. The steel door receded, then was slid manually to the side. An officer on the other side saluted.

"Good afternoon, general. There's been no Hyacinth report down here."

Teague acknowledged the salute with a nod of his head. "I'm delivering it myself, major. Nothing is to be removed until further orders. What does the duty ledger read on Colonel Birch?"

The officer turned to a metal desk that was attached to the metal wall. "Here it is, sir," he said, holding open a black leather notebook. "Colonel Birch signed out the night before last at nineteen hundred hours. He's due back in the morning. Oh seven hundred, sir."

"I see. Was anyone with him?"

The major looked again at the large notebook. "Yes, sir. Captain Stone, sir. His checkout time is the same."

"Thank you. Mr. Latham and I will be in Vault Seven. May I have the keys, please? And the combination figures."

"Of course."

Inside the metal room were twenty-two file cabinets. Teague stopped at the fourth cabinet against the far wall opposite the door. He looked at the page of figures in his hand and began manipulating the combination lock in the upper right corner of the cabinet. As he did so, he held out the page of figures for Latham.

"Save time," he said brusquely, his voice hoarse. "Locate the cabinet with the Brevourt file. B-r-e-v-o-u-r-t. Extract it."

Latham took the paper, returned to the left wall and found the cabinet.

The lock sprung. Teague reached over and pulled out the second cabinet drawer. Rapidly his fingers separated the files.

Then he separated them again. Slowly, allowing for no oversight.

It wasn't there. The file on Victor Fontine was gone.

Teague closed the cabinet drawer and stood erect. He looked over at Latham, who knelt by the bottom drawer of his cabinet, an open folder in his hand. He was staring at it, his expression one of stunned bewilderment.

"I asked you to find it, not read it," said the brigadier icily.

"There's nothing to read," replied Latham quietly, removing a single page of paper from the folder. "Except this. . . . What the hell have you bastards done?"

The paper was a photostat. It had a black border, with room at the bottom for two seals of approval. Both men knew exactly what it was.

An order for execution. An official license to kill.

"Who's the target?" asked Teague in a monotone, remaining by the cabinet.

"Vittorio Fontini-Cristi."

"Who approved of it?"

"Foreign Office seal, Brevourt's signature."

"Who *else?* There must be *two!*"

"The prime minister."

"And Captain Stone is the assignee——"

Latham nodded, although Teague had not asked a question. "Yes."

Teague breathed deeply, closing his eyes for a moment. He opened them and spoke. "How well did you know Stone? His methods?"

"We worked together for eighteen months. We were like brothers."

"Brothers? Then I remind you, Mr. Latham, that in spite of your separation from the service, the Official Secrets Act still binds you."

Chapter Fifteen

Teague spoke into the telephone, his phrases precise, his voice cutting. "From the beginning he was your man. From the day we placed him in Loch Torridon. His interrogations, the endless questions, Lübok's name in our files, the traps. Fontine's every move was reported to you."

"I make no apologies," said Anthony Brevourt on the other end of the line. "For reasons you well know. 'Salonika' was, and still remains, a highest priority of the Foreign Office."

"I want an explanation for that order of execution! It was never cleared, never reported——"

"Nor was it *meant* to be," interrupted Brevourt. "That order was our backup. You may subscribe to your own immortality, brigadier, but we don't. Air raids aside, you're a strategist for covert operations; a potential mark for assassination. If you were killed, that order permitted Stone immediate access to Fontini-Cristi's whereabouts."

"Stone convinced you of that?"

There was a pause before the ambassador replied. "Yes. Several years ago."

"Did Stone also tell you he hated Fontine?"

"He didn't approve of him; he wasn't alone."

"I said *hated!* Bordering on the pathological."

"If you knew that, why didn't you replace him?"

"Because, damn it, he controlled it! As long as he had a reason to. He has *none* now."

"I don't see——"

"You're a goddamn fool, Brevourt! Stone left us a photostat; he kept the original. You're helpless and he wants you to know it."

"What are you talking about?"

"He's walking around with an official document that gives him a warrant to kill Fontine. Countermanding it now is meaningless. It would have been meaningless two *years* ago! He has the paper; he's a professional. He intends to carry out the assignment and place that document where you can't get it. Can the British government—can *you*, or the foreign secretary, or Churchill, himself, justify that execution? Would any of you care to even *comment* on it?"

Brevourt replied swiftly, urgently. "It was a contingency. That was *all* it was."

"It was the best," agreed Teague harshly. "Startling enough to cut through red tape. Sufficiently dramatic to break down bureaucratic walls. I can hear Stone mounting his argument."

"Stone must be found. He must be stopped." Brevourt's breathing could be heard over the line.

"We've reached one area of agreement," said the brigadier wearily.

"What are you going to do?"

"To begin with, tell Fontine everything."

"Is that wise?"

"It's fair."

"We expect to be kept informed. If need be, hourly."

Teague looked absently across the office at his wall clock. It was nine forty-five; moonlight streamed through the windows, no curtains blocked it now. "I'm not sure that's possible."

"What?"

You're concerned with a vault taken out of Greece five years ago. I'm concerned with the lives of Victor Fontine and his family."

"Has it occurred to you," said Brevourt, drawing out his words, "that the two are inseparable?"

"Your conjecture is noted." Teague hung up and leaned back in his chair. He would have to call Fontine now. Warn him.

There was a knock on his door.

"Come in."

Harold Latham walked in first, followed by one of the best investigating officers in MI6. A middle-aged, former Scotland Yard forensic specialist. He carried a manila file folder in his hand.

A few weeks ago, Pear would not have walked into Teague's office smoking a cigarette. He did so now; it was important to him. Yet, thought Teague, Latham's hostility had lessened. Pear was first and foremost a professional. Civilian status would not change that.

"Did you find anything?" asked Teague.

"Scratchings," said Latham. "They may mean something, they may not. Your man here is sharp. He can lift a book off a pinhead."

"He knew where to point me," added the analyst. "He was familiar with the subject's habits."

"What have we got?"

"Nothing on the premises; his office was clean. Nothing but case work, dossiers marked for the ovens, all quite legitimate. His flat was something else. He was a thorough chap. But the arrangements of the hangers in the closets, the clothes in his bureau, the toilet supplies . . . they all indicate that Stone had been planning his departure for some time."

"I see. And these scratchings?"

Pear answered. The professional in him needed recognition. "Stone had a disagreeable habit. He would lie in bed making notes. Words, brackets, figures, arrows, names—doodling, I call it. But before he turned in he'd tear off the pages and burn them. There was nothing on it, of course, but the Yarder here knew what to do."

"There were depressions, sir. It wasn't difficult; we lifted them under spectrograph." The officer handed Teague the folder across the desk. "Here are the results."

Teague opened the folder and stared at the spectrogram. As Pear had described, there were numbers, brackets, arrows, words. It was a disjointed puzzle, a wild diagram of incoherent meanderings.

And then the name leaped up from the mass of incoherence.

Donatti.

The man with the streak of white in his hair. The executioner of Campo di Fiori. One of the most powerful cardinals in the Curia.

"Salonika" had begun.

". . . Guillamo Donatti."

Fontine heard the name and it triggered the memory locked in his mind. The name was the key, the lock was sprung, and the memory revealed.

He was a child, no more than nine or ten years old. It was evening and his brothers were upstairs preparing for bed. He had come down in his pajamas to find a book, when he'd heard the shouting from this father's study.

The door was open, no more than a foot, and the curious child had approached it. What he saw inside so shocked his sensibilities that he stood there hypnotized. A priest was in front of his father's desk, roaring at Savarone, pounding the top of the desk with his fist, his face pinched in anger, his eyes wide in fury.

That anyone could behave this way in his father's presence, even—perhaps especially—a priest, so startled the child that he involuntarily, audibly gasped.

When he did the priest whipped around, the burning eyes looking at the child, and it was then that Victor had seen the streak of white in the black hair. He had run away from the living room and up the staircase.

The next morning Savarone had taken his son aside and explained; his father never left explanations suspended. What the violent argument referred to was obscured with time, but Fontine recalled that his father had identified the priest as Guillamo Donatti, a man who was a disgrace to the Vatican . . . someone who issued edicts to the uninformed and enforced them by fear. They were words a child remembered.

Guillamo Donatti, firebrand of the Curia.

"Stone's after his own, now," said Teague over the line from London, bringing Victor's focus back to the present. "He wants you, and whatever price you'll bring. We were looking in the wrong areas; we've traced him now. He used Birch's papers and got a military flight out of Lakenheath. To Rome."

"To the cardinal," corrected Fontine. "He's not taking chances with long-distance negotiations."

"Precisely. He'll come back for you. We'll be waiting."

"No," said Victor into the telephone. "That's not the way. We won't wait, we'll go after them."

"Oh?" The doubt was in Teague's voice.

"We know Stone's in Rome. He'll stay out of sight, probably with informer cells; they're used to hiding men."

"Or with Donatti."

"That's doubtful. He'll insist on neutral territory. Donatti's dangerous, unpredictable. Stone realizes that."

"I don't care what you're thinking, but I can't——"

"Can you circulate a rumor from reliable sources?" interrupted Fontine.

"What kind of rumor?"

"That I'm about to do what everyone expects me to do: return to Campo di

Fiori. For unknown reasons of my own."

"Absolutely not! It's out of the question!"

"For God's *sake*," shouted Victor. "I can't hide out for the rest of my life! I can't live in fear that each time my wife or children leave the house there is a Stone or a Donatti or an execution team waiting for them! You promised me a confrontation. I want it *now*."

There was silence on the line from London. Finally Teague spoke. "There's still the Order of Xenope."

"One step leads to another. Hasn't that been your premise all along? Xenope will be forced to acknowledge what *is*, not what it thinks *should* be. Donatti and Stone will be proof. There can be no other conclusion."

"We have men in Rome, not many——"

"We don't *want* many. Very few. My being in Italy must not be linked with M.I.-Six. The cover will be the Court of Reparations. The government wants to control our factories, the properties. The court bids higher every week; they don't want the Americans."

"Court of Reparations," said Teague, obviously writing a note.

"There is an old man named Barzini," continued Fontine. "Guido Barzini. He used to be at Campo di Fiori, he tended the stables. He could give us background. Put a trace on him in the Milan district. If he's alive, he'll be found through the *partigiani*."

"Barzini, Guido," repeated Teague. "I'll want safety factors."

"So do I, but very low profile, Alec. We want to force them out in the open, not further underground."

"Assuming the bait's taken, what will you do?"

"Make them listen. It's as simple as that."

"I don't think it is," said Teague.

"Then I'll kill them," said Victor.

The word went out. The *padrone* was alive; he had returned. In a small hotel several blocks from the Duomo, he was *seen*. Fontini-Cristi was in Milan. The news was known even in Rome.

There was a knock on the hotel door. Barzini. It was a moment Victor both looked forward to and dreaded. The memories of white light and death inadvertently came into focus. He suppressed them as he walked across the room to the door.

The old farmhand stood in the hallway, his once muscular body now bent and thin, lost within the coarse fabric of his cheap black coat. His face was wrinkled; the eyes were rheumy. The hands that had held Victor's writhing, lashing body to the earth, the fingers that had clawed at his face and saved his life, were withered, gnarled. And they shook.

To Fontine's sorrow and embarrassment, Barzini fell to his knees, his thin arms outstretched, grasping Victor's legs.

"It's true. You're alive!"

Fontine pulled him to his feet and embraced him. In silence he led the old man into the room, to the couch. Beyond his age, it was obvious that Barzini was ill. Victor offered food; Barzini asked for tea and brandy. Both were brought quickly by the hotel waiters, and when both were finished, Fontine learned the salient facts of Campo di Fiori since the night of the massacre.

For months after the German killings, the fascist troops kept the estate under guard. The servants were allowed to take their possessions and leave; the maid who had witnessed the shooting was murdered that night. No one

was permitted to live in Campo di Fiori except Barzini, who was obviously
mentally deficient.

"It was not difficult. The *fascisti* always thought everyone else was crazy
but themselves. It was the only way they could think, and face themselves in
the morning."

In his position of stablehand and groundkeeper, Guido was able to watch
the activity at Campo di Fiori. Most startling were the priests. Groups of
priests were permitted in; never more than three or four at a time, but there
were many such groups. At first Guido believed they had been sent by the
holy father to pray for the souls of the house of Fontini-Cristi. But priests on
sacred missions did not behave as these priests behaved. They went through
the main house, then the cottages and, finally, the stables, searching with
precision. They tagged everything; furniture was pried apart; walls tapped
for hollow sections and panels removed; floors ripped up—not in anger but as
experienced carpenters might do; lifted and replaced. And the grounds were
combed as though they were fields of gold.

"I asked several of the young fathers what they were looking for. I don't
think they really knew. They always replied, 'thick boxes, old man. Cartons
of steel and iron.' And then I realized that there was one priest, an older
priest, who came every day. He was forever checking the work of the
others."

"A man in his sixties," said Victor softly, "with a streak of white in his
hair."

"Yes! That was he! How did you know?"

"He was expected. How long did the searching go on?"

"For nearly two years. It was an unbelievable thing. And then it stopped."

All activity stopped, according to Barzini, except German activity. The
Wehrmacht Officer Corps appropriated Campo di Fiori, turning it into an
elaborate retreat for the higher echelon commanders.

"Did you do as the Englishman from Rome told you, old friend?" Fontine
poured Barzini more brandy; the trembling had partially subsided.

"Yes, *padrone*. For the past two days I have gone to the markets in Laveno,
in Varese, and Legnano. I say the same to a few chosen loudmouths:
'Tonight I see the *padrone*! He returns! I go to Milan to meet him, but no one
is to know!' They will know, son of Fontini-Cristi." Barzini smiled.

"Did anyone ask you *why* I insisted you come to Milan?"

"Most did. I say only that you wish to talk with me privately. I tell them I
am honored. And I am."

"It should be enough." Victor picked up the phone and gave a number to
the hotel switchboard. While he waited for the call to be placed, he turned to
Barzini. "When this is over, I want you to come back with me. To England,
then America. I'm married, old friend. You'll like the *signora*. I have sons,
two sons. Twins."

Barzini's eyes shone. "You have sons? I give thanks to God——"

There was no answer on the line. Fontine was concerned. It was *imperative*
that the MI6 man be at that telephone! He was stationed halfway between
Varese and Campo di Fiori. He was the contact for the others, spread out on
the roads leading from Stresa, Lugano, and Morcote; he was the focal point
of communications. Where the hell *was* he?

Victor hung up the phone and took his wallet out of his pocket. In a
concealed recess was another telephone number. In Rome.

He gave it to the operator.

"What do you mean there's no answer?" asked the precise English voice that answered.

"Is there a clearer way to say it?" responded Fontine. "There *is* no *answer*. When did you last hear from him?"

"About four hours ago. Everything was on schedule. He was in radio contact with all vehicles. You got the message, of course."

"What message?"

There was a momentary silence. "I don't like this, Fontine."

"What *message?*"

"He said he might have been zeroed, but we weren't to worry. He'd reach you at the hotel when you arrived. He spotted up the car himself. It was on the road that passes the main gates at Campo di Fiori. He didn't reach you?"

Victor suppressed a desire to shout. "He didn't reach me. There were no messages for me. What car?"

"A green Fiat. The license was from Sàvona, that's on the Genoa gulf. One of the descriptions matched a Corsican in the police files. A contrabandist London believes worked for us. The others are also Corsos, we think. And *him*."

"I presume you——"

"Yes. Stone's the fourth man."

Stone had taken the bait. Apple had gone back to Celle Ligure, back to the Corsicans to find his recruits. And Apple, the professional, had removed the contact in Varese.

Eliminate the couriers. Immobilize communications. Loch Torridon.

"Thank you," said Victor to the man in Rome.

"See *here*, Fontine!" came the harried voice over the telephone. "You're to do *nothing!* Stay where you are!"

Without answering, Victor replaced the phone and walked back to Barzini. "I need some men. Men we can trust, who are willing to take risks."

Barzini looked away; the old man was embarrassed. "Things are not what they were, *padrone*."

"*Partigiani?*" said Fontine.

"Mostly Communists. They're concerned with themselves now. With their pamphlets, their meetings. They——" Barzini stopped. "Wait. There are two men who don't forget. They hid in the mountains; I brought them food, news of their families. We can trust them."

"They'll have to do," said Victor, starting for the bedroom door. "I'm going to change clothes. Can you reach them?"

"There's a telephone number," answered Barzini, getting up from the couch.

"Call them. Tell them to meet me at Campo di Fiori. I assume there are guards."

"Only a nightwatchman now. From Laveno. And myself."

Fontine stopped and turned to Barzini. "Would these men know the back road north of the stables?"

"They can find it."

"Good. Tell them to start out now and wait for me on the bridle path at the rear of the stables. It's still there, isn't it?"

"It is still there. What are you going to do, *padrone?*"

Victor realized as he spoke that he was repeating the words he had used over the phone to Teague five days ago. "What everyone expects me to do." He turned and continued toward the bedroom.

Chapter Sixteen

The lessons of Loch Torridon were always present, thought Victor, as he stood in front of the hotel desk, his arms on the marble counter, watching the night clerk carry out his request. He had demanded a car for hire in a voice loud enough to draw attention. It was a difficult order considering the hour; vehicles were hard enough to come by during the day, much less in the middle of the night. But they could be had if the money was sufficient. Then, too, the argument at the front desk was sufficiently disagreeable to alert any observer. Also, there were the clothes he wore: dark gray trousers, boots, and a dark hunting jacket. It was not the hunting season.

There were only a few stragglers in the lobby; several businessmen making unsteady treks to their rooms after long, liquid conferences; a couple arguing over one or the other's behavior; a nervous, rich youth signing in with a whore who waited discreetly in a chair. And a dark, swarthy man with the hard leather face of the sea, who was across the lobby in an armchair reading a magazine, seemingly oblivious to the hotel's night scene. A Corsican, thought Victor.

It was this man who could carry the message to other Corsicans. To the Englishman named Stone.

It was simply a matter of coordinating the upcoming sequence. To make sure there was a green Fiat on the street, probably in shadows, ready to take up a discreet position when the rented car drove away. If there was no such automobile, Victor could find reasons to delay until it arrived.

No delay was necessary. The Fiat could be seen in the middle of the next block. Captain Geoffrey Stone was sure of himself. The auto was positioned in front of Fontine's car, heading west, toward the road to Varese. To Campo di Fiori.

Barzini sat in the front with Victor. The brandy had done its work. The old man's head kept falling to his chest.

"Sleep," said Victor. "It's a long drive and I'll want you rested when we get there."

They drove through the open gates and into the long winding entrance of Campo di Fiori. Although he was braced for it, the sight of the house filled his chest with pain; hammering seared through his temples. He approached the execution grounds. The sights and sounds of that agony returned, but he knew he could not permit them to overwhelm him. The lessons of Loch Torridon: *Divided concentrations were dangerous.*

He contracted the muscles of his stomach taut and stopped the car.

Barzini was awake, staring at him. The nightwatchman emerged from the thick oak doors beyond the marble steps, the beam of his flashlight examining the car and those inside. Barzini stepped out and spoke.

"I bring the son of Fontini-Cristi. He's the *padrone* of this house."

The watchman threw the beam over at Victor, who had gotten out of the car and stood by the hood. His voice was respectful. And not a little frightened.

"I am honored, *padrone*."

"You may go home to Laveno," Fontine told him. "If you don't mind, use the north road. You probably do anyway. It's the shortest way."

"Much the shortest, *signore*. Thank you, *signore*."

"There may be two friends waiting for me at the stables. Don't be alarmed,

I asked them to drive through the north gate. If you see them, please tell them I'll be there shortly."

"Of course, *padrone*." The nightwatchman nodded and walked rapidly down the marble steps into the drive. There was a bicycle in the shadows by the shrubbery. He mounted and pedaled off into the darkness toward the stables.

"Quickly," said Victor, turning to Barzini. "Tell me. Are the telephones as they were? Is there still a line connecting the house with the stables?"

"Yes. In your father's study and in the hall."

"Good. Go in and turn on all the lights in the hall and in the dining room. Then go back to the study, keeping those lights out. Stay by a window. When I reach your friends, I'll call you from the stables and tell you what to do. Soon the Corsicans will appear. On foot, I'm sure. Watch for small flashlights. Tell me what you see."

"Very well. *Padrone?*"

"Yes?"

"I have no gun. Weapons are outlawed."

"Take mine." Victor reached into his belt and removed his Smith & Wesson. "I don't think you'll need it. Don't fire unless your life depends on it."

Thirty seconds later the lights in the great hall shone through the stained-glass windows above the huge entrance doors. Victor hurried along the side of the house and waited by the edge of the building. The chandeliers in the dining room were switched on. The whole north section of the house was a blaze of light, the south section in darkness.

There were still no signs of life on the road; no beams of flashlights or flares or matches. It was as it should be. Stone was a professional. When he moved it would be with extreme caution.

So be it. *His* moves would be cautious also.

Victor ran into the north road toward the stables. He kept low to the ground and alert, listening for the unusual. Stone might have opted for the north gates as his means of entry, but it was unlikely. Stone was anxious; he would move in swiftly, close behind his quarry, and seal off the exits.

"*Partigiani*. It's Fontini-Cristi." Victor walked down the bridle path at the rear of the stables. The few horses left inside were old and weary, the whinnies intermittent.

"*Signore.*" The whisper came from the woods to the right of the path; Fontine approached. Suddenly a flashlight beam shot out from the opposite side. From the left. And another voice spoke.

"Stay where you are! Don't turn!"

He felt the hand of the man behind him on the small of his back, holding him steady. The flashlight moved forward over his shoulder, shining in his face, blinding him.

"It's him," said the voice in the darkness.

The flashlight was removed. Fontine blinked and rubbed his eyes, trying to erase the residual image of the blinking light. The *partigiano* came out of the darkness. He was a tall man, nearly as tall as Victor, dressed in a worn American field jacket. The second man came from behind; he was much shorter than his comrade and barrel-chested.

"Why are we here?" asked the tall man. "Barzini's old and doesn't think clearly. We agreed to watch you, warn you . . . nothing else. We do this because we owe Barzini much. And for old time's sake; the Fontini-Cristis fought against the fascists."

"Thank you."

"What do the Corsicans want? And this Englishman?" The second man moved to his friend's side.

"Something they believe I have, which I don't have." Victor stopped. From the stables there was a soft, tired snort followed by a series of hoof thumps. The partisans heard it, too; the flashlight was extinguished.

A crack of a limb. A pebble dislodged under a footstep. Someone approached, following the same path Fontine had taken. The partisans separated; the stocky man moved forward and disappeared into the foliage. His brother did the same in the opposite direction. Victor stepped to his right and crouched off the path.

Silence. The footsteps scratching over the dry earth became clearer. Suddenly the figure was there, only inches in front of Fontine, outlined in the forest night.

And then it happened. A powerful beam of light burst out of the darkness, piercing the opposite woods; at the same instant there was the sudden, muted spit of a pistol, its noise contained by a silencer.

Victor sprang up, lashing his left arm around the throat of the man, his right surging beyond for the weapon, forcing it downward. As the man's back arched, Victor crashed his knee into the base of the spine. The man's breath was expunged; Fontine yanked with all his strength at the taught neck in his hammerlock. There was a snap, sickening and final. The light rolled on the path.

The tall *partigiano* raced out of the woods, crushing the light underfoot, his pistol in his hand. He and Victor plunged into the foliage, both silently acknowledging the fear that their ally was dead.

He was not. The bullet had only creased his arm. He lay wild-eyed in shock, his mouth open, his breathing loud. Fontine knelt beside him, tearing off the partisan's shirt to check the wound. The man's friend remained standing, his gun on the stable path.

"Mother of Christ! You damn fool! Why didn't you *shoot* him?" The wounded *partigiano* winced in pain. "Another second and he would have killed me!"

"I had no weapon," replied Victor quietly, wiping the blood from the man's flesh.

"Not even a knife?"

"No." Fontine bound the wound and knotted the cloth. The *partigiano* stared at him.

"You've got balls," he said. "You could have waited out of sight. My comrade has a gun."

"Come on, stand up. There are two other *Corsi* somewhere. I want them. But without gunfire." Victor bent down and picked up the dead man's pistol. There were four bullets in the chamber; the silencer was one of the best. He beckoned the tall partisan off the path and spoke to both. "I'm going to ask a favor of you. You can refuse me and I'll understand."

"What is it?" asked the larger man.

"The other two Corsicans are back there. One's probably watching the main road, the other may be behind the house, in the gardens, there's no way to tell. The Englishman will stay out of sight, near the house. I'm sure the *Corsi* won't kill me. They'll watch every move I make, but they will not open fire."

"That one," said the wounded partisan, pointing to the dead man, "did not hesitate to pull his trigger."

"These *Corsi* know me by sight. He could see you weren't me."

The strategy was clean. Victor was the bait; he would walk openly down to the circular drive and turn into the gardens at the rear of the house. The partisans were to follow him, staying out of sight in the trees. If Fontine was right, a Corsican would be seen. And taken. Or killed silently. It did not matter; these *Corsi* murdered Italians.

The strategy would then be repeated on the main entrance road, the partisans crossing diagonally far behind the embankment, meeting him at a juncture a quarter of a mile away. Somewhere between the circular drive and the gates, the third and last Corsican would be stationed.

The positions were logical, and Stone was nothing if not a logical man. And thorough. He *would* seal off the exits.

You don't have to do this for me," said Victor. "I'll pay generously, but I understand——."

"Keep your money," interrupted the wounded man, looking first at his comrade. "You didn't have to do what you did for me."

"There's a telephone in the stables. I must talk with Barzini. Then start down the road."

The surmise was confirmed. Stone had covered both roads and the gardens. And the remaining Corsicans were taken, their lives ended with partisan knives.

They met at the stables. Fontine was sure that Stone had been watching him from the embankment. The quarry was walking the killing ground; the return was painful. Loch Torridon had taught them both to anticipate reactions. It was a weapon.

"Where's your car?" Victor asked the *partigiani*.

"Outside the north gate," replied the tall one.

"You have my thanks. Get your friend to a doctor. Barzini will know where I can send a more concrete form of gratitude."

"You want the Englishman for yourself?"

"There'll be no trouble. He's a man with one hand, without his *Corsi*. Barzini and I know what to do. Get to a doctor."

"Good-bye, *signore*," said the tall man. "Our debts are canceled. To old Barzini. To you, perhaps. The Fontini-Cristis were good to this land once."

"Many thanks."

The partisans nodded a last time and made their way swiftly up the road into the darkness toward the north gate. Fontine went down the path and let himself into the stables through a side door. He walked by the stalls, past the horses and Barzini's small bedroom, into the tack room. He found a wooden box and began filling it with braces and bits and musty, framed citations from the walls. He crossed to the telephone by the door and pushed a button beneath it.

"All is well, old friend."

"Thank God."

"What about the Englishman?"

"He's waiting across the drive, in the high grass. On the embankment. The same——" Barzini stopped.

"I understand. I'm starting out now. You know what to do. Remember, at the door speak slowly, clearly. The Englishman hasn't spoken Italian in recent years."

"Old men talk louder than they must," said Barzini, humor in his voice. "Because we hear poorly, so must everyone else."

Fontine replaced the phone and checked the pistol the partisans had left him; it had been taken from a dead Corsican. He unscrewed the silencer and put the weapon in his pocket. He picked up the box and went out the tack room door.

He walked slowly down the road to the circular drive opposite the embankment. In front of the steps, in the spill of light from the windows, he paused, giving his arms a moment of rest, conveying the fact that the box was heavier than its size might indicate.

He continued up the steps to the large oak doors. He then did the most natural thing that came to him: he kicked at the right door.

In seconds the door was opened by Barzini. Their exchange was simple, without strain. The old man spoke clearly.

"You're sure I can't bring you something, *padrone?* A pot of tea, coffee?"

"No, thank you, old friend. Get some sleep. We have a lot to do in the morning."

"Very well. The horses will eat early today." Barzini walked past Victor to the steps and down into the circular drive. He turned left toward the stables.

Victor stood in the great hall; everything was as it had been. The Germans knew when not to mar a thing of beauty. He turned into the darkened south section, into the enormous drawing room towards the doors of his father's study. As he walked through the familiar space, he felt pains of anguish in his chest and the catching of breath in his throat.

He went into his father's study, Savarone's *sanctum sanctorum*. Instinctively, he turned right in the darkness; the huge desk was where it had always been. He put the box down and turned on the green-shaded lamp he remembered; it was the same lamp. Nothing had changed.

He sat down in his father's chair and removed the pistol from his pocket. He placed it on the desk, behind the wooden box, concealing it from the front.

The waiting had begun. And for the second time his life was in Barzini's hands. He could not imagine a firmer grip. For Barzini would not reach the stables. He would walk up the stable road and enter the woods, doubling back into the gardens, to the rear of the house. He would let himself in through one of the patio doors, and wait for the Englishman to come.

Stone was trapped.

The minutes dragged on. Absently, Fontine opened the drawers of his father's desk. He found sheets of Wehrmacht stationery, and methodically he placed them sheet by sheet in separate piles, a game of solitaire with huge blank playing cards.

He waited.

At first, he did not hear any sound. Instead, he felt the presence. It was unmistakable, filling the air between himself and the intruder. Then the creak of a floorboard pierced the silence, followed by two distant footsteps, bold, unconcealed; Fontine's hand moved toward the gun.

Suddenly, out of the dark space, a light-colored object came flying through the shadows toward him, *at* him! Victor recoiled as the object came into focus, trailing rivulets of blood in the air. There was a harsh slap—flesh against wood—and the horrible thing made contact with the top of the desk and rolled obscenely under the spill of the lamp.

Fontine expelled his breath in an instant of total revulsion.

The object was a hand. A severed right hand cut crudely above the wrist. The fingers were old and withered and clawlike in spastic contraction, the tendons iced at the instant of primitive surgery.

It was the hand of Guido Barzini. Thrown by a maniac who had lost his own on a pier in Celle Ligure.

Victor shot up from the chair, suppressing the revulsion that welled up beside him, stabbing for the gun.

"Don't touch that! You do, you're dead!" Stone's words were spat out in English. He crouched in the shadows across the room, behind a high-backed armchair.

Victor withdrew his hand. He had to force himself to think. To survive. "You killed him."

"They'll find him in the woods. It's odd *I* found him there, isn't it?"

Fontine stood motionless, accepting the awful news, suspending emotion. "Odder still," said Victor quietly, "that your Corsican didn't."

Stone's eyes reacted; only a flicker of recognition, but the reaction was there. "The walk you took. I wondered." The Englishman nodded his head. "Yes, you could have done that. You could have taken them out."

"I didn't. Others did."

"Sorry, Fontini. That doesn't wash."

"How can you be sure?"

"Because if there were others, you wouldn't use an old man for the last job; that's stupid. You're an arrogant son of a bitch, but you're not stupid. We're alone, all right. Just you and me and that box. *Christ!* It must have been in one hell of a hole. Enough people looked for it."

"Then you made your deal with Donatti?"

"He thinks so. Strange, isn't it? You took everything from me. I crawled out of Liverpool and made my way up, and you took it all away on a fucking guinea pier five years ago. Now I've got it all back and then some. I may hold the biggest auction anyone's ever heard of."

"For what? Old hunt prizes? Faded citations?"

Stone snapped the hammer of his weapon into firing position. His black glove slapped the back of the chair, his eyes bore through the shadows. "Don't make jokes!"

"No jokes. I'm not stupid, remember? And you're not in any position to pull that trigger. You've only got one chance to deliver the contents of that vault. If you don't, another order of execution can easily be issued. Those powerful men who hired you five years ago don't like embarrassing speculations."

"Shut up! *Stop it!*" Furiously, Stone raised the clawlike glove above the chair and smashed it down. "Those tactics won't work on me, you guinea bastard! I used them before you ever heard of Loch Torridon."

"Loch Torridon was based on *error.* Miscalculation! *Mismanagement!* That was its *premise.* Remember?" Fontine took a step backward, pushing the chair with his legs, extending his hands out in a gesture of helplessness. "Come on. Look for yourself. You wouldn't kill me before you saw what the bullet cost you."

"Move back! *Farther!*" Stone came around the chair, his immobile right hand stretched out directly in front of him like a protruding lance. His left hand held the weapon with the cocked hammer; the slightest squeeze of the trigger and the pin would spring forward, exploding the shell.

Victor did as he was commanded, his eyes riveted on the pistol. His moment would come; it had to come or there was nothing.

The Englishman approached the desk, each step the movement of a man filled with loathing and wariness, prepared to destroy at the split second of imbalance. He took his eyes from Fontine and stared at the top of the desk. At the severed, mutilated hand of Guido Barzini. At the box. At the pile of debris inside the box.

"No," he whispered. *"No!"*

The moment came: the shock of revelation was in Stone's eyes. It would not come again.

Victor sprang forward over the desk, his long arms plunging for the weapon; it had wavered with only a heartbeat, but that was all he could hope for.

The explosion was deafening, but Fontine's grip had deflected the shot. Only inches, but it was enough. The bullet shattered the top of the desk, hurling splinters of wood everywhere. Victor held Stone's wrist, wrenching with all the power he possessed, feeling and not feeling the blows delivered to his face and neck by the hard gloved hand. Stone brought his right knee up, pummeling Fontine's groin and stomach; the pistol would not be dislodged. The Englishman screamed and went into a paroxysm of frenzy. He would not, *could* not be bested by strength alone.

Victor did the only thing left for him. For an instant he stopped all movement, then yanked Stone's wrist forward as if jamming the pistol into his own stomach. As the gun was about to touch the cloth of his jacket, he suddenly twisted his body and Stone's wrist, inverting the weapon, and shoved it with his full weight upward.

The explosion came. For a second Fontine was blinded, his flesh ice cold with fireburn, and for that instant he believed he had been killed.

Until he felt the body of Geoffrey Stone collapse, pulling him downward to the floor.

He opened his eyes. The bullet had entered the flesh beneath Stone's jaw, its trajectory upward, through the skull, ripping open the top of Stone's head.

And next to the mass of blood and tissue was the severed hand of Guido Barzini.

He carried Barzini's body out of the woods and to the stables. He placed the mutilated corpse on the bed and covered it with a sheet. He stood over the body, for how long he would never remember, trying to understand pain and terror and love.

Campo di Fiori was still. For him its secret was buried, never to be known. The mystery of Salonika was a confidence Savarone had not shared. And the son of Savarone would no longer dwell on it. Let others do so, if they cared to. Let Teague take care of the rest. He was finished.

He walked down the north road from the stables to the drive in front of the house and climbed into the rented car. It was dawn. The orange summer sun broke over the Italian countryside. He took one last look at the home of his childhood and started the ignition.

The trees rushed by, the foliage became a blur of green and orange and yellow and white. He looked at the speedometer. Over eighty. Eighty-four kilometers an hour on the twisting entrance road cut out of the forest. He should brake the speed, he knew that. It was foolhardy, if not dangerous. Yet his foot would not obey his mind.

Oh, God! He had to get away!

There was a long hairpin curve that preceded the gate. In the old days—years ago—it was the custom to blow one's horn when one approached the curve. There was no cause to do so now; and he was relieved to find his foot relaxing its pressure on the pedal. Instinct was intact. Still, he took the curve at fifty, the tires screeching as he came out of the turn and headed for the gates. Automatically, on the straightaway, he accelerated. He would whip past the gateposts and swing out the road for Varese. Then Milan.

Then London!

He was not sure when he saw it. *Them.* His mind had wandered, his eyes on the immediate ground in front of the hood. He only knew that he slammed the brakes with such force he was thrown against the steering wheel, his head inches from the windshield. The car swerved, the tires screamed, dust billowed up from the wheels, and the automobile skidded diagonally through the gates, stopping only feet from the two black limousines that had converged out of nowhere, blocking the road beyond the stone posts.

His body was jolted back against the seat; the whole car shook in its sudden, violent arrest. Stunned, it took Fontine several seconds to shake off the effects of the near collision. He blinked his eyes, quickly regaining focus. His fury was suspended in astonishment at what he saw.

Standing in front of the two limousines were five men in black suits and white clerical collars. They stared impassively at him. Then the rear door of the limousine on the right opened and a sixth man got out. He was a man of about sixty, in the black robes of the church.

With a shock of white in his hair.

Chapter Seventeen

The cardinal had the eyes of a fanatic and the strained, clipped voice of a man possessed. He moved in slow, fluid motions, never permitting his audience's attention to waver. He was at once theatrical and ominous. It was a cultivated appearance, refined over the years in the corridors of the Vatican. Donatti was an eagle who fed on sparrows. He was beyond righteousness; he *was* righteousness.

At the sight of the man Victor lost control of himself. That this killer of the church could approach Campo di Fiori was an obscenity he could not stand. He lunged at the vile, cassocked figure, all sense of reason and survival and sanity itself destroyed in the instant of memory.

The priests were ready for him. They converged, as the limousines had converged, blocking his path of assault. They held him, twisting his arms high up behind his back; a hand with powerful fingers gripped his throat, forcing his head into an agonizing arch, choking off all speech, but not sight or hearing.

"The car," said Donatti quietly.

The two priests who were not restraining Fontine raced to the rented car and began the search. Victor could hear the doors and the trunk and the hood being opened. Then the ripping of upholstery and the crashing of metal as the car was torn apart. For nearly a quarter of an hour the ransacking continued. Throughout, Fontine's eyes were locked with the cardinal's. Only at the end of the search did the priest of the Curia look over at the automobile, when the two men approached and spoke simultaneously.

"There is nothing, Your Grace."

Donatti gestured to the priest whose powerful hand held Victor's throat. The grip was eased; Fontine swallowed repeatedly. His arms were still stretched taut behind his back. The cardinal spoke.

"The heretics of Constantine chose well: the apostates of Campo di Fiori. The enemies of Christ."

"Animal! Butcher!" Victor could barely whisper; the muscles of his neck and windpipe had been damaged severely. "You *murdered* us! I *saw* you!"

"Yes. I thought you might have." The cardinal spoke with quiet venom. "I would have fired the weapons myself, had it been required. And thinking thus, you are quite correct. Theologically, I was the executioner." Donatti's eyes grew wide. "Where is the crate from Salonika?"

"I don't know."

"You'll tell me, heretic. Believe the word of a true priest. You haven't got a choice."

"You hold me against my will! In the name of *God*, I presume!" said Fontine coldly.

"In the name of preserving the *mother church!* No laws take precedence over that. *Where is the shipment from Salonika?*"

The eyes, the high-pitched voice triggered the memory of years ago—a small child outside a study door. "If that knowledge was so important to you, why did you execute my father? He was the only one who knew. . . ."

"A *lie!* That is a *lie!*" Donatti caught himself, his lips trembling.

Fontine understood. A raw nerve had been exposed. An error of extraordinary magnitude had been made, and the cardinal could not bear to face it. "You know it's the truth," said Victor quietly. "*Now* you know it's the truth and you can't stand it. *Why?* Why was he *killed?*"

The priest lowered his voice. "The enemies of Christ deceived us. The heretics of Xenope fed lies to us." And once more Donatti roared abruptly. "*Savarone Fontini-Cristi* was the *communicator of those lies!*"

"What lies could *he* tell *you?* You never believed him when he told you the truth."

Again the cardinal trembled. He could barely be heard. "There were two freights out of Salonika. Three days apart. The first we knew nothing about; the second we picked up at Monfalcone, making sure that Fontini-Cristi would not meet it. We did not know then that he had already made contact with the first train. And now you will tell us what we wish to know. What we *must* know."

"I can't give you what I don't have."

Donatti looked at the priests and said one word. "Now."

Victor could never remember the length of time, for there was not time, only pain. Excruciating, harrowing, stinging, convulsive pain. He was dragged within the gates of Campo di Fiori and taken into the forest. There the holy apostolic priests began the torture. They started with his bare feet; every toe was broken, the ankles twisted until they cracked. The legs and knees were next: crushed, inverted, racked. And then the groin and stomach——*O God! He wished to die!*——And always, above him, blurred in the vision of tears of pain, was the priest of the Curia with the shock of white in his hair.

"*Tell us! Tell us! Enemy of Christ!*"

His arms were sprung from their sockets. His wrists were turned inward until the capillaries burst, spreading purple fluid throughout the skin. There were moments of blessed void, ended suddenly by hands slapping him back to consciousness.

"*Tell us! Tell us!*" The words became a hundred thousand hammers, echoes within echoes. "*Tell us! Enemy of Christ!*"

And all was void again. And through the dark tunnels of feeling, he sensed the rhythm of waves and air and suspension. A floating that deep within his brain told him he was near death.

There was a final, convulsive crash, yet he could not feel it. He was beyond feeling.

Yet he heard the words from far, far away in the distance, spoken in a chant.

"*In nomine Patris, et Filii et Spiritus sancti. Amen. Dominus vobiscum. . . .*"

Last rites.

He had been left to die.

There was the floating again. The waves and the air. And voices, indistinct, too far away to be really heard. And touch. He felt touching, each contact sending shafts of pain throughout his body. Yet these were not the touches of torture; the voices in the distance were not the voices of tormentors.

The blurred images at last came into focus. He was in a white room. In the distance were shining bottles with tubes cascading in the air.

And above him was a face. The face he knew he would never see again. What was left of his mind was playing horrible tricks on him.

The face was crying; tears rolled down the cheeks.

His wife Jane whispered. "My love. My dearest love. Oh, *God*, what have they done to you?"

Her beautiful face was next to his. Touching his.

And there was no pain.

He had been found by worried men of MI6. The priests had carried him to a car, driven him to the circular drive, and left him to die in Campo di Fiori. That he did not die was not to be explained by the doctors. He *should* have died. His recovery would take months, perhaps years. And, in truth, he would never completely recover. But with care he would regain the use of his arms and legs; he would be ambulatory, and that in itself was a miracle.

By the eighth week he was able to sit up. He concluded his business with Rome's Court of Reparations. The lands, the factories, the properties were sold for seventy-five million pounds sterling. As he had promised himself, the transaction did not include Campo di Fiori.

For Campo di Fiori he made separate arrangements, through a trusted lawyer in Milan. It, too, was to be sold but he never wanted to know the name of the buyer. There were two inviolate restrictions: The purchaser was to have nowhere in his history any connection with the fascists. Nor was he to have any association whatsoever, regardless of denomination, with any religious body.

On the ninth week an Englishman was flown over from London on instructions of his government.

Sir Anthony Brevourt stood at the foot of Fontine's bed, his jaw firm, his eyes compassionate and yet not without hardness. "Donatti's dead, you know. He threw himself off the balustrade of St. Peter's. Nobody mourns him, least of all the Curia."

"Yes, I knew that. At the end an act of insanity."

"The five priests who were with him have been punished. Three were excommunicated, prosecuted, and in prison for several decades. The other two are under life penance in the Transvaal. What was done in the church's name horrifies its leaders."

"It seems to me that too many churches permit the fanatics, then look back in astonishment, amazed at what was done in 'their names.' It's not restricted to Rome. Trappings often obscure purposes, don't they? That goes for governments, too. I want *questions answered!*"

Brevourt blinked several times at Fontine's outburst and replied rapidly, mechanically. "I'm prepared to offer them where I can. I've been instructed to withhold nothing."

"First, Stone. The order of execution has been explained; I have no comment. I want to know the rest. All of it."

"Precisely what you've been told. I didn't trust you. I was convinced when you first arrived in London that you'd made up your mind to reveal nothing about the train from Salonika. I expected you to make your own arrangements, on your own terms. We couldn't let that happen."

"Stone reported my movements then?"

"Every one. You made eleven trips across the Channel, and one to Lisbon. With Stone's help we had you covered each time. In the event of capture, we were prepared to negotiate an exchange with the enemy."

"Suppose I'd been killed?"

"In the beginning it was a risk we calculated, overshadowed by the fact that you might have bolted, made contact with regard to 'Salonika.' And in June of forty-two, after Oxfordshire, Teague agreed not to send you across any longer."

"What happened at Oxfordshire? The priest—if he *was* a priest—who led those planes in was Greek. From the Order of Xenope. Your first constituency, I believe."

Brevourt pursed his lips and breathed deeply. Admissions were being made that both pained and embarrassed him. "Stone, again. The Germans had tried for two years to locate the compound at Oxfordshire. He leaked the precise bearings to Berlin, and at the same time made his own arrangements with the Greeks. He convinced them there was a way to break you. It was worth trying; a broken man talks. He didn't give a damn himself about 'Salonika,' but the raid served his primary aim. He put a fanatic priest in the compound and coordinated the strike."

"For God's sake, *why?*"

"To kill your wife. If she'd been killed, even severely wounded, he assumed you'd turn on all things British, get out of M.I.-Six. He was right. You nearly did, you know. He hated you; blamed you for ruining a brilliant career. As I understand it, he tried to keep you in London that night."

Victor remembered the horrible night. Stone, the methodical psychopath, had counted the minutes, projected the speed of a car. Fontine reached for his cigarettes on the bedside table. "The last question. And don't lie to me. What was on the train from Salonika?"

Brevourt walked away from the bed. He crossed to the hospital window and was silent for a moment.

"Parchments, writings from the past which, if made public, could bring chaos to the religious world. Specifically, they would tear the Christian world apart. Accusations and denials would be hurled back and forth, governments might have to choose sides. Above everything, the documents in enemy hands would have been an ideological weapon beyond anything imaginable."

"Documents can do this?" asked Fontine.

"These documents can," replied Brevourt, turning away from the window. "Have you ever heard of the Filioque Clause?"

Victor inhaled. His mind went back over the years to the impartial lessons of his childhood. "It's part of the Creed of Nicaea."

"More properly, the Nicene Creed of the year 381; there were many councils, subtle alterations of the creed. The Filioque was a later addition that once and for all established the Christ figure as one substance with God. It's rejected by the Eastern church as misleading. For the Eastern church, especially the sects that followed the scholar-priest Arius, Christ as the son of God was the teacher; his divinity was not equal to God's. No such equality could exist for them in those times. When the Filioque was first proposed, the Patriarchate of Constantine recognized it for what it was: a doctrinal division that favored Rome. A theological symbol that was the excuse to divide and conquer new territories. And quite right they were. The Holy Roman Empire became a global force—as the globe was known. Its influence spread throughout the world on that single premise, this specialized divinity of Christ: *Conquer* in the name of *Christ*." Brevourt stopped, as if searching for words. He walked slowly back toward the foot of the bed.

"Then the documents in that vault," said Victor, "refute the Filioque? If so, they challenge the foundation of the Roman church and all the Christian divisions that followed."

"Yes, they do that," replied Brevourt quietly. "Collectively they're called the denials . . . the Filioque denials. They include agreements between crowns and caesars from as far away as Spain, in the sixth century, where the Filioque originated, for what many believe were purely political reasons. Others trace what they term the 'theological corruption.' . . . But if that was *all* they did, the world could live with them. Son of God, teacher, one substance. These are theological differences, subjects for biblical scholars to debate. They do more, I'm afraid. In the Patriarchate's fervor to deny the Filioque, it sent out priests to search the holy lands, meet with the Aramaic scholars, unearth everything that ever existed relative to Jesus. They unearthed more than they were looking for. There were rumors of scrolls written during the years just preceding and after the mark of the first century. They traced them, discovered several, and brought them back to Constantine. It is said that one Aramaic scroll raises profound and very specific doubts as to the man known as Jesus. He may never have existed at all."

The ocean liner headed toward the open waters of the Channel. Fontine stood at the railing and watched the skyline of Southampton. Jane was at his side, one hand gently around his waist, the other crossed in front of her, over his hand on the railing. The crutches with the large metal clasps that held his forearms were to his left, the shiny half circles of stainless steel glistened in the sunlight. He had designed them himself. If it was going to be necessary, as the doctors said, for him to use crutches for a year or more he could damn well improve on the existing product.

Their two sons, Andrew and Adrian, were with their nurse from Dunblane—one of those who had elected to sail to America with the Fontines.

Italy, Campo di Fiori, the train for Salonika were in the past. The cataclysmic parchments that had been taken from the archives of Xenope were somewhere in the vast range of the Italian Alps. Buried for a millennium; perhaps never to be found.

It was better that way. The world had passed through an era of devastation and doubt. Reason demanded that a calm be restored, at least for a while, if only on the surface. It was no time for the vault from Salonika.

The future began with the rays of the afternoon sun on the waters of the English Channel. Victor leaned toward his wife and put his face next to hers. Neither spoke; she held his hand in silence.

There was a commotion on the deck. Thirty yards aft the twins had gotten into a quarrel. Andrew was angry with his brother Adrian. Childish blows were exchanged. Fontine smiled.

Children.

BOOK
TWO

PART ONE
Chapter Eighteen

June 1973

Men.

They were men, thought Victor Fontine as he watched his sons thread separately through the guests in the bright sunlight. And twins, second. It was an important distinction, he felt, although it wasn't necessary to dwell on it. It seemed years since anyone had referred to them as the twins. Except Jane and himself, of course. Brothers, yes; but not twins. It was strange how that word had fallen into disuse.

Perhaps the party would revive it for a while. Jane would like that. They were always the twins to Jane. Her Geminis.

The afternoon party at the North Shore house on Long Island was *for* Andrew and Adrian; it was their birthday. The lawns and gardens behind the house, above the boathouse and the water, had been turned into an enormous outdoor *fête champêtre*, as Jane called it. "A ruddy, grownup picnic! No one has them anymore. We will."

A small orchestra played at the south edge of the terrace, its music serving as an undercurrent to a hundred conversations. Long tables heaped with food were organized on the large expanse of manicured lawn; two bars did brisk business at either end of the rectangular buffet. *Fête champêtre*. Victor had never heard the term before. In thirty-four years of marriage, he had never heard it.

How the years had flown! It was as though three decades had been compressed into a time capsule and shot through the skies at incredible speed, only to land and be opened and scanned by participants who had merely grown older.

Andrew and Adrian were near each other now. Andy chatted with the Kempsons by the canapé table. Adrian was at the bar, talking to several young people whose clothes were the only vague evidence of their gender. It was right, somehow, that Andrew should be with the Kempsons. Paul Kempson was president of Centaur Electronics; he was well thought of by the Pentagon. As, of course, was Andrew. Adrian, no doubt, had been cornered by several university students who wanted to question the singularly outspoken attorney who was Victor's son.

Victor noted with a certain satisfaction that both twins were taller than those around them. It was to be expected; neither he nor Jane were short. And they looked somewhat alike, but not identical. Andrew's hair was very light, nearly blond; Adrian's was dark, auburn. Their features were sharp, a combination of his and Jane's, but each with his own identity. The only physical thing they shared in common was their eyes: they were Jane's. Light blue and penetrating.

At times, in very bright sunlight or in dim shadows, they could be mistaken for each other. But only at such times, under such conditions. And they did not seek them. Each was very much his own man.

The light-haired Andrew was in the army, a dedicated professional. Victor's influence had secured a congressional appointment to West Point, where Andrew had excelled. He'd made two tours of duty in Vietnam, although he despised the way the war was fought. "Win or get out" was his credo, but none listened, and he wasn't sure it made any difference. There was no way to win for losing. Saigon corruption was like no other corruption on the face of the earth.

Yet Andrew was not a spoiler within the ranks, either. Victor understood that. His son was a *believer*. Deep, concerned, unwavering: The military was America's strength. When all the words were said and done, there remained only the power at hand. To be used wisely, but to be *used*.

For the dark-haired Adrian, however, there was *no* limit to be placed on the use of words, and no excuse for armed confrontation. Adrian, the lawyer, was as dedicated in his fashion as his brother, although his demeanor might seem to deny it. Adrian slouched; he gave the appearance of nonchalance where none existed. Legal adversaries had learned never to be lulled by his humor or his seeming lack of concern. Adrian *was* concerned. He was a shark in the courtroom. At least he *had* been for the prosecutor's office in Boston. He was in Washington now.

Adrian had gone from prep school to Princeton to Harvard Law, with a year taken off to wander and grow a beard and play a guitar and sleep with available girls from San Francisco to Bleecker Street. It had been a year when Victor and Jane had held their collective breath, though not always their tempers.

But the life of the open road, the provincial confines of a half-dozen communes palled on Adrian. He could no more accept the aimlessness of unprovoked experience than Victor had nearly thirty years ago at the end of the European war.

Fontine's thoughts were interrupted. The Kempsons were heading over to his chair, excusing their way through the crowd. They would not expect him to get up—no one ever did—but it annoyed Victor that he could not. Without help.

"Damn fine boy," said Paul Kempson. "He's got his head on straight, that Andrew does. I told him if he ever wants to chuck the uniform, Centaur has a place for him."

"I told him he should *wear* his uniform," added Kempson's wife brightly. "He's such a handsome man."

"I'm sure he thinks it would be disconcerting," said Fontine, not at all sure. "No one wants to be reminded of the war at a birthday party."

"How long's he home for, Victor?" asked Kempson.

"Home? Here? Only for a few days. He's stationed in Virginia now. At the Pentagon."

"Your other boy's in Washington, too, isn't he? Seems I read something about him in the papers."

"Yes, I'm sure you did." Fontine smiled.

"Oh, then they're together. That's nice," said Alice Kempson.

The orchestra finished one number and began another. The younger couples flocked to the terrace; the party was accelerating. The Kempsons floated away with nods and smiles. Briefly, Victor thought about Alice Kempson's remark.

. . . *they're together. That's nice.* But Andrew and Adrian were not together. They worked within twenty minutes of each other but lived separate lives. At times, Fontine thought, *too* separate. They did not laugh together as they once did as children. As men, something had happened between them. Fontine wondered what it was.

Jane acknowledged for roughly the hundredth time that the party *was* a success, wasn't it. A statement. Thank heavens the weather held. The caterers had sworn they could erect the tents in less than an hour, if it was necessary, but by noon the sun was bright, the promise of a beautiful day confirmed.

Not, however, a beautiful evening. Far in the distance, over the water near Connecticut, the sky was gray. Weather reports predicted scattered-nocturnal-thunder-showers-with-increasingly-steady-precipitation, whatever all *that* meant. Why didn't they simply say it would rain later on?

Two o'clock to six o'clock. Good hours for a Sunday *fête champêtre*. She had laughed at Victor's ignorance of the term. It was so pretentiously Victorian; the fun was in using it. It looked ridiculous on the invitations. Jane smiled, then stifled a laugh. She really *should* control her foolishness, she supposed. She was much too old for that sort of thing.

Across the lawn between the crowds, Adrian was smiling at her. Had he read her thoughts? Adrian, her dark-haired Gemini, had inherited her slightly mad English humor.

He was thirty-one years old. *They* were thirty-one years old. Where had those years gone? It seemed like only months ago they'd all arrived in New York on the ship. Followed by months of activity that had Victor flying all over the States and back to Europe, furiously building.

And Victor had done it. Fontine, Ltd. became one of the most sought-after consulting firms in America, Victor's expertise primarily aimed at European reconstruction. The name Fontine on a corporation's presentation was an industrial plus. Knowledge of a given marketplace was assured.

Victor had involved himself totally, not merely for the sake of pride, or instinctive productivity, but for something else. Jane knew it, and at the same time knew she could do nothing to help him. It took his mind off the pain. Her husband was rarely without pain; the operations prolonged his life, but did little to lessen the pain.

She looked at Victor across the lawn, sitting in his hard wooden chair with the straight back, the shiny metal cane at his side. He had been so proud when the two crutches were replaced by the single cane that made it possible for him to walk without being so obvious a cripple.

"Hi, Mrs. Fontine," said the young man with the very long hair. "It's one terrific party! Thanks for letting me bring my friends. They really wanted to meet Adrian."

The speaker was Michael Reilly. The Reillys were their nearest neighbors on the shore, about a half a mile down the beach. Michael was in law school at Columbia. "That's very flattering!"

"Hey, *he's great!* He wrapped up that Tesco antitrust in Boston when even the federal courts thought it was too loose. Everyone knew it was a Centaur company, but it took Adrian to nail it."

"Don't discuss it with Mr. Kempson."

"Don't worry. I saw him at the club and he told me to get a haircut. What the hell, so did my father."

"You won, I see."

Michael grinned. "He's mad as a bull but he can't say anything. I'm on the honors list. We made a deal."

"Good for you. Make him live up to it."

The Reilly boy laughed and leaned over, kissing her cheek. "You're outta sight!" He grinned again and left, beckoned by a girl at the edge of the patio.

Young people liked her, thought Jane. It was a comforting realization these days when the young found so little to like, or to approve. They liked her in spite of the fact that she refused to make concessions to youth. Or to age. Her hair was streaked—God, more than streaked—with gray; her face was lined—as it should be lined—and there were no discussions of a skin nip here, or a tuck there, as so many of her friends had done. She thanked her stars she'd kept her figure. All things considered, not bad for sixty . . . *plus*, damn it.

"Excuse me, Mrs. Fontine?" It was the maid; she'd come out of the turmoil that was the kitchen.

"Yes, Grace? Problems?"

"No, ma'am. There's a gentleman at the door. He asked for you or Mr. Fontine."

"Tell him to come out."

"He said he'd rather not. He's a foreign gentleman. A priest. I thought with so many people, Mr. Fontine——"

"Yes, you were right," interrupted Jane, understanding the maid's concerns. Victor did not relish walking among his guests as he was forced to walk. "I'll go see him."

The priest stood in the hallway, his black suit ill-fitting and old, his face thin and tired. He appeared awed, frightened.

Jane spoke coldly. She could not help herself. "I'm Mrs. Fontine."

"Yes, you are the *signora*," replied the priest awkwardly, a large, stained envelope in his hand. "I have seen the pictures. I did not mean to intrude. So many automobiles."

"What is it?"

"I have come from Rome, *signora*. I bring a letter for the *padrone*. You will see that he gets it, please?" The priest held out the envelope.

Andrew watched his brother at the bar with the long-haired students, dressed in their uniforms of denim and suede, medallions around their necks. Adrian would never learn; his audience was useless. They were fakes. It was not simply the profusion of unkempt hair and the offbeat clothes that bothered the soldier; those were only symptoms. It was the pretense that went with these shallow expressions of nonconformity. By and large they were insufferable; antagonistic people with unkempt minds.

They spoke so intensely, so knowingly, of "movements" and "counter-movements" as though they were participants, shifters of political thought. *This* world . . . the *third* world. And that was the biggest joke of all, because not one in ten thousand would know how to act as a revolutionary. They had neither the commitment nor the guts nor the savvy.

They were misfits who threw plastic bags of shit when no one paid attention to their ravings. They were . . . freaks, and, Christ, he couldn't stand the freaks. But Adrian did not understand; his brother looked for values where there weren't any. Adrian was a fool; but then he learned that seven years ago. Seven years ago he had discovered just how big a fool his brother was. Adrian was a misfit in the worst sense: He had every reason not to be.

Adrian glanced up at him from the bar; he turned away. His brother was a bore, and the sight of his proselytizing to that particular audience was distasteful.

The soldier hadn't always felt this way. Ten years ago when he'd gotten out of The Point he hadn't *hated* with the vehemence he felt now. He didn't think much of Adrian and his collection of misfits, but there was no hatred. The way the Johnson crowd began handling Southeast Asia, there was something to be said for the dissenters' attitude. *Get out.*

Translated: *Obliterate Hanoi. Or get out.*

He had explained his position time and again. To the freaks. To Adrian. But no one wanted to hear it from a soldier. "Soldierboy," that's what they called him. And "shell-head," and "missile-fingers," and "blast-ass."

But it wasn't the names. Anyone who'd gone through West Point and Saigon could handle that. Ultimately, it was their stupidity. They didn't simply turn off the people who mattered, they antagonized them, infuriated them, and finally *embarrassed* them. And *that* was the final stupidity. They drove even those who agreed with them into opposing positions.

Seven years ago in San Francisco, Andrew tried to make his brother see that, tried to make him understand that what he was doing was wrong and stupid—and very dangerous to the brother who was a soldier.

He'd gotten back from two and a half years in the Mekong Delta with one of the finest record sheets in the army. His company had the highest body count in the battalion; he'd been decorated twice, his first lieutenancy lasting a month before he was given his captain's bars. He was that rare commodity in armed forces: a young, brilliant military strategist from an immensely wealthy, influential family. He was on his way to the top—where he belonged. He was being flown back for reassignment, which was another way of the Pentagon's saying: *That's our man. Keep your eye on him. Rich, solid, future Joint Chiefs material. A few more combat tours—in selected areas, a few short years—and it's the War College.*

It never hurt the Pentagon to favor a man like him, especially when it was justified. The army needed men from powerful families, they had precious few.

But regardless of what the Pentagon favored or the army needed, G2 agents had shown up when he got off that plane in California seven months ago. They'd taken him to an office and given him a two-month-old newspaper. On the second page was a story about an insurrection at the Army's Presidio in San Francisco. Accompanying the article were photographs of the riot, one showing a group of civilians marching in support of the mutineering enlisted men. A face had been circled in a red pencil.

It was Adrian. It seemed impossible, but there he was! He wasn't supposed to be there; he was in his last year at law school. In Boston. But he was not in Boston, he was in San Francisco harboring three convicted deserters who had escaped; that's what the G2 men said. His twin brother was working for the *enemy!* Goddamn it, that's what they *were* and that's what he was *doing!* The

Pentagon wouldn't look upon *that* with a whole lot of laughs. Jesus! His brother! His *twin!*

So G2 flew him up north and, out of uniform, he had wandered the streets of Haight-Ashbury until he'd found Adrian.

"These aren't men, they're confused kids," his brother said in a quiet bar. "They were never even told what their legal alternatives were; they've been railroaded."

"They took oaths like everybody else. You can't make exceptions," Andrew had replied.

"Oh, come on. Two of them didn't know what that oath meant, and the other one genuinely changed his mind. But nobody wants to listen. The judge advocates want examples, and the defense attorneys don't want to make waves."

"Sometimes examples *have* to be made," the soldier had insisted.

"And the law says they're entitled to competent counsel. Not barracks drinking buddies who want to look good——"

"Get with it, Adrian!" he interrupted. "There's a war out there! the firepower's real! Bastards like these cost *lives.*"

"Not if they're over here."

"Yes, they do! Because others will begin to wonder why they're over *there.*"

"Maybe they should."

"For Christ's sake, you're talking about *rights*, aren't you?" asked the soldier.

"You better believe it."

"Well, doesn't the poor son of a bitch on patrol in a rice paddy have any? Maybe *he* didn't know what he was getting into; he just went along because the law said he had to. Maybe *he* changed his mind. But he doesn't have time to think about it; he's trying to stay alive. He gets confused, he gets sloppy, he gets *killed!*"

"We can't reach everybody; it's one of the law's oversights, an abuse built into the system. But we do what we can."

Adrian would not give him any information seven years ago. He refused to tell him where the deserters were hidden. So the soldier said good-bye in the quiet bar and waited in a San Francisco alley until his brother came out. He followed Adrian for three hours through the acid streets. The soldier was an expert in tracking stray patrols in jungles; San Francisco was just another jungle.

His brother made contact with one of the deserters five blocks from the waterfront. They boy was a Black, with a growth of beard on his face. He was tall and thin and matched the photograph in Andrew's pocket. His twin gave the deserter money; it was a simple matter to follow the Black down to the waterfront, to a filthy tenement that was as good a hiding place as any in the area.

The phone call was made to the military police. Ten minutes later three convicted deserters were dragged out of the filthy tenement, to spend eight years in the stockades.

The misfit network went to work; the crowds gathered screeching their epithets, swaying to their adolescent, useless chants. And throwing their plastic bags of feces.

His brother came up to him in the crowds that night and for several moments just stared at him. Finally he said, "You've driven me back.

Thanks."

Then Adrian had walked swiftly away to the barricades of would-be revolutionaries.

Andrew's reflections were interrupted by Al Winston, nee Weinstein, an engineer with an aerospace company. Winston had called out his name and was making his way over. Al Winston was heavy into air force contracts, and lived in the Hamptons. Andrew didn't like Winston-Weinstein. Whenever he ran into him he thought of another Jew—and compared them. The Jew he thought of was stationed at the Pentagon after four years under heavy fire in the worst sections of the Delta. Captain Martin Greene was a tough son of a bitch, a great soldier—not a flabby Winston-Weinstein from the Hamptons. And Greene didn't gouge profits from cost overruns; instead he watched them, catalogued them. Marty Greene was one of *them*. One of Eye Corps.

"Many happy returns, major," said Winston, raising his glass.

"Thanks, Al. How are you?"

"Be a lot better if I could sell you boys something. I get no support from the ground troops." Winston grinned.

"You do pretty well *off* the ground. I read where you're in on the Grumman contract."

"Nickels and dimes. I've got a laser honing device that can be adapted to heavy artillery. But I can't get to first base."

Andrew toyed with the idea of sending Winston-Weinstein to Martin Greene. By the time Greene got finished with him, Al Winston would wish he'd never heard of the Pentagon. "I'll see what I can do. I'm not in procurement——"

"They *listen* to you, Andy."

"You never stop working, Al."

"Big house, big bills, rotten kids." Winston grinned again, then stopped smiling long enough to get across his point. "Put in a word for me. I'll make it worth your while."

"With what?" asked Andrew, his eyes straying toward the boathouse and the Chris-Craft and the sailboats moored in the water. "Money?"

Winston's grin returned, now nervous, awkward. "No offense," said the engineer softly.

Andrew looked at the Jew, thinking again of Captain Martin Greene and the difference between the two men. "No offense," he said, walking away.

Christ! Next to the freaks, he despised the *corrupters*. No, that wasn't true. Next to the corrupters, he despised those who allowed themselves to *be* corrupted. They were everywhere. Sitting in boardrooms, playing the golf courses in Georgia and Palm Springs, lapping up the sauce in the country clubs of Evanston and Grosse Pointe. They'd sold their ranks!

Colonels, generals, commanders, admirals. The whole goddamned military establishment was riddled with a new brand of thieves. Men who winked and smiled and put their signatures on committee recommendations, on procurements approvals, on contracts, on overruns. Because they were understandings made. Today's brigadier was tomorrow's "consultant" or "Washington representative."

Christ, it was easy to hate! The misfits, the corrupters, the corrupted. . . .

It was why Eye Corps was formed. A very small, select group of officers who were sick to death of the apathy and corruption and venality that pervaded every branch of the armed forces. Eye Corps was the answer, the medicine that would cure the sickness. For Eye Corps was compiling records from Saigon to Washington. The men of Eye Corps were putting it all together: names, dates, connections, illegal profits.

To hell with the so-called proper channels: up the chain of command. To the inspector general. To the secretary of the army. Who vouched for command? Who for the IG? Who in his right *mind* would vouch for the civilians?

No one they trusted. So they would do it themselves. Every general—every brigadier and admiral—*anyone* who tolerated any form of deviation would be smoked out and confronted with his crimes.

Eye Corps. That's what it was all about. A handful of the best young officers in the field. And one day they'd walk into the Pentagon and take over. None would dare stand in their way. The Eye Corps indictments would hang like grenades over the heads of the high brass. The grenades would explode if the brass didn't move out, leaving their chairs for men of the Eye Corps. The Pentagon belonged to them. They would give it meaning again. Strength. *Their* strength.

Adrian Fontine leaned on the bar and listened to the intense young students arguing, aware that his brother was staring at them. He looked up at Andrew; the soldier's cold eyes held their usual veiled contempt and then glanced away as Al Winston approached, raising his glass to the major.

Andrew was beginning to wear his contempt too openly, thought Adrian. His brother had lost some of his well-known cool; things aggravated the soldier too quickly these days.

God, how they'd veered from each other! They'd been so close once. The Geminis . . . brothers, twins, friends. The Geminis were the *best!* And somewhere along the line—in their teens, in prep school—it all started to change. Andrew began to think he was better than best, and Adrian became less than convinced he was adequate. Andrew never questioned his abilities; Adrian wasn't sure he had very many.

He was sure now. The terrible years of indecision were over; he'd passed through uncertainty and found his own way. Thanks in large measure to his very positive brother, the soldier.

And today, on their birthday, he had to confront his brother and ask some very disturbing questions. Questions that went to the core of Andrew's strength.

Core? It was appropriate; the sound was right, the spelling wrong.

Eye Corps was the name they'd uncovered. His brother was on the list. Eight self-deluded elitists who concealed evidence for their own purposes. A small band of officers who had convinced themselves they should run the Pentagon through what amounted to sheer blackmail. The situation might have been comic except that the evidence was there, and Eye Corps had it. The Pentagon was not above being manipulated by fear. Eye Corps was dangerous; it had to be ripped out.

They'd settle for that. They'd hand over a blanket subpoena to the army lawyers and let them handle it quietly. As long as the army lawyers did handle it and did not cover up. Perhaps it wasn't the time for demoralizing trials and long prison sentences. The guilt was so widespread and the motives so complex. But there was one irreducible condition. *Get the elitists out of uniform; clean your military house.*

Jesus, the irony of it! In San Francisco, Andrew had blown a crude whistle in the name of military law. Now, seven years later, he, Adrian, was blowing the whistle. Less crudely, he hoped, but the law was no less specific. The charge was obstruction of justice.

So much had changed. Nine months ago he was an assistant prosecutor in Boston, happy doing what he was doing, building a reputation that could lead to just about anywhere. Building it *himself*. Not having it *given* to him because he was Adrian Fontine, son of Victor Fontine, Limited; brother of West Point's celebrated Major Andrew Fontine, immaculate warrior.

Then a man had called him in early October, asking him to have drinks at the Copely bar late in the afternoon. The man's name was James Nevins and he was Black; he was also an attorney, and he worked for the Justice Department in Washington.

Nevins was the spokesman for a small contingent of harassed, disaffected government lawyers who burned under the tactics of the most politicized Justice Department in memory. The phrase "White House calling" simply meant another manipulation was taking place. The lawyers were worried, genuinely worried. Those manipulations were taking the country too close to the specter of a police state.

The lawyers needed help. From the outside. Someone to whom they could funnel their information. Someone who could organise and evaluate, who could set up and pay for a command center where they could meet privately and discuss their progress.

Someone, frankly, who could not be harassed. For reasons more obvious than not, one Adrian Fontine fit the bill. Would he accept?

Adrian hadn't wanted to leave Boston. He had his work; he had his girl. A slightly mad, brilliant girl he adored. Barbara Pierson, B.A., M.A., Ph.D. Associate Professor, Anthropology Laboratories, Harvard University. She of the quick deep laugh, the light-brown hair and the dark-brown eyes. They'd been living together for a year and a half; it wasn't easy to leave. But Barbara had packed for him and sent him on his way because she knew he had to go.

Just as he had to go seven, eight years ago. He had to leave Boston then, too. A depression had swept over him. He was the wealthy son of a powerful father; the twin brother of a man the army paraded in dispatches as one of the brightest young lights in the military.

What was left? For him? Who *was* he?

So he fled the trappings of a lifetime to see what he could find for himself. That was *his*. It was his own personal crisis; he couldn't explain it to anyone. And he ended up in San Francisco where there was a fight, a struggle he could understand. Where he could help. Until the immaculate warrior came along and ripped the scene apart.

Adrian smiled, remembering the morning after the terrible night in San Francisco. He'd gotten roaring drunk and woke up in the house of a legal aid lawyer in Cape Mendocino sick and vomiting.

"If you're who you say you are, you can do more than any of us," said the lawyer in Cape Mendocino that morning. "Hell, my old man was a janitor at the May Company."

In the seven intervening years Adrian had tried. But he knew he had only just begun.

"It's a constitutional ambiguity! Isn't that right, Adrian?"

"What? Sorry, I didn't hear what you said." The students at the bar had been arguing among themselves; now all eyes were on him.

"Free press versus pretrial bias," said an intense young girl, stumbling over the words.

"It's a gray area, I think," replied Adrian. "Each case is judged by itself."

The youngsters wanted more than he gave them, so they went back to yelling at each other.

Gray area. Saigon's Eye Corps had been a gray area only weeks ago. Rumors had filtered back to Washington that a small cadre of young senior officers were regularly harassing enlisted personnel on the docks and in the warehouses, insisting on copies of shipment manifests and destinations schedules. Shortly after, in one of the numerous, halfheartedly pursued antitrust cases at Justice, there was a plaintiff's allegation that records had been stolen from the corporation's Saigon offices, thus constituting illegally obtained evidence. The case would be dropped.

The lawyers at Justice wondered whether there was a connection between the strange group of officers who scoured the shipment manifests and corporations under contract to the Pentagon. Had the military gone that far? The conjecture was enough to send Jim Nevins to Saigon.

The Black attorney found was he was looking for. In a warehouse in the Tan Son Nhut cargo area. An officer was in the process of illegally transcribing security-related information on armaments supplies. Threatened with charges, the officer broke, and Eye Corps was revealed for everything it was. There were eight officers; the man caught knew the names of seven. The eighth was in Washington, that's all he knew.

Andrew Fontine headed the list of those identified.

Eye Corps. Nice fellows, thought Adrian. Just what the country needed; storm troopers out to save the nation.

Seven years ago in San Francisco his brother had not given him any warning before the action started, and the sirens came screaming into Haight-Ashbury. Adrian would be more considerate. He was going to give Andrew five days. There'd be no sirens, no riots . . . no eight-year sentences in the blockades. But the celebrated Major Andrew Fontine would be out of the army.

And although the work in Washington was nowhere near completed, Adrian would go back to Boston for a while. Back to Barbara.

He was tired. And sick with what faced him in an hour or so. The pain was real. Whatever else, Andrew was his brother.

The final guests had left. The orchestra was packing its instruments, and the caterers were cleaning up the lawn. The sky was growing darker, as much because of the threatening clouds over the water as by the approach of nightfall.

Adrian walked across the lawn to the flagstone steps and down to the boathouse. Andrew was waiting for him; he had told the soldier to be there.

"Happy birthday, counselor," said Andrew as Adrian came through the boathouse door. The soldier leaned against the wall beyond the boat slip, his arms folded, smoking a cigarette.

"Same to you," answered Adrian, stopping at the edge of the slip. "You staying tonight?"

"Are you?" asked Andrew.

"I thought I might. The old man looks pretty bad."

"Then I won't," said the soldier politely.

Adrian paused; he knew he was expected to speak. He wasn't quite sure how to begin, so instead he looked around the boathouse. "We had some good laughs down here."

"Did you want to reminisce? Is that why you asked me to come down here?"

"No. . . . I wish it were that simple."

The soldier flipped the cigarette into the water. "I hear you left Boston. You're in Washington."

"Yes. For a while. I keep thinking we'll run into each other."

"I doubt it," said the major, smiling. "We don't travel in the same circles. You working for a D.C. firm?"

"No. I guess you might say I'm a consultant."

"That's the best job in Washington." Andrew's voice was laced with quiet contempt. "Who are you counseling?"

"Some people who are very upset——"

"Oh, a consumer group; isn't that nice." It was an insulting statement. "Good for you!"

Adrian stared at his brother; the soldier returned the look. "Don't dismiss me, Andy. You're in no position to do that. You're in trouble. I'm not here to help you, I can't do that. I'm here to warn you."

"What the hell are you talking about?" asked the major softly.

"A deposition was taken from an officer in Saigon by one of our people. We have a complete statement about the activities of a group of eight men who call themselves Eye Corps."

Andrew bolted upright against the wall, his face pinched, his fingers stretched, curved, immobile. He seemed to freeze; he spoke barely above a whisper, spacing his words out. "Who is 'we'?"

"You'll know the origin soon enough. It's on the subpoena."

"*Subpoena?*"

"Yes. The Justice Department, a specialist division. . . . I won't tell you the individual attorneys, but I will tell you that your name heads the Eye Corps list. We know there are eight of you; seven have been identified, the eighth is at the Pentagon. In procurement. We'll find him."

Andrew held his position against the wall; everything about him remained immobile, except the muscles of his jaw, which moved slowly, steadily. Once again his voice was low, measured. "What have you done? What have you bastards *done?*"

"Stopped you," answered Adrian simply.

"What do you know? What have you been told?"

"The truth. We've no reason to doubt it."

"You need proof for a subpoena!"

"You need probable cause. We have that."

"One deposition! *Nothing!*"

"Others'll follow. What difference does it make? You're finished."

Andrew's voice calmed. He spoke matter-of-factly. "Officers complain. Up and down the zones, officers complain every day——"

"Not this way. There's no fine line between complaints and blackmail. It's very defined, very distinct. You crossed over it."

"*Who have we blackmailed?*" asked Andrew swiftly. "No one!"

"Records were kept, evidence suppressed; the intent was clear. That's in the deposition."

"There *are* no records!"

"Oh, come on, they're *somewhere,*" said Adrian wearily. "But I repeat, who gives a goddamn? You're finished."

The soldier moved. He breathed deeply and stood erect against the wall.

"Listen to me," he said quietly, his voice strained. "You don't know what you're doing. You say you're a consultant to men who are upset. We both know what that means; we're the Fontines. Who needs resources when they have us?"

"I don't see it that way," broke in Adrian.

"It's *true!*" shouted the soldier. And then he lowered his voice. "You don't have to spell out what you're doing, the Boston newspapers did that. You nail the big fellows, the vested interests, you call them. You're good. Well, what the hell do you think *I'm* doing? We're nailing them, too! You stop Eye Corps, you're destroying the finest young senior officers in the field, men who want to rip out the garbage! Don't *do* that, Adree! *Join* us! I mean that."

"Join——" Adrian repeated the word in disbelief. Then he added quietly. "You're out of your mind. What makes you think that's remotely possible?"

Andrew took a step away from the wall; his eyes were steady on his brother. "Because we want the same thing."

"No, we don't."

"*Think,* for God's sake! 'Vested interests.' You use that a lot, 'vested interests.' I read your summation in the Tesco case; you repeated it continuously."

"It applied. One company owning many, setting a single policy when there should have been competition. What's your point?"

"You use the term negatively because that's the way you find it. Okay, I'll buy that. But I submit there's another way to look at it. There can be *good* vested interests. Like us. Our interests isn't ourselves; we don't *need* anything. Our interests is the country and our resources are considerable. We're in positions to *do* something. I'm doing it. For Christ's sake, don't *stop* me!"

Adrian turned away from his brother and walked aimlessly along the moist planks of the boathouse toward the huge opening that led to the open water. The waves slapped against the pilings. "You're very glib, Andy. You were always very glib and sure and truly confident. But it's not going to work." He turned again and faced the soldier diagonally across the slip. "You say we don't need anything. I think we do; we both need—want—something. And what you want frightens me because I've got an idea what your concept of finest is. Frankly, it scares the hell out of me. The thought of your 'finest senior officers' controlling the country's hardware is enough to send me running to the library to reread the Constitution."

"That's arrogant horseshit! You don't know them!"

"I know the way they operate, the way you operate. If it'll make you feel better, you made some sense in San Francisco. I didn't like it, but I recognized it." Adrian walked back along the slip. "You're not making sense now, which is why I'm warning you. Save what you can of your neck, I owe you that much. Get out as gracefully as you can."

"You can't force me," said Andrew scathingly. "My record's one of the best. Who the hell are *you?* One lousy statement from a disgruntled officer in a combat zone. Bullshit!"

"I'll spell it out!" Adrian stopped by the boathouse doorway, raising his voice. "In five days—next Friday, to be precise—a blanket subpoena will be served on the adjutant general of the Courts of Military Justice. He'll have the weekend to negotiate his arrangements. Arrangements *can* be negotiated, but there's one irrevocable condition. You're *out.* All of you."

The soldier started forward, then stopped, his foot on the edge of the slip, as if he were about to spring across, lunging at his enemy. He held himself in check; waves of nausea and fury seemed to pass over him and through him. "I could . . . kill you," he whispered. "You're everything I despise."

"I guess I am," said Adrian, closing his eyes briefly, rubbing them in weariness. "You'd better get to the airport," he continued, now looking at his brother. "You've got a lot to do. I suggest you start with this so-called evidence you've been sitting on. We understand you've been collecting it for damn near three years. Get it to the proper authorities."

In angry silence the soldier lurched in rapid strides around the slip, past Adrian, and out to the boathouse steps. He began climbing, taking the flatstone stairs two at a time.

Adrian moved swiftly to the door and called out, halting his brother on the border of the lawn.

"Andy!"

The soldier stood motionless. But he did not turn around, or speak. So the lawyer continued.

"I admire your strength, I always have. Just as I admire father's. You're part of him, but you're not all of him. You missed something, so let's understand each other. You're everything I consider dangerous. I guess that means you're everything *I* despise."

"We understand each other," said Andrew, repeating the words in a monotone. He started up across the lawn toward the house.

Chapter Nineteen

The orchestra and the caterers left. Andrew was driven to LaGuardia Airport. There was a nine o'clock plane to Washington.

Adrian remained on the beach by himself for nearly thirty minutes after his brother left. Finally he wandered up to the house to talk to his parents. He told them he had intended to stay the night but now thought he should leave. He had to get back to Washington.

"You should have gone with your brother," said Jane at the front door.

"Yes, I should have," said Adrian softly. "I didn't think." He said his good-byes.

When he left, Jane walked out to the terrace, carrying the letter brought by the priest. She held it out for her husband, unable to conceal her fear. "A man brought this. About three hours ago. He was a priest. He said he was from Rome."

Victor looked up at his wife. There was no comment in his eyes, and by the lack of it, there was. "Why did you wait?"

"Because it was your sons' birthday."

"They're strangers to each other," said Fontine, taking the envelope. "They're both our children, but they're very far apart."

"It won't last. It's the war."

"I hope you're right," said Victor, opening the envelope and taking out the letter. It ran several pages, the handwriting small but precise. "Do we know a man named Aldobrini?"

"Who?"

"Guido Aldobrini. That's the signature." Fontine held up the last page. "I don't think so," answered Jane, sitting down in the nearest chair, her eyes on the threatening sky. "Can you see in this light? It's getting darker." "It is sufficient." Victor put the pages in sequence and began to read.

Signor Fontini-Cristi:

You do not know me although we met many years ago. That meeting cost me the better part of my life. I have spent over a quarter of a century in the Transvaal in holy penance for an act of shame. I did not touch you myself, but I observed and did not raise my voice for mercy, which was an indecent and unholy thing.

Yes, Signore, I was one of the priests with the Cardinal Donatti that dawn at Campo di Fiori. For what we believed was the preservation of Christ's Mother Church on earth, the Cardinal convinced us that there were no laws of God or man or mercy standing between our actions and the preservation of God's Church. All our scholastic training and vows of obedience—not only to our superiors, but to the highest authority of conscience—were twisted by the power of Donatti's influence. I have spent twenty-five years trying to understand, but that is another story not pertinent here. One would have had to know the Cardinal to understand.

I am retired from my cloth. The illnesses of the African forests have taken their toll, and thanks be to Christ I do not fear death. For I have given of myself as fully as I knew how. I am cleansed and await the judgment of God.

Before I face our merciful Lord, however, there is information I must impart to you, for to withhold it now would be no less a sin than that for which I have paid holy penance.

The work of Donatti continues. A man, one of the three defrocked priests who were imprisoned by the civil court for their assault on you, has been released. As you perhaps know, one took his own life, the other died of natural causes while in prison. This third man survives and for motives beyond my comprehension, has rededicated himself to the pursuit of the Salonika documents. I say beyond my comprehension, for Cardinal Donatti was discredited in the highest circles of the Vatican. The Grecian documents cannot affect the Holy Mother Church. Divine revelation cannot be contravened by the hand of mortal man.

This defrocked priest goes by the name of Enrici Gaetamo, and he is taken to wearing the collar denied him by apostolic decree. It is my understanding that his years spent in the criminal institution have done nothing to enlighten his soul or show him the ways of a merciful Christ. On the contrary, I am told he is Donatti incarnate. A man to be feared.

He currently, painstakingly, researches every detail he can unearth relative to the train from Salonika thirty-three years ago. His travels have carried him from the yards of Edhessa, through the Balkans, over the rail routes beyond Monfalcone into the northern Alpine regions. He seeks out all he can find who knew the son of Fontini-Cristi. He is a man possessed. He subscribes to the code of Donatti. There is no law of God or man that will interfere with his "journey for Christ," as he phrases it. Nor will he reveal to anyone the objective of his journey. But I know, and now you do. And soon I shall depart this life.

Gaetamo resides in a small hunting lodge in the hills of Varese. I'm sure the proximity to Campo di Fiori does not escape you.

This is all I can tell you; it is all I know. That he will attempt to reach you, I am certain. That you be warned and remain safe in God's hands, is my prayer.

In sorrow and personal anguish for my past, I remain,

Guido Aldobrini

There was the sound of thunder over the water; Fontine wished the symbolism were not so crudely simple. The clouds were above them now; the sun was gone and the rains began. He was grateful for the diversion. He looked at Jane. She was staring at him; somehow he had communicated to her his profound uneasiness.

"Go in," he said softly. "I'll follow in a minute or two."

"The letter——?"

"Of course," he answered her unspoken question as he replaced the pages in the envelope and handed it to her. "Read it."

"You'll be drenched. The rain will get stronger."

"It's refreshing; you know I like the rain." He smiled up at her. "Then perhaps you'll help me change the brace while we talk."

She stood above him for a moment, and he could feel her eyes on him. But as always, she would leave him alone when he wished it.

He was chilled by his thoughts, not the rain. The letter from Aldobrini was not the first time Salonika had reappeared. He had said nothing to Jane for there was nothing concrete, only a series of obscurely disturbing—seemingly minor—occurrences.

Three months ago he had gone to Harkness for yet another week of corrective surgery. Several days after the operation he'd had a visitor whose appearance startled him; a monsignor from the Archdiocese of New York. His name was Land, he said. He had returned to the United States after many years in Rome, and wanted to meet Victor because of information he had come across in the Vatican archives.

The priest was solicitous; what struck Fontine was that the cleric knew a great deal about his physical condition, far more than a casual visitor would know.

It was a very odd half hour. The priest was a student of history, he said. He had come across archive documents that raised profoundly disturbing questions between the house of Fontini-Cristi and the Vatican. Historical questions that led to the break between the *padroni* of the north and the Holy See. When Victor was well again, perhaps they could discuss the past. The *historical* past. He had ended his good-byes with a direct reference to the assault at Campo di Fiori. The pain and anguish inflicted by one maniacal prelate could not be laid at the soul of the church, he said.

About five weeks later there'd been a second incident. Victor had been in his Washington office, preparing to testify before a congressional committee looking into the tax concessions enjoyed by American shippers sailing under the Paraguayan flag, when his intercom buzzed.

"Mr. Fontine, Mr. Theodore Dakakos is here. He says he wants to pay his respects."

Dakakos was one of the young Greek shipping giants, an impertinent rival of Onassis and Niarchos, and far better liked. Fontine told his secretary to send him in.

Dakakos was a large man with a blunt, open expression on his face that might become an American football player more than a shipping tycoon. He was around forty years of age; his English was precise, the language of a student.

He had flown to Washington to observe the hearings, perhaps to learn something, he said smiling. Victor laughed; the Greek's reputation for integrity was matched only by the legend of his acute business sense. Fontine told him so.

"I was most fortunate. At a very young age I was given the advantages of an education by a sympathetic but remote religious brotherhood."

"You were, indeed, fortunate."

"My family was not wealthy, but they served their church, I'm told. In ways that today I do not understand."

The young Greek magnate was saying something beyond his words, but Victor could not determine what it was. 'Gratitude as well as God, then, moves in strange ways," said Victor smiling. "Your reputation is a fine one. You do credit to those who aided you."

"Theodore is my first name, Mr. Fontine. My full name is Theodore Annaxas Dakakos. Throughout my schooling I was known as Annaxas the Younger. Does that not mean anything to you?"

"In what way?"

"The name Annaxas."

"I've dealt with literally hundreds of your countrymen over the years. I don't think I've ever run across the name Annaxas."

The Greek had remained silent for several moments. Then he spoke quietly. "I believe you."

Dakakos left soon after.

The third occurrence was the strangest of all; it triggered a memory of violence so sharply into focus that Fontine lost his breath. It had happened only ten days ago in Los Angeles. He was at the Beverly Hills Hotel for conferences between two widely divergent companies trying to merge their interests. He had been called in to salvage what he could; the task was impossible.

Which was why he was taking the sun in the early afternoon, instead of sitting inside the hotel listening to lawyers trying to justify their retainers. He was drinking a Campari at a table in the outside pool area, astonished at the number of good-looking people who apparently did not have to work for a living.

"*Guten Tag, mein Herr.*"

The speaker was a woman in her late forties or early fifties, that age so well cosmeticized by the well-to-do. She was of medium height, quite well proportioned, with streaked blond hair. She wore white slacks and a blue blouse. Covering her eyes was a pair of large silver-rimmed sunglasses. Her German was natural, not studied. He replied in his own, academic, less natural, as he rose awkwardly.

"Good afternoon. Have we met? I'm sorry, but I don't seem to remember."

"Please, sit down. It's difficult for you. I know that."

"You do? Then we *have* met."

The woman sat down opposite him. She continued in English. "Yes. But you had no such difficulties then. You were a soldier then."

"During the war?"

"There was a flight from Munich to Müllheim. And a whore from the camps escorted on that flight by three Wehrmacht pigs. More pigs than she, I try to tell myself."

"My God!" Fontine caught his breath. "You were a *child*. What happened to you?"

She told him briefly. She had been taken by the French Resistance fighters to a transit camp southwest of Montbéliard. There for several months she endured agonies best left undescribed, as she experienced the process of narcotics withdrawal. She had tried to commit suicide numerous times, but the Resistance people had other ideas. They banked on the fact that once the drugs were expunged, her memories would be motive enough to turn her into an effective underground agent. She was already tough; that much they could see.

"They were right, of course," the woman said, ten days ago at the table on the patio of the Beverly Hills Hotel. "They kept watch over me night and day, men and women. The men had more fun; the French never waste anything, do they?"

"You survived the war," Fontine replied, not caring to probe.

"With a bucket full of medals. *Croix de guerre, Légion d'honneur, Légion de résistance.*"

"And so you became a great motion picture star and I was too stupid to recognize you." Victor smiled gently.

"Hardly. Although I've had occasions to be associated, as it were, with many prominent people of the motion picture industry."

"I'm afraid I don't understand."

"I became—and at the risk of sounding immodest, still am—the most successful madame in the south of France. The Cannes Film Festival alone provides sufficient income for a perfectly adequate subsistence." It was the woman's turn to smile. It was a good smile, thought Fontine. Genuine, alive.

"Then I'm very happy for you. I'm Italian enough to find a certain honorableness in your profession."

"I knew you were. And would. I'm here on a talent hunt. It would be my pleasure to grant any request you might have. There are a number of my girls out there in the pool."

"No, thank you. You're most kind, but, as you said, I am not the man I was."

"I think you're magnificent," she said simply. "I always have." She smiled at him. "I must go. I recognized you and wanted to speak to you, that's all." She rose from the table and extended her hand. "Don't get up."

The handshake was firm. "It's been a pleasure—and a relief—to see you again," he said.

She held his eyes and spoke quietly. "I was in Zürich a few months ago. They traced me through a man named Lübok. To you. He was a Czech. A queen, I'm told. He was the man on the plane with us, wasn't he?"

"Yes. A very brave man, I must add. A king, in my judgment." Victor was so startled he replied instinctively, without comprehending. He had not thought of Lübok in years.

"Yes, I remember. He saved all of us. They broke him." The woman released his hand.

"Broke him? About *what?* My God, the man, if he's alive, is my age or more. Seventy or better. Who would be interested in such old men? What are you talking about?"

"About a man named Vittorio Fontini-Cristi, son of Savarone."

"You're talking nonsense. Nonsense I understand, but I don't see how it might concern you. *Or* Lübok."

"I don't know any more. Nor do I care to. A man in Zürich came to my hotel room and asked questions about you. Naturally, I couldn't answer them. You were merely an Allied Intelligence officer who saved a whore's life. But he knew about Anton Lübok."

"Who was this man?"

"A priest. That is all I know. Good-bye, *Kapitän*." She turned and walked away, waving and smiling at various girls who were splashing about in the pool and laughing too obviously.

A priest. In Zürich.

. . . *He seeks out all he can find who knew the son of Fontini-Cristi.* . . .

Now he understood the enigmatic meeting at the poolside in Los Angeles. A defrocked priest had been released after nearly thirty years in prison and revived the hunt for the documents of Constantine.

The work of Donatti continues, the letter said. *He currently, painstakingly, researches every detail he can unearth . . . his travels have carried him from the yards of Edhessa, through the Balkans . . . beyond Monfalcone into the northern Alpine regions.*

He seeks out all he can find who knew the son of Fontini-Cristi.

And thousands of miles away in New York City, another priest—very much *of* the cloth—comes into a hospital room and speaks of an act of barbarism that could not be separated from those documents. Lost three decades ago and hunted still.

And in Washington, a young industrial giant walks into an office and for no apparent reasons says his family served the church in ways he did not understand.

". . . I was given . . . advantages . . . by a sympathetic but remote religious brotherhood. . . ."

The *Order of Xenope*. It was suddenly so very clear.

Nothing was coincidence.

It had come back. The train from Salonika had plunged through thirty years of sleep and reawakened. It had to be controlled before the hatreds collided, before the fanatics turned the search into a holy war, as they had done three decades ago. Victor knew he owed that much to his father, his mother, to the loved ones slain in the white lights of Campo di Fiori; to those who had died at Oxfordshire. To a misguided young monk named Petride who took his own life on a rocky slope in Loch Torridon, to a man named Teague, to an undergrounder named Lübok, to an old man named Guido Barzini who had saved him from himself.

The violence could not be allowed to return.

The rain came faster now, harder, in diagonal sheets blown by the wind. Fontine reached for the wrought iron chair beside him and struggled to his feet, his arm clamped within the steel band of his cane.

He stood on the terrace looking out over the water. The wind and the rain cleared his mind. He knew what he had to do, where he had to go.

To the hills of Varese.

To Campo di Fiori.

Chapter Twenty

The heavy car approached the gates of Campo di Fiori. Victor stared out the window, aware of the spasm in his back; the eye was recording, the mind remembering.

His life had been altered, in pain, on the stretch of ground beyond the gates. He tried to control the memory; he could not suppress it. The images he observed were forced out of his mind's eye, replaced by black suits and white collars.

The car went through the gates; Victor held his breath. He had flown into Milan from Paris as unobtrusively as possible. In Milan he had taken a single room at the Albergo Milano, registering simply as: V. Fontine, New York City.

The years had done their work. There were no raised eyebrows, no curious glances; the name triggered no surprises. Thirty years ago a Fontine or a Fontini in Milan would be reason enough for comment. Not now.

Before he left New York he had made one inquiry—any more might have raised an alarm. He had learned the identity of the owners of Campo di Fiori. The purchase had been made twenty-seven years ago; there had been no change of ownership since that time. Yet the name had no impact in Milan. None had heard of it.

Baricours, Père et Fils. A Franco-Swiss company out of Grenoble, that's what the transfer papers said. Yet there was no Baricours, Père et Fils, in Grenoble. No details could be learned from the lawyer who had negotiated the sale. He had died in 1951.

The automobile rolled past the embankment into the circular drive in front of the main house. The spasm in Victor's back was compounded by a sharp stinging sensation behind his eyes; his head throbbed as he reentered the execution grounds.

He gripped his wrist and dug his fingers into his own flesh. The pain helped; he was able to look out the window and see what was there now, not thirty-three years ago.

What he saw was a mausoleum. Dead but cared for. Everything was as it had been, but not for the living. Even the orange rays of the setting sun had a dead quality to them: majestically ornamental, but not alive.

"Aren't there groundkeepers or men at the gates?" he asked.

The driver turned in the seat. "Not this afternoon, *padrone*," he replied. "There are no guards. And no priests of the Curia."

Fontine lurched forward in the seat; his metal cane slipped. He stared at the driver.

"I've been tricked."

"Watched. Expected. Not tricked, really. Inside, a man is waiting for you."

"One man?"

"Yes."

"Would his name be Enrici Gaetamo?"

"I told you. There are no priests of the Curia here. Please, go inside. Do you need help?"

"No, I can manage." Victor got out of the car slowly, each movement a struggle, the pain in his eyes receding the spasm in his back subsiding. He understood. His mind was refocusing itself. He had come to Campo di Fiori for answers. For a confrontation. But he had not expected it to be this way.

He walked up the wide marble steps to the oak door of his childhood. He paused and waited for what he thought was inevitable: a sense of overwhelming sorrow. But it did not come, because there was no life here.

He heard the gunning of the engine behind him and turned. The driver had swung the car out into the curve, and driven past the embankment into the road toward the main gate. Whoever he was, he wanted to be away as rapidly as possible.

As he watched, Victor heard the metallic sound of a latch. He turned again to the huge oak door; it had opened.

The shock was impossible to conceal. Nor did he bother to hide it. The rage inside him welled; his whole body trembled in anger.

The man at the door was a *priest!* Dressed in the black cassock of the church. He was an old man and frail. Had he been otherwise, Fontine might have struck out at him.

Instead he stared at the old man and spoke quietly. "That a priest would be in this house is most painful to me."

"I'm sorry you feel that way," replied the priest in a foreigner's Italian, his voice thin but firm. "We revered the *padrone* of the Fontini-Cristis. We placed our most precious treasures in his hands."

Their eyes were locked; neither wavered, but the anger within Victor was slowly replaced with incredulity. "You're Greek," he said, barely audible.

"I am, but that's not relevant. I'm a monk from Constantine. Please. Come in." The old man stepped back to allow Victor to pass. He added softly, "Take your time. Let your eyes roam. Little has changed; photographs and inventories were taken of each room. We have maintained everything as it was."

A mausoleum.

"So did the Germans." Fontine walked into the enormous hall. "It's strange that those who went to such lengths to own Campo di Fiori don't want to change it."

"One doesn't cut a great jewel or deface a worthy painting. There's nothing strange in that."

Victor did not reply. Instead, he gripped his cane and walked with difficulty toward the staircase. He stopped in front of the arch that led to the huge drawing room on the left. Everything *was* as it had been. The paintings, the half-tables against the massive walls, the glazed antique mirrors above the tables, the oriental rugs covering the polished floor, the wide staircase, its balustrade glistening.

He looked over through the north arch into the dining room. Twilight shadows fell across the enormous table, now bare, polished, empty, where once the family had sat. He pictured them now; he could hear the chatter and the laughter. Arguments and anecdotes, never-ending talk; dinners were important events at Campo di Fiori.

The figures froze, the voices disappeared. It was time to look away.

Victor turned. The monk gestured at the south arch. "Shall we go into your father's study?"

He preceded the old man into the drawing room. Involuntarily—for he did not care to activate memories—his eyes fell on the furnishings, suddenly so familiar. Every chair, every lamp, every tapestry and sconce and table was precisely as he remembered it.

Fontine breathed deeply and closed his eyes for a moment. It was macabre. He was passing through a museum that had once been a living part of his existence. In some ways it was the cruelest form of anguish.

He continued on through the door into Savarone's study; it had never been his, although his life nearly ended in that room. He passed by the doorframe through which a severed, bloody hand had been thrown in the shadows.

If there was anything that startled him it was the desk lamp; and the light that spilled downward over the floor from the green shade. It was *precisely* as it was nearly three decades ago. His memory of it was vivid, for it was the light from the lamp that had washed over the shattered skull of Geoffrey Stone.

"Would you care to sit down?" asked the priest.

"In a minute."

"May I?"

"I beg your pardon?"

"May I sit at your father's desk?" said the monk. "I've watched your eyes."

"It's your house, your desk. I'm a visitor."

"But not a stranger."

"Obviously. Am I speaking with a representative of Baricours, Père et Fils?"

The old priest nodded silently. He walked slowly around the desk, pulled out the chair, and lowered his frail body into it. "Don't blame the lawyer in Milan; he couldn't have known. Baricours met your conditions, we made sure of it. Baricours is the Order of Xenope."

"And my enemy," said Victor quietly. "In 1942 there was an M.I.-Six compound in Oxfordshire. You tried to kill my wife. Many innocent people lost their lives."

"Decisions were made beyond the control of the Elders. The extremists had their way; we couldn't stop them. I don't expect you to accept that."

"I don't. How did you know I was in Italy?"

"We are not what we once were, but we still have resources. One in particular keeps his eye on you. Don't ask me who it is; I won't tell you. Why did you come back? After thirty years, why did you return to Campo di Fiori?"

"To find a man named Gaetamo," answered Fontine. "Enrici Gaetamo."

"Gaetamo lives in the hills of Varese," said the monk.

"He's still looking for the train from Salonika. He's traveled from Edhessa, through the Balkans, across Italy, into the northern mountains. Why have you stayed here all these years?"

"Because the *key* is here," replied the monk. "A pact was made. In October of 1939, I traveled to Campo di Fiori. It was I who negotiated Savarone Fontini-Cristi's participation, I who sent a dedicated priest on that train with his brother, an engineer. And demanded their deaths in the name of God."

Victor stared at the monk. The spill of the lamp illuminated the pale, taut flesh and the sad, dead eyes. Fontine recalled the visitor in his Washington office. "A Greek came to me saying his family served their church once in ways he didn't understand. Was this priest's brother the engineer, named Annaxas?"

The old cleric's head snapped up; the eyes became briefly alive. "Where did you hear that name?"

Fontine looked away, his eyes falling on a painting beneath a Madonna on the wall. A hunting scene, birds being flushed from a thicket by men with guns. Other birds flew above. "We'll trade information," he said quietly. "Why did my father agree to work with Xenope?"

"You know the answer. He had only one concern: not to divide the Christian world. The defeat of the fascists was all he cared about."

"Why was the vault taken from Greece in the first place?"

"The Germans were scavengers and Constantine was marked. That was the information we received from Poland and Czechoslovakia. The Nazi commanders stole from museums, tore apart retreats and monasteries. We couldn't take the chance of leaving it there. Your father engineered the removal. Brilliantly. Donatti was tricked."

"By the use of a second train," added Victor. "Mounted and routed identically. Sent three days later."

"Yes. Word of this second train was leaked to Donatti through the Germans, who had no concept of the significance of the vault from Constantine. They looked for treasures—paintings, sculpture, art objects—not obscure writings they were told were valuable only to scholars. But Donatti, the fanatic, could not resist; the Filioque denials had been rumored for decades. He had to possess them." The priest of Xenope paused, the memory painful. "The cardinal's and the German interests coincided. Berlin wanted Savarone Fontini-Cristi's influence destroyed; Donatti wanted to keep him from that train. At all costs."

"Why was Donatti involved at all?"

"Again, your father. He knew the Nazis had a powerful friend in the Vatican. He wanted Donatti exposed for what he was. The cardinal could not know about that second train unless the Germans told him. Your father intended to make use of this fact. It was the only price Fontini-Cristi asked of us. As it turned out, that price brought about the executions of Campo di Fiori."

Victor could hear his father's voice piercing through the decades. . . . *He issues edicts to the uninformed and enforces them by fear. . . . A disgrace to the Vatican.* Savarone knew the enemy, but not the extremes of his monstrousness.

The brace across Fontine's back was cutting into his flesh. He had been standing too long. He gripped his cane and walked toward the chair in front of the desk. He sat down.

"Do you know what was on that train?" asked the old monk gently.

"Yes. Brevourt told me."

"Brevourt never knew. He was told part of the truth. Not all of it. What did he tell you?"

Victor was suddenly alarmed. He locked eyes once again with the priest.

"He spoke of the Filioque denials, studies that refuted the divinity of Christ. The most damaging of which was an Aramaic scroll that raised questions as to whether Jesus ever existed at all. The conclusion would appear that he did not."

"It was never the denials. Never the scroll. It was—*is*—a confession written in its entirety that predates all the other documents." The priest of Xenope looked away. He raised his hands; his bony fingers touched the pale skin of his cheek. "The Filioque denials are artifacts for scholars to ponder. As one of them, the Aramaic scroll, was ambiguous, as the scrolls of the Dead Sea were ambiguous when studied fifteen hundred years later. However, thirty years ago at the height of a moral war—if that's not a contradiction in terms—that scroll's exposure might have been catastrophic. It was enough for Brevourt."

Fontine was mesmerized. "What is this confession? I've never heard it mentioned."

The monk returned his eyes to Victor. During the brief silence before he spoke, the old priest conveyed the pain of his immediate decision. "It is everything. It was written on a parchment brought out of a Roman prison in the year sixty-seven. We know the date because the document speaks of the death of Jesus in terms of the Hebrew calendar that places the figure at thirty-four years. It coincides with anthropological scholarship. The parchment was written by a man who wandered blindly; he speaks of Gethsemane and Capernaum, Gennesaret and Corinth, Pontus, Galatia and Cappadocia. The writer can be no one else but Simon of Bethsaida, given the name of Peter by the man he called Christ. What is contained in that parchment is beyond anything in your imagination. It must be found."

The priest stopped and stared across at Victor.

"And destroyed?" asked Fontine softly.

"Destroyed," replied the monk. "But not for any reason you might think of. For *nothing* is changed, yet *all* is changed. My vows forbid me to tell you more. We're old men; we haven't much time. If you can help, you must. That parchment can alter history. It should have been destroyed centuries ago, but arrogance prevailed. It could plunge a great part of the world into a terrible agony. No one can justify the pain."

"But you say nothing is changed," replied Victor, repeating the monk's words, "yet *all* is changed. One cancels the other; it doesn't make sense."

"The confession on that parchment makes sense. In all its anguish. I can tell you no more."

Fontine held the priest's eyes. "Did my father know about the parchment? Or was he told only what Brevourt was told?"

"He knew," said the monk of Xenope. "The Filioque denials were like your American articles of impeachment, charges for canonical debate. Even the most damaging—as you called it—the Aramaic scroll, was subject to the linguistic interpretations of antiquity. Fontini-Cristi would have perceived these issues; Brevourt did not. But the confession on that parchment is not debatable. It was the single, awesome thing that demanded Fontini-Cristi's commitment. He understood and accepted it."

"A confession on a parchment taken out of a Roman prison." Fontine spoke quietly; the issue was clear. "That's what the vault of Constantine is all about."

"Yes."

Victor let the moment pass. He leaned forward in the chair, his hand on his metal cane. "You said the key is here. But why? Donatti searched—every wall, every floor, every inch of ground. You've remained here for twenty-seven years, and still there's nothing. What's left for you?"

"Your father's words, said in this room."

"What were they?"

"That the markings would be here in Campo di Fiori. Etched for a millennium. That was the phrase he used: 'etched for a millennium.' And his son would understand. It was part of his childhood. But his son was told nothing. We came to know that."

Fontine refused a bed in the great house. He would rest in the stables, in the bed on which he had placed the dead Barzini a lifetime ago.

He wanted to be alone, isolated, and above all, out of the house, away from the dead relics. He had to think, to go back over the horror again and again until he found the missing connection. For it was there now; the pattern existed. What remained missing was the line that completed the design.

Part of his childhood. No, not there, not yet. Don't start there; it would come later. Begin with what one knew, one saw, one heard for himself.

He reached the stables and walked through the empty rooms and past the empty stalls. There was no electricity now; the old monk had given him a flashlight. Barzini's room was as he remembered it. Bare, without ornament; the narrow bed, the worn-out armchair, the simple trunk for his few possessions.

The tack room, too, was as he had seen it last. Bridles and leather straps on the walls. He sat down on a small wooden stirrup bench, exhaling in pain as he did so. He put out the flashlight. The moon shone through the windows. He inhaled deeply and forced his mind back to the horrible night.

The shattering of machine gun fire filled his ears, evoking the memory he abhorred. The swirling clouds of smoke were there, the arched bodies of loved ones in succeeding instants of death, seen in the blinding light of the floodlamps.

Champoluc is the river! Zürich is the river!

The words were screamed, then repeated, twice, three times! Roared up at him but aimed higher than where he was, above him, as the bullets pierced his father's chest and stomach.

Champoluc is the river!

The head raised? Was that it? The head, the *eyes*. It's always in *the eyes!* A split fraction of time before the words poured out, his father's eyes had *not* been on the embankment, *not* on *him*.

They had been leveled to his right, on a diagonal. Savarone had been staring at the automobiles, into the *third automobile*.

Savarone had seen Guillamo Donatti! He had recognized him in the shadows of the back seat of the car. At the instant of death, he knew the identity of his executioner.

And the roars of fury had poured forth, up at his son, but beyond his son. Up and beyond and . . . what *was* it? What *was* it his father had done that last instant of life? It was the missing connection, the line that completed the pattern!

Oh, Christ! Some part of his body. His head, his shoulders, his hands. What *was* it?

The *whole* body! My God, it was the gesture in *death* of the *whole body!* Head, arms, hands. Savarone's body had been stretched in one final feature! *To his left!* But not the house, not the lighted rooms so viciously invaded, but beyond the house. *Beyond the house!*

Champoluc is the river. . . .

Beyond the house!

The *woods* of Campo di Fiori!

The *river!* the wide mountain stream in the forest! Their own personal *"river"!*

It was part of his childhood. The river of his childhood was a quarter of a mile beyond the gardens of Campo di Fiori!

Sweat fell from Victor's face; his breath was erratic, his hands trembled. He gripped the edge of the stirrup bench in the darkness. He was spent, but certain; it was all suddenly, totally clear.

The *river* was not in the Champoluc, nor in Zürich. It was minutes away from *here*. A brief walk down a forest path made by generations of children. *Etched* for a millennium.

Part of his *childhood*.

He pictured the woods, the flowing stream, the rocks . . . the rocks . . . the *rocks*. The *boulders* that bordered the stream in the deepest section of the water! There was one *large* boulder used for diving and jumping and lying in the sun, and *scratching initials*, and childish *messages*, and secret *codes between very young brothers!*

Etched for a millennium. His childhood!

Had Savarone chosen *this* rock on which to etch his message?

It was suddenly so clear. So *consistent*.

Of course he had.

Chapter Twenty-one

The night sky turned gradually to gray, but no rays of the Italian sun broke through the overcast. Instead, there would be rain soon, and a cold summer wind whipping down from the northern mountains.

Victor walked down the stable road into the gardens. It was too dark to make out the colors. Then, too, there were not the rows of flowers bordering the paths as there had been; he could see that much.

He found the path with difficulty, only after examining the uncut grass, angling the beam of his flashlight into the ground, looking for signs of the past. As he penetrated the woods beyond the garden familiar things came back to him: a gnarled olive tree with thick limbs; a cluster of white birches, now concealed by beechwood vine and dying spruce.

The stream was no more than a hundred yards away, diagonally to his right, if memory served. There were birches and tall pines; giant weeds formed a wall of tentacles, soft but uncomfortable to the touch.

He stopped. There was a rustle of bird wings, the snape of a twig. He turned and peered into the black shapes of the overgrowth.

Silence.

Then the sound of a small animal intruded on the quiet. He had probably disturbed a hare. Strange, he should assume so naturally that it was a hare. The surroundings jogged memories long forgotten; as a boy he had trapped hares in these woods.

He could smell the water now. He had always been able to smell the moistness when he approached the stream, smell it before he heard the sound of the flow. The foliage nearest the water was thick, almost impenetrable. Seepage from the stream had fed a hundred thousand roots, allowing rampant, uncontrolled growth. He had to force back limbs and spread thickets to approach the stream.

His left foot was ensnared in a tangle of ground vine. He stepped back on his right and, with his cane, worked it free, losing his balance as he did so. The cane whipped out of his hand, spiraling into the darkness. He grabbed for a branch to break his fall; the small limb cracked, stripping itself from its source. On one knee, he used the thick stick to push himself off the ground;

his cane was gone; he could not see it. He held onto the stick and threaded his way through the mass of foliage to the water's edge.

The stream seemed narrower than he remembered. Then he realized it was the gray darkness and the overgrown forest that made it appear so. Three decades of inattention had allowed the woods to impinge upon the water.

The massive boulder was on his right, upstream, no more than twenty feet away, but the wall of overgrowth was such that it might have been half a mile. He began edging his way toward it, crouching, rising, separating, each movement a struggle. Twice he butted against hard obstacles in the earth, too high, too thin and narrow, for rocks. He swung the beam of the flashlight down; the obstacles were iron stakes, rusted and pitted as though relics from a sunken galleon.

He reached the base of the huge rock; its body extended over the water. He looked below, the flashlight illuminating the separation of earth and flowing stream, and realized the years had made him cautious. The distance to the water was only a few feet, but it appeared a gulf to him now. He sidestepped his way down into the stream, the thick stick in his left hand prodding the depth.

The water was cold—as he remembered, it was always cold—and came up to his thighs, lapped over his waist below the brace, sending chills throughout his body. He shivered and swore at the years.

But he was *here*. It was all that mattered.

He focused the flashlight on the rock. He was several feet from the edge of the bank; he would have to organize his search. Too many minutes could be wasted going over areas twice or three times because he could not remember examining them. He was honest with himself: He was not sure how long he could take the cold.

He reached up, pressing the end of the stick into the surface of the rock. The moss that covered it peeled easily. The details of the boulder's surface, made vivid by the harsh, white beam of the flashlight, looked like thousands of tiny craters and ravines.

His pulse accelerated at the first signs of human intrusion. They were faint, barely visible, but they were there. And they were his marks, from more than half a century ago. Descending lines scratched deeply into the rock as part of a long forgotten boyhood game.

The **V** was the clearest letter; he had made sure his mark was vivid, properly recorded. Then there was **b,** followed by what might have been numbers. And a **t,** again followed by what were probably numbers. He had no idea what they meant.

He peeled the moss above and below the scratchings. There were other faint markings; some seemed meaningful. Initials, mainly; here and there, rough drawings of trees and arrows and quarter circles drawn by children.

His eyes strained under the glare of the flashlight; his fingers peeled and rubbed and caressed a larger and larger area. He made two vertical lines with the stick to show where he had searched and moved farther into the cold water; but soon the cold grew too much and he climbed onto the bank, seeking warmth. His hands and arms and legs were trembling with cold and age. He knelt in the damp overgrowth and watched the vapor of his breath diffuse itself in the air.

He went back into the water, to the point where he had left off. The moss was thicker; underneath he found several more markings similar to the first set nearer the embankment. **V**'s and **b**'s and **t**'s and very faint numbers.

Then it came back to him through the years—faintly, as faintly as the letters and the numbers. And he *knew* he was right to be in that stream, at that boulder.

Burrone! Traccia! He had forgotten but now recalled. "Ravine," "trail." He had always scratched—recorded—their journeys into the mountains!

Part of his childhood.

My God, what a part! Every summer Savarone gathered his sons together and took them north for several days of climbing. Not dangerous climbing, more hiking and camping. For them all, a high point of the summers. And he gave them maps so they knew where they had been; and Vittorio, the eldest, would indelibly, soberly record the journeys on the boulder down at the stream, their "river."

They had christened the rock The Argonaut. And the scratchings of The Argonaut served as a permanent record of their mountain odysseys. Into the mountains of their boyhood.

Into the mountains.

The train from Salonika had gone into the mountains! The vault of Constantine was somewhere in the mountains!

He balanced himself with the stick and continued. He was near the face of the rock; the water came up to his chest, chilling the steel brace beneath his clothes. The farther out he went the more convinced he became; he was *right* to be there! The faint scratching—the faded scars of half lines and zig-zags—were more and more numerous. *The Argonaut's* hull was covered with graffiti related to journeys long forgotten.

The cold water sent a spasm through the base of his spine; the stick fell from his hands. He slapped at the water, grabbing the stick, shifting his feet in the effort. He fell—glided, actually—into the rock and righted himself by pressing the stick into the mud below for balance.

He stared at the sight inches from his eyes in the water. There was a short, straight, horizontal line deeply defined in the rock. It was *chiseled*.

He braced himself as best he could, transferred the stick to his right hand, manipulating it between his thumb and the flashlight, and pressed his fingers into the surface of the boulder.

He traced the line. It angled sharply downward into the water; across and down and then it abruptly stopped.

7. It was a 7.

Unlike any other faded hieroglyphics on the rock; not scratches made by awkward, youthful hands, but a work of precision. The figure was no more than two inches high—but the impression itself was a good half inch deep.

He'd *found* it! *Etched for a millennium!* A message carved in rock, *chiseled in stone!*

He brought the flashlight closer and carefully moved his trembling fingers about the area. My God, was this *it?* Was this the *moment?* In spite of the cold and the wet, the blood raced to his head, his heart accelerated. He felt like shouting; but he had to be *sure!*

At midpoint of the vertical line of the 7, about an inch to its right, was a dash. Then another single vertical line . . . a 1, followed by yet another vertical that was shorter, angling to the right . . . and intersected by a line straight up and down. . . . A 4. It was a 4.

Seven—dash—one—four. More below the surface of the water than above it.

Beyond the 4 was another short, horizontal line. A dash. It was followed by a . . . **Z,** but not a Z. The angles were not abrupt, they were rounded.

2.

Seven—dash—one—four—dash—two. . . .

There was a final impression but it was not a figure. It was a series of four short, straight lines joined together. A box . . . a square. A perfect geometric square.

Of course, it *was* a figure! A *zero!*

0.

Seven—dash—one—four—dash—two—zero.

What did it *mean?* Had Savarone's age caused him to leave a message that meant nothing to anyone but *him?* Had everything been so brilliantly logical but the message itself? It meant *nothing.*

7—14—20. . . . A date? Was it a *date?*

My God! thought Victor. 7–14. July 14! His birthday!

Bastille Day. Thoughout his life that had been a minor source of amusement. A Fontini-Cristi born on the celebrated day of the French Revolution.

July 14 . . . two-zero . . . 20.1920.

That was Savarone's key. Something had happened on July 14, 1920. What was it? What incident had occurred that his father considered so meaningful to his first son? Something that had a significance beyond other times, other birthdays.

A shaft of pain—the second of what he knew would be many—shot through his body, originating, once again, at the base of his spine. The brace was like ice; the cold of the water had chilled his skin and penetrated the tendons and muscle tissue.

With the sensitivity of a surgeon, he pressed his fingers around the area of the chiseled numbers. There was only the date; all else was flat and unspoiled. He took the stick in his left hand and thrust it below the water into the mud. Painfully, he sidestepped his way back toward the embankment, until the level of the water had receded to his thighs. Then he paused for breath. The flashes of pain accelerated; he had done more damage to himself than he had realized. A full convulsion was developing; he tensed the muscles of his jaw and throat. He had to get out of the water and lie down. Lurching for the overhanging vines on the embankment, he fell to his knees in the water. The flashlight spun out of his hand and rolled over some matted fern, its beam shooting out into the dense woods. He grabbed a cluster of thick, exposed roots and pulled himself up toward the ground, pushing the stick behind him into the mud for propulsion.

All movement was arrested in a paralyzing instant of shock.

Above him, in the darkness on the embankment, stood the figure of a man. A huge man dressed in black, and motionless, staring down at him. Around his throat—in jarring counterpoint to the pitch-black clothing—was a rim of white. A priest's collar. The face—what he could see of it in the dim forest light—was impassive. But the eyes that bore down at him had fire in them, and hatred.

The man spoke. His speech was deliberate, slow, born of loathing.

"The enemy of Christ returns."

"You are Gaetamo," said Fontine.

"A man came in an automobile to watch my cabin in the hills. I knew that automobile, that man. He serves the heretic of Xenope. The monk who lives his life in Campo di Fiori. He was there to keep me away."

"But he couldn't."

"No." The defrocked priest elaborated no further. "So this is where it was. All those years and the answer was here." His deep voice seemed to float, beginning anywhere, ending abruptly in midstatement. "What did he leave? A name? Of what? A bank? A building in the Milan factories? We thought of those; we took them apart."

"Whatever it was, it has no meaning for you. Nor for me."

"Liar," replied Gaetamo quietly, in his chilling monotone. He turned his head right, then left; he was remembering. "We staked out every inch of these woods. We ran yellow string from stake to stake and marked each area as we studied it. We considered burning, cutting . . . but were afraid of what we might destroy. We dammed the stream and probed the mud. The Germans gave us instruments . . . but always nothing. The large rocks were filled with meaningless markings, including the birthdate of an arrogant seventeen-year-old who had to leave his conceit in stone. And always nothing."

Victor tensed. *Gaetamo had said it.* In one brief phrase the defrocked priest had unlocked the door! *An arrogant seventeen-year-old*, leaving his mark in stone. But *he* had not left it! Donatti had found the key but had not recognized it! The reasoning was so simple, so uncomplicated: a seventeen-year-old carving a memorable day on a familiar rock. It was so logical, so essentially unremarkable. And so *clear*.

As the memory was now clear. Most of it.

7–14–20. His seventeenth birthday. It came back to him because there had been none like it in his life. My God, thought Victor, Savarone was incredible! *Part of his childhood.* It was on his seventeenth birthday that his father had given him the present he had wanted so badly he had dreamed of it, pleaded for it: The chance to go up into the mountains without his younger brothers. To really do some climbing . . . *above* the usual and—for him—dreary campsites in the foothills.

On his seventeenth birthday, Savarone had presented him with an authentic Alpine pack, the sort used by experienced climbers. Not that his father was about to take him up the Jungfrau; they never really scaled anything extraordinary. But that first trip—*alone with his father*—was a landmark in his early manhood. That pack and that journey were symbols of something very important to him: proof that he was growing up in his father's eyes.

He had forgotten; he was not sure of it even now, for there had been other trips, other years. Had it—that first trip—been in the Champoluc? It must have been, but *where?* That *was* beyond memory.

". . . end your life in this water."

Gaetamo had spoken, but Fontine had not heard him: only the threat had penetrated. Of all men—all priests—this madman could be told nothing. "I found only meaningless scribblings. Childish markings, as you said."

"You found what rightfully belongs to *Christ!*" Gaetamo's words sliced through the forest. He lowered himself to one knee, his immense chest and head inches from Victor, his eyes wide and burning. "You found the *sword of the archangel of hell!* No more lies. Tell me what you've found!"

"Nothing."

"Liar! Why are you *here?* An old man in water and mud! What was in this stream? On this *rock!*"

Victor stared at the grotesque eyes. "Why am I here?" he repeated, stretching his neck, arching his tortured back, his features pinched. "I'm old. With memories. I convinced myself that the answer *might* be here. When we were children we left messages for one another here. You saw for yourself. Childish markings, scribblings, stone scratched against stone. I thought perhaps——But I found nothing. If there was anything, it's gone now."

"You examined the rock, and then you stopped! You were prepared to leave."

"*Look* at me! How long do you think I can stay in this water?"

Gaetamo shook his head slowly. "I watched you. You were a man who found what he had come to find."

"You saw what you wanted to see. Not what was there."

Victor's foot slipped; the stick that braced him in the water slid in the mud, sinking deeper. The priest thrust out of hand and grabbed Fontine's hair. He yanked viciously, pulling Victor into the embankment, forcing his head and neck to one side. The sudden contortion was unbearable; wrenching pain spread throughout Fontine's body. The wide maniacal eyes above him in the dim light were not those of an aging man in the clothes of a priest but, instead, the eyes of a young fanatic thirty years ago.

Gaetamo saw. And understood. "We thought you were dead then. There was no way you could have survived. The fact that you did convinced our holy man that you were from *hell!* . . . You remember. For now I'll continue what we begun thirty years ago! And with each crack of your bones you'll have the chance—as you did then—to tell me what you've found. But don't lie. The pain will only stop when you tell me the truth."

Gaetamo bent forward. He began to twist Victor's head, pressing the face downward into the rocky embankment, cutting the flesh, forcing the air out of Fontine's throat.

Victor tried to pull back; the priest slammed his forehead into a gnarled root. Blood spurted from the gash, flowing into Victor's eyes, blinding him, infuriating him. He raised his right hand, grappling for Gaetamo's wrist; the defrocked priest clasped the hand and wrenched it inward, snapping the fingers. He pulled Fontine higher on the ground, twisting, always twisting his head and neck, causing the brace to cut into his back.

"It won't end until you tell me the truth!"

"*Pig! Pig from Donatti!*" Victor lurched to the side. Gaetamo countered by crashing his fist into Fontine's rib cage. The impact was paralyzing, the pain excruciating.

The stick. The *stick!* Fontine rolled to his left, his left hand below, still gripped around the broken limb, gripped as one holds an object in a moment of agony. Gaetamo had felt the brace; he pulled on it, wrenching it back and forth until the steel lacerated the surrounding flesh.

Victor inched the long stick up by pressing it into the embankment. It touched his chest; he felt it. The end was jagged. If he could only find the smallest opening between himself and the monster above, space enough to thrust it upward, toward the face, the neck.

It came. Gaetamo raised one knee. It was *enough*.

Fontine shoved the stick up, driving it with every ounce of strength he could summon, impaling it into the stunned body above. He heard a cry of shock, a scream that filled the forest.

And then an explosion filled the gray darkness. A powerful gun had been fired. The screeches of birds and animals swelled in the woods—and the body of Gaetamo fell forward on top of him. It rolled to the side.

The stick was lodged in his throat. Below his neck a huge gaping mass of torn flesh saturated with blood was in his upper chest; he had been blown apart by the gun that had been fired out of the darkness.

"May God forgive me," said the monk of Xenope from the shadows.

The black void came over Victor; he felt himself slipping into the water as trembling hands grabbed him. His last thoughts—strangely peaceful—were of his sons. The Geminis. The hands might have been the hands of his sons, trying to save him. But his sons' hands did not tremble.

PART TWO

Chapter Twenty-two

Major Andrew Fontine sat rigidly at his desk, listening to the sounds of morning. It was five minutes to eight; the offices were beginning to fill up. Voices rose and fell in the corridors as the Pentagon started the day.

He had five days to think. No, not to think, to *move*. There wasn't that much to think about; it was only necessary to move out and cut *down*. Stop whatever Adrian and his "concerned citizens" had started.

Eye Corps was the most legitimate clandestine unit in the army. It was doing exactly what the dissenters *thought they* were doing, but without tearing down the system, without revealing weakness. Maintain strength and the illusion of strength. It was all important. They'd tried it the other way. Eye Corps wasn't born in Georgetown, over brandy and cigars and pictures of the Pentagon on the walls. *Bullshit!* It was born in a hut in the Mekong Delta. After he had come back from Saigon and told his three subordinate officers what had happened at command headquarters.

He had gone to Saigon with legitimate field complaints, proof of corruption in the supply lines. Hundreds of thousands of dollars' worth of equipment was being drained off all over the Mekong every week, abandoned by ARVN troops at the first sign of hostilities, routed back into the black market. Payrolls were banked by ARVN commanders, drugs bought and distributed by Vietnamese networks out of Hue and Da-nang. Millions were piped out of the Southeast Asia operation, and no one seemed to know what to do about it.

So he brought his proof to Saigon, right up to the command brass. And what did the brass do? They thanked him and said they would investigate. What was there to investigate? He'd brought enough proof to institute a dozen charges.

A brigadier had taken him out for a drink.

"Listen, Fontine. Better a little corruption than blow the whole ammo dump. These people are thieves by nature, we're not going to change that."

"We could make a few examples, sir. Openly."

"For Christ's sake! We've got enough Stateside problems! That kind of publicity would play right into the antimilitary hands. Now, you've got a fine record; don't louse it up."

That's when it started, when Eye Corps was born. The name itself said it: a unit of men who watched and recorded. And as the months went on, the four of them expanded to five, then seven. Recently, they'd added the eighth man: Captain Martin Greene, in the Pentagon. They were born of disgust. The army was led by weak-kneed whores—*women*—afraid to *offend*. What kind of stature was that for the military leaders of the strongest nation on earth?

Something else happened, too, along the way. As the records grew and the enemies within tagged for what they were, the obvious stared the men of Eye Corps in the face: *they* were the inheritors! They were the incorruptible; they were the elite.

Since regular channels didn't work, they would do it their way. Build up the records, get files on every misfit, every deviate, every corrupter, large and small. Strength lay with those who could confront the misfits and make them crawl. Make them do exactly what strong, incorruptible men wanted them to do.

Eye Corps was nearly there. Almost three years' worth of recorded garbage. Christ! Southeast Asia was the place to find it. They'd take over soon; go right into the Pentagon and take over! It was men like themselves who had the skill and training and the commitment to oversee the vast complexities that were the armed might of the country. It was not a delusion; they *were* the elite.

It was so logical for him, too. His father would understand that, if he could ever talk to him about it. And one day he might. Since his earliest memories, he felt the presence of influence, of pride, of consequence. And power . . . yes, power. It wasn't a dirty word! It belonged to those who knew how to handle it; it was his birthright.

And Adrian wanted to tear it down! Well, the spoiler was not going to tear it down. He was not going to rip Eye Corps apart.

. . . *arrangements can be made*. That's what Adrian had said in the boathouse.

How right he was! Arrangements could be made; but not any arrangements considered by Adrian and his concerned citizens. A lot would happen before then.

Five days. Adrian wasn't trained to consider the options. Practical, physical alternatives, not words and abstractions and "positions." The army would have a hell of a time trying to reach him five days from now if he was 10,000 miles away in a combat zone, involved in operations covered by an umbrella of security. He had enough clout to do that; to get over there and build that umbrella.

There was a weakling in Saigon who had betrayed them. Betrayed the rest of Eye Corps. To learn who he was—and he was one of six—was the first reason to get over there. Find him . . . then make a decision.

Once he was found—and the decision made—the rest was easy. He'd brief the remaining men of Eye Corps. The stories would be integrated, synchronized.

Even the army needed proof. And there was no way it could get that proof.

Here in Washington, Eye Corps' eighth member could take care of himself. Captain Martin Greene was steel and leather. And smart. He could hold his own against any flak leveled at him. His people had come from the Irgun, the toughest fighters in Jew history. If the D.C. brass gave him any static, he'd cut out for Israel in a second, and the Jew army would be better for it.

Andrew looked at his watch. It was a little past eight, time to reach Greene. He couldn't take the chance last night. Adrian and his civilians were trying to find an unknown officer who worked at the Pentagon. Outside telephones could not be trusted. He and Marty would have to talk; they couldn't wait for their next scheduled meeting. He would be on a plane for Saigon before the day was over.

They had agreed never to be seen together. If they met by chance at a conference or a cocktail party, both pretended they were meeting for the first time. It was vital that no connection between them be apparent. When they did meet, it was in out-of-the-way places and always by prearranged schedule. During the meetings they would combine whatever damaging information they'd culled from Pentagon files during the week, seal the pages in an envelope, and mail it to a post office box in Baltimore. The enemies of Eye Corps were being catalogued everywhere.

In times of emergencies, or when one needed the other's immediate advice, they sent word to each other by placing a "mistaken" call through the Pentagon switchboard. It was the signal to invent some excuse, get out of the office, and head for a bar in downtown Washington. Andrew had made the "mistaken" call two hours ago.

The bar was dark and cheap and gaudy, with booths in the back that afforded a clear view of the entrance. Andrew sat in a booth by the back wall, toying with his bourbon, not interested in it. He kept looking up at the entrance fifty feet away. Whenever the door opened, the morning sun burst through briefly, a harsh intruder on the interior darkness. Greene was late; it wasn't like him to be late.

The door opened again and the silhouette of a stocky, muscular man with broad, thick shoulders was arrested in the glare. It was Marty; he was out of uniform, dressed in an open white shirt and what appeared to be plaid trousers. He nodded to the bartender and started toward the rear of the bar. Everything about Greene was powerful, thought Andrew. From his thick legs to the stock of bright-red hair, shaped in a bristling crew cut.

"Sorry it took me so long," said Greene, sliding into the booth opposite Andrew. "I stopped off at the apartment to change. Then I went out the back way."

"Any particular reason?"

"Maybe, maybe not. Last night I took the car out of the garage and thought I picked up surveillance—a dark-green Electra. I reversed directions; it was still there. I went home."

"What time was it?"

"Around eight thirty, quarter to nine."

"It figures. It's why I called you. They expect me to contact someone in your section; set up a meeting right away. They probably had half a dozen others followed."

"Who?"

"One of them's my brother."

"Your *brother?*"

"He's a lawyer. He's working with——"

"I know *exactly* who he is," interrupted Greene, "*and* who he's working with. They're about as subtle as jackals."

"You never mentioned him to me. How come?"

"There was no reason to. They're a bunch of hotheads over at Justice. They were organized by a Black named Nevins. We keep close tabs on them; they mess around with hardware contracts more than we'd like. But they haven't got anything to do with *us*."

"They do now. It's why I called you. One of the six in Nam broke. They've got a deposition. A list. Eight officers, seven identified."

Greene's cold eyes narrowed. He spoke slowly, quietly. "What the hell are you saying?"

Andrew told him. When he finished, Greene spoke without moving an inch of his powerful body.

"That Black son of a bitch, Nevins, flew to Saigon two weeks ago. The matter wasn't related."

"It is now," said the major.

"Who has the deposition? Are there copies?"

"I don't know."

"Why is the subpoena being delayed?"

"Again, I don't know," said Andrew.

"There must be a reason! For Christ's sake, why didn't you ask?"

"Hold it, Marty. Everything came as a shock——"

"We're trained for shock," interrupted Greene icily. "Can you find out?"

Andrew swallowed part of his bourbon. He had not seen the captain like this before. "I can't call my brother. He wouldn't tell me if I did."

"Nice family. May the brothers live and be well. Maybe I can do better. We've got people at Justice; procurement covers itself. I'll do what I can. Where are our files in Saigon? They're the bottom line."

"They're not in Saigon. They're in Phan-thiet on the coast. In a fenced-off area of a warehouse, I'm the only one who knows the location. A couple of cabinets among a thousand G-Two crates."

"Very smart." Greene nodded his head in approval.

"I'll check them the first thing. I'm flying out this afternoon. A sudden inspection trip."

"Very nice." Greene nodded again. "You'll find the man?"

"Yes."

"Check Barstow. He's a smartass. Too many decorations."

"You don't know him."

"I know the way he operates," said Greene.

Andrew was stung by the similarity of words. His brother had applied them to Eye Corps. "He's a good man in the field——"

"Bravery," interrupted the captain, "hasn't got a goddamn thing to do with it. Check Barstow first."

"I will." Andrew smarted under Greene's pronouncements. He had to get some of his own back. "What about Baltimore? I'm worried about that."

The envelopes in Baltimore were picked up by Greene's twenty-year-old nephew.

"He's perfect. He'd kill himself first. I was up there last weekend. I would have known."

"Are you sure?"

"It's not worth discussing. I want to know more about that goddamned deposition. When you crack Barstow make sure you get every word he put down. They probably gave him a copy; see if he's got a military lawyer."

The major drank again, averting Greene's narrow eyes. Andrew did not like the captain's tone of voice. He was actually giving orders; he was out of line. But on the bottom line Greene was a good man to have around in a crisis. "What can you find out over at Justice?"

"More than that Black bastard would ever guess. We've got funds set up for the mavericks who interfere with armaments contracts. We don't care who makes a few extra dollars, we want the hardware. You'd be surprised how the lowly paid government lawyers take to Caribbean vacations." Greene smiled and sat back in the booth. I think we can handle this. The subpoena won't mean a damn thing without our records. Line officers bitch all the time, what else is new?"

"That's what I told my brother," said Andrew.

"Him I can't figure," said Greene. And then the captain leaned forward. "Whatever you do in Nam, think it out. If you use prejudice, get your facts and do it by remote."

"I think I've had more experience in those areas than you." Andrew lighted a cigarette; his hand was steady in spite of his increased irritation. He was pleased with that.

"You probably do," said Greene casually. "Now, I've got something for you. I figured it could wait till our next meeting, but there's no point in holding it."

"What is it?"

"A congressional tracer came in last Friday. From a pol named Sandor; he's on the Armed Services Committee. It concerned you, so I pulled it."

"What did they want?"

"Limited. Your rotation schedule. How permanent you were in Washington. I inserted a routine response. You were high-echelon material, War College candidate. Very permanent."

"I wonder what—"

"I haven't finished," interrupted Greene. "I called this Sandor's aide and asked why the congressman was interested in you. He checked his papers and said the request came from a friend of Sandor's, a man named Dakakos. Theodore Dakakos."

"Who is he?"

"A Greek shipper. In your family's class. He's got millions."

"Dakakos? Never heard of him."

"These Greeks are pistols. Maybe he wants to give you a present. Like a small yacht or your own battalion."

Fontine shrugged. "Dakakos? I can buy a yacht. I'll take the battalion."

"You can buy that, too," said Greene, sliding across the seat out of the booth. "Have a prosperous trip. Call me when you get back."

"What are you going to do?"

"Find out everything there is to know about a Black son of a bitch named Nevins."

Greene walked rapidly past the booths toward the entrance. Andrew would wait five minutes before leaving. He had to get to his apartment and back. His plane left at one thirty.

Dakakos? Theodore Dakakos.

Who was he?

Adrian got out of the bed slowly, one foot after the other as quietly as possible so he would not wake her. Barbara was asleep, but her sleep was fitful.

It was barely nine thirty in the evening. He had picked her up at the airport shortly after five. She'd canceled her Thursday and Friday seminars, too excited to lecture detached summer students.

She had been awarded a grant to assist the anthropologist Sorkis Khertepian at the University of Chicago. Khertepian was in the process of analyzing artifacts taken from the site of the Aswan Dam. Barbara was exhilarated; she had to fly down and tell Adrian all about it. She was intensely alive when things went right in her world, a scholar who would never lose her sense of wonder.

It was strange. Both he and Barbara had entered their professions in a sense of outrage. His was traced to the acid streets of San Francisco, hers to a brilliant mother denied her rightful place in a midwest college because she *was* a mother. A woman who had no place in the higher offices of a university. Yet each had found values that far outweighed the anger.

It was part of the bond between them.

He walked quietly across the room and sat down in an armchair. His eyes fell on his briefcase on the bedroom desk. He never left it in the sitting room at night; Jim Nevins had cautioned him about being careless. Nevins was at times a little paranoid about such matters.

Nevins, too, had come to his profession in outrage. It was the outrage that often sustained him. Not merely the frustrations of a Black man climbing over the barriers erected by a skeptical white establishment, but the anger of a lawyer who saw so much illegality in the city where laws were made.

But nothing outraged Nevins more than the discovery of Eye Corps. The idea of military elitists suppressing evidence of massive corruption for their own ends was more dangerous than anything the Black lawyer could think of.

When Major Andrew Fontine's name appeared on the list, Nevins had asked Adrian to remove himself. Adrian had become one of his closest friends, but nothing could stand in the way of prosecuting Eye Corps.

Brothers were brothers. Even white brothers.

"You look so serious. And so naked." Barbara swept her light-brown hair away from her face, and rolled on her side, hugging the pillow.

"I'm sorry. Did I wake you?"

"Heavens, no. I was only dozing."

"Correction. Your snoring could be heard on Capitol Hill."

"You lie through your legal teeth. . . . What time is it?"

"Twenty of ten," he answered, looking at his watch.

She sat up and stretched. The sheet fell away to her waist; her lovely, full breasts separated, their slow expansion, the movement of the nipples holding his eyes, arousing him. She saw him watching her and smiled, pulling the sheet over her as she leaned against the headrest.

"We talk," she said firmly. "We have three days to wear ourselves to a frazzle. While you're out during the day slaying bears, I'll preen myself like a concubine. Satisfaction guaranteed."

"You should do all those things nonacademic ladies do. Spend hours at Elizabeth Arden's, wallow in milk baths, eat bonbons with your gin. You're a tired girl."

"Let's put me aside," said Barbara smiling. "I've been talking about me all night—almost. How's everything down here? Or shouldn't you say? I'm sure Jim Nevins thinks the suite is bugged."

Adrian laughed, crossing his legs. He reached for a pack of cigarettes next to a lighter on the armchair table. "Jim's conspiracy complex remains undaunted. He refuses to leave case files at the office anymore. He keeps all his important papers in his briefcase, which is the biggest damn thing you ever saw." Adrian chuckled.

"Why does he do that?"

"He doesn't want copies made. He knows the crowd upstairs would take him off half the cases if they knew how much progress he was making."

"That's astonishing."

"It's chilling," he said.

The telephone rang. Adrian got out of the chair quickly and crossed to the bedside table.

It was his mother. She could not hide the anxiety in her voice. "I've heard from your father."

"What do you mean, you've *heard* from him?"

"He flew to Paris last Monday. Then he went on to Milan——"

"*Milan?* What for?"

"He'll tell you himself. He wants you and Andrew here on Sunday."

"Wait a minute." Adrian's mind raced. "I don't think I can do that."

"You *must*."

"You don't understand, and I can't explain right now. But Andy's not going to want to see me. I'm not sure I want to see him. I'm not even sure it's advisable under the circumstances."

"What are you talking about?" His mother's voice was suddenly cold. "What have you done?"

Adrian paused before answering. "We're on the opposite sides of a . . . dispute."

"Whatever it is, it doesn't matter! Your father *needs* you." She was losing control. "Something happened to him. Something *happened* to him! He could barely talk!"

There were several clicks on the line, followed by the urgent voice of a hotel operator. "Mr Fontine, I'm sorry to break in, but there's an emergency call for you."

"Oh, God." His mother whispered over the line from New York. "Victor——"

"I'll call you back if it's got anything to do with him. I promise you that," said Adrian swiftly. "All right, operator. I'll take——"

It was as far as he got. The voice now on the line was hysterical. It was a woman, crying and screaming and barely coherent.

"*Adrian! My God, Adrian! He's dead! He was killed! They killed him!* Adri*annnnnnn!*"

The screams filled the room. And the terror of the screams filled Adrian with a shock he had never felt before. . . . . Death. Death that touched *him*.

The woman on the telephone was Carol Nevins. Jim's wife.

"I'll be right there!"

"Call my mother," he told Barbara, as he dressed as fast as he could. "The North Shore number. Tell her it's not dad."

"Who is it?"

"Nevins."

"Oh, my God!"

He raced into the corridor and down to the elevators. He kept his finger on the button; the elevators were slow—*too* slow! He ran to the exit doors, crashed them open and leaped down the angling staircase to the lobby. He sped to the glass doors of the entrance.

"Excuse me! Pardon me! Let me through, *please!*"

Out on the curb he ran to his right, to the lighted sign of an empty taxi. He gave the address of Nevin's apartment.

What had happened? What in God's name *had happened?!* What did Carol mean? *They killed him! Who* killed him. Jesus! Was he *dead?!*

Jim Nevins dead? Corruption, yes. Greed, of course. Mendacity, normal. But not *murder!*

There was a traffic light at New Hampshire, and he thought he would go mad. Two more blocks!

The cab plunged forward the instant the light flickered. The driver accelerated, then halfway down the block came to a sudden stop. The street was jammed with traffic. There were circling lights up ahead; nothing was moving.

Adrian jumped out on the street and began threading his way as fast as possible between the cars. Across Florida Avenue police cars blocked the entrance. Patrolmen were blowing whistles, signaling with iridescent orange gloves, funneling the traffic west.

He ran into the blockade; two police officers several yards away at either side yelled at him.

"No one goes past here, mister!"

"Get back, buddy! You don't want to go in there!"

But he did want to go; he had to go! He ducked between two patrol cars and raced toward the swirling lights near a mass of twisted metal and shattered glass that Adrian instantly recognized. It was Jim Nevins's car. What was left of it.

An ambulance's rear doors were open; a stretcher on which a body lay strapped, covered completely with a white hospital blanket, was being carried from the wreckage by two attendants. A third man, holding a black medical bag, walked alongside.

Adrian approached, pushing away a policeman who held out a prohibiting arm. "Get out of the way," he said firmly, but with his voice trembling.

"Sorry, mister. I can't let——"

"I'm an attorney! And that man, I *think*, is my friend."

The doctor heard the desperation in his words and waved the officer away. Adrian reached down for the blanket; the doctor's hand shot out and held his wrist.

"Is your friend Black?"

"Yes."

"With identification that says his name is Nevins?"

"Yes."

"He's dead, take my word for it. You don't want to look."

"You don't understand. I *have* to look."

Adrian pulled back the blanket. Nausea swept over him; he was at once hypnotized and terrified at what he saw. Nevin's face was half ripped off, blood and bone more apparent than flesh. The area of the throat was worse; half his neck was gone.

"Oh, Jesus. My *God!*"

The doctor replaced the blanket and ordered the attendants to continue on. He was a young man with long blond hair and the face of a boy. "You better sit down," he said to Adrian. "I tried to tell you. Come on, let me take you to a car."

"No. No, thanks." Adrian suppressed the sickness and tried to breathe. There wasn't enough air! "What happened?"

"We don't know all the details yet. Are you really a lawyer?"

"Yes. And he was my friend. What happened?"

"Seems he made a left turn to go into the apartment driveway and halfway across, some outsized rig rammed him at full speed."

"Rig?"

"A trailer truck, the kind with steel gridwork. It barrelassed down like it was on a freeway."

"Where is it?"

"We don't know. It stopped for a couple of moments, its horn blasting like hell, then pulled out. A witness said it was a rental; it had one of those rent-a-truck signs on the side. You can bet the cops have APB's out all over the place."

Suddenly, Adrian remembered, amazed that he was able to do so. He grabbed the doctor's sleeve. "Can you get me through the police to his car? It's important."

"I'm a doctor, not a cop."

"Please. Will you try?"

The young doctor sucked air through his teeth, then nodded his head. "Okay. I'll take you over. Don't pull any shit, though."

"I just want to see something. You said a witness saw the truck stop."

"I *know* it stopped," replied the blond-haired doctor enigmatically. "Come on!"

They walked over to the wreck. Nevin's car was caved in on the left side, metal stripped everywhere, windows shattered. Foam had been sprayed around the gas tank; white globules had drifted through the smashed windows.

"Hey, Doc! What are *you* doing?" The policeman's voice was tired and angry.

"Come on, kid, get back. You, too!" A second patrolman yelled.

The young doctor raised his black bag. "Forensic washout, fellas. Don't argue with me, call the station!"

"What?"

"What forensic?"

"Pathology, for Christ's sake!" He propelled Adrian forward. "Come on, lab man, take the samples and let's get out of here. I'm beat." Adrian looked into the car. "See anything?" asked the doctor pointedly.

Adrian did. Nevins's briefcase was missing.

They walked back through the cordon of police to the ambulance.

"Did you really find anything?" asked the young doctor.

"Yes," answered Adrian, numbed, not sure he was thinking clearly. "Something that should have been there, but wasn't."

"Okay. Good. Now I'll tell you why I took you over."

"What?"

"You saw your friend; I wouldn't let his wife see him. His face and neck were blown apart with broken glass and metal fragments."

"Yes . . . I know. I saw." Adrian felt the wave of nausea spreading over him again.

"But it's a pretty warm night. I think the window on the driver's side was rolled down. I couldn't swear to it—that car's totaled—but your friend could have taken a short blast from a shotgun."

Adrian raised his eyes. Something inside his head snapped; the words his brother said seven years ago in San Francisco seared into his brain.

"*. . . There's a war out there . . . the firepower's real!*"

Among the papers in Nevins's briefcase was the deposition taken from an officer in Saigon. The indictment of Eye Corps.

And he had given his brother five days' warning.

Oh, God! What had he done?

He took a cab to the precinct police station. His credentials as an attorney gained him a brief conversation with a sergeant.

"If there's foul play involved, we'll find it," said the man, looking at Adrian with the distaste the police reserved for lawyers who followed up accidents.

"He was a friend of mine and I have reason to believe there was. Did you find the truck?"

"Nope. We know it's not on any of the highways. The state troopers are watching for it."

"It was a rental."

"We know that, too. The rental agencies are being checked. Why don't you go home, mister?"

Adrian bent over the sergeant's desk, his hands on the edge. "I don't think you're taking me very seriously."

"Fatality sheets come into this station a dozen an hour. Now, what the hell do you want me to do? Suspend everything else and put a whole goddamned platoon on one hit-and-run?"

"I'll tell you what I want, sergeant. I want a pathology report on all cranial injuries sustained by the deceased. Is that clear?"

"What are you talking about?" replied the police officer disdainfully. "Cranial——"

"I want to know what blew that man apart."

Chapter Twenty-three

The train from Salonika had claimed its last sacrifice, thought Victor, as he lay in his bed, the morning sun streaming through the oceanside windows of the North Shore house. There was no reason on earth why any further life should be lost in its name. Enrici Gaetamo was the last victim, and there was no sorrow in that death.

He himself had very little time remaining. He could see it in Jane's eyes, in the eyes of the doctors. It was to be expected; he had been granted too many reprieves.

He had dictated everything he could remember about that day in July a lifetime ago. He had probed forgotten recesses in his mind, refused the narcotics that would numb the pain because they would equally numb the memories.

The vault from Constantine had to be found, its contents evaluated by responsible men. What had to be prevented—however remote it might be—was a chance discovery, exposure without thought. He would charge his sons. Salonika was now theirs. The Geminis. They would do what he could not do: find the vault of Constantine.

But there was a piece of the puzzle that was missing. He had to find it before he spoke with his sons. What did Rome know? How much had the Vatican learned about Salonika? Which was why he had asked a man to visit him this morning. A priest named Land, the monsignor from New York's archdiocese who had come to his hospital room months ago.

Fontine heard the footsteps outside the bedroom, and the quiet voices of

Jane and the visitor. The priest had arrived.

The heavy door opened silently. Jane ushered in the monsignor, then went back into the hallway, closing the door behind her. The priest stood across the room, a leather book in his hand.

"Thank you for coming," Victor said.

The priest smiled. He touched the leather cover of the book "*Conquest with Mercy. In the Name of God.* The history of the Fontini-Cristis. I thought you might like this, Mr Fontine. I found it in a bookshop in Rome years ago."

The monsignor placed the book on the bedside table. They shook hands; each, Victor realized, was appraising the other.

Land was no more than fifty. He was of medium height, broad in the chest and shoulders. His features were sharp, Anglican; his eyes hazel beneath generous eyebrows that were darker than his short, graying hair. It was a pleasant face with intelligent eyes.

"A vanity publication, I'm afraid. A custom of dubious value at the turn of the century. It's long been out of print. The language is Italian——"

"An obsolete northern idiom," completed Land. "Court Victorian would be the English equivalent, I think. Somewhere between 'you' and 'thee.'"

"You have the advantage over me. My knowledge of languages is not nearly so erudite."

"It was sufficient for Loch Torridon," said the priest.

"Yes, it was. Please sit down, Monsignor Land." Victor gestured to the chair by the bed. The priest sat. The two men looked at each other. Fontine spoke.

"Several months ago you came to my hospital room. Why?"

"I wanted to meet the man whose life I had studied so thoroughly. Shall I speak frankly?"

"You wouldn't have come here this morning if you meant to do otherwise."

"I was told you might die. I was presumptuous enough to hope you'd allow me to administer last rites."

"That *is* frank. And *was* presumptuous."

"I realized that. It's why I never returned. You're a courteous man, Mr Fontine, but you couldn't conceal your feelings."

Victor examined the priest's face. There was the same sorrow he had remembered in the hospital. "Why did you study my life? Does the Vatican still investigate? Wasn't Donatti's cause rejected?"

"The Vatican is always engaged in study. In examination. It doesn't stop. And Donatti was more than rejected. He was excommunicated, his remains refused the sanctity of Catholic burial."

"You answer my last two questions. Not the first. Why you?"

The monsignor crossed his legs, clasping his hands in front of him on his knees, his fingers entwined. "I'm a political and social historian. Which is another way of saying that I look for incompatible relationships between the church and its environs at given periods of time." Land smiled, his eyes reflective. "The original reason for such work was to prove the virtue of the church and the error of any who opposed her. But virtue wasn't always found. And it certainly wasn't found in the countless lapses of judgment, or morality, as they were exposed." Land's smile had gone; his admission was clear.

"The execution of the Fontini-Cristis was a lapse? Of *judgment? Morality?* "

"Please." The priest spoke swiftly, his voice soft but emphatic. "You and I both know what it was. An act of murder. Impossible to sanction and unforgivable."

Victor saw once again the sorrow in the man's eyes. "I accept what you say. I don't understand it, but I accept it. So I became an object of your social and political examinations?"

"Among many other questions of the time. I'm sure you're aware of them. Although there was a great deal of good during those years, there was *much* that was unforgiveable. You and your family were obviously in this category."

"You became interested in me?"

"You became my obsession." Land smiled again, awkwardly. "Remember, I'm American. I was studying in Rome, and the name Victor Fontine was well known to me. I had read of your work in postwar Europe; the newspapers were filled with it. I was aware of your influence in both the public and the private sectors. You can imagine my astonishment when, in studying the period, I found that Vittorio Fontini-Cristi and Victor Fontine were the same person."

"Was there a great deal of information in your Vatican files?"

"About the Fontini-Cristis, yes." Land gestured his head toward the leather-bound volume he had placed on the bedside table. "As that book, somewhat biased, I'm afraid. Hardly as flattering, naturally. But of you, there was substantively nothing. Your existence was acknowledged: the first male child of Savarone, now an American citizen known as Victor Fontine. Nothing more. The files ended abruptly with the information that the remaining Fontini-Cristis had been executed by the Germans. It was an incomplete ending. Even the date was missing."

"The less written down, the better."

"Yes. So I studied the records of the court of Reparations. They were far more complete. What began as curiosity turned into shock. You made accusations to the tribunal of judges. Accusations I found unbelievable, intolerable, for you included the church. And you named a man of the Curia, Guillamo Donatti. That was the link that was missing. It was all I needed."

"Are you telling me Donatti's name was nowhere in the files of the Fontini-Cristis?"

"It is now. It wasn't then. It was as if the archivists couldn't bring themselves to acknowledge the connection. Donatti's papers had been sealed, as usual with excommunicants. After his death, they had been found in possession of an aide——"

"Father Enrici Gaetamo. Defrocked," interrupted Fontine softly.

Land paused. "Yes. Gaetamo. I received permission to break the seals. I read the paranoid ramblings of a madman, a self-canonized fanatic." Again the monsignor stopped briefly, his eyes wandering. "What I found there took me to England. To a man named Teague. I met with him only once, at his country house. It was raining and he repeatedly got up to stoke the fire. I never saw a man finger a watch so. Yet he was retired and had no place to go."

Victor smiled. "It was an annoying habit, that watch. I told him so many times."

"Yes, you were good friends, I learned that quickly. He was in awe of you, you know."

"In awe of me? Alec? I can't believe that. He was far too direct."

"He said he never admitted it to you, but he was. He said he felt inadequate around you."

"He didn't convey it."

"He said a great deal more, too. Everything. The execution at Campo di Fiori, the escape through Celle Ligure, Loch Torridon, Oxfordshire, your wife, your sons. And Donatti: how he kept the name from you."

"He had no choice. The knowledge would have interfered with Loch Torridon."

Land unclasped his hands and uncrossed his legs. He seemed to have difficulty in finding the words. "It was the first time I had heard of the train from Salonika."

Victor raised his eyes abruptly; they had been focused on the priest's hands. "That's not logical. You read Donatti's papers."

"And suddenly they were clear. The insane ramblings, the disjointed phrases, the seemingly deranged references to out-of-the-way places and times . . . suddenly made sense. Even in his most private papers, Donatti wouldn't spell it out; his fear was too great. . . . Everything was reduced to that train. And whatever was on it."

"You don't know?"

"I came to. I would have learned more quickly, but Brevourt refused to see me. He died several months after I tried to reach him.

"I went to the prison where Gaetamo was held. He spat at me through the wire mesh, clawing his hands over it until they were bleeding. Still, I had the source. Constantine. The Patriarchate. I gained an audience with a priest of the Elders. He was a very old man and he told me. The train from Salonika carried the Filioque denials."

"That was all?"

Monsignor Land smiled. "Theologically speaking, it was enough. To that old man and his counterparts in Rome, the Filioque documents represented triumph and cataclysm."

"They don't represent the same to you?" Victor watched the priest closely, concentrating on the steady hazel eyes.

"No. The church isn't the church of past centuries, even past generations. Simply put, it couldn't survive if it were. There are the old men who cling to what they believe is incontrovertible . . . in most cases it's all they have left; there's no need to strip them of their convictions. Time mandates change gracefully; nothing is as it was. With each year—as the old guard leaves us—the church moves more swiftly into the realm of social responsibility. It has the power to effect extraordinary good, the wherewithal—spiritually and pragmatically—to alleviate enormous suffering. I speak with a certain expertise, for I am part of this movement. We're in every diocese over the globe. It's our future. We are *with* the world now."

Fontine looked away. The priest had finished; he had described a force for good in a sadly lacking world. Victor turned back to Land.

"You don't know precisely, then, what is in those documents from Salonika."

"What does it matter? At the worst, theological debate. Doctrinal equivocation. A man *existed* and his name was Jesus of Nazareth . . . or the Essenian Archangel of Light . . . and he spoke from the heart. His words have come down to us, historically authenticated by the Aramaics and Biblical scholars, Christian and non-Christian alike. What difference does it really make whether he is called carpenter, or prophet, or son of God? What matters is that he spoke the truth as he saw it, as it was *revealed* to him. His sincerity, if you will, is the only issue, and on that there is no debate."

Fontine caught his breath. His mind raced back to Campo di Fiori, to an old monk of Xenope who spoke of a parchment taken out of a Roman prison.

. . . what is contained in that parchment is beyond anything in your imagination . . . it must be found . . . destroyed . . . for nothing has changed yet all is changed. . . .

Destroyed.

. . . what matters is that he spoke the truth as he saw it, as it was revealed to him. . . . His sincerity is the only issue, and on that there is no debate. . . .

Or was there?

Was this scholar-priest, this good man beside him, prepared to face what had to be faced? Was it remotely fair to ask him to do so?

For nothing has changed, yet all is changed.

Whatever those contradictory words meant, it would take exceptional men to know what to do. He would prepare a list for his sons.

The priest named Land was a candidate.

The four massive overhead blades slowed to a stop, sending metallic thuds throughout the aircraft. An airman opened the hatch and sprang the lever that swung the short flight of steps out from the undercarriage. Maj. Andrew Fontine emerged into the morning sunlight and climbed down the metal stairs onto the helicopter pad at Air Force Base Cobra in Phan-thiet.

His paper authorized priority transportation and access to the restricted warehouses down at the waterfront. He would commandeer a jeep from the officers' pool and head directly to the piers. And to a file cabinet in Warehouse Four. The Eye Corps records were there; and they would stay there, the safest place in Southeast Asia, once he saw for himself that nothing was disturbed. He had two more stops to make after the warehouse: north to Da-nang, then south again, past Saigon into the Delta. To Can-tho.

Captain Jerome Barstow was in Can-tho. Marty Greene was right; it was Barstow who had betrayed Eye Corps. The others agreed; his behavior was that of a man who had broken. He had been seen in Saigon with a legal officer named Tarkington. It wasn't difficult to understand what had happened: Barstow was preparing a defense, and if that was so, a defense meant he would testify. Barstow did not know where the Eye Corps records were, but he had seen them. Seen them, *hell!* He'd prepared twenty or thirty himself. Barstow's testimony could finish Eye Corps. They could not allow that.

The legal officer named Tarkington was in Da-nang. He didn't know it but he was going to meet another man from Eye Corps. It would be the last person he met. In an alley, with a knife in his stomach, and whiskey on his shirt and in his mouth.

And then Andrew would fly to the Delta. To the betrayer named Barstow. Barstow would be shot by a whore; they were easy to buy.

He walked across the hot concrete toward the transit building. A lieutenant colonel was waiting for him. At first Andrew was alarmed; had something gone wrong? The five days weren't up! Then he saw that the colonel was smiling, somewhat patronizingly, but nevertheless in friendship.

"Major Fontine?" The greeting was accompanied by an extension of the hand; no salute was expected.

"Yes, sir?" The handshake was brief.

"Washington cable, straight from the secretary of the army. You have to get home, major. As soon as possible. I'm sorry to be the one to tell you, but it concerns your father."

"My *father?* Is he dead?"

"It's only a matter of time. You have priority clearance for any aircraft leaving Tan Son Nhut." The colonel handed him a red-bordered envelope with the imprimatur of General Headquarters, Saigon, across the top. It was the sort of envelope reserved for White House liaisons and couriers from the Joint Chiefs.

"My father's been a sick man for many years," said Fontine slowly. "This isn't unexpected. I have another day's work here. I'll be at Tan San Nhut tomorrow night."

"Whatever you say. The main thing is we found you. You've got the message."

"I've got the message," said Andrew.

In the phone booth, Adrian listened to the weary voice of the police sergeant. The sergeant was lying; more credible still, someone had lied to him. The pathology report on Nevins, James, Black male, victim of hit-and-run, showed no apparent evidence of cranial, neck, or upper thorax injuries unrelated to the impact of collision.

"Send the report and the X-rays to me," said Adrian curtly. "You've got my address."

"There were no X-rays accompanying the pathology report," replied the police officer mechanically.

"Get them," said Adrian, hanging up the phone.

Lies. Everywhere lies and evasions.

His was the biggest lie of all; he lied to himself, and accepted that lie and used it to convince others. He had stood up in front of a group of very frightened young lawyers from the Justice Department and told them that under the circumstances, the subpoena on Eye Corps should be delayed. They needed to regroup their evidence, obtain a second deposition; to go to the adjutant general with only a list of names was meaningless.

It *wasn't* meaningless! The moment was right to confront the military and demand an immediate investigation. A man was murdered; the evidence he carried with him removed from the scene of his death. That evidence was the indictment of Eye Corps! Here are the names! This is the gist of the deposition!

Now, *move* on it!

But he could not do that. His brother's name was at the top of that list. To serve the subpoena was to charge his brother with murder. There was no other conclusion. Andrew was his brother, his twin, and he was not prepared to call him killer.

Adrian walked out of the phone booth and down the block toward his hotel. Andrew was on his way back from Saigon. He had left the country last Monday; it didn't take a great deal of imagination to know why. His brother wasn't stupid; Andrew was building his defense at the source of his crimes; crimes that included conspiracy, suppression of evidence, and obstruction of justice. Motives: complex and not without fundamental substance, but still crimes.

But no murder at night in a Washington street.

Oh, Christ! Even now he lied to himself! Or to be charitable, he refused to face the possible. Come on! *Say it, think it!*

The probable.

There was an eighth member of Eye Corps in Washington. Whoever that man was, he was Nevin's killer. And Nevins's killer could not have acted without the knowledge given by brother to brother in a boathouse on Long Island's North Shore.

When Andrew's plane landed, he would learn that the subpoena had not been served. Eye Corps was intact for a while longer, free to maneuver and manipulate.

There was one thing that would stop it, though. Stop it instantly and recharge a group of frightened lawyers who wondered if what happened to Nevins could happen to them; they were attorneys, not commandos.

Adrian would look into his brother's eyes, and if he saw Jim Nevins's death in them, he would avenge it. If the soldier had given the order of execution, then the soldier would be destroyed.

Or was he lying to himself again? Could he call his brother killer? Could he *really?*

What the hell did his father want? What difference did it make?

Chapter Twenty-four

The two chairs were placed on opposite sides of the bed. It was proper this way. It could divide his attention between his sons; they were different people, their reactions would be different. Jane preferred to stand. He had asked a terrible thing of her: to tell his sons the story of Salonika. Everything, leaving out nothing. They had to be made to understand that powerful men, institutions, even governments could be moved by the vault from Constantine. As they had been moved three decades before.

He could not tell the story himself. He was dying; his mind was clear enough to know that. He had to have the simple energy to answer their questions; he had to have the strength to give his charge to his sons. For theirs was now the responsibility of the Fontini-Cristis.

They walked into the room with their mother. So tall, so alike, yet so different. One in uniform, the other in a nondescript tweed jacket and flannel trousers. Blond-haired Andrew was angry. It was in his face, the continuous tension of his jaw muscles, the firm set of his mouth, the neutral, clouded gaze of his eyes.

Adrian, on the other hand, seemed unsure of himself. His blue eyes were questioning, his mouth slack, the lips parted. He drew his hand through his dark hair as he stared down, his expression equal parts of compassion and astonishment.

Victor indicated the chairs. The brothers looked at each other briefly; it was impossible to define the communication. Whatever had happened to alienate them had to be erased. Their responsibility demanded it. They sat down, the Xeroxed pages of his recollections of July 14, 1920, in their hands. He had instructed Jane to give them each a copy; they were to read them through before seeing him. No moments were to be lost on explanations that could be covered beforehand. He hadn't the strength.

"We won't waste words on sentiment. You've heard your mother; you've read what I've written. You'll have questions."

Andrew spoke. "Assuming this vault can be found—and we'll get to that—what then?"

"I'll prepare a list of names. Five or six men, no more; they are not easily arrived at. You'll bring the vault to them."

"What'll they do?" pressed Andrew.

"That will depend on what the vault contains, *specifically*. Release it, destroy it, rebury it."

Adrian interrupted quietly. The lawyer was suddenly disturbed. "Is there a choice? I don't think so. It doesn't belong to us; it should be public knowledge."

"With public chaos? The consequences have to be weighed."

"Does anyone else have the key?" asked the soldier. "The location of this trip on July 14, 1920?"

"No. It would be meaningless. There are only a few left who knew of the train, knew what was *really* on it. Old men from the Patriarchate; one remains in Campo di Fiori and cannot have much time."

"And we're to say nothing to anyone," continued the major. "No one but ourselves is to know."

"No one. There are those who would trade off half the arsenals in this world for the information."

"I wouldn't go that far."

"Then you wouldn't be thinking. I'm sure your mother explained. Besides the Filioque denials, including the Aramaic scroll, in that vault there is a parchment on which is written a confession that could alter religious history. If you think governments, whole nations, are disinterested bystanders, you are grossly mistaken."

Andrew fell silent. Adrian looked at him and then at Victor.

"How long do you figure it'll take? To find this . . . this vault?" he asked.

"I'd estimate a month. You'll need equipment, Alpine guides, a week of instruction—no more, I should think."

Adrian raised the Xeroxed pages several inches. "Can you estimate how large an area there is to cover?"

"It's difficult to say; much will depend on what you find, what has changed. But if my memory serves, no more than five to eight square miles."

"Five to eight! That's out of the question," said Andrew emphatically, but without raising his voice. "I'm sorry, but it's crazy. It could take years. You're talking about the Alps. One hole in the ground, a box no larger than a coffin, anywhere in a dozen mountains."

"The most logical recesses are limited; they are reduced to one of perhaps three or four passes, high above, I suspect, where we were never allowed to climb."

"I've mapped terrain in half a hundred field situations," said the soldier slowly, so courteously his words bordered on condescension. "You're minimizing an unbelievably difficult problem."

"I don't think so. I meant what I just said to Adrian. Much will depend on what you find. Your grandfather was nothing if not meticulous. He considered all aspects of a situation, and most eventualities." Victor stopped and shifted his position on the pillows. "Savarone was an old man; there was a war going on and no one knew it better than he did. He would leave nothing that was recognizable to anyone in Campo di Fiori, but I can't believe he would not leave *something* within the area itself. A sign, a message—something. He was like that."

"Where would we look?" asked Adrian, his eyes straying for an instant to his brother in the leather chair opposite him. The major was staring at the pages in his hand.

"I've written down the possibilities," said Victor. "There was a family of guides in the village of Champoluc. The Goldonis. They were used by my father, his father before him. And there was an inn north of the village. Run for generations by a family named Capomonti. We never traveled to the Champoluc without staying there. These were the people closest to Savarone. If he spoke to anyone, it would be to them."

"That's over fifty years ago," protested Adrian softly.

"Families in the mountains are closely knit. Two generations isn't a particularly wide gap. If Savarone left word it would be passed on from father to eldest child. Remember that: *child*. Son *or* daughter." He smiled weakly at them. "What else occurs to you? Questions may trigger further memories."

The questions began but they triggered nothing. Victor had traced and retraced all he could. Whatever else remained was beyond memory.

Until Jane caught something. And as he listened to her words, Victor smiled. His blue-eyed, English Jane was remarkable for details.

"You wrote that the tracks of the railroad wound through the mountains south of Zermatt and descended into Champoluc, past flagging stops. Clearings between stations for the convenience of climbers and skiers."

"Yes. Before the war. Nowadays, vehicles are more flexible in the snow."

"It seems logical that a train carrying a vault, described to you as heavy and awkward, would find it necessary to stop at one of those clearings. For it to be transferred to another vehicle."

"Agreed. What's your point?"

"Well, there are, or *were*, only so many stops between Zermatt and Champoluc. How many would you say?"

"Quite a few. At least nine or ten."

"That's not much help. I'm sorry."

"North of Champoluc, the first clearing was called Eagle's Peak, I believe. Then Crow's Lookout, and Condor's——" Victor stopped. *Birds*. The *names* of *birds*. A memory had been triggered, but it was not a memory that reached back three decades. It was barely days ago. In Campo di Fiori. "The painting," he said softly.

"What painting?" asked Adrian.

"Beneath the Madonna. In my father's study. A hunting scene, with *birds*."

"And each clearing on the tracks," said Andrew swiftly, sitting forward in the chair, "is—or was—described in part with the name of a bird. What were the birds in the painting?"

"I don't remember. The light was dim and I was trying to find a few moments to think. I didn't concentrate on that painting."

"Was it your father's?" asked Adrian.

"I'm not sure."

"Can you call?" said the major, his question less a request than an order.

"No. Campo di Fiori is a tomb without lines of communication. Only a postal box in Milan, and that under the name of Baricours, Père et Fils."

"Mother told us an old priest lives there. How does he exist?" The soldier was not satisfied.

"I never thought to ask," replied the father. "There was a man, a driver who picked me up in Milan. I assumed he was the monk's contact with the outside. The old priest and I talked most of the night, but my concerns were limited. He was still my enemy. He understood that."

Andrew looked over at his brother. "We stop at Campo di Fiori," said the soldier curtly.

Adrian nodded and turned back to Victor. "There's no way I can convince you to turn this over to the others? To responsible scholars?"

"No," answered Victor simply. "The scholars will come later. Before then, nothing. Bear in mind what you're dealing with. The contents of that vault are as staggering to the civilized world as anything in history. The confession on that parchment is a devastating weapon, make no mistake about it. No *committee* can be asked to assume the responsibility at this stage. The dangers are too great."

"I see," said Adrian, sitting back in his chair, looking at the pages. "You mention the name Annaxas, but you're not clear about it. You say the 'father of Annaxas was the engineer on the train,' killed by the priest of Xenope? Who is Annaxas?"

"In the event those papers fell into hands other than yours, I wanted no connections made. Annaxas is Theodore Dakakos."

There was a snap. The soldier was holding a wooden pencil in his hand. He had broken it in half. Father and brother looked at him. Andrew said one word.

"Sorry."

"I've heard the name," continued Adrian. "I'm not sure where."

"He's Greek. A very successful shipper. The priest on that train was his father's brother, his uncle. Brother killed brother. It was ordered by Xenope, the location of the vault buried with them."

"Dakakos knows this?" asked the soldier quietly.

"Yes. Where he precisely fits in, I don't know. I know only that he's looking for answers. And for the vault."

"Can you trust him?" asked the lawyer.

"No. I trust no one where Salonika is concerned." Victor inhaled deeply. It was difficult to talk now; his breath was shorter, his strength going.

"Are you all right?" Jane crossed quickly in front of Adrian to her husband. She leaned over and placed her hand on his cheek.

"Yes," he answered, smiling up at her. And then he looked at Andrew and Adrian, holding each with his eyes.

"I don't ask what I ask of you lightly. You have your own lives, your interests are your own. You have money." Victor raised a hand quickly. "I hasten to add that this, too, was your right. I was given no less, nor should you be. In this respect we are a privileged family. But this privilege extracts responsibilities from those who enjoy it. There must inevitably come periods when you're asked to suspend your own pursuits for an unexpected urgency. I submit to you that such an urgency now exists.

"You're separated. Opponents, I suspect, philosophically and politically. There's nothing wrong with that, but these differences are insignificant compared to what faces you now. You're brothers, the grandsons of Savarone Fontini-Cristi, and you must now do what *his* son can't do. There's no appeal from privilege. Don't look for it."

He was finished. It was all he could say; each breath was painful.

"All these years, you never said——" Adrian's eyes were questioning once again; there was awe and sadness in them. "My God, how you must have felt."

"I had two choices," replied Victor, barely audible. "To be productive or die a neuter. It was not a difficult choice."

"You should have killed them," said the soldier quietly.

They stood outside in the drive in front of the North Shore house. Andrew leaned against the hood of his rented Lincoln Continental, his arms folded across his pressed uniform, the afternoon sun bouncing off the brass buttons and the insignia.

"He's going," he said.

"I know," answered Adrian. "He knows it, too."

"And here we are."

"Here we are," agreed the lawyer.

"What he wants is easier for me than it is for you." Andrew looked up at the windows of the front bedroom on the second floor.

"What does that mean?"

"I'm practical. You're not. We'll do better working together than apart."

"I'm surprised you concede I might help. It must hurt your vanity."

"There's no ego in field decisions. It's the objective that counts." Andrew spoke casually. "We can cut the time in half if we divide the possibilities. His recollections are disjointed, he wanders all over the place. His terrain-recall is confused; I've had some experience in that." Andrew straightened up, away from the car. "I think we'll have to go back, Adrian. Seven years ago. Before San Francisco. Can you do that?"

Adrian stared at his brother. "You're the only one who can answer that. And please don't lie; you were never any good at lying. Not with me."

"Nor you with me."

Their eyes locked; neither wavered.

"A man was killed Wednesday night. In Washington."

"I was in Saigon. You know that. Who was he?"

"A black lawyer from Justice. A man named——"

"Nevins," completed Andrew, interrupting his brother.

"My God! You *knew!*"

"*About* him, yes. About his being *killed*, no. Why would I?"

"Eye Corps! He took a deposition on Eye Corps! It was with him! It was taken from his car!"

"Are you out of your goddamned mind?" The soldier spoke slowly, without urgency. "You may not like us, but we're not stupid. A target like that man, even remotely linked to us, would bring on the I.G. investigators by the hundreds. There are better ways. Killing's an instrument; you don't use it against yourself."

Adrian continued to look at his brother, searching his eyes. Finally, he spoke. Softly, barely above a whisper. "I think that's the most cold-blooded thing I've ever heard."

"What is?"

"'Killing's an instrument.' You mean it, don't you?"

"Of course I do. It's the truth. Have I answered your question?"

"Yes," said Adrian quietly. "We'll go back . . . before San Francisco. For a while; you have to know that. Only until this is over."

"Good. . . . You've got things to straighten up before we leave, and so do I. Let's say a week from tomorrow."

"All right. A week from tomorrow."

"I'm catching the six o'clock plane to Washington. Want to come along?"

"No, I'm meeting someone in town. I'll use one of the cars here."

"It's funny," said Andrew, shaking his head slowly, as if what he was about to say wasn't funny at all. "I've never asked for your telephone number, or where you lived."

"It's the District Towers. On Nebraska."

"The District Towers. All right. A week from tomorrow. I'll make the plane reservations. Straight through to Milan. Is your passport current?"

"I think so. It's at the hotel. I'll check."

"Good. I'll call you. A week from tomorrow." Andrew reached for the door handle. "Incidentally, what happened to that subpoena?"

"You know what happened. It wasn't served."

The soldier smiled as he climbed into the car. "It wouldn't have worked anyway."

They sat at a corner table in the St Moritz sidewalk café on Central Park South. They were partial to such places; they would select pedestrians and invent instant biographies.

They invented none now. Instead, Adrian decided that his father's instructions to tell no one about the train from Salonika would not include Barbara. His decision was based on his belief that were their roles reversed, she would tell him. He wasn't going to leave the country for five to ten weeks without saying why. She deserved better than that.

"So there it is. Religious documents that go back fifteen hundred years, an Aramaic scroll that made the British government go half out of its collective mind in the middle of the war, and a confession written on a parchment two *thousand* years ago that contains God only knows what. That vault's caused more violence than I want to think about. If what my father says is true, those documents, that scroll—the parchment, most of all—could alter a large part of history."

Barbara leaned back in the chair, her brown eyes leveled at him. She watched him without replying for several moments. "That seems highly unlikely. Documents are unearthed every day. History doesn't change," she said simply.

"Have you ever heard of something called the Filioque Clause?"

"Certainly. It was incorporated in the Nicene Creed. It was the first issue that separated the Western and Eastern church. The debate went on for hundreds of years, and led to the Photian schism in . . . the ninth century. I think. Which in turn brought about the schism of 1054. The issue ultimately became papal infallibility."

"How the hell do you know that?"

Barbara laughed. "It's my field. Remember? At least the behavioral aspects."

"You said the ninth century. My father said fifteen hundred years——"

"Early Christian history is confusing, date-happy. From the first to the seventh centuries there were so many councils, so much seesawing back and forth, so much debate over *this* doctrine and *that* law, it's nearly impossible to sort out. Do these documents concern the Filioque? Are they supposed to be the denials?"

Adrian's glass was suspended on the way to his lips. "Yes. That's what my father said; he used the term. The Filioque denials."

"They don't exist."

"What?"

"They were destroyed—ceremonially, I believe—in Istanbul, in the

Mosque of Saint Sophia early in the Second World War. There's documentation . . . witnesses, if I remember correctly. Even charred fragments
confirmed by spectrochemical analyses."

Adrian stared at her. Something was terribly wrong. It was all too simple.
Too negatively simple. "Where did you get that information?"

"Where? You mean *specifically* where?"

"Yes."

Barbara leaned forward, moving her glass absently in thought. Her
forehead was creased. "It's not my area, but I can find out, of course. It goes
back several years. I *do* remember that it was quite a shock to a lot of people."

"Do me a favor," he said rapidly. "When you get back, find out everything
you can about that fire. It doesn't make sense! My father would know about
it."

"I don't know why. It's awfully academic stuff."

"It still doesn't make sense——"

"Speaking of Boston," she interrupted. "My answering service had two
calls from someone trying to locate you. A man named Dakakos."

"*Dakakos?*"

"Yes. A Theodore Dakakos. He said it was urgent."

"What did you say?"

"That I'd give you the message. I wrote down the number. I didn't *want* to
give it to you. You don't need hysterical phone calls from Washington.
You've had a horrid few days."

"He's not from Washington."

"The phone calls were."

Adrian looked up from the table, past the miniature hedges in the boxes
bordering the café. He saw what he was looking for: a telephone booth.

"I'll be right back."

He walked to the phone and called the District Towers in Washington.

"Front desk, please."

"Yes, Mr. Fontine. We've had several calls from a Mr. Dakakos. There's
an aide to Mr. Dakakos in the lobby now waiting for you."

Adrian thought quickly. His father's words came back to him; he had
asked his father if he could trust Dakakos. *Where Salonika is concerned, I trust
no one. . . .*

"Listen to me. Tell the man in the lobby you just heard from me. I won't
be back for several days. I don't want to see this Dakakos."

"Of course, Mr. Fontine."

Adrian hung up. His passport was in Washington. In the room. He'd go by
way of the garage. But not tonight; that was too soon. He'd wait until
tomorrow. He'd stay in New York tonight. . . . His father. His father should
be told about Dakakos. He called the North Shore house.

Jane's voice was strained. "The doctor's with him now. Thank God he
allowed them to give him something. I don't think he could have stood it
much longer. He's had spasms——"

"I'll phone you tonight."

Adrian walked out of the booth and threaded his way between the strollers
back into the café, to the table.

"What *is* it?" Barbara was alarmed.

"Get in touch with your service in Boston. Tell them to call Dakakos and
say we missed each other. I had to fly to—hell, Chicago. On business. That
was the message for you at the hotel here."

"You really don't want to see him, do you?"

"I've got to avoid him. I want to throw him off the track. He's probably tried to reach my brother."

The path in Rock Creek Park. It was Martin Greene's idea, his selection. Greene had sounded strange on the telephone, somehow defiant. As though he didn't care about anything anymore.

Whatever was gnawing at Greene would vanish in the time it took to tell him the story. My God, would it! In one afternoon, Eye Corps had taken a giant step! Beyond anything they could have imagined. If the things his father said about that vault—the lengths powerful men, entire *governments* went to possess it—if it was all only half true, Eye Corps was in the catbird seat! Unreachable!

His father said he was going to prepare a list. Well, his father didn't have to; there *was* a list. The seven men of Eye Corps would control that vault. And he would control the seven men of Eye Corps.

Christ, it was incredible! But events did not lie; his father did not lie. Whoever possessed those documents, that parchment from a forgotten Roman prison, had the leverage to make extraordinary demands. Everywhere! An omission of recorded history, kept from the world out of unbelievable fear. Its revelation could not be tolerated. Well, fear, too, was an instrument. As great a one as death. Often greater.

Bear in mind that the contents of that vault are as staggering to the civilized world as anything in history. . . .

The decisions of extraordinary men—in peace and in war—supported his father's judgment. And now other extraordinary men, led by one extraordinary man, would find that vault and help shape the last quarter of the twentieth century. One had to begin to think like that, think in large blocks, concepts beyond ordinary men. His training, his heritage: All was coming into focus, and he was ready for the weight of enormous responsibility. He was primed for it; it was his with a vault buried in the Italian Alps.

Adrian would have to be immobilized. Not seriously; his brother was weak, indecisive, no contender at all. It would be enough to slow him down. He would visit his brother's rooms and do just that.

Andrew started down the Rock Creek path. There were very few strollers; the park was not a place for walking at night. Where *was* Greene? He should have been there; his apartment was a lot closer than the airport. And Greene had told him to hurry.

Andrew walked out on the grass and lighted a cigarette. There was no point standing under the spill of the park lamps. He'd see Greene when he came down the path.

"Fontine!"

The soldier turned around, startled. Twenty yards away at the side of a tree trunk stood Martin Greene. He was in civilian clothes; there was a large briefcase in his left hand.

"Marty? What the hell——"

"Get over here," ordered the captain tersely.

Andrew walked rapidly into the cluster of trees. "What's going on?"

"It's gone, Fontine. The whole goddamned thing. I've been calling you since yesterday morning."

"I was in New York. What are you talking about?"

"Five men are in a maximum security jail in Saigon. Want to take a guess who?"

"*What?* The subpoena wasn't served! You confirmed it, *I* confirmed it!"

"Nobody needed a subpoena. The I.G. crawled out of the rocks. They hit us on all points. My guess is that I've got about twelve hours before they figure I'm the one in procurement. You, you're marked."

"Wait a minute. Just wait a minute! This is crazy! The subpoena was canceled!"

"I'm the only one who benefits from that. You never mentioned my name in Saigon, did you?"

"Of course not. Just that we've got a man here."

"That's all they'll need; they'll put it together."

"How?"

"A dozen different ways. Locking in and comparing my checkout times with yours is the first that comes to mind. Something happened over there; something blew everything apart." Greene's eyes strayed.

Andrew breathed steadily, staring down at the captain. "No, it didn't," he said softly. "It happened over here. Last Wednesday night."

Greene's head snapped up. "What *about* Wednesday night?"

"That Black lawyer. Nevins. You had him killed, you stupid son of a bitch. My brother accused me! Accused *us!* He believed me because I believed it myself! It was too stupid!" The soldier's voice was a strained whisper. It was all he could do to keep from lashing out at the man staring up at him.

Greene replied calmly, with assurance. "You're getting the right total but the wrong numbers. I had it done, that's true, and I've got that bastard's briefcase, including the deposition against us. But the contract was so remote the people who did it don't know I exist. To bring you up to date, they were caught this morning. In West Virginia. They've got laundered money that can be traced to a company up for fraud. And we're not it. . . . No, Fontine, it wasn't me. Whatever it was, happened over there. I think you blew it."

Andrew shook his head. "Impossible. I handled——"

"Please. No burdens. I don't want to know, because I don't give a damn anymore. I've got a suitcase at Dulles and a one-way ticket to Tel Aviv. But I'm going to do you one last favor. When everything hit, I called a few friends at I.G., they owed me. That deposition from Barstow we worried so much about wasn't even in the prize money."

"What do you mean?"

"Remember the routine congressional inquiry? The Greek you never heard of——?"

"*Dakakos?*"

"That's right. Theodore Dakakos. Over at I.G. they call it the Dakakos probe. It was him. Nobody knows how, but that Greek was the one who got everything there was to get on Eye Corps. He funneled it piece by piece into the I.G. files."

Theodore Dakakos, thought Andrew. Theodore Annaxas Dakakos, son of a Greek trainman slain thirty years ago in the Milan freight yards by a priest who was his brother. Extraordinary men went to extraordinary lengths to control the vaults of Constantine. A calm swept over the soldier.

"Thanks for telling me," he said. Greene held up the briefcase. "By the way, I made a trip to Baltimore."

"The Baltimore records are among the best," said Fontine.

"Where I'm going, we may need some quick firepower in the Negev.

These could get it."

"Very possibly."

Greene hesitated, and then asked quietly, "You want to come along? We can hide you. You could do worse."

"I can do better."

"Stop kidding yourself, Fontine! Use some of your well-advertised money and get out of here as fast as you can. Buy sanctuary. You're *finished*."

"You're wrong. I've just begun."

Chapter Twenty-five

Washington's noonday traffic was slowed further by the June thunderstorm. It was one of the deluges without spells of relief that allowed pedestrians to dash from doorway to awning to doorway. Windshield wipers did little but intrude on the sheets of water that blanketed the glass, distorting all vision.

Adrian sat in the back seat of a taxi, his thoughts divided equally in three parts, on three people. Barbara, Dakakos, and his brother.

Barbara was in Boston, probably in the library archives by now, researching the information—the extraordinary information—about the destructions of the Filioque denials. If those ancient documents had been in the vault from Constantine, and proof of their destruction established beyond doubt . . . had the vault been found? A equals B equals C. Therefore A equals C. Or did it?

Theodore Dakakos, the indefatigable Annaxas, would be scouring the Chicago hotels and law firms looking for him. There was no reason for the Greek not to; a business trip to Chicago was perfectly normal. The distraction was all Adrian needed. He would go up to his rooms, grab his passport, and call Andrew. They could both get out of Washington, avoiding Dakakos. The assumption had to be that Dakakos was trying to stop them. Which meant that somehow Dakakos-Annaxas knew what their father had planned. It was easy enough. An old man returns from Italy, his life expectancy short. And he summons his two sons.

One of those sons was Adrian's third concern. Where was his brother? He had telephoned Andrew's apartment in Virginia repeatedly throughout the night. What bothered Adrian, and the admission wasn't easy for him, was that his brother was more equipped to deal with someone like Dakakos than he. Move and countermove was part of his life, not thesis and antithesis.

"Garage entrance," said the cab driver. "Here it is."

Adrian dashed through the rain into the District Towers's garage. He had to orient himself before walking toward the elevator. As he did so, he reached into his pocket for the key with the plastic tag; he never left it at the front desk.

"Hi, Mr. Fontine. How are ya?"

It was the garage attendant; Adrian vaguely remembered the face. A sallow, twenty-year-old hustler with the eyes of a ferret.

"Hello," replied Adrian, pushing the elevator button.

"Hey, thanks again. I appreciated it, ya know what I mean? I mean it was real nice of you."

"Sure," Adrian said blankly, wishing the elevator would arrive.

"Hey." The attendant winked at him. "You look a lot better'n you did last night. A real broiler, huh?"

"What?"

The attendant smiled. No, it wasn't a smile, it was a leer. "I tied one on, too. Real good. Just like you said."

"What did you say? You saw me last night?"

"Hey, come on. Ya don't remember even? I gotta admit, you was fried, man."

Andrew! Andrew could do it when he wanted to! Slouch, wear a hat, draw out his words. He'd pulled that caricature dozens of times.

"Tell me, I'm a little hazy. What time did I get in?"

"Jee-*sus!* You was flat out. Around eight o'clock, don't you remember? You gimme——" The attendant stopped; the hustler in him prevented full disclosure.

The elevator doors opened. Adrian walked inside. So Andrew had come to see him while he was trying to call *him* in Virginia. Had Andy found out about Dakakos? Had he already left town? Maybe Andy was upstairs now. Again the realization was disquieting, but Adrian felt a certain relief at the prospect. His brother would know what to do.

Adrian walked down the corridor to the door of his suite and let himself in. As he did so, he heard the footsteps behind him. He whipped around and saw an army officer standing in the bedroom door; not Andrew, a colonel.

"Who the hell are you?"

The officer did not immediately reply. Instead, he stood immobile, his eyes angry. When he did speak there was a slight drawl in his cold voice.

"Yeah, you do look like him. Put on a uniform and straighten you up and you could *be* him. Now, all you have to do is tell me where he is."

"How did you get in here? Who the hell let you in?"

"No question for a question. Mine comes first."

"What comes first is that you're trespassing." Adrian walked rapidly to the telephone, crossing in front of the officer. "Unless you've got a warrant from a civilian court, you're going to march into a civilian police station."

The colonel undid one button on his tunic, reached inside, and took out a pistol. He snapped the safety catch and leveled the weapon.

Adrian held the telephone in his left hand, his right poised above the dial. Stunned, he stopped all movement; the expression on the officer's face had not changed.

"You listen to me," said the colonel softly. "I could shoot both your kneecaps off just for looking like him. Can you understand that? I'm a civilized man, a lawyer like you; but where Eye Corps' Major Fontine is concerned, all the rules go out the window. I'll do anything to get that son of a bitch. Do you read me?"

Adrian slowly put down the telephone. "You're a maniac."

"Minor compared to him. Now, you tell me where he is."

"I don't know."

"I don't believe you."

"Wait a minute!" In his shock, Adrian had not been sure of what he'd heard. Now he was. "What do you know about *Eye Corps?*"

"A lot more than you paranoid bastards want me to know. Did you two really think you could pull it off?"

"You're way off base! You'd know that if you knew anything about me!

About Eye Corps we're on the same side! Now, for God's sake, what have you got on him?"

The officer replied slowly. "He killed two men. A captain named Barstow, and a legal officer named Tarkington. Both killings were made to look *kai-sai*—whore-and-booze oriented. They weren't. In Tarkington's case it was inconsistent. He didn't drink."

"Oh, Christ!"

"And a file was taken from Tarkington's Saigon office. Which *was* inconsistent. What they didn't know was that we had a complete copy."

"Who's 'we'?"

"The Inspector General's Office." The colonel did not lower his pistol; his answers were delivered in a flat Southwestern drawl. "Now, I just gave you the benefit of a doubt. You know why I want him, so tell me where he is. My name's Tarkington, too. I drink and I'm not mild-mannered and I want the son of a bitch who killed my brother."

Adrian felt the breath leave his lungs. "I'm sorry——"

"Now you know why this gun is out and why I'll use it. Where did he go? How did he go?"

It took Adrian a moment to focus. "Where? How? I didn't know he *was* gone. Why are you sure he is?"

"Because he knows we're after him. We know he got the word; we made the connection this morning. A captain named Greene in the Pentagon. In procurement. Needless to say, he's gone, too. Probably halfway across the world by now."

. . . *halfway across the world* . . . the words penetrated, the realization began to surface. *Halfway across the world. To Italy. Campo di Fiori. A painting on the wall and the memories of a half a century ago. The vault from Constantine!*

"Did you check the airports?"

"He has a standard military passport. All military. . . ."

"Oh, Jesus!" Adrian started for the bedroom.

"Hold it!" The colonel grabbed his arm.

"Let me go!" Fontine shook off the officer's hand and raced into the bedroom. To the bureau.

He pulled open the right-hand top drawer. From behind the colonel's hand shot out and slammed it, trapping his wrist.

"You pull out anything I don't like, you're dead." The colonel released the drawer.

Fontine could feel the pain and see the swelling on his wrist. He could not think about either. He opened a large leather case. His passport was gone. So, too, his international driver's license and his Banque Genève checkbook with the coded numbers and photograph on the flap.

Adrian turned and walked across the room in silence. He dropped the leather pouch on the bed and continued to the window. The rain outside came down in torrents against the glass.

His brother had stalled him. Andrew had gone after the vault, leaving him behind, wanting no assistance at all, never having wanted it. The vault from Constantine was Andrew's final weapon. In his hands a deadly thing.

The irony was, reflected Adrian, that the army officer behind him in that room could *help*. He could break down bureaucratic barriers, provide instant transportation;—but the army officer could be told nothing about the train from Salonika.

There are those who would trade off half the arsenals in this world for the information. His father's words.

He spoke quietly. "There's your proof, colonel."

"I guess so."

Adrian turned and faced the officer. "Tell me, as one brother to another—how did you lock in on Eye Corps?"

The colonel put away the gun. "A man named Dakakos."

"Dakakos?"

"Yes, he's Greek. You know him?"

"No, I don't."

"The data came in slowly at first. Right into my department, marked for me by name. When Barstow broke and gave his deposition in Saigon, there was Dakakos again. He sent word to my brother to get to Barstow. Eye Corps was covered both over here and over there——"

By two brothers who could pick up a phone and keep it all together," said Adrian, interrupting. "Without bureaucratic interference."

"We figured that. We don't know why, but this Dakakos was after Eye Corps."

"He certainly was," agreed Adrian, marveling at Dakakos's clarity of method.

"Yesterday, *everything* came in. Dakakos had Fontine followed to Phan-thiet. To a warehouse. We've got Eye Corps' records now, we've got the proof——"

The telephone rang, interrupting the army man. Adrian barely heard it, so total was his concentration on the colonel's words.

It rang again.

"May I?" asked Adrian.

"You'd better." Tarkington's eyes became cold again. "I'll be right next to you."

It was Barbara, calling from Boston. "I'm in the archives. I've got the information on that church fire in forty-one that destroyed the Filioque——"

"Just a minute." Adrian turned his head toward the officer, the phone between them. He wondered if he could sound natural. "You can get on a line in the other room, if you like. It's just some research I asked for."

The ruse worked. Tarkington shrugged and walked to the window.

"Go ahead," he said into the phone.

Barbara spoke as an expert does, scanning a report whose form is familiar; her voice rose and fell as salient points were enumerated. "There was a gathering of elders on January 9, 1941, at eleven o'clock in the evening at the Mosque of Saint Sophia, Istanbul, a ceremony of deliverance. According to the witnesses a consigning of holy property to the heavens . . . sloppy work here; it's all narrative. There should be direct quotes and literal translation. Anyway, it goes on to verify the act and list the laboratories in Istanbul and Athens where fragments of the ash were confirmed for age and materials. There you are, my doubting Thomas."

"What about those witnesses? The narrative?"

"I'm being overly critical. I could be more so; the report should include authorizing credentials and graphic plate numbers, but that's all academic lacework. The main thing is, it's got the archival seal; you don't buy that. You can't play games with it. It means someone beyond reproach was at the scene and confirmed the burning. The Annaxas grant got what it paid for. The seal says it."

"What grant?" he asked quietly.

"Annaxas. It's the company that put up the money for the research."

"Thanks. I'll talk to you later." He hung up. Tarkington was standing by the window, looking out at the rain. This was the man he had to get away from; he had to get to the vault!

Barbara was right in one respect. Dakakos-Annaxas got *exactly* what he paid for: a false report in the archives.

He knew where he had to go.

Campo di Fiori.

Dakakos.

Dakakos, Dakakos, *Dakakos!*

The name burned into Andrew's brain as he watched the coast of Italy go by 30,000 feet below. Theodore Annaxas Dakakos had destroyed Eye Corps for the sole purpose of destroying *him*, eliminating *him* from the search for a vault buried in the mountains. What triggered his decision? How did he do it? It was vital to learn all he could about the man himself. The better one knew his enemy, the better he could fight. As things stood, Dakakos was the only barrier, the only contender.

There was a man in Rome who could help. He was a banker who showed up with increasing frequency in Saigon, a large-scale buyer who bought whole piers, shipped the contents back to Naples and sold the stolen goods throughout Italy. Eye Corps had nailed him and used him; he had provided names that went right back to Washington.

Such a man would know about Dakakos.

The announcement came over the Air Canada loudspeaker. They would begin their descent into Rome's Leonardo da Vinci Airport in fifteen minutes.

Fontine took out his passport. He had bought it in Quebec. Adrian's passport had gotten him through Canadian customs, but he knew it would be worthless after that. Washington would flash the name Fontine to every airport in the hemisphere.

Ironically, he made a connection with several army deserters at two in the morning in Montreal. The exiled moralists needed money; morality could not be proselytized without hard cash. A stringy-haired intellectual in a GI field jacket took him to an apartment that reeked of hash, and for $10,000 he got a passport within an hour.

Adrian was so far behind he'd never catch up.

. . . He could dismiss Adrian. If Dakakos wanted to stop one of them, he obviously wanted to stop both. The Greek was no match for the soldier; he was more than a match for the lawyer. And if Dakakos didn't stop Adrian, the lack of a passport would slow him down more than enough. His brother was out of the picture, no contender at all.

The plane touched ground. Andrew unbuckled his seat belt; he would be among the first out of the aircraft. He was in a hurry to get to a telephone.

The evening crowds on the Via Veneto were heavy, the sidewalk tables under the awnings of the Café de Paris nearly filled. The banker had secured one near the service door, where the traffic was concentrated. He was a gaunt, middle-aged, impeccably dressed man, and he was cautious. No listener could overhear anything said at that table.

Their greeting was perfunctory, the banker obviously anxious to have the meeting over with as quickly as possible.

"I won't ask why you're in Rome. No address, out of your celebrated uniform." The Italian spoke rapidly in a monotone that gave no emphasis to any word and thus emphasis to all. "I honored your demand to make no inquiries. It wasn't necessary. You're a hunted man."

"How do you know that?"

The slender Italian paused, his thin lips stretched into a slight smile. "You just told me."

"I warn you——"

"Oh, stop it. A man flies in unannounced, says he'll meet only in crowds. It's enough to send me to Malta so I won't run into you. Besides, it's all over your face. You're uncomfortable."

The banker was essentially right. He *was* uncomfortable. He would have to adjust better, be more relaxed. "You're clever, but then we knew that in Saigon."

"I never saw you before in my life," replied the Italian, signaling a waiter. "*Due* Campari, *per favore*."

"I don't drink Campari. . . ."

"Then don't. Two Italians who order Campari on the Via Veneto are not conspicuous. Which is precisely what I intend to be. What did you wish to discuss?"

"A man named Dakakos. A Greek."

The banker raised his eyebrows. "If by Dakakos you mean Theo Dakakos, he is indeed Greek."

"You know him?"

"Who in the world of finance doesn't? You have business with Dakakos?"

"Maybe. He's a shipper, isn't he?"

"Among many other interests. He's also quite young and very powerful. Even the colonels in Athens think twice before issuing edicts unfavourable to him. His older competitors are wary of him. What he lacks in experience he makes up for in energy. He's a bull."

"What are his politics?"

The Italian's eyebrows once more rose. "Himself."

"What are his interests in Southeast Asia? Whom does he work for out of Saigon?"

"He doesn't work *for* anyone." The waiter returned with the drinks. "He ships middle-manned supplies to the A.I.D. in Vientiane. Into northern Laos and Cambodia. As you know, it's all intelligence-operated. He pulled out, I understand."

That was it, thought Fontine, pushing away the glass of Campari. Eye Corps had tagged the corruption in AID, and Dakakos had tagged *them*. "He went to a lot of trouble to interfere."

"Did he succeed in interfering? . . . I see he did. Annaxas the Younger usually does succeed; he's perverse and predictable in that department." The Italian raised his glass delicately.

"What was that name?"

"Annaxas. Annaxas the Younger, son of Annaxas the Strong. Sounds Theban, does it not? The Greek bloodlines, however insignificant, are always on the tips of their tongues. Pretentious, I think."

"Does he use it a lot?"

"Not often for himself. His yacht is named *Annaxas*, several planes are *Annaxas—One, Two, Three*. He works the name into a few corporate titles.

It's an obsession with him. Theodore Annaxas Dakakos. The first son of a poor family raised by some religious order in the north. The circumstances are cloudy; he doesn't encourage curiosity." The Italian drained his glass.

"That's interesting."

"Have I told you something you didn't know?"

"Maybe," said Fontine casually. "It's not important."

"By which you mean it is." The Italian smiled his thin, bloodless smile. "Dakakos is in Italy, you know."

Fontine concealed his surprise. "Is he really?"

"So you *do* have business with him. Is there anything else?"

"No."

The banker rose and walked rapidly into the crowds of the Via Veneto.

Andrew remained at the table. So Dakakos was in Italy. Andrew wondered where they would meet. He wanted that meeting very much; almost as much as he wanted to find the vault from Salonika.

He wanted to kill Theodore Annaxas Dakakos. The man who had destroyed Eye Corps did not deserve to live.

Andrew got up from the table. He could feel the bulge of papers in his jacket pocket. His father's recollections of half a century ago.

Chapter Twenty-six

Adrian shifted the soft leather suitcase into his left hand and fell behind the surge of passengers in the wide corridor of London's Heathrow Airport. He did not wish to be among the first in the passport line. He wanted to be in the middle group, even the last section; he would have more time to look around, be less conspicuous doing so. He wondered who among the scores of people in the terminal had him in their sights.

Colonel Tarkington was no fool; he'd know within minutes of the application that one Adrian Fontine was at the emigration offices in Rockefeller Center waiting for the issuance of a substitute passport. It was entirely possible that an IG agent had picked him up before he'd left the building. If no one had, he knew it was only a question of time. And because of that certainty, Adrian had flown to London, not Rome.

Tomorrow he would begin the chase, an amateur against professionals. His first step was to disappear, but he wasn't sure how. On the one hand it seemed simple: a single human being among millions; how difficult could it be? Then came second thoughts: one had to travel across national borders—that meant clearly one had to have identification; one had to sleep and eat—that meant shelter and purchases, places that could be watched, alerted.

It wasn't simple at all; not if the single human being in question had no experience. He had no contacts in the underworld; he wouldn't know how to behave if he met them. He doubted that he could approach someone and say the words *"I'll pay for a false passport,"* . . . or *"Get me to Italy illegally,"* . . . or even *"I won't tell you my name but I'll give money for certain services."* Such boldness belonged in fiction. Normal men and women did not do such things; their awkwardness would be laughed at. But professionals—the sort he was up against—were not normal. They did such things quite easily.

He saw the passport lines. There were six in all; he chose the longest. Yet as he walked over to it, he realized that the decision was amateurish. True, he had more time to look around, but conversely, so did others.

"Occupation, sir?" asked the immigration officer.

"I'm a lawyer."

"Here on business?"

"In a manner of speaking. Also pleasure."

"Anticipated length of stay?"

"I'm not sure. No more than a week."

"Do you have hotel accommodations?"

"I didn't make reservations. Probably the Savoy."

The official glanced up; it was difficult to tell whether he was impressed or whether he resented Adrian's tone. Or whether the name Fontine, A. was on a concealed list somewhere in the drawer of his lectern, and he wanted to look at the face.

Regardless, he smiled mechanically, stamped the pages of the newly issued passport, and handed it to Adrian. "Have a pleasant stay in Great Britain, Mr. Fontine."

"Thank you."

The Savoy found him a room above the court, offering to switch him to a suite on the Thames side as soon as one became available. He accepted the offer, saying he expected to remain in England for the better part of the month. He would be traveling around—away from London for much of the time—but would like a suite available during the period of his stay.

What astonished him was the ease with which he lied. It all flowed casually, with a certain businesslike assurance. It wasn't an important maneuver, but the fact that he was able to do it so well gave him a sense of confidence. He had seized an advantage when it was presented; that was the important thing. He had spotted an opportunity and acted on it.

He sat on the bed, airline schedules scattered over the spread. He found what he wanted. An SAS flight from Paris to Stockholm at 10:30 A.M. And an Air Afrique from Paris to Rome. Time: 10:15 A.M. The SAS left from the de Gaulle field, the Air Afrique from Orly.

Fifteen minutes between flights, departure before arrival, from adjacent airfields. He wondered—almost academically now—if he was capable of conceiving a deception, organizing the facts and executing the manipulation from beginning to end.

Odd things would have to be considered. Items that were part of the . . . "dressing," that was the word. Part of the ruse that would draw the proper attention in a crowded, bustling airport. He picked up a Savoy note pad and wrote:

Three suitcases—unusual.
Overcoat—conspicuous.
Glasses.
Hat—wide-brimmed.
Small paste-on beard.

The last item—the beard—caused him to smile uncomfortably, embarrassed at his own imagination. Was he crazy? Who did he think he was? What did he think he was doing? He moved the pencil instinctively to the left of the line, prepared to cross it out. Then he stopped. He wasn't crazy. It was part of the boldness he had to absorb, the unnatural with which he had to be comfortable. He took the pencil away and without thinking wrote the name: "Andrew."

Where was he now? Had his brother reached Italy? Had he traveled halfway around the world without being found? Would he be waiting for him at Campo di Fiori?

And if he *was* waiting, what would they say to each other? He hadn't thought about that; he hadn't wanted to think about it. Like a difficult summation in front of a hostile jury, he could not rehearse the words. He could only marshal the facts in his head and trust his thought processes when the moment came. But what did one say to a twin who was the killer of Eye Corps? What was there *to* say?

. . . *Bear in mind, the contents of that vault are as staggering to the civilized world as anything in history.* . . .

His brother had to be stopped. It was as simple as that.

He looked at his watch. It was one in the morning. He was thankful that he had gotten little sleep during the past several days. It would make sleeping possible now. He had to rest; he had a great deal to do tomorrow. Paris.

He walked up to the desk clerk in the Hôtel Pont Royale and handed him the room key. He hadn't been to the Louvre in five years; it would be a cultural sin to avoid it since it was so close by. The clerk agreed politely, but Adrian saw the shaded curiosity in the man's eyes. It was further confirmation of what Adrian suspected: he was being followed; questions were being asked.

He walked into the bright sunlight on the rue de Bac. He nodded, smiling, at the doorman and shook his head in response to the offer of a taxi.

"I'm going to the Louvre. I'll walk, thanks."

At the curb he lit a cigarette, turning slightly as if to avoid a breeze, and let his eyes wander over to the large windows of the hotel. Inside, through the glass, obscured by the sun's reflection, he could see the clerk talking to a man in a light-brown topcoat. Adrian was not certain, but he was fairly sure he had seen that gabardine coat at the airport two hours ago.

He started east down the rue de Bac, toward the Seine and the Pont Royale bridge.

The Louvre was crowded. Tourists mingled with busloads of students. Adrian climbed the steps past Winged Victory and continued up the staircase to the right, to the second landing, and into the hall of nineteenth-century masters. He fell in with a group of German tourists.

The Germans moved in unison down to the next painting, a Delacroix. Adrian was now in the center of the group. Keeping his head below the level of the tallest German, he turned and looked between the sagging bodies, beyond the impassive faces. He saw what he was both afraid and wanted to see.

The light-brown topcoat.

The man was fifty feet away, pretending to read from a museum pamphlet, relating it to an Ingres in front of him. But he was neither reading nor relating; his eyes kept straying up from the paper to the crowd of Germans.

The group turned the corner into the intersecting corridor. Adrian was against the wall. He parted the bodies in front of him, excusing himself, until he was past the guide and free of the group. He walked swiftly down the right side of the enormous hall and turned left into a dimly lit room. Tiny spotlights shone down from the dark ceiling on a dozen marble statues.

It suddenly occurred to him that if the man in the light-brown gabardine topcoat came into that room, there was no way out.

On the other hand, if the man entered there was no way out for him, either. Adrian wondered which of them had more to lose. He had no answer and so he stood in the shadows at the farthest end of the room, beyond the shafts of light, and waited.

He could see the group of Germans go past the doorway. Seconds later there was the blur of the light-brown topcoat; the man was running, actually running.

Adrian went to the door, paused long enough to see the Germans swing left into yet another intersecting corridor, turned right and walked rapidly toward the hall to the stairs.

The crowds on the staircase were denser than before. There was a contingent of uniformed schoolgirls entering the steps. Behind the girls was the man in the light-brown gabardine topcoat, frustrated in his attempt to pass and reach the steps.

It was suddenly clear to Adrian. The man had lost him and would wait at the exit.

There remained the obvious: reach the main doors first.

Adrian hurried down the steps, doing his best to look unhurried; a man late for a lunch date.

Out on the steps in front of the entrance a taxi was disgorging four Japanese. An elderly couple, obviously British, was walking across the pavement toward the cab. He ran, overtaking the couple, and reached the taxi first.

"Dépêchez-vous s'il vous plaît. Très important."

The driver grinned and started up the car. Adrian turned in the seat and looked out the rear window. On the steps the man in the light-brown topcoat stood looking up and down, confused and angry.

"Orly Airport," ordered Adrian. "Air Afrique."

There were more crowds and more lines but the line he was in was short. And nowhere in sight was the light-brown topcoat. No one seemed interested in him at all.

The Black girl in the Air Afrique uniform smiled at him. "I'd like a ticket to Rome on your ten fifteen flight tomorrow morning. The name's Llewellyn. That's two *l*'s in front, two in back, with a *y*. First class, please, and if it's possible, I'd like seat location now. I'll be very rushed in the morning, but hold the reservation. I'll pay in cash."

He walked out the automatic doors of the Orly terminal and hailed another taxi.

"De Gaulle field, please. SAS."

The line was longer, the service slower, there was a man staring at him beyond a row of plastic chairs. There'd been no one looking at him like that in Orly terminal. He wondered; he hoped.

"Round trip to Stockholm," he said arrogantly to the SAS attendant behind the counter. "You have a flight tomorrow at ten thirty. That's the one I want."

The attendant looked up from his papers. "I'll see what we have, sir," he replied in muted irritation, his accent heavily Scandinavian. "What would be the return date?"

"I'm not sure, so leave it open. I'm not interested in bargains. The name's

Fontine."

Five minutes later the tickets were processed, the payment made.

"Please be here an hour prior to departure, sir," said the clerk, smarting under Adrian's impatience.

"Of course. Now, there's a small problem. I have some valuable, very fragile objects in my luggage. I'd like——"

"We cannot take responsibility for such things," interrupted the attendant.

"Don't be a damn fool. I know you can't. I just want to make sure you have 'Fragile' stickers in Swedish or Norwegian or whatever the hell it is. My bags are easily recognized——"

He left the de Gaulle terminal convinced he'd alienated a very nice fellow who would complain to his colleagues about him, and got into a taxi.

"The Hôtel Pont Royale, please. Rue de Bac."

Adrian saw him at a table in a small sidewalk café on the rue Dumont. He was an American, drinking white wine, and looked like a student who would nurse a drink because of the price. His age was no problem; he seemed tall enough. Adrian walked up to him.

"Hello!"

"Hi," replied the young man.

"May I sit down? Buy you a drink?"

"Hell, why not?"

Adrian sat. "You go to the Sorbonne?"

"Nope. L'École des Beaux Arts. I'm a bona-fide, real-life painter. I'll sketch you for thirty *francs*. How about it?"

"No, thanks. But I'll give you a lot more than that if you'll do something else for me."

The student eyed him suspiciously, distastefully. "I don't smuggle anything for anybody. You'd better beat it. I'm a very legal type."

"I'm more than that. I'm a lawyer. A prosecuting attorney, as a matter of fact. With a card to prove it."

"You don't sound it."

"Just hear me out. What can it cost? Five minutes and some decent wine?"

At nine fifteen in the morning, Adrian emerged from the limousine in front of the glass doors of SAS at de Gaulle terminal. He was dressed in a long, flared Edwardian overcoat of white fabric; he looked like an ass, but he couldn't be missed. On his head he wore a matching white, wide-brimmed fedora, the cloth pulled down over his face in Barrymore style, his features in shadow. Beneath the hat were huge dark glasses that covered far more than his eyes, and below his chin was a blue silk scarf, billowing above and out of the white coat.

The uniformed chauffeur scrambled around to the trunk of the limousine, opened it, and called for skycaps to serve his very important passenger. Three large, white leather suitcases were stacked on a hand rack, to Adrian's complaints that they were being scuffed.

He strode through the electronically parted doors and up to the SAS counter.

"I feel like hell!" he said scathingly, conveying the effects of a hangover, "and I would appreciate as little difficulty as possible. I want my luggage to be loaded last; please keep it behind the counter until the final baggage call. It's done for me all the time. The gentleman yesterday assured me there'd be no trouble."

The clerk behind the counter looked bewildered. Adrian slapped his ticket envelope down.

"Gate forty-two, sir," the clerk said, handing back the envelope. "Boarding time is at ten o'clock."

"I'll wait over there," replied Adrian, indicating the line of plastic chairs inside the SAS area. "I meant what I said about the luggage. Where's the men's room?"

At twenty minutes to ten, a tall, slender man in khaki trousers, cowboy boots, and an American army field jacket came through the doors of the terminal. On his face there was a pronounced chin beard; on his head a wide Australian bush hat. He entered the men's room.

At eighteen minutes to ten, Adrian got out of the plastic chair and walked across the crowded terminal. He pushed the door marked "Hommes" and entered.

Inside a toilet stall they awkwardly manipulated the exchange of clothes.

"This is weird, man. You swear there's nothing in that crazy coat?"

"It's not even old enough to have lint. . . . Here are the tickets, go to gate forty-two. You can throw away the baggage stubs, I don't care. Unless you want the suitcases; they're damned expensive. And clean."

"In Stockholm no one busts me. You guarantee."

"As long as you use your *own* passport and don't say you're me. I gave you my tickets, that's all. You've got my note to prove it. Take my word for it, nobody'll press you. You don't know where I am and there's no warrant. There's nothing."

"You're a nut. But you've paid my tuition for a couple of years, plus some nice living expenses. You're a good nut."

"Let's hope I'm good enough. Hold the mirror for me." Adrian pressed the beard on his chin; it adhered quickly. He studied the results and, satisfied, put on the bush hat, pulling it down on the side of his head. "Okay, let's go. You look fine."

At eleven minutes to ten, a man in a long white coat, matching white hat, blue scarf, and dark glasses strode past the SAS desk toward gate forty-two.

Thirty seconds later a bearded young man—obviously American—in a soiled field jacket, khaki trousers, cowboy boots, and bush hat slipped out the door of the men's room, turned sharply left into the crowds, and headed for the exit door. Out on the pavement he rushed to a waiting taxi, got in and removed the beard.

"The name's Llewellyn!" he shouted to the Air Afrique attendant at the lectern by the departure gate. "I'm sorry I'm late; did I make it?"

The pleasant-faced Black smiled and replied in a French accent. "Just barely, *monsieur*. We've given the last call. Do you have any hand luggage?"

"Not a thing."

At twenty-three minutes past ten, the ten fifteen Air Afrique flight to Rome taxied out toward runway seven. By ten twenty-eight it was airborne. It was only thirteen minutes late.

The man who called himself Llewellyn sat by the window, the bush hat on his left in the adjacent, empty first-class seat. He felt the hardening globules of facial cement on his chin, and he rubbed them in a kind of wonder.

He had done it. Disappeared.

The man in the light-brown topcoat boarded the SAS flight to Stockholm at ten twenty-nine. Departure was delayed. As he walked toward the economy section, he passed the fashionably dressed passenger in the long white overcoat and matching white hat. He thought to himself that the man he followed was a fucking idiot. Who did he think he was, wearing that outfit?

By ten fifty the flight to Stockholm was airborne. It was twenty minutes late, not unusual. The man in the economy section had removed his topcoat and was seated in the forward area of the cabin, diagonally behind the target of his surveillance. When the curtains were parted—as they were now—he could see the subject clearly.

Twelve minutes into the flight the pilot turned off the seat-belt sign. The fashionably dressed subject in the first-class section rose from his aisle seat and removed the long white overcoat and matching white hat.

The man diagonally behind in the economy section bolted forward in his seat, stunned.

"Oh, shit," he muttered.

Chapter Twenty-seven

Andrew peered through the windshield at the sign caught in the dull wash of the headlights. It was dawn but pockets of fog were everywhere.

MILANO 5 KM.

He had driven through the night, renting the fastest car he could find in Rome. The journey at night minimized the risk of being followed. Headlights were giveaways on long stretches of dark roads.

But he had not expected to be followed. In Rock Creek Park, Greene said he was marked. What the Jew did not know was that if IG wanted him that quickly, they could have picked him up at the airport. The Pentagon knew exactly where he was; a cable from the secretary of the army had brought him back from Saigon.

So the word to take him had not been given. That it would within days, perhaps hours, was not the issue; of course it would. But he was the son of Victor Fontine. The Pentagon would not be hasty issuing any formal orders for arrest. The army did not bring charges against a Rockefeller or a Kennedy or a Fontine lightly. The Pentagon would insist on flying back the Eye Corps officers for corroborating testimony. The Pentagon would leave nothing to chance or error.

Which meant he had the time to get out. For by the time the army was prepared to move, he would be in the mountains tracing a vault that would change the ground rules as they had never been changed before.

Andrew stepped on the accelerator. He needed sleep. A professional knew when the body hungered for rest in spite of the high-pitched moment, and the eyes became aware of their sockets. He would find a small boardinghouse or country inn and sleep for most of the day. Late in the afternoon he would drive north to Campo di Fiori and find a picture on the wall. The first clue in the search for a vault buried in the mountains.

He drove by the crumbling stone gates of the entrance without slowing down, and continued for several miles. He allowed two cars to pass him, observing the drivers; they were not interested in him. He turned around and went past the gates a second time. There was no way to tell what was inside; whether there were any security measures—trip alarms or dogs. All he could see was a winding paved road that disappeared into the woods.

The sound of an automobile on that road would be its own alarm. He could not chance that; he had no intention of announcing his arrival at Campo di Fiori. He slowed the car down, and turned into the bordering woods, driving as far off the road as possible.

Five minutes later he approached the gates. By habit he checked for wires and photoelectric cells; there were none, and he passed through the gates and walked down the road cut out of the woods.

He stayed at the edge, concealed by the trees and the overgrowth until he was in sight of the main house. It was as his father had described: more dead than alive.

The windows were dark, no lamps were on inside. There should have been. The house was in shadows. An old man living alone needed light; old men did not trust their eyes. Had the priest died?

Suddenly, out of nowhere, there came the sound of a voice, high-pitched and plaintive. Then footsteps. They came from the road beyond the north bend of the drive; the road he remembered his father describing as leading to the stables. Fontine dropped to the ground, below the level of the grass, and remained motionless. He raised his head by inches; he waited and watched.

The old priest came into view. He was wearing a long black cassock and carried a wicker basket. He spoke out loud, but Andrew could not see who he was talking to. Nor could he understand the words. Then the monk stopped and turned and spoke again.

There was a reply. It was rapid, authoritative, in a language Fontine did not immediately recognize. Then he saw the monk's companion and instantly appraised him as one might an adversary. The man was large, the shoulders wide and heavy, encased in a camel's hair jacket above well-tailored slacks. The last rays of the sun illuminated both men; not well—the light was at their backs—but enough to distinguish the faces.

Andrew concentrated on the younger, powerfully built man walking behind the priest. His face was large, the eyes wide apart, beneath light brows and a tanned forehead that set off short, sun-bleached hair. He was in his middle forties, certainly no more. And the walk: It was that of a deliberate man, capable of moving swiftly, but not anxious for observers to know it. Fontine had commanded such men.

The old monk proceeded toward the marble steps, shifting the small basket to his left arm, his right hand lifting the folds of his habit. He stopped on the top step and turned again to the younger man. His voice was calmer, resigned to the layman's presence or instructions or both. He spoke slowly and Fontine had no trouble now recognizing the language. It was Greek.

As he listened to the priest he reached another, equally obvious conclusion. The powerfully built man was Theodore Annaxas Dakakos. *He is a bull.*

The priest continued across the wide marble porch to the doors; Dakakos climbed the steps and followed. Both men went inside.

Fontine lay in the grass on the border of the drive for several minutes. He had to think. What brought Dakakos to Campo di Fiori? What was here for him?

And as the questions formed, the single answer was apparent. Dakakos, the loner, was the unseen power here. The conversation that had just taken place in the circular drive was not a conversation between strangers.

What had to be established was whether Dakakos had come alone to Campo di Fiori. Or had he brought his own protection, his own firepower? There was no one in the house, no lights in the windows, no sounds from inside. That left the stables.

Andrew scrambled backward in the wet grass until all sightlines from the windows were blocked by the overgrowth. He rose behind a clump of bushes and removed a small Bereta revolver from his pocket. He climbed the embankment above the drive and estimated the angle of the stable road across the knoll. If Dakakos's men were in the stables, it would be a simple matter to eliminate them. Without gunfire; that was essential. The weapon was merely a device; men collapsed under its threat.

Fontine crouched and weaved his way across the knoll toward the stable road. The early evening breezes bent the upper grass and the branches of trees; the professional soldier fell instinctively into the rhythm of their movement. The roofs of the stables came into view and he stepped silently down the incline toward the road.

In front of the stable door was a long steel-gray Maserati, its tires caked with mud. There were no voices, no signs of life; there was only the quiet hum of the surrounding woods. Andrew lowered himself to his knees, picked up a handful of dirt, and threw it twenty yards in the air across the road, hitting the stable windows.

No one emerged. Fontine repeated the action, using more dirt mixed with small pieces of rock. The splattering was louder; there was no way it could go unobserved.

Nothing. No one.

Cautiously, Andrew walked out on the road toward the car. He stopped before he reached it. The surface of the road was hard, but still partially wet from the earlier rain.

The Maserati was headed north; there were no footsteps on the passenger side of the car in front of him. He walked around the automobile; there were distinct imprints on the driver's side: the shoe marks of a man. Dakakos had come alone.

There was no time to waste now. There was a picture on a wall to be taken, and a journey to Champoluc that had to begin. Too, there was a fine irony in finding Dakakos at Campo di Fiori. The informer's life would end where his obsession had begun. Eye Corps was owed that much.

He could see lights inside the house now, but only in the windows to the left of the main entrance. Andrew kept to the wall, ducking under the ledges, until he was at the side of the window where the light was brightest. He inched his face to the frame and looked inside.

The room was huge. There were couches and chairs and a fireplace. Two lamps were lit; one by the far couch, the second nearer, to the right of an armchair. Dakakos was standing by the mantal, gesturing in slow, deliberate movements with his hands. The priest was in the chair, his back to Fontine, and barely visible. Their conversation was muted, indistinguishable. It was impossible to determine whether the Greek had a weapon; the assumption had to be that he did.

Andrew pried a brick loose from the border of the drive and returned to the window. He rose, the Beretta in his right hand, the brick gripped in his left. Dakakos approached the priest in the chair; the Greek was pleading, or explaining, his concentration absolute.

The moment was now.

Shielding his eyes with the gun, Fontine extended his left arm behind him, then arced it forward, hurling the brick into the center of the window, shattering glass and wood strips everywhere. On impact he smashed the remaining, obstructing glass with the Beretta, thrusting the weapon through the space, and screamed at the top of his voice.

"You move one inch, you're dead!"

Dakakos froze. *"You?"* he whispered. "You were *taken!"*

The Greek's head slumped forward, the gashes from the pistol barrel on his face deep, ugly, and bleeding profusely. There was nothing that so became this man as a painful death, thought Fontine.

"In the name of God have *mercy!"* screamed the priest from the opposite chair, where he sat bound and helpless.

"Shut up!" roared the soldier, his eyes on Dakakos. "Why did you do it? Why are you here?"

The Greek stared, his breathing erratic, his eyes swollen. "They said you were taken. They had everything they needed." He could barely be heard, speaking as much to himself as to the man above him.

"They made a mistake," said Andrew. "Their signals got crossed. You didn't expect them to wire you their apologies, did you? What did they tell you? That they were picking me up?"

Dakakos remained silent, blinking from the rivulets of blood that rolled down his forehead into his eyes. Fontine could hear the Pentagon commanders. *Never admit. Never explain. Take the objective, the rest is no strain.*

"Forget it," he said quietly, icily to Dakakos. "Just tell me why you're here."

The Greek's eyes swam in his head; his lips moved. "You are *filth.* And we'll *stop you!"*

"Who's we?"

Dakakos arched his neck, thrusting it forward, and spat into the soldier's face. Fontine swung the barrel of the pistol up into the Greek's jaw. The head slumped forward.

"Stop!" cried the monk. "I'll tell you. There's a priest named Land. Dakakos and Land work together."

"Who?" Fontine turned abruptly to the monk.

"It's all I know. The name! They've been in contact for years."

"Who is he? *What* is he?"

"I don't know. Dakakos doesn't say."

"Is he waiting for him? Is this priest coming here?"

The monk's expression suddenly changed. His eyelids quivered, his lips trembled.

Andrew understood. Dakakos was waiting for someone, but not a priest named Land. Fontine raised the barrel of the pistol and shoved it into the mouth of the semiconscious Greek. "All right, Father, you've two seconds to tell me who it is. Who's this son of a bitch waiting for?"

"The other one. . . ."

"The other *what?"*

The old monk stared at him. Fontine felt a hard emptiness in his stomach. He removed the pistol.

Adrian.

Adrian was on his way to Campo di Fiori! His brother had broken away and sold out to Dakakos!

The *picture!* He had to make sure the picture was there! He turned, looking for the door of the. . . .

When the blow came it was paralyzing. Dakakos had snapped the lamp cord binding his wrists and lunged forward, his fist pummeling into Andrew's kidney, his other hand wrapped around the Beretta's barrel, twisting Fontine's forearm until he thought his elbow would crack.

Andrew countered by falling sideways, rolling with the force of Dakakos's lunge. The Greek sprang on top of him, crushing him like some elephantine hammer. He smashed Fontine's knuckles against the floor until the gun exploded, the bullet embedding itself in the wooden arch of the doorway. Andrew brought his knee up, pounding the base of Dakakos's groin, crushing the Greek's testicles until he arched his back, grimacing in torment.

Fontine rolled again, freeing his left hand, clawing the bleeding face above, tearing at the hanging flesh. Still, Dakakos would not retreat, would not let up; he slammed his forearms into Andrew's throat.

It was the instant! Andrew arched forward, sinking his teeth into the flesh of Dakakos's arm, biting deeply, as a mad dog would bite, feeling the warm blood flowing into his throat. The Greek pulled his arm up—his hand away—and it was the space Fontine needed. He crashed his knee up once again in Dakakos's groin, and slid his whole body under the giant; as he did so he shot his left hand into the well of Dakakos's armpit, and pressed the nerve with all the force he could summon.

The Greek raised his right side in agony. Andrew rolled to his left, kicking the heavy body away, pulling his arm free.

With the speed born of a hundred fire fights, Fontine was on his haunches, the Beretta leveled, spitting bullets into the exposed chest of the informer who had come to close to killing him.

Dakakos was dead. Annaxas was no more.

Andrew rose unsteadily; he was covered with blood, his whole body wracked. He looked at the priest of Xenope in the chair. The old man's eyes were closed, his lips moving in silent prayer.

There was one shell left in the Beretta. Andrew raised the gun and fired.

Chapter Twenty-eight

Stunned, Adrian took the cablegram held out for him by the desk clerk. He walked toward the front entrance of the hotel, stopped, and opened it.

Mr. Adrian Fontine
Excelsior Hotel
Rome, Italy
My dear Fontine:
    It is urgent we confer, for you must not act alone. You must trust me. You have nothing to fear from me. I understand your anxieties, consequently there will be no intermediaries, none of my people will intercept you. I will wait for you alone and alone we can make our decisions. Check your source.
                                                        Theo Dakakos

Dakakos had traced him! The Greek expected to *meet*. But where? How?

Adrian knew that once he passed through customs in Rome, there was no way he could stop those looking for him from knowing he'd come to Italy; it was the reason for the next step in his strategy. But that Dakakos would openly contact him seemed extraordinary. It was as though Dakakos assumed they were working *together*. Yet it was Dakakos who had gone after Andrew; gone after his brother relentlessly, ingeniously, wrapping up Eye Corps in a seditious ribbon that had eluded the combined efforts of the inspector general and the Justice Department.

The sons of Victor Fontine—the grandsons of Savarone Fontini-Cristi—were after the vault. Why would Dakakos stop one and not the other?

The answer had to be that he was trying to do just that. Carrots held out in front of the donkey's nose; offers of safety and trust that were translated to mean *control, confinement*.

. . . *I will wait for you alone and alone we can make our decisions. Check your source.* . . .

Was Dakakos on his way to Campo di Fiori? How was that possible? And what was the *source?* An IG colonel named Tarkington with whom Dakakos had set up lines of communication to trap Eye Corps? What other source did he and Dakakos have in common?

"Signor Fontine?" It was the Excelsior manager; the door to his office was open behind him. He had come out quickly.

"Yes?"

"I tried your room, of course. You were not there." The man smiled nervously.

"Right," said Adrian. "I'm here. What is it?"

"Our guests are always our first consideration." The Italian smiled again. It was maddening.

"Please. I'm in a hurry."

"A few moments ago we had a call from the American embassy. They say they are calling all the hotels in Rome. They are looking for you."

"What did you say?"

"Our guests are always——"

"What did you *say?* "

"That you had checked out. You *have* checked out, *signore*. However, if you wish to use my telephone. . . ."

"No, thank you," said Adrian, starting toward the entrance. Then stopped and turned to the manager. "Call the embassy back. Tell them where I've gone. The front desk knows."

It was the second part of his strategy in Rome, and when he conceived it, he realized it was merely an extension of what he had done in Paris. Before the day was over the professionals who followed him would know exactly where he was. Computers and passport entries and international cooperation made for swift relays of information. He had to make them all think he was going somewhere that he wasn't.

Rome was the best place to start. Had he flown to Milan, the IG men would dig into their files; Campo di Fiori would appear. He could not allow that.

He had asked the front desk of the Excelsior to draw up a route for a drive south. To Naples, Salerno, and Policastro, along roads that would take him east through Calabria to the Adriatic. He had rented a car at the airport.

Now Theodore Dakakos had joined the hunt. Dakakos, whose relays of information were faster than those of United States Army Intelligence, and far more dangerous. Adrian knew what the United States Army wanted: the killer for Eye Corps. But Dakakos wanted the vault from Constantine. It was a greater prize.

Adrian drove through Rome's melodramatic traffic back to Leonardo da Vinci Airport. He returned the rented car and bought a ticket on Itavia Airlines for Milan. He stood in line at the departure gate, his head down, his body slouched, seeking the protective cover of the crowd. As he was jostled forward—and for reasons he didn't know—the words of an extraordinary lawyer came back to him.

You can run with the pack, in the middle of the pack, but if you want to do something, get to the edges and peel away. Darrow.

In Milan he would call his father. He'd lie about Andrew; he'd invent *something*, he couldn't think about that now. But he had to know more about Theodore Dakakos.

Dakakos was closing in.

He sat on his bed in Milan's Hotel di Piemonte as he'd sat on the bed at the Savoy in London, staring at papers in front of him. But these were not airline schedules, they were the Xeroxed pages of his father's recollection of fifty years ago. He was rereading them—not for any new information; he knew the contents—but because the reading postponed the moment when he would pick up the phone. He wondered how thoroughly his brother had studied these pages, with their rambling descriptions and hesitant, often obscure reflections. Andrew would probably pore over them with the scrutiny of a soldier in combat. There were names. Goldoni, Capomonti, Lefrac. Men who had to be reached.

Adrian knew he could not procrastinate any longer. He folded the pages, put them in his jacket pocket, and reached for the telephone.

Ten minutes later the switchboard called him back; the phone 5,000 miles away in the North Shore house was ringing. His mother answered and when she said the words, she did so simply, without the trappings of grief, for they were extraneous, the grief private.

"Your father died last night."

Neither spoke for several moments. The silence conveyed a sense of love. As though they were touching.

"I'll come home right away," he said.

"No, don't do that. He wouldn't want you to. You know what you have to do."

Again there was silence. "Yes," he said finally.

"Adrian?"

"Yes?"

"I have two things to tell you, but I don't want to discuss them. Can you understand that?"

Adrian paused. "I think so."

"An army officer came to see us. A Colonel Tarkington. He was kind enough to speak only with me. I know about Andrew."

"I'm sorry."

"Bring him back. He needs help. All the help we can give him."

"I'll try."

"It's so easy to look back and say 'Yes, I see now. I realize.' He always saw the results of strength; he never understood its complications, its essential compassion, I think."

"Let's not discuss it," reminded the son.

"Yes. I don't want to discuss———. Oh, God, I'm so *frightened!*"

"*Please*, mother."

Jane breathed deeply, the sound carried over the wire. "There's something else. Dakakos was here. He spoke to your father. To both of us together. You must trust him. Your father wished it; he was convinced of it. So am I."

. . . check your source. . . .

"He sent me a cable. He said he'd be waiting for me."

"At Campo di Fiori," completed Jane.

"What did he say about Andrew?"

"That he thought your brother might be delayed. He didn't elaborate; he talked only about you. He used your name repeatedly."

"You're sure you don't want me to come home?"

"No. There's nothing you can do here. He wouldn't want it." She paused for a moment. "Adrian, tell your brother his father never knew. He died thinking both his Geminis were the men he believed them to be."

"I'll tell him. I'll call again soon."

They said quiet good-byes.

His father was dead. The source was gone, and the void was terrible. He sat by the telephone, aware that perspiration had formed on his forehead, though the room was cool. He got up from the bed; there were things to do and he had to move quickly. Dakakos was on his way to Campo di Fiori. So was the killer of Eye Corps, and Dakakos did not know that.

So he sat down at the desk and began writing. He might have been back in his Boston apartment, jotting down items in preparation for the next day's cross-examination.

But in this case it was not the next day. It was tonight. And very few items came to mind.

He stopped the car at the fork in the road, picked up the map, and held it under the dashboard light. The fork was detailed on the map. There were no other roads until the town of Laveno. His father had said there were large stone gateposts on the left; they were the entrance to Campo di Fiori.

He started the car up, straining his eyes in the darkness, waiting to catch a glimpse of erected stone in the wall of forest on his left. Four miles up the road he found them. He stopped the car opposite the huge, crumbling stone pillars and aimed his flashlight out the window. There was the winding road beyond as his father had described it, angling sharply, disappearing into the woods.

He swung the automobile to the left and drove through the gates. His mouth was suddenly dry, his heart accelerated, its beat echoing in his throat. It was the fear of the immediate unknown that gripped him. He wanted to face it quickly, before the fear controlled him. He drove faster.

There were no lights anywhere.

The enormous white house stood in eerie stillness, a deathlike splendor in the darkness. Adrian parked the car on the left side of the circle, opposite the marble steps, shut off the motor and, reluctantly, the headlights. He got out, took the flashlight from his raincoat pocket, and started across the rutted pavement toward the stairs.

Dull moonlight briefly illuminated the macabre setting and then disappeared. The sky was overcast but no rain would come; the clouds were everywhere above, but thin and traveling too fast. The air was dry;

everything was still.

Adrian reached the bottom step and switched on his flashlight to look at his watch. It was eleven thirty. Dakakos was not there. Nor his brother. Either or both would have heard the car; neither nor both would be asleep at this hour. That left the old priest. An old man in the country would have gone to bed by now. He called out.

"Hello in there! My name is Adrian Fontine and I'd like to talk to you!"

Nothing.

And not nothing! There was movement. A pattering, a series of scratches accompanied by tiny, indistinguishable screeches. He swung the flashlight to the source. In its beam was caught the blurred, rushing figures of rats —three, four, five—scampering over the ledge of an open window.

He held the flashlight steady. The windows was smashed; he could see jagged edges of glass. He approached it slowly, suddenly afraid.

His feet sank into the earth; his shoes crunched broken glass. He stood in front of the window and raised the flashlight.

He lost his breath in an involuntary gasp as two pairs of animal's eyes were suddenly caught in the blinding shaft. They darted up, startled yet furious, and a terrible muted screeching was heard as the creatures fled into the darkness of another part of the house. There was a crash. A crazed frightened animal had collided with an unstable object of china or glass.

Adrian breathed again, then shuddered. His nostrils were filled with an overpowering stench, a putrid, rotting aroma that caused his eyes to water and his throat to swell and choke. He held his breath and he climbed over the window ledge. He pressed his open left hand against his mouth and his nose, filtering the foul stench; he cast the beam of the flashlight over the enormous room.

The shock of it staggered him. The figures of two dead men, one in torn robes strapped to a chair, the other half-naked on the floor, were hideous. The clothes were torn by animal teeth, flesh ripped out by animal jaws, dried blood made moist by animal urine and saliva.

Adrian reeled. Vomit spewed out of his mouth. He lurched to his left; the light caught a doorway and he lunged into it gasping for breath, for air that could be swallowed.

He was in the study of Savarone Fontini-Cristi, a man he never knew, but now hated with all the hatred of which he was capable. The grandfather who had triggered a chain of killing and suspicion that in itself brought more death and greater hatred.

Over *what? For* what?

"*Goddamnnn youuu! . . .*"

He screamed uncontrollably; he gripped the high back of an old chair and threw it crashing to the floor.

Suddenly, in silence and in full knowledge of what he had to do, Adrian stood immobile and aimed the flashlight on the wall behind the desk. To the right, he remembered, beneath a painting of the Madonna.

The frame was there, the glass shattered.

And the painting was gone.

He sank to his knees, trembling. Tears welled his eyes and he sobbed uncontrollably.

"Oh, *God,*" he whispered, the pain unbearable. "Oh, my brother!"

PART THREE

Chapter Twenty-nine

Andrew pulled the Land Rover off to the side of the Alpine road and poured steaming hot coffee into the lid of the thermos. He had made good time; according to the Michelin map he was ten miles from the village of Champoluc. It was morning; the rays of the early sun shot up from behind the surrounding mountains. In a little while he would drive into Champoluc and buy the equipment he needed.

Adrian was far behind. Andrew knew he could slow down for a while, think things out. Besides, his brother was walking into a situation that would paralyze him. Adrian would find the bodies at Campo di Fiori and panic; his thoughts would be confused, indecisive. He wouldn't know what to do next. His brother wasn't trained to confront death from violence; it was too far removed from him. It was different for soldiers: It was different for him. The physical confrontation—even the bloodshed—primed his senses, infused him with an intense feeling of exhilaration. His energies were peaked, he was confident, sure of his movements.

The vault was as good as his. Now was the time to concentrate. Study each word, each clue. He took his father's Xeroxed pages and held them up, catching the morning light through the windshield.

. . . *In the village of Champoluc was the family Goldoni. According to current Zermatt records, they exist still and are scattered throughout the area. The present head of the family is one Alfredo Goldoni. He resides in the house of his father—and father before him—on several acres of land at the base of the mountains in the west outskirts. For generations, the Goldonis have been the most experienced guides in the Italian Alps. Savarone employed them frequently, and beyond this, they were "northern friends"—a phrase my father used to distinguish men of the land from those in the marketplace. His trust was placed in the former far more quickly than in the latter. It is possible that he left information with Alfredo Goldoni's father. With his death, arrangements would be made to pass this information on to the surviving eldest child—whether man or woman—as is the Italian-Swiss custom. Therefore, should Alfredo not be the eldest, look for an older sister.*

North, into the mountains—between the railroad clearings Krahen Aüsblick and Grier Gipfel, I believe—is a small inn run by the family Capomonti. Again, according to Zermatt (I made no inquiries in the Champoluc district to avoid raising suspicion) the inn, too, still exists. I gather it has been somewhat expanded. It is currently under the management of Naton Lefrac, a descendent by marriage of the Capomontis. I remember this man. He was not a man then, of course, for he was one or two years younger than I, the son of a merchant who dealt with the Capomontis. We became quite good friends. I recall clearly that he was much beloved of the Capomontis and the hope was that he would marry a daughter of the house. Obviously he did so.

As children—and young men—we never went into the Champoluc without staying at Locanda Capomonti. I have recollections of warm welcomes and laughter and roaring fireplaces and much comfort. The family was simple—in the uncomplicated sense—and extremely outgoing and sincere. Savarone was particularly taken with them. If there were secrets to leave in the Champoluc, old Capomonti would have been a rock of silence and trust. . . .

Andrew put down the pages and picked up the Michelin road map. Once again he traced the minute markings of the Zermatt railroad, his concern returning. Of the many clearings his father recalled, only four remained. And none bore the name of *hawk*.

For the hunting picture in the study at Campo di Fiori was not as his father remembered; it did not show birds being flushed from bushes. Instead, there were hunters in overgrown fields, their eyes and weapons leveled forward as hawks flew lazily above in the distant sky; an artist's comment on the futility of the hunt.

His father said that the clearings were called Eagle's Peak, Condor's Lookout, and Crow's Summit. There had to be a clearing with the name hawk in it. But if there had been, it no longer existed. And a half century had gone by; obscure railroad clearings below Alpine passes scores of miles apart were not landmarks. Who recalled the precise location of a trolley stop thirty years after the tracks were covered with asphalt? He put down the map and picked up the Xeroxed pages again. The initial key was somewhere in these words.

We stopped in the center of the village for a late lunch, or afternoon tea, I cannot remember which—and Savarone left the restaurant to check the telegraph office for messages—I do remember that. When he returned he was very upset, and I feared our trip to the mountains would be canceled before it began. However, during the meal another message was delivered and Savarone was both placated and relieved. There was no more talk of returning to Campo di Fiori. The dreadful moment had passed for an anxious seventeen-year-old.

From the restaurant we dropped by the shop of a merchant whose name was German in sound and spelling, not Italian or French. My father was prone to order supplies and equipment from this man because he felt sorry for him. He was a Jew and for Savarone, who fought bitterly against the czarist pogroms and dealt on a handshake with the Rothschilds, such thinking was indefensible. There is a blurred memory of an unpleasant incident at the store that evening. What the unpleasant incident specifically entailed, I have no recall, but it was most serious and provoked my father to quiet but definite anger. A sad anger if, again, memory serves. I seem to have the vague impression that details were withheld from me, but now, so many years later, it is only an impression and could well be false.

We left the merchant's shop and proceeded by horsecart to the Goldoni farm. I remember showing off my Alpine pack with its straps and hammer and cleats and forged double-clamps for the ropes. I was terribly proud of it, believing it signified manhood. Again there is a dim impression that while at the Goldonis' an undercurrent of distress was prevalent, but not obvious. I cannot tell you why this feeling remains after so many years, but I relate it to the fact that I had difficulty holding the attention of the male Goldonis while exhibiting my new pack. The father, an uncle or two, and certainly the older sons seemed distracted. Arrangements were made with one of the Goldoni sons to meet us the next day and take us into the mountains. We stayed at the Goldonis for several hours before leaving to resume our journey by cart to the Locando Capomonti. I do recall it was dark when we left, and, as it was summer, the hour had to be past 7:30 or 8:00.

What were the facts, thought Andrew. Man and boy arrived at the village, had something to eat, bought supplies from a disliked Jew, went to the house of the guides they were hiring, and a spoiled child was insulted because not enough attention was paid to his mountain-climbing equipment. The relevant information was reduced to the name Goldoni.

Andrew finished the coffee and screwed the lid back on the thermos. The sun was higher now; it was time to move. Exhilaration filled him. All the years of training and experience and decisions in the field had prepared him for the next few days. There was a vault in the mountains and he would find it!

Eye Corps would be paid in full.

The soldier turned the ignition and gunned the motor. He had clothing and equipment and weapons to buy. And a man named Goldoni to see. Perhaps a woman named Goldoni; he'd know shortly.

Adrian sat in the darkness behind the wheel of the stationary car and wiped his mouth with his handkerchief. He could not erase the taste of sickness in his throat any more than he could erase the sight of the ravaged bodies inside the house from his mind's eye. Or the stench of death from his nostrils.

Sweat rolled down his face, produced by tension he had never known, a fear he had never experienced.

He felt the need to vomit returning; he suppressed it by inhaling rapidly. He had to find some semblance of sanity, he had to function. He could not remain in darkness, in an immobile car for the rest of the night. He had to pass through the shock and find his mind again. It was all he had left: the ability to think.

Instinctively, he pulled the pages of his father's memories from his pocket and switched on the flashlight. Words had come to be his refuge; he was an analyst of words—their shadings, their subtle interpretations, their simplicity and complexity. He was an expert with words, as much an expert as his brother was with death.

Adrian separated the pages, reading slowly, meticulously. Child and man had come to the village of Champoluc; there were immediate impressions of discord, perhaps more than discord. *When he returned he was very upset . . . I feared for our trip.* There was the shop of a Jew, and anger. *What the unpleasant incident specifically entailed, I have no recall . . . it was most serious and provoked my father.* And sadness. *A sad anger if, again, memory serves.* Then the anger and the sadness faded away, replaced by vague feelings of distress and embarrassment; the child was not heeded by those whose attentions he sought. *The father, an uncle or two, and certainly the older sons were distracted.* Their attentions were elsewhere—on the anger, the discord? The sadness? And these obscure recollections were in turn displaced by memories of warmth, and an inn north of the village, *a warm welcome, which was like a dozen other similar welcomes.* This peaceful interlude was followed a short while later once again by vague feelings of distress and concern.

At the Capomonti inn there is little I can recall specifically except a warm welcome, which was like a dozen other similar welcomes. One thing I do remember was that for the first time in the mountains I had my own room, no younger brothers sharing it with me. It was a significant departure and I felt quite grown up. There was another meal, and my father and old Capomonti drank a good deal of whiskey afterward. I recall this because I went to bed, thinking of the next day's climbing, and later heard loud, belligerent voices below, and wondered if the noise might wake the other guests. It was a small inn then and there were perhaps three or four others registered. This concern was unusual for I had never seen my father drunk. I do not know to this day if he was, but the noise was considerable. To a young man on his seventeenth birthday, about to be given the present of his life—a real climb in the Champoluc—the thoughts of a weakened, angry father in the morning were disturbing.

It was not the case, however. The Goldoni guide arrived with our supplies, shared breakfast with us, and we departed.

A Capomonti son—or it might have been young Lefrac—drove the three of us several miles north in the horsecart. We bade him good-bye and it was agreed he would meet us at the same place late in the afternoon on the following day. Two days in the mountains and an overnight camp with adults! I was overjoyed for I knew we would make camp at a higher altitude than was ever possible with younger brothers in tow.

Adrian put down the pages on the seat of the car. The remaining paragraphs described sketchily remembered hills and trails and views that seemed to overlap. The journey into the mountains had begun.

Specific information might well lie in these rambling descriptions. Isolated landmarks might be revealed, and a pattern emerge; but which landmarks, which patterns?

Oh, God! The painting on the wall. Andrew had the painting!

Adrian suppressed his sudden alarm. The painting from Savarone's study might narrow down the location of a clearing, but what then? Fifty years had passed. A half century of ice and water and summer thaws and natural growth and erosion.

The painting on the wall might well be one clue, perhaps the most important. But Adrian had the feeling that there were others as vital as that painting. They were contained in the words of his father's testament. Memories that survived fifty years of extraordinary living.

Something had happened fifty years ago that had nothing to do with a father and son going into the mountains.

He had found part of his mind again. He was exercising his ability to think. The shock and the horror were still there, but he was passing through to the beginnings of sanity.

. . . Bear in mind, the contents of that vault are as staggering to the civilized world as anything in history. . . .

He had to reach it, find it. He had to stop the killer from Eye Corps.

Chapter Thirty

Andrew parked the Land Rover by a fence bordering a field. The Goldoni farmhouse was two hundred yards down the road, on the left; the field was part of the Goldoni property. There was a man driving a tractor along rows of upturned earth, his living body turned in the seat, watching the progress behind him. There were no other houses in the area, no other people in sight. Andrew decided to stop and speak to the man.

It was shortly past five in the afternoon. He had spent the day wandering about Champoluc, buying clothes, supplies, and climbing equipment, including the finest Alpine pack available, filled with those items recommended for the mountains, and one that was not. A Magnum .357-caliber pistol. He had made these purchases at the much-expanded shop referred to in his father's recollections. The name was Leinkraus; it had a mezuzah on the doorframe of the front entrance. The clerk behind the counter allowed that Leinkraus had been selling the finest equipment in the Italian Alps since 1913. There were now branches in Gstaad and Lake Lucerne.

Andrew got out of the Land Rover and walked to the fence, waving his hand back and forth to get the attention of the man on the tractor. He was a short, stocky Italian-Swiss, ruffled brown hair above the dark eyebrows, and the rugged, sharp features of a northern Mediterranean. He was at least ten years older than Fontine; his expression was cautious, as if he were not used to unfamiliar faces.

"Do you speak English?" Andrew asked.

"Passably, *signore*," said the man.

"I'm looking for Alfredo Goldoni. I was directed out here."

"You were directed correctly," replied the Italian-Swiss in more than passable English. "Goldoni is my uncle. I tend his land for him. He can't work for himself." The man stopped, offering no further clarification.

"Where can I find him?"

"Where he always is. In the back room of his house. My aunt will show you to him. He likes visitors."

"Thank you." Andrew turned toward the Land Rover.

"You're American?" asked the man.

"No. Canadian," he replied, extending his cover for any of a dozen immediate possibilities. He climbed into the vehicle and looked at the man through the open window. "We sound the same."

"You look the same, dress the same," countered the farmhand quietly, eyeing the fur-lined Alpine jacket. "The clothes are new," he added.

"Your English isn't," said Fontine. He turned the ignition.

Goldoni's wife was gaunt and ascetic-looking. Her straight gray hair was pulled back, the taut bun a crown of self-denial. She ushered the visitor through the several neat, sparsely furnished rooms to a doorway at the rear of the house. There was no door attached; where once there'd been a sill in the frame, it had been removed, the floor leveled. Fontine walked through; he entered the bedroom. Alfredo Goldoni sat in a wheelchair by a window overlooking the fields at the base of the mountains.

He had no legs. The stubs of his once-massive limbs were encased in the folds of his trousers, the cloth held together by safety pins. The rest of his body, like his face, was large and awkward. Age and mutilation had extracted their price.

Old Goldoni greeted him with false energy. A tired cripple afraid of offending a newcomer, grateful for the all-too-infrequent interruption.

The introductions over, the directions and the journey from town described, and wine brought by a sullen wife, Fontine sat down in a chair opposite the legless man. The stumps were within an arm's reach; the word *grotesque* came repeatedly to his mind. Andrew did not like ugliness; he did not care to put up with it.

"You don't recognize the name Fontine?"

"I do not, sir. It's French, I think. But you're American."

"Do you recognize the name Fontini-Cristi?"

Goldoni's eyes changed. A long-forgotten alarm was triggered. "Yes, of course, I recognize it," replied the amputee, his voice also changing, his words measured. "Fontine; Fontini-Cristi. So the Italian becomes French and the possessor American. It's been many years. You're a Fontini-Cristi?"

"Yes. Savarone was my grandfather."

"A great *padrone* from the northern provinces. I remember him. Not well, of course. He stopped coming to Champoluc in the late twenties, I believe."

"The Goldonis were his guides. Father and sons."

"We were everyone's guides."

"Were you ever a guide for my grandfather?"

"It's possible. I worked the mountains as a very young man."

"Can't you remember?"

"In my time I have taken thousands into the Alps——"

"You just said you remembered him."

"Not well. And more by the name than by the person. What is it you want?"

"Information. About a trip to the mountains taken by my father and grandfather fifty years ago."

"Are you joking?"

"Hardly. My father, Victor—Vittorio Fontini-Cristi—sent me from America to get that information. At great inconvenience to me. I haven't much time, so I need your help."

"It's freely given, but I wouldn't know where to begin. A single climb fifty years ago! Who would remember?"

"The man who led them. The guide. According to my father he was a son of Goldoni. The date is July fourteenth, 1920."

Fontine could not be sure—perhaps the grotesque cripple merely suppressed a sharp pain from his massive stumps, or shifted his legless clump of a body in reflection—but Goldoni *did react*. It was the *date*. He reacted to the date. And immediately covered that reaction by talking.

"July of 1920. It's two generations ago. It's impossible. You must have something more, how do you say, specific than that?"

"The *guide*. He was a Goldoni."

"Not I. I was no more than fifteen years old. I went into the mountains young, but not that young. Not as a *prima guida*."

Andrew held the cripple's eyes with his own. Goldoni was uncomfortable; he did not like the exchange of stares and looked away. Fontine leaned forward. "But you remémber something, don't you?" he asked quietly, unable to keep the coldness out of his voice.

"No, Signor Fontini-Cristi. There's nothing."

"Just a few seconds ago, I gave you the date: July fourteenth, 1920. You knew that date."

"I knew only that it was too long ago for me to think about."

"I should tell you, I'm a soldier. I've interrogated hundreds of men; very few ever fooled me."

"It wouldn't be my intention, *signore*. For what purpose? I should like to be helpful to you."

Andrew continued to stare. "Years ago there were clearings on the railroad tracks south of Zermatt."

"A few are left," added Goldoni. "Not many, of course. They're not necessary these days."

"Tell me. Each was given the name of a bird——"

"Some," interrupted the Alpiner. "Not all."

"Was there a *hawk?* A hawk's . . . *something?*"

"A hawk? Why do you ask that?" The outsized amputee looked up, his gaze now steady, unwavering.

"Just tell me. Was there a clearing with 'hawk' as part of its name?"

Goldoni remained silent for several moments. "No," he said finally.

Andrew sat back in the chair. "Are you the eldest son of the Goldoni family?"

"No. It was obviously one of my brothers who was hired for that climb fifty years ago."

Fontine was beginning to understand. Alfredo Goldoni was given the house because he had lost his legs. "Where are your brothers? I'll talk with them."

"Again, I must ask if you joke, *signore*. My brothers are dead, everyone knows that. My brothers, an uncle, two cousins. All dead. There are no Goldoni guides left in Champoluc."

Andrew's breathing stopped. He absorbed the information and inhaled deeply. His shortcut had been eliminated with a single sentence.

"I find that hard to believe," he said coldly. "*All* those men dead? What killed them?"

"Avalanche, *signore*. A whole village was buried in sixty-eight. Near Valtournanche. Rescue teams were sent from as far north as Zermatt, south from Châtillon. The Goldonis led them. Three nations awarded us their highest honors. They were of little good to the rest. For me, they provide a small pension. I lost my legs through exposure." He tapped the stumps of his once muscular legs.

"And you have no information about that trip on July fourteenth, 1920?"

"Without particular details, how can I?"

"I have descriptions. Written down by my father." Fontine withdrew the Xeroxed pages from his jacket.

"Good! You should have said so before! Read them to me."

Andrew did so. The descriptions were disjointed, the pictures evoked contradictory. Time sequences jumped back and forth, and landmarks seemed to be confused with each other.

Goldoni listened; every now and then he closed his puffed, creasing eyes and turned his neck to one side, as though conjuring up his own visual recollections. When Fontine finished he shook his head slowly. "I'm sorry, *signore*. What you have read could be any of twenty, thirty different trails. Much that's there doesn't even exist in our district. Forgive me, but I think that your father has confused trails farther west in Valais. It's easy to do."

"There's nothing that sounds familiar?"

"On the contrary. Everything. *And* nothing. Fragments of many locations for hundreds of square miles. I'm sorry. It's impossible."

Andrew was confused. He still had the gut feeling that the Alpiner was lying. There was another option to pursue before he forced the issue. If it, too, led nowhere, he would come back and face the cripple with different tactics.

. . . . *Should Alfredo not be the eldest, look for a sister.* . . .

"Are you the oldest surviving member of the family?"

"No. Two sisters were born before me. One lives."

"Where?"

"In Champoluc. On the Via Sestina. Her son works my land."

"What's the name? Her married name."

"Capomonti."

"Capomonti? That's the name of the people who run the inn."

"Yes, *signore*. She married into the family."

Fontine got out of the chair, putting the Xeroxed pages into his pocket. He reached the door and turned. "It's possible I'll be back."

"It will be a pleasure to welcome you."

Fontine got into the Land Rover and started the engine. Across the fence in the field, the nephew-farmhand sat motionless on the tractor and watched him, his vehicle idling. The gut feeling returned; the look on the farmhand's face seemed to be saying. *Get out of here. I must run to the house and hear what you said.*

Andrew released the brake and pressed the accelerator. The Land Rover shot forward on the road; he made a rapid U-turn and started back toward the village.

Suddenly his eyes riveted on the most obvious, unstartling sight in the world. He swore. It was so obvious he had not taken notice.

The road was lined with telephone poles.

There was no point in looking for an old woman on the Via Sestina; she would not be there. Another strategy came to the soldier's mind. The odds favored it.

"*Woman!*" shouted Goldini.

"Quickly! Help me! The telephone!"

Goldoni's wife walked swiftly into the room and gripped the handles of the chair. "Should I make the calls?" she asked, wheeling him to the telephone.

"No. I'll do it." He dialed. "Lefrac? Can you hear me? . . . He's come. After all these years. Fontini-Cristi. But he does not bring the words. He seeks a clearing named for *hawks*. He tells me nothing else, and that's nothing. I don't trust him. I must reach my sister. Gather the others. We'll meet in an hour. . . . Not *here!* At the inn."

Andrew lay prone in the field across from the farmhouse. He focused the binoculars alternately on the door and on the windows. The sun was going down behind the western Alps; it would be dark soon. Lights had been put on in the farmhouse; the shadows moved back and forth. There was activity.

A car was being backed out of a dirt drive to the right of the house; it stopped and the farmhand-nephew got out. He raced to the front door; it opened.

Goldoni was in his wheelchair, his wife behind him. The nephew replaced her and started wheeling his legless uncle across the lawn toward the automobile, whose motor was idling.

Goldoni was clutching something in his arms. Andrew focused the binoculars on the object.

It was a large book; but it was more than a book. It was some kind of heavy, wide volume. A ledger.

At the car Goldoni's wife held the door while the nephew grabbed the grotesque amputee under the arms and swung the carcass across into the seat. Goldoni twitched and squirmed; his wife drew a strap across him and buckled it.

Through the frame of the open door's window, Andrew had a clear view of the legless, former Alpine guide. The center of focus once again was the huge ledger in Goldoni's arms, held almost desperately, though it were a thing of extraordinary value he dared not let go. Then Andrew realized there was something else in Goldoni's arms, something infinitely more familiar to the soldier. A shaft of glistening metal was wedged between the large volume and the Alpiner's thick chest. It was the barrel of a small, powerful shotgun; a model particularly identified with warring Italian families in the south. In Sicily. It was called the *lupo*, the "wolf." It was without much accuracy beyond twenty yards, but at short range could blow a man ten feet off the ground.

Goldoni was guarding the volume in his arms with a weapon more powerful than the .357 Magnum in the soldier's Alpine pack. Briefly, Andrew focused on Goldoni's nephew; the man had a new addition to his garb. Jammed into his belt was a pistol, the large handle indicative of its heavy caliber.

Both Alpiners were guarding that ledger. No one could get near it. What was——

Christ! Suddenly, Fontine understood. *Records!* Records of *journeys into the mountains!* It couldn't be anything else! It never occurred to him—or to Victor—to ask if such records were kept. Especially in light of the years; it was simply not a consideration. My God, a half century had passed!

But according to his father, and *his* father, the Goldonis were the finest guides in the Alps. Such professionals with such a collective reputation to uphold *would* keep records; it was the most natural thing to do. Records of past trips into the mountains, going back decades!

Goldoni had lied. The information his visitor wanted was in that house. But Goldoni did not want the visitor to have it.

Andrew watched. The nephew collapsed the wheelchair, opened the trunk of the car, threw it in, and ran to the driver's side. He climbed behind the wheel as Goldoni's wife closed her husband's door.

The car lurched out of the drive and headed north toward Champoluc. Goldoni's wife returned to the house.

The soldier lay prone in the grass and slowly replaced the binoculars in the case as he considered his options. He could race to the hidden Land Rover and go after Goldoni, but to what purpose, and how great a risk? The Alpiner was only half a man, but the *lupo* in his hands more than made up for his missing legs. Too, the surly nephew wouldn't hesitate to use the pistol in his belt.

If the ledger carried by Goldoni was what he suspected, it was being rushed away to be hidden. Not to be destroyed; one did not destroy a record of such incalculable value.

If. He had to be sure, certain of his judgment. Then he could move.

It was funny. He had not expected Goldoni to leave; he had expected others to come to him. That Goldoni did leave meant that panic had set in. A legless man who never went anywhere did not race away into the indignity and discomfort of the outside world unless the motive was extraordinary.

The soldier made up his mind. The circumstances were optimum; Goldini's wife was alone. First, he would find out if that ledger was what he thought it was; then he would find out where Goldoni had gone.

Once he learned these things, the decision would be made: whether to follow or to wait.

Andrew rose from the grass; there was no point wasting time. He started for the house.

"There is no one here, *signore*," said the stunned, gaunt woman, her eyes frightened. "My husband has gone with his nephew. They play cards in the village."

Andrew pushed the woman aside without replying. He walked directly through the house to Goldoni's room. There was nothing but old magazines and out-of-date Italian newspapers. He looked in a closet; it was at once ugly and pathetic. Trousers hung, the cloth folded, the folds held in place by safety pins. There were no books, no ledgers like the one the Alpiner had clutched in his arms.

He returned to the front room. The sullen, frightened wife was at the telephone, depressing the bar in short, panicked jabs with her bony fingers.

"The wire's cut," he said simply, approaching her.

"No," the woman whispered. "What do you want? I have nothing! *We* have nothing!"

"I think you do," answered Fontine, backing the woman against the wall, his face inches above hers. "Your husband lied to me. He said he couldn't tell me anything, but he left in a hurry carrying a very large book. It was a journal, wasn't it! An old journal that described a climb in the mountains fifty years ago. The journals! Show me the journals!"

"I do not know what you talk about, *signore!* We have nothing! We live on a *pensionare!*"

"Shut up! Give me those records!"

"*Per favore. . . .*"

"Goddamn you!" Fontine grabbed the woman's straight gray hair and yanked it forward, then suddenly, brutally backward, crashing her head into the wall. "I haven't got time. Your husband lied to me. Show me where those books are! *Now!*" He wrenched the hair again, and again slammed her skull into the wall. Blood appeared on her wrinkled neck, tears welled in her unfocused eyes.

The soldier realized he had gone too far. The combat option was now defined; it wouldn't be the first time. There'd been no lack of uncooperative peasants in Nam. He pulled the woman away from the wall.

"Do you understand me?" he said in a monotone. "I'll light a match in front of your eyes. Do you know what happens then? I'm asking you for the last time. Where are those records?"

Goldoni's wife collapsed, sobbing. Fontine held her by the cloth of her dress. With a trembling arm and frenzied, shaking fingers, she pointed to a door in the right wall of the room.

Andrew dragged her across the floor. He withdrew his Beretta and smashed the door with his boot. It crashed open. There were none inside.

"The light switch. Where is it?"

She raised her head, her mouth open, the breath coming shorter, and moved her eyes to the left. "*Lampada, lampada,*" she whispered.

He pulled her inside the small room, releasing the cloth of her dress, and found the lamp. She lay trembling, curled up on the floor. The light reflected off the glass-enclosed bookcase on the opposite wall. There were five shelves, and on each a row of books. He rushed to the case, grabbed a knob in the middle and tried to raise the pane of glass. It was locked; he tried the others. All locked.

With his Beretta he smashed the glass of two panels. The light from the lamp was dim but sufficient. The faded, handwritten letters and numbers on the brown binding were clear enough.

Each year was divided into two six-month periods, the volumes differing in thickness. The books were handmade. He looked at the upper left panel; he had not broken the glass and the reflection of light obscured the lettering. He smashed it, clearing the fragments of glass away with repeated thrusts of the steel barrel.

The first volume read 1907. There was no month noted underneath; that was a system which had evolved.

He raced the barrel over the volumes to the year 1920.

January to June was there.

July to December was missing. In its place, filling the space, was a hastily inserted volume dated *1967*.

Alfredo Goldoni, the legless cripple, had outrun him. He had removed the key from the locked door that held the secret of a journey into the mountains fifty years ago, and raced away. Fontine turned to Goldoni's wife. She was on her knees, her gaunt arms supporting her shaking, gaunt body.

It would not be difficult to do what he had to do, learn what had to be learned.

"Get up," he said.

He carried the lifeless body across the field and into the woods. There was still no moon; instead the air smelled of impending rain, the sky pitch black with clouds, no stars in evidence. The beam of the flashlight wavered up and down with his footsteps.

Time. Time was the only thing that counted now.

And shock. He would need shock.

Alfredo Goldoni had gone to the inn of the Capomontis, according to the dead woman. They had all gone there, she said. The *consigliatori of Fontini-Cristi* had gathered together. A stranger had come among them bringing the wrong words.

Chapter Thirty-one

Adrian drove back to Milan but he did not go to the hotel, he followed the highway signs to the airport, not entirely sure of *how* he was going to do what he had to do, but certain that he would do it.

He had to get to Champoluc. A killer was loose and that killer was his brother.

Somewhere in the vast complex of the Milan airport was a pilot and a plane. Or someone who knew where both could be found, for whatever price was necessary.

He drove as fast as he could, all the windows open, the wind whipping through the car. It helped him control himself; it helped him not to think, for thought was too painful.

"There's a small, private field on the outskirts of Champoluc, used by the rich in the mountains," said the unshaven pilot who had been awakened and summoned to the airport by a well-tipped clerk on the night shift for Alitalia. "But it's not operational at these hours."

"Can you fly in?"

"It's not so far away, but the terrain's bad."

"Can you *do* it?"

"I'll have enough petrol to return if I cannot. That will be my decision, not yours. But not one *lira* will be given back; is that understood?"

"I don't care."

The pilot turned to the Alitalia clerk, speaking authoritatively, obviously for the benefit of the man who would pay such money for such a flight. "Get me the weather. Zermatt, stations south, heading two-eighty degrees sweep to two-ninety-five out of Milan. I want radar fronts."

The Alitalia clerk shrugged and sighed.

"You'll be paid," said Adrian curtly.

The clerk picked up a red telephone. "*Operazioni*," he said officiously.

The landing at Champoluc was not as hazardous as the pilot wanted Adrian to believe. The field, it was true, was not operational—there was no radio contact, no tower to guide a plane in—but the single strip was outlined, the east and west perimeters marked by red lights.

Adrian walked across the field toward the only structure with lights on inside. It was a semicircular metal shell, perhaps fifty feet long, twenty-five feet high at its midpoint. It was a hangar for a small private aircraft. The door opened, brighter light spilled out on the ground, and a man in overalls was silhouetted in the doorway. He hunched his shoulders, peering out into the darkness; then he stretched, stifling a yawn.

"Can you speak English?" asked Fontine.

The man did—reluctantly and poorly, but clearly enough to be understood. And the information Adrian was given was pretty much what he expected. It was four in the morning and there was no place open at all. What pilot was crazy enough to fly into Champoluc at such an hour? Perhaps the *polizia* should be called.

Fontine withdrew several large bills from his pocket and held them in the light of the doorway. The watchman's eyes riveted on the money. Adrian suspected it was over a month's pay for the angry man.

"I came a long way to find someone. I've done nothing wrong except hire a plane to fly me here from Milan. The police are not interested in me, but *I must* find the person I'm looking for. I need a car and directions."

"You're no criminal? Flying up at such an hour——"

"No criminal," interrupted Adrian, suppressing his impatience, speaking as calmly as he could. "I'm a lawyer. An . . . *avvocato*," he added.

"*Avvocato?*" The man's voice conveyed his respect.

"I must find the house of Alfredo Goldoni. That's the name I've been given."

"The legless one?"

"I didn't know that."

The automobile was an old Fiat with torn upholstery and cracked side windows. The Goldoni farmhouse was eight to ten miles out of town, according to the watchman, on the west road. The man drew a simple diagram; it was easy to follow.

A post-and-rail fence could be seen in the glare of the headlights, the outlines of a house farther in the distance. And there was a dim wash of light coming from the house, shining through windows, dimly illuminating cascading branches of pine trees that fronted the old building near the road. Adrian removed his foot from the Fiat's accelerator, wondering whether he should stop and walk the rest of the way on foot. Lights on in a farmhouse at a quarter to five in the morning was not what he expected.

He saw the telephone poles. Had the night watchman at the airport called Goldoni and told him to expect a visitor? Or did farmers in Champoluc normally rise at such an early hour?

He decided against approaching on foot. If the watchman had telephoned, or the Goldonis were starting their day, an automobile was not the alarming intruder a man alone, walking quietly in the night, would be.

Adrian turned into a wide dirt path between the tall pines; there was no other entrance for a car. He pulled up parallel to the house; the dirt drive extended far back into the property, ending at a barn. Farm equipment could be seen through the open barn doors in the wash of the headlights. He got out of the car, passed the lighted front windows covered by curtains, and walked to the front door. It was a farmhouse door—wide and thick, the upper section a panel by itself, separated from the lower to let in the summer breezes and keep the animals out. There was a heavy, pitted brass knocker in the center. He used it.

He waited. There was no response, no sounds of movement within.

He rapped again, louder, with longer spaces between the sharp metallic reports.

There was a sound from behind the door. Indistinct, brief. A rustle of cloth or paper; a hand scratching on fabric? What?

"Please," he called out courteously. "My name's Fontine. You knew my father, and his father. From Milan. From Campo di Fiori. Please let me speak to you! I mean no harm."

Only silence now. Nothing.

He stepped back onto the grass and walked to the lighted windows. He put his face against the glass and tried to see through the white sheer curtains beyond. They were in opaque folds. The blurred images inside were further distorted by the thick glass of the Alpine window.

Then he saw it, and for a moment—as his eyes adjusted to the blurred distortion—he thought he had lost his mind for the second time that night.

At the far left side of the room was the figure of a legless man writhing in short, spastic twitches across the floor. The deformed body was large from the waist up, dressed in some kind of shirt that ended at the huge stumps, what remained of the legs hidden in the cloth of white undershorts.

The legless one.

Alfredo Goldoni. Adrian watched now as Goldoni maneuvered himself into a dark corner at the far wall. He carried something in his arms, clutching it as though it were a lifeline in a heavy sea. It was a rifle, a large-barreled rifle. Why?

"*Goldoni! Please!*" Fontine cried out at the window. "I just want to *talk* to you. If the watchman called you, he must have told you that."

The report was thunderous; glass shattered in all directions, fragments penetrating Adrian's raincoat and jacket. At the last instant he had seen the black barrel raised and had lurched to the side, covering his face. Thick, jagged points of glass were like a hundred pieces of ice across his arm. But for the heavy sweater he had bought in Milan, he would have been a mass of blood. As it was, his arms and neck were bleeding slightly.

Above, through the billows of smoke and the shattered glass of the window, he could hear the metallic snap of the rifle; Goldoni had reloaded. He sat up, his back against the stone foundation of the house. He felt along his left arm and removed as much of the glass as he could. He could feel the rivulets of blood on his neck.

He sat there, breathing heavily, ministering to himself, then called out again. Goldoni could not possibly negotiate the space between the dark corner and the window. They were two prisoners, one intent on killing the other, held at bay by an invisible, unclimbable wall.

"Listen to me! I don't know what you've been told, but it's not true! I'm not your enemy!"

"*Animale!*" roared Goldoni from within. "I'll see you dead!"

"For God's sake, why? I don't want to harm you!"

"You are Fontini-Cristi! You are a killer of women! An abductor of children! *Maligno! Animale!*"

He was too late. Oh, Jesus! He was *too late!* The killer had reached Champoluc before him.

But the killer was still loose. There was a chance.

"One last time, Goldoni," he said, without shouting now. "I'm a Fontini-Cristi, but I'm not the man you want dead. I'm not a killer of women and I've abducted no children. I know the man you're talking about and he's not me. That's as clear and as simple as I can put it. Now, I'm going to stand up in front of this window. I haven't got any gun—I've never owned one. If you don't believe me, I guess you'll have to shoot. I haven't got time to argue any longer. And I don't think you do, either. Any of you."

Adrian pressed his bleeding hand on the ground and rose unsteadily. He walked slowly in front of the shattered glass of the window.

Alfredo Goldoni called out quietly, "Walk in with your arms in front of you. There's no way you'll live if you hesitate or break your step."

Fontine came out of the shadows of the darkened back room. The legless man had directed him to a window through which he could enter; the cripple would not risk the manipulations required of him to open the front door. As Adrian emerged from the darkness, Goldoni cocked the hammer of the rifle, prepared to fire. He spoke in a whisper.

"You're the man and, yet, you are not the man."

"He's my brother," said Adrian softly. "And I have to stop him."

Goldoni stared at him in silence. Finally, his eyes still concentrated on Fontine's face, he uncocked the rifle and lowered it beside him in the corner.

"Help me into my chair," he said.

Adrian sat in front of the legless man, bare to the waist, his back within the reach of Goldoni's hands. The Italian-Swiss had removed the fragments of glass, applying an alcohol solution that stung but did its work; the bleeding stopped.

"In the mountains blood is precious. Our countrymen in the north call this fluid *leiman*. It's better than the powder. I doubt the medical doctors approve, but it does the trick. Put on your shirt."

"Thank you." Fontine rose and did as he was told. They had spoken only briefly of things that had to be said. With an Alpiner's practicality, Goldoni had ordered Adrian to remove his clothes where the glass had penetrated. A wounded man, uncared for, was of little good to anyone. His role of rural physician, however, did not lessen his anger or his agony.

"He's a man from hell," said the cripple as Fontine buttoned his shirt.

"He's sick, though I realize that's no help for you. He's looking for something. A vault, hidden somewhere in the mountains. It was carried there years ago, before the war, by my grandfather."

"We know. We've known someone would come someday. But that's all we know. We don't know where in the mountains."

Adrian didn't believe the legless man and yet he could not be sure. "You said killer of women. Who?"

"My wife. She's gone."

"Gone? How do you know she's dead?"

"He lied. He said she ran away down the road. That he took chase and caught her and keeps her hidden in the village."

"It's possible."

"It is not. I can't walk, *signore*. My wife can't run. She has the swollen veins in her legs. She wears thick shoes to get around this house. Those shoes are in front of your eyes."

Adrian looked down where Goldoni gestured. A pair of heavy, ugly shoes were placed neatly at the side of a chair.

"People do things they don't think they can do——"

"There's blood on the floor," interrupted Goldoni, his voice trembling, pointing to an open doorway. "There were no wounds on the man who calls himself a soldier. Go! Look for yourself."

Fontine walked to the open door and went inside the small room. A glass bookcase was smashed, sharp fragments everywhere. He reached inside and removed a volume behind one of the shattered panels. He opened it. In clear handscript were pages detailing successive climbs into the mountains. The dates extended back beyond 1920. And there was blood on the floor by the door.

He was too late.

He walked swiftly back into the front room.

"Tell me everything. As quickly as you can. *Everything*."

The soldier had been thorough. He had immobilized his enemy, rendered them helpless through fear and panic. The major from Eye Corps had mounted his own invasion of the Capomonti inn. He had done so swiftly, without a wasted move, finding Lefrac and the members of the Capomonti and Goldoni families in an upstairs room where they were holding their hastily summoned conference.

The door of the room had crashed open, a terrified desk clerk propelled through it so harshly he fell to the floor. The soldier entered quickly, closing the door before any in the room knew what was happening, and held them all rigid at the point of a gun.

The soldier then issued his demands. First, the old ledger describing a journey into the mountains over fifty years ago. And maps. Minutely detailed maps used by climbers in the Champoluc district. Second, the services of either Lefrac's son or eighteen-year-old grandson to lead him into the hills. Third, the granddaughter as a second hostage. The child's father had lost his head and lunged at the man with the gun; but the soldier was expert and the father subdued without a shot.

Old Lefrac was ordered to open the door and call for a housemaid. Proper clothing was brought to the room and the children dressed under gunpoint. It was then that the man-from-hell told Goldoni his wife was a prisoner. He was to return to his house and remain there alone, sending his driver—his nephew—away. If he stopped to reach the police, he would never see his wife again.

"Why?" asked Adrian quickly. "Why did he do that? Why did he want you back here alone?"

"He separates us. My sister returns with my nephew to her house on the Via Sestina; Lefrac and his son remain at the inn. Together we might make each other bold. Apart we're frightened, helpless. A gun against a child's head is not easily forgotten. He knows that alone we'll do nothing but wait."

Adrian closed his eyes. "God," he said.

"The soldier's an expert, that one." Goldoni's voice was low, the hatred seething.

Fontine glanced at him. *I have run with the pack—in the middle of the pack—but now I have reached the edges and I will peel away.*

"Why did you shoot at me? If you thought it was him, how could you take the chance? Not knowing what he did."

"I saw your face against the glass. I wanted to blind you, not to kill you. A dead man can't tell me where he's taken my wife. Or the body of my wife. Or the children. I'm a good shot; I fired inches above your head."

Fontine crossed to the chair where he had thrown his jacket and took out the Xeroxed pages of his father's recollections of fifty years ago. "You must have read that journal. Can you remember what was written?"

"You can't go after him. He'll kill."

"Can you *remember?*"

"It was a two-day climb with many crossing trails! He could be anywhere. He narrows down the place he seeks. He travels blindly. If he saw you, he'd kill the children."

"He won't see me. Not if I get there first! Not if I *wait* for him!" Adrian unfolded the Xeroxed pages.

"They've been read to me. There's nothing that can help you."

"There has to be! It's *here!*"

"You're wrong," said Goldoni, and Adrian knew he was not lying. "I tried to tell *him* that, but he wouldn't listen. Your grandfather made his arrangements, but the *padrone* did not consider unexpected death, or human failing."

Fontine looked up from the pages. Helplessness was in the old man's eyes. A killer was in the mountains and he was helpless. Death would surely follow death, for surely his wife was gone.

"What were these arrangements?" asked Adrian softly.

"I'll tell you. You're not your brother. We've kept the secret for thirty-five years, Lefrac, the Capomontis, and ourselves. And one other—not one of us—whose death came suddenly, before he made his own arrangments."

"Who was that?"

"A merchant named Leinkraus. We didn't know him well."

"Tell me."

"We've waited all these years for a Fontini-Cristi to come." So the legless man began:——

The man they—the Goldonis, Lefrac, and the Capomontis—expected would come quietly, in peace, seeking the iron crate buried high in the mountains. This man would speak of the journey taken so many years ago by father and son, and he would know that journey was recorded in the Goldoni ledgers—as all who employed the Goldoni guides would know. And because that climb lasted for two days over considerable terrain, the man would specify an abandoned railroad clearing known as *Sciocchezza di Cacciatori*—Hunter's Folly. The clearing had been left to nature over forty years ago, long before the iron crate had been buried, but it had existed when father and son journeyed to Champoluc in the summer of 1920.

"I thought those clearings were given——"

"The names of birds?"

"Yes."

"Most were, not all. The soldier asked if there was a clearing known by the name of the hawk. There are no hawks in the mountains of Champoluc."

"The painting on the wall," said Adrian, more to himself than for the benefit of the Alpiner.

"What?"

"My father remembered a painting on a wall in Campo di Fiori, a painting of a hunt. He thought it might be significant."

"The soldier did not speak of it. Nor did he speak of why he sought the information; only that he had to have it. He wouldn't mention the *search* to me. *Or* the ledgers. Or the reason why the railroad clearing was important. He was *secretive*. And, clearly, he did not come in peace. A soldier who threatens a legless man is a hollow commander. I didn't trust him."

Everything his brother had done was contrary to the memory of the Fontini-Cristis as these people remembered them. It might have been so simple had he been open with them, had he *come in peace*; but the soldier couldn't do that. He was always at war.

"Then the area around this abandoned clearing—Hunter's Folly—is where the vault is buried?"

"Presumably. There are several old trails to the east that lead away from the tracks, up to the higher ridges. But which trail, which ridge? We do not know."

"The records would describe it."

"If one knew where to look. The soldier doesn't."

Adrian thought. His brother had traveled across the world, eluding the Intelligence network of the most powerful nation on earth. "You may be underestimating him."

"He's not one of us. He's not a man of the mountains."

"No," mused Fontine quietly. "He's something else. What would he *look* for? That's what we have to think about."

"An inaccessible place. Away from the trails. Ground that would not be travelled easily for any of several reasons. There are many such areas. The mountains are filled with them."

"But you said it a few minutes ago. He'd narrow down his . . . options."

"*Signore?*"

"Nothing. I was thinking of—never mind. You see, he knows what *not* to look for. He knows that the vault was heavy; it had to be transported—mechanically. He starts with something *besides* the record book."

"We weren't aware of that."

"He is."

"It will do him little good in the darkness."

"Look at the window," said Adrian. Outside, the first morning light could be seen. "Tell me about this other man. The merchant."

"Leinkraus?"

"Yes. How was he involved?"

"That answer went with his death. Even Francesca doesn't know."

"Francesca?"

"My sister. When my brothers died, she was the eldest. The envelope was given to her. . . ."

"*Envelope?* What envelope?"

"Your grandfather's instructions."

. . . *Therefore, should Alfredo not be the eldest, look for a sister, as is the Italian-Swiss custom.* . . .

Adrian unfolded the pages of his father's testament. If such fragments of truth came through the distance of years with such accuracy, more attention had to be paid to his father's disjointed remembrances.

"My sister has lived in Champoluc since her marriage to Capomonti. She knew the Leinkraus family better than any of us. Old Leinkraus died in his store. There was a fire; many thought it wasn't accidental."

"I don't understand."

"The family Leinkraus are Jews."

"I see. Go on." Adrian shifted the pages.

. . . *The merchant was not popular. He was a Jew and for one who fought bitterly . . . Such thinking was indefensible.*

Goldoni continued. The man who came to Champoluc and spoke of the iron crate and the long-forgotten journey and the old railroad clearing was to be given the envelope left with the eldest Goldoni.

"You must understand, *signore*." The legless man interrupted himself. "We are *all* family now. The Capomontis and the Goldonis. After so many years and no one came, we discussed it between ourselves."

"You're ahead of me."

"The envelope directed the man who had come to Champoluc to old Capomonti. . . ."

Adrian turned back the pages. *If there were secrets to leave in the Champoluc, old Capomonti would have been a rock of silence and trust.*

"When Capomonti died, he gave *his* instructions to his son-in-law, Lefrac."

"Then Lefrac *knows*."

"Only one word. The name Leinkraus."

Fontine bolted forward in his seat. He remained on the edge, bewildered. Yet something was triggered in his mind. As in long, complex cross-examination, isolated phrases and solitary words were suddenly brought into focus, given meaning where no meaning had existed previously.

The *words*. Look to the words, as his brother looked to violence.

He scanned the pages in his hands, turning them rapidly until he found what he was looking for.

. . . *There is a blurred memory of an unpleasant incident . . . what the unpleasant incident specifically entailed, I have no recall . . . serious and provoked my father . . . a sad anger . . . impression that details were withheld from me.* . . .

Withheld. Anger. Sadness.

. . . *provoked my father.* . . .

"Goldoni, listen to me. You've got to think back. Way back. Something happened. Something unpleasant, sad, angry. And it concerned the Leinkraus family."

"No."

Adrian stopped. The legless Goldoni had not let him finish. "What do you mean 'no'?" he asked quietly.

"I told you. I didn't know them well. We barely spoke."

"Because they were Jews? Is that the way it came down from the north in those days?"

"I don't understand you."

"I think you do." Adrian stared at him; the Alpiner avoided his eyes. Fontine continued softly. "You didn't have to know them—at all, perhaps. But for the first time, you're lying to me. Why?"

"I'm not lying. They weren't friends of the Goldonis."

"Or the Capomontis?"

"*Or* the Capomontis!"

"You didn't like them?"

"We didn't *know* them! They kept to themselves. Other Jews came and they lived among their own. It's that simple."

"It's *not*." Adrian knew the answer was within reach. Hidden, perhaps, from Goldoni himself. "Something happened in July of 1920. What was it?"

Goldoni sighed. "I can't remember."

"July fourteenth, 1920! What *happened?*"

Goldoni's breath was shorter, his large jaws taut. The massive stumps that once were legs twitched in his wheelchair. "It doesn't mean anything," he whispered.

"Let me be the judge of that," said Adrian.

"Times have changed. So much has changed in a lifetime," said the Alpiner, his voice faltering. "The same was felt by everyone."

"July *fourteenth, 1920!* " Adrian zeroed in on his witness.

"I tell you! It is meaningless!"

"*Goddamn you!* " Adrian leaped from the chair. Striking the helpless old man was not out of the question. Then the words came.

"A Jew was beaten. A young Jew who entered the church school . . . was beaten. He died three days later."

The Alpiner had said it. But only part of it. Fontine backed away from the wheelchair. "Leinkraus's son?" he asked.

"Yes."

"The church school?"

"He couldn't enter the state school. It was a place to learn. The priests accepted him."

Fontine sat down slowly, keeping his eyes on Goldoni. "There's more, isn't there? Who gave the beating?"

"Four boys from the village. They didn't know what they were doing. Everyone said so."

"I'm sure everyone did. It's easier that way. Ignorant children who had to be protected. And what was the life of one Jew?"

Tears came to the eyes of Alfredo Goldoni. "Yes."

"You were one of those boys, weren't you?"

Goldoni nodded his head in silence.

"I think I can tell you what happened," continued Adrian. "Leinkraus was threatened. His wife, his other children. Nothing was said, nothing reported. A young Jew had died, that was all."

"So many years ago," Goldoni whispered as the tears fell down his face. "No one thinks like that anymore. And we have lived with what we did. At the end of my life, it grows even more difficult. The grave is close at hand now."

Adrian stopped breathing, stunned by Goldoni's words. The *grave* is close. . . . The *grave*. My God! Was that *it?* He wanted to jump out of the chair and roar his questions until the legless Alpiner remembered! *Exactly*. But he could not do that. He kept his voice low, incisive.

"What happened then? What did Leinkraus do?"

"Do?" Goldoni shrugged slowly, sadness in the gesture. "What could he do? He kept silent."

"Was there a funeral? A burial?"

"If there was, we knew nothing of it."

"Leinkraus's son had to be buried. No Christian cemetery would accept a Jew. Was there a burial place for Jews?"

"No, not then. There is now."

"*Then!* What about then? Where was he *buried?* Where was the *murdered son* of Leinkraus *buried?*"

Goldoni reacted as though struck in the face. "It was said the father and the brothers—the men of the family—took the dead son into the mountains. Where the boy's body would not be further abused."

Adrian got out of the chair. There was his answer.

The grave of the Jew. The vault from Salonika.

Savarone Fontini-Cristi had found an eternal truth in a village tragedy. He had used it. In the end, not letting the holy men forget.

Paul Leinkraus was in his late forties, the grandson of the merchant and a merchant himself, but of a different time. There was little he could relate of a grandfather he barely knew, or of an era of obsequiousness and fear he had never known. But he was a man of acumen, bespeaking the expansion for which he was responsible. As such, he had recognized the urgency and the legitimacy of Adrian's sudden call.

Leinkraus had taken Fontine into the library, away from his wife and child, and removed the family Torah from the shelf. The diagram filled the entire back panel of the binding. It was a precisely drawn map that showed the way to the grave of Reuven Leinkraus's first son, buried in the mountains on July 17, 1920.

Adrian had traced every line, then matched his drawing with the original. It was precise; he had his last passport. To where, he was certain. To what, he could not know.

He had made a final request of Leinkraus. An overseas telephone call to London for which, of course, he would pay.

"Your grandfather made all the payments this house can accept. Make your call."

"Please stay. I want you to hear."

He had placed a call to the Savoy in London. His request was uncomplicated. When the American embassy opened, would the Savoy please leave a message for Colonel Tarkington of the inspector general's office. If he was not in London, the embassy would know where to reach him.

Colonel Tarkington was to be directed to a man named Paul Leinkraus in the town of Champoluc in the Italian Alps. The message was to be signed Adrian Fontine.

He was going into the mountains on the hunt, but he had no illusions. He was not ultimately a match for the soldier. His gesture might be only that: a gesture ending in futility. And very possibly his own death; he understood that, too.

The world could survive very well without his presence. He wasn't particularly remarkable, although he liked to think he had certain talents. But he wasn't at all sure how the world would fare if Andrew walked out of the Champoluc with the contents of an iron crate that had been carried on a train from Salonika over thirty years ago.

If only one brother came out of the mountains and that man was the killer of Eye Corps, he had to be taken.

The call finished, Adrian had looked up at Paul Leinkraus. "When Colonel Tarkington makes contact with you, tell him exactly what happened here this morning."

Fontine nodded to Leinkraus in the doorway. He opened the door of the Fiat and climbed in, noticing that he had been so agitated upon his arrival that he'd left the keys in the car. It was the kind of carelessness no soldier would be guilty of.

The realization caused him to reach over and pull down the panel of the glove compartment. He put his hand inside and took out a heavy, black, magazine-clip pistol; the loading mechanism had been explained to him by Alfredo Goldoni.

He started the ignition and rolled down the window, suddenly needing the air. His breath came rapidly; his heartbeat vibrated in his throat. And he remembered.

He had fired a pistol only once in his life. Years ago at a boys' camp in New Hampshire when the counselors had taken them to a local police range. His brother had been beside him, and they had laughed together, excited children.

Where had the laughter gone?

Where had his brother gone?

Adrian drove down the tree-lined street and turned left into the road that would take him north to the mountains. Above, the early morning sun was hidden behind a blanket of gathering clouds.

The sky was angry.

Chapter Thirty-two

The girl shrieked and slipped on the rock; her brother whipped around and grabbed her hand, preventing the fall. The plunge was no more than twenty feet, and the soldier wondered whether it might be better to break the grip between them and let her fall. If the girl snapped an ankle or a leg, she wouldn't go anywhere; she certainly could not make it down through the trails to the flat ground and the road below. It was twelve miles behind them now. They had covered the initial terrain during the night.

He could bypass the initial trails of that journey into the mountains fifty years ago. If others began the search, they wouldn't know that; he did. He could read maps the way most men read simple books. From symbols, colors, and numbers, he could visualize terrain with the accuracy of a camera. There was no one better in the army. He was a master of everything *real*, from men to machines to maps.

The detailed map used by climbers in the Champoluc district showed the railroad from Zermatt angling west around the curve of the mountains. It straightened out for approximately five miles before the station at Champoluc. The areas directly east of the final flat stretches of track were heavily traversed throughout the year. These were the first trails described in Goldoni's journal. No one concealing anything of value would consider them.

Yet farther north, at the start of the railroad's western curve, were the old clearings that led to the numerous trails specifically listed in the pages he had ripped out of the Goldoni ledger for July 14 and 15 of 1920. Any of these might be the one. Once he saw them in daylight, and studied the possibilities, he could determine which of the trails he would trace.

Those selections would be based on fact. Fact one: The size and weight of the vault mandated vehicle or animal transportation. Fact two: The train from Salonika made its journey in the month of December—a time of year when the weather was bitter cold and the mountain passes clogged with snow. Fact three: The spring and summer thaws, with their rushing waters and erosion of earth, would call for a recess in the high ground to hide the vault, enveloped by rock for protection. Fact four: That recess would be away from frequently traveled areas, high above an established route, but with an offshoot trail that could be negotiated by an animal or a vehicle. Fact five: That trail had to emanate from a section of the track where a train could pull to a stop, the ground level on both sides flat and straight. Fact six: The specific clearing, in current use or abandoned, would lead into the crisscrossing trails recorded in the Goldoni ledger. By retracing each one to the tracks and picturing the feasibility of traveling over it—in the cold and snow, by animal or vehicle—the number of trails would be further reduced until there was one that led to the hiding place.

He had time. Days, if he needed them. He had supplies for a week strapped to his back. The stump, Goldoni, the woman, Capomonti, and Lefrac and his family were too frightened to make a move. He had covered himself brilliantly. The unseen was always more effective than the observable in combat. He had told the terrified Swiss that he had associates in Champuloc. They would be watching; they would get word to him in the mountains should a Goldoni or a Capomonti or a Lefrac reach the police. Communications were no problem for soldiers. And the result of their reaching him would be the execution of his hostages.

He had fantasized the presence of Eye Corps. Eye Corps the way it had been—efficient, strong, quick to maneuver.

He would build a new Corps one day, stronger and more efficient, without weakness. He would find the vault from Salonika, carry the documents out of the mountains, summon the holy men and watch their faces as he described the imminent, global collapse of their institutions.

. . . *The contents of that vault are as staggering to the civilized world as any in history.* . . .

That was comforting. It could not be in better hands.

They were on a flat stretch now, the first elevation to the west no more than a mile away. The girl fell to her knees, sobbing. Her brother looked at him, his eyes conveying hatred, fear, supplication. Andrew would kill them both, but not for a while. One disposed of hostages when they no longer served a purpose.

Only fools killed indiscriminately. Death was an instrument, a means to be used in reaching an objective or completing an assignment, and that was all it was.

Adrian drove the Fiat off the road into the fields. The rocks ripped the undercarriage. He could drive no farther; he had reached the first of several step hills that led to the first plateau described on the Leinkraus diagram. He was eight and a half miles north of Champoluc. The grave was precisely five miles beyond the first of the plateaus that were the landmarks of the journey to the burial ground.

He got out of the car and walked across the field of tall grass. He looked up. The hill in front of him sprang suddenly out of the ground, an impromptu bulge of nature, more rock than greenery, with no discernible path on which to scale it. He knelt down and retied the laces on his rubber-soled shoes as tightly as he could. The weight of the pistol was heavy in his raincoat pocket.

For a moment he closed his eyes. *He could not think. O God! Keep me from thinking!*

He was a mover now. He got to his feet and started to climb.

The first two railroad clearings proved negative. There was no way animal or vehicle could traverse the routes from the Zermatt railway to the eastern slopes. Two more clearings remained. The names on the old Champoluc map were Hunter's Folly and Sparrow's Rook; no mention of hawk. Still, it had to be one of them!

Andrew looked at his hostages. Brother and sister sat together on the ground, talking in quiet, frightened whispers, their eyes darting up at him. The hatred was gone now, only fear and supplication remained. There was something ugly about them, thought the soldier. And then he realized what it was. Across the world in the jungles of Southeast Asia, people their age fought battles, weapons strapped to their backs over uniforms that looked like pajamas. They were his enemy over there, but he respected that enemy.

He had no respect for these children. There was no strength in their faces. Only fear, and fear was repulsive to the major from Eye Corps.

"Get up!" He could not help himself; he shouted angrily at the sight of these pampered, weak brats with no dignity in their faces.

Christ, he despised the spineless!

They would not be missed.

Adrian looked back across the ridge to the plateau in the distance, thankful that old Goldoni had given him gloves. Even without the cold, his bare hands and fingers would have been a bleeding mass of flesh. It wasn't that the climb was difficult; a man used to minimum exercise in the mountains would find it simple. But he had never been in the mountains except on skis, where tows and trams did the uphill work. He was using muscles rarely employed and had little confidence in his sense of balance.

The last several hundred yards had been the most difficult. The trail in the Leinkraus diagram was landmarked: a cluster of gray rock at the base of a crystalline schistose embankment that all climbers knew should be avoided, for it cracked easily. The crystalline rock evolved into a cliff that rose about a hundred feet from the schist, its edge sharply defined. To the left of the crystalline sheet were abrupt, dense Alpine woods that grew vertically out of the slope, a sudden, thick forest surrounded by rock. The Leinkraus trail was marked off at ten paces from the embankment. It led to the top of the wooded slope whose ridge was the second plateau: the end of the second leg of the journey.

The trail was nowhere to be found. It had disappeared; years of disuse and overgrowth had concealed it. Yet the ridge could be seen clearly above the trees. That he could see it was an indication of the angle of ascent.

He had walked into the dense Alpine underbrush and made his way, yard by yard, up the steep incline, through nettled bush and the skin-piercing needles of the pines.

He sat on the ridge, breathing heavily, his shoulders aching from the constant tension. He estimated the distance from the first plateau to be at least three miles. It had taken nearly three hours. A mile an hour, over rocks and down miniature valleys, and across cold streams, and up endless hills. Just three miles. If that were so, he had two miles to go, perhaps less. He looked up. The overcast had lasted the entire morning. It would continue on throughout the day. The sky above was like the North Shore sky before a heavy squall.

They used to sail in squalls together. Laughing as they bested the weather, sure of their abilities in the water, pitting themselves against the rain and wind of the Sound.

No, he would not think of that. He got to his feet and looked at his tracing of the Leinkraus diagram, copied from the inside binding of a family Torah.

The diagram was clear but the rising terrain beyond him wasn't. He saw the objective—due northeast, the third plateau, isolated above the sea of Alpine spruce. But the ridge he was on swept to the right, due *east*, leading into the base of yet another mountain of boulders, away from any direct line to the plateau in the distance. He walked around the ledge past the border of the dark, sloping woods he had climbed through. The drop below was sheer and the rocks beneath rose like a bubbling river of stone. The trail as marked in the diagram went from forest to ledge to forest; there was no mention of intersecting rock.

Geological changes had taken place in the intervening years since any member of the Leinkraus family had journeyed to the burial ground. A sudden shift of nature—a quake or an avalanche—had eliminated the trail.

Still, he could see the plateau. What separated him from it seemed impenetrable, but once through it—and over it—he could make out a winding trail on the higher ground that led to the plateau. It was doubtful that that had been altered. He slid down the embankment onto the river of stone, and awkwardly, trying to keep his feet from slipping into a hundred miniature crevices, climbed toward the forest of spruce.

The third clearing was it! *Sciocchezza di Cacciatori!* Hunter's Folly! Long abandoned but once perfect for removing the vault. The trail from the mountains to the Zermatt railway was passable, and the area around the tracks was flat and accessible. At first Andrew had not been sure; in spite of the level ground on either side of the tracks, the stretch was short, blocked by a curve. Then he remembered: his father had said that the train from Salonika had been a short freight. Four cars and an engine.

Five railways units could easily pull beyond the curve and come to a stop in a straight line. Whatever car the vault had been in could have been unloaded without difficulty.

But what now convinced him he was near his goal was an unexpected discovery. West of the tracks were the unmistakable signs of an abandoned road. The cut through the woods was defined, the trees in the cut shorter than those surrounding them, the brush closer to the ground. It was no longer a road—not even a path—but its former existence was undeniable.

"Lefrac!" he yelled at the eighteen-year-old. "What's down there?" He pointed northwest, where the cut in the forest sloped.

"A village. About five, six miles away."

"It's not on the railroad line?"

"No, *signore*. It's in farm country, below the mountains."

"What roads lead into it?"

"The main road from Zürich and——"

"All right." He stopped the boy for two reasons. He had heard what he wanted to hear, and twenty feet away the girl had gotten to her feet and was edging toward the woods on the eastern side of the tracks.

Fontine took out his pistol and fired two shots. The explosions thundered throughout the woods; the bullets detonated the ground on either side of the child. She screamed, terrified. Her brother lunged at him in a frenzy of tears; he sidestepped and smashed the barrel of his pistol on the side of the boy's head.

Lefrac's son fell to the ground, sobs of frustration and anger filling the silence of the abandoned railroad clearing.

"You're better than I thought you were," said the soldier coldly, raising his eyes, turning to the girl. "Help him. He's not hurt. We're heading back."

Give the captured hope, reflected the soldier. The younger and more inexperienced they were, the more hope they should be given. It reduced the fear which was, in itself, detrimental to rapid travel. Fear was an instrument, too. Like death. It was to be used methodically.

He retraced the trail from the Zermatt tracks for a second time. He was certain now. There was nothing that would prevent an animal or a vehicle from negotiating it. The ground was clear and mostly hard. And more important, the terrain rose directly toward the eastern slopes, into the specific trails recorded in the faded pages of the ledger. Light snow and layers of frost covered the earth. With every yard the soldier in him told him he was nearing the enemy zone. For that was what it was.

They reached the first intersecting trail described by the Goldoni guide on the morning of July 14, 1920. To the right, the trail angled downward into some kind of forest, a thick wall of dark green, laced with a roof of white. It seemed impenetrable.

It was a possible hiding place. That mountain forest would not be tempting to the casual climber, and without interest for the experienced. On the other hand, it *was* forest—wood and earth, not rock—and because it was not rock he could not accept it. The vault would be protected by rock.

To the left, the trail continued up, veering obliquely into the side of a small mountain above them. The trail itself was wide, on solid rock, and bordered by foliage. Boulders rose sharply to the right, forming an abrupt sheer of heavy stone. An animal or a vehicle still had space to walk or roll; the direct line from the Zermatt tracks was unbroken.

"Move it!" he shouted, gesturing to the left. The Lefrac children looked at each other. To the right was the way to Champoluc—the way back. The girl grabbed her brother; Fontine stepped forward, broke the grip, and propelled the girl forward.

"*Signore!*" The boy shouted and stepped between them, his arms raised in front of him, his young palms flat—a very penetrable shield. "Don't do that," he stammered, his voice low, cracking with young fear, his own anger challenging himself.

"Let's go," said the soldier. He had no time to waste on children.

"You hear me, *signore!*"

"I heard you. Now, move."

At the western flank of the small mountain the width of the rising trail abruptly narrowed. It entered an enormous, natural archway cut out of the boulders and led to the face of a hill of sheer rock. The geologically formed archway was not only the logical extension of the trail, but the mountain of rock beyond must have been irresistible to novice climbers. It could be scaled without great effort, but was sufficiently awesome by its breadth and height to be a good start for the higher regions. Perfect for an enthusiastic seventeen year old, under the watchful eye of a guide and a father.

But the width under the arch *was* narrow, the rock floor too smooth, especially when heavier snows fell. An animal—a mule or a horse—might cross under but there was considerable danger that hooves would slip.

No vehicle could possibly get through.

Andrew turned and studied the approach they had just made. There were no other trails, but about thirty yards back on the left the ground was flat and filled with Alpine brush. It extended to a short wall of rock that rose up to the ridge of the mountain. That wall, that short cliff, was no more than twenty feet high, almost hidden by shrubs and small, gnarled trees growing out of the rock. But the ground beneath that cliff, beneath that ridge, was flat. Natural obstructions were everywhere else, but not there, not in that particular spot.

"Walk over there," he ordered the young Lefracs, both to keep them in sight and to provide perspective. "Go into that flat area between the rocks! Spread the bushes and walk in! As far as you can!"

He stepped back off the trail and studied the ridge above. It, too, was flat, or at least appeared so. And it was something else, something that might not be noticed except, perhaps, from where he stood. It was . . . defined. The edge, though jagged, formed a nearly perfect semicircle. If that circle continued, the ridge itself was like a small, out-of-the-way platform on a small, unimportant mountain, but still high above the lower Alpine hills.

He judged the height of Lefrac's son as five-ten or -eleven. "Raise your hands!" he shouted.

Arms extended, the boy's hands were just below the mid-point of the short cliff.

Suppose the method of transport was not an animal but a vehicle. A heavy-wheeled piece of machinery, the carriage a plow, or a tractor. It was consistent; there was no part of the route from the Zermatt tracks or up the Goldoni trail that such a piece of equipment could not traverse. And plows and tractors had winch machinery. . . .

"*Signore! Signore!*" It was the girl; her shouts conveyed a strange exaltation, a cross between hope and desperation. "If this is what you *look* for, let us *go!*"

Andrew raced back into the trail and toward the Lefracs. He sped into the tangled shrubbery to the face of the rock.

"Down there!" The girl shouted again.

On the ground in the light snow, barely seen through the underbrush, was an old ladder. The wood was rotted, the steps swollen out of their sockets in half a dozen places. But otherwise it was intact. It was not now usable, but neither had it been abused by man. It had lain in that shrubbery for years, perhaps decades, untouched except by nature and time.

Fontine knelt down and touched it, pried it off the ground, watched it crumble as he lifted it. He had found a human tool where none should be; he knew that not fifteen feet above him . . .

Above him! He whipped his head up and saw the blurred object crashing down. The impact came; his head exploded in a flashing of pain, followed by an instant of numbness, a hundred hammers pounding. He fell forward, struggling to shake the effects of the blow and find light again.

He heard the shouts.

"Fuggi! Presto! In la traccia!" The boy.

"Non senza voi! Tu fuggi anche!" The girl.

Lefrac's son had found a large rock on the ground. And in his hatred he had lost his fear; holding the primitive weapon in his hand, he had crashed it down on the soldier's head.

The light was returning. Fontine started to get up and, again, he saw the unfocused hand descending, the rock slashing diagonally down.

"You little fuck! You fuck!"

Lefrac's son released the rock, hurling it into the soldier's body—anywhere, a final assault—and ran out of the snow-covered shrubbery onto the trail after his sister.

Andrew recognized the pitch of his own fury. He had felt it perhaps a dozen times in his life, and it had always been in the molten heat of combat when an enemy held an advantage he could not control.

He crawled out of the brush to the edge of the trail and looked below. Beneath him on the winding path were brother and sister, running as best they could over the slippery trail.

He reached under his jacket to the holster strapped to his chest. The Beretta was in his pocket. But a Beretta would be inadequate; it was not that accurate. He pulled out the .357-caliber Magnum he had bought at the Leinkraus store in Champoluc. His hostages were about forty yards away. The boy took the girls hand; they were close together, the figures overlapping.

Andrew squeezed the trigger eight times in succession. Both bodies fell, writhing on the rocks. He could hear the screams. In seconds the screaming subsided into moans, the writhing became twists and lurches at nothing. They would die, but not for a while. They would go no farther.

The soldier crawled back through the shrubs into the flat *cul de sac* and removed the pack from his back, slipping the straps off slowly, moving his bleeding head as little as possible. He opened the pack and slipped out the canvas first-aid kit. He had to patch the broken skin and stop the bleeding as best he could. And move. For Christ's sake, *move!*

He had no hostages now. He could tell himself it made no difference, but he knew better. Hostages were a way out. If he came out of the mountains alone, they'd be watching. *Jesus*, they'd be watching for him—he was a dead man. They'd take the vault and kill him.

There was another way. The Lefrac boy had said it!

The abandoned road west of the abandoned clearing called Hunter's Folly! Past the tracks, down to a village whose main road led to Zürich.

But he was not going to that village, to that road that led to Zürich, until the contents of the vault were his. And every instinct he possessed told him he'd found it.

Fifteen feet above.

He unwound the ropes clamped to the outside of the pack and spread the grappling hook from its axis; the prongs locked into position. He stood up. His temple throbbed and the wounds stung where he'd applied the antiseptic, but the bleeding had stopped. He was focusing clearly again.

He stepped back and lobbed the grappling hook up to the ledge. It caught.

He yanked on the rope.

The rock splintered; fragments plummeted down, followed by larger sections of limestone. He sprang to the side to avoid the falling hook; it embedded itself through the thin layers of snow into the ground.

He swore and once more heaved the hook skyward, arcing it over the ledge, far into the flat surface above. He tugged in swift, short movements; the hook caught. He pulled harder; it held.

The line was ready; he could climb. He reached down, grabbed the straps of his pack and slipped his arms through, not bothering to secure the front clamps. He yanked on the rope a last time; he was satisfied. He jumped as high as he could, thrusting his legs out against the stone, allowing himself to swing back into the rock as he manipulated his hands—one over the other—in rapid ascent. He swung his left leg over the jagged ledge, and pushed his right hand against the stone beneath, forcing his body into a lateral roll that propelled him onto the surface. He started to get up, his eyes traveling to the source of the grappling hook's anchor.

But he remained kneeling in shock as he stared at the strange sight ten feet away, in the center of the plateau. Embedded in the stone was an old, rusted metal star: a Star of David.

The grappling hook enveloped it, the prongs moored around the iron.

He was looking at a grave.

He heard the echoes throughout the mountains like repeated, sharp cracks of thunder, one right after another. As if bolts of lightning had sliced through the roof of the forest, splitting the wood of a hundred trees around him. But they signified neither lightning nor thunder; they were gunshots.

In spite of the cold, perspiration streamed down Adrian's face, and despite the darkness of the forest, his eyes were filled with unwanted images. His brother had killed again. The major from Eye Corps was efficiently going about his business of death. The screams that followed the shots were faint, muted by the forest barrier, but unmistakable.

Why? For God's sake, *why?!*

He could not think. Not about things like that. Not now. He had to think only on one level—the level of motion. He had made a half-dozen attempts to climb out of the dark labyrinth, each time allowing himself ten minutes to see the light of the forest's edge. Twice he had allowed himself extra time because his eyes played tricks, and in each case there was only further darkness, no end in sight.

He was rapidly going out of his mind. He was caught in a maze; thick shafts of bark and unending, prickling branches and cracked limbs creased his face and his legs. How many times had he gone in circles? He could not tell. Everything began to look like everything else. He'd *seen* that tree! That particular cluster of branches had been his wall five minutes ago! His flashlight was no help. Its illuminations imitated themselves; he could not tell one from another. He was lost in the middle of an impenetrable slope of Alpine woods. Nature had altered the trail in the decades since the Leinkraus mourners made their final pilgrimage. The seepage of melting summer snows had spread, inundating the once-negotiable forest, providing a bed of moist earth receptive to unlimited growth.

But knowing this was as useless as his flashlight's distortions. The initial reports of gunfire exploded from over *there*. In *that* direction. He had very little to lose except his breath and what remained of his sanity. He began to run, his head filled with the echoes of the gunfire he had heard seconds ago.

The faster he ran the straighter seemed his course. He slashed a path with his arms, bending, breaking, cracking everything that got in his way.

And he saw the light. He fell to his knees, out of breath, no more than thirty feet from the forest's edge. Gray stone, covered with patches of snow, rose beyond the dense trees and surged out of sight above the highest limbs. He had reached the base of the third plateau.

And so had his brother. The killer from Eye Corps had done what Goldoni believed he could not do: He had taken long-forgotten descriptions written down a half century ago and refined them, made them applicable to the present search. There was a time when brother would have taken pride in brother; that time had passed. There remained only the necessity of stopping him.

Adrian had tried not to think about it, wondering if he'd be capable of accepting it when the moment came. The moment of anguish unlike anything in his imagination. He was accepting it now. Calmly, strangely unmoved, though filled with a cold sadness. For it was the only eminently logical, undeniable response to the horror and the chaos.

He would kill his brother. Or his brother would kill him.

He got to his feet, walked slowly out of the forest and found the path of rock diagramed on the Leinkraus map. It wound up the mountain, a series of wide curves to lessen the angle of ascent, veering always clockwise until it reached the top. Or almost the top, for at the base of the plateau was a sheet of rock that Paul Leinkraus recalled was quite high. He had made the journey only twice—in the first and second years of the war—and was very young. The sheet of rock might not be as high as he remembered it to be, for the memory was in the context of a boy's perspective. But they had used a ladder, he recalled that clearly.

A solemn service for the dead and a young boy's sense of life were incompatible, Leinkraus had admitted. There was another way to the plateau, hardly practical for old men, but explored by a youngster lacking the proper respect for religious observance. It was at the very end of the seemingly vanished path, well past an enormous natural arch that was the continuation of the mountain trail. It consisted of a series of jagged rocks that followed the line of the narrowing summit, and necessitated sure feet and a willingness to take chances. His father and older brother had scolded him severely for using it. The drop was dangerous; probably not fatal, but sufficiently deep to break an arm or a leg.

If an arm or a leg were broken now, thought Adrian, the danger *was* fatal. An immobilized man was an easy target.

He started up the winding path, between the intermittent rocks, crouching to conceal his body below their height. The plateau was three hundred to four hundred feet above the path, the distance of a football field. A light snow began to fall, settling itself delicately on the thin layer of white that already covered much of the rock. His feet slipped continuously; he balanced himself by grabbing shrubs and projections of jagged rock.

He reached the midpoint of the climb and pressed his back into a concave flute of stone to catch his breath unseen. He could hear sounds above him, metal against metal, or rock against rock. He lunged out of the recess and ran as fast as he could, up and around the next four bends of the trail, falling once to let untrapped, unswallowed air fill his lungs, to give his aching legs a chance to rest.

He pulled the Leinkraus diagram from his pocket and checked off the curves on the map; he had covered eight, he thought. Whatever, it wasn't any farther than a hundred feet to the arch, symbolized by an inverted U on the diagram. He raised his head, his face bitter cold from the temporary pillow of frost and snow. There was a straight stretch of trail, bordered on both sides by gray, gnarled shrubbery. According to the map, there were two more hairpin curves above that stretch and then the arch of rock. He jammed the diagram into his pocket, feeling the steel of his gun as he did so. He pulled his legs up under him into a crouch and raced on.

He saw the girl first. She was lying off the trail in the shrubs, her eyes wide, staring at the overcast sky, her legs stretched rigidly in front of her. There were two bullet holes above each knee, the blood matted about the cloth. A third puncture could be seen above her right breast, below her collar bone; blood had formed a solid stream down her white Alpine jacket.

She was alive, but in such a degree of shock that she did not blink her eyes against the particles of falling snow. Her lips were moving, trembling, melted snow forming rivulets of water at the edges. Adrian bent over her.

At the sight of his face, her eyes blinked into focus. She raised her head in convulsion, coughing the start of a scream. Gently, he pressed his gloved hand over the mouth, supporting her neck with his other hand.

"I'm not him," he whispered.

The brush above them moved. Adrian whipped up, releasing the girl as carefully as he could, and sprang back. A hand edged its way over the snow—what was left of a hand. It was bloodstained flesh, the glove blown off, the fingers shattered. Fontine crept over the girl and up into the tangled, gnarled shrubbery, ripping the intertwined branches apart. The boy lay on his stomach in a bed of wild mountain grass. A straight line of four bullet wounds angled diagonally along his back, across his spine.

Adrian rolled the youth carefully over on his side, cradling his head. Once again he gently pressed a hand over a mouth in shock. The boy's eyes locked with his and within seconds Adrian's meaning was clear: He was not the killer. That the boy could speak at all was extraordinary. His whisper was nearly covered by the growing wind, but Fontine heard him.

"*Mia sorella.*"

"I don't understand."

"*Sister?*"

"She's hurt. So are you. I'll do everything I can."

"*Pacco.* The pack. He wears a pack. *Medicina.*"

"Don't talk. Save your strength. A pack?"

"*Si!*"

. . . *An Alpine pack is not a mere collection of straps and leather casing. It is a work of master craftsmanship.* . . . His father had said that.

The boy would not stop. He knew he was dying. "A way out. The Zermatt railroad. A village. Not far, *signore.* North, not far. We were going to run."

"Shhh. Don't say any more. I'm going to put you next to your sister. Keep as warm as you can."

He half carried, half dragged the boy over the grass to the girl. They were children; his brother murdered children. He removed his raincoat and jacket, tearing the lining of the jacket in order to tie the strips around the girl's wounds. There wasn't much he could do about the boy's, so he avoided his eyes. He covered them both; they held each other.

He put the heavy pistol in his belt beneath the heavy black sweater and crawled out of the sanctuary of the bushes. He raced up the path to the arch, his eyes stinging but his breath steady, the pain in his legs gone.

It was one against one now. The way it had to be.

Chapter Thirty-three

The sound of cracking came louder, hammerlike and furious. It was directly above him, above the sheer sheet of rock that sprang up, facing the small, defined plateau on the north side. The ground at his feet was disturbed; snow and earth were intermingled, footprints and broken shrubbery formed a semicircle beneath the overhang. Fragments of rock signified the method of ascent: A rope had been thrown above, with a hook attached, and the first throw or throws had not been successful.

A rotted ladder lay in the snow-laced, gray bushes, a number of its steps torn from the frame. It was the ladder Paul Leinkraus remembered. It was at least twenty feet long, on end, slightly higher than the sheet of rock in front of which Adrian crouched.

The burial ground is really a surface of shale. It cracks easily under the force of a pick to the earth beneath. The child's coffin was placed in the ground and a thin layer of concrete spread over it. The words of Paul Leinkraus.

Above him, his brother had broken through the layer of concrete described by Leinkraus. The hammering stopped; a metal instrument was thrown aside on the hard surface. Large particles of cement plummeted down, kicked by impatient feet, joining the fragments of rock on the ground and the bushes. Adrian got to his feet quickly and pressed himself into the miniature cliff. If he was seen, he was dead.

The spray of cement stopped. Adrian shivered; he knew he had to move. The cold was penetrating the black sweater, his breath formed billows of vapor in front of his face. The brief, light snowfall was letting up; a shaft of sunlight broke through the clouds, but brought no warmth.

He edged his way around the sheet of rock until he could go no farther, blocked by a projecting boulder bulging out of the mountaintop. He stepped forward onto the shrub-covered, snow-layered ground.

Suddenly, the earth gave way. Adrian leaped back and stood motionless, petrified, at the side of the boulder. The sounds of falling rock carried on the wind. He heard the footsteps above—heavy, abrupt—and held his breath so no steam would emerge from his mouth or nostrils. The sound of footsteps stopped—except for the wind, only silence remained. Then the footsteps started again—less heavy, slower. The soldier's alarm had subsided.

Adrian looked down in front of him. He had come to the end of Paul Leinkraus's path; there was only mountain now. Below, beyond the edge of broken earth and wild grass, was a drop, a wide, sweeping crevasse whose empty space separated the ground of the summit from the shallow ledge of earth across from it that led to higher regions. The crevasse was far deeper than Leinkraus remembered; it was well over thirty feet to a floor of jagged rock. The boy had been reprimanded by his elders, but not so truthfully as to frighten him, or instill a fear of the mountains.

Adrian swung his body around and, clinging to the uneven surface, inch by inch, testing each, he moved out, pressing his chest and legs into the boulder, holding whatever sharp point he could grasp. On the other side was a narrow mass of indiscriminately formed rock that angled sharply up to the flat surface of the peak.

He was not sure he could reach it. A small boy could walk on the ledge away from the immediate base of the projecting boulder; it would not give way under his weight. A grown man was something else. It had not taken Adrian's weight; it would not take it.

The distance from the central point of the boulder—where he was—to the first promontory of rock was about five feet. He was over six. If he could angle his fall, with his arms outstretched, there was a good chance his hands would reach. More of a chance if he could narrow the distance.

The muscles of his feet were in agony. He could feel cramps forming in both insteps: the strain on his calves swelled his skin, the tendons beneath arching nearly beyond endurance. He forced all thoughts of pain and risk out of his mind and concentrated only on the inches he could cover around the massive boulder.

He had gone no more than a foot when he felt the ground sinking beneath him—slowly, in minute, hypnotizing stages. Then he could hear—actually *hear*—the cracking of stone and frozen earth. He thrust out his arms at the last half second. The ledge fell away and for a moment he was in the void, suspended. His hands clutched out crazily; the wind whipped against his face in midair.

His right arm crashed over the jagged rock somewhere above him. His shoulder and head slammed into the rough, ragged surface. He clamped his hand around the sharp stone, arching his back instinctively to absorb the shock of the impact.

He swung like a puppet on the string of his own appendage, his feet dangling. He had to drag himself up. *Now!* There were no seconds to waste! No time to adjust to his own disbelief!

Move!

He clawed the uneven cliff with his free left hand; his feet pumped insanely until his right shoe caught a tiny ridge that supported his weight. It was enough. Like a panicked spider he scaled the wall of jagged rock, throwing his legs one after another over the diagonal incline, slamming his body into the base of the inner surface.

He was out of sight from above, not out of hearing. The sounds of the falling ledge brought Andrew to the edge of the plateau. The sun was behind him on his right, casting his shadow across the crevasse, over the rock and snow. Again, Adrian held his breath. He had a window on his own lantern show, played out in the now-blinding Alpine sun. The soldier's movements were not only clear, they were magnified. Andrew held an object in his left hand: a climber's folding shovel.

The soldier's right arm was angled at the elbow; the shadow of his forearm joined the shadow of his upper body. It took little imagination to visualize what the right hand held: a gun. Adrian moved his own right hand to his belt. The pistol was still there; he was grateful for its touch.

The shadow moved about the ledge above, three steps to the left, four to the right. It bent down and then stood up again, another object now in its right hand. The object was thrown off; a large fragment of cement plummeted down no more than two feet from Adrian's face and crashed on the floor of jagged rock below. The soldier stood motionless during the object's fall, as if counting off seconds, timing the descent. The last rolling spatters finished, the soldier walked away. His shadow disappeared, replaced by the harsh reflections of the sun.

Adrian lay in his recess, unaware of his discomfort, his face drenched with sweat. The curve of uneven rocks above his head swept sharply up, like a primitive spiral staircase in an ancient lighthouse. The sweep was about twenty-five feet in length; it was difficult to estimate for there was nothing beyond but sky and blazing sun. He could not move until he heard sounds from above. Sounds that meant the soldier was occupied, digging again.

They came. A loud crushing of stone, the scraping of metal against metal. Andrew had found the vault!

Adrian crawled out of his shelter and, hand over hand, silent foot after silent foot, made his way up the jagged rock staircase. The ledge of the plateau was directly above; below was no longer the crevasse but a sheer drop of several hundred feet to the winding mountain pass. There were, perhaps, eight inches between him and the open space. The wind was steady. Its sound was a low whistle.

He reached for the pistol in his belt, removed it and—as Goldoni had instructed—checked the safety. It was in upright position, locked.

He snapped it level with the trigger and raised his head over the ledge.

The flat surface of the plateau was an oval, extending thirty-five feet or more in length, twenty or so in width. The soldier crouched in the center, next to a mound of earth covered with fragments of cracked cement. Beyond the dirt, partially concealed by the soldier's broad back, was a plain wooden casket with metal borders; it was remarkably preserved.

There was no vault. There was nothing but earth, the fragments of cement, and the coffin. But no vault!

Oh, my God, thought Adrian. We were *wrong! Both wrong!*

It wasn't possible. It was not possible. For if there were no vault, the killer from Eye Corps would be in a rage. He knew Andrew well enough to know that. But his brother was not angry. He was crouched in thought, his head angled down; he was staring at the grave. And Adrian understood: The vault was below, still in the earth. It had been buried beneath the coffin, that casket its final protection.

The soldier got to his feet and crossed to the Alpine pack which lay upright against the coffin. He bent over, unsnapped a strap, and pulled out a short, pointed iron bar. He returned to the grave, abruptly knelt by the edge, and reached down with the bar. Seconds later he yanked the bar up, letting it fall on the ground, and removed a gun from his jacket. Swiftly, but carefully, he angled the weapon down into the grave.

Three explosions followed. Adrian ducked his head below the edge of the plateau. He could smell the acrid odor of the gunfire, see the billows of smoke carried above him on the wind.

And then the words came and his whole body was locked in a fear he never believed he could experience. It was the shock of the knowledge of his own immediate execution.

"Put your head up, Lefrac," was the soft-spoken command, delivered in a monotone of ice. "It'll be quicker that way. You won't feel a thing. You won't even hear any noise."

Adrian rose from his narrow perch, his mind black, beyond fear now. He was going to die; it was as simple as that.

But he was not what the soldier above him expected. Not *whom* the soldier expected. The killer from Eye Corps was suddenly, completely gripped in shock of his own. It was so total that his eyes widened in disbelief, his hand trembled and the weapon in its grasp wavered. He took an involuntary step backward, his mouth gaping, the skin on his face bloodless.

"*You!*"

Wildly, blindly, without thought or feeling, Adrian whipped up the heavy Italian pistol from the ledge of rock and fired at the stunned figure. He squeezed the trigger twice, three times. The gun jammed. The spits and smoke from the barrel-housing singed his flesh, stung his eyes. But he had hit the soldier! The killer from Eye Corps reeled backward, holding his stomach, his left leg buckling beneath him.

But Andrew still had the pistol in his hand. The explosion came; a crack of air detonated above Adrian's head. He lunged at the fallen man, crashing the jammed pistol down in the area of the face. His right hand shot out, grabbing the hot steel of Andrew's gun, slamming it against the hard surface of the plateau. His own pistol found its mark; the bridge between the soldier's eyes erupted; blood flowed into the corners of his sockets, bluring his vision. Andrew's pistol flew out of his hand. Adrian sprang back.

He aimed his gun and squeezed the trigger with all his strength. It would not operate, it would not *fire*. The soldier got to his knees, rubbing his eyes, his mouth emitting grunts of fury. Adrian lashed out his foot, catching the killer from Eye Corps at the temple; the soldier's neck arched back, but his legs shot forward, twisting, kicking, slamming into Adrian's kneecaps, causing him to lurch to the side, his knees suddenly in agony.

Adrian could not stay on his feet. He rolled to his right as the major leaped up, still wiping his eyes. Andrew sprang off the ground, hands now outstretched like rigid hooks, directly at his intruder's neck. Adrian recoiled farther, crashing into the casket at the side of the grave. The soldier's lunge was uncontrolled; the screaming pitch of his anger caused him to lose his balance, and he fell, one arm plunged into the mound of earth and fragments of concrete. The earth flew; an eruption of dirt and snow and rock.

Adrian dove over the open space of the grave; on the opposite side was the iron bar. The soldier followed; he lunged up, screaming at Adrian, his hands locked above his head into a hammer—a monstrous bird screeching in for the kill. Adrian's finger's were on the bar, and he lashed it up at the plummeting figure.

The point plunged into the soldier's cheek, stunning him. Blood burst again from Andrew's flesh.

Adrian lurched away as far as his exhausted, aching legs could propel him, dropping the bar. He saw the soldier's pistol lying across the flat stone surface; he lunged for it. His fingers wound around the handle; he raised it.

The iron bar came slicing through the air, creasing the skin of his left shoulder, tearing the sleeve half off his sweater. The shock sent him reeling back to the edge of the sheet of rock. He had brought the hand with the gun across his chest in panic; he knew the instant he did so it was the fraction of a second the soldier desperately needed. A wall of earth and stone came at him, the space between himself and the killer from Eye Corps was filled with debris. It smashed into him; sharp pieces of rock pummeled his face, his eyes. He could not see.

He fired. His hands recoiled violently from the explosion of the weapon; his fingers arched from the vibration.

He tried to get to his feet; a boot hammered into his neck. He caught the leg as he fell back, his shoulders over the edge of the sheet of rock. He rolled to his left, holding the leg until he felt the barrel of the gun against the flesh.

He pulled the trigger.

Flesh and bone and blood filled his universe. The soldier was blown off the ground, his right leg a mass of red-soaked cloth. Adrian started to crawl but he could not; there was no strength left, no air in his lungs. He raised himself on one hand and looked over at Andrew.

The major writhed back and forth, moans coming from his throat, his mouth filled with blood and saliva. He pushed himself off the ground, halfway to his knees, his eyes staring insanely at what was left of his leg. He looked over to his executioner. And then he screamed.

"Help me! You can't let me *die!* You *don't have the right!* Get me the *pack!"* He coughed, holding his shattered leg with one hand, his other trembling, gesturing at the Alpine pack against the coffin. The blood flowed everywhere, saturating his clothes. The poisons were spreading rapidly; he was dying.

"I don't have the right to let you live," said Adrian weakly, gasping for air. "Do you know what you've done? The people you killed?"

"Killing's an *instrument!"* screamed the soldier. "That's all it is!"

"Who decides when the instrument's used? *You?"*

"Yes! And men *like* me! We know who we are, what we can do. People like you, you're *not*——. For Christ's sake, *help me!"*

"You make the rules. Everybody else follows."

"Yes! Because we're willing to! People everywhere, they're not willing. They want the rules made for them! You can't deny that!"

"I do deny it," said Adrian quietly.

"Then you're lying. Or stupid! Oh, *Christ* . . ." The soldier's voice broke, interrupted by a spasm of coughing. He clutched his stomach and stared at his leg again, and then at the mound of dirt. He pulled his eyes away and looked at Adrian. "Here. Over *here."*

The major crawled toward the grave. Adrian rose slowly to his feet and watched, mesmerized by the horrible sight. What was left of his compassion told him to fire the weapon in his hand, end the life that was nearly finished. He could see the vault from Salonika in the ground; slats of rotted wood had been pulled away, revealing the iron beneath. Strips of metal had been shattered by gunfire, a coil of rope lay on top. There were torn pieces of heavy cardboard with faint markings that looked like circles of thorns around crucifixes.

They had found it.

"Don't you understand?" The soldier could barely be heard. "It's there. The answer. The *answer!"*

"What answer?"

"Everything. . . ." For several seconds his brother's eyes lost muscular control; they rolled in their sockets, and for an instant the pupils disappeared. Andrew's speech had the inflections of an angry child; his right hand extended into the grave. "I have it now. You can't interfere! Anymore! You can help me now. I'll let you help me. I used to let you help me, remember? You remember how I *always used to let you help me?"* The soldier screamed the question.

"It was always your decision, Andy. To let me help you, I mean," said Adrian softly, trying to understand the childlike rambling, hypnotized by the words.

"Of course my decision. It had to be *my decision*. Victor's and mine."

Adrian suddenly recalled their mother's words . . . *he saw the results of strength; he never understood its complications, its compassion. . . .* The lawyer in Adrian had to know. "What should we do with the vault? Now that we've got it, what should we do with——"

"*Use it!*" The soldier screamed again, pounding the loose rock at the edge of the grave. "*Use* it, use it! Make things *right!* We'll tell them we can ruin *everything!*"

"Suppose we can't? Suppose it doesn't matter? Maybe there's nothing there."

"We tell them *there is!* You don't know how to do it. We tell them anything we *want* to tell them! They'll *crawl*, they'll *whine*. . . ."

"You want them to do that? To crawl and whine?"

"Yes! They're weak!"

"But you're not."

"No! I've *proved* it! Over and over and *over again!*" The soldier's neck arched and then snapped forward convulsively. "You think you see things *I* don't see. You're *wrong!* I see them but they don't make *any difference*, they don't *count!* What you think's so goddamned *important* . . . *doesn't* . . . *matter!*" Andrew spaced out the words; it was a child's cry of defiance.

"What's that, Andy? What is it I think is so important?"

"*People!* What they *think!* It doesn't *count*, doesn't *matter*. Victor knows that."

"You're wrong; you're *so* wrong," interrupted Adrian quietly. "He's dead, Andy. He died a couple of days ago."

The soldier's eyes regained part of their focus. There was elation in them. "Now everything's *mine!* I'll do it!" The coughing returned; the eyes wandered again. "Make them understand. They're not important. Never were. . . ."

"Only you."

"Yes! I don't hesitate. *You do!* You can't make up your mind!"

"You're decisive, Andy."

"Yes, *decisive*. That's important."

"And people don't count, so naturally they can't be trusted."

"What the hell are you trying to say?" The soldier's chest expanded in pain; his neck arched back, then shot forward, mucus and blood coughed through his lips.

"That you're *afraid!*" shouted Adrian. "You've always been afraid! You live scared to death that someone'll find that out! There's a big crack in your armor . . . you *freak!*"

A terrible, muted cry came from the soldier's throat; it was at once guttural and clear, a cross between a roar of final anger and a wail. "That's a *lie!* You and your goddamned words. . . ."

Suddenly there were no more words. The unbelievable was happening in the blinding Alpine sunlight, and Adrian knew only that he would move or die. The soldier's hand was in the grave. He whipped it out. In his grip was a rope; he lurched off the ground, swinging the rope violently. Tied to the end was a grappling hook, its three prongs slashing through the air.

Adrian sprang to his left, firing the enormous weapon at the crazed killer from Eye Corps.

The soldier's chest exploded. The rope, held in a grip of steel, swung in a circle—the grappling hook spinning like an insanely off-course gyroscope—around the soldier's head. The body shot forward, over the sheet of rock, and plummeted down, its scream echoing, filling the mountains with its pitch of horror.

With a sudden, sickening vibration the rope sprang taut, quivering in the thin layer of disturbed snow.

There was the sound of cracking metal from the grave. Adrian whipped his eyes over to its source. The rope had been lashed to a steel band around the vault. The band snapped. The vault could be opened.

But Adrian did not go to it. He limped to the edge of the plateau and looked over the sheet of rock.

Suspended below was the soldier's body, the grappling hook imbedded in his neck. A prong had plunged up through Andrew's throat, its point protruding from the gaping mouth.

He filled the large Alpine pack with the three steel, airtight containers from the vault. He could not read the ancient writing etched in the metal. He did not have to; he knew what each container held. None were large. One was flat, thicker than the other two: within it were the documents compiled by the scholars of Constantine 1,500 years ago, studies that traced what they believed was a theological inconsistency—raising a holy man to one substance with God. Questions for new scholars to ponder. The second container was short, tubular; it held the Aramaic scroll that had so frightened powerful men thirty years ago that strategies of global war were secondary to its possession. But it was the third container, thin, no more than eight inches wide, ten high, that held the most extraordinary document of all: a confession written on a parchment, taken out of a Roman prison nearly 2,000 years ago. It was this receptacle—black, pitted, a relic of antiquity—that was the essence of the vault from Salonika.

All were the denials; only the confession on the Roman parchment could produce an agony beyond men's minds. But that was not for him to judge. Or was it?

He put the plastic bottles of medicine into his pockets, threw the pack down on the ground, lowered himself over the edge of the sheet of rock—next to the soldier's body—and dropped to the earth beneath. He strapped the heavy pack on his back and started down the trail.

The boy was dead. The girl would live. Together they would somehow walk out of the mountains, of that Adrian was convinced.

They traveled slowly—a few steps at a time—down the trail toward the Zermatt tracks. He held the girl so that as little weight as possible was forced on her wounded legs.

He looked back up the mountain trail. In the distance the soldier's body hung suspended against the white sheet of rock. It could not be seen clearly—only if you knew where to look—but it was there.

Was Andrew the final death demanded by the train from Salonika? Were the documents in that vault worth so much life? So much violence for so many years? He had no answers.

He only knew insanity was given unearned stature in the name of holy things. Holy wars were primeval; they always would be. And he had killed a brother for their part of an unholy war.

He felt the terrible weight on his back. He was tempted to remove the steel containers and heave them into the deepest gorge in the mountains. Broken, left to wither into nothing with the first touch of air. Swept away by the

Alpine winds into oblivion.

But he would not do that. The price had been too steep.

"Let's go," he said to the girl, gently placing her left arm around his neck. He smiled at the child's frightened face. "We're going to make it."

PART FOUR

Chapter Thirty-four

Adrian stood by the window overlooking the dark expanse of Central Park. He was in the small staff lounge at the Metropolitan Museum. He held the telephone to his ear and listened to Colonel Tarkington in Washington. Across the room sat a priest from the Archdiocese of New York, the monsignor named Land. It was shortly past midnight; the army officer in Washington had been given the private number of the museum. He was told that Mr. Fontine expected his call, regardless of the hour.

Official documentation of events surrounding Eye Corps would be issued by the Pentagon in due time, the officer told Adrian. The administration wanted to avoid the scandal that would result from charges of corruption and insurrection within the armed forces. Especially as a prominent name was involved. It did not serve the interests of national security.

"Stage one," said Adrian. "Cover-up."

"Perhaps."

"You're going to settle for that?" asked Fontine quietly.

"It's your family," replied the colonel. "Your brother."

"And yours. I can live with it. Can't you? Can't Washington?"

There was silence on the other end of the line. Finally the officer spoke. "I got what I wanted. And maybe Washington can't. Not now."

"It's never 'now.'"

"Don't preach to me. Nobody's stopping you from holding a press conference."

It was now Adrian who was momentarily silent. "If I do, can I demand official documentation? Or would a dossier suddenly appear, describing——"

"Describing in psychiatric detail," interrupted the colonel, "a very disturbed young man who ran around the country living in hippie communes; who aided and abetted three convicted army deserters in San Francisco. Don't kid yourself, Fontine. It's on my desk."

"I thought it might be. I'm learning. You're thorough, aren't you? Which brother's the lunatic?"

"It goes much further. Family influence used to avoid military service; past membership in radical organizations—they're using dynamite these days. Your odd behavior recently in Washington, including a relationship with a Black attorney who was killed under strange circumstances, said Black lawyer suspected of criminal activities. Lots more. And that's only you."

"What?"

"Old truths—documented truths—are dragged up. A father who made a fortune operating all over the world with governments many believe are inimicable to our interests. A man who worked closely with the Communists, whose first wife was killed years ago under very odd circumstances in Monte Carlo. That's a disturbing pattern. Questions are raised. Can the Fontines live with *that?*"

"You make me sick."

"I make myself sick."

"Then why?"

"Because a decision had to be made that goes beyond you and me and our personal revulsions!" The colonel raised his voice in anger, then controlled himself. "I don't like a lot of bullshit players upstairs. I only know—or think I know—that maybe it isn't the time to talk about Eye Corps."

"So it goes on and on. You don't sound like the man I talked to in a hotel room."

"Maybe I'm not. I only hope for the sake of your righteous indignation you're never put in a position like this."

Adrian looked at the priest across the room. Land was staring at the dimly lit white wall, at nothing. Yet it was in his eyes, *it's always in the eyes.* A desperation that consumed him. The monsignor was a very strong man, but he was frightened now. "I hope I never am," he said to the colonel.

"Fontine?"

"Yes?"

"Let's have a drink sometime."

"Sure. We'll do that." Adrian hung up.

Was it up to him now? wondered Adrian. Everything? Was the time ever right to tell the truth?

There'd be one answer soon. He'd gotten the documents from the vault out of Italy with the colonel's help; the colonel owed him that much, and the colonel did not ask questions. The colonel's payment was a body suspended in front of a sheet of rock in the mountains of Champoluc. Brother for brother. Debt paid.

Barbara Pierson had known what to do with the documents. She contacted a friend who was a curator of relics and artifacts at the Metropolitan. A scholar who had devoted his life to study of the past. He had seen too much of antiquity to make judgments.

Barbara had flown down from Boston; she was in the laboratory with the scholar now. They'd been there since five-thirty. Seven hours. With the documents from Constantine.

But there was only one document that mattered now. It was the parchment taken out of a Roman prison 2,000 years ago. The parchment was everything. *Everything.* The scholar understood that.

Adrian left the window and walked across the room to the priest. Two weeks ago, when his father was close to death, Victor drew up his list of men to whom the vault of Constantine was to be delivered. Land's name was on that list. When Adrian contacted him, Land began saying things to him he had never said to Victor Fontine.

"Tell me about Annaxas," said Adrian, sitting down opposite the priest.

The monsignor looked away from the wall, startled. Not by the name, thought Fontine, but by the intrusion. His large, penetrating gray eyes under the dark brows were momentarily unfocused. He blinked, as if remembering where he was.

"Theodore Dakakos? What can I tell you? We first met in Istanbul. I was tracing what I knew was false evidence. The so-called destruction by fire of the Filioque documents. He found out I was there and flew up from Athens to meet the interfering priest from the Vatican archives. We talked; we were both curious. I, why such a prominent man of commerce was so interested in obscure theological artifacts. He, why a Roman scholar was pursuing—*allowed* to pursue, perhaps—a thesis hardly in the Vatican's interests. He was very knowledgeable. Each of us manuevered throughout the night, both of us finally exhausted. I think it was the exhaustion that caused it. And the fact that we thought we knew one another, perhaps even liked one another."

"Caused what?"

"The train from Salonika to be mentioned. Strange, I don't remember which of us said it first."

"He *knew* about it?"

"As much, or more, than I. The trainman was his father, the single passenger; the priest of Xenope, his father's brother. Neither man ever returned. In his search he found part of the answer. The police records in Milan contained an old entry from December 1939. Two dead men on a Greek train in the freight yards. Murder and suicide. No identification. Annaxas had to know why."

"What led him to Milan?"

"Over twenty years of asking questions. He had reason enough. He watched his mother go insane. She went mad because the church would give her no answers."

"Her church?"

"An arm of the church, if you will. The Order of Xenope."

"Then she knew about the train."

"She was never supposed to have known. It was believed she didn't. But men tell things to their wives they tell no one else. Before the elder Annaxas left early that morning in December of 1939, he said to his wife that he was not going to Corinth, as everyone believed. Instead, God would look favorably on them for he was joining his brother Petride. They were going on a journey very far away. They were doing God's work."

The priest fingered the gold cross hanging from a cord on the cloth beneath his collar. His touch was not gentle; there was anger in it.

"From which he never came back," said Adrian quietly. "And there was no brother in the church to reach because he was dead."

"Yes. I think we can both imagine how the woman—a good woman, simple, loving, left with six children—would react."

"She'd go out of her mind."

Land let the cross drop, his eyes straying back to the wall. "As an act of charity, the priests of Xenope took the mad woman in. Another decision was made. She died within a month."

Fontine slowly sat forward. "They killed her." It was not a question.

Land's gaze returned. There was a degree of supplication in his eyes now. "They weighed the consequences of her life. Not against the Filioque, but in relation to a parchment none of us in Rome ever knew existed. I'd never heard of it until this evening. It makes so many things so much clearer."

Adrian got out of the chair and walked back to the window. He was not ready to discuss the parchment. The holy men no longer had the right to direct inquiries. The attorney in Adrian disapproved of the priests. Laws were for all.

Down in Central Park, along a dimly lit path, a man was walking two huge

Labrador retrievers, the animals straining at their leashes. He was straining on a leash of his own, but he could not let Land know it. He turned from the window. "Dakakos put it all together, didn't he?"

"Yes," replied Land, accepting Adrian's refusal to be led. "It was his legacy. He vowed to learn everything. We agreed to exchange information, but I was more forthright than he. The name Fontini-Cristi surfaced, but the parchment was never mentioned. The rest, I assume, you know."

Adrian was startled by the priest's words. "Don't assume anything. Tell me."

Land flinched. The rebuke was unexpected. "I'm sorry. I thought you knew. Dakakos took over the responsibility of Campo di Fiori. For years he paid the taxes—which were considerable—fended off buyers, real-estate developers, provided security, and upkeep——"

"What about Xenope?"

"The Order of Xenope is all but extinct. A small monastery north of Salonika. A few old priests on diminished farmland, with no money. For Dakakos, only one link remained: a dying monk at Campo di Fiori. He couldn't let it go. He extracted everything the old man knew. Ultimately, he was right. Gaetamo was released from prison; the banished priest, Aldobrini, came back from Africa dying of assorted fevers and, finally, your father returned to Campo di Fiori. The scene of his family's execution. The terrible search began all over again."

Adrian thought. "Dakakos stopped my brother. He went to extraordinary lengths to trap him, expose Eye Corps."

"To keep him from the vault at all costs. The old monk must have told Dakakos that Victor Fontine knew about the parchment. He understood that your father would act outside the authorities, use his sons to find the vault. He had to. Weighing the consequences, there was no other course. Dakakos studied both of you. Actually he had you watched for several years. What he found in one son shocked him. Your brother could not be permitted to go further. He had to be destroyed. You, on the other hand, were someone he felt he could work with, if it came to that."

The priest had stopped. He inhaled deeply, his fingers once again around the gold cross on his chest. Thought had returned to him and it was obviously painful. Adrian understood; he had experienced the same feeling in the mountains of Champoluc.

"What would Dakakos have done if he'd found the vault?"

Land's penetrating gaze settled on Adrian. "I don't know. He was a compassionate man. He knew the anguish of seeking painful answers to very painful questions; his sympathy might have guided his judgment. Still, he was a man of truth. I think he would have weighed the consequences. Beyond this I can't help you."

"You use that phrase a lot, don't you? 'Weighing the consequences.'"

"I apologize if it offends you."

"It does."

"Then forgive me, but I must offend you further. I asked your permission to come here, but I've changed my mind. I'm going to leave." The priest got out of the chair. "I can't stay. I'll try to put it simply——"

"Simply *put*," interrupted harshly, "I'm not interested."

"You have the advantage," replied Land quickly. "You see, I'm interested in *you*, in what you perceive." The priest would not be stopped; he took a step forward. "Do you think doubts are erased because vows are taken? You think seven thousand years of human communication is somehow voided for us? Any of us, whatever the vestments we wear? How many gods and prophets and holy men have been conjured over the centuries? Does the number lessen the devotion? I think not. For each accepts what he can accept, raising his own beliefs above all others. My doubts tell me that thousands of years from now scholars may study the remnants of what we were and conclude that our beliefs—our devotions—were singularly odd, consigning to myth what we think most holy. As we have consigned to myth the remnants of others. My intellect, you see, can conceive of this. But now, here, in my time—for me—the commitment is made. It's better to have it than not to have it. I do believe. I am convinced."

Adrian remembered the words. "'Divine revelation cannot be contravened by mortal man'?"

"That's good enough. I'll accept that," said Land simply. "Ultimately, the lessons of Aquinas prevail. They're not the exclusive property of anyone, I might add. When reason is exhausted, at its last barrier, faith becomes the reason. I have that faith. But being mortal, I'm weak. I haven't the endurance to test myself further. I must retreat to the comfort of my commitment, knowing I'm better with it than without it." The priest held out his hand. "Good-bye, Adrian."

Fontine looked at the outstretched hand and accepted it. "You understand that it's the arrogance of your 'commitment,' your beliefs, that disturbs me. I don't know any other way to put it."

"I understand; your objection is noted. That arrogance is the first of the sins that lead to spiritual death. And the one most often overlooked: pride. It may kill us all one day. Then, my young friend, there'll be nothing."

Land turned and walked to the door of the small lounge. He opened it with his right hand, his left still holding the gold cross, enveloping it. The gesture was unmistakable. It was an act of protection. He looked once more at Adrian, then walked out of the room, closing the door behind him.

Fontine lighted a cigarette, then crushed it out. His mouth was sour from too many cigarettes and too little sleep. Instead, he went to a coffee maker and poured himself a cup.

An hour ago Land, testing the metal rim of the hot plate, had burned his fingers. It occurred to Adrian that the monsignor was the sort of man who tested most things in life. And yet he could not accept the final test. He merely walked away; there was a kind of honesty in that.

Far more than he had shown his mother, reflected Adrian. He had not lied to Jane; it would have been useless, the lie known for what it was. But neither had he told her the truth. He had done a far crueler thing: he had avoided her. He was not yet ready for confrontation.

He heard footsteps in the corridor outside the lounge. He put his coffee down and walked to the center of the room. The door opened and Barbara entered, the door held for her by the scholar, still in his laboratory smock, his hornrimmed glasses somehow magnifying his face. Barbara's brown eyes, usually so filled with warmth and laughter, were sharp with professional involvement.

"Doctor Shire's finished," she said. "May we have coffee?"

"Sure." Adrian went back to the table and poured two cups. The scholar sat down on the chair from which Land had risen just minutes ago.

"Black, if you please," said Shire, placing a single page of paper in his lap. "Your friend has left?"

"Yes, he left."

"Did he know?" asked the old man, accepting the coffee.

"He knew because I told him. He made his decision. He left."

"I can understand," said Shire, blinking his old eyes beyond the glasses in the steam of his coffee. "Sit down, both of you."

Barbara took the coffee but did not sit. She and the scholar exchanged looks; she walked to the window as Adrian sat across from Shire.

"Is it authentic?" asked Fontine. "I imagine that's the first question."

"Authentic? As to time and materials and script and language . . . yes, I would say it will survive those examinations. I'm going under the assumption that it will. Chemical and prismatic analyses take a long time, but I've seen hundreds of documents from the period; it's authentic on these points. As to the authenticity of the contents. It was written by a half-crazed man facing death. A very cruel and painful form of death. That judgment will have to be made by others, if it's to be made at all." Shire glanced at Adrian as he placed the coffee cup on the table beside the chair and picked up the paper on his lap. Fontine remained silent. The scholar continued.

"According to the words on that parchment, the prisoner who was to lose his life in the arena on the following afternoon renounced the name of Peter, given him by the revolutionary named Jesus. He said he was not worthy of it. He wanted his death to be recorded as one Simon of Bethsaida, his name at birth. He was consumed with guilt, claiming he had betrayed his savior. . . . For the man who was crucified on Calvary was *not* Jesus of Nazareth."

The old scholar stopped, his words floating, suspended, as if broken off in midsentence.

"Oh, my God!" Adrian got out of the chair. He looked at Barbara by the window. She returned his gaze without comment. He turned back to Shire. "It's that specific?"

"Yes. The man was in torment. He writes that three of Christ's disciples acted on their own, *against* the carpenter's wishes. With the help of Pilate's guards, whom they bribed, they took an unconscious Jesus out of the dungeons and substituted a condemned criminal of the same size and general appearance, dressing him in the carpenter's clothes. In the hysterical crowds the next day, the shroud and the blood from the thorns were sufficient to obscure the features of the man under and on the cross. It was *not* the will of the man they called a messiah——"

"'Nothing is changed,'" interrupted Adrian softly, remembering the words. "'Yet all is changed.'"

"He was involuntarily removed. It was his intention to die, not to live. The parchment is clear on that."

"But he didn't die. He *did* live."

"Yes."

"He was *not* crucified."

"No. If one accepts the word of the man who wrote the document—under the conditions he wrote it. Barely on the brink of sanity, I should think. I wouldn't accept it merely because of its antiquity."

"Now you're making a judgment."

"An observation of probability," corrected Shire. "The writer of the parchment lapsed into wild prayer and lamentations. His thoughts were lucid one moment, unclear the next. Madman or self-flagellating ascetic? Pretender or penitent? Which one? Unfortunately, the physical fact that it's a document from two thousand years ago lends a credibility that would certainly be withheld under less striking circumstances. Remember, it was the time of Nero's persecutions, a period of social, political, and theological madness. People survived more often than not on sheer ingenuity. Who was it, *really?*"

"The document spells it out. Simon of Bethsaida."

"We have only the writer's word for it. There is no record of Simon Peter's having gone to his death with the early Christian martyrs. Certainly it would be part of the legend, yet there's no mention of it in biblical studies. If it were so, and overlooked, it's an awesome omission, isn't it?"

The scholar removed his glasses and wiped the thick lens with a corner of his smock. "What are you trying to say?" Adrian asked.

The old man put the glasses back on his face, magnifying his thoughtful, sad eyes. "Suppose a citizen of Rome, scheduled for a most horrible form of execution, invents a story that impugns the hated mark of an upstart, dangerous religion, and does so in a believable manner. Such a man might find favor with the praetors, the consuls, with a caesar himself. A great many tried it, you know. In one form or another. There are remnants of scores of such 'confessions.' And now one of them in its complete form comes down to us. Is there any reason to accept it more than the others? Merely because it *is* complete? Ingenuity and survival are commonplace in history."

Adrian watched the scholar closely as he spoke. There was a strange anxiety in the words. "What do *you* think, doctor?"

"It's not important what I think," said Shire, momentarily avoiding Adrian's eyes.

There was silence; it was profoundly moving. "You believe it, don't you?"

Shire paused. "It's an extraordinary document."

"Does it say what happened to the carpenter?"

"Yes," replied Shire, staring at Adrian. "He took his own life three days later."

"Took his *own life?* That's contrary to everything——"

"Yes, it is," interrupted the scholar softly. "The consistency is found in the time factor: three days. Consistency and inconsistency, where's the balance? The confession goes on to say that the carpenter reviled those who interfered, yet still at the end called upon his God to forgive them."

"That's consistent."

"Would you expect otherwise? Ingenuity and survival, Mr. Fontine."

Nothing is changed, yet all is changed.

"What's the condition of the parchment?"

"It's remarkably well preserved. A solution of animal oil, I think, pressed into a vacuum, covered by heavy rock glass."

"And the other documents?"

"I haven't examined them, other than to distinguish them from the parchment. The papers that I presume trace the Filioque agreements as seen by its opponents are barely intact. The Aramaic scroll is, of course, metallic and will take a great deal of time and care to unravel."

Adrian sat down. "Is that the literal translation of the confessions?" he asked, pointed to the page of writing in the scholar's hand.

"Sufficiently so. It's unrefined. I wouldn't present it academically."

"May I have it?"

"You may have everything." Shire leaned forward. Adrian reached out and took the paper. "The parchment, the documents; they're yours."

"They don't belong to me."

"I know that."

"Then why? I'd think you'd be pleading with me to let you keep them. Examine them. Startle the world with them."

The scholar removed his thick glasses, his tired eyes creased with exhaustion, his voice quiet. "You've brought me a very strange discovery. And quite frightening. I'm too old to cope with it."

"I don't understand."

"Then I ask you to consider. A death was denied, not a *life*. But in that death was the symbol. If you raise that symbol into question, you risk casting doubt on everything that symbol has come to mean. I'm not sure that's justified."

Adrian was silent for a moment. "The price of truth is too steep. Is that what you're saying?"

"If it's true. But again, there's the terrible absolute of antiquity. Things are accepted because they exist. Homer creates fiction, and centuries later men trace sea routes in search of caves inhabited by one-eyed giants. Froisart chronicles history that never was and is hailed a true historian. I ask you to weigh the consequences."

Adrian got out of the chair and walked aimlessly to the wall. The same area of the wall that Land kept looking at: flat, dimly lit white paint. Nothing. "Can you keep everything here for a while?"

"It can be stored in a laboratory vault. I can send you a receipt of acknowledgment."

Fontine turned. "A vault?"

"Yes. A vault."

"It could have stayed in another."

"Perhaps it should have. For how long, Mr. Fontine?"

"How long?"

"How long will it remain here?"

"A week, a month, a century. I don't know."

He stood by the hotel window overlooking the Manhattan skyline. New York pretended to sleep, but the myriad lights below on the streets denied the pretense.

They had talked for several hours, how many he didn't really know. *He* had talked; Barbara had listened, gently forcing him to say it all.

There was so much to do, to go through, before he found his head again.

Suddenly—the sound somehow terrifying—the telephone rang. He wheeled around, too aware of the panic he felt, knowing it was in his eyes.

Barbara got out of her chair and walked calmly over to him. She reached up and held his face with her hands. The panic subsided.

"I don't want to talk to anyone. Not now."

"Then don't. Tell whoever it is to call in the morning."

It was so simple. The truth.

The telephone rang again. He crossed to the bedside table and picked it up, sure of his intention, confident of his strength.

"Adrian? For God's *sake!* We've been tracing you all over New York! A colonel at I.G. named Tarkington gave us the hotel."

The caller was one of the Justice lawyers recruited by Nevins.

"What is it?"

"It's happened! Everything we've worked for is falling into place. This town is blown apart. The White House is in panic. We're in touch with the

Senate judiciary; we're after a special prosecutor. There's no other way it can be handled."

"You've got concrete evidence?"

"More than that. Witnesses, confessions. The thieves are running for cover. We're back in business, Fontine. Are you with us? We can *move* now!"

Adrian thought only briefly before he answered. "Yes, I'm with you."

It was important to keep moving. Certain struggles continued. Others had to be brought to a close. The wisdom was in deciding which.